The Taste of

Champagne Urge

WIK-ID-FICTION ©

LYNDON WALTERS

authorHOUSE®

AuthorHouse™ UK
1663 Liberty Drive
Bloomington, IN 47403 USA
www.authorhouse.co.uk
Phone: 0800.197.4150

Published by AuthorHouse   01/25/2016

ISBN: 978-1-4918-8297-9 (softcover)
ISBN: 978-1-4918-8299-3 (eBook)
ISBN: 978-1-4969-8833-1 (audio)

Print information available on the last page.

This book is printed on acid-free paper.

The Taste of Champagne Urge

WIK-**ID**-FICTION ©

Storyline, Locations, Characters and Concepts: Lyndon Walters ©

Relationships, Personal Development, Personal Performance

'I'-Coaching ©

www.lyndonwalters.com

info@lyndonwalters.com

Cover Art Concept, Characterisation and Imagery: Lyndon Walters ©

Cover Art Interpretation: Marine Lewis ©

Cover Art Illustration: Marine Lewis ©

This Book Cover is a joint Project between Lyndon Walters and Marine Lewis

Marine Lewis owns the Intellectual Property Rights for the image for the Book

Cover for 'The Taste of Champagne Urge'

Marine Lewis has given her full permission for the author, Lyndon Walters and his Publisher to use the image for the cover, any promotional materials and events with regards to his book,

WIK-**ID**-FICTION ©

'The Taste of Champagne Urge'

marinelewis@yahoo.co.uk

THANKS

Very special thanks to AYR, MCW and to the rest of my magnificent family. I love each of you unconditionally, for your unwavering faith in me, but, most of all, thank you for being uniquely you.

I am especially grateful to the artist, Marine Lewis, for taking on the challenge to produce the cover for my book. Your dedication to the Project, your perseverance, patience, for being available and your determination and focus to attend to every tiny detail which I tasked you to do so often, speaks volumes about your professionalism. I admire your awesome talent which has helped to bring the two major characters to life.

A huge thank you for giving me and my Publisher, AuthorHouse, permission for using the image for the purpose of the cover for my book and to use as promotional material at events regarding my book, 'The Taste of Champagne Urge' 'Wik-**ID**-Fiction'. This in itself is a very selfless contribution.

It is also fitting to thank my 'Universal Family', which transcends colour, race, gender, language and beliefs. You know who you are. Over the years, your personal, genuine contributions have helped to shape me into who I am, spiritually. You've helped me to enrich but appreciate my learning experiences and to fulfilling some of my purpose and mission on this planet. Our deep commitment to the core element of trust has helped each of us to develop an uncomplicated long, lasting bonding in our unconditional relationships. We have proven that it is fitting to respect our uniqueness as well as each others' cultural *'values and beliefs'*, without prejudice, whilst maintaining our own. I feel honoured that you've shared all those learning moments with me, accepting my philosophies on the importance of the principles of structure, morals and scruples.

Thanks to all the individuals, who have taken the time to listen to or read any part of these Fictional Virtual Realities Scenarios ©. Your time, interest, indulgence, feedback, unconditional commitment, consistency, resilience and patience are appreciated. I'm forever grateful to each of you.

NOTE

The locations, characters, names, occupations, organisations, environments, situations, storyline and concepts are all thoroughly fictitious. It is possible and likely probable that individuals might choose to perceive otherwise. The author takes neither responsibility nor is he in control of what or how others might choose to think or feel, what they might choose to say or do about these Fictional Virtual Realities Scenarios ©.

It must be understood that this book is not Sci-Fi but just sheer imaginative creativity of finding and utilising a virtual platform in 'The World of Space'. The language of the population of the parallel virtual planet of Asteroidia, including the exotic continents, countries and islands in the World of Space, was via vibrations and instinctive behaviours only. There is no alphabet, dictionary, vocabulary or verbal form of language. All translation necessary to explain the behaviours exhibited within the Fictional Virtual Realities Scenarios © are subject to the understandings and interpretations of the *'beliefs and values'* of the various Tribal population occupying the Royal Royal Dis-United Stately Kingdoms of Asteroidia altogether. In order to translate and reflect their behaviours, Professor Walynski, the man they called 'The Professor' and their army of official observers were beamed up from the parallel planet Earth. They were tasked to interpret those behaviours, based on each Tribe's traditional and cultural *'values and beliefs'*. It must be stressed that the translations are interpreted by way of individual perceptions only and is subject to *'human errors'* like on the parallel planet Earth, probably!

<u>Even with their best intentions, it is probable that individual perceptions might have been partially or wholly misinterpreting those behaviours like often happens on planet Earth. They may not have been accurate representations or intentions of the particular individuals to which they refer. It must therefore be concluded that some meanings or explanations might have been lost in translation, somewhat, maybe!</u>

As all behaviours were initially uploaded from Planet Earth, Hifle and Pifle had agreed that the consequences of those behaviours, not withstanding how they might impact individuals, be provided as ***<u>a 'Resource of Restorative Learning' for Planet Earth</u>***.

The Taste of Champagne Urge!

WIK-**ID**-FICTION ©

TRAILER

TRAILER

Once upon a moment in time there was a man with two brains. Their names were Hifle and Pifle. They had been conjoined mental, physical, spiritual and vibrating twins that had known each other since the moment of conception. Hifle and Pifle called themselves the mental, physical, spiritual and vibrating *'Siamese Friends'*. That's what they were most of the time. No matter how much the other attempted to disguise its thoughts, each always seemed to know instinctively what the other was thinking or doing. They were virtual *'mind readers'*. Some individuals might say that no one can actually *'mind read'* whilst others might seek to prove that they can, probably! It is a common assumption amongst individuals that *'mind-reading'* exists. Often, there are individuals who say, "I know what you're thinking", do they not? Hifle and Pifle believed that the *'mind-reading'* phenomenon is a highly skilled technical ability that transcends generations, race, age, gender, environments, situations, issues or values and beliefs.

In the case of the two brains, Hifle believed he can read Pifle's mind. Its explanation is that, through other means, like paralanguage (including body-language), individuals always state or show what's on their minds. Hifle's argument states that in doing so, individuals, through paralanguage, might be volunteering crucial information that they might have something to hide. Pifle, on the other hand, believes individuals, like those who have become experts at denying or even disguising how they might be feeling, always try to hide what's really on their minds. It sought not to be outdone by its peer brain. Pifle opens the debate to a wider audience. It questions, "what if individuals are able to master disguising or masking paralanguage or body language"?

To settle this argument between them, Hifle and Pifle both referred to the *'Lie Detector Test'* as a form of proof to both their arguments. Pifle's argument in this debate is, "as been *'proven'* on Planet Earth, the *'Lie Detector Test'* isn't an accurate science". This brain states that the test is not 100% conclusive but is based on a set of individual actions or non-actions instead. The two brains agree the function of the *'Lie Detector Test'* is limited to a set of particular patterns. They explain that, during interrogation, under 'controlled conditions', nervous impulses formulate a pattern which is perceived to indicate whether responses from individuals are said to be *'true'* or *'false'*. The *'burden of proof'* rest solely with the frequency of *'peaks'* and *'troughs'* on the polygraph display which is installed by the *'guilt-ridden'*, nervous individuals, assumedly! Hifle believes that the *'Lie Detector Test'*, being accepted as the *'truth machine'* has helped to convict many individuals of crimes that they might not have committed, maybe! It demonstrates that individuals, who believe the *'Lie Detector Test'* to be *'foolproof'*, often submit to its assumed *'efficacy'*.

On the other hand, Pifle said that individuals, who strongly disbelieve the Lie Detector's efficacy, have used a form of mind control to hide the *'truth'*. It thought that this might be done through developing a particular strategic mindset based on individuals not owning their unacceptable behaviours or negatively-charged emotions. They might have been capable of becoming oblivious of them at will, perhaps! Even when guilty, those individuals were more likely not to be convicted of the alleged crimes, sometimes, probably! Hifle and Pifle wondered how others might want to evaluate their own *'values and beliefs'* against their controversial views already cited above or against any other point, issue, situation, environment or relationship that might evolve within the Wik-**ID**-Fiction made up of Fictional Virtual Realities Scenarios © yet to be presented.

Despite their opposite views, brought about by their controversial *'values and beliefs'*, Hifle and Pifle decided to write a Classy, Epic Wik-**ID**-Fiction © Literary Docudrama Movie © made up of Fictional Virtual Realities Scenarios © together. It is about exploring what makes up relationships on a parallel virtual planet. Hifle would supply the *'stereo-hype'* and Pifle the *'stereo-tripe'*. They want to do this in order to develop the often acceptable *'imagery'* impacting those *'programmed'* and *'conditioned'* mindsets of the typical *'politically accepted'*, contrived *'stereo-types'*. These perceived *'imageries'* had more than often been referred to as *'real-to-life'*, relentlessly, perhaps! Hifle and Pifle want their movie to draw attention towards better awareness with regards to the subtlety of deliberate *'programming'* and *'conditioning'* that happens below the radar. Their Classy, Epic Wik-**ID**-Fiction © Literary Docudrama Movie © might tend to focus individual attention as to how specific objective led psychological, superficial goals are set and achieved.

The real challenge for Hifle and Pifle's Classy, Epic Wik-**ID**-Fiction © Literary Docudrama Movie © was whether it would reveal the state of the various categories of relationships, their symptoms, causes, effects and consequences especially but not necessarily exclusively when the basic, meaningful constituents, like trust or quality communication, were absent. The Fictional Virtual Realities Scenarios © would confirm the importance of each quality constituent as singular, invaluable, precise, metaphorical atoms which align themselves seamlessly into the molecular fluidity needed in order to guide relationships towards potential meaningfulness and longevity. These Wik-**ID**-Fiction ©, Fictional Virtual Realities Scenarios © were to be shot on intriguing, tantalising, imaginary, virtual locations but were to be used to expose a variety of situational, environmental, experiential *'real-to-life'* issues that even might appear similar to one's own personal experiences. They might even appear to be emotionally familiar too but might have remained unexplored, somehow! The cast represent a rainbow of colourful characters. They, individually and severally, seem aptly suitable as the *'models'* that fit the *'roles'*, probably!

The literary cameras were focused but record the pleasant as well as bizarre happenings in the foreground as well as background and peripheral features of each scenario of Wik-**ID**-Fiction © creatively described on a virtual planet. It remained parallel to planet Earth in the World of Space. On this parallel virtual planet, called Asteroidia, each of The Royal Royal Dis-United Stately Kingdoms were ruled by figurehead Kings and Queens. They ruled supreme while administration and legislation were carried out by groups called Politicrats. They appeared to be elected by the indigenous population as well as the legal immigrant residents of each Kingdom, seemingly! Conversely, there were squillionaire elitists lobby groups of influence called Poly-tricksters, who deliberately attempted to rig the results of those elections but manipulated populations with impunity. In any event, there was a Most Honourable Prime Leader in each administration.

Hifle and Pifle's Classy, Epic Wik-**ID**-Fiction © Literary Docudrama Movie © made up of Fictional Virtual Realities Scenarios © would be exposed to but directly influenced by adopting the *'values and beliefs'*, *'emotions'* and *'behaviours'* but include the relevant attitudes and mindsets practiced on its parallel planet, Earth. These were being transposed and uploaded to the parallel virtual planet called Asteroidia. The consequences that impact the relationships on Asteroidia would be beamed back to planet Earth. Hifle and Pifle think these reflective exposures of mirrored consequences, from the parallel virtual planet of Asteroidia, might act as a platform from which the greatest model of **'Restorative Learning'** for the *'victims'* of planet Earth can take place. The two brains stressed that there might even be proof that cloning and living someone else's *'emotions'*, *'behaviours'* as well as their *'values and beliefs'* is what inflate egos to become as bloated as the stomachs of those, who purposely overeat at a feast because the food is free. Hifle and Pifle were curious at minimum but intrigued potentially as to what might instigate the attitudes, mindsets and subsequent behaviours that impact relationships on the parallel virtual planet of Asteroidia, perhaps!

To better understand how *'values and beliefs'* help to supersaturate egos, shape attitudes, establish mindsets and produce behaviours which can impact relationships in either a meaningless or meaningful manner, Hifle and Pifle engaged a neutral independent researcher, Professor Walynski, of the Walynski Institute from planet Earth, to establish authentic Research and Reports in order to support the core implications of their Classy, Epic Wik-**ID**-Fiction'©, Literary Docudrama Movie ©. They also invited a Coach/Practitioner, the man they call 'The Professor' as well from planet Earth. His job is self-evident.

As joint authors, Hifle and Pifle would brainstorm alternate Wik-**ID**-Fiction ©, Fictional Virtual Realities Scenarios ©, represented by the chapters in this book, by reading each other's minds, assumedly! They agreed that neither Hifle nor Pifle wanted to devise a standard plot for the scenarios. Instead, they wanted to rely entirely on the potential creativity of their imagination, the contexts of the messages from their intuitions and the autonomic instructions from their instincts. They wrote each scenario as if they were seeing the movie through their own and each other's brains. Both Hifle and Pifle wanted to prove that they are able to read each other's mind also.

This 'Trailer' might have started the process of installing a degree of curiosity, maybe! It remains the audiences' responsibility how intrigued they might choose to become. Each chapter has the potential to test individual interest, focus and concentration beyond where individuals' had been before, probably! The power of suspense might just grip individuals so tightly that they might start to fear that Hifle and Pifles' literary visual mastery make the scenarios seem as *'real-to-life'* as they dare test individuals' imagination.

The two brains might want to inveigle individuals to live their chosen character. They have made it easy to identify the victims but have designed the Wik-**ID**-Fiction ©, Fictional Virtual Realities Scenarios © in such a way that it is easy for individuals not only to share but to live the experiences of the victims as they happen. Hifle and Pifle want individuals to sense what it feels like to be part of the various categories of relationships. They encourage individuals to indulge in practising empathy and are sure that if they have never done so before, individuals will have the strongest emotional pull towards this most important constituent relevant to all categories of relationships. It might feel so magnetic that it is likely to change how one might perceive another after that particular experience. Is it not?

Hifle and Pifle know that it is possible that some individuals might not have the strong resolve it takes to continue this journey from here on in but that it is highly probable that some individuals are at least curious enough to want to experience the first scenario, at least, maybe! They realise that each individual has the freedom to choose to continue the journey in their own time but dare them to put the book down for more than a few moments to regulate their breathing, perhaps! In making Literary Docudrama Movie ©, Hifle and Pifle have seamlessly adorned the chapters with Fictional Virtual Realities Scenarios © in this book entitled, 'The Taste of Champagne Urge' and 'Wik-**ID**-Fiction' ©. They agreed this was a huge Project and as such require independent observers to experience the magic of creation and the power of influence of these Wik-**ID**-Fiction ©, Fictional Virtual Realities Scenarios ©. Pifle agreed he'd be better at *'Producing'* the Classic, Epic Literary Docudrama Movie © while Hifle preferred to *'Direct'* it.

Sitting in the Director's Chair, Hifle was poised with the megaphone at his mouth.

"ACTION"!

The Taste of Champagne Urge!

WIK-ID-FICTION ©

PART ONE

CHAPTER 1

It was a cold January winter's day in a Kingdom called Spaceville. The flurry of acid orange coloured, fluffy, hand shaped flakes of snow had been falling for over four days continuously. Most of the roofs bore the evidence but some had collapsed due to the heavy weight. All the same, the beauty of the snow which had accumulated in the gardens and on the pavements of the streets seemed like Christmas Day in Victorian times on Planet Earth. Through lack of heating, most schools were closed. In their gardens, some children were busy making snowmen. Others threw snowballs at their friends and families who joined in the fun. Where there was an incline, the children used whatever they could to enjoy sliding repeatedly from top to bottom. High Roads and Streets were cleared with huge snowmobiles. This provided better access to commercial as well as private vehicles. The pavements were treated with *'salt'* to enable access by pedestrians. Side streets were not considered as important by local government. Although the golden sun shone, the temperature had dropped rapidly and was now 10 degrees below freezing in Lower Ghettoborough. The snow had turned from its soft slushy appearance into sheets of hardened ice latently but was glassy in appearance. It was difficult to walk on.

Individuals defied gravity but persevered to pace up and down the pavement outside The Cobblestone Arms, the local AADC, Adult Alcoholic Drinking Centre. AADCs were known on the parallel planet, Earth, as Bars or Public Houses. A garden of flowers littered the pavement not only directly outside The Cobblestone Arms AADC but also ran for 30-40 metres in each direction to the left and right of it. The little boy wearing the blue plaid flat cloth cap and strange looking suit was conspicuous to all observers. His suit was made from a horrible blue plaid tweed material. It was far too old in fashion for one so young. The style of the suit reminded onlookers of the infamous Sherlock Holmes. It had flaps at the shoulders that hung peculiarly like the oversized ears of a bloodhound but the shape of the flat cloth cap was more akin to the cartoon character Andy Capp. The crowd both inside and outside the AADC were there to pay tribute to the dead man and his family. There was hardly a hand without a drink. Some raised their glasses but murmured their individual contributions through clenched teeth. The icy cold morning meant that their breath, though being warmed by the liquor, still streamed like smoke from chimneys each time they exhaled. Trails of moisture formed patterns from their nostrils like horses having just finished their arduous morning workout on a comparatively cold morning. Those individuals outside the AADC were the unfortunate ones. They had arrived much too late to join the others in the warmth inside. The mourners were there for the sending off of the hugely popular Earl Stagg. He was a man with a huge reputation amongst the community. There was a buzz of chatter amongst the crowd outside as they busied themselves trying to keep warm. Some huddled together to enable them to do so. Most commented about the influential Earl Stagg. Though not all the conversations were complimentary, most of the mourners stated what they knew of *'The Gaffer'* as they called him. Local traffic on Vanguard High Road had come to a standstill two hours before the AADC opened. Public transport had to be diverted because of the accumulation of extra traffic attending the funeral. Police loitered around

The Cobblestone Arms AADC to ensure there was a pathway for the mourners when they were ready to leave for St Hilary's, the Local Church, where Earl's coffin would eventually be taken. It was positioned inside The Cobblestone Arms AADC, so that mourners and well wishers could show their last respects before the internment at the local cemetery. Individuals were downing booze as if it was a contest for *'The Boozy Book of Records'*. Orders were being shouted but appeared from every part of the AADC, seemingly. "Same again," was the most frequently used form of communication. The sound of the modern tills engaged in repetitively monotone 'bleeps' formed its own type of tempo, rhythm, harmonies and melodies that reminded individuals of *'digital'* Morse Coding in action. The message being funerals were viable business opportunities. Many individuals, men as well as women, had made a conscious decision to become Funeral Directors. This career was becoming even more lucrative than in the past. Independent associates like Florists, Off Licenses, Supermarkets, Banqueting Suites, Churches, Local Authority Halls as well as offices and AADCs like The Cobblestone Arms benefitted and thrived from the fact that someone had died. The oxymoron being that it takes someone to die in order to continue to keep these respective businesses alive, ironically, perhaps! Not only were there more deaths being recorded in the Kingdoms of Asteroidia but that funeral costs had been rising at dramatic levels also. It seemed less expensive to change to a healthier lifestyle in order to promote and maintain what was accepted as *'good health'*. This referred to spiritual as well as mental and physical health. Unfortunately, even though Earl could more than afford to pay for professional expertise in those areas, his embracing alcohol in order to eliminate or dissolve the haunting negative emotions and blockages, that taunted his every waking moments, finally took his life. Alcohol was not the trigger of his negative emotional experiences but it established itself as a *'programmed'* and *'conditioned'* outlet. Earl's cultural acceptance to dealing with challenges by drinking alcohol led to his addiction to the *'legal drug'*. Since he was young, Earl learnt this type of *'programming'* and *'conditioning'* through various promotions via the rigorous marketing campaigns to which he was exposed and had experienced. The strategy used by the marketers was to include *'subliminal conditioning'* through advertisements in movies as well as other resources. These highlighted the immense habitual consumption of alcohol as the typical *'solution'* to everyone's problems. Although this established practice started long before Earl was born, it seems ironic that his frequent imbibing of alcohol, affected his psyche in such a way that it rendered him an extremely highly emotional alcoholic. It is even more ironic that on the day of his funeral his friends, supporters and family were engaging in the same cultural habit that ended his life.

As a businessman, the manager of The Cobblestone Arms, Simon Crabley and others, who ran these establishments like Adult Alcoholic Drinking Centres had no option than to ensure that they profited from the sale of their stock-in-trade. Today, at the funeral of the man, who had given him the opportunity to manage The Cobblestone Arms AADC, Simon was likely to profit hugely from the sale of alcohol. As a conscientious gesture, he gave the food *'gratis'*. Sandwiches, hot sausages and pies were the food provided; compliments of the landlord, Simon Crabley. Individuals nearest to the counter scuffed at the food like gannets on a mound of rubbish. As soon as a platter hit the counter or appeared amongst the crowd, many hands appeared randomly but the food vanished as if by magic. Even in this situation where significant individuals were meant to be there for the same reason; to mourn the loss of *'The Gaffer'*, some openly exposed there propensity towards greed. Those others, who had no possible chance of getting to the counter or near where the trays appeared, shouted their disproval at those who were being inconsiderate. The staff was being kept busy all the time. As they had difficulty making their way through the bodies that filled every square metre of floor-space inside The Cobblestone Arms AADC, the staff placed several trays of food and booze along the length of Earl Stagg's metal coffin. Individuals closer to the coffin could easily access the booze, sandwiches, hot sausages and pies. Observers learnt about the rapid pace and the pressurised conditions under which the staff had to work. Never before had Simon Crabley, the landlord, been as aware of the value of his staff until today. Even though he had hired extra personnel to help him cope, Simon could see that his regular staff needed to be appreciated more in the future. Without their contribution, what might he have done on the busiest day of his career as landlord? It is ironic how such an opportunity had presented itself through the man Simon liked to call *'The Gaffer'*. His funeral was proving even more about the impact Earl was still having on the community. Simon had been the landlord for ten years. He was experienced in dealing with large crowds; especially at weekends when Association Football was being played at the local Earl Stagg Association Football Club Stadium but nothing had prepared him for the crowd that gathered for *'The Gaffer's'* funeral. Simon and his family lived upstairs The Cobblestone Arms AADC. Occasionally, he'd slip away to look through the window at the crowd that gathered outside. It seemed to be growing by the minute.

The portable toilets arranged along Vanguard High Road was an eyesore even though they were necessary but there weren't enough of them. Some male individuals, either through urgency or lack of protocol, chose the side streets to relieve themselves. It was inevitable that the intake of extra fluids was bound to find its way through individual body systems, eventually. The left hand facing side wall of The Cobblestone Arms AADC adjacent to Caviar Street leading from the Harbour-Shark Council Estate to the High Road and the trees nearby were now thoroughly splattered with urine. Even on as cold a day as this the gross stench reeked havoc with many nostrils. The pungent smell was carried by the same icy wind that sent the cold air towards those that gathered outside The Cobblestone Arms AADC. Just as quickly as the warm piss had left the individuals but impacted upon the acid orange coloured icy ground it froze in the inclement temperature.

A glass Carriage with 4 horses attached stood near the bus stop parallel to The Cobblestone Arms AADC on the far side of the High Road. The funeral Staff was all dressed in black penguin-style tailed jackets, white shirts, grey and black pinstriped trousers, black and white shiny patent spats, black silk top hats and white gloves. They were reminiscent of the characters depicted in that historic period more associated with Dickens. The glass Carriage was designed on the same lines as those depicted in western movies of the past. Two huge wheels joined by the well engineered metal cross member underneath attached to springs, supported the glass Carriage and the platform at the front for its driver and companion. The leather seating was deeply buttoned but matched the black painted frame of the Carriage itself. The horses wore black blinkers, jackets with a conspicuous motif and the highly polished leather straps that reined them to the carriage. The two female personnel atop the platform sat dutifully without conversation.

To all observers, their stiff, straight backed posture made them appear inanimate and without feelings. It was as if they were unaffected by the adverse weather conditions even though the wind chill factor had diminished the temperature to nearly 25 degrees below freezing. Significant observers commented about the two women's ability to withstand such torturous climate for such prolonged duration. Occasionally, few flakes of acid orange coloured snow randomly drifted aimlessly down towards the pavement. They fell on top of the sheets of solid acid orange coloured ice already underfoot. Individuals paced up and down as the biting cold wind help send the wind chill factor to 25 degrees below freezing. Some individuals slipped as they stamped their feet but hopped around like the dance around a Totem Pole; often depicted in old Western Movies. Every so often, staff appeared from inside The Cobblestone Arms AADC with platters of food to remind those outside that they were certainly not forgotten. Some individuals were asking the staff for cups of tea. Birdie Spring-Hip, the senior barmaid, rumoured to be Earl's mistress, assured the crowd that she'd arrange for tea to be served; especially for the funeral staff who wasn't allowed to imbibe in the drinking of alcohol. Funeral staff members sitting on the Carriage appeared to be well in need of some hot tea. It was clear that the black coats over their tailed jackets were not enough protection against the inclement weather. "You must be freezing, you poor darlings. I'll get you some tea", Birdie said. They welcomed Birdie's kind offer. "Could kill for a cuppa luv. It's parky, ain it? You wouldn't have a flask, would you", the Carriage driver asked? "Sugar", Birdie queried? "Yes please", the Carriage Driver replied. As Birdie set off towards the entrance of the AADC, some of the crowd outside voiced their opinion about feeling left out of the offer for tea. "What about us", some voices queried? As if waiting for a trigger, they were a flood of requests. This came in the form of chanting like at an Association Football Match. "We want tea . . . we want tea . . . we want tea", they chanted. Only the loud cheering interrupted the chanting. The message was quite clear and their requests echoed and could be heard by residents of the Harbour-Shark Estate that run behind The Cobblestone Arms AADC. Some residents observed that the level of the chanting and shouting sounded similar to match days at the local Stadium. Those that lived adjacent to it suffered not only from the crowd disruption but also from the noise pollution which never seemed to be addressed by the local authority. They argued that the local Stadium was not only a source of attraction for other major businesses to the community but also *"a good little earner"* for local businesses and summary stall holding entrepreneurs as well on match days. On balance, the local stadium was more than appreciated and wholesomely welcomed as a positive influence upon the community. The Stadium was owned by the late Earl Stagg. It provided much needed local jobs and other community facilitations including educational community projects for the young people. Earl Stagg Association Football Club Stadium was an asset that the little boy in the conspicuous Sherlock Holmes suite would someday own, even if he was much too young to appreciate that fact now. Even if they were rushed off their feet on this the busiest period for The Cobblestone Arms AADC, Birdie and her staff would have to meet the requests of the crowd outside. "I'll do my best", Birdie promised. When she returned, there were at least another dozen staff with her. Some had trays with polystyrene cups and some with huge Tea Urns. The crowd gathered round eager to get the hot liquid down their throats in order to get some respite from the biting cold. A separate set of staff attended the Carriage drivers and the police. Each individual appreciated Birdie, her colleagues and landlord, Simon Crabley, for their humane consideration and generosity. Conversations both outside and inside The Cobblestone Arms AADC sounded more like swarms of bees than from humans. Simon, the landlord, rang the bell. It was time to toast Earl Stagg, officially. Birdie stood at the entrance of the AADC but made the announcement over the loud-hailer. There was a lull in conversation both outside and inside The Cobblestone Arms AADC now but the odd voices kept interrupting the silence. Inside, Simon looked round to see, who the culprits might be but there was no way he could tell except for someone snitching on their friends or family members. Simon reminded the attendees that they had a singular purpose for being there and that was to pay tribute to *'The Gaffer'*. He demanded that they remain silent. Birdie relayed the same message from the entrance, via the loud-hailer, to the attendees outside The Cobblestone Arms AADC though her message was not as refined as Simon's. "Ooouuuiii, ooouuuiiii, ooouuuiiii, shush ... shut your gob", Birdie expressed. Eventually, silence was maintained. Simon instructed his staff to inform the crowd outside it was time to get their refills in order to pay tribute to Earl Stagg. When the staff had carried out his instruction about refilling the glasses of the crowd outside, they then turned their attention to the crowd inside The Cobblestone Arms AADC. "I trust everyone glasses are full. I want to drink a toast to *'The Gaffer'*", Simon said. One or two individuals were still in need of refills and they did not hesitate to say so. Simon was patient enough to allow them to have their refills then when there seem to be consensus that each was suitably ready, Simon began his tribute to Earl Stagg. "Just a few words about *'The Gaffer'*, the man who gave me this job ten years ago", he started. "Yeah, good old Earl", the crowd inside chimed. The sound of the crowd inside carried to those outside. They echoed the sentiment even though theirs were slightly delayed. On hearing the delay in the sentiments, Birdie realized that Simon's voice was not being heard by those outside The Cobblestone Arms AADC. She quickly assessed the situation. Birdie retrieved but stretched a microphone towards Simon. "Just a minute" Simon pleaded. The crowd waited silently for Simon to speak again. "I was down on my luck when I first met *'The Gaffer'*. He'd seen me nursing a pint for over an hour. As I looked into the glass of golden liquid, I began to see my situation as desperate. He came over to where I was sitting and said, ". . . you won't find your answers in there will you son"? I was touched that someone had noticed the emptiness in my life. Then he asked me if I wanted to work for him. Of course, I said yes and here I am today still landlord of this Adult Alcoholic Drinking Centre ten years to the day. There must be something significant about the whole thing, don't you think", Simon stated? The crowd roared their confirmation with Simon. He spoke into the microphone again but this time it seemed there was a disconnection. Simon looked towards Birdie but she shrugged her shoulders as if to indicate she didn't know the reason for the break in amplification. Simon looked at his watch but realised he had to carry on with the Tribute with or without the microphone. "Raise your glasses to *'The Gaffer'*. To *'The Gaffer'*", Simon said. "To *'The Gaffer'*", the crowd inside the AADC said. There was a delay once again. Some could not hear Simon's voice at all but depended on the voices of others inside to trigger their individual tribute to Earl Stagg. When they said the words, the delayed voices sounded again like repetitive echoes of the original sounds reverberating from inside The Cobblestone Arms AADC. "To *'The Gaffer'*", the crowd outside repeated. Someone started to sing "For he's a Jolly Good Fellow" and that carried throughout The Cobblestone Arms AADC. Soon the refrain was being echoed by those outside as well. The singing got even a bit more rowdy as the inebriation from the liquor took its toll upon those who'd been drinking since ten o'clock that morning. The roar was as loud as the singing at Earl's local Association Football Stadium on Match days. Soon those inside The Cobblestone Arms AADC began to file out onto the High Road. Earl Stagg's coffin was being carried from The Cobblestone Arms AADC, Lower Ghettoborough. This was to be his last visit. The Pall Bearers carried it with an air of reverence and solemnity. Journalists, TV Media Film Crew, Local and National Press Photographers as well as attendees to the funeral took pictures of the coffin being carried. Many with mobile phones used the video facility as well as took pictures of the garden of floral tributes along the pavement too. Sounds of car engines roared into life as the coffin was being loaded onto the glass Carriage on the far side of the road outside The Cobblestone Arms AADC. Some wreaths and flowers from close family members were arranged quite meticulously on top of the huge white metal coffin. Other floral tributes from other family members and particular close friends were placed to both sides of it. The rest lay where they had been placed together with other tributes like the Earl Stagg Adult and Youth Academy Association Football Club's strips and scarves. Huge pictures of Earl as a young footballer on his own and with his biological father, Raleigh Daly-Weede, thank you cards from the Earl Stagg Association Football Club members and fans as well as lighted candles shielded from the breeze by their containers assembled outside The Cobblestone Arms AADC by the many well wishers.

Brigette, Earl's wife, was ushered from The Cobblestone Arms AADC by two female chaperones. Her head, covered by the black lace veil, hung forward but she looked down towards the ground. Brigette's voice was hoarse from crying but the tears kept pouring down her face. The chaperones walked either side of her; propping her up as if she was unable to walk unsupported. There was another woman, a more matronly figure, who accompanied the 12 years old boy, Duke. His shoulders moved mechanically but his thunderous voice expressed even deeper emotions. His Andy Capp blue plaid flat cloth cap was now askew rather than being straight but the blue tweed plaid Sherlock Holmes suit with the flaps on the shoulders danced according to Duke's movement. All five individuals together entered one of the extra large black stretch limousines that had been provided for family members. Police on horseback started to arrive. There were nine police horses. Each was wearing a letter of the alphabet on the side of the horses; similar to where numbers are worn by horses at an official Race Track. The police arranged their horses in a single file along Vanguard High Road but rode in a line ahead to make a smooth path for the funeral cortege. To observers standing some distance away read the words *'The Gaffer'* spelt out by the nine alphabet letters on the sides of the Police horses.

The Bells at St. Hilary's Church started to chime. It was 12:00 hours precisely. Some of the crowd on the outside started to make their way in the direction of the church that was a mere half a mile east of The Cobblestone Arms AADC. Those others in their vehicles hurried to jockey for position in the funeral cortege. The Band, consisting of 2 x trumpets, 2 x saxophones, a flute, a tuba, 2 x large cymbals and a large bass drum made their way ahead of the two funeral Directors who walked slowly in front of the

Horse and Carriage. The whole procession was a spectacle to behold. While the Band played 'When the Saints Go Marching In' to a Jazzy feel, the solemnity of the two funeral Director's slow march brought to mind scenes from previous observations of slow marching; like trained soldiers attending the funeral of a fallen hero. The slow progress along Vanguard High Road meant that the stretch limousine carrying Duke, his stepmother and their respective chaperones lagged behind patiently. During the drive, the enormity of the carefully arranged funeral impacted further on young Duke, so much so that he broke down. He sobbed uncontrollably. His coarse voice, similar to that of his father's, bellowed but was pitiful to hear. His chaperone tried to console him but Duke resisted her efforts. He reacted badly; shoving her hands away from him but Brigette pointed out what the chaperone had intended. "Duke, she's only trying to console you", Brigette said. Duke looked over towards his stepmother, Brigette, but expressed how he was feeling inside. "Shut your gob. I wish it was you that were dead", Duke shouted. Even the limousine driver was taken aback by the comment. The matronly chaperone shook her head from side to side, indicating how she felt about the boy's comment towards his stepmother. Brigette looked on helplessly. She sensed Duke's sadness at the death of his father but couldn't fathom why he should wish that she was dead. Brigette had been a good stepmother to Duke so far. Still, she resolved that it was Earl, who had spoilt Duke but encouraged him to treat her with such disdain. Brigette recalled the many occasions when she had scolded Duke, how Earl would openly oppose what she'd said in front of him. When she tried to explain to Earl that Duke would grow up confused, he would berate, threaten or even hit her in front of the child. Now, Duke had expressed himself in front of all these witnesses that he wished Brigette was dead. The tears that welled up in her eyes were representative of her emotional state; expressing about how she was feeling inside.

Raleigh Daly-Weede was a huge 6'7" muscular man that seemed to have been a frequent visitor to the gym. He was Earl's biological father. Raleigh and Sheila Stagg were in the limousine in front of Brigette's. Sheila was not Earl's biological mother but he'd grown up believing she was until he was nine years old. It was then that Sheila told Earl the truth about him being *'abandoned'* at birth by his real mother, Myrna Mc Tittle. Earl was found in a cardboard box, placed most strategically just underneath an ATM Machine outside a popular Bank on a very cold January winter's morning when the temperature was some degrees colder than today, the day of his funeral. It seemed a coincidence that he was being buried in extremely similar weather conditions during the month of January. Earl was a typical Capricorn too not only being of a kind hearted nature, generous to those around him but also a power-hungry workaholic, with a heightened sense of obligation and duty, a pillar of society, concerned with being the best whilst having the ability to bringing his plans into fruition. He was vulnerable when Earl thought that he had a weakness. Sheila often pondered about Earl's predicament at those times. She had observed him closely since the day he arrived with her as a baby.

When the Social Workers had called her to say they had a new born baby to foster, both Sheila and her then husband, Count, were delighted. They quickly made arrangements for their new baby. Sheila had had several miscarriages previously but resolved she was not meant to bear children. Instead, she and Count wanted to foster and eventually adopt a child. This was the first stage of their dream come into fruition.

Earl was an exceptionally large but wonderful baby who was welcomed into their home as their own. They fussed about their child in the same way as most parents do with new arrivals. Sheila recalled Earl's booming voice, even when he cried as a baby. She and Count eventually converted from fostering to successfully legally adopting Earl by the time he was two years old. Count went off to war but never came back. It was never confirmed that he was killed but Count was presumed dead while on duty in a foreign land. Earl was then five years old. As a single mother, Sheila found it quite difficult without Count but she continued to love and care for Earl. Shortly after he was told the truth at nine years old about him being *'abandoned'* at birth by his biological mother, Myrna McTittle, Earl became a bully. He threw tantrums at home too but at school other children feared his *'Jekyll and Hyde'* character. Sheila was often called to school to help pacify the angry young boy. Earl kept asking about his biological father too. As a single parent, Sheila found it difficult to cope with his moods and sometimes feared how he might react to further disappointments in life. It was then that Earl was deemed by the Education Authorities to be possibly suffering from more than one condition. These were presumed to be ADHD, Dyslexia and being Bipolar. At least, this rendering of labels pacified the various teachers, who had to bear not only Earl's failure to engage in lessons but also that the assessments established what seemed like *'reasonable explanations'* for his unacceptable behaviours. After Sheila's dedicated search, it was by chance that someone purporting to be Earl's biological father came forward. He was checked out by the authorities involved. After DNA confirmation, the authorities were satisfied that Raleigh Daly-Weede, was Earl's biological father. Sheila asked Earl whether he wanted to meet Raleigh but Earl refused to see him. Raleigh's efforts to contact his son were thwarted over and over again but he never gave up. Eventually, on his 12th birthday, Earl surprised Sheila by asking her to contact Raleigh. He was ready to meet this stranger who claimed to be his biological father. Earl had a list of questions to which he needed answers. He particularly wanted to know why his father permitted Myrna to abandon him. Sheila recalled the day Earl met with Raleigh. She sat without comment with the Social Worker as the two individuals engaged in conversation. Raleigh explained to Earl that the relationship between him and Myrna was a stormy one. She was a naive and inexperienced 19 years old and he was 27 at the time. Earl and Myrna were still going through the *'novelty stage'* of their relationship. Raleigh explained in simple terms to Earl that sometimes individuals felt attracted to each other without consideration about possible consequences. Raleigh told Earl that he was attracted to the slim 6'2" model by her ungainly gait. He related that she was very attractive and that many other men were tripping over themselves to date her. Earl heard how Raleigh and Myrna got on well at the beginning of their relationship but he remained puzzled why Myrna had not told him that she was pregnant. Raleigh explained that he and Myrna did not live together. He visited her two days per week. Generally, they communicated via text, email and phone. On the weekends, when Myrna was not working away, they went out together. It was on one of those occasions that he found that Myrna had moved from the address where he used to visit. Raleigh told Earl that it was sudden and without notification. Apart from the fact that they had had a heated discussion the previous few days about where the relationship was going, he knew of no reason why she hadn't got in touch. As for her moving without notifying him, Raleigh said he was still at a loss as to why she had moved. He had no idea that Myrna was pregnant. Raleigh paused reflectively as he searched his mind for any indicators that he had missed over the years. The only thing that came to mind as the flash-backs arrived to remind him, was that during the row over where the relationship was going Raleigh seemed to remember Myrna demanding that he marry her. Earl asked Raleigh what was his answer to which he replied that he told her it was too soon to think about marriage. It was simply a matter of him not wanting to make that kind of commitment at that time. Raleigh said he was being as honest as he could with his son but it seemed all too much for the young boy. He began to cry and the Social Worker in charge abandoned the visit on that occasion. She deemed that 12 years old Earl was far too stressed to carry on. Raleigh had no choice than to agree but asked whether Earl might see him again. There was no immediate reply from the sad child. Grief-stricken as he was, Earl did sense sincerity in his biological father's voice. All that Sheila could do was be an interested observer. Over time, Earl and Raleigh saw each other more often. In fact, weekend visits became a regular feature in their respective lives. Raleigh was a scrap metal dealer. He took Earl to work with him on Saturdays. Earl was told by Raleigh that he had to earn his pocket money. He enjoyed being with his biological father. On Sundays, Raleigh would go to watch Earl play football with his local team. He bought him new boots often because Earl's feet were growing rapidly. Raleigh and Earl's relationship began to have meaning but he still hated his biological mother for *'abandoning'* him. His behaviour had improved somewhat but Earl started to hate women. By the age of fourteen, Earl and Raleigh's relationship had taken a turn for the better. Earl was learning fast how to be independent. He was learning about grafting and the rewards that were being gained by honest hard work. At seventeen, Earl was an accomplished scrap metal dealer. He then turned to scrapping motor vehicles. When he had saved enough money, Earl bought himself his first second hand Dumper Truck by the time he was 18 years old. He was impressed when Raleigh had told him the following words, "where there's muck, there's money". When Earl was able to run a fleet of Dumper Trucks, he started to invest in Adult Alcoholic Drinking Centres. He bought them but elected to let franchisee run them. Earl owned a total of 10 Adult Alcoholic Drinking Centres. While the franchisee businesses continued to help him accumulate a very healthy financial standing, Earl went on to study Media Studies. He was impressed with how the Media had helped him to find his biological father. Earl learnt to appreciate how his foster and eventually adopted parents had rescued him from a cardboard box. They had given him a home and his name. He had no good feelings or forgiveness for the woman who was his biological mother. Earl still called Sheila mom up until his last breath at 39 years old. Today, a much older Sheila was attending her adopted son's funeral. She thought of Earl as a very brave man indeed. How he had strived to overcome the issues that plagued him. He did this by working all his waking hours or so it seemed. Sadly though, Sheila had to admit that Earl never got over the fact that Myrna had *'abandoned'* him and the manner in which she had done so. It all became too much for him to conquer on his own. Earl even ignored Sheila's advice to seek professional help from those, who had the competency and skills to help him through his problems. Owning the Adult Alcoholic Drinking Centres brought him financial stability but encouraged his drinking habit even more. Sheila saw the son she had rescued turn into a very sad human over the years even though he pretended to those around him that everything was just fine. Even though he refused to accept it, Earl's depression had rendered him an avid workaholic and a chronic alcoholic. When he was drunk he became both verbally and physically abusive. Brigette was the one who paid. She suffered through the many rants and beatings, brought on through the influence of Earl's drunken binges. His emotions were triggered long before the drink passed down his throat but the effect was that she became easy target for the giant Earl. Brigette often lied over and over again to explain her bruises and even broken bones sometimes. Whenever she felt desperate enough to call for help, the community would turn their backs on her in favour of the "kind-hearted" Earl. Through the beatings, Brigette often asked for a reason why Earl chose to treat her in the way he did. She'd get the same answer every time. Silence was Earl's answer to Brigette's questions, always. Privately, she reckoned that he had become mentally deranged through depression but that he was not aware of his emotional insensitivity status. Conversely though, Earl had never laid a finger on Birdie Spring-Hip though he often verbally debased her gender too. Birdie was happy to be a *'kept'* woman so she didn't complain, well not outwardly anyway. Rumour had it that her focus was on what she might gain in kind and financially from the comfortably wealthy Earl. He had spent a small fortune on his green humanoid robotron *'dolly bird'* as he preferred to call her. Earl used to tell Birdie he was attracted to her because she didn't nag like Brigette did, apparently. Theirs were quite a blatant affair. They were often seen together very closely embraced. Earl didn't care whether Brigette knew of his alleged affair with Birdie. She was in one of the limousines behind Brigette's followed by Simon and his family. The thing that worried Brigette more so than her own suffering was how her stepson, Duke, was treating her. He had no respect for her as a person let alone as his stepmother. Earl made sure that Duke knew that Brigette was not his real mother. He had told him repeatedly, "you don't have to take any notice of this wicked witch" as he often referred to Brigette.

Duke's biological mother, Enid Staveley, had met Earl in The Cobblestone Arms AADC but was involved in a *'one night stand'* type of relationship with him. When she told Earl that she was pregnant, he blamed her for not taking precaution. Of course, the truth is that both were so drunk at the time they couldn't remember what had taken place. Even though Earl was determined to support his child, he didn't want Duke to live with Enid Staveley to whom he referred as *"a cheap slut"*. He accused her of having an affair with most of the men in the community. Subsequently, he told her that once she had given birth to their child the affair had to be ended.

Seventeen years old Brigette was Earl's live-in partner at the time. Obviously, she protested when Earl told her about Enid's pregnancy. Brigette objected not only because she felt jealous but also despised and belittled that Earl chose someone else to have his child. Being much younger and less experienced than the 27 years old Earl, Brigette sought out her rival Enid. In a jealous rage, they fought in the Saloon side of The Cobblestone Arms AADC. Despite Earl's cutting comments, Enid thought the more the pregnancy progressed the more he might grow to like her. After all, she was carrying his child. It was a naïve way to view the situation but Enid hoped a relationship might materialise between her and Earl. She was attracted not only to his wealth but also his huge 6'7" physical form. Enid's preference for tall, muscular men was brought on by her insecurities. Earl's *'live in'* partner, Brigette felt she had to stake her claim. On the night of the fight, Brigette got to The Cobblestone Arms AADC early but laid in wait for her similarly naïve rival. After a few rounds of very stiff drinks mixed with her emotional insensitivity towards Enid, Brigette finally got her chance to settle the score. As soon as 23 years old Enid entered The Cobblestone Arms AADC, Brigette started to shout at her. "Oui you . . . bitch . . . leave my man alone. He doesn't want you," Brigette bellowed. Enid shouted back in retaliation to being verbally attacked. "Sez who . . . bitch," Enid retorted? "Sez me . . . slut", Brigette replied. Their voices rose above the general buzz within the AADC but spoilt the friendly ambience that existed prior to the young females' disagreement. Barrage of words went to and fro across the ears of all whom that were present in the Saloon. The language was quite colourful indeed but the accusations flew like arrows from crossbows landing accurately at their respective targets. Some individuals listened but watched without comment while others, who wanted to see the girls fight, egged them on. Brigette walked, somewhat unsteadily, towards Enid but she stood her ground by the door. The Cobblestone Arms AADC was beginning to fill up. Hoards of people streamed through the various entrances into the spacious Saloon. It was *'Karaoke Night'* and many pretend *'Artistes'* hoped to make their voices heard but the sudden distraction had taken even Simon and his staff by surprise. Brigette staggered through the crowd; weaving her way towards where Enid was standing. Being a few years older than Brigette, Enid was confident she could handle the teenager but she wasn't ready for the liquid that flew from the glass Brigette carried in her hand. As soon as the liquid landed on her beautiful outfit, Enid launched her attack. Looking down at the soiled dress, Enid commented. "Look what you done . . . bitch", she exclaimed. There was menace in her eyes as she advanced from her position. Both women met near the south entrance but just inside the door of The Cobblestone Arms AADC. Amid much swearing and flailing arms, the two women began to physically vent their trapped emotions on each other. Shouting and screaming they grappled at each other like wrestlers in a ring. Before long, Brigette got hold of Enid's long brown hair. Her manicured extended nails dug into Enid's scalp. She grabbed Brigette by the throat but shook her violently. They tumbled through the door but fell onto the tarmac just in front of The Cobblestone Arms AADC. Passers-by as well as AADC attendees watched the two women fight. CCTV recorded the unsavoury incident. The two young women fought savagely; sometimes rolling around as if joined together like conjoined twins. Their efforts were more scratching than punching but it was a fight all the same. It was only when Simon, the landlord poured a bucket of ice cold water over them that the women seem to loosen their grip on each other. Heaving heavily, they stood facing each other. Daggers of hate were carefully aimed. It was then that Brigette made a suggestion to Enid. "You'd better get rid of it . . . bitch. I'll fight you again and again until you do. Leave my man alone. Stay away from him", Brigette threatened. "I'm having his baby . . . slut", Enid taunted. The two women continued to throw abuse at each other but both now looked bedraggled like hens with wet feathers caught up in the rain. Enid's long brown hair was just a frizzled mess and very unlike when she first appeared at the Saloon. Brigette's was not dissimilar. Her long black hair flopped over her eyes and made her look like a dishevelled ventriloquist dummy. At that point, Simon felt he had to comment. "Quit fighting girls. I don't think the Gaffer is going to like it when he hears about you fighting in his Adult Alcoholic Drinking Centre", Simon stated.

When news got back to Earl's ears, not only about the fight at The Cobblestone Arms AADC but also about Brigette's statement to Enid about aborting the pregnancy, he made her pay. Memories of his own *'abandonment'* by his biological mother sent Earl into a frenzy. He drank heavily before his brutal attack on his young live-in partner. That night Brigette felt the full force of the emotionally unstable Earl. At one time, Brigette ran from the now deranged Earl but locked herself in the bathroom. Inside, she sat on the floor crying because of the pain she was feeling, both physically and emotionally. She thought about fleeing from his cruel treatment but argued with herself about the other Earl. The kind hearted man that bought her everything she wanted. Her wardrobes were overflowing with the latest fashion clothes and footwear. Her jewels would befit a Jeweller's window display but at times like these Brigette was beginning to wonder if she might be better off in a different type of relationship. Earl's thumping on the door did nothing for Brigette's confidence but at least she knew he couldn't get in to impose the rest of this latest beating any further. This was her bathroom. Earl had his own in the huge five bed-roomed house. Brigette cried until she fell asleep on the Shagpile carpet. On awakening, she had no sense of time but Brigette recognised Earl's voice just outside the bathroom door. He was once again whimpering like a wounded dog; apologising but asking her to forgive his loutish behaviour once again. "I'm sorry my Princess. I don't know what came over me", Earl pleaded. Brigette had heard those words several times before. On previous occasions, she always relented, eventually but this time Brigette decided to ignore Earl's plea. There was a pattern to his behaviour that was beginning to show itself as obvious even to the inexperienced, naive Brigette. Earl kept banging on the door. "Open the door, my sweet. I never set out to hurt you. I must have lost my head. I'll never do that again", he begged. Again, Brigette pretended that she couldn't hear his words but found the courage to stand up. She looked in the huge mirror. There she saw an image of someone she did not recognise. Her swollen face belied her normally thin angular features. She winced at the slightest touch to the swollen areas of her face. Her arms, back and chest ached just as much and by now the bruises were becoming more prominent. Earl had fought her just like he'd have done to a man. He had completely lost control of himself. The pictures in his mind had been pictures of hate, despise, disillusionment and abandonment. Brigette's frail body and mind needed release from such suffering. In a flash she heard herself bellowing at the apologetic Earl. "You're a woman hater . . . you bastard. Why do you bother to have a relationship? I don't just want to be a kept woman. That's just like paying me to be your whore. I want to live with someone who loves me for me. You're like a spoilt kid. You need to go see someone about your problem", Brigette screamed. Earl listened but surmised that Brigette was just upset. He pleaded his apologies once again. "I'll make it up to you, my sweet just you wait and see", Earl begged. "Not this time Earl Stagg. You take me for your bleeding punch bag then you say you're sorry. If you hate me that much why don't you just kill me and get it over with. Yeah, why don't you . . . you bastard. At least you'll be free to go to your slut, Enid. Maybe a *'one-night stand'* relationship is all you're good for and she's more your type. I bet you've never laid a finger on her", Brigette raged. Earl had never heard Brigette speak like that before. It threw him for a brief moment. He was unsure what to do about her defiance. This was a new situation for the bully, Earl. He had got away with it for so long, that he didn't really know how to cope with this new situation. Usually, his women just surrendered to his behaviour but now he had to find a new solution. It bothered him much. Brigette's words had sobered him up a bit. "I said I'm sorry. What more do you want me to say", Earl asked? "Death would be better than being beaten up for your fancy woman. Why don't you just kill me . . . kill me", Brigette screamed. This time there was no response from Earl. Brigette's words had pierced him like a sword. Now he was feeling as if all the wind had been forcefully beaten out of his stomach. Earl looked down at his large hands. He stretched them out in front of him but noticed how vigorously they were shaking. He suddenly felt extremes of alternate hot and cold flushes. His face felt hot but when he touched it with his hands, they were as cold as a corpse. The sweaty palms told him it was time for another strong drink. Earl often drank to mask his emotional feelings. He had *'programmed'* himself to be like the characters in the movies. Earl had come to believe that booze was the answer whenever he needed consoling. Even though he did not know how he came to believe such a philosophy, that message was repeatedly embedded in his psyche. Brigette's determination and defiance was a new chapter in Earl's life. Never before had he been challenged in this way; especially by a woman. Earl demoted women to a lesser status than men. He ignored any characteristics that brought about any new observations of women's abilities and potential to be competent. Earl was blinded to the rise of high achievement by generations of women far and beyond his peer group. To avid psychological observers, Earl's attitude was typical of that which brought about his chauvinistic tendencies. Before Brigette's outburst, no one dared oppose the giant Earl. Whenever he was in an aggressive mode, significant others would not even dare meet his stare yet there were other times when he was likened to being like a big *'teddy bear'*. Earl was perplexed by Brigette's readiness to die rather than continuing to be his longsuffering partner. There was major confusion in his mind. Now that he was being remorseful and apologetic to Brigette, Earl seemed not to be able to see why she couldn't just put the *'quarrel'* behind her. This was new territory for him. He was betwixt and between his despise for Brigette's comment to Enid Staveley about aborting his child. He saw that as a form of *'abandonment'* but felt the longing ness to belong. On the other hand, his conscience reminded him how he chose to treat women with such disregard and dishonour. Earl truly had no idea how to cope with his current situation. Instead, he remained insensitive to Brigette's need but reverted to the type of attitude and behaviour that allowed him to hide beyond resolving the issue at hand. Whenever Earl felt a situation or problem was bigger than him, he turned to the only behaviour that he believed to be appropriate; sulking. Since childhood, Earl had always used this route whenever he couldn't get his way. Neither his loving stepmother, Sheila, his stepfather, Count nor his biological father, Raleigh, ever taught Earl that sulking was not an appropriate behaviour. They often relented to his moods instead of encouraging him to accept that other individuals have to and make choices of their own. Instead of being able to look from different sets of perspectives, Earl simply repeated the *'programmed'* and *'conditioned'* behaviours that were embedded in him. His latest response to Brigette's cry for freedom from his psychological and physical torment was to throw his hands in the air metaphorically but give himself yet another excuse to imbibe in the *'elixir'* which had become his biggest confidant. On some occasions, Earl found this temporary *'cure'* to his emotional problems had long been initiated by a culture of coercion which started when he was at Secondary School. Manufacturers of *'Alcoholic Pop'* drinks inveigled the likes of

Earl to start experimenting with alcohol from quite an early age. Cultural *'values and beliefs'* embedded but reinforced the thought that imbibing was a *'normal'* sort of thing to do. The pressure on adolescents like Earl, to "down the *'thirst-quenching'* amber liquids" or to *'graduate'* to downing *'shots'* of *'spirits'* even are chronicled through clever adverts of one type or another. Earl and others like him followed the acceptable cultural *'programming'* by frequenting Adult Alcoholic Drinking Centres as a socially accepted pastime. At times, he got involved with other forms of *'social drinking'*, like at parties, clubs or raves. Whichever of those options formulated his habit, there is no doubt that Earl became addicted through regular consumption of the *'legal drug'*. He, like so many others, seemed to follow this trend without regard to consequence on individual health or behaviours which impacted on others like the longsuffering Brigette. On other occasions, naïve individuals like Earl learnt through simple everyday *'folklore programming'* which alluded to drinking as *"drowning ones sorrows"*. He was not the initiator of such *'belief'* but instead became yet another victim to it. This he made his own. Brigette's outburst about rather *"being dead"* as a preference to Earl's brutal treatment made him respond in the only way he knew how. With her voice of defiance ringing in his head, Earl decided to stop trying to persuade the ailing Brigette to come out. "You're doing my head in. I'm going for a drink", Earl relented. Brigette heard the giant thudding footsteps going away from the bathroom then she heard the front door slam shut.

At Earl's funeral, those memories flashed through Brigette's mind as she recalled the 12 years of torturous life she had endured under the man everyone else called *'The Gaffer'*. At 29 years old, she saw things from a much different perspective from the naïve 17 years old that was searching for a *'father'* figure at the time she had met Earl. Brigette had allowed herself to be taken into an unstable intimate relationship. Earl and Brigette's relationship moved from 'hope' to *'despair'*. She could see similarities in behaviour in Earl's son, Duke. He repeated his father's mantras like "I hate you" or "I wish you were dead" quite often. The latter statement Duke had repeated earlier in the limousine. Brigette further recalled how much she'd wanted to be a strong parent to the belligerent Duke but Earl always countered her instructions. At every stage, he undermined what steps she had taken to correct Duke's unacceptable behaviours. Earl had *'conditioned'* Duke into believing that Brigette was nothing but a "scrounger".

CHAPTER 2

St. Hilary's Church was now in sight and the huge motorcade including police outriders on motorbikes with flashing blue lights but no sirens. They preceded the mounted police cordon, who rode in a line in order to spell the words *'The Gaffer'* then came the Marching Band. The two Undertakers with their traditional black top hats and tails with canes in their white gloved hands followed them then the four horses and the glass Carriage with Earl's huge white coffin. The limousines carrying Raleigh Daly-Weede and his wife Sheila followed by Brigette and Duke then Simon and Kitty Crabley, Birdie Spring-Hip and the rest of the vehicles that had set off from The Cobblestone Arms AADC. The very impressive procession snaked all the way back along Vanguard

High Road to The Cobblestone Arms AADC and beyond. Those who had chosen to walk the half a mile distance reached the Church before those who were stuck in the dense fleet of traffic. The Vicar, Reverend Sawdust-Pine, his Acolytes and a group of two dozen *'special'* attendees, waited just outside the gate of St. Hilary's Church. Its bells started to toll as soon as the horse drawn glass Carriage, carrying the giant white metal coffin, arrived outside the church. The Police Outriders on horses, the Marching Band and the two Funeral Directors were greeted by the popular Vicar. Sheila Stagg and Raleigh Daly-Weede's stretch limousine arrived first, then Brigette and Duke's, followed by Simon and Kitty Crabley's and Birdie Spring-Hip's immediately after. The Vicar spoke with the Police Outriders. Earl's coffin was retrieved from the glass Carriage. It was quickly taken into the church by some of the staff from Duke Stagg Incorporated, who were acting as Pall Bearers. Sheila Stagg, Raleigh Daly-Weede, Simon Crabley, and the two dozen *'special'* attendees followed. They were oddly dressed in long flowing brilliant white robes with full-faced hoods that completely covered their faces. The hoods were attached but designed with little slits which punctuated the mask. These slits not only facilitated breathing through noses and mouths but also were access for seeing. The other odd feature about the way the *'special attendees'* were dressed is that they all had long white ropes hanging from their waists but to one side which seemed to mimic the images of religious Monks or many versions of the legendary Friar Tuck from the Robin Hood mythology. Only those specially selected individuals were allowed to enter the church at this time. The Vicar and his Acolytes joined those selected individuals inside the church. The police on horseback had now all dismounted from their respective horses but held the reins while they stood to attention. Those on motorbikes dismounted too but entered the church as well. The church bells were significant in that they played a delayed tempo that brought an even more solemn ambience to all those present outside the now locked church doors. There were murmurs and consternation amongst the faithful mourners who had followed the funeral to this point. Some queried why they were being excluded. Others were simply dumbfounded by the unusual procedure. All this time, the cold wind fractured their resolve by the drastic rise of the wind chill. It imposed itself even more so through those that had braved the elements to walk the journey from The Cobblestone Arms AADC to St. Hilary's Church. Some were shivering but seemed as if they had taken a journey to the Swiss Alps or Alaska without winter coats or even a thought of protecting themselves against the extreme environments. Many were ill prepared mentally and physically but were deeply concerned about the icy treatment of not being informed why they were forced to wait around in the cold without explanation. All were beside themselves sharing degrees of intrigue or curiosity about the lack of information for the enforced exclusion, seemingly. Even though he was shielded from the adverse weather conditions by the warmth of the heating inside the limousine, Duke was further mystified why he was excluded from what was taking place inside the church. He raised his query with his matronly chaperone. She found it difficult to explain to the young boy. Duke's chaperone was as baffled as to what reason this part of Earl's funeral was wrapped in such mystery and apparent secrecy. Brigette avoided Duke's question by shifting her attention to her rival, Birdie Spring-Hip in a limousine behind her. She as well as Simon Crabley's wife were similarly befuddled; in their quest to fathom what was going on beyond the closed church doors. Only those inside understood the meaning of the *'ritual'* that was taking place behind closed doors for at least 20 minutes to half an hour. It was only after that period of time that the Vicar, Reverend Sawdust-Pine, re-appeared followed by his Acolytes. They led the procession of family and other mourners into the church. The coffin, now draped with a huge Spacevillean flag, was sited on the stand in front of the Alter. It made Earl's funeral seem like that of a fallen hero although the only war that he had fought was his inability to combat his psychological demons which led him to become a chronic alcoholic. Lost in that ever recurring spiral, Earl never sought nor found closure about the whereabouts of his biological mother, Myrna McTittle. Earl would never know that she too was attending his funeral. The Pipe Organ played while the mourners from various generations filed down the aisles towards the solid oak benches. These long benches with the hand carvings on the sides and the top of the backs were equally spaced in parallel rows. They started from just in front of the Alter on either side of the black and white mosaic designed highly polished marbled centre aisle but extended towards the back of the enormous church. It was approximately 75 yards in length and about 50 yards wide. From inside, the dome-like ceiling seemed to be reaching towards the sky, with nude cherubic paintings of Angels of which the artist Michael Angelo might be proud. Every seat was occupied. Some individuals without seats stood in the space between the last row of benches and the back wall of the church. Others stood in the side aisles nearer the inner walls of the church. From the outside, St Hilary's Church seemed quite a size but it didn't seem big enough to accommodate Earl's faithful followers. Because of the huge crowd, it meant that some individuals stood either immediately in the churchyard or in the street just outside the church. Inside, Vicar Sawdust-Pine spoke into the microphone but explained how the Service was to be conducted. His voice highlighted the rich resonance accomplished by the clarity of the acoustics in this vast space. All attendees were referred to the Programmes that were handed out by the volunteers. The sound of the Pipe Organ was quite engaging; especially to those who were not frequent church attendees. The short woman in the sandy coloured pill-box hat, with the plume of purple feathers looking something akin to a small version of a bird's nest resting precariously to one side of her head, looked from the back of the church. She was looking to see from whence the sound had come. The young boy next to her bore a very uncanny resemblance in height and features to young Duke. None of the mourners seemed to have noticed. Most were engrossed by the funeral proceedings. Like some others, the tall slim older woman with the black wide rimmed hat and the black mesh veil that hung just over the front rim wore a trendy black satin coat. She looked everyway like a model. The woman seemed to be preoccupied not only with surveying the paintings of Angels on the dome-like ceiling but those other images like the crucifix with the statute of Jesus Christi hanging from the cross. The lead-lined multi-coloured stained glass windows, the large and small lighted candles in gilt holders together with freshly cut flowers decorated the adjacent areas but supplemented the adornment of the magnificent building. These features added to the sombre ambience associated with funerals. Vicar Sawdust-Pine waited for the organ to finish the refrain before he began to speak. His Acolytes stood with solemn looks upon their faces. "In the name of the Father . . ." the Vicar started. ". . . the Son and the Holy Ghost", the congregation helped him complete the words. The Vicar, his Acolytes and the congregation made the *'Sign of the Cross'* upon themselves as the words were being said. To the observer, it was strange how individuals collectively started the *'Sign of the Cross'*; using their hands to touch their foreheads first followed by the touching of their bellies then from one shoulder to the other. Some people crossed themselves from right to left whilst others went from left to right. No one seemed to notice or if they did made no argument about the indifference in the patterning. The discrepancy appeared to be less important than that individuals considered themselves *'blessed'* whenever they made the sign of the cross upon themselves. "We are gathered here today because of the passing of our dearly beloved Earl Stagg. His work on this earth is over. He can do no more here. *'The Gaffer'*, as we come to refer to him endearingly, has passed on from this physical to another world. Earl heard the sound of the trumpets. May his soul rest in peace! Earl's now with the angels doing God's work. Let us pray for the repose of his soul", the Vicar stated. His words were delivered with such genuine solemnity but impacted grossly on the congregation. Duke bowed his head but sobbed silently at first. When he couldn't hold back the emotions of how saddened he was by his father's passing, Duke started to bellow uncontrollably. His coarse voice was very much like Earl's, only not yet as deep as his father's but it tested the acoustics of the high dome-like ceiling. The other boy, Duke's look-alike, standing next to the woman with the crooked sandy coloured *'bird-nest'* hat with the plume of purple feathers, sobbed then bawled in unison with Duke. It was uncanny how his voice was comparatively as deep as Duke's. Some individuals adjacent to the boy noticed but didn't think it bore any particular significance. The woman with the sandy coloured *'bird-nest'* pill-box hat with the plume of purple feathers comforted the boy as best she could. Her name was Enid Staveley. She's the young woman with whom Earl Stagg had had the *'one night stand'* relationship. The name of the boy whom she comforted was Baron. He was Duke's twin brother.

Enid Staveley had managed to keep the secret of the second child from Earl. She never told him about her discovery when she had been informed at the pre-natal scan. He was expecting only one child so Enid played along with his perception of her bearing a singular child. From birth, Enid had noticed that there were some similarities in looks of the two babies but there was evidence of differences also. She had noticed that Baron had some features more like her while Duke appeared facially to be a carbon copy of his father, Earl. As he had demanded, Enid had to hand over the child at birth. With Earl's influence, Enid knew she wouldn't have won any case for parental custody; especially in the local Court against such a powerbroker in the community. Although it wrenched her heart to give up one of her children, Enid Staveley managed to outmanoeuvre the great Earl Stagg. She moved but distanced herself away from Lower Ghettoborough in which Earl, *'The Gaffer'*, not only lived but was of great influence. Baron was born twenty minutes after Duke, apparently. Inside the church, Enid put her arms around Baron but whispered words of assurance in his ear. It was likely that she might become conspicuous to any that might have known her all those years ago but her identity was shielded by the huge frame of the dark glasses she was wearing. Her only fear was that significant others might notice the resemblance between Duke and Baron. They now looked identically the same. It was a chance she was prepared to take but Enid made sure that she stayed towards the back of the church. Strategically, she had chances of exiting before Brigette, who was positioned at the front, would have the opportunity to notice or identify her. Enid came to witness the burial of the man, who had raped her on that memorable night, made her pregnant then slandered her by referring to her as just a *"cheap slut"*. Earl did that just to save face among his worshippers. That night Enid had agreed to have a drink with the well sought after Earl in the Motel above The Cobblestone Arms AADC. Everything was going well. They laughed and drank champagne until the early hours of the morning. Earl said he had had too much to drink but didn't want to chance driving home in that state. Enid was young, naïve and innocent but agreed to spend the night with him. She remembered staggering from the settee placed at the far side of the room, where they were frolicking, towards the king-sized bed. The next thing Enid recalled was that Earl forcefully tried to remove her dress. His clumsy effort resulted in him ripping the dress from her thin body. She struggled to stop or tame the wild rage that seemed to have erupted within him on that night. Enid cried as Earl slapped her face again and again. The heavy blows brought not only her screams from the pain but also her desperate cries of rape. These were drowned out by the noise from the bizarre music of the Rock Band, *'The Mind Benders'*. They were performing below in The Cobblestone Arms AADC at the time. Enid protested as vigorously as she was able but was no match for Earl's powerful grip which was like a vice tightening around her slender frame. From her position, Enid watched helplessly but noticed the huge downpour of sweat that dripped consistently onto her from Earl's now swarthy body. His face wore contortions that befit a horror mask and he smelt like he had pissed himself some while before his vicious onslaught. In his effort to kiss Enid, the odour from his body and cigarette breath became even more stifling as Earl pressed his face towards hers. She managed to mumble that she was on her menstrual cycle but Earl ignored her, snarling like a vicious angry rabid bloodhound that had finally caught up with its prey. He pushed her roughly onto the king-sized bed, trapped her under his huge frame then savaged her most ruthlessly like a man possessed with a mission to relieve Enid of some bewitching sexual evil buried deep within her that needed to be exorcised in order to make her pure. This punishing ritualistic fantasy drove Earl into a schizophrenic act that seemed to satisfy his desire to fulfil his *'purpose'* of purging Enid of some perceived impurities. She was a virgin but found Earl's bullying approach more than just intimidating. Every thrust from his waist had intentions to cause damage and pain rather than to send messages of ecstasy. Earl kept saying the words *"bitch"* and *"slut"* while he treated Enid as the cheap whore he imagined her to be. She responded by writhing from the pain but Earl was in no mood for mercy. The vibrations of hate that he had for women manifested grossly as he repeatedly raped her throughout the time Enid was imprisoned in that room. Her tears were only a shallow representation of the hurt, suffering and shame that overcame the naïve young woman. Enid didn't deserve the reputation Earl had managed to spread about her in the community either. Now, in the church, as she looked on from the distance, Enid was experiencing the flashbacks that happened nearly thirteen years ago. She shook her head vigorously in an attempt to shift the memories from her mind but to no avail. Her only sense of relief was to be here at St Hilary's to witness the funeral of the man everyone in the community knew as *'The Gaffer'*.

Around the church, several others were affected by the sound of young Duke's sorrowful outburst and before long his crying had triggered a whole chain of emotions welled up inside other individuals. Some were crying because they genuinely missed Earl's presence but none more so than Birdie Spring-Hip. She let out a very high pitched wail before fainting; falling dramatically onto the highly polished mosaic tiled floor. Her effort was so blatantly alike an Association Football player diving deliberately in order to gain attention from the referee and all others who had borne witness. There was general consternation but Brigette was not fooled by Birdie's act. Some others rushed to her side but helped Birdie to her feet. Raleigh Daly-Weede stood next to Sheila Stagg but supported her as she, affected by the loss of her adopted son, broke down and started to weep too. The Vicar being used to conducting funerals observed the wailing and weeping but signalled for the Organist to start playing. After eight bars the Vicar signalled for the Organist to stop playing. The mourners wiped the tears from their respective faces but listened then joined in the prayers prompted by the Reverend Sawdust-Pine. "Let us read the 23rd Psalms. The Lord is my Sheppard . . . ." the Vicar started. "He leadeth me beside the still waters. He restoreth my soul . . . ," the congregation: replied. The prayer carried to the end of that particular Psalm. Brigette seemed to be inspired by that Psalm more so than the others. Her voice was most distinct amongst the rest of the congregation's; especially when it came to the part that said, "forgive those who trespass against us". Duke looked up at her. His expression bore the cynicism he was feeling inwardly towards the woman who took the place of his biological mother. He had heard Brigette saying that particular Psalm many times before but had no idea why it seemed to mean so much to her. On this occasion in particular, the 23rd Psalm rendered more comfort to the often distraught Brigette than anyone present could possibly imagine or understand. Reverend Sawdust-Pine now gave his own tribute to the popular Earl Stagg. "As Vicar of St. Hilary's, I must say that our dearly beloved Earl is a shining example of a man, who had contributed generously to our community; especially to this church. I have no idea what we would have done without his more than unselfish contributions. Let no man say a bad word about *'The Gaffer'* for the wrath of damnation might be what is reaped. We shall miss him dearly but I'm sure God will instruct his family to continue to support us in the future", the Vicar stated. He then asked that Eulogies be read by Earl's adopted mother Sheila, his biological father, Raleigh Daly-Weede and 12 years old son, Duke. Sheila was accompanied by her two chaperones. They supported the 72 year old Sheila on her way towards the Alter. She walked slowly. Sheila paused but bowed as she passed the coffin then her shoulders did that shrug which meant that she had voluntarily or otherwise began to release her innermost feelings in the form of crying. It was pitiful to watch an old lady break into such sorrowful behaviour. Her memory of the once abandoned child was just too much for the caring mother. Sheila was being comforted by her two chaperones. One whispered to her that she didn't have to say anything if she didn't feel like talking but Sheila was determined to speak to the fellow mourners. Eventually, she stood in front of the microphone that was already in place. Out of respect, the crowd both, inside and outside the church remained silent. Not even the babies made a sound. Sheila cleared her throat but began to speak. Her croaky voice told of her deep feeling of loss of the only child she had adopted. Her words were poignant and deliberate in their inflections. Sheila described the beginning and the end of her physical association with the man everyone knew as *'The Gaffer'*. Everyone heard not only of Earl's progress but also of his weaknesses as well. They heard too of his lifelong search for his biological mother, Myrna Mc Tittle, the young girl, who had abandoned him on a very cold winter's January morning 39 years ago. Sheila told of Earl's bipolar condition too and how, had it not been for Raleigh Daly-Weede, Earl's biological father, she hated to think whether Earl would have turned out to be the man they all knew and admired. "It must have been hard for Earl to control his feelings of being *'unwanted'* at birth. Whenever he had one of his turns, it was up to me to remind him that some children were even less fortunate than him. Some had been aborted at different stages because they were not wanted for one reason or another. That use to make him think a bit more positive about his mother carrying him for nine months but then he became confused as to why she would do that then *'abandon'* him. Even though she had left him on the High Street, Myrna had made sure she left him where he could be found quickly. I don't want to blame her because Myrna had her own reasons for doing what she did. In some way, although I feel fortunate to have had Earl as my son, I don't know what it feels like to have to make such a decision. Myrna Mc Tittle had wrapped him well in blankets but lined the cardboard box with enough newspaper and foil. She even provided a fleece for him to lie on. We must acknowledge that Myrna sought to offer some form of protection from the biting -15 degree temperature. I told Earl often that she might have felt insecure at the time. Even though he didn't want to accept her, Myrna probably thought she was doing the best thing for him at the time. The police did receive an anonymous call from a woman on a cell phone but the number was withheld," Sheila said. She paused. The crowd gasped as one. None of them had any idea of Earl's predicament as a baby. Even the Reverend Sawdust-Pine choked but developed a temporary coughing fit for a few minutes. Some other individuals found tears running down their faces while Sheila uncovered the mystery behind Earl's sometimes irrational behaviour. Duke was the most guttural in his sad lamentations. He was discovering the value of Brigette's caring but he still held his thoughts about her wanting his dad's money. Sheila had lost her croaky voice but now spoke with a greater air of authority. She looked at the Reverend Sawdust-Pine as if for approval for continuing her story of the life of her stepson, Earl. Reverend Sawdust-Pine gave his approval by nodding his head. He too was being educated and was more understanding of Earl's tremendous generosity. Sheila felt great relief by telling the story. Just before she continued her tribute, the sound of a mobile phone interrupted the silence. The Reverend Sawdust-Pine quickly denounced the interruption as "... a disrespect to *'The Gaffer'* ". The phone rang three or four times before he acknowledged the pulsating vibrations in his trouser pocket. They alerted him that it was his cellular phone that had interrupted Sheila's tribute. He looked flushed in the face from the embarrassment. Reverend Sawdust-Pine stared straight ahead but reached under his Cassock to silence the ringing. "I assured Earl that my late husband, Count, and I were always there for him. When Count did not return from war, he was presumed killed in action. Earl began to show his *'Jekyll and Hyde'* side of again. I viewed it was likely that Earl was feeling *'abandoned'* yet again, possibly. He was very young then but I remember that he displayed the symptoms of an individual suffering from very low esteem. At one time, Earl expressed that he didn't feel it was worth living. He said he felt scorned by his biological parents. It was then that I had the idea of using the printed Media to help in the search for Earl's biological parents. The campaign ran for several months and then there was a response. It was a very successful campaign. The printed

Media did a splendid job of work. They were very supportive and seemed genuine in their undertaking. Some of those are here today. We thank you for your sterling work", Sheila continued. She paused. Sheila looked towards Reverend Sawdust-Pine yet again for approval to carry on. He nodded his approval. This time Sheila made a very huge sigh before she continued. "When Raleigh first made contact with Earl, it wasn't the most pleasant situation for either of them but eventually Earl began to take to Raleigh. I guess he was pleased that Raleigh had made such an effort to find him. When Raleigh and I got married, Earl began to develop his potential for business and as you all know he was a talented man. His success has been due to applying himself for many long hours. I feel Earl would have wanted me to tell you all what he dared not. He wouldn't have wanted nor appreciated your sympathy but I'm absolutely certain he would accept your empathy", Sheila ended. The congregation was enthralled by the revelations that unfolded about *'The Gaffer'*. There was great applause for the old lady who had been the backbone of Earl's upbringing. The crowd continued to applaud for at least five minutes. Raleigh Daly-Weede was the next individual to speak. As he looked around the packed church, Raleigh saw a face that seemed familiar but he couldn't place where he had seen the face before. It was the tall woman who stood towards the back of the church. Raleigh had no idea why this particular woman stood out amongst the many faces that looked back at him but he had a feeling that he had met her before. He hesitated before he delivered his comments about his only child. Raleigh told the crowd that he was proud of the work Sheila and her previous husband, Count, had done for his biological son before he had made contact with him. Raleigh told them he enjoyed the times he and Earl spent together and how much he'd miss him. He said he wanted to openly apologise to his son for the *'abandonment'* by his biological mother, Myrna. Sheila was chaperoned to her seat at the front of the church. Raleigh followed behind her. It was Duke's turn to speak. His matronly chaperone stood just behind him. Duke's husky voice boomed throughout the church. Even the crowd outside the church were being deafened by his *'matured'* voice. "I miss my dad", Duke said. He could not hold back how much he was missing Earl. Duke broke down but bawled as loudly as he could over the microphone. His chaperone tried to comfort him but this only seemed to fuel his feelings of remorse. The chaperone led a broken Duke to his seat in the front row. Twelve years old Duke was inconsolable. The Reverend Sawdust-Pine rose from his seat but spoke briefly to the congregation. "I'm afraid there's just time for a few more brief comments before we have to move to another part of the Service. If any other family members or close friends have anything to say, please be brief", Reverend Sawdust-Pine warned. Birdie Spring-Hip rose but made her way towards the microphone. She spoke passionately about Earl's generosity. Birdie was followed by Simon and his appreciation to Earl for helping him out when he was down. It was more or less the same speech he'd made inside The Cobblestone Arms AADC. The police was the next to express their acknowledgement of the generous contributions that Earl had made to the *'Special Police Fund'* he had set up for them. This he had done to show his appreciation for their constant monitoring of his AADCs; especially The Cobblestone Arms where most of them spent their *'off-duty'* time. The police spoke highly of the man even they called *'The Gaffer'*. Austin Panachè, Earl's Deputy, of Duke Stagg Incorporated, Grandmeadows, Outer Suburbia, spoke on behalf of the Company. He told of Earl's genius as a businessman. "When Earl told me of all the labels that had been thrusted upon him by individual teachers/tutors at every level of his education, I began to seriously question what those individuals had hoped to achieve by telling him he was a Dyslexic or was ADHD. Yes, there were certain things Earl found difficult to grasp but don't we all? Well, at least, until someone find a way of helping us to better understand, perhaps! I've learnt today of the many unfortunate circumstances that Earl faced, not least as a young boy. It can't have been easy for him but he was determined to use the resources that worked for him. I am happy to have worked with a genius", Austin Panachè finished. There were murmured acknowledgements throughout the congregation. "Let us sing Hymn number 146, Faith of Our Fathers", Reverend Sawdust-Pine instructed. He signalled for the organist to begin. The Choir stood on the upper tier at the back of the Church. They listened to the sweet sound of the Pipe Organ then began "Faith of our fathers living still . . .". The congregation followed. It was quite a robust contribution for those, who knew the Hymn but for those that didn't they hummed along to the melodic phrases of the Pipe Organ. At the end of the Hymn, the Reverend Sawdust-Pine chanted some words in Latin. The Acolytes dressed in their red and white Cassocks added value to the Requiem Mass by responding in Latin at appropriate times to the chants of Reverend Sawdust-Pine. "Dominus Vobiscum", Reverend Sawdust-Pine chanted. "Et cum spiritum tuo", Acolytes responded. There followed a volley of Latin verses followed by many signs of the cross. The Acolytes genuflected in front of the statues and the alter but carried out what appeared to be some sequences that had their own meaning and history that was clearly more commonplace in a more recent past. Although most of the congregation did not understand the meaning of the Latin words, it made the Mass seem above ordinary and this was the purpose of this special older version of Funeral Service. Soon it was time for another Hymn. The Pipe Organ engaged once again and the Choir and those in the congregation that recognised the air either sung or hummed to the melodies again. The Service had been going for nearly two hours when the Reverend Sawdust-Pine announced that it was time for everyone, who wanted to pay their last tribute to 'The Gaffer' could do so in an orderly manner. He defined how and from which direction individuals approached and exited from the coffin; for one last look at Earl Stagg, 'The Gaffer'. When he had demonstrated his leadership in this area, Reverend Sawdust-Pine told the congregation that a collection was being held just before the coffin was to be opened. The Ushers utilized the centre aisle only to supervise the collection effectively. They passed the slotted wooden handled 'carpet-bags' amongst the congregation for their respective contributions. Reverend Sawdust-Pine encouraged individuals to "give generously". Another Hymn was being meted out by the Pipe Organist, the Choir and those in the congregation who felt able joined in. The Funeral Directors, both with canes, their assistants and the two women drivers of the horse-driven black framed glass Carriage were all dressed alike in the same type of uniform; consisting of grey trousers with black pinstripes, white shirts with black bowties, a black jacket cut above the waist but shaped at the front. At the back of each jacket the tails continued to just below the calves. Each had a collar and two huge buttons above the waist at the back. They all wore black silk top hats and black and white Spats. The Undertakers' assistants acknowledged the permission from the Reverend Sawdust-Pine to open the coffin. They removed the lid to reveal the lifeless body of 'The Gaffer'. Earl's immediate family were the first to be invited to view his body. Apart from his head which rested on the tiny pillow, Earl lay on the white quilted, silky, frilly padded interior of the large white metal coffin. In it, Earl seemed so relaxed and serene much unlike when he was alive. It appeared that, in this state, he had found solace with the many negative emotions and their respective blocks that used to visit themselves upon his hypersensitive over-busy mind. Those negative emotions and their relevant blocks that had blighted his overgenerous spirit, tormented his ailing soul, ignored his cry for freedom from confusion, wrestled with his psyche about his stinking attitude and loaded argument against every female being unworthy of the privilege of bearing a child, inveigled his mentality towards insanity but denied Earl a pathway towards happiness. It was a state of mind he had never experienced. Earl had built an exterior world of being the people's champion but his inner world suffered enormously as he was haunted by feelings of rejection, blame, denial, guilt and abandonment. Due to his monochrome way of thinking, Earl struggled to gain the clarity he sought so desperately. It was this web of confusion that kept Earl in the *'stuck state'* of extremes in which he'd been trapped. The relationship with himself was stymied by Earl's ownership of his negative ego which resulted in activating the negative thoughts and damaging cellular memories that sapped his appetite for seeking closure. Earl failed to resolve the indelible images which he'd conjured up of his biological mother. Since young, he had made the decision not to see from any other perspective. Earl focused so much on feelings of abandonment, rejection and blame that he failed to accept that his biological mother had made a decision to pass on her responsibility as a parent, unselfishly. Her methodology was rather crude, desperate and primitive in context but Earl would never know about how pure his biological mother's intentions had been. She sought to bring attention to not only herself but for the plight of mothers anywhere in the World of Space, who found themselves the victims of not only the unsupportive fathers in one context but also the irresponsible ones in another; as in her particular case. Though it wasn't her intention, Earl's biological mother managed to expose the once irresponsible Raleigh Daly-Weede towards becoming the supportive father he had turned out to be. Sheila Stagg and her husband Count had willingly accepted the giant baby Earl but welcomed him into their lives. Now, inside the walls of St Hilary's Church, Sheila, her chaperones, Earl's biological father, Raleigh Daly-Weede and Duke with his matronly chaperone were the first to view Earl's body. Duke was the first to let out the bone-chilling cry, next was the deeper baritone voice of Raleigh Daly-Weede then Sheila with her coarse throaty voice. They sounded more like Tarzan and a herd of wounded elephants being injured by poachers. The cacophony resonated so much that the vibrations caused the metal coffin to rattle against the metal stand on which it rested. The quality of the acoustics carried the sounds around the entire church but bounced itself through the open Exit door onto the ears of the mourners waiting outside in the freezing cold temperature. They too were triggered. On hearing the initial sorrowful wailing exclamations and the subsequent choruses, of the congregation inside the church, the mourners outside began to engage in the overwhelming laments. Tears were flowing down their respective faces too but not only those caused by the cold biting wind. They waited their turn patiently then began to file into the church past the rigor mortised body of *'The Gaffer'* in the coffin.

As Myrna Mc Tittle looked on at the mourners, she couldn't help but notice that the sobbing made some individuals seemed like rag-dolls being manoeuvred by puppeteers. Their body language choreographed by the movements of their rapidly shrugging shoulders emphasised their inner feelings but projected an ambience of sadness that befitted the mourning crowd. Earl's family lingered at the coffin gazing almost unbelievably at him as he lay there quite impassive to his normal active self when he was alive. They were amazed how much darker his skin had become. The skin under Earl's fingers and toenails were almost black in colour compared to his fairish skin. There was cause for consternation but each observer concentrated on mourning for 'The Gaffer'. Even Raleigh, who had before today seemed almost impervious to tears, sobbed uncontrollably. The chaperones waited for their respective charges before leading them away down the aisle, out of the church but into their respective limousines. Duke kept crying all the way to the limousine. All the people watching empathised with his feelings. Brigette was the only individual that chose not to view Earl in the coffin. She was crying too but was unable to distinguish between the reasons for her tears. Although one can imagine her sadness, none can tell whether Brigette's tears were for Earl's demise or were they tears of joyous relief, perhaps! It might well have been the realization that now Brigette had finally been freed from experiencing the brutal beatings she used to suffer at the hands of the 6'7" giant who used to be her partner. Brigette recalled more bitterness than happiness in their relationship. The Pipe Organ played solo without the Choir as the rest of the congregation, including those who spent the entire Funeral Service in the courtyard of St Hilary's Church and on the street just outside it continued to file past the coffin; each having a last glimpse at the man they called 'The Gaffer'.

CHAPTER 3

As the individuals in the funeral cortege readied themselves to continue the final part of the carefully arranged funeral, the Police Outriders preceded the Marching Band. It struck up another rendition of songs appropriately chosen to represent Earl Stagg, the local hero. They were followed by the two Funeral Directors with the canes, who marched in front of the horse-drawn glass Carriage. Even the horses strutted as previously drilled in 'slow marching'. Their knees rose with precision in unison. The stretch limousines with family members and close associates followed behind; then came the fleet from Duke Stagg Incorporated and the members of the community. Observers along the route noted the hugely spectacular funeral as the cortege proceeded towards St Hilary's Cemetery. It was within three miles of St Hilary's Church. Local traffic was diverted away from the route of the funeral. The odd motorist that chanced interrupting the flow paid dearly. Traffic police took up strategic positions along the route to the cemetery. They intervened whenever a rogue motorist or cyclist dared to defy the imposed detour. The smooth execution of Earl's funeral was the priority and all involved in its preparation remained loyal in their efforts. The Marching Band paused outside the gate of St Hilary's Cemetery just before entering. Police Outriders and those on horses arrived prior to the Marching Band but remained motionless. Ten other fully uniformed police on foot positioned themselves just inside the gates. They split into two groups; evenly spaced on either side of the entrance inside the cemetery. The Band remained outside but began to strike up a very solemn version of *'When the Saints go marching in'*. This time the two Funeral Directors with canes performed the *'Slow March'* ahead of the Police Outriders through the gate that led into the cemetery. As the horse drawn glass Carriage entered through the gates, both groups of evenly spaced police on foot either side of the narrow entrance, saluted *'The Gaffer'* on the final leg of his journey. The stretch limousines turned into the cemetery. Sheila had to console Raleigh. He was now a completely broken man. Raleigh shook as years of welled up emotions voluntarily moved him into this weakened state. For years, Raleigh had wished to apologise to Earl for his inability to fully explain the mystery that his son so much wanted to resolve within his own mind. Raleigh realized that though he had intended to, he had never apologised for his initial absence nor did he ever tell Earl that he loved him. Now, it seemed that it was too late. This reality brought on by Raleigh's conscience was playing on his mind. Sheila was rather taken aback by Raleigh's demeanour but felt that she needed to be strong to support him.

Duke was in the stretch limousine just behind Raleigh and Sheila's. Being his first attendance to a funeral, he looked around anxiously, wondering what might happen next. As he looked around at the graves, Duke noticed some with tombstones, some without, some that appeared freshly dug, others that seemed to be more ancient and in disrepair. Duke felt fear for the first time. He looked to Brigette for help. She hugged him close but embraced him. Brigette felt Duke trembling. He felt as if he was shivering from the biting cold outside but the heating inside the limousine was almost unbearably hot like being in a Sauna on a tropical island at noon. The blood had drained away from Duke's now ashen face which expressed the extent of his fears. His chaperone was oblivious to him as Duke sought the motherly comfort from the woman he despised.

The Reverend Sawdust-Pine and his Acolytes in their Cassocks dared the cold wind but headed the procession towards the Mausoleum where Earl was to be entombed. It was a huge chamber, a stately tomb, the final resting place for Kings of old. There were no expenses spared. The contributions for the funeral came by way of the local community collection arranged by Simon Crabley, the manager of The Cobblestone Arms AADC, the generous donations from Duke Stagg Incorporated as well as the Fraternity to which Earl belonged. *'The Gaffer'* was to be immortalised by those who thought of him as deserving of the very best available, even though he was dead. The Reverend Sawdust-Pine, his Acolytes, the special attendees in the white gowns with the hoods, the police, Sheila and Raleigh Daly-Weede were the chosen ones allowed to get close to the huge tomb at the beginning of the *'rituals'* that took place before the rest of the mourners were able to partake. They witness some quite strange activities which they found impossible to understand. All immediately around the large white coffin especially, the special attendees wearing the hooded white gowns with slits for seeing, breathing and talking only carried out their very *'special rituals'*. After those *'rituals'*, the Reverend Sawdust-Pine led the rest of the mourners into the other part of the service, itself a *'ritual'*, but one with which they could identify. Reverend Sawdust-Pine swung the golden vessel attached to a long gold chain forwards and backwards towards the large white coffin but mumbled even more Latin phrases to which some of the congregation from that church readily responded. The smell of Frankincense and Myrrh escaped through the perfectly drilled holes from the bell-shaped gold receptacle which housed the burning incense. Many hymns were interspersed all the way along this part of the elaborate funeral. Duke was mesmerized by the whole proceedings but seemed in awe at the action of the adults around him. When the woman in wide-brimmed black hat, who appeared to be a model, called his name Duke's attention was temporarily diverted towards his biological grandmother though he was not aware of that fact. The next voice Duke heard made him look round sharply. Baron was speaking to his biological mother, Enid Staveley, the woman with the *'bird-nest'* sandy coloured pill-box hat with the plume of purple feathers. Duke noticed the similarity in tone, inflection, diction and resonance. In fact, the voice sounded so much like his own that he did a *'double take'* at the other individual who had spoken. Both Baron's and Duke's eyes collided in the stupefied transfixed stares that seemed to seamlessly join paths but occupied the same space. In the midst of their sorrow, both Duke and Baron just seemed to know that they were related. Their smiles were enormous as they winked at each other. The boys were now distracted from the sorrowful surroundings. They moved towards each other but slipped away from the attention of those whose responsibilities were even more challenging than it first appeared. Everyone else was caught up in the elaborate and unusual ceremony. Duke and Baron just did what children do when they are bored with adult activities. Their attention span was much shorter than the adults. This meant that the boys found something else to do with their time. Before long they were running around, chasing each other, jumping on and over graves and playing hide and seek behind the tombstones. Their laughter belied the fact that the funeral was meant to reflect solemnity, lament and sorrow. Some of the attendees saw the two boys but accepted that children used every opportunity to play. There was nothing alarming about that fact.

Inside the Mausoleum significant others lavished praises about the *'The Gaffer'*. One of the senior police, the Ghettoborough Superintendent, now addressed the mourners. "We thank *'The Gaffer'* for providing the funds for the various sporting activities for the young people of this community; especially the Boxing Club. Lots of the local boys have found it to be an alternative to alleviating their anger. The crime figures are the lowest they have been since records have been kept. I can honestly say it was because of *'The Gaffer'* and his vision for the community", the Ghettoborough Superintendent closed. What the Superintendent did not say is how she had met *'The Gaffer'*. It might have been self-incriminating if Fifi Izzit was to say she had knowledge of the *'illegal'* dealings by which *'The Gaffer'* was able to afford to donate so heavily towards the *'Police Fund'*. Though he was truly an unselfish individual, *'The Gaffer'* was no saint as the Superintendent and others wanted the community to believe. Earl Stagg, like his father, Raleigh Dalyweede, was an international arms and drug dealer. Raleigh had learnt from his pink Mixed DNA Rainbow Tribe foster father, Sir Walter, how to use genuinely *'legal'* business to trade in *'illegal commodities'*. Such was the intensity of the lure for the taste of Champagne Urge. Many of the vehicles and parts that Earl had dispatched or was in receipt of from around the virtual planet were used as cover for transporting the *'hidden cargo'*. Through using *'creative accounting'*, the *'illegal financial gains'* made from the sale of *'hidden cargoes'* were never shown as *'assets'* on the company's *'Balance Sheet'* in any fiscal year. The company's hugely inflated net profit enabled Earl to *'launder'* the *'booty'* gained from dealing in those *'illegal commodities'*. Earl's situation was more than secure as he had already bought in as a franchisee member of the mighty UFO. Superintendent Fifi Izzit, herself an active member of the UFO but dubbed *'The Drug Czarine'* had personal knowledge on the amount of corruption that had brought *'The Gaffer'* his reputation of benevolence. The trading in *'Legal drugs'*, like alcohol, were not Earl's only commodity by which he had earned the enormous sums he had managed to accumulate. Ghettoborough's green humanoid robotron Superintendent had met Earl through *'Operation Drug Sting'*, in which she had posed as a prostitute. After going to a Hotel with the affable Earl, Fifi found him irresistible. She too was a *'Trophy Man'* *'hunter'*. Earl Stagg fitted Fifi's perception of the legendary *'Trophy Man Image'*, *'Mr Right'* philosophy. Fifi Izzit had a crush on him the moment she had set eyes on Earl's huge muscular frame. They had spent many hours together before she revealed her official occupation to him and her affiliation with the extremely powerful poly-tricksters from the UFO. Earl and Fifi had negotiated a deal which involved several of her colleagues too. She had committed to the relationship but had benefited financially also. Earl had bought Fifi a house and a cottage in Mid-Suburbia, Upborough, as well as showered her with many gifts including diamonds and a brand new top of the range Sports Car. Earl's commitment to contribute to the *'Police Fund'* was more than a *'trade off'* agreed with the vivacious green humanoid robotron 'Drug Czarine'.

After Superintendent Fifi Izzit's speech inside the mausoleum, the local PM, Political Member, stepped forward. She had not long been Politicrat Member for Ghettoborough. Previously, as Councillor, Janette Brayhorne, had been made aware of Earl Stagg's legal contribution to the community. His name was synonymous among all the politicrats from each of the parties in the Borough. Janette Brayhorne superseded Roy Cadish, who had retired a year before the national election. She had started out as an activist many years before but had softened her approach in order to be admitted by her peers. Janette Brayhorne soon learned that she would not be accepted in the *'seat of power'* until she relented to dampen her enthusiasm to radically change the *'values and beliefs'* of the establishment. As a radical, her visions of striving to make *'changes'* were depleted by the powerful *'political machinery'* already in place long before her great, great, great grandparents were born. When she first entered the political arena, Janette had fought against the *'status quo'* but battered herself against an *'immovable mountain'* traditionally steeped in deeply held *'philosophies'* which were most times no longer practicable in modern society. She soon learnt that hers and other modern ideas or approaches were soon recanted then usurped or recycled but adapted as all others before her had experienced. When she finally accepted that there was no possibility to even register a small dent upon the psyche of the *'solidarity'* of like-minded fraternities, Janette Brayhorne was forced to change her stance. She was now much more aware that the fraternities' existence meant recurring political decadence had been foisted, as politics, upon indigenous populations around the entire parallel virtual planet of Asteroidia. Like others before her, who had thought they could genuinely offer reasonable *'alternatives'* to the stone-aged *'one size fits all'* philosophy, Janette Brayhorne realised and acknowledged the nature of the intransient, bureaucratic, divisive ogre which still existed but defied basic logic. It was only then that Janette decided she had to relent. Her new objective was to work for change from within.

With her new her attitude and as PM, Janette Brayhorne, in Earl Stagg's Mausoleum, was proud to be the representative for her Borough. "I've been asked by the Most Honourable Prime Leader's Office to announce that Earl Stagg, the man we all know as *'The Gaffer'*, has been acknowledged by the community for the tremendous work he had put in while he was alive", Janette Brayhorne said. All the people inside the chamber nodded their heads but uttered their concurrence verbally with the PM's statement. There was also a brief interruption by the number of private conversations which had developed. Pointing to the inscription on the inlaid stone on the wall of the chamber which said, "Here lies the body of Sir Earl Stagg, known fondly by his community as *'The Gaffer'*, may he lie in perpetuity—R.I.P". Earl Stagg had been awarded a Knighthood, posthumously. "It's the least the community could do to repay *'The Gaffer'* for his selfless contributions while he was alive", the P.M continued her tribute. Some individuals wanted to be acknowledged important members of the community by their peers, for their contribution towards Earl's Knighthood. Others just patted each other on the back, shook hands or kissed on the cheek to reinforce their admiration for one another; especially those within the fraternity, who were instrumental for bringing the matter into those political chambers that sanctioned but approved Earl's *'deserved'* Knighthood. There was a huge roar within the chamber. Some of the mourners outside the chamber, who still braved the extreme cold January wind chill, heard the tremendous roaring emanating from inside it. They had no idea what was going on inside so they started to talk amongst themselves about the sudden great noise. It was quite an unusual set of events but still they stood shoulder to shoulder to cement their solidarity in honouring *'The Gaffer'*. During this period of communication, Enid noticed that Baron was missing. She looked around her but the child could not be seen. Enid asked the people standing near to her if they had seen him leave but no one had noticed where he'd gone. She began to panic. She did not know where to start looking. The tears started to run down her face as loosing her other son would cause her too much devastation. Most of the people around her busied themselves looking for the little boy in the navy blue tweed coat and the tartan scarf but he was nowhere to be found. Soon the news spread amongst the crowd and everyone was keeping an eye out for the boy. It was only when the news got to Brigette that she noticed that Duke was also missing. The panic now was multiplied many folds. The word about Duke, son of *'The Gaffer'*, being missing seemed even more significant than of Baron's disappearance. The police outside the Mausoleum immediately busied themselves organising groups to spread out to scour the length and width of St Hilary's Cemetery. Many volunteered to join the search. It meant that instead of standing in the freezing weather, individuals were now able to engage in movement that might improve their circulation whilst making a useful contribution by partaking in the search. No one inside the chamber was aware of the boys being missing. The groups set off in the different directions but called out for Duke. Brigette was the most worried because she was responsible for his welfare. In fact, Brigette felt as if she heard Earl's voice admonishing her for Duke's disappearance. The anxiety started to build up inside of her. Just the fear of the beatings she had suffered when Earl was alive brought back the sought of memories that induced her into a state of panic. Brigette rushed from place to place. She seemed quite unsteady on her feet like a boxer being disoriented by a hook to the head that was accurately on target. Whilst in this stupor, it was sheer coincidence that she bumped into Enid Staveley, the woman with the sandy coloured *'bird-nest'* pill-box hat with the plume of purple feathers. They froze but stared at each other in disbelief. It was all so surreal that they stood transfixed by the shock of meeting up again so many years after the fight at The Cobblestone Arms AADC. There they were both young girls. Enid was twenty-three years old and pregnant with Earl's children. Brigette on the other hand was 17 years old but was Earl's live-in partner. "What are *you* doing here", Brigette asked? Enid was unsure why Brigette asked the question. She thought she could sense a tone in Brigette's voice that sounded similar to that night nearly thirteen years before. They were both older now but there was a doubt on either side about the measure of emotional sensitivity intended by the other. Enid kept her eyes fixed on Brigette. She wasn't afraid of her but she had a more urgent reason for not wanting to engage in any emotional immaturity. Baron and Duke were missing and they had to find them. Enid could hear everyone shouting for Duke but not Baron. She had no time to turn the clock back; especially over someone like Earl, who had treated her so disgracefully shabby and robbed her of one of her sons for the last twelve years. "I'm looking for my sons", Enid responded. Unclear by Enid's claim about her "sons", Brigette pushed for a definitive answer. She wasn't sure what Enid meant. "My son is missing too", Brigette prompted. "I'm sorry to hear that. What's his name", Enid asked? "Duke, have you forgotten he lives with me", Brigette reminded Enid. "Well he's one of the son's to whom I refer", Enid explained. "Who's the other one then", Brigette queried? "Baron, Duke's twin brother", Enid replied. The shock was too much for Brigette. On the one hand, she didn't expect to meet up with Enid. On the other hand, the shock surprise about Duke having a twin brother stunned her even more. Brigette stared deeply at Enid but in the end seemed to acknowledge how crafty she had been. Even though she was her rival back then, Brigette had to admit to the clever way Enid had managed to outthink the legendary Earl Stagg. She was deserving of kudos for outwitting both their moody, bi-polar, revenge seeking, neurotic, ASPD, schizophrenic, physically abusing, alcoholic, serial woman hater. Brigette approached Enid with open arms but hugged her like the sister she never had but longed for. They stood in the embrace for what seemed like hours but was, in fact, only a few minutes. "After all this is over, can we meet up for a cuppa", Brigette queried? "Oh yes, let us do that soon", Enid replied. Having made amends, both women went off together to help search for the boys. It was then that they heard a greater roar than had happened inside the Mausoleum when Earl's Knighthood had been announced. There was suddenly a huge amount of chatter and cheering from all round and at one time it sounded like the roar that frequently came out of Earl Stagg's Association Football Stadium on a Saturday or Sunday afternoon League fixture when a goal was scored against the visitors in a local Derby game. Enid and Brigette walked towards the triumphant crowd that was walking back towards the Mausoleum. Both witnessed the boys being held shoulder high aloft by their rescuers. "I wonder where they were", Brigette queried? "I just want to know they are alright", Enid responded. Before long, the two boys were returned to their respective charges. Baron apologised immediately as soon as he was with his mother. Enid noticed the mud and damp patches on the children's clothes. She fussed but fidgeted with their attire as mothers do until she was satisfied they looked half decent again. As was her cultural way of cleansing the boys' faces, Enid spat on the tissue she had removed from her handbag but used it to wash the elements of mud from the boys' faces and hands. Brigette observed the caring way in which Enid handled the boys. She continued to watch but learn how Baron and his mother interacted but thought how nice it would be for Duke to interact with her in the same way. Enid at 5'5" was not much taller than her sons. She bent down to enable her to be about the same level as Baron before she addressed him. "Baron, it is unacceptable behaviour for you to wonder off like you did. You could have asked me, couldn't you? I want an apology", Enid demanded. "I'm sorry mommy. We were playing *'Bull-dog'* and *'Hide and Seek'*. I didn't see the open grave. I fell in. Duke tried to help me but I couldn't reach his outstretched hand. I told him to go get some help but he said he didn't want to leave me", Baron explained. Enid hugged Baron then reached out and pulled Duke into her arms too. They remained embraced while Brigette looked on forlornly. It was as if she had been excluded from the family hug. She watched Enid with much admiration. Duke looked up at Brigette but smiled. It was then that they noticed Duke's matronly chaperone standing patiently to escort him back to the limousine. She spoke in her very soft voice. "It all over here, can we go now", Duke's chaperone queried? Brigette asked Enid if she was coming back to the Earl Stagg Association Football Stadium initially and then after at The Cobblestone Arms AADC. Enid told her that she hadn't planned to stay after leaving St Hilary's Cemetery but now appreciated and accepted the invitation to go back to the Stadium. Brigette sought out but made arrangements for her two chaperones to travel with Simon Crabley and his wife Kitty on the journey back to The Earl Stagg Association Football Club Stadium. She told Enid that there were seats for both her and Baron to join them in their limousine. Duke's chaperone seemed surplus to requirements as the two boys chatted but played together. Brigette chatted with Enid all the way on the journey too.

CHAPTER 4

At The Earl Stagg Association Football Club Stadium, it seemed that the entire Ghettoborough had been invited. The crowd poured in from all the entrances. Because the Stadium was a public space, the police were responsible to monitor if there were any bad behaviour being displayed. The people were not allowed to go onto the pitch area. There were stalls set up in front of the seats on the athletic running track which separated the *'Field of Play'* from the crowd. The surplus of security staff were employed to marshal the crowd but ensured that each tier would be adequately served in an orderly manner. The arrangements were that the people furthest away from the pitch-side stalls were served first then the next row and so on, until the rows nearest the athletic running track were served. Hot food and drinks were provided for everyone. The enormous crowd could have extras if they wanted. The smell of the food carried around the Stadium and beyond. While people chatted amongst themselves in the Stands, music was being played over the PA system. After the multitude were fed, there was an announcement over the PA System stating that the Reverend Sawdust-Pine was about to conduct the other part of the elongated service. Further Tributes were to be made by the Mayor of Ghettoborough and some other dignitaries, who didn't have a chance to speak at St Hilary's Church earlier. There was a chance for some others from the community to pay their respects to *'The Gaffer'* too. The next announcement over the PA system was that there was to be a special Tribute from the local Police Band. Dressed in Red Tunics with golden buttons on their cuffs as well as travelling from their collars down the middle of their torsos but finished just below their waists. Some were misshaped by their huge pot bellies which made the Tunics appear too small for those individuals. All wore golden sashes draped horizontally across their chests, black trousers, white gloves, black caps with golden braiding which encircled the circumference of their heads and black boots that had *'burnished'* toecaps; befitting that of soldiers on parade ready for inspection. Each member of the band played their respective instruments with a little cards sticking up from each as they made their way to the centre of the pitch. They slow-marched in total unison but played the music that was composed specially for Earl's funeral. The formation altered in prearranged choreographed movements but eventually, whenever they were stationary, spelt the words *'Sir Earl Stagg'* then *'The Gaffer'*, alternately. It was an immense tribute which lasted a full thirty minutes. A great roar erupted in 'The Earl Stagg Association Football Club Stadium'. All the voices cheered as one. Another tribute was the *'fly-past'* by the two specially chartered aircrafts. Each had a sign trailing behind it. The words *'Sir Earl Stagg'* and *'The Gaffer'* was written in huge lettering on each of the banners. The people in the stadium cheered loudly and clapped excitedly as they saw the aircrafts appear again and again for over fifteen minutes then they turned away but disappeared into the distance. Yet a third Tribute was to be performed by the mounted Police unit, who put on a significant display of horsemanship even though there were some females in the group too. The children were especially excited to see the horses perform.

The next announcement was that of the Mayor, Myrvinne Rattatouie, who wanted to pay his personal tribute to the late Earl Stagg. He began by stating that Earl's application for the Stadium had been approved unanimously by all the parties, the incumbents as well as the oppositions of previous elections. He said that even as a councillor, Myrvinne noticed Earl's rise from obscurity to prominence over the not so recent years to the present. He punctuated his tribute with praises fit for a hero. *'The Gaffer'* had certainly brought stability to an ailing borough. The Mayor stated for the record that when the Stadium was constructed, it attracted significant business to the borough. Myrvinne Rattatouie ended his tribute to *'The Gaffer'* when he referred to the Knighthood that had been bestowed upon Earl as proof of his commitment to the community. Again, the crowd cheered loudly. They stood but maintained the cheering for at least ten minutes. As soon as they sat down, the crowd created their own tribute by instigating and encouraging the *'Mexican Wave'* all around the Stadium. Groups stood up then sat down again continuously while others cheered. They did this over and over again. It was not only a spectacle but also a means of keeping warm. Tributes from the Dignitaries and a number of locals were made. More food was being made available to the vast crowd. Once again, music poured from the PA system. The spotlights became more prominent now; welcoming the dusk. Some people with children started to vacate the Stadium as the darkness lurked on the periphery just outside the perimeter of its concrete structure.

Raleigh Daly-Weede again caught glimpse of the rather tall woman with the black satin dress and the black wide brimmed hat. Swinging her hips in a deliberate practiced manner but striding one foot in front of the other, she carried her wiry frame like a model. The woman stood inside one of the specially designed Corporate Boxes. Raleigh watched her sip from the champagne glass. She seemed to be engaged in conversation with two others, one male and a female. Raleigh's interest seemed to deepen as his curiosity enveloped his thinking. Sheila was busy enough being engaged with the number of people, who approached her in the Family Corporate Box from which she could be seen. Raleigh slipped away from their Box in order to investigate, who was the woman in the black satin dress with the black wide brimmed hat. There were some faint memories that bounced around in his head as he watched with almost voyeur-like enthusiasm. As he contemplated how to make his approach, the door of the particular Box opened. The man and woman, who were previously in conversation with the woman with the black wide-brimmed hat and the black satin coat, left the Box but headed in the direction of the *'Corporate Toilets'*. Raleigh followed his intuition but entered the Box where the woman stood alone. She was across the room from him. Raleigh stood just inside the door. He tried hard to identify the woman. "Pardon the intrusion but I have a strong feeling that we've met before", Raleigh apologised. "Are you trying to chat me up", the woman asked? The question was stunning enough to throw Raleigh's curiosity into a sense of confusion. He could hear himself babbling on about his quest to find out the identity of this woman. Her familiarity haunted but scoured his lifetime resource of memory in short, medium and long-termed categories. This mystery woman was now standing just a few metres away from him in the same space very much unlike the earlier situation at the cemetery. Sweat started to appear not only down his broad angular face but also poured from his armpits as if his amygdala had reflected his heightened state of *'fight'* or *'flight'* response subconsciously. Raleigh began to shake with anxiety and before long was feeling the power emanating from the woman in the Corporate Box. Raleigh felt weak all of a sudden but quite faint. He gripped the side of the chair next to him but was reduced to kneeling next to it as if he was in a confessional at a Catholic Church. As he looked in her direction, the woman walked slowly over towards him. "Hi Raleigh, remember me", the woman asked? Her voice was soft but evocative. It celebrated an ambience of subtle emotions but directed for effect. The voice seemed to rapidly flick through the pages of Raleigh's memory bank. Inside, the internal search engine went into overriding capacity which now brought Raleigh to a virtual role. He sifted through the frames that made up the big picture in his mind, pausing only to reflect on any one scene. There was one that stood out from the rest so he selected it for closer inspection. The sweat had now begun to feel more like a shower. He sensed his entire undergarments being supersaturated by it. Myrna stood over him tall and authoritative. She glanced down at him clasping his hands in front of his chest as if he was praying. Raleigh seemed to be in a pitiful state. Myrna seized the opportunity to humiliate him. Again she spoke. "Not so demanding now, are you Raleigh", the woman mused? There was a familiarity in that soft beguiling voice that was causative to the memories which came flooding back. Raleigh was now aware that the woman to whom he'd been attracted was Myrna, the young pregnant girl he'd abandoned. Raleigh's large eyes gazed up at her rather sheepishly but were begging for forgiveness. She was in no mood for granting him anything but the rage which had been forming within her for those many years. This opportunity was ideal for Myrna to relieve the queasiness which had threatened to erupt from a depth that felt more like a ravine. She waved her hands frantically as if she was trying to remove the thick cobwebs that were there to represent each timeframe that had expired until this moment. Enraged by the murky past but the lack of opportunity to voice how she'd truly had felt, Myrna poured out the bile that she might not have been brave enough to do when she was younger. Suddenly, without any prompting from Raleigh, Myrna shifted from the quiet, seemingly fragile, composed individual into a very animated state. Her comments too were less than complimentary. "So you thought that you could beat the baby out of me, did you Raleigh? Well, our baby is dead now but at least he managed to live for the years he did and what is important that I too survived your emotionally immature attitude. Call yourself a man eh, do you? Well Raleigh, real men don't shirk their responsibilities; especially if they have been taking advantage of a young innocent, naive girl as I was then. You *'men'*, so called, makes me sick", Myrna scolded. Raleigh recognized the anger in Myrna's voice. It was all coming back now. He could identify with the awesome brutal beating to which she referred. That night he refused to become responsible for making her pregnant. Raleigh was a *'player'* then and Myrna knew that fact. She and the other women, who besieged him and the like, knew exactly what they were getting into. Most of those women often sought after men of *'reputation'* like Raleigh. The women with these *'crushes'* were beguiled by their own perception. They often freely submitted themselves to men like Raleigh. He felt that those women who worshipped his muscular physicality, height, handsome facial features but not least his flashing smile were caught in their own web of *'programmed'* perceptions. All he did was take advantage of their naïve approach as to what makes a **'meaningful relationship'**. These women set out seeking a particular *'stereo-typical'* imagery but were entranced by them. Myrna's *'primed mind'* and naivety had captured Raleigh's attention. He, like any other *'Alpha'* male, sought to take advantage of Myrna's innocence. Raleigh gave her what she expected and more. He wined and dined her at the most expensive, exclusive Restaurants, took her to the Clubs, Raves, Cinemas, Beaches and other social events. He showered Myrna with the gifts she readily accepted. That made her more vulnerable to being exploited further. He felt that Myrna was guilty of leading him on. Raleigh did what he did with her blessing and permission. Even though on that night to which Myrna referred, Raleigh blamed her for not taking precaution against the possibility of becoming pregnant. He did throw those assertions around rather than take responsibility for not using condoms. "After that night, I came back but you had moved. What was I meant to do", Raleigh asked sheepishly? "It was three weeks after the night when we quarrelled, Raleigh. What was I meant to do, wait around for you? You never wanted the baby and you made that quite clear. I was never going to have an abortion as you had insisted", Myrna submitted. Even though he was much older now, Raleigh was still playing the victim rather than standing up and accepting responsibility for his waywardness then. He was already defeated but jousted all the same. Raleigh was shifting the blame on Myrna. "You knew I was already married when we met", he parried. "What I do know is that I had to give our son away. It was either doing that or watching him grow up without a father. The children of *'single mothers'* get enough flack from both the political and public arena.

Some have been so damaged by all and sundry, from political circles to the corporate establishments. Even poor single parents are repeating the *'stereo-typical'* mantra about themselves, amongst themselves. How pathetic is that Raleigh Daly-Weede? I wanted to avoid the slanderous tongues; those who lurk in Nurseries, Junior Schools, Secondary Schools, Colleges, to Universities and beyond", Myrna sobbed. Raleigh had no response to this passionate outburst. For the first time he was being informed about the child to whom he did not want to be a father. As if to explain her reasons further, Myrna continued to spill her *'mental vomit©'* off her chest but aimed it like a projectile towards Raleigh. "You need to understand the considerations that influenced my decision. The children of *'single mothers'* are targeted but labelled by political disinformation as being *'disaffected'*, perennially. The effect upon the targeted children is such that it is almost impossible to see a child today without some kind of label like Dyslexia, ADD and ADHD attached. Some are said to be suffering from one type of syndrome or another. That type of political bullying often leads to their esteem being diminished", Myrna instructed.

Raleigh recognised the point about diminished esteem to which Myrna alluded. His earlier experiences were filled with nothing but abuses and negative comments. Having been given away by his mother, Rita Independemente, at the age of 5 years old, Delpinius Independemente, as he was called then, lived in many foster homes. He remembered the different type of abuses he'd suffered in each of the fourteen homes in which he'd been brought up. Because of his build, Delphinius had often been abused by adult women paedophiles. They had a *'crush'* on young boys in and around those homes. At 12 years old, Delphinius suffered the indignity of abuses, consistently. He was raped repeatedly by some devious women, who had deliberately worked their way into the *'Care System'* in order to satisfy their own nymphomaniac agendas. Those women can only be described as *"being possessed"* but driven by some form of demonic spirits. Young Delphinius paid the price for his handsome features and his giant physical build. A rumour mill had been in operation about this young boy with the kind of physical features that seemed to reiterate the myth which drove their nymphomaniacs' madness. These domineering women used Delphinius as their *'sex slave'* in their sordid *'rituals'* to satisfy their individual sexual addictions. Six or seven times a day, seven days a week, he was visited by these women. No matter how many times he protested, it was always the same. The bullying adult women and their visiting associates continued to use Delphinius as their "toy boy" despite the fact he vehemently disagreed with their witch-like rituals. Sometimes, four or five of them would gather like the *'nymphomaniac vultures'* they were around the young "well endowed" boy. These women would pin his shoulders and legs while they each took turn to marvel but closely *"examine him"*. When un-aroused, this young boy's oversized physicality seemed to bring the sexual witches some form of warped sensuality which brought on some weird common thoughts that made them shiver together as if they were convulsing in unison from being exposed to extreme freezing temperature. The sounds emanating from them were just as worryingly haunting. Its resonance was maintained, like a number of owls *'oohing'* together in harmony. These cruelly domineering nymphomaniacs raped young Delphinius mercilessly but repeated this act by passing him around like a *'peace pipe'* among them from one to another in order to satisfy their own warped egos. Delphinius was chained so he couldn't run away.

The only form of activity he was allowed was to satisfy these women's sadistic *'warped-minded' seemingly grossly addictive pleasure'*.

It was not until he'd gone to live with the Daly-Weede family later that year in the fifteenth home that Delpinius was treated with some love and dignity. The Daly-Weedes encouraged him to go to school and to learn to read and write. At school, Delphinius threw tantrums both inside and outside the classrooms. He was teased about his size, complexion, the tone of his freckled skin, and his Albinism by both teachers and fellow students alike. Much as the Daly-Weedes cared for him, they didn't know how to comb his hair. They had no experience about the texture of it and so often just turned a blind eye towards its upkeep. As a consequence, it made Delphinius appear unkempt and wild. He was dubbed, *'King Kong'* by his peers but soon he was commonly referred to as such both within and outside of the school. Even though *'King Kong'* was meant to be a gorilla, the *'primed minds'* of the students went into overdrive. They threw bananas at him, daily as if he was a monkey. When he complained about his treatment, the Daly-Weedes told him to *"just ignore the comments"* while the teachers admonished him for *being "oversensitive to a bit of 'honest' fun"*. School was not a happy environment for Delphinius. His reaction to the constant bullying meant that he was always in trouble but was sent to the *'holding room'* almost on a daily basis for a whole term. The Daly-Weedes were being contacted quite often by the school about Delpinius's behaviour. As foster parents, the Daly-Weedes noticed how angry yet timid Delphinius had become. They became concerned about his diminished sense of self-worth. He no longer kept up with his hygiene. Together with the school, the Daly-Weedes agreed for Delphinius to be seen by the school psychiatrist. Even this turned out to be a problem. Instead of conducting the sessions merely on a professional level, the psychiatrist was guilty for opting to approach the young boy from a *'stereo-typical'* standpoint. Delphinius just simply refused to work with her. The final straw was when Delphinius lashed out when he was being attacked in the playground by a gang of seven boys. They surrounded him. Some kicked him while others punched him from his blindside. Each blow made him more and more irate. All the time they jeered him, by calling him "King Kong" again and again until the voices appeared like echoes rebounding inside his head repetitively. When he finally snapped, Delphinius managed to grab hold of one of the boys, who had ventured much too close for his own good. He hoisted the boy above his head with both hands but slammed him into the ground. His rage had a new impetus. It was no longer the simmering of the metaphoric molten lava that welled up inside him but a full blown explosion of his metaphoric volcano. Teachers watched the debacle but ultimately blamed Delphinius for *"overreacting"*. One in particular tried to grab hold of Delphinius but found himself being thrown as if he was on the wrong end of a wrestling match. He suffered more than a bruised reputation but insisted to the Head teacher that Delphinius be expelled from the school. With being assessed by the school psychiatrist that he had a "split personality", he was formally expelled forthwith. After hearing Delphinius's version of what happened, the Daly-Weedes complained to the Head Teacher but he said he couldn't change his mind about the expulsion. With his reputation, Delphinius drifted from one school to another until he became 14 years old. Despite his frequent outbursts at home, the Daly-Weedes decided to adopt him. In doing so, they re-named him Raleigh Daly-Weede by deed poll. Even though this was only a superficial change, it gave Raleigh a new start and a chance to escape from his previous identity. Raleigh told his new parents that he didn't want to go back to school. He started to work with his adopted father buying and selling scrap metal. Raleigh didn't want to tell Myrna about his earlier life experiences. He was too ashamed to share them with anyone but he knew in his mind how he'd sworn to take revenge on women. Raleigh also knew that he was hesitant about fathering children because of his fear that they too might suffer the form of abuse that he had suffered. The moments of reflection on Raleigh's turbulent years of his life lasted but a few minutes.

As he re-entered from his trance-like state, Raleigh began to re-engage with Myrna again in the Corporate Box. She had paused to observe the seemingly grimaced look on Raleigh's face. Myrna totally misinterpreted the furrows that appeared on his forehead but continued to reiterate the diatribe. "Raleigh, what you don't seem to realise is the type of negative impact that is visited upon young people; particularly those from single parenthood. Those parents are consistently blamed for everything that goes wrong. They are never given any kudos when their children overcome the barriers, despite the many distractions that are invented to dissuade them from knowing they are capable. The children's achievements are constructively marginalized with immense prejudice. For those whom are focused and determined enough to learn, are damned if they *'don't'* but damned if they *'do'* achieve good exam results while they are at secondary school. Each year, despite the mountainous challenges they face, some students excel in their respective annual national certificated examinations. These are set by the various educational governing bodies in order to determine the grades of competency for students in each subject. Encouragingly, the percentage of success had been rising year on year yet there are those sanctimonious critics that seem to be always lurking; ready to pounce on the students' achievements. At the time of year when the results are published, their sarcastic comments are expressed in the Media. I didn't want to have to explain to our son that he was just *'fodder'*. The individuals, who take part in the *'sniping game'*, appeared by their snide comments, to be less than student friendly", Myrna lectured. Raleigh was beginning to see that the woman he had once taken for granted had deep-rooted fears on behalf of young people. Her passionate views disturbed him because he was unable to figure out whether his birth mother might have had the same type of fears too. It entered his mind that it was hardly likely for him to find out now. Raleigh, though physically fit, was now advanced in age but wondered against all odds whether his mother could still be alive. He remembered the tone of her voice and the lisp which interrupted her speech, the freckles on her face and the tone of her skin. Raleigh even recalled that, like him, his mother used to have to shade her eyes from the sun with her hands or to wear dark glasses to do so even though she was not looking directly into it. As he grew up, he'd asked the Daly-Weedes what made him look different from others but they declined to enter into explanations. All he recalled them saying is that they loved him with all their hearts. He had no reason to doubt their genuineness. Raleigh further recalled the kind sensitive way in which they had treated him. One thing stood out most of all about the Daly-Weedes. It was that they would quickly change from their gentile, composed behaviour to becoming quite aggressive and blunt whenever they heard any derogatory comments that were directed towards him. When they died, they bequeathed the business, *'Daly-Weede and Son Scrap Metals'*, in Oudourville, Lower

Ghettoborough, the cottage in Sneersborough and the house in Higher Ghettoborough as well as a list of other assets. There was a stipulation attached to the Will. It was that Raleigh had to take reasonable good care of the two Macaw Birds, Daize and Deze. A named Vet was charged with examining the birds each month for as long as they lived. Provision was made within the Will to pay the agreed Vet fees separately from any money left to their adopted son, Raleigh. The pink Mixed DNA Rainbow Tribe Sir Walter and his wife, Lady Austragena from the white Mixed DNA Rainbow Tribe elected euthanasia together to end their long suffering from a series of strokes which left them severely disfigured but unable to retain their independence. Raleigh recalled their suffering but also their fight to survive. They had made him feel so valued and never mistreated him in any way. More than all they treated him like one of their pets. He remembered how they use to pat his head just like they did the dog. The way they expressed their endearment was no less genuine though. Raleigh soon learned what it felt like to be appreciated as part of the family. In Sir and Lady Dalyweede's final days, Raleigh wept as unashamedly as he was weeping now.

Myrna had no idea what made Raleigh cry but she witnessed the sobbing and the distraught look on his face. She too was at this moment subscribing to the myth that "men don't cry". Myrna saw it as a kind of weakness. She looked down upon the man that had impregnated her but shelved his responsibility as soon as she had confirmed the pregnancy. She listened for any challenges from the man to whom she had been so attracted but there was no form of protestation to her ranting so Myrna continued. "Raleigh, can you see the point I'm making? You're older than me with more experience but you seem to be blind to these issues, are you not", Myrna questioned? She told Raleigh that she thought it was time that *'single mothers'* be encouraged for the wonderful work they do without the absent fathers. Myrna said she couldn't possibly take credit to speak for everyone but she was sure her sentiments were being experienced by a great majority. Fired up by her intense feelings, Myrna referred to those significant others, who had consumed the indigestible snipe but readily belched the vitriolic language which seemed to re-ignite the embers of retribution and damnation thrust upon generations of children of *'single mothers'*. "Because of the *'stereotypical'* imaging purported, our children's confidence were being deliberately eroded but systematically targeted yet destroyed. Each generation suffered *'psychological abuse'* from the inoculation of *'labelling'* even within educational establishments by some significant adults who happen to be teachers. It involves a lot of people, who have no knowledge of what individual *'single mothers'* have to endure yet everyone seemed to want to have a say in our lives", Myrna continued. There was a lot of sense in what Myrna was saying but most of all her pronouncements seemed to suggest that she had thought deeply before taking the action she had done. Raleigh felt the least he could do was to let Myrna continue to say how she was feeling. He did not interrupt her. "Well Raleigh, I was not prepared to go through those slurs whilst allowing others to brand my child in the way they do other children. This had been happening over many generations prior to when I was born and still goes on today. It seems to be a *'universal sport'* but meant to demean all other relationships except for those relationships instituted by political status, like marriage, for example", Myrna stated. At this point, Raleigh queried what Myrna meant by the previous statement. He asked her to help him understand better what she was alluding to. "Marriage is sanctioned by the *'status quo'* as the *'ideal'* platform from which *'successful relationships'* are birthed but what's the universal divorce rate confirming about lack of longevity? Ask yourself that question and choke on the answer. Single relationships can work. There are many that have done but no official figures had ever been produced because of *'men' like you'*", Myrna sneered. Raleigh explained that his marriage had dissolved into a pitiful divorce between him and his money-grabbing green humanoid robotron wife, Etna. The divorce was described as *"marriage irretrievably broken down"* but the truth is they were never compatible as a couple. Etna had targeted but forced herself upon the then naïve Raleigh. She was much older than him but reminded him of his experiences as a young boy. He did not explain to Myrna what had taken place. All he said was that his wife needed a *"Toy Boy"* to satisfy her nymphomaniac urges. After a while, Raleigh started to seek to share his virility with younger women. Etna was more like a *'motherly'* figure to him. They had nothing in common except for his hard-earned money and the assets his adopted parents had bequeathed him. Raleigh remembered how Etna had filed for divorce when she couldn't extract any more money from the then extremely popular entrepreneur. He was not only king of the *'Breaking'* business but also bought and sold property and cars. Etna managed to extract half his fortune as a settlement in the bitter divorce. Raleigh explained that the Court, run mainly by green humanoid robotron Judges, had awarded her money and property he had earned before meeting the scheming green humanoid robotron Etna. He confided that he thought the law encouraged the Etnas of this world to seek and destroy naïve men like him. Myrna felt no pity for how Raleigh was treated by his wife. She had saved up all of her frustrations, disappointments, anger and the other negative emotions which she had experienced for the moment she had hoped would present itself, one day. That day was now. She ignored Raleigh's sad story but continued to rant even more. "Serves you right, you're just a dog, Raleigh. You men use women too. A woman gets pregnant and the likes of you have never been made to be responsible within your own family unit let alone outside it. So, what's your answer to responsibility? Run away from the challenge. What did you do Raleigh? When I was most vulnerable, what did you choose to do? Run away but abandon mother and child. Where were you Raleigh when we needed you most, where were you? Actively playing the part of the *'stereo-typical'* absent father and that's before our child was born even", Myrna raged. Raleigh was feeling ashamed of his non-compliance with the then pregnant Myrna. His face bore the embarrassment that contorted his handsome features into a saddened demeanour. Tears started to roll down his cheeks. Raleigh wiped them away with his huge hands. They looked like shovels. There was a very long pause before Raleigh responded. "I'm sorry I let you and our son down but I did *'man-up'* when I saw the advert in the newspaper. We had meetings and I did explain to Earl about our staggered relationship as best as I could", Raleigh drawled. "I trust you did explain to him the options you left me once you knew of my pregnancy. Did you explain to him that the one option you chose was to abort him? This day would then not exist, would it Raleigh", Myrna demanded? He hung his head in shame but stared at the floor. Raleigh had no argument which could counter anything that Myrna threw at him. "You make me feel so guilty", Raleigh submitted. Myrna heard his comment but she was in no mood to surrender her grasp from around his metaphoric throat. Instead, she stuck in but twisted the metaphoric knife a bit more.

Sneering at Raleigh she steered the reference to herself briefly before tearing in to him again. "No one else knows how devious you are. I suppose you can't help being a rat escaping from one hole but seeking another and yet another to crawl into and hide. You're an expert at playing the role of *'King Rat'* and attempting to do so again now, aren't you Raleigh", Myrna pressed? Raleigh murmured something. It was not clear what he was saying but Myrna heard the words *'loss'* and *'pain'* mentioned. These words seem to fire her up more rather than pacify her. Raleigh looked awkward just standing there gazing at the beautiful Myrna. He only sought to find her because he wanted to see whether he could rekindle their friendship or at least to be able to share conversation about the loss of their child. Instead, he found a woman so enraged that he was no match for her mood. "I'm pained by my loss then and now. How can that be resolved? Guess you're happy with your 50% sperm contribution to the revered son we made together. Look at you, you disgust me; trampling upon my naivety, using me the way you have. All those years Raleigh Daly-Weedw, all those years I've spent drowning in my tears while you plugged the gaps between the other women's legs with your giant dick. That's all you have to go with your muscles and athletic frame but it certainly doesn't make you a man. I feel sorry for the women, who make the same mistakes again and again reeling off fantasy according to how we've been *'programmed'*. The kind of man I'm searching for must be that special individual, who can give me more than muscles, brawn, looks and other physical features we women have become accustomed to expect. The perennial *'stereo-typical'* images to which women seem attached do not guarantee longevity in relationship terms. I Coach that now to vulnerable individuals", Myrna emphasized. It was as if Myrna had stored but rehearsed these deeply felt feelings in order to deliver such a tirade of admonishment to the defenceless Raleigh. The power of a now reconciled Myrna established her mental occupation with the changes she had had to make during the years which separated both her and Raleigh's previous meeting so many years ago. Whilst he emulated the role of a giant wimp, Raleigh's memory had long since whizzed him back to the days to which she referred. His recall of taking her for granted and the rough treatment to a younger Myrna Mc Tittle magnified itself through her rant at him. He was well and truly weakened by Myrna's onslaught. For the ever so gentle soft-spoken Myrna Mc Tittle to display this kind of explosion of emotions was not typical of her normal behaviour. Raleigh was feeling like when the nymphomaniacs had bullied him. He got down on his knees but begged Myrna's forgiveness. She poured the balance of the champagne from her glass over the now whimpering man in front of her. His huge frame seemed to be shrinking into a rapidly diminishing enfoldment into the foetus position. As Myrna looked down, she saw Raleigh place his left thumb into his mouth but suckled from it like a baby seeking contentment from a *'dummy'*. She then emptied the content from the bottle she held in the other hand. The mixture of his supersaturated sweaty swarthy body and the champagne marinated both Raleigh and Myrna's nostrils in the hot Corporate Box. Because of the reinforced tinted glass panelled structure, the heating was meant to defrost the colder outer surface but inside it felt like the tropics at high summer. Myrna had expounded her pent up wrath without compromise and all her *'mental vomit ©'* had erupted but emptied its content all over the unsuspecting Raleigh. She looked at him in his current helpless state but began to see how her strong words and undaunted '*emotional retribution*' had affected him. Raleigh was reduced to metaphoric rubble, literally just like an unwanted multi-story block of flats that had imploded. It was pitiful to see such a huge '*hunk*' diminished to the state in which Raleigh had found himself. The tall slender frame of Myrna McTittle sat on the floor next to the morally wounded Raleigh Daly-Weede but cradled him towards her bosom. They looked like a picture of the biblical '*Holy Mary*' cradling a much older '*Jesus Christi*' in her arms, only Myrna was much younger than Raleigh.

CHAPTER 5

For the ever so gentle soft-spoken Myrna McTittle to display this kind of explosion of emotions was not typical of her normal behaviour. When she was younger, Myrna had been a very successful model. Tall, slim and wiry she had often swung those hips in her exaggerated walk down many Runways to the delight of many designers and fans. Myrna's near breakdown from depression started shortly after she had abandoned Earl. It played on her mind but consistently dragged her into states of feelings she had not known existed before. Myrna was thoroughly traumatized by her decision. It affected her while she was awake. Myrna was awake more often than she slept. Because of her busy mind, arousal brought on her condition of Insomnia. It was an almost too familiar experience which lasted for over two years. As if that wasn't bad enough, Myrna slipped into owning and experiencing consistent negative emotions. Anger, hurt, sadness, disappointment and shame she wore like a third skin. Confusion, anxiety, judgement, procrastination and guilt were some emotional blocks that followed her around like a shadow, often. Day after day Myrna allowed these negative emotions and blocks to dominate but she adopted an attitude that led her close to the abyss of ruination. Her self-esteem plummeted to the darkened crevices of the deepest mental ravines. With not much support, Myrna failed to access the resources that she needed to help her confidence. She carried a heavy conscience about her desperate situation. Feelings of resentment, abandonment and anger subscribed to her low self-worth in such a way that made Myrna plunge headlong from a cliff, metaphorically. Her decent began like a small snowball which had gathered momentum but increased in energy on its way down towards the foot of her situational mountain. It seemed there was no other way but down until she met a young man, known as "The budding Professor". He was merely three or four years older than Myrna. The young man was a Counsellor and Mentor. His coaching style was exclusive in technique, skill and execution. This meant that "The budding Professor" did not just have a sterile objective. His significant unique technique reinforced yet guaranteed each client unique well-formed outcomes. As a Coach and Practitioner, "The budding Professor" specialized in three main areas. These core areas were 'Relationships', 'Personal Development' and 'Personal Performance'. "The budding Professor" was a disciplined man. He was famed for his direct approach yet he remained reflectively curious, empathic, flexible, trustworthy but with integrity. "The budding Professor" encouraged those same attributes among his clients too. It is rumoured that he dedicates six and a half hours each day to research. In doing so, it enabled access to new

'Tools', fresh insights, perspectives and continuous learning opportunities. Myrna had told him what she had done but expressed how guilty she felt; blaming herself for having to make the decision to abandon her son. The depression had kicked in but almost ruined her chances of becoming a top model. She improved with each session but soon was able to dump her obsession with guilt and blame. Within a few months, Myrna started to turn herself around. She gained the highest accolade from the modelling fraternity and was well on her way to a very successful career, subsequently.

In the specially designed Corporate Box, Raleigh Daly-Weede was still being affected by the verbal drubbing dished out by Myrna. He seemed to be in a permanent state of malaise as he wallowed in the sea of self-pity. He stared blankly ahead of him into the vast unknown but sobbed like a spoilt child throwing a tantrum. Tears flowed down his face like dripping taps in need of new washers but his nose showed evidence of opaque moisture of a very different consistency which trickled but slithered like a snail along its path. The cloudy muck, after leaving his nostrils, lingered in the rough two days stubble that protruded from the skin underneath Raleigh's nose but pretended to act as camouflage in that area above his upper lip. Thick greyish slimy mucus tinged by yellow and red streaks, closely aligned, oozed profusely from both nostrils. It was as if the mucus was deliberately being poured slowly from a vessel from within. The crawling motion of it gathered enough pace and force then reached but trailed over the curved ridge of Raleigh's upper lip. Being forced by irregular expanse and rhythm of breaths which rendered the multi coloured mucus as a gooey mass that had the potential to actively prolong its journey into and between both lips, the snot mounted then disappeared under Raleigh's lower lip. The two trails continued towards their unknown destinations, randomly pausing at times into almost a standstill but somehow managing to gain restored movement until sliding under Raleigh's clean-shaven chin. The mass of fluid energy continued until arrival upon Raleigh's thoroughly supersaturated black lapel of his jacket, tie and previously well laundered white shirt. Eventually, seemingly like the accumulated mass of molten lava from volcanoes, the awful, unsightly gel came to rest, settling beyond any further movement. There was no attempt by the hapless Raleigh to do anything about his predicament but Myrna, either through pity or for reason only she could confirm, slipped her hand into her handbag which hung in place over her shoulder by the thin red leather strap. Myrna fished for the packet of tissues but removed a few. She dutifully wiped the muck from Raleigh's nose and lips but kissed him lightly. At first, there was no reaction but in what seemed like minutes but was in fact a matter of seconds, Raleigh acknowledged the feathered kiss as a token of humane acknowledgement that Myrna's anger had now dissipated but was not permanent. The delay had given Raleigh time to realize that he needed to recover from his current situation. As he glanced up at Myrna, she noticed the sadness in his eyes. She even perceived that the look in Raleigh's eyes seemed genuine enough to convey a sense of apology to her. There was not much more she could do but to console Raleigh and just hold him close to her. Myrna looked down at the man with whom she had had a brief affair earlier in her life. She wondered how she could have once believed in such a weak character. Myrna realized that her own perceptions had been something she had chosen to gravitate towards but came to believe as reality. She was now experiencing the fact that the *myth* was just that and nothing more. In this situation, Raleigh proved to be just as vulnerable as any other human. Apart from his awesome athletic body, handsome features, chiselled jaws, dazzling smile, big dick together with her perceptions of the programming towards which she had gravitated, there wasn't really much to him that was superior. Myrna now realised that Raleigh had flaws like everyone else. She had been conditioned by the folklore that had become a legendary mythical imagery of the ideal partner, the *'Trophy Man'*, *'Mr. Right'*. At that time, she was young and naïve enough to be convinced that hers and Raleigh's relationship might have led towards the storybook ending she had read or heard about. Being thwarted by her own experiences, such belief Myrna now acknowledged to herself as unrealistic and false. She was learning that the *'stereo-tripe'* and *'stereo-hype'* were yet another form of segregation that was invented by those, who sought to destroy the confidence of less athletic build individuals even. This Myrna now realise might have driven other individuals into great depths of low self esteem. The myths were more than a form of imperative class-ism. Some insecure women might have chosen to worship the legendary *'stereo-typical'* image because they found it psychologically comforting. Arguments were deduced from the myth by some women to support the notion that the *'stereo-typical'* athletic build males offered a better form of physical security than the skinnier male. Myrna's experience had alerted her that the *'programmed'* perceptions were fast losing their appeal or effect when it came to what is really important within relationships. There were still some remnants of other perceptions that still stayed with Myrna. Since her experience with Raleigh at that young age and subsequent intimate relationships, she still had a particular reason to hold him in high esteem. Like all other *'programming'*, Myrna was taught that she had to pay homage to the man who took her virginity. As a consequence of this myth, all Myrna's other intimate relationships suffered then failed, subsequently. She found that she was inextricably permanently chained to Raleigh Daly-Weede for taking her virginity. Even though her memory of that day was more about pain instead of pleasure, Myrna was still susceptible to the influence of the myth. Raleigh's approach was based upon his *'programmed'* *'values and beliefs'*. He too had experienced the type of myth that led him to believe that women like Myrna were there to be conquered. Raleigh knew of the myth about the obsession women had about men with his type of build. In addition, he considered himself as being handsome too. This drove Raleigh and men like him on a singular lifelong quest. As far as he was concerned, he was irresistible. His rationale was simple. Women had to be ready to have sex with him or he would just walk away but find another that did consent. At 27 years old Raleigh had bought the naïve 19 years old young adult Myrna a gold chain as a gift. She accepted it but smiled at him with a most admiring look on her face. Raleigh placed the gold chain around Myrna's neck. She raced to the mirror. Myrna commented appreciatively about how she felt. Raleigh told her he was happy that she liked the gold chain but what happened next took Myrna by surprise. He felt Myrna needed to reciprocate his generosity by making herself available for sex. Raleigh had used this ruse on many occasions previously and had successfully conquered the grateful recipients. On this memorable occasion, he had premeditative thoughts about this scenario. Raleigh had decided that he was not accepting a negative response from Myrna. Another notch on his dick was all he cared about. Feeling grateful for the gift, the naïve Myrna leant forward but kissed Raleigh lightly on his lips. This stirred Raleigh into action. Myrna was unprepared for what happened next. Feeling encouraged by the kiss, Raleigh drew Myrna closer to him. He hugged her tightly to his huge frame. Her slight build was enveloped by Raleigh's excessive musculature. Myrna found it hard to breathe even. She realised that he was aroused beyond what she had intended. Raleigh groped her breast with one hand whilst placing the other under her dress. Myrna reached down to discourage the hand beneath her dress. In doing so, her hand brushed against his thighs. It was then that she felt the bulge that was trying to escape from Raleigh's trousers. Whilst strongly protesting her non-commitment to engage in sexual intercourse, Myrna managed to get both her hands between them but pushed firmly upon Raleigh's chest. While separated temporarily, Myrna told him firmly that she didn't want to go beyond the kiss. Raleigh was disappointed that she was "playing hard to get" and he told her so. Myrna told him she didn't feel ready to have sex with him. After all, she hardly knew him. In a fit of temper, Raleigh told her that he knew she wanted to have sex with him and that she should quit playing with his emotions. Before Myrna could respond to his outburst, Raleigh pushed her onto the carpeted floor but placed both her hands above her head. Myrna squirmed, wriggled but was no match for the 105 kilos giant. She weighed a mere 55 kilos. Raleigh pinned both her hands with one of his huge shovel-like hand but lay on top of her. The next thing Myrna knew was that she felt Raleigh's big dick entering her vagina. She can't remember giving him permission to have sex with her. When she said no, she meant no. Raleigh just kept repeating that he knew she was "just playing hard to get". He also told her that he knew she couldn't resist his big dick and so he forced it into her. Myrna's account was quite different but she was so smitten by Raleigh's muscled body, his dazzling smile that she felt drawn to him and his big dick. She too believed the myth that a big dick guaranteed satisfaction, apparently. On this occasion, it didn't prove anything but painful. The myth was yet another which Myrna had overheard from family members and friends alike as she grew through the various life stages. Despite her prolonged protest, Myrna had no choice than to succumb to Raleigh's sexual advances. In spite of her trepidations about what the sexual experience might turn out to be, Myrna suffered the ignominy of being raped repeatedly on that occasion. Subsequently, each time that Raleigh visited her after that memorable night, he replicated the same behaviour. Even though Myrna kept protesting, she still hoped that a relationship might develop between her and the *'stereotypical'* *'Trophy Man'*, *'Mr. Right'*. On one of his visits, Myrna told Raleigh that she was pregnant. It was then that he disclosed he was a married man. Raleigh demanded that Myrna "abort the baby". His visits became more infrequent until he faded out of her life. Despite being 19 years old and left in this awkward situation, Myrna decided to ignore Raleigh's advice.

Earl was born at home on that fated day. Myrna, with no prior experience, struggled through the awesome pains without medical intervention or supervision. She had been having contractions for over 39 hours. When Earl had decided to make his entry into this world, Myrna pushed and panted instinctively. She bore the agony of childbirth all by herself. Myrna felt exhausted by her experience but persevered all the same. She used pillows to dampen the sounds of her screaming as frequently as was necessary. Myrna committed to cut the umbilical cord with the brand new pair of scissors that she had purchased a month before. There was not much time to contemplate about the baby. Myrna heard him cry. She hugged her baby for as long as it took to breastfeed him, which was about twenty minutes. Myrna didn't want to get too attached to the baby. She carefully wrapped him in the warm clothing she had purchased a few weeks before his birth. The cardboard box was next to the bed. It had already been prepared. Lots of foil and newspaper lined the inside of the box. The sheepskin fleece lay on top of the foil and newspaper. Myrna carefully wrapped the baby in two woollen blankets. She covered his head with a hat and the hood from the outfit she had bought the previous day then placed him in the box. Myrna removed her winter coat and the matching woollen scarf from the hook behind the door. She called the local cab service then waited for its arrival. Within ten minutes, she and the baby in the box climbed into the back seat of the cab but headed for the Main Street. The cab pulled up where she had directed the driver to stop. It was just near to the local Banks. The driver asked if Myrna wanted him to wait but she told him not to.

After the birth of their child, Myrna sought to resolve with getting on with her life without Raleigh. It was tough. She was always haunted by the way he had ducked out of his responsibility to father their child. It was not an easy decision to abandon their son but one that Myrna had thought through prior to doing so. Indirectly, the Media kept her informed that her baby had been found initially. Subsequently, Myrna was delighted to learn of Sheila and Count's generous contribution towards her son. She had also seen the appeals in the Media about the need for Earl's biological parents to contact Sheila Stagg but Myrna chose to remain anonymous. She feared that Earl would not understand the reasons behind her decision, so she deliberately remained anonymous. All through the peaks and troughs of depression and mood swings she'd experienced, Myrna had managed to monitor Earl's progress from afar. She kept her finger on the pulse but tracked his rise to prominence. Again, it was through the Media that she'd learnt about his death and funeral arrangements.

Now, in the specially designed Corporate Box she had purchased, it was the heavy snoring that notified Myrna that Raleigh had stopped sobbing. His whole body shook as he drew on his in-breath. Echoing as it did, within the spacious Corporate Box, the sound was already becoming unbearable. In his more relaxed state the tall mesomorphic somatotype seemed much heavier than when Myrna first started to cradle him. She struggled to get Raleigh to shift his position in order to enable her to free her arm. It was becoming deadened by his weight. Myrna called his name but gently at first. When there was no response apart from the snores intensifying by degrees of decibels, Myrna raised her voice to a pitch that indicated she was getting a bit impatient with Raleigh. She nudged, pushed, harassed and harangued until Raleigh grunted acknowledgement that he was coming back to consciousness. He opened his eyes as if he was peering cautiously before opening them wider. Myrna told him of her discomfiture with the deadened arm. Raleigh looked concerned but eased himself into a position to enable her to free the trapped arm. Myrna had no feeling in that arm temporarily. "Oh Raleigh, I can't feel my arm. Don't think it's broken, do you", Myrna queried?

Raleigh took the affected arm but massaged it gently at first then applied a more rigorous routine. His huge hands surrounded but caressed Myrna's thin arm. Within a short period of time, she could feel the blood flowing again in that arm. She looked up at him as if he'd performed some miracle but bent gently towards him. She kissed him gently on his forehead in appreciation for the attention he had shown. As Myrna retreated from Raleigh, she noticed his muscular body and his flashing smile but once again she weakened to the myth to which she had become accustomed. The self-conditioning of the myth reinforced but quickly triggered her feelings about the man who took her virginity. Myrna voluntarily chose to revisit those feelings of being 'turned on' in Raleigh's presence. She rose from her position on the floor but walked over to the Bar area in the Corporate Box. Myrna removed another bottle of champagne from the silver ice bucket but invited Raleigh to join her. He too rose from the floor. Standing for a few seconds as if to re-check his balance before walking over towards where Myrna was standing. She used the remote to draw the curtains around the inner perimeter of the Corporate Box but beckoned for him to sit on the large beige curved four seat sofa. Raleigh took his glass of champagne and sat down. Myrna sat close to him but held her glass out in front of her. They toasted the achievements of their son. "Who would have thought our son would have been given a Knighthood", Myrna asked? "Who indeed", Raleigh responded? "Raleigh, I've called you several names over the years. I've called you a bastard and worse but you still do it for me. You're still as handsome as the night we met and your body is still so muscular and firm. I must tell you that I've still got feelings for you Raleigh, after all these years. Did you know that", Myrna asked? "To be honest, I didn't think you'd want to see me ever again let alone have feelings for me. I'm flattered", Raleigh confessed. "You took my virginity, Raleigh. You gave me my first sexual experience. Should I not feel grateful or indebted to you", Myrna asked? Remembering what really happened Raleigh was more than surprised to hear Myrna speak so encouragingly about that particular night. He remembered tricking Myrna into the room, overpowering then raping her most mercilessly. Myrna sensed Raleigh's hesitation. "Don't worry Raleigh, I won't tell anyone what really happened. After all, it's none of their business, is it? Our son has brought us together on this day. Don't you think it was meant to be? Let us drink a toast to our son, drink up", Myrna chirped. They raised their glasses but drank the toast to their son. Raleigh looked at his watch but realized how long he had been away from Sheila and the others. "Is that the time? I'm sorry Myrna but I'll have to go before they send out a search party for me", Raleigh apologised. "Are you going back to the Adult Alcoholic Drinking Centre afterwards", Myrna queried? "Yes, but we'll have to be discreet. You know the wagging tongues and all that", Raleigh warned. "I'll be there but don't worry, I won't make myself too obvious", Myrna replied. Raleigh rose from the sofa. His tall 6'7 muscular frame towered above Myrna's 6'2" frame. They stood close until she gripped him around his waist but pulled him into her. Raleigh could hardly resist her. He buried his lips upon hers but groped her breast firmly. Soon the two of them were off into a different zone. She was still hot for him and him for her. Myrna pulled him onto her as she fell backwards onto the sofa. She reached down but felt the huge bulge that was now throbbing to its own tempo. Myrna gripped but squeezed it firmly. Raleigh feeling encouraged adjusted himself but released his throbbing dick from the stricture of his boxer shorts but sought to implant it into Myrna's vagina. She managed to adjust herself but turned 180 degrees but now lay on top of him. They petted heavily. This sent Raleigh into a greater state of excitement. He grabbed her hand but begged her to let him enter her. "No Raleigh, it's my turn to do the raping. You'll just have to take it as I give it to you", Myrna confirmed. Her voice was soft but controlled. She stroked his shaft repeatedly from its base to its tip slowly and lightly with the back of the nail of her index finger. He wrenched his body but felt the spasms of sensations rushing through it. Myrna then climbed on top of Raleigh. She inserted the tip of his dick inside her but generated some movement. It was her turn to make him desire her greatly but restrict him from being in control. Myrna brought him to a point where Raleigh sensed that he wanted to explode but she withdrew his dick from her vagina and watched it do its throbbing dance. He gripped Myrna's shoulders, pulled her roughly towards him, kissed her ravenously but begged for full penetration. Again Myrna denied him his request. She climbed off but replenished the glasses with more champagne. "Let us have a bit of fun Raleigh. After all it has been a long while. Let us not rush any of this. It might be another long while before we meet again", Myrna implored. Raleigh lay on his back but sipped from the glass. His throbbing dick stuck out of his trousers but raged for inclusion. Myrna completely ignored it but proceeded to speak to Raleigh about how lonely she'd been without him over the years but particularly how she found it impossible to maintain any meaningful relationship since that time. She confessed that the myth that drove her *'mental conditioning'* about allegiance to whom took her virginity made her not feel as deeply about lusting after any other man. In fact, Myrna described herself as feeling as if she belonged to Raleigh. She described her allegiance to him as being like an *'item of property'* like a *'chattel-led slave'* to her Master.

Raleigh was surprised by Myrna's revelation. He had had many other relationships like hers since then and really didn't care a damn about what had happened so many years ago. As a man, Raleigh went out to *'conquer'* in order to satisfy his lust and that was all there was to it. Getting some pussy was the aim of the game. Commitment was never an item on his agenda. To Raleigh, one pussy was more or less the same as another. It was the ultimate target and keeping score was the thrill. Intrinsic motivation was never a problem to Raleigh or his kind. Trendy appearance was as much lure as materialistic embellishments like silver and gold rings, chains, bracelets and earrings. These were the baits that hooked the underside of the female admirer's psyche. Alcohol added to the lifting of their spirits. Charm was a highly skilled weapon to the *'hunter'* but the art of communication known as *'the gift of the gab'* or *'lyrics'*, commonly, engaged yet often mesmerized the intended prey. Once hooked, promises, whether futuristic or immediate, though these were as plentiful as fireworks at an annual national celebration, were used as *'bait'* to ensure to reel in the catch. The skill of the *'hunter'* meant that the *'hunted'* kept this game alive because they too were *'hunters'* in their own right seeking their degree of perceived satisfaction. The *'spy'*, *'counter-spy'* ideology remonstrated by two *'consenting'* individuals meant that the ultimate prize, sex, was procured more frequently than openly acknowledged. In fact, most times there was little or no subtly involved. As long as they could get it and as often as they could was their only interest. Raleigh thought that women, like Myrna, made themselves vulnerable. As far as he was concerned, he didn't make her or any other woman a promise to commit to a long-termed relationship. Myrna and the others like her were the ones doing the chasing. They lust just the same as men. Raleigh's way of looking at women like Myrna was that their own perception of "having a crush" or being *'drawn'* towards men like him was not some kind of divine right with which they were born, but just *"their inner yearnings of lust manifesting"*. He felt that Myrna and others like her ought to get a grip of the way they think. Instead, they needed to accept the reality of their individual egotistical mental contrivance of such a mindset. After all, Raleigh concluded that if Myrna and women like her preferred to believe their own *'stereo-hype'* about the *'magnetism'* of attraction between a man and a woman being anything else than *'heat'*, then they must be ready to suffer the consequences just like any other animal species. The *'magnetic pull'* was the *'attraction'* or *'distraction'* which alerted one to the other. This is so whether initiated by the man or woman. It is simply nothing less or more than what had been acknowledged subsequently as *'THE LUST FACTOR'*.

Swallowing but digesting the *'stereo tripe'* and believing the *'stereo-hype'*, which has been perpetrated throughout generations, meant that the reasons given by women like Myrna for *"having a crush for"* and *"being drawn"* to men like Raleigh set their own standards. It is a self-fulfilling philosophy. Those women must take full responsibility for the situations in which they find themselves. Raleigh thinks that children with absent fathers must question but demand to be told the truth by those mothers, who choose not to explain to them about the true reasons for their fathers' absence. He feels the responsibility for bringing a child into the world started with a sexual act by both parents. Raleigh reasons that most men might not even have known that they were fathers. This might be due to the casual engagement by both consenting individuals at the time the child was being conceived. Just like four-footed animals, Raleigh claims that chance meetings, like *'one night stands'*, do happen, more often than disclosed. These were initiated by nothing else but what's known colloquially as *'a crush'* for the other individual. The *'crush'* is nothing less than sheer unadulterated act of lust. Raleigh was of the opinion that some women chose to commit themselves to these meaningless relationships based on their own perceptions and beliefs about the myths. In fact, he firmly believed that any research could easily confirm his findings. His experiences had taught him that those women, who chose to make themselves available to him and other men like him left themselves open to being exploited with their permission. They did this in order to satisfy some peculiar perceptions of those *'values and beliefs'* that they had cultivated within their own minds. Men like Raleigh actively sought those women, who think or behaved like Myrna and the others do. As far as Raleigh was concerned, he helped himself to what was available at the time. Those women flung themselves at him, offering their vaginas freely and he obliged by fucking them. Raleigh saw them as no different to whores. To him, the only difference is they didn't have a pimp driving their objective. They did that job themselves. Myrna, and the women who think like her, didn't hang about on street corners necessarily but they went to Hotels, Motels, Parks, Cars and remote or darkened areas to be fucked. There was no other consideration. That is what they were seeking and that's what they got. As for satisfaction, that's another story altogether but that is left up to the imagination. Raleigh reasoned that all this nonsense about looks, shapes, body size, height, weight and size of genitalia were the madness that drove some women to cheapen themselves towards being *'closeted whores'*. He insisted that it was up to Myrna and others to sort out their narrow-minded egos, tainted attitudes and subsequent degraded, diminished mindsets of low self-worth.

In the specially designed Corporate Box, Myrna saw that, through conversation, she'd managed to distract Raleigh enough. His dick was not so erect now. In fact, it listed to one side like a drooping flower which had lost its appeal but caused it to appear lopsided. It was not yet dead. Some leakage of sperm drained from the opening at the top. It looked gooey but smelt slightly raw. Myrna grabbed hold of Raleigh's dick again at the root with one hand. She began to slap it with the other hand while she manoeuvred to resurrect its erection. Raleigh sensed that Myrna was in charge though he just wanted to come. He wrenched according to the spasms of pleasures he was experiencing. When Myrna thought Raleigh was ready to re-engage, she asked him to stand up. When he did so, she turned her back to him but bent over towards her toes. She invited him to enter her. Like the stallion he was famed to be, Raleigh gladly accepted Myrna's invitation. As soon as she felt his re-entry, Myrna started her exaggerated movements. Using her hips, Myrna made her bum cheeks tremble like a human earthquake. Those seemingly voluntary practiced shaking movements by Myrna sent Raleigh wild. He raised his tempo but drove home his initiative, borrowing deeper, much deeper and yet deeper still into the fleshy surface like a miner's drill borrowing for diamonds. They were both sweating profusely now from the temperature in the Corporate Box and from their individual exertions also. Myrna's cooing sound coinciding with Raleigh's deep-throated roaring added to the *'Ecstatic Chorus'* that was happening in the Corporate Box. It wasn't until they heard the voices of Myrna's two previous guests apologising for interrupting that Raleigh and Myrna realised the door had been left unlocked. Wrapped up in their passionate stirrings, they carried on grunting and humming their harmonies to their own melodic vibrations regardless, until exhaustion.

Posthumously, Earl's ethereal body floated above them but observed his biological mother and father copulating at his stadium, on the day of his funeral. His visit was unannounced, unexpected and unseen but he was present throughout every leg of the relay that coordinated the entire funeral adulations let alone this ironic moment. Raleigh and Myrna, having satisfied their lust for each other, collapsed onto the sofa but laid there for a while. She was more than excited by the feelings which swept over her; resting cosily on Raleigh's muscular frame entwined with her own slender frame. Raleigh enjoyed Myrna's hot passionate advances which served as the trigger that released those pent up years of sexual desires which Sheila could not necessarily evoke nor maintain. After all, she was not as forthcoming with the passionate lustful type of loving that Raleigh and men like him found challenging and exciting. Sheila's green humanoid tribal heritage meant that she was quite cold and not as sensual or seemingly obsessed as Raleigh. She was from an era and cultural background that possibly had sex as *"a matter of duty"* rather than from a passionate standpoint. Sheila rationed her sexual need to maybe once per week like her assigned *'bath-nights'* which she executed on a predetermined night and time. Her systemic schedule demanded that on Thursday nights only, Raleigh ready himself for sex by 20:23 hours precisely for the foreplay which Sheila directed but insisted take no more than ten minutes followed by insertion immediately afterwards. Despite the level of enjoyment and Raleigh's longevity in maintaining an erection, Sheila insisted that the act should end by precisely 20:56 hours. That gave her four minutes to log the occasion in her diary and to say her prayer before falling asleep precisely at 21:00 hours. Otherwise, Sheila Stagg was likely to suddenly develop a *'headache'* just when Raleigh was really in the mood. She was older too but was unaware where Raleigh went on his so called long walks during weekdays or his long visits to *'friends'* that lasted until the early hours of the mornings. Sheila knew nothing of his arrangements when he went away for weekends. Raleigh knew the kind of women' who made themselves available to him, what they wanted from him and his insatiable quest to conquer. Some of these women were nymphomaniacs. Most had never experienced an orgasm or felt they had managed to achieve *'fulfilment'*, perhaps! In desperation to have that *'elusive sensual experience'*, some women hankered after the *'stereo-tripe'* that prolonged the *'stereo-hype'* about *'stereotypes'* like Raleigh, whose physical attributes they perceived guaranteed satisfaction, assumedly! Raleigh was a most virile *'stud'*, who accepted those women's massaged egos but elected to play the *'game'*. Because of the proverbial *'values and beliefs'* with which some women chose to *'programme'* and *'condition'* their minds, men like Raleigh need not have a brain. As far as those women were concerned that was a *'bonus'* to their twisted fantasies. Those drove their insatiate mental arousals which needed to be reconciled in their quest for *'satisfaction'*. This they claim to reach through perception of cloned mindsets about not only having a *'crush'* on but also to throw themselves at the mercy of studs with physicality like Raleigh. Whatever else he did, Raleigh kept himself busy with other women six days a week but made sure he was always available on his and Sheila's *special night*. That was enough to keep her contented.

CHAPTER 6

The Cobblestone Arms AADC was not sufficient for the huge crowd that left from the stadium but had turned up for the final leg of Earl Stag's funeral arrangements. Simon Crabley, the landlord, and his staff were in for a very busy night. The crowd gathered like worker bees around a hive. The buzzing of the voices travelled way beyond the confines of the AADC. Simon and his staff had to ask the patrons to shout their orders. Some people, unable to get inside, gathered outside the front of the Adult Alcoholic Drinking Centre on Vanguard High Road. At the rare of The Cobblestone Arms AADC, facing the Harbour-Shark Estate, there was a huge play area for children. Swings, slides and climbing frames were scattered amongst the tables and chairs for parents to enable them to supervise their children, whilst they enjoyed their favourite tipple. That area at the back of The Cobblestone Arms AADC was packed solid, so much so that the children hardly had any space to play. Adults were not sensitive to the children's presence. Some were careless about their language and habits like smoking. The passive smoking ban was strictly adhered to inside but not in front of nor at the back of The Cobblestone Arms AADC. Some people had to wait a very long time before they could get their orders in. Simon Crabley and his staff were sweating profusely just trying to keep up with the orders. There was a sound which caused everyone to be silent. It was the feedback from the microphone from which Birdie Spring-Hip was about to speak. Two or three times the feedback from the microphone deafened the crowd inside The Cobblestone Arms AADC. Finally, the volume was lowered enough to enable Birdie to make her announcement. "Ouiiiiii, Ouiiiiii, you lot are too selfish. You can see we're struggling to serve but some people are hugging the bar. Once you get served, move away from the bar so others can be served? It doesn't need brain surgery, does it", Birdie shouted? It was quite a stern demand but fair. The announcement should not have had to be necessary but it was a long day and those, who were regular drinkers, seemed to want to make up for their *'sacrificial abstinence'* earlier in the day. They were being selfish but were shamed into embarrassment. As soon as those guilty of hugging the bar moved away, there was a charge by the next group towards the bar by those who were as keen to quench their thirst too. Birdie Spring-Hip was in charge of the extra staff that had been hired for the day. She was a good organizer but her ego was hugely inflated. Birdie had a tendency to overact her role. She perceived that being in charge made her seem important to others. When Birdie approached Enid Staveley at the back of the AADC, she had no idea that Enid was Duke's mother. Birdie's comment about Duke's behaviour was enough to unnerve her rival Brigette but she didn't cater for the overprotective Enid. "I don't know who you think you are talking to about my children like that. Have you any idea how little space there is for them to run about and play", Enid asked? "I wasn't talking to you. I was talking to his mother", Birdie replied. As she said the words, Birdie indicated that she was referring to Brigette. She smiled broadly before responding. "Some people need to get their facts right before they get into other people's business", Brigette chided. She looked at Enid but smiled broadly. Enid smiled back. The two boys weaved their way towards where Brigette and Enid stood. "I'm hungry. I want a burger", Duke demanded. "Me too and something to drink", Baron concurred. "We'll have to wait until the next set of food is brought out. You would have thought they would have served children first", Brigette criticised. She looked directly at Birdie when she made the last comment. That was a deliberate snide remark aimed at the egotistical Birdie Spring-Hip. She was embarrassed by the comment that Brigette had made but decided to challenge anything that she said. Birdie wanted to respond to the challenge because she felt confident about being able to manage the frail looking Brigette. "Some people want to watch what they are saying about how things are arranged. I'm in charge and if you don't like it you can leave with your spoilt kid", Bridie sniped. Her comment was aimed at Brigette because she knew that Brigette used to be Earl's live in woman and that Duke was Earl's son. There was jealousy and bitterness in Birdie's voice when she spoke. That was enough for Enid. She didn't have to listen to Birdie's acid remarks about her child. Enid approached Birdie but confronted her about her statement. "If you have something to say about my child say it to my face", Enid challenged. Birdie was taken aback by Enid's confrontation. Her comments were aimed at Brigette not Enid. Birdie was confused and shocked. "I wasn't talking to you. I was talking to her", Birdie pleaded. "Yeah, but you were talking about my son, weren't you", Enid challenged. "Duke's your son", Birdie asked? "Yes, they are both my sons". If you talk about them in a derogatory manner again then you've got me to face", Enid finished. Birdie did not say another word. She hurried from the back of the AADC to get some more food. There was something that told her that Enid might be more than she can manage. Enid was stockier than Brigette even though she was shorter than her. There was definitely a seed of doubt that was sewn in Birdie's mind that warned her not to challenge the meaner looking woman. Brigette and Enid laughed together. "Did you see the look on her face", Brigette asked? "Yeah, she got a shock, didn't she", Enid responded.

The boys had wandered off towards the other children with whom they were playing earlier. Brigette and Enid watched them interacting. Soon Duke had got into an altercation with another boy. It appeared as if they were arguing about whose turn it was to go onto the slide. Enid and Brigette did not interfere but kept glancing over towards them. Soon they heard Duke's heavy voice. He seemed to be challenging but spoiling for a fight. As they looked over to see exactly what was going on, Enid heard Baron's heavy voice join in the argument. By the time the women began to weave their way over towards the children, Baron had already thrown the first punch and pandemonium had set in. Parents were shouting for the boys to stop fighting. Duke had heard the derogatory comment calling him the 'A' word. He grabbed the purple coloured Mixed DNA Rainbow Tribe boy, who had made the degrading remark by his collar, but swung him from side to side like a rag doll while Baron repeatedly punched the pink coloured Mixed DNA Rainbow Tribe boy. Both of the boys with whom they were fighting were at least two years older and taller than them. Some of the women closer to the boys screamed. "He's got a knife", a woman's voice shouted. On the other side of the mesh wired fence that divided the Harbour-Shark Estate and The Cobblestone Arms AADC, a white coloured Mixed DNA Rainbow Tribe boy about sixteen years old seemed to be egging on the fourteen year old purple coloured boy to stab Duke. "Shank him Hartly, shank him", the white coloured sixteen year old inveigled. Enid and Brigette couldn't believe what they were hearing and before long there seemed to be thirty or so boys about fourteen to sixteen years old on the other side of the meshed wired fence that separated the Harbour-Shark Estate from the back of The Cobblestone Arms AADC. They were agitated but jumping up and down and shouting. Duke pushed the purple coloured boy away from him. The purple coloured boy raised his arm and that was when Enid and Brigette saw the knife. It glinted under the bright lights at the back of The Cobblestone Arms AADC. "Stop them before they kill someone", a female voice implored. Duke watched the purple coloured boy as he rushed towards him. He was frightened but not afraid. Baron had knocked the pink coloured Mixed DNA Rainbow Tribe boy out cold but Duke kept his eye on the knife all the time. When the purple coloured boy stabbed at him, Duke managed to dodge the blade but kicked the offender in the shin area of his standing foot. When it came into contact, the hard leather soled shoe with the steel toecap Duke was wearing sounded against the boy's tibia. The impact was immediate. Pain surged through the purple coloured boy's leg as swiftly as voltage through copper wiring. Although he couldn't be sure until having his leg x-rayed, the purple boy's leg was possibly broken by the force and intention in which the kick was delivered. It hurt enough for the boy to drop the knife. In his effort to stab Duke, through momentum the purple coloured boy lost his balance but tumbled to the ground. Like in the movies, when the weapon has gone to ground, the perpetrator began to crawl towards where the knife had fallen. In an effort to stop the purple coloured boy from retrieving the weapon, both Duke and Baron set upon him. Each delivered kicks with such venom that the thudding into the boy's ribs sounded like the striking of bass drums with padded sticks. The muffled sounds were quite distinctly opposite to the high pitched shrieking coming from the boy on the ground each time a kick from Baron or Duke found its target. Hoards of other Mixed DNA Rainbow Tribe coloured boys from the Harbour-Shark Estate, including the white coloured boy, who had passed the knife through the fence to the purple coloured boy from his tribe, stood on the other side. When the gang members saw how one of their colleagues was being beaten by Duke and Baron, they started to shout threats at the two brothers. The gang members seemed animated in the way they were behaving. Some backed off from the fence but ran towards it in great numbers and at speed to generate enough force to break the fence down in order to visit their revenge upon Baron and Duke. Others attempted to climb the fence in order to help their colleague. The noise was now unbearable but all the adults in the Play Area went over to quash the disturbance. The multi-coloured Mixed DNA Rainbow Tribe Harbour-Shark Estate Gang was more than a neighbourhood nuisance. Many of those boys had already been to Youth Correctional Establishments (Prisons) or had been given Anti Social Behaviour Orders, ASBOs. Some of them were excluded permanently, others temporarily, from their respective schools. Most of their parents had attended Earl's funeral earlier in the day and were regular patrons of The Cobblestone Arms AADC. Some were inside whilst some others were at the front of the Adult Alcoholic Drinking Centre, unaware that their sons were involved in a gang attack on Earl's sons. The sounds of the police sirens were not far away. It meant that someone had called the cops. Their imminent arrival was enough for the now not so brave gang members to desist from climbing the fence. As some of them disappeared from the scene, threats were hurled back at Duke and Baron. Gunshots were heard as the thirty or so boys ran in different directions on the huge Housing Estate. Enid and Brigette were shocked at the assault on the two boys. Other individuals commented about the gang's behaviour but swore allegiance to Earl's son, Duke. Many had no idea that Baron was his brother although they had seen the similarity in the build, height and looks of the two boys. Birdie Spring-Hip stood with tray in hand and mouth agog. She had heard but witnessed only the end of the chaotic furore. Birdie knew something had happened but wasn't sure about the details. Many people went up to Birdie to get some of the food from the tray but she said it was for "Duke and the other boy". She went over towards where they were standing. Enid and Brigette were standing next to them but were engaged in finding out what had taken place before the fight. Duke spoke first. He told Brigette and his mother that the older purple and pink coloured Mixed DNA Rainbow Tribe boys were "mean" to him. They kept teasing him about his blue plaid *'Andy Capp'* flat cap and the blue plaid Sherlock Holmes suit with the shoulder flaps that reminded them of *"bloodhound's ears"*. The purple and pink coloured boys told Duke he looked like "a cartoon character" from a different time zone in his "blue plaid *'plus-four'* suit and cap". They questioned from which area he'd come then deliberately got in his way each time he tried to get on the swings or slides. The pink coloured boy that Baron had knocked out had pushed his hand down his own baggy trousers but said that he had a gun and that he would shoot him. Baron didn't wait to see the gun. He knocked the pink coloured boy out cold using several martial art punches. Another boy had rushed towards Baron while his back was turned to him. Duke explained that's when he had grabbed the purple coloured boy by the collar but started to shake him vigorously. When he'd pushed him away, the white coloured boy gave the purple coloured boy from his tribe a knife and began to shout, ". . . shank him Hartly . . . shank the f . . . . ng *'A'* ". Duke said he kicked him as hard as he could in his shin. He said he had seen his dad do that to a man before so he did the same. Brigette and Enid congratulated the boys for looking out for each other. A blue coloured Mixed DNA Rainbow Tribe boy, who remained neutral, warned them that the gang would try to get them another time. He told Duke and Baron that they were now *"targets"* and that the gang would use every opportunity to get them. Birdie

Spring-Hip stood transfixed at what she'd heard. She had only been gone some ten to twelve minutes but what had developed was quite serious. Birdie would have to alert Simon Crabley about the incident. Baron and Duke took the burgers and drinks from Birdie. They bit into their food like ravenous young pups that were tasting food for the first time. When Simon Crabley heard about Duke's predicament, he announced the incident over the microphone. There was a huge outcry from the inebriated crowd for revenge on behalf of '*The Gaffer*'. The crowd at the front also heard the news and joined in the passionate remonstrations about "cleansing the community" of the likes of the Mixed DNA multi-coloured Harbour-Shark Estate Gang. Some of these individuals had already decided that they would "swing for '*The Gaffer*' ". A posse of men was rounded up but headed for the nearby Harbour-Shark Estate. Some carried baseball bats, some planks of wood or pieces of metal like piping whilst others were armed with bottles, beer glasses, knives and other assorted weapons. The lighting on the Estate was not very good in certain areas but the lighting that reflected from the back of The Cobblestone Arms AADC was extraordinarily bright. Police saw the two hundred or more vigilantes from the AADC as they searched for the boys that had started the trouble with Duke. Conversely, the families attending the final leg of Earl Stagg's funeral that lived on the Harbour-Shark Estate formed their own posse to defend those members of the Harbour-Shark Estate Gang who happened to be their children. They didn't agree with what their children were getting up to but refused to stand by and watch their children be attacked by the vigilante gang. The shouting reinforced by the amount of drinks that each side had had became more like the thunderous eruptions when a goal was scored at Earl Stagg's Association Football Stadium. The police called for backup as the size of both posses started to swell. Individuals were ready to war against their next door neighbours, with whom they had sat or stood together moments before the trouble started amongst the boys. Threats were being traded from either group. This gave strength to the boys from the Harbour-Shark Estate Gang. They joined their respective relatives in the awesome confrontation. Some threw bottles and other missiles in the direction of the police. Sporadic gunshots were fired into the air. Even the police ran for shelter. More police sirens could be heard and before long the entire Estate was surrounded by the ARU, Armed Response Unit, of the police. They and those in Riot Gear with batons, helmets and shields stood in solid formation ready to battle with the posses. Some of the police came to the fence to find out what had taken place. When someone said that it was Earl's son that the boys wanted to attack, the police was taken aback. Earl had personally invested not only money but a great deal of his time rescuing some of the boys from the Harbour-Shark Estate. One or two had graduated from the Earl Stagg Association Football Academy at The Earl Stagg Association Football Club. He had initiated the pathway for previous boys to the Academy. They had graduated but moved on. Some were currently with other Association Football Clubs. They spread across the different Leagues and Divisions. Others were currently training with youth and junior squads. The police were aware of the increase in violence on the troubled Estate. Drug dealing was rife on the Harbour-Shark Estate as most of the young adults sought to feed their young families or sought independence from their respective families, who were mostly on State Benefits.

The police called to the Estate was employed by the privately owned *'Ethnic Stereotypes'* Special Unit. It was in charge of the crimes committed by those ethnic *'stereo-types'* against their own. These ethnic *'stereo-types'* were, seemingly by implication, *"more dangerous"* than any other *'type'* of criminals. They needed "to be approached with more aggression and numbers than the *'ordinary'* criminals", apparently! There was no doubt of the likelihood that there were some extremely dangerous individuals amongst the *'stereo-types'*. Some of them manifested into the *'stereo-typical imagery'*, regrettably so but did it mean that each criminal had the same degree of intent as another? The debate continued throughout the generations on the parallel virtual planet. Some of the *'stereo-types'* didn't seek to eliminate the image being painted by significant others but lived it instead. In fact, some chose but seemed to enjoy the notoriety associated with the *'City Cowboy'* image whilst others were being bullied or directed by Gang Orientation Scientists, Operators and Practitioners into the criminal lifestyle by default. One typical example of this was known as the UFO's Cult-Induced Post/Zip Code Wars. According to the *'Post/Zip Code'* in which they lived, young adults, youths and juniors latterly assembled in large groups on the street corners but violently challenged each other frequently. Sometimes, the challenges were serious enough to cause real damage. At times, individuals were maimed physically and mentally by the bizarre bullying attacks in the streets; sometimes resulting in deaths. It was a real problem within local precincts, neighbourhoods, districts and boroughs. Politicrats seemed not to want to accept the messages which pointed to the underlying reasons for the madness on the streets. What used to be peaceful communities were breaking up into different factions which now warred on a daily basis. Fear had assured that social relationships were deteriorating into shambles. There was real lack of quality communication and emotional sensitivity amongst families and communities let alone with any other. The blinkered *'drive'* and *'focus'* was about raising the *'anti'* to the most dangerous levels of incessant deep-seated raging rivalry that had not only threatened to decimate relationships amongst families, friends and, in this case, neighbours, who were backing the *'wrong-doings'* of their children and other family members but also to establish the type of intensely corrupted mentality, which had been encouraged by the UFO and their affiliates, the Gang Orientation Scientists, Operators and Practitioners. This precariously high level of *'denial'* was not yet measurable on any scientific scale.

Now, on the Harbour-Shark Estate, whether it were those individuals, who were there on behalf of the son of *'The Gaffer'* or to defend their family members, who were caught up in UFO's Cult-Induced Post/Zip Code Wars, both sets were just as keen and ready to commit to display ASPD, Anti Social Personality Behaviour, with as much schizophrenic unremorseful violence as they needed to apply. It was a *'them'* versus *'us'* situation. The vigilante gang knew their action would be applauded by both central and local politicrats. They did this in order to gain cheap political *'acclaim'*. Vigilante gangs had often claimed to be acting "on behalf of the *'good'* citizens of the communities". While their cause sounded plausible enough, a great many were motivated by their veiled inveterate prejudices. Although bigotry was their staple mentality, some claimed that, as a group, they wanted to exercise their *'power'* as citizens "to carry out *citizen's arrests*" on behalf of the particular communities. Most individuals in the communities were tired of the senseless madness known as the UFO's *'Cult-Induced'* Post/Zip Code

Wars, commonly, but they feared that these *self-appointed vigilantes' 'citizens arrests'* might be serving a different *'purpose'* that was more covert, perhaps! Communities feared the *vigilantes' 'missions'* might be carried out with the type of stinking attitudes and heavily partisan toxic bigoted mindsets that might have a premeditated propensity against ethnic groups. Their approach would leave no margin for error about the predictable result of such attempts to *'arrest' 'protesting suspects',* who might be *"wrongfully arrested"*. Driven by the predetermined prejudiced perceptions of the *'assigned'* Marshals, many young *'suspects'* had been shot to death even within seemingly *'secure' 'gated'* communities. The *'Laws'* that permitted such behaviour by those *'self-appointees'* were themselves being manipulated by seasoned *'Legal Eagles',* whose agendas were no less suspect than those of the offending vigilante gang members, who had made the decision to pull the trigger, probably! Even though it would take the operation of another's brain to know what they were thinking, the enablement by *'Law'* to murder any *"suspicious looking character"* either because of their attire, ethnicity or both meant that the offending inveterate bigot vigilante gang member could cite the intensity of their perceived fear as being *"just cause"* for choosing to squeeze the trigger. The Law didn't seem to take into account that, despite advising vigilantes not to continue their pursuit of *'suspects',* those vigilante gang members had often ignored those *'orders'* from relevant *'Emergency Operators',* who had been contacted by them but chose to aggressively stalk, like trackers, but hunt down to entrap or provoke a defensive reaction from perceived assailants.

Most communities agreed that politicrats could act more positively towards supporting new fairer initiatives. There were outreach workers better qualified and with more meaningful intentions than the vigilante *'gangs'* towards the young people. What they needed were holistic approach where thoughts, feelings and situational or environmental experiences were being taken into account. These outreach workers had excellent contacts with the young people in the communities in Spaceville including those on the Harbour-Shark Estate. Instead of being empowered to help the *"disaffected"* young people, so-called, to turn away from crime, the outreach workers were being marginalized by those in authority. These workers were well respected by those young people, who were struggling with extremely low self worth, esteem and confidence issues. They felt vulnerable yet exposed to the violence within communities too. The political elements failed to protect the young people from those, who preyed on their naivety, but left them most vulnerable to the predators. Instead, those in authority viewed the troubled young population from the same narrow fixed perspectives that they had held perennially for as long as their tunnelled visions were initiated. What politicrats had done previously and was continuing to do currently were to deliberately ignore all other ideas or perspectives but the ones they had held as *'gospel'* for as many years as *'gospels'* had existed, seemingly!

In Spaceville, there was one politicrat, who was qualified to earn the respect from the people on the Harbour-Shark Estate. In the recent national election, the community of Ghettoborough had voted for her to represent them as their PM, Political Member, for that particular borough. Amongst her other strengths, Janette Brayhorne had worked as a volunteer youth worker previous to her existence as a Councillor and currently as PM for Ghettoborough. While she was travelling home, Janette had heard the news about the confrontation with the two groups on the *'Breaking News'* via the national radio station. She stopped the car but made a couple of phone calls before deciding to go to the Harbour-Shark Estate. This Estate came under her ward. There was no other individual better qualified to answer the media about the problems she knew existed on the Estate. By the time she made her way back towards the Harbour-Shark Estate, the news media were already there. They sought to get an angle for the disturbance. The journalists and reporters spoke with the police as well as some local people, who were living on the run-down Estate but the reasons given for the disturbance were fluctuating and as controversial as first reports always are. The 'Riot Police' stood three rows thick between the two sets of posses. Their stance kept the two posses apart. The Armed Unit went from block to block on the run down Estate to see whether they could find the individuals who had fired guns into the air.

Inside The Cobblestone Arms AADC, those who had chosen to stay put despite Simon Crabley's announcement were immersed in conversations about possible new owners of The Cobblestone Arms AADC now 'The Gaffer' had died. Simon Crabley had not yet been notified but spoke of his concern too. He thought that Sheila Stagg might be in charge even temporarily at least. It was then that Raleigh Daly-Weede arrived in the Saloon Bar. He beckoned for Simon to come towards him. Even though he too had a very heavy voice, Raleigh managed to keep it in a low tone. Simon nodded and gesticulated often but no one else could figure out what was being discussed. Raleigh turned but walked away from the bar. Simon walked back towards the regulars but said nothing about the discussion. Raleigh slipped through the crowd but headed up the stairs towards a room in the Motel above The Cobblestone Arms AADC. He had secured that room for him and Sheila. His considerate action meant that she could get away from the crowd but have a chance to rest. That is what she did before he took her home. Now that he was back, Raleigh decided to go back to the room. About ten minutes after he returned to the room, Simon sent up the order they had spoken about in the Saloon Bar. The rapid knocks on the door alerted Raleigh that the drinks he'd ordered had arrived. He opened the door slightly but accepted the silver bucket with the ice, the two bottles of champagne and the two glasses. Birdie Spring-Hip wanted to bring the tray into the room but Raleigh told her it was not necessary. She was like a reluctant stray pet that was yearning to get closer but go home with its rescuer. Birdie Spring-Hip looked up rather sheepishly at the statuesque figure and looks of a matured version of her perception of Adonis. Raleigh's eyes followed Birdie's as they went slowly down the middle of his torso but came to rest and focused on the front of his trousers. Raleigh noticed her tongue flickering like that of Maori Warriors in their tribal dance. "Are you sure I can't do anything for you", Birdie chanced? Raleigh was focused on the woman he wanted to be with and knew that her arrival was imminent. He thanked Birdie for bringing the champagne up from the bar area but placed a large tip in her hand. Her eyes widened but she smiled sheepishly before disappearing down the stairs. Raleigh placed the tray on the table in the corner of the room then removed his jacket and tie. He reclined on the bed but propped his head up with a couple of pillows. The next knock on the door seemed to be expected. He didn't even move but used his heavy voice commandingly. "Come in", Raleigh encouraged. The hinges on the door were not the only things needing lubrication. Myrna Mc Tittle eased into but stood in the doorway. The smile on her face told its own story. Raleigh stood up but walked towards her. He pushed the door shut but pressed up hard against her. They stood in close embrace until Raleigh turned the key in the door. He took Myrna by the hand but led her towards the bed. They sat down but kissed over and over again. Raleigh was breathing rather heavily. His heart raced with excitement. Myrna quickly unbuttoned his crumpled shirt. Raleigh's hairy chest was exposed. Myrna stroked his chest but played with the patch of hair which ran provocatively way past his navel and below. He seemed to be in playful mode. She brushed her hand against the front of his trousers but found that Raleigh's was well aroused. Myrna stroked it from outside his trousers but felt the heat emanating and the throbbing became more regular. In the meantime, she was having her own rhythmic spasms that caused her to become quite moist. There was even more heat being generated from between her legs. Raleigh's hand searched below Myrna's waist too. He felt the moisture and knew that it wouldn't be long before they could both explore the passions that had been aroused between them. "Fancy a drink", Raleigh asked? "Oh, yes please Raleigh", Myrna replied. He crossed the room in rather hurried steps. Myrna sidled up to him. They stood close while Raleigh poured the champagne into the two glasses. He wrapped his hand around her slim waist. She melted into his arms but smiled at him provocatively, winking as he flashed her one of his dazzling smiles. "You're such a handsome man Raleigh. No wonder we women fall for you. You don't even have to say a word. Just your smile alone is enough to let us fall at your feet", Myrna complimented. Raleigh placed his hand under Myrna's chin but tilted her mouth upwards towards his. Bending forward, he met Myrna's lips with the most delicate of kisses that seemed to last forever. Lost in those enchanting lingering moments, they stood unmoved for what seemed hours but were in fact a few minutes, savouring every moment of that passionate kiss. Soon, Raleigh unbuttoned Myrna's black satin coat but slipped it past her shoulders onto the floor. The thin black dress she was wearing had stuck to her like a third skin but exposed the figure that had won her so many plaudits in the world of modelling. Raleigh's *'Lust Factor'* rose in quantum calibrations that indicated he was experiencing a meteoric ascent way past his threshold. His egotistical desires remonstrated how much he needed to satiated his immense abnormal sexual appetite without any form of resistance. He was transcending latently through that type of trance which progressed by quantum degrees way beyond thinking. These autonomic feelings were seamless but rendered Raleigh towards becoming impulsive in his behaviour. His focused ambition was to quench the sexually ravenous Myrna's apparent lust. Raleigh Daly-Weede can testify that he only felt this way when he was in Myrna's company more so than in any other woman's presence. She had this mesmerising effect upon his psyche but made him feel much younger than his age. Raleigh kept his body fit from the daily exercise routines that he practiced. Myrna could not have chosen a physically fitter sexual partner but she was about to experience some tricks Raleigh had learnt from other experiences over the years they were apart. When Myrna unzipped his trouser but allowed it to fall to the floor, she could see not only Raleigh's ugly polka dot boxer shorts but also his huge dick that was protruding through the split down the front. It was standing firmly to attention but made him and his huge dick appear like a guard presenting arms at an army inspection. Raleigh's eyes pierced through Myrna's thin dress. His imagination seemed to be rapidly catching up with the recent past event in the Corporate Box at the Earl Stagg Association Football Stadium. As Myrna used her hands to casually ease the dress over her shoulders, Raleigh felt compelled to help with the undressing. In his clumsy way his assistance rather delayed the process than help. His hands moved swiftly towards Myrna's bust but fondled her breasts with his rough palms. It seemed to send spasms of varying voltage of *'electrical'* currents through her body. Myrna shivered from the warm sensual feelings that signalled her yearning to fulfil the sexual void that had built up over the years and since her last relationship with the more than competent lovemaking techniques that Raleigh alone seemed to possess. Both Raleigh and Myrna made their way over towards the bed. She lay on her back while he lay on top of her. They caressed each other. The foreplay was an extended one which they both seemed to be enjoying immensely. Suddenly, Raleigh started to slide gently down Myrna's body until his lips met with her breasts. He kissed them all over then used the tip of his tongue to titillate her nipples; sending Myrna into a spiral of deeper sensual passionate state. Raleigh's method seemed to be much more effective than he was able to control. The magnitude of sensations travelling through Myrna's body was confirmed when she grabbed hold of the back of his head but pressed his face towards the affected breast triggering the sensations at the time. Her wiry body kept reacting to the new thrills that she'd never experienced before. Myrna felt a grateful recipient to Raleigh's expertise. Next, Raleigh reached down but brought the champagne bottle from where he had strategically placed it on the floor beside the bed. Myrna watched as he poured the champagne all over her breasts before pretending to lick it like a dog from her breasts. She didn't quite understand what made Raleigh do what he was doing but she observed his very strange behaviour. Myrna couldn't say she enjoyed that part of the petting. After licking the champagne from her breasts, Raleigh continued to slide even lower down Myrna's body but she felt even more uncomfortable about him getting lower than just below her navel. Myrna grabbed Raleigh's hair but gripped it firmly enough for him to stop. "Raleigh where are you going", Myrna queried? "Don't stop me now, Myrna. Let me show you how it's done. Just lay back and enjoy it", Raleigh offered. "No Raleigh. I don't like what I think you're about to do", Myrna protested. Raleigh was disappointed by Myrna's objection but he didn't say much. He sat on the edge of the bed with his hands covering his face. Raleigh seemed disappointed that Myrna had stopped him from showing her what he thought might be her biggest *'thrill'* yet, probably! She sensed his disappointment but wanted to re-engage on her terms. Myrna gripped Raleigh around his waist but assured him by stroking his dick with the side of her index finger while resting her head upon his thigh. Raleigh felt encouraged by her caressing him in the way she did. He turned himself towards her but moved his dick closer to her mouth; more than hinting for her to commit. Myrna had no hesitation than to withdraw her head away from where it was resting. As a principle, she found it disgusting that Raleigh even suggested the lewd act. As far as Myrna was concerned, she had always been against such pornographic acts. She strongly objected to Raleigh's assumption that she might be happy with this advance as well. Having not been refused before, Raleigh found Myrna's objection more than a distraction. He displayed his annoyance at her refusing to involve herself in this part of his foreplay. "Oh Myrna, don't be a prude. Lots of women and men do this all the time", Raleigh protested. "That might be so but I have a choice, don't I? I'm not a porn star whore, Raleigh. Save those choices for your women who accept them", Myrna told him firmly. Raleigh sulked for awhile. He got up but walked across the room to fetch the glasses. On his return, Raleigh sat on the edge of the bed. He poured the golden liquid from the bottle next to the bed. Raleigh handed one glass to Myrna but supped from the other. Myrna still wanted to have sex with him but wanted to discount the acts with which she felt less than comfortable. Her reactions had stopped Raleigh from his intended move. He started to think that she was odd compared to the other women he'd been with over so many years that welcomed the sort of attention he was about to visit upon Myrna. Raleigh was more than put off by her protestation. She pushed him aside then got up from the bed. Raleigh looked puzzled as Myrna walked towards the door. "Where are you going", Raleigh asked? "Where is the toilet", Myrna countered? "It's down the corridor, third door on the right", Raleigh replied. Myrna slipped on the black satin coat over her naked body but turned the key. She wrenched the round gilt plated knob on the door then walked through it. Raleigh was puzzled at Myrna's behaviour to some of his advances. He assumed that his recent approach was a *'natural'* progression to foreplay but had not met any resistance in all the years that he'd been engaging in sexual involvement. Every film he'd seen whether on DVDs or at the Movies portrayed the male borrowing between the female's legs and her involvement in fellatio as an acceptable *'culturally correct'* *'normal technique'* in foreplay pre-empting the insertion of the penis into the vagina. This was Raleigh's first experience of a woman objecting to what seemed *'normal'* to him. He thought that Myrna's exposure to sexual intercourse must have been very limited indeed. Raleigh looked down at his big dick which wasn't as erect as earlier in the foreplay. It had shrunk in size but drooped precariously like a neck that had been broken but hung to one side. Still Raleigh desired for Myrna had not subsided. He was beginning to think about how long since she'd gone to the toilet. It must have been at least half an hour. Raleigh looked towards the door with deep anticipation but all he could see is the skimpy dress Myrna had left lying by the door. He strained his ears to try to detect whether he could hear her footsteps along the carpeted landing. There was no sound apart from the noise that came from the Harbour-Shark Estate. It was strange how he had taken no notice of that earlier on. His focus was on Myrna and the plan they had made whilst intermingling with the others, who had assembled for the last leg of the proceedings arranged for their son's funeral. Raleigh got up from the bed but walked over to the window. He could see the activities taking place. The police completely surrounded the areas of the Estate that he could see. Standing on a box was Janette Brayhorne. She had a megaphone in her hands. Although Raleigh couldn't hear properly what she was saying, the crowd on both sides seemed to be cheering her comments and the police seemed a little more relaxed yet alert. By her gesticulations, Janette Brayhorne appeared like the typical old fashioned politician, standing on her soapbox delivering some kind of a speech to her audience. It was when Raleigh heard the creaking of the door that he suddenly turned around to see Myrna walking through it. He could not hide his renewed excitement at her arrival but she didn't seem too happy with herself let alone him. Raleigh walked swiftly over towards Myrna but she extended an arm to prevent him from touching her. "Don't touch me Raleigh Daly-Weede", she said. Her words were delivered with deliberate inflexions and the tone was scornful. Raleigh was flummoxed by Myrna's new behaviour. He looked stunned as if he'd been hit over the head with a baseball bat. Raleigh shook his head as if to clear it from the frosty reception he was receiving from the very sexy Myrna. He tried to make light of the situation. "Women", Raleigh said. Thinking that might have appeased Myrna into being rational again, Raleigh reached for the champagne but pour her and him a glass each. Myrna took the champagne but did not appear any happier. "Sit down Myrna. Don't you feel well? Did someone upset you? What happened", Raleigh queried? "Yes, something happened but it happened before I had walked through that door to go to the toilet. You treated me like I was some type of cheap slut you'd just picked up in a red light area. How dare you Raleigh Daly-Weede? How dare you take me for granted, again", Myrna demanded? Raleigh didn't expect this tirade of admonishment from Myrna and he didn't want a repeat of the verbal lashing he'd received in the Corporate Box. Everything had been going so well until he indicated that he wanted to borrow into her vaginal area with his mouth like a pig into swill. The second time was when Raleigh indicated what he had wanted her to do. Myrna did not approve of such sexual techniques. Those two moments were causative to her declaration of disapproval and subsequent coldness towards him. Myrna had a different feeling now for the handsome, muscular built, chiselled jawed Raleigh Daly-Weede. She was in no mood for his sweet talk or even his flashing smile. Myrna spoke to him with not much respect. "Raleigh, what would have happened if I was young enough to be seeing my menstrual cycle at the time when you chose to borrow your head between my legs? How might you have managed if I had let you have your way and I had come on while you were down there? Imagine, that's where you wanted to put your mouth just moments ago, was it not", Myrna fumed? Raleigh hung his head like a man having been exposed in public for some things that he'd rather remain private. Myrna's acid remarks were heavily underlined by her scathing tone. Despite her beauty, she managed to keep a rather serious countenance which clearly demonstrated the level of disgust she was feeling towards him. There was really no answer that Raleigh could offer to satisfy the bizarre scenario that Myrna painted. While he paused to contemplate the arguments for and against Myrna's theoretical assumptions, Raleigh realised that he had never before thought about the possibilities to which she was alluding. It was a chastening experience for the careless Raleigh. While he relived the flashbacks of his frequent sexual experiences over the years, Raleigh was beginning to see the point that Myrna felt so strongly about. She was not finished with her assessment of Raleigh's behaviour or intentions towards her. "Is this what you've been getting up to over the years? I suppose you wouldn't know if any of your cheap whores ever come on while you carried out your seemingly choreographed ritual on them. I suppose if I had let you have your way you might have wanted to kiss me again too, wouldn't you", Myrna fumed? There was just no escape route for Raleigh, whether from Myrna or his conscience. Compared to the next round of probabilities that she asked him to assess, the impact of Myrna's previous words were tame, relatively. "Raleigh, it is men like you who cause women like me to go off sex. How dare you kiss me when you must have found your way borrowing amongst the legs of all the other women with whom you've had sexual intercourse? You might have syphilis, gonorrhoea, herpes or one of those diseases. I was aware of diseases being spread by consenting individuals via sexual organs but never considered it could by mouth, possibly! Don't you think Raleigh that it is highly probable to take sexual diseases from one woman but pass on to the next via your mouth? Aren't you worried about your health? I am about mine. I'm having a check up as soon as this coming Monday", Myrna admonished. Raleigh was dumbfounded by the implications. For the first time, he realised that the sexual trends to which he'd attached himself might prove to be directly impinging on the status of his health. He had never even thought about questioning whether his sexual habits were his own preferences or some others *'values and beliefs'* to which he'd attached himself or adopted, even. Myrna's words ricocheted but rebounded again and again until her voice seemed to be emanating but became the voice from within his head. It was dauntingly maddening. He used the heel of one hand to hammer against the voice, which seem to hauntingly mock him like the bullying echo which seem to be increasing not only in volume but also with repetitions. Raleigh felt he had to defend himself from the many aspersions that were being sent his way. "You're the only woman that's ever complained. Everybody does it, don't they? What makes you different", Raleigh fired back? This was not a good strategy for Raleigh to use to counter the lambasting he was receiving. Similar to her extended outburst in the Corporate Box earlier on, Myrna was more than ready but comparatively determined not only to complete her rant but to rivet the point of principles in which she truly believed. She remembered the *'traditional teachings'* from her grandparents when she was coming up towards puberty. Grandma/Nan and Grandpa had sat her down to teach her the lessons of becoming of age. Myrna remembered vividly when Grandma/Nan stated that Myrna could learn everything about sexual intercourse from animals. "They know no other way than what is instinctively natural", Grandpa had finished. Reeling from the disgust and disdain she felt towards Raleigh, Myrna felt overcome by the fear that she had caught some form of disease from him. Raleigh could see that he was being disposed of in a way he was not used to. He was realising that he had never been challenged like this before by any woman. Apart from his experiences with those older women, who had abused him in the foster homes, Raleigh had never felt as challenged by any woman before. He was always able to choose those, who he might want to conquer; including a much younger Myrna. Raleigh sensed that the adult Myrna was a much different proposition. She had gumption and a much stronger character than he'd bargained for. Being used to taking the younger Myrna and other gullible younger women for granted, Raleigh was feeling out of sorts. His feeling of indifference began to make him uncomfortable. He responded in the only way he knew how. In one desperate last attempt to convince Myrna of what she was missing by not partaking in his *'programmed'* and *'conditioned'* ritual, Raleigh decided to hit back, literally. He switched from the charming hunk into the manic abuser like his son Earl. Without warning, Raleigh struck Myrna across her jaw with the back of his large hand. The blow registered on the right side of her face sending her tumbling to the ground. Myrna saw a constellation of stars even though she was not looking up into the sky. The only image that eluded her was that of the sound of chirping birds that might have completed the imagery linked to being knocked out. The intensity of pain registered like a momentary electric shock. Myrna was disoriented for awhile until she felt those shovel hands of Raleigh's around her neck. She realised he was attempting to choke her out and Myrna heard the commentary as he raged. "You've got some front telling me what to do. What makes you think you're better than the other women with whom I've been? You're just a bitch like any other bitch," Raleigh commented. His remarks were cynical to say the least but it reflected the turmoil that Myrna's action and words had stirred up inside him against the women who had used him as a sexual slave when he was twelve years old. She, in the meanwhile, was struggling to survive. Physically, Myrna was no match for the super fit 105 kilograms 6'7" giant but she was fighting back as best she could. Myrna in her plight for survival recalled something she had learnt. She could not say where or even when she had learnt it but she remembered the voice saying, ". . . scratch your attacker. Even if you don't survive, you would have provided enough DNA for the investigators . . .". Myrna followed the advice she remembered. She scratched Raleigh's face with her nails leaving a superficial scarring on the right side of his face. The burning sensation from the scratches made Raleigh wipe the right side of his face with the palm of his left hand. He saw the blood. The distraction gave Myrna the only opportunity to use one other desperate method to save her life. In the moment when Raleigh sought to investigate the burning sensation on his face, Myrna placed her hand between her and Raleigh's thighs but reached for his big dick. With as swift a movement as she could muster, Myrna joined 'the bell ringer's union'. Having grasped Raleigh's big dick but yanked it with all the strength she could muster, Myrna tugged again and again as if she was trying to remove it from its socket. His very deep baritone voice carried not only to the floor below but also across to the Harbour-Shark Estate, probably! Raleigh removed his other hand from Myrna's neck immediately but rolled to one side to see if he could free himself from her firm grasp. With even more leverage, Myrna used both hands to yank even harder. This time Raleigh sounded as if he was auditioning for the role of Tarzan. Birdie Spring-Hip wanted to go up to the Motel to investigate the agonizing sounds that was coming from upstairs The Cobblestone Arms AADC but Simon Crabley insisted it was none of their business. Raleigh begged Myrna to stop the tugging but she refused until he agreed to desist from the physical abuse. Myrna told him she hadn't finished saying what was on her mind but warned that she would be forced to take legal action against him if he dared to hit or attempted to choke her again. Raleigh agreed. He sat on the edge of the bed looking rather forlorn. Myrna was so angry that she had not noticed the taste the salty blood in her mouth. The bruising on the inside of her mouth was caused by the blow from Raleigh's giant hand. Myrna seized this opportunity to tell Raleigh how insanely 'programmed' and 'conditioned' she believed he'd become by living someone else's *cultural* 'values and beliefs' rather than seeking to set standards for himself. Myrna continued to focus on the subject before the frenzied attack by Raleigh. "Raleigh, you and men like you and those women, who engage in such lewd acts need to have some kind of psychiatric treatment. You might have all the attributes of the stereotypical 'Mr. Right'; the muscular body, the chiselled jaws, the athletic build, even the money and the dazzling smile but you're less than what I'm looking for in a man. You and the likes of you are just disgustingly sad specimens, who know you're incapable of staying with natural lovemaking techniques. Animals do. It is patently clear that you have to depend on these quirky practices to satisfy your ego", Myrna complained forcefully. Raleigh's head was swimming by her forthright remarks. He recognized the difference in Myrna's mood and so did she. Myrna turned but swiftly walked away from Raleigh towards the table in the corner. She lifted but carried the silver ice bucket over towards the bed. She threw the contents over the naked Raleigh. He started to shiver not only from the cold impact of the contents from the silver bucket but also the intense dressing down he was receiving from the deeply incensed Myrna.

Raleigh was beginning to feel quite despondent about his demise. Just when he thought he was rekindling his old flame, the metaphorical hurricane winds and rain had not only dampened his enthusiasm towards Myrna but had thoroughly extinguished the smouldering embers that were revived in the Corporate Box earlier in the day. "I'm hoping you have ingested enough incurable germs that will cause you to suffer torturously while you die a very slow death. I'm wondering how much enjoyment you'll get out of those memories that haunt those moments. May you rot slowly from inside, you sad excuse of a man. Real men don't need to lower themselves (pardon the pun) to such depths to enable them to satisfy women like me, who prefer natural intercourse compared to what might be offered in sleazier environments like where you learnt your techniques, seemingly! Goodbye Raleigh, I trust I never set eyes on you again. You disgust me. I feel so awfully sick just sharing the same space as you", she implied? Myrna McTittle turned but strode towards the door. She stepped over the previously tight-fitting dress without reference to it but grabbed hold of the gilt edged round knob. Myrna yanked the door towards her, stepped through it with much haste and urgency but slammed it shut with such rage that the un-oiled hinges seemed to forget to squeak when those two actions were executed. Raleigh was dumbfounded by Myrna's revelations. He sat staring at the tight-fitting dress that was the only memento he would have to remind him of the gorgeous Myrna McTittle. In this moment, Raleigh had relinquished all hopes of ever seeing let alone engaging with the tall, slim, hauntingly beautiful, tantalizingly sexy Myrna again. There was a sad, empty feeling of the permanency indicated by the way they had said goodbye, which puzzled the handsome, athletic build, chiselled jawed Raleigh with his flashing smile. It doesn't matter how old one is, being dumped isn't only a devastatingly crushing feeling. The fact is that it can linger for a while longer when it becomes apparent. Despite them having the attributes of the *'programmed'* mythical *'Mr. Right'*, Raleigh and men like him can be *'resisted'* by strong women like Myrna. As a last infliction of the preciseness of her verbal incisions, Myrna had delivered a measured farewell. Her words were deliberate, her sentiments deepened and her message suitably designed for Raleigh and men like him to ponder, perhaps!

CHAPTER 7

After the funeral, Duke started to miss his father's physical presence enormously. He was a very sad boy indeed. Duke still didn't get on with his stepmother, Brigette. She offered him comforting words, a shoulder to cry on, and even cuddles but Duke refused her even more. Brigette was beside herself with her private grief, let alone being shunned yet again by Duke. He had started to play truant from School. When the school contacted Brigette, she was stunned. At the school's request, she made appointments, one after another, to try to resolve what could be done to encourage Duke back to school. On one occasion, he told the Head Teacher that Brigette was the cause of his not attending School. It was a straightforward lie and he knew it but the School had a responsibility to investigate Duke's comments. Brigette was visited by Social Workers approved by the Education Department. They visited the home but questioned Brigette about her relationship with the youngster. It was then that they realised Brigette was not Duke's biological mother. They also learnt how Earl had helped to condition the boy into showing her no respect. The female Social Worker asked Duke what he wanted to do about his issues with Brigette. He told them that he wanted her out of his life and that he'd never show her any respect as long as he was forced to live with her. In fact, he was quite adamant about getting her out of the house and his life. "Where do you want to live", the female social worker asked? "I don't want to live anywhere else. This is my house. I love it here but I don't want to live with this dozy cow. She's a scrounger", Duke stated. "I understand you are feeling upset but it seems unfair to call Brigette names, don't you think", the female Social Worker continued? Duke looked down towards the floor then mumbled to himself. The female Social Worker thought she had heard Duke say the 'f' word. "I'm sorry, I didn't get that", she said. He remained silent but still looked towards the floor. The female Social Worker noticed Duke's body language. He seemed to be getting tired with being questioned. "O.K. young Duke, I'll visit again next week just in case you change your mind", she said. Duke did not look up but instead ran off towards his room. The female Social Worker told Brigette that she would check on them the next week to see if there was any improvement. Brigette walked both Social Workers to the door before commenting on how she was feeling about the whole situation. Tears rolled down her face as she expressed the effect of Duke's perception and treatment of her. "I can't believe how he could say those mean things about me when all I've offered him is love and care", Brigette sobbed. The female Social Worker told Brigette that she was not able to comment on whether Duke was lying but she would monitor the situation closely. "Let's get him back to school then see what can be done", the female Social Worker ended. Throughout the visit, the male Social Worker had remained silent but seemed to be making copious notes on his *'Me-pad'* © during the entire interview. As they turned to walk away down the pathway, he engaged with his colleague but shared his observations with her. Brigette closed the door but went back into the lounge. There, Duke sat spread across the settee but hindered her from being able to sit on it. She looked down at him but he wouldn't shift his position. "Get out of the way, I can't see the telly", Duke demanded. Brigette held her ground. She felt that Duke had gone way past the limit. The way he addressed her was as if he was speaking to one of his peers. Brigette knew she would have to let him know in no uncertain terms that his behaviour was more than unacceptable but that she herself had to remain calm yet emotionally sensitive. Duke was adamant that he could speak to Brigette in this derogatory tone like his father, Earl used to. There were strands of Earl's behaviour coming from this young boy. "Didn't you hear what I said ... bitch? Get out of my way, I can't see the telly", Duke barked? To Brigette these words were a mere echo of Earl's voice resonating through his son. Even though Duke's voice was not yet as deep as his father's, it still bore the hallmark as far as diction, accent, intonation, pitch and vitriolic sarcasm. It proved how, driven by negative ego, consistent programming can help to form conditioned patterns that influence individual behaviour. Brigette was being tested beyond where she'd been before but didn't quite know how to cope with this brash young boy. It was clear he was testing just how far he could push her. "Duke, don't speak to me in that manner. Your behaviour is not acceptable", Brigette jousted. "I can speak to you how I want and there's just nothing you can do about it", he boasted. "I don't have to put up with your nonsense", Brigette said firmly. "Well if you don't like it you know what you can do, don't you", Duke sneered? His caustic remarks broke Brigette's resolve. She felt emotionally angry at the boy but held back from telling him about his stinking attitude. Brigette stood her ground but glared at him without further comment. When their eyes met, Duke felt the anger through her stare. He tried a new approach. "Do you want to hit me? Go on then, hit me", Duke challenged. Brigette was almost losing control and all that was going through her mind was to slap him as her stepfather used to do to her whenever she was cheeky to him. Then she recalled that's what drove her away from her home. His physical abuse was too much in the end for her to want to stay. She'd run away from home twice before meeting Earl. At that time, he offered her refuge but then it turned out he was worse than what she had run away from. On reflection, the anger she was now feeling was not at the boy but at his father for encouraging Duke's rude behaviour. Brigette resolved that this in-fighting between her and Duke could only end up with her feeling even more distressed. It was while she was contemplating what it might feel like to be able to release the burdensome weight that seemed to pin her down like a submissive hold in wrestling but sap her of energy that Brigette experienced what is known as a 'light-bulb' moment, commonly. Overwhelmed by her attempts to *'mother'* Duke, Brigette was beginning to see what made him seem to resist. She needed to start to communicate her understanding of Duke's predicament. Brigette accepted that she was not his mother. For the first time, Brigette acknowledged that it seemed more meaningful not to deny Duke's resistance towards her as his mother but instead help him to understand his feelings. This was a new approach. Suddenly, she found herself empathising with Duke's position. Here he was fatherless but with her, the last person he seemed to want to be with. She wondered what he must be experiencing. After all, Duke was very close to his father. He worshipped the ground Earl walked on. He could do nothing wrong in Duke's eyes. In fact, Earl had never let Duke think for himself. Before walking away, Brigette spoke to Duke but with more understanding. "Duke, I understand you are missing your father terribly. I'm so sorry you are feeling the way you are", Brigette said. He had placed his hands over his ears but not firmly. Duke heard every word that Brigette had uttered. He also heard the sincerity in which those words were said. They were genuine and from the heart. Even Duke could not discount the tone of Brigette's voice but he continued to pretend he didn't hear. "Did you hear me Duke", Brigette asked? He hesitated before commenting. "Yeah, whatever . . . this is boring", he replied. "If we are going to live in the same house, we will have to find a way to communicate better, don't you think", Brigette queried? "Talk to the hand", Duke replied. "That's rude. You'll have to do better than that to improve your communication with me", Brigette said boldly. "You're boring", Duke retorted.

The next day the School telephoned to ask why Duke was not in school again. Brigette didn't know and she told them so. "He got up, had his breakfast but left for school. I'm not sure why he's not there", Brigette told the Deputy Head Teacher. "You are aware that if your child is continuously absent from school you can be taken to Court, don't you", the Deputy Head Teacher asked? Her voice was cold and unsympathetic. There was no indication that she might consider the circumstances that might have been causative to Duke's absence from school. The Deputy Head was simply being insensitive in her approach. Brigette was stunned by the announcement. How could she be taken to

Court when she had no knowledge of what was in Duke's mind at anytime? It was only when the Deputy Head Teacher spoke again that Brigette realized she hadn't answered the question. "I suppose I'll have to bring him to School to ensure he arrives but it doesn't guarantee he'll stay, does it", Brigette reasoned? The green humanoid robotron Deputy Head was unrelenting in that she just repeated robotically the earlier words as if she was a scheduled recording programmed on *'repeat mode'*. Brigette told her what she believed was within her power to do. "I'll bring him to school as often as I can but it isn't practical to do that everyday. I'm going back to work soon", Brigette responded. "Well that's your responsibility. Rules are rules. We have to abide by them even when we don't agree with them, don't we", the Deputy Head Teacher commented? The tone of the Deputy Head suggested that she was not only unimpressed with Brigette's answer but also un-empathetic towards her demise. As far as the Deputy Head was concerned, it was a matter for the Courts to decide not her. The coldness in her communication warned Brigette that she could become not only another statistic but also the type of headline that might expose her to even more ridicule and judgement than she had experienced before. She was well aware of how the printed and television Media might portray her to the world. All the inconvenience and finger pointing could become unbearable. Brigette did not know quite how to respond to this situation. After she returned to work, Brigette couldn't guarantee that Duke would attend school. She put the phone down but wondered where Duke might be and what was he getting up to. Brigette got dressed quickly but left the house. She had no idea where she was going but wandered along the pavement. Brigette arrived at The Cobblestone Arms AADC but stood just outside it. One or two individuals going to and from the Adult Alcoholic Drinking Centre said hello. Some mouthed their condolences but none stopped to speak directly with her. Brigette found herself walking towards the entrance. Inside, she sought out Simon, the Landlord. "Hello there, come and have a drink. What will you have", he asked? "I don't want a drink. I need to talk to you", Brigette said. "I need a break anyway. Will you have lunch with us? Kitty was asking after you. She'll be glad to see you. I'll tell her you're here", Simon said. Brigette welcomed his invitation for lunch and the fact that she'd have another female to talk to. She moved away from the bar but lingered by the Slot Machine.

Brian Edgeworthy, the local Bookmaker, was having a drink with his mates but his attention shifted to Brigette. He told his friends that he'd always fancied her and that he was going to try his luck now Earl had passed. "Don't you think it's a bit early? I mean Earl's just gone some weeks now," one mate said. "Nonsense, she's a sure bet. Odds on favourite to say yes to my proposal", Brian Edgeworthy boasted. He walked over to where Brigette was standing but introduced himself. "I'm Brian Edgeworthy, the local Bookmaker. I'm sorry to hear you've lost your husband recently. As a matter of fact, ever since the funeral I'd been meaning to come and have a chat with you", he commented. "A chat with me", Brigette queried? "Yes", Brian Edgeworthy replied. "What is it you want to see me about? I don't even know who you are", Brigette reminded him. "That's what I want to talk to you about. I figure you must be wanting some company; especially at night. You're much too young to be the weeping widow. Fancy me do you", Brian Edgeworthy asked? Brigette was least in the mood for this bore. She looked him up and down but did not comment. Brian mistook that for a *'come on'* look. "If it is money you want, I've got plenty of it. I know you're used to nice things and I'll make sure you're never short. I'll keep you in the way you're accustomed just like your late husband did. You won't be wanting for anything", Brian Edgeworthy assured. Brigette thought that the Bookmaker had an over-inflated opinion of himself. He seemed to think that she was available and that his money would win her over. Brigette was not interested in his comments, his money or him but she did ask a question. "Why me", she asked? "Because I fancy you something rotten and I'm sure you'll grow to like me even if you don't at the moment. With my money, I'm irresistible and you'd be foolish not to take up my offer", Brian Edgeworthy said boastfully. "I'm sure there are more women of your type out there, who would jump at your proposal but I'm still in mourning in case you hadn't noticed", Brigette said disdainfully. Finding a new partner was the last thing on her mind. She was not thinking of starting a new relationship on the rebound as some others might tend to do after being made *'free'* from a violently abusive relationship. Brigette had enough problems keeping up with being responsible for Duke let alone taking on a pompous creep like Brian Edgeworthy. She looked past him towards where Kitty and Simon were standing beckoning her to come over to them. It was a well timed intervention because she was getting really tired of the boring, insensitive Brian Edgeworthy. Brigette tried to walk past him but he blocked her way. She, with pity in her eyes, looked scornfully at Brian Edgeworthy before walking round him towards where Kitty and Simon were standing. When Brigette arrived with them, Simon asked her why she looked so upset. Brigette explained about the boring Bookmaker. Simon wanted to go over to speak with him but Brigette did not want a confrontation between Simon and one of his patrons on her behalf. Instead, she started to tell them about the difficulty she was having with Duke. They all sat at the table that Kitty had selected. It was far enough away from the patrons to ensure some privacy. When Brigette started to cry, Kitty hugged her but offered some comforting words. Simon was gutted for the vulnerable Brigette. He told her that he too was concerned about Duke. "I've seen him roaming around the streets with a group of other boys. The first time I noticed him loafing on the streets during school time, I confronted Duke and the other six boys with him. I asked them why they weren't in school but Duke mentioned that they were late going back after having lunch at the infamous burger restaurant. There was no reason for me to doubt the boys but last week I saw him in a crowd of twenty or more. Something is not right. I told Kitty I am becoming suspicious of what he's getting up to, didn't I Kitty", Simon confirmed? She acknowledged Simon's testament but suggested Brigette and Duke come to dinner on Sunday next. Kitty stated that it was both her and Simon's weekend off. She suggested they take a ride to a secluded restaurant which was bordering on the edge of Upper Ghettoborough in Town and Greensborough, Suburbia. "You'll enjoy getting away from it all. Simon and I go there as often as we can. Can you imagine the peace of Greensborough compared to the contrasting liveliness that Ghettoborough has to offer", Kitty asked? There was a certain hint that Simon and Kitty might prefer to live in Suburbia but still welcomed working with the buzz and nightlife that Lower Ghettoborough offered. Brigette didn't have a peaceful environment in which to look forward. There seemed to be no change in her circumstances. Life before Earl's passing was filled with uncertainties and now life with Duke seemed much the same. She asked Simon and Kitty if they could tell Duke about their concerns about his playing truant. They assured her that they would. Lunch was served. They ate almost in silence except for the odd reference to who might be taking over from *'The Gaffer'*. Brigette told both Simon and Kitty that she had no idea. She could tell that Simon and Kitty were concerned as to who might now be in charge and whether their tenancy was indeed safely assured under the old arrangements. There was no written contract that existed. It was just a "gentleman's agreement", so to speak, between Earl and Simon that had existed over the years. Neither Kitty nor Simon had any idea that Earl might die so suddenly. They were truly worried about their own situation. Simon asked Brigette to let him know if she heard any rumours as to who's in charge. The lunchtime regulars began to pour into The Cobblestone Arms AADC. Simon signalled that his and Kitty's break was now over. They had had an early lunch in order to make themselves available for the expected rush upon the popular AADC. Birdie Spring-Hip cavorted herself amongst the regulars, stopping every now and again to perform her version of lap-dancing in order to excite the men who came to have that experience. Brigette left The Cobblestone Arms AADC not too clued up on how she was going to handle Duke but she was grateful to Simon and Kitty for listening. The new information about what he was getting up to meant that Brigette's task was even more circumspect. She needed to confront Duke about his errant behaviour at home, in school and on the street. When Duke did not come home by 00:00 hours that night, Brigette waited up for him. She worried where he might be or what he might be getting up to. Brigette sat with her head in her hands because she had no experience of how to handle the likes of Duke. He was far from being an adult but he seemed to behave as if he thought he was. Brigette had noticed that many younger people did not seem to want to be children like when she was younger. Some children tended to want to view the process of being a child as a sign of weakness. Brigette began to wonder if it was a case that a great number of the recent generations of parents seemed to want to grow their children up as their *'friends'* rather than being their parents. It would mean that the laissez faire approach to parenting was preferred. The rigours of structure seemed to have been substituted for the lack of accountability. Duke's lack of structure started with Earl's disdain for it. By spoiling Duke, he eroded yet demeaned the value of structure that Brigette had offered at the time when it was meant to be reinforced by both of them as parents.

It was 00:17 hours when Brigette heard the key in the front door. She walked towards the hallway to ensure that Duke knew she was aware of the time he chose to come home. He looked blankly at Brigette as if she did not exist. Duke said nothing. Brigette could smell the mix of *'skunk'* weed and alcohol which lingered in the hallway. "I know you were not at school today. Where have you been all day Duke", Brigette asked? Her voice was assertive and to the point. Duke tried to walk past her without the courtesy of answering but she stood firm. "Out, ain't it", Duke offered feebly? Brigette didn't want a *'tit-for-tat'* situation. She delayed the next question while she counted to ten. Watching how unsteady Duke was on his feet, Brigette tried to contain the conversation to refer only to today. "What have you eaten all day", Brigette queried? "Burgers and chicken with chips", Duke offered. "I didn't give you any lunch money today so where did you get money to buy food", Brigette pressed. "I've got friends, don't I", Duke lied? He was feeling a bit groggy from the combination of the *'legal'* and *'illegal'* drugs he had consumed. Duke felt that if he didn't sit down, he might fall flat on his face. Again, he tried to walk past Brigette but she was resolute that she didn't care about how the teenage Duke felt about being questioned. It was his 13th birthday but that didn't give him the right to treat

Brigette the way that he did. Today's confrontation as all the others previously was about responsibility and accountability. Brigette was adamant that Duke ought to understand that he needed to change his attitude. It stank even more than the stench of the illegal drug, cannabis. The *'skunk'* weed, as it was rumoured, had a very strong distinct smell. Brigette wondered whether Duke and others like him needed to smoke it. She felt quite *'high'* just on the smell that emanated from his breath and clothes. As for the alcohol, Brigette remained puzzled what made it exempt from being recognized as a *'drug'* too. She wondered whether it was because it was deemed *'legal'*, *perhaps!* Apart from imparting its influence upon individual behaviours, Brigette deduced that, like any other addiction, it was self-evident that the *'legal'* drug proven to be just as destructive towards individual health. She questioned what was behind the *'reasoning'* of governments all over the World of Space to openly ignore the obvious damage caused by the legalisation of this powerfully harmful *'legal'* drug? Brigette couldn't be sure. She was absolutely certain though that singularly or as a combination, alcohol and the *'skunk'* weed had to have some adverse effect upon the way individuals felt and behaved. The longer Brigette prevented Duke from going up the stairs to his bedroom he began to behave more like his father used to. Duke's impatience with his stepmother manifested into the tantrum he now displayed. The volume of his voice was now at a very high level and the swearing spilled from his mouth in an outpouring of dastardly foul language that might best befit someone whose vocabulary was more limited than Duke's. He had heard it all before when his father, Earl, used to attack the then naive Brigette. Duke was drunk but there was no excuse for some of the names he called her. When Brigette countered back, Duke threatened to physically harm her. She lost her assertiveness but succumbed to the verbal abuse and physical threats of violence against her. Brigette relented because she was afraid that Duke might beat her in the same manner as how his father before him had done. Duke had witnessed his father doing so many times before and in his present state was quite capable of copying Earl's treatment of her. This was just another episode of the many confrontations that kept happening frequently between the caring Brigette and the uncaring Duke. He grew more and more belligerent until Brigette allowed him access to his bedroom. The next day, Brigette tried to awaken Duke so that he could be taken to school but to no avail. He seemed to be in the land of *'Nod'*; far beyond normal sleep. Duke was simply exhausted. He slept until well after 14:00 hours. Later that morning, Brigette had been contacted again by the Deputy Head Teacher, who informed her that she had not consolidated her responsibility to bring Duke to school on that day. The Deputy Head notified Brigette that she had advised the Education Department about Duke's continued absence from school. She told Brigette that she had emailed Duke's record of absence to the Department, as proof of the Deputy Head's recommended action against her. Due to Brigette's lack of *'parental responsibility'* to ensure a minor child, namely, Duke Stagg, aged 13 years old, attend an educational establishment, she was alleged to be negligent in her role as guardian. She was told that the Education Department would confirm that Brigette be summoned to attend Court to answer the charge. Subsequently, Brigette suffered the ignominy of having to attend such a Court. She was found guilty and fined quite heavily because of Duke's consistent lack of attendance to school. The law under which Brigette was taken to Court was passed under the reign of the previous Government of Spaceville. It confirmed that parents or in Brigette's case, guardians of children, who frequently played truant from school would be taken to Court once they had received an official letter from the Education Department. It was authorised under that law to invoke fines or imprisonment on those parents or guardians whom were found guilty in Court. The vision of that government was to force parents to be more responsible for their children's attendance to school. There was inter-party agreement about the general theme about responsibility but the objections arose when *'reasonable'* or *'extraordinary personal circumstances'* were summarily dismissed despite protestations from eminent legal commentators. They demonstrated that (1) the law could not isolate any *'reasonable steps'* contributed by parents or guardians to ensure their children went to school, (2) it was derelict of the law to assume otherwise unless it could prove that the parents or guardian deliberately collaborated with the child not to attend school, (3) in the case of illness, having to fulfil a doctor or hospital appointment or other reasons deemed appropriate by the Education Department or particular school, (4) the law was being *'unreasonable'* if it didn't take into account personal events that might be beyond those reasonable measures that parents or guardian might not have anticipated or have control over. There was great turmoil when the law was proposed but it was carried through the political channels despite the chorus of legal objections from established legal eagles to current legal eaglets. Clovis Damnation, the individual, who had proposed the law, together with the other headline seekers, had collectively refused to understand that there were other possible reasons why individual students might be unavailable to attend school. There was no consideration how the stigma of Court action might impact on the families in the limelight of headline news. The invention of that particular law without leaving room for extenuating circumstances meant it turned out to be the most idiotic of political blunders, sanctioning heavy fines and possible prison sentences to parents and guardians like Brigette. At least, she was in a financial position to afford the payment of the heavy fines but it was grossly unfair on those other single parents, who were on minimum wages or State Benefits, possibly. There was a risk that families might be broken up if single parents, especially, had to be imprisoned because they genuinely lacked the ability to pay the extremely exorbitant fines. The previous leader of Spaceville, Constance Ignoble, and her government had won over her political cronies with the idea but failed to impress the population at large with such an un-empathetic, inconsiderate law. Hence, her government was ousted because they had flaunted the opportunity to enter into or establish meaningful communication or relationships with Spaceville's population.

What became more popular was the idea tabled by Janette Brayhorne P M, Political Member for Ghettoborough. She won the votes of the Harbour-Shark Estate and most of Ghettoborough by countering the previous Government's stance on two major points. These were (1) education and (2) single parents. Janette Brayhorne championed but affirmed her interest on those two points by taking the opportunity to strategically research the thoughts and comments of the young people and their parents in Ghettoborough. Her manner on the doorsteps was a holistic approach which included the thoughts and feelings of the constituents. Janette Brayhorne's canvassing was a huge success. For the first time, constituents felt that their comments were being valued rather than ridiculed by some politicrats previously and now. They chose to embellish their candidacy with political stereo-tripe and stereo-hype. It led to sensational headline seeking approaches for short-termed popularity amongst those whom wallowed in the demeaning of members of the communities. These were targeted as scapegoats for the particular political candidates involved. Unlike Janette Brayhorne, those politicrats and their supporters were bent on a mindset which glorified the thought of having a snipe at less fortunate individuals. They did this rather than taking into account the real needs of the people. Janette came across as more genuine than the fast-talking individuals whose missions were to ignore the messages of the communities but had chosen to consistently tread on them instead. As a Councillor, Janette had been very popular with the community when it came to using her influence to diffuse or resolve local discrepancies. On the doorsteps, she was committed to act as a conduit between the community and local government. When Janette won the seat as P.M for Ghettoborough, she pledged in her victory speech to press for (1) the possible revision of how the Education Department viewed the importance of the main stakeholders, the students, (2) to highlight the need to review individual's preferences for learning as a priority in order to allow those individuals 'equal opportunities' for learning within educational establishments (3) to seek a platform to highlight the positive contributions of single parents and their importance in that role (4) how to encourage single parents to take responsibility for initiating structure within their respective families and (5) establishing mentors to empower small groups of single parents in each community. Janette Brayhorne established that there was more than one reason behind her victory speech when she was declared as P.M for Ghettoborough. She was strongly against fining and imprisoning parents or guardians but remained dedicated to having the un-empathetic law rescinded. The results of Janette's research during her pre-election canvassing had exposed the myth behind why some students, locally, were showing a lack of interest in schools. These children wanted to make clear that some teachers were exceptional in the way they planned and executed the lessons. Conversely, they complained strongly about those teachers that didn't represent themselves well enough to command or gain the respect that they so often demanded from students. Some said they played truants because they were bored in class. They reported that the boredom was caused mainly because (1) the method of teaching was not appropriate to their preference or style of learning (2) they didn't feel challenged educationally in the classrooms. Duke was one of those students that found school boring. He was not intrinsically motivated because he didn't feel educationally challenged nor a stakeholder. He and students like him felt less than valued by some individuals who happen to be teachers. These had not been emotionally sensitive towards students' individual needs. This often led to the diminution of individual self esteem particularly.

Duke's behaviour reflected how low his level of self esteem had plummeted in spite of the recent loss of his father. He stated his intense dislike for Brigette. She agreed with the Social Work Department that both her and Duke could no longer live under the same roof. The Social Work Department suggested that Duke be placed in foster care for a trial period of six months to see if his behaviour improved. During those six months, Duke was placed with no less than five foster parents. None could tolerate his emotional explosions for more than short periods. There was no change in his lack of interest in school either. Duke was asked to attend a local 'Referral Unit' initiated, sanctioned and approved at national government level by the previous administration. At those 'Referral Units', students behaviours deteriorated rapidly. Their chaperones' responsibilities seemed to be limited to being in charge of the students cigarettes. They condoned both emotionally unintelligent and immature behaviours without consequences rather than agreeing and working with students to plan strategies which might enable them to set realistic goals let alone achieve them. More often than not the growing hoards of students hanging around these *'Referral Units'* without involvement in structured activities ended up with students' physical absence at some time of the day. Very many physical confrontations happened on site or just outside those *'Referral Units'*. This often led to hoards of youths grouping together according to what they found in common. For example, Duke's group found that each of their mothers or fathers was totally or partially excluded from their lives. Other groups identified with their common issues too. What Janette Brayhorne was learning from her continuing surveys was that each group were being formed by the patterns mentioned above. She was being enlightened further that there was no migration from one group to the other. Each group became a *'family'* unit but was dedicated to looking out for each other no matter what the environment, situation, circumstances or consequences even. It was most difficult to separate these groups once their allegiance was formed and cemented.

CHAPTER 8

D uke was part of a group that found the risks of *'street-life'* more thrilling and challenging than school. He and his brother Baron led a gang. Like any other gang in the World of Space, they identified themselves by the tattoos that they agreed to wear. Duke told Baron that he'd copy the design of the tattoo their father, Earl, used to display on his upper right arm. He told his brother that his father referred to it as *'Clout'*. The members of the gang wore the tattoo as identification and to prove their solid individual commitment towards a common cause. They felt the need for the challenge to implement a type of *'graduation'* process which moved them from being just a group, who shared a common issue to becoming the *'stereo-typical'* street gang. Duke and Baron decided their gang was to be called 'Clout'. Each group member had to commit to an agreed set of rules. The rules of *'The Three Musketeers'*, "One for all and all for one" was the number one rule and, "watching each others' back" was the number two rule. 'Clout' meant to impact in a very big way. They studied how others before them had gained notoriety by the exposure that was afforded them through national media and social websites. These they used strategically to enable recruitment of individuals from the same ethnicity. Like other gangs in the World of Space they used the news media as an educational base. Duke, Baron and their colleagues witnessed the daily footage of news that seemed to allude to sanction yet support and glorify the rise of anarchy in other Kingdoms, exotic continents, countries and islands in the World of Space. Unlike the anarchists in those other Kingdoms, exotic continents, countries and islands often referred to in the news, Clout had no political ambitions to overthrow their governments. Instead, the lessons learnt in principle meant that Duke and Baron could plan to formulate strategies of how to overthrow the powerful influence of the brown, purple, pink, white and blue Mixed DNA Rainbow Tribe Harbour-Shark Estate Gang or any other in neighbouring precincts, neighbourhoods and boroughs in Lower

Ghettoborough. Since meeting up with his twin brother, Duke, Baron started to play truant from school too. He did this so he could be with Duke more often.

Their mother, Enid, was summoned to Court in Brazenborough to explain Baron's continued lack of attendance to school. The law, being a national piece of legislation, impacted on her too. Unfortunately, Enid could not afford to pay the exorbitant fine like Brigette did and so she was actively serving time in prison. Baron was now in the charge of Social Services. They decided to let him live with foster parents during Enid's 3 years sentence, imposed on her by the Court. Baron hated living with foster parents in Brazenborough. Unlike his brother, he was used to structure and enjoyed living with his mother. It was Earl with whom he was angry. As far as Baron was concerned, Earl had not only rejected but also abandoned him. He had never met his father or known much about him until the day of his funeral. Enid had not hidden the fact that he had a father but had decided to stay away from Earl. With his powerful influence, she thought he might take her second child away like he did Duke. Prior to their living with foster parents, both Duke and Baron had swapped cell phone numbers and were actively communicating with each other each day. They also used the social websites and free Apps to update on their individual experiences with foster parents and more. Brigette had no idea that Baron and Duke were seeing each other nor was she aware that Enid had gone to prison. She had called the cell number that Enid had given her but to no avail. Brigette often longed to speak with Enid. It was only on the day that Duke was injured in a street fight that Brigette heard of Enid's imprisonment. From the report in the media, some brown, purple, pink, white, and blue Mixed DNA Rainbow Tribe boys from the Harbour-Shark Estate Gang had chased Duke through the streets but manage to cut him under his left cheek with a knife. Baron, who travelled from Brazenborough to Ghettoborough each day, apparently stabbed the boy who injured his brother. He used the same knife that he had recovered from the purple boy who wanted to shank his brother, Duke, on the night of the 'pasa-pasa' or 'beef' with the boys at the back of The Cobblestone Arms AADC on the night of Earl's funeral. Baron was arrested and charged with attempted murder. The story was headline news and it appeared on television too. The media savaged Baron's reputation and upbringing but they spared Duke much of the blame. He, being the son of the posthumous local hero, Sir Earl Stagg, was protected by his father's reputation. The media, not being aware that Baron was Duke's twin brother but saw him only as an *'ethnic stereotype'* slaughtered Baron as a rogue and a thug. He was portrayed as a typically vicious street gang member. Baron's tattoo was highlighted to convince the readers of his commitment to a criminal fraternity and lifestyle. There were several other charges linked to him too like public affray. The media had found the link between Baron's mother, Enid and her being sentenced to prison. Typically, they made use of that story to castigate Enid as "the stereo-typical, utterly worthless, scourge-of-the-earth, non-job-seeking, benefit-dependent single mother". Brigette cried for Enid, because she knew the stories about Baron and Enid were not true. She also knew of the fight that had happened with Duke, Baron and the boys from the Harbour-Shark Estate Gang, in the back of The Cobblestone Arms AADC just a few weeks prior to this incident. Brigette also remembered the other young boy, who had warned Baron and Duke that the Harbour-Shark Estate Gang would seek revenge for their colleagues who had received the beating from them. His injury was not life threatening but Duke was left with a scar under his left cheekbone that, apart from the intervention of plastic surgery, he would take with him to his grave. Even though Duke no longer lived at the address at which Brigette was residing, he used it conveniently in order to curry favour whenever he was involved with the police. It didn't matter if it was the daily experience of being stopped and searched or whether he deserved to be questioned by them because he had committed a crime. Duke soon realised what other youngsters like him, in Ghettoborough, Brazenborough and the other boroughs affected by gang culture had to endure. What he was learning most is the frequency with which individuals were being stopped and searched, principally because of their ethnicity. From another perspective, Duke had to agree that the dangerous violent gangster lifestyle to which the likes of Clout were so attracted, was causative to keeping the *'stop and search'* campaign alive. Curiously, being a *'thug'*, living in the *'fast lane'* and the reckless *'ride or die'*, *'kill or be killed'* lifestyle seemed to be an attraction to youngsters in gangs like Clout and those on the Harbour-Shark Estate. It spread like an epidemic that was fast becoming into a pandemic. The mental infection was viral in that it seemed to be affecting youngsters from places as diverse as Brazenborough and Ghettoborough in Town to Greensborough, Sneerborough and Snideborough in bordering Suburbia. The likes of Poshborough, Snobsborough in deeper Suburbia, the Village of Urgington and particularly Champagne Valley, being much further away in distance from the likes of Ghettoborough, seemed to be exceptions to the street-life scenario. Crimes of other sorts were being committed in those other places but were never highlighted in case that type of news *'stained'* their prestigious reputations. Apart from areas like Poshborough, Snobsborough, the Village of Urgington and Champagne Valley, it seemed that most of the rest of Spaceville was fast deteriorating into the crime capital of the World of Space. Not even the 5th rated exotic continents, countries and islands were as dangerous as Spaceville now. In Lower Ghettoborough in particular, gang warfare exploded into an hourly occurrence. Reputations gained massive *'Street-Credits'* but were fast becoming more important than the life of another human.

Professor Walynski indicated that Research had identified that the cold-heartedness being displayed by individuals was not a sign of mental toughness but instead "a mixture of Schizophrenia and ASPD, Anti Social Personality Disorder. Together, these rendered individuals prone to violence. The main elements that characterises ASPD are blatant disregard for following the rights or welfare of others and that they break the law, consistently. Significant individuals display a sense of immunity towards feeling remorse. This seemed to render those individuals impervious to reasonable behaviour", he explained. Their commitment to this cold-heartedness did not even seem to make them aware of how they were triggered to display such behaviours. Any intervention, like Counselling, Mentoring or Coaching in their earlier years might have helped individuals like Duke and Baron to identify the triggers that made them so emotionally insensitive and unfeeling. Coaches like the man they called 'The Professor' became aware that *fear* had stood out as the most likely trigger in most of the case histories to which he can refer. He also pointed to what he called ". . . an astronomical level of *'bullying'* that had hit our communities". He said it was the most common factor to which individual clients referred. The man they called 'The Professor' stated that individuals complained of being bullied at home, work, educational establishments, on the streets, on social websites and technological devices like cell phones too. Many youngsters, particularly in Ghettoborough, who resisted but did not volunteer to join one of the gangs like Clout or The Harbour-Shark Estate Gang, were often targeted on their travels to and from schools, colleges, Universities and, in some cases, work. The level of intimidation ranged from being threatened if they didn't steal or bring information about their parents' bank accounts to the gangs, to being roughed up, physically. Others were forced to become drug runners or to peddle guns and ammunition on behalf of the gangs. The consequence of bullying impacted greatly in many ways upon the families within the communities of Ghettoborough and Brazenborough in particular. Some youngsters were so psychologically distraught that they chose to commit suicide rather than continue to live with the incessant bullying. Others reacted in the opposite way. They chose to become even meaner bullies than the ones who initiated the behaviour against them. The man they called 'The Professor' was at a loss to understand what made this viral mental disease invisible to those who had the means to wipe out this epidemic. Bullying had not only just become a form of *'culture'* but was *'politically accepted'* as such. The man they called 'The Professor' was flummoxed as to what could possibly be blinding others, with influence, from seeing the obvious *'mental viral germ'* that was spreading not only in Spaceville but around the entire World of Space. He is adamant that if *fear* can be eliminated from our lives then bullying can be permanently eradicated. Through fear, modern bullies were becoming even more vicious than their perpetrators who visited it upon them. The consequences meant that many more individuals like Baron and Duke were becoming more violent because of the trauma of fear they had experienced when they were being bullied at a younger age. Another *'Breaking News'* item tells of yet another family in distress from the recurring violence. In Asterodia, it was becoming an hourly occurrence. Somewhere in the World of Space there were families burying their children on a more regular basis because of the continuous *'pasa-pasa'* and *'beef'* amongst youngsters in particular. In the affected precincts, neighbourhoods and boroughs in Spaceville, there were now public technological meters on permanent display. These accurately count the hourly and accumulated number of deaths caused by the ultra violent UFO's 'Cult Induced' Post/Zip Code Wars as they happened throughout each year, month, week, day, minutes and moments even. The Security Forces issued the statistics in order to demonstrate the rise in the level of street violence in the various, neighbourhoods, precincts, districts and boroughs. Each day, the news was riddled with the madness that was not only emotionally draining to the grieving families, who were losing their children across the virtual planet of Asteroidia but it was robbing Kingdoms like Spaceville of the natural resources for talent, potential, abilities and capabilities also. The Gang Orientation Scientists, Gang Mentality Scientists and Gang Orientation Practitioners were the real *'Brain Snatchers'*. Subliminally, they loomed even larger than the ghostly shadows reflecting the continuous reign of terror. This voracious appetite for bullying existed across the World of Space. There were no remedial efforts towards its consequences, until it had impacted upon the intended victims. Their traumas seemed to have morphed into a type of surrender to its burdensome weight. From another perspective, Baron, Duke and the other youngsters displaying questionable violent behaviours were being boosted by consistent skilfully embedded messages being implanted, farmed and harvested to the detriment of the *'offended'* by the *'offender'*. Some of these embedded messages were being deliberately projected by predators towards the likes of individuals, who chose the gangs as their replacement families. What some young individuals didn't seem to be mindful of is that they were representatives of their original families and that their behaviours were often deemed as being not acceptable by them. In the World of Space, the advent of the Gang Orientation Scientists and Gang Orientation Practitioners meant that there were awesome sophisticated 'mind-games' which lay much deeper beyond the appearance of the 'fun' activities. These torturous stimuli were hugely provocative but inveigled these gang members to hunt in packs to gain readily available accolade, 'Street Credits' and the associative reputations in order to move up to the next level of criminality. Like Pavlov dogs, the subtle programmed and conditioned stimuli had generated a new army of 'pretend' anarchists, who were being deliberately mentally inoculated but encouraged to commit to developing the type of toxic mentality in order to commit to execute 'Ethno-Genocidia'. The likes of members of Clout and The Harbour-Shark Estate gangs were 'fair' game for the Gang Orientation Scientists and Practitioners. In the Royal Royal Dis-United Stately Kingdoms of Asteroidia, the demographics had proven this 'target market' to be the most susceptible to a new spawn of mutant 'mind-games'. Self-help 'ethnic cleansing' was one of those 'mind-games' being installed, under the radar, in the Royal Royal Dis-United Stately Kingdoms of Asteroidia. It was rife and very much alive to those, who were mindful of its existence, functionality and purpose. In a matter of a few years, the Royal Royal Dis-United Stately Kingdoms of Asteroidia would rid itself of those ethnic groups the *Ghetto Mental Terrorists* predators had determined to eradicate. They did this by encouraging the continuance of the madness known as the UFO's Cult-Induced Post/Zip Code Wars.

Preaching from the stone-aged *'Bible of Bigotry'*, Daryll Fastfamousse, Editor of the printed newspaper, The Orion Argument and his poly-tricksters cronies had woven a sense of fear into the psyche of his audience. He had consistently infiltrated the indigenous population's minds by spreading his fear-mongering, poisonous, inflammatory bile ever since the first set of 'invited immigrants' had started to arrive from the far off exotic continents, countries and islands. In the Kingdom of Spaceville where he lived, Daryll Fastfamousse spent a great deal of time actively inciting the population. On the television 'Talk Programme' called 'The Time for Questions', Daryll Fastfamousse seized the opportunity to launch his political career by devaluing ethnic minorities yet again. He referred to them as, *"the weeds in your garden"* and *"a plague of pest worst than those of the biblical locusts"*. When questioned by the chairman, Sidney H. Porkeatre, of the 'Talk Programe' to clarify what he meant by his insidious 'asides', Daryll Fastfamouse openly stated that, should he become part of the ruling government at the next election, his singular 'mission' was to continue to massage the already over-inflated egos of the 'pseudo-patriots', play on their emotions, reiterate his bigoted message but inflame the misplaced passions of those individuals, who happened to subscribe heavily to his kind of pre-stone age rhetoric. Swept up with his self-importance, Daryll Fastfamousse activated his venomous, toxic vitriolic diatribe like a volcano that had lied dormant for many years but had started to belch off the poisonous 'mental sulphuric acid fumes' into the atmosphere. Referring to ethnic immigrants, Daryll Fastfamousse raged, *"If you want to get rid of vermin, get rid of the younger ones first, by any means necessary, then impede, by inoculation, the females from breeding, and their population would diminish permanently"*, he inveigled. Some from the audience and those in their homes and other environments watching the programme, who agreed with Daryll Fastfamousse's corruptive, asinine remarks, cheered wildly. Most of those audiences, who agreed with Daryll Fastfamousse's racist bile, lived in deep suburban Boroughs like Snobsborough, Highborough, Snideborough, Upborough and the Village of Urgington though some lived in urban Boroughs amongst and were, in some cases, partners or spouses with the ethnic populations against whom they railed. Of course, on the virtual parallel planet, seasoned bigots like Daryll Fastfamousse were *'free'* to use the *'language of hate and incitement'* without consequence. Whether what he meant by the words ". . . by any means necessary" indicated that he was a part of or a full member of the Ghetto Mental Terrorists, Ghetto Mentality Engineering Scientists, Gang Mentality Practitioner, Gang Orientation Scientists, or Practitioners', Daryll Fastfamousse might want to take *'credit'* for the explosion of madness, called *'Ethno-Genocidia'*, probably! This was what Clout, the multi-ethnic Harbour-Shark Estate Gang and others were practicing through the virtual *'game drills'* embedded in their minds. In reality, these *'game drills'* were being perpetrated and executed via the UFO's Cult-Induced Post/Zip Code Wars. Although they appeared to be virtual in content and interaction, the most effective *'quality'* of these *'game drills"*, which the Mixed DNA, brown, purple, pink, white and blue coloured Harbour-Shark Estate Gang and the Albino Clout Gang were playing as *'fun'* activities, went under the radar at the subconscious level. It meant that the subtle subliminal messages were being delivered but populated through the experience of playing just a *'virtual game'* as an innocent *'pastime'*. These seemed to have had a myriad of *'conditioning'* influences upon the likes of Baron, Duke and their peers. In the Kingdom of Spaceville, this type of *'conditioning'* was also contained in the music they listened to, the ultra violent films and instructive cartoons they watched. Effectively, *'subliminal entrainment'* operated at the *'unconscious levels'* but actively impinged upon the way individuals were being patterned to think and behaved, subsequently. When prompted, individuals like Duke, Baron and their peers were being instructed to *"finish them off"*, *"eliminate"*, *"seek and destroy"*, *"run them over"* or *"blow up"* the perceived *'enemy'* in order to enable access to the next level. By the constant repetitions of *'drills'*, members of Clout, The Harbour-Shark Estate Gang and their peers became skilled in dexterity at carrying out the *'games'* instructive challenges but which render them acutely yet effectively more immune to empathy, sensitivity and remorse. Outside that virtual space, like Pavlov's dogs, egos were being alerted to the triggers but engaged in mindsets which sought to be rewarded for individual efficiency in *'finishing off'*, *'eliminating'*, *'seeking and destroying'* the perceived *'enemy'* in reality. The man they called 'The Professor' explained that "when the *'fight'* or *'flight'* response system was in a state of arousal, the perceived *'enemy'* felt the full force of the fear that initiated the process. In this state, the *'adrenaline rush'* took over and all *'drills'* which happened at a virtual level previously switched on to neural automation in reality. The body's autonomic system in full operation rendered each individual liable to respond without preamble towards achieving the ultimate commitment until **'Game Over'** for the victims in the virtual world. At that point, the 'player'/gangster possibly being unaware of the high state of distress it took to overcome the challenges from one level to another, automatically copies the formatting *('drills')* until **'Game Over'** for the <u>real victims</u> in the 'World of Reality'", he insisted. Duke and Baron testified that their cold-hearted stinking attitudes, toxic mindsets and schizophrenic ASPD behaviours transcended from the *'virtual world'* to the *'world of reality'*. It was quite easy to see how the likes of Baron could stab the boy, who injured his brother, Duke, without feeling any remorse. The man they called 'The Professor' stated that the *'mind-games'* were not limited or exclusively applied only to the virtual games. In fact, he concurred with Research from the Walynski Institute which stated that a great percentage of young individuals in Youth Offending Units and Prisons, who had got caught up in the serial predators' nets, reported that their experiences included *'activities'* like watching particular cartoons, which gave blatant instructions to defy authority. These were only two examples of the array of stimuli that was known amongst youngsters on the streets as the technological *'buzz'*. The likes of Duke and Baron *gained* their *'stripes'* by causing as much havoc, death and destruction as each could make in as little time as possible. Getting into gangs was the young individuals' new *'high'*. Reputations for *'Street Credits'* were the *'psychological medals of honour'* that individuals in UFO's Cult-Induced Post/Zip Code Wars were seeking, even posthumously. It was rumoured that some 'City Cowboys' and 'City Soldiers' as they had been reputed to be by their peers, were being buried with *'Guards of Honour'*, *'Gun Salutes'* and had their weapons placed inside their modern metal artistically decorated coffins as a mark of *'respect'* from their fellow gang members. This ritual was representative of their contribution in the *'self-help'* *'Ethno-Genocidia'* reflected by the UFO's Cult-Induced Post/Zip Code Wars. As twisted as that might sound, the virtual planet of Asteroidia was beginning to steep in its own juices of the new madness. What the UFO had failed to plan for is that *'Genocidia'* knew no ethnicity or barriers. The bigots, who had formulated but installed the Ghetto Mentality Terrorists, Ghetto Mentality Engineering Scientists, Gang Mentality Practitioners, Gang Orientation Scientists, Operators and Practitioners, had not catered for the backlash of karma. It was no time to celebrate someone else's demise but even young green humanoids was beginning to find the *'excitement'* of the perilous *'fun activities'* attractive. They were installed by the UFO to act as serial *'profiling agents'* but were colloquially known as the *'Neighbourhood Watch Monitors'*. Driven by Daryll Fastfamousse's *'bloodthirsty rants'* in his self-sponsored television and radio adverts, that title had boosted the *'Neighbourhood Watch Monitors'* already super-inflated egos but rendered their warped *'over-biased mindsets'* as being superior in breeding and class to ethnics, who lived within those neighbourhoods. Most had more than ambitions to join Spaceville's Security Personnel Forces. These groups of self-appointed individuals were being trained by them. Even though the principle of having *'Neighbourhood Watch Monitors'* in neighbourhoods might have been a fairly reasonable idea, some had morphed into heavily partisan *'Vigilante Groups'* but began to act with more *'official'* authority than their remit provided for but with immense political impunity. *'Neighbourhood Watch Monitors'* were allowed to be *'armed'* when they were patrolling their respective neighbourhoods, especially those in what was known as *'gated communities'*. As a consequence, many innocent ethnics had fallen *'prey'* to Daryll Fastfamousse's instructions to *"shoot first but question later"* fear-mongering philosophy. Many ethnics were being challenged unfairly most times because they fitted the *'stereo-type'* *'model'* which the *'profilers'* adjudged to be *"threatening"* to the neighbourhood. Even green humanoids, who had not become robotrons, identified with but integrated with the *'ethnic culture'*. They too suffered at the hands of the *'Vigilante Groups'*. Because of the way the young people chose to dress, especially in what was called *'hoodies'*, indigenous as well as immigrant ethnics from all tribes were being gunned down too by over-eager *'Vigilante Groups'*. They could not tell the difference in ethnicity under the *'hoodies'*. The indigenous young people of all tribes and the immigrants loved the same type of music, sports, films and cartoons in which their peer ethnic groups were involved. They were committed to the same technological *'blurb'* that seeped into their minds too, actively destroying the *'artificial'* filters that had been put in place over millennia by bigots to separate them from their ethnic peers. Some indigenous youngsters from other tribes had learnt that the children of the indigenous ethnic as well those of immigrants, who were born in Spaceville, in the same hospitals, gone to the same nurseries, junior and secondary schools or academies or later attended the same colleges, universities, or apprenticeships. In some cases, they chose to work together even. Some belonged to mixed gangs like the Mixed DNA Rainbow Tribe, smoked the same *'skunk'* weed, felt similar low self-worth, esteem or confidence, did the *'shankings'* and *'gun'* crimes while representing the same *'endz'* as their peers from all tribes in Spaceville. Daryll Fastfamousse and his cohorts might have been unable to sleep comfortably at nights if only they knew that his heavily partisan rhetoric had no impact on this new generation, who wanted none of the segregation, prejudices or bigotry of the past. They especially did not want to be separated from their peers no matter what their origin. These new generations did not see colour or religion. They experienced the friendships they valued highly. The 5th rated and the 1st rated *'worlds'* were now merging into a type of fusion, which might render Daryll Fastfamousse and his heavily partisan cohorts as a type of *'species'* older than fossils that might be found by palaeontologists on their next dig, probably! The epidemic *'mental germs'* and *'demons'* that had been released by his beloved UFO with the intention to decimate particular ethnic populations over the entire World of Space did not discriminate their *'hosts'*. Young individuals like Duke, Baron, members of the Harbour-Shark Estate Gang and their peers were mere *'pawns'* in an awful *'mad experiment'* in which they had no idea they were involved.

As the years went by, Brigette have had to put up with raids on the house in which she lived. Duke still had keys but accessed entrance to the house. Between the age of 13 to 17 years old, Duke had become so immersed in criminal activities that he used the house to hide the drugs, guns and ammunition he was selling. After serving 3 years in a youth prison and bound by his allegiance to their gang, Clout, Baron's reputation on the street was enormously powerful. Even in the youth prison, Baron's tattoo was cause for concern as it identified him as a member of the now notorious gang, Clout. Unlike any new prisoners who would have normally been bullied, other prisoners feared Baron. When they approached him, they did so cautiously but told him the stories they had heard from their colleagues, who had visited them before his incarceration. Duke and Baron's reputations were gaining them *'respect'* amongst the criminal *'fraternity'*. Like in the infamous movies, Duke and Baron were referred to as *'Super Dons'*. Because of their statuses, Clout's reputation was more popular in those neighbourhoods, precincts and boroughs in Spaceville that were being affected by street crime. Even from rival gangs, Clout's *'Street Credit'* had begun to manifest but was being commuted through the social websites much swifter than Duke and Baron had imagined. Even though they were now older in age, those members of the Harbour-Shark Estate Gang were now being very wary and watchful of Clout. Some members wanted to make peace with Duke and Baron for fear of not only their safety but also those of their families. Baron and Duke as individuals but Clout as a gang were notorious for their attitudes towards *'family cleansing'*. The purple coloured boy, who had stabbed at Duke in the back of The Cobblestone Arms AADC on the night of Earl's funeral, was reported to have attempted to take his own life rather than face the anticipated revenge from Duke and Baron. He had already been kidnapped but tortured by some Clout members. They deliberately released him so he could tell the tale to his peer members of what to expect from Duke and Baron. Both had the temper of their father, Earl. What angered them so? Uncannily, like most serial killers, it was the feeling of abandonment and rejection that haunted them so relentlessly that there was no respite from their busy brains even when they were able to sleep. Duke felt abandoned and rejected by, his mother, Enid. Baron felt abandoned and rejected by his father, Earl. Strangely enough, the brothers never discussed their feelings with each other but it was that common element which seemed to trigger but maintain their determination to self-destruct.

It was the timely intervention of Sheila Stagg's illness and subsequent hospitalisation that brought Raleigh and Duke together. Sheila, the caring grandmother that she had become through fostering and eventually adopting Earl requested that Duke come to see her in hospital. She had watched the news many times on television and read the printed media as well. Sheila was worried that Duke would waste the massive inheritance that Earl had bequeathed to him in his Will. She and Raleigh were left with power of attorney to confirm Duke's rights to his father's hard earned fortunes. There was no mention of Baron in the Will. Raleigh had visited Brigette. She told him of the odd visits that Duke was making to that address. Raleigh left a letter under the door of the room which Duke previously used as his bedroom. More than four days had passed without any contact from Duke. He had retrieved the letter on one of his mysterious visits to the house. At first, he threw the letter amongst the rest of the items on the floor but eventually he picked it up. When he read the content, he was quite shocked surprised to see that his grandmother was ill. It impacted on him greatly. Duke did love Nan as he called her. He decided to call the cell phone number that Raleigh had written in the letter. It was about 23:00 hours when Duke called. The phone rang quite a few times before Raleigh answered. "Hello", he said. "Granddad, it is Duke", he responded. Raleigh was very pleased to hear his grandson's voice. The joy in his voice boomed its way through the technological airways. He quickly told Duke about Sheila's health. "Sheila wants you to come to visit her. Do you think that's possible", Raleigh asked? "Yes granddad. I would feel guilty if anything happened and I didn't go to see Nan", Duke replied. They negotiated a day and time that suited them both and where they would meet. Duke had asked Baron to accompany him on the visit. At first, he refused. Baron was sensitive about invading his grand parents' lives but Duke insisted that his twin brother join him on the visit. On the day, Raleigh arrived to pick up Duke. He introduced Baron but did not explain who he was. Raleigh spoke with them generally but he did puzzle about how uncanny it was that they so resembled each other. Raleigh was a bit reticent about taking this other boy with them to see Sheila. He knew the reason Sheila had requested Duke to come to see her. The last thing they wanted was for some *'stranger'* to learn about their private business but he didn't tell Duke. On their journey to the hospital, Raleigh couldn't help telling them what he thought.

"You look like twins. If I didn't know better I'd say you are brothers", Raleigh commented. Both Baron and Duke laughed but didn't confirm nor deny Raleigh's statement. He kept looking into the rear-view mirror at the boys sitting in the back. On one of those occasions, the car swerved recklessly as Raleigh fought with the idea that Baron was Earl's son. He wondered if his son had impregnated two women at the same time. Knowing his own reputation with women, Raleigh mused with the idea so much so that it occupied his mind completely. He was entranced by the idea but not focused on his driving. The car drifted but Raleigh corrected his error in time. The oncoming vehicle had to swerve violently to avoid a collision with the careless Raleigh's vehicle. The driver of the other car stopped but hung out the window. He swore but gesticulated by pointing his finger like a gun in a menacing manner, as if he was indicating he would shoot Raleigh. Duke and Baron looked at each other but smiled. Duke was the first to speak. "Stop the car granddad. We'll deal with this fool", he pleaded. "It's not worth arguing. It was my fault for drifting. I suppose I might have felt just as angry. Let him have his tantrum moment", Raleigh said calmly. The other driver was a much younger man than Raleigh but older than Baron and Duke. On the other side of the road, he followed slowly in the line of traffic which was creeping ahead towards the traffic light in the opposite direction until he had to stop. Raleigh held his hand up acknowledging that he was in the wrong but indicated that he was sorry. The driver of the other vehicle carried on ranting. Raleigh hadn't noticed that Duke had slipped out of the car on the nearside but he did see Baron open the rear door from the offside. It was then he saw Duke as both he and Baron swiftly approached the raging driver. It all happened too quickly for Raleigh to stop the boys. He witnessed the awesome power of the two boys. It wasn't long before the raging driver was curled up on the ground. Baron kicked him several times in the rib area while Duke stamped on the fingers that he had pointed at his granddad. They just as quickly returned to the car but urged Raleigh to drive on. He was aware of Duke's reputation and his leadership of the gang Clout but he was more aware now of the awesome way in which they dealt with adversaries. After all, he had just witnessed it but he had a duty to get Duke to the hospital to see Sheila. They travelled for the rest of the journey without comment. Soon, Duke and Baron could see the entrance to the Highbrow Hospital, Upborough. Raleigh turned the car in through the gates but headed for the car park. It was relatively empty. Raleigh chose a parking bay. The three of them alighted from the car but walked the short distance to the Ward in which Sheila was. As they entered, they were greeted by the staff. They seemed to know Raleigh. He flashed his magnetic smile but headed for the private room which Sheila occupied. It was about 15 yards along the corridor. When they arrived, Baron said he'd wait outside. Raleigh was happy that Baron was being considerate but Duke wanted him in the room. Raleigh reminded the boys that Sheila was quite eager to see Duke but he didn't want Baron to feel like an intruder so he decided to wait outside with him. As Duke entered, he saw Sheila. She looked as if she was asleep. He walked up to the bed but spoke quite softly. "Nan, it's your grandson, Duke. Are you awake", he queried? Sheila was not asleep but opened her eyes. Her smile was broad and inviting. She opened her arms wide, welcoming Duke lovingly. He bent over but hugged his grandmother affectionately. They remained in the embrace until Sheila whispered his name. "Duke, oh Duke, it's so lovely to see you. I thought I'd never see you again", she said. "It's lovely to see you again Nan. Why are you here", Duke asked? Sheila hesitated before she replied. "Old age is catching up with me. I am a bit worn out now. The doctors say I've got three months to live", Sheila admitted. "Three months", he asked rhetorically? "How do they know how long you can live", Duke asked? He was shocked. For the first time since his father's death, he felt a jolt in the pit of his stomach and a huge lump of sadness in his throat. His eyes started to well up with tears. The thought of losing his Nan so close to his dad was devastating. There was a human side to the cold-hearted, tough young *'senior'* gangster leader after all. Duke sobbed but looked deeply into Sheila's eyes. For a moment he felt rather hopeless but without the type of power that he felt when he was with his gang. Then he decided to tell her about Baron. "Nan I've got some good news for you", Duke declared. "Pray tell me young Duke. Are you giving up being in a gang? What makes you want to do that when you've got so much going for you", Sheila asked? Duke ignored his Nan's questions but blurted out his *'good news'*. "Nan, I have a twin brovver", he said proudly. Sheila asked him to repeat what he had just told her. It wasn't as if she didn't hear him but the news seemed more like a myth than being real. "Tell me I am not talking to you in my sleep. Did I hear you say you've got a twin brother", Sheila asked? As if she couldn't help herself, Sheila fired the inevitable question. "Where did he come from", she asked directly? Before Duke could answer, Sheila asked yet another question but this time it was a rhetorical one. "Twin brothers don't just happen, do they", she murmured? "He can tell you himself Nan. He's outside", Duke enthused. It was too much for Sheila to take in both set of news. She gasped deeply as she struggled to accept the *'good news'*. It wasn't that she was unhappy to learn that she had another grandson but she wondered why Earl wouldn't have told her. Sheila asked yet another question. "Does Raleigh know of this other boy, your brother, I mean. By the way where is Raleigh", she queried? It was as if the joy of seeing Duke had relegated Raleigh to a delayed thought in order of importance. This wasn't true of course but seeing Duke had overwhelmed Sheila so much that there seemed no necessity for mentioning her husband. She told Duke that she had some very important news for him but queried how she could tell him now his twin brother was present. Duke assured her that he and Baron were very close and that he had no secrets from his brother. Sheila warned that Baron could possibly be an impostor but Duke quickly refuted those comments. He assured his grandmother that he knew that Baron was his twin but challenged her to see for herself. Finally, she acceded to Duke's argument. He turned quickly, walked towards the door. Duke disappeared from Sheila's view. He told Baron to go into the room without him or Raleigh. At first Baron hesitated but then he caught on to the reason behind Duke's thinking. He wanted to see if Sheila could tell them apart. Baron entered the room but walked up to the bed. He said nothing but looked at the woman who was his grandmother. She looked back at him but asked what was happening. "Where is your brother Duke", Sheila asked? Baron remained silent but was feeling a bit awkward about the situation. He didn't want to impersonate his brother nor did he want to lie to his grandmother. Baron smiled but walked back towards the door but signalled for Duke to come back into the room. Sheila's eyes widened as if she was seeing doubles. She was. "Good God, you're twins. How did Earl manage to keep this away from me? I would never have thought he would have done such a thing. There must be some feasible explanation. Get Raleigh in here", Sheila demanded. When he arrived by her bedside, Sheila asked Raleigh what he knew about Baron. He told her honestly that he was learning about Baron for the first time too but that he had no doubt that he was Earl's son. It was fortunate for them that they were in a private room for the next part of the conversation was undoubtedly not for public consumption. Baron revealed that he was told he had a father but that the first time he met him was some weeks ago when Earl was being buried. There was huge silence around the room as the others tried to understand what it must be like for Baron. After about fifteen minutes of silence the other bombshell was dropped. Duke told a similar story to Baron's, only his was about meeting his biological mother, Enid, for the first time too at his father's funeral. Sheila and Raleigh heard these revelations for the first time. They were dumbstruck. There were no words that were satisfactory in such personal experiences. Raleigh was grateful to Sheila for using the media to find him. At least, he had met and was involved in Earl's life, subsequently, albeit when he was 12 years old. Sheila looked up at Raleigh as if she could interpret his feelings. He, Baron and Duke looked at each other but extolled their appreciation to the woman who was responsible for bringing them together. They hugged Sheila together but smothered her with kisses until she begged for a break. Even when Raleigh and Duke had let go of her, Baron clung on to the woman who he'd just found. When Duke told him that Sheila was told that she only had three months to live, Baron bawled unashamedly. He could not understand how it was possible to find his grandmother after such a long time but might soon lose her in as short a time as three months. Sheila and Raleigh on the other hand were more than happy to meet the grandson they never even knew existed before today. The sound of Baron's heavy voice bawling had alerted the staff. There was a knock at the door. Raleigh went to open it. A doctor, the Nursing Sister and two nurses were standing there looking concerned. Raleigh asked what they wanted. The Nursing sister said she heard crying in the room but wondered if Sheila's condition had worsened. Raleigh explained that the family was upset at hearing that Sheila might die in three months. He thanked the staff for their concern then returned to family business. Sheila wanted to know what was causative to Baron and Duke being part of a gang. It was Duke that answered first. He told of his despair of not knowing his biological mother. He had developed a real hate for her. Baron said much the same thing about Earl. They both said they had felt abandoned and rejected by each of their biological parents. Duke said he realised that he was a bit more fortunate than Baron because their biological mother was still alive. Their father, Earl is dead. Baron had no chance now to meet or speak with him. Both Raleigh and Sheila stated that they still didn't understand why Earl would have chosen one but not the other. They decided to request that Baron ask his mother to get in touch with them. Raleigh and Sheila assured him that Enid was not being judged but that they felt they needed to clear up as much as they could before Sheila passed on. She pushed the buzzer to alert the staff. One nurse arrived with them quickly. Sheila ordered tea and biscuits for each of them. The nurse exited the room but returned quickly with the refreshment. After the consumption of the tea and biscuits, Sheila decided to tell the boys about the Will that was bequeathed to Duke. They described the special terms and conditions Earl had insisted be invoked. Both Sheila and Raleigh said they held power of attorney jointly. This meant that they could instruct the lawyers of the new set of facts about Baron. When Sheila told Duke about the extent of his inheritance, he stated that he wanted to share it with his brother equally. It was a very huge statement which represented the solidity of their relationship. Earl had stipulated under the terms and conditions that Duke inherits the five bedrooms house that he lived in when he became 18 years old. At 20 years old he inherits The Cobblestone Arms and two other Adult Alcoholic Drinking Centres. When he becomes 25 years old, he inherits another seven Adult Alcoholic Drinking Centres and Duke Stagg Incorporated. There was an array of other businesses which he accumulates at various stages. Some ownership coincided with current arrangements while others didn't. Altogether, Duke was to be a very rich man. Earl made sure that Duke understood that he could not sell the five bedroom house for ten years. Simon Crabley is to stay as landlord of The Cobblestone Arms AADC for another ten years. Duke Stagg Incorporated was to remain the prestige family business. It must never merge, be taken over or be sold. In order for Duke to access ownership, he would have to have attended University and acquire the relevant degrees before he could become owner. Duke must be trained for seven years by the current Board members led by Alan Panaché. He must conduct the business in the manner how Earl preferred. Duke must prove his business prowess to the Board over 10 years before he could make changes of his own. Mary Allsorts must remain as Secretary until she decides to give up her post or retires. Duke must keep the business at the top level at all times he's in charge as owner. These were very well thought out strategies but would prove very challenging for Duke. Baron was learning not only how rich his father had become but how focused and determined he had become when he was alive. On the day of Earl's funeral, Baron had learnt how much impression he had made on the community of Ghettoborough. It also meant that if he was willing to share equally with Duke, Baron would have to attend University too but aim to succeed in business. He looked at Duke. It dawned on both of them that the time for being in a gang was to be terminated. It was a very futile *'business'* in which to be involved. There were no guarantees that they could accumulate half of what their father had done by being involved in street life. Even if they did, they realised they might not be free to enjoy their *'illegal earnings'*. Both Duke and Baron had already worked out that reputations on the streets only lasted for as long as they did. The likelihood that someone from inside the gang might become jealous or tire of them being at the top was a real consideration that could not be ignored. It only takes one member, who feels disgruntled, to hatch a plot to oust the leader. This was a common occurrence amongst groups and especially gangs. Even in the violent films that they watched so avidly with frequency, there was animosity that pre-warned of the inevitable dethroning to come. The law too had become more sophisticated and was technologically driven, currently. It was more than just possible that both might end up with long prison sentences. Silently, Duke and Baron contemplated that to enable them to enhance their reputations they would have to become more vicious than they already were amongst not only with their rivals but within their own gang too. It seemed likely that either or both of them might end up behind bars for long periods or possibly never be free to pass their illegal earnings on to their families. They were both conscious that their 18th birthdays were imminent. There was no time like the present to make a decision whether they continued as notorious gangsters because that's what they were fast becoming. The prospect of earning big money from the sale of drugs, guns and ammunition was a real possibility. Both Baron and Duke had been initiated since they were in junior schools but remembered being bullied into that situation then. Now all they were doing was repeating a pattern over which it seemed they had no control. Baron and Duke felt the same about their respective parent that they had thought had rejected and abandoned them. Their deeply felt anger had been dissipating rapidly the longer they spent with family. Each was beginning to feel responsible for their individual behaviours instead of owning them. This was a vastly different experience for each of them. They had begun to resolve that there was no further need to stay as angry as they had chosen to be. Duke and Baron learnt how they had gained by being angry. They had used it as an excuse for how and when they exhibited their unacceptable behaviours. As they stared in each other's eyes very deeply, both Duke and Baron knew that there had to be a rapid change in their individual mentality, attitude and mindset. There were no words to be said. Earl had spoken to his children from beyond his grave. Raleigh and Sheila remained quiet while they observed their grandchildren as the reality of the enormity of responsibilities drove home the initiative to both Baron and Duke. When they next spoke, Raleigh and Sheila told Baron and Duke that Earl's last instructions were that the Will would become null and void if this further request was not adhered to consistently. The last instruction was that Duke should seek out the services of the Spiritual Holistic Coach, the man they called 'The Professor'. Duke must book an initial appointment but follow up on the appointments as and when the man they called 'The Professor' directed. This stipulation was irreversible in content and context. Raleigh fished the paperwork from the folder that was in the cupboard next to Sheila's bed. She spoke to both Baron and Duke. "Now boys, if you agree to what Raleigh and I have explained to you, it means you have to sign the legal documents that Raleigh is about to hand to you. It is legally binding and must be returned to the lawyers for their records. Only sign it if you have no doubt about your commitment to the terms and conditions your father invoked", Sheila explained. The boys voiced their commitment before agreeing to sign the paperwork. Raleigh pressed the buzzer. When the nurse came in, he asked that the Doctor and the Nursing Sister come to witness the document. The nurse turned on her heels but left the room. Within two minutes, the Doctor and the Nursing Sister entered the room. Sheila asked them to witness the boys signing the document. They did. Sheila sighed but said she felt extremely tired. Raleigh, Baron and Duke watched as she closed her eyes but seemed to instantly drift off into sleep. The Doctor and the Nursing Sister seemed concerned. They asked the boys to remove themselves from the side of the bed so that they could examine the frail old woman. The doctor placed the stethoscope upon Sheila's chest while the Nursing sister felt for the pulse on her wrist. They both looked at each other. The Doctor shook his head to indicate that there was no sign of a heartbeat while the Nursing Sister confirmed there was no pulse. The Doctor opened Sheila's eyes but shone the light into it but there was no sign of dilation. He looked over at Raleigh but murmured that he was sorry. The boys protested but Raleigh said Sheila had suffered enough already. He agreed with the Doctor that she didn't want to be resuscitated should the inevitable happen. It was hard for the boys to understand but Raleigh had promised his wife that he would honour her request. Duke and Baron were shocked by the enormity of the situation. Duke in particular was glad that he had decided to come to see her today and Baron was grateful to his brother for inviting him to come with him. Their deep voices were like the baritones in a choir as they expressed their sorrow through crying. Raleigh just kept shaking his head from side to side while the tears rolled down his face. The snot had started on its journey again like it did a few weeks prior in the Corporate Box at the Earl Stag Association Football Stadium.

CHAPTER 9

Duke inherited his father's five bedroom house and staged access to a generous lump sum on his 18th birthday. There were to be further acquisitions as he grew older but specific terms and conditions were attached. It was the best present that Duke received on his very special day. Earl's Lawyers had sent the letter to inform him of his father's instructions by way of Earl's Will. Duke read the letter but smiled broadly as he did so. Everything that Raleigh and Sheila had told him and Baron was being confirmed in the letter from the lawyers. Arrangements were made for Duke to visit the Lawyers, Planit and Planit Limited, who represented Earl's Estate. Duke had arranged for him and Baron to meet Raleigh there but first he wanted to settle the score between him and Brigette. The house was now his. Duke now had the power to get Brigette out of it. When he and Baron arrived, Duke found a letter just inside the door. It was hand written but addressed to him. There was no postage stamp on the envelope but there were a couple of special notes written on it. One said *'Personal'* and the other said *'By Hand'*. Duke examined it carefully then showed it to Baron. He handed the letter back to Duke but encouraged him to open it. Inside, there were three handwritten pages. The writing was neat. Baron asked Duke to read the letter out loud. He did. "Dear Duke, I am writing to you to clear up quite a few points . . ." it started. The letter went on to address some of the huge misunderstandings that happened between Duke and Brigette. Baron listened attentively. What he heard was such a moving story. Who else would have sacrificed their life in the way the letter described the writer? Both Baron and Duke learnt that their father was also a troubled man. He thought his mother had abandoned him too. In fact, they now know that Earl went to his grave having not met or known the whereabouts of his mother. Baron rolled his eyes towards the ceiling. Even though he never met Earl until the day of the funeral, Baron told Duke that he felt more fortunate than their dad. They both empathised with him but the biggest revelation was the part Brigette had played in Duke's life. When they realised that not only was she a mere child of 17 years old when 27 years old Earl met her but also that Brigette was forced to look after Duke since the day he left hospital as a baby, tears started to roll down Duke's face. All the time he had behaved atrociously; calling Brigette names and telling her she was a scrounger as he was programmed and conditioned to do. There was some remorse welling up inside the young man. Baron whistled when he heard the part about the beatings but wondered if his father would really physically strike a woman. When he thought of his mother, Enid, Baron knew that he would have had to confront his father on that particular issue and it wouldn't have been a discussion. Duke knew he had witnessed such beatings and they were frequent too. Even now, he could hear Brigette's voice in his head, begging for someone to help her. Duke was a young boy then but didn't understand that his father was suffering from deep depression and alcoholism. The end of the letter was the real clincher. It stated that, although Earl had mistreated her badly, at times Brigette saw him more like a wounded bear rather than a deliberately viscous man. His wounds were as deep as his depression. Brigette stated that she only knew this because she had found a letter written to him from the man they called 'The Professor'. In the letter he stated that he was concerned about Earl's depression and alcoholism. The man they called 'The Professor' said he had no experience to work with alcoholics but thought that Earl needed to go to see a psychiatrist instead. He wanted Earl to be assessed about the seriousness of his depression and alcoholism. The man they called 'The Professor' was a Coach with a holistic approach, who believed in spiritual development. Earl needed the services of a Psychiatrist, rather urgently, in order to find out if he was bi-polar as well as suffering from deep depression. Brigette ended the letter by thanking Earl for his generosity in leaving her a lump sum in his Will. This letter was to say goodbye to the boys. Brigette said she had booked a ticket and would be leaving soon to go to start a new life in a foreign country. She instructed where Duke could find her set of keys for the house but encouraged him to do something decent with his life. The letter ended with these words . . . "all my love, Brigette". No longer was Brigette to be the target of his tantrums or the other behaviours that Duke had chosen to use against his loving stepmother. She was now out of his life. For the first time, Duke realised that Brigette had genuinely cared about him as an individual and about his welfare, specifically. She had insisted that structure was a necessary part of development, especially from a young age. Ironically, Duke realised that, despite the fact that Earl had spoilt him when he was younger, his instructions under the Will was about the importance of structure. Duke was becoming more aware of how much further he might have advanced as an individual had he listened to Brigette. Baron witnessed the impact of Brigette's letter on his brother. He put his arm around his shoulders, hugged him tightly, but commented. "All that happened but it's where we go from here that matters brov", Baron assured. Duke agreed but was honest enough to admit that he was feeling guilty about how wrong he had been in his perception of Brigette. Both he and Baron proceeded to look around the house. They went from room to room. Finally, Duke found what used to be Brigette's set of keys. He gave them to Baron. "That's yours brov. We each own half the house. Which half do you want", Duke asked? Baron stated that he would decide later. For now, all he wanted to do was get some food before they left to go to the appointed Lawyers, Planit and Planit. Duke agreed but pointed out that they also had to plan their birthday celebration too. He opened the refrigerator but was surprised that there was so much food in it. He told Baron. They placed the packaged meals into the Microwave machines. Within minutes, the two young adults sat down to eat. They laughed and joked but threw bits of food at each other as if they were still in their pre-teenage years. Baron's cell phone interrupted their horseplay. "What's gwaning", Baron answered? "Got something for you, interested", the caller asked? Baron did not recognise the voice so he ended the call. Duke asked him who it was that had phoned. Baron kept silent. Duke was aware that Baron was trying the number that called but he kept the phone close to his ear. When the voice answered, Baron spoke. "Got something for you, interested", he asked? Baron did the same as before. He ended the call. The phone rang again. Baron put the phone to his ear but said nothing. The voice named a rendezvous and a period of time as twenty minutes. Baron got up from the table but went into Duke's *'old'* bedroom. He removed the gun from where he had hidden it. Baron checked the clip then pushed the gun inside the front of the baggy name brand jeans he was wearing but took an additional clip with more ammunition with him. Duke begged his brother not to go but Baron said that the individual had asked for the confrontation and that he wasn't backing down. Duke reminded his brother about the visit to their Nan and the new responsibilities that challenged them. Baron was adamant that he couldn't loose face to the punk who had called him out. He had already opened the door and was just leaving when the shots rang out. Baron fell to the floor. Duke rushed across the hallway, just in time to hear the screeching of the car which raced away into the distance. He saw the model of the car but had no time to get the registration of it. Duke looked down at Baron then he saw the blood. His heart was racing with the anger he felt towards those, who had shot his brother but Duke was even angrier with Baron. He felt, intuitively, that Baron should have listened to his warning. Duke held him under his arms but dragged him back into the house. The trail of blood streaked along the wooden panelled floor. Duke called Baron's name. He looked at Duke but did not reply. "Where does it hurt", Duke asked? "It's only a graze brov. It is nothing to worry about", Baron said. "Did you see who it was", Duke asked? "Yeah brov, I can't believe Chirpy 'the bird' thinks he's a bad boy. Since when did he become a bad boy brov", Baron questioned? "Brov, you know how it is on street. You don't have to be a bad boy. Sometimes, cowards have to prove themselves to their leaders just like the brovs in Clout. It's no different. Whoever wrote the script just needed to write the words "do as I do" next to it because it's the same in every gang", Duke stated. Baron raised himself off the floor but looked at the wound in his arm. It was just a flesh wound. The bullet did not directly enter the muscle. In fact, it remained lodged into the solid wooden door, only Baron and Duke had not noticed. Blood still poured from the wound but the injury didn't seem to be as serious as the gushing blood indicated. Baron whipped his bandana from around his neck but made a tourniquet above the wound on his left arm. Duke supplied the tissues but applied the necessary pressure to the wound in order to stop the oozing of blood. Between them, Baron and Duke cleaned up the wound. They found a First Aid Box in what used to be Brigette's bathroom. Using some gauze and bandaging, they managed to keep the wound clear of any possible infectious contact. Duke copied the bandaging of his left arm, the same as his brother, Baron. Duke looked at his watch but told Baron that they would have to leave soon to keep the appointment with Planit and Planit. Baron finished cleaning up then he changed his shirt. Duke changed into a matching shirt too. When they were ready to leave, Duke asked Baron to leave the gun at home but he insisted that there was now a better reason for him taking it with him. Baron encouraged Duke to do the same. Duke took his brother's advice but tooled up the same as him.

Like most children on the virtual planet of Asteroidia and other galaxies in the World of Space, Duke and Baron were introduced to guns since they were very young. It was part of the deliberate subliminal programming and conditioning that drove the *'beliefs and values'* of using guns, discriminately or otherwise. At toddlers' age, Duke and Baron, like millions of others over the World of Space, had been given their first lesson in **'Gunology'**. Most parents saw a water pistol as a *'suitable'* yet *'harmless'* **'gift'**. It was considered as *"harmless"* and it was *"suitable"* because only water ever came out of the nozzle. Many parents joined in the *'fun'* of spraying or being sprayed by their children with the seemingly *"harmless"* *"toy"*. Duke and Baron, like other children, at about 6 or 7 years old, eventually *'graduated'* to the *'cap-shot'* gun when a sound is necessary to hold their attention. At about 8 to 10 years old, the *'cork-shot'* gun becomes the option. As the nail strikes the explosive that lies just beneath the thin sheet of paper on the inner side of the cork, the sound of the explosion coincides with the cork being propelled from the nozzle. It travels as a projectile across a distance. Duke and Baron's interest at that age was now about accuracy in *'hitting a still target'*. At 11 to 12 years old, the likes of Duke and Baron were inveigled by parents to *'hunt' 'moving targets'*, like rabbits or other animals, with their *'BE-BE'* guns then wallow in the *'fun'* of watching the wounding animals suffer while they flee. Baron, Duke and others like them, used their *'BE-BE'* guns to injure other children. They often end up in Court. All of that *'programming'* over those earlier years was being ably *'reinforced'* by the violent films they were encouraged to watch and the *'ultra violent' 'games'* they chose to play, often without supervision on their personal consoles. At times, the children learned, under the *'tutelage'* of irresponsible parents, who often found it *'fun'* to share in the *'gruesome eradication'* demanded by the *'rules'* of the *'games'*. Having earned enough *'credits'* enabled the *'players'* to move up another level. "Whilst there was an argument about using the games on the consoles for improving *'spatial awareness'* and improving *'spatial intelligence'*, the *'learning' 'under the radar'* at the subliminal level inoculated the *'players'*. The *'post-hypnotic'* messages had the ability to numb individual player's emotional sensitivity but exchanged it for a type of *'pseudo-pleasure'* instead. In the virtual game there didn't seem any need to be *'emotionally sensitive'* but whenever the players transferred their *'primed minds'* and *'corrosive mentalities'* into *'real-life'* scenarios, there was always a danger that it was impossible for individuals to distinguish how to react differently in *'real-life'* situations or environments, especially when reacting through fear", Professor Walynski declared.

To carry a *'real gun'* as a defensive or offensive weapon in areas like Lower Ghettoborough had now become the automatic choice. This was not a quantum leap for the Harbour-Shark Estate, Clout or those others gang members scattered around the virtual planet of Asteroidia. The likes of Baron, Duke and their peers were *'mentally primed'*, *'strapped'* and ready to "*terminate*" their *'pseudo-enemies'* or *'frenemies'* as they were called. This they did without any feeling of emotional sensitivity. To be *'terminated' 'in action'*, by individuals, who followed the *'post-hypnotic'* subliminal instructions of their *'puppeteers'* meant that there was no remorse being felt by those delivering the fatal wounds. "Their sympathetic nervous systems had been breached but they had become impervious to feeling any form of empathy towards the individuals they had wounded or eliminated. Haunted by severe *'mood swings'*, the *'programmed and conditioned'* serial psychopathic schizophrenic behaviours of the *'ultra-insensitive'* socially excluded *'stereotypes'* often didn't understand how they were being *'mentally kidnapped'* and *'subliminally manipulated'* by *'significant others'*. Their only interest was to gain financially from the huge *'mental ransoms'* they demanded from those naïve individuals, often with much premeditated prejudice and menace. The *'mental kidnappers'* inveigled the *'enmity'* amongst individuals like Duke and Baron from Clout, the Harbour-Shark Gangs and others around the virtual planet to become deeply involved in criminal activities. In doing so, those attracted to and being actively involved in the crazy UFO's Cult-Induced Post/Zip Code Wars chose to tote guns and knives out of fear of becoming targets themselves. Like all *'cult-driven'* philosophies, the *'street disciples'* were unaware that their *'belief systems'* had been subtly but severely breached by the recurring post-hypnotic *'subliminal sermons'* being instigated but delivered expertly by the appointees of the UFO's Gang Orientation administrators. The self-appointed *'city-cowboys'* continued to settle their *'petty disagreements'* known as *'pasa-pasa'* or *'beef'*, indiscriminately. They did this in order to gain the attention they sought to boost their notoriety", Professor Walynski's Forensic Psychiatric Research explained. Baron, Duke and others like them seemed to have become almost immune to the harm that happened whenever they chose to use knives or guns to injure someone, sometimes fatally. There were no *'Crime Prevention Projects'* in place that really addressed **'the culture of criminal behaviours'** that seemed to be attracting the children of Spaceville. Influenced by special interests contributors like the UFO's Ghetto Mentality Terrorists and Ghetto Mentality Engineering Scientists, amongst others in their hierarchy, to influence naïve individuals, who chose to engage with the type of challenging *'activities'* and *'pseudo-entertainment'* which gave specifically tailored instructive subliminal messages to maintain their *'bravado'*. Driven by fear, what these *'mentally conscripted'* young volunteer recruits, who sought *'Street Credit'* or to become *'A' Blisters*, failed to understand, were that they had become **privately and politically owned *'indentured mental slaves'*** to the chaotic illusion of *'infamy'* known as the UFO's Cult-Induced Post/Zip Code Wars. These youngsters had been distracted into the *'business'* of the *'Fast Lane delusions'* known as the *'ride or die'*, *'live fast, die trying'* mindsets in order to quench their humungous thirst for the taste of Champagne Urge. The younger generation were so entranced by the subtle embedded post-hypnotic subliminal messages that they had come to believe were their own thoughts. All over Spaceville and the 5th rated exotic continents, countries and islands, the younger generations had hardly noticed that they had been carefully *'selected'* through a form of *'mental culture'*, aided and abetted, by an *'educational system'* that had deliberately and politically discriminated against their best interests as incumbent *'stakeholders'*. To help youngsters avoid what was obvious even to the simplest of minds, the educational authorities could have sought innovative teaching methods to inspire those students, who did not feel they were either *'stakeholders'* or *'educationally challenged'* within the particular educational establishments they attended. Instead, The Royal Royal Dis-United Stately Kingdoms of Asteroidia collectively chose not to acknowledge the *'needs'* of the students. They failed to see the urgency for looking from new perspectives but chose to deliberately ignore the small *'leaks'* in the metaphoric pipelines until the enormity of the floods manifested. The custodians of the children of the virtual planet of Asteroidia's education were *'united'* in the condemnation of those children's *'needs'* but had actively contributed to the **_'educational assassination'_** of such huge resources of potentialities and abilities. They did this by using a type of segregation (suspensions and expulsions) which highlighted the students' errant behaviours rather than helping them to enhance their capabilities. Through an inflexible model that had proven to be more than inadequate perennially, the politicrats and poly-tricksters continued to recycle the same old *'stone-aged rhetoric'* to address *'new generational needs'*. The mindsets of those *'anoraks'* used the antiquated model to debase the uninspired students' breeding, demeaned their values, self-worth and capabilities but purposely corralled and directed their thinking towards subservience. This approach prevented the young generations of the virtual planet of Asteroidia from using their genial talents in meaningful ways but drove them onto the streets, instead. Feeling rejected, abandoned, disillusioned, hopelessly low in self-worth, esteem and confidence but driven by fear, the young generations all over the virtual planet of Asteroidia sought to partake in the senseless UFO's

Cult-Induced Post/Zip Code Wars. Even though their choices were not rationally weighted in their favour, the young generations found a rather *'twisted excitement'* by being in charge of their hopelessness and a false sense of security in numbers. Each seemed to wallow in their own whirlpools of emotions which flooded their brains but rendered them *'worthy'* of working towards a common *'goal'*, assumedly! Even though they thought it gained them the reputations of being *'hardcore'*, the UFO's Cult-Induced Post/Zip Code Wars did expose their superficial psychological need for recognition, even posthumously, perhaps! The man they called 'The Professor' stated that "those younger generations, who had chosen the UFO's Cult-Induced Post/Zip Code Wars as the new *'activity challenge'* towards which they were attracted, were entrapped in a most vicious cycle. Their only guarantee was that the bullying *'offenders'* would end up in the land based *'Human Zoos'*. Those that had been slaughtered through the madness of the UFO's Cult-Induced Post/Zip Code Wars would end up in the new privately manufactured *'designer coffins'* and buried under the earth in the same graves where *'human grave-diggers'* had been made obsolete by privately owned mechanical machines. Such was the guaranteed frequency of *'Ethno-Genocidia'* that the advent of mechanical diggers and their operators had become the only *'efficient'* practice of the *'modern'* funeral. Parents, other family members and friends were no longer able to mourn or grieve by the gravesides of their beloved and the singing of hymns were no longer to be *"tolerated"* or heard over the humming of the engines of the mechanical diggers", he commented. The man they called 'The Professor' further stated that "when those messages like, *'ride or die'*, *'live fast, die trying'*, were being subtly implanted in the minds of the younger generations, it is possible that they might well be responsible for the young generations' stinking attitudes, toxic mindsets and subsequent insensitive, cold-hearted behaviours displayed by individuals in gangs", he added. Those individuals involved in the UFO's 'Cult-Induced' Post/Zip Code Wars seemed not only to accept the senseless extremely violent modes of conduct but also they seemed to believe it was necessary to re-enact the *'roles'* of their *'heroes'* in the ultra violent movies they choose to watch repeatedly. Some accepted the *'values* and *beliefs'* or the chillingly deliberate violent explicit lyrical messages of those subservient *'models'*, who best befit the slavish *'Uncle Tom'* and *'Biblical Concubine'* *'roles'*. As long as their taste for Champagne Urge were being satisfied, these self-appointed *'role models'* didn't seem to mind that their *'dutiful allegiance'* to which they subscribed or reinforced were producing more cold corpses for PODA, Private Organ Donation Organization, in the Royal Royal Dis-United Stately Kingdoms of Asteroidia. The *'Uncle Tom'* *'models'* were being replicated, whenever the *'ultimate virtual destroyer'*, as portrayed in the violent games they chose to or were inveigled to *'play'* on their respective consoles, seemingly! Though places like Lower Ghettoborough seemed to attract more attention from the media, these violent atrocities were not exclusive to it but instead were being perpetrated across the length and breath of the World of Space. Oftentimes, the younger generations of Spaceville generally, but particularly those from Lower Ghettoborough, were treated like the *'stereotypical imagery'* that had been portrayed by individuals like the green humanoid robotron profiler, Daryll Fastfamousse. He seemed as if he had a penchant for inveterate bigoted views towards some ethnic group or other, by default, probably! Sadly, the UFO's Cult-Induced Post/Zip Code Wars did not help to negate his bigoted perception. In fact, it fuelled even moderate commentators to back the mantra of bigots like Daryll Fastfamousse. The UFO's Cult-Induced Post/ Zip Code Wars were bad for everyone including the innocent victims, who had got caught in the cross-fire between the feuding gangs. All age groups were affected but older folks felt intimidated more and were afraid, literally. Fear from the gangs' reputations, which preceded them and their subsequent actions had begun to fulfil not only the *"prophecy"* of the bigots but also reinforced the seemingly *'prophetic'* *'stereo-typical images'* Daryll Fastfamousse and his followers had constructed. The UFO's Cult-Induced Post/ Zip Code Wars meant young individuals were restricted in movement from one borough to the next. Sometimes, even within the same boroughs, young individuals could not visit other areas but risked life and limb when they did. This quickly spread but infiltrated communities like Brazenborough, Sneersborough, Snideborough as well as some parts of Yupborough. Each day, the fear of any young person was to become a victim, dead or alive, perhaps!

The issues, situations, conditions and environments that were causative to those younger generations feeling so low in self-esteem, less than valued or not a stakeholder in schools, forced them to abandon their obvious potentials and abilities. In the 1st rated Kingdom of Spaceville and similarly in the exotic continents, countries and islands, more youngsters fell into the trap set to destroy them. Street violence rose rapidly but was in itself responsible for the many fatalities in the communities. Each was stated as an *'isolated case'* by the *'Ethnic Stereotypes Unit'* which dealt with *'Ethnic on Ethnic'* crimes only. Due to the senseless madness of the UFO's Cult-Induced Post/Zip Code Wars that prevailed, whenever there was another fatality, it seemed the ideal opportunity for families to come together in their communities. They could then actively seek to find a resolve to this dastardly infectious mental disease. It appeared to be worsening with each headline in the printed media or the *'breaking news'* items on television. Though the violence was impacting on all within communities, there were some individuals, who preferred to turn a blind eye with regards to getting involved with seeking a solution. As long as it wasn't their children involved, it didn't seem to matter to some individuals. Conversely, when their child was accused of being involved in criminal activities, especially as being part of a gang, some parents and guardians went into deliberate acts of denial about their children's behaviours. The consequences of those children's actions were never considered until the day they had to be escorted from freedom to join the others in what's known commonly, in Spaceville, as the *'Human Zoos'*, called prisons on the parallel planet, Earth. Even then, prison as an intended deterrent, did not appear any longer to have the same impact on those committing crimes. What had been intended as a deterrent in order to send the message of intimidation had now become *'New Colonies'* with an ever increasing population. In Spaceville, some of the sentences that were meant to discourage individuals from being involved in crime, sounded more ridiculous than the people who uttered them. Though the idea of sounding tough was, in itself, meant to establish the permanency of the occupant's stay behind bars, sentencing any individual to anything from 100 to 1000 years is simply impracticable and made the laws of Spaceville seemed like something that might get few chuckles at the movies.

Instead of rehabilitation, the likes of Baron or any other gang member, who had served terms in the *'Human Zoos'* openly testified that *'street reputations'* were enhanced but rose to a much higher level. It was deemed as some kind of *'Street Credit'* to be incarcerated, apparently. With the access afforded them via social websites, criminals confirmed the *'status'* of their *'street reputations'* to an even bigger audience in the World of Space. Reputations, for "serving time *'inside'"*, had been *'idolized'* in the past, is currently so and might be in the future too, possibly! Even though that is an unfortunate yet regrettable occurrence, it really cannot be ignored by the likes of 1st rated Kingdoms like Spaceville. In the World of Space, Spaceville's own reputation was suffering, especially abroad, because of the increase fear of violence. A drop of 46% in Leisure and Tourism proved that it's once magnetic attraction and reputation had slid deeply into a modern day distraction that rated it amongst the 5th rated exotic continents, countries and islands. Spaceville appeared in the top ten on the World of Space *'Worst Countries List'*. Visiting famous sport individuals had first hand experience of being kidnapped for ransom or suffered consistent burglaries upon their properties and persons. The real fear was the frequency of violence on the streets. These were being perpetrated by gangs, like Clout and The Harbour-Shark Estate Gangs. Their reputations, as gangs, had caught on much quicker than a bush fire can spread. Individuals like Duke and Baron, who begot fearsome *'street reputations'* were ready, and *'tooled up'* with awesome warlike hardware and technological resources to broadcast their cruel insensitive actions within microseconds of committing any criminal act. When individuals were unable to do it themselves, their colleagues or families assisted with the broadcast. Each day, Baron and Duke and many others like them were *"strapped"* and ready to kill or be killed. They lived in a time where they were forced, by default, to become *'adults'* the moment they were born. It seemed that transitioning through the life stages, from being a baby becoming a toddler, a young child, a pre-teenage child, an adolescent and then into adulthood had been relegated into antiquity. This new image created by the *'modern parents'* referred to their children as *'mini-adults'*. These creators of this new imaging had their own reasons for wanting to refer to children as such, probably! The man they called 'The Professor' pointed out that "those, who had ascribed to but had supported the creation of these absurd new words, like *'little man'*, *'mini-adult'* and *'kid-hult'* ought to be committed not just to the *'stock'* as in olden days but to be *'water-boarded'* until they confessed publicly about the insane intentions they have for their children".

Duke used to be referred to by those parents like Earl, who had chosen to use those so-called *'endearments'* to describe their children. What parents like Earl were not aware of was the messages being conveyed by those *'sentiments'* and the inevitable consequences somewhere down the line, probably! Earl had witnessed how Duke's behaviour was tainted by his insistence in inveigling the child to address and treat his stepmother, Brigette as if they were on *'equal terms'* as adults and not child to parent. She wanted to implement structure in Duke's life but Earl constantly rebuked her for doing so. Duke was not encouraged by Earl to be responsible for his behaviour. Instead, Earl had made him feel as if he was *'an adult'* rather than *'a child'*. Duke had no reference then or as he grew up to ever being a child. The confusion in his mind between the *'mixed messages'* he had received from both Brigette and Earl made Duke feel he had a responsibility to go out to *'earn'* and become the *'man of the household'*. He was being treated as a child by Brigette but as an adult by his father, Earl. It were these contradictions that had contributed toward his "unacceptable behaviours" that resulted in him being suspended consistently and excluded subsequently from secondary school, permanently. It had started much earlier in his life when Duke attended Nursery School. His father, Earl, allowed the life stage *'child'* to wear two gold earrings in the shape of guns, one in each ear, a thick linked solid gold chain that was much too heavy for his *'immature bone-dense'* neck, an ornately jewelled branded watch, expensive name brand trainers and sagging baggy trousers many sizes too big. Duke was even encouraged to match the way his father, Earl, walked with that perceived distinctive swagger at crawl pace which announced that he was happy as being perceived as a tough, no-nonsense thug. It seemed ridiculous and dangerously irresponsible for Earl to dress the then four year old Duke in that way but left him vulnerable also. As an adolescent, Duke had carried these *'thug-like'* behaviours onto the streets where reputations for psychopathic schizophrenic antisocial personality disorder behaviours warranted *'respect'* from peers involved in the crazed *'Ethno-Genocidia'* known colloquially as the UFO's Cult-Induced Post/Zip Code Wars.

Through traumatic *'Life Experiences'* like losing a child through the senseless street violence, some parents were becoming more aware of the type of approach being used to achieve *'ethnic cleansing'* through *'Ethno-Genocidia'*. They now better understood the psychological subliminal techniques and the type of *'programming'* and *'conditioning'* of their children minds, seemingly, perhaps! Parents on the virtual planet of Asteroidia were accepting that there was a need to monitor and manage the type of games, films, cartoons and music to which their children had been attracted otherwise the deliberate *'mental infiltration'* might well result in more parents burying their children rather than the other way around. The man they call 'The Professor' stated that, "if the madness mentality trend was allowed to continue without parents taking active roles of heavily investing in their children's future by putting in meaningful structures in place for them then, even at the current rate, it is inevitable that soon bigoted individuals like the hugely financially influential poly-tricksters like Daryll Fastfamousse's heavily biased *'prophetic'* rhetoric might continue to be fulfilled. If so, it was likely that the total annihilation of ethnic groups and other indigenous generations, who shared the same lifestyle as their ethnic colleagues, friends and families might manifest if the UFO's Cult-Induced Post/Zip Code Wars were allowed to continue. Generations of ethnic groups would disappear forever from the Kingdoms of Asteroidia initially and from the World of Space, eventually. It seemed likely that, in their quest to develop, inoculate and astutely maintain the infestation of a particular toxic mindset amongst the younger ethnic generations, the green humanoid robotron population's subliminal *'programmers'* and *'conditioners'* miscalculated that, without the ethnics to continue to provide the major basic building blocks and expertise in the art of survival, they needed to consider the inevitability of their own extinction, at least. The green humanoid robotrons considered being able to lie and deceive themselves about their mental cerebral aberrations caused them to block natural responses, expose their inadequacies to think outside their *'blinkered views'* on *"breeding"*, *"superior racial classification"* but made them exempt from being affected by their severe psychopathic, psychiatric psychoses altogether, somehow!

As far as Duke and Baron were concerned, their earlier experiences had influenced yet necessitated their decision to carry and use guns as an assumed representation of power. The fear of being eliminated by another, suffering similar degrees of fear, was a real issue amongst younger individuals. Fear had now become the new *'language of communication'*, especially amongst gangs like Clout and The Harbour-Shark Estate Gangs.

The local Private Cab Service supplied the car that Duke had ordered. As soon as they heard the horn being blown, Duke peered through the window. He exited first. Having scanned for any suspicious vehicles or characters, Duke then signalled for Baron to join him. They entered the cab but asked the driver to "step on the gas". The car screeched its way from the stationary position but hurtled along the street. Its acceleration had turned it into a dangerous projectile in the narrow street. The little girl who, had carelessly wandered from the pavement into the road on the bicycle, had no idea how close she came to being run over. The driver swerved to avoid the collision. He just managed to negotiate between avoiding contact with the little girl and running over a mother pushing her baby in the pushchair across the *'zebra/striped'* crossing. She was well in her rights to cross at that time as indicated by the flashing signal for pedestrians indicating that it was still safe to cross. The private cab driver managed to swerve around the woman and her baby on the crossing but broke through the red stop light regardless. It was only when they heard the siren that caused the driver to check his mirrors to establish whether it was his car that was being pursued by the mobile Security Forces. Duke and Baron turned to look through the rear window. They saw the flashing blue light snaking its way through the traffic behind them. Duke told the driver to pull over. As he slowed the vehicle down, both Baron and Duke exited the moving vehicle from the nearside like stuntmen in the movies. The driver stopped the vehicle further along but turned to look at the boys. By the time he heard the volume of the siren much closer and saw the flashing light in his rear view mirror, it was inevitable that the driver was being pulled over. The boys mingled with the crowd at the bus stop nearby but keenly watched the interaction between the mobile Security Forces and the cab driver. He exited from the car but seemed to be explaining what Baron and Duke already knew had happened. A bus arrived at the stop but obscured their view. The two or three minutes seemed more like half hour's wait. Duke looked at his watch again but indicated that they might be late for their appointment with Planit and Planit in Upper Ghettoborough. It was the sound of a car horn that alerted their attention. Baron looked towards from where the sound was coming. It was then that he saw Raleigh's flashing smile. Baron nudged Duke but pointed towards the car. The young adults quickly moved from the bus stop towards Raleigh's car. As they climbed in, he greeted them. "Seems we're all running a bit late", Raleigh surmised. "Baron and I were in a cab but it got stopped by the mobile Security Forces. Glad you happen to be passing by granddad", Duke explained. Raleigh was proud that his grandsons seemed so keen to get to the appointment on time. He expressed his appreciation. Raleigh told Baron and Duke that his next appointment after Planit and Planit was with the Undertaker to see their Nan, Sheila. He asked the boys if they wanted to accompany him but they said they too had previous arrangements which couldn't wait. It wasn't true but they didn't want to tell Raleigh that they couldn't bear to see the dead body at the Undertaker. It was strange how these so called cold-hearted gangsters could not bear to see the dead bodies of relatives in the morgue or at the Undertakers but could unfeelingly gun down each other in the streets. Some even filmed the scenes on their cell phones but boastfully shared these insane acts with others on their social websites in order to bolster and embellish their criminal reputations. There were many questions that remained unanswered. What of the mindsets which sought to inoculate the younger generations with fear but drive them towards satisfying their negative mindsets with behaviours that relegated others' lives as being unimportant and utterly meaningless? They appeared to be driven by spite and revenge yet remained immune towards empathy and compassion. What seemed to be highlighted was that those *'adult'* individuals, some of whom happened to be *'parents'*, that knowingly supported these *'children'* into crime, were themselves lacking emotional intelligence and maturity, specifically. The man they called 'The Professor' commented that "excellent observers might want to add that negative egos drove the obstinate and atrocious attitudes which manifested in the type of mindsets which drove those errant behaviours, being experienced by communities", he explained. During their individual Sessions, Duke and Baron had told him that from as early as junior school, they had experienced being bullied which might have been causative to them feeling extremely low in esteem. Being bullied might have initiated their slide into the entrance of the mental pit called fear. This negative emotion often led to them feeling less than valued. The man they call 'The Professor' said of their feelings of low esteem and those of feeling being *'less than'* valued seemed to have impacted their lives greatly in negative ways that had led to their errant behaviours. Others, who felt like Baron and Duke, were having similar experiences too. Raleigh signalled but pulled over into the nearside lane. He stopped outside the office of Planit and Planit. He asked Duke and Baron to go into the office while he found a parking space or meter. The young adults alighted from the car. They entered the office but went up to the reception to announce their arrival. Duke checked his watch before he spoke. There were still twelve minutes left before their appointment. The receptionist warmly welcomed the brothers. She smiled at them in admiration but also with curiosity as she challenged herself to tell the difference between the two. The receptionist accepted Raleigh as being present as well once Baron had informed her that he was parking the car. The young adults walked over towards the seats provided. There were two other individuals waiting to be attended. Raleigh arrived with about two minutes to spare before the time of the appointment. He flashed his dazzling smile at the receptionist before going over to his grandsons. Raleigh had hardly sat down before they were asked to join the lawyers representing Earl's Estate. After the formal introductions, Raleigh handed over the legal document to the lawyers that Duke had signed before Sheila died. He told them that Sheila had met and approved Duke's wishes to share the proceeds of the Will with his brother Baron in the proportion of 50% each. The lawyers told them that, while they acknowledged the request, they had no authority legally to alter Earl's original Will. They suggested that if Duke wanted to make his statement legal then he could have an Affidavit drawn up, signed and witnessed. They agreed and it was done. The official reading of the Will confirmed the details that Sheila and Raleigh had told Duke in Baron's presence. At the end of the reading of the Will, the handshakes meant that the formalities were over. Baron, Duke and Raleigh exited the offices of Planit and Planit. They walked for about five minutes before they reached Raleigh's car. Duke asked Raleigh to drop them off at The Cobblestone Arms AADC. He said that he too was going there in order to assure Simon of Earl's insistence that he remain as landlord. They drove without much comment for the rest of the journey. As they turned into Vanguard High Street, Baron spotted Chirpy 'the bird' ahead of them. Baron nudged Duke. He asked Raleigh to pull up. They told him they would meet up with him in a matter of moments. Raleigh drove off. Baron and Duke had one hand tucked inside the front of their baggy jeans. Their gait meant that they both walked with a slight stooping motion but with a swagger that denoted their status as being 'bad'. They were rapidly decreasing the distance between them and Chirpy 'the bird'. His hand was also tucked inside the front of his baggy grey track suit bottom but he was unaware of the twin brothers behind him. Suddenly, Baron and Duke started to run towards their target. As they approached him, they removed their hands from the front of their baggy jeans. With swift strokes they both attacked Chirpy 'the-bird'. It was too sudden for him to react. Baron pointed the gun to Chirpy's head but pulled him from the High Street into the nearest side street. They pistol-whipped him. The blood was pouring from the wounds on his head. Chirpy 'the bird' quickly told the brothers, who had sent him to 'assassinate' Baron. "Thought you would earn your stripe by taking me out Chirpy, did you", he asked? Baron hit him again on the shoulder with the butt of his gun while Duke removed Chirpy's gun from his track suit bottom. He was now lying on the road from the beating. His head was swimming round but he heard the message from Duke and Baron. "We are only sparing your life because you've now become our 'carrier pigeon'. Try taking me out again and you'll die", he warned. "Tell your man to meet us later if he wants to settle the score. Let us see how tough your leader is. We are ready to die, is he", they asked? They kicked Chirpy 'the bird' a few more times. He was no longer a threat to them so they left him bleeding in the gutter. Baron and Duke walked casually away from Chirpy 'the bird' as he drifted into unconsciousness. The women watching from the windows opposite saw the beating but dared not interfere for fear of repercussions. All they did was call an ambulance for the young man, who lay injured in the gutter. Duke and Baron arrived at The Cobblestone Arms AADC in time to see Raleigh just leaving. He told them he had to go to the Undertaker to see Sheila. Baron and Duke said their goodbyes to their granddad.

CHAPTER 10

S imon Crabley greeted Duke and Baron with a great deal of enthusiasm. "Raleigh told me you two are brothers. You do look alike. I told Kitty at the funeral that you look like twins. You are, aren't you", Simon asked? Baron nodded. Duke told Simon about wanting to celebrate their birthday at The Cobblestone Arms AADC. "It'll be a pleasure. Do you want a band as well", Simon asked? Duke told him they wanted to make arrangements for their act to perform. He also told Simon about the type of equipment that was required for the performers. "Don't you worry young Duke, I'll take care of it straight away", Simon responded. He was always an accommodating individual. He preferred to be of service rather than focus on himself. Another of Simon's qualities was that he was very appreciative of those that empathised with his situation. For Simon, his eternal hero was Earl Stagg. He considered Earl a "Godsend". Even in his Will, he ensured that Simon was well looked after by the executors of his Will. Though in all honesty, Simon was worried about what might happen between the young adults' gang Clout and the neighbouring Harbour-Shark Estate Gang, he was more than keen to ensure that Duke and Baron's birthday party was a huge success. It was going to be a 'Champagne

Party'. After all, champagne was that drink, which denoted it to be a perceived *'class above the rest'*. Most individuals in the World of Space were programmed and conditioned to believe that other drinks were below the level of champagne. Imposing its superiority by reputation or branding for appropriateness of being chosen as priority over 'the rest' of the alcoholic drinks, champagne, by its sheer presence, relegated all other drinks to the *'subordination league'*. A programmed urge had been created for its preference, presence and taste in all celebrations. The most incongruent image is that of an athlete or other sports personnel being given the *'customary'* bottle of champagne as a token gift by sponsors. It is questionable as to what the intention of the particular sponsor is, is it not? If Sports Science is to be adhered to, after physical exertions of such magnitude, athletes need to replenish their depleted energies, after their performances, with *'muscle friendly foods'* and Sports Drinks. At any celebrations where alcoholic drinks were to be consumed, champagne seemed to be selected to represent the quality of intention for both the hosts and their guests. At Baron and Dukes' 18th birthday celebrations, champagne has been chosen as the preferred alcoholic drink. Simon enquired how many people were invited but wrote swiftly on his notepad as he calculated how many bottles of champagne he should have available. Just before they exited The Cobblestone Arms AADC, Simon asked about whether he should hire security to exclude individuals they didn't want at their party. Baron and Duke agreed but told him that they too had catered for their personal security.

That evening Duke and Baron celebrated their birthday at the local AADC, known as The Cobblestone Arms. There were more people at the party than Duke and Baron had anticipated. Some of the females, who seem to outnumber the males, wore very skimpy outfits with low bust-lines that almost invited their voluptuous breasts to pop out like the cuckoo bird from the cuckoo clock or at least such was the expectations by the *'breasts specialists'*, who ogled at them. The male individuals were spoilt for choice, so much so that they adopted the polygamous mode in order to satisfy their egos. Each of them was surrounded by at least two or three females. They giggled with every opportunity but some cavorted themselves but managed to wiggle their bodies provocatively like a peahen in heat parading or prancing around in order to gain even more attention. Some of the girls shrill voices tried unsuccessfully to speak above the loud music that emanated from The Cobblestone Arms AADC. Simon Crabley had retained the services of the faithful Birdie Spring-Hip. She kept the extra helpers on their toes. There was not a group without a bottle of champagne on their particular table. The urge to guzzle the free champagne seemed quite a commonplace habit with the guests. Everyone was at it. The imbibing of the perceived premier alcoholic drink had quite profound effect upon individuals. Even Baron and Duke wore smiles that they didn't recognize as their own. These were installed by the merriment and jollification that effused from the recreational drugs and the guzzling of the finest wine at their 18th birthday celebration party. The Harbour-Shark Estate Gang saw the activities of the guests, who gathered at the back of The Cobblestone Arms AADC. Some of their members wanted to spoil the fun for those individuals. There were no other reasons for them to want to spoil the party other than that they were experiencing feelings of jealousy and spite. Others wanted to spoil Baron and Duke's party in order to drive fear into the guests just for the hell of it. Those members of the Harbour-Shark Gang were unable to contain their lack of emotional intelligence, maturity or both. They anticipated gaining some kind of *'enjoyment'* in spoiling things for their rival, Clout. The Harbour-Shark Estate Gang was unable to have any negative effect on Duke and Baron's party. Apart from arrangements made by Clout to monitor the guests, Simon Crabley had employed some of his off-duty police friends as security guards around the periphery. That included the area on the other side of the fence which separated The Cobblestone Arms AADC from the Harbour-Shark Estate. The arrangement ensured that dodgy individuals were kept at bay. At a distance, gunshots were being fired into the air by the Harbour-Shark Estate Gang in order to intimidate or even inveigle a response from Clout. When the on-duty police were summoned by their off-duty colleagues, they made their physical presence on the rundown Estate more than obvious but perused the periphery continuously, as well. The troublemakers soon dispersed. Their plan had been thwarted by the unexpected continuous police presence. Duke and Baron's Champagne Party carried on without incidence from outside but within the confines of The Cobblestone Arms AADC some individuals had got themselves into drunken fits of temper. These sporadic behaviours were soon quashed by security but when individuals tried to repeat the pattern they were simply given the option to leave voluntarily of be thrown out forcefully. There was to be no compromise. Baron and Duke's party had summoned enough urge for the taste of the finer wine but the smell of skunk weed attacked the nostrils of all those, who ventured within half a mile of The Cobblestone Arms AADC. The plumes of smoke erupting from the rear of The Cobblestone Arms AADC rose above it like the exhaust fumes from the top of an industrial kiln or the signal to signify that a new Pope had been approved at the Vatican. Both off-duty and on-duty police kept a low profile because they didn't see any drug being peddled. Instead, they surmised that individuals, like Duke, were using it for *'personal use'* only. Well, they could hardly have arrested Sir Earl Stagg's son at his 18th birthday bash for as *'minor'* an offence of smoking a spliff on what was assumed to be his premises. Baron did not smoke spliffs. He enjoyed smoking a pipe instead. It was a stranger shape than *'peace pipes'* but was not dissimilar for its purpose. The deliberately deep inhalation of the smoke from the burning substance via the mouth but being exhaled through the nose in streaks of smoke which resembles the trail, known as *'drag'*, created behind aeroplanes. All through the night until the early hours of the morning, the music bleared out but was a nuisance to some families on the nearby Estate. A complaint was lodged with the Local Government's Anti Social Behaviour Unit. It arrived outside The Cobblestone Arms, AADC. There, the ASB Unit were met by Simon Crabley. He explained whose party it was but assured them that the Local Government had been informed about the party. Simon didn't feel he could jeopardize his tenancy by telling the incumbent owner what to do. He told the white Mixed DNA Rainbow Tribe lead worker that if he wanted to speak to Duke then he alone will bear the consequences. The lead worker insisted that he had come to investigate the noise nuisance. He said the sound from The Cobblestone Arms AADC was many decibels above the permitted level and that he would have to seize the equipment. Simon knew that Duke would not take too kindly to the lead worker's insistence but he had no choice than to direct him to Duke. When the lead worker announced who he was, Duke pulled hard on the spliff but blew the smoke into his face. As the worker recoiled, the intensity of the smell of the skunk overpowered him. The other Clout members began to push the lead worker from one to the other just like when they surround a target on the street. They didn't hit him but just the glare from each of the Clout gang members involved was enough to warn the insistent worker that he was way in over his head. When they thought that they had drummed their message home, some members of Clout lifted the lead worker but threw him out into the street, literally. His pride was as bruised as his body that had hit the hard surface with quite a thud. The worker's colleagues, who had returned to but stayed in the van realised how fortunate they were to stay put in the vehicle. When the lead worker managed to drag himself up from the road, he dialled the local police to assist him to execute his duty. They asked the lead worker for the location but assured him that they had police within the area monitoring any violent activities. The celebrations carried on way into late morning. Duke, Baron and their friends got absolutely drunk during the celebration.

The young adult, Duke, had drunk so much champagne, he paid for his overindulgence; especially the next day. His head seemed as if it was weighted down by blocks of concrete. Irregular rhythms played on his temples, nape and forehead. Duke's mouth had a most sickly taste; mainly from the intermittent vomiting that had taken place. His vision was impaired severely by the many images that appeared whenever he opened his eyes. The glare from light affected him too; so much so that he developed a sort of squint in preference to opening his eyes in the normal way. After several attempts to get off what appeared to be a spinning bed, Duke relented to staying with that motion. He dared not attempt standing up. It was only their groaning that brought to Duke's attention that there were others with him in the same bed. "Who the bloody hell are you", Duke asked? His deep-throated voice had more of an edge to it than normal. The three women giggled but didn't answer. They just lay there, unashamedly. One of them curled up close to Duke as if she was a pet waiting for her master to stroke her head. The other two wore smiles that appeared to be permanently painted on their faces. Duke looked from one to the other through his squint but tried to assess how the women got into his bed. He did not recognise any of them. It was too much effort to quiz them any further. Any form of rational thinking did not help the throbbing in Duke's head. The woman closest to him threw one of her legs across Duke's then shuffled until she lay on top of him. "Want some more honey", the woman on top of Duke teased. The two others giggled but seemed as if they too wanted to join in. Duke started to feel excited by the woman's movement but his head kept reminding him of a different set of priorities. "Not now. Get me some coffee. Got to get rid of this bloody headache", Duke said? "Anything you say Romeo", the woman on top of Duke replied. She rolled off him then worked her way into a standing position on the floor. She swayed a bit before disappearing in one direction. A few moments afterwards she returned to the bedroom. Duke looked at her through squinted eyes. "Where's the bloody coffee", he demanded. "Keep your shirt on. I had to go to the loo. Anyway, this is such a bloody big house. One could get lost just looking for the kitchen", the woman standing parried. She then sauntered off in another direction. The other two women in the bed sidled up to Duke. One placed his head into her lap but massaged his temples. The other rested her head close to his chest while she stroked the hairs on it. The throbbing in Duke's temples began to subside and he started to feel slightly more relaxed than he did earlier. He was beginning to like this treatment. The two women continued to weave their magic on Duke. He offered no defiance to the pampering. As soon as he was getting used to the attention being meted out by the two women in his bed, the first woman walked in with some mugs of coffee. The steam was a welcoming sight let alone the aroma that infiltrated their nostrils. The first woman sat on the carpeted floor but the two others sat on the edge of the bed either side of Duke. Each sipped from their respective mugs, simultaneously. Soon the coffee had some effect on the previously ailing Duke. He burped loudly. It seemed all the bubbles he had swallowed the might before had exploded into the belch but sounded like a thunderclap just before a storm. All the women giggled but said the word "pardon" at the same time. A few more sips and the aches started to drift from Duke's head. "How do you feel now you've got that off your chest", the woman sitting on the floor asked? "Bloody marvellous", Duke replied. He felt a little more alive than he had earlier. Duke stood up. His penis was quite erect. One of the women sitting on the edge of the bed noticed but commented. "Where are you going", the woman asked? "Where do you think", Duke retorted? His voice sounded a bit brighter now and he was beginning to feel a bit more himself than before. On his return, Duke sipped from the mug again repeatedly before placing the empty mug on the floor. The three women giggled together but started to converse amongst themselves. By way of introduction, the woman sitting on the floor spoke first. "My name is Gordy, what's yours", she asked? The other two women sitting on the edge of the bed introduced themselves as Mari and Joseté. They engaged in small talk. "Do you think he is as rich as he said he is", Joseté asked? Mari said she thought he was well off but not as hugely rich as Duke made out to be. Gordy didn't seem to care to put a value on Duke's riches. As far as she was concerned, rich meant rich and that was all she needed to understand. The women were all sitting together on the carpeted floor now. They were facing the direction from which Duke had disappeared but he approached the bedroom from another entrance. Duke stood there but listened to the women's conversation. Not only did he learn their names for the first time but also how much they knew about his apparent changes in fortune. Duke cleared his throat then commented. "You seem to know more about me than I you", Duke stated. The women, as one, turned to where they heard his coarse voice. Unanimous giggles were the only response from them. They looked from one to another but with none of them volunteering to tell Duke how they manage to have slept in his bed altogether. Joseté was the first to make a move towards Duke. She walked deliberately but paused a few feet in front of him. His gaze focused on her huge breasts. She was about a 44D cup. Duke hardly noticed Gordy as she too sidled up to him as well. Mari had the sweetest voice but it unsettled his focus on Josete's breasts. The women's naked bodies brushing up against Duke's by way of shaking hips, belly dancing and deliberate handling excited him further. He didn't try to resist their advances but seemed ready for the frolicking to which the women were alluding. It was obvious what the women intended. Soon all three women were busy caressing the now aroused Duke. They led him back towards the giant bed. Soon Duke was being tormented by the various explicit sexual exploitation of his body. The women seemed to be enjoying Duke's encouragement. When Gordy grabbed hold of him much more firmly she pushed Duke away from her. He ended up on his back. Joseté quickly climbed on top of him. She sat astride Duke but her waist gyrated gently at first, but increased the revolutions per minute. This action resulted in movements which started a pattern of more furious rhythmic motions. Its centripetal force kept the momentum at a constant furious rate much like a Hula dancer.

From Duke's perspective, Joseté reminded him of a cameo from a Rodeo show. Her bucking and writhing was reminiscent of those associated actions. Clamped between her loins, Duke began to notice the effects of Joseté's frantic movements as she galloped home towards her desired outcome. Not only could he feel her sudden jerking motions but also those of his own body too as he yielded to the climax of the release he too was experiencing. Duke was aware of his own coarse voice moaning and groaning; joining in harmony with Joseté's persistent cooing. There was a sudden crescendo to the sound dynamics but Duke was too far gone into the land of ecstasy to notice whether the other two women's voices had join in the chorus. What he did notice though was the sudden hush that followed. The quiet in the room was so conspicuous that each was now aware of their own breathing. Joseté lay slumped on top of Duke with her head nestling upon his hairy chest. Her long hair flopped partially across his face. They all lay motionless for some 30 minutes before Gordy stated that she was feeling hungry. Duke told her there were some sandwiches and a bottle of champagne in the fridge. She set off to get them. Joseté seemed quite comfortable atop Duke but Mari kept whispering into his left ear. He listened to the sweet nothings that she uttered but her voice seemed to have a mesmerising effect on him. Looking up at the ceiling, Duke begun to weigh up how enjoyable his birthday had turned out. Here he was being attended to by three beautiful women, who were giving him their full 100% undivided attention and he was enjoying their company. It was Mari's voice that brought Duke back from his dream-world. "Do you live here on your own", Mari enquired? Her voice was gentle and soft but demanded a response. "Yeah", Duke replied. "Don't you get lonely", Mari asked? Duke avoided answering the question by stating that he had to go to the toilet. He exited the room. It was about ten minutes before he returned. The girls had no idea that it was Duke's brother, Baron. They queried where he had been but all the girls got was a quizzical look. They noticed that his penis was quite erect as he entered the room. Gordy pulled a bit closer to him now but indicated that she was on heat. Grabbing his penis firmly, Gordy welcomed its erection. She backed onto him but directed it inside her. Her movement had provoked the very strong thrusts with which he responded. Gordy actively encouraged him in his movement. Joseté stroked his back while Mari nibbled his ear. Gordy reached backwards with her hands but played with Baron's hair. This seemed to drive him crazy. With every thrust, he was grunting like a hog but hurried towards his finish line. The girls did not know about Baron. He had swapped places with his brother. They kept swapping places practically all day until the women were exhausted. The girls commented on Duke's assumed sexual longevity. He rang the local Pizza shop but ordered pizza for the women and an extra large one for 'himself', assumedly. When the doorbell rang, Duke had to pull on his boxer and jeans quickly. He glanced through the window before opening the door but grabbing the pizzas. Duke tipped the delivery man but returned to the room where the girls were laying around on the carpet. He placed the pizzas for them in the middle of the floor before exiting the room with his extra large one. "Aren't you eating with us", Joseté asked? "Just putting some away for later", Duke lied. When he returned, the girls witnessed Duke tucking into the pizza. He joined them on the carpet. They chatted for a while then Duke told them they would have to leave. Mari wanted to see Duke again but the others protested and accused her of being selfish.

CHAPTER 11

I t took Baron and Duke almost another two years before each had come to realize how fortunate they were to be still alive. Both had recklessly entered into a lifestyle that had demanded they stay enslaved to the street-life to which they had become attracted. It overwhelmed many young people like Duke and Baron without them even knowing how they had managed to get involved. Although Earl's request, via his Will, was for Duke to go to see the man they called 'The Professor', Baron too had become as curious as his brother. The second phase of Duke's inheritance was soon to manifest. He had to show recorded proof of his attendance to the man they called 'The Professor' to the lawyers, Planit and Planit. They were legally bound to follow Earl's Will precisely as stated. After their first three visits with the man they called 'The Professor', both Duke and Baron began questioning whether they had to continue to act like the robotic humans they were becoming. The young adults were beginning to learn more about themselves. Encouraged by the man they called 'The Professor' to view from different perspectives, Baron and Duke started to examine their individual behaviours. Each agreed with the man they called 'The Professor' that their behaviours were *'infantile'* and that their lack of quality in communication was a huge barrier towards meaningful relationships, indeed. The man they called 'The Professor' asked them to define what they understood by the terms *'emotional intelligence'* and *'emotional maturity'*. He could see them wince as the challenge exposed Baron and Duke's acceptance of their weaknesses in both these disciplines. The negative emotions which Baron and Duke chose to feel and display, the man they called 'The Professor' referred to as the *'Vex Factor'*. He explained that it was often causative to them being entrenched in conflicts not only with peer groups but also with the law.

With the advent of technology, the law being more informed was catching up with criminals and pseudo-criminals alike. Dawn raids by the CSF, Civilian Security Forces, were not only better planned but warrants were now more available to them so that entry into premises was now not hindered because of lack of authority but instead were appropriately justified, seemingly. Many members of Clout like Henry 'the hook', Pete, 'the hammer', Trojan 'the horse' and 'crazy' Bobby had been tried, found guilty of the vicious crimes they had committed and sentenced to long stretches in prison. All those potential talents would now never be realized nor would those abilities ever be engaged into something more meaningful or possibly fulfilling. There were deterrents other than the long sentences, which had been meted out to peer gang members like 'crazy' Bobby and the others. These seemed to have huge impact upon on Duke but Baron, in particular.

Spaceville was being told that it had to do something about its rocketing crime rate or lose possible membership and be excluded from the UO DIS-UK, Union of Dis-United Kingdoms to which it belonged. One of the deterrents announced by the UFO, United Fraternal Organization, through their associate politicrat members, was that it had introduced *'Floating Prisons'*. These were huge ex-Cruise ships that were no longer used for that purpose. Their original capacity was meant to house approximately 4000 individuals. After being re-modelled, each of these ships had the capacity to accommodate up to 8000 prisoners, potentially but not including crew or supervisory prison staff. The UFO stated further that floating prisons had now been installed to compensate for the overflowing number of individuals whom voluntarily chose to apply, via their *'Criminal CVs'*, to be part of prison population. With the floating prisons, there were massive restrictions implemented. Unlike the land based prisons which seemed to be fast becoming established as HPRS, *'Human Potential Refuse Sites'*, the floating prisons had a more sinister reputation. Those prisoners were not allowed any phone-calls or visits. Because there were no way of contacting individual prisoners, who were taken to these floating prisons, proving their continued existence on board was becoming a more mysterious challenge. Rumours were spreading all over Spaceville that those prisoners on the floating prisons were being used for *'experiments'* within the scientific field. One investigating journalist, Marje Proopfield, challenged the Prime Leader of Spaceville to justify the political *'denial'* to the allegations that (1) the floating prisons were privately owned (2) that the prisoners on board these ships had become prisoners through entrapment engineered by corrupted Enforcement Officers engaged by influential poly-tricksters and (3) as *'properties of the governments'* of the KOA, Kingdoms of Asteroidia, those prisoners had voluntarily agreed to be *'organ donors'*. The allegations went on to say that organs were being removed from those prisoners without their consent but sold via the recently established *'Private Organ Donors Association'* or PODA as it was called, again privately owned but wholly funded by *'Human Organ'* magnate poly-tricksters. The article went on to protest that, even as a prisoner of war, there were Conventions to which countries had to adhere. Marje Proopfield asked the question, "how is it justifiable for any government to sanction such underhand practices, be they on terra firma or on the high seas"? It was the latter part of that question that seemed to justify the UO DIS-UK position on the allegations. The official response from them was quite profound indeed. The Most Honorable Prime Leader Donnakeye Tailles stated that she wanted to make it clear that the ruling and directives about the floating prisons had come from her boss the UFO, United Fraternal Organization. As Prime Leader, she and her government were obliged to obey and carry out directives ordered by the UFO. The UO DIS-UK was the oversight body that reported back to the UFO. Its ruling meant that, neither Donnakeye Tailles, nor her government, had a choice in the matter. "The UFO and subsequently the UO DIS-UK are the upper echelons of authority on the virtual planet of Asteroidia. They rule supreme over each Kingdom's governments and that includes Spaceville's", the Most Honorable Prime Leader, Donnakeye Tailles explained. A source that represented the UO DIS-UK confirmed the Prime Leader's statement. The UO DIS-UK was quoted as saying that "within the context of the Dis-UKAC, Dis-United Kingdoms of Asteroidia's Constitution, **'Article 666'** states that, (1) when caught and convicted via *due process*, any individual, who chose to live a life of crime had made a conscious decision to become a prisoner (2) when they became prisoners those individuals chose to abandon their human rights (3) prisoners are the property of the governments of Asteroidia. They are not allowed to dictate where they were being accommodated and for that reason volunteered to recant their legal rights to challenge the governments on any issue with regards to comfort or otherwise whilst serving their sentences". Even Janette Brayhorne realized that the ruling and directives had not come from her government but from a more powerful source than she or any other individuals or groups dared not challenge on their own. The UFO, United Fraternal Organisation, was the powerful private body of poly-tricksters lobbyists that not only configured the amalgamation of but had the power to rule over the RRDIS-USKA, Royal Royal Dis-United Stately Kingdoms of Asteroidia, of which Spaceville was one. It dictated what laws applied to the allied group of Kingdoms in the region. A lot of families were complaining about the lack of contact with prisoners but the Media supported the UFO in their action, generally and specifically too. One green humanoid robotron poly-trickster Editor, Daryll Fastfamoussè, of the most popular daily printed media, The Orion Argument, was quoted as saying that ". . . businesses in Spaceville are moving to the neighbouring Kingdoms in the Union because of its extremely high crime rate". His quotation expanded onto the crime figures. Daryll Fastfamoussè presented statistics that proved "ethnics were the greater population of land based prisons" but championed the cause for "the government of Spaceville to place ethnics onto floating prisons". He was adamant that if the government of Spaceville took his advice, it could save itself from exclusion from the powerful UFO. Daryll Fastfamoussè was wearing his poly-trickster hat at the time, of course. Rumour had it that he was seeking to become personal advisor to a very famous politicrat in opposition to the current government. To measure the impact Daryll Fastfamoussé had on the public, he was invited to appear on the weekly Political Talk Programme, The Time for Questions on STC, Spaceville Television Corporation. It featured individuals from politicrats, authors, poly-tricksters, sports personnel, actors, printed media as well as television journalists, individuals from the world of entertainment, and a variety of other so-called VIPs to discuss the major points of current affair news that was considered worthy at the time. Prior to his appearance, Daryll Fastfamoussè had conducted a poll that seemed to confirm his and the UFO's stance on floating prisons. Places like Champagne Valley, the Village of Urgington, Snobsborough, Snideborough, Sneerborough, Upborough, Brazenborough and even some parts of Upper Ghettoborough overwhelmingly sanctioned the clarion call by Daryll Fastfamoussé. He had stricken so much fear into the people's hearts and minds that Darryll Fastfamoussé was now looked upon as a type of 'champion' instead of the green humanoid robotron partisan poly-trickster that he was. The whipping up of hysteria was not new nor was it Daryll Fastfamoussè's alone but his timing was precise enough to make him appear not as the inveterate bigot that he was but genuine, seemingly! Some like-minded individuals, who sensed the opportunity to reinforce their perennial narrow-minded stone-aged views about 'ethnics' not only displayed their savage mindsets but also pounced upon yet ripped their prey to shreds with venomous verbal talons which drove fear into the minds of the population of Spaceville. Despite the vitriolic bile that was being spouted by Daryll Fastfamoussè and his avid supporters, the UFO's 'Cult Induced' Post/Zip Code Wars and their violent stereotypes were real issues for Spaceville. The intimidating behaviours, displayed by the few impacted upon the majority but began to seriously cramp the freedom of those individuals, who sought to journey into other boroughs for work, education or social events. These were not the only crimes that were being committed within the affected boroughs in Spaceville but the Post/Zip Code Cult-Induced Wars were being highlighted because of the unparallel level of violence that they brought with them. The representatives from the ESU, Ethnic Stereotypes Unit, part of the CSF, Civilian Security Forces responsible for EoE, Ethnic on Ethnic, crime only, informed the Political Talk Programme, The Time for Questions, of its importance and why it had been initiated and assigned by the previous government of Spaceville. The justification for its birth said enough about the type of approach the previous government had taken. Instead of investigating what had brought on this Post/Zip Code War *'trend'*, the ESU adopted a policy to *'isolate'* these criminal incidences, perpetrated by *'ethnics against ethnics'*, as if they were far worse than those perpetrated by green humanoid robotrons against their own and others besides. The ESU justified their psychiatric criminal *'prognoses'* and *'diagnoses'* about particular *'ethnic orientations'* by simply highlighting how deeply their Neuro-bigotry characteristic *'traits'* were buried within each individual involved in the Unit. According to their *'cultural'* *'values and beliefs'*, individuals within the ESU had a particular bond which was specially formulated by their collective allegiance to what they perceived to be *"politically 'correct' and 'acceptable' 'gang oriented'* mentality and behaviours towards *'ethnic minorities'*, *'wittingly'* or *'unwittingly'* ", perhaps! The *'tactics'* chosen by them to defeat the UFO's Cult-Induced Post/Zip Code Wars were pathetic minimally but bore no real consideration for the unnecessary loss of ethnic lives. When it was a green humanoid robotron child that was being maimed or slain by *'shanking'* or *'guns'*, there was quite a different approach and outcry compared to when an *'ethnic'* child had had a similar fate. Like some of the green humanoids, who had chosen not to associate with the *'robotron mentality'*, the ethnic population did not asked to be *'isolated'* or *'specially treated'* but only that no form of bigotry was to be applied when their children had been maimed or slain. Either way, it was a huge loss to families in spite of their origin, humanoid or ethnic but the CSF "lessons learned" mantra were always the same. Their tactics remained like some "outmoded trend", reactive rather than being proactive, always. Its efficacy was questionable. There never seemed to be any preventative measures being debated or researched to which the Unit was seen to commit. Instead, the ESU appeared to spend most of its time always sending out *"sympathy"* to the aggrieved families. As genuine as their sentiments might have been, it was proof that there was no active preventative measures or fresh ideas welcomed or in place to combat what was now moving from being epidemic to pandemic waves of madness being visited upon the maimed, slain or murdered *'victims'* of crime across the entire virtual planet of Asteroidia. In Spaceville, the ESU's existence was being justified, supported and reinforced by the likes of Daryll Fastfamoussè in his *'after dinner speech'* at the Civilian Security Forces Annual Dinner and Dance held at The Penitentiary Hotel in Yupborough.

What Daryll Fastfamoussè and his colleagues failed to discuss at the dinner was the existence of a Hierarchical Organisation Chart which showed the hierarchy in rank order and their remit. A whistleblower, PC Percy de Parrot, at the risk of being sanctioned severely by his peers and bosses, exposed the extremely powerful influence of the UFO. He explained that they were at the apex followed by the UO DIS-UK then the GMT, Ghetto Mentality Terrorists and the GMES, Ghetto Mentality Engineering Scientists. Those were the *'Top Ranks'* in order of seniority and significance. Next, the *'Middle Rank'* consisted of the GMP, Ghetto Mentality Practitioners, the GOS, Gang Orientation Scientists, the GOO, Gang Orientation Operators and the GOP, the Gang Orientation Practitioners. The *'Lower Rank'* was the GCCEO, Ghetto Celebrity CEOs and the GCE, the Ghetto Celebrity Entrepreneurs. The *'Lowest Rank'* was the GSE, Ghetto Sodomy Entrepreneurs which consisted of SR, Serial Rapists and SP, Serial Paedophiles. These had been installed by the once covert *'phantom organisers'* to catalyse *'the process of elimination'* using *'Ethno-Genocidia'*. This they did via the UFO's Post/Zip Code Cult-Induced Wars. PC Percy de Parrot said that those vulnerable youngsters, often being referred to as being *'disaffected'*, were being encouraged, through the practice of *'Ethno-Genocidia'*, to eliminate the ethnic populations from the virtual planet of Asteroidia and ultimately the World of Space. The *"blue whistleblower"* as he was referred to by his employers stated that he had found files marked **'Highly Classified Information'** and **'Top Secret'** which described there was a deliberate movement in place towards the *'self-elimination'* of particular ethnic groups. PC Percy de Parrot from the Mixed DNA Rainbow Tribe explained the content of the files. Schools were to drive those students classed as *'being disruptive'* onto the streets through summary suspensions and eventual expulsions instead of finding out and reasonably addressing those children's *'needs'*, like **'preference for learning'**. The *"blue whistleblower"* said he was unsure whether the schools had been seeking to find out what was causative to the students' disruption without the heavy political prejudices which drove their decisions to throw them onto the streets. PC Percy de Parrot stated that in spite of the schools and their bosses, the Education Departments were not only jointly guilty of shirking their responsibilities but also instigated the disruptions inside the classrooms by failing to understand that education was more than what the institutions offered academically. Despite the cold-shouldering which he was experiencing from his colleagues and the threats from more senior sources, PC Percy de Parrot was willing to be the *'sacrificial lamb'*. He said he had received death threats even within the confines of the canteen at work. The *"blue whistle blower"* continued to disclose the information he had found. PC Percy de Parrot stated the rest of the *'Highly Classified Information'*. He explained the remit of each rank of the UFO. The GMP, were the *'Recruiting Agency'*, summarily. So that there was a seamless transition into the world of crime, the *'Recruiting Agency'*, the GMP ensured the order of subordinates, under their charge, were maintained. The Gang Orientation Scientists recruited and organised the GOP. These were the young adult gangsters. They, in turn, recruited and organised the youths. The youths recruited and organised the juniors. Bullying, whether in the form of threats, roughing up or beatings, was the main base of the intimidating indoctrination ritual. It was a sure way of getting individuals to conform. Once the initiating process had been installed, the next step was to *'convince'* individuals of becoming *'Ghetto Drug and Arms Entrepreneurs'*. This was the role of the GOP, GCE and the GSE. These were being trained by GMES. Ghetto Celebrity CEOs were a gradation at a much higher level than the Ghetto Celebrity Entrepreneurs. They were being treated as *'a cut above the rest'*. GMS, Ghetto Mentality Scientists trained the more established of them. Those individuals, who had been recently converted from being merely GCE and GSE bought in as franchisees at a higher level.

On the virtual planet of Asteroidia, *'The Kudos Effect'* meant that these individuals had reached an uncanny similar position as the historic *'house slaves'* as directly compared to the *'field slaves'* on the parallel planet, Earth. On one hand, the *'field slaves'* were deliberately worked harder and for longer hours with few or no *'privileges'*. They were more radical in there approach and argued for improvement in their circumstances but were constantly reproached severely by their masters for questioning their situations and environments. On the other hand, the *'house slaves'* were pathetically ultra submissive and would *"do anything"* to impress their masters. The *'field slaves'* detested the *'house slaves'* slimy, subservient mentality. "Yes Massa, I'll do anything for the privilege of *'licking your boots clean'"* was the *'house slaves'* repetitious *'self-talk'*. Their snitching viper-like tongues could make a *'shoe-shine boy'* redundant! These individuals had been following the same entrancing repetitious *'hook lines'* and mesmeric melodies as that of the legendary *'Pied Piper'*, until Coda. Year after year, they wore their badges and medals of *'dishonour'* with pride, accepting their *'Judas Awards'*, with much glee, mirth and aplomb for the privilege of appearing in the perennial **'Mind Movie'**, *'A Part of my Brain has Gone Missing'*, **Part '666'** recurring, probably!

In Ghettoville, Lower Ghettoborough, Spaceville, unlike all other entrepreneurial businesses which required capital, *'Ghetto Entrepreneurship'* required no capital layout but plenty *'sheep'* instead. Individuals, who were temporarily suspended or permanently excluded from schools, fitted these *'roles'* and were the major targets, initially. The new recruits, in their respective gangs, worked for the *'Gang Orientation Unit'*. Together, they *'modelled'* but were the *'models'* that fulfilled the *'roles'* of their favourite gangsters and were actively taking the *'rap'* for their *'new lifestyle'*. Most found it like auditioning for a part in a movie and that's how they were encouraged by the Gang Orientation Scientists, Operators and Practitioners. They trained them how to exploit their respective communities. The gradation spiral continued until they lost total respect for themselves and their families. Most had to prove themselves by stealing from their families and communities. Once the individuals past those *'tests'*, they were trained to become *'street assassins'*. They acted out their *'roles'* as *'City Cowboys'* and *'Bounty Hunters'* in the *'reality' 'street movies'*, *'modelling'* heinous criminal behaviours in order to receive their *'medals of dishonour'*, albeit sometimes posthumously. Grieving parents became *'victims'* as a result of the *'fashionable trend'* know as *'Ethno-Genocidia'* being practiced by generations of young people. They were maiming and slaughtering each other on the streets. When they were obviously emotionally traumatized by the loss of their loved ones, the ESU used the victims' families to demonstrate their *'importance'* to communities. After the crimes had been committed, the ESU used the media to appeal to the grieving families and friends of the bereaved as their **'only means or source of detection'** available to them. On other occasions, the ESU would have well publicized *'Dawn Raids'* which more often than not turned out to be visited upon the wrong addresses. These *'Dawn Raids'* were always *'headlines'* and *'breaking news'* but the apologies, if any, were so miniscule, it was harder to find than the metaphoric *'needle in a haystack'*. At times, when the UFO's Cult-Induced Post/Zip Code Wars gangs and their members were caught, the grieving families and their communities were grateful and relieved that the guilty offenders would be imprisoned.

Because of the advent of the UFO's Cult-Induced Post/Zip Code Wars *'gang culture'*, there were occasions, when the ESU shot down some innocent victims, who they claimed had been carrying *'dangerous weapons'*. On some occasions they had been mistaken. The population did not argue over the times the ESU had been justified to genuinely discharge their weapons, when they were certain there was a threat to them or other members of the public but what the population did not understand was the 'cover up' 'gang culture' which seemed to run throughout the ESU like a computer devised 'worm' which was deliberately planned, agreed, fostered and initiated but used to corrupt entire internet systems. Bereaved families grieved the loss of the many 'innocent victims' whom were being consistently 'taken out' by the ESU with much inveterate prejudice 'wittingly' or 'unwittingly'. They did this because of the psychopathic Neuro-profiling mindset that existed amongst them. What was more galling to the bereaved families and the communities in which they lived was that this was happening much too regularly. They needed salient explanations from the 'Political Committees', who were charged to extract information about the repetition of 'barefaced lies' that were being spouted from the 'higher ranks' of the ESU as if they were 'facts'; in order to justify their insensitive behaviours.

The CSF support for both Daryll Fastfamoussè's proposal and the UFO's commandments about floating prisons, which was to be used to mainly house prisoners from 'ethnic' backgrounds, was no great surprise. The Chair of the Political Talk Program, The Time for Questions, which was filmed in Snobsborough, lost control as the audience voiced their raucous approval of the proposed remedies to the senseless madness named the UFO's Cult-Induced Post/Zip Code Wars. To those, like Duke and Baron, watching on television, it was hard to disagree with those sentiments to rid the Kingdoms but especially Spaceville of the negative psychological and sometimes psychopathic behaviours of intense bullying, increasing maiming and killings. They had lived that style of living and their gang Clout was as guilty of partaking in those highly charged seemingly schizophrenic behaviours, which drove the stabbings and shootings in the UFO's Cult-Induced Post/Zip Code Wars. Those individuals were singularly and collectively responsible for the existence of the ESU. They could choose to behave more reasonably and seek help to rid them of the devilment that not only occupied their minds but drove their crazed behaviours. From another perspective, it can be argued that Janette Brayhorne's surveys had provided compelling evidence that (1) a provision of structured activities and (2) increasing quality mentors and coaches in secondary but particularly junior schools were the type of resources required to help those young people whose self esteem were low.

Individuals like 'crazy' Bobby, was himself a type of 'victim', who had fallen prey to the GOO. He wasn't really crazy but the shy individual acted out being crazy to gain the reputation that saw him re-offend all the way through his childhood to him becoming an adult. Many of his victims, who happen to be still alive, can testify to the crazy behaviours that got 'crazy' Bobby locked away on so many occasions. Because of his low esteem issues, Bobby Joe Insole, 'crazy' Bobby, was always angry. No one knew that he was the only surviving member of three brothers. He was one member of a triplet. Bobby Joe Insole lost his two brothers and both his parents in a house fire. He has been carrying that guilt around for all his life because he was the young 7 year old, who was playing with the lighter that his father had left carelessly where he could reach it. Bobby Joe Insole kept flicking the lighter. At first, it was a small flame like when his father was lighting a cigarette. He fiddled with the cheap throw away lighter then flicked it again. This time the flame had increased in height. Even though he was frightened, Bobby was fascinated that the flame could be increased by the little button to the side and it was only halfway. He could see his brothers fast asleep in the beds beside his. Bobby lifted the bedclothes but flicked the lighter again. This time the flame seemed to shoot much further into the air. By the time he realized it, the bedclothes were already alight. He dropped the lighter but jumped out of the bed. Bobby was shocked at the rapidity of how quickly the fire had spread. The shock had rendered him numb, temporarily. He ran to get water to put the fire out. By the time Bobby had ran downstairs to the kitchen to fetch a glass of water to put the fire out, the entire top floor was ablaze. He panicked further when he opened the windows downstairs to let the smoke out. This extremely frantic 7years old child heard the roar of the angry flames, felt the extreme heat emanating from the roaring furnace upstairs but was engulfed by the thick smoke. Bobby Joe Insole heard the screams of his parents and his two brothers. There was nothing he could do apart from getting through the front door to ask the neighbours to help. By then, it was too late. The sounds of the fire engines still play a part in the flashbacks that live inside his head. Growing up with his aunt and his cruel uncle didn't help. He blamed Bobby for his brother's death and was responsible for the name 'crazy' Bobby. His uncle told everyone that Bobby was crazy and that he had killed his family. Even when the school suggested intervention to help to free Bobby from his recurring nightmares, his uncle refused. He treated Bobby with disdain but continued to spread the vitriolic rumour around. His uncle reminded Bobby Joe Insole constantly that his action had robbed him of his brother.

Both Duke and Baron learnt about the floating prisons while watching the Political Talk Programme, The Time for Questions. Earlier, they had both watched a Documentary Newsreel that had engaged them thoroughly too. It was in response to the Tourism Ministry's threat to distance the ailing Spaceville from the rest of the UO DIS-UK, Union of Dis-United Kingdoms. On the Documentary Newsreel on television, it was reported that the Most Honorable Prime Leader of Spaceville, Donnakeye Tailles and her Senate Cabinet had held urgent meetings since the news had broken about the possible migration of businesses away from Spaceville to its peer Kingdoms within the Union. She announced new tough measures to show her intention of not only ridding Spaceville of its current criminal image but also vouched to return the Kingdom to its previously pristine reputation. This proposed legislation was meant to be fast-tracked through the Commons Senate. It stated that all dangerous prisoners; meaning all individuals, and including those involved in gangster-ism that had committed gross crimes like terrorizing their communities with guns and knives, murder, kidnapping, rape, paedophilia, arson, grievous bodily harm, actual bodily harm, any form of threatening behaviours like bully-ism made themselves liable to be (a) transported to the 'floating prisons' or (b) be sanctioned to report for duty for the frontline in the wars around the World of Space. In either case, those prisoners were to be afforded no pay but only the most meagre amenities. The ethos of the new legislation, *'one strike and out'* was intended to thwart re-offending. If individuals re-offended, it meant that they had chosen to volunteer to be transported to the 'floating prisons' or to be conscripted but would remain permanently *'in service'* to the Ministry of Defence. They were to be made available for duty whenever and wherever they were requested to go to fight for and on behalf of the UO Dis-UKA, Union of Dis-United Kingdoms of Asteroidia. Those individuals would continue to be *'in service'* until they exhausted their term of sentence. This piece of legislation had unanimous cross party approval. There was a caveat that was attached to the new legislation and that meant that the new legal custodians, the CSS,

Civilian Security Services, would have to apply new standards instead of the current ones which allowed rogue individuals within the service to get away with corruption and prejudices. Those had remained latent but frequently unaccountable factors within the ways of how the old service used to be administered under the previous government. These new standards meant that each community was able to assess the quality of service they received from the Civilian Security Services. Local Government was empowered to collate the information from its diverse residents but feed the result back to the communities on a quarterly basis. The community stakeholders now had a meaningful influence over some of the unfair shenanigans that had happened in the past under the Security Body then known as the CSF. Minister for Communities, Janette Brayhorne, insisted that these new standards were important to the communities, which were being served by the Civilian Security Services. After all, it was their local taxes that funded the individual Service. It was agreed that a *'pilot period'* of one calendar year was sufficient to measure the effectiveness of the new project. Success was no longer to mean that massaged statistics would appear in the media to boost over-inflated political egos. Instead, each member of the Civilian Security Services would be empowered to enhance their performances according to more reasonable written outcomes. The man they called 'The Professor' was drafted in to demonstrate how *'Paired Training'* can affect a much higher level of performance for each individual employee as well as a group. Significantly, each member of the Civilian Security Services was now being reminded that they were employed by their communities to secure them from crime. Crimes perpetrated by members of the Civilian Security Services were to be included too. For example, entrapment, framing, bullying or any other deliberate connivance in order to secure convictions was now outlawed by this new legislation. As Janette Brayhorne pointed out, "no individual in Spaceville was immune to these new Laws . . . . we are all citizens of Spaceville. None of us are above the Law and should strive to uphold it like any other citizen in our communities". In the House of Commotions, Donnakeye Tailles was being grilled by the opposition about the new caveats in the new legislation. Opposition Leader, the Honorable Secon D. Hanshuzā, parried that seeking to ask the Civilian Security Services "to be treated *"just like 'ordinary citizens'"*", was tantamount to *"reducing their 'powers'* amongst the communities in which they are serving". There was the customary roar of laughter and jeering which in itself audibly resembled the kind of rambunctious behaviour that resonated with a group of disapproving individuals at the ancient Coliseums on the parallel planet, Earth. The Honorable, Secon D. Hanshuzā further argued that the communities would come to disrespect those agents of the Civilian Security Services "because of their having to *'account'* for sometimes errant behaviours by rogue individuals within the Services". Shouts of "who's to blame" and "clean up your own backyard" were being chanted all around the Chamber by the ruling government members. The echoes hauntingly reverberated around the Senate Chamber just as the Honorable Secon D. Hanshuzā was about to respond to the deliberate acidic retorts. Donnakeye Tailles told the opposition Leader that she could not understand why he and his colleagues didn't agree with the proposal for new legislation but reminded him of the list of *'tragedies'* that had taken place under his leadership in the previous government. The volume of laughter filled the Senate Chamber and the choir of voices with its acoustics added to the derision of stupidity from the opposition Leaders' statement. Shouts of "sit down" and "you're an embarrassment to the House and the communities" were being bandied about, until the Chairman of Proceedings called for *"order"* to be restored. "Let the Honorable gentleman speak", the Chairman pleaded but even his voice was being drowned out by the overwhelming avalanche of roaring laughter by the huge majority of the ruling party. The Honorable Prime Leader of Spaceville had meant to come down tough in order to detract from the inevitable drainage of businesses away from Spaceville. That would only have manifested into a spiralling financial depression that Spaceville could ill-afford to entertain. Images of long-termed unemployment would not only mean the end of the ruling government but also the disengagement from the trusting relationships within the communities that had brought Donnakeye Tailles and her colleagues the overwhelming landslide victory that had brought their Party into power. Those champagne moments still loomed large yet encrypted in the memories of all Donnakeye's trusted members of her government. Those with and without portfolios had celebrated with champagne together with their respective supporters at the time the ruling government triumphed over the bloated egos of the opposition. There was also the consideration that, if the Honorable Prime Leader Donnakeye Tailles and her colleagues did not address the current situation with severe but fair measures, the government could have encountered the wrath of the all powerful Inter-Kingdom Council for Ethical Standards. That could mean total oblivion from the world of politics altogether. Baron and Duke listened intently but wondered how these Laws and Spaceville's Donnakeye Tailles' government legislations might impact on those, who had already re-offended. They were even more concerned for individuals whom were long-termed prisoners; especially those who had committed crimes as members of Clout.

Prior to the news about the new legislations with regards to conscription and floating prisons, Duke and Baron had attended a weekend Seminar presented by the man they called 'The Professor'. The theme was The UFO's Cult-Induced Post/Zip Code Wars. Baron and Duke learnt that the UFO's Cult-Induced Post/Zip Code Wars were a deliberate invention by the UFO via the likes of their subordinates, the GMT and the GMES. The UFO's Cult-Induced Post/Zip Code Wars on the virtual planet of Asteroidia were fashioned deliberately to lure young people *(puppets)* into a culture of *'virtual living'* via their consoles. It was a highly subtle way of invading the privacy of young individuals' psyche but controlling the depth of *'programming'* and *'conditioning'* that was taking place at an unconscious level subliminally in the name of *'entertainment activities'*.

Professor Walynski's Research exposed the conduit between how behaviours from the *'virtual world'* were transferred over to behaviours in *'everyday life experiences'* via those *'entertainment activities'* that impacted behaviours in an insensitive but meaningless way. This psychological scientific feat had not only become an addictive *'mental drug'* but also grooved then implanted embedded subliminal post-hypnotic commands to the young individuals' minds. These influenced but transposed those behaviours from the *'virtual world'* into *'real actions'* and *'reactions'* in the *'real world'*. Professor Walynski said that "bringing individuals to a *'high state of arousal'* as finely tuned as professional athletes' preparation before competition meant that the youngsters involved in the UFO's Cult-Induced Post/Zip Code Wars were being deliberately targeted but forced to *'compete'* violently against each other (*'endz'* to *'endz'*) until the **_inevitable 'end'_**, whatever form that took! It did mean that the youngsters had to confront or be confronted just like the *'challenges'* they faced in the *'virtual games'* to move up to a higher level on a daily basis. The young individuals were guaranteed to replicate the subliminal post-hypnotic commands indelibly encrypted into their psyche. These were imparted via the subliminally coded post-hypnotic messages they received from these robotic violent virtual console games, the genre of music in which they chose to partake and the repetition of violence in the films they chose to watch, which excited them but made *'being violent' seem a perfectly 'normal' occurrence*, maybe! With the daily repetitive drills, which fired their fragile nervous *'hair-triggered' 'reaction times'*, those young individuals' *'primed minds'* were more than *'ready' to react adversely towards any level of 'fear' which they might perceive as dangerous"*. Apart from *their poor diets of 'fast foods'*, the youngsters actively sought to be involved in the *'Ethno-Genocidal'* UFO's *'Cult-Induced'* Post/Zip Code Wars. During any real or perceived confrontation, the youngsters developed massive increases in *volumes of adrenaline; causing instantaneous unusual high rise in their blood pressures, racing heartbeats, 'anxieties' and 'panic attacks' through fear*. The Professor Emeritus researcher stated that the installation of such high levels of fear amongst the various *'endz'* was the singular mission of the chief *'puppeteers'*, the UFO. The expressed purpose of their envoys, the GMT and GMES with their subordinates the GMP, GOS, GOO and GOP, was to trigger young individuals *'fight or flight'* autonomic response systems, subsequently. The green humanoid robotron UFO's singular intension was to *'regulate'* but remotely *'manage'* these response systems through intensifying the level of fear via the grotesque *'Ethno-Genocidal'* UFO's Cult-Induced Post/Zip Code Wars. Professor Walynski further explained to whom he referred as the *'scientific missionaries'* of *"virtual 'fun' entertainment"*. He said that the UFO and their accomplices had infiltrated the psyche of the youngsters by stealth by first announcing themselves as *'scientific missionaries',* who had come to work in communities with the *'disaffected young individuals'*, so called. Once they had managed to gain the confidence of the youngsters, the UFO had started to implement the Ghetto Mentality Regime Programme but had changed into *'mental mercenaries'* by sleight whilst developing the ultimate *'Street Militia Model'*, the UFO's Cult-Induced Post/Zip Code Wars, wittingly or unwittingly!

The genial Professor referred to the many thousands of interviews he had with incumbent young adult and adolescent prisoners through PORF, the Prison Online Research Facilitation available exclusively to The Walynski Institute. Professor Walynski said that he wanted to be able to share his findings with the scientific oversight body, SOB, in The Royal Royal Dis-United Stately Kingdoms of Asteroidia. He wanted to enlighten the youngsters and their parents that the *'bait'* of *'superficial accreditation'* known as *'Street Credits'* for abominable, thoroughly insensitive behaviours, which were totally unacceptable, was part of the young individuals' *'fraternal initiation'*. Once the young individuals were initiated, they had to show *'allegiance'* to their respective gangs by proving that they *'had their backs'* or to carry out a totally senseless, insane attack on rivals or even someone within their communities, who expressed that they did not want to join the gang. At each level of *'destructive mastery'*, the youngsters received superficial titles, badges and awards. In his speech at The Walynski Institute, the eminent researcher used a metaphoric example to simplify his meaning. Professor Walynski said, "it was like watching a *'Western Cowboy Movie'*. A bunch of hoods would ride into town spoiling for a fight. They would be strong in numbers and would reeked havoc amongst the particular community in that town. The gang would rape, pillage and plunder but bring their unacceptable, chaotic, reckless behaviours into the lives of the people in that town without mercy or care. Some would die but the rowdy gangs would replace those *'collateral damages'* with new eager naive individuals, who were excited by the wanton way of life that seemed attractive at that time. Similar to the pattern of the UFO's Cult-Induced Post/Zip Code Wars, the rowdy gangs would keep repeating those same behaviours from town to town doing exactly the same thing again and again. From the Western Movie Cowboys' perspectives **'Life'** was considered as *'cheap'*, had *'no real value'* and was carelessly *'taken for granted'*. Similarly, though their means of transportation were not necessarily horses but instead vehicles with engines, the *'City Cowboys'* on the virtual planet of Asteroidia sought recognition by reputations. Titles of *'infamy'* like *'Shodda'*, was fearsome enough to gain recognition amongst peer groups in the UFO's Cult-Induced Post/Zip Code Wars let alone the perceived *'enemies'* or in street terms *'frenemies'*. Badges like *'Street Creds'* were accumulated by perpetrating some awesomely bizarre, cold-hearted action or actions to prove how emotionally insensitively cold they had become. This included the mandatory custodial incarceration at youth or young adult level. Awards for misplaced understanding of the word *'Respect'* were also part of the *deliberate 'psychological trickery'* that made the experience of the younger generations on the virtual planet of Asteroidia seemed like an *'accolade of achievement'"*, he explained. In summing up, Professor Walynski's closing argument stated that, through the *'Carrot and Stick'* approach, the targetted young individuals were being forced into acquiring an enormous thirst for the taste of Champagne Urge. In order to do this, the naïve individuals *(puppets)* had to compete in a most vicious environment under constant pressure. They traded in *'illegal commodities'* that they had either ripped off from rivals or for which they were in debt to their suppliers. Under this high level of stress, those young individuals hoped to gain pecuniary accumulation of wealth on which they paid no tax nor could legally justify. Trained by their *'mercenary masters'* *(puppeteers)*, the Royal Royal Dis-United Stately Kingdoms of Asteroidia's *'City Cowboys'* *'primed minds'* had been *'drilled'* to achieve a similar finely tuned *'hair-trigger reaction time'* as that of an elite 100 metres Olympic sprinter.

According to their *'culture'* of *'beliefs and values'*, hoards of marauding eager technocrats on the virtual planet of Asteroidia had made a conscious decision to invent violent technological "*'fun' activities"*, so called. These might have been subliminally mentally anaesthetizing at minimum; destroying any form of emotional feelings of remorse when individuals chose to obey the post-hypnotic *'virtual behavioural instructions'* like *"finish him off"*. The post-hypnotic command had been latently transposed over into *'real' life* situations and environments in order to settle petty issues. Technological technocrats, who invented the "'fun' activities", were either not aware of the damaging effects their *'virtual living'* was having in preparing young individuals minds to repeatedly reinforce but practice those unacceptable behaviours from their consoles or that the patterning had been transferable into *'real-life scenarios'*. Professor Walyski commented that if they were aware then either they are not taking responsibility for their *"marvelous inventions"* or have come to realize, without regard, that **_"the marketplace is not the product but the mind"_**, probably! The eminent researcher had invited comments from the technological technocrats but they abstained from responding to the question he had posed. That question was quite simple. It was, whether it was important to them to weigh up the effect their "*fun*' activities" might be having upon the mentalities of the young individuals, who were their *'target market'*?

The Commons Senate had received Professor Walynski's Report via the astute Member of Communities, Janette Brayhorne. All technological virtual game giants all over the Royal Royal Dis-United Stately Kingdoms of Asteroidia were summoned to appear before the Commons Senate to determine whether the manufacturers of the "*fun' entertainment activities*" would voluntarily review the scientific allegations referred to in Professor Walynski's Report. It had implied that with the consistent diet of *'stereo-tripe'*, the entrapment of the philosophy of the *'stereo-hype'* and, through the external manipulation of their *'target market'*, the technological technocrats were instilling but reinforcing "*an immunization against emotional sensitivity*" into the mentality of the typical *'stereo-type'*. The young individuals, who chose to identify with the *'politically accepted'* typical *'stereo-type'* had unfailingly rehearsed but been exposed to patterning those unacceptable behaviours of *'virtual living'* from their consoles repetitiously. Those same psychologically trained principles of ill-tempered, abominable behaviour patterns had been triggered yet were being converted, transposed and applied into *'real life'* situations and environments all over the World of Space. Each *'real life'* challenge was met with well over-dramatized panic actions or reactions to perceived threats, learnt from the repetition of *'game-play'* allegedly. These perceived threats were triggered most times by simulated levels of fear which were way off the scale. One after another, the *'shankings'* or *'itchy trigger-fingers'* were applied on the streets of places like Spaceville and the rest of the Royal Royal Dis-United Stately Kingdoms of Asteroidia. Such was the *'psychological blueprint of fear'* which was being unleashed upon the *'susceptible minds'* of the youngsters within communities, who were being attracted to the *'greed'* over *'need'* philosophy of the UFO's Cult-Induced Post/Zip Code Wars.

Baron and Duke were learning that *approved token 'models'*, who served particular approved token *'roles'*, known as Ghetto Celebrity CEOs and Entrepreneurs were carefully being selected to inveigle them and other young individuals into *'entertainment activities'* that seemed to be more challenging. Those *'Role Models'*, so called, were made to appear as a fulfillment of the mythical *'rags to riches'* stories. Their *'achievements'* in reaching the eagerly sought after champagne status, made them the *ideal 'models'* to be emulated but they had never found it necessary to explain the challenges of becoming an *'insider'*. Mingling with or amongst the perceived highly fashionable and especially inspirationally impressionable constellation of stars was more appealing than the seemingly uninteresting, unexciting alternative *'meaningful structured'* lifestyle. Duke and Baron were becoming even more aware that some of the choices they had made were setting them up for a *'pre-determined predictable outcome'*. They were learning from the Ghetto Celebrity Entrepreneurs that living in the *'fast lane'*, selling drugs, guns and ammunition could possibly gain them some quick money but the more they pillaged from their rival peers and communities made it become a more dangerous occupation than they had probably first reckoned. It was beginning to dawn upon the brothers that *'greed'* over *'need'* would only lead to their possible deaths or long-termed imprisonment. Baron and Duke knew now that the perspectives on their current situation had to change.

Baron, who had already served time in theYOCC,Young Offenders Correctional Centre, and his twin brother, Duke, had more than one reason for wanting to make a change in the way they had chosen to live, previously. Being in a gang was never going to challenge their immense potentials nor fulfill their wealth of abilities. His and Baron's choice of the way they had chosen to live their lives had started out with how lesser valued they were feeling about themselves then. Each was missing a vital parental link. The man they called 'The Professor' had pointed to their immensely inflated negative egos that had initiated then drove the attitudes that had manifested into the type of mindsets which fashioned their negative emotional behaviours. Tinged with levels of despondency about not knowing what their purposes or missions were meant to be, both Baron and Duke were heading down an ever decreasing one-way spiral towards destruction. Sadly, the downward spiral they had chosen was affecting others lives as well as their own. Baron and Duke began to realize that there was more to living their lives than just being angry with others all the time or to engage in *'tit-for-tat'* infantile behaviours. What they were learning from their visits to the man they called 'The Professor' was that discovering their talents was a far better use of their time than being an occupant of a very restricted space like a prison cell in the *'Human Zoos'*. The man they called 'The Professor' encouraged but challenged Duke and Baron to *finding the treasures within themselves*. This concept seemed to hit a note with the brothers. They were beginning to resolve how they were going to get the best out of themselves. As requested by Earl, if Duke wanted to reap the benefits of the Will, he had to agree to and apply the terms and conditions stipulated by his father. Having already acquired some property and adequate lump sums, Duke was more than keen to fulfill the other instructions. He knew his father was quite a shrewd businessman but longed to emulate him. Duke was more than aware that Earl's legacy was left to him initially but now included his brother Baron. Frequent visits to the man they called 'The Professor' meant that their new learning was impacting on each of them. Encouraged by their Coach, Baron and Duke began to question their pungent attitudes of the past but acknowledged information about themselves that just seemed to arrive with them. The brothers began to shed their infantile behaviours but sought to replace them with striving to be more emotionally intelligent and matured.

Baron told Duke that he was going to College to study Drama. Duke said he wanted to follow in Earl's footsteps eventually but he preferred to study Computer Science at College. Both Baron and Duke told the man they called 'The Professor' that they had signed up to go to College but in other Boroughs. They had made their decisions. It would mean that they were distanced from the immediate infantile behaviours of the gangs. It didn't mean that they had given up on their friends but that they had made emotionally intelligent and matured decisions to start to pave a new chapter in their lives. After two years at College, both Baron and Duke achieved distinctions in their chosen subjects. During the next three to four years they studied but successfully achieved distinctions yet again. Baron graduated from Holygoodyā and Duke from Bastardé Universities. He, having followed the terms and conditions set by his father's Will, regularly attended DSI each weekend but learned the rudiments of the business under the watchful eyes of Alan Panaché, the man Earl had assigned to be his mentor. At the age of 25 years old, Duke became the owner of DSI, Duke Stagg Incorporated.

The Taste of Champagne Urge!

WIK-**ID**-FICTION

PART TWO

CHAPTER 12

Asteroidia had adopted a quota system to bring in immigrants from the far off lands in the World of Space. Because of their tropical environments these far off lands were termed as exotic continents, countries and islands. Asteroidia needed these indentured workers to do the work that Asteroidians didn't want to do for one reason or another. Each year the Kingdoms of Asteroidia would determine to draft in a fixed number of immigrants. It was a lottery where each group was landed. The immigrants had no choice where they ended up geographically in Asteroidia. Many families were separated but scattered around Asteroidia as they eagerly accepted the jobs they were offered. It may sound crazy to leave such paradise continents, countries and islands to come to live in Kingdoms with such varied and unpredictably harsh temperatures. In Asteroidia the temperatures could vary from an average 30 degrees Celsius in the summertime to a minus 20 to 40 degrees below freezing point in wintertime. This might include something known as wind chill factor too. Tangerine coloured frost, lilac coloured mist and purple coloured fog, sometimes freezing, were other elements that were uncommon for the immigrants from the far off lands. Snow and hail fell from the sky all over Asteroidia. Hail were irregular shaped hard blobs of ice varying in sizes like small pebbles to large stones and sometimes as big as small pineapples. Snow was acid orange coloured hand-shaped soft fluffy flakes that fell but just as quickly melted immediately, sometimes. At other times, it lay on the ground but became slushy then melted away. There were times when it stayed frozen into sheets of solid ice for days and sometimes weeks or even months. People had to get around but had no alternative than to walk, run and drive on solid ice. Winter sports like Skiing were played on the solid ice. These were relished by Asteroidians. The only comparison for what it was like for the people from the far off lands is like having to convert from shorts and bikinis to wearing socks, scarves, mittens, gloves, boots, hats, coats and underclothing called 'long johns', in these extremely inclement temperatures. It was like converting from basking in the sun at 90 degrees and above to suddenly having to adapt to minus temperatures like Inuit Indians, formerly called Eskimos, on the parallel planet, Earth.

The governments of Asteroidia deliberately chose to pay immigrants at a cheaper rate than indigenous Asteroidians. Even though the immigrants were asked to work at least twice or sometimes up to four times as hard as Asteroidians, they were grateful for the frequency of work. In their continents, countries and islands in the far off lands, there was not an abundance of regular work. Oftentimes, the people in the far off lands had communities that worked together. In doing so, each family contributed towards the efficient sharing of basic needs like the provision of food. What is commonly known as 'Cook-outs' in the Kingdoms of Asteroidia was a daily occurrence in the far off lands. This was no more or less than simply sharing what was a tradition. When Asteroidians visited those exotic continents, countries and islands, they copied what they had witnessed but called it 'Cook-outs'. Theirs was only an occasional event that took place in warm weather only. In some geographical areas of Asteroidia, the activity of 'Cook-outs' known as 'Quebarbies', was a hugely successful social event. Even though the governments of

Asteroidia had invited this indentured labour force from the far off lands to do the work Asteroidians had clearly refused to do, some of the indigenous Asteroidians were against the arrival of immigrants on the grounds of ethnicity. The Neuro-classist mentality had been initiated but maintained all over the Kingdoms of Asteroidia. Immigrants or their presence were not welcomed. As a consequence of their arrival, conflicts soon arose. Some green humanoid robotron politicrats opposed to the new arrivals used disinformation in order to excite inflammatory verbal and physical abuses against the immigrants though all they were guilty of was of being a different ethnicity. Those perpetrators stirred up the hornets nests, so to speak, by summoning their inveterate feelings towards *'foreigners'* as they often referred to the immigrants. Because they were skilled in the art of programming and conditioning via misinformation, politicrats used those *'cheap tactics'* to score cheap political points, whenever it suited them. These tactics had been proven over generations to guarantee but impact most efficiently upon the fears of the indigenous people all over Asteroidia. Soon, there were neighbours, who became hostile towards the immigrant population for just living next door, being on the same street, the same neighbourhoods, precincts, districts and boroughs. At work, the immigrants were threatened, berated, bullied but altogether totally humiliated by their green humanoid robotron colleagues and those in senior positions. Some immigrants were told plainly to "get back to where you once belong". It was a harrowing experience to be invited yet not experience feeling welcomed or accepted. These were everyday occurrences that were typical responses all over the Royal Royal Dis-United Stately Kingdoms of Asteroidia. In Lower Ghettoborough, Spaceville, where there was a greater concentration of immigrants, they were rounded up by green humanoid robotron officers of the law. By day, they'd be accused of loitering with intent even when standing waiting for public transport at bus stops or at train stations. At night, stopping to look into shop windows was a crime, seemingly. The distraction or in some instances attraction of images on a screen on television in a shop window was quite a different experience for most of these immigrants from the 5th rated exotic continents, countries and islands. Oftentimes in their 5th rated exotic far off lands, their only other experiences of being able to view a television might have been to gather with others in their respective local communities around the only set available to them collectively. With the freedom to view this modern phenomenon in Spaceville, immigrants from those exotic far off lands would often stare into the future when they might be able to afford to purchase one of the televisions for them and their families. Their dreams were often shattered by the accusations by officers of the law. They perceived the immigrants, individually or severally, were contemplating breaking into these shops, apparently! Many immigrants suffered at the whim of opposing officers of the law. Through judgment, based on their individual and cultural prejudices, they deemed the immigrants as "very suspicious characters". Competition was rife amongst those law officers, whom joked about the part they were playing to systematically debase the new arrivals to their shores. Often, during their canteen breaks or on their respective beats within the communities, those law officers compared yet boasted about their personal records of intimidating behaviours. They even discussed the *'unwitting'* racial slurs which surfaced either verbally or through physical action. This practice occurred especially when individual immigrants protested their innocence or annoyance at the number of times per day that they had to endure that type of experience. Most immigrants were emotionally battered but were shocked surprised by such behaviours and the high-handed levels of intimidation meted out by those law officers, without recourse. Other immigrants, who protested most vigorously, suffered not only emotionally but also physically too. Individual immigrant testified to experience feeling "the full *'force'* of the law" on those occasions. Such was the application of an apartheid system being practiced in places like Painsville, Odourville and Ghettoville in Lower Ghettoborough. This meant being set upon by *'gangs'* of law officers to boost the number of arrest in order to fill their remitted quota. They often sought to justify this type of behaviour by stating that they were "attempting to *'restrain'*" each individual immigrant that had lived that experience. Even when CCTV captured the whole scene from initial approach to action taken by law officers, cases against such abuse of power would later be pardoned by the *'Justice' System*. Individual law officers were either re-instated or, in most cases, promoted but retained. The *'words'* of the law officer was sacrosanct and gospel as opposed to those of the abused immigrant. A comment from the law officer like "they (meaning the immigrant) were up to no good" was often enough for Magistrates to find the immigrant guilty. Exorbitant fines too were well out of proportion to the alleged *'crimes'* of suspicion. Many immigrants spent much of their hard earned wages on fines for the perception of those green humanoid robotron serial Neuro-bigoted law officers. Apart from the fines, the immigrants were beginning to find out that they were accumulating criminal records they didn't deserve. Their good conduct reputations were being cancelled out and subsequently ruined by those rogue officers of the law that woke up, found themselves in a bad mood or who chose to establish their individual or collective prejudices, *'wittingly'* or *'unwittingly'*, against the arrival of immigrants. They also were learning that, in Asteroidia, as immigrants, they had no rights.

Some individuals like Amos Oddball had been through that type of treatment when he first arrived in Spaceville, Asteroidia. He and his friends lived in a place called Ghettoville, Lower Ghettoborough. They recalled having to fight physically and mentally against such prejudices. Whether at work, on the street or at the addresses where they lived, Amos and his friends' experiences were daily occurrences. After surviving the living in Spaceville for two to three years, Amos started to realize that not all the people of Ghettoborough including some reasonable individual law officers were of prejudiced views. Some of the people spoke to him pleasantly and made him feel welcomed in his community, though the ones with the *'plastic smiles'* with the covert agendas highlighted themselves. Amos was never one to let his guard down but he felt it was time to send for his wife, Dorothy. When she arrived, they lived in the one room dwelling with hardly any decent amenities in Ghettoville but he was happy that Dorothy was with him. The Oddballs, Dorothy and Amos, arrived in the host country thinking that they might carry on their respective careers. Dorothy was a bespoke seamstress. She'd learnt under the watchful eyes of her own mother, who was the well known district seamstress back home in the far off exotic island. Her clientele included the local Parish PM and all the major Celebrities within the Parish. There were other eminent individuals like female doctors, nursing sisters, teachers and the entire local Bank's female staff members. Amos was a farmer. He was used to handling the soil as well as raring the animals that he was used to tending. Both Amos and Dorothy found the unfamiliarity of Town living quite strange yet they were the typical hard working family all the same. Amos and Dorothy Oddball scrimped and saved as much as they could from the small wages they earned, in Spaceville, as bus driver and factory worker respectively. After two years of her arrival, Dorothy gave birth to their son, Raymond. On the day when their baby came home, both Dorothy and Amos decided that it wouldn't be healthy for their child to grow up in that one room. The damp walls showed the fungus in dark patches, whilst the broken window pane was reinforced by cardboard and duct tape. The shared bathroom and kitchen facilities meant there were always jostling amongst other tenants to use the one cooker in the kitchen, the one bathroom or the only indoor toilet. There was another toilet at the far end of the garden but it had no heating and in the winter the water froze so it couldn't be flushed even if one was desperate enough to use it. Dorothy and Amos busied themselves seeking new accommodation with at least two rooms and adequate facilities but it was quite a struggle. Some of the adverts on the Newspaper Shops advertising accommodation had their own restrictions. Some read *'no dogs, no visitors and no immigrants'*. It was as stark as that in reality. Raymond was never without a cold and was frequently having to go to the doctors because of the damp in the single room. Amos and Dorothy were suffering too from the dank conditions. In particular, not many people from the far off lands owned their own houses. Friends told Amos and Dorothy that, of the few that did own their own houses, a great majority from the Tribe of Hawke treated their own people even worse than the green humanoid robotrons did. There were complaints of gross overcharging from those landlords in most cases. Some wanted the less fortunate individuals from the Tribe of Hawke to bow down and worship them. One of Amos' friends, from the Betting Shop, told his story about a work colleague renting him a room but provided him with a cooker on the landing of the first floor which was situated just outside the door of the room he was renting. Amos' friend stated that he had to plead with the landlord to turn on the hot water so he could have a bath. When the landlord chose to do so, he made Amos' friend feel like a nuisance rather than a paying tenant. One of Dorothy's friend told of her experience of a landlord from the far off lands, who had made an unusual approached to her. He ask Dorothy's friend to befriend him. This he did while her husband was at work. When she refused his repetitive requests for sex, the landlord gave them notice to leave his premises within days. Dorothy's friend and her family became homeless with their two children for over eight months before they could find accommodation again. The couple survived the harsh winter days with the help of genuine friends and family members, who rotated their stay at great risk to themselves being dismissed from their own accommodation. She told Dorothy that sometimes it would mean that all four of them had to stay at different addresses in order to have the basic needs like shelter and food. Dorothy and Amos were currently living in a house owned by a couple from the same far off lands. Their current experience was personal testimony but which matched the stories they were told by some others. It was nigh on impossible for Amos and Dorothy to secure any other accommodation easily but they never stopped searching. Amos registered with the local council housing. They told him that he didn't have enough points to qualify for one of their flats. Amos and Dorothy's doctor wrote a letter to confirm that this family was in poor health especially the child, Raymond. The nursery reported that they too were concerned how often Raymond was being ill with a cold. In fact, they stated that he was never without a cold. The Nursery staff said they were so concerned about Raymond's health that they decided to send a social worker to view the conditions under which the child was living. Dorothy took these letters and the report from the social worker's visit to the Council. They in turn visited the Oddballs but bore witness to the extreme damp walls which were now thoroughly covered in dark green fungus. The plaster had started to fall off in clumps all around the room. The officer attending was more than appalled at the condition of those areas of the house he could see let alone the room in which the Oddballs occupied. Within one week of the Council's visit, Amos and Dorothy were told they had enough points. Having waited more than five years, the Oddballs were sent to view two flats but were told that if they refused both, the Council would not offer them another choice. The Oddballs made their choice. It wasn't ideal accommodation but they were grateful to the local Council Housing for at least agreeing that the room they had previously occupied was not fit for living in. Amos couldn't get over the fact that they lived on the 18th floor of a 21 story building but the Oddballs were grateful for small mercies. At least, they had heating and hot water, two bedrooms, a lounge, a small kitchen, bathroom and toilet but most importantly they didn't have to share with any other tenant and there were no damp walls. Amos and his friends decorated the flat and lay the carpets and vinyl. The lounge, kitchen and two cupboards were downstairs while the two bedrooms, toilet and bathroom were upstairs. Though the accommodation was more expensive than the cost of the one room, the Oddballs kept much healthier than before. It wasn't long before Dorothy had gone back to work at the factory. She worked as much overtime that she could and so did Amos. Both worked long hours but depended on Child Minders to collect Raymond from the Nursery then but subsequently from Junior School too. Trusting to leave their child in the care of complete strangers was a worry for both Dorothy and Amos. In their far off lands, extended families and others within their communities were ready and available to take on these tasks and often without expectation of payment. Amos and Dorothy could be assured of the quality of care and the reliability of the individuals, who did these tasks as an additional representation to the fabric of the community. In Spaceville, Dorothy and Amos's experiences were nothing like those of their exotic island. This was a huge sacrifice to trust total strangers with your child's welfare while striving to earn extra money for his future. Dorothy and Amos made these sacrifices whilst they were in the host country to enable them to give *'young'* Raymond *"ah gud upbringing"*. On his days off Amos could be seen with his friends in the Betting Shop, hoping for the *'win'* which could help them pay the crippling bills. Sometimes he and a few friends would gather at his rented Council flat to *'reason'* or play dominoes. Amos was a rough man and a strict disciplinarian. He had often commented to Dorothy about his expectations of their son. "Ah doan waan Raymond fi tun wutlis. Tell di bwai fi guh study im book insted ah walk street wid im fren dem", Amos often told his wife. Dorothy was different in her approach to life. She was a lively, jovial woman who did not let anything bother her. Dorothy saw life in her particular way. Close family ties were the most important things in her life. Often, Dorothy had to placate her husband whenever the next door neighbour knocked their door to ask them to stop Raymond, the child, from kicking the ball against the wall or whenever Amos played his stereo system. On occasions when Amos thought he had been reasonably thoughtful towards his neighbours, in ensuring that the volume was low but was still being pilloried by some of them, he would get into a rage. "Doant bi suh ignorant Amos, whey wi fi duh when yuh gaan ah jail? Who Raymond gwein hav fi look up tuh", Dorothy would ask him? There was pressure "fram maawning til nite" from some neighbours but Dorothy somehow managed to keep Amos under control. Dorothy and Amos attended The Apostolic Church, whenever they could. On Sunday mornings, in church, Amos sung in his deep baritone voice. Dorothy, unfortunately, had one of those voices that sounded more like scraping a nail against glass. "Dorothy, people who cawn sing too good fi keep dem voice low", Amos would often tease his wife. "Leave mi alone Amos, yuh try fi drown out evrybady else wid yuh hoarse voice," Dorothy would respond. The Oddballs were not, what one would call, devout Christians but they believed that God was there to be praised for helping them to survive the awesome struggles through life, let alone overcome some of the trying times they were experiencing in a *"fahwren"* country. They raised Raymond in the *Traditions* and *Culture* they themselves had been brought up in. Amos *'lectured'* Raymond many times about sticking to his *cultural* foods. Whenever young Raymond refused to drink the *'banana porridge'*, Amos would scold him. "How yuh tink wi survive dis long? Yuh tink is jus lucky wi lucky", Amos asked his son? It was Amos, who prepared breakfast and he would insist that Raymond consume the very last drop. "Doant waste food son, some doan hav nun", Amos reinforced.

The Oddballs were very proud of their son who, at 16 years old, successfully attended Coleport College in Greensborough but passed the exams required to go on to the prestigious Bastãrdé University in Snideborough. Amos and Dorothy waited for Raymond to complete his first year at university before deciding to go back to the exotic far off land. They were sure it was the right time for them to return to their native land but promised to return for the Graduation Ceremony. Both were disappointed that they had been so badly treated in a *"fahwren"* land. With the sun a constant reminder of their return to paradise, the Oddballs quickly re-settled in their community. Amos returned to farming and Dorothy to being a seamstress again. After settling back to their indigenous surroundings, they noticed that some things had changed. There was a new culture creeping into their community.

Other arrivals in Spaceville were the Boguses, Constantino and Dian. Constantino Bogus, CB, was born in Spaceville and was a product of a second generation mixed DNA relationship between an indigenous female mixed DNA Spacevillean, Eartha Contemptious and a Tribe of Hawke immigrant Constantinus Adolphus Bogus from one of the exotic far off lands. In the earlier years, he, like others from those exotic lands, were actively encouraged by the then governments of Asteroidia to leave their more exotic sunnier climates to live and work in one of the Kingdoms of the virtual parallel planet of Asteroidia. Constantinus was grateful to be invited to work abroad yet again. In his paradise island, there were few opportunities to secure long termed work on a regular basis. He had no choice where in Asteroidia he would be placed but that didn't matter to him. Constantinus was more grateful for the opportunity to have more financial security than he would have had in his home country. He was a strong, fit, healthy man in his early forties. Constantinus had experienced going abroad to another large country closer to his exotic island that occasionally issued visas to recruit *'Farm Workers'* to harvest sugarcane and cotton. There, he and his colleagues toiled for seven days per week but received three and a half days pay only each week. Constantinus, like some of his colleagues, wanted to protest against this unfair practice. Those who voiced their opinions were swiftly quietened but suspiciously disappeared overnight. They were never seen again. That was more than a warning to anyone whom did not approve of the underhanded mystery. It was grossly unfair how Constantinus and his colleagues were treated but three and a half days pay for *'farm working'* was much more than what Constantinus earned from the occasional work on his paradise island. He learned not to complain. Constantinus saw his contract through until it was time to return to his paradise island. He now had an opportunity to go to live and work in Asteroidia. Spaceville just happen to be where he had been disembarked.

Constantinus was attracted to an indigenous Spacevillean woman named Eartha. They married within the first 18 months of his arrival. On the birth of their baby, Constantino, they celebrated with much champagne on his arrival into the World of Space. Two months after Constantino's birth he was christened. At the christening, there were even more champagne celebrations. Eartha's father liked Costantinus but her mother had and showed her reservation for the unison between him and her daughter. Some of Eartha's mother's family openly ignored Constantinus at the wedding and again at the christening too. Baby Constantino's arrival seemed to act as a conduit between Eartha's mother and Constantinus. Gradually, he was allowed to visit Eartha's parents' home in Highborough, providing they arrived after dark. Constantinus was allowed to stay for one hour with his in-laws but leave Constantino and Eartha overnight, returning the following night to collect both of them. Constantinus did not feel comfortable with the arrangements but agreed to the terms so as not to upset his wife Eartha. She argued with her mother and all the other family members, who were being difficult towards Constantinus. Eartha's mother was a very domineering woman. She even bullied her husband constantly. Eartha's father was so obedient he might as well be the family pet. He seemed not to have any backbone. Eartha challenged him to stand up to her mother and the others but her father elected not to do so. Constantinus told his wife that he didn't know how much more he could bear but she assured him that she loved him. This assurance quelled Constantinus' simmering volcano. In spite of the unacceptable behaviours of her mother and those family members, who mistreated Constantinus, Eartha showed her allegiance to her husband. It meant that her parents could not have access to condition their child, Constantino, into partisan *'values and beliefs'* against which she was rebelling. Eartha agreed with Constantinus to send their child to the exotic far off island from which he'd emigrated. After a couple of visits to the exotic island to meet Constaninus' family and friends, Eartha reinforced her commitment. She had learnt that it was a traditional habit of some of the people from the far off lands to send their children back to close family members, especially grandparents. The purpose was that Constantino be steeped in the traditions of the particular exotic island. Eartha agreed in order to punish her mother for trying to drive away the man she loved. At the age of five years old, Constantino was taken back to his father's exotic island to live with his grandmother. Eartha enjoyed the welcome she received from Constantinus' family and friends but looked forwards to visiting the exotic island each summer holiday to bask in the sun in order to deepen her tan. She loved the food and the lifestyle of the indigenous people. Eartha found the Spacevillean culture boring, lifeless and pretentious compared to the happy approach of the exotic islanders. She too was from a mixed background but she had never been given the opportunity to visit her father's far off land. Earlier in her life, Eartha's mother and her family preached the doctrine of hate but asked her to despise *"foreigners"*. Eartha not only wondered how her mother could entertain such prejudice but also how her father managed to put up with those partisan views when he too was from mixed heritage background. She stood firm in her own belief that she would weigh up the pros and cons for herself. Eartha was so determined to rubbish the mantra she had been taught since young that she actively sought to deliberately engage with a *'foreigner'*. Constantinus Bogus had become her lover, friend and husband. They remained deeply in love with each other. On their visits each summer to the far off island, the exotic islanders worshipped Eartha and her friends. Having been previously ruled by the Kingdoms of Asteroidia, the friendly indigenous people truly believed that Eartha's heritage was far superior to their own but she would tell them that wasn't so. On their return from their annual two weeks holiday in the exotic islands back to Spaceville, Asteroidia, Eartha and Constantinus started to give Constantino an opportunity to spend three weeks of his summer holidays with them since he became 10 years old. Constantino continued to live on the exotic island with his grandmother from his father's side. He went to school and college there. He was a qualified engineer like his uncle wanted him to become. Though Constantino, learnt the local dialect, traditions and culture of the far off island while growing up there, he chose to return to his *'roots'* for fear of losing his beautiful woman to a more daring indigenous islander. They were very bold in their approach and Constantino feared that their sheer persistence might persuade his gorgeously stunning woman to be swooned by an indigenous Cassanova. Constantino's insecurities prevailed but stymied his growth in self esteem. Over the years, Constantino had returned to Spaceville intermittently to visit his parents prior to his permanent return with his gorgeous wife from the far off exotic island. It was her first trip abroad. Her name was Dian Bogus, formerly Diana Marie Biblethon. They lived in Lower Greensborough, Spaceville. It rested just on the edge of Brazenboruogh to the south, Highborough to the north, Sunnyborough to the east and Ghettoborough to the west.

In Diana Biblethon's life, dreams and illusions of grandeur were her only escape. Her earlier years consisted of extreme poverty. Those days were memories Diana, as she was then known, wanted to completely erase from her life. There were times when Diana had a single cracker for dinner followed by a mug of water. Such were the realities of being a pauper. Her parents were so poor financially that they couldn't confidently promise to provide a meal each day for themselves let alone their only child. At the age of 14 years old, Diana set out to secure work. She found a job, working as a *'Domestic Servant'*, for an affluent family in her home country. In comparison to the modern version of *'Home'* help (an *'Au Pair Girl'*) a *'Domestic Servant'* was a slave, literally. A typical workday meant that Diana started at 05:30 hours but worked through until 22:00 hours each day for six days per week. Official breaks were not offered nor encouraged. Even the natural functions of individuals, like going to the toilet, were monitored and timed by her employers, Mr. and Mrs. Cactus. Deduction were taken from her wages if she overstayed the permitted 5 minutes to use the toilet or used more than one x 5" square sheet of grease-proof type paper to clean herself after excreting natural waste. The Cactus' were by name and nature *'spiky'*, at least. They lived in the suburbs with their four children, 11 years son old Aloe, 14 years old daughter Vera, 16 years old son Hornie and 6 years old daughter Sandy. Ninety years old granddad, Desert, lived with the family too. As employers, they treated the young Diana like a *'skivvy'*. Dildo and Macka Cactus utilized intimidating behaviour and demeaning intonations whenever they needed Diana's attention. Sometimes, they would whistle or bang the table with anything that was available. Diana likened their mannerism and tones similar to that of a dog's owner giving orders to a wayward pet. This happened everyday but especially when the Cactus' were entertaining other family members and friends. Diana heard the blasé debasing comments too. As she was regarded as illiterate, the Cactus' and their friends did not hide their feeling for her. It was as if Diana was a lesser human being, somehow. The daily tasks were arduous most times but demanded efforts beyond what was reasonable for one individual to accomplish. Young Diana toiled hard for the meagre pay she received sometimes. Some weeks, after deductions for *'infringements'*, Diana received partial or no pay. The Cactus' never explained about their random decisions. Oftentimes, she wanted to give up but kept going in spite of the shabby treatment. Despite her concerns, Diana carried on working with the Cactus' all the same. She dusted, cleaned, scrubbed and polished floors. Diana had to wash all the family's clothes by hand. This caused her hands to look more shriveled than the Cactus's eldest family member, grandfather Cactus, who was closely approaching his 90th birthday. At 14 years old, young Diana with the *'wrinkled'* hands was expected to iron all the washed clothing too, including underclothing and socks as well. Clearing up after the family of seven, cooking and serving meals three times a day plus snacks made for a very weary Diana. At that time, whenever Diana told them how exhausted she was feeling, the green humanoid robotron Cactus's considered those many tasks as being *"all in a day's work"* as they often reminded her. Though her job was more than a little challenging, Diana resolved that she had no immediate alternative to her situation. She knew that she would require written *'Recommendation'* from a previous employer to enable her to gain further employment. Diana had other reasons for staying on at the Cactus's too. Even though she was trapped in a job that gave her no satisfaction, Diana took pride in her work. It gave her the independence she needed but most importantly Diana spent time away from the whims of her cruel parents. From another perspective, she was also able to contribute towards the upkeep of her parents, who were wholly dependent on her infrequent meagre wages, literally. Whenever she was at home, things were no different to her being at work with the Cactus family. Each day was like going from work to work but not being appreciated in either environment. Diana still had to cook when she came home as well as scrub and clean up after her parents too. It wasn't as if they couldn't help themselves. Rebbecca and Obediah Biblethon believed in designating duties to *'help'* young Diana understand the traditional rudiments necessary for her personal development, apparently. Travelling to and from work, provided the only break between shifts at work and at home. Obediah and Rebecca's intentions were genuine from one perspective but had been overdone on too many occasions. Obediah's philosophy was to rule with the iron fist while Rebecca remained his shadow, never questioning the caustic remarks or the beatings suffered by Diana at the hands of her cruel father. On more than one occasion, when Obediah had drunk some of his favourite Whisky from "fahwren", he'd order Diana to re-do areas of work that she had spent time carefully applying more than a little effort. Whenever Diana dared to comment about the clearly unnecessary repetition of tasks, she received the typical biblical *"spare the rod and spoil the child"* comment from her mother. This was Rebecca's way of justifying the necessity for yet another imminent beating for Diana from Obediah. As if this was not enough torture for the young girl, Rebecca and Obediah forced Diana into Christianity too. She'd felt bitter that she had no choice but there wasn't a lot Diana could have done about it then. Sundays were meant to be her *'day of rest'* in everyway possible but the church was of more significance to her parents. Every Sunday, both Rebecca and Diana joined others, who arrived dutifully, a couple of hours before the morning services began. It was incumbent upon young Diana to get involved with the rigid routine of *'Church Duties'*. She had to help her mother, Rebecca, dust the benches and clean the church floor. They adorned the church with flowers and lit the candles too. For Diana, that meant she couldn't afford to have a *'lie in'* on a Sunday morning. She had to attend two church services each Sunday; one in the morning and one in the evening. 'Sunday School' fell in between the two services but was repetitively long and boring. The repetition of the same biblical stories had lost their magical appeal. The only miracle Diana believed in was to be able to fulfill her dreams. Those were her only imaginary taste of freedom. In her mind, Diana lived in a world where neither her parents nor the Cactus' were allowed to invade. She was determined to lift herself from the strict Christian upbringing too. Diana perceived it as the major factor that *'blighted'* her life. These repetitious chores and super-saturation of religious dogma became the main cause of Diana's rebellious inner feelings. She swore on the Bible that she would go in a totally opposite direction from the church as soon as she could, possibly. This kind of thinking served as a catalyst but introduced Diana into the world of vanity instead; that *'world'* deemed as *"sinful"* by her parents. Rebecca and Obediah lived their lives through the Bible. "Thou shalt not covet thy neighbours' goods" was the most repeated yet reverentially held commandment/philosophy of the Biblethon's household, then. Diana didn't covet but instead scrimped and saved from her meagre earnings to enable her to escape to the *'freedom'* she believed she needed and deserved. She readily broke some of the commandments/philosophies when she left home on her 21st birthday. It was customary to consider 21 years old as being an adult. Diana left the Cactus's employ with good written recommendation on that same day. They were reluctant to let her go but after 7 years of enforced servitude, the Cactus' realized it would be senseless not to recommend Diana's dedication and loyalty.

She'd moved in with Constantino Bogus, CB, as he preferred to be called. At 38 years old, he was seventeen years her senior. Although CB loved carpentry, he was forced by his uncle to become an Engineer, like his father before him. CB served an apprenticeship in Engineering and was working regularly at a large Engineering Firm. He and Diana lived in the one room that CB had rented a couple of years before meeting her. Their room was one of many made available to tenants in the tenement yard. The dwellings were small but tightly spaced. Most of them were built at ground floor level except for a few. Five of those dwellings had two floors but offered one bedroom and one sitting room on the upper level, a toilet and a tiny area known as a 'Kitchenette' at ground level. Three single rooms on a block at ground level which had access to a shared space called a Communal Veranda. There were ten other single rooms in the yard. These were random additions that the landlord saw as additional income potential only. CB and Diana lived in one of those single 10'6" x 9'0 rooms situated directly in front of the only three-story Block. It housed 12 rooms but had better facilities with 4 x showers, 4 x toilets and an area at the end of the main corridors for washing clothes by hand. CB and those tenants living in the main yard had separate out-buildings. These were one compact communal kitchen, two communal toilets and a single standpipe which towered above the cistern below it. Inside the cistern, green slimy morass clung to its sides, while the thick carpeting on its floor grew randomly across the drain-hole. When clogged, the water rose to the height of the cistern but became stagnant. The putrid, unsightly body of water would remain for days and sometimes weeks until Diana decided to use straightened wire hangers or strips of wood to clear the blockage for the pungent water to run out through the drain-hole. Diana volunteered to set an example for others to follow. She poured *'sugar-soap'* in and around the slimy green morass cistern then scraped it thoroughly. After removing the offending content from the cistern with a makeshift scoop, Diana used a rough yard broom to scrub the inner walls with more *'sugar-soap'* and water until the concrete could once again become visible. All single room tenants and those who lived in the three room block shared the use of the cistern and the other communal facilities at the other end of the yard with Diana and CB. Instead of being grateful to Diana for her sterling effort to alleviate the possible threat from an infestation of mosquitoes, a gang of women and men cursed her mercilessly. Diana's efforts were not appreciated as she thought it might. Diana had hoped that others might be grateful and her effort might set an example how all the users could strategize to rotate the duties to clean the cistern. The other tenants, who were meant to share its use, told Diana in no uncertain terms that her considerations were not welcomed. They saw her as a "show off" trying to make them feel guilty. Some gathered as one against her. They cursed Diana in a most disgraceful bullying manner but offered to fight her for showing them up. Diana found the experience of living in a tenement yard quite threatening and claustrophobic. Her experience was extremely different from having a yard where the only occupants were Diana and her parents. Her experience of sharing communal showers did not prove hygienic. She found that there was no arrangement for their upkeep either. Neither were there any clear arrangements amongst the other tenants for the use of the communal kitchen. Diana found the daily squabbling amongst the users a much frightening experience. Oftentimes, individuals fought literally for the use of the limited facilities but the overcrowding and disorderly way in which individuals went about resolving the situation brought much intimidation and chaos. CB urged Diana to stay away from particular individuals but encouraged her to engage with the selected few he could trust. After all, CB had been exposed to his neighbours for two years prior. He'd learned from bitter experiences but most of all from his astute sense of observation. CB also knew that the men, who had verbally cursed Diana, were only doing so because they wanted to have sex with her. They had started to openly comment but pester her from the very first day that she moved in with him. She had gone to the standpipe to fetch some water but was surrounded by six men. They all were squabbling amongst themselves as to which one of them had a right to "mount her". The women, who had set upon Diana, surrounded her as a group as well but their reason for the intimidation was one of jealousy. Even their live-in partners were openly commenting about the physically beautiful Diana. Some of the women were complaining that she had no right to the mixed DNA CB with green eyes. They complained that they wanted to have a *"fair-skinned child by him"*. Those women didn't hide the fact that they were on *'heat'* for the tall muscular built *'Trophy Man Image'*, *'Mr Right'*, with the *"big job"*.

It took three weeks after her 21st birthday for Diana to secure a new job. This time she started working for a foreign Diplomat and his family; again as a *Domestic Servant*. Now with 7 years experience, Diana managed to negotiate less working hours but with a small increase in pay and marginal breaks in between tasks. She started at 06:00 hours in the mornings but now finished at 20:00 hours at nights instead. Her tasks were many and varied but in a more orderly way. The foreign Diplomat, Alan Mc Aburr-Bushe Cowitche and his family spoke more civilly to Diana than the Cactus' had done. The Mc Aburr-Bushe Cowitche's showed her their schedule from the start and she was allowed to input with regard to making decisions, sometimes. Though the hours were still long, Diana felt appreciated in her new job. The children spoke to her nicely but asked her advice about what they should wear or whether she thought one was being fair to the other. Diana felt a part of the family. The eldest of the Diplomat's children was Celia. She was eighteen. Diana and Celia spent quite a lot of time together. They often sat on the ground under the Guineppe fruit tree. Diana and Celia exchanged stories about their lives. At one time when Diana was telling her story, Celia stopped her. She began sobbing when Diana told her how the Cactus' had mistreated her. Celia told Diana that she felt the Cactus's were wrong in their attitude towards her. Diana too broke down crying when she remembered how the Cactus' expressed their disdain for her being born out of wedlock. She confided to Celia that they treated their cats and dogs better than her. Diana told Celia that she would remember her experience at the Cactus' for a very, very long time. Celia and Diana's friendship blossomed. The two young women shared many *'secrets'* for each other. It was their friendship that started Diana's dream of being in the Film World. Alan and other members of his family were persuaded by Celia to allow Diana a planned *'day-off'* every fourth week of each month. On those *'days-off'* Celia and Diana went to the Movies together. Even while she toiled away at her job, Diana's imagination kept her in the world of Movies. She and CB talked often about her dream to be a Movie Star. Each time Diana mentioned her dream and that was often, CB agreed that she had more than great potential to enable her to fulfill it. CB agreed because he was besotted by his beautiful younger partner with whom he lived.

Officially, Diana had changed her name from Diana Marie Biblethon to Dian Biblethon. In doing so, she had hoped to shake off any memories of her younger days but especially those of her cruel parents, Obediah and Rebecca. Dian Biblethon married CB a year before they emigrated from the exotic island. Theirs was a grand wedding. Dian was dressed resplendently in the traditional white wedding dress. There were four Bridesmaids. They carried the long train behind the physically beautiful, shapely, buxom bride with the *'Film Star'* looks. Dian seemed as if she was a heavenly angelic apparition just visiting in a cameo role subtly triggering the flashing cameras. The video captured her angelic countenance reflecting the pride and joy she was feeling inside. Dian had managed to attract the admiration of the curious and some jealous observers, who stared, pointed but commented about the picturesque scenery of the wedding. Friends and family members mingled but gathered together in celebration of the newly married couple. CB looked admiringly at his young bride but felt a huge sight of relief that he had managed to dissuade his bride's attention from the wily, pestering indigenous competitors. Now the ring was on her finger, CB felt they might start to *'respect'* Diana as a married woman but not flirt with her anymore, probably!

Both 'the Bogus' and the Oddballs' parents had emigrated from their *'Homelands'* in search of the jobs they thought were *'plentiful abroad'*. They tried hard to *'inspire'* their children to *'better'* themselves. "Mek yuhself inna smaddy" was a common phrase often used, in both households, to the respective child. As far as raising the quality of their lifestyles, both the Oddball and Bogus families hopes and dreams had, comparatively, been the same, though the maps of their individual lives turned out to be quite different. Amos and Dorothy's rural upbringing and cultural *'beliefs and values'* obeyed different *'life references'* to the Bogus'. They preferred an urban lifestyle in while Amos and Dorothy preferred more of a village lifestyle. While the Bogus family found it easier to adapt to the new culture and *'values and beliefs'* in the host country, Spaceville, the Oddball family did not enjoy having to sacrifice their traditional *'values and beliefs'*. Unlike Raymond's parents, Dian Bogus, chose to stay in the host country, Spaceville, instead of returning back to the far off exotic island from which she had emigrated. She commented most convincingly about her considered preference to make Spaceville her permanent home. "Mi cuddnt guh back dey, my child hav more opportunity over yah", Dian told her friends.

CHAPTER 13

Dian worked hard as an Auxiliary Nurse at the Saintly Angels Hospital in Central Greensborough. Her husband, CB worked three shifts, namely 06:00 to 14:00 hours, 14:00 to 22:00 hours and 22:00 to 06:00 hours alternate weeks at the Hover Cars Factory in Brazenborough. Dian had persuaded her husband to buy a house on mortgage in lower middle class Lower Greensborough. The wages paid by the Hover Cars Factory was not enough to pay the heavy mortgage, provide for CB's only child, Sandra, and Dian's extravagancies as well. Each week, he would find some hours to work as a mini-cab driver in upper middle class Highborough between the few hours of sleep that he afforded himself. Dian did not see it as her responsibility to do more than the weekly household shopping from her wages. The rest she tucked away for a *"rainy day"*. In their relationship, CB maintained a more docile role than Dian. She dictated the priorities in their home. Being 17 years older than her, CB privately feared that he might lose his buxom *'film star'* looking wife with the voluptuous shape to a more handsome younger man. CB recalls the times when he and Dian met some of his work colleagues at the local supermarket in Lower Greensborough. He never told Dian but he had noticed how his colleagues looked at her. Their reaction had warned him that he was looking much more like an older brother than her husband. CB had heard the quips at the factory from work colleagues about their perception of Dian's looks and shape. The whispers sometimes made him so angry. CB felt like exploding but he kept his cool all the same. He was insecure about his retaining Dian's interest but became quite jealous. In the far off exotic island from which Dian had emigrated, competitors had contested lyrically, materially and most times physically for her attention. There, it had become like a hunting game where the hunter does anything in order to capture the quarry notwithstanding risking getting caught by the snares that they themselves might have set. Once trapped, it was quite possible that the hunter then became the hunted. Diana, as she was known then, played innocent but most of the time had teased and encouraged her suitors that she was *'fair game'*. Such were the contradictions which surrounded but drove this particular relationship between CB and Dian. She had not been involved in any previous relationship apart from a singular fleeting enforced encounter with the gardener when she worked for the Cactus'. Diana, as she was known then, had noticed how much the gardener seemed to be attracted to her. She teased and tantalized him but every time he got close, Diana ignored him deliberately. She listened to but heard the flirtatious comments he'd been making whenever she was within earshot. Diana often sidled up to the gardener but brushed against him deliberately. She even allowed him to hug her but then she asked him if he thought he had what it took to win her undivided attention. The gardener wanted more than just being able to hug her occasionally. On more than one occasion, Diana increased the stakes in this high risk game she was playing with the gardener. She would ask him to accompany her to the bus stop when she finished work. At times she would kiss him on his forehead as a sign of appreciation but his imagination was now being viewed from his perspective. On a particular day when the Cactus' were away, the gardener had forcefully grabbed but pinned Diana to the ground. As he lay on top of her, she could sense his anxiety as his rough trembling hands navigated their way over her body. One groped her right breast while the other found its way under her dress; eagerly trying to rip her knickers/panties off. All this time his sweaty face and the stench of his foul breathe, smelling like an un-emptied cigarette ashtray, came closer to hers. He kissed her now open mouth. Diana tried to resist but was no match for the strong sinewy frame that entrapped her. Apart from the sudden grunting and jerking of his body, Diana could identify another musty smell that was different from the gardener's cigarette smelling breathe or the profusion of perspiration that flowed down his face and swarthy, frowsy seemingly unwashed body. It was when she felt dampness on her thigh that the gardener relented. Just as quickly as he had assaulted her, he arose. Diana not only saw the wet patch on the front of his trousers but also his embarrassment. She laughed at the gardener's demise but taunted him by commenting negatively towards his effort. "You shouldn't take on what you can't manage", Diana jibed. She was not sure whether the stupefied look on the gardener's face represented a twisted sense of attempting to live his fantasy, the disappointment of his failure to penetrate her because of his premature ejaculation or the embarrassment in spite of it. During the ordeal, it seemed to the gardener he had trapped her for hours but in reality it was a matter of but a few moments. Diana's dominance in the relationship between her and CB grew from the encounter with the gardener so many years ago. It taught her how vulnerable men were to her physical attributes. Diana had learnt so much about inflicting humiliation upon the *'Alpha'* male, who was careless enough to expose any frailty about their submission towards her beauty. Her flirtatious moments manifested into a quest to tease, tantalize or torment the likes of self-confessed *'romantic addicts'*, like CB, to her magical presence. His seemingly erstwhile desire to hold on to his woman, because of his fantasies about Dian's *'film star'* physique and looks, made CB seem weak rather than thoughtful. He had *'captured'* the young Diana but took her to his lair. CB was unaware that Diana's willingness to move in with him was one of convenience only. Part of her attraction to him was the fact that he was older. She saw his being older as a sign of perceived maturity and security. Diana sought solace from both financial and physical perspectives. Culturally, she was driven by a given set of deeply misguided cultural *'values and beliefs'* which rendered Diana's naive commitment to believing that CB was the ideal *'Trophy Man'* physical specimen of *'Mr. Right'*. His muscle bound body befitted the tall athletic image that can be found in virtually all the mythical teachings (programming) and folklore throughout the virtual parallel planet of Asteroidia. Legend had it that the perceived image of the ideal *'Mr Right'* was the one any woman needed to enable her to feel secure, apparently! In the exotic continents, countries and islands, other myths about men fed into the cultural psyche of those women, who chose to believe in them. Women, like Diana, chose to believe that men with *'fair skin'* but, particularly those with mixed DNA like CB, were considered and believed to be *'superior'* to men with melanin-induced very dark skin. Other mythical *'attributes'* like *"straighter pretty hair"* were embedded but had become a cultural *'belief'* that had been programmed and conditioned many generations long before Diana was even conceived. The validation of the mentality behind the myth that *"straighter or curly hair"* was of *"superior quality"* to the texture of men with *'lamb's wool'* type hair; as quoted in 'Songs of Solomon' in the Bible, had been passed onto every generation over previous millennia and would carry on beyond the present one, probably! CB's light green coloured eyes, were accepted as being *"more attractive and powerful"* than Dian's own brown eyes. Thin-bridged noses were yet another folklore that reinforced the myth about *"high class breeding"*. All of these subservient embedded programming and conditioning had attracted Diana to CB. In fact, he had met very little resistance when he first approached her. Like most women from the Tribe of Hawke, these women often drooled over men with a certain build and *"high class breeding"*, like CB's, seemingly! Because of that type of egoist mindset, women like Diana were *'switched on'* but experienced an intense overheated orgasmic state they refer to as *'crush'*, in the presence of men like CB. He was considered an eligible *'catch'* that the women determined made him qualify as their *'ideal partner'* to sire their children. Diana offered little or no resistance when CB first approached her. She was feeling even more secure when she learnt that he was a qualified engineer by trade notwithstanding his locally infamous reputation of being a Record Producer also. This was a time that Diana was convinced that *'The Heavenly State'* was not to be entered only via the church but that God could and had provided her with *'fast-track answers'* to each of her individual prayers. Diana had prayed silently both night and day to be liberated from her cruel parents, Obediah and Rebecca as well as the cruel Cactus' but more than all she believed that God had provided her *'ideal'* man too.

Unlike CB introverted characteristic, Diana was clearly extroverted. For the most part, she was more likely to be emotionally insensitive to others needs over her own; especially CB's. Diana grew even more knowledgeable about the *'crush'* that he had on her. She played with his one-sided loyalty. Living in Lower Greensborough, Dian had come to learn how to trap her husband into saying *"yes"* to her next extravagant adventure. She knew not only when but also how to tame her honest husband. The reality was that Constantino Bogus, CB, had married a perennially physically beautiful woman, the then Diana Biblethon, whom he boasted looked like a *'Movie Star'*. CB was not only permanently entranced and obsessed by her stunning physical beauty but often commented how her figure was a constant reminder of his vision of his *"Exotic Mona Lisa"*. He carried her picture in his wallet all the time. It was an instant reminder of what *he was missing* while he slaved away at the extra jobs he had to do to keep up with Dian's incessant unreasonable demands. The other picture CB carried with him was that of his *'wonder'* child, Sandra. He and Dian saw her as *"a gift from God"*. Dian was a healthy woman but had seemed *'unable to become pregnant'*. She had told CB that she wanted to try the new 'IVF Sperm Bank' Treatment. Privately though, she believed in but deliberately sought a *'surrogate'* father to sire her baby. This idea of *'surrogacy'* was being flouted around in the media and being further embedded into women like Dian's mind via promotional adverts. Like everything new, the idea seemed appropriate for some women, who aspired to become pregnant the way nature had planned it rather than via *'unnatural'* sourcing. It did mean that fostering and adopting were no longer optional priorities and that the population of orphans would increase massively but no one would want to take away the joy of birth from any mother. Just when it seemed as if traditional relationships were being replaced by the new technological scientific *'miraculous'* advancement, the 'IVF Sperm Bank Treatment', another route of impregnation was being conjured by the poly-tricksters. For the women, who chose not to immediately latch on to the 'IVF Sperm Bank Treatment' route, the poly-tricksters had advanced yet another money-spinner. This was another *'Win/Win'* scenario if ever there was one but for whom! The *'Adultery'* Commandment was being given short shrift. It was relegated to being *"just an incidental biblical reference"* only. Instead of saying "thou shalt not commit adultery", it was now legal and *'politically correct'* to say *"thou shall go forth and sew thy wild seed with much gusto and purpose for the benefit of our financial abundance"*. These new *'gods'* openly defied the biblical commandment but were making a statement that it was prudent to *'blaspheme'* with impunity as long as it was profitable, maybe! In Spaceville, polygamy had been resurrected but was rife once again and being *'legally'* encouraged too. Women, like Dian, accepted that the men they chose to sire their *'surrogate'* children could sew their wild seeds with freedom and blessing under the protection of the law.

On the subject of IVF and *'Human Surrogacy'*, no controversial input against the *'profitable trend'* was being encouraged nor tolerated by the producers from the stage-managed umpteen *'Talk Shows'* on radio or television about the subject. Programme Presenters, with heavily partisan producers, gave specific instructions to their switchboards and technological monitors. Their orders were to deflect or block any other approach, argument or perspective than what they wanted their captive audiences to perceive as being the *'majority consensus'* of opinions which represented the population of Spaceville and the rest of the Royal Royal Dis-United Stately Kingdoms of Asteroidia. This type of monitoring and screening was more prevalent than the population of Spaceville or the rest of the virtual parallel planet was aware of. Politically contrived Jingoism was what those producers incited in order to justify their nullification of any other arguments in the *'one-sided debates'*. The producers engineered the statistics artificially but presented their *'politically correct'* ruse as being genuinely *'patriotically'* very heavily in favour of the *'status quo'*. It was easy for producers to manipulate those programmes but never engaged in genuine debates to present a genuinely balanced set of arguments. According to their remit, political bias or personal one-sided arbitrary cultural *'values and beliefs'*, the presenters, producers and their programme makers had invented a format that was disingenuous to the integrity of not only Spacevilleans but also the entire population of the Royal Royal Dis-United Stately Kingdoms of Asteroidia. In Spaceville, the monitoring personnel simply did what they were ordered to do. They informed the caller/contributor that *"the producer had decided that your point of view is not relevant"*. This kind of strategy was installed, driven and sponsored by the poly-tricksters whose agendas were to use the oils of compassion to massage the egos of those individuals who were in favour of surrogacy and IVF treatment. They did this in order to generate *'emotional anarchy'* against those, who dared to disagree with the programmed and conditioned *'tunnel-vision mentality'*. The seemingly patriotic clamour and backing for those *'sexual farmers'* as well as the *'purveyors and the practitioners of the sleight,* were being paid handsomely to carry out their adventurous artificial or natural *'surrogate promotions',* seemingly! There was no room afforded from any other perspectives, like scruples, moral arguments or views, to be entertained. Every window and door was slammed shut tight in the faces of those, who wanted to engage in the debates. Poly-tricksters delved even deeper into the metaphoric *'honey pots'* because there was nothing sweeter to savour than their overestimated, super-inflated, superlative egos which were focused on their insatiable dehydrated thirst for the taste of Champagne Urge.

CB was unaware of Dian's involvement in the *'surrogate saga'*. She had already been defying the "thou shall not commit adultery" commandment for some time but was frequently enjoying more than flirtatious moments with the younger men she fancied more than the amiable older CB. Whilst enjoying her freedom to commit to surrogacy, it was then that Dian had told CB about the 'IVF Sperm Bank Treatment'. She was covering her tracks in case she fell pregnant for those sires, who were seriously entranced by her mesmeric beauty. They were enough *'worker bees'* buzzing around her *'honey-pot'*. Dian was *'hot'* and she knew it. She had become ultra promiscuous. These younger men, with whom she flirted and copulated, were more virile than the exhausted CB and they chanced to use aphrodisiac stimulants that turned them into young stallions. CB was relegated to Dian's dependable financial resource but deemed as "too old" and "too eager". Dian's sexual needs were far beyond CB's capabilities or even what he could ever imagine. Her nymphomaniac tendencies had made her become careless about whom she chose as sexual partners. For well over 15 months, CB's prolonged, enforced celibacy did save him from the knowledge of Dian's exposure to PID.

When CB first learnt about Dian's arrangements to have the new technological 'IVF Sperm Bank Treatment', she left him no room for argument against her plan. He was meant to feel as if her not being able to get pregnant was his fault. Dian told him there was something wrong with his sperm but made him feel more than inadequate to father a child by natural sexual intercourse. Dian had sent him to the Urology Department in Saint Angels Hospital, where she worked, to test his sperm. The humiliation was huge for the rather shy CB. He remembered some of the nurses with whom Dian worked pointing at him but whispering among themselves. As Dian was the domineering partner in this relationship, she opened all the mail that arrived at their address. The one with the result of CB's sperm did not convey good news. He was asked to return to the hospital to furnish more sperm on three more occasions. The next time CB visited, he wanted to know why he had to give so many samples. The 'IVF Sperm Bank' personnel explained that Dian had made the requests. She wanted to make sure they had not mistaken the previous results, apparently! The Urology Department had found nothing wrong with CB's sperm. It was Dian's wretched plot to further demean the affable yet naïve CB. She told the personnel in the Urology Department that she couldn't understand that, if there was nothing wrong with CB's sperm, how come she hadn't got pregnant by him. They could not answer her question but acceded to her repetitive requests. On this occasion, CB told the personnel that he was not happy to go the *'Masturbarium Booths'* provided in order to produce sperm. He found it embarrassing. When Dian had confirmed the pregnancy, she decided to stop working. CB spent a great deal of money on private medical treatment, including a private visiting midwife, whenever Dian was home. The confirmation of a daughter via the scan had given Dian enough time to plot how she would use Sandra. Dian had long determined what her child would become even before she was born. Unlike Dian, who attracted the Media to her *'longsuffering'*, CB dressed *'incognito'* in a huge pair of dark glasses and an enormous Mexican sombrero on the day of Sandra's birth. Dian was interviewed and her *'story'* was mentioned on the front page of the local newspaper, 'The Weekly Expressionist'. Pictured with CB, Dian held Sandra aloft as directed by the newspaper photographers. It looked more like a scene from the movie 'Roots'. The headline, *'Heavenly Intervention'* was pathetic and the story being sensationally but extravagantly overplayed. According to Dian's input, the newspaper confirmed the importance of the advancement of *'technological intervention'*. Dian received a small *'lump sum'* payment for the article.

Aiming to bring into reality her unfulfilled life's ambitions, Dian aggressively targeted Sandra towards *"fame and fortune"*. In doing so, she overcompensated but began, consciously or unconsciously, to drift into re-living her *'life'* through her daughter. While growing up, Dian's singular dream was "to be a Movie Star". On the exotic island from which she had emigrated, she had shown great potential in the church community Plays in which she used to partake. Dian pushed her daughter, Sandra, into every children competition weeks after her birth. Sandra was *'Baby of the Month'* in the local Community Competition. She was only six weeks old at the time. Already having the edge over less *'experienced'* candidates, Sandra had appeared in newspapers, on boxes of oats and baby food packets. Advertisers were licking their fingers at the prospect of counting the financial profits. With pictures and adverts of babies, like Sandra, money was generated from the sales of branded products that were understood to be *"good for babies"*. By the time Sandra was two years old, modeling, ballet schools, advertising agencies, and others had composites of the *'child star'*. Sandra's smile had, apparently, caused chaos amongst the various Branded Toothpaste Producers, BTP. Their adverts alerted other subscribers to Sandra's *'Star'* qualities. Pressures built up as the popularity of the *'child star'* grew. Sandra's quick rise towards stardom influenced but persuaded other mothers. They repeated the *'rhetoric'* they were picking up from their respective agents about the importance of attending various shows in order to exhibit their babies in the various parades from which *'judges'* chose *'winners'*. Some mothers potential *'lateral'* thinking started to become tarnished but immune to sensibility. There was a rush for mothers to secure specialist agents; *"people who understood the business"*. This link would ensure that the agents remained the conduit through which advertising businesses communicated with the mothers. Professional agencies squabbled, threatened but utilized *'shady'* tactics often in order to win the right to bind Sandra to a 3 year contract. Her green humanoid robotron agent from the Tribe of Babylon was first to Dian's signature. Being aware of the competition, he simply asked her to sign the contract. She wanted to know the terms and conditions. "I need to take it home to my husband", Dian had told him. "Never mind about him, you can sign it. The company won't be too pleased about you running off to get it signed," the agent had responded. Dian felt pressured by the agent's reaction. She insisted that he give her time to read and digest the information. "That's not fair, you mean I don't get to read it before I sign", Dian queried? The agent stared at her but commented. When he did, he told Dian about the effort and inconvenience he'd put himself through to get this seemingly lucrative contract on her behalf. "Do you know how much trouble I went through to get this contract for you", the agent snapped? Dian felt guilty for putting the *"nice important man"* through any inconvenience. Though she was unhappy about the situation in which she found herself, Dian humbly apologized then signed on the *'dotted lines'* indicated to her by the agent. These types of contracts were extremely hard for individuals from Dian's ethnicity to secure, apparently! It was a *"once in a lifetime"* opportunity the agent had led her to believe.

Mothers, like Dian, didn't see it as *'auctioning'* their children to the highest bidders. She, and mothers like her, touted their children from venue to venue where *'baby models'* were being examined for their *'photogenic'* qualities. Sandra's popularity was being spread via the various campaigns. Some others were becoming envious about her success. They perceived that their lack of opportunity was due to Sandra's rise in attracting the attention of the influential investors. This was becoming evident but showed in the negative feedback that Dian was receiving from some of her competitors. At one particular gathering, Dian was awaiting instructions from the agent when an apparently envious parent attention to Dian and her friends. "Oui you, I want a word with you", the green humanoid woman's voice bellowed. She walked hurriedly but directly towards where Dian was standing. Her friends sensed the imminent threat in the way the woman was approaching Dian. They urged her to walk on but she stood her ground. Dian could see the onlookers gathering. Everyone was observing how briskly the woman was striding towards her. They anticipated a *'bust-up'* between Dian and the green humanoid woman from the Tribe of Babylon with the *'ponytail'* hairstyle. She was now about six feet away when she started her onslaught on Dian. The woman's venomous expletives were structured, not only to irritate but also to get under the skin of the receiver. "Why did you have to turn up", the woman with ponytail asked? Surprised by the attack, Dian countered. "What do you mean", she asked? "Couldn't you miss just one competition? Give us *'others'* a chance, couldn't you", the woman with ponytail parried? Dian was rather taken aback by the woman's negative attitude. Sandra was upset from the shouting around her. She tried to say something but no words came out. Dian was much too aroused now to notice. All her attention had been drawn away from Sandra to this irritating distraction. Intimidated by the woman's threatening behaviour, Dian snapped back at the woman. "What's it got to do with you in which contest I enter my child", she asked? Dian couldn't have been quite sure what answer would satisfy her but she was angry enough to want to defend herself and her child's right to be there. Suddenly, the woman with the *'ponytail'* openly tried to snatch Sandra away from Dian's grasp. Some of her friends came back to stand by her side. "No way", Dian shouted. She pulled

Sandra behind her but, with clenched fists, approached the woman. Dian snarled but swung a punch at the woman. The blow connected with the woman's jaw. "You bitch", the woman with ponytail squealed. She retreated but held her jaw. Then, as if spurred on by the blow, she came forward again but tried to grab Dian by her hair. She warded off the offending hand. Both women grappled each other like wrestlers. The two women snarled, hissed and swore volumes of *'un-printable quotes'*. They struggled and tussled but neither could get a clean blow in. The women shouted abuse at each other and clawed their way unto the ground. Quite a crowd had now gathered to see the spectacle. Audience participation was high. Some encouraged, some condemned but some others were animated into motion. One overexcited onlooker punched the man next to him but swiftly apologised. "Sorry", the male onlooker said. "Don't do it again, though", the other man warned. Ringed around the competitors, the crowd became even more excited. Dian was the fitter of the two feuding women. She sat atop the woman with the *'ponytail'*, uttering words of admonishment while she punched out her anger. "My madda sey, nuh mek nubaddy beat mi", Dian kept repeating. Her accent had changed to her native language. No longer was she speaking with *'grammatical correctness'* but instead in a language that had long been spun to be *'politically incorrect'*. The significant crowd was *'enjoying'* the action but had split themselves into two distinct groups. One group sided with Dian while another sided with the woman with the *'ponytail'*. When she was in control of the fight there was shouts of, "go on" or "bastard" by her supporters. When Dian took control of the fight there were shouts of, "yes" and "give it to her good, sister". Either way, all the children were involuntary witnesses to an event they did not chose to attend. There had to be some explanation to the lunacy that took place at a competition for children. It was only when a voice shouted "cut" that everyone realized that filming was taking place. "That's fine. I think we've got everything", the voice of the green humanoid robotron director interrupted. They had all been part of a filming that surprised everyone. The crowd started to buzz with a new excitement but Dian demanded that her agent "sort this whole thing out". "I didn't sign a contract to do a film, did I", Dian insisted? "You did", the agent said calmly. Before anyone else could say anything, the director spoke. "The new advert is quite innovative. It wants to portray many real life situations on screen", he stated. "I wasn't told about that when I signed the contract", Dian insisted. "You should have read the fine prints", the agent warned. There was a dry tone to his words. A few moments passed before either spoke again. "Anyway, you and your girl are the stars of this advert. What have you got to complain about? Cheer up, enjoy it and welcome to the world of the *'big times'*", the agent stated. His voice was chirpy. He was smiling now and looking quite excited. Dian was still angry at not being informed properly but somehow the mention of stardom, for Sandra, pacified her a little. "Do we get movie rights too", Dian pressed? "We can all look forward to the fat cheques in the post each quarter", the agent added. "Every three months", Dian quizzed? "Most definitely", the agent confirmed. The woman with the *'ponytail'* came over to Dian, but apologized. She told Dian that she was an actor. The woman hugged Dian but wished her and Sandra good luck.

Dian truly loved her daughter, apparently, but believed wholeheartedly that she was doing the *'rite ting'* for her 'San San', as she preferred to call Sandra. Doing the "rite ting" was a kind of philosophy sought after but practiced by most parents from the far off exotic lands. They were not the originators of such philosophies and practices but they soon adapted to vying for such activities to which they considered the "rite ting". Each had learnt but copied from the other. Most of Dian's colleagues and friends entered their children in similar competitions too. They hoped that the *"fame and papilarity"* would be a start to a *better future* for their children. Previous experience of hardship had taught these parents harsh *'lessons'* about the state of being without sufficient monetary stability. These parents from the far off exotic lands did not want their children to have the same type of negative experiences they had endured. *'Proceeds'* from competitions and contracts were astutely managed by these parents. Many, like Dian, opened bank accounts for their children but planned to provide them with the *'surprise package'* when they reached young adulthood. It was meant to give those children a "start in life". Even when their efforts were portrayed as genuine, none of the parents involved thought of any consequence at the time. Most saw their efforts as creative opportunities to help bridge the financial *'gap'* for the next generation, so to speak. None wanted to be outdone or left behind. Some others specialized in certain areas like *'Ballet'* while others went from one activity to another, relentlessly. It became an obsession to individuals like Dian. She treaded in the footsteps of many others before her. Each individual sought to exploit *ways* of gaining financial stability for them and their children. "Wi hafe mek sure wi children get di bes", those mothers exclaimed. At six months old, Sandra had appeared in newspapers, on boxes of Oats and Baby Food packets. By the age of seven Dian had relaxed Sandra's hair but plastered her with *'make-up'*. "Yuh haffe inna di fashion child, oddawise yuh caan win di contest", Dian assured her daughter. At eight, Sandra was the star performer at the local Carnival. It was a hot sunny summer's day when dozens of families strolled around aimlessly, while the children ran about playing happily. Sandra could only watch but not join in the fun. She was not allowed to join the other children in case she "ruined the *'make-up'*" and the costume Dian had bought her for the Carnival. Dian didn't wish to be cruel but focused only on Sandra's appearance "in front of the Judges". At eleven, Dian Bogus sent Sandra to a school in Upper Highborough, not only because she wanted her to attend a Grammar School but also to have the opportunity to rise above the mediocre standard offered by the local Community School in Lower Greensborough, where Sandra's true friends attended. Dian didn't have any idea what kind of impact her forceful way was having on the naive Sandra. This new school and these new *'friends'* were having more negative influence on Sandra than Dian or her husband CB, were aware.

Dian Bogus was a domineering woman, who wanted her daughter to have everything; even those things which were *unnecessary* sometimes. She spoilt Sandra by doing everything for her instead of letting her have her own experiences. Dian did not encourage Sandra in the kitchen as most of the people from the exotic continents, countries and islands. Whenever Sandra offered to wash the dishes or wanted to help to make the *dumplings,* Dian would find a reason to object. One of those reasons was her visual recall of her own shriveled hands when she had worked for the Cactus'. "Yuh wi ruin yuh hands", Dian told Sandra repeatedly. CB was more than grateful for his daughter. He doted on her. CB told his friends that he'd do as many jobs as he could to guarantee enough funds "for Sandra's education and welfare". Both he and Dian were totally in unwavering agreement on that issue and Sandra was made aware of that fact since she was young. Dian had sought out and chosen the typical institutional religious grammar school for Sandra to attend. Saint Halo High Apostolic Grammar School in Upper Highborough, Suburbia was perceived as the ideal type of school for the naturally bright students. Its *'pass rate'* was in the high 90s. There were many parents, who wanted their children to go there. Dian was a bright student herself but, because of *'political bias'* in her home country, she was denied the opportunity to go to a grammar school. As far as Dian was concerned, she wanted her child to have the best. It is what Sandra was afforded. Dian Bogus' *'indoctrination'* easily diluted but more importantly superseded any perceptions young Sandra might have had for herself. She was ambitious for her daughter. Dian was typical of some parents who, seemingly having failed to fulfill their own *'needs'*, injected their *'renaissance'* through their children instead. Her intentions were well meant but Dian's methodology might have been causative to ruining Sandra's life. Because of her *'phobia'*, Dian drilled her daughter into *'airs'* and *'graces'* that were both estranged to her own traditional values but unsuitably too synthetic in context compared to her original cultural background.

CB was a dutiful father and husband. That was all Dian thought of the dedicated man she'd married but never failed to tell him how much she loved him when it was convenient for her to do so. Dian knew not only when but also how to taunt her *'honest'* husband. Her *'film star'* looks were not her only *'assets'*, but was the *'first'* attraction to the mild-mannered CB. Dian had *'style'*, a stunning figure and she knew how to use it to rouse his inner feelings. All the time Dian had been two-timing her husband for a long time but maybe he would never have guessed. She played with CB's acceptance that she was young and needed to go out with friends of her own age. Sometimes, CB suspected that Dian might have felt tempted to be in the company of younger men but he dared not comment in case she threw one of her tantrums. CB was more than aware that it might mean him going without sexual activity for however long Dian decided to punish him for his transgression if he dared even joke about such a thing. Instead, he threw himself into any other odd jobs he could find to earn money. When he was still living in the exotic island, CB had abandoned the engineering job but fulfilled his own dream of becoming a skilled carpenter. That was before he returned to the country of his birth. CB surmised that there was demand for his type of work in Spaceville but he never managed to secure a full time job in either engineering or carpentry.

Dian never really loved CB but instead settled with him because he was *'steady'* and a hard worker, who complied with her every demand. Each year she *'ordered'* CB to have the outside of the house repainted, change the front door, completely re-decorate the inside, re-carpet the entire house, replace the entire household contents and buy her a new car. This did not depend on the state of these things but merely a perennial *'exercise'*. When CB challenged the justification of such seemingly waste of funds, Dian went into a strop but commented. "CB, we have to keep modern", she preached. She had her own *process* for exacting fresh financial resources from her hard-working husband. CB suffered many nights of *'discomfiture'*. At times, Dian would lure him into bed, teased by sidling up and lying close to him. She seduced him until he'd begin to *'lose control'*. Dian would then choose the *'right'* moment to turn away from CB's amorous advances. "Stop CB, I don't want to" or "not tonight CB, I have a headache", Dian often told him. The agony would often make the normally cool CB comment about the *'torture'* he was going through. "Dian, you're not being fair. I'm a human being. I need a little loving like others do", he would say. Dian would kiss his lips tenderly but turn away from him. She'd smile though he couldn't see. He'd snuggle up to her tightly to let her realize how aroused he'd become. "I'm your husband. Don't I have a right to feel the way I do", CB would ask? "Try counting sheep and drift off to sleep. The feeling will go away", Dian often replied. While the sarcasm sunk into CB's wounded pride, Dian would then wriggle away from his arms. She knew the next few moments would be CB's weakest. Dian was confident that her husband would react the same way every time. She waited with baited breath until CB spoke. Dian had this act to such precise timing. His words would come out at that precise moment. Dian mouthed his synchronized response on cue while her back was turned to him. "What can I buy you to take your headache away, darling", CB would plead? Now Dian would sink her metaphorical talons in a bit deeper into his flesh. "Oh, you want to buy me something, darling? Is that a promise", Dian asked? "I've got some extra jobs that have been waiting for a while now. I'll find the time to get them done", CB would reply. Dian would turn around, hug him but encourage CB to lie on top of her. She would feel his excitement but knew at this point he was more of a sprinter than an endurance athlete. Once CB's volcano had erupted, Dian would be aware his *'heat'* had subsided. She'd allow him to fall asleep where he lay. Conversely, Dian used another tactic when she was on heat. She would literally rape CB when it suited her but if he was too tired to respond, Dian would often accuse him of *'sleeping around'*. CB's reply was always the same. "When would I have time to go sleeping around and with whom", CB: asked? Dian's merciless demands led to many heated arguments between them, all of which CB lost to Dian. She would orchestrate the mood before physically abusing the mild mannered CB. While thumping him repeatedly in the chest with both hands, Dian would often comment. "You're no good to me if you can't satisfy my needs", Dian would taunt. "You're not being reasonable. I am just coming off a heavy shift. I'm simply tired", CB would parry. Dian would then start stamping her feet like a naughty child; throwing not only tantrums but objects around the room. On one particular occasion, CB ducked just in time. The vase with flowers still attached smashed against the bedroom wall. "You're going to wake up our daughter. What will she think of us", CB asked? Dian decided to twist the metaphorical knife. "Are you sure she's your daughter", she mocked? Dian knew what the result of such a cutting remark would do to her husband. It felled the normally laid back CB. For a moment he couldn't speak at all but felt this strange pressure welling up inside his head and chest. He was aware that his heart had stopped beating for a few moments. CB was so angry he could not respond with the words that his mind wanted to say. He was aware that his mouth had opened and closed several times but no sound emanated from him. CB started to shake like a frozen mountaineer at wintertime without shelter on the top of the Himalayas. The rage had made him as without feelings but his eyes bulged from their sockets like a mouse whose head got trapped trying to reach for the cheese. All this time, Dian kept sewing more doubts not only to CB's ability to be sexually active but also to his virility as well. This was one step too far. CB collapsed like a broken branch from a tree that had been struck by lightning. There was no bending at the jointed areas, instead CB just toppled forwards like a wooden statue until he hit the floor. He started convulsing. The spasms were irregular but CB was foaming at the mouth. The noise further disturbed

Sandra, the anxious child, who had long since had her ears pressed up against the door listening to her mother questioning her father's performance. Dian stepped over CB's fitting body but went towards the door. She hissed like the snake she was but murmured that she could get her satisfaction elsewhere. As Dian pulled the door open, Sandra fell onto the floor in front of her. "Oh my God, Sandra, what are you doing out of bed", Dian asked? She had been too obsessed with her own needs to realize how loud the quarrel had been. Dian reached down to pick up her daughter but Sandra shied away from her; recoiling as if Dian's touch might just render her unclean. "Don't be frightened San-San, daddy is only having a fit", Dian offered. The comment was delivered with such casualness that it seemed inappropriately cold and insensitive towards the afflicted CB. Having not had any previous experience of witnessing her dad in such precarious situation, Sandra started to think of the worst scenario. Amid the verbal exchanges, she had figured that her parents were not only having a disagreement but having heard the vase crash against the wall determined that some physical exchanges might have taken place. Sandra was unsure how her dad ended up on the floor but challenged her mother as to what outcome might be expected. "Is daddy going to die mommy", Sandra asked? The tears rolled down her face and she could not control the bellowing that followed. "Your daddy has always suffered from 'fits', even before you were born. He'll soon be alright", Dian said. This did not reassure the nervous Sandra. After all, she was a *'daddy's girl'*. It was clear to Dian now, even more so, than Sandra had ever shown before. CB stopped fitting but raised himself enough to sit up. He had a stupefied look upon his face. CB didn't seem to remember falling. "What am I doing down here", he asked? Sandra ran towards him. "Daddy, daddy, why are you on the floor? Are you alright", she asked? Sandra hugged him tightly while he sat on the floor. Dian left the room. When she returned she had changed from her negligee into street clothing. "Look after Sandra until I come back", Dian said. "Where are you going mommy", Sandra asked? "San-San I'm going to get some fresh air. Mommy needs it", Dian lied. With that, she walked towards the front door. It slammed shut. Both CB and Sandra could hear the car roar off into the early morning. It was 03:20 hours when Dian left.

CB had worked too many inconvenient shifts, which effectively meant that he didn't see too much of his daughter. He loved her dearly and would defy illness and adverse weather conditions to attend "di lickle job", as he often referred to it. "CB, Sandra waan anada pair of shoes fi match di yellow dress yuh buy har las week. Di Modelling Competition is nex Saturday", Dian demanded. CB complained about feeling extraordinarily tired. He told Dian he was feeling much too weak to even get out of bed but she showed no empathy for the normally consistent workaholic. During the week leading up to the fatal day CB and Dian had quarrelled frequently about the extra money she had demanded. "Ah fi yuh pickney, git up, guh ah wuk, bout yuh sick", Sandra had heard her say. To enable him to buy his daughter yet another pair of fashion shoes even though she had *twelve* good pairs at the time, CB worked *'overtime'* yet again. He collapsed from severe exhaustion at the Hover Cars factory but could not be resuscitated. Sandra lost her father and Dian her husband CB. He died with Dian's cruel dig that had planted the seeds of doubt whether Sandra was his child or not. She looked more like Dian than him but CB treated Sandra as his own. What Dian didn't know on the night she had delivered that mind-shattering blow was that CB had died wondering how many children would be sired by him, via the 'Sperm Bank' posthumously! Was Dian inseminated with his sperm? These questioning thoughts, together with severe distress from Dian's emotional insensitivity, had raised CB's *'stress'* level and subsequent abnormal high blood pressure but was causative to his heart attack.

CHAPTER 14

Trendy, curvy, tall, beautiful, but unpredictable, are a few of the words Raymond Oddball used whenever he had the opportunity to describe his girlfriend, Sandra Bogus. Raymond had a crush on her the moment he saw her and was happy that Sandra liked him too. When she walked, her lithe, sleek, slender frame reminded Raymond of a tall wispy tree swaying gently in the wind. Sandra was neat, intelligent but intrinsically motivated to be successful! Her ambition was to be rich. She longed for the life that she had seen in the Soap Opera DVD, *'RJ Sallad'*. Sandra used to watch it when she was younger with her mother. They never missed an episode. The story was about living life at the 'Top'. Dreams of awesome financial power, celebrity connections, cocktail parties, cruises, palm beaches and the kind of status that would keep her in the limelight eternally is all Sandra wanted from life. Nothing else could pacify that dehydrated thirst for the taste of Champagne Urge which haunted her day and night. This limelight *'charade'* attached then hooked itself onto the underside of Sandra's psyche. Its diffusion layered her whole inner being but sharpened her awareness to the ladder of opportunities that could lead to the achievements of her dream. Layer by layer, Sandra planned the foundation to a lifestyle that always seem to constantly loiter while she was awake but kept recurring even while she was in the slumberous state of sleep. Striving to be rich was at the core of her psyche. It remained the central focus of her existence.

Raymond was besotted by his woman's physical beauty and was internally obsessive whenever he saw her *'flirting'* with other young men. They had met at Coleport College. Their magnetic attraction, sheer impulsive, commonplace *lust* started in a most peculiar way. One day, whilst they were in the college canteen, Raymond was trying to avoid being scalded by a spilt cup of hot tea. Sandra was standing in the queue behind him at the time. Raymond trod on Sandra's toes, accidentally. Maybe it was just sheer embarrassment or Raymond's empathy for her situation that brought them together. Realizing what he had done, Raymond swiftly turned around to apologize but when he opened his mouth nothing came out. He tried again and again but the sound of the words he was trying to say could still not be heard. Mesmerized by Sandra's physical beauty, Raymond found himself staring deeply into her large cornflower blue eyes. Those eyes didn't seem to befit her deep black melanin body but heightened the mystique which had started to manifest in his mind. The pleasantly shocked surprised Raymond was not only deeply intrigued but also entrancingly fascinated by his chance discovery. He perceived that Sandra might be wearing contact lenses. This only drew him deeper into those mysterious eyes. As he tried to fathom whether her eyes were natural, all sorts of exciting thoughts encompassed his brain. Raymond's heart was pounding with excitement and anticipation. He thought of all the things he'd come to believe about the stereotypical *'Mrs. Right'*. The common folklore was being confirmed by Sandra's physical attributes but Raymond cannot remember any mention of the colour of eyes. Now that he was close to this outstandingly beautiful young woman, Raymond had already decided he wanted her to be his girlfriend. Sandra scanned Raymond's athletic build but sensed all his musculature wrapped around her body. She felt her heart skip not just one but several beats. Sandra was aware of her pulse racing at a pace she'd not experienced before. She knew then that she wanted to get close to Raymond. Both seemed to have entered into a trance-like stare; whilst trying to express verbally how they felt for each other. Tears were flowing from the ailing Sandra's eyes but she was unaware of their existence. There was something about the way these two people were looking at each other that told its own story. Sandra bent down to remove the shoe to examine her bruised foot. Raymond stooped to help her. He could see where his foot had left the bruise. Raymond tried once again to apologize but the words still failed to come out. Now that he was closer to Sandra, Raymond's heart was racing even more; thudding against his chest like repetitive waves against a wall. He sensed that Sandra wanted him to be closer to her. Raymond was tempted greatly by Sandra's neat mouth and even smile. A bolt of lightning surged through his body and without preamble, Raymond found himself leaning forwards helplessly. He kissed Sandra lightly on her cheek then put his muscular arm around her slender waist but helped her into a standing position. On impact, there were several volts of electricity that passed through Sandra's body too. The tingling sensations rendered her helpless in Raymond's strong arm. For those moments they both forgot about their environment but stood like long lost lovers in the middle of the canteen floor. Some mischievous students cleared their throats deliberately hinting at the couple. Sandra allowed Raymond to support her towards a chair. "Sit down ... I'll get some ice", Raymond told her. Sandra liked the way Raymond was fussing over her predicament but she wondered why he had kissed her. "Why did you kiss me", Sandra asked him directly? "I was just trying to make up for the damage I'd done", Raymond said genuinely. "Did I say you could kiss me", Sandra asked? "Well no ... but ..." Raymond's voice tailed off. Suffering huge embarrassment, he ventured to put things right between them. Not only did Raymond bruise Sandra's foot with his size 14s but he also kissed her without being invited by her to do so. He was feeling a bit of a fool. Raymond was wondering why he'd lost control of himself. "Can I make it up to you", Raymond asked? "How are you going to do that", Sandra retorted? "I'll take you to dinner if you let me. Will you", Raymond pressed? As if someone had unhinged her jaws, Sandra sat open mouth for some moments. She felt herself come over faint. Quite a few observers were interested in what was happening between the two individuals. They weren't whispering but speaking in excitable tones. It was clear that the chemistry between the two individuals were mixing quite well. Raymond and Sandra were having more than just a casual chat. Both of them heard the comments from others but they didn't seem to care. "Oh, please say yes", Raymond insisted. Regaining her composure a little, Sandra tried to play hard to get but inside she had already decided to accept Raymond's invitation to the proposal for dinner. All the same, she tried once more to appear unsure. "With you ... but I don't even know you", Sandra teased. "You could get to if you really wanted to", Raymond pleaded. She stared at Raymond up and down. "You must think I'm an easy target ... maybe I've already got someone ... maybe your girlfriend wouldn't approve", Sandra jousted. "I have female friends but I don't have a steady girl friend. What about you, have you got a boy friend", Raymond countered? Sandra did not reply but smiled wryly at him. One of the students who were taking interest into Raymond and Sandra's public courting was Samish Galango. He had previously sized up the beautiful Sandra. It was exactly three weeks to the day when Samish met the beautiful Sandra. It was raining on that day. Sandra had an umbrella but began to walk towards the canteen. Samish was getting ready to negotiate the fifty yard sprint to the canteen when he noticed that Sandra had the umbrella. He asked if he could share the umbrella with her over the distance. She said yes. Samish was immediately smitten by her unusual piercing cornflower blue eyes. He said as much but Sandra was used to people commenting so much so that she began to feel like a bit of a *freak* by the frequency of comments. Samish was no different and the look of astonishment on his face was about on par with the others. Even the lecturers commented about the colur of her eyes. Sandra seemed always to have to explain that her dad, CB, was third generation mixed DNA descendant. His eyes were light green but not as piercing as Sandra's. Because her skin colour was as dark as her mother's but she inherited her eye colour through her father's genes, Sandra couldn't understand why all the fuss. One lecturer assumed they were contact lenses but asked her to remove them as she was distracting the other students. It didn't matter how many times she explained it, there was always someone else that wanted to know. Since that time Samish Galango had an obsession with trying to date the beautiful Sandra but to no avail. He was determined for her to be his girl. Now he made a play to dissuade her from accepting Raymond's proposal. "What about me taking you to dinner instead", Samish chimed? Sandra looked up but smiled at him. Samish was a handsome young man too but Sandra didn't get the same feeling for him as she did for Raymond. He was much taller and bigger in physique than Samish. Raymond fitted Sandra's stereotypical '*Mr. Right*' ideology. She could sense that something was brewing. Sandra looked at Raymond and then at Samish. The cold stares that passed between them needed no words. It was like sitting in the Coliseum awaiting the fate of the two gladiators. The onlookers wanted to see the action and so they egged on the two young men to do battle. By now, mobile phones were used to spread the word and before long there was standing room only inside the canteen. Raymond and Samish squared up to each other. Forehead to forehead the two young men, like two Rhinos in the wild, vied to establish their authority. Neither gave an inch. With their oversized trousers hanging just below their bum cheeks, the two highly testosterone young adolescents sneered but tried to gain ground from each other. There was chanting of "fight, fight, fight" from the eager observers who wanted to see more action but Raymond and Samish pressed even harder for space. Up to then, the two young men were trading the usual short forms of communication. "What", one asked? The other repeated the same word in a more aggressive manner. "What"? This was repeated several times and began to sound like two individuals without much more to their vocabulary. Both were sweating profusely as if each had just completed a half marathon. The crowd continued to inveigle the two individuals even more. "Who's he, punch him", a voice prompted. The rest of the baying crowd made their suggestions too. Some of which indicated that things were getting a bit more serious than when it first started. "If she was my girl, I'd mash his face", another voice commented. "This is foolish. I'm not a prize", Sandra pleaded. She tried desperately to stop them but they wouldn't even listen to her. The canteen staff shouted at them from behind the counter but neither Samish nor Raymond could hear them. Even the thunder that rolled heavily, announcing the inevitable bad weather that was brewing up outside, was not heard by the raging combatants. Raymond took the first step to command authority. He raised his hands but pushed Samish in his chest. It was quite sudden but caught Samish unaware. He stumbled backwards but he didn't fall. The crowd pushed him forwards towards the advancing Raymond. They grappled like wrestlers inside the human ring that surrounded them. Both were grunting almost as loudly as the rolling thunder. Raymond was the taller and bulkier of the two young combatants but Samish was a street fighter. His techniques were not as polished as Raymond's though his efforts were as determined to impart pain on his opponent. Sandra saw when Samish brought his knee up into Raymond's groin. She heard him groan as contact was made. He let Samish go but reached him with a martial art punch to the chest that sent him sprawling onto the floor. The crowd was enjoying the action. "Fight, fight, fight" the crowd chanted. Both men needed time to recover from the respective blows they had received. Raymond was the first to move again. This time he moved forward swiftly but intended to crush the fallen Samish but he managed to roll swiftly away from Raymond's intended kick. The crowd, excited by the skill of both men, begged for more. "More, more, more", the crowd bayed. They sounded more like a crowd watching a bullfight encouraging the matador to kill the bull. Encouraged by the cries, Samish managed to get to his feet. He reached into the front of his baggy jeans where he carried his knife. Raymond saw Samish's hand go inside the jeans but didn't give him any time to withdraw his weapon. Samish received three rapid blows to his chest. It was like watching the infamous Bruce Lee perform. Raymond's rapid blows happened too quickly for Samish to take shelter. He coughed, spluttered then spat a reddish fluid from his mouth. Samish's contorted face told its own story about the pain he was feeling. His knees buckled then he fell, face first, onto the canteen floor. "Did you see that", one young man asked? He looked at Raymond who now stood over his fallen foe, Samish. The knock out blows had silenced the crowd too. One could hear a pin drop had it not been for the repetitive sound of thunder which added the background sound effect. Gradually, the crowd started to disperse, each casting a final glance towards the figure on the floor. It was clear that Raymond was a martial arts specialist. There was no mistaking his superior technique during the combat for Sandra. She sat with her head hung, staring at the floor. Raymond was heaving heavily from the exhaustive efforts he'd expanded. The canteen staff rushed out from behind the counter to attend to Samish. He lay on the floor; his neck resting at an awkward angle. His breathing was shallow and irregular but he was still alive. The staff tried to reassure Samish. They told him that they had called for an ambulance. Raymond made his way over towards Sandra. He put his arms around her. "Why did you have to fight with Samish", Sandra asked him directly? Before Raymond could summon an answer Sandra spoke again. "I'm nobody's prize. I want you to know that" she insisted. Raymond wasn't quite sure what to say. He was feeling quite uncomfortable by Sandra's comments but secretly he was glad he beat off the competition from Samish. He had been made to work harder than he had anticipated but had been outdone by a superior puncher. Some of the crowd had started to comment on what they had just witnessed. "I think we'd better go", a voice commented. "Why", another voice: asked? "I don't want to be called as a witness", her colleague replied. The canteen staff continued to tend Samish while waiting for the ambulance to arrive. Its siren was quite distinctive. Senior staff members from the college rushed in to enquire what had taken place. Raymond sat quietly with Sandra. While the ambulance staff attended to Samish, Senior College staff members spoke with Raymond. They suggested that he would have to talk to the police about the incident. When they arrived to question Raymond, Sandra stood up for him. She told how Samish deliberately provoked Raymond into action. "There're lots of witnesses", Sandra defended. The cop told Raymond that it was possible that Samish might want to bring charges against him. Raymond knew his father would be angry with him for *"bringing disgrace upon the family"* but he was sure his mother would be more empathetic towards him. The police spoke with Samish but he assured them he did not want to bring charges against Raymond. Sandra was relieved to hear Samish say those words. Since that chance meeting, Sandra and Raymond had been having an *'affair'*. She liked him because he made her laugh and his vivid imagination caught her in awe each time he spun another of his *'rhythmic'* rapping. Sandra often repeated the parts she could remember even when she was away from him. Raymond continued to excite Sandra with his wit but most of all he was a good listener too. On many occasions, Sandra told Raymond bits and pieces about her life; those that pitched her towards this burning urge to succeed. He was keen on Sandra because he thought that she was the *'perfect model'*. Sandra was his *idol, his ideal* woman, his *'Mrs. Right'*. Raymond observed how her body swayed when she walked, the way she smiled, her soft spoken, sweet-talking voice, the colour and texture of her skin and particularly her very inviting cornflower blue eyes. In fact, Raymond was mesmerised by the *seriously* beautiful and elegant Sandra. Mentally, she had a strong hold over the naïvely obsessed Raymond. Outside of college, Sandra and Raymond saw each other frequently. He liked to take her to the cinema, parties, barbeques and sporting events.

After leaving Coleport College, Sandra and Raymond carried on to the prestigious Bastãrdé University where they set out to fulfill their respective academic potentials. Raymond studied Sports Science and Sandra chose Advertising and PR. She and Raymond had often swapped chapters of their lives but identified many similarities about their parents' experiences in Spaceville. Raymond was always encouraged by his parents, Dorothy and Amos, to make decisions for himself. While growing up, Sandra learned under the *'tutelage'* of her mother. Sandra copied but matched Dian's behaviour traits avidly but had learnt those patterns that she had come to claim now as her own. She was grown up now and had bought a house in Brazenborough from the proceeds of the portion of the Will that her father, CB, had bequeathed to her. She lived with Raymond at her house. Sandra chose to stay away from her domineering mother, whom she thought, had driven her father to his early grave. She set off in pursuit of a career. Sandra wanted desperately to be successful and had dreams of becoming an 'A' Blister celebrity. She saw herself as above the *'un-ambitious'* people so called. Her mother, Dian Bogus pleaded with her to stay away from such individuals. Dian saw individuals who didn't go on to higher academic achievements as *"un-ambitious"* and *"dunces"*. She didn't seem to understand that some people had different preferences for learning nor that each was unique and that is what being an individual means. Dian also failed to understand that some individuals' needs were about creating rather than subjecting themselves to the stricture of logical sequencing. Some of Dian's own friends came in for a barrage of negative comments from the *"lady with the 'Film Star' looks"*, as CB often referred to her.

She was in the habit of harshly criticizing but quickly abandoning those individuals that were suffering *'hard-times'*. Tricia Mc Niggle was accepted as a close friend of Dian's. She was even rumoured to be her shadow. Trisha was notified via email that she was no longer employed. It had come as a huge shock to the loyal worker. She read the contents of the email but past out. The sudden shock had rendered her hapless. Over the months that went by, Trisha's savings dwindled more rapidly than she might have anticipated. Her marriage, which was already rocky, completely disintegrated. Trisha suffered even more humiliation when her son accidentally injured another boy while playing association football/soccer at college. The injured boy's parents had no private health insurance. They accepted the empathetic financial gift from Trisha. It helped to pay the cost of the privately arranged life-saving operation for the boy but it left Trisha almost penniless. She was a proud woman. Trisha didn't want to be considered as a *'sponger'* but she needed assistance from the government. Becoming dependent on the meagre social benefits, Trisha found life a stressful experience. Because of her situation, Dian dropped her friend of more than 20 years. Growing up with Dian and her application of her narrow-minded *'values and beliefs'*, Sandra was exposed to every nuance of her mother's class-ist preferences. She couldn't help than to adopt some if not all of those reinforced daily conditionings.

Sandra and Raymond discussed how they saw the world. She saw the world through rose-coloured glasses but Raymond was a bit more circumspect and cautious. His perspectives were drawn from a different set of *'values and beliefs'*. His parents, Amos and Dorothy came from a different background than Dian. Although the Oddball's philosophy directed Raymond towards striving for the getting the best out of himself, he was taught not to hang his hat where he couldn't reach it. His was from a more structured upbringing than Sandra. Both Raymond's parents were just as ambitious for their child. The least they wanted him to do was to work hard at a career that he felt could challenge him enough to keep him motivated yet fulfilled and which paid him well for his expertise. Consistency was the principle that was driven home despite the career he might prefer to choose.

CHAPTER 15

After graduating from Bastârdé University, Sandra secured a job, as Assistant Public Relations Officer, with a major company, DSI, Duke Stagg Incorporated. It was a 'Quoted' Company on the Stock Market and had held its status amongst the 'Majors'. At the interview, the genial Sandra had impressed Duke straight away but not her immediate supervisor, Andy Mann. He was the Senior Public Relations Officer and would be Sandra's immediate boss. Andy Mann did not hide his feelings for the young woman. He sniped at the *'validity'* of her qualifications. "Given access to the right type of technology anyone could produce one of these", Andy said cynically. He examined the 'watermarks' on the certificates that Sandra had produced. Inexperienced and eager to prove Andy Mann wrong, Sandra clashed with him at the interview. "St Halo High Apostolic Grammar School is the only grammar school in Upper Highborough. I'm sure it wouldn't take you long to find it in a search engine", Sandra retorted. Andy Mann was not used to applicants, especially females, replying in this manner. He signalled to Duke to end the interview but he liked Sandra's instinctive reaction to the situation. Duke particularly liked the calm, confident way in which she had quietened Andy Mann. Duke restarted the interview when he asked Sandra how she would manage to travel to work. "It's quite a distance, isn't it", Duke enquired? "I'll be here at eight o'clock every morning", Sandra replied. "What happens if you overslept", Andy Mann dug in? "I'm quite confident I'll be here at eight o'clock each day according to my contract", Sandra said. She reinforced the point she'd made before but adding just enough to deflect the determined Andy Mann. He had jousted with Sandra on two occasions and on both she'd managed to humiliate him. Duke could sense the intensity of the situation but he was most impressed by the feisty Sandra. "You'll do", Duke said. Sandra smiled and Duke was immediately struck by her persona. "The Press will love her, don't you think", Duke asked? His secretary, Mary Allsorts backed Duke's *'judgment'* but reminded him of the 'Temp' who only stayed for a week. "It was one of her *'type'*", Mary Allsorts warned. Duke shrugged off the suggestion quickly and pointed out why he approved of Sandra. "How many applicants have we had for this post", Duke asked Mary directly? "We've interviewed over a hundred so far but we're down to four short-listed possible candidates", Mary advised. Andy Mann was foaming at the mouth because he saw how Duke had kept his eyes fixed on Sandra all the time he was conducting the interview. When Duke winked at Sandra, Andy Mann was desperate to distract him from hiring her. The truth is that Andy felt threatened by Sandra's qualifications. He ribbed Duke about having to pay Sandra more than him. Andy suggested that Sandra's attendance to the prestigious Bastärdé University "makes her over-qualified for the post". "Ms. Bogus, we wouldn't be able to afford your salary", Andy Mann added cynically. Mary Allsorts cleared her throat as a signal of agreement with Andy Mann. Duke had noticed the tone in Andy Mann's voice. The *'code'* was open enough for Sandra to pick up too. She glared at Andy Mann sternly but restrained herself from any verbal reply. Between them, the interviewers had put Sandra, the interviewee, through the *'accepted'* line of questioning but they could not divert her from her singular aim, to join DSI. Duke asked Mary if she had any other questions. Mary surprised Sandra with the question she chose to ask. "Are you married", she asked directly? The secretary's voice was formal but cold. Sandra turned her head towards Mary Allsorts. She was quite poised when she replied. "That's personal and has nothing to do with the efficiency of my standard of work", Sandra challenged. Again Duke was impressed with the way in which she responded. He seized that opportunity to have a tea break. "We'll adjourn to reach a decision, would you wait outside please, Ms. Bogus", Duke asked? As she rose, Duke noticed Sandra for the first time in profile. He was stunned at his own reaction. "I'll come to get you when we've decided", Duke said. He rose from his chair, tripped as he went pass Andy Mann, who was sitting to his right. Duke diverted past the desk and hurried to open the door for the elegant Sandra. She was smiling now quite sheepishly; rolling her eyes around then winked at Duke. It was while Duke was closing the door that he heard the slight sniggling going on between Mary Allsorts and Andy Mann. He was aware of Andy Mann's whispered comment but he did not alert them. Returning to his desk, Duke asked Mary to prepare some refreshments. "Two sugars", Mary Allsorts asked? Duke confirmed he wanted two sugars. "White Coffee, please Mary and don't forget the biscuits", Andy Mann chimed in. Mary made her way over to the far side of the office where there was a sliding door. Inside, she arranged the bone-china cups and saucers on the large solid gold tray. Mary Allsorts was a well-practiced *'tea-maker'*. She'd been making the tea since she first started with Duke's father, Earl Duke Stagg. While Mary made tea, Duke took the opportunity to remind Andy Mann about the earlier comment he'd overheard. Duke was furious that Andy would want to snipe behind his back. "I want a little chat with you Andy", he said. Andy Mann saw the concerned look on Duke's face. "Listen Andy, I'll have you keep your nose out of my personal life. What I do is my business. It ain't got nothink to do with my wife, Mary or you. At least you could be man enough to say it to my face", Duke said sternly. It was Mary Allsorts chiming that broke the silence that followed Andy's little chat with Duke. "Tea is served", she said. Mary placed the solid gold tray on top of the hugely ornate desk. Andy Mann eyed the assortment of cakes and biscuits that were *necessary* accessories at tea-break. He sat up for a moment, rubbed his hands together then shuffled forwards in his chair. Duke's eyes followed Andy's *'focused'* gaze. He'd zoned in on the creamed donut pastry. That was a particular favourite with all three of them. Mary practiced *protocol* and allowed Duke to have first choice. As far as Mary was concerned, she had already abandoned the idea of tasting the tempting pastry. Andy reached out to remove the creamed donut from the tray but was hindered from doing so, by Duke's action. He stood up and forcefully blocked Andy Mann from achieving his aim. "Have some manners, I saw it first", Duke said. He moved swiftly to take the creamed donut from the tray. Mary listened but watched the two men squabble and fight for ownership of the pastry. She smiled to herself but likened them to school-aged children in a canteen situation. The two men stood nose-to-nose but glared at each other. "You should see yourselves", Mary Allsorts croaked. She choked on another nicotine-induced breath. Andy's jaws tightened as he sulked but Duke staked the final claim to the savoury pastry. "This is mine", Duke said. He proceeded to bite off a huge chunk of the donut. His huge angular jaws, seemingly a chisled piece of sculpture, replicated a chewing action similar to that of cattle, in profile, chewing grass. Duke savoured the taste of whipped cream, syrup, sugar and the dough, altogether. Mary empathized with Andy's feeling but remained silent while the two men sorted out their indifference. Defeated, Andy sat down but sipped the coffee. He watched grudgingly, as Duke ate the donut. "I'll have a couple of biscuits", Andy Mann commented. "One", Duke reprimanded. Andy stared at him but remained silent. Mary tried to say something but suddenly broke into a coughing fit. The rattling sound concerned both Andy and Duke. "Are you alright Mary", Duke asked? The spasms had rendered Mary unable to speak. Each time she attempted to take a deep breath, it seemed to trigger the cough even more. Andy came to the other side of her but started to slap Mary's back. "Do you want some water", Andy Mann asked? She shook her head. "Give her some air", Duke shouted. Andy began to cuddle Mary. She was feeling comforted by Andy's empathetic arms but Duke was unaware of her *'need'*. Mary managed to get a few words out through several gasps. "I'll be ... all ... righ ... t ... in ... a min ... ute" Mary Allsorts said. Her constant sniveling added to Duke's concern. "I told you to go see the old doc", Duke said. He handed Mary a box of tissues that was on the desk. She cleared the yellow mucous from her nose and throat unto tissue paper. Mary folded the tissues but placed them on the desk, next to her cup of tea. She indicated that she had recovered sufficiently enough to carry on. Mary spoke to Duke and Andy. "If only you could see yourselves, like Tom and Jerry", Mary Allsorts finished. Duke giggled at Mary's analogy. He remembered the famous cartoon. Duke, seeing himself as 'Tom' and Andy as 'Jerry', deliberately jerked his head back then proceeded to shove the balance of the donut into his mouth. He used the heel of his hand to ensure that none of it was wasted. Duke didn't bother to work his molars too much this time, instead he preferred to hurry the process of getting the rest of the donut into his stomach. Swallowing hard, like a snake its prey, Duke ingested the contents. "Mmmmmh, that was great, thanks Mary. You know how to treat a boss", Duke commented. He looked over again at Andy Mann. The insinuation had further impacted on him. Having been allowed just one biscuit, Andy complimented Mary about the "great coffee" she'd made him. Mary blushed with well-earned pride. She reminded Duke that they hadn't yet reached a formal decision "on the applicant, Ms. Bogus". Duke told them that he was in favour of Ms. Bogus joining the company. "I think her confident manner is what I'm most impressed with", Duke continued. Andy Mann was the next one to comment. He pressed home the points he'd made before but in particular he said Sandra seemed too "cocky for her own good". Turning towards his secretary, Duke asked her opinion. Mary had observed Duke's special efforts to make Ms. Bogus feel welcome. In her mind there was no doubt that Duke had found a new *'quarry'*. "Well, I've known you long enough to know when your mind is made up", Mary said cautiously. Duke was getting bored with his colleagues. "You've got no balls", Duke mumbled under his breath. Both Mary and Andy were very efficient employees but that's all they were. They had no spirit, Duke thought. He looked at Mary and Andy but thought to himself that the company could do with a new image. Sandra was the bright spark Duke needed to improve the company's profile. "Is there any tea left Mary", Duke asked? "Yes", Mary croaked. "Well, lets call Ms. Bogus in", Duke advised. He rose from his chair again and went past Andy Mann. This time Andy Mann made sure he gave him enough room. Duke walked quickly across the office towards the door. He opened it. Duke waited for Sandra to walk through but she stood just in front of him. Sandra placed herself close enough to Duke but without touching. He looked up into her large cornflower blue eyes. Duke experienced the mesmeric effect they had on him. Sandra could see Duke melting and chanced to brush against him as she strode forward into the office. Duke was aroused by this action. He hesitated for a moment before shuffling back to his desk. Duke seemed a bit flush in the face and Mary and Andy noticed. He kept quiet, deliberately restraining himself from commenting about Duke's rising embarrassment, which was very noticeable. "Sit down Miss Bogus, would you like some tea", Duke asked? "May I", Sandra asked? Duke signalled that it was alright for her to "have a cup of tea with us". Mary reminded Duke that she'd only brought three cups and saucers. She offered to go to fetch another. "Ms. Bogus can have my cup. You don't mind drinking from my cup, do you? Sugar, Duke asked? "Two please", Sandra replied. Duke poured then placed the cup of tea in front of her. He waited for Sandra to have a couple of sips of the tea before announcing his final decision. "Congratulations Ms. Bogus, you are hired", Duke said. "Thank you", Sandra replied. She looked across at Andy Mann, who sat with a glum look on his face. He was seething about Duke's decision. Andy felt that he should have been able to choose his *'underling'"* and not Duke but his decision was final and Andy Mann was clearly aware of that fact. They discussed and agreed contractual issues with Sandra, while she finished her tea. As she went to place the empty cup down, Sandra saw the two strands of hair that was sticking to the inside of the cup. She used her extended nails to remove them from the dregs of tea leaves that formed a pattern along the side and at the base of the cup. Sandra looked up at Duke. Realizing that Sandra was concerned about the hairs in the cup, Duke intervened immediately. "It won't harm you", he assured her. Sandra seemed satisfied with Duke's explanation but chose to comment on the brand of tea instead. "Darjeeling", Sandra asked? Duke smiled. "Yes", Duke replied. He rose from the desk and went past Andy Mann yet again. "Let's show you around", Duke said. They walked towards the door. Mary and Andy trailed behind. When they entered the open-planned, area Sandra noticed the overwhelming stony silence that greeted her. The members of staff only stared blankly at her. Two of them though started to whisper but pointed as Sandra walked through the open-planned office. Duke whispered to Mary and then left for his office. The secretary showed Sandra around and indicated where her desk would be situated. The whispering became deliberately louder than normal whispers. "Hawk at her, is she the new Temp or something", a staff member asked another? "What's Mary doing, showing her Manny's desk", another staff member asked? Andy Mann's facial expressions, nodding, winking and the jerking of his head to one side to indicate a *'coded'* message that Sandra had got the job. The staff seemed to understand quite clearly what Andy Mann meant by his peculiar mannerisms. "This is my new assistant. That makes her your new supervisor. She went to St Halo High Apostolic Grammar School and the prestigious Bastārdé University", Andy Mann mocked. "I'm not working under her", a member of staff stated. Sandra could hear the comments quite clearly and was disturbed by the open sniping that was being allowed to take place. Neither Mary nor Andy seemed shock at the comments. They just ignored them. Sandra needed some clarification as to whom the staff was referring. "Are they talking about me", Sandra asked? Mary shrugged off the question. "They're upset that Manny is gone. He used to make the tea for them and buy them biscuits", Mary explained. She turned to Andy for some support but he turned away and walked past Sandra. He stood behind her but at a slight distance away. Sandra was focused on getting an explanation from Mary but failed to see the antics that Andy was getting up to behind her. He was gesturing like an adolescent prankster to his captive audience, who in turn started to chant. "Manny, Manny, Manny", the staff members chanted over and over again. Some staff pounded a staccato beat to the count of three, on the desks. The chant of "Manny, Manny, Manny," followed the three beats. This type of *'chanting'* one would probably associate with the game of association football, aka soccer. Sandra looked helplessly to Mary but she only confirmed why Manny was so popular with the staff. "He was a lovely man. Manny was *'like you'*, you know", Mary told Sandra. "I won't be making the tea", Sandra stated firmly. "That's what you think, duck. Andy loves his tea", Mary Allsorts said. She smiled as she said the words. Sandra wanted to straighten out these priorities with Duke. She told Mary. "Mr Stagg will be engaged for the rest of the day. He won't have a break for the next couple of hours at least. Are you willing to wait that long", she asked? "Well I'm not starting until I have a word with Mr. Stagg", Sandra said. She turned and walked away from the open-planned office. Sandra could hear Andy Mann's voice amongst the laughter. The impact of the strange experience brought currents of mixed memories to the fore. Sandra remembered her experiences at St. Halo High Apostolic Grammar School, where she was blamed unfairly on a number of occasions or forced to do chores that other students weren't asked to do. Similarly, she'd complained to her mother, Dian, but she had given Sandra no more support than Andy or Mary. Sandra paused where one aisle intersected with another. She was unsure which way to go but had to make a decision. Sandra turned left. The first office door appeared after about 20 yards down the long corridor. Sandra could hear the sound of other footsteps behind her but she didn't look back. Mary Allsorts had suspected that Sandra was hurt enough to want to get to Duke. The sound of Mary's leather soled shoes carried through the corridors. Sandra strode quickly down the long corridor towards the office looking for Duke's nameplate. As she approached the door, Sandra could hear Mary's croaky voice ringing through the corridor. "You can't go in there", Mary advised. Sandra didn't bother to knock but instead wrenched the handle but walked straight through Mary's office into and through the middle office that led through to Duke's. She grabbed the handle of Duke's door but pushed it open. Sandra stood with mouth agog. Duke and a woman were in a very precarious position on top of the desk. The woman saw her but started to push Duke away. He was unaware of Sandra's presence but continued to seek pleasure. "Don't stop me now", Duke said. His voice was coarse naturally but it sounded hoarser than Sandra had heard it earlier. The voice from her right made Sandra aware that someone other than those she'd already observed was present in the office too. She saw the tall man who sat in the chair. He got up but approached her. "Are you my partner", the tall man asked? He then reached out to touch her. "Keep your hands to yourself. Don't you dare touch me", Sandra instructed. She brandished her extended nails and the man recoiled. "Touchy, who've we got here", the tall man asked? Duke recognized Sandra's voice. He turned to look. "JH Christ, Ms. Bogus how did you get in", Duke asked? "Never mind, I won't be staying", Sandra replied. She turned to go but Duke stopped her. "You can't go now, well not until I've had a word", he pleaded. Duke adjusted his clothes then shuffled quickly over towards her. The woman on the desk was sitting on it now. She hung her head but stared at a pattern in the carpet. The woman was feeling quite disappointed that Duke had abandoned her. He placed his hand gently around Sandra's waist but ushered her into the office that separated his and Mary's. She was holding on to her desk, breathless from trying to catch up with the determined Sandra. Duke listened to Sandra's comments about how she was treated by the staff. "Ignore it. I must say I'm disappointed with the way you handled that. You'll have to get used to taking a bit of flack at times", Duke advised. Sandra looked stunned, for that was not the answer she was expecting. "I beg your pardon", Sandra exclaimed. Duke was not one to mess around. He would say what he wanted to say then let the other person worry about it. Sandra's furrowed brow made Duke soften his line. "Now tell me you'll prove that I made the right decision", Duke continued. Mary had recovered from her breathlessness but walked into the middle office. She saw Duke and Sandra standing close, in conversation. Mary couldn't hear what Duke was saying but she knew Sandra was assured by the way she was nodding her head up and down like a performing horse at a circus. "Oh Mr. Stagg, I tried to stop her but I couldn't", Mary commented. Duke looked up but turned towards Mary. He chose and directed his words carefully. "Tell the staff to be nice to Ms. Bogus, will you Mary", Duke said. "I want my own office. I'm not sitting in the open-plan with the rest of the staff", Sandra demanded. Duke turned to Sandra then smiled. "Your wish is my command, Ms. Bogus", he added. She was satisfied by the assurances given by Duke. Sandra thanked him then left. Mary turned to go but Duke stopped her. "Er, a word in your ear, Mary", Duke said. She braced herself for what was to come. Mary had started to prepare for it while she was recovering in her Office. She knew of the special arrangements between her and Duke. He reminded

Mary that he could stop the special *'bonus'* he was paying her, if she couldn't keep to their "little agreement". The *'bonus'* wouldn't be missed by Mary but the prestige of working for DSI meant more to her. "I'm sorry Mr. Stagg", Mary said sheepishly. "Come, come, now Mary, Mr. Stagg is a bit much, ain't it? Don't start sulking", Duke said. Mary indicated that she wasn't. Duke issued her with fresh instructions. "Get rid of that scrubber and her boyfriend then straighten up my office, it's a bloody mess. Oh, open the windows, it don't half pung in there. I'm going to The Old Frigate AADC", Duke advised. He set off on his journey. Walking down the long corridor, Duke's gait was one that bore that particular swagger which indicated that he was in a hurry to get to his destination. He hummed but his quick shuffling steps carried him along as if he was gliding just above ground level. Sandra was on Duke's mind. He replayed the scene where she had deliberately brushed against him in the doorway while he stood to let her by. "What a bird", Duke exclaimed. He spat in both palms of his hands then rubbed them together. It was a peculiar cultural habit but he did this often when he felt challenged. "F . . . . . g beautiful . . . . . Exotic, yes", Duke mumbled to himself. He punched the air in similar fashion to an association football/ soccer player. Duke felt the vibration of the cell phone in his pocket. He removed the tiny phone from the pocket but placed it at his ears. "Hello, Mary what's up", Duke asked? "The young woman said she wanted more money and the boyfriend said he's going to the newspapers about your "breaching the agreement", Mary told him. "What agreement", Duke asked? "What agreement", Mary Allsorts echoed? "He promised me a partner but she didn't seem to fancy me", the woman's boyfriend said. Mary related the man's concerns to Duke. It was always difficult to tell if Mary was crying but Duke sensed that she was crying. "You been crying, ain't you? Who upset you, it's not Andy and his bloody moaning, is it", Duke asked? As Mary began to explain why she was crying, Duke could hear the woman's boyfriend's voice in the background. He heard him call Mary, "an old crow, an f . . . g old goat and a silly moo". "I'll fix his business Mary sweetheart. Tell that f . . . g 'git' to leave you alone. Tell him to be a man and meet me over at The Old Frigate AADC", Duke threatened. "I don't want to. I can't talk to him Duke", Mary submitted. Duke listened carefully. "Get the smart Alex on the phone", Duke ordered. Mary told the man that Duke wanted to talk to him on the phone. "What does he want to talk to me about", the tall man asked? "Mr. Stagg is the boss", is all Mary said. Duke waited for a while then he heard the voice. "Hello", the tall man said. "Listen, you little fool, you can't hurt me. You can't hurt Duke Stagg. I've got too much clout for that", he emphasized. There was a spell of silence. "So what", the tall man asked? "So, someone gets squashed like a bothersome fly. You know what I mean, Harry Bragman", Duke emphasized? Again the silent pauses were getting under Duke's skin. "Scared now, are you? Cat got your tongue", Duke jeered? "How did you know my name", the tall man asked? The woman's giggling alerted Duke's rage. "Listen here, Harry Bragman, I know who you are and where you live. You've got a daughter and a son. Does your skinny wife know what you do? I'm giving you a chance to get out of this. I'll give you and your girlfriend another 50 SPCU each and you both walk free, deal", Duke wagered? He could hear the garbled sounds disguised for whispering and the gleeful chant from the woman. "Yes", she exclaimed. "O.K. that's a deal", Harry Bragman replied. "Let me speak to Mary", Duke ordered. "Yes, Mr. Stagg", Mary croaked. "Give them another *'wonner'* and they'll go", Duke advised. He waited on the phone until he heard Mary's voice again. "Thank God, they're gone", she exclaimed. "You alright now",

Duke queried? "I need a cup of tea and a cigarette", Mary replied. "That's just what you need Mary", Duke encouraged.

CHAPTER 16

He hung up. Mary changed the sign outside her office door to 'OUT'. She made herself a cup of tea. It was strong but had a colour similar to mud. Mary had a few sips of the hot liquid then lit a long, slender, brown cigarette. She pulled hard on it. The fire from the cigarette glowed but appeared to run swiftly upwards towards her lips. Mary pushed her chair back but placed her feet upon the desk before releasing the acrid smoke out into the air. Soon the office looked misty enough to earn a place in an epic movie. "That's better", Mary Allsorts exclaimed. She sipped some more tea. Someone tapped the door. Mary jumped. She took her foot from off the desk. Mary waited but heard the tapping again. She swished at the clouds of smoke that now saturated not only the office but also her clothes. Although Mary was not aware of it, her clothes wreaked of the compounded odours, gathered accumulatively since Mary woke up. Her first cigarette was at 06:20 hours just after her first cup of tea and her last was always just as she climbed into bed at night. She habitually followed this routine for the last 46 years. The tapping at the door started again. Mary decided to invite the person in. "Come in", she croaked. The door opened. Andy Mann came in. "Hello Mary", he said. Andy Mann spoke in practiced gasps that changed tones frequently but sounded as if he was commentating on a horse race. Mary waved him in but she did not speak. "Is his Majesty back from The Old Frigate AADC yet", Andy jeered? "Not yet", Mary replied. "Time for a ciggy then", Andy Mann indicated. He removed the packet of cigarettes from his trouser pocket. Andy lit one but quickly drew the nicotine into his lungs. He made rings with the smoke. Some were huge while others were tiny but neat. "Any chance of a cup of tea", Andy Mann asked? "Yes, if you're making it", Mary Allsorts replied. Mary lit another long, slender, brown cigarette. She and Andy caught up on the debacle in Duke's Office earlier. "That man was awful to me Andy, bloody awful", Mary told him. Andy slapped his left fist into his right palm. "I could get a few of my friends to sort him out", Andy Mann offered. "You can tell where he's brought up. His language was blue and his aggressive attitude got me down. At one time I swear he was going to hit me", Mary said. "I'll get Geoff O'Cape to deal with the matter, he'll sort him out", He's a strong man. Andy Mann assured. He took two or three quick pulls on his cigarette. The long ash fell onto his trouser on its way down to the floor. Andy paced around then decided to switch the electric kettle on. "Mary, what did his majesty have to say about it", Andy Mann asked? "He talked to the boyfriend on the phone", Mary Allsorts replied. The mist of smoke was getting thicker and the office was foggier now. Neither Andy nor Mary could see each other clearly. "Can't see if the kettle is boiling", Mary Allsorts queried? It's boiling all right, now", Andy Mann replied. He flicked the switch to turn off the kettle. "Do you want a cuppa", Andy Mann asked? "A strong cuppa, please luv", Mary Allsorts replied. The ringing of the phone made Mary jump. She searched through the wall of smoke but managed to locate it. "Duke Stagg Incoporated", Mary Allsorts announced. She listened for a short while then responded. "Mr. Stagg is out of the office, Mrs. Stagg", Mary said. They exchanged the cursory greeting then Mrs. Stagg asked Mary to remind Duke to ring her "as soon as he can". After Mary hung up on Mrs. Stagg, she phoned Duke's cell phone. He felt the vibration of the phone in his pocket. Duke removed the tiny phone from the pocket but placed it at his ear. "Hello", Duke said. Mary gave him the message from his wife. "Oh, she'll have to wait in the queue like everyone else, thanks Mary", Duke replied. He hung up. "Lets have a re-fill", Duke demanded from the male attendant? He placed the glass on the table. The attendant told Duke that he was off duty. "So what are you doing behind the bar", Duke queried? "I'm just waiting until the other attendant arrives. She's late", he said. Duke looked at the temporary bar attendant then shook his head. "Get me a drink then", he demanded. He placed his hands on both sides of his head but wiggled his fingers, then jeered like a primary school pupil. "Naa, na, na, na, naa, who's an awkward bastard then", Duke jeered? Unexpectedly, the bar attendant rushed over to where Duke was seated. The young attendant placed his forehead close to Duke's, in a manner likened to two bulls confronting each other *'head to head'* in an arena. "What, what . . . who you looking at . . . what", the attendant: exclaimed. Duke was not sure he understood the attendant's behaviour but he sensed when he was being challenged. He reached out for the glass on the table. Once in hand, he brought it up to the attendant's face. "Do you want this", he asked? Duke was serious about his intention. He pressed hard enough for the attendant to back off a little but he stood close enough to Duke. Still seated on the chair, Duke lifted then stamped the heel of his shoe on the attendant's toes. The sudden pain brought the attendant into a bent position. Duke used his large head to batter the attendant's face. He placed one hand over his face but raised his other hand in submission. Duke stood up then followed up his *'head-butt'* with a swift kick to the attendant's groin area. He delivered a left hook with his stubby fist, sending the attendant reeling across the floor. He bumped into tables and chairs on his way down to the floor. "That'll teach you, you mad 'git'", Duke expressed. The small crowd watched attentively as Duke delivered the *'lesson'* to the young bar attendant. Shakeef Bin Mc Fluggle was a young student, who had taken the bar post as one of the two part-time jobs that he attended. As he tried to cover the two jobs in between getting his university assignments done, Shafeek was under great financial strain. The student's high stress level had manifested itself in the odd behaviour he had displayed but Shafeek had taken on the wrong man. When it came to fighting Duke was ruthless. Ever since he was young, he was grown street-wise and tough. Duke had to survive the streets back then and they were never safe. He stood over the motionless figure then shaped to kick him. "Jesus, Mary, Joseph, that's enough", someone shouted. "He's dead", someone else shouted. Duke noticed that the student was hardly moving but he stepped away. He walked back towards the original table. The crowd had milled around the body on the floor. There was an assortment of suggestions as to what to do. One woman rushed behind the bar and came back with a bucket of cold water. "Mind out", the woman's voice ordered. The crowd parted to let the woman through. She poured the cold water on Shafeek's face. The water managed to wash away some of the blood from his face but there was a more damp area behind his head as he lay on the carpeted floor. The blood soaked area concerned everyone who witnessed it. "Did someone call an ambulance", a voice asked? "Yes", another replied. "Quiet", someone shouted. The Old Frigate AADC was silent. One woman purporting to administer *'mouth to mouth'* resuscitation stopped but listened to Shafeek's chest. She could hear the faint beating of his heart. Though it was irregular, it indicated that Shafeek was alive. The woman placed her ears close to his nostrils to listen to his breathing, alternately looking at the rising of his chest. When she was satisfied with her primary findings, the woman spoke to the young student. "Can you hear me", the female First Aider asked? Shakeef did not respond verbally. "What's your name, luv", the female First Aider continued? She lifted the lids of both of Shakeef's eyes but saw the idle stare in them. They were not focused sufficiently to indicate full consciousness. Duke had helped himself to more brandy from the bar but was observing the scene from a distance. The sound of the ambulance brought a sudden buzz of conversation and Duke could hear the odd comments about the intensity of force used. "It wasn't necessary, the head butt was enough", a voice said. The doors to the AADC opened and the paramedics announced their arrival. "Where is the patient", voice of one paramedic asked? They saw where the crowd had gathered but moved towards them. When they parted they saw the woman still working furiously to restore Shafeek's condition. "We'll take over now", the paramedic said. The female First Aider pressed her lips on Shafeek's for the last time but blew with renewed hope that he would recover from the relapse he'd experienced while the paramedics were on route to the Old Frigate AADC. They began to examine the young student as he lay on the carpeted floor.

It was the ambulance siren that had alerted the manager of The Old Frigate AADC to come downstairs from the flat above. He'd heard the voices and the tumbling but he was not concerned about "a few remarks", as he'd told the female attendant with whom he was 'sharing a few moments'. He had told Shakeef what to do if anyone became a bit overbearing. "Just don't take any notice of them. Give them more of what they are drinking, you know . . . more of the same. It will soon shut them up," Cedric had instructed. Strangely, the manager's accent was quite similar to that of Andy Mann's. The short gasps and flat whispering voice sung every word uttered. "What the bloody hell is going on down here," Cedric asked? He looked genuinely concerned when he saw the paramedics. They were examining the pulse at the base of Shafeek's neck. "What's his name? Does anyone know his name", the paramedic queried? A plastic mask was placed over Shakeef's face. The other end of the long tube, attached, led to a small oxygen bottle. Cedric looked around for some of the familiar faces but each deliberately avoided direct eye contact with him. The manager, Cerdic Rudderman-Snyde, ran a good AADC. He did not need bad publicity. "Did anyone see what happened," Cedric asked? His eyes traced an arc around but no one stepped forward nor offered an explanation. He walked over but approached a paramedic. "Is he going to be alright," Cedric queried? Sweat was pouring from the manager's furrowed brow. He mopped it with the large white handkerchief he took from his pocket. "He's in a bad way, we'll have to inform the police", the female paramedic stated. Cedric submitted that the paramedics had a job to do though he tried to persuade them to "wait and see". Duke waited for the paramedics to leave then he summoned the manager over to the table where he was sitting. "Here, Cedric, over here", Duke said. He used his head to indicate his verbal command. Cedric walked over to Duke's table. He told Cedric what had happened but insisted that Shakeef had "attacked" him. "He asked for it", Duke said stubbornly. "When the old bill gets here, would you do me a favour and explain it to them", Cedric implored? "Yes mate", Duke replied. Most of the crowd had been reduced to just a few people, who had waited to see what was going to happen when the cops arrive. They didn't have long to wait, the sounds of the sirens told of their imminent arrival. The first cop appeared through the door on the left of where Duke was sitting. He asked for the manager. Cedric stepped forward and confirmed his status in the The Old Frigate AADC. "What happened here mate," one cop asked? Cedric explained his absence "at the time of the incident". Other cops had arrived from other entrances of The Old Frigate AADC. They questioned the other people that were still present. One of the cops asked Cedric if he knew how the boy got hurt. Cedric advised the cop should speak with Duke. He further explained Duke's fame and importance. He was pointing directly at Duke. Both Cedric and the cop walked over together. "Hello guv", the cop said. "Hello mate", Duke replied. "I understand that the boy attacked you", the cop stated. "Yeah, little twerp, got what was coming to him, insolent little bastard", Duke said confidently. Another cop took Duke's comments a bit more seriously but came over and stood next to his colleague. "Asked for it, did he", he asked? "Yeah, think he was tough but I showed him", Duke said. "Well unless he wants to bring charges, we won't be bothering you again, Mr. Stagg", the first cop said. "I owe you one, does your wife like champagne", Duke retorted? "Yea, not half", the first cop replied. "And my wife too", the second cop pressed. They left the AADC. Wiping his forehead with the large white handkerchief, Cedric commented. "Phew, I'm glad that's over. Let's have a drink", he suggested. Duke agreed. "Little bastard, was he", Cedric asked? "He had an attitude problem. Got to knock it out of them", Duke insisted. "I had a feeling about that boy", Cedric stated. He filled the two glasses with a rich brandy. The clinking sound of the glasses together indicated Cedric and Duke toasting the *'lesson'* meted out to young Shaffeek. Other individuals, who had remained to see whether Duke would be arrested, cleared their throats in unison. Duke looked over but waved at them. "Give them a drink, would you", he encouraged. "This one is on me", Cedric insisted. He announced the free booze and immediately got reactions from each one of them. Some were now smiling but confirming openly that Duke "did not provoke the situation". He was happy to hear the testament of the witnesses. "Can't stay chatting all day Cedric, got work to do", Duke stated. The others, led by Cerdic Rudderman-Snyde, toasted their hero, Duke. He raised his glass high into the air before signalling his farewell from the AADC. "Down the hatch", Duke said. He emptied the contents of the glass down his throat. The strong liquor burnt a trail down the back of his throat. "Cor, this is bloody good brandy, Cedric. Where did you get this", Duke asked? "New Supplier, nudge, nude, wink, wink", Cedric announced cheerfully. It was nearly lunchtime and The Old Frigate AADC had started to fill up again. Cedric busied himself getting ready for the *'happy hour'* crowd. The young female attendant, with whom he'd spent "a few moments" earlier, helped clear the previously used glasses, plates and empty bottles away. Another two other female attendants joined the shift. "We're one short today girls. Young Shakeef has gone and injured himself", Cedric explained. "Was he meant to be in today", one female attendant asked? "He'll work when I tell him to", Cedric stated firmly. "That's it mate, you tell 'em who's Boss", Duke retorted. He winked at Cedric before leaving The Old Frigate AADC.

CHAPTER 17

Duke's cell phone started to vibrate again. "Hel-lo, who's that", he asked? When he heard his wife's voice, Duke spoke to her as if she was a nuisance caller. "I haven't got time for your childish behaviour", Dora parried. "You silly cow, what do you want", Duke asked? Dora Stagg was used to her husband by now. She had been called those names many times before but today she was in no mood to put up with Duke's barrage of abuse. "Don't you talk to me like you're addressing one of your *'common-a-garden' slags*", Dora said. "It's that time of the month again, is it", Duke enquired? Dora did not put up with Duke's jibes. Instead she lambasted him. "You did not come home again last night. Where were you", she demanded? "Stop nagging, woman", Duke teased. Dora was in no mood to *'play'*. "Duke Stagg, you are a disgrace. Imagine your son is in hospital but you couldn't care about what goes on at home", she stated. "What's the use? You've turned them against me. They are your sons not mine", Duke retorted. "Artificially inseminated, was I", Dora asked? Her comment was deliberately laced with sarcasm. When there was no immediate answer from her husband, she hung up abruptly. "Hello", Duke said. He realized that Dora had hung up. "Silly Moo", Duke murmured. The phone started to vibrate again as soon as he placed it in his pocket. Duke placed the phone to his ear again. This time it was one of his *'flusey'* girls. "Hello . . . oh, hi Chloe . . . no I can't, I've just left The Old Frigate AADC. What do you want", Duke asked? "I want you, gorgeous man", Chloe told him. She was in the mood to charm the over-generous Duke. Chloe was an unfortunate individual, who had complex life experiences that had rendered her very low in self-worth, esteem and confidence. She did not love herself but sought to abandon her natural potential and abilities. Chloe not only lost her 13 years old teenage brother to the maddening UFO's Cult-Induced Post/Zip Code Wars but sought the comfort of an older step-brother, who assured Chloe's mother that he would help Chloe through her *'troubled experience'*. This older step-brother had come over from the exotic continent from which Chloe's grandparents had originally emigrated. Thirty-six years old Sam Fyeman had been given a six months visa on compassionate grounds to visit Spaceville to attend his step-brother's funeral and to help console his family. He took the then 16 years old Chloe into his confidence. She never had an older brother or father figure around so Chloe welcomed his assurance. She really knew nothing about him least of all his imprisonment for being part of a notorious gang called *'The Solderers'* back in his exotic continent. Sam Fyeman had spent seven years in a Category 'A' prison for gang-rape in the exotic continent from which Chloe's grandparents had emigrated. He had groomed the 16 years old teenager but waited for his opportunity to show his *'real intentions'*. Sam Fyeman started by intimidating young Chloe. He beat her then hugged her but apologised for his behaviour. Sam Fyeman would seek Chloe's sympathy by playing the victim. This he did by crying while he told her of the *'sad life'* he had experienced since he was a young boy. No sooner than when Chloe started to feel sorry for her step-brother, he started to fondle her intimately. Chloe was confused by the mixed messages being sent by her step-brother. She refused to have sex with him. "You're much older than me and you are meant to be my step-brother", she protested. This only made Sam Fyeman angrier. He was used to intimidating young girls but forcing them to have sex with him. When they refused, he would physically beat them by punching and kicking them. On more than one occasion, many young girls had their bones broken or had adhesions after being brutally attacked by the vicious *'emotionally immature'* Sam Fyeman. In his exotic continent, this type of behaviour was a daily *'ritual'*. Older men relentlessly pestered young girls to have sex with them. This psychopathic trait to select then stalk these young girls was as ritualistic as a hobby. It was quite similar to a hunter's quest to *'conquer'* but was often something those men kept score of and boasted about in their communities. These men did this to satisfy their super-inflated egos about their *"right to conquer"*. It was a type of *'cultural ritual'* that has been handed down through generations. They had not invented but copied and continued this age-old insensitive behaviour without questioning since that same act was initiated by the invading green humanoid robotrons slave masters, decades before the likes of Sam Fyeman was conceived even. Being born into the *'cultural values and beliefs'* about men's dominance over women, Sam Fyeman and others like him feasted on the *'stereo-tripe'* without questioning, believed the *'stereo-hype'* with a passion but became the *'stereotype'* latently. Back in his homeland, Sam Fyeman had witnessed his father treating young girls in the same way in which he was behaving. Sam Fyeman didn't agree with the way his father treated the young girls then yet he grew up repeating the same behaviour because he chose to own rather than be responsible for his own behaviour. He was a real nasty piece of work. Sam Fyeman had no scruples or moralistic structural reference. On the day when he decided to get more than *'sisterly love'* from his step-sister, Chloe, Sam Fyeman started the *'ritual'* by punching and kicking her before his vicious sexual assault. He threatened that, if Chloe told anyone what had taken place, he would kill her. Chloe froze with fear. As she cowered in a corner, she planned how she might be able to escape from the torturous experience but Sam Fyeman had done this kind of thing before. He told Chloe that he knew exactly what she might be thinking. She found herself sobbing but offered no resistance when Sam Fyeman made sexual approaches to her. Like an obedient child, Chloe succumbed to his demand. This was repeated for most of Sam Fyeman's six months stay in Spaceville. Chloe even became pregnant for the notorious rapist. When she told him, he punched her in her stomach repeatedly but kicked her in her crotch while she was on the floor. Sam Fyeman was a psychopathic *'professional bully'*. He made sure he did not leave any marks on Chloe's face or hands. She had a miscarriage but lost the baby. With the inflation of his negative ego, Sam Fyeman was becoming careless. He bullied Chloe into becoming his *'gofor'*. Amongst sexual pornographic *'asides',* she was ordered to cook his food as well. Chloe had thought of poisoning her step-brother but could not find it within herself to do so. Sam Fyeman had become so confident that Chloe was now like *'putty in his hands'*. On this occasion, he went into the kitchen to complain about how long Chloe was taking to prepare his meal. "You must give me my dinner precisely on time", he demanded. "I'm not your slave", Chloe heard herself retort. She had no idea from whence the response had come but she heard herself rebelling about the tactics of the bully. Sam Fyeman had had his fix of cocaine moments earlier. He was addicted long before he arrived for his stepbrother's funeral. Sam Fyeman had made contact with other drug users since his arrival but stole from his stepmother's purse to satisfy his addiction. In the kitchen, he used the back of his hand to strike his stepsister across her face with a swinging blow. Chloe cowered but held her jaw. It felt as if it was dislocated by the thickset muscular bully. His eyes stared wildly way beyond Chloe's presence but told of the menace that was rising up inside him. Chloe held her jaw but looked at him with as much hate as a look could transmit. "You had better hurry up", he warned. Sam Fyeman towered over her. Chloe hung her head like an animal that was being tamed. The knife Chloe was using to dice the onions fell from her hand onto the floor. As she bent down to pick it up, she felt a kick into her crotch from behind. Confident that Chloe had to accede to his demand Sam Fyeman hurried to confront her face to face. She began to rise from picking up the knife from the floor. "I said to hurry up with my food", Sam Fyeman yelled. His belligerent act elicited a reaction from Chloe but not one he had expected. Chloe Dibidibi was tired of the physical and mental bullying and the sexual abuse that she had suffered since Sam Fyeman's arrival. It was in rising that she made the decision to plunge the 12 inch kitchen knife into Sam Fyeman's stomach. He let out a cry like a victim from a Hitchcock movie but grabbed at the knife. His hand was bleeding from the cut he inflicted upon himself in his effort to remove the blade from his stomach. It was plunged far deeper than even Chloe had been aware of. The blade had travelled with such velocity that it had embedded itself some eight or nine inches by the sheer force Chloe had generated. Sam Fyeman's face contorted into a kind of expression which showed surprise and dismay all at the same time. There was no further sound from the serial bully's mouth but his lips curled as he attempted to mime whatever it was he was trying to say. Sam Fyeman staggered but fell backwards. He lay on the tiled kitchen floor wearing the type of mask he had seen on the many victims who had suffered or fallen at his hands. The blood oozed from his stomach into the air like water from a fountain but Sam Fyeman would not be able to bully anyone else anymore. This is how Chloe Dibidibi was able to free herself from the emotional and physical bully.

She was found not guilty by jury of the charge of pre-meditated murder in the Brazenborough's Central Criminal Court. As Chloe Dibidibi exited from the court, she was cheered by the massive crowd of mainly females. Many had followed the case via printed and TV media. Some had listened attentively to the case from the public gallery over the four weeks. They too had been abused but had been humiliated further when they had reported their ordeals to the police. Some were asked awkward questions in court by barristers and judges alike about personal information like "how many times a week do you have sex"? In most of the cases, those same *'representatives of the law'* refused to punish the perpetrators. Outside Brazenborough Central Criminal Court, journalists from the written and television media interviewed Chloe. As she told her story to them, the chorus of cheers exploded from those, who had never had a chance to defend themselves when in similar situations. Chloe's instinctive reaction against Sam Fyeman was a kind of release for those women, who had been weighted down by pent up feelings over time. Chloe was their heroine. It wasn't the first time that she had been raped. At 11 years old, Chloe was kidnapped on her way home from school but was subjected to being gang raped by teenage gangsters, who claimed to be *'repping their endz'* in a part of Brazenborough that was in conflict with another gang that was *'reppin their endz'* where Chloe just happened to live. It was an awfully bizarre emotionally insensitive experience for Chloe and the other girl, who had to suffer at the hands of the *'mentally deranged'* gangsters. After her aweful ordeals, Chloe felt cheapened by those *'life experiences'*. She felt she was of no further *'use'* than to satisfy men like Duke for a fee. Chloe did this in order to maintain a lifestyle that was modelled by the *'role models'* she admired. Her quest for *'make up'*, bling, branded goods, *skin lightening'* and hair *'straightening'* products was her personal statement of how inferior she felt about her significantly natural very dark melanin skin and tradition. Chloe had been abused by a variety of individuals from different ethnicities. None were pleasant experiences but she was especially pained at being abused by individuals from her own ethnicity in particular. There was confusion in her mind as to her ID. Chloe started to swallow and digest the *'stereo-tripe'* about *"a lighter skin tone"* being a *'preferred option'* to her natural original darker skin tone. Even in her family circles, this programming and conditioning was repeated like a mantra as far back as Chloe can remember. Though this *'stereo-tripe'* was established generations before the now 21 years old Chloe was conceived let alone born, it seemed to rivet itself to the cultural underside of the psyche of most individuals from the exotic continents, countries and islands. Chloe Dibidibi had undergone a series of *'reconstructive surgeries'* to *'enhance'* her appearance. It was a culturally contrived *'model'* which was being *'sold'* as the programmed and conditioned typical socially acceptable *'stereo-type'*. In fact, young Chloe had entered the *'Cloned Barbie of the Year'* contests repeatedly but was still not yet being viewed or as yet deemed *'light-skinned'* enough *'model'* to fit the *'stereo-hyped'* socialite *'role'*. There was always something that didn't quite meet the *'standards'* of the *'judges'* who pontificated at these events. Thadius P Henpicker was her Sex Surrogate Agent. His agency catered for but had many young girls queuing at those events to satiate the sexual *'appetites'*, *'needs'* or *'fantasies'* of many rich, very rich and extremely rich men, who were able to select from the throngs of women dressed only in thongs. They made themselves available to be ogled at, accepted, rejected or be physically examined by their *'auctioneers'* for rent or sale. Chloe and some of her colleagues were paraded virtually on, TWS, Technological Whorehouse Sites. One of those was called AS, Anonymous Selectors. Girls were selected by men of *'high financial repute'*, whether politically or from Corporate Bodies, for display as *'Escorts'* at Commercial Events, particularly. Chloe had got caught up in the social quagmire which established her as a modern day *'Kept Woman'* known as *'concubines'* in days of the biblical Jesus Christi. They earned a hell of a lot more than the *'nine to fivers'* and was able to maintain the *'false images'* their *'troubled minds'* had perceived them to be. Some, like Chloe, were used as *'drug mules'*.

She was just letting Duke know that her mission to the exotic continent had been successful and that she was now back in Spaceville. He did not want Chloe to reveal the reason for her call. Duke knew she was a bit careless sometimes and he just couldn't take that chance. "Not now Chloe, this is not a good time. I've got to get back to the office. I'll see you later, Duke retorted". She wanted to tell him about how much she had enjoyed the wonderful *'free holiday'* trip that he had sponsored and that she was happy to have joined the *'mule train'*. Although she understood that Duke was unable to have a long conversation with her, Chloe wanted to inform him that she had no problems with either Customs in the homeland of her grandparents or on her return. As instructed, she had deposited the return *'cargo'* at her current destination, Stache Airport, in Sunnyborough, Spaceville. Before he hung up, Duke asked Chloe to just say the code words. "Only jack asses bray", she confirmed.

After hanging up with Chloe, Duke reflected on his wife's sarcastic comment about his lack of interest in his son's situation. Although Duke acted as if he didn't care, news of his son's hospitalization did disturb him but he was even more upset at his wife, Dora, for hanging up on him. Duke was approaching the street upon which his business was established when he heard the sound of a car horn. He turned his head to look. The cops, who had attended The Old Frigate AADC, were smiling and waving at him. Duke waved back. One

Cop put his head out the window but commented. "Don't forget my wife's favourite tipple", he reminded. Duke smiled to himself but realized that he would have to keep to his promise or be forever haunted by his kind gesture. The cops sounded the horn again then, with siren blazing, sped off through the light traffic. Duke waved the police goodbye and just as quickly turned his attention back to yet another phone call. This time it was Mary. "Duke, Ms. Bogus just called. She won't be able to start until next week", Mary told Duke. "Did she give a reason", he queried? "Yes, her new car won't be ready until the end of the week. She has just been told by the showroom", Mary told him. "Can't we arrange some transport for her in the mean time", Duke asked? "I suppose we could but Andy thought it's just as well she won't be able to start 'til next week. It will give him time to sort out a few things", Mary explained. He said he needs more time to prepare her new office. "I'm not interested in what he thinks. Ask Ms. Bogus to ring me, would you Mary, Duke counselled? "At the office or on your cell phone", Mary queried? "My cell phone is best. I'll be back in the office later this afternoon. Tell my chauffeur to have the car ready in five minutes, please Mary", Duke stated. Mary contacted the chauffeur. "Sam, Mr. Stagg is on his way over to you, o.k.", Mary stressed. "O.K. Miss Mary", he replied dutifully. Sam placed his cell phone in his pocket but prepared himself for the man he secretly called, *'Lord Clout'*. Sam saw Duke as he approached the building. The limo was immediately put into drive and headed towards him. Duke stood but waited for the limo to arrive. Sam pulled up, alighted from the car then opened the door for him. "Hello Mr. Stagg, how are you today, sir", Sam enquired? Duke acknowledged Sam's concern. "I'm fine Sam, take me to Braniffy", Duke said. "Sure Mr. Stagg", Sam replied. He climbed in behind the steering wheel and set off for Braniffy Champagne Company down by the Yellow Bird Wharf. Braniffy was a specialist Champagne Company owned by a family of Quadruplets. Three brothers and one sister ran the company. When he was younger, Duke and the family had lived and played together on the same streets in Ghettoborough. The friendships had lasted because of the special bond between them. They had shared past days together having fun but also they shared the *'secrets'* of the other side of their lives. People living on that side of the Yellow Bird Wharf controlled all that took place in that area but did not welcome *'strangers'*. They didn't want to live or mingle amongst them. Every stranger would either have to run the gauntlet or suffer a practiced routine that mentally and physically challenged the individual into *'heroism'* or *'martyrdom'*. Sam did not like to go to that particular area. The risk was emotionally high but Sam could not help the rush of adrenalin as memories of his miraculous escape came flooding back. At 18 years old, he had been chased down those same streets near the Yellow Bird Wharf. Sam had been invited to play in a game of association football/soccer for his friend's team. It was commonly known as a *'no go'* area for Sam and his *"lot"* as they were referred to by the residents, who lived in and around the environs of Yellow Bird Wharf. Sam was young and naïve at the time and his love for the game of association football/soccer had been the stimuli that lured him into entering that particular area. While he was on the pitch, the *'anti-ethnic'* green humanoid robotron *'cultural gangs'* from the Tribe of Babylon had been brazenly intimidating. Even though all the population in that part of Ghettoborough were not all green humanoid robotrons, they were typically representative of a *'tunnel-vision' toxic mindset* which had been programmed and conditioned by inveterate *'values and beliefs'* against people from the Tribe of Hawke in particular. This psychological bullying had been allowed to fester for millennia but multiplied virally without oversight over generations. Sam and his friends from the

Mixed DNA Rainbow Tribe were the targets on this particular day. The intimidating behaviours manifested when some green humanoid robotron *'supporters'* threw bananas on the pitch. Some team members told Sam to *"ignore them"*. He tried to focus on the game but was unsure whether it was his summary skills or the bullying of the green humanoid robotron *'supporters'* that drove the behaviours of the opposition team on the pitch. Whether he was on the ball or off it, Sam's memory of that experience was one of being targeted by members of the opposition. Off the ball, the verbal abuse seemed to come from every opponent all over the pitch. On the ball, elbows were registering much too frequently. Tackles that came in were high and well over the top. The green humanoid robotron referee also ignored each of the possible leg-breaking tackles on him. Threats came from the opposition manager, the substitutes as well as some in the crowd. On one of the occasions when Sam was being tackled, he decided that the opponent had deliberately intended to break his leg. Writhing in pain, Sam saw the area where the skin had been totally removed by the offenders' studs. The area of contact on his knee appeared white and to the bone. It took some time before the blood started to ooze then poured from the wounds made by the metal studs from the opponent's boots. The two-legged tackle had been deliberately aimed but connected with Sam's knee-bone. He had been down for a while but the referee shouted abuse at him. He referred to his ethnicity in a derogatory manner but said Sam was faking how badly injured he was. The referee did not stop the game. Even the team Sam was playing for showed no concern about the physical and verbal abuse to which he had been exposed. As he hobbled off towards the green humanoid robotron manager of his team, Sam received the worst of the abuses. He came over to Sam but told him to "get on with it". Sam pointed to his damaged knee and the blood. "Contact Sport", his green humanoid robotron team manager replied. "Did you see the tackle", Sam asked? "50-50", the team manager replied. He tore into Sam but accused him of letting the team down by walking off the pitch. He told Sam to get back on it if he knew what was good for him. "I can't stand quitters", the team manager bellowed. More jeers from the crowd tested young Sam's ability to control how he truly felt at that time. Walking gingerly, Sam made his way back onto the pitch. More bananas were thrown at him and not all were ripened ones. To compound Sam's inner rage, the referee came over towards him but accused him of *'diving'*. He awarded a *'free kick'* to the opposition instead. Sam realized that he should not have punched the referee but he reflected he was at the end of his tether then. This *'no go'* area had an even more gruesome history than Sam's own experiences during the football match. Whilst standing at the bus stop after the game, he and his friend had been set upon by a gang of green humanoid robotron bigots. Sam told his friend to run but set off in pursuit of preserving his life. His friend froze but was fatally wounded at that bus stop by the gang. They were known as Neuro-xenophobes even by other green humanoids in their local community. Even though the police was aware of the gangs' repetitive intimidations, maiming and fatal slayings, they failed to secure legal prosecution against them.

Sam was now an adult but, to date, none of the perpetrators had been brought to justice. After all those years, the police say they do not have enough evidence against the gang. Sam did not have any choice whether to revisit Odourville, Ghettoborough, or not. His job as Duke's chauffeur meant everything to him. Sam looked in the rear view mirror at Duke. He could see him flicking through the pages of a document, which he'd retrieved from the briefcase that was on the back seat of the limo. Sam saw Duke's brow elevate then he saw him nod his head several times before breaking out into a smile. He had been working with Duke long enough to safely assume that *'Lord Clout'* was pleased with what was in that particular document. Duke removed the cell phone from his pocket but started to dial. He put the phone to his ear but started to talk. "Allan Greencorke", Duke demanded. The operator on the other side acknowledged Duke's request. "Hold for a moment please", the operator said. While he was holding for Allan Greencorke, Duke heard the background music over the phone. It was a song that he knew. He smiled as he remembered, when as a young boy of 17 years old, he used to play it on the piano at his local AADC. "Allan Greencorke", the voice boomed. "Allan, you bastard", Duke replied. Allan recognized the voice at the other end. "Duke, you rascal, how are you mate", Allan asked? "I'm alright, how are the boys", Duke asked? "They're still about, you know. Jack 'the jeweller' is in again", Allan commented. "What's he gone down for this time", Duke asked? "Jewellery, you know how passionate he is about his precious jewellery. It's a weakness for poor old Jack", Allan confirmed. "I'm coming over to see you", Duke stated. "Anytime mate", Allan said. "Got to go now, see you later", Duke said. He hung up. "Sam, put on one of your CDs, would you", Duke requested. "Yes, Mr. Stagg", Sam replied. He selected a CD that he knew Duke liked to hear. "Turn up the bass", he pleaded. Coming from the speakers, the thumping of the bass made Sam nod his head to the reggae music. Duke could see Sam's cap moving up and down. The vibrating of the phone alerted Duke to his next call. Putting the tiny phone to his ear, he talked excitedly to the person on the other end. "Ms. Bogus I thought you could start straight away", Duke asked? "I need my car to get there but it won't be ready until the end of the week", Sandra explained. "What would you say if I sent you a limo until you get your car", Duke asked? Sandra was shocked surprised that Duke would want to do that for her but she knew Raymond would be suspicious about such an arrangement. "A limo, that's sweet of you Mr. Stagg but I don't think my boyfriend would like that", Sandra told him. "Jealous, is he", Duke teased? Sandra was not sure why the Boss of DSI was paying her so much attention. The doorbell made Sandra jump. She was not expecting anyone. "Mr. Stagg, would you hold on please? Someone is at the door. It's probably the postman", Sandra said. She walked towards the solid front door. Sandra unlocked it by rotating the key that was already in the door. She wrenched the handle then pulled the door inwards. "Ray, what are you doing home? Is something wrong", Sandra asked? Though Raymond was taken aback by her reaction, Sandra was genuinely surprised. "Are you alright Sandy", Raymond asked? "Yes, I'm on the phone to my boss. I'll talk to you in a minute", she said. Sandra made a special point of pecking Raymond on the cheek but she evaded his open arms. Her large cornflower blue eyes were fixed on him. Raymond couldn't think of a reason but sensed that Sandra was acting strange. Duke teased her about "the jealous boyfriend". She said little but listened while Duke tried to convince her to "start immediately". Sandra saw the anxious look on Raymond's face. She told Duke that she would like to help but was determined to give herself a chance to catch up with a few things she needed to do while waiting for her car to arrive. "O.k, I'll be expecting you at 08:00 hours on Monday next", Duke stated. He hung up. Sandra just caught up with Raymond as he started to turn away from her. He had just reached the front door when Sandra pinned him against the wall but expressed her message of *'love'*. She held him quite tightly as if she was trying to prevent Raymond from leaving. "Can't you stay for a minute Ray", Sandra asked? Raymond was sulking a bit. He felt Sandra's greeting didn't feel or sound the same, somehow. "Well, you were busy and I didn't know how long you would be on the phone", Raymond lied. "Have lunch with me", she said. "I need to get back", Raymond explained. "Share my lunch with me. It should arrive soon", Sandra pleaded. Raymond looked at his watch. It was 13:53 hours. He had to get back to work within 45 minutes. The journey at that time of day would take at least 40 minutes. Raymond would need to travel amongst light traffic to reach his destination on time. The doorbell caused both of them to jump. They both looked at each other before Raymond finally opened the door. He stood in the doorway as the rider of the moped raised his helmet. "Meal for Ms. Bogus", the boy said. He was about sixteen years old. Raymond paid for then took the meal. He slipped a tip in the boy's hand. "Thanks", the boy said. He then turned away. As soon as the front door was shut, both Sandra and Raymond went into the kitchen together. Sandra opened the foil container but removed the white piece of cardboard used to cover the food. It was Raymond who got the fork. He looked at his watch again but announced, "I'll have to go", Raymond said. "Just have a little with me, please Ray", Sandra pleaded. She rolled her eyes at him and he froze in his track then turned back to take a mouthful of the food. "Now, I really have got to go", Raymond said. He walked towards the front door. Raymond exited from the house. Sandra was happy that Raymond had returned to his normal composure seemingly. She enjoyed the rest of the food then poured herself a cup of coffee from the percolator. Sandra sat on the stool with the white painted rattan seat. She contemplated not only the prospects of the job but also the reactions from the other staff members. Sandra pondered how she might cope with such hostility yet she felt assured that Duke would tend to back her. She was confident that he would, providing she could convince him that her actions or comments were strictly professional and viable. Her contract had given her direct control over the staff but Sandra would report to her boss, Andy Mann. She read the copy of the contract to re-confirm her understanding of it. The terms and conditions were clear and binding. Sandra took a few more sips of the coffee then reached for a small note pad and a pencil. She wrote quite swiftly but soon filled many pages with ideas of how to get the best out of the staff. Sandra still felt intimidated by their behaviour. After finishing the coffee, she went into the lounge. Sandra searched for and found a book on 'How to get the best out of your staff'. She scanned the contents page until she found the chapter she needed. Sitting in the recliner chair, Sandra eased it until she felt comfortable. Because Sandra was keen on finding a solution to the blatant *'disapproval'* of her appointment, she studied the book earnestly. When her cell phone rang, she looked at the screen. It was another call from Duke. She stared at the screen but decided to answer it. "Hello Mr. Stagg", Sandra said. Her voice was stern yet professional. Duke noticed but preferred for Sandra to feel relaxed with being less formal. "Duke please", he replied. As Duke awaited a response from Sandra, there was a brief silence. Without waiting for her response, Duke fired another question which caught her completely off guard. "Can I call you Sandra", he asked? "We are meant to have a professional relationship, aren't we", Sandra tested? Duke did not want to upset her. He submitted temporarily, at least. "When I get to know you better, may I call you Sandra", Duke pleaded? Sandra was cautious in her response "I'm sure you didn't just ring to ask me that, Mr. Stagg, she dodged. Duke was astounded how Sandra cleverly re-routed his intentions to her advantage. He liked that feisty trait which she exhibited so effortlessly. To Duke, Sandra would make an ace PR Consultant. "I rang to see if I could help to speed up the delivery of your new car", Duke fished. "How is that possible", Sandra queried? "It's called clout. People either have it or they don't. I've got plenty of it", Duke persisted. "Let me think about it", Sandra insisted. "All you need to do is . . ." Duke started. Their conversation was interrupted once again. She hadn't heard the rest of what Duke had to say. Sandra paused. She heard the sound of keys at the door but Raymond had gone to work. "Mr. Stagg, I'll have to go, I think someone is trying to get in my house", Sandra whispered. Her voice was soft anyway but when she whispered her sweet voice did something to Duke. He flushed but suddenly started sweating. Duke placed the cell between his ear and shoulder, using his hands to loosen his tie but undo the first button on his shirt to ease his excitement. "Don't hang up", Duke shouted. He then lowered his voice to a whispered tone too. Duke's baritone voice belied his short physical stature but it did easily attract attention. When he didn't get a response from Sandra, Duke commented yet again. "Are you there Ms Bogus", he enquired? Sandra leaned from the room but peered at the door to see who was trying to get in. She slid from the lounge into the kitchen but armed herself with a knife from the draw in which cutlery were stored. Sandra stealthily eased her way to stand in the hallway nearer to the front door. The sudden pounding on the wooden door inflicted more fear in both Sandra and Duke. He too could hear the thumping sound over the phone. Duke panicked when he thought someone might be harming Sandra. He was eager to find out. "What the hell was that? Ms Bogus are you all right", Duke asked? Sandra did not reply but kept her stare on the place where the lock was situated on the door. She could hear Raymond's voice now. "Sandy, open the door", Raymond shouted. It was then that Sandra realized that the security lock was engaged. As shocked as she was to hear Raymond's voice, Sandra was puzzled why he had returned so soon. She moved forwards to disengage the security lock then pulled the door open. "I've been knocking for at least ten minutes, were you asleep", Raymond asked? He rushed pass Sandra but went upstairs. She stood in a quandary as to what was going on. "What's the matter Ray", Sandra asked? He did not reply. She followed him upstairs. Sandra rushed into the bedroom but Raymond wasn't there. Sandra heard the toilet flush. She smiled. Raymond came onto the landing. He noticed that Sandra had the cell phone in her hands. "Been on the phone that's why you couldn't hear me", Raymond teased. Sandra remembered that Duke was still holding on. "Hello Mr. Stagg, are you still there", she queried? "Still waiting patiently for your answer about the car", Duke said. "Oh, I can't give you an answer at the moment, I'll have to think about it", Sandra replied. She looked at Raymond. After learning that Mr. Stagg had phoned again, Raymond looked at Sandra with indignation. He sensed a bad vibe about the repeat phone-call. Suspicion overwhelmed him. "If you would rather be on the phone all day I might as well go out again", Raymond said dryly. "Jealous, is he", Duke jibed? Sandra decided to take the initiative to end the phone call. She heard a few more mumblings from Duke including an invitation to dinner before she started the job. "Anyway, I'll have to go", Sandra strained. She pressed the red button on the cell phone. Sandra sidled up to Raymond but stood looking into his eyes. She knew her stare was stronger than his and soon Raymond began to turn his attention from anger. Sandra eased the buttons on his shirt but pushed herself closer to him. Clinging tightly to his larger frame, Sandra kissed Raymond on his lips then immediately turned away from him. She headed for the bedroom. Raymond warmed to the invitation. He caught up with Sandra just before she entered the room. Raymond swept her off her feet but carried her over the threshold. He placed her on the bed but bent to kiss her. Sandra pulled on Raymond's open shirt and he toppled unto her. Both were urgently preparing to enter the pathway to blissful emotional experiences when the doorbell rang. It rang haphazardly in long and short bursts. The impatient *'imposter'* was not welcomed at that moment by Raymond or Sandra. They tried to ignore the interruption but the bell continued to ring. There was a heavy knocking of the letterbox following the long and short bursts on the bell. As their focus had been disturbed, Sandra and Raymond decided to see about the urgent *'request'* for them to open the door. Raymond was still trying to appear decent when he opened the door. Sandra trailed behind him. Rage engulfed them as the four Jehovah's Witnesses brandishing the new Monthly Edition of *'Awake'*, stood looking embarrassed as they observed how much Raymond was sweating and the oddly buttoned shirt; showing the collar as higher on one side. The more advanced of the four had a brief glimpse of the sweaty Sandra in her see-through negligee. The Witness cleared her throat but continued to quote biblical verses. Neither Raymond nor Sandra found enough patience, at that moment, to attend to *'christian values'*. "Excuse us, we're busy", Sandra exclaimed "We're busy doing God's work, what are you busy doing", the Jehovah's Witness asked? Neither Sandra nor Raymond welcomed the Witness' cynical tone or her implicit reference. "Shut the door Ray", Sandra instructed. The Jehovah's Witness seemed impervious to both Sandra and Raymond's feelings. She didn't move. Raymond shut the door all the same. He phoned his job but asked his colleague to cover for him. Raymond lifted his gorgeous woman back over the bedroom threshold once again in order to resume where they had left off.

Chapter 18

Raymond was a Physical Instructor and a fine athlete. He was Sandra's ideal *'fantasy'*. Raymond was her idea of the *'Trophy Man'* type, the legendary *'Mr. Right'*. Raymond remembered how Sandra used to look enviously at the other girls at Coleport College and Bastärdé University, who dared to approach him because of his personality, handsome facial features and physical build. Sandra had her claws in Raymond and would not give him up unless she chose to. She realized that it was impossible to change Raymond's popularity amongst the women. Most of them, who lived in the community, showed that they fancied Raymond, openly. Sandra had shown her claim to him when they visited the local market. She and Raymond wandered through the market until Sandra saw a pair of fashion shoes that she liked. "Look Ray, do you like them", she asked? Sandra pointed excitedly to the pair of red name brand fashion shoes displayed in the window. "Yeah, try them on, I'll buy them for you", Raymond offered. As far as he was concerned, his highly melanin elegant angelic heavenly *'Mona Lisa'* deserved anything that he found affordable. There was no dispute in his mind how much he wanted to shower Sandra with gifts and as often as he could. "Did you see the price", Sandra queried? Raymond pulled her close to him but hugged her tightly. He stared into those bewitching large cornflower blue eyes, which he found so mesmerizing, before confirming that Sandra's wish to own a pair of those name brand shoes was about to be realized. Raymond guided his *'Mrs. Right'* towards the entrance of the shop. They stepped over the threshold and into the shoe shop displaying the name brand fashion shoes.

Inside, the assistants were busily attending to the many customers who were rapidly reducing the shop's stock. Sandra tried to get the attention of one of the assistant. The young woman, about a year older than her came over but immediately turned her attention to Raymond. She was attracted to him but was brazen enough to do it in front of Sandra. It was as if she was invisible. "Whey yuh ah sey", the shop assistant asked? She meant for Sandra to know how much Raymond had impacted her. The shop assistant kept smiling, rolled her eyes but repeatedly licked her lips, shook her hips violently to indicate how much of a *'crush'* she had on the handsome hunk specimen who stood in front of her. Sandra was none too pleased about the assistant's peahen display of being on heat that she was witnessing. Before Sandra could react to the whims of the wayward assistant, she flaunted herself yet again. "Yow baby, mi hav supmn fi yuh. Whey uh hav fi mi", the assistant teased? Raymond was not really interested in the assistant but he wanted to comment back in the cultural vernacular that she was using. Raymond responded in a form of greeting to acknowledge he was from the same type of heritage as the assistant. "Yuh is a *'hot girl'*, yeah", Raymond parried? They laughed together. The assistant approved of the language in which he had chosen to respond. They chatted briefly together then Raymond tried to introduce Sandra to his new *'friend'*. Heaving heavy sighs as she looked jealously at the assistant, Sandra had drifted away from them. Raymond sensed what was going on so he tried to pacify Sandra's tantrum. "Sandy, this is my *'friend'*. Ask her about the shoes", Raymond said. It was obvious to Sandra that Raymond was no friend of this brazen assistant. Sandra was off-handed about the introduction. In fact, she didn't want to meet Raymond's *'friend'* at any time. Sandra found her behaviour reprehensibly too common and daring. "Don't bother, I thought assistants were supposed to serve customers not transfer sexual intentions to them", Sandra fired acidly. The assistant took offence to Sandra's comments. She quizzed Raymond about his woman. "Wha yuh woman ah try fi sey", the assistant asked? He didn't want to seem as if he was taking sides so he remained silent. Sandra looked long and hard at the assistant. Arrows of hate, projected into flight by sheer weight of jealousy reached its target with precision. The assistant received the message when Sandra snarled angrily but bared her long talons inferring the kind of physical damage she wanted to inflict upon the assistant. The shop assistant's final comment on the matter warned of her observation of the stability of Raymond and Sandra's relationship. It was a passing shot that sent a direct message to reflect her feedback as boldly and honestly as she was allowed to express her observations of Sandra's behaviour. "She mite as wel chain yuh 2 har", the assistant exclaimed. Sandra heard the comment but was satisfied that her message had got through to whom she perceived as a *'brazen hussey'*. Satisfied that she had made her claim to her *'Mr. Right'*, Sandra restated her enquiry about the pair of name brand shoes that had drawn them into the shop. It wasn't as if she was still interested in the pair of shoes anymore but she found another opportunity to reinforce her claim on Raymond. This time her comment was meant to be silently transferred. It was Sandra who took the initiative this time. "I want to try the red name brand shoes in the window", Sandra demanded. "What size", the assistant enquired? "Size twelve", Sandra responded. The assistant confirmed her interest in the sale by turning to retrieve the size Sandra had specified. She sat down on the little padded bench in the middle of the floor. When the assistant returned, Sandra dragged the shoes from her hands but tried them on. Turning to Raymond, she asked for his approval. "Do you like them Ray", Sandra asked? He was ashamed by the unnecessary attention they were receiving from the other people in the shop. His embarrassment was reaching to a point that was more than being a little uncomfortable. All Raymond wanted to do was speed up the sale. "Yeah", Raymond replied. Sandra could sense the level of discomfiture both Raymond and particularly the assistant was feeling. She deliberately delayed her confirmation by strolling up and down in the pair of red name brand shoes but posing in front of the mirror occasionally for effect. The assistant was getting impatient as it was obvious that many other prospective customers were growing in numbers rapidly. Some had been attracted into the shop by the earlier loud exchanges between the two women. The assistant asked the inevitable question. "Do you want it", she asked? Sandra stared from the assistant to Raymond to the pair of red name brand fashion shoes and back again several times. She sidled up to Raymond but kissed him passionately on his lips before voicing her approval. "Yes", Sandra snapped. "How are you paying", the assistant asked? Sandra removed the wallet with credit cards. At first, she removed the Gold credit card then returned it to the wallet. Next, she removed the Platinum credit card from the wallet. Raymond intervened but commented. "I said I'd buy them for you Sandy. Let me buy them for you", he pleaded. Sandra had to get her last shot at the unprepared assistant who might not have been aware how she was being played by Sandra's wicked ruse. She made her final verbal comment. "If I still mean as much to you before we entered this shop, Ray honey then you can pay for the pair of shoes", Sandra responded. Raymond paid for the fashion shoes with his Platinum credit card. The assistant was humbled in as many ways as Sandra had orchestrated. Her final action about whose company Raymond preferred was yet to come. When the assistant returned with Raymond's Platinum credit card, Sandra took it from the assistant but placed it in the wallet with the rest of her credit cards. Her comments were interesting too. "You won't need this card until you feel you must buy me yet another expensive present, Ray darling, will you", Sandra asked? It was only a rhetorical question but it was effective. Sandra hugged Raymond but kissed him again before walking in the direction of the exit. The last warning to the assistant was the reminder what might happen if she persisted to fling herself at Raymond. Sandra turned but looked directly at the assistant but held up her talons to her lips. She blew on them like cowboys do to their smoking guns in *'Western Movies'*. She and Raymond talked about the incident while they travelled back from the market. He pointed out to her that it was just a cultural exchange between him and his *'friend'*, the assistant. "Our partnership must be built on trust Sandy", Raymond reinforced. Sandra argued that when the boot was on the other foot, Raymond had shown different levels of jealousy too. "Don't tell me that. Look how you wanted to fight the guy in the supermarket who paid me a nice compliment. You're just as jealous", Sandra retorted. Raymond did not agree with Sandra's assessment. "That was different, he was talking to you as if you're a *'loose woman'*", Raymond countered. Sandra stayed silent for a while then she challenged him. "Do you think I'm a *'loose woman'* Ray", she enquired? "Lets not fuss Sandy", Raymond replied. He sighed but breathed deeply. Even though Raymond wanted to end the feud about which of them were the more jealous, Sandra wanted an answer to her question. She pressed him for an answer. "You haven't answered my question", she insisted. Raymond had had enough of the bickering. He declared that he did not want to prolong the squabble. "Look Sandy, we live together so that is a silly question. Let us just forget it", Raymond advised. They drove for a while in silence. Sandra told Raymond that she was hungry. She ordered him to stop at a particular restaurant. They did. Sandra ordered a full dinner. She tucked into it immediately. Raymond was hungry too but he preferred eating at his friend's restaurant. Between mouthfuls, Sandra tried to persuade Raymond to order a dinner. His response highlighted one of the core differences in their relationship. "I told you before Sandy, I like to eat my own type of food. My daddy insisted I do and he is right. The other foods do not agree with my stomach. I'll pick up something on the way home", Raymond replied. He took out his cell phone and began to dial. Sandra could not hear the responses to Raymond's requests but she heard his response. "About half an hour", he said. Raymond pressed the red button to end the call. It didn't take long for Sandra to finish her roast beef and two veg meal. The apple crumble with custard disappeared just as quickly as it had been placed before her. Raymond paid and they continued on their journey. Even though it was a bright sunny day, the roll of thunder alerted that rain was inevitable soon. When it started as light shower, Sandra commented on the elongated shape of the crystal clear drops but also the acid orange coloured polka dots that decorated each drop. It was as if they were transparent mini-balloons filled with water but with the acid orange coloured polka dots on the outside of the balloons. The journey to Raymond's friend's restaurant, 'Mouth-Watering Ethnic Cuisine', took exactly forty minutes. Sandra said she would wait outside in the car. Raymond objected. "I want you to meet my friend who runs the business", he said. Raymond opened the passenger door. Sandra's compromise was conditional. "OK, but promise you won't stay long chatting", she insisted. Inside the restaurant, Sandra saw a large flyer on the counter for the *'Miss Brass & Beautiful'* Contest. She picked it up but dreamed of entering. Raymond had gone towards the counter to greet his friend. Unlike Sandra, he accessed the washroom to wash his hands before sitting down to eat. Raymond had already placed his order with the owner. Before long, the smell of curried goat and rice filled the restaurant but also wafted through the open doors of the restaurant too. It was tempting not only to passers-by but also even to those others already tucking into their meals inside the restaurant. The strong identifiable smell of the curry was so overwhelming that Sandra seemed to be longing to taste it. She asked Raymond but he warned her that it might be too hot and spicy for her. Sandra could not resist the temptation. Raymond gave her the fork. Sandra tasted it. She enjoyed the taste but for the pieces of scotch bonnet peppers that lay betwixt and between the highly spiced gravy. Sandra begged Raymond to get her some iced water to quench the burning in her mouth. He and the others, who watched Sandra's reactions, laughed loudly at the way she used her hand like a fan to indicate not only the heat emanating from the plate but also that which was generated by the highly spiced cuisine. Like a crying doll, tears flowed from Sandra's large cornflower blue eyes. Her nose ran as free as an open tap but heat escaped from her crown. Sandra was grateful to the females who offered her tissues to stop her embarrassment. After Raymond finished his meal, he ordered a big glass of Sorrel and ginger with lots of ice. Having recovered from her ordeal, Sandra showed the flyer to Raymond. He shook his head but commented. "No way, you'll only wear a bikini when I'm with you", Raymond stated. "Oh Ray, let me try, I might even win and become famous", Sandra pressed.

Raymond was firm with his reply. "No Sandy", he said. He was pleased that Sandra wanted to be a winner but not the way she seemingly wanted to expose herself. Even though Sandra was aware of how Raymond felt about her exposing herself to all and sundry, she had displayed time and time again that "Sandra gets what Sandra wants". Raymond had begun to notice a few flaws in his *'little diamond'* but he didn't want those flaws to ruin their relationship. He idolised Sandra but was blinded by her *stunning facial beauty* and *physique.* Both of those attributes kept him under her spell. They left the restaurant but travelled to the Ghettoville Community Centre near where they lived. On their arrival to the local Community Centre, Raymond's *'bona fide'* friends expressed their approval of Sandra's physical beauty. They teased him. "Yuh lucky to have "ah woman like dat. Some man wudda tek life fi hav a woman like dat", 'Gold Digga' Herman commented. With comments like that, Raymond was feeling proud of himself for choosing the seemingly delectable, Sandra. Other friends teased him about his physique. They too were conditioned to believe in the culture of facial *'looks'* and apparent *'physical attributes'* that seemed to be the yardstick by which their relationships were being measured. "Me waan know whey she si pon yuh", Rafael teased. Every one of his friends, who were present at the Ghettoville Community Centre, had something nice to say about the shapely, bustylicious and outstandingly naturally beautiful Sandra Bogus. Everyone, except for DJ Herbie and 'Screwface' Frankie had made the encouraging comments. Rafael pressed for their opinions. Rather than upset his friend or simply to dodge the onslaught of criticism that was bound to be aimed at him, 'Screwface' Frankie declined to comment against the perceived norm. "Mi nuh have nuttn fi sey", he replied. Unlike 'Screwface' Frankie, DJ Herbie was respected by the others as a deep thinker. His words were not criticised but were considered by most as wisdom but was rather sought after, often. He made a subtler point but with succinct distinction. "Beauty is not only pon di outside", DJ Herbie retorted. When the music came on, they changed the conversation. Rafael got up from the chair but started to dance the *skank.* The others moved their heads to the lively reggae beat they were used to. DJ Herbie went to do his stint over the microphone. Music was in *'session'.* The heavy bass line walked across the floor while the other accompaniments thrilled the users within the Ghettoville Community Centre. In order to socialise with his friends, Raymond visited the Centre on Thursday and Friday of each week. He and his friends often shared a joke or two but listened to the music they loved. *'Reasoning'* was considered by his friends and colleagues as a *'Therapy'* that worked for them. Raymond wasn't going to give that up not even for the irresistible Sandra. Previously, he had asked her to accompany him to the Centre to meet some of his friends but she had refused. Today, he was shocked at Sandra's remarks. "I have got time for you Ray but some of your friends are not my *'type'* ", Sandra stated. Raymond was outraged by her comment. Dismissing his friends as if they were beneath her, Raymond found quite offensive but he tried not to show his contempt for her narrow-minded *'class-ist'* approach towards them. Raymond felt a cold chill come over him. Even Sandra felt his body shudder as she sidled up to him. Looking deep into his eyes, she smiled but hugged Raymond around his waste. She seemed unaware of her insensitivity towards him. Raymond was unsure how to handle Sandra's snobbery. He looked at her blankly but DJ Herbie's words began to resonate in his head. "Listen Sandy, I welcome your friends so what's wrong with mine", Raymond asked firmly? "I just don't trust them. Their behaviours are *'child-like'*. They are loud, rude but always making lewd comments when they see me. I don't understand the way they talk but their gestures are quite clear", Sandra explained. Raymond felt a twinge of jealous rage rise within him. "Which one, just show me", he enquired. Sandra sensed that Raymond's voice had a new serious edge to it when she implicated his friends but she did just the same. "All of them . . . well except for the one you call DJ *'thingy'*. He's creepy, doesn't say anything just looks straight through me as if he can see into my soul", Sandra complained. Raymond tried to justify the difference in cultural *'values'*, *'beliefs'* and approach. He thought that Sandra needed to have a more open mind but accepted that people coming from different backgrounds might choose not to see from her perspective.

"Even those from the same cultural backgrounds behave differently", Raymond explained. Unlike Sandra's friends, Raymond's were from a more open way of living. Their preference for open yet extreme expressionism was an indelible theme that became a proven *'therapeutic tool'* for those individuals. Their everyday survival depended on their individual ability to lessen the impact of the most mundane situations and environments. Traditionally, his friends' relationships were often built on the daily banter and perceived frivolity to which Sandra referred as *'child-like'* behaviours. Because of Sandra's misunderstanding of Raymond's friends' background and culture, she saw them as being below her *'moral'* standards. Their *'values'* and *'beliefs'* seemed quite distant from those that her mother had taught her as being superior, comparably. Sandra became suspicious of Raymond's friends mannerisms and intentions. Her comments confirmed the constant repetitious programming and conditioning of the *'stereotypical images'* that had been carelessly sewn into her psyche by her mother and those significant others. Over time, their influence seemed to have shaped Sandra's *'values and beliefs'* system. Her egoist mindset seemed to have isolated her from the possibilities of having any new meaningful relationships, especially with individuals from different cultural backgrounds like Raymond's friends. As far as Sandra was concerned, DJ Herbie was as much a plebian as the other useless *"idle jubbies"* against whom her mother had warned.

On the Sunday afternoon when DJ Herbie visited her and Raymond's home, Sandra treated him badly. She didn't greet him when she opened the door. When DJ Herbie asked for Raymond, Sandra just stood aside but used her head to indicate he could come in. She waited for him to enter but refused to speak to him. Instead, Sandra looked him up and down but held her nose as he went past her into the hallway. DJ Herbie's clothes and breath carried the smell of the spliff he was smoking in his car on his way to see Raymond. He was not aware how much impact the smell can have on those who did not approve of smoking. Raymond had heard the doorbell but hurried down the stairs. He welcomed his friend but directed him into the lounge. Raymond offered DJ Herbie some light refreshment but he refused. They sat but chatted about music and the Radio Station. When DJ Herbie asked to use the toilet, Raymond directed him up the stairs. When he got there, DJ Herbie was faced with three doors. He opened one but put his head around the door to confirm whether it was the toilet. It wasn't. That was the bedroom. Sandra gasped as if she'd been face to face with a wild beast in the jungle. DJ Herbie mumbled an apology but shut the door quickly. His visit to the toilet was becoming even more urgent. DJ Herbie's selection now was down to choosing from two doors. He made his selection but again this was not the toilet. It was the bathroom. He slammed the door shut but reached for the handle on the only door that he had not previously opened. It was the toilet. DJ Herbie entered. Unbeknown to him, Sandra had been keeping an eye on him. When he came out from using the toilet, DJ Herbie re-entered the bathroom to wash his hands. As he exited from the bathroom, DJ Herbie met with Sandra on the landing. She was standing just outside the bedroom. "You just wasted my water by washing your hands. Are you suffering from OCD", she criticized. DJ Herbie looked at her quizzically but did not comment. He made his way back down the stairs to the lounge to rejoin his friend Raymond. DJ Herbie told him what happened. Raymond realised he had not specified to his friend which door led to the toilet and he was aware that Sandra's cultural habits were more akin to the green humanoid robotrons. While DJ Herbie had gone to the toilet, Raymond had selected some CDs that he wanted to play for his friend to approve for his show later that day. DJ Herbie listened to the music attentively. The next time he needed to go to the toilet, DJ Herbie found that Sandra appeared not from the adjoining room but from the kitchen downstairs. She followed him up the stairs but waited for him to complete his mission before escorting him back down the stairs. DJ Herbie did not feel comfortable with her looking at him disdainfully either but that was beyond his control. When he re-entered the lounge, Raymond could see DJ Herbie's countenance had changed to an even more sombre look. Even though he'd sat down again, DJ Herbie seemed uncomfortable. He kept fidgeting, sighed deeply but kept hissing. He got up from the plush sofa. "Wha di time", DJ Herbie asked? Raymond sensed but wanted to know what had happened to make DJ Herbie feel so uncomfortable. "Yuh caan guh yet, mi ah guh play di tune fi yuh", Raymond commented. "Naw man, bring it dung ah di Radio Station", DJ Herbie replied. As he exited from the lounge door which led towards the hallway, Raymond wanted to know what made DJ Herbie want to leave in such a hurry. "Whaappen Herbie", Raymond enquired? He was concerned about his friend's change of mood. DJ Herbie was angry and tired of being handled with such suspicion. "Cho, si yuh lata", he said. DJ Herbie did not even give his friend Raymond the cultural touching of fists, which was a cultural form of welcome when they met but a sign of leaving valued company in a respectful way also. He got into his car. Something was wrong and Raymond wanted to know what it was that had angered his friend so immensely. The car sped away to the accompaniment of screeching tyres and the scent of burning rubber emanating from the asphalted road. "Sandy, what did you say to my friend when he had left the room to go to the toilet", Raymond asked her directly? "I didn't say a thing, cross my heart and hope to die Ray honey", Sandra lied.

CHAPTER 19

Duke Stagg was the boss whose genius Sandra admired. He was clever and very quick to spot an opportunity. His method of problem solving was unique. Often times, it would be just a hunch but Duke was accurate more often than not. Sandra was one of Duke's targets. They both bore an appetite for the extreme and he knew it. Duke tantalized his prey with the *'high-life'* strategy. His strategy was to promise as much as he thought would suffice the particular individual. Tactically, Duke played everything by ear. His game-plan was never always the same. He'd zone in on an opportunity at the drop of a hat but just as soon abandon the woman if she didn't want to play his games to his rules. Duke's vast general knowledge on a variety of subjects, some as ancient as the Latin language, made him popular. His technological knowledge about computers and other *'mod cons'*, was quite outstanding. Duke had studied computer technology at college. He used modern technological knowledge to impress his women. Sandra lingered on his every word but was drawn towards this strange character. Unlike Sandra, Doris Bendlow was attracted to Duke because she had seen him on TV and was *moved* by his dazzling performances. In his younger days, Duke had appeared on and was the winner of many Television Quiz Shows like *'Minds of the Masters'*. Sandra was too young to know about Duke's early successes on TV though she vaguely remembered her mother mentioning Duke's name. His preacher-like manner could convince any audience that the world isn't round. Unlike Raymond, Duke's battle-hardened upbringing made him appear brash. He oozed brashness and power. Duke called that "clout". He 'wined' and 'dined' his women, introduced them to his many influential friends but bought the women extravagant, expensive presents in order to solidify the affairs. Duke targeted women like Sandra for particular reasons. Like Raymond, physical beauty was Duke's first attraction. Wooing women was almost a hobby. The women he chose didn't *"need to have too much between the ears"* or at least that's what Duke would assume. Voluptuous, rotund women like Doris Bendlow fitted his assumption readily yet the slender model-type women like Sandra presented him with another kind of challenge. Both Doris and Sandra had quite a lot of hair and that hit a high note on Duke's private vetting system. Even though Duke was aware of the horse mane type hair which often appeared as real or natural even, he knew that some women were not naturally blessed with long flowing hair. Duke played along with the women's *'barbie-likeness'* fantasy. He loved to engage in conversations with his friends and colleagues at the AADCs about his status as a *'womanizer'*. This was a kind of ritual that the *'boys'* spent their time talking about. It was just idle chatter, something to past the time away. Duke's friends and colleagues knew that he'd always talked about getting himself an "exotic bird". They often teased him about it. One night, while he was imbibing with his friends and colleagues, one of them offered some information regarding *'exotic birds'*. "I found you a Parrot Duke. Is that exotic enough for you", Matt asked? Duke was not impressed with Matt's meaning of 'exotic birds'. Duke voiced his displeasure. "Now you're being bloody silly, Matt", he countered. On another occasion, Matt told Duke that he found a "Macaw bird" in his garden. "It had a note attached to its leg", Matt joked. "What did the note say, Matt", a voice asked? "Take me to Duke", Matt replied. "That's a good one", one of the liquor assistants quipped. There were screams and much laughter. Matt's guttural laugh, punctuated with heavy *'smokers' cough'*, sounded more like the deep Tuba section of a Salvation Army Band. Duke could not control the roar that followed the cryptic remarks that Matt and the others had made. Triggered by Matt's humour, *'Sod's Law'* meant the entire AADC seemed to erupt all at once. Duke decided to join in the frivolous laughter but resolved, privately, that he'd find his *'exotic'* woman. He swore he'd make Matt and the others eat their words.

The feisty Duke Stagg decided to utilize some of the late *working* nights to demonstrate his *genius quality* to his *'exotic bird'*, the eager Sandra. She needed his important contacts to enable her to achieve her goal. Immersed in her *'rich dreams'*, Sandra went into uncontrollable spasms whenever she watched any Soap Operas about fame and fortune. She'd seen how the *'Top'* people on TV and in the News Papers built their careers. Ever since she was introduced to the glitzy lifestyle by her mother, Sandra developed an *'urge'* for that type of lifestyle. Her mother had seen to that. Dian lured her daughter into a world Sandra hungered for but clearly didn't understand. She was a good student, who was aiming for the top as quickly as she could. Her aims and objectives were crystal clear. Sandra would seek, encourage but cling on to anyone, who she established as influentially powerful enough to help her on the road to stardom. That's all she ever desired since she was young. It was easy for the likes of Duke to entrance young women, like Sandra, into his *lair*. He had practiced his techniques on other naïve women for many years. A compliment here and there was a common part of his portfolio. His status and clout as company boss was an exciting challenge for any young woman seeking the dizzy heights of fame. To be seen in the company of celebrities like Duke was only one important ingredient which women, like Sandra, used to structure their own careers. Late *'working'* nights were more convenient than the daytime for *both* Duke and Sandra to express their passion more explicitly. That night when Duke lured Sandra into his office, he hinted at promoting her *"in the near future"*. He produced a partially filled bottle of his favourite, expensive champagne, 'Champagne Urge' Mark 1. Sandra was sly and coy but pretended to be surprised when Duke offered her champagne. "Oh Duke, you'll spoil me. To what do I owe this honour", she asked? "Let us celebrate your achievement within the company so far", Duke explained "I've only been here a short while. The others might get jealous", Sandra parried. She made eyes at Duke but expressed her meaning by flicking her tongue like Maori Warriors in their celebration dance, licking her lips, flapping her eyelids rapidly then finished with a wink. Duke knew the meaning of Sandra's actions. He was stunned at how willing she was to accommodate his *'need'*. Duke's pulse rate accelerated irregularly and he twitched as spasms passing through his body made him aware how much he wanted Sandra then. Duke flushed with embarrassment. He flattered her with this compliment. "Ms. Bogus you're quite a *'looker'*, if you don't mind me saying so. You don't mind, do you", Duke asked? Sandra was comforted by the compliment. She smiled. Duke poured the two glasses of champagne then re-corked the bottle. He handed one of the glasses to Sandra. "Cheers", they exclaimed as they touched glasses. The slight clinking sound of the touching glasses signalled the permission to taste the bubbly liquid. Sandra felt the bubble tickle her nostrils as she sipped from the long stemmed glass. The taste made her mouth feel dry. "Nice", she said. "You like it then", Duke enquired? "Bit peckish though", Sandra said. Duke was leaning on the desk. "Shall I order a meal in", he asked? "I'm not that hungry, just peckish", Sandra replied. Duke walked towards the fridge in the corner of the office. He removed a plate with small biscuits and an ornate dish with caviar. Duke brought the plate and the dish over to the desk. He motioned to Sandra. "Tuck in", Duke encouraged. Sandra crammed the first biscuit, covered with the fish eggs, into her mouth. The salty taste reminded her taste buds of her addiction to salt. "Mmmmmn, real caviar", Sandra exclaimed. Her face wore a beaming smile. Duke stayed silent but watched the amateur Sandra devour the *'treat'* he'd offered. "Salty", Sandra said. Her comment was rhetorical. "Have some more champagne to wash it down", Duke advised. He continued to refill the glasses again and again. Sandra drank the champagne as if it was a glass of 'pop' drink. She started to giggle then looked over the rim of the glass at Duke. He and the walls of the office seemed to wobble at times as Sandra struggled to focus on any one object. Duke was feeling merry too but he was still focused on his objective. During their conversation, Duke kept inferring about promotion prospects within the company. He told Sandra that he'd already noticed the professionalism in her work. She was impressed that Duke, the boss, had taken notice of her professionalism. "I'll drink to that", Sandra beamed. This time her enthusiasm caused her to gulp rather than sip the bubbly drink. It didn't take long to have an effect on the naive Sandra. A few glasses later, she was giggling to everything that Duke said or did. When he reached up to grasp her breast in his huge hands, Sandra felt a tingling that sent her body into spasms. "Oh Duke", Sandra purred. Leaning towards him Sandra pressed herself up against him. This closeness triggered Duke. He started to fidget but couldn't keep his hands still. With very swift movements Duke stroked Sandra's body. He sensed that she was responding to his every whim. Feeling confident he was about to achieve his objective, they staggered hand in hand across the office floor towards the desk upon which the ice bucket was placed. Duke was beyond control of himself. It was Sandra's 'guttural' groaning that had set Duke off. She had faked yet another orgasm when she sensed Duke was beyond control of himself. Sandra popped the cork and Duke's 'advances' poured all over the lovely but gullible Sandra. He had quickly galloped his way to satisfaction. Duke was spent. Sandra was far from satisfied. Though Duke had just had sex with her, she yearned for those orgasmic satisfying feelings usually experienced when making love with Raymond. Both Sandra and Duke were both lying on top of the desk. His breathing was fast and irregular. Sandra listened but turn from the position on her back to look if Duke was alright. She could hear his heart pounding against his chest. Sandra was concerned about Duke's heavy panting. "Are you alright Duke", she asked? "I'll be alright in a minute", he managed to reply through gasping breaths. Sandra sat up then stood to straighten her dress. She looked down but used her hands to dust some of the crumbs from the small crackers. Her hands felt something other than the crumbs. It was damp and slimy. She looked helplessly at Duke. "Where do you keep your tissues", Sandra asked? "Middle drawer", Duke instructed. Sandra went around the desk but pulled out the middle draw. It fell onto the floor. All the contents spilled but scattered around haphazardly. Sandra saw the bottle of *'potent'* pills amongst the debris. The label said *'Stallion'*. Her hands were shaking as she reached for the bottle. "Did you take any of these today", Sandra asked? Duke had forgotten that the pills were in the middle drawer. He didn't want Sandra to know he was taking tablets to boost his libido but now that she knew Duke was willing to explain. "Only bought them today, I was going past the chemist/drugstore anyway", he defended. Duke didn't give Sandra a chance to respond before commenting again. "Don't think I needed them, do you", he queried? Sandra was not going to answer that question. Knocking Duke's ego was not in her game-plan. Instead, she threw the question back for him to answer. "Do you", Sandra countered? She continued to wipe the mess from her dress. The caviar had spilt but Sandra had not noticed before. "It's getting late Duke. I'll have to go soon", Sandra reminded him. Duke was breathing normally now but still excited by Sandra's nearness, his heart was still playing an irregular pattern on his chest. Duke savoured his involvement with his ravishingly beautiful exotic bird. Sandra implanted a kiss upon his brow. Duke reached up but groped her breasts. "Are you sure you have to leave now", he asked? "I have to go", Sandra insisted. She strode but walked away without looking back. Duke managed to get down from the desk. He adjusted his trousers then took the bottle with the remainder of champagne over to the light blue deeply buttoned rolled arm chaise lounge. Duke sat there contemplating whether he should bother to go home. He knew his wife would be waiting up for him but felt he had to finish off the *'bubbly'*. Duke sipped the flat champagne but still sensed Sandra's presence. He put his feet up on the chaise lounge but started to replay the previous moments in his mind for a while longer. The ringing of the cell phone startled him a little. Duke got up from the chaise lounge but walked over to the desk. He picked up the cell phone. "Hello", Duke said. "Shall I wait up for you", Dora queried? "Dora, are you still up, he asked? "Yes I was waiting up for you. Since he came from school, the little one has been feeling a bit poorly", she advised. "He's faking it. Doesn't like school, that's what it is", Duke assured her. Dora tried to explain that she had taken the child to the doctor and that she was advised to keep him at home for a few days. "Oh dear", Duke said offered. His tone was cynical. Without waiting for Dora to respond, Duke added a bit more vitriolic cynicism. "The little bleeder wins again. I'm getting tired of his moods, aren't you", he finished? Dora knew that Duke had been drinking again. She was annoyed that he had shown very little empathy towards her or the child. "When you're sober you might want to examine your approach towards the children", Dora told him firmly. "Can we talk about it another time", Duke asked? It wasn't as if he had conceded the argument but Sandra was still on his mind. "Look Dora, I'm leaving in a few moments. I'll see you in about an hour and a half", Duke said. He hung up. Duke finished the flat champagne then staggered towards the side of the desk. He placed the glasses on it but took up his briefcase from the floor. Duke pressed the cell again but summoned his chauffeur. "I'm coming down", he said. Duke shuffled towards the lifts but waited for one to become available. He could still smell the perfume Sandra was wearing. The odour lingered until the lift arrived. Duke took one more sniff before going into the lift. He started to hum to himself. The lift travelled quickly to the ground floor. Duke alighted from the lift and was promptly met by the chauffeur. "The limo is just outside, Mr. Stagg", the chauffeur stated. Sam took the briefcase from Duke but promptly stepped aside for him to go first. He watched his employer stagger towards the limo.

It was embarrassing for Sandra to look Duke in the eye the next day. For quite some time now she was committed to his every *whim*. Sometimes he would completely shut her out of his daily routine knowing that she would be eager to answer his next call. Sandra wanted to get a commitment from the elusive Duke but his experience at playing on women's *weaknesses* made him in charge. His plan was to bait her until she grovelled to him. Duke managed to surprise the gullible Sandra yet again. He deliberately went to Andy Mann's office although he knew he had sent him on an errand outside of the office. Duke glanced in Sandra's direction but noticed how her eyes followed him from her immediate boss's office. "Would you be working late tonight Ms. Bogus", Duke teased? "Sure Mr. Stagg", Sandra replied. She looked at her watch wandering if she could catch Raymond before he left for home. Sandra was hoping that he would not come to meet her that evening. When she strode towards Duke's office she was determined that she would end this affair promptly. It had started but Sandra didn't like how she had been ignored and treated, as just another *'conquest'*, by Duke. She paused to glance at something that attracted her on Mary Allsorts' desk. She had long gone home but Sandra noticed the vase of flowers which was prominently placed there. She mumbled to herself. "Perhaps it's her birthday", she said. Sandra flicked the attached card with her extra long nails. The writing was definitely Andy Mann's. Sandra could indeed recognize his writing. After all, he did send her several memos each day. Sandra frowned but continued towards Duke's office. She passed through the other office; the one just behind Mary Allsorts'. Thinking Duke was there alone, she continued to approach his office. She shouted. "Duke" Sandra queried? He didn't respond. Sandra knew he must have heard her. She listened if he was in conversation on the phone. Sandra called out a bit louder this time. "Are you in there Duke", she exclaimed? Sandra proceeded to advance towards his office door. Duke saw Sandra as she approached. He raised his hands in order to indicate that someone else was in his office. Sandra looked to her left as she entered Duke's office. She could see Andy Mann, her immediate supervisor, leafing through some Reports. Sandra was bursting to get to the point she had come to make. She had planned to tell Duke that she would bring the whole sordid affair out into the open if he planned on just using her. Sandra wanted guarantees. She expressed herself angrily through clenched teeth but lowering her voice so Andy couldn't hear. "You can't use me like that, you bastard", Sandra said. Duke looked up but smiled. He sensed that he would have to calm Sandra down. Duke decided to play with her ambitious nature. Looking directly into Sandra's eyes, Duke spoke to her. "When I talked to you the other night about promotion I meant it", he said. "Just wait until Andy goes I'll tell you all, ok", Duke said. His tone was professional and his voice was calculatingly toned low but Sandra was feeling used. She couldn't control her anger. Again Sandra spoke through clenched teeth. "Get rid of him for God's sake, I can't stand that man", she demanded. Duke was sterner with her now. Raising his voice enough for Andy Mann to hear, Duke spoke in a tone Sandra was hearing for the first time. His deep baritone voice boomed but threw her into confusion. "Sit down, Ms. Bogus, please", Duke ordered. His voice sounded more officious than before. Sandra obeyed like the obedient pet. She found herself sinking in the chair opposite Duke's desk. Sandra crossed her legs as she sat down. Duke was distracted by her presence. His eyes followed the movement of her legs. He put away the pen that he was holding in his hand but sat back in the deeply buttoned, winged, red leather chair. It had a straight back, rolled arms and 4" high deliberately distressed bulbous wooden legs. Gold nails decorated the outer edges of the back, the wings, front of the rolled arms and down the front of the chair, stopping just before the bulbous spun wooden legs met with the upholstery. Duke sat forward now, on the large red latex cushioned seat. He tried to look relaxed but he was just as eager to get rid of Andy Mann. "Now let us find out what Andy has come up with", Duke said. "Well Andy", he prompted. Andy Mann had been told about his promotion. He was now Chief Press Officer. He would remain as Sandra's boss though she too was being promoted to Public Relations Officer. She didn't know it yet. Duke's Chief Press Officer spoke. "We're on schedule as usual but there's still the *'Priority List'* to sort out", Andy replied. Duke made a specific enquiry which he had not previously discussed with Andy Mann. "Have you put Ms. Bogus' name on the list", Duke asked? "No Duke", Andy replied. Duke gave him new instructions. "Be sure to make arrangements for Ms. Bogus to be included in the next Newsreel", Duke ordered. He saw the look on both Andy Mann's and Sandra's faces. Duke got up from his chair but left the office. Sandra was numb from shock. She was not expecting Duke to openly overrule Andy in front of her. Sandra could not speak for a while but she noticed Andy's facial reaction. His was more than a puzzled look. Andy Mann was Duke's right hand and he knew it. He also knew the pranks that Duke got up to with his female workers but it was none of his business. Andy Mann used Sandra's efficiency but he didn't like her. "I don't know if Mr. Stagg thinks I can work miracles", he moaned. Without waiting for any comment from Sandra, Andy continued his objection towards her inclusion in the imminent Newsreel. "Everything is already fixed for the next Newsreel, why should you be included", Andy questioned? His tone was condescending but represented his true disgust about having Sandra included in the Newsreel. Andy Mann's further objection came from a different reference point located much deeper in his psyche. This expression exposed the real reason behind his whole approach to Sandra. "We don't want your *'type'* at the shoot", Andy snorted. Sandra was adamant that Andy justify his statement. "What *'type'* are you referring to", Sandra questioned? Andy Mann paused then delivered even more abuse. "Gutter *'type'* like you", he replied. His response was clearly disdainful but dismissed Sandra as the perceived enemy. Andy's expression was reinforced by his deep resentment for the *'type'* to which he referred. His preconceived assumptions were not necessarily based on facts but rather a programmed and conditioned acceptance of a set of *'beliefs and values'* to which Andy Mann had come to believe was his own. He had never queried how others came to those prejudiced views about the *'types'* he had been conditioned to despise. Andy chose to remain blinkered in his world of spiteful emotional insensitivity and hate. Sandra was beginning to get a better understanding why Andy despised her so much. She was more aware of his xenophobic remarks which he seemed unable to contain.

Those same categories of remarks Sandra had experienced previously at Saint Halo High Apostolic Grammar School, in particular. There, she had received this kind of treatment from peer groups and teachers alike. Some peer students had even felt her coccyx area to ascertain whether she was *"growing a tail"*, apparently! Others, including teachers, teased her about her melanin skin. They called her *"burnt toast"*. When Sandra complained to the green humanoid robotron Head of Year, Kirsty Allin, she was told that she was being "over-sensitive" and that the others *"didn't mean anything by it"*. The green humanoid robotron Head Teacher, Adelaide Bullocks, berated Sandra for *"making a fuss"* and said her complaint was about *"much to do about nothing"*. Adelaide Bullocks said of the perpetrators that they were *"just being friendly"*. Sandra's daily journey from and to the *'Government Approved'* private premier educational establishment meant that she had to endure this type of behaviour for five years continuously. Her mother did not help either. When Sandra was seeking some support to remedy the daily bullying, her mother, Dian, told her daughter to *"just ignore them"*.

In Duke's office, Sandra told Andy how she was feeling about his prejudiced view. "You've got a mental problem. You need to seek psychiatric help", she taunted. The green humanoid robotron, Andy Mann, was choked by Sandra's inference to him being mentally deranged. He hit back in a way he thought might inflict some damage to Sandra's confidence. "You think you're so special because Duke is showing you attention. He'll just use you like the others", he warned. Sandra glared at him. She threatened by showing him her talons. "Keep your comments to yourself", Sandra warned. Neither she nor Andy was aware that Duke overheard their comments to each other. He had stood for awhile in the middle office which separated his from Mary Allsorts'. Duke's return prevented more abuse from either commentator. He wasn't going to take sides. Duke needed both Andy and Sandra but for different reasons. "Now, now children", he interrupted. "I'll see you later Duke", Andy said. He turned but left the office immediately. Sandra was upset. She was vulnerable to Andy Mann's remark because she was already in an angry mood with Duke. Sandra complained about Andy Mann's attitude towards her. Turning to Duke, Sandra appealed to him. "Why can't that man keep his comments to himself", she asked? Her *'mascara'* mixed tears, trickled down her face and her large cornflower blue eyes begged for an answer. Duke removed the crumpled handkerchief from his side pocket but handed it to Sandra. She dabbed her eyes, wiped her nose then put the handkerchief on the desk in front of her.

CHAPTER 20

D uke, in an uncontrollable fit, began to laugh. His booming laughter carried to the floors immediately below his office but Henry Hardcase, security personnel, only heard it as a loud disturbing noise and he took his job seriously. His loyalty was well beyond the call of duty but he wouldn't even listen to his colleagues whenever they tried to tell him so. Henry was an ignorant man. He was not the sort of person, who could be persuaded by anyone else other than Andy Mann, Mary Allsorts or Mr. Stagg. Henry was that sort of irritating character that would bamboozle proven scientific laws on personality traits. Duke's laughter had sounded like an uproar to him. The sound travelled down the stairwell. Henry didn't even bother to discuss his concern with his colleagues around him. Instead, he decided to investigate the perceived disturbance alone. Confronted with the choice of whether to use the lift or stairs for his ascent to the upper floors, Henry decided on the latter. There were six flights of 6 steps, 7 turnings off the relative landings and a straight flight of 12 steps before anyone, using the stairs could get to Duke's office. At first, Henry selected to use three steps at a time but soon dropped his pace down to taking them one or two at a time. Though his legs and body started to complain about the demands on them, Henry's breathing was exceptionally smooth after much exertion. He had trained hard at the Snideborough Army Complex where Duke sent his security staff. At Henry's initial interview, Andy Mann had told him what was expected of him when he qualified as one of Duke's personal security staff. "With this job you'll need not only to be fit but ready to die if anyone tried to injure Mr. Stagg", Andy Mann had demanded. Henry had confirmed Andy Mann's meaning. "You mean a *'bullet catcher'*, Mr. Mann, don't you", Henry confirmed? Like his colleagues, he agreed to those terms and conditions. Henry Hardcase became top student of his group. The army supervisors were so impressed with Henry they even tried to recruit him at 30 years old. This was almost two years ago. Henry had negotiated about 16 of the 48 steps when he heard the second phase of the disturbance. Sandra had misunderstood Duke's reason for laughing. She had already perceived that he was taking her for granted before she had entered the office. Being spoken to by Andy Mann in the way he did had put Sandra into a real foul mood. She raised her voice to a much higher level when she addressed Duke. "What's so funny Mr. Stagg? I'm going to sort out our little problem, now", Sandra screamed. Henry heard the perceived threat to the man who he is meant to protect. His legs were going up and down like pistons now but he wasn't making as much progress as he'd been before. Henry wished he'd chosen the lift now. Beads of sweat had left its trail along the marble stairs; easily contravening any Health and Safety Regulations normally upheld by the company. His blue uniform reeked nauseatingly of a mixture of Henry's sweat, after shave cologne and body odour sprays altogether. Almost *'high'* on these *'scents'*, Henry began to feel a bit dizzy. He was feeling thirsty too. Henry stopped at the next convenient landing, the one just before the straight flight of 12 stairs. He needed to regulate his breathing. Henry was heaving and puffing now as he panicked about getting to Duke on time. Drenched and dripping in sweat, Henry's light blue shirt could now be wrung and put out to dry. He fiddled with the blue tie that he had so far refused to loosen. Henry was afraid that he would be considered as being *"out of uniform"* by doing so. Andy Mann had advised him that the tie was considered "part of uniform, no matter what the weather". Henry understood that to mean that he was not allowed to remove his tie no matter the circumstances. He might have felt a bit of relief at this particular time had he chosen to loosen his tie just a little. Henry thought so but did not dare risk his job. Though his breathing was not yet regular, Henry persisted in negotiating the final flight of stairs that gave access towards Duke's office. He rather dragged himself up with the aid of the banister. The top landing led to Mary's office. Henry could only get to Duke's office through Mary's, then the middle office that separated hers and Duke's. As he entered the secretary's office, Henry could hear Duke's voice. "Ok I'll put my hands up", he said. Henry saw Sandra pointing but advancing towards Duke. She was reacting to his ignoring her. Duke backed away with his hands in the air; playfully portraying total surrender. His dramatic impersonation of a man surrendering to a threat seemed real to Henry Hardcase. He could not see, from where he had entered, whether Sandra had a weapon in her hand. Henry perceived that she presented a threat to Duke's well being. As far as he was concerned, there was an imminent threat to his boss's life. The security man from the Tribe of Hawke did not wait to see anymore, he aimed the handle of the gun towards Sandra's head. Duke rushed forward but instinctively grabbed the security man's arm but shouted. "No Henry, don't do that", he pleaded. Sandra looked round but saw the gun as Duke wrested it from the security man's arm. With mouth opened wide and eyes bulging she screamed as loudly as she could. Her voice sent a chill down Duke's spine but not Henry's. He was insensitive to Sandra's screaming fit. The only thing he wanted to do was shut her up but Sandra kept on screaming. Other security personnel could now hear Sandra's screams. They wondered what Henry was doing upstairs. Two or three of them were on their way up. Unlike Henry, they chose the lift. Sandra was in a shocked state, temporarily. Her contorted facial expressions resembled that of a moving mask. Duke shook Sandra gently at first, then again but this time more violently. "Pull yourself together. Shake it off, Ms. Bogus, shake it off", Duke demanded. He was aware that the other security personnel on the lower floors had heard the wretched sound. He knew they would soon be joining their colleague, Henry Hardcase. Duke didn't want that scenario to happen. Shaking Sandra didn't appear to help. Duke panicked. As if the embarrassment drove him into an insane moment, he slapped her face with the back of his hand then he slapped her again with the palm side.

"Shut it, I tell you", Duke scolded. He was angry. The last slap was a bit stronger than the first but sent Sandra crashing to the floor. Duke looked at Henry but commented. "Women", he exclaimed. Looking at Henry Hardcase, he continued to complete his comment about women. "You've got to show them who's boss, don't you", Duke asked? Sandra lay slumped on the floor. Stunned by Duke's brutality, she recoiled away from him but kept her eyes on both him and Henry Hardcase. Sandra held her face but tested her jaws. She shook her head to clear it. Sandra was now more conscious than she was earlier but mystified as to how she ended up on the floor. She could not remember falling. Both Duke and Henry helped her unto the chaise lounge. Duke retrieved the crumpled handkerchief from the desk where Sandra had left it after drying her tears that were triggered by Andy Mann's stinging comments. Some inner tissues having been damaged by the blows to her jaws, Sandra took the crumpled handkerchief to wipe the trickling blood from her mouth. She wiped the blood from the corners of her mouth. Sandra asked Duke what had happened? He ordered Henry into action. "Get her some water", Duke ordered. Henry went to the huge water cooler, took a plastic cup from the holder but filled it with water. He walked hurriedly across the office then gave it to Sandra. She took it without commenting but she looked, suspiciously at Henry Hardcase. Duke had escaped from his moment of insanity but was now a bit more rational and sympathetic towards Sandra. "Are you alright now Ms. Bogus", he enquired? He noticed the empty look on her face. She tried to get up but Duke persuaded her to stay on the *'chaise lounge'*. "Just lie there for a minute or two. Have a little kip", Duke encouraged. Henry Hardcase felt he had to apologise for his part in the dramatic performances that had taken place earlier on. He started to apologise. "It was all my fault Ms. Bogus. I thought . . ." Henry Hardcase stated. His voice trailed off before he could complete his apology. Sandra looked at him angrily but commented. "Did you hit me", Sandra asked? Duke looked sheepishly towards her. "It was me Ms Bogus, you were in shock. I had to slap your face", he explained. Sandra didn't complain. Duke wanted to be alone with Sandra and told Henry Hardcase so. Dismissing the security personnel, Duke instructed him to leave. "Miss Bogus needs a bit of quiet. Close the door on your way out, Henry", he said. Duke could hear the lift but chanced that Henry would intercept his colleagues before they got to his office. As Henry walked towards the door, Duke fired another salvo. "And another thing Henry, change your uniform, will you? You don't half pong", he criticised. He waved Henry away. "Not a word to anyone Henry, not a word", Duke warned. "No Sir", Henry Hardcase assured. Duke looked down on Sandra lying sprawled across the chaise lounge. Her long legs were a temptation to him. They hung over the edge and her large cornflower blue eyes gleamed with the reflection of the lights above her. She smiled at him. Duke was encouraged and eager to *apologise*. He also wanted to show Sandra how sorry he was about having to slap her face. Duke knelt beside Sandra but fussed over her. "Would you like some champagne", he asked? His manner was more polite than earlier. "Yes", Sandra replied. Duke crossed the office to where the Drinks Cabinet was positioned. He held the stems of the two champagne glasses between his fingers on one hand but wrapped his other arm around the solid gold champagne bucket that housed the ice and the bottle of Champagne Urge Mark 1. "Is there anything to eat", Sandra asked? "There are some sandwiches in the fridge left over from the Board Meeting", Duke said. "That's a few days ago though", Sandra replied. "There's nothing wrong with them. I had some earlier on", Duke testified. He put the gold bucket of iced champagne on the floor next to Sandra then went to the fridge to fetch the sandwiches. "Got prawn and mayonnaise, beef and mustard, turkey, salmon, crab spread, a couple of eggy ones with mayonnaise", Duke announced. "How is the beef done", Sandra asked? "That's a bloody silly question, ain't it", Duke asked? His comment was cynical. "There's only one way to eat beef", Duke assured. "That's what I'll have, what are you having", Sandra asked? "I think I fancy the eggy ones", Duke said. His voice was chirpy. "They're nice but they smell a bit", Sandra reminded. "The champagne will take care of that, won't it", Duke retorted? He sat on the floor next to the chaise lounge. Sandra sensed what was about to happen but she had only smiled at Duke in appreciation for saving her from the insensitive Henry Hardcase. It seemed the whole situation had changed now. What should she do? What could she do? Sandra asked herself these questions. Remembering the snub after the last event, she decided to make Duke pay. She would take him to his threshold and then refuse to let him make love to her. Now was her chance to turn the table on him. Make him *beg*. She pouted her lips at him enough to encourage him to kiss her. Duke did not need a second invitation. He crushed her lips with his own but kissed her passionately. In their act of 'French-kissing', some remnants of the smelly hard boiled "eggy" sandwiches transported themselves from Duke's mouth but entered Sandra's. She felt the lumps but chose to ignore them. The pungent stench from Duke's breath smelt like 'stink bombs' in a chemistry laboratory but Sandra's only focus was to excite Duke. Like a leech, he chose to savour the 'bloody' taste of the almost uncooked bloody beef within the sandwich Sandra had chosen to eat. Both Duke and Sandra satisfied their cannibalistic addictions. She hugged him close with one hand but stroked his back with the other. Now Duke was on fire groping her mercilessly. Sandra knew he was out of control. This was the moment she chose to take her revenge for being snubbed. "Not so fast Duke", Sandra said. She pushed him away from her, coyly. "Don't stop me now", he pleaded. "Raymond will be here shortly", Sandra whispered. She rose from the *'chaise lounge'* but straightening her dress. As the passion rose within him, Duke implored her. "Have some more champagne", he recommended. They had both had a few glasses of champagne but it seemed to be affecting Duke more than Sandra. He was pleading now. "We have to talk", Duke implored. Changing to a more formal tone of voice, Sandra told him that she agreed with him. "You're right Mr. Stagg. We need to have a serious chat. That is what I came to see you about", Sandra inferred. Duke feared from the sound of her voice, that his new *conquest* might end the affair. He had enjoyed their previous meetings where he was allowed free access to do as he pleased with the stunningly beautiful Sandra. Now she had managed to change things round to her advantage. Duke was more than humble in his desperation to put things right. "Let me apologize for bursting out in laughter earlier on. I wasn't laughing at you but instead with you", Duke explained. Without waiting for Sandra to comment, he continued his diatribe about Andy Mann. "Andy gets on everyone's nerve but he doesn't mean any harm. He has experience and gets his work done", Duke added. Sandra was determined to hint at her own efforts. "Does he ever mention how he manages to present such quality work", she hinted? Duke was sorry he'd bothered to mention Andy Mann because this was leading to a discussion about him but eroding his chances. "Have some more champagne", he insisted. Duke poured more champagne into the glasses yet again.

"We can discuss Andy another time Sandra", he pleaded. Duke was not a man to subtly insinuate his intentions upon his target. He always went straight for the throat or rather straight for the crotch might be a more apt phrase. Sandra glanced at him but pretended she was embarrassed by his comment. Without waiting for her to reply, Duke spoke again. "I don't half fancy you", he said. "I don't know what you mean Duke", Sandra parried. It was almost a fixation with Sandra to toy with her victims but Duke was impatient. First he offered to feed her the champagne. She played along with that. Duke used his other hand to stroke her legs. "I'm not a loose woman, I'll have you know", Sandra responded. Duke was very excited now and he began to loosen her blouse. He clumsily undid a few buttons at the top but reached into her bosom. Sandra placed the glass on the floor but held Duke's hand in appreciation. She helped him unto the chaise lounge on top of her. Duke was now snorting like a raging bull charging at the matador. He was rough and awkward but Sandra didn't mind. She was impressed how much Duke wanted her. Teasing him beyond his threshold, Sandra dug the talons on her other hand into Duke's back as she pretended to climax. He could feel the pulse in his neck dancing and his chest sounded as if his heart was trying to get out. Sandra noticed how his nostrils flared like that of a horse after a race. While running her fingers through his hair, Sandra accidentally scratched Duke's skull with her talon-like fingernails. Clutching the back of his head, Sandra pressed Duke's face towards her breasts. She also had another reason for clutching him so close; to muffle Duke's grunting. He was not complaining. Duke collapsed from his efforts in Sandra's arms. This was partly due to his drunken state and partly from him feeling spent from the huge explosion below his waist that he had experienced in his moment of triumph. More likely, his collapse might have been due to the excessive demands the fitter, younger 24 years old Sandra managed to extract from Duke's 57 years old body. He could easily have been her grandfather. Sandra didn't think about the age difference. She'd watched the RJ Sallad Video many times. It had implicated that if Sandra's urge was superlatively strong enough then she should use whatever approach seemed appropriate to guarantee her the outcome she desired. What seemed to be important was to get on the 'Gravy Train' any which way she can even if it meant selling her soul to the devilment which guided her inflated ego. Having passionately been engaged, both Duke and Sandra lay there together. He felt good about having access to the stunningly beautiful Sandra despite the huge difference in age. He had succeeded in conquering the gorgeous Sandra yet again. The phone in Duke's office rang. He didn't want to move from his position on top of Sandra but he relented when it rang for the fourth time. He made his way over to his desk but spoke into the phone. "Yes Henry ... who ... yes I'll tell her ... thank you", Duke said. He relayed the message from Henry Hardcase to Sandra. "Mr. Raymond Oddball is here to see Ms. Bogus", Duke mimicked. "Oh, I'd forgotten about him", Sandra commented. Duke smiled but groped her breast again. "I'll have to go now", Sandra said. She straightened her blouse, walked over to the desk to retrieve her handbag. "This whole episode has left me drained", Sandra said. "Take the morning off and I'll see you at the Press Conference before the shoot ... good night Ms. Bogus", Duke teased.

Sandra strode past Duke, stopping only to glance back to wink at him. Having completed the *'overtime hours'*, Sandra exited from Duke's office but headed for the lift. There was no one else in it and Sandra quickly arrived on the ground floor. When the door next opened, she saw Raymond waiting in the foyer. "Hey, how are you Sandy", Raymond asked? He preferred to call her Sandy. Without looking at him she replied. "Rough day Ray, rough day", Sandra offered. They strode past the last of the security personnel and out through the exit to the car park. Raymond smelt the drink on her breath but he didn't say anything while he was inside the building. Outside, he offered to drive. "Do you want me to drive", Raymond asked? "No Ray, I want to drive", Sandra replied. "You can't drink and drive Sandy. You are in no state to drive", Raymond counseled. Sandra insisted that she was well within her limit. "I make my own decisions, right Ray", she reminded. Sandra got behind the wheel but waited for Raymond to get in. He'd hardly closed the door when she pressed hard on the accelerator. The Sleek Coupe lurched forward rapidly causing them to pitch backwards in their seats. The tires screeched loudly as the car accelerated away towards the exit. "Wait for me to fasten my seatbelt", Raymond pleaded. Sandra remained quiet. The Sleek Coupe was quite a nifty car. It could do 0-60 in very few seconds. Soon they were zooming along at 80 mph along the dual carriageway. "Slow down, Sandy", Raymond urged. Sandra was feeling guilty about her affair with Duke. She hadn't intended to use Raymond like this but her superlative urge for the champagne lifestyle she craved had got Sandra in this situation. There was some traffic ahead. Raymond thought that Sandra needed to slow down. The dual carriageway that they were driving on narrowed because of repairs being carried out. Because of these repairs, the previous six months had seen traffic tailbacks regularly. Raymond was feeling a tinge of fear. "Slow down Sandy", Raymond begged. Sandra kept driving erratically. She drifted from one lane to the other, recklessly. The Sleek Coupe snaked its way in and out of the slow moving traffic. At times Sandra had to brake suddenly. It was as if Sandra was on a mission to kill them both. As soon as they had passed the bottleneck, the tires screeched but smoked when Sandra pressed hard on the accelerator yet again. Raymond tried to get hold of the steering wheel when Sandra's Sleek Coupe seemed destined to hit another car. This time she did not brake but instead forced the other car to pull violently to one side in order to avoid crashing into her Sleek Coupe. In trying to avoid crashing into the Sleek Coupe, the driver of the other car lost control but caused it to crash into yet another vehicle. Raymond pleaded with Sandra but it was as if she had a death wish. "Stop Sandy, look what you have done", Raymond scolded. Sandra hissed through her teeth but pressed sharply on the accelerator yet again. The car lurched forward causing both their heads to go backwards. "It was his fault anyway, he should've looked where he was going", Sandra goaded. Raymond knew that, in this sort of mood, Sandra was unapproachable. He remained silent but he was very worried about his own life and that of his unpredictable girlfriend.

At the traffic lights Sandra glared at the motorist who kept revving his engine. Raymond could sense the dare. "Ignore him Sandy", Raymond advised. There was no point in him saying anything. Sandra's mind was already made up. She slipped the car into gear but balanced the clutch and the accelerator at *'biting point'*. As the lights changed, she released the clutch and pressed the accelerator but the other car still raced ahead. Sandra, who had a passion for motor racing, weaved in and out of traffic until she was level once again with her opponent. She smiled sarcastically at him, steering closer, pushing him towards the pavement. Raymond was angry now. He was shouting at Sandra to stop the car so he could get out. "If you want to kill yourself go ahead but let me out", Raymond demanded. Sandra ignored him but carried on racing. Caught up in this madness were a couple of cyclists, who fell as they tried to get out of the way of the two crazy motorists. The other driver had his head turned towards Sandra as he jockeyed with her for the limited space in front of them. Neither Sandra nor the other driver wanted to give way to the other. When he saw the bicycle it was much too late. Braking and swerving he tried hard to avoid contact. The rear wheel of his car crushed the bicycle. Sandra looked from the rear view mirror of her car just long enough to see the tangled wreck. Another passage of silence passed for the rest of the Sandra and Raymond's journey. He was beside himself with rage but had decided to play the submissive role to the stubborn, spoilt woman with whom he lived. Finally, they arrived home. Sandra parked the car in the usual place in front of the house. They sat in the car for a while in contrasting moods, both totally angry but for different reasons. Raymond was the first to break the silence. "What's wrong Sandy? Something is eating you. What is it", he asked? When there was no answer he tried again. "Are you angry with me", Raymond prompted? Sandra just looked straight ahead. They got out of the car. Across the street a man was greeting his friend in a loud tone. Raymond recognized the voice but turned to acknowledge the greeting. Sandra tugged at him. "Come on Ray, I can't stand that guy", she complained. "You can't stand any of my friends", Raymond retorted. His sarcastic remark was more than obvious. Raymond pushed the first key into the door. Sandra's response was a bit delayed but she made her point all the same. "Whey yuh ah seh baby love", Sandra mimicked. Raymond's *'friend'* had tried to chat up Sandra. Raymond's jealousy came to the fore. He wanted to find out when and how they had come into contact. Sandra ignored Raymond's enquiry. Instead, she commented on her day. "Oh what a day, what a rotten day", Sandra exclaimed. They entered the house. Once they were inside, Raymond tried to soothe Sandra. "Sit down Sandy and don't try to talk, let me help you relax", he suggested. Raymond proceeded to massage her neck muscles gently. Sandra's tensed body started to respond to the gentle massaging. She was also encouraged to do some gentle breathing exercises. Raymond was an expert at releasing tension both sexually and otherwise. In his athletic world, he was used to good stretching and breathing techniques. Soon Sandra felt calm and relaxed. "Shall I run you a bath Sandy", Raymond asked? "No Ray, I'll have a *'wash'* instead", Sandra insisted. That was one of the things that puzzled Raymond about Sandra. Since he moved in with her, Raymond can't figure out why Sandra prefers to have a *'wash'* when she could just as easily have a bath or a shower. The overpowering strong perfumes and deodorants she always wore did affect his breathing too but Raymond always avoided telling Sandra. She would have called him a chauvinist. Raymond was opposite in character to the fiery and often feisty Sandra. His role in this relationship was simply to be there for Sandra and to shower her with gifts, love, care and affection in that order. He was blinded by her astounding beauty, superb physique and great desire to succeed in her chosen career. Some of the other girls he knew didn't seem to have the same enthusiasm or ambitions, like Sandra did. "Have you eaten much today Sandy", Raymond asked? "No. Let us have a *'take away'*. You choose", Sandra replied. "Which restaurant shall we try tonight", Raymond asked? "Your choice Ray, I'm just hungry", Sandra replied. Raymond lifted the cell phone from his hip but dialled. "Yeah, I want two . . . can you hear me . . . two" Raymond stated. He peered at the phone in disbelief but mumbled something about forgetting to charge the battery. "Lend me your phone Sandy", Raymond requested. Sandra went to the bedroom but slipped on her frilly negligee before returning to join Raymond in the lounge. They sat on the lime green sofa holding hands. She told him about Andy Mann's insulting behaviour. "He hates me. He's a consummate racist", Sandra declared. "Do you want me to talk to him", Raymond enquired? "No Ray, I can handle him", Sandra replied. The tone of the doorbell was crisp and loud. Raymond headed towards it with haste. "About time", Sandra said. Raymond opened the door. With two large boxes held out in front of him, the carrier commented. "Two large pizzas for Mr. Oddball . . . that'll be . . ." the carrier said. Raymond pushed the money in his hands but told him to keep the change. "Thank you sir", the carrier exclaimed. Sandra and Raymond sat at the kitchen table enjoying their pizzas through light conversation. She told Raymond some exciting news. "I'm going to be on T.V.", Sandra boasted. Raymond was very excited too. His woman appearing on TV was quite a feat. He couldn't wait to tell his work colleagues and friends. Raymond did not wait for Sandra to tell him the fine details. He started asking questions one after another. Sandra responded eagerly. "Tomorrow I start late then I arrive for a big Press Conference. Still later there's filming which will be part of the News", Sandra drooled. "I'll tell everyone I know to watch the News", Raymond enthused. Before Sandra could react to Raymond's immediate support, he asked yet another question. "How did you swing it Sandy . . . you can tell me, can't you", Raymond asked? As if to give his approval, he winked at her. Sandra's response to his last question was in the negative, jokingly. "No I can't tell you Ray . . . top secret. You wouldn't even be able to guess", Sandra stated. Thinking about the *'Overtime Overtures'* with Duke, she smiled. Even tough Duke had sexual intercourse with her, Sandra felt dissatisfied. Only Raymond could quell her fire. "Coming to bed Ray", Sandra encouraged. As she made her way up the stairs towards the bedroom Sandra beckoned Raymond with a teasing finger indicating she wanted him to follow after her. As far as Raymond was concerned, he felt teased each time he thought about Sandra let alone be near her. He was next to Sandra within a few seconds. Raymond looked into her beautiful large cornflower blue eyes and his heart melted like butter on any hot surface. In bed, Sandra tempted him greatly then rolled away from him. Raymond felt the urge to be even closer to his ideal woman. He didn't want to be teased anymore. Raymond crushed Sandra's breast close to his bare chest. She responded just enough to get him to his threshold then told Raymond she had "something important to say". "Not now Sandy we have more urgent business to take care of right now", Raymond submitted. The truth is Sandra was ready too but she felt guilty now about her fling with Duke. She wondered whether Raymond would notice. Sandra had heard her mother, Dian Bogus and her friends saying things like that when she was a little girl. This was the first time since they've been together that Sandra had gone with another man. Guilt was present on her mind. She didn't really know how to handle this type of situation. Raymond sensed her uneasiness. "What's the matter Sandy, you're trembling. Are you feeling ill", Raymond asked? He had no idea how much of a conniving bitch his Tribe of Hawke 'Cloned Barbie', Exotic Mona Lisa really was. "No, I'm just yearning so much for you, Ray. Can't you tell", Sandra lied? She had no explanation for the reason why she chose to lie to Raymond but he was too infatuated with the stunningly beautiful woman who was his partner. Raymond swallowed Sandra's lie hook, line and sinker.

They huddled together in a tangled mass of tissues, cartilages, muscles and bones together gyrating and grunting as if they were in pain. With their pleasures exploited and fulfilled, both Sandra and Raymond were feeling good. "You show so much understanding Ray", Sandra complimented. "Yeh", Raymond replied. They lay awake laughing and joking until sleep took control. Raymond did not hear the feint sound of the telephone but Sandra did. "Hello", she drawled, "who is this", Sandra asked? "I know about you and Mr. Stagg", the voice said. Sandra was quite taken aback by the revelation. The shock rendered her more awake than she had been before the phone rang. "Who is this", Sandra asked? She was trying to identify the muffled voice. The caller hung up. Sandra found herself shaking uncontrollably but she dare not awaken Raymond. Snuggling up to him for comfort, she hugged him very tightly but fear gripped even tighter and the night seemed to last twice as long. Sandra couldn't help wondering what would have happened if Raymond had been awake and how many people knew of her fling with Duke? Those questions kept gnawing away at her. Was this punishment for her infidelity? Sandra had not intended to go all the way with Duke but she didn't realize how much he had wanted her until that moment. She had only meant to tease him a little? They both wanted something for nothing but got caught in the 'old trap'. Tonight, Duke's lust had surfaced again while she was lying on the chaise lounge. Sandra had noticed his flared nostrils and his direct heart thumping approach towards her. Duke wanted her again. The excitement in his eyes had told her so. Horror filled Sandra's thoughts as she realized how exposed she was to extortionists. Should she come clean now with Raymond or play the waiting game? Sandra decided to do nothing until she had a chance to talk to her best pal, Pamela Labrishe. She was her mentor, confidant, the 'older sister' type friend. Many times in the past, they had shared personal 'secrets' together. Maybe they could arrange to meet soon, Sandra thought! Morning seemed a long way off and so the agony had to be borne for yet a while longer. Raymond, in contrast, was enjoying a well-earned rest. Exhausted from his recent physical efforts, he was now sleeping like a baby. Sandra lay beside him. She was resting on her right elbow. Her neck was at a slight angle but her head rested in her palm. She savoured the previous satisfying moments then drew closer to Raymond. Sandra rested her head on his bare chest but drifted off to sleep as well. Blissfully serene together, they lay there on top of the duvet. Raymond's dream was pleasant and fulfilling but Sandra's was more of a nightmare. She dreamt that her mother, Dian had caught her and Duke in bed together at the Hotel Welcome. The dream was vivid enough for it to awaken Sandra's natural reactions while she slept. Sweat was oozing from every pore in her body. Both Raymond and Sandra's bodies stuck together with the profusion of her sweat. She reeled away from Raymond but continued to roll until she stopped herself from falling off the edge of the bed. In her nightmare, Sandra was screaming but in reality, it sounded more like an owl 'ooing' in the night. Sandra could still see the figure of her mother, Dian, as she stepped into the Suite at the Hotel Welcome. "San San, what're you doing here with this man, she asked? Where is yuh husband or Ray as you call him", Dian asked? Sandra did not reply. She'd wished for a hole to hide in but there wasn't any. "Who does this maid think she's talking to? Do you know her? I'll get her fired", Duke boomed. Sandra tried to plead for the 'maid' without saying the woman is her mother. "Maybe if we all calm down, we'll be able to have a calm conversation", Sandra offered. Duke looked at Sandra as if she had gone mad.

"Pleading the case for chambermaids now, are we", he jeered? Have you gone out of your mind" Duke asked? There was a derisory tone about the way he expressed the word 'chambermaid' as if their job status made them inferior. She reminded Duke that he had told her that his friend Doris Bendlow was once a chambermaid too. That was where he first met her. In reality, it was *lust at first sight* for them both, Duke and Doris, the 'chambermaid'. He had made sure to keep close contact with the bustylicious Doris even after their first encounter. Duke adored her 'bit of rough' type image, her long curly hair and her *common* laughter. Sandra was not privy to that knowledge but she objected to how he spoke to her mother. She had no idea that 'mom' worked at the Hotel. A chambermaid's job is what she was doing. The confrontation between Duke and Dian developed into a most bizarre scene, with Dian Bogus throwing a bucket of cold water over Sandra and Duke, while they were still in the King-sized bed. Duke had stood up to remonstrate with Dian. By doing so, he exposed himself to her. She had more of a fiery temper than even Sandra could imagine. Dian was no saint. When she was younger, she was cautioned at the local Magistrate Court. Dian had injured a man who tried to assault young Sandra at the bus stop. Dian had taken off one of the six-inched 'stiletto-heeled' shoe but had pummeled away at the man with it until he fled. She was seething now that Duke had told her mother to "F ... Off" but called her a name that was closely associated with bigotry. Dian had experienced much of that in the past. Her reactions now were automatic but precisely attuned. She felt embarrassed about the revelation about her daughter. "Since you're both in your birthday suits, let me *"baptise you"*, Dian had threatened. She then carried out her version of baptism while dumping the contents of the bucket on them.

In her dream Sandra felt the water as being hot, hence the 'ooing' sound she was making. It was not loud enough to awaken Raymond. Sandra was very aware of the sweat that washed over her body. She turned onto her back but lay on the 'sweat-soaked' part of the duvet. Sandra tossed and turned for a while but she could not settle enough to go back to sleep. Raymond's snoring was helping to keep her awake. She could feel the heavy throbbing in her chest as her heartbeats raced into quicker spasms. The dream had shaken her badly and its vividness caused her, even in a semi-conscious state, to shiver involuntarily at times. Sandra was not aware of how much time had passed between her falling asleep and awakening by the nightmare. She sat up in the bed but shook her head from side to side then opened her large cornflower blue eyes even wider to confirm she was now fully awake. Sandra couldn't see the figure of her mother anymore but she looked around to discover that it was Raymond lying next to her and not Duke. Sandra smiled cynically to herself then lay on top of the sweat-soaked duvet once again. She didn't care if it was 'sweat-soaked', because she was in her bed. Sandra snuggled up to Raymond once again. She was just beginning to feel a bit more relaxed when Sandra heard the shrill sound of the doorbell. She swung her head round to look at the clock.

CHAPTER 21

" Six forty ... who the hell would call at six forty in the morning", Sandra mumbled. As she rose from the bed, Raymond stirred but flung his arm across the spot where she had been lying. Sandra had eased herself out of the bed, tiptoed towards the window overlooking the street but peered downwards. The angle was too acute for her to see the caller. Two more sharp bursts on the bell awakened Raymond. "I'll get it Sandy", Raymond said. Thinking it was the first time it had rung, Raymond stumbled out of bed. Sleep was still in control of his body. Raymond's gait was clumsy. He wiped the sleep from his eyes with the heel of his hands but blinked several times. Sandra was hanging out of the window but she was not engaged in conversation. "Who is it Sandy", Raymond asked? He crossed the room but headed for the window from which Sandra was looking. "That's the strange thing Ray there isn't anyone there", Sandra replied. Still half asleep, Raymond could not rationally figure out what was going on. "Someone must have pressed the wrong bell. Come back to bed Sandy", he pleaded. Sandra made her way towards the bedroom door. "Can I get you some juice Ray", Sandra asked? "Yes Sandy, I feel a bit thirsty", Raymond replied. Sandra made her way hurriedly down the stairs, tripping as she saw an envelope lying on the carpet. "Too early for the postman", Sandra whispered. The envelope was unsealed. With trembling hands, Sandra eagerly ripped it open. She read the contents. 'IT WILL COST YOU TO SHUT ME UP' was the message. There was neither signature nor further instructions. Sandra gasped. Her breathing was highly irregular as she glanced towards the stairs. Sandra was determined to see who had dropped the note. She summoned some courage before opening the door but she didn't see anyone apart from the young couple just passing by. The young boy swung his head round in Sandra's direction. His attention had been drawn to her near nakedness. Sandra wore a 'see-thru' negligee that exposed her slender body. She did not seem to be aware of the distraction or attraction she was causing until the young man expressed his approval. His 'wolf-whistles' had caused his girlfriend to clip him round his ears with her handbag. "You've got some front", she scolded. "Can't I look", the boy asked? He tried to hug his girlfriend but she pulled away from him. The girl started to break into a trot. "Leave me alone", she fussed. The boy caught up with his girlfriend. "You know I love you", he reassured. The boy wrapped both his arms around his girlfriend but kissed her every time she tried to say something. The girl surrendered to his ploy. They both embraced until his girlfriend was calmer. The boy and girl laughed together but set off again down the road. Sandra quickly discounted the couple but advanced towards the gate. She looked left and right but there wasn't anyone else around. "Who's there Sandy", Raymond asked? Standing on the top of the stairs, Raymond's voice carried through the open door. Sandra went back inside. "I don't see anyone", she replied. Sandra slammed the door shut to confirm she was back inside. Raymond was fully awake now but desired the gorgeous Sandra again. His appetite for her was immense. "Come back to bed Sandy", Raymond pleaded. Gripped with fear, Sandra headed for the kitchen. She tucked the envelope and its contents in her slippers. Raymond leaned over the banister. "What's keeping you Sandy, are you going to let me die of thirst", he joked? For the first time Sandra felt an emptiness in the pit of her stomach but she knew she had to compose herself before going back upstairs. When she did, Sandra handed Raymond the glass of juice. Raymond sipped from the glass but his intention was to get Sandra back into the bed. He held her close but rocked her from side to side gently. Sandra could sense what Raymond had in mind but she did not encourage him. "I could take the morning off to stay with you until you're ready to go", Raymond pressed. "No Ray, I need to be alone to prepare for my day", Sandra insisted. Raymond's lust for his ideal woman, at this time, was precariously high. It was difficult for him to erase this singular emotion but he was experienced enough to understand Sandra's feelings and priorities. "Ok Sandy, I can wait", Raymond whispered. He hugged Sandra gently against his body but saw the anxious look on her face. "Are you feeling alright Sandy, you seem a bit nervy", Raymond queried. Sandra wanted to confess about her affair. The thoughts in her mind were not sparing in their critique. On the one side Sandra felt guilty about cheating on Raymond but on the other side, the urge for celebrity status fought most viciously against the guilty feelings. Sandra eased away from Raymond. All the time, she deliberately avoided eye contact. Raymond felt foolish as he stared at his empty arms. "I'm going to have a shower", Raymond exclaimed. He went towards the bathroom. Sandra kept looking at the time. Raymond's reactions told her that he still cared about her. He was in more of a stupor now than when he had stumbled out of bed earlier but not from sleep. Raymond was experiencing those emotional moments which identified the agony experienced by individuals when the level of lustful urge within was not satisfied but which followed a decline for permission to enter into sexual intercourse. Sandra went into the kitchen. She put more coffee into the percolator. Sandra knew that Raymond loved the taste and smell of coffee. She felt she wanted to make up to him so Sandra decided to make Raymond's breakfast. She broke the four eggs separately into the frying pan. Sandra remembered that Raymond liked his eggs *'sunny side up'*. She smothered the hot toasts with so much butter that some of it ran down the side of the crusts. Raymond smiled as he returned from the shower. He was singing now while he dressed for work. Sandra heard the baritone voice as it poured out a rendition of the Barry White's single. The lyrics he emphasized were. "You're the first, you're the last, my everything". Sandra felt better now that Raymond was in this mood. They ate breakfast together. Raymond slipped his hands across the table but held Sandra's. He squeezed them gently. "Thanks for breakfast, Sandy", Raymond said. He winked at her then smiled. "We'll finish our little business later", Raymond hinted. Sandra made sure she kissed Raymond gently on the forehead the moment he rose from his chair. She thought the least she could do was to keep his hopes alive. He looked at his watch to check the time. "I have to go Sandy. See you later", Raymond commented. He had hardly gone through the front door when Sandra started to dial on her cell phone. Someone picked up the other end. "Hello", the voice said. "Is that you Pam", Sandra asked? "Hi, how are you doing girl . . . hit the big times yet", Pam chimed. Sandra didn't mind fooling around but she was scared about the latest threat which she had received earlier. There was a hint of anxiety in her voice. "Pam, I need to see you, I've got to talk to you", Sandra pleaded. "Seems like heavy stuff . . . tell all girl, tell it all to your big sister", Pam concluded. She deliberately spoke with an *'American-style'* accent. Pam could hear the anxiety in her friend's voice. Sandra laughed at Pam's ability to use varying accents whenever she felt the need to do so. "Could you come over for a couple of hours? I need to talk to you", Sandra pleaded. "You make it seem like you are in real trouble", Pam continued. This time, she said it with a *'Chinese-style'* accent. "Big story to tell girl but I can only talk to you", Sandra moaned. Pam was having fun with her friend. She discerned that Sandra was urgently requiring an empathetic ear but she still clowned around. "Could it not wait until later? I'll have to cancel my appointments", Pam teased? When there was no reply, Pam stopped fooling around but returned to her normal accent. "O.k. Sandra I'll be round as quickly as I can", she assured. Pam dialled a minicab number. On the way to Sandra's, Pam stopped to buy a potted plant for her friend. She knew how much Sandra admired potted plants. Sandra had enough in her house already but one more wouldn't hurt, Pam thought. She spent time asking the shop assistant for information but finally chose the potted plant that she knew Sandra would appreciate. Returning to the minicab, Pam learnt that she would be charged waiting time. "How much extra", Pam asked? The driver made her aware of the minicab fare structure. "It's calculated per minute", the cab driver argued. They agreed to differ but continued on the journey once Pam had assured the driver that she would pay the extra on top of the normal fare.

Pam, like Sandra, was a graduate but with plenty of *'life-experiences'*. She too had been a *'high flier'* but was made redundant two years ago. To date, she had made dozens of applications but was turned down most of the time. Some of the interviews she had been to were just a mere exercise in statistics for the *would-be* employers. Oftentimes, the one post would attract over 400 applicants. Only twice had she been short-listed and on both of those occasions Pam was told that she was too old, at thirty-three. Now, she was reduced to being dependent on 'The Benefit Agency'. Since the test case against the local government department, Pam was not able to secure another job. That was no surprise as her case was highlighted but featured in the national as well as local newspapers for some months. As far as Pam was concerned, she thought the unfair verdict had brought her the wrong kind of publicity. Still, her bubbly personality kept her afloat. When Pam arrived at Sandra's house she noticed the front door was ajar. She pushed the door but cautiously peered around it. Pam stepped into the hallway. "Is it that bad", Pam asked? Sandra did not answer but beckoned for Pam to follow her into the kitchen. She could see the worried look on Sandra's face but Pam remained silent while Sandra talked. Pam handed her the potted plant. Sandra took it but was more eager to continue talking. She told Pam about her fling with Duke. At the end, Pam asked Sandra whether she would tell Raymond. "No way ... I don't really love Duke but he's head over heels about me and very generous towards me. I don't want to loose him", Sandra confessed. Pam listened but she did not approve of Sandra two-timing Raymond. She felt that Sandra's unquenchable thirst for fame and the taste of Champagne Urge would eventually trap her into carrying on the seemingly sordid affair. "You know the saying, can't have your cake and eat it", Pam warned. "Look Pam it just happened, I only meant to tease Duke but now he can't keep his hands off me. Did I do the wrong thing", Sandra questioned? "I'm your friend. Stop it now before it's too late or you'll lose Raymond", Pam warned. Sandra shook her head to indicate that she would not change her mind about continuing the affair with Duke. "Don't tell me you have a crush on Duke, it could never work", Pam advised. "Pam you've got no idea how rich this man is. He also has clout, lots of it", Sandra drooled.

Pam stayed quiet. By her silence Sandra knew that Pam was making her strongest statement yet. "I know you mean well but think about it. He's the boss. If anyone can influence my career he can", Sandra determined. Pam knew Sandra wanted to be successful. She was hell-bent on impressing the people around her. Pam knew Sandra was playing a dangerous game also. They walked towards the kitchen. Sandra poured two cups of coffee from the percolator. She put them on the kitchen table. Sandra picked up a cup and saucer but walked over to the other side of the kitchen. Pam remained where she stood. Sandra was sipping the hot liquid when the landline phone in the kitchen started to ring. Deep in thought, Sandra was disturbed by the sudden loud noise. She jumped but dropped her cup of coffee on the floor. Some of it splashed onto the slacks she was wearing. Sandra bent down to pick up the broken cup and saucer that had separated into large pieces. The splinters found their way all around the floor. "Take a hold of yourself Sandra. It's only the telephone", Pam soothed. When she refused to pick up the landline telephone receiver, Pam could tell there was something else on Sandra's mind. The phone kept ringing until Pam picked it up. "Hello . . . oh it's you gorgeous man", she replied. "It's Raymond", Pam whispered. "I don' want to talk to him now", Sandra whispered. She used her hands to indicate a negative response to Pam's prompting. "Sandra just popped out for a moment. Can I get her to call you back", Pam asked? After Pam hung up, she encouraged Sandra to tell her why she didn't answer the phone. It was then that Sandra showed Pam the note she had received earlier. She stood with her mouth opened. "Get yourself a private detective girl this is more than we can manage", Pam advised. Sandra looked up at the kitchen clock. She hadn't realized till then that she was fast running out of time. Sandra did not want to be late for a previously arranged appointment. "I'll have to talk to you later Pam, I can't afford to be late for the Press Conference. I'll be on TV tonight . . . don't miss the 19:30 hours News. I'll have to hurry now. Excuse me while I get ready", Sandra stated. Pam read the note again but wondered how Sandra might cope with the demands. She told Pam she was ready to go. They left together. Sandra dropped Pam home but started on her journey to work. The traffic was crawling along and that made Sandra edgy. She tuned her car radio to the national station so she could listen to the Traffic Report. When it was announced, Sandra decided that she would get the train instead. There was a station about two hundred yards down the road. Sandra tried to see if there had been an accident but she could see nothing unusual like flashing lights. She wound down the window and listened if she could hear sirens but the heavy droning of the Lorries drowned out all other sounds. It had been raining earlier so the roads were wet and slippery. One impatient driver, driving on the other side of the road, overtook Sandra's car at a ridiculous speed. His car skidded but swerved as he attempted to get to the next side street over on the right. This was reminiscent of Sandra's own erratic driving the night before. She noticed that some drivers were hanging out of their windows too, looking at the maniac performance. Both the driver of the car and the oncoming lorry were at fault for what happened next. The bright lights of the lorry must have blinded the manic car driver; whose *'death-wish'* mission was almost completed when he collided into the oncoming lorry. It didn't seem as if the driver of the car could have survived such a tremendous impact. There were sounds of crushing metal. The loud thudding sound and screeching of metal along the tarred road, metal barriers and the street lamp post, best reflect the scene that Sandra witnessed. The bizarre accident happened so fast that it was hard for Sandra to take it in but nevertheless she felt numb from the experience. Some other people had been affected too. One woman got out of her car but ran along the pavement. She ran in one direction, stopped then proceeded to run back in the direction in which she had started. Most everyone left their respective vehicles unattended to see if they could help. Many were shocked into complete silence whilst others were shouting contradictory advice to each other. The lorry driver must have been flung through the windscreen of his cab. His now motionless body lay contorted as if he was a rubberized version of a real human. Only the blood that trickled from his nostrils and ears indicated that this torso had once been alive. Conversely, the body of the car driver could hardly be seen from the now immobile, compressed metal which, moments before, had displayed its capacity as a moving personnel carriage. Those who got closest insisted that the trapped car driver was still alive. It was difficult to believe that he could still be alive. Because of the lines of traffic on both sided of the street, the emergency vehicles were finding it difficult to get through. The relevant Services sirens played the familiar *'Emergency Blues'* in the distance. Their flashing lights highlighted the grave difficulties they were having in getting to the scene of the accident. Drivers on both sides of the road were given permission to mount the pavement in order to create enough space for the emergency vehicles to gain access to the scene of the accident. Ambulances, fire engines and the police arrived. Each driver or passenger told their version of how the accident happened. It meant further delay for everyone, particularly for the now nervous Sandra. She cursed herself for choosing the wrong route. Sandra could now be late for the Press Conference and the Newsreel Shoot. She resolved that fate is what it is. Sandra decided to return to her car but practice some of the breathing exercises that Raymond had taught her. Gradually, her head began to clear. She tried to figure out how she could dig herself out of this messy situation. The ringing tone of her cell phone made her jump but sent new glimmers of hope. "Ray", Sandra said. No one answered. The line went dead. Sandra was desperate to contact anyone who could get her out of this situation. I'll phone Ray, he'll know what to do, she decided. Sandra dialled furiously then placed the phone to her ear. It kept ringing for a while but there was no answer. "Damn, where could he be", Sandra asked herself? She dialled her friend Pam. This time it took quite a few rings before a voice answered. "Pam it's me Sandra", she said. Sandra proceeded to tell her friend about the accident. "Now I'm stuck and don't know what to do. "I've been trying to call Ray but to no avail", Sandra explained. "Ring your boss instead maybe he'll have a solution", Pam advised. This sounded the most sensible thing to do, Sandra thought. "Thanks a million Pam, someday I hope I can return the favour", she concluded. The next phone call she made was to Duke. His secretary took the call. "Mr. Stagg's office", Mary Allsorts answered. "Mr. Stagg please Mary . . . Sandra Bogus . . . I'll hold", Sandra agreed. She said a silent prayer as she waited for Duke to respond. "Keep holding. I'm connecting you to Mr. Stagg as soon as I can, Mary Allsorts advised. She was the diligent secretary who worked for Duke's father, Earl, in the past. Duke was instructed through his father's will for her to be retained her to continue under his leadership. Mary was thin and scrawny with huge yellow teeth decorated with tobacco stains. She had a nasty cough that sounded like the noise from a broken exhaust. Her ghostly voice belonged to a crypt but she had experience and efficiency as a secretary. Mary had no other love but her job, her mansion and her cat, Bill. Some whispered rumours that often floated around the offices, indicated that Mary was married to her cat, the job and her riches. Once it was said that Mary was so rich that she fed Bill champagne for breakfast and dinner. Some said her husband died alone in a Nursing Home of malnutrition because Mary thought more about the cat than she did him. She put the call through to Duke. "That young lady wants to talk to you. I don't want to interfere but she sounded pretty upset. I can hear it in her voice", Mary continued. "Yes, yes, thanks Mary, put her through, Duke said. "Duke Stagg", he boomed. "Duke it's Sandra Bogus. I'm having a bit of a problem getting in to work", she explained. Sandra spoke so softly that Duke found it difficult to hear. "I can't hear you properly", Duke commented. Sandra managed to get her story across, eventually. "Are the police still there", Duke asked? "Yes, and they'll be here for quite some time", Sandra replied. "Leave the car where it is. I'll arrange to get it to your house", Duke advised. As soon as she hung up, Sandra abandoned her green Sleek Coupe but headed for the Train Station. Sandra looked eagerly at her watch. It would be a very tight squeeze to get to the Press Conference on time. Sandra walked quickly. At one time, she even broke into a trot. Sandra knew Andy Mann would find it quite amusing if she showed poor time management. He would use it against her when it was time for her Assessment because, technically, she was still 'on probation'. As Sandra attempted to go through the barrier, the guard asked to see her ticket. "Ticket please, ma'am", the guard asked politely? Sandra could see the train on the platform. Some of the doors were still open but she knew it was a matter of minutes before it left. She couldn't miss this train. It was her last hope of getting to the conference on time. "I'll pay on the train. I have got to be on that train", Sandra said. Her communication was firm. She smiled coyly at the guard. While he was busy admiring her beautiful body and mesmerizing large cornflower blue eyes, Sandra walked through towards the platform. She hurried along towards the train before the guard could change his mind. Sandra boarded the train but walked through to the First Class carriage. Some people looked up as she entered the carriage. "Are you lost dearie", one green humanoid robotron woman enquired. Sandra ignored the woman's comment but went past her. The woman spat on the back of Sandra's dress then summoned the guard. She beckoned for him to come towards her. Bending his head to listen above the sound of the train, the guard heard the woman's concern as she whispered into his ear. "Ok Madam, I'll check", the guard replied. He did not hesitate. The guard from the Tribe of Hawke approached Sandra straight away. She was still trying to get a seat in the sparsely occupied carriage. Each time Sandra thought she'd found a seat, she was barred from sitting down. The excuses ranged from "seat taken", "gone to the toilet" or even bluntly told to "find another seat". The most explicit comment was "I just don't want you to sit next to me". The guard stood next to her now and he tried not to sound too anxious. "Have you got a ticket madam", the guard questioned? "Well no, I told the other guard at the gate that I would pay when I boarded the train. He didn't object, do you", Sandra asked? By now Sandra was frustrated at the treatment she was experiencing. She cursed both drivers of the accident for her predicament. The guard tried to humiliate Sandra. "You have no ticket and there are no seats. What would you like me to do, call the police or have you thrown off the train, madam", the guard threatened. The woman, who had asked the guard to question Sandra, laughed loudest when he overplayed his authority. Sandra was not intimidated by the puppet in uniform. Instead, she waited until the laughing had died down then she countered. "Your observation must be limited. I offered to pay", Sandra declared. The guard was hurt by Sandra's remark about his limited observational skills. Pandering to his green humanoid robotron segregationists' captive audience, the guard was resolute in his condemnation of Sandra. He chose to ridicule her further. In his attempt to impress his captive audience in the carriage, the guard even raised his voice several pitches. "How would madam like to pay, cash or credit card", the guard asked? His cynical remark catalysed the venomous humiliation of Sandra. Following his *'stand up' 'uncle tom'* act of disdainful rhetoric and the high pitched tone in which he used to address Sandra, the guard could not control the volume of laughter that followed. From a kneeling position on the floor the guard competently emulated the late actor/comedian Norman Wisdom. The guard's impersonation of Norman Wisdom's infectious style was well worthy of an acclaim for the highest stage or movie award. Sandra not only heard but experienced the impact of the exploitation of voices as the whole carriage erupted with laughter. Being the enforced elected target for humiliation, Sandra felt like jumping from the moving train but her instincts told her to battle on. She waited for the laughter to subside enough to retaliate with effect. Amongst the odd chuckle coming from those few, who were still finding pleasure in the cheap thrill, Sandra reached inside her handbag but took out a long folder of credit cards. She let them dangle from the plastic wallets quite deliberately. Turning to the guard, she addressed him directly. "Guard, it seems you are taking no responsibility for doing your job. You are a representative of the company for whom you work. I'm sure your employers won't be happy to know that you've chosen to include using the commuters as a form of entertainment. When you've finished enjoying yourself at my expense, you may now choose to charge one of these credit cards as payment for my fare", Sandra said. Her delivery was aimed at the attitude of the guard. Her tone was at a level which oozed class but more so the message was succinct and effective. The level of disdain was more than apparent. Sandra was aware that her inferences were scorching enough without being abrasive or to be considered by the stereotypical green humanoid robotron serial profilers as being aggressive. She watched the jaws drop around the carriage but more so how much more quiet the ambience had become. Several of the segregationists hid their faces in their newspapers. For those who had no newspaper with which to hide suddenly found the terrain an alternative means of focus but altogether expressions were changing *'post haste'*. The woman, who had initiated the spectacle, now buried her head in the Financial Newspaper she was pretending to read. Sandra could see the flushed look of embarrassment on the guard's face. He came up to her but selected a credit card from the long plastic wallet. Sandra removed the credit card for the length of the transaction but put it back before refolding the long plastic wallet. She placed the wallet back in her handbag. Sandra was not finished with the guard as yet. When he handed her the receipt, she looked him straight in the eyes but demanded he find her a seat in the carriage now she had paid her fare. Sandra was surprised how many offers for seats were being volunteered. Bags were being moved but placed in the overhead compartments that were available from the start. The guard wanted to help her place her hand luggage in the overhead compartment but Sandra refused his help. She just had one more thing to communicate to the hapless guard. She told him. "Give me your name and badge number. I'll be making a formal complaint to your superiors", Sandra ended. She took a note of the name on the badge and the relevant ID number. Sandra plucked the ticket from the guard's hand but put it in her handbag then dialled a number on her cell phone. When the voice at the other end answered, she asked for Duke. "Duke Stagg, please Mary", Sandra said. "Duke here Sandra, where are you now? Did you manage to get sorted out", he asked? There was urgency in his voice but Sandra could not tell if that was just concern over her or the fact that she might arrive late for the Press Conference. "I've had a bad start but I'll make it to the Press Conference yet", Sandra confirmed. "Press Conference", Sandra repeated. It wasn't as if Duke hadn't heard her the first time but Sandra wanted the green humanoid robotron people in the carriage to know that she was a woman of importance. Sandra told Duke about the humiliation on the train. "I couldn't even get a seat earlier. I'll probably have to duck out of the conference if I'm too tired but I'm still up for the Newsreel Photo Shoot. Could you ask Andy to prepare to attend if he gets a call from me at the last minute? Thanks Duke, see you later", Sandra concluded. The people on the train were silent now; each pretending not to take any notice of her conversation with Duke. The man with the huge 'handlebar' moustache whispered to his colleague who sat in front of him. "You don't think she was talking to the real Duke Stagg, do you", he asked? "It could be. She mentioned Press Conference. That would be the real Duke Stagg, Media Magnate Extraordinaire", the other man replied. "Rather", the man with the 'handlebar' moustache exclaimed. Sandra found that some seats were now made available to her. She managed to secure a window and aisle seat together. The train controlled by magnetic technological engineering glided above the tracks but hurtled along at 150 miles per hour for a while. Sandra heard the sound of a symphony of snoring which began to infiltrate the carriage. The guard came along the carriage with refreshments. "Tea, coffee, drinks", he repeated. He didn't look directly at her but the guard stopped by the seat Sandra was occupying. "Would madam like some refreshments", the guard asked? His manner was polite this time. "Yes, I'll have one of those Rumbabas", Sandra replied. She pointed to the huge donut-like tasty pastry treat. The smell of the coffee had triggered the addiction within her and she couldn't resist it. "Give me a large cup of coffee as well", Sandra ordered. She removed the Gold Credit Card from its holder but presented it to the assistant. "I've been instructed not to collect any money from you for refreshments. Please accept it as compliments of 'The Train Company Madam'", the guard explained. Sandra knew that Duke had made the appropriate phone-calls. "Clout" is what Duke called it. After she devoured the Rumbaba and coffee, Sandra phoned Raymond. The reception was patchy. "I'll tell you all tonight Ray", Sandra ended. As she got closer to her destination she gazed out the window at the beautiful green scenery of the suburbs and the large mansions that sat on acres of prime land. Sandra knew that people like Duke and Mary lived in those types of houses. She was determined that one day she too would live in such luxury.

CHAPTER 22

A lot of people had gathered for the Press Conference but Sandra busied herself making sure the prepared script was in order. Duke had a way with the journalists, especially those who tried to trip him up on every occasion. It was all one big game to him and he had an answer for everything. "That's enough gentlemen. It's time for lunch wouldn't you agree", Duke teased? A great big roar came from most of them as they hurried to get to 'The Feathered Fish' AADC. They reminded Sandra of her primary school days when everyone rushed to be first in the dinner queue. Inside 'The Feathered Fish' AADC, people were drinking as if the only sustenance in life was booze. Duke made sure Sandra's glass was always filled and he kept breaking away from his friends to show her a lot of attention. "Duke they might notice", Sandra fussed. "They'll be too drunk to notice. Drown away your bad start to the day", Duke quipped. "After the filming, I'll have to leave a bit sharp, can I give you a lift somewhere", Duke asked? "That'll be fine . . . thanks", Sandra replied. The journalists and photographers exchanged conversation while they gulped their favourite tipple. Boisterous laughter and idle chatter filled the air but Duke's attention was diverted to the scantily dressed barmaid, Doris Bendlow. She was flirting with almost all the men. When Duke eased his way to the bar she pretended that she'd hardly noticed him from the rest. Duke was trying hard to attract her attention but she still continued to ignore him. A drunk reached over but tried to kiss her. She slapped his face. All the others laughed but commented. Some said it was unfair for her to tease and then decline. "It's my life, I'll choose for myself", Doris said. Seizing the opportunity to get her attention, Duke interrupted her focus. "How about me", he teased. Doris looked over at him. "Only if you're rich", she replied. There was a loud roar of laughter as she sidled over to where he was sitting. She pushed her face quite close to his. "How rich are you", she asked? Duke was embarrassed because he wasn't ready for that type of question. Doris had thrown him offline. He looked around for help but could only find an anxious press daring him to reply. What a scoop that would be. One journalist couldn't bear the suspense any longer. "Go on Duke tell us what you're worth", he encouraged. Doris realised what she had started but tried to quash Dukes' embarrassment. "Leave him alone you sharks, I thought this was lunchtime", Doris quipped. She shook her hips from side to side like a practiced belly dancer but licked her lips again and again while winking at Duke. Andy Mann, walked over to Duke, leaned over but whispered something in his ear then handed him an envelope. Duke ripped it open and started to read the note. It said, 'I KNOW ABOUT YOU AND SANDRA BOGUS'. Duke felt weak and he started to sweat a little. "What is it Duke", Andy Mann asked? Duke didn't answer but his eyes searched the crowded AADC for Sandra. "Andy I've got to go, take care of things here", Duke ordered. "Do you want me to deputise this evening", Andy Mann enquired. "I'll be there", Duke replied. On his way out, he bumped into Sandra. "Come with me", Duke said urgently. Sandra had not seen or heard Duke so shaken before so she just followed. Outside, they walked silently for a while. "We'll have to stop seeing each other", Duke exclaimed. Shivers of cold currents ran through Sandra's body as the thought of being dumped surged to her brain. She stayed silent but angry. Sandra was wondering what the next detail of bad news might be. Duke was angry too because he had not yet exhausted his lust for the beautiful Sandra. "What have I done and why so suddenly", Sandra asked? "Extortion that's why", Duke said. "That's a big assumption, isn't it Duke", Sandra fumed. It was only then that Duke realised what Sandra might be thinking. "No, no, I don't mean you my sweet. I mean someone is trying to . . .", Duke said. He hadn't finished explaining to Sandra but pulled the envelope from his pocket. "Read this" he ordered. Sandra stopped as she recognised the similarity of the message. "Duke I got one too", she squirmed. "When", Duke enquired? He seemed more frightened now even more so than he had been earlier. Extortion was not something he had to deal with often but he knew he had to solve the mystery before it ruined his name, family and business. "If the press gets hold of this, I'm ruined", Duke explained. "What about me" Sandra reminded? "Yes, and you too", Duke empathised. "We'll discuss it more fully later", he hinted. "Duke I'm frightened", Sandra exclaimed. They entered the huge office block. Its Gothic appearance blended in with the not so far away hills. Each went back to their respective office needing work to eliminate their immediate demise. There was a memo from Andy Mann on Sandra's desk. It described the order of priority for the filming. Sandra phoned Raymond to remind him to watch the news. "Record it for me Ray", Sandra instructed. Her day had been a nightmare so far but nothing would stop Sandra from her pride of place at the filming. She gazed momentarily from the only window in her office. Attracted by the sound of a motor bike, Sandra looked out towards the private road in front of the building. She saw the leather suited figure crouched on the bike as it left the parking area. It was a courier. A few minutes later the office messenger brought her an envelope. It was addressed as *'Personal'*. Sandra was slightly puzzled as she wasn't in the habit of receiving personal mail at work. When she opened it, the note said 'NOW YOU BOTH KNOW THAT I KNOW'. She put it in her handbag but strode towards Duke's office. Mary looked up from her desk. "Mr. Stagg is on the phone to his wife. He doesn't want to be disturbed. Do you want to leave a message", Mary Allsorts asked? Mary's stern manner had upset Sandra before. She knew that Mary could be quite cold towards her but now she was handling her like unwanted company. It was as if she was Duke's guard dog rather than his secretary, Sandra thought. In answer to Mary's question, Sandra would not be put off by her. She fashioned a reply. "No, he asked me to come to see him at this time", Sandra lied. She didn't wait for Mary to respond. Sandra spoke again. "Could you tell him I'm here", she insisted. "O.K. but he can get pretty angry if he's on the phone to his wife", Mary insinuated sarcastically. Though the stress on the word wife seemed deliberate, Sandra ignored the comment. She was anxious to show Duke the note. Once inside Dukes' office, Sandra pulled out the note. "Another one Duke", Sandra said. "Snap", he replied. He tossed yet another note on the desk. Sandra picked it up and read it. 50,000 SPCUs OR I'LL TELL YOUR WIFE—INSTRUCTIONS TO FOLLOW—NO COPS'. Sandra gasped but slumped into the chair. "Would you like some water", Duke asked? "I just want this to stop", Sandra replied. Duke could sense the weary tone in Sandra's voice. He told her that he had already hired a private detective to investigate who was sending these notes. "Sit tight, don't give up", Duke assured her. He could see that Sandra was broken by the ordeal. He was worried too but had decided that he would fight to the end. His daddy had built this company and he had to keep it even if he had to use *'unusual methods'*. The telephone rang. It was Mary announcing the arrival of Andy Mann. "Five minutes, I'll be ready in five minutes. Damn, I almost forgot the filming", Duke said. "Sandra, we have to be careful. Please don't stand close to me at the filming just in case . . .", he warned. "That's already been taken care of by Mr. Mann", Sandra said. She sounded quite disappointed. Outside the building, Duke pointed Sandra to a separate car. The uniformed chauffeur stood by its open door. She sat motionless for the first ten minutes of the journey deep in thought about the events of the day. Somehow, she would have to present the company's image at the filming while she suffered on the inside. Was this the price she would have to pay for success, she asked herself? Sandra needed to talk to someone other than Duke so she phoned Pam. There was no reply for sometime then Pam's voice penetrated the silence. "I am glad that I finally got you", Sandra exclaimed. She didn't wait for Pam to respond before speaking again. "Were you busy? I can call back", Sandra apologized. "Just a little bit", Pam said. Sandra could hear Pam panting. She sounded as if she had just finished a race. "What's wrong Pam", Sandra queried? "Nothing, just busy at the moment", Pam replied. Sandra thought she could sense that Pam would prefer her to call back. She made an excuse then hung up. "Are we almost there", she asked the chauffeur? "We should be there in another 20 minutes or so Ms. Bogus", the chauffeur replied. Sandra was a bit suspicious and a bit paranoid about the chauffeur's knowledge of her name. "How did you know my name", Sandra asked? "Mr. Stagg told me ma'am", the chauffeur replied. The convoy of cars eventually arrived at the TV Station. A lot of security guards were present. They busied themselves to prove their efficiency. Some journalists were trying to get an interview with Duke but his personal human *'guard dogs'* made sure that they kept their distance. He preferred to joust with them verbally. Duke knew that they had limited time before the broadcast. The bright lights and cameras seemed to appear from every angle. Presenter, Arnold Letterhead, probed with many loaded questions but Duke was equal to the challenge. Sandra's wish had come through at last. It was Duke who had made it possible. She looked over at Andy Mann and, at that moment, hated him for wanting to exclude her. However, she also acknowledged to herself that his input had also made this possible. They stayed in the Hospitality Room for a little while then started separately to go their own ways. Duke and Sandra were among the last few to leave. "Good night Ms. Bogus, the chauffeur will take you home", he said. "Good night Mr. Stagg", Sandra replied. She made her way to the limo. During the journey home, Sandra noticed that some parts of the dual carriageway were unlit. The water from the steady drizzle on the tarred road made mirror-like reflections onto the windscreen. It seemed for a long while that theirs was the only vehicle on this side of the carriageway. Occasionally, another vehicle would pass in the opposite direction. Sandra felt lonely but longed for conversation. "Is there any music in this limo", Sandra asked? "Yes Ms. Bogus, would you like me to turn it on", the chauffeur from the Tribe of Hawke enquired. Jazz was never Sandra's favourite music but it would at least punctuate her long lonely journey. However, fear reared its ugly head again when the limo suddenly started to sway, slither and slide. "What are you doing", Sandra screamed? "I'm sorry Ms. Bogus but we seem to have a puncture on our hands", the chauffeur replied. Sandra became even more paranoid than before. Fear gripped her tightly. "Not our hands, your hands", Sandra said. The chauffeur was angry with Sandra too but in his capacity it would have been foolish to argue with her. "I'll see to it straight away Ms. Bogus. There's a spare in the back", the chauffeur replied. Sandra looked out into the darkness but wandered how he would be able to see to change the wheel. She was scared. When the phone rang Sandra's loneliness disappeared. "Hello Sandy", Raymond said. "Ray, it's good to hear from you, where are you . . . did you see the News", Sandra asked? "One question at a time Sandy", Raymond advised. "Yes, I saw you", he replied Raymond sounded excited by it all. "Did you record it Ray", Sandra asked? "Yes Sandy, I did. What time will you be home", Raymond enquired? Without waiting for her to answer, Raymond fired at her again. "By the way your car is parked across the road but you're not in it. The puzzle deepens", Raymond added. "I am stuck on the dual carriageway in a chauffeur driven limo, how's that for class", Sandra teased? "Been given the star treatment huh", Raymond implied. "That was the idea but some clever chauffeur chose to drive over

a nail or something on an unlit part of the carriageway. How's that for star treatment",
Sandra asked? "You sound desperate, shall I come to get you", Raymond asked? "I must
be at least 50 miles from home but I'll soon find out if this chauffeur knows how to change
a wheel. Don't wait up Ray. I'll awaken you when I finally get home", Sandra concluded.
"O.K. Sandy, see you then", Raymond ended. Sandra's patience with the chauffeur had
just about reached breaking point. Peering into the darkness she could only see the small
light from the torch lying on the verge where the chauffeur had placed it to enable him
to see. Sandra pounded the bullet proof glass with clenched fist but the chauffeur couldn't
see nor hear her. She needed to know why he was taking so long to change the wheel. As
far as she was concerned, he was just like one of Raymond's friends; lowly paid and not
ambitious. The jazz music was her only companion for the moment but she didn't like that
either. Fear gripped her as she thought about the many times she had read that people had
disappeared in lonely places. Their bodies were sometimes unidentifiable when found.
Sandra had noticed the way the chauffeur had looked at her but she couldn't be sure what
he might do. Sam, the chauffeur, didn't like Sandra either. He knew there were others
before her and there would be others when Duke had grown tired of her. After what
seemed an eternity, Sam Cleverman, put the damaged wheel into the back of the limo. He
too was a bit testy. After all, he was now thoroughly soaked by the steady drizzle and his
back ached from the long bending. It had taken him more than half an hour in poor light
to change the wheel. He slammed the boot shut. The long wait and fear of the unexpected
had affected Sandra's reasoning. For reasons only known to her, she thought Sam had gone
to the boot for an axe. This thought filled her with hysteria so she started to scream
uncontrollably. "H-E-L-P . . . MURDER . . . SOMEONE HELP ME PLEASE", Sandra
bellowed. Sam heard her but knew that if he had tried to calm her down he would be
blamed for whatever happened next. He was in no mood for this nervous woman. Sam
was hurt by her implication but attended to what he was paid to do. The rest of the journey
was an embarrassment to both.

Raymond timed his return to the house he was sharing with Sandra. An envelope
was lying on the carpet. He picked it up but glanced at it. There was no name or address
written, just the words 'BY HAND'. Raymond opened the envelope but whistled as he
read the note which said 'I KNOW ABOUT YOU AND PAMELA LABRISHÈ'. Who
could it be, he wondered? Pam and Raymond did not set out to be lovers. After all, she
was Sandra's best friend. Their friendship blossomed in spite of Sandra's infidelity. Tired
of Sandra's lack of cooking skills, Raymond had to make do with *'take away'* food every
day. He neither found them filling nor particularly nutritious yet he did sometimes enjoy
the odd pasta meal. His cultural foods were rice and peas, bananas, greens, dumplings and
various types of yams. These were the type of meals he enjoyed at Pam's. At least she was
never guilty of trying to knock him out with perfumes that Raymond deemed capable of
being used as anesthetic in a hospital operating theatre instead of gas. When he poured his
heart out to Pam one evening, Raymond described how he sometimes regretted moving
in with the beautiful Sandra. "I feel I've made the wrong decision Pam", Raymond
confessed. Pam empathised with his position. She knew Sandra was two-timing Raymond
but she couldn't say anything to him about it. Pam had decided to be available if Raymond
wanted her. Raymond opened his heart to Pam. "I'm dying inside. Sandra doesn't like my
friends. They can't visit me at home. She looks down on them, my culture and traditions

as not being worthy. Sandra doesn't or can't cook me a traditional meal. I need a woman who understands and caters for my cultural needs. I need a woman who understands me for who I am instead of whom she wants me to be; an image of some unknown myth called 'Mr. Right'. I don't want to be a *'Trophy Man'*. Sandra is naïve. She can't see that the women, who say they are her friends, are parasites. They enjoy spending her money. She has wasted large sums of money chasing *'rainbows'* that were never even there. These women are loose women. They are into living the type of living that belongs to *'Sin City'* only. I am no longer allowed to comment about these leeches. Sandra gets upset with me. In fact, sometimes she can be a bitch", he complained. Pam had never heard Raymond speak like this before so she cradled his head in her arms "You poor man. You must have been going through hell", Pam empathised. Raymond, who'd longed for this style of caring, melted to Pam's caress. That is how it happened some two months ago. Pamela Labrishè was lonely too. She didn't have a job or a man. The men with whom she had been friendly in the past used her because of her generous and kind nature. Now that she was just about surviving on government benefits, her loving and caring wasn't enough for them. They wanted money and sex. She was relatively attractive and great fun to be with. At least Raymond had told her she is. Her fall from the *'high life'* was a blessing in disguise. She too had blazed a trail to the end of the rainbow but came crashing down with a bump after she was unexplainably made redundant from her job as a social worker. Pam had also lost the case against the local government. Both of these major events in her life acted as contributory factors towards her now realistic view to life. Raymond knew that she was still ambitious. Pam was making great efforts to get herself another job, which would enable her to free herself from dependency of government benefits.

Raymond Oddball loved Sandra Bogus because of her looks and shapely physique in the main but he could hardly resist the advances of those other women who flocked him. His face was not necessarily a pretty picture but he knew that the women, especially Sandra, loved him because of his muscular athletic physique; most women's and her fantasy of the legendary 'Mr. Right'. Raymond also knew that having a steady job would promote him still further in their estimation of him being the *'perfect'* partner, though his intelligent brain was surplus to their requirements. He was not the innocent besotted lover that Sandra imagined. In fact, he was a very deceptive man who pretended to be Sandra's lapdog. Oftentimes, he played the passive role just to let Sandra believe she was in charge. Raymond figured that while she was being so wrapped up in herself, Sandra would never notice anyway. He knew that job status, thrills and fame, in particular, was all she sought from life. Sandra could never just survive like so many less fortunate women have to but he admired the genius in her as an academic. Yes, Raymond Wilberforce Oddball was a sly cheater too but Sandra's dilemma and late nights were his outlet. Pam was now his focus. He'd left Pam's but got home before Sandra did. He was just finishing his shower when he heard the keys in the door. Sandra saw the light on in the bathroom. "Hi Ray", Sandra shouted. "Come and join me Sandy. The water feels good", Raymond encouraged. He was trying to inveigle her into the shower. "I'm too tired even to eat, I'll have a *'wash'* now and shower in the morning", Sandra replied. He was disappointed by Sandra's response. Raymond had images of both of them having a romantic shower together. His imagination had preceded Sandra's arrival. Raymond's desire for his *'Cloned-Barbie Trophy Woman'*, *'Mrs Right'* drove his ego onto a higher level. He could sense Sandra's warm body next to his but the thought had aroused his manly probe to attention. The involuntary throbbing needed to be quelled or Raymond could remain haunted by the feeling that seemed to have overwhelmed him. The hot shower did not only seem even more invigorating but also seemed to act as a trigger for his lust towards Sandra's physical involvement. "Sandy, you'll feel much fresher . . . come on the water is just right", Raymond pleaded. "Ray, I'll have a *'wash'*," Sandra said sharply. Raymond's ego crashed faster than a penis from a premature ejaculation. His probe was now a mere ornament dangling from its attached site; much reduced in size. He knew Sandra would not change her mind so he desisted from carrying on about it. Sandra's insistence to *'wash'* instead of showering or bathing was getting to him. Surely it was quicker to shower than it was to have a *'wash'*, he pondered. One day it might just be the thing that split them apart. By the time Raymond finished his shower and climbed into bed, Sandra was asleep. He had wanted to talk to her about her day, the filming, the press conference and the traffic delay earlier in the day. They never seem to spend enough quality time together anymore, Raymond thought to himself. He lay awake thinking about their lack of compatibility lately. He pondered how many people did he know, who weren't compatible but firmly believed that money could buy happiness? He had first hand experience that philosophy was wrong. Money was only a means of paying the bills. It did not, necessarily, guarantee him or anyone else happiness. Sandra and Ray earned particularly good salaries. Their total overheads were merely chicken feed compared to someone like Pam's. Raymond was happier with her than Sandra. Pam was not physically as attractive as the stunningly beautiful Sandra but she brought out other characteristics in Raymond that might have laid dormant within him forever. He tossed around in bed yearning for the loving Pam when his mobile began to ring. "Yeah", Raymond drawled. "I'm lonely Ray", Pam said. Raymond's pulse raced even faster now than when he desired Sandra while he was in the shower. Pam's distinctly husky voice had a certain magical intonation that Raymond found irresistible. "Can you come over for awhile", Pam enticed. "Yeah sure", Raymond replied. He dressed quickly but rushed out to his car. Neither his impulsive action nor the screeching tyres disturbed the weary Sandra. Raymond's heart played an eager rhythm against his chest but his mind was focused on the caring Pam. Several green lights later he was parked outside her flat. He did not press the buzzer but instead opened the entrance door with the key she had given him. He hurriedly opened the door to the flat. As he stepped into the hallway, he could hear the sound of reggae music playing at an extremely low volume but audible enough for both him and Pam to hear. She was dressed in a transparent negligee, which seemed to highlight her assets. Pam advanced towards him. "Oh Ray", Pam exclaimed. She pulled him closer to her. "I wish you could be here every night", Pam exclaimed. Raymond kissed her passionately. "That might soon be possible", he said. "You make me feel alive again Ray", Pam said. She clung to Raymond like a vine wrapped round a tree trunk. The sparkle in her eyes was mixed with tears of joy which ran down her cheeks. Raymond brushed them away with his fingers. "Don't cry baby, don't cry", Raymond whispered. They lay entwined in each others arms until they fell asleep. There was no way back now. Raymond would no longer have to eat *'take away'* foods every night nor wait for Sandra's *'headaches'* to go. When he awakened, Raymond showered and made breakfast for him and Pam. He placed the tray on the small table next to the bed. Pam awakened to his gentle kiss but smiled when she saw the hard dough bread and the plate of ackee and salt fish meal. "My, my Ray and you can cook too, I must be the luckiest woman in the world", Pam said. He looked at his watch but reluctantly told Pam that it was time he left for work. As soon as he got into his car, Ray turned on the radio. The bass vibrated from the customized speakers at the back while the crisp rhythms poured from the front ones. DJ Herbie played only 'Roots and Culture' at that time of the morning. Raymond tapped the steering wheel with one hand while he nodded his head up and down. The ringing of the mobile was barely audible. "Yeah", Raymond said into the phone. "Well Ray, my bed was empty for most of the night, where were you", Sandra demanded? Her voice sounded shrill. Raymond was tempted to tell her it was over but he sensed how highly strung she sounded. He did not hate Sandra, only her outlook on life and the sharks she kept as friends. "My battery is going flat. I'll call you back later Sandy", Raymond cautioned. With that he switched off the phone. "Bu-yaka", Raymond exclaimed. He tossed the mobile on the passenger seat.

CHAPTER 23

D espite her fling with Duke, Sandra felt she owned Raymond. He had never spent all night away from home before and that made her angry. She did not like his friends, who she felt were not ambitious enough about improving their lives. Sandra scorned their very existence and thought her status would be diminished, if Raymond did not free himself from their company. They were not allowed to visit Raymond at her house. As far as she was concerned, they were to blame for his mysterious absence last night. Sandra did not even consider that Raymond was growing tired of her constant nagging, inability to cook, preference for *'take away'* foods, unpredictable moods, naive perceptions, and mannerisms. Sandra's passion for masking her body odour with body sprays, preference to have a *'wash'* instead of bathing or showering, was a definite turnoff from the beautifully structured woman the naïve Raymond used to view as his 'Mrs. Right'. He was developing an allergy not only to the *'body sprays'* Sandra used but also the *'air fresheners'* which confronted but restricted him from breathing too deeply whenever he was home. On top of all that, Raymond found that snuggling up to Sandra in bed was just as stifling not because of the intensity of their physical embraces but the various chemicals it took to maintain her hair. Sandra was always at the *'hair dressers'* having her seemingly *'fatigued'* hair *'perm'* to *"liven it up"* or to have it *"relaxed"*, apparently! Raymond knew that Sandra desired for her naturally beautiful hair to appear like that of the green humanoids. The *'novelty stage'* of their relationship had expired. A more matured Raymond was beginning to realize that Sandra's reasons for working late so frequently was beginning to wear thin; especially now she had her own chauffeur. Even though they still had very strong physical attractions for each other, Raymond was more than convinced that both him and Sandra had different *'values and beliefs'*. They wanted different lifestyles too. Later that morning Sandra tried to contact Raymond again on his mobile but the line was constantly engaged. This made her even angrier. Andy Mann queried why she was moping about the office and not doing any work. "Why did you bother to come in", Andy Mann sniped? Sandra, still preoccupied by her predicament, lashed out at him. "Get off my back", she warned. Andy knew she was fiery but he did not anticipate the venom in her voice. "Ms. Bogus I can issue you with a conduct warning if you don't calm down", he scolded. Andy Mann was trying to show his seniority. "Do what you want you little twerp", Sandra replied. All the other staff in the open plan office heard them. Two junior clerks peered around the open door. They wanted to see what would happen next. Neither Sandra nor Andy noticed. They were too busy getting at each others throats. "You slag", Andy Mann jeered. Sandra, hurt by his latest comment, slapped him with all her might. "How dare you", Sandra exclaimed? The blood was running down the side of Andy's face but he felt a burning sensation. He grabbed his jaw in his hand but ran out of her office. Sandra's carefully manicured extending nails had almost ripped his jaw open. It was like being slapped by a bear's claw. Sandra was panting heavily. Her well formed bust was heaving up and down. Someone must have summoned Henry Hardcase, the security guard. He came to restrain her. As he approached, Sandra threatened him with her extra long talons. "Don't even try it", she warned. Henry was just about to summon help when Duke walked in. "I'll take care of this", he assured Henry. "Ms. Bogus would you come to my office now please", Duke said. His voice was stern. As they walked past the general open planned office, the staff were whispering and pointing. Sandra halted briefly but glared at them. There was immediate hush. Mary Allsorts did not look directly at Sandra. She craned her scrawny neck to one side instead, making sure to avoid Sandra's staring gaze. "Shall I hold all your calls Mr. Stagg", Mary Allsorts searched? "Yes Mary . . . and a pot of tea would be fine", Duke said. He and Sandra entered his office. "I want you to sit down and take time to compose yourself before you tell me what happened Ms. Bogus", Duke said. He spoke in a very officious voice. Sandra was very quiet. Duke observed how beautiful Sandra looked even when she was angry but he was anxious to know what could have caused her to react in the way she did. Andy Mann had gone down to see the nurse in the medical room. "You'll need to get a tetanus injection Mr. Mann", the nurse told him. She cleaned the deep wounds but applied some antiseptic cream. Andy Mann continued to relate to the nurse how he came to be injured. "She must have long nails", the nurse observed. "Bloody talons if you asked me", Andy Mann replied. Mary Allsorts arrived at Duke's office with the pot of tea. She pushed the trolley as near as possible to the desk. "Would there be anything else Mr. Stagg", Mary asked? "No thank you Mary", Duke replied. As soon as Mary had gone out of the office, Duke got up from his desk and poured two cups of tea. He handed one to Sandra but started supping from the other cup. "Have you calmed down enough to tell me what happened out there", Duke asked? "He called me a slag and I reacted, that is all there is to it", Sandra complained. Duke was in a predicament. He wanted to show sympathy towards Sandra but at the same time he wanted to remain loyal to Andy. "I know that Mr. Mann is not your favourite person but after all he is your supervisor", Duke confirmed. "Does that give him the authority to mistreat his staff", Sandra countered. "Of course not but you have the right to complain through the proper channels, don't you", Duke questioned? Sandra was not only an academic she was feisty too. "Surely he would have had to justify his remark", Sandra queried. Duke was no match for the determined Sandra. He sat back in his chair wondering if he had bitten off more than he could chew. "Will you go to lunch with me", Duke asked? Sandra stayed silent but looked at him. "I've got something to tell you which cannot be discussed now. Just say yes and I'll tell you where to meet me", Duke continued. "I'm not hungry", Sandra replied. "You might not be but you'll be happy with what I've got to tell you", Duke hinted. He wrote something on a piece of paper and handed it to her. "I'll need to talk to Mr. Mann as well. If you start your journey now I'll meet you there as soon as I can", Duke advised. She got up and left. Duke watched as the swaying of Sandra's slender body mesmerized him even more. He dialled a number on his private phone. "Hotel Welcome", the voice answered. "Duke Stagg here, I'd like to reserve a table for two for a business lunch", Duke replied. "Sure Mr. Stagg, what time should we expect you Sir", the voice enquired. "A Ms. Sandra Bogus will arrive shortly please make sure she's comfortable until I arrive", Duke hinted. "Yes Sir", the voice ended. Sandra was still seething at Andy Mann's slur but she felt satisfaction when she recalled how she had slapped his face. The fact that she almost ripped his face open with her nails was purely accidental.

She arrived at the Hotel Welcome but sat outside in the car park talking to Pam on the cell phone. Sandra told her every detail. "You should have kicked him in the balls as well", Pam encouraged. The conversation went on for quite some time. "By the way Raymond stayed out all night with his no good friends", Sandra complained. "Men are strange", Pam replied. "I can't understand it. Raymond has never done that before", Sandra moaned. Pam remained silent. "Well Pam why do you think he did it", Sandra asked? "I don't know. Maybe he just wanted to be with his friends for a while. Maybe that's his way of telling you he needs to get out more often on his own. Maybe you could tie him to the four poster", Pam suggested. They laughed together. It was the first time she had laughed heartily for sometime. "Pam I'm having lunch with the boss at this plush hotel, the Hotel Welcome. Tell you all about it later," Sandra boasted.

The uniformed doorman, from the Tribe of Hawke, blocked her path as she attempted to enter the foyer. He spoke to her as if she had strayed off course. The doorman's arrogance preceded his negative emotional behaviour. "I'm sorry ma'am you can't come in here", he stressed. "Why not", Sandra asked? "Hotel rules", the doorman snapped. Sandra looked at him as she would have done one of Raymond's friends. "Well how comes you are allowed to work here", Sandra countered. The doorman reminded her of the other puppet on the train. This one had clearly some notion that his uniform or remit allowed him the power to speak to prospective clients from the Tribe of Hawke as he had chosen to do. The doorman seemed to relish the fact that he was allowed to speak to Sandra the way he did yet he didn't seem to have the ability to fathom the Neuro-profiling, 'programming' and 'conditioning' that had set him up to demonstrate his ignorance so openly. "That's different ma'am. I'm allowed to work here but we don't cater for 'riff-raffs'", the doorman spouted. Sandra was already in warrior mode. She could have proven to the doorman that he was not as tough as he portrayed he was. Sandra decided to sit in her car but observe how many more people the doorman would regard as 'riff-raffs' but to whom he'd refuse entry. As she walked back to her car, she noticed how conspicuously it looked on its own in the car park yet others who were arriving were being pampered and escorted from their respective vehicles. She was so bitterly disappointed to be rendered unwelcome that she hardly noticed Duke's limo arriving. He spotted Sandra sitting in her green Sleek Coupe in the parking area and immediately knew something had gone awry. "Over there Sam", Duke ordered. The chauffeur drove over towards the part of the car park where the Sleek Coupe had been parked but melancholy Sandra was already moving away. The Sleek Coupe skidded to a halt only when the limo crossed its path. Sandra sat with her head down thinking it was all her fault. Duke hurried from the limo but held the Coupe's door open for Sandra to get out. "Where are you going Ms. Bogus", Duke asked? "Mr. Stagg I've changed my mind about lunch", Sandra said. "Not until you tell me what happened I hope", Duke enticed. "I was refused entry by the doorman. Hotel rules he said", Sandra explained. They stood looking at each other for a while until Duke broke the short embarrassing silence. "At least allow me to right the wrong", he pleaded. This time the doorman did not try to stop Sandra from entering but instead stepped aside but lowered his head politely in reverence. Both Duke and Sandra entered. She noticed the mainly sage green with streaks of black marbled floor and walls. There were over ornate pearl coloured chandeliers which hung elegantly from the matching painted ceiling. The reception desk hosted the seemingly super-efficient staff whose uniforms had the logo of the Hotel and their individual name tags attached. All the staff seemed to be trained to be *'client friendly'* except for the overzealous member' who had refused Sandra entry on her own earlier on but call her *"riff-raff"*. It was clear that his super-inflated ego had led him into a false sense of importance against one from his own Tribe. The arrogance with which the offending doorman had spoken to Sandra seemed to have been derived from his subtly initiated *'programmed'* and *'conditioned'* *'values and beliefs'*. This led him to believe he was in a *'position of power'* to profile anyone from the Tribe of Hawke as *'riff-raff'*. The doorman felt empowered, like the green humanoid robotrons, to assume that *'stereo-typical imagery'* about individuals from the Tribe of Hawke especially. The *'uncle tom'* clone had come to believe in the *'stereo-hype'* and *'stereo-tripe'* about the *'stereo-type'* that had influenced his perception. Subsequently, on Duke's arrival, that same member of staff had confirmed his *'lapdog subservient mindset'*. It made him appear as if he wanted to get down on his knees but lick Duke's feet. Sandra was aware of such individuals since she was young. Her mother, Dian, had referred to them many times throughout her life stages as *"uncle toms"*.

The people passing through or lounging in the foyer smiled when Sandra and Duke entered. Some were pointing towards them but commenting under their breath about the mismatch in age difference. Few sniggered for different reasons which were not openly expressed. Sandra told Duke but he just told her to ignore them. Their curiosity deepened as Duke and Sandra was greeted and surrounded by the staff. The Maitre D' recognised Duke Stagg immediately. "Good afternoon Mr. Stagg may I show you to your table Sir", the Maitre D' asked? His slimy manner irritated Sandra but she managed to desist from commenting. They were ushered over to the area marked 'RESERVED'. Sandra noticed the name tag on the Maitre D's jacket. It said Claude Spinaché, Maitre D', Hotel Welcome. He pulled out a chair and motioned for Sandra to sit down. He did the same for Duke. "Champagne Urge Mark 1, Mr. Stagg", the Maitre D' asked? Duke approved the choice of the Maitre D'. He snapped his fingers and a waiter arrived promptly. "Champagne Urge Mark 1 for Mr. Stagg", the Maitre D' commanded. All this was like a dream to Sandra. Never before had she been waited on in such style. Duke smiled as he saw the wonderment in her eyes. It was like a child let loose with too many choices. "We could do this every day if you wish", Duke said. "So, this is what being rich is about", Sandra asked? Duke smiled but did not comment. Sandra noticed that she was the centre of attention but did not know why. Some people were blatantly pointing and whispering but Duke assured Sandra that they were only admiring her beauty. "Now you will appreciate why Duke Stagg wants to be seen in your company", he lied. Her head began to spin, not yet from the Champagne Urge Mark 1 but from the flattery flowing from Duke's lips. As she wasn't familiar with the language on the menu, Sandra let Duke choose the food. Three or four waiters continued to attend their table at the crisp orders of Claude Spinachè, the Maitre D'. The table was filled with smoked octopus, lobsters, squid, caviar and a range of other foods Sandra had never heard of, seen nor tasted before. It all seemed too much food for just two people but, not wanting to waste Duke's money, Sandra decided that she would eat as much of each as she could. There was conversation and laughter galore and more Champagne Urge Mark 1 to be poured. Sandra was a bit tipsy from the unusual champagne but she still maintained a healthy appetite. "Now can I try some of the delicacies that you mentioned", Sandra asked? There was a separate menu for these. Duke signalled for the Maitre D' to come over. Although she didn't understand the language of the menu she persisted that she should choose. "Which would you like", Duke asked? "Can I try all of them", Sandra giggled. "Sure, why not, we'll have the lot", Duke agreed. The Maitre D' retreated from the table. Inside the kitchen there were flaming pots, steamy pots, enamel pots, shiny metal pots, special glass pots and a busy chef who barked orders to several people. The whole scene would be best described as organized chaos. Organized meant that all the Menus were carefully planned. Chaotic, as the staff busied themselves preparing the various dishes for final approval. The chef barked the orders for the delicacies Duke and Sandra had ordered. "Kangaroo steak, rare . . . curried stewed bush rat . . . rhino steak, rare . . . escargot, chewy . . . pigs liver cooked in wine . . . earthworms, parboiled, tender . . . selected lizards' tongues, marinated in vinegar and succulent sheep eyes, in jelly . . . times two for Mr. Staggs' table". The Maitre D' led the posse of waiters over to Duke's table with the delicacies but Sandra couldn't wait to get started. She tried everything Duke told her to, except for the sheep eyes. "I can't eat that Duke", Sandra said. "Why not", Duke asked? "They are looking at me", Sandra squirmed. "Sandra darling, it's an aphrodisiac it's good for you", Duke replied. She still hesitated but Duke assured her further. "I ate it didn't I", Duke asked? Sandra closed her eyes then swallowed, hard. "Come on. Wash it down with some more Champagne Urge Mark 1. A good year don't you think", Duke enquired. Thinking Sandra was a famous fashion Model, a girl of about 17 years old came over to their table but asked for her autograph. Duke approved the signing because he didn't want to disappoint the young woman. When the girl had moved away Duke broke the news he'd forgotten to tell her. Sandra was now officially the Public Relations Officer for DSI. She would be moving into Andy's old Office and she could recruit an assistant for her old office. That was the first of the good news. He did confirm that Andy Mann had been made up to Chief Press Officer. Andy Mann would be having an office on the other side of the building. He would still be Sandra's boss but would now liaise with Sandra through his PA most of the time. "That would mean you both would only have occasional contact", Duke explained. Sandra smiled broadly. She was relieved that she would not have daily contact with Andy Mann. Duke broke the next bit of news. He confirmed to Sandra that he had arranged for her to model some exclusive garments for a friend who owned a fashion agency. He told her that he had booked adjoining suites for both of them and that the show would take place later on that evening in the same hotel. Sandra's eyes almost popped out of her head because modelling came a close second to her PR career. Influenced by the type of magazines she bought, Sandra had always thought of herself as a centre page model. "Suppose they like what they see", Sandra asked? "It would be good PR", Duke replied. "Wow, Duke I love you even more now", Sandra exclaimed. "I'll have to phone Raymond", Sandra said. Duke did not answer but smiled. He listened while she explained to Raymond why it was necessary for her to be absent from their bed tonight. "Just get yourself a *'take away'*. Yes, I've been drinking. Yes, it is part of my job. Good night Ray", Sandra ended. "Men", Sandra exclaimed. Raymond was furious with Sandra not necessarily for her absence but because of the way her job robbed them of the chance to see if they could have resolved their problems. His mind conjured up the worse scenarios of Sandra and Duke. He was fed up with her *'working'* so many late nights. Still, he had Pam who cared deeply for him. Their affair was coming on stronger each day. Raymond picked up his car keys but stormed out the door then drove recklessly until he arrived at Pam's. In the car park he noticed a middle aged man loitering. Raymond took a second glance when the man struck a match. He cupped his hands as he lit the cigarette. The man wore a felt hat pulled down over his face like a detective in a black and white movie. He kept fidgeting but pacing up and down. Raymond paused as the man approached him. "Forgot my keys", the man said. He kept tapping his head repeatedly as if to indicate he has an empty brain. Raymond opened the entrance door but stepped in. The man tipped his hat but walked pass him in the corridor. Raymond pushed the key into the inner door but entered the Flat. Pam was smiling broadly while she approached him with open arms. She greeted him ecstatically. Pam hugged Raymond tightly, resting her head upon his chest. She cuddled up to him. "Hungry", Pam asked? "Famished", Raymond exclaimed. "I thought you might pop in so I cooked you some dinner", Pam said. Raymond felt welcomed. He washed his hands in the bathroom; not like Sandra, who regularly washed hers in the kitchen sink. Pam and Raymond sat at the table talking while they ate. Sometimes, whenever Sandra's name was mentioned, they would look at each other and giggle. Pam cleared away the dishes then invited Raymond to join her in the lounge. The landline phone rang. Instinctively, Raymond reached out to answer it but Pam managed to get there first. "Hello", Pam said. She indicated with her finger that it was Sandra on the other end. "Pam you'd never guess what happened to me today", Sandra asked? She sounded quite excited. "Did everything go to plan", Pam asked? "I'm going to be a model", Sandra chimed. "What about your other job", Pam asked? "I've been promoted to Public Relations Officer with my own assistant but there is more. Duke don't mind if I do both. Soon, I won't only be the talk of the town but instead the talk of the world. Duke is going to see to that", Sandra boasted. Pam wanted to know where Raymond would fit into Sandra's plans. She asked her directly? "Where does Raymond fit into your busy life", Pam quizzed? Sandra laughed scornfully at Pam's question but commented. "If he loves me he's got to be prepared to take me as I am. Duke loves me as I am and that's all that matters right now Pam", Sandra replied. Pam remained quiet. "You there Pam", Sandra asked? "I don't know what to say", Pam confessed. "Say congratulations girl, Sandra's made the big times. Got to get my beauty sleep before my first Runway", Sandra chirped. Pam heard the dial tone. She eased over to Raymond's side and huddled up to him. She was trying to distract him from what he had heard.

"What was that about fitting Raymond into her busy life", he asked? "Gives us more time together Ray", Pam replied deviously. She got up from the sofa but brought back a gold chain. It didn't cost her much but it was gold and she had bought it for Raymond. He bent his head forward as Pam placed the chain around his neck. The ringing tone of the cell phone punctuated their peace. "Yeah", Raymond said into the phone. "Ray, it is Sandra. I'm sorry about today, I had too much champagne and it got to my head", Sandra explained. "Yeah", he replied. "You only talk to me like that when you're angry. What have I done to upset you", Sandra probed. When he didn't answer she tried to smooth things over. "No matter what happens between us you'll always be my 'Mr. Right'", Sandra whispered. "Yeah, but I don't want to be 'Mr. Right' Sandy. I don't want to be yours or anybody else's *'Trophy Man'*", Raymond countered. He switched the phone off. Sandra was less upset than Raymond thought. She looked around at the luxurious suite. It had marble walls, gold plated fittings and plush carpet. "Eat your heart out Raymond Oddball", Sandra exclaimed.

CHAPTER 24

The phone rang. "Hello", Sandra answered. "Will you come over to my suite or shall I come over to yours", Duke inveigled. "Duke, stop teasing me and come over", Sandra said. Her voice was provocative. Her invitation indicated her acceptance to be visited by Duke. The adjoining door swung open. Duke staggered in. His tie hung loosely to one side, his crumpled shirt hung partially outside his trousers. Sandra saw Duke's glazed eyes and the silly grin which seem to be painted on by a face-painting artist. She realised that he was drunk. "Duke", Sandra gasped. She sprang from the bed, naked. Excited by her velvety, highly melanin naked body, Duke lurched forward then swayed. He steadied himself enough to continue to stay standing. Sandra leaned her tall frame against Duke's comparatively diminutive figure but led him back to his suite. "Lay down, you might feel better later", Sandra suggested. "Sandra, do you know .... how long .... I ... I ... I ... I ... I've been ... trying to ... to get one of you ... exotic birds", Duke asked? "No", Sandra replied. She chose to ignore what was Duke's meaning of *'exotic birds'*. She put his revelation down to him being intoxicated. Sandra decided to play along with Duke's disclosure. "How long", Sandra queried? "All my, all my ... life" Duke replied. He was in a bad way. Duke lay with his head hanging over the side of the bed. Sandra diverted his attention briefly. "Tell me about your wife, you never talk about her", Sandra searched. "She looks after ... af ... ter the ... children well but ... but ... but she's an ... awful bore", Duke said. There was no sense of emotion in his voice. His wife being an efficient mother with the children seemed to sum up his assessment of her. "Is she beautiful", Sandra pressed? "As beau ... tiful as ... t ... t ... t ... the back ... of a ... bus", Duke spluttered. Before Sandra could respond to his cruel description of his wife, Duke spoke again. "You ... you ... you're ... most beau ... ti ... ful", Duke continued. Within minutes he fell asleep. Sandra lay next to him on the huge round bed. If viewed from an aerial point, Duke's diminutive figure seemed like a dot. It was the choking cough which alerted Sandra to Duke's predicament. "I ... f ... eel s ... ick", Duke moaned. Sandra dragged him by his feet across the customized bed. It was large enough to sleep four or five people comfortably. She stooped from her waist to Duke's height. Sandra placed one of Duke's arms around her neck and one of hers around his. Bending to accommodate Duke's lack in height, compared to her 6'2" frame. It made Sandra appear like the picture of a hero rescuing a wounded colleague but seeking to find a safer environment. She struggled with him towards the en suite bathroom. Duke bent over the sink heaving and retching. His stomach contents gushed out with as great a force as a ruptured pipe leading from an oil well. The mirror above the sink also bore the evidence of the slime he once ate as food. Sandra thought he was dying and wanted to help him. The putrid smell befitted that which emanated from cesspool tanks. "Duke, shall I call a doctor", Sandra enquired. "No Sugarcake, I'm feeling better already, he replied. Duke wiped his mouth with the back of his hand but turned round to face her. "What a mess", Sandra exclaimed. She grabbed a new white fluffy towel but walked over to the sink. The sheep eyes which Duke had swallowed whole was staring back at them. She remembered her doubt about eating that particular *'delicacy'* and now her own stomach was churning violently wanting to start its own eruption. Sandra felt nauseous. Cold sweat washed over her and she began groaning from the griping pains in her stomach. Duke's sheep eyes reflux triggered her imagination. Inside her gut, Sandra saw her succulent *'delicacy'* looking around, like a voyeur, inquisitively surveying the inner workings of her stomach. She too started to wretch violently but began to empty the contents of her stomach into the sink as well. Because Duke's contribution had already blocked but filled the sink, Sandra's caused an immense overflow onto the white carpet. The putrid smell was further intensified many folds. There was also a strong smell of methane gas, caused by them farting, permeating the already foul air. It was fortunate that Duke was not smoking one of his cigars. A naked flame might just convert the beautiful Hotel Welcome into a derelict sight! After each wretch, Sandra commented. Her intermittent delivery likened itself to the sporadic interruptions to commentary on a cell phone with poor reception as the signals alternate between masts. "Oh . . . D . . . u . . . ke, I'm d . . . yi . . . ng. Get . . . m . . . doc . .", she pleaded. "You'll be fine", Duke assured her. Feeling relieved about shifting their bulk loads in and around the sink, wall, mirror and carpeting, Duke supported Sandra back to his bed. Opposite to the image of the much taller Sandra carrying the more diminutive Duke like a hero with an injured colleague, it made it seemed like Duke was carrying Sandra like a deflated life-size plastic doll hanging over his broad shoulder. The effect from the colic weakened them both so much so that the only thing Duke and Sandra could do was lie motionless until sleep freed them from the agony they were suffering. The room stank of the putrid mess. Within moments, as if deliberately released through the small opening of the window, a swarm of about two hundred bluebottle flies were attracted to a feast of smelly vomit. Despite the summary buzzing from the infestation of flies, both Sandra and Duke slept on. It was about three hours later that they awakened. Sandra woke first, then Duke. They both became aware of the stiflingly awful smell and the swarm of flies. "What are we going to do Duke", Sandra asked? "We are calling in the bloody chambermaids. That's what we're going to . . . do. It is their job to clean up, ain't it", Duke replied? Never before had Duke given credit to the value of ancillary workers, like chambermaids, so accurately. Even Sandra was reminded of the dream she had about her mother as a chambermaid in the same hotel. There was a more valuable lesson for both but for Sandra in particular.

Those lowly '*un-ambitious*' people like chambermaids can be real valuable in a time of crisis like this was. She sensed that without the existence of somebody wanting to do such mundane jobs like rubbish collection operators and chambermaids, not only the Suite in Hotel Welcome but also the entire planet might seem quite a different place, perhaps! Sandra and Duke were learning that there were lessons here to be learnt about appreciation of the value of all workers but especially those, who were at the sharp end keeping our environments tidy, clean and less smelly too. Duke picked up the phone. "Reception", the voice said. "I need 'Room Service'. Send me some chambermaids with buckets and mops, will you, Duke demanded". Sandra and Duke literally crawled across the huge hand made carpet in the connecting door to the other suite. They closed it behind them. Finally, they managed to get on the bed. "Let us get some coffee", Duke suggested. "Can I order it Duke", Sandra asked? "You don't have to ask for approval Sandra, my sweet. Do what you like", he told her. She picked up the phone but ordered the pot of coffee for two. Duke looked at the digital clock resting on the shelf near the headboard but realized that the Grand Fashion and Modelling Show would soon begin. He tried to stand up but fell back onto the bed. "J.H Christ, I didn't realize how weak this thing makes you feel . . . damn colic", Duke said. "Wait for the coffee Duke", Sandra suggested. She put her hands around Duke but hugged him close. Sandra chose to ignore the lingering smells of putrid puke, stale cigar smoke and his body odour which fused together. He, in turn, chose to ignore the smell of her unwashed frowsy body which reeked of stale sweat, volumes of stale perfumery and body sprays. Both chose to ignore their unwashed mouths which stank enough to encourage the repeated visits from the flies which had emigrated from the other suite while Duke and Sandra were making their way through the connecting door. Sandra reassured Duke of her empathy and caring. She stroked his head affectionately. "Never mind my little sugar dumpling, your exotic bird will look after you", she whispered. Duke seemed to like hearing that kind of talk. He placed his head on Sandra's lap but snuggled up to her like a pet to its owner. There was a rap at the door. "Come in", Sandra commanded. Sandra pulled the duvet cover over their naked bodies but stayed in bed. The waiter placed the trolley with the coffee at the foot of the bed. "Coffee for madam", he said. The stench from the other suite drifted underneath the adjoining door to attack the waiter's nostrils. The smell reminded him of the rubbish dumps he used to visit as a child when he was in his own country. The waiter exited the suite as quickly as he could. Duke sipped the hot coffee quickly. "I've really got to go", he said. "You can't go Duke", Sandra advised. "Why not", Duke asked? "Your clothes are in the other suite", Sandra reminded. "Damn, the show starts in half an hour but I can't go like this", he exclaimed. Duke pointed to his nakedness. Sandra laughed but teased. "Why not Duke, it would be good PR", Sandra jibed. She put on her black laced negligee, which was a permanent passenger in her car since that first night with Duke. Sandra knew she looked desirable in the provocative outfit. Entering through the connecting door she noticed that the stench had gone from Duke's suite. The flies had all emigrated except for those in her suite. Everything was neatly in place and the bed was remade. Sandra slid the giant built-in wardrobe door but began selecting Duke's attire. "It is ok Duke you can come in now. The chambermaids have gone", Sandra stated. Duke, who by this time was feeling more awake after the coffee, raced across to embrace Sandra. "You look gorgeous in that negligee where did you get it", Duke asked? Sandra responded to his embrace but completely ignored his question because she knew Raymond had given it to her as a birthday present. They raced each other to get to the sink. There, Sandra had a wash before Duke then rinsed her mouth with the branded mouthwash. He cleansed his mouth with a chewing gum. "These are better than the mouthwash", Duke insisted. He pointed to the packet of gum. Sandra smiled but did not comment because she had complete faith in mouthwashes. They dressed as quickly as they could, all the time glancing at the clock. Duke wore his black dinner suit with cummerbund, a dazzling white shirt which didn't show the wrinkles under the jacket, new cuffs, stiff white collar and a black 'Dicky Bow' tie. He wore black brogues on his size 14 feet. Earlier, Duke had arranged for some outfits to be delivered to Sandra's suite prior to her arrival. She wore a peach outfit which had a pinky shade to it. Sandra slipped her arms into the open gown, wrapped it around her tightly but tied the short broad streamer which was attached at the waist. She wore high heeled peach coloured shoes, large pearl earrings, matching glittering pearl lipstick and eye shadow which she said *'enhanced'* her good looks. Sandra carried a small matching handbag made from a collection of lizard skins with a thin strap across her shoulder too. Duke told her she looked *"special"*. He looked at her with eyes widened as if he was seeing the manifestation of an angel appearing before him. "Shall we go gorgeous", Duke asked? Sandra smiled but slid into his inviting arms. Her face beamed a smile. They entered the Auditorium. Women and men alike looked at Duke's stunning partner as they went by. Men whistled and women cooed their approval of the stunningly beautiful shapely Sandra Bogus. The standing ovation reinforced Sandra's impact on the crowd of celebrities, fashion designers, agents and the media who were present. Excited by the ambience of the room, Sandra commented. "Oh Duke", she exclaimed. He escorted her to the dressing room where other beautiful women assembled. "I'll leave you to it. See you later", Duke said. Though he was reluctant to leave the *'stunner'* behind, Duke began to exit the dressing room. As he exited, Duke blew Sandra a kiss. All the girls were chattering amongst themselves. They exchanged opinions about the different designs and colours. Some were giggling even when there was nothing to giggle about. There was an air of excitement and nervous expectations. A woman dressed in a pale green linen frock raised her arm. The girls carried on their chitter-chatter. "Now girls, lets have some silence. SILENCE PLEASE", the woman pleaded. When total silence was established, the woman began speaking again. "Girls, there are VIPs out there just waiting to see you strut your stuff. You need to walk with poise and assurance but don't be afraid to strut your stuff", the woman encouraged. She looked across towards where Sandra was sitting. "Oh, you must be the new girl Duke talked about". "Come over here and let me see if you're as beautiful as Duke says", the woman encouraged. Sandra walked over but stood in front of her. The woman looked her up and down and then asked her to do a twirl. "You'll do just fine", the woman said. She winked at Sandra.

The trumpeter blasted a fanfare in the Auditorium which signalled the start of the Grand Fashion and Modeling Show. Dressed in their new outfits, many of the girls, who had preceded Sandra onto the Runway, looked quite a picture. Sandra, wearing a tightly wound sash of translucent acid pink coloured silk, was the best picture of all. Her outfit was a singular length of silk which was meticulously wrapped around her body from bust to buttocks but passed through her legs, ran up her back then draped over her shoulder. There was enough of the sash left for Sandra to use to tease the baying crowd. She had eight inch high heeled shoes, earrings, matching shade eye blush, lipstick, stewardess type hat and her talon-like nails were painted to match as well. The crowd erupted into a frenzy the moment Sandra entered the Runway. "Wow, who's that", a voice asked? "I don't know but she's a *'stunner'* ", another voice replied. Many voices asked similar searching questions but Sandra was enjoying her moment with no sign of nerves. She pranced, posed and suggestively seduced the now rabble crowd. Shrill whistles and crude comments thickened the air. A form of disorder set in. There were urgent negotiations going on in the ring beneath the stage encouraging that kind of atmosphere more akin to horse racing circles. Flash bulbs were rapidly exploding and video cameras followed her in every direction. Sandra's extremely long legs strode one in front of the other, accentuating the spring-like movement of her narrow hips and huge backside which was propelling Sandra into her forward motion. The audience which sat directly in front of and those, who was positioned to both sides of Sandra, were held captive to her hypnotic performance. She paused but tempted and tantalized the men especially with the loose end of the silken outfit. Sandra deliberated pouted those exciting lips as she offered to unwrap the length of silken material to reveal what was beneath the wrapper. She did this by rotating her body around, deliberately slowly, in order to continue the mystique she was creating in the audiences minds. There was uproar amongst the crowd. As any other rowdy crowd, they were becoming out of control. Even members of the same organizations pushed and shoved or obscured the other; all vying for Sandra's attention. Shouts and sounds of wolf whistling were interspersed together with the guttural operatic cries of howling wolves on the prairie. Some from the crowd nearer the Runway threw large denominations of paper currency and their cards unto it. At one point, the lights were deliberately dimmed and a conical spotlight above Sandra's head followed each and every step that she made. This was done in order to reflect not only the glow from the reflective yet translucent acid pink single length sash outfit but also allowed Sandra to sparkle like the diamond she was being discovered to be. At another point during her appearance, the Auditorium was thrown into complete darkness. This was previously arranged by Duke. There was a collective "ooooh" at the sudden darkness. As she began to exit the Runway, a horizontal spotlight was deliberately aimed but focused at Sandra's backside to highlight her *'little wiggle'* as Duke called it. The acid pink translucent single sash wrap glowed in the darkened Auditorium once more but only this time making Sandra's backside look like two Siamese giant glow worms bobbing up and down, like buoys on the surface of the ocean. This was followed by the collective "aaaahs" coming from the interactive audience. Sandra was a class act. She unloaded her natural flowing coordinating movements which swept the Fashion and Modeling Industries into ascending spirals of cyclonic currents. Sandra's seismic performance occasioned both the Fashion and Modeling industries to transcend from one state to another latently; rendering this new position incomparable to any before it. Her sensational impact catalogued her arrival into the Annals of both the Fashion and Modeling Industries' Events History. This was taking Sandra from an unknown quantity to towering towards her stratospheric rise all in a matter of a few minutes on the Runway. Her sensational presentation altered the dynamics relating to Fashion and Modeling. Sandra Bogus didn't know it yet but she was already way above and far beyond any of her current peers. The headlines and articles in the printed media were already preparing to turn Sandra Bogus into the biggest money spinning sensation. She might well go on to prove to become unstoppable! With the entire Auditorium in complete darkness, Sandra began to walk slowly towards the direction of the exit. She had provocatively started to unwind from the singular length acid pink sash outfit along the length of the Runway. The top half of her body was partially exposed as far as the upper part of her voluptuous breasts. She teased the audience still further by twirling again and again along the full length of the Runway as she headed towards the exit. Each revolution unwound the singular length acid pink sash outfit some more revealing more of Sandra's peach textured melanin body but leaving the length of the singular sash to lay behind her by the time Sandra was completely out of sight. When the lights went on again, the audience could now see the length of acid pink sash that Sandra was wearing moments before laying there along the Runway. It lingered there for some moments provocatively suggesting that Sandra was now completely naked. The roar from the audience confirmed that they approved of the suggestive artistic dare which Sandra so competently implied. Shouts, whistles and coordinated stamping of feet spoke volumes about the new Runway sensation. On exit, the remaining girls crowded around Sandra to celebrate her most successful debut. "Thank you", Sandra said. Duke was the only one she really had in mind. She wondered if he too had applauded ecstatically. Sandra's effort to find him from the rest of the crowd came to no avail but she knew her Duke was out there watching with approval of his 'exotic' bird.

Advertising and Marketing agents fussed but sneered at each other's offer but the woman, Candie Posie, whom Duke had put in charge as Chief Negotiating Officer, displayed the kind of auctioneering technique and skill which guaranteed astronomical bids to market the lovely 'exotic package' which had caused panic amongst rivals. "I'll guarantee she'll be a millionaire within three months", one of the agents said in response to some of the other offers that were being made. By the time Sandra made her second appearance, she brought out just as much appreciation from the buzzing crowd. She wore a spherical shaped dress made of pure lace. Apart from its unique shape which fitted from her slender neck to precisely seven inches below her bum cheeks, Sandra's long slender legs, arms and her shoulders were left exposed. The horizontal yellow hoops intricately blending into the black dress and the black skull cap with artificial feelers made Sandra appear like a 'Queen Bee'. This was a daring piece of innovation by a young college student designer. The aesthetic values triggered the humming of approval from the busy 'Worker Bees' in the audience. Sandra's carrying of her own honeycomb in her hand suggested she was overflowing with honey. This lifted the spirits of all, who could see the thinking behind the designer's artistic impressionism. Sandra did justice to the designer's intention of creating a fresh 'buzz' around a new genre in fashion designs. Still and video cameras were once again clicking and recording the advent of a new star. The audience was chanting Sandra's name. Arguments amongst the rival feuding agents had now changed about Sandra's time-span to becoming a millionaire. A female agent challenged her rivals that Sandra would become a millionaire within one month not three as previously suggested by a peer agent. Another parade of Models on the Runway meant that the variety of designs was causing agents to scuffle amongst themselves about the range of outfits on display. Sandra watched as her peers bravely exhibited their experience in working the excited audience. The woman in the lime green linen dress stood next to her but commented on the techniques Sandra's peers were displaying. She also pointed out the difference in the atmosphere in the Auditorium. The woman reminded Sandra how much she has the audience in the palm of her hands. It was nearly time for Sandra to do her final walk down the Runway. The audience gave the other girls a generous round of applause but they eagerly awaited Sandra's appearance. Candie Posie praised the other girls for their contributions. She baited the crowd by delaying Sandra's final appearance. Candie Posie had been in the modelling business for over ten years. She knew how to get the best reactions from an audience. The chanting warned how impatient they were becoming. Sandra's final appearance was imminent. Her entrance brought the biggest response from the audience yet. The Auditorium's high roof confirmed the acoustics. All the lights were turned off except for a few along the length of the Runway. Her entire smooth, slender melanin torso was exposed except for those parts that were covered by Sandra's skimpy sky blue shiny taffeta top and 'pum-pum' shorts. They suggested more than a hint of summer. The top started just above her bust but barely went past the nipples of her breasts. It exposed the underside of them. The skimpy sky blue shiny taffeta 'pum-pum' shorts started from Sandra's hip but attached itself like another skin. Because it fitted so snugly at the front, the 'pum-pum' shorts further accented the long jaws of Sandra's genital area and made it seem like the jaws of a vice grip. The other end of the tightly fitting shorts fitted just over her bum cheeks at the back. Sandra's tremendously long legs were accentuated by the scarcity of clothing. She wore dark blue sandals trimmed with a flash of sky blue. Earrings, eye shadow, lipstick, painted nails matched the shiny taffeta top and the 'pum-pum' shorts. Sandra wore an extra large sky blue plastic empty spectacle frame to draw attention to her large cornflower blue eyes. Her shiny taffeta skimpy top and 'pum-pum' shorts glowed in the darkened Auditorium. The audience cheered wildly. Wolf whistles and guttural hound dog howls surfaced but resonated in the huge Auditorium. Sandra's lazy long legged strides up and down the Runway sent the audience into wild exuberance, inciting dreams of being with her on a desert island. Her final performance anchored Sandra's presentation to the audiences' psyche but gave the crowd more than they could bear. In their twisted minds some individuals conjured thoughts of pornographic acts with the stunningly beautiful Sandra. Others were now literally fighting each other over derogatory emotional comments that threatened the safety of women, as a whole, who chose to wear skimpy outfits that were as revealing as Sandra's. Some deeply religious-minded worshippers soon found they were more addicted to lustful thoughts of the flesh than the *'heathens'* they often preached against. Held in awe of the *'bedeviling image'* of the provocative, mesmeric Sandra, many religious devotees had started to revise their solemn oath towards a life of celibacy. In acknowledging their weakness for the flesh, they began to mumble their confessions while praying for forgiveness from their Gods for their lewd thoughts that seemed to emanate from a much deeper ravine of their minds. They recited the ending of 'The Lord's Prayer', "lead us not into temptations...", like a mantra, as loudly as they could amongst the rowdy worldly clamour from those others, who wanted to physically connect sexually with the *'A' Blister* Model elect. Unknown to the others, the excitement had caused some other physical reactions amongst the now rabble crowd, who had lost control not only over their thoughts but also their bodies. The temptation of intimacy with the provocative Sandra was causative to some weak-minded individuals ejaculating upon themselves as mysteriously as in a *'wet dream'*. But for the sensual feelings, there was no other warning of the release of the slimy semen which seemed to have oozed but appeared without control. It soiled the boxer shorts and trousers of the men. Some females in the audience and from the Dressing Room Candie Posie were having similar experiences to the men but their soilage was not as apparent as the men. In the Auditorium, both genders were triggered into confrontational reactions over the sensational Sandra Bogus. The intensity of the turmoil which developed frightened the girls who were backstage. They could hear the loud exchanges and see the physical actions and reactions that resembled a bar fight that had gone out of control in a Saloon Bar in a Western Cowboy Movie. One man was so angry that he punched a woman, with whom he didn't agree, in the face. "I'll say what I'd like about women in skimpy clothes. I can say what I'd like to do to her if I want", the angry man complained. "You filthy beast", the woman retorted. She was brave enough to strike him back with her handbag. Some women fought among themselves too. They grappled hair, removed wigs but expressed their desire to be with the stunningly beautiful Sandra. It was some time before the security staff was able to stop the feuding crowd from what seemed like rioting. An announcement came over the public address system. "We are appealing to everyone to calm down. Let us try to resolve the problem together", the voice appealed. At times, some so called *'adults'* exhibited childish behaviours in the Auditorium. Some people sat down but then stood up again because others hadn't. It looked like a scene from a kindergarten classroom. After another *public address* message threatening to revoke membership, the rowdy crowd began to calm down but returned to their seats.

Waiters and other members of the Hotel Welcome staff witnessed the whole debacle. They had worked at many previous fashion shows before and had seen lots of unusual *behaviors* but this ranked as the most belligerent compared to the previous shows. Even though the arguments for and against the crude suggestions which started this melee, Sandra remained calmest of all. She was still locked into the high level of adulation she had been receiving throughout her first experience of being a model. Many from the crowd were now busy on their cell phones making contact with their respective bosses in the quest to sign the "new Sensational Wonder girl". Sandra Bogus was an *instant hit* with the press too. They assured Duke and his friend, Candie Posie, the Chief Negotiator, from the Fashion Art Interpreter Agency that they would make Sandra a *household* name by the following day. Even though Sandra had not yet been offered a contract by any agency or their representatives, Duke's appointed female negotiator, Candie Posie, now estimated that she was confident that Sandra had already become a millionaire. During the celebrations which went on late into the early morning, Sandra wanted Duke to pose with her for the camera but he refused. "It's not the right time Sweetheart. The Press will have my guts for garters", Duke whispered. She was clearly disappointed but was seeing from a much narrower perspective than Duke. He had the experience that Sandra did not yet have. "When will it be the right time", Sandra pressed? "I'll tell you when it's the right time", Duke assured. "OK Duke, you're the boss", Sandra relented. Amongst the myriad of thoughts swirling around in her mind like a carousel out of control, one particular thought prioritised itself for selection. It was more one of those questions that required deep concentration before answering. What about Raymond? What would happen between them now? There was no doubt that she needed Duke's riches and clout but he never really satisfied her female *needs*. Each time she deliberately faked an orgasm just to impress Duke but with Raymond it was different. He knew how to quell a *woman's 'fire'*. Raymond was worth holding on to even if he couldn't compare to Duke's clout or financial status either, Sandra mused. As far as PR was concerned, Duke and Sandra both had a successful evening.

They managed to slip away from the rest of the entertainment. Craftily, neither Duke nor his Chief Negotiator, Candie Posie, agreed any deals in the Auditorium. Duke's experience as a businessman taught him not to sign too quickly. Here, he had a new chance to improve his clout status, riches, popularity and contractual options while fashioning a new life for and with his exotic bird. Unlike Sandra, Duke was confident that she wouldn't have time for the athletic Raymond while she was busy fulfilling her contractual engagements as the Top Model in Poshborough. Duke was aware of his own shortcomings but intended to bridge the gap (no pun intended) by dazzling the extraordinarily beautiful Sandra with riches and fame. He reasoned that no woman could resist those two things in life. He was also cocksure (again no pun intended) that, given the chance, most women would gladly be more than willing to swap places with his exotic bird. Once inside the Hotel Suite, Duke pushed Sandra to the floor and, in a frenzied act, started to rip her clothes off, but Sandra was not ready for such passion with Duke. One, she knew it wouldn't last too long. Duke was always "too hasty". Two, Sandra's mind was still back in the Auditorium experiencing the grand ovations of her newly found zany fans. Duke saw this as a moment for Sandra to show her appreciation and gratitude for his master class and stroke of genius. Still, Sandra remained numb to Duke's needs. "There is no greater high than the feelings I'm having right now Duke. Thanks to you. I'm also so overwhelmed that not even sex comes close", Sandra advised. "I can't help it if I want you so badly, my sweet", Duke panted. His 'smarmy' approach reminded Sandra of a dog begging for attention. She pushed him away as gently as she could. "Not now Duke, I need to have a wash", Sandra said. Duke was in no mood to be put off his focus. He started to insinuate that Sandra was flirting and maybe that was what was on her mind. "I didn't like the way you were chatting to that handsome young man for such a long time. What's his name", Duke raged? His tone was gruff and demanding. Sandra remained silent because she was beginning to understand some of Duke's 'spoilt child' tactics when he couldn't get what he wanted. She pouted her lips but pretended she was sad. Sandra looked up at him with an expression of 'innocence' but Duke didn't react to her ploy. He displayed more than a hint of jealousy that Sandra did not expect. Grappling her arms, he pinned her to the floor. "What's his name? Tell me his name", Duke bullied? "Oh Duke, you're jealous. I cannot believe that you could be jealous", Sandra implied. At this moment her female instincts told her that Raymond would have been better company and more understanding at a time when she needed him to be. Raymond would have been more romantic and matured in his approach. As if on cue, Duke got up but removed some DVDs from his briefcase. "Let us have a look at these. They might just put you in the mood", he challenged. From his cultural 'beliefs and values', this was Duke's way of turning Sandra on. Watching 'blue movies' was Duke's way for getting into a heightened state of sexual readiness but it really did nothing for Sandra. She was bored with those movies and she had told him so previously too. Initially, she didn't want to try any of the things Duke hinted from the movies but he told her that was the price she'd have to pay to get to the top. Reluctantly, Sandra agreed to Duke's wishes. He seemed to get something from it but she wandered though how some men like Duke managed without these pornographic episodes. Natural lovers like Raymond didn't seem to need this type of unnatural ritual.

CHAPTER 25

L over boy Raymond was relaxing with Pam. Though Raymond's comparison was only in his mind, he found her more affectionate than Sandra. Mentally, Sandra did not stimulate him as much as Pam but then she couldn't compare with Sandra's outstanding physical attributes or facial beauty. Raymond was enjoying the best scenario any man could ever dream of. He had a real stunner, who engaged his ego sexually and prestigiously but also a more matured affectionate woman, who catered for his other needs. These included the ethos of his *cultural 'values and beliefs'*. Pam's level of conversation engaged yet stimulated Raymond's brain but helped him to see from many other perspectives. The ringing tone of the cell phone imposed once again. "Yeah", Raymond answered. Pam looked up anxiously with eyes which begged him not to move. "Where? What time? . . . I can't leave now . . . maybe tomorrow . . . yeah", Raymond said. He was really hoping it would have been Sandra on the phone so that he could have vented his feelings. Pam squeezed Raymond but whispered in his ear. He hugged her tightly when he asked her how she felt about children. "They are fine when they have support", Pam answered. Raymond kissed her cheek but smiled. "I'll take care of my children", Raymond vouched. "Would you like children Ray", Pam asked? "Yes", I love children", Raymond replied. "I'd love to have your children Ray", Pam said. Raymond kissed her gently again but fondled her tenderly. He told Pam that he would be a good father to his children. "I know that Ray", Pam assured. She had been experiencing morning sickness but wasn't yet sure it was the right time to tell Raymond. She wanted to be sure before breaking the good news yet she worried how Sandra would react. Being her best friend, Pam felt a twinge of guilt. She knew how jealous Sandra was and that she wouldn't give Raymond up easily.

The next morning Raymond listened once again to DJ Herbie's cultural selections on his way to work. He was happily driving along when he spotted one of his friends at the bus stop. Raymond pulled over to the side but waited for his friend to join him. "Want a lift", he asked? "Yeah", his friend replied. He climbed into the passenger side of the Series 6 high performance car. The friend voiced his admiration for the type of vehicle Raymond was driving. "Wicked car Ray", the friend chimed. Raymond smiled but kept nodding his head to the music. His friend unfolded the newspaper but started to search for his favourite page. When he saw Sandra's picture on the centrefold, he whistled but commented. "Your girl looks like she hit the big times Ray", the friend enthused. Raymond did not want to discuss Sandra at that moment and was still unaware why his friend had made that comment. When his friend next spoke, it drew a caustic comment from Raymond. "She looks good man", the friend insisted. Raymond heard the words but remained focused on his observations of the rush hour traffic whilst listening to the music. It wasn't until his friend's second comment that Raymond chose to respond. "She looks real good. You are one lucky guy", the friend exclaimed even more enthusiastically. Raymond smiled but still kept focused on the car ahead of him. Twice the driver of the vehicle in front of him had signalled to turn right but hit the brakes then drove on straight ahead. Raymond was wary of the driver's indecisions. The driver filtered to the left but continued straight ahead, again. Raymond thought if only he could get past the immediate vehicle in front of him, he could probably pay more attention to what his friend was saying about Sandra. His opportunity soon presented itself. At the next traffic light, Raymond pulled level with the offending driver. He glanced across at the driver. The young woman was oblivious of being observed by Raymond. She was too busy talking on her cell phone to notice. The delay at the traffic light was very short. Raymond accelerated away from the lights before the young woman even noticed that the lights had changed. It was the sounds of car horns which alerted Raymond's attention. As he looked through his rare view mirror, he could see the woman in the car but it wasn't moving. Raymond had no idea why but the young woman's car had stalled. The impatient drivers behind her car told of their impatience and possible indignation. "If she was my woman she couldn't expose herself like this", the friend warned. It was then that Raymond took his eyes from the road momentarily to glance at to whom his friend was referring. Sandra's picture loomed from the page. It was a colour picture of her in the shiny taffeta sky blue skimpy top which barely covered one half of each breast and the 'Pum-Pum' shorts that seemed as if it was glued to her body. Now Raymond understood better what his friend meant. His high performance Series 6 started to drift from one lane to the other but heading towards the crowded bus stop. "Watch what you doing man", his friend shouted. With quick movements of his hands, Raymond managed to correct his error just in time. The other motorists did not hesitate to let Raymond know how they felt. The cop several cars behind didn't actually see what had happened. Raymond was again in full control of the vehicle. He was still shocked surprised at the provocative picture on the centre page of the national newspaper. The headline read " 'Pum-Pum' Shorts Sensation Causes Riot". A long article by the side of the picture told of the wolf whistles, the hound dog howls and the fights that took place in the Auditorium of the Hotel Welcome in Poshborough. Raymond was not only angry at Sandra for posing in the paper but also because she had not bothered to tell him. As soon as Raymond dropped his friend off, he phoned Pam. "Have you seen this morning's newspaper", Raymond asked? He was rather blunt. Pam could sense the unease in Raymond's voice. She instinctively knew it was something to do with Sandra but didn't know what it was specifically. All she could do is to be there for Raymond. "No Ray, why", Pam asked? "That bitch has finally done it", Raymond replied. The anger he communicated was so intense but was a new experience for Pam. She didn't even think Raymond was capable of sounding so angry. "Done what", Pam asked? "Just buy a paper and you'll see", Raymond said. He was completely stunned and his mind was bombarded with lots of unanswered questions. Why didn't Sandra tell him she had changed her job and why modelling? How long had Sandra been modelling? Was she sleeping around? Raymond had heard so many stories about models and they were not complimentary to say the least. He had no real knowledge about them but the rumours suggested that they had to compromise themselves in order to get anywhere in that particular occupation, apparently! Raymond could neither prove nor disprove the allegations but at this moment, without any proof, he was ready to accept the rumours as true. Now, Raymond began to feel almost unclean to have been involved with the seemingly secretive Sandra. Pam sensed his unusually angry mood. It worried her greatly but she had a fair idea what had caused him to react in this manner. Pam slipped across to the newsagents on her Estate but they were sold out of morning papers. It took many visits to other newsagents before Pam was able to obtain a copy of a national newspaper with Sandra's picture on the front and centre pages. On the front page, she was shown on the runway in the stunning translucent acid pink single length silk wrap teasing the wild eyed audience. It reminded Pam of a Lion Tamer at a Circus daring the wild animals into temptation. On the centre page was the more daring picture. Sandra was in a most provocative pose in the shiny sky blue taffeta top which started just above her breasts but just about covered her nipples. The top exposed the bottom half of her rather voluptuous breasts and the explicit 'Pum-Pum' shorts berely covering her bum cheeks from the rare but highlighted the imprint of her vaginal area onto the tightly fitting skimpy shorts. The newspaper stated that grown men caused near riotous scenes not only in an effort to unwrap the gorgeous newcomer on the front page but also those, who brawled openly but made their lewd intentions known when Sandra appeared in the utterly provocative skimpy top and 'Pum-Pum' shorts. The journalist covering the story confessed that he too found himself being swept along with the crazy melee. At home, Pam tried to ring Sandra and then Raymond but both their cell phones were engaged for more than an hour. Later in the day, Pam managed to contact Raymond. He told her that he hadn't seen the newspaper with the two pictures of Sandra. Raymond said that one picture was enough to make him feel the way he does now. He assured Pam that he was on his way back to her flat. "Don't let her hurt you anymore Ray", Pam advised. "I just can't seem to get things together at work", Raymond said. He told Pam of his near crash earlier that morning when his friend showed him the centre page spread while he was driving. "We'll talk about it when you come home", Pam assured. Raymond told Pam that he couldn't continue the conversation on the cell phone because he was driving. He struggled to control the car rationally. It swayed from side to side. Raymond's mind was in turmoil. He weaved in and out of lanes by overtaking on the inside as well as the outside of the slowly moving traffic. The music inside the car had increased by several decibels higher and it blared through into the streets from the opened windows. This seemed to disturb the green humanoid robotron cop on foot patrol some 100 or so yards ahead. He spotted Raymond in the high performance Series 6 car but suddenly darted out onto the road in front of the moving vehicle. Raymond was alerted by the sudden movement but pressed hard on the brakes. The screeching of the tyres drew attention from passers by. There were only inches to spare when Raymond finally managed to stop in front of the cop. This created more problems than Raymond could possibly imagine. The cop rushed to the driver's side. He told Raymond to turn the music off but because of the volume of the music, Raymond did not hear clearly what the cop said. He, thinking that Raymond was being awkward, removed the pepper spray from his hip. Raymond turned away from the cop in order to turn the music off. The cop misinterpreted his movement. When Raymond turned back towards him, the cop pointed the canister with pepper spray but released it into his face. Whilst still recovering from the shock and the burning effect in his eyes, Raymond yelped loudly. The cop opened the door on the driver's side of the car but dragged the defenceless Raymond out of it. "Turn around and put your hands on top of the car then spread your legs", the cop ordered. Raymond was seething with anger but was more concerned about his temporary blindness caused by the pepper spray. He was genuinely struggling to carry out what the cop had ordered him to do. The cop used his foot to help Raymond follow his orders to spread his legs. He frisked Raymond thoroughly but told him to remain in the same position. Raymond heard the cop requesting *"back up"* as he spoke into his 'walkie-talkie' radio. "I've just nearly been run over by one of them *'lot'*. Officer needs help. He's a big, extremely aggressively looking beast. Hurry", the green humanoid robotron cop agitated. Within minutes, Raymond could hear the sound of the *'Siren Orchestra'* getting closer. The adrenalin began to flow and his heart seemed to beat faster. Raymond had no time to think about Sandra now. His thoughts recalled that one of his friends had died in similar circumstances 16 months before. When the other green humanoid robotron cops arrived, two of them took Raymond to the back of the car but started to question him all at the same time. It was confusing because Raymond was hardly given time to answer one question let alone another. The first cop pushed past the others but began to hit Raymond with his truncheon. He made some foul and degrading comments while he carried out the beating. "Tried to run me over . . . you bastard", the cop judged. He kept repeating the same thing as he hit Raymond again and again. Sometimes it was on his body but at other times the blows were aimed on his shoulders and head. In the meantime other cops from neighbouring boroughs had turned up to assist their colleague, who had sent out the distressing 'SOS' coded alarm. Passersby witnessed twenty-one police vehicles at the scene. Apart from the cop, who had initiated the summary panic message, the rest joined their colleagues in the admonishment of Raymond Oddball. They bundled Raymond to the ground. Using the plastic ties, they cuffed his hands and legs but forced Raymond to lay face down on the road. One of the cops from the Tribe of Hawke placed one foot on Raymond's neck while others kicked him all along his body but particularly in the rib area. Whilst engaging in the assault on Raymond, one cop was heard to ask him how he could possibly afford such an expensive car like the Series 6. Raymond screamed like a banshee when two insensitive green humanoid robotron cops shocked him simultaneously with their tazers. Despite the passersby witnessing the deliberate unprovoked manic attack on Raymond, the cops continued in the kicking and sometimes stamping all over the defenceless Raymond. His cries for help were ignored completely as the cops prolonged the kicking and stamping on Raymond again and again. As if the attack was not enough to vent their inveterate feelings, each green humanoid robotron cop from the Tribe of Babylon and the two from the Tribe of Hawke took turns to spit on Raymond. The astonished crowd mumbled their disapproval at the treatment of the young man but they dare not openly say how they felt for fear of the same treatment. Some used their cell phones to record the over-the-top actions on the lone figure on the ground. The cops from the firearm unit arrested the middle aged woman, who was recording the vicious assault from her front garden. She was pushed to the ground and her cell phone was smashed against the tarmac but stamped on by the huge boot of the cop, who had snatched it from her. He and another wrenched the physically challenged woman's arm but handcuffed and took her away in one of the vehicles with a cage. Some of the other individuals, who were recording, managed to escape being arrested by losing themselves among what was now a large crowd of witnesses. Exhausted from their efforts, four cops lifted the giant Raymond but threw him into the cage at the back of one of the vehicles. Some of the irate motorists sounded their approval but the crowd which had gathered wondered what he had done to deserve the beating he received. Some said he was driving like a maniac while others assumed that he was a *'drug dealer'*. "Look at the car he was driving. He's bound to be dealing in drugs", an observer said. "Or owe a lot of money to some finance company", another observer countered.

At the station, Raymond was asked to empty the contents of his pockets. After giving a sample of DNA, Raymond was photographed and fingerprinted. The Duty Sergeant/

Deputy Sheriff whistled when he saw the diamond ring Raymond had bought for Pam. He had bought it two days before but was waiting for the right moment to dazzle her with it. "Did you steal this", the gruff voiced Sergeant assumed? Raymond was feeling too much pain to bother to answer the envious cop. His ribs were very sore and his shoulders felt as if the bones were piercing through his skin. The back of his neck was stiff not only from tension but also from the bruising from the size 14 boots of the cop from the Tribe of Hawke had deliberately placed there. Raymond's ribs ached even more with every step that he took and his breathing was laboured. His eyes were still on fire. He asked to see a doctor but his request was denied. The four burly cops flanking him sneered, sniped but hurled even more abuse. Raymond was in no state or position to argue. Finally, the cops stopped outside a cell. They opened it then pushed Raymond inside. The cops slammed but locked the door. Each one took a little peep through the spy hole as if to confirm he was still there. Raymond must have drifted off to sleep because when he awakened the cell was dark. The floor was cold and there was a smell of stale urine but he couldn't be sure from whence it came. Raymond heard the jingle of keys as the cell was opened but he couldn't see the faces of the people who entered in the darkness. The only light on in the cell was that of a torch carried by green humanoid robotron Sergeant/Deputy Sheriff Gruff. "Are you awake", a voice asked? "Yes", Raymond confirmed. "Tell us what we want to know and we'll leave you alone", Sergeant/Deputy Sheriff Gruff demanded. That was the voice that Raymond recognized. It was that of Sergeant/Deputy Sheriff Gruff. He was the Station's Duty Sergeant/Deputy Sheriff. His mannerism matched his gravel voice and his weather-beaten antique distressed leathery skin enhanced by his deeply furrowed brows and his heavily calloused hands. Sergeant/Deputy Sheriff Guff's mean and uncompromising approach was reflected in what he expected from the rookies whom carried out his orders without question. His stern voice was direct and demanding. "Where did you get the diamond ring? Tell us why you stole it", Sergeant/Deputy Sheriff Gruff searched. In his reply, Raymond defiantly expressed his disgust by the way he chose to answer. It was short but inferred his impatience with the Sergeant/Deputy Sheriff and his colleagues. "I didn't", Raymond grunted. "Get the chair", Sergeant/Deputy Sheriff Gruff ordered. The shuffling of feet well contrasted the once silent cell. Sergeant/Deputy Sheriff Guff's rookies surrounded Raymond but dragged him up off the floor. The Sergeant/Deputy Sheriff positioned the chair where he wanted it then the rookies pushed Raymond onto it. They placed his hands behind the chair but cuffed them then secured his feet with rope to the legs of the chair. Fear shot through Raymond's mind. Flashbacks to the times when he and Sandra were once inseparable kept the images of her picture in the skimpy outfit on the center pages of the national newspaper. It had got him into his present situation. Raymond wished he hadn't stopped to pick up his friend. He was soon brought back to his current environment. The rookies, one from the Tribe of Hawke, a blue one from the Mixed DNA Rainbow Tribe, one from the Tribe of Duke and the others from the Tribe of Babylon were well practiced in the method used to extract information from individuals. They shone the light from the torch directly into Raymond's sore eyes. When he flinched but turned his head, one of the rookies grabbed his hair but yanked his head back. The voice from behind warned him not to move. Sergeant/Deputy Sheriff Gruff asked the same questions over and over again. The idea was to continue asking until Raymond confessed to the crime implied. The stern voice of Sergeant/Deputy Sheriff Gruff suddenly changed to sounding *friendly*. This was part of the tactic often employed to confuse suspects.

The *'good'* cop *'bad'* cop form of eliciting information was a typical form of questioning. *'Roughing up'* a suspect then *'seeming reasonable'* at other moments were meant to coerce the suspect to admit to the crime the cops had already concluded they were guilty of. "I'm a reasonable man. Just come clean. Confess and we'll go away", Sergeant/Deputy Sheriff Gruff lied. Raymond was not impressed by any of the techniques the cops used. He was just frightened. When the cops could not get Raymond to confess to stealing, they left as abruptly as they had arrived leaving him still cuffed and bound to the chair. Raymond felt the warm fluid on his legs and realised that he had uncontrollably peed himself. He heard the jingling of keys yet again but now his fear suddenly turned to defiance. For the first time the cops switched on the light in the cell. Six rookies and Sergeant/Deputy Sheriff Gruff entered yet again. He spoke first. His tone had changed yet again. This time both his body language and voice warned Raymond about the intention of the quick revisit to the cell. "We'll ask you again, did you steal the diamond ring", Sergeant/Deputy Sheriff Gruff interrogated? "I bought it two days ago", Raymond replied. "You mean you stole it two days ago", a rookie cop accused? Before Raymond could reply Sergeant/Deputy Sheriff Gruff chimed in. "We're wasting our time. Work him over. He'll soon tell us", he ordered. The rookies' reactions to the Sergeant's/Deputy Sheriff's command were immediate and well coordinated. Like a pack of wolves, surrounding their prey, they moved ever so much closer, menacingly honing in for the *'kill'*. Raymond sensed that the militia style movement was meant to intimidate. His premonition reinforced the sudden fear which swept over him. Raymond found himself suddenly praying to God. When there was no response from God, his resolve started to weaken. The cops' intentions were more than imminently inevitable. Raymond voiced his fear as loudly as he could manage. "Nooooooooooooooooooo", he shouted. The rookies started to wrap the wet white towel around his already sore ribs. They each took turn to punch him several times. Raymond felt each cops intended intensity of intimidation. He grunted after the delivery of each blow much the same as any victim whom had experienced being tortured at the hands of any gang. Raymond had long gone way past his pain threshold. He was now close enough to admitting to a crime he had not committed. The cops kept the pressure on. They continued to beat Raymond until he drifted into a state of unconsciousness, mercifully. Each blow was now much the same. Raymond just sat with his head slumped, not caring what would happen next. The cops had exhausted themselves on working over the innocent Raymond. Sergeant/Deputy Sheriff Gruff halted the beating but only because he too was thoroughly exhausted from the 45 minutes of nonstop intense punishment. He commented to the rookies. "Sleep depravation next", Sergeant/Deputy Sheriff Gruff commanded. His message to Raymond was just a warning that they hadn't finished their *'investigation'*. He could expect them to visit him again later on. "We'll be back", Sergeant/Deputy Sheriff Gruff threatened.

Pam was anxious that several hours had past since Raymond had told her he was on his way home yet he had still not arrived. Earlier, he'd sounded so angry Pam wondered if he had gone directly to confront Sandra. She rang his cell phone. When there was no answer, Pam rang the landline number at Sandra's house. There was no reply from that either. Suddenly, she had a feeling that something had gone wrong but she knew Raymond would have phoned by now. All through the night, Pam stayed awake hoping that Raymond was alright. After all, she was bearing his child. Pam was in a place she's not been before. This time she decided to ring Sandra's cell phone. "Hello", Sandra answered. "Sandra, it is Pam. I thought of phoning you earlier but I couldn't", she lied. "Oh Pam, thank you very much. Did you see the pictures girl? I drove them wild. They were tripping over themselves to unwind the '*Wrap*'. Some of them started to fight when I wore the 'Pum-Pum' shorts, Sandra boasted. "What did Duke say", Pam pried? "Oh he loved every minute of it and of course it didn't only make the tabloids. Duke said the offers are pouring in even from overseas", Sandra gloated. "I'm happy for you but was Raymond", Pam asked? "He hasn't phoned me yet, I suppose he's upset because I didn't tell him", Sandra admitted. She said it so airily as if she was referring to a spoilt child, who was likely to throw a tantrum if he couldn't have his way. "Well, you have to do things the way you want but I think you're driving him away from you", Pam insinuated. "Ray will never leave me. He loves me too much", Sandra disagreed. "Hope things go well for you. Keep in touch", Pam said. Sandra was enjoying the '*high life*'. She was sitting in the Jacuzzi while she dialled Raymond's cell-phone. "Hello", a voice said. "Ray honey, will you forgive me for not telling you about the pictures which appeared in the national papers this morning", Sandra asked? Sergeant Gruff/Deputy Sheriff was stunned by the revelation, he put his hand over the mouthpiece but exclaimed. "It's her, the '*beauty*' who was in this morning's papers", he confirmed. "Are you listening to me Ray", Sandra queried. Sergeant/Deputy Sheriff Gruff selected to continue the call in the hands-free mode. "I'll make it up to you Raymond Oddball just you wait and see. I'll buy you the Series 6 GTI convertible with extra wide wheels and with gold rims", Sandra promised. Still, there was no response from her prompting so she hung up. Sergeant/Deputy Sheriff Gruff looked at the others. He couldn't hide his surprise. He put the phone down as if it was burning his hand. "Would you believe it? A jerk like that with such a gorgeous bird", a brown Mixed DNA Rainbow Tribe rookie cop insinuated? He kept shaking his head from side to side in disbelief. "The diamond ring might have been bought after all", another rookie cop suggested. Armed with this fresh information, Sergeant Gruff/Deputy Sheriff and his other militia trained rookies visited Raymond yet again. This time they decided to use the '*good cop*' gentler approach. Raymond heard the jingling of keys once again. The fear had never really left him but it resurfaced with greater surge. His hands were still cuffed and his legs still attached to the chair by rope. As the cops re-entered the cell, Raymond looked under his eyes at his interrogators. His head hung to the side. None of the cops could understand the foolish grin on Raymond's face. Surely, he was not happy to see them. Raymond was not smiling. It was a grimace brought on by the anticipation of another beating and the pain he was experiencing. Even his breathing caused him pain. Raymond waited for the cops' next act of bullying aggression towards him. Sergeant/Deputy Sheriff Gruff was highly curious about the response he received when he made the call to Sandra. He fired the question at Raymond. "Who is Sandra Bogus", he asked? Raymond paused before answering. That caused Sergeant/Deputy Sheriff Gruff to repeat the question. "Who is Sandra Bogus", he asked again. Raymond was a broken man from both sets of ordeals. Even though he felt immense pain from his physical trauma, he was hurt at a deeper level by Sandra's picture in the national newspaper. Raymond came pretty close to denying that he knew her at all. Sergeant/Deputy Sheriff Gruff asked for a third time. Raymond still didn't give an answer. "I'll ask you one more time. Who is Sandra Bogus he asked yet again? "She's my girlfriend", Raymond replied. "Would you like to ring her to tell her you're here", the stern voiced cop asked? Raymond had very little to say to Sandra. The hurt and embarrassment were still too fresh in his mind. "Not particularly", Raymond responded. This seemed to throw the cops. They were confused as to why

Raymond didn't want to ring his girlfriend. Sergeant/Deputy Sheriff Gruff asked cynically. "You don't want her to know you're here", he queried? Raymond's arms and legs had no feelings. He felt hopeless but challenged the cops to finish the job so he could be relieved of both forms of suffering. All he wanted was to be left alone. Raymond dared the cops to do their worse. "Look, either finish off what you come to do or just leave me alone, let me die in peace", Raymond responded. Sergeant/Deputy Sheriff Gruff switched his tactic yet again. He ordered his rookies to loosen the rope from Raymond's feet and the cuffs from his hands. Both Raymond's hands and feet were numb and his ribs hurt even more with every breath. He tried to stand up from the chair but the numbness in his legs caused him to fall awkwardly onto the hard floor. In his state of despair, Raymond asked for some medical assistance. Grimacing after each word he managed to get his request across. "I wa . . . aant a doc . . . . tor", Raymond pleaded. "We'll see what we can do", Sergeant/Deputy Sheriff Gruff replied. He turned but abruptly walked out of the cell. The rookies trailed after him. Much like a slithering snake, Raymond dragged himself along the hard floor towards the mattress in the corner. Though it was only a few feet away it took quite a while for him to get to the mattress. When he got there, it took several attempts before he was able to get on top of it. The mattress proved much more comfortable than the cold hard floor. Still, the rancid smell of stale urine followed him around. Because of the horrendous beating, Raymond could not find a comfortable position. By the time he had noticed the cell phone sitting in the corner of the cell, Raymond decided it would take too much effort to move from the cozy comfort of the mattress to retrieve the phone. Raymond continued to make adjustments to his position. He decided to lie on his back but prayed for the pain to stop. Raymond was also weakened from lack of food. He had not eaten since breakfast. When the burly Sergeant/Deputy Sheriff Gruff arrived with the doctor, Raymond begged him to send him to a hospital. "I'm going to give you something for the pain", the doctor said. He pushed the needle into Raymond's arm. After examining him, the doctor told the cops that Raymond was bleeding internally and would die if he didn't get to a hospital immediately. "Can't you patch him up until we release him", Sergeant/Deputy Sheriff Gruff asked? "I can't perform miracles, this man will die if you don't follow my advice", the doctor concluded. He and Sergeant/Deputy Sheriff Gruff left the cell together. One of the younger cops threw the cell phone unto the mattress but commented. "Call your fancy woman and get her to take you to the hospital", the cop challenged. Raymond picked up the cell phone. He managed to dial Pam's number. When she answered, Raymond begged her to come to the station quickly. "Why are you at the station", Pam asked? "No time to explain just get a minicab quickly", Raymond pleaded. He started to drift off into unconsciousness again but this time from the injection. Pam heard no more from Raymond. She started to cry the moment Raymond had stopped speaking. She dialled his cell phone again but it seemed to be engaged, constantly. Pam dialled the mini cab office. "No cars for at least twenty minutes", the Controller replied. This caused Pam to panic. She dialled other minicab numbers but again to no avail. Pam found herself shaking as if she was having a chill. Raymond was in trouble and she had to help him by whatever means. Pam had no choice but to call Sandra. When she answered Pam told her that Raymond had asked that she pass the message on. "Why didn't he phone me directly", Sandra asked? "I don't know but he sounded real bad", Pam confirmed. "Why can't the cops take him to the hospital themselves", Sandra asked? "Look Sandra, I don't know but if you have to have a debate about it you might as well ignore his call for help", Pam blurted out. Sandra phoned

Duke and told him she had to attend to an emergency and that it concerned life or death. "Use my chauffeur if it's that urgent", Duke suggested.

CHAPTER 26

S am Cleverman pulled up in front of the Hotel Welcome within minutes of the call. They drove swiftly through the light traffic arriving at Painville Police Station within an hour. All the cops' heads turned in the same direction as soon as Sandra entered. Their wish had come through. Standing in front of them was the girl on the front and centre pages of the national newspapers. Sergeant/Deputy Sheriff Gruff was first to ask for her autograph, "It's for my grand-daughter", he lied. "Ms. Bogus how nice to see you in the flesh", a blue rookie cop from the Mixed DNA Rainbow Tribe said. "Where is Raymond now", Sandra asked? "We'll get him for you ma'am", Sergeant/Deputy Sheriff Gruff grovelled. He motioned with his head for the rookies to get Raymond. Sam Cleverman stood dutifully to the side awaiting further instructions but when he saw Raymond being carried out he cringed with a sudden pang of sympathy. Sandra did not recognize her 'Mr. Right'. "What happened to him", Sandra asked? Raymond recognized her voice but was past caring. He just wanted to get to the hospital. His face was swollen from the bruising he received when making contact with the hard tarred road and the kicking in the van. He was grunting all the time now and the tears ran down his face. "He's dying. Get him to a hospital", Sandra shouted. The cops refused to take responsibility for getting Raymond to the hospital. "It would be quicker for you to take him yourself instead of waiting another hour for an ambulance", Sergeant/Deputy Sheriff Gruff lied. The truth is he didn't want the attention of the public drawn towards the station. Sandra collected a paper bag with Raymond's belongings but instructed Sam to go as fast as he could to the hospital. "Don't let him die Sam, don't let my Raymond die", Sandra sobbed. When they arrived at the Community General Hospital, Ghettoville, the emergency room was crowded with people suffering from different ills yet Sandra was able to get immediate attention for the ailing Raymond. Her morning appearance in the national newspapers had stood her in good stead. Even the overworked doctors and nurses couldn't help feeling pleased that the new star was there with them in real. "We have to admit him and operate straight away he's bleeding inside", the Consultant reported. "I'll pay if I have to, just save him", Sandra pleaded. "Don't worry Ms. Bogus I'll do the operation myself", the Consultant assured. Raymond was taken to the operating theatre immediately. When Sandra realized the full enormity of Raymond's condition, she too felt faint. Turning to Sam, she started to sob. He felt helpless because, although he felt sympathy for Sandra, he did not want to abuse his position by hugging her. Sam remembered how she had spoken to him that night on the dual carriageway. "I'm sorry ma'am", Sam said. His sentiments were genuine. When he next looked at Sandra, Sam was moved by the blank look on her face. She reminded him of a lost child. "Maybe Mr. Stagg would know what to do", Sam suggested. His suggestion seemed to revive her. "Good idea Sam", Sanda said. She rang Duke. Her voice made him aware of an emergency. "Duke I've got a real big problem and I need a lawyer pronto. Can you recommend one", Sandra enquired? "Where are you", Duke asked? "I'm at the Community General Hospital, Ghettoville", Sandra replied. Duke did not wait to hear why she was there. He started to curse Sam Cleverman and said he was sacked immediately. His perception was that Sam had somehow been negligent in his duty but had had an accident causing Sandra to be injured. "I'm coming over myself", Duke assuredly. "No Duke, that isn't necessary. I'm not hurt. Just give me the lawyer's number. I'll explain later", Sandra pleaded. She promptly phoned the lawyer, who told her he would meet her at the police station within half an hour. She left her cell number with the Ward Sister but headed for the police station. On the way there, she surprised Sam by asking him what he would do in such a situation. "I'd make those cops pay", Sam replied. "Raymond is a good man Sam. He is not the type to get in trouble. Something is odd about the whole thing", Sandra said. "I hope the lawyer is good Sam. I hope he's good", Sandra said. Sam thought it was strange hearing her say that about Raymond yet he knew she was having an affair with Duke. "Women", Sam mumbled.

Sandra's family was hardly a feature in her busy life but her mother, Dian, had approved her friendship with Raymond. Dian Bogus loved 'Ray Ray' as she preferred to call him. She used to tell Sandra to "look after him good". 'Ray Ray' had a lot of time for Dian too. He would often send her flowers on Mother's day or on her birthday. Now Sandra had to tell her mother that he was seriously ill in hospital. She reached the number which was programmed into her cell phone. "Hello mom, how are you", Sandra enquired? She was cold and matter of fact in her greeting but her mother was excited that her daughter remembered to ring her. "'San-San' is it really you? Why yuh throw mi away like dat", Dian asked? "Just busy mom, just busy", Sandra replied. "We see you in the papers this morning. All di men in di Paper Shop was whistling when dem si yuh picture", Dian responded. "Mom I'm afraid I've got a bit of bad news", Sandra hinted. She told her mother about Raymond's life saving operation. "Duh all you can for your poor husband", Dian replied. She would always refer to Raymond as Sandra's husband even though they weren't really married. "I'll let you know the moment he comes out the theatre. Bye mom", Sandra concluded. Sam Cleverman parked the limo in front of the police station. "Should I wait outside ma'am", Sam asked? "No Sam, come inside with me, you're a witness to Raymond's condition", Sandra replied. A successful top class lawyer from a City law firm was waiting inside when Sandra and Sam entered. "Hello Ms. Bogus, my name is Hilton Fairly. Mr Stagg asked me to help you anyway I can", he indicated. The lawyer shook Sandra's hand as if he'd just met a Queen. Sandra told him all that she knew. "Mr. Fairly I want you to ask all the right questions. I need to know how he came to be here in the first place", Sandra instructed. The duty Sergeant/Deputy Sheriff Gruff was not very helpful to the lawyer. He skipped lots of important details in regards to Raymond's injuries. "You were on duty when Mr. Oddball was arrested, weren't you", Hinton Fairly asked? "Yes", Sergeant/Deputy Sheriff Gruff replied. "What time was Mr. Oddball arrested and on what charge", Hinton Fairly queried. When he'd established those details, Hinton fired the first *'stinger'*. "What was Mr. Oddballs' state of health when he was brought into the station", Hinton Fairly asked? "What do you mean", Sergeant/Deputy Sheriff Gruff countered? "Let me put it simply", Hinton Fairly stressed. Pausing briefly before he exploded the bombshell, the lawyer wanted to establish Raymond's health status when he arrived at the station. "Did Mr. Oddball require a doctor on his arrival at the station", Hinton Fairly searched? The stern voiced Sergeant/ Deputy Sheriff Gruff took umbrage to this line of questioning. "Look, I only do my job. I don't go about examining criminals. I'm a policeman, not a doctor", he retorted. Hinton was used to awkward people like the stern voiced Sergeant/Deputy Sheriff Gruff. By his reply, the canny lawyer had already found out what he wanted to know. "I must tell you Sergeant/Deputy Sheriff Gruff that I'm not happy with the answers you've given me. We'll be taking legal action against you and any other officers involved in Mr. Oddball's condition whilst in your care", Hinton Fairly said. He led Sandra out to the limo and told her that he would start proceedings against the police the next day. "I'll be in touch as soon as I have something positive to tell you. It will be a long hard fight. They'll never admit liability. They normally settle out of court, eventually", Hinton Fairly warned. The lawyer headed towards his car. Sandra instructed Sam to take her back to the hospital. Inside the limo, Sandra asked Sam if he wanted to phone his family to tell them he was working late. "They'll understand ma'am, it's my job", Sam said. She phoned Pam and told her about Raymond's condition but Sandra was surprised to hear her reaction. "Oh God, please don't let him die", Pam screamed. Without waiting for Sandra to respond, Pam spoke again. "Did they beat him, did they beat him", Pam asked? "Yes they did, he's bleeding inside and only stand a 50/50 chance of staying alive. I'm on my way back to the hospital now", Sandra reported. Pam started to cry uncontrollably then hung up on Sandra. She knew Pam and Raymond were very good friends and that she was a very emotional person but Sandra had never heard Pam react like this before. Sandra put it down to shock. The paper bag with Raymond's things was still resting on the seat beside her. Sandra picked it up but looked inside. She checked that all his credit cards were there then Sandra spotted the small box with the ring inside. It brought a smile to her face to think that Raymond was keen to adorn her with yet another present. She knew it could never compare with anything Duke could afford but all the same Sandra thought it was a nice touch. She put the cards and the box with the ring into her hand bag. Sam pulled up at the Community General Hospital. Inside, the nurse told Sandra that the Consultant Surgeon had not yet finished operating. "Mr. Oddball's injuries are quite severe. He's very badly hurt and it will take several hours to complete the operation", the nurse said. Sandra was visibly shaken. "He's bleeding inside and has five broken ribs but the consultant is doing the operation himself. He's a very good doctor", the nurse assured. "You'll need to sign the consent form. Come this way", the nurse advised. Sandra beckoned Sam to follow her to the nurses' office. She signed the necessary form but returned to the waiting area with Sam. There they sat in silence for a long time observing the new casualties as they arrived. Sam saw someone he knew being brought in on a stretcher. The man's wounds were very apparent. "Good God", Sam exclaimed. "Do you know him Sam", Sandra asked? "Yes ma'am, he's my neighbour", Sam replied. "Go on Sam, I won't be leaving for a while", Sandra said. She spoke with a hint of sympathy in her voice. Sam thanked her but walked over towards the stretcher. He lent over and began talking to the man. Sandra could not hear what Sam was saying yet she noticed his head moving from side to side; signalling disbelief. When Sam came back, he told Sandra what his neighbour had told him. "He was attacked by two Pit Bull Terriers while out jogging", Sam reported. Still shaking his head from side to side in disbelief, Sam described some of the injuries that his neighbour had endured. "Why aren't they treating him immediately", Sandra asked? "They just don't have enough staff to attend to him right now, poor man", Sam said. Sandra was always an impulsive person and on this occasion she was no different. She strode into the nurses' office to complain. The nurse explained the priority situation at the hospital. "If the man was a private patient he could be seen straight away. I don't make the rules I just follow them Ms. Bogus", the nurse continued. Sandra saw the look on Sam's face but realized that he couldn't possibly afford to pay. "I'll pay, get someone to see him straight away", Sandra instructed. "Yes Ms. Bogus", the nurse replied. Sam was most grateful for the humane action Sandra had shown and promised to repay her at a later date. "It's no problem Sam. I couldn't just sit here and watch him die in front of my eyes", Sandra stated. There was no more to be said so they sat there once again in total silence. This time, both Sandra and Sam were sharing a common form of grief. Each of them from opposite ends of the social status but nevertheless waiting anxiously for whatever fate had to offer to their respective friends. The busy hospital staff seemed exhausted as they toiled to reduce the ever increasing number of casualties. There were babies, toddlers, pensioners and all other age groups uneasily awaiting their turn to be seen. One junior doctor was overheard complaining to his colleagues about the many hours he was asked to work even though he had hardly had any sleep. Sandra began to dose as her extraordinary night began to take its toll. Sam was tired too but dared not fall asleep on duty. "I'm going for a walk Ms. Bogus I'll be outside if you want me", Sam told her. "OK Sam", Sandra replied.

When Pam walked into the 'Waiting Area', Sandra did not see her because she had dosed off again. Pam looked around searchingly for Sandra. She was not sure how she would explain the reason for being there. The Consultant Surgeon approached Sandra. "Ms. Bogus", he called out. Sandra jumped as she opened her eyes and saw the Consultant Surgeon approaching her. "Is he alive", she asked? "Yes Ms. Bogus, he's alive and very lucky that you brought him here in time. The operation was successful and he's now in the recovery room. You'll only be allowed to see him for a short while when he comes onto the ward", he concluded. Sandra felt great relief. "Thank you doctor", Sandra said. Pam stood with jaws clenched. She was squeezing back the emotions which had started to rise inside her. Sandra sounded genuine when she spoke with the Consultant Surgeon. Pam approached her from behind. "Sandra", she whispered. Sandra turned round quickly, in disbelief. She hadn't expected to see Pam there. "Pam what are you doing here", Sandra asked? Pam sensed the suspicious inference. "I'm here as a friend of both you and Raymond. I can leave if you don't want me here", Pam retorted. It was Sandra who was feeling guilty now. "I'm sorry. I didn't mean it the way it sounded. It must have sounded awful. Thank you for coming Pam", Sandra apologised. Both women entered into the whole sorry saga of how Raymond ended up in hospital. Pam squirmed but flinched as she listened. "I'll be going to see him shortly, will you come with me", Sandra asked? "Yes", Pam replied. Her heart was racing in anticipation. The doctor, who attended to Sam's neighbour, came over but told Sandra that the man died during the operation. "I'm afraid he'd lost too much blood. There was nothing we could do for him", the doctor apologised. Pam looked at Sandra then asked if the man was also arrested. "No, Sam just happened to recognize him when he was brought in. Apparently, he was attacked by two Pit Bull Terrier dogs while out jogging. Sam's bound to be very upset", Sandra said. Refreshed from the cold night air, Sam entered the 'Waiting Area' but rejoined Sandra. "Any news Ms. Bogus", Sam asked? "Sit down Sam and meet my good friend Pam", Sandra replied. "Pamela Labrishè, meet Sam Cleverman, my chauffeur. Sam Cleverman, meet my friend Pam", Sandra said. "Any news about Mr Oddball or my neighbour Ms. Bogus", Sam pressed? Sandra did not know how to tell him that his neighbour had died while he was outside. "Mr. Oddball is recovering after his operation but I'm afraid your neighbour didn't make it", Sandra confirmed. Sam had known his neighbour for more than three years. He was one of the first to welcome him when Sam moved into their street. They weren't living in each others houses but held a healthy respect for each other. Now, he would have to be the one to tell the man's wife that he had died. "I've got to make a phone call Ms. Bogus, will you excuse me ma'am", Sam asked? Both Pam and Sandra heard the remorse in his voice. "Use my phone Sam", Sandra offered but Sam Cleverman was not a presumptuous man and he was still only the chauffeur. "Thank you but no thank you ma'am", Sam said. He looked sheepishly embarrassed. "It's ok Sam, go ahead, take it", Sandra pleaded. Pam could not believe this was the same Sandra, who would normally look down on people like Sam. She seemed to have changed. Sandra would normally be thinking of him as lowly and non-ambitious. Sam moved away from Sandra and Pam. He didn't want them to hear his broken voice as he transmitted the sad news to the man's wife. Sam did not want to abuse the favour but he had to explain what he was told by the man before he died. The man's wife was distraught. At one point Sam thought she may have passed out by the shocking news. "Hello . . . Miss 'D', are you still there", Sam asked? He was concerned whether she was alone at the time of receiving the bad news. "Sam, whey mi fi duh? How mi ah guh get tuh di hospital. Mi nuh noah mi way good pon di train", Miss 'D' explained. Sam gave her directions to the hospital. He explained that technically he was still at work and didn't know if he would still be at the hospital when Miss 'D' got there. Sam walked back towards where Sandra and Pam were sitting. "How is she", Sandra asked? "Well, she didn't take it too good but she will be coming to identify the body", Sam explained. "Thank you Ms. Bogus", he said. One of the nurses came over to tell Sandra that Mr. Stagg was on the hospital phone wanting to speak to her. "Could you tell him I'll return his call, thank you", Sandra asked? She walked towards the exit. Outside, she spoke to Duke on the mobile. "Hi, Duke honey, I'm sorry I couldn't get back to you before now" Sandra apologised. "That maybe but Hinton Fairly said the cops told him your man is in big trouble", Duke retorted. "They can't treat Raymond like that and hope to get away with it", Sandra countered. "I know, but you've still got business to attend to. You're famous now and your public demands your presence", Duke stated. "I just can't leave until I speak to him", Sandra replied. Duke could hear the determination in her voice but decided to put his foot down. "He's in the best place at the moment, wouldn't you agree", he challenged? Sandra was fuming because she always liked to have the upper hand but this time she was caught in the web of her own success. Duke did not get to where he was today by allowing others to dictate to him. On top of that, he felt jealous that Raymond was receiving her 100% attention. "I've booked a photo session for you tomorrow. You need to be at Grant Favours' Studios precisely at 12:00 hours", Duke instructed. Sandra listened then responded sarcastically. "Do you mean I've got a whole day to rest Duke", Sandra parried. He sensed that Sandra was smarting from his lack of sympathy for her situation. Duke tried to smooth things out. "I know you must be very tired but these arrangements were made before your present predicament and there are penalties for cancellation", Duke explained. "What about Sam, he must be tired too", Sandra asked? "He's your chauffeur now my sweet", Duke injected. "The battery is dying Duke. I'll call you again when I can", Sandra assured. When she returned to the waiting area Pam was not there. "Where is my friend gone Sam", Sandra asked? "I'm sorry ma'am I don't know", Sam replied. "Well she couldn't have just disappeared", Sandra said sarcastically. "I must have dosed off ma'am. I didn't mean to", Sam apologised. "Never mind Sam, I almost forgot how many hours we've been without sleep", Sandra said. She realized how edgy she was becoming through lack of sleep and stress. However, she told Sam of the arrangement for the next day. "I'll put it in my diary ma'am", Sam replied. It was the wailing which made them look towards the entrance door. Sam's neighbour, Miss 'D', supported by members of her family entered the hospital. All the other people in the waiting area were drawn to their arrival by the wailing and mourning too. "Where is mi husband? Somebody show mi mi husband", Miss 'D' pleaded. Sam, not waiting for Sandra's permission, jumped up but approached the distressed woman. "Take it easy Miss 'D', take it easy", Sam empathised. She rested her head upon his broad shoulders but exclaimed. "Oh Sam, if yuh neva dey yah mi wuddn't noah wha happen tuh him", Miss 'D' stated. Sam tried to console her. "Him sey anyting before him ded Sam? Him sey anyting", Miss 'D' asked? The purple Mixed DNA Rainbow Tribe nurse with the mole on her nose came over to help console Miss 'D' but showed her the way to the mortuary. Sandra looked on helplessly but thought that she could have been in a similar situation if Pam had not called her to get Raymond. The shocking thought of dealing with funeral arrangements made her shiver but brought home to her how alone she was in her own little world. After all, it was her choice to be distanced from her family and true friends in the selfish search for fame. Duke, Raymond and Pam were the only friends she had apart for the *'sharks'* who wanted to see her fail. It was Raymond who had warned her about the parasites, she pondered. When Pam reappeared she was crying as if someone for her had died. "Where have you been, I thought you had abandoned our friendship", Sandra said. "It's Raymond. He can't speak. It seems like he's getting a stroke", Pam said. She explained to Sandra that, while she was outside on the phone to Duke, the nurse had come to tell them that Raymond was struggling to come out of the anesthetic. "I looked outside to see if I could find you but you weren't there, so I followed after the nurse. "Oh Sandra, what have they done to him", Pam asked? "Take me to Ray. I want to see him", Sandra pleaded. They went towards the narrow gap which Pam had discovered as a short route to the ward. "This way Sandra", Pam instructed. "Did he say anything at all", Sandra asked? "He just about mumbled the word *'ring'* that's all. It doesn't make any sense. I asked him who I should ring but he couldn't reply". Pam explained. "Do you think he's going to die Pam", Sandra asked? "Don't be so negative, Sandra", Pam replied. Raymond's torso was swathed in bandage up to his chest. His head and the sides of his face were also bandaged but the front of his face particularly was disfigured by the swelling and bruising. "It will take time", the doctor assured them. "How long", Sandra queried? "Oh, we can only guess that his ribs will mend within eight to twelve weeks and the swelling will start to go within a few days but the real problem is the coma. Some people do recover in time but we mustn't rule out the possibility that he might never speak again", the doctor warned. Pam gasped unashamedly.

"He was conscious when we brought him in", Sandra said. "Perhaps if you had used an ambulance he might not be in a coma right now", the doctor countered. "Would it have made a difference", Sandra asked? "Of course, one can't be sure but at least he would have been able to get medical assistance earlier", the doctor: explained. "His head was busted all over, do you think the blows caused the coma doc", Sandra probed. "We don't know if the head injuries caused the coma", the doctor said. "Is he going to become a *'vegetable'* ", Pam asked? The doctor just shrugged his shoulders. Sandra started to sob. Worried that their Ray might never be the same again, she and Pam hugged but cried on each others' shoulders. Pam envisaged her child without a father though Sandra's thoughts were centred on his physical attributes. "I'm sorry I'll have to ask you to leave now but you can come back later to see if there is any change", the doctor: stated. The two women huddled together. Silently praying for Raymond's speedy recovery, they walked quietly back through the narrow gap until they reached the waiting area once again. "Take us home Sam", Sandra pleaded. He did not need them to tell him that Raymond was in a bad way. As they approached the limo, Pam noticed that Sandra was shaking badly. She was trying hard not to cry in front of Sam when she informed him about Raymond's comatose state. In a voice croaky and hoarse, Sam expressed how he was feeling. Inside, he was experiencing conflicting emotions. One set of emotions was the sadness he felt for Miss 'D' and her family but the other was the deep anger he felt towards the cops for beating Raymond into a coma. "Where to ma'am", Sam asked? "Hotel Welcome", Sandra replied.

CHAPTER 27

P am tried to resist but Sandra insisted that her friend should spend at least the next few hours with her. "You have no pets or babies at home. Let us spend some time together Pam. After all, we're almost sisters", Sandra confirmed. "Mr. Stagg is not going to be pleased about that", Sam murmured. He was discreet enough to whisper those words to himself. After all, he didn't want to jeopardise his position or his career. Sam was struggling to keep his eyes open as the limo glided in the direction of the posh hotel. Pam noticed the enormous expanse of land which surrounded each mansion but wondered what life must be like for the occupants of those thoroughly expensive buildings. Poshborough was much deeper into suburbia than those other boroughs on the outskirts of Ghettoborough. Pam had no reason before now to visit this part of Spaceville. She began to feel uncomfortable and out of her depth. "Are you sure it'll be alright for me to stay at that posh hotel", she asked? "You'll be my guest", Sandra assured. "Where will Duke sleep", Pam asked? "Duke will sleep in his own suite", Sandra replied. From about half a mile away, Pam could see the grand building bearing the name Hotel Welcome. She realized that even a pot of coffee in that place could make her bankrupt for life. "Sandra, it must cost an arm and a leg to stay in this place", Pam commented. Sandra smiled briefly but didn't answer. Soon, Sam was pulling up in front of the Hotel Welcome's main entrance. He got out but opened the doors for Sandra and then Pam in that order. Her experience of the enormity of the grand building was most overwhelming. She gazed at it in sheer amazement. There were attendants in uniform standing at the entrance as if they were part of the decoration. Their three quarter length fawn coloured jackets with dark brown epaulettes, collars and cuffs made the attendant look official. The matching fawn coloured cap with dark brown braid around the full circumference of the individual attendant's head was offset by the dark brown peaks. Matching brown shoes completed the full uniform. All that was left was for the attendants to carry out the functions of their remit. They became animated whenever guest appeared. Observing the building and its surroundings, Pam hesitated to move from the spot where she was standing. Sam stood dutifully until Sandra gave him orders to leave. Looking straight at her chauffeur, Sandra addressed him. "You need to get some rest too Sam. I'll call you later", she instructed. Sandra turned away from Sam but headed for the large glass doors where the attendants were standing. Each was on either side waiting to welcome the next guest in. Pam followed. The same brown Mixed DNA Rainbow Tribe doorman Sandra had met the first time she had visited the Hotel Welcome was on duty. This time his manner was more submissive than dismissive. His negative ego seemed to have hibernated leading to a more docile, almost subservient attitude. He bowed but welcomed Sandra and her guest, beckoning politely for them to enter. "Welcome Ms. Bogus", the doorman said. Sandra smiled at him sarcastically because she hadn't forgotten how he had treated her on her first visit. In the foyer, many people started to murmur but point towards Pam and Sandra as they entered. Pam felt embarrassed but whispered to Sandra. "I told you I shouldn't have come. Those people are pointing at us. They must think we couldn't possibly be able to afford to stay in a place like this", Pam surmised. Claude Spinaché, the Maitre D', came over but asked Sandra if she would sign a few autographs for the people who were pointing towards her. "They enjoyed your show Ms. Bogus", Claude Spinaché stated. "Sure Claude", Sandra replied. She scribbled on the napkins which she knew they would keep as souvenirs. Loud applause resounded around the foyer. Sandra waved towards the crowd but headed for the lifts. The attendant inside noticed how Pam was scrutinizing the carpeted ceiling and walls of the lift. "Anything wrong ma'am", the attendant queried? Pam didn't need to reply. Sandra answered the attendant. "No, just take me to my suite", Sandra reprimanded. Pam could not understand how they had arrived at another floor as she didn't feel the lift move. She realized they must have done because they stepped out into yet another '*world*' when they vacated it. The deep piled carpeting underfoot made Pam feel as if she was floating on air and the decorations around including the massive chandeliers reminded Pam of scenes in a movie. At the Hotel Welcome, this was real. Looking down the long corridor which seemed to last forever, they stood outside the Suite. Sandra observed how cautious Pam was when they entered it. Absorbing the plush interior, Pam's eyes scanned every detail of the giant suite but she didn't say anything. "Welcome to my Suite sis. Make yourself at home", Sandra chimed. Contrasting to Pam's unease with the huge extravagance, Sandra seemed at home in the luxurious setting. She chose to lay sprawled across the large expanse of handmade carpet. Pam looked at Sandra quizzically. "Why are you laying on the floor", Pam enquired? She was trying to figure out if Sandra had misjudged where the bed was located. "Raymond taught me that whenever I'm distressed, I should lay flat on my back on the floor for about twenty minutes", Sandra explained. "Does it work", Pam queried? "Why not try it and see for yourself", Sandra suggested? Pam joined Sandra in the ritual. They lay there in complete calm. Both of them experienced the stress draining away from their weary minds and bodies. Pam wondered why Raymond had not bothered to show her this form of relaxation but then she recalled that most of their times together were never as stressful. When they had recovered, Sandra got up but picked up the phone. She requested 'Room Service' to "bring a pot of coffee, a menu and some extra towels" to her Suite. Sandra commented how much she was appreciating Pam's friendship. "It's nice to have a friend like you Pam", Sandra said. "Why", Pam asked? "You're dependable, that's why", Sandra explained. Pam smiled. "We should be talking about poor Raymond, not me", she offered. "That reminds me, I must ring my mother to tell her about Raymond's status", Sandra stated. She picked up the landline phone. When her mother answered, Sandra went through the normal formalities but Dian told her how much she had been thinking about Raymond since she learnt of his being hospitalized. "'San San' I've bin worried bout 'Ray Ray'. Las nite I had a bad dream bout im", Dian stated. "Your dream is accurate mom, he's in a coma", Sandra confirmed. "Blessed Father, yuh si mi dying trial", Dian exclaimed. Before Sandra could respond, Dian asked the prickly question. "So what really happened to him? Was he in an accident", Dian queried? Sandra knew that her mother would probe until she was told the full details. She related the story as she knew it. "That's all I know, I'll keep in touch, bye mom", Sandra finished. As if she was relieved to get off the phone with her mother, Sandra ended the call abruptly. She wiped her brow. "Phew", she sighed. The knock at the door signalled the arrival of the coffee, menu and extra towels. Sandra met with the waiter but instructed him to come into the Suite. He asked where she wanted the trolley with the coffee to be placed. A female attendant was right behind the waiter. She presented the fresh towels but placed them in the bathroom area. The waiter also presented the menus from which Sandra and Pam could make their selections. He took their orders. When both the attendant and waiter had vacated the Suite, Pam spoke to Sandra. "I'll need to shower but I don't have a change of clothes", Pam stated. "That's not a problem", Sandra replied. She beckoned for Pam to come over to the enormous built-in wardrobe. It ran the full length of an entire wall of the Suite. Sandra slid the giant sized doors aside displaying far more clothes than both she and Pam could wear if they both changed three times per day for a year. Pam's jaws dropped in disbelief. She simply could not come to terms with the need for anyone to have this amount of clothes. Sandra's way of looking at the manifestation of abundance was very casual. She made Pam aware of her attitude towards the excessive resources of choice of attire. "Welcome to the *'high life'* sister. Take your pick", Sandra invited. "There must be several dozen outfits here", Pam exclaimed. "You'll find undies/smalls over there", Sandra directed. She pointed to another section of the enormous wardrobe. Pam's attention was being directed towards some of the interior shelving units on the upper tiers and drawers on the lower tiers. Sandra continued, like a guide, to direct Pam on a tour along the 40 ft wall filled with the different outfits from which she could choose. She told Pam that Duke had provided them. Pam's comment was significant and appreciated by Sandra. "Duke must love you more than words can say. Why don't you marry him and give me Raymond", Pam probed. "Duke can't give me everything. You know what I mean", Sandra asked? She had no idea that Pam did or was beginning to get to know what she meant. Pam allowed herself to savour those romantic moments she had experienced with Raymond. Both Pam and Sandra laughed together for the first time since Raymond's demise. They finished their coffee. The waiter rapped on the door firmly but waited for instructions to enter. On receiving permission to do so, he pushed the trolley in with the food that Pam and Sandra had ordered. "Oh, we're not ready to eat at the moment. We'll let you know when we are", Sandra instructed. The waiter acknowledged the instructions but turned and left the Suite with the trolley of food. Sandra suggested that Pam and her do some activities before dinner. "Fancy a swim", Sandra asked? "Why not, I'll race you", Pam replied. Sandra and Pam both chose swimwear which they wore under their gowns. They approached the area where there was a huge swimming pool. Sandra dived in first then Pam. This was reminiscent of the friendly competitions they use to have earlier in their friendship. Some of the people from the Tribe of Babylon already in the pool came out just as soon as Pam and Sandra entered. They talked among themselves but pointed towards Pam and Sandra. Pam noticed but she couldn't be sure whether Sandra had. After their swim, they lay side by side on the loungers by the pool but beckoned for the waiter to come to them. "What will you have Pam", Sandra asked? "I fancy some pineapple", she replied. "That will be a large brandy and a large pineapple juice", Sandra instructed. "No, I fancy real pineapple not just the juice", Pam corrected. The waiter repeated the order. "One large brandy and a whole pineapple coming up ma'am", he said. "Oh waiter, would you bring me the phone please", Sandra requested? "Yes Ms. Bogus", he replied. Pam and Sandra discussed Raymond's comatose condition before ringing the hospital. They agreed that Pam would visit Raymond every day until Sandra could get the time off from her many engagements to visit him herself. Then Sandra phoned the minicab office local to Pam's flat but instructed them that she, Sandra Bogus, would be responsible for the account. "Were you the bird in the papers", the controller asked? "Yes", Sandra replied. "Now, that's all fixed", Sandra said to Pam. The waiter returned with the order and placed it beside them. "Will there be anything else madam", he enquired? "That will be all for now", Sandra said. Having dismissed the waiter, Sandra decided to relax in the Jacuzzi. As they headed over towards it, Pam was having another of her *'craving'* moments. She expressed her request verbally. "I fancy some smoked herring and crackers", Pam said. Sandra signalled for the waiter again. Pam's request seemed to have confirmed Sandra's suspicion. She asked Pam directly. "Huh, first real pineapple now herring and crackers, are you alright girl", Sandra teased? "May I take your order madam", the waiter asked? Pam repeated her *'crave'*. The waiter, from the Tribe of Hawke, thinking he knew the type of crackers Pam wanted, politely hinted that the brand was not catered for at this hotel. "I don't think we stock the type of crackers your friend wants madam", the waiter said. "Any type of crackers will do", Sandra snapped. "I'm sorry madam", the waiter said. He bowed his head as he retreated. Pam didn't want to tell Sandra the waiter was right but she hoped he would be able to find a brand that was similar in taste to the one she craved. "These waiters are too presumptuous", Sandra assumed. "It's alright. He was just trying to be efficient. That waiter is from the paradise island that I come from. He knows the brand of crackers to which I referred. Leave him alone", Pam defended. They laughed together. "Tell me Pam, who is this guy you've got? You're so secretive. I hope you're going to introduce me to him", Sandra hinted. "Oh, he's very shy. He wouldn't like that", Pam lied. "You're not being fair. I told you about Duke", Sandra teased. "I know but it's not the same because he's really shy", Pam parried. "Old school friend is it", Sandra probed? "Oh, leave it for now Sandra, leave it for now", Pam deflected. "OK I'll leave it for now but do you promise to tell", Sandra probed? The waiter's arrival helped to distract Sandra's interest into investigating about Pam's intimate partner. There was a folded note and an envelope on the tray. Sandra read the note but told the waiter to tell the chef that the brand of crackers he recommended is acceptable. She handed the envelope to Pam. She waved the envelope away as if trying to discourage a bothersome fly. "It can't be for me. Only you know where I am", Pam insisted. "I think it's strange too but your name is written on the envelope. Do you want me to open it for you", Sandra asked? Both looked at the envelope suspiciously. "No, I'll open my own mail", Pam stated. She retrieved the envelope from Sandra. Again, she scrutinized it thoroughly before opening it carefully. Inside, there was a note. Sandra wanted to know what was inside but she didn't want to pry into Pam's private affairs. She noticed the shock surprised look on Pam's face. "What's the matter Pam", Sandra asked? Pam mouthed a reply back to Sandra but the words did not come out. "Waiter, a glass of water", "What's wrong Pam? You look like you've seen a ghost", Sandra queried? Pam remained silent but still looked quite stunned. Sandra was now more concerned than ever that Pam had not said anything for about ten minutes since she read the note. The waiter brought the glass of cold water and a bucket of ice. Sandra fed Pam like a child with the water. "Drink this. You'll feel better", Sandra coaxed. She tried to see if she could read the note, but Pam, now refreshed by the cold drink of water, crumpled it in her fist. She got up from the lounger but beckoned for them to go back to the Suite. "What about your herring and crackers", Sandra asked? Pam could not speak. Walking back from the Jacuzzi, a few onlookers saw the look on Pam's face but wondered what might have happened. Some were whispering in each others ears but none of them asked what was wrong. Sandra put a comforting arm around Pam as she led her back towards the Suite. It was Sandra who chose the fish dinner with wine for both of them. "How long", Sandra asked? "Dinner will be served in fifteen minutes madam", the waiter replied. Sandra and Pam spent the rest of the time preening in front of the mirror. Sandra told Pam how she slapped Andy Mann's face when he had called her a slag. Sandra told how the extended nails had almost ripped his face off. Pam, now recovered from her ordeal, asked earnestly. "What did Duke say", Pam probed? "Oh, he knows me and Andy don't exactly see eye to eye", Sandra replied. She explained that Duke was aware of Andy Mann's feelings about her distinctive qualifications. She told Pam that she believed Andy Mann felt she threatened his position. The knock at the door signalled the arrival of dinner. Sandra opened the door but pointed where she wanted the waiter to leave the trolley. "Just leave it over there", Sandra said. Pam and Sandra sat down to eat. "The wine is good, you should try it", Sandra prompted. "Can I have something else instead, something soft", Pam asked? "I know you love to drink, why don't you want the wine", Sandra pressed? "I've given up drinking", Pam replied. "Since when", Sandra teased? "Since some weeks ago", Pam countered. As if to reinforce Sandra's suspicion, Pam pointed to her belly. They laughed together once again. Sandra asked the chef to bring Pam a non-alcoholic drink.

Neither Sandra nor Pam was ready for Duke's entry. The connecting door flew open and there he stood with the largest bouquet of flowers either had ever seen. "Flowers for Ms. Sandra Bogus", Duke chimed. He thrust the bouquet towards her. "Oh, Duke, they're lovely. Thank you", Sandra purred. He came over to her but hugged her tightly. It was as if he was trying to stop her from escaping. Pam felt awkward. "Shall I leave the room", she asked? Wrapped up in their self interests, neither Duke nor Sandra seemed to have heard her. Duke totally ignored Pam's existence. He pushed Sandra to the floor. Panting like a demented rapist, he started to display his lack of control. Sandra's deeply tanned skin may well have been the catalyst which had started it all. Duke kept stroking her face and commenting how the texture and colour of her skin excited him. They rolled about on the floor as if they were glued together. Pam thought it strange that Sandra did not discourage him. However, it was either the knock at the door or exhaustion that stopped Duke from his crazy few moments. The waiter handed Pam the drink but exited quickly. When Duke stood up, Pam noticed his wild eyes. Duke's face was flush and his podgy belly heaved up and down from the exertion. His crumpled suit did not befit the image Sandra had painted about her rich lover. He was a swarthy little man with no real personality. Pam could see his hair, normally held down with 'Petroleum Jelly' (Vaseline), now sticking out all over the place and made him look more like a *mad* ventriloquist dummy. As if to calm Duke down, Sandra quickly changed into a less revealing outfit. She introduced her friend. "Duke this is my best friend Pam", Sandra said. She pointed towards Pam but Duke just ignored her presence but carried on staring at Sandra as if he would attack her again. She too was aware how aroused Duke had become but there was nothing new about his behaviour. In fact, this was quite a normal reaction when he was in Sandra's presence. "That's enough Duke. I'm not in the mood now anyway. There is plenty of time later on", Sandra advised. Pam could hear the level of control in Sandra's voice. Duke did not seem like the nice boss whom Sandra had boasted about. Instead, he appeared as if he had no control over his lust for Sandra. Duke left just as suddenly as he'd arrived but still not acknowledging Sandra's friend. Pam was more embarrassed than Sandra. She was getting used to being Duke's *'exotic'* bit on the side. "Now you see why I can't let Ray go", Sandra teased. "Why is he so hot? Doesn't he have a wife", Pam asked? "Yes, but she's only as beautiful as *'the back of a bus'*", Sandra replied. Pam wanted to know more about Sandra and Duke's affair. "Do you let him *'paw'* you like that all the time", Pam asked? "Poor Duke, he's just very emotional. He hardly gets any attention at home", Sandra replied. Pam reminded Sandra that they needed to call Sam to take them to the hospital. She did. "How long before you get here Sam", Sandra asked? "An hour ma'am", he estimated. Pam took this opportunity to gossip a while longer. "Well girl, tell me how you got into modelling", Pam enquired? "It was Duke's idea", Sandra replied. "How are you going to manage two jobs", Pam asked? "Duke doesn't mind. "Seriously, I like to excite the crowd", she confessed. "Mind they don't get beyond control like Duke", Pam teased. They probed further into each other's life until Raymond became the main focus once again. "I won't be able to stay long at the hospital tonight because I've got to catch up on my beauty sleep. Duke arranged an early photo session for tomorrow morning and I need the rest", Sandra commented. "Don't you care about Raymond", Pam asked? "Sure, but the hospital is the best place for him Duke said", Sandra replied. "You seem to say those words without any feelings for the man you say you can't do without. Don't you think he's worth more than you're offering", Pam pressed. Her reaction hit a point about having a consideration for his current state. It made Sandra feel guilty. "All we can do is sit and wait", Sandra added. "And pray", Pam stressed. When Sam arrived, both Sandra and Pam were ready. "Your chauffeur is outside madam", the receptionist advised. "OK, we're on our way down", Sandra replied. In the foyer, some of the other guests were attracted to Sandra and again she was asked for more autographs. One man asked if he could have a photograph of her. "Not at the moment", Sandra replied. She continued to smile all the time while making her way towards the exit. She and Pam met Sam outside. "Right on time as usual", Sandra commented. "Yes ma'am", Sam replied. "Take us to the hospital Sam", Sandra ordered.

Inside the limo, Pam asked Sam how Miss 'D' was doing. "She's still very distraught and confused ma'am", Sam replied. "Poor woman", Pam said. Sandra reminded Sam about the arrangements for the photo session. "What time would you want me to pick you up Ms. Bogus", Sam asked? "How long will it take from the hotel to Grant Favours' place", Sandra asked? "About forty five minutes ma'am", Sam replied. "I'll be ready by eleven o'clock", Sandra hinted.

CHAPTER 28

The conversation had lulled by the time they arrived at the hospital. Sandra and Pam alighted from the limo. They walked through the narrow path that led to the ward where Raymond was admitted. Some of the patients were barely awake in bed awaiting their visitors while others, like Raymond, just lay there motionless. Sandra and Pam approached the bed where, the once fit, Raymond lay propped up but swathed in bandage. Sandra bent over him. She whispered. "Ray, it's Sandy. Can you hear me", Sandra queried? There was no sign of recognition in Raymond's staring eyes. "Pam, he doesn't even know we're here", Sandra exclaimed. Pam held Raymond's hand in hers. She too spoke to him. "Raymond, Raymond, listen to me. If you can hear me, squeeze my hand", Pam encouraged. She was surprised that he responded but she definitely felt him squeeze her hand. "Sandra he can hear", Pam said. Sandra gasped but held Raymond's other hand. "Oh Ray, if you can hear Sandy, squeeze my hand", Sandra pleaded. She could not honestly say that she felt a reaction. Sandra looked around her helplessly. A nurse on the ward was summoned. The nurse hurried over to Raymond's bedside. "Has Mr. Oddball shown any sign of recovery at all", Sandra enquired? "There has been no change since last night. Would you like to talk to the doctor", Nurse asked? "Yes", Sandra replied. The doctor, who came to see them, introduced himself as the Senior Consultant Neurologist, Mr Headley Skully. Having been told of Sandra's concern about Raymond's non-progress, he decided to explain the degree of injuries Raymond had suffered. "Would you come with me? I'd like to show you the x-rays", Mr Headley Skully said. Both Sandra and Pam followed him. The x-rays showed severe fractures to Raymond's skull and several broken ribs. "It is these areas of the skull that gives us cause for concern", Mr Headley Skully explained. He pointed to particular areas, known as the frontal and temporal lobes, with the end of his pen. The doctor further explained that, because Raymond had received heavy blows to these particular areas of his head, his chances of recovery would be slow, if at all. "I think it would only be fair for me to tell you that because of those injuries it is likely that Mr Oddball will probably loose parts of his memory. The brain itself is swollen and, if it continues to do so, he might become a *'vegetable'* ", Mr Headley Skully ended. His delivery was quite forthright but honest. It left no doubt as to the massive damage that had been done to an otherwise physiologically fit individual before the assault upon his person by that gang of cops. They had a premeditated *'stereo-typed'* image of individuals from the Tribe of Hawke. The ASPD schizophrenic official government neuro-profilers had meted out **_'just this'_** instead of *'justice'* to a typically perceived *'stereotypical'* image rather than assess what possible threat Raymond could possibly have been to such huge numbers of cops. He was only one individual against the huge number of cops in attendance, who had responded to the coded 'SOS' call from their colleague. After all, Raymond had been de-oriented by the pepper spray, handcuffed and searched before the 'back-up' 'gang' had arrived. Their behavioural approach was no different to that of the Post/Zip Code 'street' 'gangs' in Spaceville, comparably. Even after the cops' arrival, Raymond had been tazered on more than one occasion but was in no position to pose a 'threat' to any of the cops. When Mr Headley Skully had finished explaining the bare facts about Raymond's possible quality of recovery, both Sandra and Pam gasped. Because Sandra perceived that she might never again hope to be sexually stimulated or satisfied to the same degree as she had experienced before with Raymond, her gasp was one of sheer exasperation, while Pam perceived the worse case scenario for their child. The last thing she wanted was for their child not to have a father. The doctor saw how the news had impacted the two women. He reminded them that he and the staff would take good care of Raymond. "We have a wealth of dedicated specialist staff looking after him. We do this routinely, especially in the Intensive Care Unit", Mr Headley Skully reassured. Both Sandra and Pam stood dumbfounded but wore expressions of grief and despair. The Senior Consultant Neurologist, Mr Headley Skully, could tell them no more. He was summoned by the noise coming from his bleeper. Turning away from the two women, the doctor spoke into his cell phone. Pam and Sandra saw him hurrying towards the exit. They walked back to see Raymond again before leaving. Pam and Sandra stood helplessly over him staring down in hope. Sandra bent over but kissed Raymond on that part of his face that was exposed. Pam held his hand. "See you Raymond. I hope you can hear me", she said. Again, Pam felt the feeble squeeze acknowledging that Raymond has chosen to respond. This time Pam did not tell Sandra. Looking back occasionally over their shoulders, the women walked away from the bed but headed for the exit. The walk back through the narrow path brought them back to the Casualty area where Sam was waiting. "Where to ma'am", Sam asked? "Take Miss Labrishè home, then take me to the Hotel Welcome", Sandra instructed. Sam heard the glum tone of her voice. Sandra spoke further with Pam. "Do you promise to see Ray every day", she queried? "Oh yes Sandra, I promise I'll see him every day", Pam assured. Sam interrupted their conversation but asked Pam to confirm the route which she wanted him to take. Pam explained to Sam where she wanted him to go. She asked him to confirm that he knew the particular Estate. "Is it the Estate on the right near the petrol station Miss Labrishè", Sam enquired? Pam confirmed his reference meant the Elementary Estate to which she referred. "If Raymond needs anything, anything, just call me", Sandra reiterated. "Ok", Pam confirmed. They travelled swiftly through the light traffic.

Sam indicated to turn into the Estate. While waiting to turn, he could see a group of teenage youths gathered on the road inside the Elementary Estate. Sandra and Pam saw them too. "Why don't they find something to do", Sandra commented. Her voice sounded fearful. "Are you afraid", Pam asked? Sam turned into the Estate entrance slowly. He had to keep his speed low because of the 'humps' in the road and the straggling group of youngsters, who seemed not be in a hurry. Sam was patient but Sandra was showing great impatience with the youngsters. She gave Sam particular instructions. "Blow the horn Sam, keep blowing it until they move", Sandra ordered.

Pam intervened. She pleaded with Sam not to. He showed a lot of patience and skill as he weaved his way through them. Some of the youths crowded the limo when it stopped but peered through the window to see who was inside. Two of the youths had friendly bets about the mystery person inside. They started to argue in the way they were culturally accustomed. Like the green humanoid robotron's culture into which she had been *'programmed'* and *'conditioned'*, Sandra *'profiling'* mindset was to perceive the youths' *'behaviour'* to be *'threatening'*. "They seem hostile. Is it safe to come out of the car", Sandra asked? Frustrated with Sandra's inference about the young people, Pam challenged her perception of the young people's behaviour. She had more knowledge of young people and was more *'young people friendly'* than Sandra. Pam had worked with young people, when she was a social worker. "They are just *'mouthing'* each other Sandra. It's our custom. Don't pretend you don't know", Pam criticised. Sandra did *'know'* but those young *"idlers"* were whom her mother, Dian, had often referred to as being "worthless". She too was a typical *'profiler'* of *'stereo-type'* images. The youths spoke loud and were very dramatic in their actions, always. Pam assured Sandra that the youngsters were boisterous but not a threat. Being humbled by Pam, Sandra then asked Sam to open the door. There was music blasting out from the party on the fourth floor. A lot more people gathered near the entrance door of the block. Some were waiting for the opportunity to get into the building. Although Sandra was quite scared, she wanted the youths to see that she was a friend of one of their residents on the Estate. "I'll come in with you Pam", Sandra offered. Both she and Pam climbed from the limo but walked towards the entrance door. Some of the youths started to approach them. Sandra became paranoid but viewed them suspiciously. "Aren't you scared Pam", she asked? "No, not really, I do my thing and they do theirs", Pam replied. "How are you Miss Labrishè", one Boy asked? "Fine Ricky", Pam replied. Some wolf whistles made Sandra even more nervous but as she looked round a loud voice shouted. "There she is. That's super model Sandra Bogus", the loud voice exclaimed. More whistles, loud cheers and comments made Sandra smile with relief. She waved to them then proceeded to accompany Pam in through the door. "I wouldn't have come out if I was on my own", Sandra commented. "The youths won't bother you. They're just being curious. These boys don't see a limo on this Estate every day. It is quite a novel experience for them. Seeing you might just give some of them a boost", Pam advised. Outside, Sam was struggling to win a conversation with some of the local youths. One of them wanted to bet him that his secondhand car could perform better than the limo. "I'll race you on the dual carriageway", the youth challenged. Sam roared with laughter as he tried to explain mechanical facts to the youths. Some of the youths' friends tried to pressure Sam into accepting the bet but he laughingly declined. One of them asked Sam if he could get him a job. "I would if I could but I can't", Sam answered. They teased Sam for awhile but stood aside as Sandra approached. They watched Sam open the door for her as she got in then they cheered again. Sandra smiled and waved at them from the window. "Take me home Sam, Hotel Welcome", Sandra ordered. The cheering got louder as the limo turned but headed for the exit.

Inside, the flat Pam pulled out the envelope from her handbag and with shaking hands read it again. How could she suppress this news and for how long? "Oh Raymond, I wish you were here with me now", Pam exclaimed. She read the note aloud this time. "Landed in Spaceville dis mawning. Come tuh si yuh. Yuh neighbour sey yuh gawn fi visit smady ah di hospital. Mi ah leve yuh dis note. Mi ah stay at Aunt Rose place. Phn yuh lata. Yuh sista", Carmen. Pam left her flat but walked the short distance down the hallway to George's flat. She rang the bell. George's wife, a middle-aged woman, known locally as Antie Merkle, opened the door. "Cum in Pam. Yuh get di note", Antie Merkle asked? "Yes, how did you know where to find me", Pam asked? "George cum ah di hospital but yuh did leve aredy. Im phn fram di hospital fi sey dem tel im dat yuh gawn wid yuh model fren, di one ina di newspapers. George tel dem sey it waz a *'life or deth'* situation. Dem giv im di address weh yuh fren lef wid dem. Yuh noah George, der isn't anyting im wudn't duh fi yuh. I tink im fancy yuh", Antie Merkle said. She and Pam laughed loudly at the teasing. She continued to brief Pam. "I tel im dat im cud leave it unda yuh door but im insis im hafe get it 2 yuh. Im drive al di way out 2 di Welcome Hotel I tink dem cal it", Antie Merkle explained. She always said things the wrong way round. "Hotel Welcome, Antie", Pam corrected. Antie Merkle wasn't really Pam's biological aunty but she addressed her that way to show *'cultural respect'*. Now Pam understood better how the note got to the hotel. "Suh how is di sick? Is it dat young man who bin comin regular", Antie Merkle enquired? Pam didn't really want to discuss Raymond with her because she knew Antie Merkle loved to gossip. "You'll like Carmen, Pam deflected. "She seem 2 be a lively girl", Antie Merkle observed: "Well, thank you and George for getting the note to me", Pam commented. As she exited from Antie Merkle's flat, Pam commented further. "Tell George I'll buy him a drink when I get my next benefit payment", Pam said. She made her way quickly towards her flat. Inside, Pam started to notice how much she was missing Raymond. She was just getting used to having him around. Pam turned on the stereo but started to select some CDs she and Raymond used to play together. The songs brought back a lot of happy recent memories. Pam recalled the times when Raymond and her danced to these songs. All of those times brought Raymond's presence into the room. When the phone rang, Pam picked it up quickly as if expecting bad news. "Mi finally get hold ah yuh" Carmen said. Pam was truly excited to hear her sister's voice. "Carmen ah yuh", Pam queried? The two exchanged a lot of *'chit-chat'* for a while then Carmen explained about her earlier visit and meeting Pam's nice neighbours. She confirmed she had received the note. "How long is your vacation", Pam asked? "Six months sista, six long months", Carmen replied. "When are you visiting me", Pam asked? "Sooner dan yuh tink", Carmen replied. The phone was disconnected. Pam seemed pleasantly puzzled for awhile. She remained in a trance-like state for some moments but happily recalling those wonderful times growing up with her sister Carmen in the far off exotic island. Then Pam recalled how the family always supported each other, especially through so many hard times. The entrance buzzer distracted Pam's momentary reminiscing. She was not expecting anyone at that time of night. Pam pressed the button but asked cautiously. "Who is it", Pam asked? "Is me Carmen, I'm outside. Open di door", she instructed. Pam hurried to press the release button. She and her sister, Carmen, met in the hallway. They hugged endearingly. Displaying dramatic scenes of happiness, they separated then hugged again. Now they held each other at arms' length away but asked the same question of the other, simultaneously. "Is really you", Pam asked? "Yes is me. Is really yuh", Carmen asked? It was quite sometime after this emotional meeting of sisters took place before Pam acknowledged the young man with the cell phone and car keys in his hands. He stood patiently in the background as if he was invisible. Carmen apologized to him but introduced him to her sister. "Meet Natty Hawke, ah gud fren ah mine and personal chauffeur", Carmen said. Natty Hawke made a fist but touched his chest and nodded to Pam. "Greetings", Natty Hawke said. Pam tried to copy the *'greetings'* but she got it *'slightly'* wrong. They all laughed at Pam's imitation of Natty Hawke's style of greeting. Once they got indoors, they sat down and began to recall the earlier days and events that surrounded Pam and Carmen's younger life. "So how is Mommy", Pam asked? Pam and Carmen had the same biological father but not the same biological mother. Carmen lives with but refers to Pam's mother as Auntie Jean on the far off exotic island. "Auntie Jean is fine", she replied. "What about my daughter? How is she", Carmen enquired? "Darsna is fine. Mi niece is growing fast. She waan yuh fi cum visit har", Carmen reported. The two sisters entered into their focused zone but Natty Hawke didn't mind being left out of the conversation. He was simply admiring the level of love among the two sisters. Occasionally, the sisters would seize an opportunity to engage in conversation with Natty Hawke. "Hawke, yuh noh how mi feel suh guilty dat wi ah ignore yuh. Yuh noh nuttn cudnt guh suh", Carmen apologized. Natty Hawke just remained silent but smiled to acknowledge Carmen's reassurance. Pam could see that Natty Hawke and Carmen liked each other. They kept giving each other that *'look'* which described more than fondness. Pam offered them some 'Sour Sop' juice. Carmen seemed curious that this tropical fruit was available in Spaceville. "Unnu get 'sour sop' ova yah", Carmen asked? "Yes, in the tin", Pam replied. Her remark was a cynical one. Natty Hawke added his measure of sarcasm too. "Is not the same doah", Natty Hawke hissed. They chatted for more than an hour before Natty Hawke left. The two sisters chatted until 04:00 hours. Pam told Carmen about her and Raymond's affair. She explained how it started. It was not just a *'love at first sight'* thing but she confessed that he had made a good impression upon her. Pam told Carmen that she was in a *'funny'* situation. She confided that she and Sandra were good enough friends. Pam said she valued the *'friendship'* as priority to Raymond's appeal to her but that she knew that Sandra was cheating on Raymond. She explained every detail to Carmen. Pam said that it was just a matter of time before Sandra and Raymond would have split up. "Sandra noah wat hapenin", Carmen asked? "No, not yet", Pam replied. "So, wat if di baby look like im daddy", Carmen queried? Her brows were furrowed and the look upon her face bore many more salient questions. Pam did not reply. "Sista yuh mus noah wat yuh doin, but it sound like truble 2 mi', Carmen advised. "Let us get some sleep. We have a long day ahead", Pam explained. They stayed silent till they wandered off into deep restful sleep.

At 10:00 hours, Carmen was the first to awaken. She woke Pam. They showered, dressed, baked a corn meal pudding, prepared a meal and ate before calling the minicab. Pam instructed the driver to take them to the Community General Hospital. When they were going past the police station Pam showed Carmen where she thought Raymond received his injuries. "That was the place where Raymond was beaten", Pam implied. The white Mixed DNA Rainbow Tribe cab driver heard everything that was said. "They stopped one of our drivers the other night and beat him too. He's from your tribe", the driver commented. Carmen was far different to Pam. She was a woman of action. "I think people should sue them", Carmen suggested. The minicab driver began to laugh. "You can never win. It's just politics, just politics", the driver explained. They seemed to be approaching the Community General Hospital from a different route to the one Pam was used to. "Do you know the way to the hospital", Pam asked? "Yes, I know where it is", the driver replied. "You should have turned off this road a long time ago", Pam said. "Passengers, you always think you know more than the driver", he snapped. "Stop the car", Pam ordered. He pulled up near the curb. "Look, I don't know if you are a new driver but you are taking the long way round", Pam said. She was fuming at the cheat. Pam expressed her concern about the driver's intention. Carmen's cultural upbringing meant that there was no need for subtlety when someone was cheating. She only knew one way to say it and she did. "Tief, bax di bwai", Carmen threatened. She cursed him. Carmen called him some names he didn't even understand. The driver could see that Carmen would fight him if he didn't get back on the right route. He did a u-turn but headed for the hospital. Carmen kept cursing him all the way, until he pulled up in front of the Casualty Area. "How much is it", Pam asked? He was tempted to put on the extra mileage but one look at Carmen's face made him change his mind. The driver told the correct amount. "It's on account and don't forget to collect me in three hours", Pam instructed. They entered the Intensive Care Unit through the narrow path. Pam and Carmen saw some staff standing around Raymond's bed. Pam's heart skipped many beats. She wondered what they might be concerned bout. "Hello Raymond, can you hear me", the doctor asked? Pam's heart jumped suddenly. She walked hurriedly over to the bed. "What's wrong with him", Pam asked? "We think he can understand us", the doctor replied. Pam peered at Raymond's eyes through the bandage. She thought she saw them flicker. Pam blinked a few times. She was quite sure it wasn't an illusion. Pam held Raymond's hand. "Hello Raymond, this is Pam. Do you recognize me", she asked? She felt Raymond's feeble grip. It was the same as she had felt the day before. The staff could see by her reaction that Raymond recognized her. "We'll be back in a while", the doctor said. The rest of the staff followed him away from the bedside. Pam smiled at Raymond. "Well done Raymond, well done", she praised. Pam couldn't see his lips under the bandage but she knew he was smiling. Carmen looked on in silence. She was admiring her sister's dedication and support to Raymond. "This is my sister Carmen. She'll be spending six months with us", she explained. Carmen looked at the drips, monitors and the breathing apparatus attached to Raymond but wondered if he really stood a chance to recover. "Im cawn brede pon im own", Carmen asked? "I don't know", Pam replied. "Sum peeple nuh noh how lucky dem is", Carmen commented.

CHAPTER 29

P am held Raymond's hand again but asked him if he was hungry. It was a nice easy code that Pam and Raymond had worked out. One squeeze denoted 'yes' and two for 'no'. He squeezed her hand only once. Pam got up from his bedside but went towards the general office area. Carmen could see from her body language that her sister was arguing with the nurse. She and Pam walked back together towards the bedside. There, the nurse made some adjustment to the 'flow valve' on one of the drips. Pam wanted to know why she had made the adjustment. "This is liquid food in this drip. The valve to regulate the flow can only be adjusted according to hospital procedure in regards to how rapidly it flows", the nurse explained. Carmen was impressed but Pam was not. As soon as the nurse left the bedside, Pam told her sister that she was going to query everything even if the staff thought she was a nuisance. They sat at the bedside for about three hours watching over Raymond. Pam had to leave because the minicab was due to arrive soon. She and her sister said goodbye to Raymond. Carmen and Pam exited through the same narrow path which led to the Casualty Area. There, they found the driver waiting. He drove the route that Pam directed. As Carmen and Pam got near to the police station, Pam asked the driver to stop. "I've got to go in there", she explained.

Inside, she asked the green humanoid robotron cop sitting nearest the Reception Area whether he could tell her about Mr. Oddball's car. He stretched out his legs, ignored her but pretended to be reading a book. "Yuh def. Yuh nuh er smady ah talk tuh yuh", Carmen demanded? Because of Carmen's loud questioning of the cop sitting at the nearest desk to Reception, both the green humanoid robotron female and male Sergeants looked out from around the partition further in the open plan designed office. "Is there a problem", the female Sergeant asked? Pam explained about the offending cop but the female Sergeant ignored her. She went back behind the partition. Both Carmen and Pam stood at the Reception Desk for quite sometime until Carmen struck again. This time she swore even more than she did in the cab. The offending cop was suddenly on duty again. He was swearing back at them but gave them a lot of other verbal abuse. "I'm cautioning you that if you swear again you'll be arrested", the cop closer to the Reception Desk said. Carmen was even more incensed but she didn't want to be arrested. The cop turned his attention to Pam. He addressed her specifically. "What do you want", the cop enquired? Pam asked him about Raymond's car. "Who are you, his mistress? That other bird is his woman, isn't she", the cop jeered. "Look, I have full permission from Ms. Bogus to make this enquiry", Pam countered. The cop scratched his head roughly before responding. "I don't know anything about the car. It weren't me that arrested him", the cop stated. "Wel whey di cop dat arrest im", Carmen enquired? "Hey you, stay out of it. This is between me and his missus", the cop inferred. He pointed towards Pam to establish to whom he was referring. She raised her voice as well, indicating that she too was loosing patience with him. "Now just calm down and tell me again", the cop said. Pam went over it once more. The cop walked over to the partition but pretended to speak to the Sergeants. Pam and Carmen waited patiently for at least another hour before another cop, one from the Tribe of Hawke, came over to them. He wanted Pam to go over the story yet again but this time she snapped. "I'm not repeating it all over again. What do you take me for", Pam asked? The second cop laughed. He shrugged his shoulders. "It's up to you", the cop from the Tribe of Hawke stated. Carmen led her sister away from further humiliation. "Cum on Pam. It's no use. Dey playing ah game. Wi not getin anywhere", Carmen advised. Both sisters exited the station but headed for the minicab. The driver made sure he told them how much extra it would cost for *'waiting time'*. Neither Pam nor Carmen cared about what he was saying. She was ready to go through all that had happened in the police station again but Pam indicated that she didn't want the driver to know her business. "Lovely evening", the driver prompted. He was trying to engage in conversation with Pam and Carmen. They remained silent for the rest of the journey home. Arriving outside the Estate where Pam lived, she saw her neighbour, George. He said hello to the minicab driver. "Ah hope yuh not overcharging mi family", George warned? "Now, would I do that George? Would I George", the driver retorted? He laughed but drove off. George opened the entrance door. He bowed but motioned for Pam and Carmen to enter. "Ladies first", George said. In the hallway, he asked them if they were coming to see Antie Merkel. Pam declined. "Not tonight George, wi got a few tings fi sort out", Pam said. "Mi undastan", George said. Pam and Carmen said goodbye but closed the door. Inside, they reflected about the varied happenings of the day. Pam was still angry at the crude behaviour of the cops at the station. She and her sister had been humiliated but could do nothing about the treatment they had received. "Wat I doan undastan is how dem seniors mek dem get weh wid it", Carmen queried? The landline phone rang. Carmen answered. She had a similar tone of voice to her sister Pam. "How is my man", Sandra enquired? "Who dis", Camen asked? Sandra thought Pam was fooling around. She began to poke fun at her. "You've seen my man today, didn't you", Sandra enquired? "Look woman, mi nuh noah who yuh tink yuh is? Wat mek yuh ah phn dis house acusing peeple. If yuh man is er is cause im doan fine yuh attractive anymore an im wanna be wid me", Carmen said. "Hey Pam, lighten up. It's me, your friend Sandra, remember me", she asked? The surprise in her voice alerted Carmen that she was offending Pam's friend. "Mi sary, yuh waan talk tuh Pam. Ol awn mi wi get har fi yuh", Carmen apologised. Pam only heard her sister's end of the conversation but she could tell it was Sandra on the other end of the phone. She delighted that the misunderstanding had taken place because Pam knew the day would come when she might have to talk to Sandra like that. "Hello, this is Pam", she assured. "Who the hell was that? She nearly bit my head off. Has she got a guilt complex", Sandra queried? "You just met my sister, Carmen. I told you she looks like me but she has a quicker temper", Pam explained. "Why didn't you tell me she was coming over", Sandra asked? "I only found out when we were at the Hotel Welcome together. Remember the note I received? Carmen's date of arrival was what the note was all about", Pam explained. "Call yourself a friend, do you", Sandra teased? Pam remained silent. "You could have told me then", Sandra pressed? "OK Sandra, if you say so", Pam interrupted. "How is my Ray", Sandra asked? "He's progressing slowly", Pam replied. "Can he talk yet" Sandra asked? "No", Pam said. "When you go to see him again give him my love", Sandra said. Pam thought that might make Raymond more ill but she didn't say that to Sandra. "I will", Pam replied. She looked skywards as if seeking forgiveness for her hypocrisy. The entrance buzzer sounded. Pam signalled for Carmen to answer the intercom but she didn't seem to understand how to operate it. "Hold on Sandra, there is someone at the door", Pam explained. "Who is it", she asked? "Natty Hawke and Aunt Rose", Natty Hawke replied. Pam pressed the release button but met them in the hallway. Carmen smiled at Natty Hawke while Pam hugged Aunt Rose. "Come in, come in", Pam said. Carmen sat beside Natty Hawke while Aunt Rose sat close to Pam. They were deep in conversation when Pam realized she had left Sandra hanging on the phone. Carmen was closest to the phone so Pam told her to tell Sandra she'd ring her back later. Carmen and Natty Hawke were looking deeply at each other releasing that body language which suggested they wanted to be alone. He put his arm around her shoulder but pulled her towards him. "Dem in love", Aunt Rose told Pam. She used her mouth to indicate the young couple. "Is about time she found someone nice", Pam added. "Wen yuh two getin married", Aunt Rose asked? "We nuh believe in dat Aunt Rose", Natty Hawke replied. "Wat yuh believe in", Aunt Rose pressed? She proceeded to lecture young Natty Hawke and her niece Carmen on the merits of marraige. "Look pon me and mi husband. Wi married fi forty eight years now and still love each other di same as di first day wi meet", Aunt Rose expressed. "Times change Aunt Rose, nowadays, is nuh longer ah disgrace fi jus live 2geder. One time dem use fi tell wi sey is a *'sin'* fi live 2geder widout marriage. 2day everyone proud ah dem *"love child"*. Even rich people who not married hav *'love children'*", Natty Hawke argued. Pam laughed but did not comment. Carmen listened to the banter going to and fro then commented. "Aunt Rose, statistic sey more peeple getin divorced dan getting married nowadays. How yuh explain dat", Carmen queried? Aunt Rose knew that no amount of lecture would divert Natty Hawke and Carmen from what they intended but she had to show her dislike of statistics. "Blasted statistics, it doan mean anyting, dem invent dat fi confuse yuh brain", Aunt Rose said. They all laughed together heartily. Pam was disappointed that Raymond was not present to enjoy the cultural banter which he longed for, seemingly. Living with Sandra had literally erased his cultural roots from his everday living, somewhat. Once Raymond was indoors with Sandra, he programmed himself to adopt the type of *'culture'* which Sandra accepted as her own. Raymond's urge for sharing in the richness of his parents' *'traditional culture'* was being compromised. This he sacrificed in order to satisfy his *'superlative urge'* and to quench his lust for his *'Exotic Mona Lisa'*. Such was the intensity of lust for the stunning physically shapely and facially beautiful Sandra Bogus. Pam brought some drinks and some cornmeal pudding that Carmen had made earlier. "Mmmm, dis is wat I cal real cornmeal pudding. Ah can taste di coconut milk ina it", Natty Hawke praised. Carmen smiled. "It mus taste nice. "Ah me mek it", she explained. "Is important fi hav ah woman who can cook", Aunt Rose chimed. "A wife perhaps", Natty Hawke teased. They laughed again heartily. When Natty Hawke and Aunt Rose were ready to leave, Pam and Aunt Rose hugged each other while Natty Hawke embraced Carmen lovingly. "Is gud 2 si yuh. Tek care Aunt Rose", Pam said. Carmen and Pam escorted Aunt Rose and Natty Hawke to the vehicle. They said their goodbyes. Natty Hawke opened the door of the 13years old green Transporter in the dimly lit car park. The front spoiler coupled with the broad wheels enhanced the sporty features of the car. Its tinted windows contrasted the streaks of red and gold flashes along the sides and on the bonnet. As they drove away, Pam and Carmen could hear the deep sound of a blown exhaust. In the distance, the car backfired but Carmen thought it was something else. "Gunshot", Carmen exclaimed. "Yuh tink is *'home'* yuh dey", Pam asked? The explosive sounds were coming from Natty Hawke's Transporter.

Pam remembered that she had to return Sandra's call. She dialled the number that she retrieved from the landline phone. The number rang for a while before there was an answer. "Hotel Welcome", the voice said. "Ms. Bogus please", Pam replied. "Ms. Bogus doesn't want to be disturbed at the moment unless it's urgent", the receptionist replied. "I must talk to her. Tell her it's her friend, Miss Labrishé", Pam instructed. It took a while before Sandra answered the phone. Pam heard her crying. "Pam this is not a good time to talk to me right now", Sandra sobbed. Pam thought it was bad news about Raymond. "What happened to Raymond", she asked? "It's not Raymond Pam. It's Duke. He passed out earlier and I don't know what to do", Sandra wailed. "What happened", Pam asked? "No time to explain. I'm too desperate for good advice", Sandra replied. "Get a doctor. I'll ring off now but don't forget to let me know what happened", Pam encouraged. She hung up. Sandra's predicament presented her with a huge problem. First, she had to get a doctor then she had to inform Duke's next of kin. This was a very testing time for the popular Super Model. If Duke died, the Media would be tempted to write a story about her, Sandra thought. Though some seemed not fussed about her friendship with Duke, she knew that some of his colleagues only tolerated her. Grant Favours had warned her to get a Press Agent to handle that side of things but Sandra was a stubborn individual. She wanted to handle that side of things for herself. Once she had dug her heels in, it would take a great deal of convincing for Sandra to change her mind. Now the urgency to get an Agent was also part of her anxiety. Sandra knew that questions would be asked as soon as the story about Duke got through the grapevine. In the course of her own career, Sandra had learnt of scenarios which were similar to hers. She had also read many case histories in the magazines and other Media News that she digested on a daily basis. Sandra remembered that one of Duke's rivals in the Business, Harold Gawky, had it in for Duke. Harold Gawky was sore with Duke when he refused to help him slander a particular PM. He had never forgiven Duke for what Harold called disloyalty. Not only was Sandra intimidated by Harold Gawky but also feared his friends too. They were known as the sharks in the business. Sandra feared that, without Duke and his clout, her career would be ruined. She tried to shake the haunting premonition from her head but concentrate on her more immediate problem. Getting Duke a doctor was to prove very difficult for Sandra. She had never spoken to him about his doctor. Sandra didn't even know the name of Duke's doctor. She puzzled for a few moments then decided to ring the Reception Desk. "Can you get a doctor up to Mr. Stagg's room", Sandra implored? The receptionist was stunned by the request. It was a very unusual one. "Just a moment madam", the receptionist replied. Sandra waited on the line for the receptionist to come back to her. She glanced at Duke then looked away quickly. "Is madam still there", the receptionist asked? "Yes", Sandra replied. The brown Mixed DNA Rainbow Tribe manager of the Hotel wants to talk to you", the receptionist advised. He handed the phone to the manager. "Let me speak to Mr. Stagg", the manager demanded. "He can't come to the phone", Sandra replied. "Well, take the phone to him then", the manager barked. He reminded Sandra of the Hotel's reputation though she didn't understand what that had to do with her request for a doctor. Sandra couldn't fathom what would make the manager say what he did. She soon learnt the meaning behind the cynical remark. "I don't want to attract an ambulance at the front of the Hotel", they manager warned. "Well, what if there's no choice", Sandra asked? "It's not the done thing. We don't want to alarm the rest of our guests. They are all prestigious clientele but have reputations to protect", the manager fired. Sandra fidgeted with the flex attached to the phone then she boldly retorted to the manager's slight. "If Mr. Stagg dies in your Hotel, you will have to answer to the Media and not me", Sandra implied. Her comment shook the manager. He was truly angry now. The manager knew who she was but didn't care for Sandra to threaten his position. "Don't you talk to me like that", the manager ranted. He aborted the call abruptly. It wasn't long before Sandra heard the rapid knocking at the door. She walked quickly over towards it then stopped. "Who is it", Sandra asked? "Open the door", the voice on the outside of the door boomed. Sandra recognized the tone of the arrogant manager. It was unmistakable. She hesitated then turned the handle but peered round the door. Two men stood in the doorway.

One was the manager and the other said he was a doctor. She let them into the Suite. They made their way over to where Duke was laying on the floor of the Suite. The green humanoid robotron doctor, from the Tribe of Babylon, examined him. Sandra was embarrassed because Duke was still naked. His podgy belly hardly moved and his eyes stared wildly, looking into oblivion. "Is he dead doctor", Sandra asked? The doctor ignored her question but asked one of his own. "How long ago did you say he passed out", the doctor asked? His features were grim. It reflected his behaviour. Sandra was confused because she had not noted the time. "I don't know", Sandra replied. "You were with him, weren't you", the doctor sneered? "Yes . . . but . . ?", Sandra stuttered. The doctor looked directly at the manager. "Never mind, we'll have to get him off to the hospital", the doctor decided. Sandra was pleased to hear that Duke would get to the hospital but she was not prepared for the doctor's next comment. "You're not his next of kin, are you", the doctor asked? His tone was cryptic and his manner abhorrent. He dropped his biggest bombshell. "I know Mrs Stagg quite well. She's a decent woman. Does she know you're with Mr. Stagg", the doctor insinuated? This revelation made Sandra shudder. She felt a chill pass through her body but curled up into the embryonic position on the enormous water bed. The doctor staggered Sandra with another of his remarks. "I don't suppose you and Mrs Stagg are friends, are you", the doctor taunted? His cynical remarks were measured but effective. As if one-upmanship had to be achieved, the doctor delivered yet another blow. Both the manager and the doctor looked scornfully at Sandra but it was the doctor, who wagged his finger at her, as if he was scolding a child. "Have you met Mrs. Stagg's children", the doctor asked? That such abuse could take place without redress made Sandra feel enraged. She did not reply. Feeling totally numb from the embarrassment and humiliated by the strange experience, Sandra was aware of angry feelings within her that were coming to the surface. She realized too that her affair with Duke would not be as smooth as she had first thought. The doctor summoned the ambulance. He and the manager stayed in the Suite. There was a brief wall of silence then the manager used his head to signal the doctor to come over to the other side of the Suite. They had a long whispered conversation. Sandra was aware that she was the main focus of the whispered conversation. The manager and the doctor both took turns to point or indicate with extreme jerking of heads in her direction. At times, the manager giggled while he looked at her. Sandra ignored them but went over to where Duke was laying. She lifted his head but placed it on a pillow then Sandra covered Duke with the huge duvet. "A bit late for that now, isn't it", the doctor commented. He took every opportunity to have a pop at Sandra. She was tired of the caustic comments but this time, she reacted. "Duke chose me. Have you got a problem with that", Sandra asked? The doctor became even more critically spiteful. His reply catapulted but registered even more venom. Turning directly to Sandra, he expressed his innermost feelings. "I don't know why Duke would want to waste his time with your *'type'* when he could easily wave his hands and be surrounded by a crowd of beautiful bevvys from his own tribe", the doctor criticised. The degree of scorn was apparent. Sandra had endured the one-sided jibes for long enough. She could not hold back any longer. "Duke loves me and he won't be pleased when I tell him what you said", Sandra warned. "If he makes it", doctor implied. There was a knock at the door. It signalled the arrival of the ambulance staff. "Hold on while I put his clothes on", Sandra said. She hurriedly dressed Duke. After the green humanoid robotron ambulance staff entered the Suite, Sandra made an announcement. "As Duke's Official Public Relations

Officer, I'm asking on his behalf for discretion. There will be no news to the Press about this incident nor will there be any information concerning his whereabouts", Sandra warned. She looked quite serious and her voice had taken on an officious tone. The manager started to giggle again but the doctor nudged him but whispered some advice into his ear. The doctor could not resist firing one last insult at Sandra. "Who's going to inform his wife", he asked? The ambulance staff looked at Duke and then Sandra. "Dirty bastard", the ambulance staff member mumbled. Sandra heard the comment but was unsure whether it was meant for her or Duke. So as not to alert the other guests, Duke was carried to the ambulance via the Service lift discreetly, apparently. Sandra tried to go into the Service lift with Duke but one of the ambulance staff told her that there was "not enough room" for her to fit in. She strode hurriedly towards the regular lifts. All three lifts on one side were on upper floors but the lifts on the other side were on the basement floor. Sandra pressed all of the buttons but waited anxiously. "Come on, come on", she mumbled. Sandra was becoming more impatient. She paced one way then another until she heard the chime when one of the lifts finally arrived. It was on the other side of the hallway. Sandra ran over towards it then jumped back as a young couple, inebriated by booze, staggered from the lift. They swayed but stumbled forward. The man had a heavy accent. He opened his mouth but made a mumbled sound. The smell from his breath told Sandra that he'd been vomiting. She shielded her nose from the putrid stench. Sandra was not sure if the booze and the vomiting were the only cause of the man's offensive breath. She tried to go past the man and his partner but they ended up doing the *'excuse me'* dance. Each got in the other's way every time they moved. "What floor is this", the woman asked? Her speech was heavily slurred too. Sandra did not immediately understand what the woman was trying to say. She wasn't in a patient mood anyway. Sandra was truly concerned about Duke. Her impatience with the couple was implied in the cynical question she asked them. "Going down", Sandra asked? She strode towards the lift. The couple seemed to be undecided what they wanted to do. She kept her eyes on the couple but stepped backwards into the lift. "Are you coming in", Sandra asked? The couple talked slowly and at times walked in a direction towards the lift then away from it again, as if it was a game. "That's it", Sandra exclaimed. She pressed the button that read 'Ground Floor'. She smelt the putrid vomit in the lift. When she looked round, Sandra saw the mess that the drunks had left on the side and floor of the lift. The contents of their stomachs lay on top of the carpet. Sandra tried not to breath but that was a difficult task. It seemed to take a long time for the lift to reach the ground floor. As a last resort, Sandra tried pinching her nose to block the sickly smell but she found that task impossible because of her extended nails. Finally, the lift stopped and the doors opened. Sandra exited from it. Her long slim legs carried her gracefully even though she was walking hurriedly. Outside, she asked the door attendant to get Sam's attention. He noticed Sandra standing just outside the entrance of the Hotel. Sam drove the limo over to where she was standing. Sandra was in a hurry. She did not wait for Sam to open the door for her. Sandra let herself into the limo. She ordered Sam to follow the ambulance. He noticed the grim look on Sandra's face. "Is Mr. Stagg dead Ms. Bogus", Sam asked? "No Sam, at least I don't think so", Sandra replied. "Play me some of that jazz music Sam", she ordered. The ambulance had already left the Hotel. Its siren sounded far away. Sam turned right outside the gate but accelerated quickly away from the Hotel. The limo glided through the light traffic until Sam could see the ambulance ahead of him. It intermingled in an out of the traffic and so did the limo. Sandra pressed Sam to go even faster. "Keep up with the ambulance Sam", she ordered. Sam was a very advanced driver. He managed to keep the ambulance in his sight. Sandra was thinking aloud. She was murmuring while trying to work out how she could get the bad news about Duke to his wife. Sam would know, Sandra thought. After all, he used to be Duke's chauffeur in the past. "Sam, you do know where Mr. Stagg lives, don't you", Sandra enquired? "Yes ma'am", Sam replied. "You will have to go to his house and tell his wife what happened", Sandra instructed. "I don't know what happened but I'd be prepared to tell her that he is in the hospital Ms. Bogus", Sam corrected.

CHAPTER 30

There was the odd build-up of traffic here and there but generally both the ambulance and the limo arrived at the Poshborough University Teaching Hospital, in pretty quick time. At the hospital, Sandra had seen the same green humanoid robotron senior consultant when visiting Raymond at the Community General Hospital, in Ghettoville, Lower Ghettoborough. He extended his hand. "Hello Ms. Bogus we meet again", the senior consultant said. Sandra shook his hand politely. "I'm here to see Mr. Stagg, my boss", Sandra explained. "Well, that's not the rumor round here. Nudge, nudge, wink, wink, my lips are sealed", he stated. The senior consultant smiled but squeezed Sandra's hand firmly as if to indicate they had an agreement. She was a bit confused as to what he meant by his words and strange behaviour. Sandra soon learnt how much he knew about her. "I know all about you. In fact, the doctor, who accompanied Mr. Stagg from the Hotel, is a colleague of mine. He has kept me up to date about what happened in the Hotel Suite", the senior consultant confirmed. Sandra wanted the earth to open and swallow her up. Before she could recover from the information being exposed by the senior consultant, he spoke again. "You'll be interested to know that young Mr. Oddball has made a little progress lately", he stated. "Huh", Sandra said. The senior consultant's last comment disturbed Sandra's concentration. Raymond was the last person on her mind. "I'll be seeing him soon", Sandra replied. The nursing Sister, Chrissy Walker, interrupted their conversation. She addressed the senior consultant. "Could I have a word Mr. Pain", Sister Chrissy Walker asked? Both of them moved away from Sandra but spoke in hushed tones. "Thank you Sister", Mr Pain said. She turned but walk away from them. As he approached Sandra again, Mr Pain scratched his head. "We'll have to do some test on Mr. Stagg", he confirmed. "Can I see him", Sandra asked? "Not straight away, some of my colleagues are examining him at this moment. Protocol dictates that we'll have to inform his next of kin. Have you got their phone number and address", Mr Pain enquired? "I'll write it for you. Excuse me", Sandra replied. She looked round for Sam. She saw him standing on the other side of the 'Waiting Area'. Sandra started to make her way over to Sam. She signalled for him to come towards her. When he did, Sandra asked Sam for the details Mr Pain had requested. She wrote the details on paper from her little notebook. Sandra walked back over to where Mr Pain was standing. She gave him the piece of paper with the information on it. He thanked her. Mr Pain walked towards Sister Chrissy Walker's office. There, he instructed her that under no circumstances should Sandra be allowed to see Duke before his immediate family. She had no idea what had been discussed. Sandra sat alone in the 'Waiting Area'. Because he didn't feel comfortable inside the hospital, Sam had asked permission to return to the limo. He had heard the whisperings but noticed the gesticulations towards him and Sandra's presence. Some green humanoid robotron serial bigoted individuals removed themselves when Sandra sat down. This was Poshborough. There weren't many from the Tribe of Hawke living there. Those that worked in Poshborough were mainly ancillary workers. It was as if they were drafted in to do the work that Poshborough residents chose not to do. It was quite apparent that Sandra was not welcomed in the hospital. She continued to sit in a row of seats on her own. All the others around her were either pretending she did not exist or that she was infected with some incurable disease. Her isolation was being enjoyed by the Neuro-bigoted green humanoid robotron doctor whom had accompanied Duke to the hospital. Sandra didn't notice him at first but she recognised the tone and cynicism in his voice. "Not so chatty now, are you Miss Bossy Boots? No one to talk to either, have you noticed? You're not welcome. We don't want your *'type'* here", the doctor warned. He made sure that others in and around the 'Waiting Area' could hear what he was saying to Sandra. She was being belittled with a vengeance. Sandra looked long and hard at the doctor before responding. She too raised her voice enough for the others to hear. "You seem to find me an easy target, don't you? I know you're going to regret this when Duke has recovered. I'll see to it that he singles you out for special treatment", Sandra retaliated. The doctor did not seem concerned about Sandra's threat. He chuckled when he next spoke. "You'll probably have to sleep in your car tonight because the manager at the hotel will not be allowing you to stay in the Suite while Mr Stagg is in the hospital. How's that for Public Relations", the doctor jeered. Sandra took a deep breath. She seemed confused by the personal attack.

Her mother, Dian, had never taught her about individuals like these yet Sandra had been treated this way before. She recalled her experiences at St Halo's High Apostolic Grammar School were much like now. Only there, it was a daily occurrence. Students, teachers, support workers and even parents had chosen to make comments to and about her. She was not welcomed in Highborough then. Her daily travelling from and to school was made more than just a touch uncomfortable. Sandra had suffered racial abuse and segregation at this level before but her mother, Dian, like so many from the Tribe of Hawke, who had become subservient apologists for the behaviour of the green humanoid robotrons serial Neuro-bigotry, had told Sandra to *"just ignore them"*. Sandra had always wondered what made her mother, Dian, think it was that *'easy'* to *'just ignore'* being *'verbally abused'*; being *'bullied'* but treated as if she was carrying some sort of incurable infectious disease or somehow being *'less than'* in *'class'* in comparison to the perpetrators. That type of Neuro-profiling had started when Sandra was quite a young child. Her mother, Dian, had refused to let her choose a doll that looked more like the Tribe of Hawke. Dian had wrenched the doll that Sandra had chosen from her hands but forced her to have a green humanoid doll, instead. Through her actions then, Dian might not have realized that she was helping to reinforce the practice of Neuro-profiling, maybe! Each day, for as many years as she had spent at the prestigious grammar school, Sandra was made to sit on her own in the canteen. There, the isolation meant that Sandra had been given a particular utensils; cup, glass, plate and cutlery too. She used those for all the years she had spent at Saint Halo's. Sandra had to wash them herself after each meal. She was often pilloried when she rinsed the soapy liquid from the utensils and cutlery. The green humanoid robotron woman in the canteen complained that Sandra was wasting water but asked her why she couldn't do the same as them. In the playground, Sandra walked around trying to find someone to play with or with whom she could have conversation. The only time anyone would want to engage with her was when she was prepared to accept that her brain was smaller and inferior to her peers or accept that she was somehow inferior to them because she was from the Tribe of Hawke. Apart from those times, Sandra's experience was a torturous one. She had no friends at St Halo High Apostolic Grammar School. It was just as if her mother, Dian, had thought that the perpetrators would disappear by Sandra choosing to *'ignore'* the daily taunts about her colour, hair, lips, mouth not to mention her eyes. Children and adults alike used to tease her by asking if Sandra had a brown set at home to better match her skin colour. Even the dreaded 'N' word was a constant description too. An "F . . . ing 'N'" was the chant in the playground when Sandra's peers sung "There's a brown girl in the ring, tra la, la, la, laa" . . . This constant refrain transposed into ". . . there's an F . . . . ing 'N' in Saint Halo's High, lets get rid of her". Being called and treated as the *'defaulted misfit'* had hurt Sandra deeply. Those deep wounds had rendered her without confidence in herself. Some of those wounds had now scarred over but left raw underneath. Sandra lived those taunts in her sleep as well as each and every waking moment. The perpetrators were not all children. Some were adults too. They haunted her relentlessly through the ironically named *'social websites'* and via electronic devices like cell phones too. Neuro-bigotry was *'trendy'* then for the green humanoid robotrons. They displayed it from nursery pre-schooling through to old peoples' homes. Like the *'social cancer'* it was, Neuro-bigotry led to Neuro-profiling in various environments and situations. Even those individuals, who were classed as *'green-collar'* workers, many of whom were *'authority figures',* practiced this type of toxic mentality covertly, overtly, wittingly and unwittingly too upon the likes of Sandra. Even as a young adult, those *'daymares'* and *'nightmares'* had caused her moments of anxiety and panic attacks. The bullying taunts she had received via text messages and on the various *'social'* websites had left her feeling suicidal at times. Sandra kept those thoughts away from her domineering mother, who was emotionally insensitive to her *'needs'.* She had confided in her father, CB. He was the only one that seemed to empathise with how Sandra was feeling about being treated in such a derogatory manner as a *'social misfit'* by those who targeted her. CB had approached Dian about Sandra's concerns. Dian threatened CB that if he caused a fuss at Saint Halo's High but jeopardised Sandra's attendance to the prestigious grammar school, she would make sure he went without sex for the rest of their marriage. CB loved his daughter but he was entranced by Dian's physical attractions. He sacrificed his daughter's obvious concerns for his superlative urge for the promised fragmented moments of sexual release that he might have with his 'Movie Star' wife.

Neither Dian nor CB was aware that it was only Sandra's brilliant brain, high absorption rate, precocious potential, unlimited abilities and her insatiable appetite for learning that had kept her at St Halo's High Apostolic Grammar School for those years. Even when some teachers marked her work unfairly, Sandra was able to justify her arguments against those teachers' *deliberate mistake.* Being the only student from that particular tribal ethnic background to have attended the exclusive Saint Halo's High Apostolic Grammar School, in Highborough, she was conspicuous by her appearance. Sandra practiced a form of self-loathing that was not physically noticeable. Its mental scarring was cutting much, much deeper than she might have realised. Instead, since her teenage years, she beat up on herself consistently. Her self-worth was lower than a snake's belly to the ground. On an Evaluation Scale of 0-10; ten being extremely worthy and zero being not at all worthy, Sandra rated her being worthy as **-10** at the opposite end of the scale. Her self-assessment, being a huge minus quantity, meant that Sandra determined that she was not good enough or worthy of being treated as other than someone else's *'possession'*. Whilst her *'internment'* into and subsequent *'initiation'* over those turbulent years at Saint Halo's High Apostolic Grammar School, Sandra was being *'programmed'* yet *'conditioned'* to experience feeling as if being *'used'* was *'normal'*. She contemplated going onto the streets as a whore so that she might make herself available to give *'pleasure'* to whichever men could afford the type of *'service'* they wanted her to provide. Sandra had done her research but became scared when she observed, witnessed but questioned how others with seemingly similar low self-worth were being treated by their *'pimps'* and *'madames'*. She resolved that she might just go ahead anyway but hoped that her *'pimp'* wouldn't be as abusive as others had told of their experiences. Sandra realised that she might have to *'mix'* with individuals that her mother had previously referred to as being *"below her status"*.

When she had met Raymond at Coleport College, was the day Sandra made a final decision that being on the streets was not her way out. Raymond's interest in her, gave Sandra new hope but it didn't solve her depression. Many of her temper tantrums and angry outbursts were a result of feeling as if she was being judged by others. This was a particular trigger. Individuals like Andy Mann felt the consequences of their slight towards her. Sandra was a volcano simmering but waiting to erupt. Duke was no match for the genial, highly sexual, glamorous, Super Model but he provided the type of financial security and clout that Sandra needed. With that and Duke's seeming admiration for her, she began to see it as important to be accepted by him and his contacts. Sandra perceived that the image of being a *'social misfit'* would gradually fade into insignificance as she climbed the career ladder. She hoped to quench her thirst for the taste of Champagne Urge whilst striving to fulfill her dreams of becoming an 'A' Blister celebrity.

Now, whilst sitting alone in the 'Waiting Area' of the hospital, Sandra sat with her head in her hands reviewing but comparing the similarities of her experience at Saint Halo's to her current situation. It was only a few days ago that she was recognized and accepted by all, who had seen her in the national newspapers, seemingly! Sandra was being hailed as Super Model Extraordinaire then. Here in Poshborough's University Teaching Hospital, none wanted to be associated with her now. Sandra was fast realising that, despite her astronomic rise in financial abundance and strive for fame as an 'A' *Blister* Celebrity, she was no one *'special'* in Poshborough or so it seemed. She had begun to realize that her closest confidant was loneliness. Its isolating qualities sapped the energy out of the excitement she had felt prior to this *'green cloud'* that was descending over her. Sandra desired to learn how to have clout like Duke did. She wandered if it was a singular technique or skill or groups of those to initiate clout. Sandra saw it as important to seek how to gain this seemingly elusive power over others. With it, she would have the potential to influence others at will like Duke does, maybe! Sandra was mesmerized by the thought. While she was contemplating how she might be able to use that type of influence to her advantage, she heard her name. As Sandra looked up, she saw Sam. "Are you alright Ms. Bogus", he enquired? Sandra appeared more than happy to see him like a dog its master. She got up but walked towards Sam. Sandra was smiling now, broadly. She greeted him as if meeting up with a long lost friend. "Oh Sam, it's good to see you", Sandra exclaimed. Sam was unsure about Sandra's approach. He stood there dutifully but wondered what he had done to warrant the unusual greeting but most of all, the huge smile. Sam sensed this unusual behaviour did not fit the model (no pun intended) he had experienced before. "Are you feeling alright Ms. Bogus", Sam queried? "I've never felt better or happier in this moment. You're so dependable Sam. That's what I find fascinating about you. You always arrive at the right time, right on cue as the saying goes", Sandra assured. Sam was becoming more suspicious by the minute. He took a step back to enable him to observe Ms. Bogus from a distance. Sam believed the picture might become clearer if he gave himself a bit more space. He turned to go but Sandra told him she needed him to keep watch for Mrs. Stagg. "You will let me know when Mrs. Stagg arrives, won't you", she enquired? "Yes Ms. Bogus", Sam replied. "Gee Sam, it's stuffy in here. I think I'll go outside for some fresh air", Sandra commented. She walked with Sam back towards the limo. He went to sit inside it but she stayed outside. Sandra started to dial on her cell phone. When Pam answered, she spilled everything. Sandra told her best friend about the treatment she'd received from the manager of the Hotel Welcome, the attending doctor and the ambulance staff at the hotel. "Now everybody knows about me and Duke", Sandra sobbed. "I did warn you but you wouldn't listen", Pam reiterated. Sandra continued to reveal how she was treated by Mr Pain, how she was being ignored by hospital staff and cold shouldered by the people, who left her isolated in one row of seats in the 'Waiting Area'. She also told Pam that she wasn't sure of how Duke's wife might react. "What am I going to say to his wife when she arrives? I dare not leave before she comes as that would only raise suspicion", Sandra explained. "Just tell her that you came out of loyalty to your boss. After all, you're not only the firm's but also Duke's personal PR person", Pam offered. She really had no sympathy for Sandra but she wanted things to work out between her and Duke. This was purely from self interest. Pam did not want the union between Sandra and Raymond to rekindle. The only way she could ensure Sandra's decline in interest in Raymond is by encouraging her to warm towards Duke. Pam made a few suggestions that she thought might help Sandra. "Have you thought about ringing Duke", Pam encouraged. "You're a true friend. Why didn't I think of doing that", Sandra queried. She told Pam she would call her back. Sandra dialled Duke's number. It rang for a while then went on to voicemail. She was disappointed. Sandra was becoming despondent about being left totally alone in a situation in whicn she had no real input. After returning to the 'Waiting Area', Sandra redialled Duke's number once again. It rang until it went to voicemail once more. She was just deciding to ring Pam again when her phone rang. The sound of the ring tone was modern but very much not something with which people in the 'Waiting Area' could identify. They glared at Sandra as one. She appeared foolish as she mouthed her apologies for not putting the phone on silent. Sandra's excitement soon overcame her embarrassment. It was Duke's number that came up on the caller ID. "Hello Duke. How are you feeling", Sandra asked? "I'm fine", Duke replied. Sandra explained that she had to give his details to the hospital staff. Duke thanked her but wanted to apologise for not contacting her sooner. He told her that his wife had been "nagging on the phone". Duke asked Sandra of her whereabouts. When she told him that she was still at the hospital, he wanted to know why she hadn't come to see him. "I couldn't find anyone willing to communicate with me. Everyone seems so stand-offish", Sandra complained. "They were giving you the run around, were they", Duke asked? When Sandra confirmed that was so, Duke told her that heads would roll for the indiscretions. She told him that Sam was the only person that spoke with her since Mr Pain did. Duke told her that his wife was on her way over but to brace herself for further snide remarks. He told Sandra he would ring her back in ten minutes. She seized that opportunity to ring Pam. When she answered, Sandra thanked her for the suggestion then she filled Pam in. She explained that Duke had spoken to her. "What did he say", Pam asked? "He's alright thank God. He told me he had too much to drink at a business lunch which he had attended earlier in the day", Sandra explained. She had to break away from her conversation to speak with Sam. He had come back from the car to tell Sandra that his colleague, who was Mrs Stagg's chauffeur, had alerted him that they were already here. They must have approached from a different entrance because Sam couldn't see the other limo. When Sandra rejoined her conversation with Pam, she told her that a middle-aged woman in a fawn linen suite was approaching them. "Hold the line Pam. Let me see what this woman wants", Sandra cautioned. The middle-aged woman asked if she was Ms. Bogus. Sandra looked up at the stranger but acknowledged that she was. "I'm Sandra Bogus", Sandra confirmed. "Can I talk to you privately", middle-aged woman asked? The tone of her voice alerted Sandra but they walked away together to the side away from the crowded 'Waiting Area'. After speaking with Sandra for a brief moment, the woman escorted her and Sam along the corridor which led to the private rooms. They arrived outside the private room where Duke occupied. Sam stopped. "I'll wait out here ma'am", he said. In the private room, Sandra saw a chubby faced woman, from the Tribe of Duke, dressed in an outdated blue check suite. The steady gaze from her beady eyes seemed to suggest she was expecting Sandra to be much older. "You must be Ms. Bogus, Duke's assistant PR person", Mrs. Stagg asked? "The Company's and Mr. Stagg's Personal PR Officer", Sandra corrected. She extended her own hand in a gesture to appease the awkward moment. Sandra had often asked Duke what his wife looked like but now she could see for herself. Never mind Duke describing his wife as looking like "the back of a bus", this woman was clearly the benefactor of his entire estate. Mrs. Stagg ignored the intended handshake but proceeded to ask where the near fatal moment took place. "Be careful Ms. Bogus, my wife thinks that I'm flirting with all the women I meet", Duke warned. "Duke, I can speak for myself", Mrs. Stagg scolded. Sandra was embarrassed to be face to face with Duke's wife. He watched the two women as they silently fought each other with stares and eyes that burned with hate. Mrs. Stagg knew that Duke's popular status brought him close to many women but she hadn't figured on someone as beautiful as Sandra. Mrs. Stagg stared menacingly at Sandra. "You could have chosen better, Duke", Mrs.Stagg criticised. "Leave it out Dora", Duke bullied. Mrs. Stagg expressed all her pent up feelings. She laid into Sandra. Looking her up and down, she communicated how disgusted she was with her. "Duke, you must have been desperate. In which red light district did you find this one", Mrs. Stagg sneered? "What is all the bloody fuss", Duke asked? Sandra was angry with the woman, who stood in front of her. She had to stay passive while Mrs. Stagg debased her character. Sandra could not lash out at her as she did with Andy Mann, her immediate boss. Mrs. Stagg was determined to have at least one more swipe at her. "Duke, I will forgive you for the affair you had with the Au Pair but not *'this'*, she said pointing at Sandra. I want a divorce", Mrs. Stagg stated. Her statement was acid enough to cut through any blockage that stood between them before today. Having got that off her chest, Mrs. Stagg got up from the chair but strided briskly away from Duke's bedside without looking back. The embarrassment and frank comments were too much for Sandra. She burst into tears. Duke tried to comfort her. "Don't take any notice of the old bag. She doesn't mean it. Dora flies off the handle every now and again because she knows it's finished between me and her", Duke soothed. Even those words didn't seem to comfort Sandra. She sat at his bedside with her head in her hands wondering whether the affair was worth continuing. "That's it Duke", Sandra blurted out. "Don't be so silly. I still love you", Duke replied. His suggestion was for Sandra to endure the torrent of insults despite his assurances. Sandra's hurt feelings were deeper than he thought or knew. "No Duke, I could understand her not liking me but those comments went straight through me. They are demeaning, defamatory and wounding to my reputation. Now, I'm the *reason* for your divorce", Sandra sobbed. Even as she cried, Duke's lust for Sandra outweighed the prospect of being without her. He could tell that only firm resistance would bring Sandra back to her senses. "You cannot leave just like that", Duke warned. "Why not", Sandra asked? "You are still under contract", Duke replied. The ploy seemed to shock Sandra back into a state of understanding. "OK Duke, have it your way but then you'll have to marry me when you get the divorce", Sandra demanded. "Definitely, my sweet", Duke replied. Sandra told Duke what the doctor had said about the manager of the hotel locking her out of the Suite while he was not there. "I'll fix that too", Duke assured her. He started to dial the hotel. When the receptionist answered, Duke demanded to speak with the manager. The receptionist asked Duke to hold. When he came back, he said the manager had gone off duty. Duke insisted he be contacted by him within twenty minutes. "If he doesn't, he'll have me to deal with", Duke challenged. He told Sandra to ask Sam to take her back to the Hotel Welcome. He assured her that he would be discharged after the compulsory 24 hours monitoring had expired. Sandra smiled broadly but kissed Duke lightly on his forehead. He grabbed Sandra. Duke held her close to him but commented. "No one is going to take my exotic bird away from me", he assured. With that Duke groped her voluptuous breast with one hand before releasing her. Sandra found a new reason for believing in the man, who could satisfy her champagne urge. She glanced at him from over her shoulder but asked one final question before exiting the private room. "Duke, will you show me how to have clout", Sandra asked? "Only when you are ready to commit to the code of clout", Duke warned. Sandra met Sam outside the private room. He was waiting patiently. Sam had witnessed the worried look on Sandra's face before she entered the private room, seen the angry look on Mrs. Stagg face when she had exited. He puzzled but became more curious as to what might have happened inside the private room that made Sandra look so happy once again. "Take me back to the Hotel Welcome", Sandra ordered. As she walked up the long corridor heading back towards the previously uncomfortable ambience in the 'Waiting Area', perpetrated by those serial bigoted individuals, who had excluded even the thought of her presence, Sandra was lifted by Duke's promise to marry her. This buoyed her with a new confidence that made Sandra's strides as if she was floating on air and with the broadest of smiles. The people in the 'Waiting Area' turned their heads as one to witness the power of Duke's exotic bird. As soon as she exited the 'Waiting Area', Sandra was back on the phone with Pam. "Pam, I'll be grateful to you forever, for helping me when I felt so down", Sandra assured. Pam was interested whether the woman in the fawn linen suite was Duke's wife. She couldn't hold herself back from asking the question. "Was the woman in the fawn linen suite his wife", Pam probed? "No, that was the hospital manager, nice woman", Sandra explained. Pam was grateful for the update. They ended the conversation shortly afterwards. Carmen's only interest was to find out one piece of information that she seemed curious about. She asked her sister. "Yuh tink di wife bax har face", Carmen asked?

CHAPTER 31

The next day Sandra phoned Duke to find out what time he wanted her to collect him from the hospital? By the tone of his voice, she could hear a sense of disappointment. "What's wrong Duke? You don't sound happy to hear me. Is something wrong", Sandra queried? "The doctor said he needs to run some more tests. They want to monitor me for at least another 24 hours", Duke stated. "Oh no, I thought you said the late lunch was the cause", Sandra implied. "I don't want you to worry. I'll be alright", Duke assured her. "I'll come down to see you if that is alright. I don't want to argue with your wife again", Sandra inferred. "She is coming back with one of the boys. The other one is away at university. I've told her it's not worth him coming. There is nothink wrong with me", Duke revealed. "So what do I do? What time is best to phone you again", Sandra queried? "Forget about today, it's just a lot of fuss about nothink", Duke stated. "If you say so", Sandra said. They said their goodbyes. Sandra phoned Pam immediately. "Duke is still in hospital for at least another 24 hours. I can't spend all day at the hotel alone. Can I come to visit you", Sandra asked? The connection from the phone was severed. Sandra looked at the cell phone but wondered what had happened. She redialled Pam's number but it was unavailable. Now Sandra didn't know what to do. The landline phone began to ring. Sandra darted across the huge Suite towards the bedside table on which it stood. She thought it was Pam or Duke. "Hello", Sandra said. "This is the manager. I wonder if you could find some time to have a meeting with me today", the manager enquired? Sandra noticed that his tone was quite more amicable than when Duke had collapsed in the Suite but she was unsure what made him call. "We have nothing to discuss. What is it you want", Sandra demanded? "I believe that there are some facts you need to know. It's important that I tell you about them. Please Ms. Bogus, you need to know about these facts. I would be grateful if you could find the time to have this meeting with me", the manager pleaded. Sandra was still suspicious about the manager's intentions but she was curious enough to find out what was so important for her to know. She thought she would make him wait for her answer. "I'll let you know", Sandra responded. "As soon as you can please", the manager begged. Sandra phoned Pam. She told her of the manager's request. Pam said that she should challenge him but record the meeting on her cell phone secretly. Sandra thanked her but asked what had happened while they were on the phone last. Pam told her about the intermittent connection problems that she was having with her phone. "This cell phone handset is old. Though it is normally reliable for the purpose of enjoying the basic functions, I believe the provider is monitoring my calls", Pam surmised. Sandra laughed loudly but played down the possibility. "Why would they want to monitor your calls? You're not an enemy of the Kingdom, are you", Sandra questioned? "No, but we are all being treated as though we are, are we not? My sister told me she knew that random monitoring was a fact. I'm definitely not an enemy of the Kingdom", Pam confirmed. Both Sandra and Pam laughed heartily together. "By the way, talking of enemy of the Kingdom are you not interested in how Raymond is anymore? You hardly mention his name since this Duke episode", Pam searched. "It's not easy leading this double life. I need Ray sexually. He fills my soul and sends me into those orgasmic moments Duke cannot. On the other hand, Duke fills my financial needs more than I ever thought any one man could. I'm so close to fulfilling the *'Spacevillean Dream'*. I've got to keep going. Ray might come back into my life someday. Who knows", Sandra confessed. "I hope you will remember that you chose to abandon Ray for Duke and what he means to you. No one else has chosen to lead this double life but you. Are you saying that you are gambling that Raymond is going to wait around until you've decided when you've fulfilled the *'Spacevillean Dream'*", Pam challenged? "I don't mean to Pam. I want the best for Ray. He's so handsome, quite a hunk of a man and he's a great lover. Who would want to give up such a nice man? I'd be mad to want to do that, wouldn't I", Sandra confessed. At first, Pam listened without comment but then she spoke. "You know me. I am saying it as I see it", Pam warned. "Pam, Ray will never leave me. He's obsessed with me but I have to live the *'Spacevillean Dream'*. The truth is Ray won't be able to give me the financial security that I want or need. He surrounds himself with *'deadbeats'*. Ray doesn't like my friends. You're probably the only one that he seems to get on with", Sandra confessed. Pam was beginning to see where Sandra wanted to be. Her goal was clear. Sandra's superlative urge was stronger than Raymond could provide her with but she still needed Raymond sexually it seemed. "I hear you Sandra. Duke's obviously your choice but you still need Raymond to fulfill your sexual needs. Is he aware of that", Pam searched? "My priorities keep changing each day. I love Raymond for certain reasons as I've stated. There's no other man that can do what Raymond does for me sexually but he will never have the type of clout that Duke has. Raymond has surrounded himself with what my mother use to refer to as *'yaga-yaga'*. They are holding him back but he can't see it", Sandra accused. "When did you make such a decision", Pam asked? "I've known for a while now what my dreams are. I need to be up there girl rubbing shoulders with the stars. They have got it all. Don't you see how important it is to be an *'A' Blister* Celebrity? *'A' Blister* don't only get invited everywhere. *'A' Blister* go everywhere. People adore them. *'A' Blister* have clout. I want to have all that and more. That is one thing I can thank my mother for. She riveted this kind of thinking into my head as far back as I can remember. She didn't make it. I've got to", Sandra confessed. "I hear you are sending mixed messages. You know what happens when people do that, don't you? They receive them back many folds. Is that what you want", Pam pressed? Sandra heard the words but ignored the message that Pam prophesied. Duke's promise to marry her had bolstered Sandra's hopes of realising the *'Spacevillean Dream'*. It was the same as her dreams since as far back as Sandra can remember. "I'll go to see the manager then make my way down to you. We can finish this conversation over coffee", Sandra confirmed. Both of them agreed it was crucial to clear up what plans Sandra had for the future. From Pam's point of view, she was happy that Sandra was forcing Raymond away from her and into her arms. They ended the call. Pam wanted to know the reason behind Sandra's confidence that Duke might want to continue the relationship. As far as she knew, he had a wife and children. Duke was rich but could have as many Sandras as he wished. More than all, Pam wondered how Sandra might cope if Duke wanted to end the affair.

Sandra picked up the phone from the bedside table but requested to speak to the manager. The receptionist seemed alarmed about her request. "Is everything alright Ms. Bogus", she enquired? Sandra was in no mood to answer. Pam's message was seeping through. Sandra was confused as to how much she might be hurting Raymond. She saw this as an opportunity to examine her conscience. Sandra saw things in 'black' and 'white'. It was either this way or that way. There was no grey area of meaningfulness interspersed in between. "I'm still waiting", Sandra reminded. "Yes ma'am. I'll get him for you", the receptionist assured. The next voice Sandra heard was that of the manager. "Yes Ms. Bogus, Sherman Tanker at your service", the manager announced. "I'll be leaving shortly. What is it you wanted to talk to me about", Sandra asked? Her manner was abrupt but demanded the manager get straight to the point. "Please come to my office. What I have to say to you is confidential. It's more private here", Sherman Tanker assured her. Sandra agreed but hung up the phone. She gathered her things but headed for the lifts. There was one immediately available. On her arrival on the ground floor, the manager was waiting by the Reception Area. He smiled profusely but bowed gracefully from his waist as if he was greeting a head of state. "Come with me please Ms. Bogus", Sherman Tanker encouraged. They walked the short distance to his office without comment. The manager opened the door. He waited for Sandra to go in. Once inside, he pulled out the chair but beckoned for her to sit down then he made his way round to the other side of the desk. Sandra took Pam's advice. She slipped the cell phone out of her handbag but pressed record. The manager looked very uncomfortable but began to break out in sweat. At first, he used the back of his hand to remove the first appearance of sweat then as it started to flow, the manager started to fiddle with his tie. Sandra looked on but kept on recording. She was becoming more and more curious the more uncomfortable he appeared. As if he was suffering from verbal constipation, the manager had still not said a single word. Sandra cleared her throat to ensure that he saw her look at her watch. She was becoming impatient with his calling this meeting but had said nothing so far. Sandra remembered how cocky the manager was when he and his colleague were in the Suite. The derogatory behaviour he had encouraged was surely lacking in protocol but broke every rule on professional performance. She seized upon the manager's weakness but decided to take revenge on him for allowing not only the doctor, who had come to attend to Duke but also his failure to address the ambulance staff that had made the derogatory comments about her. Sandra got up from the chair in which she was sitting but went round to the other side of the desk. She grabbed the manager by the collar but dragged him towards her like a bully. His eyes bulged as if they were about to pop out of their sockets. Sandra reprimanded him. "You little piece of shit. You're not so brave now, are you? Your little friend *'Dr. Nasty'* isn't here to back you up. Thought it was powerful to insult my breeding, huh. What made you do it", she questioned? Hanging like a rag-doll from Sandra's firm grip, the manager burst into tears but begged for forgiveness. "It was Dr. Tarzan Sono-Fabitch that made me do it", Sherman Tanker confessed. "You could have refused, couldn't you", Sandra inferred? "No. You don't understand. You have no idea what these people can do or how far they will go to ensure their deeds are carried out. "What deeds, Sandra queried? "Ms Bogus I can't tell you everything but you've got to believe me. You don't know what that man can do. He has power over me. Now he's managed to get Mr Stagg angry. He said when he comes out of hospital he is going to take me to the *'torture room'* and sort me out then fire me from my job. Please Ms. Bogus can you ask Mr. Stagg to have mercy on me? I've got four children and a wife and I can't afford to lose my job", the manager begged. Sandra was happy to hear Duke was going to make him pay for the racist insults and those other inferred defamatory aspersions that the manager, his colleague and the ambulance staff had thrown at her. Though she was stunned to hear about the *'torture room'*, Sandra needed to hear more about its location. "Where is the *'torture room'*", she asked? "It's on the basement floor Ms. Bogus. Please tell Mr. Stagg that I will do anything he wants without question but please, please don't take me to the *'torture room'* and don't fire me. I'll even take a lesser job if that's what he thinks I deserve but don't fire me. I couldn't take the humiliation", the manager implored. Sandra could see that Sherman Tanker was a broken man. He was no further threat to her. She let go of his collar. He fell to the floor in a crumpled heap. Sherman Tanker looked dishevelled and his sweaty body mixed with stale body sprays made the room smell like a sweatshop in Odourville, Ghettoborough. Sandra turned off the recording but phoned Sam. She asked him to collect her from the reception area in about twenty minutes. Sherman Tanker, the manager stood with his head looking down to the floor like a naughty child, who had been scolded by an adult but put in the *'naughty corner'*. Sandra ordered him to take her to the basement floor to show her the *'torture room'*. He protested. "Why not", Sandra questioned? "Mr. Stagg wouldn't like it. I took an oath that I wouldn't say anything to anyone about it", the manager reasoned. "You told me about it, didn't you? How much worst off are you going to be", Sandra queried? "Please, don't let me do it. You don't know Mr. Stagg like I do. He can get very angry and he has lots of friends that are just as mean", Sherman Tanker revealed. Sandra was determined that this might be the only opportunity she might have to see the *'torture room'*. She approached the manager aggressively again but showed him her talons. "How would you like these across your face? I'll cry out for rape when I exit your office to justify why I have your DNA under my nails. Do you think you'll have a job ever again anywhere", she challenged? Sherman Tanker could not figure the worst of the two evils he was facing. Either way he'd be humiliated but made to suffer the consequences of his own fears brought on by one set of threats or another. It was really a matter of 'heads I win, tails you lose' sort of scenario. Sherman Tanker succumbed to the pressure that Sandra imposed upon him. "You must agree not to tell Mr. Stagg that I showed it to you", he pleaded. Sandra and Sherman Tanker left his office together. He directed her towards the service lift. Both Sandra and the manager exited from the lift on the basement floor. They walked along the long corridor past the various doors until they came to the end. There were a series of tunnels which extended in different directions. The tunnels had no light except that which came from the small torch that the manager removed from his pocket. Sandra wasn't sure she wanted to continue the journey. "What kind of place is this? Where do these tunnels lead", Sandra queried? "Each tunnel leads to the various *'torture rooms'* Ms. Bogus. I'll only show you one", the manager said. "Give me the torch", Sandra demanded. Sherman Tanker handed it over to her. He guided Sandra along one of the secret tunnels. When he got to a huge iron door, the manager asked Sandra to shine the torch on his key ring that he wore on his belt. He tried a few keys until he found the one that opened that door. It took him a lot of strength to open the huge solid iron industrial door. It was covered with a rather flaky faded washed out green coloured paint. The exterior seemed to have been aged by layers of dust even though there was a damp smell which seemed to linger but alerted the nostrils of it haunting presence. There was a rectangular border pattern of flat plate metal on its outer edges measuring about 18 inches in width, with a matching flat metal cross-member which divided both its height and width precisely. It 3 huge hinges measuring approximately 12 inches each with protruding solid iron supports nearer the stone wall of the cave-like environment that appeared to have been hewn to shape the walls that supported it. The creaky sound reminded Sandra of the horror films she used to watch on DVDs. Sherman Tanker instructed Sandra where to shine the light. They walked down some steps before being confronted by a huge metal gate. They went through it but down some more steps where they were confronted with yet a huge unpainted metal gate and yet more steps leading deeper downwards. When Sherman Tanker approached the fifth huge metal gate, Sandra started to feel as if she was being lured into a trap. "Wait a minute. We've gone through four huge metal gates and a thick metal door at the beginning. Where is all this leading? It's getting colder the deeper we've gone. I demand you tell me exactly what you think you might gain by this expedition", she demanded? Her mind was primed and ready. She knew exactly how she would destroy this brown Mixed DNA Rainbow Tribesman, who had already proven his subservient mindset. Sherman Tanker had displayed a streak of self-righteousness, previously in the Suite with, the man he called Dr. Tarzan Sono-Fabitch and the ambulance staff, who had attended when Duke had become ill. Sandra decided that she would pluck out his eyes like she did to the pot-bellied Security man at Brigadier Tank Alpino's Club, The Pharmacy. She even thought of imprisoning Sherman Tanker beyond one of the huge unpainted metal gates as repayment for his act of indiscretion in the Suite. From his position on the level looking up at the taller figure of Sandra as she paused on the steps above him, Sherman Tanker felt a chill. Staring into Sandra's large cornflower blue eyes when she was angry was even more mesmeric. She was contemplating how to destroy her *'prey'*. She was focused but crouched like all felines do as they prepare to attack their *'prey'*. The level of fear which Sherman was feeling made him cower even more so than in his office earlier. There, Sandra had rendered him as inanimate as a straw-filled scarecrow being taken out into the field in order to frighten the birds away. Sherman sensed the intensity of Sandra's potential feline power. She was feeling a bit exposed to be in this underground tunnel with a man that had clear advantages over her. Sandra wanted to know how many more gates existed. She reminded the manager of her talons. Sherman Tanker was shaking like leaves on a tree on a windy day. He expressed how daunting it must seem to someone, who didn't know the *'torture rooms'* existed let alone a fearfully strong female. Sherman assured Sandra that he had no ill intentions towards her but felt compelled to tell her about the existence of the *'torture rooms'*. After the fourth inner gate, the manager directed Sandra on a tour around one of the crypts. It had a dank smell and the stench of burning and rotting flesh also. Sandra saw some white gowns hanging from some pegs embedded in the wall. Like the pegs, there were chains embedded in the walls and a wooden stand with a thick rope that was tied in a noose. There was a guillotine with dried up blood on it and a piece of bone which seemed to be part of a skull attached to its razor sharp thick metal blade. An old solid wooden table was positioned with some chains at the head and foot of it. Some hand and foot irons cuffs, an iron poker, a giant box of matches, some used as well as stocks of unused injection needles, industrial gloves, disposable plastic butchers' aprons, boiler suits with hoods, an acetylene torch and several bottles of oxygen, adorned the cave-like environment. There was also a stone fireplace with old ashes and some bones, which looked like fingers and toes. This completed the blood splattered stone floor and walls. It was an eerie setting; enough to convince Sandra of the manager's account of torture. He looked at her but begged Sandra to say nothing to Mr. Stagg. After closing the fourth gate behind them, they set about climbing the final set of stairs but exited from that particular *'torture room'* altogether, finally. Sandra was completely stunned to know that such a place existed but began to question her naivety about what Duke really meant by *'clout'*, perhaps! She asked the manager how many of these *'torture rooms'* existed. He told her he didn't know but he would imagine from deduction there must be as many as the number of keys on the bunch. Both she and the manager made their way back to the service lift but returned to the Reception Area of the hotel. Sam was waiting dutifully as usual. They both left the Reception Area but headed for the limo. Sandra gave Sam instructions. "Take me to Miss Labrishé's", she ordered. "Yes ma'am", Sam confirmed. "Turn on that jazz Sam", Sandra requested.

The journey to Painsville, Ghettoborough was without conversation between Sandra and Sam. He didn't mind. Sandra spent the time reflecting on the manager's fear of Duke, the *'torture rooms'*, the evidence and the fact that those crypts exist. She thought how strange it was that the *'torture rooms'* were situated at the basement area of the huge prestigious Hotel Welcome. What was Duke involved in that she was yet to find out? Sandra began to look beyond Duke's financial clout. She was so naïve. Sandra had no idea that *'clout'* involved more than just riches. There was so much she didn't know about Duke. Who were those *'mean friends'* of his to whom the manager referred? Sandra reflected on how petrified he had become when talking about what he had witnessed. It was as if what the manager had witnessed in the *'torture rooms'* haunted him so much that he had become fearful of offending Duke. His image began to seem like her *'torturers'* at Saint Halo High Apostolic Grammar School. It wasn't the same type of torture but Sandra could identify with the degree of fear as experienced by all *'victims of torture'*. She was becoming more aware of the effect of any sort of torture. As with her personal experience of being tortured by her peers, teachers and parents alike at Saint Halo's for so many years, Sandra began to realize how it drives individuals to extremes beyond their thresholds. When her threshold was being breached by the constant bullying, she had contemplated suicide. Sandra could easily identify with how rapidly individuals can deteriorate into a downward spiral. She started to become more conscious of the questions that were flooding into her mind. Those questions were reflective but Sandra's depth of curiosity made her feel grossly uncomfortable about what she did not know. She needed answers to the many questions which remain unresolved. Sandra began to wonder what happened to the individuals that were being tortured in the crypts below the splendid building of the Hotel Welcome. Whose bones and ashes remained in the stone fireplace? Why were there so many doors to the *'torture rooms'*? All these questions remained unanswered. Sandra was totally intrigued. The limo glided along the expressway. There was traffic but well spaced enough to enjoy the green scenery and the huge mansions which seemed so tiny compared to the amount of land space which surrounded them. Sandra's dream involved owning at least one of these mansions in deep suburbia like Poshborough. She wondered if she might be accepted by the other rich and famous people there. Even with the idea of owning and living in one of those mansions could not detract Sandra from thinking about the images being conjured in her mind with regards to the subject of torture. She felt that being isolated like she had been throughout her grammar school days and again at the Poshborough University Teaching Hospital recently was, by gradations, examples of a form of torture. Sandra reasoned that the intention to intimidate, by whatever means, was the initiator that led to the act of torture. She was never told of her mother's days of being tortured by the Cactus' or that her grandparents' cruelty to her mother also amounted to a form of torture. The real question burning a trail upon her psyche was where were the *'statistics of victims of torture'* kept? How many homes and institutions were secreting acts of torture? Who were the custodians of the *'history of torture'*? Sandra was haunted by the disturbing questions which kept popping into her consciousness. She needed some answers in order to satisfy her intrigue. Sandra became very tense but could not settle. Images of horrible scenarios kept appearing and reappearing. Even the beautiful jazz that would normally help her to feel relaxed seem to elude her conscious mind. Sandra had no idea that Raymond had been a victim of torture too. She was unaware that he was being hospitalised as a consequence of a form of torture. Sandra drifted off into a type of comatose state in which she remained until awakened by the voice of her chauffeur, Sam. "We have arrived at Miss Labrishè's Estate ma'am", he announced. Sam watched from the rearview mirror as Sandra began to stir. She yawned and stretched as if she had been asleep for hours. Sam watched as Sandra opened her large cornflower blue eyes widely as if to ascertain that she was fully awake. She shook her head as if trying to clear her brain of some memory that she wanted to get rid of that instance. Sam was now more aware of how strongly attracted he was to Sandra. At that moment, he was tempted to risk all but tell her how he felt being always in her company. Sam had had many thoughts of *'bedding'* the gorgeous female that seemed to haunt his overactive imagination each moment of his waking day. He wanted to tell Sandra how many *'wet dreams'* about him and her since he became her chauffeur but Sam was also aware that he did not have the resources to quench her seemingly enormous thirst for Champagne Urge. Sam climbed from the limo but opened the door for Sandra to alight. The huge cheering and clapping took both of them by surprise. Before they could approach the security door of the Elementary Estate in which Pam lived, Sandra and Sam were surrounded by adoring fans. Each fan wanting an autograph or to have their picture taken with Sandra. It was the huge commotion that alerted Pam and Carmen. They peered through the window which looked out onto the street that led to the Estate. There, they saw Sandra and Sam in the midst of the crowd. Neither of them had expected the reaction but Sandra revelled in the adulation all the same. Some of the youngsters, who had challenged Sam to race against the limo on a previous occasion, asked for his autograph too. He hadn't realized that being

Sandra's chauffeur had made his signature as valuable as hers. Not wanting to appear as if he was celebrity, Sam told the boys that he would need Sandra's permission to fulfill their request. She granted it and in those moments, Sam became a celebrity instantly. Pam and Carmen watched from the security doors. Pam called out to Sandra. "When you finished with your fans can we get on with visiting Raymond", she reminded? Sandra was relieved that Pam had come to rescue her. She announced to the crowd that she would sign more autographs and pose with them for pictures the next time she returned to the Estate. They accepted Sandra's offer but allowed her to go to Pam. Some of the youngsters thanked Pam for having such a celebrity visit their Estate. Carmen kept quiet but observed the iconic status that Sandra represented. Pam escorted her friend into the flat.

Sam stayed with the limo and the youngsters, who engaged him in several challenges yet again. None of which he accepted but Sam was grateful for the banter. He thought about his once 'home alone' son, who was of a similar age to these boys and girls. Sam had often wondered if he too had being involved in some sort of group or gang. He didn't want to think so but by the nature of his job and the irregular hours that he had to agree to work did keep him and his son from enjoying the quality time that kept parental relationships afloat. Many parents like him lived in a time where inconvenient hours of work had kept them from spending quality time with their children. The consequences rendering them targets for Ghetto Celebrity CEOs, Entrepreneurs, Ghetto Sodomy Entrepreneurs, Gang Orientation Operators and Practitioners. With regards to his only son, Sam became saddened by the facts. He couldn't hide the tears that began to run down his face. The youngsters were perplexed as to why the seemingly jovial Sam was crying. He didn't seem soft but those were real tears. The youngsters were curious. They questioned Sam. His response shocked them. Sam told them that his only son had died a few years ago. The story was common amongst youngsters of that age group. When questioned further, Sam related his memory of his son's death. He told of how his son was bullied consistently by a gang, who was trying to recruit him to sell drugs and arms for them. He was 14 years old at the time but most of the recruiting bullies were between 17 and 19 years old. His son had not told him about the bullying threats to his own life and Sam's. As a consequence, when his son could take it no more, he hung himself in his room. Sam told of the horrible discovery on the night he found his son dead. He started to sob but became broken by the sad memories. Sam cried unashamedly in front of the group. They tried to console him but he blurted out some strong words that registered with the group. ***"If you're being bullied, tell your parents. Please don't hold on to the threats by yourself. Share it with your parents. Even if there is nothing they can do about it, give them a chance to at least be aware of what you're going through"***, Sam pleaded. The boys and girls were shocked at Sam's revelation. What they didn't know is how they had helped him to release this pent up feeling he'd been carrying for more than four years. It was the first time Sam had discussed it with anyone. He told them that he didn't want to see them going down the same route wasting their lives instead of aspiring towards striving *meaningfully* to achieve. Sam reminded them that they were more than capable of achieving with fulfillment. He continued to establish that they, like his son, are diamonds waiting to be polished. Some of the boys showed their appreciation by coming over to Sam but patting him on his back. Some didn't make any verbal contributions but accepted that he cared enough about them to share the story about his young son's sad experience with them. A number of those fourteen year olds and younger were aware of what Sam's son had gone through. Many were being bullied too and being recruited but forced into selling drugs and arms for the older boys. Some even sold drugs and arms for the rogue cops that visited the Estate. Sam told the boys and girls that he would consider being a mentor to them on his days off. They accepted. He returned to sit in the limo. The boys and girls wondered off but kept looking back towards the limo. Sam sat listening to the jazz music which was a kind of therapeutic activity for his mind.

Inside the flat, Carmen, Pam and Sandra enjoyed coffee but spoke about the importance of keeping updated about Raymond's progress. Pam kept pushing that her intuition was alerting her towards the urgency that they needed to be at the Community General Hospital instead of idly chatting in the flat. Pam instructed Sandra that she should go now to see Raymond. She told her that she and Carmen would follow later. They had some family business to attend before coming to the hospital. "OK Pam, I'll go to see Ray now. What would I do without you? You're my only friend", Sandra ended. Pam escorted Sandra to the limo. As she climbed in, Pam reminded Sandra that she and Carmen would meet her at the hospital. Sam tooted the horn but waved to the group of boys and girls as the limo moved in the direction of the exit from the Elementary Estate. They acknowledged Sam's farewell. Inside the flat, Pam told Carmen about Sandra's dilemma about living a double life. She expressed her opinion about the woman she kept referring to as not knowing her ID. Carmen didn't hold back on how she felt about anything or anyone. She was extroverted but frank. It was that to which Natty Hawke found attractive about her. Carmen's no nonsense approach suited his rebellious characteristics. Pam knew her sister's candid approach but always sought her opinion. On this occasion, Pam wanted to know how Carmen felt about Sandra's feedback to the consequences of her double living. "Gud, she waan all now she got all. Mek har deal wid it harself", she responded. Carmen told Pam that she preferred to take the minicab instead of travelling to the hospital with Sandra. Carmen found Sandra an odd individual. It was nearly time for the minicab to collect Pam and her sister to take them for their second visit to the hospital. They had another piece of cornmeal pudding and a drink before the buzzer went. Carmen operated the intercom. "Who is it", she asked? "Minicab", voice at intercom replied. "Wi coming out now", Carmen advised. Both sisters exited the flat. As soon as the key turned the lock in the door, Antie Merkle stepped out into the corridor. "Mi wi keep ah eye fi yuh", she reassured. "How's George", Pam countered? "George is George, im gaan guh look fi im fren dem", Antie Merkle replied. "See yuh later, Antie", the sisters chimed. As they approached the minicab, both Pam and Carmen noticed the driver was different from the 'cheat' they had previously. "Don't badda fi guh di long way round", Carmen warned. "Why not 'baby-love', it wudda gi mi time fi lyrics yuh off", the driver said. As the car moved off, the driver flashed a smile in Carmen's direction. They travelled in silence for a while. As they drove by the police station, Pam looked directly at it. She recalled her ordeal with the insolent green humanoid robotron and the '*token honorable stereotype*' officers inside the station. Pam wondered how they could treat individuals like Raymond in the way they did but was not answerable to anyone for their errant behaviours. She conversed with Carmen. By her accent, the cab driver realized that she had only just arrived in the country from the far off exotic island where he was born. The driver was keen to show Carmen a '*good time*' in Ghetoborough. "Wat yuh doin dis weekend", the driver asked? "Staying away from you", Carmen replied. Pam and Carmen looked at each other but burst out laughing. They murmured some references about the driver but laughed yet again. He looked into the rear-view mirror but assumed that Carmen fancied him somewhat. The driver assumed that's what the women were laughing about. For the rest of the journey, both of them ignored his further attempts to woo Carmen. They pulled up outside the Casualty Area. "Don't forget fi collect wi", Carmen reminded. They got out of the car. "How could I", the driver replied. He looked admiringly at her when he made the comment. She liked the attention too but Natty Hawke was whom she preferred. He was not the *'smarmy'* type. As they walked through the narrow gap that led to the ward, Pam pleaded with Carmen not to tease Sandra about the situation they had discussed. When they arrived on the ward, they saw her sitting with head bowed at Raymond's bedside. "Hi Sandra, what happened", Pam enquired? Sandra hardly looked up. "He still doesn't recognize me", she moaned. A nurse came over to the bed but told them that each patient was only allowed two visitors at a time. "Mi wi wait outside", Carmen offered. Reflecting the strain she was under, Sandra still sat with her head down. As if she felt defeated, Sandra told Pam that she was going to sit in the limo to gather her thoughts. She left abruptly. Carmen took the opportunity to return to her sister's side. Pam's attention was focused on Raymond. She held his hand while she asked him several questions. He used the code they had worked out to respond. Pam moved her hand in front of his face but his eyes did not follow the hand. She was desperate to find out if Raymond could see. "Can you see me Raymond", she asked? Her heart sunk when Raymond squeezed twice. "Can you remember anything", Pam asked? This time he squeezed only once. "Very good Raymond", Pam encouraged. Carmen noticed the *'liquid food'* drip was almost empty. "Dem shud replace dat drip now", Carmen hinted. Pam agreed but walked towards the general office area to confirm if the drip would be replaced immediately. "As soon as we can", the nurse responded. Pam returned to the bedside. There, she sat holding Raymond's hands in hers, talking to him all the time. "Er she come, dat bitch", Carmen warned. Sandra walked towards the bed. She was looking tired and drawn but smiling. They all looked round when they heard the groaning sounds coming from Raymond. Pam and Carmen both looked puzzled. Sandra was the first to respond. "What's the matter Ray, are you feeling pain", she asked? She knew he couldn't answer verbally. Pam and Carmen were worried too but none of them could figure out what was wrong. "Get the nurse", Pam ordered. Sandra hurried over to the general office area but talked to the nurse about their concern to Raymond's sudden groaning noises.

CHAPTER 32

The nurse bleeped a doctor. "The doctor is coming to see Mr Oddball", the nurse assured them. At the bedside, the four women wore worried expressions. The nurse tried to look calm but when Raymond closed his eyes she hurriedly checked his pulse and blood pressure. The doctor arrived soon afterwards. He asked the nurse some questions then asked Sandra, Pam and Carmen to leave the bedside. Two more doctors arrived. The female one was the most senior. She ordered the nurse to pull the screen around Raymond's bed. All Sandra, Pam and Carmen could hear were the murmurs from the staff and the increase in volume of Raymond's groaning coming from behind the screen. "Don't die

Ray", Sandra pleaded. Pam held her tummy as she heard intermittent loud grunts interspersed with the groaning. Carmen felt a lump in her throat. The three women huddled together in the middle of the ward but waited for someone to tell them what was going on. None of them saw Sam approaching. "A word please, Ms. Bogus", Sam said calmly. Sandra looked at him angrily as if she didn't want him to disturb her. "What is it Sam", she barked? He told her that Duke had phoned to ask where they were because he couldn't get through to her phone. "What do you mean he couldn't get through to my cell phone? It didn't ring", she retorted. Sandra busied herself looking into her handbag for the phone. To her shocked surprise, she couldn't see it. She gasped but panicked. Sandra threw the full content of her handbag onto the hospital floor. She stooped but rifled through the accumulated items but the tiny phone was nowhere to be found. Sandra remembered the recording she had made of the conversation with the manager of the Hotel Welcome. She didn't want that to be found by someone else. Sandra started to panic. She asked Sam to return with her to the limo. He walked while she ran. The sound of her long strides echoed on the hard flooring but made it sound like a singular horse on early morning gallop on a frosty morning on the moors. Pam and Carmen looked at each other momentarily. "She can't leave now", they both declared. The declaration was far too late. Sandra was already exiting the ward with Sam in her wake. He hurried along as fast as he could. His footsteps sounding like a delayed echo responding to Sandra's *'clipdy clop'* sounds. Some of the other visitors were moaning about the loud chatter that had been taking place in the middle of the ward. One visitor took it up on himself to show his displeasure. The green humanoid robotron man approached Carmen and Pam. Pointing in Pam's face with a wagging finger, the man expressed how he felt about the loud chatter in the ward. "This is a hospital, not a common room", the male visitor admonished. Carmen was ready to tell him to mind his own business but Pam begged her not to comment. Some other visitors moaned about "foreigners receiving free hospital treatment" before returning to the bedsides of the patients they had come to visit on the opposite side of the ward. The nurse opened the screen but went past Carmen and Pam with a bedpan. The stench lingered long after she had gone. "He's had a little motion", the senior doctor explained. "Why was he groaning", Pam asked? "So would you if you had busted ribs and you were constipated. It was important for him to pass the bruised blood so we gave him an enema to soften the poo", the senior doctor replied. All three doctors left together. Pam was the first to return to Raymond's bedside. She held his hand but asked if he was feeling better. His eyes were opened again and a single feeble squeeze confirmed that he was. The sound of the heel of Sandra's boots echoed on the hard floor once again. She had noticed that the screen had been withdrawn. Sandra hurried along to get to Raymond's bed. She joined Pam but held his other hand but asked if he recognized her. He squeezed her hand twice. Unaware of what had taken place after she had vacated the ward in search of her cell phone, Sandra uttered a loud yelp of joy that Raymond had chosen to respond to her question. Mistakenly, Sandra thought his response meant yes. "He squeezed my hand twice", she enthused. Pam did not want to disappoint or dampen Sandra's moment of excitement so she chose not to decipher what the code meant. Sam waited awkwardly in the middle of the ward. He did not know whether to leave or stay. Carmen reminded Sandra that he was waiting. "Dat poor chauffeur standing dere all alone in di middle ah di ward", she commented. Sandra apologized but said she had to leave yet again. She gave no explanation. "Oh, I'll be back as soon as I can", Sandra said. Pam nudged her sister, as if to remind her that Raymond could hear their conversation. "It mite b beta fi yuh if im doh wat ah gwaan", Carmen insisted. She pointed to her belly to indicate that Pam should tell Raymond that she is pregnant. "Not now Carmen, not now", Pam pleaded. The nurse returned to change Raymond's *'liquid food'* drip. She explained to Pam that the *'feed'* did cause constipation but that it was the only way Raymond could be fed at the moment. She said when it was necessary they would give him another enema to help free his bowels. "Do you think he'll ever recover fully", Pam asked? "You'll have to ask the neurologist", the nurse replied. "By the way, Mr. Oddball had another visitor earlier but he didn't stay long", she stated. "Who was it", Pam asked? "He said his name was DJ Herbie, do you know him", the nurse asked? "Yes", Pam replied. The nurse left the bedside. "Raymond did you know DJ Herbie came to see you", Pam asked? He squeezed her hand once. Pam was excited. First, that Raymond's friend, DJ Herbie had come to see him and also that Raymond had recognized him. Carmen reminded her sister that the minicab was almost due to arrive. "We'll come back tomorrow, Raymond", Pam assured him. They walked through the narrow path back to the Casualty Area where they met Sam. "Where is Ms. Bogus", Pam asked? Sam told them that he didn't know. Pam asked if she was in the limo but he confirmed that Sandra was not in the limo. Pam puzzled where Sandra might be. All Sam could say is that he saw her speaking with a doctor but that both had disappeared from his view. Pam asked Sam to tell Sandra that they had left the hospital. The minicab driver waited for them to finish their conversation before announcing his presence. They said goodbye to Sam before exiting with the minicab driver. "Minicab at your service", he prompted. Again, the driver's full attention was directed at Carmen. This time Carmen noticed the gold chains and the rings on every finger. His clean-shaven face matched his clean-shaven head that was partially hidden under the baseball cap. The driver wore the latest fashioned clothes and branded trainers. "It luk like yuh waan tek mi awn. Weh yuh can duh fi mi? Yuh hav money", Carmen asked? She didn't want to encourage the driver but she liked the attention he was paying her. "Baby, fi yuh I'll swim di ocean or climb di highest mountain al ina di same day", the driver stated. "Den yuh ah guh bi too tiad fi duh nuttn else. Yuh ah guh fal asleep", Carmen teased. "When you two have finished courting each other I'd like to go home", Pam said. They left the hospital but soon approached the road that went past the police station. "Stop at the police station", Pam ordered. The driver advised Pam about the solid red lines and their implications. "Drop me off and park somewhere else but I need to go in there", Pam stated. Carmen followed Pam into the station. "Can I help you ladies", the green humanoid robotron cop asked? Pam asked about Raymond's car. "Let me see", the cop said. He looked through the information on the computer. "Here it is. Raymond Wilberforce Oddball arrested for reckless driving, noise nuisance, suspicion of burglary, resisting arrest, driving a motor vehicle at an officer and suspicion of drugs. Articles found on his person are two different sets of house keys (hence the burglary charge), an assortment of money, an expensive branded gold watch, one notebook and a stolen diamond ring. That's it", the cop finished. "You've got to be wrong. Raymond wouldn't do any of those things you've just described", Pam said. The cop laughed. "Your *'lot'* are always pleading innocence but my Commissioner knows what he's talking about", the cop said bluntly. "What about his car? You still haven't told me about his car", Pam insisted. "That's at the Forensic Lab undergoing tests", the cop retorted. Another green humanoid robotron cop

Pam and Carmen had seen on their previous visit, walked up to the desk. He stared at Carmen. "I can't hear you swearing today. Learnt your lesson have you", the other cop implied? Pam nudged Carmen but hinted that she shouldn't reply. "Come on sis", Pam instructed. They left the police station knowing for certain, Raymond was in big trouble. The minicab driver noticed the change in their mood. "Where to now", he asked? "Take us home", Pam replied. "Tun up di music," Carmen ordered. "You like good music", the driver queried? He fulfilled Carmen's request. She moved rhythmically to the bass. "Yes", Carmen replied. Pam was in a more sombre mood but she too nodded her head to the beat. The music started to take priority over all their problems. They drove through the heavy traffic until the crackling of the *'two way'* radio interrupted. "Anyone near base", the voice of the minicab controller asked? "Echo 38 approaching Elementary Estate near petrol station, over", the driver replied. "58, Birdness Close, let me know when P.O.B", the minicab controller ordered. "Roger", the driver replied. They could see the entrance to the Elementary Estate 50yds away but there were a greater number of cars than usual. "Damn traffic", the driver moaned. He was cursing the slow movement of the traffic in front of him. He indicated but pulled out then drove the 50yds to the entrance on the wrong side of the road. "What ah driver", Carmen commented. She was responding to the dangerous manoeuvre but she somehow enjoyed the thrill of danger. Carmen had come from a background where people risked their lives and others by simply being reckless. Inside, the Elementary Estate the car went too quickly over the first hump in the road. "Take it easy driver", Carmen shouted. Pam started to hold her belly. Without commenting, the minicab driver immediately slowed down. After negotiating the other humps more slowly, they parked about 15yds away from the main entrance door. It was being obstructed by the scattered formation of the huge metal and plastic Refuse/ Dumpster bins. As Carmen and Pam alighted from the car, the driver commented. "See you later baby love", he said. As he drove away, the driver popped his head through the window but smiled and whistled at Carmen. Pam heard the landline phone ringing long before she opened the door to her flat. Carmen was first to it as if she was expecting a call at that time. "Hello", she said. "Is that Miss Pamela Labrishè", the voice asked? "Dis is har sista", Carmen replied. "Oh, do you live there too" the voice at the other end probed? "Hold on", she replied. She placed her hand over the receiver. Carmen told Pam about the questions but handed her the phone. "This is Pamela Labrishè, who am I talking to", she asked? "Benefit Agency Investigator, Allan Baitman", the voice on the other end replied. Pam's brow furrowed as she tried to figure out why the Benefit Agency Investigator would be ringing her at this time. "Can't you phone during office hours, I've only just come in and I have several things to do", Pam argued. "We've been tipped off that you are not the only one living at your address. My investigations confirm that a man is living there. He let me in through the entrance door of your Estate a few nights ago then opened the door to your flat with a key. We'll be writing to you in regards to your claim", Mr. Baitman ended. "Those bastards", Pam shouted. She slammed the receiver down. Pam told her sister why the man had called. Carmen tried to calm her older sister down as she ranted on about the heartless system would deny Raymond, her lover, the freedom to visit her. "Do dey spy on yuh ina dis country", Carmen asked? "Yes", it is called the *'Big Sister System'* Pam replied. "Don't dey tink yuh need a man", Carmen asked? "They don't care", Pam replied. "Mek wi eat. Mi ah starve", Carmen exclaimed. She washed her hands in the bathroom upstairs but came back and headed towards the kitchen. Over dinner, Pam told her sister how humiliated she felt about the Local Government spying on her. "It's as if I don't have a right to my own private life", Pam exclaimed. ***"Livin abraad ain't easy,*** I cudn't liv unda dis kinda stress", Carmen concluded. The intercom buzzed. It sounded as if someone was trying to play 'Chopsticks' on glass but with a flat tone. "I wonder who that could be", Pam asked? She pressed the button on the two-way intercom system but enquired. "Who is it", Pam asked? The voice was female but seemed to be rambling on. Pam was unable to determine the owner of the voice so she replaced the handset. The intercom buzzed again continuously as if someone had made a decision to keep the tone at an annoying duration. Pam was not pleased. This time she determined to let the individual know that their persistence was becoming a nuisance to her. "What do you want", Pam shouted. This time the voice was male but he identified himself to her. "It is Sam, Miss Labrishè", he responded. Pam had worked herself up to such a temper that she was unable to relate to the name. "Sam. I don't know any Sam. Who the hell is Sam", Pam demanded? "Ms. Bogus's chauffeur", Sam replied. Pam was in total shock as to why Sam would want to visit her. After all, she had never encouraged Sam to visit her, especially at this time of night. It was 00:20 hours. Pam still thought it was some kind of hoax by someone who wanted to gain access into the flats. It was a regular ploy by individuals, who had come to visit others but either was unsure of the address or just randomly demanding access to satisfy their reasons for wanting entry. Pam was suspicious. She told her sister Carmen so. "Mek mi guh open the door. Mi wi get im fi justify wha mek im ah pres yuh buzzer dis early ina di mawnin", she challenged. Before Pam could respond the intercom buzzed once again. This time Carmen picked up the intercom phone. "Yuh waan smady in yah. Mi ah cum open di door fi yuh. Anyting yuh get yuh deserve", Carmen threatened. Pam pleaded with her sister. "It might be a druggy. Be careful Carmen", Pam pleaded. Her warning was too late. Carmen had already exited from her flat. Pam followed after Carmen but was shocked surprise to see Sandra in the foyer. She muttered words that neither Pam nor Carmen understood. Sam apologized for buzzing the intercom at that early hour but insisted he was only doing his duty. Pam stepped back open mouthed because Sandra looked as if she had been drinking heavily. "Come in Sam", Pam said. Without him, Sandra would not have made it from the limo. Sandra staggered in followed by Sam supporting her. "Who let you into the building", Pam asked? "Your neighbour George", Sam replied. Carmen looked at Sandra then at her sister. "Yuh fren suppose fi bi ah famous model. Dis ah di fren wey luk down pon peeple less fortunate dan harself", Carmen asked? "Not now Carmen, can't you see she needs help", Pam confirmed? "Shi nuh drunk, shi only ah pretend", Carmen expressed unsympathetically. Sandra could hear the voices but she couldn't think clearly. "Dukes' wife looks . . . li . . . ke . . . the back of . . . a bus", Sandra mumbled. She laughed an empty laugh. Sam was embarrassed about the whole spectacle. "Do you want to go back to the Hotel Welcome Ms. Bogus", he asked? "Leave her here. She'll be alright", Pam countered. "Ms. Bogus has an appointment tomorrow morning at 11:00 hours. I'll be here at 10:00 hours", Sam said. He got up from the armchair. "Ill remind her about the appointment when she wakes up", Pam assured Sam. She opened the door for him. Sandra moaned and groaned as if she was in pain. "Give me a hand Carmen, lets take her upstairs", Pam urged. "Whey shi gweing sleep. Shi naw sleep wid mi", Carmen declared. Before Pam could respond, Carmen spoke again. "Leave her pon the settee/couch", she instructed. Pam did not want to argue with her sister so she agreed. "Get two pillows and some cover for her", Pam ordered. Carmen walked slowly across the room through the lounge door but headed towards the stairs. She heard a more urgent message. "Bring the bucket quickly", Pam ordered.

CHAPTER 33

After Sandra settled down, Pam and Carmen went to bed. During the night Sandra kept tossing and turning as if haunted by a bad dream. When she started to scream, Carmen rushed downstairs to see what was wrong. Sandra was sitting up staring but pointing towards the window. Somehow, they had forgotten to draw the curtains but a man's face was there vividly peering through. Carmen, dressed only in her nightdress raced through the door and out through the main entrance. Outside, she saw a man crouching by the trees still peering through the window. "Hey yuh is a *'peeping Tom'*? Yuh gwein get whey *'peeping Tom'* deserve", Carmen shouted. As he turned round, Carmen kicked him in the stomach then in the crutch. He grunted as he felt the sharp pain. "Dat wil teach yuh fi peep thru windows, you thief", she screamed. Alan Baitman may have been an investigator but none of his other missions would be as memorable as this one. Carmen wasn't finished yet. She grabbed his right arm as he raised it in defence but twisted it until he surrendered. "Please stop, I'm Alan Baitman, Benefit Agency Investigator", he pleaded. Pam approached them. "What's happening out here", she asked? Pam was puzzled why her sister was outside in her nightdress and she wondered who the man was. "What happened", Pam asked? "Mi ketch dis tief dat's what hapen", Carmen declared. "No, I'm Alan Baitman . . .", the *'peeping Tom'* repeated. "Shut up. Yuh is ah tief. Mi ketch yuh ah try fi bruk ina mi sista flat. Yuh beta kanfes", Carmen threatened. Some of the neighbours were peering from their own windows. One had already formed her own opinion of what she thought happened. "It's a lovers tiff", she reported. Sandra watched the whole scene from the window. The swirling clouds of drunkenness in her head had disappeared and she was fully aware of Carmen's actions. She noticed that Carmen was a martial arts expert too. Her precise movements and selected areas of attack confirmed that. "Hold him until the police arrive", Sandra suggested from the window. "There is no need for the police, I'll go quietly", Alan Baitman surrendered. "Gud, doan come bak unles yuh waan sum more ah di same", Carmen threatened. She feinted yet another kick towards his crutch. Carmen deliberately did not make contact this time but Alan Baitman, anticipating the pain, grunted all the same. He looked a beaten man as he dragged himself towards his car. Pam now knew this was the man who had spoken to her earlier on. "Come on in sis, you'll catch a cold", Pam advised. She guided her sister Carmen back towards the entrance door. Inside, the three women discussed the whole thing again from beginning to end. Pam went to the kitchen to make some tea. She asked Sandra if she wanted some. "After that I'll need something stronger, have you any brandy", Sandra enquired. "Yuh nuh tiad ah drink", Carmen asked? She didn't give Sandra anytime to reply. "Yuh come yah drunk. Now yuh soba but di fus ting yuh waan is ah drink agin. Sum peeple neva lern", Carmen admonished. Sandra was seething inside but sensed that her long fingernails would not be sufficient to combat the younger, more agile Carmen. "It was only meant to be a joke, that's all", Sandra jousted. As they sat drinking the hot mint tea, Pam told Sandra what Sam had said. "He said, he'll be here at ten", she conveyed. "Another photo session at Grant Favours", Sandra replied. Rapidly the conversation drifted from Alan Baitman to Duke. "Tell me what Duke's wife said when you met her", Pam asked? Sandra wanted to tell her friend what took place at the hospital but she was too embarrassed to discuss her personal affairs in front of Carmen. Somehow Sandra sensed that Carmen would have a sarcastic comment or two to offer. "That's not important at the moment. I'll tell you another time", Sandra dodged. Pam realised that it wasn't the right time so she asked Sandra if she had gone back to see Raymond before she left the hospital. "I couldn't", Sandra replied. "We went to see the police about his car but all we received were insults", Pam reported. "Let them keep the car. I'll buy him another one", Sandra replied. "Dats not di point", Carmen interrupted. Sensing that her sister was getting impatient with Sandra, Pam ventured to explain. "Listen Sandra, Raymond is in lots of trouble. The charges are very serious", Pam stated. "Duke said Hinton Fairly is the best. I'm sure he will be able to make the Judge see sense", Sandra confided. "Since mi dey yah, mi si ina di newspapers an pon TV how Judges look pon di Raymonds ah dis world", Carmen exclaimed. "What do you mean", Sandra asked? "Two of the charges are drug dealing and theft of an expensive diamond ring", Pam explained. "They are wrong. I can swear that Raymond is not involved in such things", Sandra defended. "Yuh mus bi livin pon ah different planet. Yuh doan noh sey wi gilty til prove innocent", Carmen enquired? "That maybe true where you come from but here one is innocent until proven guilty. I'm confident under our law, Raymond will receive a fair trial", Sandra justified. "Dream awn", Carmen responded cynically. Pam was getting tired of the tedious naivety coming from Sandra. She yawned and stretched. "We're all tired and stressed out. Let us get some sleep", she implied. "I could do with a couple more hours myself", Sandra replied. "I'll put a new toothbrush and some fresh towels in the bathroom for you", Pam advised. The two sisters made their way upstairs. Sandra made sure the curtains were drawn this time before stretching out once again on the settee. Within minutes they had all fallen asleep.

When the doorbell rang Pam looked at the digital clock radio which rested on the headboard. It was 08:10 hours. "I wonder who that could be", Pam questioned? Still half asleep, she put on her dressing gown but made her way down the stairs. She looked in on Sandra but she was still asleep. The bell rang again. Pam opened the door. Antie Merkle was standing there with George behind her. "Come in", Pam invited. They entered the flat but headed for the lounge. "I'm sorry you can't go in there, lets go into the kitchen instead", Pam declared. The kitchen was only big enough for two peole to fit in comfortably. However, they squeezed their way in. "Las nite mi si yuh sista giv ah man sum tumps and kicks. Wats going on", she queried? Pam patiently explained that Carmen thought the man was a thief. "She tink is 'bak home' she is", Antie Merkle asked? As some memories flooded back to her earlier days, Antie Metkle laughed uncontrollably. "Wen I wz young, di whole community used 2 beat di thief", she recalled. George and Pam saw the funny side and laughed as well. "Carmen has always been a brave girl", Pam confirmed. "George pick up im machete fi cum help but mi stop him cause yuh sista didn't seem fi need any help at all. She can hangle harself", Antie Merkle continued. They all laughed again. "It's finished with now", Pam confirmed. "If im cum bk im hafe ansa tuh mi", George emphasised. As they made their way back towards the door, Antie Merkle pointed towards the lounge. "Why yuh nuh mek yuh sista sleep upstairs", she queried? Pam did not correct Antie Merkle's assumptions. Instead, she smiled as she ushered George and Antie Merkle towards the exit door. "I will", Pam replied. Carmen had heard the whole conversation as she lent unto the rail on the landing upstairs. She made her way down the stairs. "Gud mawning sis", Carmen exclaimed. "Hi Carmen, did you manage to get some sleep", Pam asked? "Wha dem waan suh erly ina di mawnin", Carmen asked? "Antie Merkle doesn't miss a trick. She said both she and George saw what happened last night", Pam replied. "Mi er wha George sey be4 im leave. Yu tink im mean wha im sey", Carmen asked? Pam gazed absently into the hallway. "Yes, I think he means it", Pam replied. Both Carmen and Pam showered but dressed before preparing mackerel and green bananas for breakfast. The smell of food drifted into the hallway but carried through to the lounge. Sandra was unaware of the tantalizing smells that tickled nostrils but excited taste buds. Pam and Carmen's mouths were *'watery'* from sheer anticipation of tasting the nutritious, delicious, natural foods of which they had become accustomed. They were from a far off exotic island where consumption of these foods was an everyday occurrence and the benefits to good health remained automatic. Carmen did not waste the opportunity to raise this point with her sister. She was keen to confirm that Pam had not detracted from her natural food. "Suh unnu eat di same diet as bk home ova yah", she asked? "Not all the time", Pam replied. This did not seem to satisfy Carmen's curiosity. She taunted Pam with another comment towards the availability of exotic fruits. "Mi did si sum mangoes di odda day but dem ah nuh di same as bk home mango", Carmen queried? Pam was feeling home-sick now. She chose to silence the taunts from her sister. Pam chose to respond to her sister in the language that would also convey how she was feeling about having her choice restricted. "Whey wi can duh bout dem tings deh. Fiwi peeple cum yah tinking everyting is di same as bk home but yuh si fi yusself. It nuh easy awn yah", Pam concluded. The choice of language had the impact Pam had intended. There was no other way to convey the huge sacrifice that she and other immigrants from their respective exotic continents, countries and islands had to make in order to live abroad. Carmen empathized with Pam's lamentation. She reached into the pot with the cooked food and the frying pan with the mackerel. Carmen used the fork and spoon to remove a small amount of each but placed these on a small plate. Pam watched her sister pick up the food from the small plate with her hands. She teased Carmen about their earlier days back on the far off exotic island where *'forks'* were a luxury item. Again, Pam decided to stay with the island language. "Yuh memba how we used 2get 2geder an cook food bk in dem days", Pam asked? As they reminisced, the memories flooded back momentarily. Carmen savoured the salty mackerel and the unique taste of the green bananas. She used her fingers to remove the remnants of the bones that survived the action of her molars. Carmen looked up at the clock in the kitchen. "Wha time yuh fren gwein wake up? Is 09.20 hours aredy. Di chauffeur sey him ah cum 10:00 hours", she commented. "Mek mi wake har", Pam agreed. She made her way towards the lounge. Pam knocked on the door but called out. "Sandra, are you awake", Pam enquired? "Yes, I'm awake", Sandra replied. "It's 09.21hours Sam will be here soon", she reminded. There was no other verbal response. The door opened but Sandra stood in the doorway. She smiled at her friend. "Thank you for letting me stay overnight", Sandra said. She started to walk towards the kitchen. Carmen stood in the kitchen doorway like a guard on duty at a Palace Gate. "Suh yuh naw guh ah di bathroom guh brush yuh teeth", Carmen asked? "Can't I do it in here", Sandra asked? "Naaah, dats why dere is a bathroom", Carmen rebuked. Pam joined in the damning of Sandra's assumption that her *'cultural'* way of life was not at all similar to theirs. "Not in my kitchen sink, you should know that Sandra", Pam confirmed. Sandra did not reply but instead made her way upstairs to the bathroom. "Dat gal nasty doah", Carmen stated. "Is how yuh parents bring yuh up Sis. Har mada is one ah dem who adopt the *'fahren culture' 'values and beliefs'*. Yuh wudda surprise how fiwe people dem change from our traditional *'values and beliefs'* to what dem perceive to be superior", Pam crtitcised! She shrugged her shoulders but used her mouth to indicate that she was referring to Sandra. They both looked at each other then smiled. "Mi ah guh inna di lounge fi pick up di duvet", Pam confirmed. Carmen followed Pam into the lounge but immediately opened the window. She used her hand to fan her nose. The strong smell of perfume infiltrated their nostrils. "Mek wi get some air inna di place", she gasped? They anxiously awaited the draught of fresh air from the open window in order to expel the noxious smell of perfume from the lounge. Pam and her sister quickly cleared away the duvet and pillows. "Finish off di food Carmen wile mi tek dem tings yah upstairs", Pam instructed. They heard the toilet flush but Pam strained her ears to try to identify the trickling of the bathroom taps. There was no such sound. On her way down the stairs Sandra walked passed Pam. "You have to wash your hands if you're going to touch anything in my kitchen" Pam warned. "Oh, I forgot", Sandra replied. She returned to the bathroom. This time Pam did hear the trickling of the water from the bathroom taps. She smiled but felt her body shudder as she thought about Sandra. Before she had completed her journey down the stairs, a sharp smell of quite expensive perfume preceded her entrance into the kitchen. The smell of the perfume burnt the inner parts of Carmen's nostrils. "Dat perfume is very strong, wha yuh cal dat", Carmen asked? "Gynasium No. 5, very expensive", Sandra replied. "It smells more like an unwashed armpit to me", Carmen critised. "Maybe you wouldn't like the even more expensive one which they call *'Skunk-Pee'*. It's reported to be an extract from that animal. It's very much in vogue but at 2000 SPCU a bottle, it's a bit too expensive for me at the moment. I'll probably be able to afford it after my next contract", Sandra commented. "Tell mi yuh doan mean the black and white animal", Carmen queried? "Yes, that's exactly what I mean. I don't see anything wrong as long as it's expensive. That's all that matters to people who want to follow the trend of the moment", Sandra said nonchalantly. Carmen looked at Sandra then at Pam, who stood just outside the kitchen door. "'Sis, is yuh friend alright upstairs", she queried? "Sandra is addictive to trends", Pam replied. Carmen looked up to the *'heavens'* but mumbled some words under her breath. "We cook sum mackerel an green banana fi brekfas. Yuh waan sum", Carmen asked? "No, I can't eat that" Sandra replied. Offended by the mere suggestion in Sandra's voice, Carmen confronted her. "Why not", she asked? "Yuk. The teachers at primary school told me it is *"dirty food"*. My mother used to try to force me to eat it but I told her I didn't want it", Sandra responded. She removed the lids from both the pot and the frying pan but looked scornfully at the food. "Wel fimi food ain't dutty", Carmen snapped. "It is true what Sandra said Carmen. From nursery through to junior school, the green humanoid robotron teachers say those things to children of ethnic parents, who've emigrated to this country. I don't know with what authority they claim they have over us. I went through the same procedure but they had no influence on me", Pam explained. "My neighbour told me that is what they told her child too. She can't get her child to eat our traditional foods anymore", Pam finished. "Dem green humanoid robotron teachers dem mad. Fimi food ain't dutty. Fimi grand parents and fiwi ancesta dem ah nawm dis kinda food since dem bawn. It nuh kill nun a wi yet", Carmen declared. Pam and Carmen laughed loudly together while they each cherished the memories of the taste of their particular favourite dishes. Sandra broke Pam and Carmen's journey along their individual memory trail. "Have you any coffee", she asked? "Jus dun", Carmen teased. "Ignore that last comment but you'll have to make it yourself", Pam replied. She handed the bottle of grounded coffee to Sandra but instructed Carmen to turn the fire under the kettle. It didn't take long to boil again. Sandra poured the hot water into the cup but stirred briskly. She put two measured teaspoons of the brown sugar and stirred again. "Yuh want milk inna dat", Carmen offered? "No thanks. I prefer my coffee black. It keeps me wide awake", Sandra countered. "Yuh mean yuh get ah '*high*' from the coffee", Carmen suggested? The buzzing noise of the '*intercom system*' at the front door alerted them. "Oh that must be Sam. It's exactly 10:00 hours", Sandra declared. As she was caught between taking a sip from the cup and placing it unto the worktop, Sandra spilled the coffee over the worktop. Rushing to pick up her handbag from the lounge, she apologised. "I'm sorry I've got to go", Sandra explained. "Wha bout di mess? Yuh nuh hav nuh servant awn yah", Carmen criticized. "Sorry, no time, see you Pam", she apologized again. Sandra exited. "She's ah real mess. How yuh talarate har", Carmen asked? "That is Sandra Bogus. Take her as you see her", Pam replied. Sam was waiting attentively beside the car. "Good morning Ms. Bogus", he chimed. "Am I late Sam", Sandra asked? He opened the door for her. "No maam", Sam replied. He closed the door then got in behind the wheel of the limo. Sam eased it gently along the road leading out from the Elementary Estate unto the High Street. As the limo got closer to the end of the road, Sam saw the blue flashing lights but there was no siren. He had to wait until the police cars turned into the Estate before he turned right onto the High Street. "I wonder who is expecting a visit", Sam mumbled. Sandra glanced at the two cops as the cars passed. The journey to Grant Favours' Studio would take a mere 20 to 30 minutes, Sam thought. He drove carefully as usual, utilizing his many years experience to great effect. Sam could not have known that the riders on the scooters filtering to exit at the next turning ahead on the right would suddenly decide to continue straight ahead instead. This put him in a challenging situation. Sam had tried to anticipate the scooters exiting. He pressed on the gas for the limo to go past them on the left side of the lane. Its extra-ordinary length was already halfway across the roundabout. The three scooters seemed certain to collide into the right side of the limo. Sandra looked anxiously as the scooters hurtled towards the rear door where she was closest to. There seemed to be no time for adjustments from the scooter riders. Sandra curled up into a ball, shrieked loudly but anticipated the inevitable crash. As he advanced further into the roundabout, Sam chanced that the car on his left further along, waiting to join the roundabout would not attempt an entry into it. The driver of the four-wheel drive vehicle sat patiently as he willed Sam to accelerate. The driver observing the scene encouraged Sam by blowing his horn to get his attention. Sam did not need any further encouragement than to know that, if anything happened to Sandra, while she was in his charge, he would be in big trouble with Duke. Pressing harder on the gas, Sam took the limo around the arc he had to cover then wrenched the steering wheel to the left to exit the roundabout. The sharp wrenching of the steering wheel caused the limo to swerve awkwardly. It negotiated its sudden change in direction with the left side of the limo lifting itself off the road. The screeching had attracted the attentions of all those who witnessed the seemingly reckless limo driver. Sandra did not hear nor feel the anticipated bang into the side of the limo. She was now being thrown like a singular parcel in an empty vehicle from left to right and then from right to left in a sequence of momentary motions without volunteering to do so. She still shrieked loudly but remained in the crouched position. Some observers had seen only the erratic movements of the limo but were totally unaware of the antics of the scooter riders. The woman with the two little fluffy dogs talking to the old man on the sidewalk pointed at the limo but commented. "That driver must be drunk to be driving like that, don't you think", the woman assumed? "Bloody mad drivers", the old man replied. He bent down to stroke the dogs. "Who's a good boy then? Who's a good boy then", the old man repeated? The dogs smelt then licked the old man's hand. As they did so, he shifted his attention from dog to dog. The woman told him that both dogs were female. "Both bitches then", the old man confirmed. Returning to the subject about the driver, the woman seemed intent to keep the conversation fresh in the man's mind. "It's those stunts they see on television, ain't it", she queried? The old man ignored her comments, patted the dogs on their heads then walked off. "See you Betty", the old man said. He adjusted his flat cap. It lay neatly upon his head. The man folded his newspaper, placed it under his arm but marched away like a soldier in a movie, whistling a merry tune after a successful mission. Sam's mission was not a memory but simply a matter of calling upon all his skills, techniques and experiences to bring the limo back under full control. It lurched from lane to lane. Sweat was pouring off the animated Sam now as he manoeuvred the steering of the oversized vehicle. His heart was pounding loudly, thumping his chest as if it was beating out a message on a drum. There was a yellow sports car behind on the outer lane that was rapidly diminishing the distance between it and the limo. Its huge size was positioned awkwardly in both the middle and the outside lanes. The driver of the yellow sports car could see that there would not be enough space or time to overtake the limo but continued to forge along all the same. Sandra had only just braved it to look up from her crouched position when she saw the other difficult situation confronting them. She started to shriek uncontrollable once again. In order to avoid the approaching yellow sports car, Sam had to make yet another desperate swing to his left then corrected the steering again. The limo was now stable and on a straight path down the middle lane. Sam looked across as the yellow sports car sped past him just moments after the drastic manoeuvre that stabilized the limo back unto a straight path. As the yellow sports car whizzed by, Sam saw a young girl of about 14 years old behind the steering wheel. Sam's first thought was that she must have taken the car without permission. He shook his head in disgust at the unlicensed driver. Sandra waited until she felt comfortable with the limo's line then she sat up normally. She asked Sam to explain the unusual set of circumstances. "What is happening Sam", Sandra asked? Sam related to her about the two instances of narrow escape. "How far away are we? Will we still make it in time", Sandra fussed.

CHAPTER 34

Her voice wore fear in its tone. At times, Sandra fidgeted, fussed with her hair but glanced at herself repeatedly in the small mirror that she carried with her everywhere. "How do I look Sam", Sandra asked? He glanced into the rear view mirror. Sam wanted to say "sizzling and sexy" but had to adjust his secret admiration because of his position. "Sssss . . . mart as usual Ms. Bogus", he replied. Sam really wanted to tell Sandra the truth. She looked gorgeous but Sam did not want to seem too familiar.

Secretly, he really fancied Sandra and hoped that, through some strange coincidence, she would eventually be his woman. "I'd really like to care for you", Sam mumbled. Sandra overheard the words "to care for you" but not the rest of Sam's mumbling. "What was that Sam", Sandra asked? He glanced through the rear-view mirror again, to take another look at the woman he privately hoped to 'rescue' from his overall boss, Duke. "Just thinking aloud, ma'am", Sam lied. "Won't be long now before we get to the place Ms. Bogus", he added. The limo filtered right but Sam had to slow down rapidly as the bus in front of him stopped suddenly. In front of the bus a 'Learner' driver had stalled the car. The instructor sat passively but observed the old woman as she fidgeted and fussed over what to do. It was her first lesson and she was unfamiliar with the gears. She managed to put the car into neutral. Without sinking the clutch, the old woman tried to put the car into gear again. A crunching noise could be heard over the noisy engine of the bus. The instructor was calm. "I can't get the car into gear", the female learner fussed. "Clutch first", the driving instructor reminded. The woman was sweating now but felt embarrassed about her incompetence to engage the gear. Her instructor remained calm and patient. He reminded the old woman once again of the purpose of the clutch. "You need to press the clutch to the floor", the instructor advised. Sounds from the horns of impatient drivers penetrated the air. The driver of the white van which was travelling in the same direction as the limo was obstructing the box with the yellow diagonal lines. He had jumped the red light and now because of the flow of traffic travelling in the opposite direction of the limo, the white van just sat in the yellow diagonal box. When the lights had changed, access to the traffic coming from the left hand side of the four way traffic junction of the main cross road was unable to continue forward. The selfish action of the driver of the white van caused a heavy tailback of traffic on that side of the main road. Lots of 'road ragers' identified themselves by demonstrably cursing, swearing but pressing the horns of their vehicles in sheer frustration of the inactivity caused by one inconsiderate driver. Even when the lights changed in favour of the traffic in front of the limo, it stood stationary. The bus and the 'Learner' driver remained in the same position too. When the traffic light turned red again, the driver of the white van completed the right turn but continued on his journey. The driving instructor pressed the clutch of the 'dual pedal' car but encouraged the woman to "try again". This time she engaged the 1st gear and when the car was at its 'biting point' the woman released the handbrake. The car lurched forward but stalled yet again. Sandra was now feeling the butterflies in her stomach as she became more and more impatient. She kept looking at her watch. Sam remained coolest of all because he knew that Grant Favours place was a matter of about 3 minutes away. The bus had just begun to amble forward when it had to stop abruptly again. The sounds from the horns of the impatient drivers continued but were no longer a 'staccato' rhythm. Instead, they were more in the order of maintained notes. Sandra was stirred by the panic started by the impatient drivers. "Are we going to be late Sam", Sandra queried? "We still have about 17 minutes to get there", Sam assured. He glanced again into the rear view mirror but he saw the anxious look on Sandra's face. "Cheer up Ms. Bogus, we'll get there on time", Sam reassured. The bus started to move forward again after the patient instructor had managed to persuade the old woman that she could drive the car. One driver travelling in the inner lane stuck his two fingers up at the old woman in the 'Learner Driver' car. He also swore at her. She couldn't hear him but the sound of the horn from his car made her aware of how he felt about her. Sam followed the bus as it turned right off the main road. It then filtered left but stopped at the bus stop. Sam indicated but overtook the bus. He was approaching the pedestrian crossing with the Pelican lights when he saw the woman with the push-chair and the two little children who were walking beside her. Sam stopped the limo before the crossing. The driver of the car travelling in the bus lane was busy talking on his cell phone. Whatever was being discussed, the driver thought was funny. He threw his head back but laughed heartily at the comments from the other person enjoined in conversation. Sam could see the errant driver and vehicle through his near-side mirror. He pressed his horn in staccato fashion but hoped that the sound might alert the driver of the possible bizarre catastrophe ahead. Sandra responded to Sam's odd behaviour. "What's going on, Sam", Sandra asked? "It's that fool over there on the cell phone", Sam replied. Generally, he was a very quiet, polite person, who seemed always in control during testing situations but now Sam seemed anxious, impatient, angry and animated. The errant driver was oblivious of Sam's help. He continued to talk but there was no response from the other end. The driver removed the phone from his ear. He looked at it to check what had gone wrong but threw it on the seat next to him. The errant driver realized that the power from the battery in the cell phone had drained away. Sam sounded the horn once again. All the time he was keeping half an eye on the offending vehicle and half an eye on the woman with the push-chair and the two children crossing. Sam's focus was to warn the driver of the possible danger. The woman and her children had almost gone past the width of the giant sized limo. Sam saw one child suddenly run off in front of the mother. He turned anxiously around to look at the driver's reactions towards the new danger. Sam was shocked surprised to hear the screeching of brakes. By the time the errant driver had seen the imminent danger, it was almost too late. The mother with the pushchair and the children narrowly managed to escape from injury just in time. Fate had played its part, Sam thought. He eased the limo back into motion but signalled to the left. They arrived outside Grant Favours Studio with a little time to spare. Sam parked the limo. Sandra climbed from the car. Duke and Grant Favours were anxiously awaiting her arrival. She knew how much fuss Grant had made of her the first time. She had anticipated that he'd be pounding the pavement anxiously awaiting her arrival. Sandra did not expect Duke. "Sandra, darling", he cried. He rushed forward to hug her tightly. "Thank you for helping me get rid of the scourge of my life", Duke exclaimed. She was quite taken aback by his sudden outburst in front of Grant Favours and the general public. Duke didn't give Sandra time to speak. "Marry me please Sandra, marry me", Duke implored. Grant was very patient but he had a business to run. "Come on lovebirds, I've got a Studio to run", Grant reminded. Duke reluctantly let Sandra go then patted her on the backside. "See you later Sugarcake", Duke said. He was smiling from ear to ear as he watched his *'wife to be'* walk slowly away with his friend, Grant. "Sam take good care of Ms. Bogus, won't you", Duke stressed. "Yes Sir, I will", Sam replied. He watched Duke walk towards his own chauffeur driven limo. Grant Favours walked with Sandra towards the entrance of the Studio. Inside, Sandra went to the Dressing Room to change into the dress that Grant had asked her to wear. He had provided staff to do the *'make-up'* but he'd ordered them to stay in the Dressing Room until he needed them. "Stay out of the way", Grant demanded. Sandra exited from the Dressing Room. She looked a real

'Glamour Gal'. She was dressed in a long, tight-fitting antique gold coloured dress. It was *'Royal'* in its line but modern in its plain shiny surface. The sleeves were three quarter length but shaped like part of the costume from 'Dr. Who'. The bust-line was pointed and full but the neckline was cut low enough to tantalize. Sandra was also adorned with a golden mesh Tiara and long golden mesh fingerless gloves. Grant had paid particular attention to Sandra's hands and noticed the passion she had displayed for naturally grown long nails. They were as hard and sharp as a falcon's talons. The dressing room attendants painted Sandra's nails in matching antique gold too. She posed for Grant under his expert direction. He was very fussy about small details. Oftentimes, he would come from behind the camera to adjust a wrinkle or two in her outfit. It must have been the long Evening Dress which made Sandra seemingly tantalizingly irresistible. Her deeply tanned, cool, dark shaded velvety skin stood out as totally contrast to the antique gold shiny dress. Grant couldn't hold back the rapid endearing comments that he showered on her. He had carefully prepared the Studio before Sandra's arrival. Grant had arranged seven flashing lights around the room. Each was a different colour. These lights were all directed toward the mirrored walls. Grant was famous for his unusual photos. Sandra gazed at her reflection and felt pleased with the way she looked. She spun and pirouetted like a Ballerina on her toes in the diamond-encrusted shoes that Duke had dropped off for her. The sparkles from the shoes, blended with the many coloured lights, entering the mirrors at different angles, refracting and reflecting into several rainbows. These rainbows fused into a new kind of exciting light show. It cast itself like a sparkling *'aura'* from the mirror back into the Studio. This sparkling *'aura'*, on its reflection, surrounded Sandra but made her own 'aura' seemed to glow with a blinding brightness that would force Duke and all from the Tribe of Duke to have to revert to dark glasses. Grant had already started clicking away. "Feel free", he encouraged. Sandra smiled. "Lift your chin a little", Grant instructed. The instructions were more demanding than Sandra had thought but she was coping well with the Photo-shoot. According to Grant, Sandra was *"a natural"*. He was excited by her more than any other model he'd worked with before. Grant took pictures of Sandra from every possible angle. Some were quite normal but some others were suggestively rude, Sandra thought. Grant rushed from behind the camera to make yet another adjustment to the neckline of the dress. His hands were trembling now quite severely and Sandra noticed how profusely he was sweating. She looked sympathetically at him as he melted in front of her like butter on hot toast. Grant fidgeted with the neckline of the dress then in one mad uncontrollable moment, he ripped the top part of the dress from her. Sandra's voluptuous left breast tumbled from behind the torn dress and was now fully exposed. "Eureka", Grant shouted. He sprinted back to take dozens of pictures of the shocked Sandra. Puzzled by Grant's action, Sandra was looking down at the exposed breast. He had given her no notice or reason for his unusual behavior. "Grant", Sandra shouted. "Don't speak now just do as I tell you", Grant advised. "Look left, now turn slowly towards me, head up slightly, hold it . . ." Grant continued. The instructions and subsequent flashes from the camera were coming thick and fast now. Sandra obeyed. Excited by his subject, Grant's breathing became quite laboured and shallow subsequently as if he was being asphyxiated. His breath now came in rapid short gasps as if they were his last. Showered in sweat, Grant kept crossing his legs like a child waiting to use the toilet. The studio was hot from the lights but Sandra, who was wearing a long Evening Dress, did not seem as flustered about the heat as Grant. She began to feel a little frightened. Sandra decided to ask Grant if he was *"alright"*. His shirt was supersaturated but stuck to him as if he had been caught in a heavy downpour of rain. "I'll be alright in a minute", Grant replied. An entranced look upon his face betrayed the twisted thoughts that were going on in his mind. Grant's upper body began to shiver like a dog, who had just escaped from being dumped in a pool of iced cold water but his lower body seemed to convulse into a backward and forward set of incontrollable spasms. The patches of moisture appearing down the front of his trousers matched the gasps signalling a type of release, perhaps! A stupefied silly grin signalled some degree of accomplishment appeared over Grant's countenance. "Have a break now while I have a look at these pictures", Grant instructed. "Why did you rip my dress", Sandra enquired? She looked down at the one exposed breast. Grant was in a hurry to exit the Studio. He looked over his shoulder but responded to Sandra's question. "Artistic interpretation", Grant replied. Grant disappeared swiftly through an inner door. Sandra hurried back to the Dressing Room but changed into the dress she had worn to the Studio. She thanked the *'make-up'* staff but left a note for Grant to say she had gone to lunch. Outside, she asked Sam to take her to a restaurant. "I'm famished", Sandra said. "Sure ma'am, what type of food would you like", Sam asked? "Something simple and quick", Sandra replied. Sam opened the door for her. He knew of the rumours about Grant and models but he couldn't disclose such information. It wasn't his place to do so. "How did your session go, Miss Bogus", Sam searched? Sandra wanted to tell him about Grant's strange behaviour, especially about the torn dress but she held back from telling Sam about it. "Lets just say it was a new experience", Sandra replied. Sam closed the door gently. After taking his seat behind the steering wheel, he drove the limo away from Grant Favours Studio. Sam knew there were a lot of restaurants from different cultures in that area. He turned right and was soon close to the pelican crossing where the errant driver had caused him those earlier anxious moments. About 150 yards later, Sandra glimpsed at the different signs above the restaurants. "Stop Sam, that Chinese restaurant will be fine", Sandra stated. Sam pulled up just past the restaurant in front of The Wayward Rock AADC. He climbed out but walked towards the rear door of the limo. As he held the door open for Sandra, a couple of green humanoid robotrons from the Tribe of Babylon known as the Squareheads, standing outside the AADC, taunted Sam about his uniform and his race. "Go home", they shouted. Sam tried to ignore them. He knew that they were deliberately baiting him. Any wrong move now could signal that trait which might trigger but expose the worst in an individual like Sam.

When he was a younger man, Sam had met with this type of serial bigotry many times before. He remembered the beatings that some of his friends had got from those, who practiced the *'madness philosophy'*, racism. Though, most prominent in his mind was the killing of some youngsters in this and the peripheral surrounding areas. Sam recalled that 13 years previous there was a report about a birthday party where, amongst others, 13 youngsters had perished in a house fire alleged perpetrated by a group of green humanoid robotron Squareheads. Apparently, the alleged perpetrators were irate neighbours, who had objected to their neighbours from the Tribe of Hawke, hosting the birthday party for the young girl and her friends. It was reported that there was forensic evidence that a tin of paint thinners and a handmade lighted fire stick ablaze had been thrown through a window at the back of the building which led to a green humanoid robotron Squarehead's back garden. The report further commented that the police had stated "the evidence was only circumstantial". There was no proof, who had taken the offensive action to throw the tin of paint thinners and a handmade lighted fire stick ablaze through the window while the party was going on. It was revealed that during the case against that particular neighbour whose house backed onto the building that had been set alight by the introduction of the tin of paint thinners and the handmade lighted fire stick ablaze, the police admitted that the said green humanoid robotron neighbour is a self-confessed member of the serial Neuro-bigoted green Squareheads gang. Before the fire had been started, he had called that particular police station on more than four occasions on that night to complain about *"that 'lot' having another noisy party"*. Sam was seething with anger then and still felt a sense of "one *'law'* for *'them'* and another set of *'laws'* for *'us'*" recurring for those 13 years. Over that time span, individuals from all Tribes, had demonstrated hugely. They did this by organising marches on each anniversary. They did this to commemorate the children who were lost in that awesome inferno caused by a most deliberate act by either a singular perpetrator or with accomplices who had aided and abetted the perpetrator. In response to those demonstrable outcries, the green humanoid robotron police tried to *'frame'* one individual from the Tribe of Hawke'. They did this in order to justify their pallid, disinterest and lack of *'responsibility'* or *'commitment'* to solving the *'genocide'* that had happened 13 years ago. In a nutshell, this Police *'Cover-Gate'* episode demonstrated a *'lack of will'* to lead a genuine investigation on behalf of the 13 youngsters and others, who had been maimed or had perished in the fire. On each anniversary, it had been regularly reiterated that there was enough forensic proof that the fire had been started deliberately.

In this moment while he was being set upon, Sam felt that in the absence of *'justice'* every individual had the *'humane right'*, as a natural survivor, to revert to basic instincts whether to *'fight'* or *'flee'* when presented with adversity. Surrounded by the serial profilers, Sam's only option left to him was to *'fight'*. He wanted to punch the troublemakers but Sam felt he had to withhold his feelings for another time. After all, he was at work. Sandra sensed that trouble was brewing. She stayed inside the car. "Let us go Sam. I'm not that hungry", she pleaded. He shut the door for Sandra but glanced at the green humanoid robotron Squareheads, who had verbally abused him. One of them reacted violently towards Sam. He saw the blow aimed at his head but didn't see the broken beer glass until the last minute. Sam ducked like a boxer, who sees a blow too late but parried with his arm. The jagged glass ripped through his uniform but sliced Sam's upper arm. He lashed out at the attacker but managed to throw him off balance. Sam swung a right cross to the green Squarehead's jaw. He went crashing to the ground. Sam's momentum and anger allowed him to follow up with a kick to the ribs. The green Squarehead winced. Soon a crowd, mainly from the AADC, gathered around. One big mouth shouted more abuse but encouraged the other green Squarehead to "rip him apart". "Go on, finish the f . . k . . g N . . . . r bast . . . off Bill", the voice encouraged. Sam waited for the other green Squarehead to advance towards him. He swung a kick which collided with the attackers' own effort. Both men cried out as their shin bones met. Sam took longer to recover than the green Squarehead who, seizing the initiative, tried to grapple with Sam on the sidewalk. He held Sam by the throat but tried to strangle him. They fought for a while, bouncing on and off the limo. The pain in his shin was still there but Sam saw this whole episode now as a *'life'* or *'death'* situation. He fought like a man desperate to stay alive. It was the green Squarehead's turn to feel the full force of Sam's punches. They came more rapidly as the fight went on. Sam's left hook made him feel proud. He recalled his earlier years when his parents use to take him to boxing lessons. Most vividly, Sam remembered the instructions from his then coach. "The hook followed by the uppercut is sure to see your opponent go down", he had encouraged. Being young and naïve then, Sam had asked his coach a question. "What happens if he doesn't go down", he had queried? "Repeat the dose until he does go down. Make that your motto", the coach had advised. Those were the consistent instructions he would hear then. The coach's voice and words echoed through Sam's mind. Sandra saw the first green Squarehead creeping up behind Sam. She knew she had to do something. "Look out Sam", Sandra cried. She found herself stepping from the limo. Sandra was angry enough to let her claws go to work, deliberately this time. The green Squarehead squealed but reeled away as the extended nails ripped his jaw open. Now the situation had changed for the attackers. Sam had laid one out cold with his infamous right cross and now another was running for cover from the angry Sandra. The two green Squareheads were unable to defend themselves against the duo. They were not in a position to encourage others to join in the fight. The crowd was a noisy, rowdy, bunch throwing individual racial comments like confetti or rice at a wedding. Two men from the Tribe of Hawke were working on a building site on the other side of the street. They had heard the commotion but weren't the only ones that did. Some of their colleagues, from the Tribe of Duke and the Mixed DNA Rainbow Tribe, heard the swearing and racial comments that were coming from the group outside the other AADC, The Gung-ho Tavern a few doors away from The Wayward Rock AADC from which the first set of green Squareheads had come. The Tribe of Duke, the Tribe of Hawke and the Mixed DNA Rainbow Tribe joined forces but hurried across the street. Each carried something to protect himself.

Three green humanoid robotron motor bikers from the Tribe of Babylon had already got off their machines but were tensing and flexing their muscles in defence of the green Squareheads. They were from a notorious gang called The Bevvy Boys. "Who we got here then, Miss Amazonian Warrior", one biker asked? The bikers took a slow, deliberate, carefully rehearsed approach towards Sandra. They were attempting to surround her from different angles. She saw the heavily tattooed arms with insignias representing a particular set of *'values and beliefs'*. Sandra was forced to listen to the vitriol of derogatory language, laced with venomous spite delivered with unbridled deliberation. The bikers each had a *'weapon of destruction'*. Other onlookers saw the chain that one of the bikers carried in his hand. He started to shake the chain threateningly whilst moving towards Sandra. "Call the Police", a voice shouted. It came from the curious crowd that was quickly assembling. The sounds from the cell phones pads were playing 'Symphonies', 'Minuets' and 'Etudes' as the dramatic moments got more tense. "I hate you F . . . ing N . . . rs", a green Squarehead's voice shouted out. The ambience was a busy bout of insults and reactions. Screeching tyres signalled that more people had become interested in 'The Urban Street Movie' that was taking place. One of the Bevvy Boys biker with the chain was approached by one of the workers from the building site across the street. "Hey bwai, leave di sista alone", one from the Tribe of Hawke challenged. "Your Sister, is it", the biker countered? "Yeh and my sister too", one other voice from the Tribe of Hawke replied. He advanced his position towards another of the bikers. Those from the Tribe of Duke and the Mixed DNA Rainbow Tribe showed allegiance with the Tribe of Hawke. "Er mate, we're with them", six individuals from the Tribe of Duke confirmed,. They pointed towards the two men from the Tribe of Hawke. "We are with the Tribe of Duke and the Tribe of Hawke, the four individuals from the Mixed DNA Rainbow Tribe stated. This latest announcement by the Mixed DNA Rainbow Tribe seemed to confuse both the Bevvy Boys and the green Squareheads. "But you look more like us than them", one of the Bevvy Boys commented. The puzzled look seemed to muzzle the rest of what he was going to say. It was just like how a muzzle on a dog stops not only its bite but also its bark. This admission of oneness thwarted the attack on Sandra. The *'oneness code of conduct'* from the three other tribes seemed to disturb the green humanoid robotrons Bevvy Boys bikers and Squareheads alike. They were angry that the three tribes had joined forces against them but they were especially angry at those, who they assumed might have been on their side. "F . . . . ng N . . . . . r L . . . r", whose side are you on", both bikers shouted? The men from the Tribe of Duke, the Tribe of Hawke and the Mixed DNA Rainbow Tribe moved closer towards the biker, who had shouted the latter remark. He started to move towards his bike. "Come on, lets go", he suggested. The two others were reluctant to withdraw from the conflict situation. "Lets do 'em Irke", the biker with the chain insisted. He was sneering at the men from the Tribe of Hawke but they too could not be described as calm. All the men from the three tribes were brandishing metal baseball bats and more. The baseball bats weren't new ones. By the many dents that haphazardly decorated them, bore signs of previous usage. Irke cranked the pedal and the bike with twin chrome mufflers on both sides, roared into life. They spat out immeasurable carbon monoxide fumes into the air. Those fumes were thickest into the faces of the chaotic crowd standing close by even though they were just onlookers. A woman from the crowd, who had stopped to observe the behaviour of the rivals, feinted when she inhaled the fumes. "It's her asthma", the woman's husband croaked. His chesty murmurings did indicate that he too was experiencing a form of breathing difficulty. The man was significantly smaller than his wife, who had past out. He was about 10 and she approximately 22 stones. "Madgie, did you use your inhaler this morning", he enquired? Madgie struggled to reply but managed to confirm that she had. She was gasping for breath as she lay on the pavement. The man kept talking to her. Irke and the rest of the Bevvy Boys bikers thought this was as good a time to make their exit. Placing his index and little fingers into his mouth, Irke produced a very sharp, shrill whistle. The other two bikers acknowledged the signal but proceeded towards their machines. They cranked the other two bikes into action but created even more fumes. The thick cloud blasted its way into the faces immediately behind them. As the volume of carbon monoxide increased, Madgie's breathing became more laboured, irregular, ill-timed spasms. The crowd outside The Gung-ho Tavern AADC jeered Madgie, the woman who had feinted. "Come off it, she's faking it", one voice commented. "Seen the state of her? I bet she will cop it. Ten will get you twenty", the other voice chimed. The bets escalated, diminishing Madgie's demeanour. Even in her traumatized state, Madgie could hear the un-empathetic comments and she felt anxious but determined to prove them wrong. Sandra looked from one scene to another. On one side Madgie, her concerned husband and the small group made up of the Tribesmen. The other was the jeering group outside both AADCs. This group was known as *'micky takers'*. They would pick on, taunt and tease until the subject had run out of patience and was triggered into action or decided to run a hundred yards quicker than the current sprint world record holder. Unless you're ready to die or go to jail for a long time, the latter option would always be advisable. The drunken crowd started to retreat towards the AADC. As a parting shot, one drunken man said something about Sam then the others joined in. They made up a song about a chauffeur. Sandra snarled, screamed at but advanced towards those who still threw abuse at Sam. She felt quite shielded as the amalgamated union of tribesmen added their vocal support on her behalf. Sandra thought there was enough protection around for her and Sam to make their exit. "Let us go Sam", Sandra ordered. She looked round but Sam was slumped upon the car, feint from the exertion and the rapid loss of blood. The sleeve of his gray uniform was now a deep reddish-purplish colour. It was soaked with Sam's blood. Sandra struggled to get him in the car. He weighed a bit more than Sandra might have expected. She stood astride Sam's torso but passed her arms under his armpits. Sandra pulled but dragged until she was exhausted. She was at a loss of what to do. Sandra thought of calling on the tribesmen but they reminded her of Raymond's friends. Sandra's class perceptions of Raymond's friends dissuaded her from asking for help to put Sam into the limo. The few green Squareheads, who stood just in front of The Wayward Rock AADC, were in conversation about Sandra's efforts to get Sam into the car. The bets started yet again. "I'll bet you ten SPCU she can't lift him into the car", one voice teased. "Twenty she gets him in", another voice countered. Sandra's struggle seemed too much to do on her own. She looked round for the tribesmen but they had turned their attention back to Madgie. In fact, they were genuinely unaware of Sam's predicament. The limo had not been parked straight so the tribesmen could not see Sam from the position from which they had approached. When asked where Sam had disappeared to, one from the Tribe of Hawke had told the other in their cultural way what he thought Sam had done. "The chauffeur look like him duck out", one from the Tribe of Hawke said. Confirmation of the common belief was circulated through to the colleagues from the Tribe of Duke and the Mixed DNA Rainbow Tribe.

Previously, Sam had turned the limo into the space, in anticipation of the driver, who had signalled to pull out. She had changed her mind but decided to stay put. This caused the limo to stick out into the street. Sam was towards the rear door. Sandra managed to get his upper body into the limo. She stood astride him again lifting, heaving and pushing until a greater part of Sam's body was into the limo. Exhausted from her efforts, Sandra had to rest again. The extra exertion made her feel very tired. Sandra remembered what Raymond had taught her about good breathing. She put the learning into practice. Soon, her heart rate started to get closer to its regular beat. Sandra saw that the blood had ruined the upholstery and the carpet but there was nothing she could do about that now. All her thinking was focused on getting Sam to the hospital Sandra went around to the other side of the limo, held Sam under his armpits but pulled him unto the back seat of the blood-splattered limo. "I'll get you to hospital Sam, just hold on", Sandra pleaded. She climbed into the driver's seat but drove the limo back to Grant Favour's place. He was waiting outside for her but started to wave excitedly as the limo pulled in.

Grant took one step back as Sandra climbed from the driver's seat. "Grant, Sam's hurt. Where's the nearest hospital round here", Sandra asked? He saw the blood on her clothes but re-directed her away from the *'prestige'* area. "You'll have to take him to one nearer to your place", Grant replied. "He's bleeding badly. Sam needs immediate medical help. Where is it", Sandra demanded? Grant went to the limo but peered through the window. Sam lay motionless. Grant saw the blood-splattered plush upholstery. "Duke's going to do his nut when he sees the mess", Grant insisted. Without a further word, Sandra got back into the driver's seat of the limo but sped off. She wanted to phone Duke to tell him what had happened. In her haste to help Sam, Sandra had left her handbag and cell phone at the rear of the limo. Sandra thought about stopping to get her cell phone but she dare not waste anymore time. She needed to get Sam to hospital immediately. Sandra couldn't understand Grant's reluctance to direct her to the nearest hospital but she was determined to do her best for the dutiful Sam. "Talk to me Sam", Sandra shouted. There was no response from the seemingly gentle Sam.

CHAPTER 35

When that didn't work, Sandra turned on the CD player but increased the volume to try to alert Sam. There was still no response. Though she struggled to stop herself from crying, tears started to roll down her face. "First it was Raymond then Duke, now Sam. Why me", she queried? Sandra reflected how the fight started. "Poor Sam", she exclaimed. Sandra glanced yet again at his motionless body now partially on the floor of the limo. The rest of his body was still on the back seat but was situated in a twisted position. Sam's head was almost resting on the floor. He looked awkward. Sandra handled the limo quite expertly but the length of the vehicle sometimes caused her to misjudge the pavements. After the third bump with pavements, Sandra tended to drive closer to the middle of the road. She was a strong-minded person but Sandra was nervy about Sam's chances. "Talk to me Sam", she shouted. Sandra glanced back from time to time. A lorry was parked in the bus lane. The hazard lights were flashing, indicating that the vehicle was stationary. One bus had pulled up close to it but the driver had allowed adequate room to vacate the bus lane. Another bus travelling behind it was beginning to pull out from the bus lane into the path of the limo. Sandra saw a car coming from the other direction at the same time. Her options were to either slow down or try to overtake the bus in front of her that was pulling out from the bus lane. Sam's groaning alerted Sandra's decision-making. She stepped on the brake sharply. The limo pitched forward from the severity of the sudden pressure being applied to the brake. Sandra stopped the limo in the middle of the road but turned to look at Sam. "You're alive, talk to me Sam", she pleaded. The sound of a horn brought her attention back. When Sandra looked round again the buses had moved on further down the road. She pressed the gas pedal but drove the limo smoothly along. Sandra could see a turning but she was unsure if it was the correct one that led to the hospital. The sound of the siren from an ambulance confirmed the route. Sandra had to pull over quite a bit to enable the ambulance to go past. She turned right but followed the ambulance along the road. Sandra waited for it to turn into the hospital then she followed. As she pulled up in front of the

Casualty Department, Sandra observed the nurse with the mole on her nose making her way towards the entrance. The nurse smiled but waved at her as she climbed from the limo. "Where is that handsome chauffeur of yours today", the nurse asked? "Help me please", Sandra pleaded. She told the nurse that he was in the back of the limo needing urgent attention. The nurse peered through the rear side window but reacted immediately. "I'll get the some help", she commented. The nurse saw the bloody interior and Sam's body now completely slumped on the floor of the limo. Sandra opened the rear door nearest to the emergency entrance but removed the cell phone from the handbag. It was now smothered with blood. She quickly pressed the preprogrammed number. "Duke Stagg", he answered. Sandra told him very quickly what had happened, including Grants' refusal to help. "Poor bastard, stay there, I'm on my way over", Duke instructed. Once inside the 'Accident and Emergency' Department, there was a lot of medical language being used that Sandra did not understand but the urgency that the staff showed confirmed that Sam was in a bad way. A drip was attached to Sam's arm as they wheeled him off to theatre. Sandra tried to phone Pam but the phone just kept on ringing. She went back into the 'Waiting Area' but was desperate for company. Apart from Duke or Pam, there wasn't anyone else for her to talk to. For the first time, she began to feel alone and she suddenly recalled the last time she and Raymond had quarrelled. He had told her then that" . . . you are going to feel it one day when you don't have nobody to talk to . . . People who're only for themselves are going to find loneliness closer than their shadow". Sandra was momentarily in a trance. She shook her head from side to side, trying to rid herself of Raymond's voice. The voice she heard in reality was not that of Raymond's. "Hello, it's you again", Mr Pain confirmed. Sandra looked up. "Hello doctor", Sandra replied. "What happened to your chauffeur, was he getting fresh with you", Mr Pain asked? His tone was cynical but Sandra responded. "No, ignorant green humanoid robotron Squareheads attacked him", she explained. The last thing Sandra wanted was some clever remarks. She was just not in the mood for that sort of thing but the green humanoid robotron Mr Pain pressed home his snide comments all the same. His inference was not welcomed by Sandra.

Pam and Carmen arrived at the hospital. They were utterly shocked to see Sandra there. "What happened to Raymond", Pam asked? Sandra noticed how worried Pam looked but she was far too exhausted to challenge her friend about what was bothering her. "It's not Raymond. It's Sam", Sandra replied. "What happened", Pam asked? Sandra went over the story once again. She described how brave Sam had been even though his life was in grave danger. When she mentioned her part in the fight, Carmen started to clear her throat sarcastically. Sandra was incensed by the snide response. She glared at Carmen. Sandra had gathered that Carmen didn't like her. "Don't take me for granted. You should see me when I'm really angry", Sandra warned. Pam didn't want to see the confrontation between the Sanda and her sister Carmen. She appealed to their better judgement. "Calm down girls, we need to be together on this", Pam encouraged. Sam's blood had soiled Sandra's dress but she hadn't noticed at the time. "You've got blood on your dress", Carmen prompted. Sandra looked down at the ruined dress. "Oh my God", she exclaimed. A few other people in the Casualty Area looked at her strangely. One whispered into her companion's ear. He got up but spoke into his cell phone. Pam saw the way how the man was looking at Sandra but nudged Carmen. She was sitting nearer to the man. Carmen listened to his conversation. "Hello police I want to report a murder", the man reported. He gave his name but told the police that the suspect was at the hospital Casualty Department covered in blood. Carmen did not wait to hear the rest of the conversation. Instead, she came over to where Sandra and Pam were sitting. "Pam, that man just told the police that your friend committed murder", Carmen warned. Pam's shock response made Sandra ask why Carmen was whispering? "I think you should call your lawyer right now", Pam warned. "My lawyer, what for", Sandra asked? She was suspicious about Pam's comment. "Jus duh it. Save yuhself sum *aggravation*", Carmen warned. Having been through the trauma earlier on, Sandra was a bit edgy. She snapped at Carmen and Pam. "Call yourself friends", Sandra complained. Carmen didn't particularly like the inference but she knew that the police were on their way. "Duh it fi yuh owna gud. Tell har sis", Carmen pleaded. "That man just told the police that you have committed murder. Call your lawyer now", Pam warned. Sandra was puzzled how the man could have come to such a conclusion without even asking her what happened. She asked Pam to point out the man then she walked over to him. As he cowered beside his companion, the green humanoid robotron's face turned a paler shade of green. "Stay away from me", the man shouted. "Find out your facts before you interfere in other people's business", Sandra shouted. She then raised her hand to slap his face. Pam stopped her from hitting the man. She pointed out that others were watching. Archie Hingepin, from the Tribe of Hawke was the security personnel on duty that evening. He reminded Sandra of Henry Hardcase. Archie was just as 'keen' as Henry to impress his employers by ensuring that he embarrassed individuals from his own tribe in particular. He had heard the shouting but came to investigate. Archie had seen Sandra raise her hand so he came directly to her. "Can you keep the noise down? This is a hospital not a marketplace", Archie Hingepin said. Sandra and Pam started to walk away from him but he followed them. "Anymore violence and I'll have to ask you to leave", Archie Hingein told them. Neither Sandra nor Pam objected to him doing his job but they did not like him poking Sandra in her chest. "Get your hands off me", Sandra warned. She stood up to face him. He pushed her back into the chair. She leapt up and without thinking ripped his jaw with her claws. "I told you to get your hands off me, you creep", Sandra wailed. Archie grabbed his jaw but let out a cry that would befit a wounded bear. A crowd gathered around. Some of the staff, who had heard the yelp, rushed in the direction of the crowd. Green humanoid robotron Nursing Sister, Irenie Stumpington, made the call to the police. "Quick, they are wrecking the place", she pleaded. Pam knew that if the police arrived, Sandra would be as good as dead. She had read many reports in the media about people from the Tribe of Hawke dying on their way to police stations and she remembered that Raymond was only yards away. He was a victim of the awesome brutal beating he had suffered at the hands of the police. "Quick Sandra, you've got to get away", Pam said. She detailed Carmen to cause a distraction while Sandra made her escape. Outside, Sandra climbed into the limo but started to move slowly towards the traffic light at the end of the road leading from the hospital. The red light seemed to stay on for a long time. Sandra tapped impatiently on the steering wheel. She stared blankly through the windscreen. Still the lights did not change. Her nerves could not take it for much longer. She strained to suppress the impulse to jump the light. The police sirens dissuaded her impulse. Five vans and four cars passed the limo in the opposite direction. The lights changed to green. Sandra pressed the accelerator. The limo lurched forward then stalled. Sandra panicked but fumbled with the keys before the limo kicked into life again. This time she eased the limo forward but turned left at the lights. Sandra proceeded along the light traffic. She pushed at the steering wheel as if urging the limo to go faster. Sandra reached out but picked up the cell phone from the open handbag. She pressed the pre-programmed number. "Duke Stagg", he bellowed. Sandra explained what had taken place at the hospital. "All this is driving me mad", she cried. "What happened", Duke asked? She told him all the details she could remember. "Where are you now, my sweet", Duke asked? "I'm going to my house. Can you call Hinton Fairly", Sandra asked? "I'll get you the best, my angel", Duke quipped. "What about the police", Sandra asked? "Don't worry, I'll sort it out. You stay at your place. I'll meet you there", Duke assured her. He was near to the hospital but he didn't bother to tell her. When Duke arrived, there was a crowd outside the Casualty Area looking down onto the road.

Pam's sister, Carmen, was about the same build, height and colour as Sandra. Though she had dark brown eyes, no bloodstain on her dress to fit the description made by the informant nor extended fingernails to tie her to the claw marks on Archie Hingepin's face, Carmen's height, build and ethnicity was sufficient description for the green humanoid robotron police to arrest Carmen. The crowd kept looking at the way the police was handling the figure on the floor. "Move away", the cop ordered. "Don't do her like that. She hasn't done anything wrong", Pam cried. The cops ignored Pam's plea. They kept on administering the headlock and the arm wrenching. Carmen was a strong fit girl. In order to free herself from the *'strangle-hold'* being brought to bear upon her, she flinched one way then another. Carmen's instinctive effort was a futile one. When her body went limp, Pam cried out. "Yuh kill har", she shouted. Pam collapsed unto the floor. Some of the medical staff among the crowd had seen what had happened. "Move away from her, move away", the nurse with the mole on her nose ordered. She bent over Pam but slapped her face hard enough to revive her. As she came round, Pam could hear the sound of the police vehicles driving away. Duke followed them out but headed for Sandra's place. Carmen had told the cops what she thought of their aggressive approach. She had remonstrated dramatically with her arms to demonstrate how Archie Hingepin had aggressively prodded Sandra in the chest. It was at that moment, that she naively prodded the green humanoid robotron police Sergeant with the stern voice in his chest to show how Archie Hingepin had done it. "Like that", Carmen had explained. Pam sat in the Casualty Area looking into the cup of tea that the nurse had given her, pondering her sister's demise. "Assault on an officer", is what the Sergeant added to the other charges. The last half an hour had drained Pam of any energy that she had earlier on. Her thoughts were like a broken jigsaw puzzle with pieces missing to complete the picture. Pam could not afford a lawyer. The only person who could help her was lying in the ward near the end of the narrow passage. She had a small current account which she barely kept in credit. There was no collateral to secure a loan. Now her mind was in turmoil but she still had Aunt Rose, perhaps! Pam phoned her. Natty Hawke answered the landline phone. "Greetings", Natty Hawke chimed. "Hello Natty, is Aunt Rose dere", Pam asked? He could hear a change in her voice. "Wha wrong wid yuh voice. Yuh hav ah cold", Natty Hawke asked? Pam explained about Carmen and the cop. "Babylon brutality", Natty Hawke boomed. "Natty, Carmen neva duh nuttin wrong but the cop sey shi too aggressive. Shi tel dem sey dem bias", Pam explained. "Just dat", Natty Hawke asked? "Wel, yuh noah fiwi peeple talk wid wi hands but di cop put dat dung tuh violent behaviour", Pam continued. Natty Hawke was not acting as calmly as when Pam first met him. He swore that 'Babylon' would have to pay for their transgression upon his woman. Having been assured that Natty Hawke and Aunt Rose would help to free Carmen, Pam hung up the phone. She dialled Sandra's cell phone number. The speed of the response threw her. "Hi, it's me Pam. Where are you", Pam asked? She explained about Carmen's demise. "I want to go to bail her out but I have to wait until Aunt Rose and Natty Hawke arrive" Pam explained. "No need, I'll call Hinton Fairly. I've only just found his card", Sandra assured. "I wouldn't have enough money to pay such a top lawyer", Pam explained. "What are friends for if they can't help when you're in a crisis? I'll help you with the expense", Sandra countered. Pam was grateful but said she would only accept Sandra's '*offer*' if it was treated as a *loan*. Sandra wanted to repay Carmen for taking the rap for her. She insisted that she would fund the total amount for Hinton Fairly's service. When Pam protested, Sandra reiterated that she appreciated the sacrifice she and her sister had made on her behalf. "My career would have been ruined and my dreams would have been shattered totally had it not been for you and your sister. At least give me the opportunity to show my appreciation", Sandra declared. "When you put it like that, I can hardly refuse", Pam confirmed. She told Sandra she would phone again then returned to her seat to await Aunt Rose and Natty Hawke's arrival.

CHAPTER 36

Duke stopped on the way to buy some flowers and champagne for Sandra. He was smiling to himself at the thought of being alone with her again. His chauffeur, Calvin Poser, was busy arguing with the eager traffic warden pointing out that the parking ticket would not be paid. "Move bwai, wi nuh pay parking fine. Dats fi di lickle people like yuh", Calvin Poser boasted. When Duke walked back to the limo, the chauffeur opened the door but bowed before he commented to the warden. "Now yuh undastan whey mi mean", Calvin Poser confirmed? Duke was pleased to hear him talk to the warden like he did. He was further pleased to hear Calvin defending his property. "Good boy Calvin, good boy", he remarked. Even though Calvin was taller than Duke, he bent his head so Duke could pat it like a pet. It appeared as if this was a regular '*treat*' for the seemingly subservient Calvin. Though he was from the same far off exotic island as Calvin, the warden observed how ready he was to commit on behalf of his boss. The fact that the limo was parked illegally on double red lines didn't seem to matter to Calvin. These red lines prohibited all other vehicles except for emergency and public transport vehicles from stopping. The warden also thought that Calvin was showing off to curry favour with his boss. After the ritual of having his head patted, Calvin Poser seemed to indicate that he approved of Duke's action towards him. "Thank you boss", he replied. After opening the door for Duke, Calvin got back into the limo. He drove over the level crossing then turned right into the street towards the houses near the parade of shops. Calvin Poser saw the other limo from a distance. "What number is it boss", Calvin asked? Duke told him. They pulled up about twenty yards from the other limo. As Duke got out, he noticed Sandra's green Sleek Coupe covered in parking tickets. He whistled as he gathered them in both hands. "Take the other limo back. Have it cleaned up", Duke ordered. "OK boss", Calvin replied. Duke waited for him to get into the limo but hesitated when the chauffeur started running back towards him. He wanted so much to be with Sandra that he became impatient with Calvin's delay to move the unclean limo. "What now", Duke asked? Gasping for breath, Calvin could hardly get the words out. "Boss you have to come and see for yourself", he declared. They both went back to the unclean limo. "Look boss", he said. Duke followed the direction of Calvin's finger pointing through the glass. Duke saw the tramp sitting in the back seat of the unclean limo. "Get him out of there", he ordered. Duke swore as he ranted and raved at the indignity of their discovery. Curled up on the large back seat of the unclean limo was a tramp hugging a bottle of booze in one hand, guardedly! His other hand hugged the puppy that was also cozily asleep. They both appeared to have been on the road for a awhile. The tramp's clothes and the puppy's coat bore the grime from the streets. It seemed to have lost bits of its hair in patches. His skinny frame would have exposed his ribs just the same even if his coat was not damaged. Duke became very flushed in the face and at one moment started a coughing fit which seemed to last for a full five minutes. The young *'tramp'* stirred but peered up through sleepy eyes. His unwashed face and un-brushed nicotine stained teeth greeted Duke and his chauffeur just as Duke had finished spluttering. The *'tramp'* smiled broadly as he noticed their attire. He may have been labelled as a *'down and out'* but his brain still worked. Duke did not want to speak to him directly because that was below his dignity. Calvin threatened the tramp. "Cum outta di boss car before a bruk up yuh an yuh mawga dawg", Calvin threatened. Unknown to ignoramus like Calvin, despite their situations, issues and environments, tramps were *'survivors'*. They were impervious to threats especially from negative emotional subservient individuals like Calvin Poser. Indeed, he seemed to be *'poser'* by name and a *'poser'* by nature. He was clearly unaware that *'tramps'* were only in the position they were in due to some traumatic event that had rendered them without *'hope'* even. The greater *'hardships of living'* covered the salient facts that they too are human but had a home, family, friends and possibly a job just like anyone else. The *'tramp'* was thinking that, given the same *'set of circumstances'* surrounding his life, the like of the boastful Calvin could never have survived like he has, possibly! Duke saw that short of grabbing hold of the *'tramp'* and his dog but throwing them back on the streets, the only way round getting them out of the limo was to negotiate with the tramp. "Offer him some money", Duke ordered. "Money boss? Gi mi di money an mi wi show im dat im hafe cum otta di limo. Im feisty boss", Calvin declared. Duke reminded Calvin that he wanted the process to be speeded up. "Yes boss", Calvin submitted. He tapped the window to attract the tramp's attention. "Ten SPCU if you come out", Calvin said. He waved the ten SPCU note as he spoke. The tramp closed his eyes but put his head back down on the seat. He pretended to go back to sleep. Tapping harder on the glass the chauffeur increased his offer. Calvin's offer went up progressively in denominations of ten. "Twenty … thirty … forty", he auctioned. The tramp continued to ignore him but still pretended to be asleep. A police siren sounded close by. Calvin started to panic. "The blood boss", he shouted. Duke realized what Calvin was trying to infer. "Offer him five hundred", Duke advised. "Five hundred boss? I don't even get that in a week", he stated. "Yes, five hundred", Duke snapped. The chauffeur still hesitated but looked strangely at his boss. "Get on with it. I've got a very important appointment to attend", Duke snapped again. "It just doan mek any sense being a chauffeur. I'd be beta off being a tramp", Calvin replied. "Are you complaining? After all I've done for you Calvin, you choose to complain. It can be easily arranged for you to become a tramp. When you can't get a job, you'll soon be happy just to survive let alone eat. Now get on with it", Duke ordered. He was confused and angry that he was wasting valuable time, which might be better, served with his exotic bird. "Look, I don't know what your grouse is but I wish you would settle the immediate problem first", Duke stated. The chauffeur hissed his teeth but carried out his boss' instructions without further outburst. When the tramp heard the figure five hundred mentioned, he was ready to settle immediately but neither Duke nor Calvin had noticed. The tramp did not want to appear too eager. He waited until he heard the chauffeur's voice once again. He sat up, stretched and yawned then, with his tobacco stained teeth, smiled once again at them. He nodded his head in agreement to the offer. As he shifted to get out of the limo, the puppy began to whimper but wagged its tail. It did this to draw attention that it was hungry. Duke heard the whimper and it moved his heart. He made an offer which further confounded the jealous Calvin. This time, Duke spoke to the tramp directly. "A thousand SPCU and I keep the puppy", Duke bartered. As he got out of the limo, the tramp looked at the puppy's skinny frame, stroked his head a few times then handed the dog to the chauffeur. He was heartbroken to be separated from his puppy but a thousand SPCU was hard to refuse at any time, let alone when he had no idea from whence his next meal might be coming. The tramp hands trembled greatly as he took the money then walked away. He never looked back to show the tears which were freely flowing from his eyes. Duke sensed that the separation might have triggered some deep emotions. He thought he would reassure the tramp that the puppy would be well looked after. He shouted after the tramp as he continued to walk away. "I'll give him a home, what's his name", Duke asked? "Tramp", the man shouted back. The tramp disappeared amongst the bustling crowd frequenting the parade of shop and then into the distance. Whilst still holding the puppy, Calvin felt the warm fluid against his skin. He looked down on his uniform. It was soaked with the puppy's urine. "Look what di lickle dawg duh boss. Him piss pon mi", Calvin exclaimed. "They say it is good luck", Duke chimed. "The pee-pee smell wrenk. How can it be good luck boss", Calvin protested? His indignation at Duke for paying the tramp a thousand SPCU and being pissed upon by his "little mawga dawg" was too much for Calvin. His voice was raised above his normal loud way of speaking. Tramp was trembling as if he was cold but he was frightened of Calvin's outburst and being in the company of strangers. Turning to his chauffeur, Duke reached out but took the puppy. "I'm giving my Sugarcake Flowers, Champagne and a puppy. What more could she ask for", Duke asked rhetorically? He sent Calvin on his way before setting off on his short journey towards Sandra's house.

Anxiously awaiting his arrival, she was on edge all the time. Sandra saw Duke as he crossed from the other side of the street. She could hear the sound of his leather shoes on the tarmac street, then the pavement and along the gravel pathway from the gate as he made his way towards her front door. Sandra was already behind it. She timed Duke's imminent arrival to perfection. He was caught out by the sudden opening of the front door. Sandra stood there with open arms to welcome Duke. He had never been welcomed home by his wife Dora in all the years that they had been together. This was a new experience for the randy Duke. "Sandra honey", he exclaimed. Duke spoke in such a loud voice as if he was overplaying a part in a Play. The hug was suffocating but Sandra did not feel the same enthusiasm as Duke did. Still, Sandra clung to him like vine around a tree, helping to prolong the embrace. Sandra led Duke into the lounge. "Welcome to my humble abode", she said. Duke placed the flowers and champagne on the table but handed her the puppy. She put Tramp on the floor. "Don't leave him there. He's a special gift for you. You'll need company through the lonely nights while you're not with me", Duke offered. "Where will he sleep", Sandra asked? "In our bed of course, my sweet", Duke replied. His reply was nonchalant as if this was customary in every culture, assumedly! Sandra's focus was on her immediate situation. She wanted everything cleared up before Duke got into too much of a romantic mood. "Listen Duke, let us sort out one problem at a time. What about the police", Sandra asked? "I don't think you need to worry too much about them. The police have their suspect. It's in the bag as they say", Duke enthused. "What about Sam", Sandra asked? "Again, no problem, a woman called Miss D answered the phone. She's going to see him later. Now, can we relax and enjoy our time together", Duke queried? He got up but started to pull the wire from around the cork on the bottle of champagne. "Get the glasses Sugarcake", Duke ordered. He was excited that his brand of champagne, Champagne Urge Mark 2, might be as effective as Champagne Urge Mark 1 had been at the Hotel Welcome some while back. Duke blew into the glasses to remove the dust that had settled in them before filling their glasses with the green champagne. As they supped away at the champagne, Sandra told him about Grant Favour's crude behaviour in the studio. Duke laughed heartily but assured her that Grant had been a lifelong friend and that he was not capable of what she was suggesting. Sandra was angry because she misunderstood why he laughed or what he meant by his comment. "Are you saying he didn't do it", Sandra searched? Her brow took on the furrowed look of disbelief at Duke's casual reply. He put his arm round her assuredly but kissed her chin gently. "Grant's a bit of a rascal but he's harmless. He knows I'd break his frigging fingers if I think he's going too far plus I know his *'secret'*. I wouldn't let anyone hurt you darling", Duke assured. He was eager to get on with his intended plan but Sandra was still stalling, seemingly. Unbeknown to Duke, she was having flashbacks of the scene where Sam got injured. She alerted Duke about them. "Duke I'm having terrible flashbacks even as I talk to you. "Stop making such a fuss. Sam will live", Duke confided. "The thought of Grant refusing to help, I don't want to go back there", Sandra affirmed. "Grant's alright I tell you. He just didn't want you to be embarrassed at the other hospital. Grant should have told you that membership is at a premium there", Duke explained. "Have you anything for the puppy to eat", Sandra queried? "No, I only just bought him from the tramp that was sleeping in the limo. You had left it open", Duke explained. Sandra held her head in her hands. "A tramp, do you mean that Duke" Sandra asked? She looked at Duke as if he had just told her another of his famed *'whoppers'*. This time she wanted to know of any permanent plan for the puppy especially the type of food to buy. "Duke what are we going to do about the puppy", Sandra reminded. "The shops are still open. Run along and see if you can get him some food, won't you", Duke suggested? The puppy whimpered but sidled up to Sandra's feet. He put his cold nose to her foot but sniffed around for a while then he raised his leg but peed on her leg. She felt the flow of warm fluid against her leg but looked down in disgust. "Duke look what he's done", Sandra exclaimed. "Lovely, that means he likes you", Duke retorted. Sandra frowned at first then, engaging with tramp's eyes, she agreed he was a loveable puppy. Sandra bent down to stroke its head like how Duke had stroked Calvin's. "Naughty boy", Sandra commented. "Take him with you", Duke suggested. "What's his name", Sandra asked? "Tramp, got it", Duke replied. He chuckled at the wisdom of the previous owner in naming the dog same as he was called as a person. "Takes a certain sense of humour to do that", Duke commented. He heard the front door slam shut. He also heard Sandra's footsteps as she walked away from the house but down the pathway towards the street. He chuckled to himself as he thought about the surprise he had in mind for his exotic bird. His friends had commented how fortunate he was to be going out with such a pretty woman. Duke would be the first to admit that he was no *'oil painting'* but he was infatuated with Sandra, mesmerized by her beauty, impressed with her efficiency and lustfully out of control for her body. Duke rubbed his hands together as he paced across the room. He giggled, wiggled, shouted "Whehey" then started a type of jig where it involved a hop to one side, a jump backward then forward and a very vigorous shake of the hips. When Sandra returned, she was bearing a shopping bag piled high with an assortment of different brands of dog foods. Tramp seemed to sense it was time to eat. He danced around yet barked happily when the tin was being opened. "Now to find something to put it in", Sandra murmured. Duke sized up Sandra's dilemma but held out a plate he had selected before her and Tramp's return from the shops. "Give it to me", Duke enthused. He placed the food on the plate but gave it to the puppy. Duke put the fork, which he had used to remove the sticky jellied food from the tin, into the kitchen sink. The ringing tone of the cell-phone pierced the short silence. "Hello", Sandra said hesitantly. "Two thousand SPCU bail", Pam shouted. She sounded as if she was having a nervous breakdown. Sandra sensed the desperation in her friend's voice. "Oh my God, I forgot you were going to be ringing back", Sandra apologised. "Aunt Rose and Natty Hawke can only afford one thousand SPCU between them. Is the loan still on", she asked? "No, there's no loan. I owe you and your sister a debt of gratitude. Did Hinton Fairly come", Sandra enquired? "Yes he's here, do you want to speak with him", Pam asked? "Yes", Sandra replied. She told Hinton Fairly that she would be responsible for the two thousand SPCU. Pam came back on the phone to thank Sandra for her help then hung up. Duke, copying the style of the tramp in the limo, pretended to have dosed off. The puppy licked his face but Duke didn't budge until Tramp pulled at his large ear which stood out conspicuously from the side of his head. Sandra looked on in amazement at the mischief Tramp was getting up to. "Don't you think he's cute", Duke asked? "Yes, tomorrow I'll have the vet check him out", Sandra replied. Tramp was certainly entertaining. He barked at every strange sound he heard. The puppy chased round and round the plush sofas then tried to reach the sash which hung from the heavy curtains. He wandered in and out of the lounge as if he was a child exploring his new home. Duke had now managed to get Sandra to slip cosily into his arms while Tramp entertained them further. The effect of the champagne they had drunk so far brought out the worst in Duke. His roving hands caused the merry Sandra to flush with that tingling excitement which turned her from the recipient gentle female into the uncontrollable *'bitch'* which Raymond often experienced. She dug her nails into Duke's back hoping that he would respond. In her search for that ultimate satisfaction which each woman sought so desperately, Sandra displayed foul mouthed language which shocked even the well travelled Duke. He had raised her hopes yet again but he could not quell her fire like Raymond could. Displaying the frustration she felt, Sandra pushed Duke away from her. Tramp was there yapping away, trying to gain their attention but neither of them took any notice of him. Sandra was too frustrated to care while Duke was still trying to find yet another excuse for letting her down once again. Duke was used to sprinting his way towards his own goal without concerning himself about Sandra's need. He took his annoyance out on the puppy. Tramp did what was natural. He barked but Duke found him an easy target for his inadequate performance. "Shut up", Duke snapped. "Don't shout at him. It's not his fault", Sandra retaliated. Duke's flushed face told of the embarrassment he was feeling. Still, he was determined he would never let Sandra go. The only thing he could do to ensure continuity was to remind Sandra about his wanting her to be his wife. "I'd like you to meet my children before we get married", Duke declared. He looked at Sandra from the corner of his eyes. At times like these and that was often, Duke found it difficult to look Sandra in the eyes. She remained silent and her face looked glum. All she could do was to reminisce on the athletic Raymond's performances but compared them to Duke's. Sandra reminded herself that, by choosing the influential, financially abundant Duke, she had made a clear decision towards achieving 'The Spacevillean Dream'. Duke knew of his strengths but fought to come to terms with his *'weaknesses'*. Lust was his biggest *'weakness'*, possibly! He could not control this superlative urge which was to *bed* as many women as his fame and riches could buy. Like most men do, Duke believed in polygamy. He realized that the sanctity of marriage was not enough to manage the *'superlative urges'* of his *'over-inflated'* ego. Some of the women like Doris Bendlow would have him believe that he had satisfied their needs. They lied to themselves even. Whether it was the exotic Sandra Bogus or the rotund Doris Bendlow, Duke seemed to be unaware that they often faked orgasms. While pretending to be happy with their cohabiting partners or husbands, these women secretly gorged themselves with secret love affairs in search of experiencing the ultimate ecstatic state of orgasms. Men like Duke pretended that they knew that they were actively giving women what they wanted but often underestimated the most desired element which was their sexual *'need'*. It's only in moments like that he was being made aware that what he offered sexually was not catering for the woman's *'need'*. Duke was insensitive to Sandra's need. He tried to appease her frustration. "Let us have some more champagne", Duke piped. Sandra's ripped dress fell to the floor as she stood up to reach for the bottle. It was half filled with the now tepid champagne. In an attempt to deflect the level of her frustration Sandra sought another type of *'buzz'*. She raised the bottle to her head but guzzled the expensive aerated, effervescent wine as if she was drinking water. The loud burp sent Tramp running for cover behind the plush sofa. Duke had never seen Sandra drink champagne like that before. "What's the matter my angel", Duke asked? She did not reply but instead collapsed onto the floor in front of him. The bottle smashed as it hit the floor. Duke was himself in a state of drunkenness but he snapped out of it when his exotic bird crumpled to the floor. Duke saw the stupefied look upon Sandra's face. It told him that she was now in a different world. "You bloody fool", Duke sighed. As he pondered what to do, Sandra began to murmur but the words were incoherent. Tramp sniffed at her frowzy body then proceeded to lick her face until she began to stir. Sandra's head was still swirling from the effects of the warm champagne.

She opened her eyes but closed them quickly as she couldn't make out clearly which of the dogs was Tramp. As she began to choke on the bubbles trapped in her throat, Duke sat her up. Sandra leaned awkwardly like a pantomime performer pretending to lean against a wall as Duke went to get her some water. He too was still unsteady on his feet. Duke stumbled even more as he tried to hurry to revive his exotic bird. Duke spilled most of the water from the glass. "Here, drink this", Duke encouraged. Sandra supped the plain water until another burp exploded into Duke's face. The foul smell mixed with her frowzy body. The stench from the unwashed dog and Dukes' sweaty body lingered in the lounge for a long time. Duke was unaffected though Tramp dashed for cover a second time. Duke beckoned for the dog to come towards him. "Here boy", Duke encouraged. He lay next to Sandra on the long piled carpet. Duke cuddled her with one hand but stroked Tramp with the other until they all fell asleep.

A sudden blast of the doorbell stirred Tramp into a barking fit. His young voice was hardly a threat. "Yap, yap, yap", the puppy barked. The barking was close to Sandra's ear but registered in her head. It seemed to anger her. She wafted airily at the puppy but soon realised what she had done. When the swinging hand registered, Tramp yelped. Unintentionally, Sandra's claws dug into the puppy's already damaged coat. He whimpered continuously while the doorbell played in a different key. "I'll get it", Duke shouted. He dragged on his trousers then flung the door open. Carmen gasped. Duke looked wild and intimidating. His hair was sticking out all over the place, reminding her of the straw doll she used to have as a child. "Who do you want", Duke asked? His tone was dry but suggested he didn't want to be disturbed. Carmen was expecting Sandra to open the door. "Sory, wrong house", she replied. Carmen stepped back but looked Duke up and down in amazement. As she walked back towards the gate, she looked back once again. Carmen was puzzled that the number on the door coincided with that which Pam had given her but she wasn't expecting Duke to be opening the door. Pam and Aunt Rose sat in Natty Hawke's car some yards from Sandra's gate. Carmen went back to the car but asked Pam to confirm the address. "Yuh sure ah di numba sis", Camren asked? "Yes, mi sure. Mi cum yah al di time", she replied. Pam offered to go back with her sister. Carmen stopped her before they got to the gate. She told how the man at the door had no shirt on and how his open zipper exposed his private part. Carmen also revealed that she had heard a dog barking. "Ah dawg? Sandra ain't got nuh dawg", Pam expressed. Her surprise about the dog was more than apparent. Carmen assured her sister that she did hear a dog barking at the address. "Yes, mi hear ah young dawg ah bark", Carmen confirmed. "Sandra wuddn't hav Raymond frens inna har house let alone ah dawg. Yuh probably er di dawg nex door", Pam countered. She accompanied Carmen back to Sandra's house. They pressed the doorbell. Duke, now with a shirt on, returned to the door. He was resolute that this time he would get rid of the caller who dared to further disturb his night with his *'wife to be'*. When he opened the door, Duke remembered Pam from that time at the Hotel Welcome. "Oh it's you? Sandra's resting at the moment", Duke lied. Pam didn't believe him but she didn't want to push. "Can you ask her to get in touch with Miss Labrishé as soon as possible", Pam instructed. They turned to walk away when Sandra, now more sober than before, appeared at the door in her night robe. She was in the act of tying the sash as she invited them in. "Come in", Sandra said. Pam and Carmen bumped into each other as they turned towards where the voice was coming from. "Come in before the neighbours think you're those church people", Sandra encouraged. Duke led the way into the lounge. He sat next to Sandra on one of the plush sofas. He stared straight at Carmen and Pam who sat opposite. The frowsy smell still lingered in the room. Carmen's eyes scanned the room immediately but there was no clue apart from the flowers which still laid on the table and the broken champagne bottle on the floor. She whispered into Pam's ear what she thought had taken place before their arrival. "Well how did everything go", Sandra enquired? "As you see we're here. Anyway, we're not staying long because someone is waiting for us in the car", Pam advised. "Would you like something to drink", Sandra offered? She beckoned Pam to follow her into the kitchen. Tramp had hardly noticed them come in. He was busy rolling over on his back in idle play. The blood and hair on the wet tea cloth resting on the worktop dissuaded Pam from accepting the drink Sandra had offered. Then she saw the carrier bag full of tins of dog food resting on the kitchen table. "A dog Sandra", Pam asked? She eyed the *'mutt'*. He stopped playing but turned and started to yap once again. Pam was always scared of dogs. She ran out of the kitchen when Tramp bared his teeth and growled. He ran after her. Carmen heard the sudden commotion then saw her sister enter the lounge at speed with the puppy yapping at her heels. "Move", Carmen shouted. She raised her foot threatening to kick the seemingly vicious puppy. Tramp stopped in his tracks as Carmen shouted at him again. "Move before I . . .", Carmen dissuaded. "Keep the noise down he won't hurt you", Duke shouted. He was on the other side of the large lounge but he started to move menacingly towards them. Sandra did not want the confrontation because she remembered how she witnessed Carmen had beaten Alan Baitman. She decided to call the puppy towards her. "Here Tramp", Sandra said. She tapped her side like a pedigree owner at a famous dog show. Sandra lifted him from the floor. He showed his appreciation by licking her face all over. Carmen found that disgusting. In her culture in the far off exotic islands, dogs were not allowed indoors let alone licking someone's face. Carmen was learning that different cultures had different rules for the way they chose to live. "Oh my God, did you see that", Carmen exclaimed. She tugged at her sister to make sure she hadn't missed what had happened. Duke took offence to Carmen's reaction to Sandra allowing the dog to lick her face. "What's wrong with that", Duke piped? With mouths agog, both Pam and Carmen looked at him at the same time in disbelief. They didn't wait for Sandra to show them out. They rose from the settee in unison as if it was a pre-arranged agreement. "We'll see you Sandra", Pam commented. Both sisters made their way through the lounge door hurriedly. Tramp followed them out into the hallway but hurried their exit by yapping at them. Duke was relieved to hear the front door slam shut. Pam and Carmen ran from the house as if they were being chased by a rabid dog. As they entered the car, Aunt Rose wanted them to explain why they were running from Sandra's house. Natty Hawke looked at his watch. Smiling at them, he reprimanded both Pam and Carmen for letting him and Aunt Rose wait around. "Soon come huh. Mi shudda noah betta", Natty Hawke commented. Unlike Natty Hawke, Aunt Rose sat patiently. She listened to the younger ones banter. "Mi cook dinner fi all ah wi", Aunt Rose prompted. This was Aunt Rose's way of conveying her message. She too was fed up with the waiting around. "OK Aunt Rose, wi gwein tek yuh home now", Natty Hawke confirmed. Carmen looked at Pam but commented. "What ah nasty woman yuh famous fren is. Yuh did smel di musty smell inna di place and si di lickle mange dawg ah run all ova di place", Carmen blurted out. "Yuh shudda si di tea cloth wid di blood and di dawg hair pon it", Pam criticised. She shook her body as if she felt a sudden chill. "Jezebel", Natty Hawke shouted. The conversation lasted all the way to Aunt Rose's place. Inside, Pam and Carmen washed their hands in the bathroom instead of in the kitchen sink as Sandra did while they were at her house. They scrubbed their hands extra carefully, hoping that they did not catch any germ from the puppy's presence. Carmen said she was concerned for the puppy. She had noticed the dirt on his coat and the patches of hair that made him appear as if he was moulting. "Yuh did si di dirt pon di dawg coat and di way im hair ah drop out", Carmen asked? "Wanda whey she get di dawg from", Pam asked? "Tramp, dats ah funny name fi ah dawg", Carmen added.

The sound of Aunt Rose's voice alerted them that dinner was ready to be served. Natty Hawke sat next to Carmen. He started to reminisce about the treatment she had received from the police. "Nearly lost mi princess", Natty Hawke mused? He shook his head from side to side. Carmen smiled at him but did not comment. Words were not necessary. After the maltreatment she had suffered at the hands of the police, Carmen's eyes showed her appreciation for being alive. She rubbed her bruised wrists where the cuffs had been placed. "Still hurt ah bit", Carmen sighed. Natty Hawke held unto her hands lightly. Aunt Rose reminded them that Carmen had to appear at the magistrate court by 10:00 hours the next morning. "Mek wi all get some rest. Wi hav ah early start inna di mawning", Aunt Rose advised. "Wi can't sleep yet Aunt Rose", Natty Hawke teased. "Why not", she asked? "Wi jus eat. Wi mite get indigestion if wi lie dung too early", Natty Hawke replied. He pointed toward his belly indicating that he had had his fill. They all laughed together. "Mi still ah guh ah mi room and leve yuh young peeple alone, goodnite", Aunt Rose said. She headed for the bathroom. Pam sat with Natty Hawke and Carmen for a while discussing the traumatic times they were going through. She stressed how she was unable to visit with Raymond because of the police assault on her sister. "Poor Raymond, im mus tink wi feget him", Pam commented. Carmen reminded her sister that it was not possible for her to do more than she had done. "Yuh can't duh nuhmore", Carmen assured. "Just cool", Natty Hawke added. Pam decided to leave the two 'lovebirds' alone. "Good nite, si yuh inna di mawning", Pam said. Left alone, Natty Hawke wanted to review how Carmen came to be targeted by the police. He urged her to relive the awesome moments. "Tell mi agin wha happen 2deh", Natty Hawke prompted. Carmen explained the whole scene ending with the part leading up to Sandra's escape. "After shi push thru di crowd and wi sure shi gawn, me and Pam siddung away from di odda people dem. Wi er a big commotion, den di police storm in like dem come fi capture wild animal. Dem hav gun an riot shiel", Carmen explained. "Den", Natty Hawke prompted.

CHAPTER 37

Carmen told him how the police approached her and Pam when the coward man and his companion and several others had pointed them out. "Den two police rush mi and pin mi tuh di floor. One sey "bruk har han. Mi try fi explain and demonstrate how di security man poke Sandra inna har ches. Is jus ah bak home way. Ah was jus trying fi show di policeman how but im tek it di wrong way. Afta dat, dem tek mi outside. Dem jus ah swear at mi al di time. Sum ah di oddas ah tel mi fi leve dem country and ah cal mi *'Tardie leader'*. Ah doan even kno wha it mean. Natty, mi holiday ruin. Mi cum yah fi spend sum quality time wid mi family and frens but dem ah insis dat mi involve inna some kind ah drugs ring. Mi cawn undastn dem people yah. It look like dem possess by demons. How can people tel suh much lie? Dem jus mek up wat dem waan sey. It nuh seem like dem responsible fi dem behaviour", Carmen expressed. Natty Hawke was filled with anger but he couldn't hold back from saying how he truly felt about the incident. He knew that Carmen's was not the only story with a similar *'plot'*.

The cops' approach and behaviour was an everyday occurrence in Ghettoville. Natty Hawke spoke with the passion of a man incensed. "Babylon mus fall", Natty Hawke shouted. "Ssssh", Aunt Rose indicated. "Dem lick you", Natty Hawke asked? "No, but dem push mi round like a set ah bullies in a playground. Dem ah challenge mi fi poke each ah dem inna dem ches. Den two *'butch looking'* woman police tek me inna ah room fi strip search me. Dem was awful to mi Natty. Dem feel up inna mi like dem ah search fi mi womb", Carmen declared. Re-living the whole experience again, it became too much for Carmen. She started to sob. Natty Hawke was more furious now. Straining every muscle in his neck, he spoke with uncontrolled emotions. Natty Hawke's voice reached maximum volume and as the anger raged inside him, sweat started to pour from his forehead. He took off his *'crown'* but shook his long dreadlocks. It appeared as if they were being moved by hurricane winds. "Strip search yuh? Wha fah", Natty Hawke questioned? "Dem sey dem was looking fi drugs. Whey poor mi fi get dem suppmn deh from. I'm ah law student", Carmen finished? Again Natty Hawke fumed cynically. "Dem always assume", he confided. Still emotionally involved by re-living the embarrassing moments, Carmen began to shake as she tried to stiffle the tears back. Her emotions got the better of her too. "Wha mek dem suh bitta Natty, why", Carmen screamed? She was pleading with him for a logical explanation. Natty Hawke didn't pretend to know the cops' answers but he did his best to explain in a way that he knew Carmen would understand. "Is jus Babylon system Princess, just Babylon system, seen", Natty Hawke finished. Carmen cried unashamedly for at least ten minutes. It had begun to release the tensions which had built up inside her. She rested her head upon Natty Hawke's chest but continued to talk until they both surrendered to the fatigue and stress.

Aunt Rose was the first to awaken at 06:30 hours. She tried to awaken Pam. Aunt Rose shook her a little but Pam did not respond. She shook Pam a bit firmer but commented. "Court day, it is court day", Aunt Rose reminded. Pam awakened. She knew how worried Aunt Rose was about the whole matter. "Don't worry Aunt Rose, leave it to Mr. Fairly. Sandra asked him to represent Raymond as well", Pam assured. "Mr. Fairly is not God, only the Lord can conquer the devil and his children", Aunt Rose countered. She had hardly had any sleep herself. Aunt Rose prayed through the night for her dear niece, Carmen. Pam rang Sandra as she had promised to do. "Hello", Sandra said. Pam sensed that Sandra had not been awake for long. "Did I wake you", Pam asked? Sandra yawned helplessly. "I'm sorry, I didn't get much sleep. Duke and I quarrelled after you and your sister left", Sandra explained. "I'm sorry if we embarrassed you. I know he doesn't like a hair in my head", Pam accepted. "He'll calm down", Sandra replied. Pam told her about the imminent court case. Sandra told her that she couldn't make it. "I'm going to be busy today. Tramp needs a bath and I'll also have to take him to the vet", Sandra explained. Pam realised that Sandra would not change her mind. "I've got to go. I'll call you when I can", Pam promised. The smell of the dumplings, fritters and plantains Aunt Rose was preparing for breakfast, made Pam feel hungry. "Is breakfast ready yet", Pam teased. "You can come and help sweeten the porridge", Aunt Rose countered. Pam smiled. "Aunt Rose you haven't changed a bit", Pam stated. She smiled again as she picked up the spoon from the drawer. "Natty, is Carmen awake", Aunt Rose asked? "Yes Aunt Rose, we wake up long time", Natty Hawke replied. He and Carmen headed for the bathroom to brush their teeth then came into the kitchen. "I smell food", Natty Hawke said. As he pushed his head round the half closed door, Natty Hawke commented again. "Aunt Rose mek di bes dumplings I've ever tasted", Natty Hawke enthused. Aunt Rose looked at Pam but winked her eyes. She addressed Natty Hawke without looking directly at him. "Don't badda wid yur sweet talk flattery. Yuh can only hav six dumplings like everybody else", Aunt Rose warned. Even Carmen laughed at Aunt Rose's banter with Natty Hawke. She announced her arrival in her cultural way. "Good mawnin", Carmen said. Concerned that the ordeal of the serious charges pending might have kept Carmen awake through the night, Pam ventured to ask how her sister slept. "Did you get any sleep", Pam asked? "Very little but I've just finished meditating and I don't feel any stress now", Carmen replied. Aunt Rose was pleased to see the difference in her. Last night Carmen was very angry but now all her anger seemed to have died or at least so it appeared. Inside, Carmen had not forgiven the police for their drastic actions. The ordeal had given her a much clearer picture of what life was like for her sister and others who lived abroad. "Wha time wi ah leve", Carmen asked? "Bout ah hour", Natty Hawke replied. "Aunt Rose, ah need fi sample di food. Gimme jus one ah di dumpling fi nibble", Natty Hawke pleaded. "Yuh can nibble on one if you is a goat", Aunt Rose reposted. Natty Hawke removed one of the dumplings from the large plate with one hand while he indicated how hungy he was by rubbing his belly with his other hand. They all sat down at the table near the window that faced the back garden. The potted plants decorated the window-sill but caused the curtain to hang awkwardly. As he tried to get an extra fritter from the large plate in front of them, Natty Hawke complimented Aunt Rose's cooking yet again. She was nervous about going to court. Aunt Rose fidgeted with the handle of the large enamel mug she used for all her hot drinks. "What time is it", she fussed? "Is o.k Aunt Rose. Wi stil hav enuf time fi get dey", Pam assured. Carmen and Natty Hawke both reached out at the same time for the last dumpling on the plate. They smiled at each other but decided to share it. "Just like husband and wife", Aunt Rose teased. They all laughed together. The ringing of the landline telephone interrupted the lighthearted moments. "I'll get it", Carmen offered. "Hello, yes . . . hol on. Pam is di lawyer man, missa Fairly", Carmen said. Pam made her way towards her sister but took the phone. "This is Pamela Labrishé", she confirmed. "Miss Labrishé, the police advised my office that your sister should bring her passport with her to the court", Hinton Fairly advised. "Why, what's happening", Pam asked? "I don't know but I would advise her to comply. I'll be there about 09:50 hours", Hinton Fairly ended. Aunt Rose saw the puzzled look on Pam's face. She became a bit paranoid. "Wha hapn, wha hapn", Aunt

Rose queried? Pam shook her head as if to clear it from a numbing blow. Natty Hawke hugged Carmen tightly but she remained calmest of all. Pam finally told them of the newest demand from the police. "Passport? Why? She is here legally", Aunt Rose pressed. None of them could understand the demand but they were advised by Hinton Fairly to comply. Aunt Rose hurried to her bedroom. She took her diary from her handbag that was resting on the pedestal table in the corner of the room. "Get mi di phone", Aunt Rose demanded. She returned to the kitchen. Aunt Rose found the number for which she was searching. The phone rang twice then she heard the recorded voice that said, ". . . the caller knows you're waiting . . . .". Aunt Rose tapped her foot rapidly to a beat which was rhythmic yet unknown to the others in the kitchen. She did this habitually whenever she was very upset as if it was a tic. "Councillor Broome-Weede", the voice announced. "This is Rose Culture who used to work for you. Do you remember me", Aunt Rose enquired? "Rose . . . Rose, oh yes, Rose Culture, yes I remember you", Councillor Strawberg Broome-Weede confirmed. Aunt Rose could not understand his hesitancy in recognizing who she was but she related Carmen's situation as briefly as she could. Ignoring the urgency of the situation, Councilor Broome-Weede, like the worm he was, started to wiggle out of any commitment to the *'case'* against the police. "Seems a little complicated. I think the best advice I can give you is to employ a lawyer. I know a very good one I could recommend", Councillor Broome-Weede stated. "She already has a lawyer to deal with the police charges but why are they asking for her passport when she is here legally", Aunt Rose pressed. "I'm afraid I really don't know", Councillor Broome-Weede replied. Rose Culture, formerly Rose Labrishé, was a nice woman but she had not lost that tenacity which she had used to help Councilor Broome-Weede to mount his campaign for election. "I am sure if you really wanted to you could help in some way", Aunt Rose pressed. Councillor Broome-Weede stayed silent for a while. His memory was being refreshed by Aunt Rose's stern stance on his position. Councillor Broome-Weede remembered how hard Rose had driven the Team that she had led in the canvassing for votes on his behalf. "Keep me informed. I'm sure there's something I can do, ok Rose", Councillor Broome-Weede finished. "Wen fiwi peeple dem get somewhey inna life dem always feget who help dem get deh. Come mek wi guh", Aunt Rose criticised. In the car, Natty Hawke crunched the gear into reverse to enable him to negotiate around the vehicle in front of him. The crunching noise disturbed Aunt Rose. "Wha dat", she asked? "Di clutch slipping Aunt Rose. It mek dat funny nize wen mi put di car inna reverse but is awrite inna di odda gears. We'll get dere", Natty Hawke assured. Pam and Carmen remained silent but they too were a little bit anxious about what might be awaiting them at the court. The rest of the journey was totally silent except for the few times when Natty Hawke had to brave the challenges linked to any motorist, who was in a hurry to get from point 'A' to point 'B'. In this particular occasion, Natty Hawke demonstrated how he learnt to deal with threats from other motorists to his life while driving. The motorcyclist, who suddenly cut across Natty Hawke's path, was such a threat. He jerked the steering wheel to his left just about avoiding the rear wheel of the cycle. "Move bwai. "Yuh si dat, yuh si dat", Natty Hawke repeated. As the motor cyclist accelerated away, other vehicles behind screeched their tyres to an abrupt halt. Pam and Carmen each reacted differently to the sudden confusion which almost ended their lives. Aunt Rose was on her fourth prayer to God. She mumbled over and over that she had lived a clean life but asked God's forgiveness for the time she assumed that Pam, then a high-flyer, might turn out to be like Sandra. Natty Hawke just kept saying that, if fate defined that it was time to pass over, he was ready. "If is Jah will is Jah will, I and I doan fear dat, cause Zion is I and I destiny", Natty Hawke declared. After another few miles, they saw the huge ugly building. Some people were rushing towards the entrance of the building, suggesting that they were late. Aunt Rose was concerned if they were late for Carmen's appearance in front of the dreared Magistrate. She experienced moments of anxiety. "Wha di time", Aunt Rose fussed? "09:50 hours", Carmen replied. They met a worried looking Hinton Fairly on the steps outside the building. "We're a bit late", Pam apologised. "The Magistrate will not be happy if we're late. Trust you brought the passport", Hinton Fairly asked? Pam looked at Aunt Rose, who in turn looked at Carmen. Natty Hawke saw the puzzled look on all their faces. "Yes, I've got it", Carmen commented. "Hurry", Hinton Fairly encouraged. "What happens now", Pam asked? Hinton Fairly went over to the Reception Desk. He spoke to the cop standing behind the desk. Carmen noticed that a group of people, gathered around a type of bulletin board, were being approached by one of the cops who were present at her arrest. When Hinton Fairly returned, he told them that they had to hurry as their case was the first on the Agenda. Aunt Rose commented. "This place makes me shiver", she said. The shuddering she was experiencing were the spasms that made her dance involuntarily. Led by Hinton Fairly, they all arrived outside court No. 2 in time to hear Carmen's name being announced. "Quickly", Hinton Fairly said. Shortly afterwards a voice said, "be up standing . . .". The arrival of the Magistrate and the two advisors took their place on the rostrum. They sat behind the desk in a particular order. The Magistrate sat in between his two advisors. One was of male gender and the other was of female gender. The Clerk of the court made the usual statement then proceeded with the 'swearing in'. The Magistrate, Altiman Knowall, read the charges out aloud. "Carmen Labrishé you are charged with 1) suspicion of murder, 2) grevious or actual bodily harm to one individual, namely Hospital Security Officer, Mr. Archie Hingepin, 3) inciting violence in a public place, 4) public affray 5) assaulting a police officer, 6) resisting arrest, 7) drug dealing and 8) being a member of an international drug cartel 'The Tardies'. How do you plead", the Magistrate asked?

The enormity of the overstated charges bore the type of distress upon all of Carmen's family but to Aunt Rose in particular. It was because she had vouched for Carmen as a person of exceptionally good character that made Spaceville Immigration Department grant Carmen with a visa to travel to spend time in the country. Aunt Rose was aware of the heavy financial penalty involved if Carmen was proven to be other than whom she had vouched for. Her house was the collateral. Aunt Rose had offered it as a guarantee to the affadavit that she had signed. It would be tragic if Aunt Rose was to lose the house which she and her husband had worked so hard to own. They had made huge sacrifides by sweating, scrimping, saving, peering their figurative heels and toes to enable them to pay for the house entirely over 25 years period on mortgage. Aunt Rose's house could now be taken away as a forfeit to the agreement which she had made with Spaceville Immigration Department. Everything rested on the result of this case against her niece, Carmen Labrishé. Carmen made sure she looked straight at the Magistrate when she answered. "Not guilty", Carmen replied.

Ghettoville's Crown Prosecutor, Rip Tearup, representing the *'Crown'* and the Kingdom of Spaceville, began with the charge for "assault on a police officer". His whole premise was to establish the alledged *'Tardie leader'* not only to be of violent character but also to show Carmen to be "having no respect for authority. "Did you poke PC Clone in the chest in the Casualty Department of the local Ghettoville Community General Hospital on the date mentioned", Crown Prosecutor pressed? "He asked me to demonstate to him how the security man poked a woman in the chest", Carmen replied. "So you admit that you poked the officer in the chest yet you plead not guilty", Crown Prosecutor insisted. "Your honour, my learned friend should know a "not guilty" plea should be directed to the Higher Court where my client would be able to defend herself in front of a jury", Hinton Fairly advised. The brown Mixed DNA Rainbow Tribe Magistrate, who saw himself as a honourary green humanoid robotron, spoke with both of his advisors. One of them was a white individual and the other a pink individual from the Mixed DNA Rainbow Tribe. The Magisrate, Altiman Knowall, confirmed Hinton Fairly's argument. A date would be set for Carmen's new trial in the Higher Court. One of the cops passed a note to the Clerk of the Court, who in turn passed it on to the Magistrate. He sat up much straighter in the chair. His bifocal glasses magnified his already large eyes. "Carmen Labrishé you are a visitor to this country yaw", the brown Mixed DNA Rainbow Tribe Magistrate confirmed? "Yes", Carmen replied. The Magistrate glared at her over the rim of his bifocals. He demanded Carmen address him as *"your honour"*. "Yes what", the Magistrate demanded. Carmen obliged the brown Mixed DNA Rainbow Tribe Magistrate's ego. "You were asked to bring your passport to this court. Have you got it with you, yaw", the Magistrate queried? His advisors leant but whispered in each of his ears. The Magistrate listened to the advice from his advisors. All the time they were shaking their heads from side to side as if to indicate their disapproval of something known to them exclusively. Carmen reached into her handbag, withdrew the passport but handed it to the Clerk of the Court. He in turn passed it to the Magistrate. On inspection, he showed it around to his advisors. They each intricately examined it before handing it back to him. "Do you understand the terms under which you had been granted permission to visit in this country Miss Labrishé, yaw", the Magistrate asked? Carmen could hear and sense the venomous intonations in the voice of the Magistrate. She counted herself fortunate that the Magistrate was not the immigration officer she had met at the airport. "Yes your honour", Carmen obliged. The Magistrate handed the passport back to the Clerk of the Court who, in turn, handed it to Carmen. "Be up standing", the Clerk of the Court said. The Magistrate, Altiman Knowall and his Advisors rose from their high backed, deeply buttoned leather chairs. They exited from the court glancing back briefly over their shoulders disdainfully at Carmen. Hinton Fairly lent over towards but engaged with his legal rival. He expressed to him his objection to the unnecessary comments from the Magistrate. "That was a little below the belt, wasn't it", Hinton Fairly suggested? "We'll do battle in the Higher Court Hinton. How's your dear wife", Crown Prosecutor, Rip Tearup, enquired? They shook hands then Hinton caught up with Pam and the others. "It'll be a few months before the actual case comes up. I'll be in touch", Hinton Fairly assured. Carmen and her family exited the Magistrate Court but headed for the car park.

Natty Hawke saw the two policemen as they hovered around his Transporter car. Their body language warned him that they were not there admiring the red, gold, and green colours on his 13yr old vehicle. As they reached the vehicle, one policeman approached Natty Hawke. "Are you the owner of this car", the cop asked? "Yes", Natty Hawke replied. "Can I see your driving licence", the cop asked? Natty reached into his back pocket but withdrew an old brown leather wallet. As he opened it to remove the licence, a small flat plastic bag fell to the floor. The police did not even look at the document they had requested. All of a sudden their focus now was on the flat small plastic bag with the singular button in it. "Against the car, spread your legs. Place your hands on your head", one voice ordered. As Natty Hawke turned to face the car, he remembered an incident he had seen in a News report on TV that was similar to his own experience. Even though the CCTV footage had shown that the man did not try to resist, that man was beaten senseless by a pack of police officers. Natty Hawke felt the hands as they roughly frisked him from head to toe. His sense of justice rose within him. "Babylon", Natty Hawke shouted. "What did he do", Pam asked? "Shut it", another cop ordered. He reached for his 'two-way' radio. The cop mumbled into it. Soon some police vans and cars entered the car park with sirens wailing. A small crowd, mostly from the street, had now gathered to see what was happening. The excited cops, who had only just arrived, sent them back out into the street. "Clear the car park", the other cop shouted. The crowd started to video the scene. The police pushed the people physically towards the gate. A lot more police gathered around Natty Hawke now. Some prodded him with their batons hoping that he'd respond like their perceived 'stereo-type' to their dare. Somehow, Natty Hawke managed to control himself from trying to defend against the provocation. "Read him his rights", Inspector Grievance ordered. The arresting cop mumbled some words, in an accent Natty Hawke didn't understand. They led him to one of the vans. With his hands cuffed behind him with the plastic type cuffs, Natty tried to climb into the van but one of the cops, who was impatient, used his foot to push him in. He fell awkwardly onto his face on the floor of the van. More police piled into it. Some helped to drag him further inside. They sat both sides of him taunting and insulting him about his 'way of life'. One tugged his locks while pressing his foot into his neck. Natty Hawke shifted around to find the most comfortable position he could. "Stay there", the cop shouted. All ten police vehicles arrived at the back of the Ghettoville Police Station where Natty was again roughly handled. They shifted him from the floor of the van into a standing position on the tarmac. "In there you", one cop's voice ordered. He was pointing towards a grilled door. Natty Hawke hesitated. The cop with the pepper spray pointed the canister towards him but pressed the nozzle. Natty Hawke felt the burning sensation in his eyes. His whole face felt quite hot as if it was on fire. Natty Hawke screamed as his eyes met with the acidic chemical. Pain and the likelihood of blindness started to set in. Despite the pain and suffering, Natty Hawke remained defiant to the obvious injustice being perpetrated towards him. "Babylon must fall . . . Jaaaaaaah Raaaaastaaaafari", Natty Hawke repeated. The voices around him were hysterical with laughter then he felt them push him in one direction then another as if they were playing a particular game. "Have you searched him yet", Sergeant McToughe asked? "Yes Sarge but he had nothing on him", the rookie cop replied. "Well, search him again. You might find something on him this time", Sergeant McToughe prompted. The eager rookie was hasty to gain *'Station Credits'* among her colleagues. She removed a small plastic bag from her own boots. "Look Sarge", look what I've found", the rookie cop enthused. She handed the plastic bag to the Sergeant. "Good girl, you'll make it yet. Charge him with possession of cannabis. That's what you Rastas smoke, isn't it", Sergeant Toughe finished. Natty Hawke didn't hear what charge they had fitted him up with. He just wanted some water to wash away the pepper spray from his face. They led him into an area where he was allowed to wash his face after being fingerprinted, photographed and DNA samples taken. Natty Hawke could barely see the flash from the camera. He felt quite ill and exhausted from the hassle he was receiving. "Take him to the cell", the duty Sergeant ordered. With his hands still cuffed behind him, the cops held him by both elbows. They dragged Natty Hawke all the way to the cell like a heavy sack of stones. On reaching the cell the cops deposited Natty Hawke into it. "In there", the cops said. They slammed the door after him.

Aunt Rose, Carmen and Pam had witnessed the treatment to Natty Hawke in the car park at the Magistrate Court. Pam had phoned Sandra on her cell phone. This time she could not hold back the tears which flowed down her face. There was no mascara added to those tears because Pam was a *'natural'* girl. She explained what Aunt Rose and her sister Carmen had also witnessed in the car park at the Magistrate Court. "Sandra, they were waiting by his car deliberately", Pam explained. Sandra was not one who believed the police ever did anything wrong. "Pam I know you're upset but I don't think the police would go that far", Sandra parried. Pam's anger rose rapidly. She told Sandra in no uncertain terms what she thought of what she had said. "I know you don't like people like Natty Hawke but a big woman like Aunt Rose wouldn't lie about something like that", Pam retorted. Sandra felt ashamed because she knew Pam's aunt to be a decent woman. Though she had never met him, Sandra didn't care much for people like Natty Hawke or his *'type'*. "I'm sorry to hear about your friend but what can I do, would you like another loan", Sandra offered. "I'm forced into yet another situation where I can't refuse but I'll pay you back every penny I owe you", Pam confirmed. "Which station is he at", Sandra asked? "We don't know. Get Hinton Fairly onto it. He'll know what to do. I'll phone you as soon as we get back to Aunt Rose's house", Pam concluded. Sandra valued Pam as her only friend and she had no intention of losing her. She quickly dialled Hinton Fairly's cell phone number. "Hinton Fairly", he answered. Sandra explained what Pam had told her. She stressed how concerned Pam seemed on the phone. "OK, I'll see what I can do", Hinton Fairly replied. "Let me know the outcome as soon as possible", Sandra stressed.

CHAPTER 38

Tramp was at her feet whimpering. Sandra bent down to pick him up but he backed away from her. "Here Tramp, come to mommy", Sandra said. She motioned for him to advance. He ran towards the front door then barked at it. "What's the matter baby? Who is there", Sandra asked? Tramp kept on yapping. He ran back to Sandra, barked once, but returned to the door. This time, she followed him and there on the doormat she found an envelope. She looked at it curiously. It was addressed to her. The envelope looked *'offical'*. Her long nails acted as the opener. Reading eagerly, Sandra saw the part which said, "... and we would like to offer you the opportunity of appearing in our advert". Sandra danced her way back to the lounge while imagining her picture on every billboard. "Yes", Sandra shouted. She thumped the air. That gesture of a most significant accomplishment like a golfer celebrating achieving potting a hole in one. The total sum offered, which included royalties on each product, endorsements built up the apparent financial abundance beckoning, made Sandra's head spin. She started to jump up and down like a field athlete, who had just managed to achieve breaking a world record. "I'm rich, I'm rich", Sandra shouted. Tramp joined in what he thought was a game, yapping as he rushed from place to place in the room. "Come here Tramp. You've brought me good luck", Sandra said. She hugged the now immunized dog. Grant Favours had done his job. His agency had succeeded in winning Sandra a major modelling deal with a major Credit Card Company. The initial letter indicated that there was no hesitation in choosing the really gorgeous Sandra. An appointment with hers and their legal representatives was arranged to ensure the best deal for Sandra. The ringing of the landline telephone interrupted their joyous moment. "Hello", Sandra purred. "My darling, has Grant been in touch", Duke's voice boomed. "Duke, oh Duke, where are you? You're a genius. How did you manage this scoop? This calls for a celebration", Sandra encouraged? "Not far away", Duke replied. Tramp started to yap once again. "Tramp wants to talk to you", Sandra said. She held the receiver close to the dog's mouth. "Speak to daddy Tramp", Sandra encouraged. As if Tramp understood Sandra's instructions, the little dog started to yap excitedly at the sound of Duke's voice at the other end of the phone. It was the sound of the key in the front door that alerted both Sandra and the dog that someone was entering the house. Tramp rushed towards it before Sandra could react. He scratched but barked with excitement. Tramp ran into the room but tugged at Sandra's slippers then returned into the hallway. "Who is it Tramp", Sandra asked? "It's me honey. Give me a hand, would you", Duke asked? He patted the dog's head like he does to Calvin Poser whenever he approves of something he had done to which Duke approved. Sandra ran to embrace him. "Thank you Duke, thank you, thank you, thank you", Sandra exclaimed. She hugged him with expressed emotions. "Steady on", Duke said. He loved every bit of the fuss Sandra was making of him. He started to do his little *'wiggle'* again as if her embrace had injected new life into his whole being. "I told you I'd make you famous. Now will you marry me", Duke asked? His chauffeur stood dutifully behind his boss waiting to unload the crates of Champagne Urge Mark 3 from the limo. The crates got heavier the longer Calvin Poser had to wait. His subservient manner was apparent. "Where do you want me to put them boss", Calvin Poser asked? "Just there", Duke implied. He pointed randomly to a place in the hallway. The chauffeur unloaded the twelve crates then asked his boss what he should do for the rest of the day. "You're on standby. I'll call you when I'm ready", Duke replied. He had eyes only for Sandra. Hardly noticing that Tramp had gone out, he shut the door. No sooner had he done so, the doorbell rang. Annoyed at being disturbed, Duke flung the door open. Standing there looking rather annoyed stood his chauffeur, Calvin Poser. "Boss look what he did", the chauffeur said. He held the little dog at a distant away from him. Tramp had urinated on Calvin's leg. Duke saw the funny side as he took the dog. "Some say it's good luck", Duke commented. He burst out laughing before closing the door behind him. He shared the joke with Sandra. They both laughed. "Lets celebrate the beginning of a wonderful partnership", Duke suggested. He opened the first bottle of Champagne Urge Mark 3. "How did Grant do it", Sandra asked? "Those pictures of you in the torn dress made them dizzy. I understand that their marketing people refused to look at any other agency's entry the moment they saw you. Just think there'll be calendars, billboards, TV adverts and interviews. The sky is the limit Sugarcake", Duke explained. Sandra was so excited she began to shake with expectation. Even Tramp was momentarily forgotten by them until Duke pulled Sandra unto the floor. With trembling hands, he tugged at the skin tight knitted *jump'* suit she was wearing. He tried to rip it off her "You're so beautiful. I can't keep control when I'm with you. Haven't you noticed", Duke asked? Sandra did notice how he was sweating profusely as the excitement brought out his true personality yet again. Duke became more frustrated with his failed attempt to rip her *jump'* suit. Losing complete control, he grabbed the opening at the top but ripped Sandra's suit from her body. "Oh Duke, we can't", Sandra warned. She hoped it was enough of a hint for Duke to understand it was that time of the month but he insisted. "I didn't come all this way for nothing", Duke snapped. His flushed face displayed the waves of fantasy, which ran through his mind. He persisted with having sexual intercourse with her while she was on her period. Tramp thought they were playing a game. He observed the strange murmurs and moans. Duke sprinted once again to relieve his superlative urge then rolled to one side. Sandra still lay on her back. Tramp ran to and fro playfully around her then tried to mimic what he had seen Duke do earlier. "Go on boy. Get some in", Duke encouraged. He sat back to enjoy the spectacle. "Get away, naughty boy Tramp", Sandra said. She pushed the dog away but again her long nails accidentally dug into his body. As she rose from the floor, Sandra rebuked Duke for encouraging the dog to mount her. He thought it was funny. They argued briefly. "Duke how could you", Sandra fumed. She was totally embarrassed not only by Duke's insistence to satisfy his ego but also for encouraging the dog. "Where's your sense of humour", Duke criticised? He swigged some of the flat champagne from the bottle then passed it to Sandra. "This was meant to be a celebration", Duke said. "Sometimes you go too far Duke, like today", Sandra replied. "My darling, sometimes you can be a bit naive. I only meant for us to have some fun", Duke quipped. "What about Tramp", Sandra asked? She was referring to the dog's previous antics. "He was having fun too", Duke replied. He giggled but reached again for the bottle of flat champagne. "We're having a party tonight. I've invited a few friends over, you don't mind do you", Duke asked? "You should have asked me first Duke", Sandra replied? "Well, it's too late now to cancel. Everyone will be here by 20:00 hours. I've arranged for some more champagne and food to be sent here by 19:00 hours", Duke continued. Sandra was both shocked surprised yet confused by the news. She couldn't speak for awhile. "What's the matter, cat got your tongue", Duke teased? "I'm just not in the mood for a lot of people today. That's all", Sandra whispered. Her mood swings at this time would have been so predictable to the more considerate Raymond but Duke seemed unaware. She had hoped he would have understood her condition. "Cheer up, you'll feel great later on. Being the centre of attention and all that my sweet", Duke chirped. They sat on one of the plush sofas completely naked while Tramp licked the top of the champagne bottle which was resting beside them. Duke noticed the dog licking the bottle. He went to the kitchen but returned to the lounge with a cereal bowl. Duke poured some of the champagne into it. "Here boy", Duke encouraged. The eager dog quickly lapped up the flat champagne. "He loves it", Duke exclaimed. He poured more champagne into the bowl. Sandra too was amused at her dog drinking champagne. "Eat your heart out Mary Allsorts", Sandra exclaimed. "What was that", Duke enquired? She ignored him but continued to speak to the dog. "I bet that's the first time you've tasted champagne", Sandra said. She stroked the dog. "If only his previous owner could see him now", Duke commented. Suddenly, he had a brainwave. "That's it", Duke shouted. Sandra, knowing the genius of her lover, tried to encourage him to tell her what he was thinking. She stroked his untidy hair while sidling up to him. "What is it Duke, honey? Tell your Sugarcake" Sandra whispered. She pouted her lips enticingly then blowing gently into his ears. Duke quickly submitted to her advances. This time Tramp watched from the floor. At first, Duke and Sandra's moans, groans and erratic movements made the little dog anxious. The inebriation from the Champagne Urge Mark 3 made Tramp have blurred vision. He was unsure what to do. His attempts to join in were thwarted by the many images he could see in front of him. Tramp used his paws to try to clear his visions. Sandra's slender body was wrapped around Duke. She held his huge head with both hands. Sandra pulled Duke's head closer to her voluptuous bosom as if she was cradling a broken bag packed with shopping. At this heightened stage, Duke wouldn't have cared if he had died from asphyxiation by being smothered by his exotic bird's breasts. He'd often told his friends that he'd probably *"die on 'the job' one day"*. When they queried what made him not care if he did die on *'the job'*, Duke explained that he would "die happy". Duke's friends knew those words might even reappear one day on his Epitaph. Tramp could hear Duke shouting the word *"bitch"* several times as he made his final charge towards his target. The grunts and groans had taken a particular pattern but increased in volume. Sandra joined in actively shouting her cries of simulated satisfaction. She knew how much Duke wanted to please her. Sandra wanted him to know how grateful she was for using his clout to give her the opportunity to become closer to fulfill the Spacevillean Dream. At times, Sandra seemed to be the lead voice in the *'Duet'* performance. She shouted Duke's name at regular intervals with him responding in grunts only. Sandra further exploited Duke's superlative urge, lust, by heaving her huge busts but particularly gyrating and thrusting her narrow hips. She thrust those hips provocatively both backwards, forwards and sometimes sideward in a coordinated motion similar to that of a professional belly dancer. The rolling movements of her belly thrust Duke into a different gear. These more passionate moments did find Duke pressing on the gas rather recklessly as if Sandra's slender body was without bones. She used her feminine expertise to full advantage. Soon, Duke raised the vocal register by roaring himself to victory. His hoarse baritone voice resounded all around the room and beyond. It effectively cued Sandra into sounds of emotional parity with Duke. Writhing as if she was in spasms and cooing like a pigeon, Sandra helped Duke towards his final charge for the line. She joined him in the last few bars of the *'Ecstasy Chorus'* until Duke collapsed on top of her. Sandra bent to nibble at Duke's large ears. She nibbled like a goat, feeding on leaves from a tree. Sandra realized that, for the first time, Duke managed to maintain his erection for a prolonged period. That helped Sandra towards a satisfaction that still was less thrilling than being with Raymond but was an improvement from Duke's standpoint. She was unsure what was causative to Duke's new found *'staying power'*. Sandra wasn't sure but she gave credit to Duke's new Champagne Urge Mark 3. Time and time again Tramp's attempts to join *'mommy'* and *'daddy'* on the plush sofa, was thwarted by his inability to judge both height and distance. The little dog felt lonely but deserted. Tramp started to whimper. He whimpered so much that Duke reached down to pick him up. All three cuddled but lay closely together. The room appeared to be spinning a bit faster now that their enormous physical efforts and the light-headed, dizzy feelings, courtesy of the Champagne Urge Mark 3, rendered them immobile. Sandra tried to shift her body to make herself more comfortable but Duke was already heading towards that great spiral which takes one swiftly to sleep. He was snoring heavily now. Tramp put his paws over his ears to try to dampen the frustrating sound. Duke's heavy frame pinned Sandra to the plush sofa. From her position, all she could do is to watch the ceiling go round and round. She tried to focus on the huge chandelier on the ceiling but that made for quite a different experience. The glitter from the over-ornate diamond crystals were mesmerizing enough when one was sober but the sparkling, spinning chandelier, glittered but seemed to dance around. The over-embellished gold chain from which it hung also played its part in hypnotizing Sandra. Soon, even with her eyes closed, she could still see the glitter and the sparkle of the many bunches of diamond crystals. Each trimmed along their shape, by gold. It was 18:20 hours when Duke stirred. He put his foot down onto the long piled carpet while looking back at Sandra who cuddled Tramp closely to her chest. Duke didn't want to wake her but it was nearly time for the arrival of the things he had ordered. He tried gently to awaken her. "Wake up Sugarcake. It's nearly time for your party", Duke whispered. Sandra didn't stir. The phone rang. Duke answered it. "Hello", Duke said abruptly. "Can I speak to Sandra", Pam asked? "She's asleep", Duke said. "OK, I'll phone back later", Pam replied. "No, don't phone back later. She'll be busy", Duke stated. Pam was shocked by his reply. She hung up the phone. "Dat man is suh rude", Pam reported. "Which man", Aunt Rose asked? Carmen looked directly at Pam but shook her head vigorously indicating that Pam shouldn't tell Aunt Rose. "It don't matter Aunt Rose", she replied. "Yuh young peeple suh secretive", Aunt Rose surrendered. They laughed together. "Talking bout secrets, yuh cudn't tel mi seh yuh pregnant", Aunt Rose asked? Carmen's mouth opened wide but Pam looked sheepishly towards her aunt. "Ah was waiting fi di right moment", Pam replied. "Suh, who is di fawda", Aunt Rose questioned? Again Carmen shook her head at her sister. Natty Hawke did not join in the conversation but he was enjoying the banter all the same. He sighed heavily as he pondered how he would have coped with a night in jail. Carmen hugged him. "Neva mind Natty, dem caan get wey wid it everyday", she assured him. *"Ah hope wen yuh guh bak home yuh can tel dem whey wi ah guh thru every day ina fahwren land"*, Natty Hawke instructed. "Ah tru, wen wi deh back home, wi er sey unnu deh yah ah live 'high life'", Carmen confirmed. "Sum ah dem tink di streets ova yah pave wid gold", Pam added. "Well, ah wudda bi ah rich woman if dat was tru", Aunt Rose chimed. "An ah wudn't bi ah di whim ah di Benefit Office", Pam added? "Evry day dem pounce pon wi an call wi 'scroungers' an batta wi dung", Natty Hawke contributed. Carmen reminded Pam to ring to see how Raymond was doing. "Tank yuh sis", Pam replied. She connected with the hospital. "How is Mr Oddball today", Pam enquired? "He's very chirpy today", the nurse replied. This threw Pam. She was expecting to hear the well rehearsed meaningless phrase, "as well as can be expected" again. Given that Raymond was in a coma, she was unsure the nurse was referring to him. "Chirpy, are you sure nurse", Pam queried? "Yes, it's a miracle but he can talk now. He's out of the coma", the nurse reported. Pam thanked the nurse then hung up. She raised both hands skywards but expressed her relief at the good news. "Tank yuh fawda", Pam exclaimed. Aunt Rose, Carmen and Natty Hawke looked over at Pam when she made the exclamation. They rejoiced in the good news about Raymond's miracle recovery. Pam was so happy. She did not care whether Aunt Rose knew he was the father of her child. "Tank yuh God, mi child wi hav im fawda", Pam beamed. She dialled the hospital again. Pam asked the nurse if it was possible to speak to Raymond on the phone. The nurse said that it was possible if Pam phoned the mobile public phone on the ward. She explained that it could be wheeled over to Raymond's bed. Pam asked for the number of the mobile ward phone. She dialled the number but waited patiently for Raymond to pick up the phone. When Pam heard his voice, she choked but was overwhelmed with joy. "Hello", Raymond said. Pam was now absolutely sure the nurse had given her the correct information. She started to cry. Raymond heard her voice. He assured her that he had come out of the coma the previous night. Raymond explained that the pain to his ribs seemed worse but he was just happy that he's still alive. Pam conversed with him for about 15 minutes. She expressed her love for him but told of the progress of her pregnancy. Raymond said he felt better just hearing her voice. Pam asked if it was alright to tell Sandra about his recovery. He sanctioned it but confirmed that it wouldn't make any difference between his and Pam's relationship. Raymond assured Pam that he was a much happier man living with her. He explained that being in hospital had given him time to reflect. Raymond told Pam that as soon as he recovered fully, he wanted to marry her. She wept unashamedly at the prospect of becoming Mrs. Oddball. At last, Pam would be able to stabilise in a meaningful relationship. She told him that there was a bit of family problem that was hindering her from visiting him. He told her to do what she had to do. "We still have the rest of our lives to spend together", Raymond assured her. Pam was floating on a cloud by the time she hung up with Raymond. She had visions of them walking down the aisle together. After confirming that Raymond was able to communicate once again, Pam dialled Sandra's cell phone. It rang for a while.

CHAPTER 39

"Hello", Sandra's sleepy voice replied. "It's me, Pam. I phoned today but I was told you were asleep", she said cynically. "I've only just awaken. What time is it", Sandra asked? "Nineteen thirty five hours", Pam replied. "I'll have to call you back tomorrow girl. Duke arranged a celebration party which starts at twenty hundred hours", Sandra explained. "What are you celebrating", Pam asked? "I've been chosen to be in an advert for a major Credit Card Company, I'll tell you all about it tomorrow. Sorry, I've got to go, I can hear Duke coming down the stairs", she concluded. "Aren't you getting ready Sugarcake", Duke asked? Shaking his head as if he wanted it to fall off, he jumped and pranced awkwardly in front of her. "Where's Tramp", Sandra asked? She looked around the room as if she was looking for a lost child. "Tramp, Tramp, here Tramp, here boy, Sandra searched. "He's out of it. I've put him upstairs in our bed", Duke said. He laughed uncontrollably. His podgy belly shook violently to the reverberation of his laughter. Sandra made her way up the stairs. As she entered the bedroom, she stood back as she saw how Duke had placed the tiny dog on the pillow. He looked lifeless for one moment then Sandra witnessed him being sick on the pillow. The griping made the dog wretch. "Tramp", Sandra said. Partly from anger and partly through concern, she lifted the little dog to her chest. He gratefully licked her face. "Duke", Sandra called. He ran swiftly up the stairs. "What's the matter Sugarcake", he enquired? She showed him the pillow. He looked at his watch. "Leave it. Your first guest will arrive any minute now. You should be ready. You're the host", he said. Duke turned but went back down the stairs. By the time Sandra had finished her *'wash'*, the doorbell rang. She rushed to put on the new outfit Duke had brought with him. Sandra removed it from the bag quickly. She knew Duke treated her like a queen but she never would have thought he'd even go near a shop which sold African outfits. They were transported to the virtual planet of Asteroidia from planet Earth. "Wow", Sandra exclaimed. On her way down the stairs, Grant Favours looked admiringly at her as he reached for his camera. The flash exploded and she found herself posing to Grant's direction once again. "Let us take one of you and Duke together", Grant suggested. Sandra remembered the last time she tried to take a picture with Duke he had told her that he would say when it's the right time. In as sweet a voice as she could muster Sandra popped the question. "Is it the right time Duke", she asked? "Yes, my Queen", he replied. They posed together. Sandra looked elegant and royal in her 'African Queen' Outfit and Headwear. Her deeply tanned skin blended subtly, against the red, gold and green outfit. Wrapped around Sandra's tall, slender frame, the outfit accented the uniqueness of her body movements. Her long strides caused her swaying hips to constantly baffle those who continuously observed this mesmeric, biomechanical feat. Duke, with his podgy belly, thin legs and large feet, in his oversized Dasheki outfit would have made Natty Hawke swear. They took many family pictures with Tramp. He found the flash a bit frightening. "One more", Duke kept saying. He fussed about how the white Dasheki suit with the red, gold and green flashes made him look. "Can you see my tan", he asked his friend? "It makes you look brilliant, a good contrast I'd say. How long did you stay under the sunlamp", Grant asked? "Until I almost cooked", Duke replied. His loud laughter boomed out once again. More people began to arrive rapidly. Soon, the lounge was filled with people Sandra hadn't met before. Duke made sure he introduced each one to her as soon as they arrived. "This is Sir Ivanhoe Goldfeet", Duke said. He owns the Credit Card Company that is giving you the contract to advertise their card. He introduced the elderly man to Sandra. She handed him the glass of Champagne Urge Mark 3. He sipped it but commented. "I've not tasted this brand before, what is it", Sir Ivanhoe asked? "It's Duke's own brand, Champagne Urge Mark 3. Very potent", Sandra declared. "You're coming up in the world young Duke", Sir Ivanhoe commented. He saluted Duke before making his way into the crowded lounge. Grant Favours came into the hallway where Sandra and Duke were standing. "Parties are all about atmosphere. How about some music", he asked? Sandra and Duke both looked at each other. "I don't have more than a few CDs", Sandra explained. "I came prepared", Duke assured her. He smiled broadly as he headed for the lounge. Sandra was just welcoming other guests at the door when the sound of the noise from the lounge made her jump. Duke's selection was a poor excuse for music but the guest didn't care. "Nice party", a woman said. She jerked her body but, with her finger, beckoned at her companion. "Please come in", Sandra said awkwardly. She had no idea who they were. The next guest gave Sandra quite a shock. "Hello is Duke here", Doris Bendlow asked? She pushed past Sandra at the door. Her oversized breasts trying desperately to escape the restriction of the skimpy knitted top she was wearing. Sandra remembered how Duke had tried to get Doris's attention in the AADC that day but wondered why she was invited. All the people Duke had invited were now present. They ate the food and drank Champagne Urge Mark 3. Duke stopped the pounding music to draw attention to the reason for the celebration. "Ladies and gentlemen, we have among us a beautiful young woman whose career is about to take off to astronomical proportions. Grant has managed to help her secure a contract with our good friend Sir Ivanhoe Goldfeet. He is here, give him a round of applause", Duke prompted. The people shouted their approval but sung the refrain, "He's a jolly good fellow" Sandra was encouraged to kiss Sir Goldfeet. She did. Duke asked her to kiss all the other men, who themselves, were VIP contacts she daren't ignore. Sandra was passed around, from one to another, like the *'parcel'* in the game *'Pass the parcel'*. Men and women were quite stunned by her beauty. They all made a big fuss about her. Some of the men were whispering into her ears. One blew into her ear and she giggled a lot with him. The comments were not always good wishes. One woman overheard her husband suggesting wife swapping with Sandra. "Denver, don't forget I'm here", she scowled. "I was only making small talk my dear", he said apologetically. He winked at Sandra while squeezing her hand. The man's wife smiled cynically but called Sandra a bitch through clenched teeth. Doris Bendlow was busy making small talk with most of the men. She told as many dirty stories as she could remember, ensuring to demonstrate each tiny detail. "I say, she's jolly", one of the men commented. He nudged his friend as he roared with laughter at Doris' common antics. Each movement she made ensured attention to her visible assets. When the music started again, Doris gyrate her hips like a 'hula' dancer. "My God, she can't have any bones in her body", one of the older men exclaimed. Doris didn't care whose party it was. She just wanted to be the centre of attention at all times. She made her way over to where Duke was standing. She demanded he dance with her. This made Sandra angry but she didn't want to upset her VIP guests. Duke was uncaring in the performance he put down with Doris. In fact, his tan began to redden under the humid condition and the formulated champagne. He waved the half filled bottle as he flitted from place to place. Doris reached out but hooked arms with Duke but attempted to drink from the bottle as married couples do. "She's drunk", one woman said. Doris joined in the chain but performed this rather rowdy ritual. It moved in one direction then to the opposite direction. Every now and then the participants hopped on one leg raised their knees in unison in the air but shouted *"oui"* quite loudly. The woman's description of Doris' state did in fact apply to most if not all of them in the lounge. Some others, who were either standing in the hallway or coming back from using the toilet, breached the line to join in. Sandra was not familiar with the dance so she stood almost alone looking on at the high spirited movement. A man, who had been stalking her all night since his arrival, grabbed Sandra by her waist but forced her to partake in the jollification. "I say, come join in. Don't be such a stiff shirt, what" he chimed. His reddened cheeks bore the hallmarks of a type of flushing which indicated that he was thoroughly sizzled from the Champagne Urge Mark 3 like the rest of Sandra's enforced guests. Her neighbours paid the price of the shouting of *"oui"* as the group celebrated the ritual dance around the imaginary totem pole. "Come on, join in", he insisted. The man used the opportunity to pinch Sandra on one of her bum cheek. She looked at him over her shoulder but ask him not to. He pretended that he didn't hear but carried on to fondle her ass. He patted it but groaned as if he was gaining some form of pleasure from his strange behaviour. Sandra was trapped but could not free herself from the assault. She used her hand to slap the man's hand but he insisted she "enjoy" the experience. Colonel Calder Upride was the culprit. He was well known by his colleagues as a *'ladies man'*. The colonel had a funny way of living up to the reputation. His wife observed as he continued to fondle Sandra's backside. She let him know in no uncertain terms that she was aware of his behaviour. "Calder, rein yourself in", she demanded. "I'm just having fun", he declared. The colonel's upper dentures slackened when he tried to laugh. It sounded more like he was choking on a morsel of food that had gone down too suddenly. Nobody heard the doorbell for a while but eventually someone asked Sandra to answer the door. When she did, two policemen addressed her as if they had come to raid the party. She enquired why they were there. They told Sandra that they were asked to come to that address about a disturbance. "Well, as you can see officer there is no disturbance here", Sandra defended. The cops handled her coarsely but accused Sandra about her *"lot"* always having noisy parties. They insisted it cease immediately. She giggled foolishly from the effects of the champagne. The other policeman peered closely into her face. "Sarge don't you know who this is", the rookie exclaimed? The Sergeant looked her up and down. Upon recognition he answered. "Yes I do", he said. "Can we have your autograph", the Sergeant pleaded. "I haven't got a pen", Sandra replied. Again, she giggled like a hyena. "I'm sure you can come in for a moment while I search for a pen", she encouraged. The rookie cop was quite excited. "We can't pass up an invite like that, can we Sarge", he enquired? "It must be our lucky night, a few minutes won't hurt", the Sergeant agreed. "Have you got any of that Rum", the Sergeant asked? "This is a champagne party", Sandra declared. She gave each of them a bottle of Champagne Urge Mark 3 and glasses. "Help yourselves, there's food over there", she encouraged. She pointed to the buffet. The two cops couldn't believe their luck. They gorged themselves with food. "What's this Sarge", the rookie asked? "Who cares, they are eating it. Make sure you get some for later", he ordered. Both the Sergeant and the rookie wrapped some sandwiches in serviettes but put them in their pockets. Duke was smoking a spliff. The skunk's aroma was extremely strong. The cops noticed it. The rookie cop got excited but drew the Sergeant's attention to Duke and the spliff. "Sarge, Sarge he's smoking a spliff", the rookie cop told the Sergeant. "Ignore it son ", the Sergeant replied. Doris Bendlow made sure she included the cops in her continuous cabaret. She took off their hats but placed one on her head. The other she put on Duke's head. Bending at the knees in some sort of ritual, Doris spoke. "Evening all", she teased. It meant something to the cops. They laughed. The Sergeant's eyes were focused only on Doris' huge breasts each being the size of large cantaloupes. They jutted out but stretched the knitted top to its limit. The implanted breasts were not only the Sergeant's main attraction but his imagination had increased with the effect of the Champagne Urge Mark 3. It certainly had an aphrodisiac quality. What the Sergeant felt below his waist was certainly not his truncheon. His desire for the rotund Doris was driving him wild. "Come over here darling", he joked. He walked over towards her but joined in the chain dance with Doris while the young rookie looked on. At exactly 02:00 hours, Duke stopped the music to make another announcement. "We have something to tell you", he started. Duke beckoned Sandra to his side. Everyone gathered round to hear what Duke wanted them to. He produced a ring box. "This beautiful young woman is going to marry me. All my life, I've wanted an exotic bird. Now, I've got one. Ain't I lucky", Duke asked? He was flushed with pride. Most of the crowd encouraged him to continue. "Look at her stunningly beautiful, slim, tender, young body in her 'African Queen' outfit", he said. All the guests, except for Doris, cheered. She looked on with immeasurable jealousy and hate but she knew how Duke might react if she tried to sabotage his plan. He walked around Sandra, like a slave auctioneer, pointing out all the other details which attracted him to her. He reached up on tiptoes but opened her lips with his stubby fingers, which he had just used to scratch his crotch inside his boxer shorts, then proceeded to *'sell'* his exotic bird to his friends. "Strong teeth", he concluded. The crowd, including the cops, cheered loudly. Turning directly towards Sandra, Duke handed her the box but commented. "You're mine now Sugarcake. This is for you", he declared. The people in the room gathered closely as Sandra was about to open the box. "It's just got to be diamond", one woman commented. The woman's guess was accurate. The large encrusted diamond ring brought sharp intakes of breath and also drew general comments of well wishes. However, some, like Doris, wore *plastic* smiles. "You're a very lucky girl. It must have cost Duke a few hundred thousand SPCUs", one female guest complimented Sandra. "A million", Duke corrected. The sharp intake of breaths was more than a draught of wind comparably. It was more like the suction created by a very powerful vacuum cleaner and even more conspicuous now than before. Doris's flushed face turned as deep in colour like a beetroot. Some of the guests started to make comments to show they didn't mind being in Sandra's company. "You're alright but it's the others", one woman commented. "I can't understand some of your people but you are eloquent", another woman commented. She patted Sandra but stroked her upper arm like she would her pet. Sandra was unsure how to respond to the women's comments but she didn't feel too comfortable by them. She chose not to comment as Duke might accuse her of being "too thin skinned", maybe! The first woman's eyes widened as she saw the huge stone. "Thank you Duke. First Tramp now this", Sandra whispered. She hugged him close to her. "You can have anythink you like, my queen. I tell you what, tomorrow you can go out and choose a new house. I'll pay cash whatever it cost", Duke told her. Sandra's head was already spinning from the powerful effect of Champagne Urge Mark 3 but she heard Duke clearly. Her thoughts reflected on the houses she had seen in the leafy suburbs like Poshborough from the train on the day the manic driver had crashed into the lorry. Doris Bendlow had guzzled enough Champagne Urge Mark 3 to be in the mood to demonstrate even more why she was invited. Duke had told her that he wanted her to entertain his friends. This she did without effort. Holding Sir Ivanhoe Goldfeet by his tie she led him into one corner of the room then she placed herself close to him but purred. Sir Ivanhoe had not been purred at for a long time and he quickly melted to her whims. Two of the younger women grew jealous of Sandra's rhythm to the music. They pushed their way into the middle of the floor but demonstrated the art of 'hula' dancing without limit or decorum. The brazen women plunged themselves unto the men they chose to help them exhibit what was now becoming a pornographic circus. Duke tried to get into the act when he attempted to follow Sandra's polished "little wiggle" but there was no synchronisation to the beat he was dancing to. His whole emphasis reminded Sandra of a toddler hearing music for the first time. She could remember her young cousin Tara, at the kiddies' birthday party, jumping about but shaking her head as if she wanted it to fall off. Sandra had laughed then at the effect the music was having on the child. When the chain dancing started again someone treaded on a body in the corner. Under the attention of Doris Bendlow, Sir Ivanhoe got far too excited. The exertion from Doris' demanding *'dirty dancing'* moves had taken its toll on the advanced aged billionaire. He had fainted. Sandra rushed over to him. "Sir Goldfeet. Sir Goldfeet", she shouted. Sandra and the others were concerned about his irregular breathing. "Duke, Duke I think he passed out. Maybe we should open the windows", Sandra cried. "Raise his head", one woman advised. "Put him in the recovery position", another suggested. Doris wanted to revive Sir Ivanhoe Goldfeet with mouth to mouth resuscitation but Duke thought that he might have a heart attack if she came that close to him again. Doris left the room. Duke took off but placed his folded Dasheki top under Sir Ivanhoe's head. That was just a temporary measure. "Get a pillow", Duke instructed Sandra. She staggered her way through the crowded lounge into the hallway where people were coupled together. Some were blissfully unaware of Sir Ivanhoe's demise. They were too busy smooching and petting each other. Sandra struggled to weave her way through the maze of bodies strewn along the stairs. Finally, she reached the landing where live orgies were taking place. Sandra stepped over the bodies on the landing in front of her bedroom. The door was slightly ajar. She heard groaning coming from her bedroom. Inside, she discovered the reasons for the groaning in her bedroom. Doris Bendlow and the Sergeant were engaged in an act that was too gross to describe. It can only be left to the imagination. "Not in my bed", Sandra screamed. Totally forgetting the reason for the party, Sandra dragged Doris Bendlow from her bed. She slapped her with each hand in a synchronised exhibition of a woman enraged. Doris grabbed her face but squealed as she backed away from the enraged host. She stared at the palms of her hands which were covered in her own blood. Doris looked at Sandra's hands to see if she was holding a knife but instead she saw the claws which had torn into her face. Sergeant Clueless was hurriedly trying to prevent what he saw as *'actual bodily harm'*. "Calm down, calm down", he shouted. At the same time, he was trying to retrieve his trouser. Sandra saw his mouth move but could not hear above the commotion of voices and the thumping of the loud music. She thought he was trying to protect Doris Bendlow but Sandra was angry enough not to care who he was. As far as she was concerned, at the time when she discovered them in her bed, the Sergeant *"was not in uniform"*. He stumbled as he made his way towards Sandra. She felt threatened. Stepping aside she, like Carmen had done to Alan Baitman, kicked the Sergeant violently in his crotch. The tears were an embarrassment but Sergeant Clueless could not control the pain he felt from the blow as he sunk slowly to the floor. Sandra kicked him again and again until he pleaded, "I surrender". "Get out of my house", she ordered. As he pleaded for her to be patient while he made himself *'presentable'*, Sandra hovered over him menacingly until he crawled through the bedroom door on all fours before making his way hastily down the stairs. Sandra slammed the door shut but turned to Doris. "Now you", she expressed. Doris Bendlow was now crouching in the corner like a trained puppy. "Don't hurt me anymore. Please don't hurt me anymore", she pleaded. Sandra grabbed her by the neck of the knitted top, now bloody from the wounds, but pulled Doris into a standing position. All the Champagne Urge Mark 3 Sandra had drunk seemed to make her more ill-tempered and impatient. "This is my house and my party", she reminded the timid Doris. Sandra was in a foul mood.

She ripped the blouse from Doris' body. "You're nothing more than a common slut. I don't know why Duke invited you here. He must have been drunk at the time", Sandra raged. She didn't know it but she sounded just like Mrs. Stagg talking to or about her. Doris was hurt by Sandra's remarks. After all, Sandra did not really know her. Doris had been in many fights before and was still alive. She decided that Sandra had shown her best. Doris decided that Sandra's remarks were uncalled for. By the time Sandra noticed the white powder on the foil paper on one of the bedside tables, she couldn't stop Doris from sniffing it. As if rejuvenated by the white powder, Doris felt braver now than she did moments before. "You bitch. You've got your hooks so deeply into Duke he thinks the sun shines from your blue eyes. You're just as much a slut as me. At least, I'm willing to admit it but you keep pretending you're better than the likes of women like me. You're nothing but a *'kept woman'* yourself and that means you're a *'closeted whore'* ", she jeered. Suddenly, Doris pounced. She grabbed Sandra by her long black hair. She was not ready when the seemingly cowering Doris launched her attack. Sandra fell backwards as she tried to avoid Doris' sudden movement towards her. She had a weight advantage over the slender Sandra. They tumbled around the bedroom. Doris now had the upper hand. With renewed strength from the white powder, Doris knelt astride the shocked Sandra, who was now being pinned to the floor. "I'm going to make sure your pretty face will never grace the billboards. I hate your *'lot'*. You've come over here but think you own the place", Doris exclaimed scornfully. She raised the champagne glass she had picked up while she was cowering in the corner.

Duke had grown impatient waiting for Sandra to fetch the pillow. He left Sir Ivanhoe with his colleagues to see what had delayed Sandra's return. By the time Duke managed to wade through the smooching couples in the hallway, on the stairs and the bodies engaging in orgies on the landing, the two women had been wrestling for some time. Duke entered the bedroom in time to see Doris sitting astride his gorgeous exotic bird. Doris had her hand in the air. In it was a champagne glass. Duke was just in time to save his exotic queen. He grabbed Doris' hand with the glass but wrenched it violently until the glass fell unto the carpet. Doris screamed as loud as a wounded elephant. She moaned, sobbed but whimpered in such sequence that Duke was now feeling quite guilty about the force he had used but he had to take whatever steps he could to save Sandra from being scarred permanently by the envious Doris Bendlow. "Come on girls, don't spoil the party", he dissuaded. "Whose side are you on, Doris asked? Her tone befitted that of a child. Doris continued her tantrum act until she had Duke's total attention. She had to be restrained by Duke. Sandra was seething with anger. That was not only due to the fight with Doris but also because she felt Duke had gone soft on her offender. Sandra leapt towards Doris and they ended up in a tight clench. They rolled around in unison. When their rolling ball action ceased, Doris' weight advantage was once again why she managed to get on top of Sandra. They were panting heavily now, Doris more so than the fitter, leaner Sandra. Doris was swearing all the time. "You f . . . ing slag, stick to your own and leave Duke alone. He only wants you on his arm as his exotic mistress . . . Think you're special, don't ya? You're just a decoration, Duke's Miss Fluesy. So there, you . . . hoity toity bitch, she raged". Duke knew that Doris was jealous of Sandra. Her racist implication was a revelation for him. Duke couldn't tell if the words, *"stick to your own"* uttered by Doris, came from an inveterate racist perspective. Was it the drugs that brought these feelings to the fore, he wondered? Duke had been under the illusion that Doris' mannerism against Sandra was the typical female competitiveness of ownership, he understood as jealousy. He became more curious about what each of the women really felt about what it means to be with him. Duke took most women for granted but there was something about Sandra that magnified his urge to be constantly in her company. He also realized that, after his declaration about wanting to marry the gorgeous Sandra, the presentation of the huge diamond ring had got up Doris' back somewhat. Duke needed to find out what had driven Doris and Sandra to be at each other's throats, literally. "What's going on", Duke asked? He pulled the jealous Doris from atop his precious Sugarcake. "I'm going to kill her", Doris shouted. She wriggled to be free of Duke's restraining hold. "Now stop you two", he shouted. Duke separated the two women. He now stood in between them like a referee in a wrestling match keeping the opponents apart. Duke manoeuvred Doris around Sandra but told her to stay in the room. "Stay put", he ordered. Duke removed the key from the inner side of the bedroom door. He locked the door from the outside leaving Sandra inside fuming to herself for allowing Doris to get the better of her. She paced up and down the room like a caged tiger wanting to avenge the humiliation she had suffered at Doris' hands. Tramp was hiding from the noisy, chaotic party crowd all night. While all the action had been taking place, he had stayed on top of the laundry basket. Tramp's whining during Doris' and the Sergeant's sexual encounter and the vicious fight between *'mommy'* Sandra and Doris remained a frightening experience for the little dog. Even *'daddy'* Duke had not seen him atop the laundry basket. In fact, for those periods of time Tramp was trembling nervously from feeling frightened all the time. He ran over to Sandra when she bent her head but cried from the frustration of being locked in the bedroom of her house by her lover. She could hardly hear the yapping above the music which had seemed to get louder and crazier. Even her polished wiggle could not stand the pace of the irregular beat though Sandra imagined Duke jerking his head as if he wanted it to drop off. Tramp made sure Sandra could see him. She finally picked up the little dog but cuddled him. Tramp was about the only one Sandra could tell her sob story. "Man's best friend. Women's best friend too", she commented. Sandra kissed Tramp. The little dog was excited to be back in her company. He showed his appreciation in the only way a dog knew how. Tramp washed Sandra's face with his tongue. The taste of the sweat, perfume and make-up interrupted his taste buds. The little dog stopped licking her face. Sandra hugged Tramp closely but wished she was in Raymond's arms once again. She allowed herself to think of Raymond at that moment because somehow she felt a degree of comfort from doing so. He was still her *'comforter'* whenever Sandra felt abandoned. With Tramp for company, she became less aware of her imprisonment. "Tramp, why have you been hiding from mommy", she asked? Sandra looked deep into the little dog's eyes.

CHAPTER 40

S he looked out through the window onto the street. It was light enough now to see without the street lamps. The double-parked cars made her realize how big a party she was having. A couple of youths, returning from their own party looked towards the house where the irregular music was coming from. They were laughing but pointing at something which amused them. Sandra could not see from the window of her bedroom on the first floor what was so amusing immediately below in the recessed area on the ground floor. When the youth crossed the street but hovered outside the fence near the gate, Sandra guessed there was something unusual happening. She heard the banging of the front door several times and the sound of loud cheers. In the front garden she saw two men as they grappled and fought while some others crowded round them. None of them tried to stop the men from fighting except for the woman with the red handbag, who got more animated the longer the fight went on. Tramp started to yap at the angry men. Sandra opened the window but shouted for the men to stop fighting. "Shut up you" one from the drunken crowd shouted. Sandra noticed how many of her neighbours had gathered to view the spectacle. Some just watched while others commented. Two or three other skirmishes were going on inside the lounge but Sandra was unable to see for herself. Still, without his Dasheki top, Duke finally appeared. Sandra could see the sweat pouring from his tanned body but she wondered if he had been keeping Doris 'happy' while she was locked in her own bedroom. "Duke", Sandra shouted. He looked up. Signifying exertion, his podgy belly was heaving up and down. "Not now", he shouted back. Duke tried to pull the fighting men apart. He swaggered from side to side as he tried again to stop the two men. They had been seen sniffing a white substance from foil paper all the way throughout the party. The two men argued loudly but seemed determined to die for whatever reason they were fighting. "If I say she's mine, she's mine", one said. The man squeezed harder on the other man's throat. When his singular effort failed, Duke asked the others to help him separate the combatants. "Give us a hand. Let us get these bloody idiots apart before they kill each other", Duke pleaded urgently. Someone had called the police but was told by them that *"the address had already been 'investigated' "*. They had not found anything wrong. It was the seventh call that brought the police back to the address. One police car turned up with two cops inside. They were not the same ones who had called before. These approached the gate hesitantly until they saw the youths outside the fence. Striding more purposefully, the cops tried to apprehend a couple of them, who refused to move on their order. Many of the onlookers could see that the youths weren't involved in the melee. "Leave them alone", one woman shouted. Several others joined in. They repeated it like a mantra until the police freed the youths they were hassling. Duke was the first to approach the cops when they entered through the gate. "It's nothing unusual. We were having a nice party until these two started to fight over Doris", he managed to explain. He turned but shouted for Doris to come forward. "Over here Doris", Duke ordered. He jerked his head to one side to reinforce his order. The crowd parted for her. The people on the street began to laugh as she made her way towards Duke like an obedient child. Both cops looked at each other as Doris approached. Sandra had ripped her top from her earlier. Bare feet and wearing only a skirt, Doris distracted more than the two cops. Loud cheers and wolf whistles came from some sections of the crowd outside the gate. The youths in particular commented loudly about her appearance, but brazen Doris couldn't see what all the fuss was about. The two cops ogled at her assets as she asked Duke why he wanted her to come forward. "What do you want darling", Doris asked? Sandra heard Doris' words but continued to be an observer. Duke told her to explain to the cops how the fight had started. "Don't bother, I think we can use a bit of imagination on this one", the senior cop commented. "I'll sort it out", Duke said as he patted the Sergeant on his back. The younger of the two cops was still mesmerized by the busty Doris' large cantaloupe sized augmented breasts. She pressed hard against him. The younger cop believed his luck had changed. Even though Doris was much older than him, he was eager to explore the rotund Doris and her assets. "When do you finish your shift", she teased? Duke openly rebuked her. "Give it a rest Doris", he ordered. Most of the VIPs, including the two men, who had been fighting, started to go back inside for fear of sleazy comments from the press. Sir Ivanhoe Goldfeet tried to cover his face from the video camera which was pointing in his direction. Under Duke's instructions, the young cop pursued the man in the grey chauffeur suite with the camera. They lost him in the large crowd. Calvin Poser was partially hidden in the crowd but Duke had seen his chauffeur too as he filmed the ugly scene. It confirmed what Duke's private detective, Alan Baitman, who was himself employed by central government as a private investigator into benefit fraud, had told him about his own chauffeur. Calvin Poser was the extortionist, who had been sending the threatening cryptic notes. Duke knew that now for sure. He thought his chauffeur, Calvin Poser, was working under the instructions of his wife, Dora. It was reported to Duke by Alan Baitman that they had become more than just *'familiar'* with each other. Duke Stagg watched as the young cop, disappointed at losing his *prey*, turned on the crowd outside the gate. "It's all over, go home", he said angrily. The young cop added insulting abuse as he gestured his intention. Some of the crowd began to move away but apparently not fast enough. The young cop snapped. He struck out with the long baton at those nearest to him. He wielded it with enough venom and intent to cause permanent harm. One of the unfortunate victims was Sandra's next door neighbour. He was trying to explain that the path to his house was blocked by the others. Sergeant Benjamin Clawhammer and his colleagues, who were called to the *"riot scene"*, joined their colleagues to compete in the power game they often played. Soon, panic set in and the once orderly crowd began to run in every direction. Some shouted and screamed as they tried to escape the blows raining down on them. Many were trampled underfoot as they stumbled and fell. Duke and Doris, both topless, watched from Sandra's front garden. She retreated from the upstairs window the moment the first blow found its target. "It's none of our business Tramp", she said. He whimpered his disagreement. Tramp trembled so much that Sandra thought he had caught a chill. She placed the dog on her pillow then covered him with the duvet. Sandra pushed her head through the window again but this time shouted for Duke to come up to the bedroom. "Duke it's Tramp", she said. Sandra beckoned frantically with her arms. He turned but made his way through the open door. His effort to run up the stairs was thwarted by the drunken bodies strewn haphazardly along its path. Finally, Duke hurdled over the others on the top landing. He reached into the shallow trouser pocket for the key. When he couldn't find it he threw his heavy shoulders against the door. One effort was not enough to shift the solid mahogany door. Duke felt the sharp pain as he made contact with it again and again. "What's the matter Duke", Sandra asked? "I've lost the bloody key", he explained. "Look in the garden, it could have fallen out", Sandra said patiently. Duke eventually made his way back downstairs to the hallway where Doris stood dangling the key in front of him. "Give it here Doris", he said bluntly. She laughed in his face but carried on teasing with the key. "Now I've got something you want. Come and get it", she teased. She enticed Duke to grapple with her. "Doris, give me the bloody key", Duke shouted. He grabbed her as she tried to go into the crowed lounge. Duke was shorter than Doris so, when she raised her hand into the air, his face was at the same height as her augmented bust. These acted as a further shield but made it more difficult for Duke to retrieve the key. Doris brought her hand down swiftly but smothered Duke with a bear hug, suffocating him with her assets. "Now precious, are you going to get me a modeling job too like your fancy woman upstairs", Doris bullied? He tapped the wall behind her like a wrestler, who was signalling for surrender. When Doris released Duke, he was gasping for air. His flushed face expressed more than his highlighted tan. Before handing him the key, Doris threatened, "I've got witnesses".

Sandra was finally freed from the confines of her bedroom. She was eager to see what was happening in the lounge. Most of the guests, still clutching individual bottles of Champagne Urge Mark 3, were either propped up against the wall or lying on the floor with glazed expressions. A few were still waltzing around on the same spot although the music had stopped. When two people tried to resurrect the chain dance, they found that Sandra's patience was running out. She looked at her watch. The time was 07:42 hours. Doris Bendlow tried to undress the influential Sir Ivanhoe Goldfeet. "Duke, do something about this", Sandra said firmly. He was tired too but eager to be alone with his exotic bird. "OK the party is over", Duke announced. The man with the ill-fitting dentures raised his unfinished bottle but commented. "Bloody good party Duke", he confirmed. He fought to keep the top denture from falling to the floor. Some of the people began to leave, slowly. Sandra started to busy herself clearing up the empty glasses and bottles. "Give us a hand Duke", she said firmly. "Oh leave it until we wake up", he replied. Duke said goodbye to his friends, who were staggering towards their cars like beaten boxers returning to their corners. One of the women guest tried to open one of the three bottle banks which stood in a row on the pavement not far from Sandra's house. "That's not your car you silly cow", Duke shouted. He called a minicab to take Doris home. As the last of the guests left the house, Duke spoke with Sandra. "Thank goodness that's all over, did you enjoy yourself", he enquired? "All except for the orgies and that vulgar woman with the cop in my bed", Sandra replied angrily. "Oh Doris, she doesn't mean any harm. She likes to have fun, that's all", he defended. "Fun, you call it, fun when people use my house like a brothel", Sandra fumed. "It happens all the time at our parties. You'll have to get used to it. Ever heard the saying if you can't beat them join them", Duke reiterated? Sandra realized that was part of the price she'd have to pay in her quest for fame and celebrity status. "I'm tired, I'm going to bed", she replied. She picked up Tramp from the buffet table where he was finishing off the left-overs. Both Sandra and Duke made their way upstairs to the bedroom. He flopped onto the bed and immediately started to sleep. Sandra lay beside her husband to be and her dog until she too fell asleep.

Later that same day, at 14:22 hours, Pam pressed Sandra's doorbell but there was no reply. She kept pressing the bell until she heard Tramp's yapping. The little dog yapped until Sandra stirred. "Quiet Tramp, you'll wake daddy", Pam heard her say. She lifted the brass knocker but hammered until Sandra opened the door. She was shocked surprise to see Raymond standing there. "Hello Sandy, can I come in", he asked? His voice was calm. Sandra froze. Her jaws dropped. She kept her mouth opened as wide as a dentist would approve. The shock had rendered her speechless at first. Raymond was the last person Sandra might have thought to be ringing her doorbell. She had no idea he had even recovered from the coma let alone be fit enough to be appearing like the 'prodigal lion' returning to his lair. Eventually, Sandra was able to comment. "What are you doing out of hospital", she asked? "It's only for a day", Raymond replied quietly. Thought I would pop round to see you and thank you for saving my life", Raymond explained. Sandra was wide awake now. She began to realize that this wasn't just a bad dream. Having been busy chasing around with Duke, Sandra had ignored the 'crippled' Raymond. All of Duke's suggestions came flooding rapidly back into her head. "Forget him, he's a bloody cabbage. He's no good to you or himself", she remembered him saying. His words were more like a tsunami of memories as they rushed back from a not too distant past. Sandra remembered that was the first time when Duke had asked her to marry him but she had refused. "Why not", Duke had asked? When she mentioned Raymond, Duke snapped and had suggested she "pull the bloody plug, you'll be doing him a favour".

The ambulance staff helped Raymond to stand. They were keen to return to the hospital. "We can't leave him standing here", one of them told Sandra. They needed a decision to be made. "Can I come in Sandy", Raymond asked again? Sandra was hesitant, still looking at him as if he was a version of the biblical 'Lazarus' returning from the grave. She pondered how Duke might react if he woke up to find Raymond in the house. A number of questions started to flood into her mind. Would he get angry, take back the large diamond ring but just walk out of her life forever? How would she explain to Raymond why Duke was there? Sandra's mind was in a quandary. For the first time, she was being forced to decide between her need for the tall, muscular specimen, Raymond, or the short, rich, influential, unattractive Duke. Sandra didn't want to lose either but it was being made clear that she couldn't have them both. Somehow, Sandra genuinely wished Raymond would make a full recovery even if he was just available to quell her fire whenever she needed him. Duke's money and influential clout were what he had to offer. Sandra had spent many frustrating moments longing for the loveable Raymond. She could see how weak his eyes looked. Sandra made her decision. She used to share this house with him. Sandra couldn't find it in herself to refuse to allow him to speak with her for a few moments. It wasn't as if he was asking to return permanently. At least, she could defend her decision if Duke started to complain. Sandra agreed Raymond could come in. "Sure Ray, but please forgive the state of the place", she apologized. Sandra remembered how neat Raymond used to keep the place. She was embarrassed at the mess the house was in. Raymond noticed the little dog that was yapping at him as if he was an intruder. He wanted to sit down so badly he didn't care what the dog thought of him. Slowly, he made some small steps towards the door with the help of the ambulance staff. Pam walked in behind them. She knew Sandra would be upset that she hadn't given her notice of Raymond's arrival. Once inside, he noticed the champagne bottles, cigarette butts, spliff ends and the bits of foil paper which some of the guests had thrown carelessly on the floor. There were also one or two syringes scattered all around. The carpet was completely ruined with the spilt drinks too. Raymond tripped on an empty bottle as he tried to get to the plush sofa. "Some party", one ambulance staff commented. They glanced at the many unopened bottles of Champagne Urge Mark 3 perched on the long sideboard on the other side of the room. Sandra's smile was only superficial. She was seething underneath at her friend Pam whom she had helped financially many times without hesitation. Her anger came out as soon as the ambulance staff had gone. They said Raymond would have to return to the hospital the following day. Sandra couldn't hold back. She turned to Pam but released her anger. Sandra spoke in the language that she had learnt from her parents. "How yuh cudda duh dis to mi", she yelled? Her natural language preference was the indicator to the eruption which was about to follow. Sandra did not want to spell it out while Duke was around but she knew that Pam fully understood to what she referred. "Yuh backstabber", Sandra fumed. Pam knew what she meant. Sandra advanced towards Pam. She knew an angry Sandra was lethal but Pam was not going to sit there and be dictated to over Raymond. "Look Sandra you're so busy fulfilling your dreams that you don't remember the people who really care for you", Pam said firmly. They carried on arguing bitterly until Raymond called a truce. "If I'm causing so much inconvenience I would rather go back into hospital", he said quietly. Raymond was embarrassed that the two women were talking as if he wasn't there but he was learning all the time. He looked at the watch Pam had bought him earlier. Raymond looked directly at Pam when he spoke. "It's time for my tablets", he reminded. Pam removed the two small brown bottles and the two large plastic packets that contained the huge bright yellow and deep red bullet shaped antibiotic capsules from her handbag. She read the instructions on the labels then proceeded to open them. Pam removed one normal sized white and then a sickly pink tablet from the two brown bottles and one large bright yellow and one deep red capsule from the plastic packets. "I'll get some water", Sandra said. "I don't need any water", Raymond said firmly. He didn't trust Sandra's hygienic qualities even when they lived together. Raymond remembered the times he used to try to persuade her that it took less time to shower than to 'wash'. Having the dog in the house was against his cultural upbringing. He also remembered the times when he was tired of having to come home to a sink full of dirty dishes. Raymond was not going to trust Sandra to get him a drink, not even water. The musty stench inside the lounge lingered in his nostrils. He tried hard not to breathe but this placed more pressure on his still sore ribs. Raymond pleaded with Sandra. "Could you open the window please", he requested? Duke had sat quietly on the stairs listening to the voices in the lounge. He had heard the bitter words between Sandra and Pam that indicated their friendship was over. Pam was angry too. Sandra accused Pam of "two timing" her. "Yuh supposed to be mi fren but look wat yuh dun. Yuh tief mi man", Sandra shouted angrily. "Well, he's mine now. You didn't lose Raymond. Instead, you drove him into my arms", Pam jeered. Duke giggled with delight. Sandra was deeply wounded by Pam's remarks. She hit back at Pam. "How long yuh tink im gwein stay wid yuh? Raymond is a trendy guy an I know yuh naw guh able fi afford fi tek im guh ah swanky restaurants like I used to", Sandra insinuated? Pam knew that if it was one thing she couldn't take from her 'friend' was the way Sandra perceived money to be the highway to true happiness. Pam blurted out their long held secret about Duke, Sandra and the sordid pornographic affairs they had had in the office during those times when she had been wooed by Duke. Pam told Sandra, in a very serious tone of voice, that Andy Mann was right to call her a slut and that Raymond didn't need her. Pam was quite deliberate in her delivery. In a measured response she spoke more calmly than before. "Raymond needs a caring, compatible woman, who can have his children to whom he can teach his tradition and culture. There are many other men like Raymond out there searching for a good family life but they don't want concubines like you", Pam retaliated. Sandra was crying now. Her groaning cry reminded Raymond of a cow bellowing. As the truth began to burrow through her mind, Sandra begged Pam to cease the barrage of words that simply ripped her apart. The truth appeared too much for her to take. Eventually, Sandra acknowledged Pam as her only true *'friend'* who had never been afraid to tell her the truth even at the risk of ending their friendship. Sandra apologized profusely to Raymond for cheating on him and begged his forgiveness. "I didn't mean to cheat on you Ray but I am trying to improve my standard in life and you couldn't afford it. I know I hurt you deeply but please try to understand", she begged. Raymond had noticed the huge diamond ring. He knew it was over between him and Sandra. Raymond told her in a quiet voice that he could never forgive her. "We want different things out of life Sandy. I'm sure you're aware of that now. We'll see you often on TV or in the newspapers, billboards and magazines like the ones you used to read when we were together", he reminded. Raymond felt a lump in his throat as he recalled how he still felt about Sandra's natural, physical beauty. She felt humbled by Pam and Raymond's cutting remarks. They made her feel cheap and very much like "a loose woman". There was no way Raymond would want Sandra back now. Somehow, it had worked out better than Duke had hoped. He would finally get his exotic bird all to himself to feed her Champagne Urge until she comes round to his way of life or until Doris Bendlow became as famous an *'A' Blister* as Sandra, perhaps!

CHAPTER 41

The extraordinarily potent, Champagne Urge Mark 3 was being launched. Duke had tested it at the engagement party at Sandra's house. All the guest had shown curiosity in the unusual effects of the aphrodisiac quality champagne that had rejuvenated not only Sir Ivanhoe Goldfeet but also the instant effect it had on the likes of the Sergeant and Doris Bendlow to name a few. Braniffy had come up with the formula that Duke had requested. Other samples were sent to hotels, wine bars and all the AADC's that Grant had targeted. The response was more than overwhelming. The demand had increased production at Braniffy's so much so that they were making arrangements to have new plants throughout the entire Royal Royal Dis-United Stately Kingdoms of Asteroidia. Duke was more than delighted with the huge impact that his new champagne was having all over Spaceville and beyond. He arranged for a huge celebration dinner and advertising strategy which featured Sandra. With her most recent impact in the breathtaking dazzling outfits at the Auditorium of the Hotel Welcome, which had captured mammoth interest in the glamorous Super Model, Duke made sure he invited the printed and TV Media to record this huge event. There was a 'Pay-Per-View' option available to all within the virtual planet including the far off continents, countries and islands too. Parallel Planet, Earth, was linked into the feed within its own time zones. The advert for the aphrodisiac champagne was to be fashioned from this spectacular event. After the huge Celebration Dinner they'd enjoyed earlier in Sandra's honour, Duke made sure there was more than enough Champagne Urge Mark 3 around for everyone to satiate their particular taste buds. He never missed an opportunity to promote his own brand. Sandra stood in front of the first of the Giant Jeroboams. They were arranged in the shape of an 'S'. The hollow Jeroboams were crafted a month before, initially from rough sketches made by Grant Favours, while he and Duke were having a drink in 'The Upside Down' AADC, near Duke Stagg Incorporated. Duke had recalled seeing *'glass-blowing'* done at seaside towns not far away from where he used to live as a child. Even his good friend Grant had first doubted whether it was possible to fashion hollow giant bottles as tall as the 6'2" Sandra by means of the art of glass-blowing. At the time, even Grant was too timid to tell Duke that his idea seemed impractical. Together, Duke's intuition and Grant's artistic brain alloyed to bring about the innovative design for the alleged extraordinarily potent aphrodisiac Champagne Urge Mark 3. It was an ambitious concept but turned out to become an even more outstanding artistic event. Grant was clever enough to re-design the outfit on the label as it appeared on a bottle of champagne. Like any bottle of champagne the dark green background reflects the dominance of the antique gold colour label. Sandra's hands, neck and legs were coloured the same shade of green as a bottle of champagne. Except for her left breast, her body as far as her upper thighs and her face was coloured in gold. Sandra's cornflower blue eyes remained to reflect the true colour of the new Champagne Urge Mark 3. After all, it was her eyes that first inspired the concept that Duke and Grant had concocted between them. The concept of cornflower blue champagne was an original idea. On the labels of the 6'2" Jeroboams and subsequently on the bottles of Champagne Urge Mark 3, Sandra's picture showed her in the same golden outfit that Grant had torn in order to expose her left breast. It matched the stunning picture from Grant Favours's *'Breastgate'* fame in the *'Ooooppzssz' Magazine*. Ever since Grant Favours had published the infamous *'left breast'* episode, *'Breastgate'*, Sandra's popularity had soared to 'Celebrity' status. This new phenomena had started when Grant had launched the Glossy Magazine, 'Ooooppzssz'. His artistic interpretation and implementation meant that Grant deliberately used the flashing coloured lights into the mirror to create an image of an aura around Sandra to make her appear like a *'heavenly'* being. The highly imaginative picture with the torn dress exposing the singular breast seemed to have excited but had caused a great stir amongst some individuals that craved for provocative photos to satiate their personal *'shortcomings'*. Grant's clever ruse had started an auction amongst the mighty moguls all over the virtual planet of Asteroidia and beyond. The photo on the Magazine had made Sandra seem as if she was an 'angel' in *'Art Deco'* type shiny tight-fitting long evening dress. Because of her deeply tanned skin against the antique gold dress, the exposed breast was further accentuated. *'Suitable'* adjectives were twisted but molded to enhance the intention of such a clever piece of *'Creative Artform'*. The first set of sales figures indicated that publication of the magazine had broken all records within the first few days but Sandra's ascension amongst the 'A' Blisters was comparably quite meteoric. Never before had a magazine caused so much stir over the singular exposure of a breast. *'Breastgate'* was something that had hit not only the Media headlines in Duke's country but also almost usurped by foreign 'News Media' too. They helped to boost the sales of the 6'2" *'life-sized'* plastic *'Breastgate Dolls'* that were made available for those individuals, who wanted to privately satisfy their *'superlative urges'* for the voluptuous, buxom, stunningly beautiful Sandra. She was now *'international property'* in more ways than she had set out to be. Grant knew there was a market for his twisted humour. Duke had harboured Grant's *'ideas'* because he "didn't see anythink wrong" in what he was doing. In fact, Duke quite enjoyed whatever Grant suggested. Neither Duke nor Grant really cared about what anyone else thought of their twisted provocative suggestions, how it impacted on women or who it affected. They both shared but reflected their *'values and beliefs'* about a *'typical type'* of *'cultural acceptance'* that presupposed the *'life-sized'* plastic dolls were *"just a bit of 'harmless fun'"*. Both Duke and Grant were *'professional'* businessmen and that's all there was to it. Their philosophy was to increase their financial abundance "by any means necessary". Prompted by Duke, the only difference to the original photo, Grant Favours had removed the sleeves from the shoulders and shortened the length of the dress for the label of the potent aphrodisiac Champagne Urge Mark 3. As this version of the dress barely covered Sandra's bum cheeks, it made her seem much more sexually alluring but very risqué. The provocative image solicited the type of attention which not only initiated attraction towards the product being sold but was a compelling distraction from the competition. This type of philosophy was a well worn psychological pathway often used in Advertising and Marketing to lure potential clients into buying the product. The outrageous dress portrayed on the label was not only suggestively revealing but adhered to Sandra's delicate, slender figure like another layer of skin. Duke had made that suggestion because he knew the effect Sandra's picture and exposed breast would have in distracting attention away from the other champagnes on any shelf or in any other adverts. It was all part of the *'presentation'*. Sandra recalled Duke's Herculean effort to ensure everything ran smoothly. The media acknowledged Sandra's performance very favourably, indeed. They tussled but shoved each other about, trying to get the best photos or filming positions to capture an image of the *'hottest'* rising Star. Duke had warned off a couple photographers, who dared to attempt to place their cameras under Sandra's ultra revealing mini outfit. Individuals from the world of Media displayed uncouth behaviour. They squabbled and babbled amongst themselves. Some volunteered but shouted out their innermost thoughts. Most comments were witty and were meant to amuse, generally. Significant others though pushed way past the barrier. "Hey Sandra, I'd love to pop your cork. How about you and me going upstairs", one of the guest photographer's suggested. Duke put an immediate halt to that individual's stupidity. He nodded to Geoff, 'the rhino'. He nodded to Pete, 'the hammer'. He walked over to Frigit 'the mouse'. She walked over then whispered to Barney, 'the owl'. He made signs like the man on TV who gestures betting odds about horses. Henry, 'the hook' saw the signal. He jammed the hooked extension of his arm rapidly against the individual's ribbed area. The man was alerted to follow Henry's nodded instructions. He obeyed but walked in the direction that was indicated. Barney, 'the owl' used movements of his head to indicate that the man should come over to him. Frigit 'the mouse' escorted the man until she reached Pete, 'the hammer'. He used his head to nod the direction in which the man should travel. When he reached Geoff 'the Rhino', the lights went out. It was just briefly, but when it came back on again the man could see Duke approaching swiftly. "What did you say to my exotic bird", he bellowed? Sandra knew what was coming but the hapless individual didn't. He could see the angry look on Duke's face but tried to defend his comment. "Duke, it was only meant to be a joke. Where is your sense of humour", the man asked? Duke whispered to Geoff 'the rhino', to take the man down to the crypt on the basement floor. Though she could have handled the photographer herself, Sandra was so grateful for Duke's interference. The rest of the evening went as well as planned. Grant, Duke and others were to be complimented highly for their professionalism for planning the dual event. Both the launch of the extraordinary potent aphrodisiac Champagne Urge Mark 3 and Sandra's career had morphed into one seamless extremely successful event. All the agencies were well represented and the launch had been successfully beamed live via satellite into the millions of homes around the virtual planet of Asteroidia and to Planet Earth too.

Sandra and Duke had returned to the Suite they had reserved at the Hotel Welcome. As she looked across the huge Suite, she thought for one moment that Duke was struggling to maintain his balance. Sandra wasn't sure whether her imbibing the Champagne Urge Mark 3 was causative towards her perception of Duke's imbalance. "Duke, are you alright", she queried? He couldn't hear her. Duke was too busy singing his favorite song, 'I can't get no satisfaction'. His movement was typical of the type of music he enjoyed. Duke sometimes stamped his foot then he pretended playing a guitar. He swayed but grimaced as if he was feeling pain, emulating his heroes. His right hand pretended to hold the chords necessary for the accompaniment to his version of the classic. His left hand pumped up and down in a vertical plane as if he was getting the most distortion that he could get from the instrument. Duke's hollering carried around the Suite as he stomped and twitched in front of the large mirror affixed to the wall. His deep baritone voice sounded more like an un-tuned Double Bass being played rather poorly by a tone deaf learner. Sandra was getting a bit concerned about the volume. Soon the sound of the telephone startled both Duke and Sandra. He shouted for Sandra to answer the landline phone. "Get the phone then", he instructed. She reached out but picked it up. "Is Mr Stagg alright", the voice queried? "Someone said they heard shouting sounds coming from your Suite", the voice of the receptionist continued? "Yes, he's fine. Thanks for asking", Sandra replied. "Who was it", Duke asked? "It's just a courtesy call from reception", Sandra replied. "What do they want", Duke asked? "Oh, nothing, you know how they like to pamper you", Sandra lied. She knew Duke would make a scene if he thought someone had complained about his *'singing'*. "Shall I order us something to eat? I feel famished", Sandra insisted. "You must be joking. You can't be hungry after that spread earlier. Where do you put all the food you eat", Duke asked? Sandra smiled but avoided answering the question. Instead, she offered to get him a cup of coffee. "Yeah, why not, are you having one", Duke asked? "I fancy a snack. That Alligator steak was nice. Perhaps I'll have a sandwich with my coffee, shall I order one for you", Sandra asked? "I prefer the *'old joey'* kangaroo steak. It has more blood in it than the alligator. That's much too fatty", Duke replied. Sandra picked up the telephone. She placed their order. Duke finished his *'act'*. He attempted to walk towards the huge bed on which Sandra lay. She slithered like a snake towards the part of the bed that was furthest away from Duke. Sandra's action was quite deliberate. She'd heard Duke's *'hint'* during his performances, once at the Celebration Party and now in the Suite. His message was clear. Sandra was aware how disappointed Duke might feel if she told him she was not in the mood but she wondered if he might empathize with her feelings too. Duke noticed Sandra's movement but had premeditated thoughts he wanted to put into action. He smiled broadly as he staggered towards the huge bed. The sidelights were soft but cast his silhouette onto the shag-pile carpet. This was the same Suite they had stayed in before. The memory of Duke being taken out on a stretcher loomed largely on Sandra's mind. She recalled the remarks that had been made about and to her by the manager of the Hotel, the doctor who was friends with Duke's wife and the paramedics. She didn't want a repeat of the nightmare she had suffered at the time. It was all coming back now. The humiliation had rendered Sandra temporarily impotent. She had no feelings for sex. All the time, Sandra worried how Duke might react. When he was in a good mood, Duke was an extremely kind individual. He would almost habitually go *'over the top'* to woo his exotic bird. There seemed to be no limit to his kindness but Sandra also recalled that Duke didn't take the word 'no' with the same spirit. She wanted to show her appreciation for the great Celebration Party but she really didn't feel in the mood. Duke was in the mood. There was not going to be any excuse tonight. Sandra had not been in the mood, lately. Yesterday, her reason for not being in the mood was another of those headaches that Duke didn't want to understand. Sandra was growing tired of having to explain why she was not in the mood.

Recently, the demand on her had been less than fair. Her Celebrity status meant that she had to commit to many engagements. She'd mentioned to her agent, Jane Dunnit, that she was feeling extremely tired. Sandra told her that she needed a break but Jane told her starkly, ". . . that is the price of fame. The only need you have is to fulfill the engagements to which you are contracted". Jane had explained that it was to be assumed that Celebrity careers were brittle but hinged on what contracts and contacts demanded. "Accede to the power that control your career or die", was the agent's motto. Sandra was now a household name but was kept extremely busy. Gruelling schedules meant that Duke didn't see her much. After all, Sandra was not only *'flavour of the month'* but also *'flavour of the year'*. Magazines, media adverts, billboards and social websites were just some of the other exposure that had been made available to her. Jane never spared using these *'reminders'* to keep Sandra concentrated. She was not a personal friend of Duke but had been recommended by Sandra's sponsor, Sir Ivanhoe Goldfeet. He'd told Duke that Jane was the best and that was good enough for Duke. Sandra had complained to him about the way in which Jane spoke to her. He'd told Sandra that she was being oversensitive. "I'm not getting involved with arguments between two women", he'd said.

Duke was now about four feet from the bed. His eyes were almost closing now from the tiredness that had crept up on him. He stumbled a few times. Duke stopped but tried to keep still. "Whoa", he exclaimed. He could feel himself trying to retain his balance. Sandra looked on through 'sleepy' eyes. She felt drained. Duke moved towards the bed again, this time casting a giant shadow across the bed. It was gigantic compared to Duke's real size. The sounds of the background music from a Hitchcock Movie flashed through Sandra's mind. There was a knock at the door. Duke and Sandra jumped when they heard the sound, then they laughed at the same time. "It must be the waiter with the sandwiches and the coffee. I'd forgotten about the order", Sandra said. It's not like you to forget food, petal", Duke remarked. He'd called her *'honey'*, *'precious'*, *'darling'*, *'Sugarcake'* and *'my exotic bird'* before but this was the first time he'd called her *'petal'*. This seemed to make Sandra begin to feel guilty about not being in the mood. She decided that she had to please Duke, if not only for the Celebration Party but for him thinking of her as such a fragile thing, like a petal. It was at that moment Sandra decided that she would have sex with Duke but that she would need to fake orgasm once again. There was a slightly louder rap on the door. Sandra slid her naked body under the sheets but the outline of her body still showed that she was naked. Duke was still wearing his black trouser with the black cummerbund. His white shirt was slightly soiled from the staining from spilt Champagne and caviar. The shirt was unbuttoned halfway down his body. A part of it was partially pulled from the trouser but flopped loosely over the cummerbund. Duke had rolled the sleeves of his shirt up to his elbows in order to have a *'wash'*. The black tie hung untidily from one strap trapped under the stiff white collar. Duke staggered towards the door. Both he and Sandra could hear the voice of the manager when he spoke. "Mr Stagg, are you awake", he asked? There was a hint of anxiety in the manager's voice. Sandra felt a chill run through her body. Duke banged the heel of his left hand on one side of his head a few times then shook it from side to side, in an effort to clear it. "Duke, don't open the door", Sandra warned. The fear and anxiety in her voice penetrated Duke's drunkenness. "What", he asked? "I just have a bad feeling about you opening the door, that's all", Sandra pressed. Duke shook his head some more. "Do you think something's going to happen to me? Oh petal, that's a very sweet thing for you to think of me", Duke said. His voice indicated that he was in one of those *'sloppy'* moods. Duke felt a warm glow come over him. He had noticed Sandra's lack of encouragement earlier but this seemed the ideal time to woo her with his charm. Sandra's concern sent Duke's hope rising. Sandra sensed this when Duke shouted the words *"whe-hey"*, thrusting his fist into the air like an Association Footballer, celebrating a goal. Duke had managed to reach the door. He opened it but took the trolley from the manager. Duke thanked him but ask the manager to bring him two bottles of the extraordinary potent Champagne Urge Mark 3 and two golden ice buckets. The manager looked at Duke's rather dishevelled appearance but obeyed the instructions like the subservient slave he had become. Duke had broken his *'cocky'* arrogance which he had displayed towards his exotic bird. He had not told Sandra that all the perpetrators had paid dearly for their stance towards her but Duke had made them all visit those crypts on the basement floor. "Yes, Mr Stagg, straight away sir", the manager replied. He bowed with a form of reverence but walked backwards away from the door as if he was in the company of Royalty. Sandra heard the tone of the manager but was unaware about his new behaviour. Duke pushed the trolley over towards the huge bed. They both scoffed at the sandwiches like gannets on a rubbish pile. Sandra sidled up to Duke but hugged him. "Thanks Duke", she said. "What for", he asked? "For everything", she replied. Sandra was acknowledging how much Duke was contributing towards her superlative urge; that of being in the company of the *'Champagne for Breakfast, Lunch, Tea and Snacks in between Snacks Society'*. Here she was with a highly competent competitor in the champagne industry. Sandra realized that, despite the established brands, Duke's range of Champagne Urge was special. With its cornflower blue colour, the current Mark 3 was bound to buck the trend not only with the younger generation but it also promised to re-energise that older demographic whose relationships were previously on the wane. As she fondled Duke, Sandra could feel a new firmness as if he was ready to initiate a new mission. The manager arrived with the two bottles of Champagne Urge Mark 3. Upon being alerted that the manager had arrived, it was Sandra, not Duke, who hurried to retrieve the guaranteed aphrodisiac. She was becoming hopeful that at last Duke might be able to satisfy her needs, probably!

CHAPTER 42

It was a Sunday morning and Duke had hardly had any sleep. The excitement of going on holiday was the motivating factor that got Duke out of bed long before six o'clock. Tramp was as snug as a 'bug in a rug'. He nestled up to Sandra. Because he had been trembling earlier, she wrapped her long slender arms around him. Sandra thought the dog might be having a cold. Duke looked at them and felt it almost a sin to awaken the *'couple'* but he was in the mood for mischief. At first, he thought of shaking them gently awake but there was no time to delay the adventure that he had planned for Tramp and Sandra. An adventure at the seaside might bring them closer than before. Going on holiday was the sort of thing that families did each year, commonly. He banged the 'gong'. "Come and get it" Duke shouted loudly. Tramp was the first to respond. His yapping would have awakened an entire household let alone just Sandra. She sat up quickly, snarling and snapping as if she was being attacked. Duke's chuckling made her more irritated. Though he did not know why, Duke had been noticing a shift in Sandra's behaviour. She had been more moody than before, fancied very strange combination of food at odd hours of the night but seemed to have a brighter glow than before. In the mornings, she would be sick, sometimes violently. At other times, she was so much sweeter to him than before. Sometimes, Sandra clung to Duke but made him feel as if she couldn't do without him. To Duke, it seemed such a mystery as to why each mood lasted for a set period of time. Sandra's moods were unpredictable and they frequently threw Duke off balance. This was the main reason why Duke wanted to have this short break with her and Tramp. While Sandra and Tramp got dressed Duke made breakfast. "Come on, let's get to the Airport. I can't wait to get on that plane, can you", he asked? Sandra was in one of her moods. She didn't particularly care to move let alone bother to get on a plane. Sandra felt nauseous. Her stomach was churning around and around. The room seemed to spin every now and again. Duke had tuned the radio on to his favourite waveband but was now not noticing Sandra's lack of response. While he dished up breakfast, he danced to the music. His dance consisted of lots of irregular movements. Sometimes it seemed as if Duke was in a 'Rugby Scrum' while at other times he seemed to be trying to take off from the floor. He would stoop slightly then explode into a great plyometric leap similar to that of a Long Jumper but without good technique or skill. His dance was as unpredictable as winning 'The Lottery'. Sometimes Duke would hop on one leg at a time then just as suddenly land on both feet as if he was practicing 'Hop Scotch'. The pulsating thin beat of the music was impacting on both Sandra and Tramp. He scampered but hid under the huge Oak Sideboard. Tramp put his paws in a manner that suggested that he was covering his ears from the noise. Sandra's head was throbbing violently. She felt like screaming. Her efforts would have been very feeble because the light-headed feeling resulted in her fainting. Sandra felt as if she was being pulled, in an arranged manner, towards the floor. Instinctively, she put her hands out in front of her to save from smashing her head on the floor. It was a frame-by-frame *'action replay'* type of experience for Sandra. Duke did not see her fall nor did he hear the thudding sound as she crashed to the floor but Tramp was aware. He rushed over to Sandra but started to show concern. Tramp licked her face; sending the slimy, frothy saliva all over Sandra's face but she did not reach out for him as he expected. When Sandra didn't stir, Tramp raced round past the Breakfast Bar that jutted out enough to obscure Duke's view. He jumped, growled and barked but Duke took Tramp's behaviour the wrong way. "You're excited then, who's going on holiday boy", Duke asked? He stroked and patted the dog's head but Tramp was still acting up. Duke reached down and picked up the little dog. "Come and sit with Daddy", he said. Cuddling the dog to near asphyxiation, Duke walked towards the Breakfast Bar where he had placed their breakfast. "Come on then, what will you have", he asked the dog? "Feast your eyes on that lot, you couldn't get a more splendid breakfast in the Shelly Beach Hotel could you boy", Duke asked rhetorically? Tramp was hungry. He wagged his tail happily. Duke put the little dog on the table. "Go on boy, have some grub", he encouraged him. Tramp was not fussy about which plate of food he ate from. He scurried over and started to lick the runny eggs. Some of the yolk flashed up into Duke's face as Tramp enjoyed breakfast but it was the sausages that he went wild on. Tramp got hold of the sausages in every plate. "Leave some for your mom", Duke shouted. He grabbed a couple of the sausages from Tramp's mouth. "Your mom will be angry with you and she has a right to. Look what you did to her breakfast". Naughty boy", he finished. Duke threw the two partially eaten sausages back onto one of the plates. "Where is your mom? She's taking a long time to get dressed", Duke commented. He put the dog on the floor but got up from the stool. "Let's go and find mommy", Duke said. He followed the dog until he saw Sandra on the floor. "Oh no", Duke shouted. His heart was racing fast. He could feel and hear the thumping sound on his chest. Duke rushed over towards Sandra. He bent over her. "Darling what's the matter", he asked? Sandra moaned. "I just felt faint. I don't know what happened", she replied. "Shall I call an ambulance or will a stiff brandy do", Duke asked? Sandra tried to sit up. At first, she didn't feel she had the strength to push herself from the floor but gradually her head cleared enough to encourage her to get up. Duke tried to help. He was puzzled and felt a bit guilty that he had not been aware of Sandra's demise. "I'm sorry, darling. I didn't know", Duke said sincerely. "It's ok Duke, how were you to know, she queried"? Sandra was on her feet now. Looking down at Duke, she smiled and touched his face. "You're such a *'fusspot'*. I'm alright, really", Sandra assured him. Tramp was feeling rather left out and he decided to gain some attention. He barked a few times and then started to stand on his hind legs. He was performing for them. Tramp was quite a *'show-off'* too. He began to flip over and over then he rolled to one side then the other and unto hind legs again carefully tucking his front paws onto his chest. It made him appear like a Meerkat that had been alerted to the arrival of a hawk. Duke and Sandra applauded the 'Act'. They had sent Tramp to *'Pet Drama School'* for Acting Lessons. Duke reminded them that they needed to start out for the Airport. Sandra had some juice and the two remaining pieces of sausages that Duke had retrieved from Tramp's mouth. Sandra told Duke that she couldn't lift her suitcase. He tried to lift the case but it was impossible for him to lift and move it at the same time. Duke's strong short arms could lift the suitcase but he wasn't tall enough to move the enormous suitcase that Sandra had chosen to take.

"What's in it", Duke asked? They fussed as to the best way of getting it out of their new house in Poshborough. Duke took his and Tramp's suitcases out to the vehicle.

A brand new golden 'Four Wheel Drive' vehicle was parked just outside. It gleamed in the bright golden morning sun. The new chauffeur had done a very excellent job. Tramp jumped in the moment Duke opened the door for him. Sandra wore a 'loose-fitting', thin, see-through floral dress, a wide brimmed hat, 'Designer' dark glasses and sandals with long lilac coloured leather straps that she wrapped around her slim legs up to the height of her calves. The pattern had a *'crisscross'* shape to it. Sandra looked elegant as she sat in the driver's seat. She posed for Duke to see. He was busying himself taking photos of Sandra, Tramp and the golden 'Four Wheel Drive' vehicle. "This is another present, darling. It will make your new neighbours jealous", Duke told Sandra. "What's this one for", she asked teasingly? "Just being you my sweet, for just being you", Duke piped. He knew that the news about putting Doris Bendlow in the New Advert could be very hard to discuss with Sandra. Duke had bought Sandra this latest present to pave the way to that inevitable subject. After asking the new chauffeur to "take a few snaps of us together", Duke ordered him to "get the heavy suitcase and don't be long. We've got to get to the Airport on time", Duke reminded him. It seemed unfair that Duke would want to treat the new chauffeur in that way, Sandra thought. She told him so. "Leave him alone Duke and let's get going", she urged. Duke mumbled to himself. "Lazy bastard, where's he been all morning? I bet he's having it off with that new 'Au-pair' girl we've just hired". Sandra smiled because she knew Duke fancied the girl too. She had noticed how many times he went to her room to see "how she was getting on". Duke had been up to her room to teach her the *'language'* and to find out if "there was anything else she needed to make her feel at home". Sandra had come to realize that she would never be able to tame Duke but instead commented cynically about his lustful attention to the 'Au Pair' girl. When the chauffeur returned with the suitcase, Sandra gave him a tip and particular instructions that Duke didn't like to hear. "Take care of the new 'Au Pair' for us while we're away. Take her out somewhere like the Zoo or the 'Wax Works' place. Take her somewhere interesting", she instigated. Sandra looked over at Duke, who was now sulking a little. "Keep your filthy hands off the Au Pair. I don't want you spoiling her", Duke said loudly. When Sandra cleared her throat deliberately, Duke began to laugh. "I was only joking Sugarcake. Just poking fun at our friend here", he chuckled. Sandra pressed the gas and the golden 'Four Wheel Drive' vehicle lurched forward. Tramp was yapping as he would whenever he was being driven. Duke peered through his dark glasses to take the glare from the golden sun away but reached over but picked up the little dog from the back seat. "Come and sit with mommy and daddy", he commented. As they drove along, Sandra told Duke that she had a lovely surprise for him. Immediately, he wanted her to tell him what it might be. "It can wait", Sandra said teasingly. There was no other traffic in either direction for at least 10 miles. Duke kept chatting to her about Tramp and his antics. "Let him steer for awhile and see how clever he is", Duke prompted. Sandra was reluctant. Duke assured her that Tramp had recently learnt this *'new trick'*. She allowed Duke to place the little dog between her legs on the seat. Tramp immediately stood on his hind legs but placed his front paws on the sensitive power-steering wheel. Sandra often needed only light contact with the power-steering wheel for it to change direction. She couldn't see any harm in allowing Tramp to show off the *'new trick'* he had learnt at the *'Pet Drama School'*. With some assistance from

Sandra, Tramp steered the vehicle accurately for at least a quarter of a mile. "That was excellent Tramp, just excellent. I bet no other dog can do what you just did", Sandra commented. She turned her head slightly towards Duke. "When did he learn that trick", she asked? "Tramp learnt that while you were away", Duke replied. He looked up into the sky but commented. "Nice day for a family outing, wouldn't you say", Duke asked rhetorically? Sandra was enjoying her new 'Four Wheel Drive' vehicle. There was hardly a sound coming from it. At times, it was only the sound of the tyres on the varied road surfaces that gave feedback to confirm the vehicle was moving. As Sandra looked around across the farms and fields on either side of the expressway, she saw the freedom the animals were enjoying in those open expanses of space. Sandra also further appreciated the furrowed grounds being prepared as a foundation to implant seeds for new growth. Bales of hay and the huge barns adorned the environment. Tramp was now asleep and so was Duke. The queasy feeling overcame Sandra again but not to the extent of fainting. She pressed the button which operated the electric window on her side of the vehicle. Sandra had hoped to do the type of breathing which Raymond had taught her when they used to live together. When she did inhale deeply, Sandra smelt a very pungent odour which suggested that pigs were being kept on some of the farms nearby. The acrid smell wafted into the vehicle causing Duke to rise from his nap. He looked at Sandra then at Tramp accusingly as if one or both of them had passed wind in the vehicle. His broken nose twitched as the smell became more overpowering. "J.H Christ it don't half pong. This smell reminds me of Henry Hardcase", he criticised. Sandra smiled because she too agreed that Henry Hardcase had a very peculiar smell. She remembered it well and the night when his sweaty presence had highlighted his lack of hygiene. Tramp began to stir. Duke lifted him up to the window to show him the Control Tower which could now be seen at a distance. "Look boy, we're nearly there", Duke said excitedly. They soon approached the roundabout from which they needed to exit to go into the tunnel that led to the Car Parking facilities. As Sandra drove through the tunnel, she started to feel a sense of excitement about going abroad on holiday with Duke and Tramp for the first time since they've been together. Duke looked over towards her and he could see her pleasant smile. "You're going to enjoy Costa Del Shell", he assured her. The sign directed them to the 'Long Term' Car Park. There, they parked but alighted from the vehicle. Duke told Sandra to wait while he got an attendant to "fetch the luggage". The attendants drove vehicles that reminded Duke of 'Golf Buggies'. The difference was that these vehicles hovered above the ground. Like a child, Sandra was mesmerized by the elevation of the 'Golf Buggy' type vehicles hovering above the ground. She commented on the experience. "Your new vehicle has that type of facilitation too", Duke assured her. "Cool, why didn't you say before", Sandra queried. "I wanted you to make that discovery for yourself but now you're enjoying the experience, I thought I would tell you about it", Duke confirmed. Sandra knew that Duke did not compare physically with Raymond but he had a very shrewd way of making up for his 'shortcomings', she thought. Duke, Sandra and Tramp were transported to the Departure Lounge. There, they went over to the *'First Class'* area but checked in. Sandra told Duke that the smell of the coffee from the Coffee House was irresistible. She fancied a large "Presso" as she called it. Apart from its unique blend, Sandra liked the 'Presso's contrasting image of the dark body with the white frothy top. They sauntered towards the Tia Coffee House which boasted 'Tia' as the 'Best Coffee on the Planet'. It is rumoured that it can only be found high up in the mountains on a particular tropical paradise island. Even Tramp had coffee too but his was iced instead of hot like Sandra's and Duke's. The little dog lapped up his treat but by repeatedly licking his lips, indicated that he wanted more. Such *'addiction'* by a dog seemed quite unusual but said a lot for the taste of the unique coffee. Duke looked up at the computer screen which showed the flight schedules. He told Sandra that they needed to start preparing to board the plane. When they did, Duke, Sandra and Tramp sat upstairs in the area reserved for 'First Class' passengers only. There, they experienced more *'privileges'* than those other passengers travelling in the 'Economy Class' Section *'beneath'* them. The motion of the moving plane startled Tramp. He began to shiver. "Are you cold boy", Duke enquired? Even before being asked, the attending Stewardess produced a blanket as if by magic. Such was the level of personal attention that was being afforded to those travelling *'First Class'*. As the whining of the engine indicated the advent of 'lift off', Sandra closed her eyes but prayed silently that Duke would be happy when she related the *'good news'* she had managed to guard so well to date. Duke showed Tramp the Control Tower from the window. "Look boy, it's the Control Tower", he exclaimed excitedly. The attending Stewardess smiled at them but asked if Sandra was scared of flying? Duke saw the grimaced look on Sandra's face too but was concerned. "What's the matter Sugarcake? Are you scared of flying", he enquired? "No, I need to go to the toilet", she responded. Sandra released the seatbelt but rushed passed the Stewardess. She tried to tell Sandra that passengers were required to remain in their seats until instructed to do otherwise but it was to no avail. Sandra had already entered. Inside, she wretched but vomited all the coffee, juice and the remainder of the sausages that Duke had salvaged from Tramp's mouth. As she looked down at the pan, Sandra saw the contents but smelt the sour vomit. She was reminded by association about her ordeal at the Hotel Welcome when the sheep eyes looked back at her. The movement caused by the air turbulence distracted Sandra from distinguishing the heavy thudding against the toilet door. Shaken by the heavy turbulence, she felt even worse than before. Cold sweat washed over her but made Sandra's nauseous feeling seem almost permanent. She flushed the toilet but remained in there for a while longer. After the turbulent movement had subsided somewhat, Sandra could now distinguish the heavy thudding on the toilet door. It seemed urgent. Sandra was unsure how long she had been in there. Not wanting to appear selfish, she opened the door. There, Sandra saw the Stewardess on the other side of it. She looked concerned. "Are you alright ma'am", she asked? "Yes", Sandra replied. She went back to find Duke looking anxiously at her. "What's the matter Sugarcake", he asked? "Felt a bit queasy", she replied. Tramp yapped his concern too. Sandra took the little dog from Duke. He licked Sandra's face in appreciation. Duke offered her some champagne and caviar but Sandra told him she wasn't hungry. The rest of the flight was without anymore queasiness or incident. Sandra fell asleep again. Duke ensured that Tramp did not disturb her. This aircraft was the Supersonic type. It was reported to break not only the sound but the *'zone barriers'* too. They had been made to fly at nearly 1000 miles per hour making long-haul flight to far off continents, countries and islands easily reachable and in much lesser time than the ordinary aircrafts. After four and a half hours flight, the plane began its decent. Duke held Tramp by the window but spoke directly to the little dog. "Look at that, can you see the Control Tower, boy", he asked? Duke pressed the little dog closer to the window then pointed towards the taller building on the left. It stood out above the scattered lower buildings, which constituted basic houses, a few small businesses including independent small motels, two banks, one local hospital and a clinic. The little dog placed its paws on the window, yapped but wagged its tail as if he understood. The plane turned 180° and now Duke could see the taller buildings on the other side that were, at first, not in view. Duke saw the Del Shell Hotel before the landing was completed. It appeared to be a round Castle engulfed in a waterfall of blue and pink lights. They flashed on and off intermittently. "Look boy, isn't that just a beautiful site", he prompted? The varying colours of neon type lights were reflecting from lamps arranged on the underside of the crown of the building. The Castle 'Style' Building had many small lamps all around so that the effect of the neon lights cascaded down the sides unto the floor. This fusion of lights mixed, merged then diffused into a kind of *happening* that nobody can accurately define. An announcement signalled that the plane was about minutes from landing at the Del Shell Airport. Sandra, Duke, Tramp, the Airline Staff and the other passengers felt the heat from the golden sun. The landing gear was engaged. There was a sudden bump and screeching of tyres allied to the whining sound of the engines as they decelerated. After touchdown on the runway, the plane taxied towards where the passengers were to exit. Duke awakened Sandra. "Wake up darling, we've landed. Tramp's been keeping my company while you rested, ain't you boy", Duke quizzed? It seemed the little dog understood and he started to tug, playfully, at Duke's shirt with his teeth. Sandra didn't say much. She yawned and stretched but told Duke she was "feeling tired". "You'll have all the time you want to sleep once we get to the hotel", Duke acknowledged. They alighted from the plane but edged their way along with the rest of the passengers through the narrow isle. They smiled but complimented the Airline staff whom they had kept busy by their many requests and, sometimes, demands. Sandra's long floral 'see-through' dress had caught the attention of many who were on the flight. As she strode down the steps of the plane, Sandra now held the attention of most of the men and particularly some selfish, jealous women too. At the bottom of the steps, some came closer to admire her sheer physical beauty. One touched her but reached out to feel the texture of her hair. "It is one of those new fashion wigs", one woman commented. "It would suit you. Ought to get one", the other replied.

The pilot, resplendent in his uniform with badges and medals on his chest, extended his arms but bowed. "Captain Plantain ma'am, did you enjoy the flight", he enquired? Smiling coyly, Sandra replied. "Yes, thank you". "May I escort ma'am", the Pilot asked politely? Sandra told him that she was already being escorted. "I don't see anyone with you", he insisted. Captain Plantain didn't wait for a reply. "Allow me to buy you lunch sometime or preferably let me make you breakfast", he said confidently. Sandra sensed that it was time to stop this one sided conversation. "I'm with someone", she said quietly then looked round for Duke and Tramp. They were separated from her by mere coincidence. As they walked down the isle in the plane, Duke had stopped, politely, for a woman and her child to get out from their seat. She in turn had done the same for a couple of others further along. Duke and Tramp had no choice in the order of how they alighted from the plane. Captain Plantain realized that he was being cold-shouldered by Sandra but he left with a parting comment. "You might need me before too long", he stated. The Captain turned but walked away from her. Sandra could not see the look on the Captain's face. It was one of resentment from being snubbed but, more importantly, he figured what he was going to do to lure the outstanding beauty to him on a different occasion. Sandra looked, longingly, for Duke and Tramp to appear. She didn't have to wait much longer. Duke was hugging Tramp while they made their way down the steps. Sandra was relieved to see Duke in particular. She, somehow, felt alone and abandoned. "Did you forget something", Sandra asked him? Duke explained what had happened. They wandered into the Airport Building and joined one of the queues. Duke was sweating profusely from the heat. "Dam, it is hot and sticky", he commented. Tramp's tongue was hanging out and he panted pleadingly for a drink of water. The little dog whimpered but looked up at Sandra who was now holding him. Duke summoned a Luggage Attendant but slipped some money in his hands. "I need to get some water for the dog, understand", he asked? The Luggage Attendant looked at Duke but smiled. His teeth were not necessarily the best set of *'chops'* around. The brown staining indicated that which was caused by tobacco but, without DNA, one could never be sure. It might have been caused by certain chemicals in the water even. Duke looked at Tramp. He saw that the dog was listless and had stopped whimpering. Indeed, he looked as if he'd gone off to sleep. "Look, you dumb bastard, go and get me some water for the dog", Duke demanded. He mimed the whole time while he delivered the words but the Luggage Attendant kept on smiling, bowing and generally worshipping Duke. He was getting tired of not being able to make himself clear. "The money, give us some back. The extra was for you to fetch me the water for the dog", he insisted. Duke tried to take some of the money back but the Luggage Attendant retreated. He bowed several times then bent down but kissed Duke's feet. All the other passengers looking on were amused at the simplicity of the Luggage Attendant. He looked up from Duke's feet with eyes that told a story seldom heard on Duke's side of the 1st rated world. The sadness in the local man's eyes reflected his humble surroundings. It was quite astonishing for some of the children in the queue to see such a spectacle. One nine year old child asked his dad, if Duke was of "Royal Heritage"? His dad pointed at Sandra but whispered in the boy's ear, "No son, I don't think so", he replied. The cynicism and embellished chuckling tone of his voice indicated that he thought his son's question quite funny. Another local worker approached the first local man, who was kneeling at Duke's feet like a tame puppy. His large sorrowful eyes looked towards his fellow worker. Both spoke in their local dialect. Duke looked from one to the other because, by the volume of delivery and the animated body language, they seemed to others to be having a disagreement. Suddenly, the man rose to his feet but gestured towards the other worker. He could understand and speak a little of Duke's language. They swapped places. Duke explained very slowly to the new man that he wanted some water for the dog. "He's parched", Duke said impatiently. "You want water, yes", the man asked? He was smiling at Duke just like the first attendant but he didn't move an inch. He held his hand out to indicate that he too wanted a tip. The cheek of the second attendant to ask for a tip made Duke become less than patient with the second man. "Ask your friend to share the tip I gave him. Neither of you have done anythink to deserve it", he scolded. Duke lost his temper but started to fuss over the difference in language. "Why can't they have people who understand us", he asked some of the other people? They laughed with Duke. Each was interested in the debasing of the local men.

Most of those others, who had been processed by the immigration staff, were looking on from the other side of the huge area. Duke's deep baritone voice was raised to a higher level in volume and his words were mostly *'blue'*. When the local man repeated one of the swear words to Duke, he *'flipped his lid'*. "Listen you smelly underling, understand this", Duke derided. He swiftly approached the second attendant, grabbed him by the ear but marched him off in the direction he had come from. "There's plenty of water here, show me the bathroom you ignorant *'git'* ", Duke told him. It was the man's squealing that had made the reluctant Airport Police come over to Duke. One pointed the gun but aimed it at his chest. "You stop, yes", the cop told Duke. He let go off the man's ear. "Ok, you tell me, where is the toilet, yes", Duke mocked? The guard was not amused. Duke was worried about the look in the cop's eyes. His narrow eyes were trained on Duke's huge gold chain. Another cop approached Duke. Sandra was caught up between watching from afar like the others while improving her position in the queue. She had hardly realized how rapidly the queue had progressed since the upheaval with Duke and the two attendants. A deep bass voice almost sung the words, "Passport". Sandra's attention had been drawn towards the interaction between Duke and the cops. Turning suddenly, her elbow crashed into the Custom Officer's face. "Oh, I'm so sorry", she said embarrassingly. There was no blood but the pain had already registered. No amount of apologies could erase the anger the Custom Officer felt at being *'stricken'*. He glared at Sandra but murmured some words in his native language. Before handing the Custom Officer her passport she copied Duke, "it was an accident, yes". He looked at the passport suspiciously then summoned his colleague over to his desk. One then another then another, came over to the desk. They conversed. As they did, each took turn to look at Sandra but then look away again. She tried to explain that she was with Duke but the Custom staff was not interested. One male officer confronted her with the passport but showed her the picture of Tramp. "That's you, yes", the man said laughingly. "Oh dear, I made a mistake. That's Tramp, my dog", Sandra explained. She too could see the funny side. Rustling around in her huge branded handbag, Sandra found her own passport. She gave it to the Immigration Officer but commented. "It's the right one this time", she confirmed. Again, the Immigration Officer wore the same type of frown as before. "You have visa, yes", he enquired? "No, I don't need one, do I, she asked? The Officer insisted that she did need a visa. "No visa, I don't let you come in", he said forcefully. Sandra could not believe she was hearing those words but the serious look on the officer's face made her feel uncomfortable. The Immigration Officer and his colleagues had decided that Sandra was "trying to enter the country illegally". "You have passport for dog, but no dog, yes? You have passport, no visa, yes", the Officer continued. Sandra had no answer to disprove the Immigration Officer. She didn't understand much of the local language herself but she understood the word "police". The crackling of the 'two-way' mobile communicators brought Sandra's attention to the activities of the Airport cops. They talked busily into their mobile communicators perched on their shoulders. The Airport cops swooped in from all different directions. They made it seem as if the entire airport was under siege by terrorists.

Two huge female cops escorted Sandra towards the area reserved for *'Detainees'*. As she looked around her, Sandra tried to fathom what happened to Duke and Tramp. She remembered how the cop had pointed the gun at Duke and she knew his temper but she didn't hear any gunfire. He was busy trying to convince the two cops why he'd held the attendant by his ear. "Get water for dog", Duke insisted. When there was no common understanding between them, Duke started to mime an urgent request to go to the toilet. "Ah", the cop said; bowing his head several times to indicate he understood. "You savvy then", Duke said cynically. The cop used his gun to indicate in which direction Duke should go. He tried to hurry. His short strides quickened a pace but soon Duke was running with the dog held out in front of him. He weaved in and out of the straggling crowd until he saw the sign. Inside, he plugged a hand basin but turned on the cold tap. Duke held the little dog so he was able to drink the water then he splashed some of the cold water on his own face and neck. "Bleeding heat, it's a killer, Boy, it's a killer", he told the little dog. Duke's shirt and shorts were now quite soaked with both water and sweat. "Let's go and find mommy", Duke told the dog. They exited the toilet area and begun to make their way back towards Immigration Control. Most of the desks were vacant now as most passengers had been *'processed'* and were on their way to begin their holiday. The female Immigration Officer beckoned Duke to her desk. "Passport", she asked? "I don't need one", he said but brushed her hand aside. "You need passport", the woman told him. Duke looked searchingly for Sandra. "Have you seen a tall woman in a floral *'see-through'* dress and a wide-brimmed hat", he asked? The female Immigration Officer ignored his question. She pointed to Tramp. "Quarantine", she asked? "No thanks, he's had his 'shots'", Duke retorted. The Officer told him to "wait". She spoke on the phone to her supervisor.

An announcement requesting Duke to get in touch with the Airport Information Office broke the stalemate, suddenly. The voice said, "Would Mr. Duke Stagg, co-owner of Del Shell Hotel Chain, please contact Airport Information. Your chauffeur is waiting for you in the Arrival Lounge". "That's me. Let me use your phone", he demanded. The woman handed him the phone. "Get me information", Duke said into the phone. When the voice on the other end answered, Duke bellowed into the phone. He threatened that he would withdraw his financial support from Costa Del Shell. The operator asked him to hold on. After a few minutes, several cops arrived to escort the important visitor to his Hotel. Even the cop, who had trained his gun at him earlier was now bowing and saluting profusely. They whisked him and Tramp through the building and into a golden coloured stretch limousine. There were several outriders and a long procession of startled workers, who were pulled from their *'Siesta'* time, to make up the numbers. Duke was more comfortable now that everyone on the island knew that he'd arrived. The influential Grant Favours had already made sure that Duke's reputation had long preceded his arrival. Grant was waiting with Beth Tittye and some others. A small band played a version of Duke's country anthem in his honour. "Grant you old bastard, you set this up didn't you", he asked? "Where's my favourite model, couldn't she make it", Grant asked? Duke told him about Sandra's disappearance. "I don't know what happened but she just disappeared and nobody knows where she's gone", he complained. "Let me deal with it", Grant offered. He went back into the Airport building. After talking with the Senior Immigration Officers, Grant was led toward the area for *'Detainees'*. Sandra was more than pleased to see Grant. She wept unashamedly but told him she wanted to fly back to her home country. "Tell Duke I'm not staying in this hellhole", she blurted out. Sandra described to Grant how she, Duke and Tramp had been treated. "Duke and Tramp are fine, they are waiting for you outside", Grant assured her. Some of the other detainees were asking Grant to help them as well. He told them he couldn't.

CHAPTER 43

S andra and Grant went outside the Arrival Lounge to find Duke and Tramp pacing around near the limousine. She was surprised to see the entire Flight Crew, including Captain Plantain, standing with the local crowd. Some of the children were waving Del Shell Flags but singing in traditional local dialect. Duke saw Sandra but rushed to meet her. He was carrying Tramp under his left arm. The dog bolted from Duke's grip but hurried even faster towards Sandra. She reached down to pick him up. The little dog wagged his tail rapidly but yapped as if to show his excitement in being re-united with her. "Come to mommy", Sandra encouraged. When she lifted him up, Tramp helped to remove some of Sandra's dried tears. He seemed to enjoy the salty taste which Sandra had tasted some moments before she was rescued from the humiliation of being assembled like unwarranted luggage to be shipped out from the paradise island which was much closer in ethnicity to her than Duke. At the time of the immense questioning and aspersions about her seeking illegal entry into an island not dissimilar in culture to her mother's, Sandra's anger could not be satiated. This was a completely new type of experience which rendered her without the resources to repel the unfair allegations and physical abuse that she had suffered. Sandra was interrogated by both male and female immigration officers. The very tall but muscular *'butch'* type individuals were summoned to take her for *'internal examination'* in case she happened to be a "drug mule", assumedly! Apart from the humiliating insinuations, the internal search was carried out without empathy but with a physical rigour that would not be fair to be carried out on farm animals let alone a human being. The search was carried out wholly under the instructions of the 'Director of Search'. She was a sad, crude, insane thoroughly *'programmed'* and *'conditioned'* specimen of a human. Charlady Uppers was brown and from the Mixed DNA Rainbow Tribe. She was in line for promotion but wanted to impress her superior, white ex-army Sergeant Cyndy Broekenheart from the Mixed DNA Rainbow Tribe too. Before she joined the army, Cyndy had made a decision to have the type of surgery which converted from being male into female. Her gender was now not in question but she seemed to have maintained the mindset of a man! Even Cyndy found it difficult to act or behave differently. Power was her game and she used it to the detriment of subordinates like Charlady Uppers. Sergeant Cyndy Broekenheart installed immense fear but imposed her insane mood swings upon those who come up against her. There were no exceptions. It depended upon the hue and intensity and duration of her moods, swings and duration. These varied immensely but were dangerously schizophrenic at times. Colleagues, family and friends ran scared of her. Cyndy's approach to her job was much, much more than her remit but, because the results she generated were statistically heavily in favour to the department, Cyndy was allowed to ride *'rough-shod'* over individuals. She was allowed to carry out her role without supervision. When Sandra had commented angrily about her painful experience, Cyndy Broekenheart slapped but scolded her like a child with an errant behaviour. Cyndy had held Sandra by the shoulders but shook her as if she was ridding her of some unholy spirit or uncleansed aura. It was then that Sandra had started to cry. She had wanted so much to use not only her talons but also her martial arts expertise on this seemingly demented bully.

Duke was unaware of the treatment that had been dished out on his exotic bird. Instead, he seemed to be lapping up the adulation that was being thrust upon him. It was Beth Tittye that shouted "tally ho" to signify the start of the journey from Del Shell Airport to the prestigious Del Shell Hotel. It was reserved for tourists only. As often depicted in old black and white *'western'* movies of past generations and current colour ones, the indigenous population from the 5th rated exotic continents, countries and islands were accepted as the cooks (now renamed chefs) and general ancillary workers. It was as if, according to programmed and conditioned *'values and beliefs'*, all indigenous populations from those exotic environments not only perceived themselves to be but also were perceived as such by significant others as being defaulted as *'culturally correct' 'stereo-types'*, seemingly! These *'models'* fit those *'roles'* and those *'roles'* fit these *'models'*, quite significantly, probably!

The motorcade was making its way from the Airport towards the Del Shell Hotel. Six Police outriders on motorbikes headed the motorcade. They preceded the golden coloured stretch limousine with Duke, Sandra and Tramp. It had two small flags at the front signifying their importance. In the limousine behind Duke's was that of Beth Tittye and Grant Favours. The third limousine carried the Minister of Tourism and his wife followed by a fourth limousine with the Ambassador from Spaceville to Costa Del Shell. Three Diplomatic Representatives of Costa Del Shell followed in the fifth limousine. Some of the crowd consisted of school children. They were dressed in their uniforms. Others who cheered on the important Celebrity visitor, Duke, and his companion, Sandra, to Costa Del Shell were members of the local *'rent-a-crowd'*. Strewn for at least half a mile on either side of the coast road which led from the Airport, the crowd cheered loudly. Sandra was swept up in the moment. She was feeling quite honoured by the seemingly adorable indigenous people of the holiday island. Duke saw the childlike expression on Sandra's face but nudged her. He reminded Sandra of his immense influence. "Now you know how effective clout is, don't you", he inveigled? Sandra kissed his forehead. Encouraged by Sandra's long arms which seemed to be wrapped around his neck like a *'friendly'* python, Duke commented once again. "Someday, you'll be worshipped like this on your own", he assured. The motorcade eased its way towards the destination of the Del Shell Hotel complex. After about twenty minutes, Duke and Sandra saw the magnificent building. It stood out from the low-lying partially derelict buildings in the distance. Those seemed to be dwarfed by the monstrosity of a modern 1st rated 15 story block rising out of the ground like a spectre standing predominantly alone, seemingly! Duke rubbed his hands together as if he was rubbing fire sticks in order to create a spark. Sandra had noticed this behaviour before. She understood it to mean that Duke repeated this action whenever he sensed the potential for huge increase in his financial opportunities. "Grant's on the ball", he exclaimed. It was the first time that Duke had seen the building in which he had invested. Grant and Beth Tittye were the speculators but Duke was the major investor. Erecting the buildings had provided work for some local people but the majority of the workforce was drafted in from Spaceville. Still, the politicrats and poly-tricksters of Costa Del Shell were grateful for Duke's investment. It was an ideal getaway for individuals from places like Spaceville.

Tourism was the main trade for Costa Del Shell. On their arrival at the Del Shell Hotel, Duke and Sandra encountered yet another set of heroic welcome from the attentive uniformed staff. They used animated movements representative of some folklore dance aligned with their painted smiles that resembled those on the inanimate 'Bone China Dolls' displayed in the Souvenirs Booths inside the Del Shell Hotel. The Minister of Tourism hurried to greet Duke as he alighted from the golden coloured stretch limousine with the small flags attached on both sides of the bonnet. The six accompanying police together with another ten, who had already arrived at the hotel and the Diplomatic Contingent, formed a *'Guard of Honour'*. They saluted Duke and the Minister of Tourism whom walked side by side just ahead of the lone figure of a bewildered Sandra. While Duke conferred with the Minister of Tourism, she had been relegated in order of importance to an *'also ran'* position. As she tried to fathom what seemed more important to Duke than her, Sandra stared blankly into space. She didn't even notice the efforts of Captain Plantain, who had somehow joined the *'Guard of Honour'* at some stage. Grant Favours and Beth Tittye moved swiftly towards her but joined Sandra, eventually. They explained the reason for the protocol but confided that the Minister had some urgent business to discuss with Duke.

Even though the local people of Costa Del Shell really enjoyed the meagre increase in employment prospects brought about by tourism, there was strong protestation about the clash of *'cultural values'* between Spacevilleans and the indigenous population. They didn't mind the traditional seafood stalls, funny mirrors, 'one-arm bandit' machines, ghost train rides or even some of the new up-market technological computer games. Some welcomed the new look 'Designer Beach' atmosphere consisting of 'Beach Malls' which catered for 'Fast Food' outlets, 'AADCs' and 'Dog Tricks' Shows to name a few of the more innovative ideas that had started to appear on the traditionally exotic island. These were at minimum tolerable. The main protest was against the 'Mini Casinos', 'Strip Joints', 'Shooting Galleries', Nude Beach Parties, 'Dancing Pole Showcase Extravaganza' Competitions and Escorts like Kerry O'Ki, who were fast becoming the main *'Showstoppers'*. Dozens of visitors to the island were not able to resist these particular distractions. The *'Showstoppers'* had the influence of a giant magnet. Mesmerized by the *'stereo-hype'*, a growing number of young people were drawn to these *'attractions/distractions'* even when they didn't necessarily want to be there. The great fear of many local parents was the influence and impact these strange behaviours were having upon the younger people of Costa Del Shell. The authorities turned a *'blind eye'* towards the complex in general.

Duke explained to the Minister that Grant Favours had his blessings and was in charge of and responsible to generate the new businesses on the island. He reminded the Minister that he was not happy about the amount of negative publicity that was being levelled at them. Grant had complained that the groups, Scruples United and Moralist Inc. had challenged the insipid looking Favours about the issue of the *'culture of hedonism'* which was being forcefully marinated into the psyche of the population of the far off exotic paradise island. These behaviours and alien *'values and beliefs'* were being transported as *accepted workable cultural 'models'* from the parallel planet, Earth, initially but being sanctioned by the entire Royal Royal Dis-United Stately Kingdoms of Asteroidia as *'harmless fun' according to their 'values and beliefs'*. It never seemed to be considered that some of those *'accepted workable cultural models'* from the parallel planet, Earth, might be *'unacceptable'* at minimum but considered as *'downright offensive'* to the indigenous population of exotic continents, countries and islands like Costa Del Shell. There seemed to be an abominable behavioural 'tic' from these *'traditional mercenaries'*, who like the historical character Columbus, claimed to have *'discovered'* Costa Del Shell. On arrival, under the guise of being *'missionaries'*, they lived amongst the indigenous population but taking the indigenous population's almost subservient but nevertheless selfless generosity for granted. The *'Missionaries of Cultural Adjustments'* elect reconnoitered the terrain for commodity resources, psychoanalysed the population, infiltrated their psyche but weighed up when it was time to bring in the *'traditional mercenaries'*, like Duke, to overwhelm the naïve youngsters with choosing the *'new cultural models'* which fit the *'new cultural roles'*. The like of Duke was able to do this through the medium of tourism. It was the typical *'catch 22'* situation for the 5th rated exotic continents, countries and islands, like Costa Del Shell. They needed tourism to help boost the much needed *'foreign currency'* and *'provision of jobs'* in exchange for the often overt subliminal programming and conditioning that was taking place under the radar on behalf of the likes of *'cultural missionaries'*, like Duke Stagg and his accomplices, Sue Allen-Stokeley, Beth Tittye and the dedicated Grant Favours. All this had been previously planned from the initial introduction of the pioneering *'cultural missionaries'*. They deliberately obliterated all indigenous traditional 'values and beliefs' but forcefully installed their *'brand'* of alien *'values and beliefs'* as the *'new'* and <u>only</u> *'cultural standards'*, by which the exotic environments should adhere, apparently!

Any individual or group objecting to this *'raping'* of indigenous traditional *'cultural values and beliefs'* had been given *'short shrift'* by the *cultural mercenaries'* caustic rebellion against those traditional *'morals'* and *'scruples'* which were being embraced by the older indigenous generations but had been installed over previous millennia. On the paradise island of Costa Del Shell, the indigenous people publicly outlined their intention to demonstrate opposition to what they claimed was poisonous but threatened to erode millennia of traditions and culture of the Del Shellians without regard. These were being implemented by interloping GSE, Ghetto Sodomy Entrepreneurs, in particular. They were using the *'airstream'* of a vital industry known as tourism to exploit the minds and lifestyle of the indigenous people. Moralist Inc. stated strongly that they welcomed tourism but took umbrage to being forced to accept the title of *'Sin Island'*. The toxic pornographic mentality was being soaked up into the minds of the younger generations like water to sponge. Super saturation was now the status being experienced but affecting a younger and younger generation, perennially. Moralist Inc. underground newspaper, 'AH-SUH', was an internet-based blog site. It evoked responses from viewers not only in Costa Del Shell but also from other groups protesting about the same issues around the entire 'Royal Royal Dis-United Stately Kingdoms of Asteroidia as well as other exotic islands, countries and continents. 'AH-SUH' further protested about the technological games which portrayed violence and evil as *'fun'* as well as pornographic DVDs and a selection of CDs of *'modern'* music with subliminal corruptive degrading and violent lyrics. Initially, these were being deliberately and aggressively introduced by the GMT, Ghetto Mentality Terrorists, the GMES, Ghetto Mentality Engineering Scientists and the Gang Orientation Scientists from the 1st rated Dis-United Stately

Kingdoms. Those *'cultural mercenaries'* were in Costa Del Shell on a recruitment drive to *'blood'* (pun intended) some locals into this *'new toxic lifestyle'*. These practices were fast diminishing the value of life on the once paradise hideaway but had proven to be having a devastating cyclonic effect upon the traditions and cultures of indigenous populations across the World of Space altogether. Children were being used as the proverbial *'guinea pigs'*. They were being exposed to these viral *'mental diseases'* that were being deliberately thrust upon them. Along each life stage, they were being led into the green humanoid robotrons' reckless and uncaring alien *'lifestyle'* which promoted and continually reinforced but demanded that they have no respect for themselves, their peers, parents, adults or even authorities.

Scruples United added that *'manufactured'* *'Role Models'* were being engineered by an element of the organized network which included the GMT, Ghetto Mentality Terrorists, the GMES, Ghetto Mentality Engineering Scientists and the GMP, Ghetto Mentality Practitioners. Their *'jobs'* were to design and designate the *'roles'* of Ghetto Celebrity CEOs and Ghetto Celebrity Entrepreneurs in the creative industries but to inveigle the youngsters into this new *'fast lane'* to *'ride or die'* or *'die trying'* this *'toxic cocktail mentality'* in order to achieve the *'Spacevillean Dream'*. Ghetto Sodomy Entrepreneurs jobs were to *'groom'* but entice young people towards accepting and embracing pornography and paedophilia as being *'normal'*. Gang Orientation Scientists installed fear physically and subliminally. Gang Orientation Operators directed Gang Orientation Practitioners as to how to create turmoil through chaos, what level of intensity of physical *'bullying'*, and when to instill fear, through the *'rumour mill'*, amongst the UFO's 'Cult-Induced' Post/Zip Code Gangs. This encouraged individuals to eliminate each other under the umbrella of *'bravado'* to earn *'Street Credits'* through the UFO's Cult-Induced Post/Zip Code Wars madness. These Ghetto Scientists, Gang Orientation Operators and Practitioners joined forces as core elements of the Ghetto Mentality Terrorists' entourage across the exotic continents, countries and islands. Their remit was specific. It was to encourage chaos through fear amongst families, friends and communities "by any means possible" as sanctioned by the green humanoid robotron politicrats and poly-tricksters, like Secon D Hanshuze and Daryll Fastfamousse, respectively.

Scruples United further stated that the indigenous young minds started to believe the *'stereo-hype'* and *'stereo-tripe'* being fed to them so consistently that alluding to living the perceived *'stereotypical image'* in the *'fast lane'* had become more exciting than indigenous traditional and cultural activities, comparably. This 'distraction/attraction' relegated parental structure as merely an inconvenience at minimum but a *'nuisance'* factor altogether. Armed with the constant barrage of subliminal commands of significant others, parents had started to become an unimportant *'incidental'* in the scheme of things. Scruples United warned that those perpetrators were risking the wrath of King Karma in the Kingdom of Spaceville.

Moralists Inc stated that the *'processes'* of *'Neuro-profiling'* and *'Neuro-bigotry'* meant that the GOS, Gang Orientation Scientists were in syncopation with the GCCEO, Ghetto Celebrity CEOs and their subordinates the GCE, Ghetto Celebrity Entrepreneurs. Their derisory and violent subliminal lyrics in turn activated the Ghetto Sodomy Entrepreneurs whose job it was to debase young individuals; robbing them of their innocence, worth, confidence, esteem, evaluation of self-worth and most importantly

'ID', maybe! This form of *'programming'* and *'conditioning'* said to be more effective than *'water-boarding'* echoed but resonated with gross reverberations until *'Coda'*; repeating such effect on a kind of *'mental loop'* until *'Fade-Out'* (death) as was evidenced by the wanton waste of lives in the madness created called the UFO's Cult-Induced Post/Zip Code Wars. These *'civilised'* *'Practitioners of Gloom and Doom'* were allowed to operate with impunity but were being presented as *'Role Models'* to the youngsters. Moralist Inc., Scruples United and 'AH-SUH' had great support (over 10 million *'hits'*) in less than a week across the expanse of The World of Space.

Parents who had lost their children either to the *'Human Zoo'* Community or to the *'Funeral Assembly'* seized the opportunity to register what it feels like in terms of being emotionally drained by the seemingly irreversible *'mental pandemic'*, the UFO's Cult-Induced Post/Zip Code Wars. They had proven to be more devastating than the biblical *'locusts'* plague. Some parents complained that it seemed as if their children were not being empowered or enabled to choose which *'way of life'* they might prefer. Instead, they seemed to be forcefully *channeled* down a *'One-Way Mental Alley'*. As far as the *'politically correct'* mantra about *'Role Models'*, the editor of 'AH-SUH' posed two major questions which were left open for debate, apparently. (1) What *'model'* fits which *'role'*? (2) Which *'role'* fits what *'model'*? Scruples United not only confirmed their agreement with Moralist Inc. but also drove home the biblical story of Judas Escariot and the thirty pieces of silver philosophy. They claimed that the *"Modern Judas'"* were not dissimilar in intent but sold their *'stereo-hype'* and *'stereo-tripe'* for 'Titles', 'Trophies' and 'Statuses' which were worth financially more to them today *"for services rendered"* than the proverbial *'thirty pieces of silver'*.

Scruples United said it was more like *'thirty million'* pieces of silver, gold, platinum or diamonds even. They brandished their opposition upon religious grounds. Scruples United cited Hedonism on their paradise island as an integral part of the typical change in traditional *'values and beliefs'* to which they objected. They had seen Hedonism as providing male and female concubines, et al. They were driven out of the Temple by an enraged biblical Jesus Christi but rendered as being unscrupulously blasphemous, maybe! Massage Parlours being opened next door to schools, Scruples United referred to as the *'serpents'*, with the type of latent *'deadly venom'* to which there was no antidote. Brandishing a copy of Moralist Inc and Scruples United's physical Local Newspaper, The Shoreline Gazette, the groups had approached their local, MCA, Member of Cultural Adjustments, to consider the plight of younger people who attended the local Salute and Bow Junior School. It was situated not too far away from the Del Shell Hotel complex. Their major objection was against the proposal to implement Pole Dancing as a suitable activity three times a day. At the beginning of each day in Assembly, these junior school children were to be inveigled to partake in this immoral pornographic adult activity. It would be repeated at the end of the school day as well as being made available as an *'after school activity'*.

Beth Tittye, previous Head Teacher of the original Salute and Bow School, in her home country, Spaceville, had vigorously campaigned against Moralist Inc. while the insipid Grant Favours railed against Scruples United. In Beth Tittye's letter to the Minister of Tourism, she wrote, "Young people will not be affected adversely by the popularity or success of our local entrepreneurs", she guaranteed. This message was further augmented in an extract from her *'Annual Address to the Nation'* courtesy of the Department of Tourism. With a young local girl by her side nodding throughout her speech like a mechanical dummy, Beth Tittye stated, "My job is to encourage young people, like Kerri O'Ki, to develop her wonderful talent and skills". What Beth Tittye failed to comment on is that the *'skills'* to which she was referring was Kerri O'ki doubling up as an Escort Girl and Pole Dancer together with her role as *'Local Ambassador'* for recruitment of others like herself from the poverty stricken exotic paradise island. Another extract from Beth Tittye's speech referred to the reason she was backing the type of work she was providing for the likes of Kerri O'Ki. She said, "that way we, as a wider community will be rich enough to dissuade poverty from taking any foothold in our type of society". Beth Tittye had learnt a lot of *'mental reinforcement techniques'* when she trained as Head Teacher for the Salute and Bow School in Spaceville. Part of those techniques was the deliberate prolonged hesitation before stressing or switching for another purpose. She needed the *'hushed'* crowd to take in the other side of her *'Annual Address'*. This time there was a greater surge of riptides of under-currents with which Beth Tittye wished to sweep away the *'nuisance'* factor from anyone who dared to complain against her or current colleagues, Sue Allen-Stokeley and Grant Favours. He was an ex-student of the original Salute and Bow School back in Spaceville.

Now, with the audience salivating like Pavlov's dogs anxiously awaiting her delivery, Beth Tittye drilled much deeper into their psyche even without them being aware of the subliminal techniques that they were experiencing. Similar to the Ghetto Celebrity CEOs and Ghetto Celebrity Entrepreneurs, who had announced their mental dexterity of this psychological technique, Beth Tittye focused on zooming into the audience's vulnerability. Another excerpt from her *'National Address'* stated, "Some people have deliberately tried to undermine our community by moaning unnecessarily about *'modern concepts'*. Those are the ones who wish to spoil our *'fun'*", she protested. Without any attempt to hide her contempt for such *"moaning minnies"*, Beth Tittye pulverized the efforts of the opposing Groups. She questioned not only the reason behind their existence but encouraged the indigenous population to question whether those groups had *"their country's interest at heart"* or any real part to play *"in this 'modern' community setting"*?

Beth Tittye knew that she could stir up real hate amongst the younger population. Some of whom had already started to strip away the old traditions for the *"live fast, die trying"* philosophy that had found its way into their minds via the *'modern role models'*. They had invested *'stereo-tripe'* through their *'stereo-hype'* but remained oblivious to the consequences. These were not only partaking in the dismantling of centuries of great works that had been done long before the 'Ghetto Celebrity CEOs' grandparents were conceived but also the subtle devastation of those traditional principles passed like a baton from one generation to the other. The younger generations ever increasing negative super-inflated egos seemed to adopt a less than healthy disregard for what sacrifices had been made by previous generations to ensure their presence upon the parallel virtual planet of Asteroidia.

Some *'conscientious'* tourists had either some morals, scruples or both but remained empathetic with the views of the protesting groups. These supporters loved the quaint look and feel of natural paradise rather than the contrived model that Beth Tittye, Sue

Allen-Stokeley, Grant Favours and Duke were shaping. Beth Tittye saved her most acid remarks for those visiting empathisers. She referred to them as *'do-gooders'*. "They come over here *to change us from whom we are* or appear to be. We like the business that Shelly Beach and its associates are bringing to <u>our area</u>. Those *'moaning minnies'* can get on the next plane or back into their little shells". She broke off but chuckled to herself. "Pardon the pun . . . Shelly Beach, got it", she chuckled. Beth Tittye squealed with delight. It was what she termed as *"common wit"* amongst *"people of like minds"*. It seemed as if the moment had overtaken her better senses. Beth Tittye had lost all of her composure. Her laughter carried all the way to the back of the Auditorium. The echo seemed to rebound with the reactive force of a ball being hit hard against the wall of a squash court. Beth Tittye's very strong hoarse baritone voice sounded quite similar to that of Duke's. The only interruption to her operatic laughter was the intermittent coughing fits that confirmed her habitual smoking. Beth Tittye's breathing was laborious but signified that she was having a respiratory problem. Her eyes were filled with tears that seem to appear either through sufferance from a histamine allergy or the joy of laughter. Her huge yellow and brown stained teeth not dissimilar in size to that of a horse were exposed for all to see, especially by those individuals who were watching the *'Annual Address'* on Television with high definition. They could also see her eyes squinting so rapidly now, that they appeared as if Beth Tittye's eyelids were being animated in a 'Betty Boo' cartoon. Her REM, Rapid Eye Movements, was not too dissimilar to that of the flapping of bat's wings on 'take-off', comparatively. Despite the protestation from some dissenters, those visitors who were in agreement with Grant Favours and Beth Tittye's philosophy of forcefully *'modernizing'* this paradise island roared their approval. Beth Tittye told the audience to choose whether they agreed the need for Hedonism, Massage Parlours, Pole and Lap Dancing in particular, at the Del Shell Hotel or on near Shelly Beach. "You're either for us or against us", she declared. First she asked, "Who's against us". All the audience present did not agree but, those who didn't, abstained from stating how they truly felt because they sensed they were being outnumbered by those who were attracted to what was on offer.

The former Head Teacher of the original Salute and Bow School, back in Spaceville, knew how to work an audience. She was now ready to show not only those present but also sent her core message to those watching on television across the paradise island and beyond that Moralist Inc. and Scruples United were wasting their energies protesting. Beth Tittye reinforced hers and Grant Favours' stance about encouraging more tourists to Costa Del Shell. She pointed out that she and Grant weren't the only ones on a *'mission'* installing *'Sin Continents'*, *'Sin Countries'* and *'Sin Islands'* across the Royal Royal Disunited Stately Kingdoms of Asteroidia.

Beth Tittye stated that competition existed amongst the various Kingdoms to impose their Nation's *'values and beliefs'* upon those continents, countries and islands perceived as primitive. She confessed that this egoist mindset had been inherited but passed on through generations since the Buccaneers on Planet Earth. They had pillaged, ravaged, plundered and raped similar exotic continents, countries and islands many millennia before the parallel virtual planet of Asteroidia was known to exist. Beth Tittye said she was motivated not only by the financial rewards but also that she felt a sense of power to have control over the shaping of an entire population's mindset. She confirmed that Grant and her were just two of the multitude of *'cultural missionary converters'*. They were going around the virtual planet rapidly ensuring that even remote places were not impervious to their dominance. Beth Tittye likened the *'act of persuasion'* to that of *missionaries* spreading religion to what was perceived then too to be *'primitive people'*. She talked about those primitive people as needing *'guidance'* from a source whose *'values and beliefs'* (standards) were considered as being superior to the indigenous population of those 5th rated continents, countries and islands. Again, Beth Tittye paused before her last act. She had already embedded her commands through subliminal messaging upon the psyche of the attentive audience. These included individuals watching on television, listening on radio, computers, phones and other technological devices as well as those who were in the Auditorium. Beth Tittye delivered the final nail in the audience's mental coffins when she asked this question, "Who is with us"? The captive audience in the Auditorium began to applaud loudly but stamped their feet to show their approval. They chanted Beth Tittye's name over and over again. The insipid Grant Favours appeared as if from nowhere but encouraged the now rowdy audience, "Three cheers for Beth Tittye, three cheers for Beth Tittye, three cheers for Beth Tittye". Over and over the crowd kept repeating her name. Even those who were watching or listening on the various media devices away from the Auditorium did the seemingly standard obligatory highly choreographed *'standing ovations'*. They sometimes appeared like Seals along the shorelines of the Galapagos Islands. These *'ovations'* seemed to have lasted for as long as ten minutes in duration but were not dissimilar to staged political campaigns on Planet Earth. As one, the audience in the Auditorium waved mini versions of Shelly Beach Flags but held up prepared posters confirming their allegiance with the new plans for Costa Del Shell.

"She's some bird ain't she", Grant commented to one of his colleagues. At the same time as feeling quite elated, Grant was aware of what Media was going to do with such popularity. This was *'Manna'* from Costa Del Shell. The *'New Heaven'* that the 6'3" overlarge, square shouldered, flat backside, thin legged, overly buxom, unshapely *'angel'*, Beth Tittye, had come to help defend. Her popularity by the majority of tourists had already brought her to *'Celebrity Status'*. Grant was an ace opportunist and he was already formulating how to further promote Beth Tittye. Soon there would be *'Ten things you need to know about Beth Tittye'*. There would be a book and, most possibly, a Movie or TV 'Soap Opera' Series about the previous Head Teacher of the Salute and Bow School in Spaceville. Solid offers were already manifesting themselves into the minds of those who were charged to *'make things work'*. Grant Favours and his other colleagues at the Ministry of Arts and Finer Arts in Spaceville would come to defend Grant Favours Inc., a multi-billion company that had proper political 'Lobby Status'.

While Beth Tittye's Annual Address was going on, Duke was still engaged in a 'tell-it-all' meeting with the Minister of Tourism for Costa Del Shell. His Report had already reached Duke while he was in Spaceville. Now, the Minister would have to explain those areas which concerned Duke. The Tourism Minister, the Honorable Altiman Begi-Begi was a pro-Duke fan. His brief from the government was to create and accommodate new opportunities for the paradise island. He assured Duke that he was ready and willing to help crush the protest against the *'attractions'* which were bringing the much needed foreign currency into the island. Duke was adamant to erase any opposition to Grant and Beth Tittye's influential strategies. Altiman Begi-Begi relayed Costa Del Shell's Governor's concerns about demolishing any threats that could possibly dissuade tourists from the type of experiences with which they preferred. "Let me tell you Mr Duke that the Governor is beside himself with what he refers to as the nuisance element", the Honorable Begi-Begi assured. "Well, look Altiman I can't see what the problem is. If you want me to deal with it, I know just how to install fear into those bastards", Duke threatened. Altiman Begi-Begi understood the local people much better than Duke. He acknowledged their concerns but decided he was not going to put his career in danger or, least of all, offend Mr Duke. All the same, some of the protesters were either long-standing friends and in some cases family members even. Altiman Begi-Begi's idea was to call a series of meetings but considered that he could persuade his people to abandon their protest. He felt he could make them see Tourism as a *'cash cow'* with the false pretences that there was *"opportunity for all"* rather than being an ogre. His philosophy was to win over the avid protest leaders. In this way, their followers would dwindle and effectively all protest might be abandoned. "I'll arrange a meeting with the leaders of Moralist Inc. and Scruples United. I know my people Mr Duke. They will come round to our way of thinking", he assured. The response from Duke was not what Altiman Begi-Begi was expecting. In fact, he was quite taken aback by Duke's aggressive response. "Do what? Have a meeting then another meeting and another meeting about the first two meetings. No way is that going to solve the problem. You know something Altiman, you talk tough but you haven't got the guts for the fight, have you", Duke raged? It took quite several moments before Altiman Begi-Begi was able to regain his composure somewhat. Before he could re-assemble his thoughts, Duke twisted the metaphoric knife with the kind of force that rendered the Minister to get on his knees in front of the powerful Mister Duke. This made Duke angrier. He glared menacingly at him then pointed his stubby index finger in the Minister's face. "You are a spineless bore that's what you are. Who goes round arranging meeting with the enemy? You're a bloody joke. Get off your knees", he ordered. Altiman Begi-Begi pleaded with Duke to give him a chance to negotiate with his people. "Everything is a compromise Mr Duke", he offered. "I don't have to compromise. I've got clout. That always works. Get the cops to pick up the trouble makers and bring them to the basement floor of the Del Shell Hotel. I'll show you how to deal with dissenters", Duke insisted. The Minister had no idea how ferocious Duke could be or what was so significant about the basement floor but he had no alternative than to obey his master and carry out his wishes. "I will do what I can Mr Duke", the Minister assured. "You'll do more than that Altiman. You'll do what I tell you. If you still want to be Minister of Tourism by the end of the day, you will have those protest leaders here within the next hour", Duke threatened. With that, he ended the meeting abruptly but left the room.

Duke was in no mood to spend his holiday concerning himself about opposition to these lucrative business opportunities. Their potentialities were limitless and he knew it. He thought that the protesters were short-sighted about the element of job creation. Duke refused to see their concerns from any other perspectives than the *'values and beliefs'* he saw as *'normal'*. He didn't allow himself to consider that the indigenous population of the Costa Del Shell had different perspectives from his own. Blinded by insolence for the 5th rated island but driven by the egoist relentless mindset, Duke and his Spacevillean colleagues pursued a policy of installing their will and culture upon the population of the exotic island of Costa Del Shell. As he exited the building where the meeting had been held, Duke placed the huge dark glasses on his face to shade his eyes from the glare of the golden sun. Protecting his eyes from the glare of light was like a daily ritual for Duke and people from The Tribe of Duke. When he didn't protect his eyes from the glare of bright light, especially brilliant sunshine, it seemed to adversely affect Duke and those from his particular ethnicity. This was his first visit to Costa del Shell but already he was being familiarized with what his enormous contribution had managed to bring about on the paradise island. In partnership with some much smaller investors, Duke owned Costa Del Shell. He climbed into the waiting golden coloured stretch limousine but glanced up at the Large Shelly Beach Hotel Complex and the Spacevillean Flags which were not only proudly aloft the huge complex but signified the fusion of the two cultures. The Flags were Badges of Honour but proved publicly that there was consent at government level to exploit the vagaries of the meaning of Tourism. It took less than ten minutes for Duke to arrive back at the Del Shell Hotel.

On alighting from the limousine, Duke hurried towards the Reception Area. He announced his name to the smiling subservient buffoon who kept bowing. "We know who you are mister Duke. I give you best worker", the uniformed personnel announced. He talked in his language to the Bell Hop who was standing a few yards away. "Take mister Duke to the King Suite", the receptionist ordered. Both Duke and the Bell Hop walked over to the lifts. They disappeared from view as the door closed. The receptionist picked up the phone but spoke into it. "Mister Duke is here", he announced. The voice at the other end thanked the receptionist. The 15th floor was reserved for the rich and famous exclusively. When Duke alighted from the lift, the manager of the Del Shell Hotel was there waiting for him. He saluted then bowed from his waist so much so that his torso was now parallel with the floor like Jeeves the butler. Another lift opened. A waiter with a trolley bearing a large bottle of champagne in a golden bucket with ice, a dish with imported caviar and small biscuits were wheeled along the long corridor to the King Suite reserved for Duke. The manager placed the entry card into the slot. The waiter pushed the door open but stood aside for Duke to enter. He did. The trolley was left where Duke ordered the waiter to leave it. As the manager turned to leave, Duke asked which Suite Sandra had been given. The manager looked puzzled. "Who is this ... eh, Sandra", he queried? Duke looked stunned by the question. "Have you gone bonkers", he asked? The manager sensed the seriousness of Duke's enquiry but was rather taken aback. "Bonkers? What is bonkers, mister Duke? I don't understand", he confessed. Duke's anger was beginning to surface. "Did you not see a woman in a see-through floral dress, a wide brimmed hat with a dog", Duke stressed? The waiter seemed to have the information that the manager didn't. He signalled to the manager. The manager saw the look on the waiter's face but asked Duke to allow the waiter to speak. "What do you know that your manager doesn't", Duke asked? He was beginning to sense that something had happened. "The woman with the dog was asked to leave because we don't admit dogs in the Del Shell Hotel", the waiter explained. Duke had heard enough. "That's my missus and my dog you blundering idiots", he raged. The manager and the waiter had no place to hide their embarrassment. "I apologise", the manager said. He fell on his knees then bowed maybe half a dozen times from his waist. "We are not used to seeing many people like her at the Del Shell Hotel, mister Duke. That is why we sent her to the motels on the other side of the island. It is true what the waiter said about not allowing dogs into the Del Shell Hotel. Where would he sleep? It is not our custom to have dogs in the house. Here on Costa Del Shell the dogs stay outside. In our culture, a dog is a pet not a member of family", he stated. The manager's honesty ought to have been taken into account by Duke but his next comment was a new experience for the manager. "You pompous little ass, do you not know that I own your island? My missus and our dog are staying here at the Del Shell Hotel in this Suite. I'm paying for it not you or any of your people. If you know what is good for you, you better have my missus and my dog here pronto. Do you hear? Pronto, you savvy", Duke raged? With that, he dismissed the manager and the waiter by physically pushing them through the door then slammed it so hard that the sound could be heard by others along the corridor.

CHAPTER 44

Sandra and Tramp were re-united with Duke. There were apologies not only from the manager of the Del Shell Hotel but also Altiman Beg-Begi, the Minister of Tourism. He also assured Duke that he had managed to convince the leaders of Scruples United and Moralist Inc. to rethink about protesting against the Massage Parlours, Pole Dancing, Lap Dancing and the whole Hedonism on the island. Duke's rage had already started to subside and so he accepted Altiman Begi-Begi's alternative solution with regards to Scruples United and Moralist Inc. In a phone call from the Governor of Costa Del Shell, Duke was told that there was a ceremony being arranged for him to have the Key to the Island within a few days. He was assured that the printed and television media would be present to inform the population of Costa Del Shell about his importance. Duke, Sandra and Tramp celebrated the news by ordering another bottle of champagne before lunch. They wandered towards the beach. Sandra stopped at one of the novelty shops to purchase some souvenirs. Duke bought some 'rock' candies. This was Sandra's first experience of the seaside attractions. She was particularly fond of the ice cream cones with the sticks of flaky chocolate, the splash of red syrup and the sprinkled multi-coloured decoration that enhanced its artistic appearance. Even Tramp enjoyed an ice cream cone too. He licked the cold sugary ice cream but chewed the empty cone. Duke gave Sandra one of the rock candies. She was surprised at how brittle and chewy it was. Sandra was fascinated by the words 'Shelly Beach' which appeared on the inside of the rock candy. "How do they do that Duke", she asked? Gradually, Sandra, Duke and Tramp made their way unto the beach in the early afternoon with the bottle of champagne and a few sandwiches they had ordered from the Del Shell Hotel to take with them. It was while they were on the beach enjoying themselves that the little dog had wondered off. Tramp was enjoying himself too, feasting from the many generous sponsors of food. The smell of burning flesh from the beach barbeque stall had attracted him. Most of the people were, at first, oblivious, of the little dog. "Yap, yap, yap", Tramp barked. He was trying to get attention from a pair of *'lovebirds'*. They seemed to spend most of their time kissing and smooching. Some life-guards were mingling with the crowd; showing off their ultra-tanned skins and body shapes. One man was so burnt that his skin was dry and peeling. His female partner wore a skimpy orange outfit, little more than the size of a handkerchief, to cover the lower half of her body and the top being the width of three parallel shoe laces together, supporting her unnaturally enhanced protruding breasts. She had a slim neck but a rather big head and her dentist might have been proud of the gleaming whiteness of her precisely *'engineered'* superficially whitened teeth. They were so perfectly aligned that bookies would have been hard pressed to offer anything more than 1/100 on odds prediction of when she would next smile. Everything about this woman was *'perfect'* to the programmed and conditioned mind of the observer but she had a very nasty kind of tone to her laughter. It was grainy, hoarse and very *'common'*. The man with her carried a surf board in one hand. When the woman started to cling to him more closely, he let go of the surf board. It was on its way down to the sandy shore but in its path was the little dog. Tramp's agility and natural instinctive reaction saved his life and he knew it. Without any warning, Tramp sunk his teeth into the man's ankle. He growled but pulled at it. The man danced around and around, trying hard to shake the little dog from his foot. The scene was now seen as humorous. Soon, throngs of people were attracted to the spectacle. Duke and Sandra were amongst the first ones to arrive. The crowd became unruly but pushed and shoved to get the best position to view the spectacle. A pair of size 14 feet trod on Duke's foot. He winced but swore loudly. Duke hopped about as if he was dancing around a Totem Pole then hobbled until the pain had begun to subside. Sandra suggested that Duke soak his injured foot in the sea-water. "It'll be soothing anyway. Come on, try it", Sandra encouraged. "He's a bloody fool, wearing boots on the beach", Duke said. Sandra readily agreed. "He should watch where he's putting his feet", Duke moaned. The man could not have heard him above the chaotic crazy environment that had developed. Some had empathy with the man whose ankles were being tested for *'bite-ability'* by the little dog. The surfer, tried everything he could to shake the dog from his foot but he was making no progress. His leg began to feel tired and numb. The man had been swinging the little dog around on it for more than two or three minutes. His current efforts had clearly not worked and suggestions were coming from a distance of about 10 yards away. Everyone was close enough but not too close. Some people were suggesting that Tramp was a *"rabid dog"*. Being a scientifically engineered mini Pit Bull Terrier, the dog's jaws seemed to be locked in place for such a long time that Duke, jokingly, bet another man 1000 Del Shells that Tramp was capable of holding on "for at least another five minutes". It was as if Duke had flicked a switch on. Offers started to come thick and fast. The cacophony of shouting voices did not make it any easier, for Duke or Sandra, to hear the *'bets'*. This betting *'ring'* had started from one loose remark by Duke but now it had taken on the same enthusiasm as an annual Horse Race on Planet Earth like 'The Grand National' or 'The Kentucky Derby'. The whole scene reminded Sandra of those market places to which her mother, Dian, used to take her, when she was a young girl. Duke was a touch embarrassed at how easy people parted with their money, but still the flood of money kept on coming in from the *'bets'*. His short stubby fingers held many Del Shell *'notes'*, folded expertly between them. "1/20 on odds is all I will pay, if you win", Duke reminded the people. Sandra stored the takings in the large name-branded fashion handbag with the logo that she carried around with her. The *'contest'* between man and *'beast'*, even as tiny a *'beast'* as Tramp, concluded to be a very uneven one. The loudest scream came from the woman with the even set of gleaming white 'chops'. She reached for the *'surf-board'* but the people who now stood on it refused to budge. Whether through novel, educated and scientific methodology or simple 'guess-*ology'*, some had already lost their money. Others were still *hopeful* because they had placed their *'bets'* a bit closer to Duke's time. The injured man had passed caring anymore. There was no feeling in the injured foot anyway and by now he was already determined to focus on raising his pain threshold. All he could feel now was deep anger for the little dog and its owners. The pilot, Captain Plantain, had agreed to be the *'Timekeeper'*. He took pride when he announced that it was fast approaching Duke's estimated time. "Countdown to the end of the five minutes set by mister Duke, 10, 9, 8, . . . 3, 2, 1, time", Captain Plantain shouted. Sandra and Duke celebrated the win. Some of the people cheered him. They appreciated his opportunism. "Like taking candies from babies", Duke boasted. He waved then bowed to his audience. Sandra went over to free the man from his torment. She talked gently to the little dog and then attempted to release his jaws by pressing an area on his face. The dog was himself exhausted from the *'activity'*. "Tramp let go of the man's foot", Sandra said. The little dog released the man's foot. Tramp began to nestle up to Sandra. She stroked his head and then picked up the little dog to cuddle him. "You made me and daddy a lot of money today", Sandra said. She let the dog lick her face again and again. Some of the froth from the corner of Tramp's mouth remained for a while on Sandra's cheek. "Who's a good boy then", she asked the little dog?

There was a blast from a trumpet. All the peoples' attention went from the injured man to the direction of the trumpeter. It was Captain Plantain. A fanfare was sounded then Beth Tittye used the megaphone to tell her message. It sounded something like the muffled announcement from PA systems of the past at some mainline Train Stations on Planet Earth. Because of the interference, which punctuated the delivery, the information was inconsistent. The voice was very nasal and patchy. "The 'Synchronized Snorkeling Contest' will be held in one hour. Registration for entry must be made at the kiosks over there on my right", Beth Tittye emphasized. There was a rush towards the kiosks indicated. Many people thought it a lovely idea to snorkel but 'Synchronized Snorkeling' was unheard of previously. Captain Plantain rested the Trumpet on the table next to Beth Tittye. She proceeded to spell out the Terms and Conditions of the Contest. "You may carry a harpoon gun with you but you will restrain yourself from firing unless it is the particular fish that is specified on the chart indicated in the Information Leaflet. Entrance fee for the competition is 10,000 Del Shells. The money should be deposited with the staff at the Kiosks. Beth Tittye indicated the direction with her hand. At the end, you will enter your catch for scrutiny by the Judge. He is a local man who knows these fish well. Each incorrect *'catch'* will cost you another 2500 Del Shells so hunt carefully. No *'catch'* means you forfeit your deposits", she warned. Beth Tittye was enjoying this official status as she uncovered the huge Trophy, shaped like a fish that would be handed to the winner. She had come to Costa Del Shell on a '10 day' break with her friend, Sue Allen-Stokeley 3 years ago. They had never been questioned by nor have they ever applied to the Costa Del Shell Immigration about extending their stay but Sue had opened an AADC quite close to the border of the Tourist Village. She owned half-shares in three seedy Brothels and two Motels on the far side of the island. Captain Plantain owns the other half-shares.

Sue used to work on the buses in her home country while Beth was a Head Teacher at the *'Salute and Bow'* School in Snideborough, Spaceville. Since that '10 day' break, both had stayed on, in Costa Del Shell, to flourishing careers. Beth Tittye's talents were geared towards the Promotion side of Marketing. She handled all 'Promotions', for the Del Shell Hotel chain. Grant Favours had scouted her talents when Beth promoted Sue's AADC, 'The Wooden Barrel'. Single-handedly, Beth Tittye created more interest into the lucrative 'AADC Business'. The indigenous population had abandoned their traditional harsh local drink for the imported foreign liquor. Sue Allen-Stokeley bore testament of the locals' craving for foreign liquor and cigarettes. With Beth Tittye and Sue Allen-Stokeley's insatiable appetites for opportunism and enormous thirst for the taste of Champagne Urge, even Costa Del Shell's traditional brew was being processed abroad in Spaceville but being recycled and sold in foreign bottles to the indigenous people. Their own tobacco was being re-packaged and re-branded but was now available at higher costs too. Sue Allen-Stokeley and Beth Tittye had it all sewn up. They were being assisted by the indigenous people who kept exposing one traditional secret after another to tourists, voluntarily. This *'freedom of information'* gave the likes of Beth Tittye and Sue Allen-Stokeley the means to exploit not only Costa Del Shell's local traditions but also the people's naivety too.

Kerri O'Ki was the main attraction. She was a local girl who enjoyed reading 'Glossy' Magazines, which Grant Favours brought to her shores. Kerri's mind was made up. She wanted to be a famous model like the ones in the magazines. Beth Tittye had chosen her as an Escort to *'entertain'* the VIPs who visited the Del Shell Hotel. This arrangement meant that Kerri could financially afford and had a bit more money than other local girls. Grant had specially requested that Kerri be part of the *'Presentation'*. Beth Tittye held the megaphone to her mouth once again. She told the crowd that she was handing over to Kerri O'Ki, ... a lovely local girl". She is the perfect *'role model'* for her people", Beth Tittye ended. Kerri O'ki took the megaphone and spoke into it. She did this deliberately slowly as Beth had previously prompted her to do. "Synchronized Snorkeling is very good, yes", she asked? "Yes", the crowd bellowed. "The winner will be my escort at the Midnight Disco. You can dance with me ... every song, yes", she teased? Kerri O'Ki began moving her waist like a *'practiced belly dancer'*. There was a huge roar from the captive crowd. "Only if man wins, yes", Kerri confirmed. "If woman wins, the Captain will be escort, yes", she asked, searchingly? Captain Thursday Plantain stepped forward, bowed and displayed a huge grin. Giggling, Kerri O'ki put the megaphone down on the table. She turned towards Beth Tittye. "How I do, Madame" Kerri asked? Beth Tittye quickly ended the conversation with a stern glare but commented in a low voice. "Don't call me Madame in public", she scolded. The Captain challenged the girl. He spoke to her in their local dialect and told her to apologize to "Miss Beth". The girl apologized. Beth Tittye took up the megaphone again but summoned Grant Favours and Duke to come up to the platform. When they finally nudged their way up to the platform Beth Tittye introduced them as the "Architects of Modernity" to Costa Del Shell. She pointed at the Hotel Del Shell and further commented. "Let us give a great welcome to Grant and Duke for their pioneering spirits. Great Entrepreneurs have great foresight. These men are trailblazers for this island. Because of them, local people can get work, isn't that wonderful", she asked casually? "Ladies and gentlemen I give you the Saviours of Costa Del Shell", she added. The crowd was ecstatic in their praises for Grant and Duke. The applause was interspersed with shrill whistles. Beth handed the megaphone to Duke, who had indicated that he wanted to say something to the crowd. "Earlier my dog bit a man. I'm sorry about how things turned out. I'll see to it that the man is properly looked after. That's all", he concluded. Duke handed the megaphone to Grant but he just waved to the crowd. They left the platform to mingle with the crowd once again. Sandra was proud of the action that Duke had taken over the man who had suffered the injury. She prompted him to ask Grant to take the man to the local hospital for treatment. "I'll pay him off", 2,000 Del Shells ought to do it, Duke suggested.

The harpoon guns, snorkeling gear with flippers were a necessary part of the tools required for the competition. Beth Tittye had made provision for these tools to be hired by participating competitors. Some of the local helpers distributed the snorkels, flippers and harpoon guns to the more than willing participants but that was only after they had paid the inflated hiring fees to Sue Allen-Stokeley who was in charge of collections. She handled the accounts for all the AADCs, Brothels and Motels as well as Beach Collections. Before long, dozens of people were snorkeling happily hunting for the catch that might prove to be the winner. Beth Tittye pointed to the gullible tourists that fell for such hype. "Easy money", Grant responded. He, Beth Tittye and Sue Allen-Stokeley knew that most of the fish shown in the leaflet would never be found in those waters so close to shore. Some tourists were busy on their hired jet-skis while others exploited being dragged behind a fast moving craft suspended by a rope. The bungee jumpers took their daring jump on the beach. There were those who bet on the snail races too.

Some others wanted to explore the island to see whether they might be able to purchase and use illegal drugs. A number of female tourists came especially to examine, by experience, the folklore about exotic men's sexual habits, physical attributes and longevity. Rumours had spread abroad faster than a bush fire and Costa Del Shell bore the hallmarks about the daily '*Sex-a-thons*' that took place on the island. More than seventy per cent of the tourists who visited Costa Del Shell were women. They appeared like flocks of birds or shoals of fish daily. Each individual seeking some sort of '*ritual*' that had been fabled long before the religious 'Ten Commandments' were invented. It seemed to challenge the meaning and restriction implied by the word '*adultery*' which appeared as one of the '*don't philosophies*' embodied within those 'Commandments'. The legend of polygamy had been around even before the fabled '*Adam and Eve*' appeared in the so called '*Garden of Eden*', wherever that was! Its geographical location had never been explained in terms of its latitudinal position and longitudinally on any map on Planet Earth. It surely did not apply in the 'Virtual World of Space'. There was mention though about the normalcy or social acceptance of men from the 'Tribe of Hawke', who had dwelt with many women from the year dot without any knowledge of the existence of the word marriage let alone '*adultery*' or even the intervention of 'The Ten Commandments'. This practice carried on through the ages but was referred to as late as when the fabled '*Henry the 19th*' reigned on the virtual planet of Asteroidia, apparently! In '*Their-Story*', it had not been established if Henry's '*Lust Factor*' was due to him being a generational product of the original custodians of polygamy, the Tribe of Hawke. They were the first tribe recorded to have lived on the virtual planet, or was Henry a product of a more '*politically and socially acceptable*' Mixed DNA Rainbow Tribe. Henry was more likely to have gained his *'dual-ethnicity'* through an enforced mixed DNA merging from the *'slavery mentality'* that came with the advent of the arrival of the green humanoid robtrons from another galaxy. Since their arrival, the green humanoid robotrons from the Tribe of Babylon, who had invaded the virtual planet of Asteroidia, had enslaved the minds of the people from the Tribe of Hawke. They became fearful of the invaders from the Tribe of Babylon but began to condition their own minds with the mantra they were forced to repeat several times over until they had convinced themselves that "theirs were not to wonder why but theirs was but to do or die", assumedly! The effect of buying into this *'philosophy'* was so powerful that the green humanoid robotrons from Tribe of Babylon immediately became aware of how naïve and vulnerably addicted the people from the Tribe of Hawke were to buying into subservience. Usurping the mental power from the larger population of indigenous people, Tribe of Hawke, the lesser population of green humanoid robotrons from the Tribe of Babylon took control of the parallel virtual planet of Asteroidia. As they couldn't breed as fast as the Tribe of Hawke, The Tribe of Babylon decided to strategise but exploited the indigenous Tribe. In the absence of IVF, the Tribe of Babylon studied but practiced the original versions of *'sex surrogacy'*. Henry and his generation were the first of the Mixed DNA Rainbow Tribe made up of a male donor from the green humanoid robtron *'slave master's genes'* and that of their targeted *'sex surrogates'* from the Tribe of Hawke. The female donor's genes came, through *'the act of rape'* perpetrated by the green humanoid robotrons upon the black Tribe of Hawke, whom they met on their arrival on the parallel virtual planet. By logical sequence, Henry's Tribe of Hawke mix in his DNA was proof enough to fathom how he managed to *'maintain'* his fabled giant erectile *'tool'* and unbounded stamina, like those traditional indigenous men from the Tribe of Hawke, in order to *'service'* the *'needs'* of his 19 *'wives'* and countless concubines in any one day, probably! He would have had to be ready to absolve himself from the guilt-label called 'Sin' (if it had been invented then) in order to focus on his intended *'purpose and mission'*, perhaps!

For the traditional indigenous men from The Tribe of Hawke, their reputations were at stake and none dared to relent from keeping this folklore alive on the paradise island of Costa Del Shell. In pursuit of this legendary experience, the women tourists' premeditated thoughts drove them to boldly seek after those colloquially known as *'rent-a-dicks'*. They scoured the beaches daily but hired themselves out to any of those desperate women with foreign accents. These women were more than prepared to avail themselves to the local *'stallions'* who awaited them. The *'rent-a-dicks'* paraded themselves openly but guaranteed to keep the folklore alive through demonstrating their capabilities to maintain an erection and stamina for a whole day, without ejaculating, maybe! Whether the folklore was partially or wholly maintained can only be measured by the repetition of visits from those women with foreign accents, who had not only heard about it but had actively lived the ritual on previous occasions. They had come back for more, again and again, seemingly! The re-visits seem to be a testament that was not *'old'* or *'new'* but *'true'*, probably!

Male tourist to the exotic island of Costa Del Shell were more prone to wanting to sample the local liquor for their raw unprocessed strengths and the myth that it had aphrodisiac qualities. Some tourists came specifically to sample the *'high-grade'* drugs that were grown on the paradise island. Others requested only those chemicals that had been imported to suffice or maintain their addiction. Daily, these tourists could be seen negotiating one *'high'* after another according to their preferences. Costa Del Shell was experiencing the beginning of a new *'dawn'* or *'twilight'*, even. Drunken visitors performed like *'untrained animals'* but never seemed to have any respect for the indigenous population, their traditions or culture. The visitors' attitude were more about reminding the indigenous population about their dependency upon a singular industry, tourism, which was rudely and forcefully imposed upon them. It is true that, since the arrival of the tourists on islands like Costa Del Shell, there was new impetus to improve the financial status of the local community and the whole island, subsequently. Foreign currency was needed on the paradise islands to increase not only the GDP but also individual *'coffers'*. As pointed out by the political opposition, there were huge sacrifices that the exotic continents, countries and islands like Costa Del Shell had to make in order to accommodate the *'all important'* tourists.

For every new Hotel Complex that was needed to cope with the new influx of tourism, it meant that there was a new refuse problem to resolve. There would come a time when the island would not smell like paradise anymore because of the huge mountains of rubbish which could not be recycled but was creating airborne diseases. The health of the indigenous people were deteriorating rapidly too. Children and old people were the most affected demographic. Likewise, new planning to manage natural human waste (excrement) had not been taken into account. The overflow had now begun to be released into the ponds, brooks, lakes and rivers on the island or the once beautiful emerald green ocean that surrounded it. The floating mass of excrement looked like a massive spillage of oil from a tanker that had run aground. At first, the *'slick'* of excrement just seemed to sit on top but the wading birds, marine animals, the coral reefs as well as the fishing industry were being affected adversely and being destroyed at worst. Because of the super hot temperatures experienced in the region in which Costa Del Shell was located, the stench carried for miles around the island and across the seas to the neighbouring islands too. From an Arial view, it was reported that, the increase in the fly population was so great that the massive *'slicks'* of excrement drifted for miles but appeared to be visited by colonies of *'bluebottles'* that descended upon the flotsam jettisoned from the broken cesspool walls into the water table and beyond. It had long been breached and was now in this condition because, over a great number of years, heads of government had purposely ignored the threat to human and marine health. There was excrement coming out of the taps in and around the once exotic island. These were just two of the major problems that seemed to have escaped previous and current government. Apart from mosquitoes, which thrived in the environments described, the population of the swarms of flies far exceeded that of the humans that lived on the exotic island. The new threat was real and needed urgent attention. Politicrats and poly-tricksters pockets and bank accounts were bulging with the *'back-handers'* they had received for ignoring the inevitable breaches of cesspool walls and the seepage caused by the oozing from the old corroded rusty broken metal pipes into the water table. Anyone, who was anyone, was subject to and became recipients of the volume of corruptive practices that had crept into the island's indigenous people's minds and hearts. It had now become customary to be known as working for one of the people with clout.

Even the police stopped the visiting Del Shellian emigrants on holidays in their own continents, countries and islands to ask them, who they were "working for"? When they replied that they were visiting but not *'working'* for *'anyone'* on the island, the emigrants were roughly treated but discouraged from completing their stay. Similarly, even returning residents were being hounded by some indigenous people who had not travelled abroad. Some individuals had travelled abroad but had made a conscious decision not to live there. Both of these groups didn't welcome the returnees. On Costa Del Shell and other exotic islands like it, there was a greater segregation that had been encouraged by politicrats and poly-tricksters. They were wary that, with their much broader experiences, returnee residents might have meaningful influence on the indigenous population. That meaningful influence might help the indigenous population to see how they have been used as *'pawns'* in the political games. The indigenous population, who had not traveled, had been persuaded not to trust the patriotism of the returnee residents. This fear was easy to initiate because it was true that some individuals had chosen to abandon the countries in which they were born. Those claimed to have *'crossed over'*. Even though those individuals had made their decisions, the critics of returnees needed to understand better that there were some individuals, who had remained faithful in their hearts, minds, bodies, souls and spirits. These were die-hard patriots, who consistently made great sacrifices in order to gain opportunities to improve themselves educationally and to put themselves in a better financial position. Others had chosen apprenticeships and training for the trades they wanted to work in. The indigenous population in exotic continents, countries and islands like Costa Del Shell needed to become better aware that returnee residents were not a burden to the island nor were they unpatriotic by choosing to live abroad. Returnee residents can help the indigenous individuals, who had not travelled, to better understand how they can improve from being in a state of subservience and narrow-mindedness to realizing that they are capable of fulfilling their potentials and abilities. Those individuals, who marginalized the returnee residents, need to address their own *'prejudices'* and *'judgments'* against the returnees but make clear their meaning of patriotism, also. Some indigenous individuals were less *'patriotic'* than those returnees they were accusing. Those judgmental individuals were being *'unpatriotic'* by *'selling out'* to the *'highest bidders'*, who could afford to line their pockets and bank accounts in exchange for the brutal suppression of their own people. Returnee residents to Costa Del Shell and the other exotic continents, countries and islands in the region just wanted to be able to come home to gather that traditional *'feel'* again that they had sacrificed in order to maintain their families both abroad and in their respective exotic continents, countries and islands of birth. It somehow never occurred to those judgmental individuals, who were ready to criticise returnee residents but did not question those significant others that helped to plant such ridiculous ideas into their minds against their own natural born islanders. They needed to understand that the real patriots were those, who were willing to seek and gather more *'intelligence'* about how the indigenous population had come to practice 'beliefs and cultures' which they had *'inherited'* rather than forged themselves.

The separation of dwellings for returnee residents in Costa Del Shell and the other exotic 5th rated continents, countries and islands was a deliberate ploy to isolate them from settling amongst the indigenous population. They were being treated more like *'lepers'*, who were being quarantined. Instead, the returnee residents were forced to live in *'communes'* known as *'Gated Communities'*. The tourists were more welcomed on these exotic islands like Costa Del Shell much more readily than the indigenous returnee residents. Costa Del Shell was fairly new to this type of exposure compared to some of the other exotic continents, countries and islands, that were celebrating more advanced anniversaries of becoming *'Sin Continents'*, *'Sin Countries'* and *'Sin Islands'*. The behaviours and seemingly contrived attitude and treatment towards returnees were very similar across the exotic continents, countries and islands on the virtual planet of Asteroidia. It was as if they were *'being punished'* for seeking to live their experiences. What the critics needed to understand is that those returnee residents had learnt more about those 1ˢᵗ rated Kingdoms, that had pretended to be or even assumed to be *'superior'* in class to the 5ᵗʰ rated exotic islands, countries and continents. Without the knowledge and subsequent expertise of the likes of returnee residents, the 5ᵗʰ rated exotic islands, countries and countries were left open to further *'exploitation'* from the likes of Duke, Beth Tittye, Grant Favours and Sue Allen-Stokeley. Costa Del Shell was becoming a replica of those other 5ᵗʰ rated exotic islands, countries and continents. They had swallowed the *'bait'* from the likes of Duke and his bullying cronies. They knew and were experts at imposing their will upon a naïve and vulnerable indigenous population, who were desperate to earn an honest living to enable them to provide for their families.

The opposition political party, Moralist Inc and Scruples United were not against Tourism. If they did they would be foolish to do so. Their protest was about their government being more in charge of the type of *'activities'* and *'behaviours'* that took place at those resorts that catered for tourists. Moralist Inc, Scruples United and the opposition political party wanted the *'seedier activities'* to cease forthwith. Their influence was such a strong magnet for desperate individuals, who were being led like the proverbial lemmings following the Pied Piper blindly. On Costa Del Shell, it was common for dozens of young girls to assemble at establishments made available for them by local *'Ghetto Sodomy Entrepreneurs'*. Their business was to compete to become *'super-pimps'* on behalf of the tourists. Most of these local *'Ghetto Sodomy Entrepreneurs'* groomed these young women. They led the young girls and women between the ages of 11 to 17 years old to believe they were entering *'dancing contests'* in order to win prizes. That was how Kerri O'ki was spotted. Grant Favours had scoured the island of Costa Del Shell with some of the local men, who assured him they were "in the business". He was whisked around the island. Grant was eagerly accepted but encouraged to come to view *'The Dancing Hall Queenbees'*. He saw the dozens of young girls who had assembled for the weekly events. They were being encouraged by their *'hosts'* to put on a display for the "man from foreign". The camera crew followed in order to record and document the potentiality for establishing a base for *'Sin Island'*. Grant Favours had his own views about women but carried on in the *'fun'* events. The performers put on an extra *'show'* for the "man from foreign". The young girls were told that "this important man" might be able to provide them with *'work'*. In an attempt to impress Grant, the local *'Ghetto Sodomy Entrepreneur'* ordered the girls to give Grant a sample of the type of dancing he was about to view in the *'contest'*.

One young girl about 14 years old climbed unto Grant's 6'5" standing body but attached herself to him like a monkey to a tree. Whilst still clinging to him, she expertly turned herself upside down so much so that, instead of clinging to his torso with her hands as before, the young girl was now using her hands to cling to Grant's thighs. All the other young girls were jumping up and down as children do in a school playground but shouting "...'69', give it to him girl. Go Ker-ri, go Ker-ri, go Ker-ri". There was high frequency shrieking. Grant's face was completely obliterated from view by the girl's lower body. As the camera scanned the rabble crowd, they turned towards it; vibrating their bum cheeks to the same sort of oscillation wave lengths as their colleague who was still attached to Grant Favours. Even after the music had stopped, the act carried on for yet another few minutes. After his experience with Kerri O'ki, Grant was ready to view the contest to see who was to be *'The Dancing Hall Queenbee'*. The local *'Ghetto Sodomy Entrepreneur'*, Pimpè Ernel V1, created a display as if he was daring Grant to copy his sexual insinuation. Pimpè Ernel V1 chose a young volunteer with whom he displayed a routine that seemed to be choreographed in preparation to amuse the male tourists who wanted to be *'entertained'* by the local young girls. Under the instructions of the 'Ghetto Sodomy Entrepreneur', <u>effectively the owner of the 'dance troupe'</u>, the young girls put on a display which defied the maturity of their life stages. Most were scantily dressed but paraded themselves like vibrating machines. To vibrate their bum cheeks rapidly seemed to be the craze that formed the core of the competition. This display of particular sexual insinuations through *'dance'* might be considered a creative art form or just plain sensual suggestions like peahens shaking their feathers to signify that they were on *'heat'* in the mating season. When Grant started his rather awkward rendition, the local entrepreneur shouted into the microphone, "Jeeezaas Christ". It was a cry of approval that the tourist had managed to emulate his mentor that he was fully engaged with the young girls who were being interviewed (exploited) for *'suitability'*. Grant jigged but tried to mimic the girls as well as their host, Pimpè Ernel V1. Both he and Grant negotiated the terms and rate after Kerri O'Ki was adjudged to be the most impressive *Dancing Hall Queenbee'*. Having been sold like the *'slave'* she had become, Kerri O'Ki left with Grant to start her *'career'* under the tutelage of Madame Beth Tittye.

Other tourists watching the spectacle were encouraged to learn of these *'holding cells'* for vulnerable young girls like Kerri O'Ki. Like Grant Favours, others were ready to negotiate terms with Pimpè Ernel V1. A short stocky bespectacled swarthy looking man sought the ear of the local *'Ghetto Sodomy Entrepreneur'*. He commented that he was only interested in very young girls and boys. Pimpè Ernel V1 summoned his Aide, Scarlet, but whispered into her ears. She told the man to follow her. Scarlet took the tourist through some bushes and a well trodden pathway where there was but a splattering of the moonlight that managed to seep through the thick bushes and canopy of trees. "Where are you taking me", the man asked? "Don't worry, you are safe with me. I take you to get your very young girl and boy", Scarlet assured. Soon the tourists could see what looked like an old wooden Barn. After contacting someone by cell phone, Scarlet led the tourist to the door. She rapped hard on the door to a particular code. A huge woman with an extremely large behind and a jockey's whip appeared when the door opened. She greeted Scarlet but smiled broadly at the tourist. The woman's smile was warm and welcoming. Both the swarthy tourist in his ill-fitting khaki shorts which seemed two sizes too small for him, a brightly coloured floral shirt that seemed to have survived from the days of the flower power movement in the 1970s on Planet Earth and his bifocal spectacles, which seemed to have survived several centuries, made him look awesomely suspicious. The man and Scarlet entered the old wooden Barn. The tourist's eyes seemed to bulge with delight as he saw the array of young children that looked curiously almost timidly at him. There must have been forty to sixty of them. These were little boys and girls between the ages of four to eight years old. "Take your pick", the woman with the jockey's whip shouted. The tourist was rather spoilt for choice. His eyes enlarged as he realized that he had found the harem that he was promised months ago whilst booking his ticket back in Spaceville. Finally, the woman cracked the jockey's whip but called out the young 6 year old girl and a 4 year old boy that the tourist had selected. The shy young children seemed frightened but walked unsteadily forward as the woman's voice prompted them to hurry along. Another crack of the whip found the young children gripped by fear jogging forwards to be further assessed by the stranger. The selected children started to cry. "Don't cry. I'll look after you", the man assured. "You have to pay first", the woman with the jockey's whip bellowed. "For how long", the tourist queried? "That's up to you. What can you afford? These young ones are pretty expensive. We take huge risks in order to cater for your needs", the woman commented. "How much for one hour", the tourist queried? "20 thousand Del Shells each", the woman replied. The tourist tried to barter with the woman but after several cracks of the jockey's whip while the huge framed woman walked menacingly towards him was intimidating enough for the 5'5" grossly obese swarthy tourist. It was not apparent whether it was the intimidation or the excessive heat that caused him to sweat but the tourist produced an odour which seemed to attract the flies. Even the huge framed woman and Scarlet agreed he smelt like the polluted pond not far from the barn. The tourist paid promptly. With his outdated floral shirt and ill-fitting shorts thoroughly saturated, the tourist stood there with the young children by his side. "Where do I go", he asked? "Outside and as far into the bushes as you can get. We don't want to hear the crying. If you are one minute over the time you've paid for, the fee doubles", the large woman with the huge backside and the jockey's whip warned. With that, she opened the door for the stranger to leave with the children. He hesitated in the doorway long enough to take one more glance at the children he was leaving behind. He saw the fear in their eyes. Both girls and boys were being corralled in the old wooden Barn waiting to be sold to any paedophile that had the money to pay for their services. This was the lifestyle that had begun to appear all over the new 'Sin Island' of Costa Del Shell and the other exotic continents, countries and islands in the region.

The tourists were protected by the Del Shell government. Even when they committed crimes like this, the tourists were made to pay a measly fine or easily pardoned when they happened to be taken to court if they ever were! It is likely that the offending tourists were often let off with a possible 'warning'. Whenever the odd case of serious charges were brought against a tourist from one of the 1st rated Kingdoms of Asteroidia, representative politicrats and poly-tricksters would openly, actively get involved but threaten to take harsh steps against the 5th rated continent, countries and islands and made them appear to be the offenders instead. There was no register of paedophiles accessible to immigration whether at the Airports nor Sea Ports of Costa Dell Shell or the other exotic 5th rated continents, countries and islands in the region. As long as all the exotic destinations' eggs were in the one basket, perpetrators of these crimes would be re-admitted the next time they chose to visit the exotic islands like Costa Del Shell.

On this occasion, the smelly, swarthy tourist, who had selected the little children from the barn, Jamie Pilchard-Fishe had a singular reason for purchasing the children. He was an eminent award winning investigative journalist from Spaceville. Jamie Pilchard-Fishe was making a documentary film to highlight the plight of innocent children in the various exotic continents, countries and islands, like Costa Del Shell. The investigative journalist was in agreement with the likes of Scruples United and Moralist Inc. His documentary film would also prove beyond doubt that children from these exotic resorts were not only being systematically abused by individual tourists but also by representatives of official established organizations like some Church Pastors, Vicars and Priests, Scout and Girl Guides Leaders and their affiliates most of whom had deliberately targeted but conned their way into those Organizations for the sole purpose of practicing paedophilia in those exotic 5th rated continents, countries and islands like Costa Del Shell. The documentary would also expose the fact that children were being groomed in those exotic continents, countries and islands *'for sale'* by local 'Ghetto Sodomy Entrepreneurs' like Pimpè Ernel V1. Unbeknown to Grant Favours, the woman with the jockey whip, Scarlet and Pimpè Ernel V1 were being filmed secretly by the hidden camera which the journalist, Jamie Pilchard-Fishe, carried on his person. He left the island the next day with the little children. Jamie Pilchard-Fishe purchased tickets over the internet for the young children, who he told immigration was his adopted daughter and son. The award winning journalist was more than confident that his story about the young children's passport had gone missing from his hotel room would be believed by immigration both in Costa Del Shell and in Spaceville. After all, Jamie Pilchard-Fishe was a household name around the virtual planet of Asteroidia let alone in Spaceville.

CHAPTER 45

Many people preferred to stay in the cool water even though the golden sun's rays were spreading the warmth. There was no wind. The stifling heat had sapped their energies; even those, who dared to seek some form of shelter under the thatched roofed fake Obis that housed the obligatory table and selection of free booze. Many of the fake Obis were consistently *'serviced'* by a series of females dressed in grass skirts and beads only. They stepped lightly bare feet across the hot silver sand, swayed from side to side; carrying their hips as late as possible. Trays were carried with poise and gesture. Girls winked their way into the hearts of their guests and promised *'gratuities'* were severally returned. Some of the girls were specially selected as *"alternative entertainment"* for the visitors. Waiters and waitresses danced their way through the crowded beach to ensure that food was plentiful for their guests. Some men and women wore casual uniforms of oversized 'T-shirts and shorts. Duke stopped one waitress who was carrying a tray of honey melons. "Over here my dear", he urged. When the girl came over to him, he removed two melons but placed them under her oversized T-shirt but commented sarcastically. "Quite an improvement, wouldn't you say", he teased laughingly. The waitress was embarrassed but dared not protest about the uncouth tourist for fear of loosing her job. "That told her, didn't it", Duke chuckled? He caught the look on Sandra's face. It suggested that his crude attempt at his type of cultural humour was an embarrassment amongst the indigenous people. By the look of consternation on the faces of the waitress' colleagues, it was clear that the young woman had suffered from Duke's action. "That wasn't very nice", Sandra commented. Duke was impervious to emotional sensitivity. Like his father Earl, he was just a brash spoilt individual who thought that others had a problem if they couldn't see from his 'perspectives'. "It's just a bit of fun", ain't it, he submitted? Sandra did not pursue the matter. She was buried in the sand. Tramp lay on top of the *'sand coffin'* and, every now and again, moved forward to repeatedly, lick Sandra's face. Duke looked down on his exotic bird. "Let's go for a boat ride and leave this noisy lot" he suggested. "I can't go anywhere until you and Tramp free me from the sand", she reminded him. As soon as Duke started to dig, the little dog showed his master how it should be done. Barking and digging as if he was enjoying the task, Tramp helped to free 'mommy' from the sand tomb to which she had been relegated. Sandra had become the amusement of Duke and anyone else who was interested. She raised herself into a sitting position. Sandra dusted herself down. Some of the wet silver-sand still clung to those parts of her body that was exposed. In the bright golden sunshine, the grains of sand contrasted against Sandra's naturally smooth very deeply tanned melanin skin. It was in complete contrast to the silver coloured sand. Some of it was trapped inside the skimpy bikini outfit that Sandra was wearing. As she stood up, Duke's heart started to pound uncontrollably. The couple nearest to them heard the rapid beats against his chest. To them, it sounded like horses hooves against a hard frosty surface on a morning gallop. Maybe it was the angle at which Duke was standing but Sandra appeared to him like an angelic apparition. Flashbacks of their more passionately intimate moments together came flooding back and Duke desired her at that moment. He had consumed at least two bottles of Champagne Urge Mark 3. Duke was sure that it was Sandra and not the potent Champagne that caused his heart to palpitate with such rapidity. Sandra had this kind of effect on most men that set eyes on this most beautiful, proportionately well sculptured delightful female specimen. Her slender waist was more accentuated not only by her buxom, voluptuous breasts and magnificent wobbly attractively large backside but also the way how Sandra seemingly deliberately delayed the movements of her swaying hips to a type of rhythm. It was as if her mesmeric aura managed to capture yet transfer its willingness onto a man's psyche but offered to bring about the maximal rate of lust factor that was possible. Perhaps the 'new' aphrodisiac ingredient in the Champagne Urge Mark 3 was more potent and responsible for Duke's enormous appetite for sexual involvement. He knew that he desired Sandra now with more urgency than he had experienced before. Duke swiftly closed the small distance between them then pounced upon her, knocking her down to the floor like in a Rugby or American Football players' tackle. Sandra was aware of Duke's impatience. She didn't want to disappoint him but she preferred not to be the spectacle and talk of Costa Del Shell. "Not here Duke, please", Sandra implored. "How can you refuse a man his right", Duke asked? "Not here Duke", Sandra whispered. Nobody would have noticed or cared because they were busy enjoying themselves too. Duke told Beth Tittye to look after Tramp until they returned from the boat ride. "Just make sure he goes when he wants to and he'll be fine", Duke advised. Beth Tittye took the little dog in her arms and started to stroke his head. "Lovely dog", she purred. Sandra kissed Tramp goodbye then hugged Duke around his shoulders. He hugged her around her waist. Both strolled off towards the Marina. "Darling, I don't half fancy you now", Duke told her. "It won't be long Duke, honey", Sandra said, encouragingly. "Can't wait", he pleaded. They stopped to kiss and cuddle. Duke's 'jerky' movements began to warn Sandra of his loss of control. She pushed him away gently but still held his hand as they walked towards the Marina.

The local man, who Beth Tittye had nominated to manage the Marina, was a tall skinny man about 6'4" whose gaunt face made him seem to fit the role of a wanted man, in a 'cowboy' movie. He was unshaven and rough looking had large eyes which sat inside the deeply sunken eye sockets, high cheekbones with sunken jaws, and a long thin angular face. His mouth looked like that of a rodent with matching shark type teeth that seemed as if they were filed into those pointed shapes deliberately, perhaps! "A boat squire", Duke demanded? The manager offered Duke a selection of standardized motor boat but he refused them. Sandra's eyes scanned around until she saw the more modern boat that seemed to say "hire me". "That one's nice Duke", she said excitedly. Sandra pointed at the newest model of motor boat that was on display. Its aerodynamic shape stood out from the rest. "Fast boat, yes", the manager inferred. "You want driver, yes". I get you good driver, yes", the manager continued. He uttered some other words, loudly, in local dialect and another man appeared. Although he had the same kind of dark melanin skin tone, he didn't have quite the same appearance as the seemingly indigenous people. The man was as tall as the Manager of the Marina but was a much younger man with a more pleasant feature. Sandra thought he was quite handsome but he didn't have the muscular features like Raymond did. She had a crush on him secretly. Both men chatted quickly and the thin scrawny manager ordered the other man to drive the powerful boat. "I give you best driver mister Duke", the manager assured him. Duke looked at Sandra and she nodded to indicate approval. "He'll do", Duke confirmed. They climbed unto the boat and before long started to move gently away from the jetty. A trail of water indicated the 'skin friction' and 'drag' experienced by the body of the boat. A sharp turn to the left meant that the boat was heading for deeper waters. The sea was calm enough for a smooth ride. "Just drive until we tell you to stop", Duke told the local man then he turned to Sandra. "We spend some time below deck, yes", he mimicked. Led by Duke, they quickly slipped out of the driver's sight. He cut the speed of the boat and more or less just drifted along with the tide. He was aware of the reason Sandra and Duke had gone below deck to satisfy their need. The driver relaxed his grip on the wheel he used to direct the boat. Complacency was creeping into the man's manner in handling the boat and soon it was drifting in a haphazard way. It sometimes veered to the left before he casually corrected its direction. From time to time it appeared that he had nodded off for a short while but neither Duke nor Sandra could see the bottle of local 'spirit' drink in his pocket. The local 'spirit' drink was a very strong kind of 'Poteen' mixture that seemed to blaze a burning trail upon the throats of those who dared to try it. It had a certain type of 'revenge' that the drinker would be made aware of, especially if it was hurriedly consumed. The local man looked out to sea but inhaled the salty air into his lungs and blessed himself several times then bowed; moving his head rapidly up and down. He started to increase the speed of the boat suddenly. Duke and Sandra were startled by the sudden jolt. "What's he up to", Sandra queried? She stood up. "I'll tell him what for" Duke replied. The boat lurched again, this time causing Sandra to slip backwards and fall unto the lower deck. "I'm going up there", Duke shouted. They hurried back onto the deck. Trying to keep his balance as the boat veered off to the right then to the left, Duke set off towards the front of the boat, "I'll kill the sweaty bastard", Duke implied. No sooner than when the driver became conscious of the zigzag pattern the boat was taking, that it started to go in a circular motion instead. Sandra was feeling queasy and light-headed but Duke was too enraged to notice. The driver took another swig at the bottle and savoured the taste of the *'acidic'* brew. He grimaced and contorted his face into a type of mask that would befit the face of a carnival masquerade. When he looked out to sea again, the driver was unsure whether the waves were getting bigger or was it his imagination playing tricks. He was keen to make things right but the harder the driver tried to correct his errors the more the boat seemed to be going out of control. Because of the surge of waves slapping unmercifully against the sides of the lightweight speedboat, the driver was not sure that they would make it back to the Marina. He was trying desperately to drown his sorrows with the local concoction. The drink had registered hugely. It numbed his brain, freezing his ability to think clearly but rendered the boat driver into a state of ineptness. He had entered into a strange *'world'*. Double vision was only one phase of the strange experience he was having. The boat driver's head was spinning now and only the fresh breeze, blowing directly into his face, kept him from falling off the *'edge'*. He struggled to hold concentration for more than a few minutes at a time. His judgment and timing were grossly affected. When an unexpected huge wave crashed against the side of the boat causing it almost to capsize, the boat driver began to panic. He, Duke and Sandra were sent crashing to the deck. They tumbled around from side to side but also up and down according to which crest of wave that had impacted on the underside of the lightweight glass-fibre speedboat. More alertness was required but there was none forthcoming from the unstable boatman. The boat pitched and rocked with the new currents when the wind suddenly appeared. It surprised the local man but now it was gusting at 60-80 mph. It whistled an eerie tune and the sea groaned its disapproval for being taken for granted. The boat swayed and bobbed up and down some more; depending whether it was caught on the crest of a wave or in a trough. It was like a scene from the film 'Shipwrecked' or even 'Mutiny on the Bounty'. Duke paralleled this experience to those old movies. He longed to throw the driver overboard. The gale force winds lashed the boat continuously now and the drunken driver panicked even more. Unbeknown to Duke, they had ventured too far from the beach but had just about enough fuel to get back to the jetty. The driver looked at the gauge but he could not understand why the needle didn't move anymore. After all, it was quite a new boat but no one had checked the fuel before they set out to sea. The driver rubbed his eyes with the back of his hand a few times because he couldn't decipher whether his judgment was being impaired by the booze or the howling wind. It took Duke quite some time to negotiate the small distance. He was battered and bruised by the howling wind but was still sore at the driver. They could all now hear the sound of a much bigger vessel ahead. The foghorn was unmistakable and the size of the lump of grey metal was quite outstandingly realistic. The gigantic lump of metal brought into focus the fragility of the speedboat; should there be a collision. Though it was in the distance, any contact would have been the end to those in the small boat. The large vessel was a fishing vessel trawling for fish. Wide-eyed and staring, the driver of the speedboat shook his head again and again to clear it from the influence of the booze now that he realized he should stay clear of the large vessel. The pressure of responsibility dawned on the driver of the speedboat and so he tossed the empty bottle over the side. Duke clambered up towards him. He stumbled like a *'drunk'* himself as the waves and the wind made his journey more difficult to complete. His head ducked down and turning almost sideways, Duke braved the elements but made slow progress towards the drunken driver. The local man was unaware of Duke's progress towards him. Sandra, being buffeted by the wind too, made her way towards the direction of the driver as well. She called after Duke but her voice was pitched against the wind. Sandra had a fair idea what Duke had in mind and she feared that he could commit murder. They were being battered by the strong winds and at times were taken quite a few steps backwards. Sandra decided to lie face down on the deck and crawl towards Duke while his low centre of gravity did place him at a slight advantage. The strong waves made the boat rock from side to side then it pitched backwards then forwards like a bucking rodeo horse. Sandra started to scream, as it seemed sure she would go over the side of the boat but Duke couldn't hear her. In fact, he did not expect her to nor was he aware that she was following him. The *'implant'* done by the Trichologist had blown all over the place in the wind and made him appear like a crazed, manic killer in a 'Hitchcock' movie. All that this scene needed was the music to complete the drama that was taking place. The driver was now mumbling some sort of prayer to himself when Duke finally caught up with him. Duke kicked the man in the back of the leg and as the sudden force made his balance unstable, Duke grabbed the local man by his shoulder but swung him round towards him then he sent his stubby fist flush into the man's face. "I'll teach you, you slimy bastard", Duke commented then he smelt the booze. He hit the local man again but this time *'kneed'* him in the crotch. The driver winced and muttered many prayers but he did not attempt to fight Duke. Instead, he started to cry and beg. "A thousand pardons, mister Duke, a thousand pardons", he pleaded then bent down and kissed Duke's feet. "Get up, you sniveling little guttersnipe", Duke ordered. The boat driver stood uprightly now, still bowing and praying to him for mercy but Duke was relentless in his condemnation. "You hurt my missus, you slimy bastard. Do you have a license to drive this boat", Duke asked? The man continued to offer even more *'pardons'* but Duke kept on hitting him. He punched the driver in his kidneys. The driver reeled away from Duke. This time the punch had made its mark. The driver 'doubled' over but held his side. The pain was becoming more excruciating. As he bent down but placed his hands over his kidney, the boat driver remembered that he had a knife in his pocket. He saw that with no resistance being offered from him, Duke was becoming more reckless. In his moments of being beaten into despair, the boat driver thought of timing Duke's next foray then stabbing him in the stomach. Because of the prolonged torturous beating, the driver felt his action would be justified. He was a bit more sober than a few moments before. Though on reflection, the boat driver withdrew his desire to stab Duke. He remembered that he had signed a contract with his boss, Beth Tittye to report any abuse by tourist. She had assured him that any incident would be "looked into". The boat driver also remembered one of his colleagues who had settled the score with a tourist previously. Beth Tittye had him sent to the crypt but he had not been seen since her instruction was carried out. Duke kicked the boat driver in the shin and then chopped him in his nape as he bent forwards. The driver tumbled to the floor. Encouraged by the man's inability to fight back, Duke kicked the boat driver again and again in the rib area, while he was on the floor then stamped on his head as if he'd meant to send it through the deck. The stamping on the man's head was a behaviour Duke had carried with him from the gang culture that was a *'trademark'* from the UFO's Cult-Induced Post/Zip Code Wars. "Get up and fight like a man, you worm. I can't stand worms", Duke raged. Sandra finally caught up with the enraged Duke. Even she was concerned as to why Duke was still beating the boat driver. He had been doing so for at least ten minutes without any resistance from the stunned local man. "Darling, don't let this little shit cause you to go to prison. You'd have more to lose", Sandra encouraged. She hugged him and rubbed his face with her slender hands. Duke was now in a strange mental situation. He was extremely angry with the driver yet Sandra's comment and action made him think. He had so much contempt for the "slimy bastard" that he expressed another comment that sent shivers down Sandra's spine. "I'll kill him", Duke raged. The driver was not in any condition to offer protection from the torture he was under. "Temper, temper", Sandra warned. Duke was grateful for Sandra's intervention because he knew no limits when it came to fighting. All he remembered was his time on the streets when his emotions and moods were switching from one moment to another like the lights on an agility display board.

The foghorn sounded again several times. It brought Sandra and Duke's attention to the fact that no one was in charge of the boat. Duke couldn't see over the stern because of his lack of height but he knew how to drive the boat. The tall Sandra could see that the Trawler was getting closer and sailing directly towards them. "Where's that madman going", she asked? Duke told her to get behind the wheel. "I'll guide you", he assured. Sandra was confident that Duke could get them out of the situation. There was no other choice. "Look at the wheel as if it were a clock. Each minute represents one degree turn", he advised. "Turning right is clockwise and left anti-clockwise, got it, yes", Duke advised. Sandra stood astride the local man, who was still lying on the deck writhing in pain while Duke shouted more instructions. Sandra's long hair flapped about in the swirling winds even more and made her appear to Duke as if she were an Amazonian warrior. Tasked with *'manning'* the boat, Sandra concentrated on Duke's commands. "Left 10 degrees hold that course, full speed ahead" were just some of the instructions that Duke spat out. The Trawler's Skipper had seen the speedboat but wondered why it would be this far adrift from the jetty! He signalled to the small boat but Sandra didn't understand the code of the flashing lights. "Duke, I don't know what they mean", she queried. "Just stay out of his way, can you do that", he asked? The wind had just as suddenly dropped again as it did when they first started out and the sea was calmer. The Trawler pulled up alongside and the people on board looked down on them. One excited fisherman nudged his colleague but pointed. Sandra mistook the man's concern as a greeting but he was pointing at the local man below her feet. All the faces that stared down at them seemed less friendly than Duke and Sandra had anticipated. Soon, the fishermen were shouting and gesturing towards them. They flung fish at them. "What are they doing", Duke, feeding us like animals", Sandra raged? "Maybe they're just trying to be friendly, ignore them", Duke counselled. What Duke and Sandra did not know is that Duke's cruelty, to the driver, had been noticed. The Captain, of the fishing vessel and the crew were local women and men too. Through binoculars, they had witnessed the awesome beating that Duke had dished out on one of their own people. They had no idea why the driver was being beaten but they did not feel good about it. The crew shouted their disapproval together and the sound of the many voices were thunderous enough to spring Duke into action once again. "Hard right 30 degrees", he shouted. "This type of boat will outpace them", Duke encouraged. Charged with this new responsibility, Sandra played 'footsie' with the accelerator. The craft seemed to glide over the water. It skimmed over the surface at many more knots than the Trawler could manage and soon it was quite a distance away. "Good girl", Duke encouraged. "They would have lynched us", Sandra mentioned. The groaning of the local man reminded Duke that his tortured opponent was still alive. Sandra tried to disentangle her feet from him but she couldn't. She timed the kick to perfection. "Get from under my feet. You make me uncomfortable", she commented. The man was no longer drunk. He had only wished that Duke hadn't treated him like he did. The elected boat driver realized how much 'clout' Duke had on the island but he began to plan how to get even if he remained alive. Duke had found a box and was now standing on it. "There it is", Duke shouted. The familiar jetty, from which they had started out, was now only a matter of two or three miles away. Sandra pressed harder on the accelerator because the speedboat seemed to be slowing down. "Faster", Duke shouted. He was now standing with one foot atop the edge of the boat. The other foot stood firmly on the box. Duke uttered a kind of 'memory gem'. "Half a league, half a league, half a league onward", he kept repeating. He placed his left hand outwards for balance but pointed with his right, as if he was leading a 'Cavalry Charge'. The engine started to splutter and soon their progress towards the jetty slowed in pace. "The boat is out of gas", Sandra interrupted. Duke hesitated before he replied. "Just our bleeding luck, ain't it", Duke exclaimed? He looked towards the beach but he couldn't see clearly. Duke thought about Tramp for the first time. "Little devil, I'm sure Beth's looking after him", he mused. "Duke the gas, what are we going to do about it", Sandra asked pointedly? "Hang on, I'm not Einstein you know, I only look like him", Duke replied jokingly. "Well I'm not sleeping out here with no sharks tonight", Sandra moaned. "I'll get us out of it. Have I ever let you down", Duke questioned? He turned to smile with Sandra but from the corner of his left eye he caught a glimpse of the injured boat driver. Turning back to Sandra Duke pointed to the local man. "He'll go and get it". Sandra was puzzled as to whom Duke was referring. "Who will go and get what Duke, honey", she questioned lightly? "Him over there, old Alberto, he can swim to the jetty and get help for us", Duke said casually. Sandra sighed deeply before reminding Duke what he'd done to the local man. "Look at him Duke, he's nothing to us but to his people he's somebody. When he tells them how you beat him, seeing his injuries, they're bound to feel empathy towards him. What becomes of us Duke, what becomes of us", she reasoned? Duke had always admired this particular quality in Sandra. "You're no mug", he said assuredly as he considered the implications Sandra had pointed out.

The Beach Resort was full to capacity. Bookings had exceeded the previous year. Duke could only depend on the support of his friends, Grant and the other dozen or so that were on the island. He was in a corner and he had to get out of it with credibility. Duke held his head down but Sandra was wise enough not to break his concentration. She looked longingly towards the beach. Sandra couldn't see clearly what was taking place but she had keener ears for music than Duke. She could hear the music from the steel Pans and the drumming from local musicians. Sandra could tell because the music sounded nothing like in her home country. She longed to 'party' but would have to wait for Duke to chew over current events. His greatest asset in business was as a *'problem solver'*, a *'trouble shooter'*. His decision-making is far superior to his peers. Duke would come up with an answer that would *'eliminate'* the problem once and for all. He would have preferred to have the gas brought out to the boat for what he was planning would need a full tank and reserve too. Duke had planned to take the boat driver far out to sea and drown him. He had planned to say the local man attacked them and a fight ensued whereby Duke had to defend Sandra and himself from the drunken local man. He knew that the people on the Trawler would report the fight. Duke figured that the local people would be ashamed that one of their men had attacked him, a man of such importance, and Sandra. The local people were committed to welcoming valuable guest, like "mister Duke", upon the island. After all, they needed the foreign currency. Their currency, the Del Shell, wasn't worth the paper it was printed on nor was it worth the metal utilized to produce small change. Because the Del Shell rate had been devalued so grotesquely, the local people preferred and used only the highly valuable foreign currency that the likes of Duke and his people brought to the shores of Costa Del Shell. Duke had long realized that 'clout' was much more of a tool than Sandra might imagine. He planned for him and Sandra to play the role of the *'caring couple'*. Duke would pretend to be extending compassion and empathy for the boat driver's family. He had further planned to give the man's family 50,000 Del Shells as a kind of insurance *'pay-out'*. Showing such compassion, he thought, would endear the locals to him and Sandra. Snapping his fingers together like a performer playing 'castanets', he exclaimed, "I got it". When Duke told Sandra what he had thought of doing, she flatly refused to take part. "I love you Duke, darling, but that's asking too much of me. I couldn't take part in cold-blooded murder. It's alright for you to just shrug your shoulders and say "many famous people have done similar deeds and got away with it but I can't. That does not solve our current situation", Sandra defended. Duke knew Sandra would hold onto the principles that she so eloquently stated but he hadn't thought of anything else than to terminate the witness. "We could say he tried to mug us while we were out at sea, couldn't we sweetness", Duke searched? "I'm hungry", Sandra told Duke. "We've got some of that champagne left, I'll get it", he said. Duke started to move towards the rear of the boat. He had set himself a distance where he knew, if the driver tried to make a run for it, he would stand a good chance of deterring him from carrying out an escape. Duke stopped suddenly, turned, looked at the boat driver. "Changed my mind Sandra honey, I don't trust Alberto over there", he said pointing at the injured man. Alberto, as Duke called him or the slimy bastard, had propped himself up against the side of the boat. So now he was seated in a position where he could see Duke if he tried to approach him again. He had listened intently to all the conversations, watched the body language; especially when Duke was celebrating seeing the jetty or was enjoying the *'Cavalry Charge Scene'*. Either way, Alberto observed enough to know he was not far from home. His only problem was that Duke had forbidden him to stand. He was at that same time adopting a strategy for escape from the cruel "mister Duke, yes". Excitement had entered his mind when he saw Duke heading for the rare of the boat. Sandra, being a woman, would be easy to overcome, he assumed. His main plot was not to attack Sandra. The local boat driver rather fancied her but only wanted to have the opportunity to go over the side, to safety. Having practiced since he was a young boy, he was a very strong swimmer. Alberto had done this distance for fun over and over again. Duke had somehow put paid to Alberto's plans. If Duke didn't go to the rare of the boat then Alberto's chance of escape would be impossible.

It was the deep voice of the scrawny manager that interrupted their thoughts. Duke heard the man call his name, "mister Duke" but he couldn't understand the rest of the message. "What's he saying", he began to ask the local man but he soon abandoned the question when he remembered the local man could not understand his language. Duke walked towards him but Alberto started to withdraw even further to the side of the boat from fear that Duke might attack him again. The crackling of the radio made it impossible for any of them to decipher clearly what was being said though Duke heard the manager's voice repeat his name again, "mister Duke". "Gimme that walkie-talkie apparatus over here", Duke demanded but the boat driver pretended that he didn't understand. Duke stretched over the man and removed the two-way radio from its cradle. "Why didn't I think of this earlier on", he asked rhetorically? Placing the radio close to his mouth, Duke shouted into the mouthpiece. "Garcia, we need some gas, got it . . . over", Duke said slowly. That was not the man's name but Duke felt it important to give him a name. When there was no reply Duke sent the message again but he changed it slightly, "Garcia, we need some gas, got it . . . yes", Duke mimicked. "Mister Duke", the voice said then trailed off again. The crackling was unbearable now but Duke kept on. "Mayday, mayday, Garcia, this is mister Duke here, no gas, mayday". There was another effort from Garcia but it was too weak for anyone to pick up clearly. Duke kept his eyes on the boat driver all the time he was talking into the radio. "I don't trust you, you shifty bastard", Duke cursed as the man looked up towards him. He walked backwards as he made his way towards the back of the boat, not trusting to turn his back on the boat driver. Duke picked up some of the fish that the trawler crew had so unsparingly thrown at them. "Looks like we're shipwrecked for a while might as well make the most of it," he told Sandra. He handed her the raw fish and when she squirmed, Duke reminded her of the many dishes of 'Sushi' they'd had, previously. The contact with the manager of the Marina had raised all their hopes slightly for a while but now they were feeling deflated by the lack of good quality reception. For a while even the boat driver felt there'd be a chance to be rescued by his friend, the manager of the Marina. He was frustrated by the bad reception too but he was used to it.

Garcia, as Duke would call him, paced up and down his little office wondering why the boat was so late back. He knew that Beth Tittye would hold him responsible if anything happened to "mister Duke". Garcia had had some contact. He was feeling a bit happier than he was before. Garcia sat on the rough stool but contemplated his next move. He lit one of the large Cuban-type cigars and rested his back on the wall of the office. His feet were on top of the table. He blew large as well as small smoke rings but day-dreamed *'the rescue'*, its implications and about that chance Beth Tittye had promised him abroad. She had told him that she would send him to Spaceville to study Marine Engineering but he knew so much about engines that he didn't think there was much anyone else could teach him about them. Garcia thought of the possibilities of working abroad and sending money for his wife and seven children. In his present job he was earning a mere 10,000 Del Shells per month. Allowing 1000 Del Shells per head of family, the rest was eaten up by the 2000 Del Shell rent he had to pay Sue Allen-Stokeley for the small house he needed for him and his family. Garcia would have seen the speedboat if he'd spent more time outside of his office but it and the title of Manager made him feel important. The cigar had gone out but he'd hardly noticed. Garcia tried to pull hard on the unlit cigar. He paused and looked at the stub of rolled tobacco leaves in his hand then lit it again. Garcia took yet more smoke into his mouth, pondered the possibility of taking his family away from a life of degradation of poverty then exhaled the smoke. The crackling of the radio made him jump as he returned to reality. "Garcia, if you can hear me, come out of your blasted hut and stand on the jetty", Duke demanded. Garcia placed the cigar in the corner of his mouth, looked at the two-way radio but cursed to himself. Any translation of his mumblings would exhibit the same degree of frustration as Duke or Sandra might have experienced in their own jobs. Garcia allowed the *'broken'* two-way radio to fall from his hands. It hit the side of the small wooden table he used as a desk and tumbled onto the sand floor; still dangling from its own flex. He ventured outside and for the first time in nearly two and a half hours, looked out to sea. Garcia was looking into the setting sun that was quickly disappearing below the line of the ocean. Shading his eyes from the reflections on the water, Garcia could make out the shape of the speedboat. He jumped, waved frantically but shouted, "Mister Duke, mister Duke". Some observers of this behaviour, in isolation, might have thought Garcia strange at least or that he had gone completely mad, whilst others, in the know, might feel empathy towards the worried man. Garcia had continued to work way beyond the hours he was being paid for but he could not let "Miss Beth" down. He just had to stay until "mister Duke" was accounted for. He raced along the jetty back to his office where he once again tried to contact Duke on the broken two-way radio. The excitement had overwhelmed the poor man. Garcia entered into the prayer *'mode'*, bowing his head in humility and giving thanks to his God for the *'miracle'* he'd prayed for. He had now decided to drive one of the other boats out to the speedboat he'd lent to Duke. Garcia took a huge torch, some life-saving rings attached to rope, two bottles of brandy and a fresh cigar with him. It took a few goes before the engine started but Garcia was happier now. He said some more prayers then lit the huge cigar. Duke saw the flickering from the jetty and told Sandra about it. She was tucked up under the tarpaulin, shivering in the evening breeze. The boat driver, Alberto, was cold too but he remained vigilant as the evening closed in. His fear of Duke was immense but he knew that, under the shadow of darkness, anything could happen. He prepared himself mentally for that time when he would make one almighty effort to go over the side. Duke had seen some huge fins in and around the waters where they were but Alberto was not aware of that particular fact. Duke didn't want to add to Sandra's fear so he kept it to himself.

The water was a bit choppier now and the strong irregular motions of the waves sometimes caused the boat to bob about recklessly. Sandra complained of feeling queasy again and Duke wanted to know what was happening. "Are you sure you're alright", he quizzed? He didn't give her time to reply. "You've been feeling queasy quite a lot lately, haven't you", Duke pressed? You are working too hard. We'll have to find time for more *'mini-breaks'* together", he advised. Sandra was happy about Duke's concern for her and she told him so. Sandra also told Duke that she was far too queasy and cold to discuss it and "it's far too personal for us to discuss with strangers", Sandra added diplomatically. Duke was overwhelmed by his passion for money. "I hope you haven't got a *'little bun'* in the oven", Duke replied. "That would just spoil everything that I've planned for you and don't forget the contracts that you've signed", he warned. Sandra felt as if her stomach was doing somersaults and she was feeling lonely now though Duke was by her side. She had thought that Duke might have reacted happily to news about her pregnancy but the thought of him rejecting *'their child'*, sent shock waves through her whole being. "How could you say such a thing Duke", Sandra retorted angrily? "Don't be a silly girl, do you know how much you are worth to the Industry", he asked pointedly? Without waiting for Sandra to reply, Duke told her openly, "billions sweetheart, bloody billions". "You can't have children now. You'd be throwing away a very long lucrative career. Can't you see that sweetheart", he asked? He didn't wait for Sandra to acknowledge or digest any of the information he was imparting. "It's only the other day Lord Fixit, Sir Ivanhoe Goldfeet and Sir Lawrence Dundus paid you a lot of compliments and suggested you take a star role in a new Soap Opera Series on television. I wanted to surprise you but, as it has come out, I might as well tell you now", Duke stated. There was no time for Sandra to reply as they could hear the sound of the engine of the other boat. Sandra's queasiness was no longer priority. She swiftly threw the tarpaulin aside but stood looking at the slow progress the other boat was making towards them. Duke jumped onto the box but started shouting, "over here, over here". Sandra joined in the shouting but her thin voice was covered by Duke's louder, coarser voice. They could see the light from the huge torch Garcia was pointing into the darkness. The light blue moonlight had failed to shine through the dark red clouds that sabotaged the natural heavenly light.

CHAPTER 46

In their excitement, they forgot the boat driver, Alberto. He knew that Duke could not hit him now while his colleague was so close. He got up into an upright position but tried to free his legs of the cramped feeling. At first, Alberto stumbled around, fell a few times then held on to what he could until he could feel 'tingling' as newly released blood slowly flowed back into his legs. Alberto had to shake them vigorously for a while before he felt his legs were strong enough to walk on. His face was now quite swollen from the beating that Duke had given him. His left eye was almost shut and the dried blood that trailed from his nostrils had darkened but stuck to the tracks they had formed. His side, where he had been hit in the kidneys, reminded him of the discomfiture and pain that he'd felt when he first received the blow. Alberto was now aware that his disability might just make it more difficult for him to escape. He listened to the droning of the engine of the old rescue boat but its approach was causing the speedboat to react strangely. It rocked, swayed and pitched awkwardly as the waves from the rescue boat, violently, crashed against it. Alberto fell backwards but skidded across the deck. Duke and Sandra went through similar experiences; both were sent tumbling to the deck too. With the motion of the boat, Sandra fell awkwardly then rolled over unto her back. Duke, in turn fell from the box but he had a softer fall than Sandra. He was lucky that the crumpled tarpaulin cushioned his fall. As Garcia pulled up alongside the speedboat, they collided. The thudding of the rescue boat unto the speedboat had thwarted any attempt, by each of the individuals, to get up. Garcia's demise was much different from the others. "Mister Duke, mister Duke", Garcia shouted as he struggled to maintain some sort of control over what was happening to the rescue boat. It had rebounded off the speedboat when they had impacted. The rescue boat had slid horizontally and then started to tilt unto its side. Water had entered the boat via the courtesy of the rogue waves that were, themselves, dancing to some irregular rhythm. Garcia had to let go of the torch and it disappeared in the same way as his hopes of staying alive, seemingly. The howling winds had swept away his desperate cries for help. There was no moon and the dark red rain clouds had set in. They were rolling around haphazardly as the winds, at altitude, forced the clouds into continuous confusion. Thunder boomed and lightning sent free electrical currents into motion, without care. The lightning was the only form of light. The low dark red storm clouds seemed to hang a bit closer to the surface of the water and made them appear like drapes hanging in a theatre scene. Garcia began to panic as the water rushed in over the side of the rescue boat. He prayed to his god for forgiveness for all the *'wrongs'* he'd done. Though he was in dire trouble, Garcia said prayers for his woman and their children. He even said a prayer for "mister Duke", his woman and Alberto his friend. He was quite sincere for he knew that his time had come and that for "mister Duke" and others, their hopes of survival might be lesser than they might be thinking. Garcia knew these waters and the weather more than Sandra and Duke. For the first time Sandra witnessed Duke panicking. He mumbled to himself as he held on close to her as a child would to his/her mother. "Whatever happens, I want you to know that I've left you something in my Will", Duke told her. He was trembling now, not only from the freezing conditions but also from inside. Fear had a special way of visiting individuals and Duke was no exception, though, if he could have bribed it, he would have done, perhaps! Duke had sensed fear before, when he was being bullied at junior school but he had always managed to fight back, whatever the circumstances. This time Duke was a broken man. There was no fight left within him. The situation was scary enough to cause any individual to reflect over vast collection of memories; especially those that remained vivid over time. As Duke flicked through the pages of the great tomes of his past, he acknowledged to himself that he was being humbled by nature. Duke had reached a point in his life where there was no hiding from the truth anymore, however blunt it manifested itself. He realized that no amount of clout could counter the hazards of natural catastrophes like what they were experiencing now. Fate was a great leveller. His, Sandra and Alberto's hopes of survival were very thin and he knew it. "Looks like we've had it, sweetheart", Duke mumbled vaguely. Sandra's response was rapid and certain. "Well, I'm not going to sit here and die", Sandra countered.

No one else, apart from Grant Favours and Beth Tittye, knew they were still out there. Beth Tittye was too committed, by way of directing events, to focus on Duke and Sandra alone. Tramp had caused great stir and conversation by performing for an audience. Grant Favours had taken it up on himself to produce this extra bit of entertainment for the crowd, who patiently awaited their special guest, Duke Stagg. Grant knew that Duke and Sandra were sometimes almost inseparable and that he, in particular, had downed a lot of the Champagne Urge Mk 3, while they were on the beach. It occurred to Grant that something was not quite right. Duke loved adulation and publicity. He had agreed with Grant to use the opportunity to help promote the new potent Champagne. Beth

Tittye came over to where he was in conversation with about a dozen or so people. They were standing around him. Some giggling almost foolishly, while others were giving signals that everyone was "having a swell time". "Isn't it wonderful", one woman commented. "I'm definitely coming back next year", another stated. The loud music drowned out half the conversations but nobody cared. Beth Tittye finally managed to get Grant away from the crowd. "I don't want to panic you but don't you think Duke and that girl should be back by now", she asked bluntly? "I was just thinking the same thing myself", Grant replied. They walked hurriedly towards Beth Tittye's office. Inside, they talked about gathering the people and announcing their concern about the late arrival of the majority owner of the Del Shell Hotel Complex. They would use his importance as the major reason for the bravery and heroism they would be asking from the volunteers. Having agreed the strategy, Beth and Grant returned to the guests. Beth asked the DJ to turn the music off then took the microphone from its stand. She addressed the crowd. "We are concerned because Duke would never stand up his guest, would he now", she asked rhetorically? The crowd were at first resentful that the music had been turned off but they were shocked into reality and they realized that a man's life was more important than frivolous antics which made them happy. There was a great buzz of hurried conversation everywhere in the hall. Grant took the microphone from Beth and told the people about the reward involved. "10,000,000 Del Shells will be paid cash if any group or singular individual rescued Duke. No questions asked", Grant assured them. Captain Plantain was amongst the first to respond. "Let's rescue mister Duke, yes", he challenged. In the confusion that followed, Tramp ran off from the stage. He was tired of the chaotic scene that had developed. The crowd was truly oblivious of the little dog and they were being careless where they put their feet. Tramp was only a small dog anyway but might have been trampled underfoot. He worked his way through the maze of feet; whimpering all the time but nobody could hear him. The most likely explanation for his whimpering could have been that he was scared by the uproar and probably his missing 'mommy' and 'daddy' too. Neither Duke nor Sandra was aware of Tramp's situation or that his and Sandra's absence had started such a rush to rescue them from the possible watery grave that they faced.

Sandra crouched down low but tried to make progress towards the side of the boat. "Be careful sweetheart", Duke cried. He followed her in the same crouched manner. The two of them braced themselves against the side of the boat. "Hold on, Duke", Sandra warned as he slipped back a few paces. "I'm alright, grab the side of the boat", Duke instructed. He could not see over the side but he instructed Sandra to relay the details of her observations. "Can you see Garcia", Duke asked? "I'm not sure but his boat is listing to one side", Sandra replied. The thought that Garcia had drowned sent new fear through them. "Can you see the light from the torch", Duke questioned? "No", Sandra replied. Duke's heart sunk and a lot of memories kept flooding back. His life had many chapters, each of which was, in volume, a complete book in their own right. Duke could feel his feet trembling. His body moved in irregular spasms and his lips trembled like an alcoholic, in remission, craving for a drink. Duke was aware that his feet were cramped but his lips moved involuntarily. The wind had suddenly dropped a bit and the rocking of the boat was no longer as severe as before. Duke, Sandra and Alberto had been stranded now for well over two and a half hours. Sandra was crying shamelessly because she also realized that the possibility of being rescued was looking bleaker by the minute. Duke tried to console her but Sandra, protected by the darkness, let out a 'blood-curdling' scream. It was long and shrill; sending even more shivers down Duke and Alberto's spines. He kept as quiet as he could because, although he could still hear the droning from the engine of the rescue boat, Alberto sensed that something had happened to Garcia. Alberto was intimidated by the awesome moods of the weather too. Its unpredictability was a constant reminder to a man like Alberto that humans really have no power except of their minds. He prayed silently, over and over, for his good friend, Garcia.

Though he and his rescue boat had taken a battering, Garcia was still hanging on despite the odds. He had a red and white 'ring' around him with one end of the rope attached to one of the hooks on the side of the boat. His legs were cramped and without feeling, his hands were so cold he could not feel his grip on the rough sisal rope. It had already severely bruised Garcia's palms but he was clinging on all the same. As he summoned strength from a greater depth than before, Garcia's resolve was to stay alive. He gripped the rope and, with as much strength as he could muster and hauled himself a little bit further onto the partially submerged boat. Sandra's eyes were a little more accustomed to the darkness now but she blinked several times as she tried to confirm if she had seen movement on the rescue boat. She wanted to be sure before she raised Duke's hope. Cautiously, Sandra told him that she saw some movement below. "I think it's him Duke, I think it's him", she repeated. Duke could not believe Garcia had survived but the news sent a slightly warmer feeling through his mind. "Are you sure you can see him down there", Duke queried? Sandra looked away for a moment then tried to re-focus on the rescue boat again. "I'm sure he is Duke, honey. I wish we had a torch though", Sandra stated intriguingly. Duke wrapped the tarpaulin tighter around them. "Never mind darling, we'll get out of this together or die together, won't we sweetheart, Duke asked? Alberto's sudden sneezing fit broke Duke and Sandra's conversation. In the darkness, their heads turned towards each other and their mouths dropped simultaneously. "Alberto", they both exclaimed. Whilst their attention had been taken by their quest to survive, Duke and Sandra had left themselves exposed. Alberto coughed, spluttered and sneezed continuously for at least 30 seconds. His condition seemed consistent with someone who was having the first signs of flu. Sandra drew Duke's attention to Alberto's predicament. "Let him cover with the other end of the tarpaulin Duke, its big enough to give him some shelter", she pleaded. Duke agreed with Sandra that the ordeal was borne by each of them and that it would be at least a good gesture to offer the boat driver minimum 'human rights'. "Ok, poor bastard must be freezing, yes", he joked. Sandra giggled too. "He'll have to wait until I can see him though. I don't trust Alberto an inch", Duke added. The breeze became lighter, barely ruffling the waters now. The dark red storm clouds were clearing and a hint of the light blue moonlight meant that visibility was somewhat improved. Duke approached Alberto. This time Duke did not call him names like *"slimy bastard"* but instead called him by the name he had given him. "Alberto, you don't sound too good, go on, take that end", he encouraged. Alberto watched as Duke demonstrated what to do with the tarpaulin. He understood Duke's offer but he did not take it up straight away. Alberto waited until Duke retreated sufficiently. He was grateful for the late offer and was thankful for the small mercy Duke was bestowing upon him. Sandra was pleased too that Duke had yielded to her suggestion. "Thank you Duke, honey", she said casually. A sudden flash of lights from the beach caught their attention. Sandra told Duke that she could see several boats, with flared torches, in the distance. As the speedboat was now more stable than before Duke placed the box by the side and stood on it. "Who needs Garcia now", he asked cynically? Sandra looked down into the rescue boat again and she could see Garcia clearly now. He had expelled a great deal of energy in his efforts to avoid being drowned. Though his thin sinewy body had taken a hefty beating from the strong currents and brutal encounters with the boat, Garcia's mental fortitude was well beyond what would be expected by scientists in Spaceville, assumedly. In reality, Garcia had gone way beyond his own mental and physical thresholds. He was thoroughly exhausted but had climbed back onto the stricken boat. Unlike Duke and Sandra, Garcia had no tarpaulin to keep him warm but he prayed even more than he'd prayed before and he gave thanks to his God for saving him from drowning. He also prayed to his God to save "mister Duke", his woman and his friend, the man Duke named Alberto.

Sandra was impressed by Garcia's survival. She acknowledged to herself that Garcia must have been guided or fated to survive. Her mother, Dian Bogus, had been a firm believer in an almighty power and had reminded Sandra about such power, repeatedly. "San-San, if yuh ask di Almighty fi guidance it will always be dere", Dian used to tell her. Sandra told Duke that her head was spinning from all the action that was taking place and that she was feeling queasy again. "This is all too much for me Duke", she moaned. "Quit bloody moaning, we're all in the same boat, ain't we", Duke asked firmly? "How could you think of puns at a time like this, Duke", Sandra asked disappointedly?

The flared flotilla of boats still seemed far enough away and even though Sandra and Duke were made aware of the enthusiasm of the people on board, they became impatient and on edge. So, when they heard the sound of a foghorn coming from behind them, it distracted their attention once again. Duke looked further out to sea from whence the sound originated. Aided by the clearance of storm clouds and the light from the bright bluish moonlight, Duke could see the huge lump of grey metal heading in their direction. "J. H. Christ, the bastards are coming at us" he exclaimed. Sandra could see the anxious look on his face. They were left in a grave dilemma. On one side, it looked as if the flotilla of boats would arrive too late to save them. On the other side, the fishing Trawler's sheer size was intimidating enough but seemed much closer than it actually was in distance. From Duke and Sandra's position they could only look from the Trawler to the flotilla of boats coming from the direction of the beach. The movements of Duke and Sandra's heads reminded one of watching a tennis match. She was extremely fearful at this stage. "Lets try and swim towards the boats", Sandra exclaimed. Memories from the past came rushing by. Each carefully parcelled like articles on a conveyor belt. Sandra reflected on her younger days when she and Raymond were both at Coleport College together. Their romance had been triggered by events and then they became lovers. Raymond was still her best lover to date. Sandra still carried his image, most vividly, around in her mind. Duke had no such romantic memories except for the time when he had told Doris Bendlow that he loved her. He didn't really mean it but those words had paved the way for the start of their everlasting sordid affairs. Privately, Duke thought that Doris more typified the type of personality that he most enjoyed being around, socially but not professionally. Duke and Sandra both recalled the earlier reactions of the fishermen. When Sandra reminded Duke, he took immediate action. Duke saw the life-saving belts that were attached to the rescue boat. "Garcia", "throw us a couple of those belts, will you", he shouted? Duke mimed his message while he said it. Garcia looked up and smiled. It was an extremely joyous moment in his life. Garcia felt relieved that "mister Duke" was still alive. During the violent behaviour of the wind and waves, Garcia could not be sure whether Sandra, "mister Duke" and Alberto had been washed out to sea. Confident now about Duke's survival, Garcia exclaimed assuredly. "Mister Duke, mister Duke, you live . . . yes". His voice was broken and hoarse yet there was a hint of relief in it. Sandra smiled at Garcia but he was unaware of her well intentioned smile. Instead, his whole concentration was geared towards rescuing "mister Duke". Garcia wielded the life-saving ring, like a lasso, but attempted to get it to "mister Duke". His hands were cold and numb but Garcia kept trying. It took at least four attempts before Garcia could throw the first life-saving belt high enough for Duke to get hold of it. He placed the first ring over Sandra's head, the following ring around himself and threw the third in the direction towards Alberto. "Cop hold of that", Duke said. The Trawler sounded its foghorn repeatedly. After several blasts, an enormous roar from the flotilla of boats from the opposite side got even louder than before but rivalled the sound of the foghorn. Comparatively, the scene took on a likeness to frivolous, fun-packed scenes at Association Football Matches. A foghorn would sound then 120,000 fans would roar back; consequently diminishing the significance of the foghorn. Duke could hear the people from the flotilla shouting his name and he knew that Beth Tittye and Grant Favours were behind the rescue attempt. Garcia heard the voices too and acknowledged to himself that Miss Beth would have participated in this rescue attempt. Although he did not know about the reward, Garcia considered it his duty to rescue "mister Duke". Garcia had experienced Miss Beth in an angry mood before and he didn't want that same experience again. Most of all, Garcia didn't want to be considered as incompetent. It would have hurt his pride. He was determined to carry out the rescue himself. Sandra and Duke watched the brave man as he skillfully attempted to displace the rest of the water from inside his boat with his bare hands. Every sinew, muscle and mental power was instinctively summoned to enable Garcia to complete his task. He beckoned for Sandra and Duke to make their way unto his boat. Sandra was the first to lower herself onto the rescue boat. Being tall she didn't have too much trouble, apart from slipping a couple of times. Duke's transfer would have been reasonably smooth too had the Trawler not sounded its foghorn again. He had turned his head towards the irritating sound just as he started to clamber over the side of the rescue boat. Duke swore as he hit the deck. "Must have a word with Beth about that blasted Trawler", Duke piped then he spoke to Garcia. "Took your time, didn't you", Duke commented? Garcia was praying again. He kept bowing to Duke saying, "Mister Duke, I save you, yes"? He handed Duke the two bottles of brandy. Duke's eyes bulged when he saw the booze. "This Garcia is quite a smart so-and-so after all, isn't he", Duke asked? He quickly unscrewed the top but gulped the booze. Duke handed Sandra the bottle and told her to "get that down ya". Sandra was tempted but refused the drink. She remembered the meaning behind the queasy feelings. "I'd rather not", she said politely refusing Duke's offer. "Don't know what you're missing, sweetheart", he commented. He could feel the burning sensation in the back of his throat. Duke ordered Garcia to head for the beach. He impressed upon

Garcia that he would give him 100,000 Del Shells if he got him and Sandra to the beach, safely. "...and don't stop 'til you get there", he chimed. 100,000 Del Shells was an awful amount of money to a man of Garcia's current status. It was almost a year's wages. Garcia showed concern for his colleague, Alberto, as well. "Mister Duke, my friend, driver of Speedboat", Garcia insisted. He did not want to disobey orders from "mister Duke" but he remained concerned about Alberto, his close friend. "I understand, yes", Duke replied. He pointed towards the slow flotilla of boats coming towards them. "They'll take care of him, yes", Duke assured him. Garcia was not totally convinced, even though there was 100,000 Del Shells on offer but he did not dare argue with one as important as "mister Duke", yes! He turned the rescue boat around and started his journey back towards the jetty. They had travelled only a short distance away from the speedboat when they heard an almighty crash. Looking round they saw the Trawler but not the speedboat. It had disappeared from view altogether and so did Garcia's good friend, Alberto. The Trawler continued on its reckless path; heading for its main target, the rescue boat. Duke urged Garcia to "step on it" but the old boat was not made to travel as fast as the speedboat that had just been destroyed. The flotilla of boats was getting closer to the rescue boat. They had started out in orderly formation but, because of the threat from the Trawler, were no longer a disciplined convoy. Instead, they got into each other's paths. The terrified escapees threw their flamed torches into the water, each heading back towards the beach.

Garcia's rescue boat took rather a zigzag pattern in its attempt to avoid the fishing Trawler. Sandra looked much paler than her normally deep tanned self while Duke tried even harder than before to convince Garcia to get them to safety. "Here", he said as he removed the huge diamond encrusted gold chain from around his neck but placed it around Garcia's. The manager of the Marina was most impressed by Duke's generosity but his own life was also at risk and he longed to be with his family. Weighted down by the heavy diamond encrusted gold chain, Garcia found it quite difficult to keep his thin, scrawny neck straight. He did not know the true value of the piece of jewelry but could guess that if a man as important as "mister Duke" wore it, then it should have immense value. Garcia peeked through the corners of his eyes at both Duke and Sandra. He observed the scary masks of fear on their faces but wondered why they had left his friend, Alberto, on the Speedboat. "Mister Duke, mister Duke, where my friend", Garcia asked sadly? Sandra was feeling quite queasy again but this time it was a matter of conscience that was causing the nauseous feelings to revisit. The tears began to fill her eyes. Duke saw those tears but kissed Sandra's cheek. "Don't be upset, sweetheart. We can't change anythink now", he offered. Duke knew Garcia's comments had triggered this latest bout of tears. He patted Garcia on his back and told him of his own experience of "losing a good mate". Duke recalled the time when he was fourteen. He had found his friend, John Crowe, dying in the gutter. John and his twin Jim were Duke's very close friends and he remembered how he'd felt when John gave up his last breath. His brother Jim Crowe survived but became even a bigger bully altogether than his brother John. Jim was strong-minded but hell-bent on *'influencing'* the feeble minded by force. He had even more clout than the then young Duke though not as streetwise as him. In reply to Garcia's last question though, Duke emphasized that the gift of the diamond encrusted gold chain was only a token offer of thanks to him for saving their lives. "See, that won't make up for the loss of your mate, Alberto, but you'll never look back now.

This chain is the only one of its kind. It's immensely valuable and will bring you many Del Shells. Wait and see", Duke encouraged. Garcia clearly didn't understand much of Duke's words but he realized by the urgency of his miming, that Duke was worried about his friend's absence. There was a brief pause before Duke spoke again. "You can tell the people Alberto died while doing his duty, yes", he said. This latest statement by Duke did not explain whether Alberto had volunteered to stay on the speedboat. It did not pacify Garcia's anxiety about his missing friend but he had already decided he'd sell the chain. He'd give half the proceeds to those he knew as Alberto's family. Garcia looked at Duke but smiled. His mind wandered briefly as he looked down at the solid, diamond encrusted, gold chain. How much was the chain worth? Garcia had no idea but somehow he knew that, if a man as important as mister Duke wore it, then it could be worth a few thousand Del Shells, at least.

Some from the flotilla of small boats had already made it back to shore and had joined those others who had stayed on the beach. The torch bearers on Shelly Beach moved unto the concrete Walkway that led from the beach out to sea. As seen from the beach, the design of the Walkway was a horizontal line of about 60 yards wide parallel to the shoreline of the beach. Both ends were being supported by two parallel right angled supports about 45 yards in length at either end which joined the horizontal line but linked it to the shoreline. Each block that built both the horizontal and parallel right angled lines at either end leading from the shoreline were made up of 9 x 5' square concrete blocks. There was heavy meshing surrounding the lower parts of the complete structure, effectively keeping out unwanted visitors like sharks for instance. The Del Shell Hotel had advertised itself as the safest beach in that part of the world. Those Walkway areas were filled to capacity with people bearing torches, even though the full moon had now fully manifested itself.

Garcia had managed to steer his rescue boat to a calculated safe area; one in which he knew the Trawler could not follow. Now safely betwixt and between some of the older boats mooring in and around the jetty, Garcia steered expertly through them towards the huge concrete structure. The crowd noticed the change in direction of the Trawler. Collectively, they cheered loudly. Now they could see that Garcia's expertise had secured Duke's safety, the crowd continued to shout enthusiastically. Duke and Sandra were waving back at the cheering crowd but Garcia, being a very humble man, remained low key. Tears of emotion overwhelmed his otherwise gaunt appearance but immediately displayed the humility within Garcia's being. Sandra, Duke and Garcia looked behind them but saw that the Trawler was indeed veering away now; changing direction just in time to avoid crashing into the jetty and the remainder of boats that had been left there. "That was bloody close. Well done Garcia", Duke said. Garcia smiled and mumbled through clenched teeth. Neither Duke nor Sandra heard or cared what Garcia was saying. Duke turned to Sandra but hugged her tightly. "We live to tell the tale, Sugarcake", he said and smiled at her. "Just", Sandra replied. Garcia fell to his knees and offered prayers of thanks to his God for getting them to safety. He had managed to save the very important "mister Duke" and his woman from the jaws of death. Least of all, Garcia thought, his God had managed to save his life as well. The rescue boat drifted with the gentle tide, sometimes bumping into the scattered boats mooring in the waters close to the jetty. Several foghorn blasts soon brought their attention back to reality but they needn't be alarmed as the Trawler was heading back out to sea.

Beth Tittye, Grant Favours and Captain Plantain were amongst the first of the crowd to shout their mode of approval for the heroic Garcia. "He's a real hero", one voice shouted out. "Three cheers for the man who saved 'mister Duke' and the future of Costa Del Shell", shouted Captain Plantain. He wanted his comments to reflect how proud he was of his fellow islander for his skill and deep determination to complete the rescue but he also wanted to sing his approval for "mister Duke", yes! The thing with people like Captain Thursday Plantain was that his subservience to the perception of the Duke image came out via the way in which he expressed himself. One of the people who sensed this overdone *'Loyalty Syndrome'* was Grant Favours. He was a master of overplayed roles. In his profession, everything always had to be to clichéd formulae. To enable individuals to capture empathy from their audience almost by way of a type of commercially psycho-analytic blindfolding, all roles had to be grossly overplayed. With his captive audience totally immersed in *'Spin'*, Grant was competently able to manipulate them and be in complete control of every situation. That certain over-exuberance in tone was what Grant heard in Captain Plantain's voice. He indicated to Captain Plantain that he needed to "tone it down a bit". Duke was the first to be assisted up onto the parallel concrete structure. People rushed to hug him and slap him on the back. "You had us worried for a while", Grant said. He hugged Duke tightly but almost too affectionately, perhaps! "What would we do without you", Beth Tittye asked? She crushed him towards her huge frame, kissing him on both cheeks. This was more a custom of the host nation but Beth Tittye thought the greeting reflected warmth and endearment. Duke was feeling quite elated by the warm greetings that he was getting from his friends and the crowd. He looked over towards the two outer Walkways and realized that staff as well as holiday makers alike gathered, waiting to greet them. There was a slight altercation along the narrow structure. A woman was trying to get through to see Duke but she didn't want to wait her turn in the queue. "Let me through to him" she insisted. Other people who were in front turned on her but ordered her to wait. "You'll have to wait like everyone else", a man told the woman.

Beth Tittye made the first move to help the next person onto the concrete structure. Shouts of "he . . . ro" made the moment extra special. Garcia was smiling from ear to ear but he did not seem as enthusiastic as the others. As he looked out to sea, Garcia could not hold back the tears. He cried unashamedly but fell to his knees. "Give him some air", Beth Tittye ordered. She thought Garcia had collapsed. He knelt on the concrete platform and openly thanked his God for completing the rescue but he also promised his God that he would return to try to find his friend, Alberto. The crowd watched patiently until Garcia had finished praying. He stood up and glanced out to sea again. Sandra watched from the rescue boat. She longed to be helped unto the concrete platform too. Duke's elation and Garcia's dramatics had taken the people's attention. Sandra felt abandoned. Duke did try to make his way back to her but he'd wandered too deeply into the crowd. It was travelling in one direction only and that was back towards terra firma, unto the sandy beach. Sandra wondered why Duke hadn't come to get her out. "Can somebody give me a hand, please", she pleaded. Though they were within touching distance, not even one person from the crowd acknowledged Sandra's plea. To them, she was not important. It was as if it was deliberate, she thought. Sandra remembered how she gained attention when she was younger. Often times, when Sandra wanted attention then, she would stamp her feet and scream until she was noticed. Sandra took a deep breath but bellowed out a blood-curdling cry for "heeeeelllllpppp". Duke identified the sound of Sandra's voice immediately. "That's my sweetheart, Sandra", he commented. Duke told the people to "shut your bloody row, be quiet" and they obeyed. The silence held demonstrably long enough for Duke to reply to Sandra's plea. He was quite astounded how the people parted to enable him to go, unhindered, to his sweetheart's side. His short legs were pumping like pistons yet the flip-flops tended to slow him down a bit. "Just coming Sugarcake", Duke kept repeating. One woman, who couldn't get a clear view of him, unwittingly, edged her way into Duke's path. He moved away from the entranced woman but bumped into some of the others on the side of the platform. That action caused a few people to topple over the safe side and into the water below but Duke would never have known. Sandra felt extremely proud that at last Duke's action to rescue her, would gain her authenticity amongst both the holiday makers and indigenous people of Costa Del Shell. As he got closer to her, Duke tripped on one of the flip-flops that had got caught under his feet. This caused Duke's balance to be unstable. He pitched forward and headlong over the side where the old boats were moored. Duke's belly-flop caused a huge splash and he felt the impact of the water against his body. He let out a cry that indicated he was hurt. Some water had got into Duke's mouth. Gulping for air, he swallowed some of the salty water but disappeared from the view of the observers.

"Oh no", Beth Tittye cried. "Oh my god", Grant Favours responded. He was wringing his hands nervously and crossing his legs as if the excitement was causing him a kidney functional problem. The reaction of Captain Plantain though was quite commendable. Dressed in his pilot's uniform, adorned with medals, he dived in to save Duke. The Captain's braided peaked cap was still attached to his head even after he'd entered the water. He swam stylishly towards where Duke had fallen. His head bobbed up but then he went under again, this time for much longer. Sandra was feeling queasy again but this time even Duke would have been empathetic towards her. He was running to help her but now his life was endangered by the fall. Sandra turned away from the parallel structure, ran across the deck of the boat to the other side but pulled herself up and over the side. She swam under water with her eyes open. Sandra blinked rapidly as the strong salt water burnt her eyes. She was determined that she would save Duke. Sandra had to come up to get some air. She took another deep breath before she dove again. Sandra could see that one of Duke's legs was caught. He was struggling to free himself from the tangled meshed nets that were part of the rubble, often off-loaded into the sea. Sandra's technical competency in the breast-stroke worked to Duke's advantage. She reached to the place where Duke was shackled but worked to free him. Duke's lungs felt as if they were about to explode. He needed air desperately. Sandra worked quickly. Having removed the netting, Sandra patted Duke's foot. He used his legs like flippers but advanced towards the surface. Captain Plantain had reached the surface before both Duke and Sandra. He saw when Duke and then Sandra broke the surface. Captain Plantain swam towards them. Duke, Sandra and Captain Plantain were all strong swimmers but the force of ebbing tide caused them to drift away from the parallel structure. All three of them treaded water but held a brief conversation. The Captain was pointing toward the shore. Sandra and Duke visibly nodded their approval to his suggestion. Duke Sandra and Captain Plantain swam across the tide towards one of the 'L' shaped ends of the concrete structure. The previously shocked crowd was now cheering wildly again. As Captain Plantain looked towards them he noticed how the clapping motion of the crowd reminded him of the colony of seals that lived on the other side of the island. Sandra was slightly ahead of the others. She appeared to be gliding through the water, her sleek aerodynamic figure intermingling with each atom of water particle. Duke was second in line, doing the *'western crawl'* style swim stroke. Captain Plantain reverentially trailed behind both Sandra and "mister Duke".

When she saw the fins coming out of the water, Beth Tittye shouted out the first warnings. "Shark, shark", she cried. These warnings were echoed by the rest of the crowd too. Many varieties of advice were offered to the trio but that was all the crowd could do, literally. Using his short stubby arms like oars in a famous annual boat race back on Planet Earth, Duke led the race towards the shore. He had caught up but gone past Sandra. Captain Plantain heard when Duke had said the words "everyman for himself". Although he didn't understand what Duke meant, Captain Plantain knew all about survival. Several powerful butterfly swim strokes brought him close to the others in a very short time. Garcia jumped back into the rescue boat but maneuvered through the old boats once again. He positioned the boat in between the fins and the trio giving them more time to escape. The noise from the engine of the rescue boat disturbed the sharks and gave the trio a real chance of escape from the marine carnivores. Now that the trio were safely out of the shark-infested water, Garcia returned to his office to fetch another torch. He headed back out to sea to search for his friend, Alberto.

Sandra, Duke, Beth Tittye, Grant Favours and Sue Allen-Stokeley celebrated until the early hours of the following morning. There was an abundance of Champagne Urge Mark 3 for all to rekindle their inner drive for sex. Kerri O'ki repeated the *'Dancing Hall Queenbee'* vibration dance movement to the delight of the visiting tourists. As Ambassador, Kerri O'Ki drafted in some other young girls whom joined her in the extravagant sexually implicit movements. Many of the female tourists engaged in copying Kerri O'Ki's *'Dancing Hall Queenbee'* movements as best they could. Even though some looked rather awkward but showed not as much flexible fluency, all seemed to enjoy exhibiting and flaunting what they had to flaunt. They were encouraged by the new attention they were getting from their respective partners and admirers alike.

Beth Tittye and Sue Allen-Stokley got into a fit of jealous rage over the overbearing charm and attention each was getting from Captain Plantain. In order to placate the two women, Captain Thursday Plantain ended up in a threesome compromise with the two Spacevillean tigresses. There was no limit to their superlative thirst for satisfaction. Whether it was the potency of Champagne Urge Mark 3 or by some other means only known to the islanders, Captain Plantain managed to preserve the folklore about exotic men's longevity. Sue Allen-Stokeley had been his regular visitor but the often ignored Beth Tittye was the most demanding of Captain Plantain's energy. Hidden behind that huge awkward frame was a real woman with needs just as genuine as those others, like Sue Allen-Stokeley, who was purporting to be the *'finished'* article by default or by *'re-design'*. She had sunk to a very low level, probably. Women like Sue Allen-Stokeley had made deliberate choices to be mentally and physically *re-sculptured*, perhaps! With the advent of the *'Human Engineering Facilitation'*, these women chose to make those decisions to re-construct their natural bodies, shapes and images. The man they called 'The Professor' stated that some individuals like Sue Allen-Stokeley were rather low in self-worth, diminished in self-confidence and self-esteem. The Walynski Institute's Report showed that "not many women or men with such extremely low self-worth saw *'Human Engineering Re-sculpturing'* as *'self-harming'* but it is a fact that it is". Through his Research, the man they called 'The Professor' drew references to those individuals psyche that had been breached by the relentless slants (programming and conditioning) as to how one should look or be. Professor Walynski stated that the Walynski Institute's Study had implied that over 73% of the individuals, who took part in the National Survey on the parallel virtual planet agreed that not even the biblical ***Jesus Christi*** had been known or expected to perform such *'miracles of perfection'* as the new self-proclaimed modern ***'Human Gods'***. In The Walynski Institute's Journal, Professor Walynski stated that 'HERO', the *'Human Engineering Re-sculpturing Organisation'*, had created a new industry through an extremely effective form of psychological *'politically accepted trickery'* known as the *'sleight of subliminal indoctrination'*. Similar to religious *'conversion'*, it targets the *'Belief Systems'* of individuals. Its aims and objectives seemed not dissimilar to that which had been used in the *'modelling industry'* in previous generations but had the same type of addictive *'post-hypnotic'* impact upon the human psyche. The *'neural profiling'* process was applied so subtly that individuals believed that they were the ones making the decisions to seek the ***'perfect body structure'***.

On the virtual parallel planet of Asteroidia, ***'neural self-harming'*** was becoming far too frequently accepted as being *'normal'*, probably! Professor Walynski stated that individuals who believed that they were making their own decisions were being duped. They were being persuaded by *'subliminal messaging'* about the *'superficial trend'*. He questioned the stability of the mental well being and the states of those individuals' minds at the time of their decision to have reconstructive surgery to re-sculpture their bodies. He raised the argument for debate but referenced the same type of *'values and beliefs'* which brought about *'Bulimia Nervosa'* and *'Anorexia'*. These two sets of evidence pointed to decisions being made by targeting individuals with extremely low self-worth. They were being asked to conform to a particular psychological *'stereo-tripe'* *'Gospel'*. The bearer of such ***'Good News'*** did not only shout it out but also inveigled individuals to become *'converts'* to the serialised popular *'stereo-hype'* about "the importance of seeking the ultimate in *'perfectionism'*". The *'stereo-type'* *'models'* who fitted those *'roles'* sought the ultimate in *'perfectionism'* from their ***'Human Gods'*** but were representative of the *'politically accepted'* *'Role Model'* Socialites. While the majority of the *'wannabee'* Socialite *'converts'* had to resort to loans from family members, friends, colleagues or other financial resources, the *'real'* Socialites cavorted their affable financial abilities to choose to address their *'imperfections'* through body re-sculpturing (*'self-harming'*), publicly. These individuals bore the *'hallmarks'* of their ***'Human Gods'*** as testaments in order to infer 'HERO', Human Engineering Re-sculpturing Organisation, as being *'authentic'* and *'normal'*. The man they called 'The Professor' said he too had weighed up the number of Case Histories to which he referred. They proved Professor Walynski's Study to be on point. The man they called 'The Professor' commented further about the states of minds of individuals, who no longer loved themselves. He said those individuals were making such a statement, when they made decisions to abandon their *'natural body form'* but selected to *'recreate'* the perception of who they were being inveigled to become, instead. Both these eminent genial men said that what the *'converts'* did not know is that the captains of the re-sculpturing industry were being heavily financed by squillionaire puppeteers poly-tricksters and their puppets, the politicrats. They often hailed the *'Human Gods'* as *"pioneers"* and as the ideal *'models'* who fit the particular *'roles'*. They rewarded them publicly with awards and titles also.

In concert with the man they called 'The Professor', Professor Walynski carried out a survey called 'Planet Survey'. This included both 1st Royal Royal Dis-United Stately Kingdoms as well as 5th rated exotic continents, countries and islands. Since publishing their findings, they also featured extracts of interviews with some of the individuals, who admitted that, at the time of making the decision to physically re-invent newer versions of themselves, their self-worth were extremely low indeed. Some reinforced that their minds were far too busy and they hadn't acknowledged or understood their reactive depressive states of minds. It seemed inevitable that, without meaningful interventions, some individuals had found it quite a struggle to think clearly let alone made such life changing decisions whilst they were being dragged deeper into spirals of decline. Significant others complained that they felt invaded by the *'new look'* stranger but complained that at times it was like welcoming home an *'imposter'* into their homes

Some others were adamant that they had made the right decisions and that they had no regrets because they didn't like the *"old physical versions"* of themselves anyway. The Walynski 'Blog Site' bore even more testament as significant others weighed in with their comments. Largely, there was a split between the *'pro'* and *'anti'* arguments about the importance of 'HERO', the Human Engineering Re-sculpturing Organisation. Both sets of arguments were accepted as valid by The Walynski Institute. Significantly though, parents on both sides of the debate confirmed they no longer recognised the children they birthed or nurtured. Some children said they no longer recognised their parents. Significant individuals said that they had accepted the change to their body forms in order to convey a much deeper message. This they reported as a *'cry for attention'*. Both the man they called 'The Professor' and Professor Walynski hinted at a need for individuals to be become more aware of any loss in confidence, their levels of esteem and their evaluations of self-worth. They ask individuals to seek expertise in these areas to enable them to maintain reasonable mental health and well being.

The expansion of the *'philosophy of perfectionism'* in itself was a statement being made by the *'disciples'* who preached it but foisted it upon the psyche of the *'converts'* elect. Professor Walynski said that "as long as individuals thought they needed *'re-sculpturing'* they might be making statements that for whatever reason (1) they made a conscious decision not to love but reject the *'old physical version'* of themselves instead (2) their perception of imperfection/perfection was confirmation of their level of *'delusion'* (3) they had surrendered to a particular *'mentality'*, willingly or unwillingly (4) that they had ceded control of who they are to someone outside of themselves. In order to substantiate these arguments, the man they called 'The Professor' referred to some Case Histories. He said, "individuals slid into *'reactive depression'* through some traumatic *'Life Experience'* events which had rendered them devoid of or with little or no *'self-worth'*". The written feedback from his seminars allowed for anonymity and so individuals, who felt like *'victims'* of troubling *'Life Experiences'* were more than willing to share with him. The man they called 'The Professor' said that the trend towards this new expression of *'self-harming'* was very worrying. He said the pattern seemed to be the same all over the World of Space, including the exotic islands, countries and continents. As *'new resources'* were being made available to *'help'* individuals towards *'correcting'* *'imperfections'*, apparently, there were concerns from significant others about each generation, who were following the seemingly *'normal'* recurring practice of re-sculpturing their bodies!

More women like Sue Allen-Stokeley were being deliberately driven to unquestionably accept someone else's *'values and beliefs'* of what they should look like. Through aggressive advertising, many like her, had swallowed the *'stereo-tripe'* but was easily persuaded to believing the *'stereo-hype'* about the *'stereo-type'* imagery that was being demanded of them through a process called and Neuro-bigotry by the green humanoid robotrons. Sue Allen-Stokeley and others like her had no idea that they were being fed these *'stereo-tripe'*, *'stereo-hype'* and *'stereo-type'* mental imagery through the embedding of subliminal messaging known as Neuro-profiling. It was causative to inveigle individuals to *'voluntarily'* submit themselves to the *'values and beliefs'* of an industry that had been formed to prey on their vulnerabilities, probably! Captain Plantain found Sue Allen-Stokeley's *'model'* nigh on being intrinsically irresistible and she found his defined firm muscular body the type of image she'd come to accept as her ideal *'Trophy Man Image'*, *'Mr Right'*. Beth Tittye had found that under Captain Plantain's uniform was the revelation of a very well honed *'model'* specimen. It was the type of image that women like her only dreamed of let alone fitting into a *'role'* of being next to him in bed. Sue Allen-Stokeley didn't know it yet but Beth Tittye was well stirred up by the sensual excitement she had experience but was focused and determined to have it repeated more frequently; sooner rather than later. What Captain Plantain didn't know is how exacting a fired up Beth Tittye might prove to be, maybe!

Although the rest of the holiday had gone rather well for Duke and Sandra. The only sad news was that Tramp had gone missing. Duke and Sandra cried for two days and Beth Tittye begged them to forgive her. She was determined to find the dog but offered 120,000 Del Shells of her own money as an incentive to find the dog. Neither Duke nor Sandra blamed Beth Tittye. They understood how difficult it must have been to concentrate on Tramp while arranging the flotilla of volunteers to attempt to rescue them from the likes of the fishing Trawler boat and the sharks. Grant Favours had made the entire government of Costa Del Shell aware of the hunt to find the missing dog.

CHAPTER 47

Duke's return to Spaceville meant that he had to carry through the promises he had made to Sandra while on holiday in Costa Dell Shell. They had purchased a mansion in Poshborough. Their nearest neighbour was at least a mile away. Sandra felt grateful to Duke for his generosity but she now had new demands too. She told him that she wanted to be his wife. Duke was beside himself by such revelations. He wanted to get rid of the *'old dragon'*, the woman *"with a face like the back of a bus"*. Even though his current wife, Dora had his two children and had astutely handled the money with the expertise of an accountant, Duke found Sandra more attractive to be with. Well, for one she was much younger than him and he prided himself to be seen next to this extraordinarily beautiful model of his ideal woman. Her status as super model and 'A' Blister actress did boost his image too. Duke knew that Sandra was everything any man would want, probably! He also felt threatened by Raymond's athletic body but feared that if he didn't pamper Sandra immensely, she might return, as most women seem to tend to do, to her first love, who took her virginity. There was no way that Duke was going to let go of his exotic bird, especially not now that she had agreed to marry him. Duke felt he had waited so long to hear these words. He was more than determined now to end his association with the boring Dora. Duke had come to dislike everything about her. Dora didn't dress like Sandra nor was she as ambitious as her. The delay in the divorce had made Duke edgy with his wife. She taunted him each time they met. "I suppose you spent the night with that little Miss Whore no. 1 again, didn't you", Dora incited? "Stop your nagging, woman ... sqquaak, sqquaak", Duke jeered. He made faces and sometimes threw fits of tantrum as if he was a child. Duke didn't wait for Dora to respond. Instead, he poured more gas on the flame. "Why is this dam divorce taking so long? It's more money, is it? O.K I'll fix it. I'll move out and leave you and the kids here in the house but I want to see my kids", he continued. Dora felt his sarcastic remarks were to be challenged so she decided to reciprocate. "That's if they want to see you", Dora replied. She was a very intelligent woman and Dora knew that Duke was jealous of her academic achievements. Dora also knew that whenever she reflected back the intensity of sarcasm, Duke would begin to launch a more personal verbal attack. He hesitated then commented. "I hate you. Look at you dressing the way you do. You dress like a *'hippy'*, you do. I bought you pearls but you choose to wear them bloody beads instead. I can't take you anywhere without people pointing you out", Duke ranted.

It was not just the words but the frequency and intensity of Duke's last comments that seemed to break this dedicated woman's spirit. The personal attacks had worn down her defence. Dora Stagg was in tears now. She hung her head as she wept. Her shoulders were hunched and Dora covered her ears as if to soften the sound of Duke's harsh criticism. Anguished and pained by the feuding, she looked at Duke and for the first time desired to be with someone else, permanently. Dora yearned for that someone, who might be able to appreciate her for whom she truly was. She was a plain, unfussy woman, who didn't find riches a route to happiness. Dora Stagg considered happiness a treasure seldom found amongst people, generally. Although when they first started courting, she was 10 years younger than Duke, Dora knew that he didn't marry her for her looks. She had hoped that over time her talent for watching the pennies and her common-sense approach might capture Duke's attention. "It'd be a matter of a few years 'til you start to love me", Dora had told him when they had first met. Now she was aware that Duke would never let go of the type of women to whom he was attracted or by whom was attracted to his riches. "I know you hate me Duke but I don't know why. Why Duke, why Duke, why", Dora asked repeatedly? He reached into his briefcase but pulled out a copy of 'Ooooppzssz' Magazine. He threw it on the floor in front of her. The picture of a much greener airbrushed image of Sandra with the exposed breast looked back at Dora from the floor. "Have a look at that. You haven't even got anything like this, have you", Duke asked boastfully? This bold affront was a deliberate ploy to upset his wife. Duke knew that flaunting Sandra's picture in front of Dora would be a painful experience but he didn't care. He had hoped to trigger her into speedier action about the divorce. Duke was desperate to make Sandra his wife. He wanted to humiliate Dora into submission. She was hurt by Duke's blatant reminder of her smaller breasts which he had told her reminded him of "two fried eggs". Dora decided to deride Duke's prized *'possession'* and to demean the importance he attached to his incumbent catch. "It's only a photo, I don't see why you men have to get so excited over a photo", Dora countered skillfully. She knew that Duke was baiting her but she was determined to belittle his efforts to upset her anymore. Because Dora did not succumb to the baiting, Duke got into a fit of temper. "Shut your gob before I . . .", he threatened. He looked at the position of his hands on his wife's throat. "I ought to ring your bloody neck, you slut", Duke raged. His eyes stared but reflected the depth of hate he was feeling. Dora now appeared like a piece of junk he had discovered during spring cleaning that he needed to place in the dumpster. Her eyes started to bulge.

With the intensity of rage rising to a much higher level, Duke revealed that he was aware of the relationship between Dora and her chauffeur, Calvin Poser. "Hanging out with my old chauffer now, are we? That's your type I suppose. I'm tired of people telling me that they see you and him smooching in the car. I'll teach you . . . you cheap bitch", Duke growled. There was a hint of jealousy and a hint of cynicism in the tone of his voice. Dora had taken a fancy to the pushy chauffeur.

Alan Baitman, the Private Investigator hired by Duke, had reported to him about Dora and Calvin spending many wild nights together. What Duke didn't know is that Dora had a superlative urge too for being in the company of an exotic man. She too had needs that she believed an exotic man could fulfill. The rumours that men from exotic continents, countries and islands were renowned for their penises being of a more generous length and girth and that their rhythmic *'dance'* were more alluringly sensual, led women like Dora to seek them out. Women like Dora had superlative urges to experience the manifestation of their deeply hidden orgasmic challenges. Duke had taken the woman with "the face like the back of a bus" for granted for too long. He failed to realize that she too had feminine needs to be fulfilled. Dora found that Calvin lived up to the stereo-typical reputation of the men from the far off exotic continents, countries and islands. Calvin was to Dora what Raymond was to Sandra. Calvin's foreplay was much different. His techniques were from a more natural progression to Duke's more programmed and conditioned pornographic preferences. Duke's wham, bam, thank you ma'am sprint never satisfied the adorable, caring, patient, dependable wife. Calvin made Dora feel good by paying her a lot of compliments. Apart from telling her how much she was appreciated, he also threw her the type of compliments that every relationship needed in order to survive. Dora felt that just existing like a piano accompaniment in the marriage was not a necessary element in the composition of the type of *'marriage model'* she had aspire towards She didn't feel that Duke and her were in *'synch'* with each other.

Being physically battered by Duke, the *'wife beater'*, did not do anything for raising Dora's self-esteem, either. Duke's constant derogatory remarks sapped her self-worth often. Dora had remained in the marriage for the children's sake. She wanted them to have a stable background. Dora had seen or heard of too many children who had only one parent. She didn't want to be a *'single'* parent. Her aspirations were driven by the various *'single parent'* groups, which she supported but were often criticized and ridiculed by the emotionally insensitive Duke. Dora was never shown any appreciation by Duke for her resolve and dedication to their relationship. Calvin made her feel appreciated. He was tender and understanding with her. Dora was enjoying the relationship with her *'exotic'* man while Duke was busy wooing his *'exotic'* bird. Now being caught up into his emotional tempest, he was loosing control. Duke squeezed Dora's neck a bit tighter. She struggled as she saw the twisted look upon his face. Dora feared Duke's *'old'* personality trait was returning.

As a young man, Duke's jealousy drove him to quite cruel exhibitions of deep rage. Once when they were courting, Duke and Dora were dining in a posh Hotel with several other young hopefuls, who were competing for few places with Elite Media News. They were the giants every young hopeful would have wished to work for. Duke had kept his eyes on the young man, who had stopped to give young Dora a Rose. He snatched it out of the man's hands but grabbed him by the large tie he was wearing. As the man grasped for air, Duke stuffed the flower, worm and all, into his mouth. "That will teach you ... you cheeky bastard", Duke had said. His stubby arms were strong and his huge fist crashed into the man's face. Both men grappled but fought like dogs in the wild. Duke found the man quite a handful. They struggled, tilted but swayed until they tumbled unto the table. Some people screamed as items like the thin stemmed champagne glasses and bottles crashed to the floor. Some individuals were either too embarrassed or fearful to comment openly. Others started to make their way out of the Dining Suite. While the two men struggled and fought like snarling dogs but striking without care, the captive audience was helpless. The sound of the two men's grunting and groaning mixed in with the peripheral screams, technical advice, betting as well as empathetic and opposite comments about Duke permeated the Suite. Some thought he was a show-off and a bully. Some hoped that someday someone would test him to his full capacity and beat him at his own game, probably! Others commented about expected behaviour, protocol and ethics. "Someone stop them", a voice shouted. The two men rolled around, each battling to gain control. A woman screamed at Duke but accused him of lacking in class. "Young man, you can't do that sort of thing here", a matured woman scolded. Her piercing voice had got to Duke. Glancing over his right shoulder, he responded. "Leave it out you dozy cow ", Duke sneered. While he was being distracted by the woman's comments, the man seized the opportunity to push Duke away from him. He used both hands with as much force as he could muster. Duke lost his balance but went hurtling to the side. He slid across the table and as other guests dodged for cover, Duke crashed into a woman, who was rooted to her seat through fear. Screams of anguish, pain and suffering filled the air as Duke completed his fall to the thickly carpeted floor. His momentum had carried him at such swift pace that he had no time to stop himself for looking such a fool. He looked up from the floor to the many faces that seem to drift in and out of focus in a haunting way. Duke shook his head to clear it but his vision continued to be affected. The blurred periphery all seemed so senseless and unreal. He tried to raise himself from the floor but gave up after several attempts. His actions mimicked a boxer, who had been stunned by an unexpected blow but didn't know when to quit. Duke attempted to get up but the room, people and furniture seem to be a seamless whirl that rendered him into a dizzy stupor. He couldn't see clearly so he lay there on the floor staring at the seemingly revolving ceiling. A waiter with tray in hand stood transfixed at the spectacle. He appeared to be frozen in motion. The look of consternation on his face revealed the impact the physical altercation between Duke and the man with the swarthy complexion. On the waiter's tray were several small plastic bottles of ice cold water.

Dora was flattered that her suitor had found her attractive enough to offer her the flower. This was something that Duke had never done. He was more sexually driven rather than pampering her with things like flowers. All the same, she felt strongly that a man had bothered to pay attention to the likes of her. She was even now still unsure what made Duke start to court her. Dora's experience had always been one of being deliberately avoided, unselected or even being despised even from pubescence to adolescence during her secondary school days. This carried on during her college and most recent university experience. Despite her intelligence and academic achievements, men would generally not find her physically attractive. On this occasion, Dora was having undiluted mixed feelings. These consisted of her managing to achieve being flattered by the suitor, who saw her as worthy and being fought over. Of the two men fighting over her, one of those men was her boss, Duke. They had been dating. When Dora recovered from her moments of reckoning, she grabbed a couple of bottles of the iced cold water from the waiter's tray but started to pour them on Duke's face. At the same time, she tried to reactivate the waiter back into taking action. "Could you open some bottles for me . . . please, please", Dora implored? The waiter, as if being awakened from a freeze-frame mode back into action, responded to Dora's pleas. Together, they managed to get Duke to react. When he did, Duke responded in the only way he knew. He was neither apologetic nor grateful. "What are you trying to do, drown me? Stop pouring water all over me", Duke squealed. "Duke, oh Duke you're still alive my love", Dora cried. The tears were genuine but Duke still managed to dent Dora's true concerns. "Stop fussing woman, I'm alright", he retorted.

Duke declined any help that was offered to help him to get up off the floor. "I can do that for myself, thank you", he added cynically. After a few slips, Duke managed to get up partially from the floor then the pain in the back of his head registered. It exploded so powerfully that he could not control himself from screaming out. "J.H Christ, my f ★ ★ ★ ★ ★ g head is coming off. Duke grabbed the table for support but grimaced. His face had yet a deeper hue than his natural albino yellowish colour. Dora was quick to go to his side. She asked what she could do. "I don't know, you think of something . . . anything as long as this headache stops. Get me some pills, get me some pills", Duke pleaded. He placed his hands at the back of his head but carefully touched it to see if there was any blood. Duke was surprised when he did not see any blood. "You dozy cow . . . don't just stand there, go look at the back of my head . . . see if it's f ★ ★ ★ ★ ★ g busted", Duke demanded.

Dora Stagg was a dutiful kind of young woman. She was beginning to learn not to challenge Duke at the wrong time. Dora moved around him but saw the huge swelling at the back of Duke's head. She did not comment straight away. "Come on", do you see any blood", Duke asked impatiently? Dora did not see any blood but she told him she was concerned with the size of the swelling. That part of Duke's head must have been tender, Dora thought. She wouldn't dare to touch it. On the way down to the carpeted floor, Duke had cracked his head upon the bulbous part of the table leg. He stumbled around, defiantly refusing help from people, who just wanted him to calm down and wait for the ambulance. "I'm alright . . . where's that bastard", Duke shouted? He swiveled from side to side. He held his head in both hands as his own voice reverberated in it so violently that Duke started to do a kind of jig that copied steps from the 'Highland Fling'. The people who gathered around commented but they were all aware of Duke's predicament. He still couldn't see clearly and this bothered him somewhat. He decided not to argue but he kept mumbling. "I'm going to kill that bastard", Duke exclaimed. He repeated these words like a mantra but the man had long made his escape while everyone else was attracted to Duke's demise. The ambulance had arrived to take him to hospital. As time passed, Duke overcame his injury. Dora Stagg was disconcerted by the obvious lack of control in the man she admired but hoped to love. His depth of anger and rage did make her shiver and would again whenever Dora sensed that Duke was truly angry.

In this moment in their lounge, she was in no doubt as to how angry he was about her delaying the divorce proceedings. Dora had suffered in silence for a very long time. She knew now that, with his hands around her throat, Duke's deep anger and rage had resurfaced. As time went by but particularly at this latter stage of their lives together, it seemed to impact deeply as their relationship deteriorated irretrievably, seemingly! Dora's eyes were bulging from the pressure on her throat. She felt a throbbing in her temples and a sense of abandonment. Dora had hoped that at least one of the children might have heard the row between her and Duke but they were playing loud music. The pulsing and thumping drowned out any hope.

Buck Stagg, the older child, once told his daddy that he would kill him "if you ever make mom cry again". Duke had clipped him around his ears to "teach him a lesson". At 7 years old, that was Buck's first run in with dad. He had since grown to hate his Dad. Now that he was 18 years old, Buck had resolved that he would live away from home while he attended university. He was enjoying a short break to be with his family, especially his younger brother, 14 year old, Ryan. The twanging of guitar and the banging of drums meant that it was not possible for Buck or Ryan Stagg to hear the awful row that was taking place between mom and dad downstairs. Dora was now desperate to free herself from the madman, Duke had become. Desperation had become her closest ally and Dora knew she had to do something extravagant to free herself from his firm grasp. She grabbed Duke's hair but pulled as hard as she could manage. His toupee was no longer a secret. Dora was surprised to find the handful of hair in her hand. As she stopped to puzzle whether she had managed to pull the clump of hair from its roots, Duke punched her in the face with his huge fist. Dora could take no more of this type of treatment. She threw the clump of hair onto the floor and as Duke bent to pick it up Dora raised her knee, bringing it crashing into Duke's face. The blood from his busted nose oozed freely down his face. He looked up from the floor expecting her to withdraw but somehow Dora begun to act more like a cornered animal, scratching and snarling. The froth from her mouth splashed all over Duke's face as Dora let fly with comment as well as action. "Do you treat your fancy women like this" Dora scowled? Without waiting for Duke to respond, she expressed just how she was feeling. "I'm tired of your bullying", Dora added. Duke was still defiant even though Dora's reaction had puzzled him. "Shut it", Duke replied. He blocked the fingernails aim at his face. Duke grabbed his wife in a bear hug, pulled her to the ground but rolled over on top of her. Dora realized that she had no more respect for the man, who called himself her husband. Duke could not cope with this new person Dora had become. She was ever so passive before but now it was as if this was her last stand. He decided to change tactics. It would have been almost a year since he had approached Dora for sex. As he pressed up against her, Duke could feel himself rising. "How about a bit of rough", he asked? Dora Stagg did not fancy Duke anymore. In fact, she was most insulted by his suggestion. Every thread of passion had been carefully clipped over the years she had been suffering. Dora was beginning to get used to the kinder romantic approach that her friend, Calvin Poser, the chauffeur, had displayed. He was not like Duke, who believed he always knew best what she wanted from sexual intercourse. She didn't need sex from the impatient Duke and she thought it was time to tell him so. "You've never managed to satisfy my needs before, why do you think you could do it now", Dora remarked cuttingly? Duke was deeply wounded by her remarks. He tried to force himself on her. Using his free hand to raise her dress, he fumbled but fought to take her panties/knickers down. "You know you need me. How long has it been", he asked? Dora was not amused. In fact, she could have cried out for rape but she thought that would not make the point she really wanted to make. Instead, she told Duke the words she knew would wound him even more and for a long time. "Your idea of lovemaking is yesterday's news. Women need to be satisfied. Your wham, bam, thank you ma'am approach has never done anything for me. I have needs you can never fulfill if you live for another fifty years", Dora told him firmly. That remark seemed to touch a raw nerve. He flinched as he replied. "You ungrateful bitch", I gave you two children", Duke retorted. The fact that Duke even suggested sex left Dora cold and un-aroused. The blood from his broken nose dripped onto Dora's face. She squirmed but twisted until Duke shifted himself to one side. Dora brought her left knee into Duke's groin. He grunted but doubled up in pain. His face became an even deeper hue. Dora was now almost enjoying her battle with Duke. She got up from the floor quickly but advanced towards the retreating Duke. Dora Stagg was more than incensed at his presumption. She was determined to reinforce the message. Dora knew Duke would have forced himself on her despite the fact that she had insulted him. This time the blow was aimed lower but it was't necessarily physical. "You're no longer the special person in my life. I have found myself a 'real' man, someone who makes me feel good", Dora jeered. Duke had never been snubbed before. He was neither emotionally intelligent nor matured. Duke didn't know how to handle this type of situation. He lurched forward but grabbed Dora's throat with both hands again. This time he pushed her against the huge solid dark oak sideboard. With her back towards the sideboard, Dora seized the opportunity to grab the small wooden carving of a 'Doctor Bird' that Duke had brought back from one of his famous holidays abroad. The carving was small enough to fit into her palm. Its shape included the sharp pointed beak that protruded enough to cause damage. Dora would have preferred to be able to simply scream for help but Duke's firm grasp told her that this time he did mean to kill her.

She had never believed in violence as a means to settle any argument. Most of her life, Dora had belonged to one group or other that opposed the use of violence. It was her devoutness to this present group, 'Peaceful Millionaires', which caused rifts between her and Duke. The Group's impact was much more effective than Duke wanted to admit. He was incessantly hypercritical of his wife's profile, as Assistant Chairperson of the Group. During the many campaigns with which Dora got involved, she bothered to identify with a lot of women, commonly. She had gained a lot of solid support from the public. When a morning 'Phone In' Radio Presenter had asked the public to vote whether they agreed with Dora's philosophy on "Peace as a more justifiable alternative to War", Dora Stagg received a massive 72% per cent 'Yes' votes in favour of her views. Long before they were married, Duke had voiced his opinion about such groups. "I despise you, your views and your 'Earthty' friends. You go about wanting to save the world but you haven't managed to make a dent on political views, yet", Duke had exploded. He had turned his cynical *knife* with a sadistic twist. Duke had always seen Dora as a "stupid cow" with a face "like the back of a bus".

When he was a young man, it was commonly accepted then that "the wife" was only a necessary accessory to a man. Women were reduced to little more than slaves who, coincidentally, bore their husband's children, dutifully. A *'housewife'* is what Duke called her. He preferred the *"dolly-birds"*; the *"tasty birds with legs up to their armpits"* as Duke and his friends often referred to them. Ultimately, he desired but mingled with the likes of Doris Bendlow and several others like her. He referred to them as *"common as muck"* but his preference for such women was because he knew they needed *"a bit of rough"* as he often boasted to his friends in the AADCs. Doris was the *'darling'* with the customers. She would tease them often beyond their threshold for patience. It was when the drunken *'Traveller'* could take no more provocation from Doris but attempted to reach over to grab her breasts that Duke had stepped in to play his 'role' He had knocked the *'Traveller'* out cold. "He asked for it . . . Doris don't mean no harm . . . it's just a little fun", Duke had told the packed AADC. He dusted his hands as if he had just handled something dirty.

Those women like Doris were no comparison to the obedient Dora. Duke's only reason for marrying her was because he was sure she would be the staunch partner, one eager to bear his children. They would become *'heirs'* to his multi-billion Empire. "Stay home and look after the kids. That's your job", he would often order whenever Dora tried to find even a 'part-time' job in the past. She was quite happy to stay home with her children while they were young but Dora felt that they were of an age when they needed their independence. She had told Duke that her self-confidence would be raised from the level she felt at that time but he didn't understand or care about how she felt about anything. What Duke said was gospel. His commitment to their relationship was less than hers. As far as Duke was concerned, she was *"an ugly so-and-so"* who had to obey his commandments. The rows between her and Duke had got to a stage where they were jousting with each other, each trying harder to hurt the other with more acid personal comments than before. They traded insults rapidly. Duke was simply a *'replica'* of his father. Pausing for a few moments, he looked at his wife as if she was the *'old enemy'*. Duke delivered the words Dora knew was imminent. "That's it, I want a divorce", he exploded. "Suit yourself Duke Stagg because you'll never find anyone as loyal as me again", Dora warned. She said it with such certainty because Dora had seen some of the women with whom Duke had been associated. It was common knowledge that people had begun to whisper about the likes of Duke and Sandra's affair but Dora had played the 'role' of the 'perfect' wife and mother. She had kept up the appearance of the devoted wife until lately. Duke and Dora's life had deteriorated long before Sandra came along but any slim chance of making up had totally evaporated since. Dora referred to Sandra as "Slut no. 1" and Doris as "Slut no. 2". She had a name for all the ones previously as well that she knew about.

As the physical struggle between Duke and Dora continued, she was fading in and out of consciousness now, desperately needing to get some air into her lungs. She decided that this was her best moment to strike out at Duke's persistent bullying. Dora hit Duke on the side of his head with the carving of the 'Doctor Bird'. Again and again Dora Stagg pounded Duke in his head until he freed his hand from her throat. Gasping for air, she laboured to regulate her breathing. As the much needed oxygen rushed to her brain, Dora felt quite dizzy at first then her head began to clear a little. Dora realised that, for the first time since they have been together, she had the upper hand on the mighty Duke. He was cowering away now like a boxer, who knew s/he had been hit by a 'good punch'. Duke looked as uncoordinated but staggered around aimlessly like a cow suffering from mad cow disease. He was beginning to see several Doras but could not be sure what made them seem so distant at times yet so uncomfortably close at other times. His consciousness was waning faster than Dora's had been earlier. The thumping pain in his left temple made him wince even to breathe. Each footstep from either Dora or Duke sounded as if he was being hunted by elephants and Dora's voice seemed denser, coarser but more hauntingly ghostly than it actually was. There was only one way to stop this seemingly vicious attack. Duke was on the ropes now hearing 'Hitchcock's Staccato Discordant Symphony' while he hung on like a boxer that prayed for that one punch from the opponent to put him out of his misery. Even in his younger day, Duke had never suffered such a beating. "You've lost it Dora. Calm down woman", Duke pleaded. Whilst trying hard to ward off the blows that Dora was now piling on, Duke continued to experience double vision. With each blow that she delivered, Dora felt a sense of freedom that she had not felt before. Although she didn't know it, Dora had begun to release all those pent up feelings over so many years. Those feelings were pretty complex. The hurt, beatings, loneliness, resentment, feeling abandoned, being discarded, disparaged, feeling belittled, used, taken for granted but treated with scorn and disdain had lowered Dora's evaluation of her self-worth. The accumulative effect was like a volcano bubbling like molten lava over the years but had come to a point of eruption. Dora surprised herself that these feelings had arisen to the point where striking out was giving her a warped sense of pleasure as she pounded the now hapless Duke like a huge mortar in an oversized pestle pounding one grain of maize. Each blow represented freedom from a different tier of experience, which she had previously chosen to block from release or had put to the back of her mind. Dora had lost total control of her faculties but was temporarily in a state of madness. Her superlative urge was to get even with the emotionally insensitive Duke. She thought of the earlier years when Duke's emotionally immature acts of jealousy were unbounded and even a smile at a stranger had him reacting like she was one of his 'possessions' rather than an equal partner in the relationship.

Earlier in their partnership, Dora had gone out but joined up with a women's group for battered women and rape victims in order to share her experience with others. She was stunned to learn Duke's behaviour was so commonplace amongst co-habiting as well as marital relationships. The testimonies from diverse ethnicities highlighted a need for not only raising but maintaining the debate to provide more education and learning at a much earlier life stage in order to prevent such mental and physical abuses from continuing to take place generation after generation. As a *'battered wife'*, Dora was learning that using this serious issue as a *'political football'* was not an option. She wanted to champion the need for *'emotional sensitivity'* to be a subject to be studied from Secondary School age through to Phd level. Dora presented research from 'The Walynski Institute' and a collection of Case Histories from the man they called 'The Professor' to bring more weight to her argument about the subject which bore her personal experience. The genial Professor Walynski had been the pioneer, who had been urging successive governments around the Royal Royal Dis-United Stately Kingdoms to begin to address the issue by implementing *'Emotional Sensitivity Studies'* as a most urgent addition to the School Curriculum. He saw it as a necessarily meaningful subject. The eminent Professor Emeritus opined that in doing so, there was much to be gained from reducing all forms of irrational behaviours to drastically reducing bullying, initially, probably! As Dora continued to campaign, she became more and more aware that her and the eminent Professor's efforts were being deliberately stymied by influential poly-tricksters and their puppets, the politicrats alike. Their *'values and beliefs'* had driven their self-serving interests to continue to use *'Human Zoos'* as the *'one size fits all'* answer to what was deemed all over the entire parallel virtual planet of Asteroidia as a *'mental pandemic'*. By default, those politicrats and their puppeteer masters reinforcement of the antiquated philosophy was already centuries old and spreading like an uncontrollable virus well out of control in the present millennia. Despite the strength of opposition from the mighty poly-tricksters and their subordinates to her and Professor Walynski's sensible proposal, Dora had not only managed to establish funding for the groups with which she was engaged but secured the support of the man they called 'The Professor', also. He gave the groups innovative 'Tools' with which to start their individual journeys towards coming to terms with their bizarre *'Life Experiences'* but supported them towards striving for closure as well. Duke had raged at her but took Dora to a crypt at the Hotel Welcome. There, he tortured her until she had agreed not to give any information to the media about him abusing her. Duke told Dora, in no uncertain way, that he could not afford for his bullying, abusive behaviour to come to light in the public domain. He said that kind of information might tarnish his or the companies image and reputation but most of all would diminish the amount of clout he had managed to establish over so many years. "It's just not the *'done thing'*. I can't imagine me without clout. I would become a laughing stock and that I cannot afford to be. If you so much as think about washing our *'dirty laundry'* in public, they won't even find your bones in the crypt", Duke had threatened.

In her present predicament, Dora recalled Duke's words about teaching her a lesson. She realized that this was the moment to reverse the *'role'* that fit the *'model'*. Dora seized the opportunity to let Duke experience what it was like to be on the receiving end of the type of treatment he had given to her over the years. "I'll teach you a lesson for a change Duke", Dora jeered. At last, the freedom to give Duke a bit of his own medicine overwhelmed Dora so much that she kept swinging wildly now. Some of the blows were far off target and these wasted efforts were now making her arms tired. The repetition of the blows now disturbed the trance-like state that Duke was in. At times, it appeared to Duke that Dora had many heads as a Hydra and as many tentacles as an Octopus. Dora's shrieking voice now began to sound like a cheap tuneless violin being played for the first time by an over-keen tone deaf novice. The room was now spinning out of control, or so Duke thought. That was the last memory that he would recall. Duke was out cold. Dora looked down on the man, who had made her life hell but was tempted to finish him off there and then. It took a lot of effort and energy to defeat the mighty Duke. Many men had tried and failed but it was worth doing. Dora had succeeded to put into practice that which she had feared to do before. Thoroughly exhausted from the fight, Dora sat on the floor and wept. These were tears of relief not sorrow. She was glad Duke had finally decided to divorce her. Dora understood that Duke could ruin her easily but she had past worrying about what Duke could do. She touched her neck as if to confirm the beads were no longer there. They were scattered all around on the floor. Dora Stagg watched Duke's chest heave up and down in short irregular patterns while her own breathing was still affected by the long drawn out battle. Duke had slumped into unconsciousness. As he lay awkwardly on the floor, Dora spoke again. "Please Duke I don't want to fight anymore. It's painful for the children too. They know what's going on, they're not fools", Dora advised. When Duke did not respond she began to feel sorry for what she had done though she felt a kind of release, now that she had conquered the bully. In her hands she still grasped the 'Doctor Bird' carving. It was totally covered with blood. The protruding beak had snapped and was now only a half of the size it was originally. Dora tried to release the wooden carving but it stuck to her palm. The sticky blood had begun to dry now and Dora felt silly holding the wooden bird. She shook her hand gently at first but began panicking when the carving didn't drop to the floor as she had expected. Dora looked over at Duke but his face had gone from a deep hue to a very pale, pasty colour. The pale green plush carpet was supersaturated with the dark coloured blood. Dora tried to rouse Duke but there was no response. "Duke it's not time to play games, answer me, answer me", Dora fretted. When there was no response, Dora started to scream as loudly as she could. "I've killed him, oh my God I've killed him . . . help somebody . . . anybody". "Buck . . . Ryan . . . heeeeellllllppppp", she screamed. Dora Stagg was shaking terribly now because, for the first time, she thought that she had killed Duke. She cried uncontrollably. Each time she piled the blame unto herself.

It was sheer coincidence that Buck and Ryan had stopped playing the loud music. They heard their mother's screams. Both raced down the stairs to see what was happening. Though Dora was not aware of it, the door was locked from the inside. Buck and Ryan shouted together. "Open the door mom, what's going on in there", they asked? Ryan, the younger son, peered through the keyhole. "I can see the key. It's still in the lock. Buck give us a sheet of the newspaper", he urged his brother. Buck retrieved a newspaper from the rack in the hallway. Ryan slid the sheet of newspaper under the door then expertly used the blade of his penknife to slide the key from the lock. It fell unto the sheet of newspaper then Ryan skillfully drew the piece of paper through the space between the carpet and the bottom of the door. "Clever", Buck commented. After unlocking the door they pushed it so hard that it banged against the solid oak sideboard behind it but sprung back at them. Buck stopped it with his arm, instinctively. Dora Stagg was sobbing like a child, who had been punished for being *'naughty'*. "Mom, what happened, why is

Dad laying on the floor? Is he dead", the boys asked? Duke's broken nose was twisted and hugely swollen. It reminded his sons of a Toucan's beak. The children observed the splattering of blood all around the room but particularly the many holes that was drilled into Duke's skull by the protruding beak. The wooden bird was still attached to Dora's palm by the sticky blood. "My God", they exclaimed. Dora was now suffering from latent shock but could not give a lucid explanation. "Mom, we'll have to get him to the hospital", Buck said. Ryan began to sob. "Are they going to arrest our Mom", he asked? "I don't know Ryan, I don't know", Buck replied.

It was the sound of the doorbell that startled them. The impatience of the visitor only added to the panic that was setting in. "I am guilty . . . guilty of killing him. He drove me to it . . . he tried to kill me for his fancy woman", Dora confessed. Buck had established that Duke was still breathing. "He's not dead", he assured his mom but he too was in a quandary. Should he answer the door or pretend there was nobody at home? What if it was a neighbour? How long had the fight gone on for? Did Dad really plan to kill Mom? Had mom gone crazy through jealousy? Buck had to make a lot of grown up decisions fast or he might lose both parents. He poured a double measure of brandy. "Drink this", he ordered. He held his mother's head back and literally poured some of the brandy into her mouth. The strong liquor had immediate effect. Soon Dora was holding the glass herself in the other hand. She gulped yet another mouthful then quietly asked them to see who was at the door. Ryan started to go towards the door but hesitated when Duke started mumbling. "What's he saying", Ryan asked? The piercing sound of the doorbell and the thumping on the door made Dora and the children jump. "I'll see to it", Buck said. He walked towards the door. Buck heard the flat sneer-like flap of the letterbox then footsteps disappearing down the gravelled pathway. He picked up the card from the floor. It indicated that there was a parcel to be collected from the local Sorting Office. Buck peeped through the 'spy-hole' just in time to see the postman getting into the red van. "It's alright, he's gone", Buck told them. Ryan took the empty brandy glass from his mother but asked if she needed some more. Buck had only just noticed the marks around his mother's neck. "What happened to your neck? Did dad try to strangle you", he asked? "Yes, at first I thought he was just trying to scare me but when I saw his eyes bulging I realized he meant to kill me", she sobbed. "He must have meant it because he locked the door with the key. Didn't you know the door was locked" Ryan chirped in? Shocked by that revelation Dora bowed her head. "So he really meant to kill me this time", she whispered to herself? Ryan and Buck were just as devastated by the reality of the situation. "Why does he want to do that when he could just walk away", Dora asked? Duke still lay on the floor. His face was now swollen beyond recognition. "Get some ice from the 'fridge' Ryan", Buck said urgently. Duke's head was now the shape of a green skinned melon. He had a large skull anyway but this was quite grotesque. "I don't like the way he looks, we'll have to get him to a hospital", Buck implied. "Call his friend Dr. Scapelovic, he'll know what to do", Dora suggested. They were all very concerned now because Duke was now struggling to breathe. Dora told Ryan to dial the number but that she would speak to the doctor. The telephone rang for a while. "He's not home mom", Ryan said anxiously. "Try his cell phone", Buck suggested. This time the phone rang twice and the voice said, "Dr. Horace Scapelovic". Ryan held the phone to his mother's mouth. "Horace, it is Dora. There's been an accident, can you come to the house", she pleaded? "Sure Dora, in about 20 minutes", he replied. "Hurry", Dora cried.

Horace Scapelovic was older than Duke but had remained loyal to his young friend despite the difference in their age. Dora knew she could depend on him. It seemed much longer than 20 minutes but Horace Scapelovic didn't let himself or them down. Ryan heard the car pull up in the drive. "It's him mom. It's Dr. Scapelovic", he chimed. Buck rushed to open the door. "Young Buck, how are you getting on in university, well I trust", Dr. Scapelovic asked? Buck smiled nervously but showed Dr. Scapelovic to the room. "Good God, was it burglars that did this", he asked? "Is Duke alive Horace,", Dora asked timidly? Dr. Scapelovic saw Dora's neck too. "They tried to kill you as well, I see", he assumed? Quickly he placed the two ends of the stethoscope into his ears but started to examine Duke. Dr. Scapelovic turned but looked at Dora and the young men. The look on his face told them that Duke was in a very bad way. "It's the blows to his head", he indicated. Dora looked away but the boys hugged her to show their allegiance. "My dad is a bully Dr. Scapelovic. He's been beating mom for a long time now but she always made excuses for him. He would always have had to have a 'skin full' before he felt that he'd had a good time then mom pays for all his frustrations", Buck explained. "I hate him", Ryan added. Dora reached up but held her children's hands. Dr. Scapelovic pointed out that one of the wounds had pieces of the broken beak in it. "Dora, there is nothing I can do here. Duke needs to go to hospital right away if he's to have any chance at all", he counselled. "We don't want the neighbours to know, how can we get him to the hospital, Horace", Dora asked? "It's the chauffeur's day off and I'm not in a state to drive", she finished. "I'll drive mom", Buck offered. He took the spare keys from the hook in the hallway and drove the blue limo around the large building. Buck entered through the back door to join the others. Ryan and Dora held one leg, Buck the other and Dr. Scapelovic held Duke under his arms. From the position in which Duke was laying, it meant that his head was farthest away from the door. This posed a problem for them. Buck, Ryan and Dora's combined strength was inadequate to pull Duke towards the door. Conversely, Dr. Scapelovic was a giant; standing at 6'7" and weighing a hefty 25 stones to Duke's 5'5" and 20 stones. "We'll have to turn him around before we can attempt to get him through the door", Buck suggested. "It's a big risk", Dr. Scapelovic told Dora and the young men. It took enormous effort to carry out the first task. They were forced to rest for a while before attempting to take Duke to the limo. "This can't be helping him. It could make his condition worse", Dr. Scapelovic warned. He looked down at Duke, furrowed his brow but scratched his head. Dr. Scapelovic put his ears close to Dukes nose but listened earnestly. Reaching hurriedly for the stethoscope once again, he proceeded to listen to Duke's chest. The others sensed that something serious was awry. "You'll have to call an ambulance, I'm afraid", he said ruefully. "Is he dead", Ryan asked? "No, but he'll be lucky to survive. He lost too much blood", Dr. Scapelovic replied. "I killed him", Dora sobbed. "Nonsense mom, you were only defending yourself", Buck consoled. Dr. Scapelovic had heard the remarks but he was busy giving directions to the Emergency Services operator. She recognized the name of the celebrity doctor. "I don't need to remind you that a discreet approach is recommended, my dear", he asked pointedly? "The ambulance is on its way doctor", the operator finished. Dr. Scapelovic asked for a blanket to cover Duke. Ryan raced away to retrieve a blanket. Dora was trembling now quite uncontrollably. She felt quite weak. "Mom", Buck said then he knelt down beside her and put an arm around her shoulder. Ryan returned with the blanket and helped Dr. Scapelovic to cover Duke with it. Dr. Scapelovic's cell phone rang. He put the phone to his ears and listened then spoke into it. "You're round the back, are you", he asked? As promised, there was no siren. Buck let the paramedics in. They hurried to Duke's side. "Oxygen", one ordered. They attached the mask over Duke's face. "How long has he been like this", another asked? No one was sure not even Dora. "We're going to need an air ambulance. We've set up the necessary drips but he needs to get to the hospital immediately", the senior paramedic explained. There was no hiding anything from the neighbours now. Dr. Scapelovic gave the nod and the call was made. "Ten minutes, rear of the building", the senior paramedic confirmed. "I'd better move the limo", Buck said. One paramedic left with him to move the ambulance further away from the back door too.

The humming sound of the air ambulance could be heard and the shuddering of the building as it landed. The vibrations affected the figurines on the shelves along the wall and made them dance. The paramedics expertly placed Duke on the stretcher but carried him from the building. Once the air ambulance had taken off, Dr. Scapelovic urged Dora to go to the hospital too. "You can travel in the road ambulance. The young men can travel with you. I'll be right behind you", he assured her. They left the house for the hospital.

CHAPTER 48

There was no action from the Crown Court against Carmen for the alleged crime at the Ghettoville Community General Hospital. Subsequent to a complaint from a member of the public that an ethnic woman had someone else's blood all over her, the police had to attend to ascertain whether the allegation was true. Upon their arrival, the Security Guard, Archie Hingepin, had complained that Carmen had assaulted him. When asked by the police if he was sure, he had replied that he couldn't tell the difference between *"that 'lot'"* but he was sure Carmen was the one from a group that had pushed him in the chest area and had promised to "put his lights out". They had arrested but charged Carmen for (1) Public Affray (2) Disturbing the Peace (3) Grievous Bodily Harm to the particular Security Guard, Archie Hingepin (4) Threatening behaviour against the Security Guard (5) Assaulting a police officer (6) Obstructing a police officer and (7) Resisting arrest. After viewing the CCTV footage from the Community General Hospital, the jury found Carmen not guilty of any of the charges. The Judge, Lord Justice Tribesman, in the Higher Court, Central Greensborough, commented that the Prosecution ought to have advised the police that they had no case.

Carmen had returned to her exotic island nearly thirteen months ago. She was returning to Spaceville not only to visit her family again but to accompany Pam's daughter, Darsna, who was born on the Elementary Estate, Painsville, Lower Ghettoborough, in Spaceville. She had been growing up in the far off 5th rated exotic island with Pamela's mother. Ten years old Darsna seemed tiny as she exited from the

Immigration Department. She looked eagerly through the small breaks in the wave of human traffic in front of her walking down the main aisle towards the Arrival 'Waiting Area' on the ground floor of the Cryptic Airport, Brazenborough. The buzz of the mixture of different languages being spoken around Darsna was a particular thrill for her. She had an interest in languages since she was a very young child. Her aunt Carmen was a little distance behind her. She was struggling with the luggage trolley. It seemed to pull severely to the left when being pushed forward. Carmen swore to herself but some other passengers walking through did hear her comment. "You don't have to swear", a woman commented. She tossed her hair with the hand that was free of luggage then flicked her hair to one side. The woman did this several times as if it was a tic. It wasn't the first time that Carmen had noticed that type of behaviour. She pondered over the woman's comment then reacted. "Hey you", Carmen called out. The woman had, whether by choice or having to keep up with the flow of human traffic, increased the distance between Carmen and herself. The trolley distracted Carmen from her target. Feeling frustrated by the interrupted progress caused by the inefficiency of the trolley, she stopped altogether. Carmen stood for a brief moment in order to steady herself from the effort of trying to keep the trolley in a straight line. The jolt and comments from behind startled her. "Bloody foreigners, get out of my way", the voice said. The impact was causative to the pain Carmen now felt in her lower back but the word *'foreigner'* hurt even more. "Who the . . .", she started to say. Carmen swung round. She held the pained area of her back with her right hand but swung her left elbow as she turned. It was held high and was deliberately searching for the side of the individual's face that was behind her. The impact was complete when Carmen's elbow registered its intent into the individual's temple. He could not have been expecting it. The man, Iven Lambtroski was a chauvinist. He'd relished in telling stories of his hate for women. At his local AADC, he had often referred disdainfully to the barmaids as *'bimbos'*. Iven's partner, Rosie Darnwood walked next to him like an obedient dog. Her head was down and she stared at the floor all the time. Rosie was Iven's 'Gofor'. She struggled with the faulty trolley similar to the one that Carmen was using. It was loaded to the top with luggage. Rosie toiled to maintain steady progression but the burly Iven chose to let her continue to struggle. Earlier, when she'd asked him to help, his response was more than insensitive. "Keep going woman, you'll soon get the hang of it", he had instructed. Carmen, the woman whom he faced now was no 'lapdog'. This was a woman whom cowards like Iven had never crossed before. By the time Iven realized what was happening, he found himself on the floor. Some other passengers had stopped but observed the event happening in front of them. Iven lay on his back. Carmen kicked him between his legs. He yelped like a wounded coyote singing falsetto in an animal choir. Carmen followed up with two short kicks to Iven's ribs. He hummed like the bass section of an Orchestra.

Darsna had lost sight of her aunt Carmen against the flow of human traffic. As she started to navigate her way back towards her aunt, it had become a difficult experience for the child. Darsna dragged her bag along the floor. It was near one of the yellow 'slippery floor' signs where the man with the golf bag tumbled but fell to the floor. Darsna had played the *'excuse me'* dance with the oncoming stranger. He went to his right when Darsna went to her left. She changed over to her right but the stranger now moved to his left. At one point, Darsna had perceived that the man was trying to hinder her from going forwards. She was just thinking to kick him in his shin to free herself from the *'nuisance'*. It was at that moment that the stranger changed tact. As he approached the yellow sign, he tried to get past it before the oncoming Darsna. When the stranger saw the bag being dragged behind her, he tried to sidestep it. This action forced the stranger to attempt to hurdle the yellow 'slippery floor' sign. His front leg straddled the obstacle. It was clear of the yellow sign but his trailing leg caught the top of it. Momentum carried him forwards forcefully as he tripped. The stranger was a tall man. Darsna could not be sure of his height but she witnessed the stranger's dramatic journey to the floor, which reminded her of a tall tree being felled on her exotic far off paradise island. Those who clearly saw what had happened made Darsna's pathway much clearer.

She heard her aunt's voice before she even got to where Carmen was being *'restrained'* by the Airport Security staff. They pinned her to the floor. There were seven people around Carmen with more arriving in that background. The uniformed personnel were too busy apprehending Carmen to hear what the old couple with the wide rimmed straw hats and Khaki Safari type apparel had to say. They appeared to be explaining something to the security staff. Most of them ignored the old couple. "We were witnesses to what had taken place between the man and the woman who you've got on the floor", the old woman said. One male staff responded without looking around. "Can't you see we're busy? Go away, we can't talk to you now", he discouraged. The couple moved a few yards away from the *'restraining'* officers. Carmen had resisted when they first came along but only instinctively. The security staff each appeared responsible for keeping Carmen from *"harming herself"*. Darsna shouted at them. "What are you doing to my aunt", she queried? "She's your aunt, is she", a male member asked? "Yes", Darsna replied. "Well, maybe you can tell us if your aunt is mad", he said. Darsna was hurt by the remark. "Why do you say that", she queried? It was then that Darsna was able to comprehend some of what had happened while she was separated from her aunt. The old couple came over but stood next to Darsna. "We've tried to help but they won't listen to us", they complained to Darsna.

A white Mixed DNA Rainbow Tribe female member, who arrived with the current mob of supporting security staff, heard the conversation. She came over but spoke with the couple. They told her their story. The female member assured the couple that they could go now that they had told their story. The old woman was concerned that Carmen be set free. "It was gross provocation", the old man said. Before turning away from the scene altogether, the old woman gave Darsna a piece of paper. She'd ripped it from the small diary in which she had made notes concerning the incident both she and her husband had witnessed. Finally, they turned but set off in the direction of the 'Waiting Area'. Darsna noticed how alone and helpless she felt. She hung her head as she contemplated the dilemma in which she'd found herself. The female member of the security staff who had spoken last to the old couple approached Darsna. "You'd better come with me love", she said encouragingly. Darsna was only 10 years old but, having grown up in the exotic far off paradise island, she was more matured in thinking and smarter than her age. "Where are we going", she asked? The female security guard was taken aback by Darsna's response. She backed away from the woman's outstretched hand. "We'll look after you until your aunt comes out of jail", the woman said casually. "Why is she going to jail", Darsna asked? "She attacked another passenger", the woman said.

"What about the witnesses? I heard them tell you that my aunt was defending herself against a bully. I saw you write down their statements", Darsna said. "What witnesses, where are they", the woman asked? When Darsna insisted that she saw the woman writing the couple's statements, the female security staff denied that there was any such couple let alone a statement. "You're imagining it love", the female security worker responded. Darsna couldn't figure out why the woman would lie when she clearly had the old couples' statements. The woman removed the small pad from her pocket. She held it out then asked Darsna, do you mean this? The female security member ripped the top sheet off the pad but only managed to tear a second sheet with it. The woman rolled the paper into a ball then tossed it towards the refuse bin. It was situated some 5 to 7 yards from where they were standing. The woman laughed when the paper found its way into the bin. She punched the air. "What did you see me write", she asked? "Now come with me", the woman demanded. Her face had suddenly contorted from a laughing mask to a very serious countenance. The female member of security staff spoke with a harsher almost demanding bullying tone. "There'll be no trouble if you come with me quietly", she stated. Darsna was alarmed by the woman's change in behaviour. She was feeling scared. "My mother wouldn't want me to go with strangers", Darsna proffered. "Mother, who is she when she's at home", the woman asked? Darsna was mystified by the strange way the woman phrased the question. "My mother is waiting for me to come out. If I'm not out soon she'll come looking for me", Darsna commented.

As if Darsna and her mother practiced ESP, Pam appeared in the now scanty aisle. Darsna saw her first. Pam wore anxiety on her face, like a veil. "Mom", Darsna shouted. All the previous disappointments had shrunk into insignificance. Pam hugged her daughter. Tears of joy rolled down her face. Pam lightly pushed Darsna away from her momentarily. She held her daughter at arms length looking longingly into her eyes. "You've grown. Let me look at you", Pam said. The excitement in her voice revealed Pam's inner feelings. Over eight years she'd applied for Darsna to rejoin her. This moment was special to both mother and daughter. For Pam it meant that the long fight with immigration had been worth it. For Darsna it meant even more than Pam would dare to guess. The re-union wasn't planned to be this way but at least Darsna had arrived. There would be opportunities for Pam and her daughter to start to get to know each other better. "Where is my brother, I can't wait to meet him", Darsna said? "He's outside with daddy", Pam replied. Darsna felt confident and strong in her mother's presence. "How come they let you come in", Darsna asked? "I couldn't see you or Carmen come out. I ask the security man at the other end if I could come to see what was delaying you", Pam said. "He must be very important to give you permission to come in", Darsna prompted. "Your dad knows him", Pam said.

She saw the many security staff around someone on the floor. "Where is your aunt", Pam asked Darsna? It was then that Darsna was jolted back to reality. She pointed towards where the airport security staff had gathered. Pam was shocked surprised. She wanted to know what was going on. Pam approached the mob surrounding her sister. "That's my sister you've got down there. She's no criminal. What are you doing to her", Pam demanded? The female member of staff, who'd been talking with the old couple and Darsna, came forwards. She engaged in a heated conversation with Pam. "I want to speak to your manager or supervisor", Pam demanded. When the woman went back towards her colleagues, Darsna broke away but retrieved the crumpled paper that the woman had thrown in the bin. No one else turned up to speak with Pam. She removed the cell phone from her handbag. "Ray, ask your friend if he could get the supervisor to come and help Carmen. They have her on the ground", Pam explained. "What", Raymond exclaimed. He spoke with his colleague, who was situated nearer the exit. Both of them walked swiftly. Raymond was holding Rasdan in his arms as he approached Pam and Darsna. This was the first time she'd met Raymond and her brother, Rasdan. They both looked the same as the photos Pam used to send to Darsna. Raymond's friend went over to his colleagues but enquired why Carmen was being restrained. They told him that she was being violent and had assaulted another passenger. He told them that he knew the family and that there must have been a genuine reason for Carmen to act the way she did. Raymond's friend asked to speak with the offended passenger but he had carried on the moment the security personnel had apprehended Carmen. One of the security personnel had seized Carmen's passport to *"run a check on her"*. Surprisingly, there was information of a *'previous offence'* on the record. This was a complication for Carmen.

The pink Mixed DNA Rainbow Tribe security personnel said that he had alerted the green humanoid robotron airport police and that they were on their way. Soon, five burly male and three female police started to come towards them. They seemed robotic in their approach. Armed to the teeth with their militia style assault weapons, pepper spray canisters and dogs, the airport police made it seem as if the airport security was being breached by terrorists. Carmen was feeling very uncomfortable from being restrained in the one position. She complained loudly that it was unnecessary for so many of the members of security to continue pinning her to the floor. She protested loudly but her timing could not have been more inappropriate. The green robotron airport police indicated that they would take over from the security personnel restraining Carmen. As they prepared to change restrainers, a blue Mixed DNA Rainbow Tribe member of the police sprayed the pepper spray into Carmen's eyes then they set upon her as if they were trying to restrain a vicious animal, like a crocodile, from escaping. Carmen screamed but it was to no avail. Darsna witness the cruel way in which her aunt was being handled but couldn't understand why. Pam cried but protested about how her sister was being treated. Raymond had had first hand experience at the hands of police but had spent several months in hospital because of his experience with them. He knew that, because of his muscular build he would be set upon if he protested too strongly. Instead, he started to dial his lawyer but the phone just kept ringing.

There was a lot of confusion. The dogs were barking, Carmen was screaming from the excruciating pain she was experiencing. The pepper spray made her eyes feel as if they were set on fire from beyond the sockets. Rasdan witnessed the cruel actions upon his aunt but started screaming too. Pam's could take no more of the madness. Her quick thinking brain forced her into action. She selected Sandra's number from her contact list on her cell phone. The phone rang but went through to voicemail. She was desperate to make contact with Hinton Fairly, the lawyer who had defended Carmen before. She left a brief message that there was an urgent situation and for Sandra to call her back. The brutalism from the airport security previously and subsequently by the airport police continued against her sister. There was no one to whom she could appeal except for Raymond's friend. He had no authority over the airport police. When Carmen continued screaming was when the dog handlers allowed the dogs to intimidate her further. Even though they were on leaches, the handlers let them hover and scowl at the defenceless Carmen. She was too frightened to move. The foam from her mouth signified that she had gone into a different mental zone. She started to convulse. Carmen's eyes rolled around in her head but she tossed her head from side to side like the woman in the film 'The Exorcist'. Carmen's body went into irregular spasms similar to those that Sandra's father C.B used to experience when he was alive.

It was the sound of Pamela's cell phone that punctuated the confusion. She looked at the phone. It was Sandra returning her call. "Thank God", Pam said. Her prayers were being answered. "What do you want now", Sandra asked? Her voice was blunt but showed the spite she still carried against Pam for *"stealing"* her lover, Raymond. "I'm not sure I should be talking to you after what kind of friend you've proven to be", Sandra sniped. "Look Sandra, this isn't the time or place for us to settle old scores. I need a lawyer. What was his name, Hinton something", Pam said. "Oh, you remember who helped you when you were down but you still stole my man", Sandra stressed. "You chose to let him go. If I didn't take him somebody else would have. Grow up Sandra. You chose to let him go. You're more of a Judas than I am. Look, I don't need any of this now. All I want is the lawyer's number. Can you give it or not", Carmen raged. Her voice was quite stern.

Raymond looked on but understood that Pam was talking to his ex-lover, Sandra. She had never heard Pam speak to her like that before. Sandra could sense that something serious had happened. When she next spoke, Sandra gave Pam the number she wanted but stressed that she would be willing to help if Pam needed a loan. The truth is Sandra was bitter about losing Raymond to her best friend but she knew that, apart from that, Pam was the most genuine friend she had ever had. Right now, Sandra could do with a friend like Pam. "Let me know how you get on, girlfriend", Sandra ended. After she hung up, Sandra rang Hinton Fairly herself but gave him Pam's cell phone number. Her cell phone began to ring. Pam answered. "It's Hinton Fairly. Miss Bogus told me you have another urgent problem to deal with", he said. Pam explained what was happening at Cryptic Airport in Brazenborough. She told him the security guard had stated that some record of the case against her sister was still being held on file. Hinton explained how that happened but needed to ring off in order to inform the airport police of the facts.

For Pam and Raymond to witness this act of barbarism was bad enough but not as bad as Rasdan and Darsna being present when all this violence against their aunt was going on. The scene was bizarre. It was like something out of a movie. When one of the police answered his walkie-talkie, he told the others to withdraw from Carmen. They went into a huddle away from everyone else but then walked away from the scene without explanation or apology. The security members were also withdrawn when their burly senior personnel appeared but told them to let Carmen go. "There will be no charges against you", she assured the bewildered Carmen. Raymond's friend signalled that they could go but he was not allowed to engage with them any further. It was as if everything had gone back to *'normal'* except for the traumatic experience that had been witnessed by Pam, Raymond and the children but most of all for Carmen who had lived it. Pam hugged her sister with one hand while hugging Darsna with the other. Raymond was in charge of the trolley with the unpredictable set of castors. Both sets of luggage became the perfect seating for Rasdan who hitched a ride to the Car Park.

Carmen was suffering from spasms but complained that she felt moments of cold chills. Her eyes were still smarting. Carmen told Pam she needed to get some cold water to wash the spray from her eyes. They went to the toilet so Carmen could wash her face before exiting the Arrival Lounge. Raymond joined the long line of people, who were waiting to pay for their parking tickets. This was done automatically via the machines provided to dispense this service. Although the machines were meant to speed up the process, it took Raymond about ten minutes before it was his turn to use the machine. Pam, Darsna and Carmen had gone ahead of him to start the car so that Carmen could keep warm. Rasdan stayed with Raymond. He was still sitting on top of the luggage.

There was a confrontation between Raymond and some others in the queue, who had become impatient with him. Raymond could not find the ticket to insert it into the machine. He searched all of his pockets but the ticket could not be found. Raymond did not want to have to queue again and so protested his priority with the others. They objected to his obstruction to use the machine while he searched the same pockets yet again only to find that the ticket still remained unfounded. Raymond tried to ring Pam to see if she had it but there was no signal in that part of the building. Frustration boiled over and the man behind Raymond pushed him but commented. "Move aside", the bully demanded. Raymond did not want to have an altercation with the man but he felt he had to teach him a lesson. He turned the peak of his baseball cap to the back of his head but pointed his fingers like a gun at the man. Some others including his son, Rasdan, had noticed Raymond's behaviour. The others in the queue chose not to argue with this muscular specimen. Raymond was acting the stereo-typical image of what his ethnicity was perceived to be. In doing so, he had not only highlighted but driven a level of fear and intimidation into the minds of those who believed in the stereo-typical imagery. The man that had pushed Raymond seemed to be a gym enthusiast himself but declined to back down. He stepped forwards towards Raymond and before the others could blink moved his forehead closer to Raymond's. The man placed his forehead onto Raymond's. They pushed back and forth like two rhinos using their foreheads to gain ground in order to establish territory. Raymond was in no mood to play this silly game known in school playgrounds as the *"what"*, *"what"* scenario. One individual would say "what" then the other would show even more attitude by saying "what". The man's breathe was as off-putting as a communal toilet that had not been cleaned. Raymond used his hands to push the man against the machine with a lot of force. He placed his right hand into the front of his oversized jogging bottoms as if he was reaching for a concealed weapon. "I got something for you", he threatened. The man withdrew immediately but kept his eyes firmly on Raymond's right hand. He hadn't noticed that his baseball cap was on the floor. A woman from the Tribe of Hawke, who was also waiting in the queue, told him. As Raymond reached down to pick up the cap, he saw the parking ticket on the floor next to it. Raymond remembered then that's where he had placed it on his way into the Arrival Lounge. He made his payment but turned to thank the woman from the Tribe of Hawke. As he walked towards the car park, he took his hand from inside his jogging bottom but said something to the man who had challenged him. "Today is your lucky day. You had better sleep on the same side you slept on last night", Raymond threatened. He carried on towards the car without any further incident. Once Raymond had loaded the luggage, he exited the car park but headed for the expressway towards home. Pam commented on the time it took for Raymond to rejoin them. Before he could explain to her, Rasdan told about the incident with his father and the man from the Tribe of Babylon.

Carmen was exceptionally quiet. Raymond switched on the CD player. The reggae CD had the effect he wanted. Soon he was bowing his head to the vibrant beats. The whole ambience in the car changed from the seemingly glum to an upbeat spirited one. Even the traumatised Carmen was reacting to the inspirational cleverly mixed, genius production, crisp rhythm section, repetitive melodic bass line, 'rights and *truths*' lyrics, driving tempo of the drums, subtle integrated harmonies and the haunting horns section that makes reggae music the dominant force it had become in all the Kingdoms of The Royal Royal Dis-United Stately Kingdoms of Asteroidia in the World of Space. While they listened to the rest of tracks on the 'Roots' CD, all the occupants of the car continued to experience the enriched quality of ambience within.

When Raymond spotted the flashing blue lights somewhere in the distance through his rear view mirror, he had no idea of its destination but kept checking their progress in the fast lane. He had not broken any traffic rules so to him there was nothing to concern himself about. Raymond watched as the three police vehicles whisked by soon followed by an ambulance in their wake. When the next sirens were heard in the distance Raymond saw the two fire engines too. "Some accident ahead", Pam exclaimed. Raymond had turned his head around to speak with his children. It was only but a brief glance but in that short space of time fate might have dealt them a very unlucky hand. "Raymond, look out" Carmen shouted. His head swivelled towards the front. All he could see was the brake and flashing lights of the car in front of him. Raymond stepped onto the brakes and clutch but engaged second gear. The car screeched and skidded towards the one in front of it. Having travelled its full braking distance, when his car came to rest, Raymond had broken out into a sweat. He realised that one moment of indiscretion had almost cost them their lives. The car had come to rest about eight or nine inches from the car in front. As he quickly flicked on his flashing lights too to warn the driver behind him, Raymond looked into his rear view mirror to establish how helpful his warning had been to the car behind him. Fortunately, that car was at a greater distance from theirs than his was to the one in front of him. Rasdan and Darsna had pitched forwards but banged their heads on the back of the front seats. Neither of the children was wearing a seatbelt. Mercifully, apart from the impact with the seats, they were not hurt badly.

All the traffic on the expressway came to a halt. The acid orange coloured snow started to come down at a much faster rate and before long everywhere had this light acid orange florescent glow. Darsna, who had never seen snow before marvelled at its beauty but wondered what it might be like to walk on or even play in it. Rasdan was asking to go out to have a snowball fight. He was far too young but did not understand why it was inappropriate for him to have a snowball fight on an expressway. Pam asked Raymond if it was safe to go to the boot to retrieve some snacks and drinks they had brought with them for the children. He opened the door but looked ahead to see if the traffic had started to move. It hadn't. Raymond could see the blue flashing lights in the distance ahead. He retrieved the snacks and drinks from the boot for the children but went back inside the car. The CD was still churning out the music. Raymond had sometime to ask

Darsna how she felt about leaving the exotic far off paradise island. She told him exactly how she felt. "I feel happy but I feel sad. I don't know how to explain it but that's the way I feel. I miss grandma and all my friends but I'm happy to see mom again, meet you and my brother", she stated. There was no complication in this young girl's answer. Darsna was expressing truly how she was feeling. The others listened to what Darsna had to say. Rasdan wanted to know what time it was in the exotic far off paradise island and what was the name of Darsna's friends. "I have quite a lot of friends. You want me to tell you all their names", Darsna asked? "Yes", Rasdan replied. Darsna, Raymond, Pam and Carmen laughed together. "What so funny", Rasdan asked? "I have got a lot of friends. It would take all day for me to tell you all their names", she consoled. Rasdan thought about what his sister said. He stayed silent for awhile then asked a different question. "What's the name of your best friend", he demanded. "Trevonne", Darsna replied. Rasdan hissed his teeth but asked yet another question. "Trebonne? What kind of tupid name is that", he asked? His mispronunciations and his stark response to the unfamiliar name was not all that triggered the laughter that emanated. It was more the look of incredulity and the manner in which he said the name that was more noticeably funny. There was great laughter in the car. Raymond was rolling about behind the wheel. "Rasdan, yuh nuh easy", Carmen said. They continued to enjoy the banter between brother and sister.

None, including Raymond, had noticed that the cars in front of them were now in the distance ahead of them. It was the blowing of horns from the less than patient drivers of the vehicles behind that had alerted Raymond to restart their journey. The falling acid orange colour snow had decorated the fields, barns and houses that could be seen on either side of the expressway. Rasdan told his sister about the cows and horses he'd seen on their way to the airport. Darsna told him she couldn't see any cows or horses but asked him if he had imagined them. "I saw them when we were coming to meet you at the airport", Rasdan assured. "Well, where are they now", Darsna teased? As is typical of any 3 year old, Rasdan gave the only truthful answer he could. "I don't know", he replied. Darsna stayed silent for awhile then she spoke to Rasdan again. "Do you know what a memory gem is", she asked? "No", he replied. Darsna asked if he wanted to learn one. "Yes", Rasdan replied. "Hey diddle, diddle the cat and the fiddle the cow jumped over the moon. The little dog laughed to see such fun and the dish ran away with the spoon" Darsna recited. "Darsna, what's a fiddle", Rasdan asked? She explained that it was a musical instrument. Darsna demonstrated how it was played. Rasdan gave her a look that suggested more than his considered opinion. No one inside the car was prepared for his response to the memory gem. "Cats can't play fiddles? I've never seen or heard a dog laugh and cows can't jump over the moon", he told her. Again, it was the manner in which Rasdan said the words that was comical. He was showing how advanced he was for his age. The uproar of laughter within the vehicle made even Rasdan laugh. He was only laughing because the others were. Tears were streaming down their faces. Then, to cap it all, Rasdan turned to his father for confirmation. "Daddy, have you ever seen a cow jumping over the moon? Tell my sister to stop telling me tupidness", Rasdan persisted. "You mean stupidness, don't you son", Raymond asked? "Yes, tupidness", he continued. Raymond was almost losing control of the car. His belly laughter was infectious and by now all within the car were in stitches. Carmen shook her head but commented "Nuh body nah guh fool disya one yah. Pam di bwai brite eeh", she commented. Somehow the children had managed to help the adults change their states. As they neared the exit of the expressway, Pam asked Raymond to take them to Aunt Rose before they went home. Carmen used Pam's cell phone to call Natty Hawke.

When they arrived at Aunt Rose's house, Raymond blew the horn to alert her. After a few moments the door opened. Aunt Rose stood in the doorway but beckoned for them to come in. Dressed in his winter coat, gloves and red, gold and green scarf, Natty Hawke came out to greet them. Darsna wore the winter coat Pam had brought to the airport. She felt what it was like to walk in the snow and Rasdan threw a snowball at his sister. Inside, Aunt Rose made much of young Darsna and Rasdan. Raymond hugged Aunt Rose but greeted Natty Hawke. Carmen hugged him in a more prolonged embrace after she had greeted Aunt Rose. Pam felt at home as usual. She made herself available to help share the dinner. Rasdan asked if he could play in the back garden with his sister after dinner.

Carmen related to Aunt Rose and Natty Hawke what had happened at the airport. Aunt Rose said it was typical of how they treated people from their ethnicity. Natty Hawke was unforgiving but swore that he would make them pay for their indiscretion. There was really nothing he could do and he knew it but it felt good venting his anger towards the green humanoid robotron *"suppressors"* as he referred to the *"Babylon system"*. He hugged his beloved but expressed his frustration with the way people from the Tribe of Hawke were being treated. Rasdan had hardly finished his dinner before he started to press his parents to allow him to play in the garden with his sister. Raymond and Pam realised their excitement. Darsna wanted to have a new experience of playing in the snow with her brother, Rasdan. Eventually, they were excused from the table. The draft coming from the back door was soon noticed by those inside the lounge. Pam went to close the door. She witnessed the joy of her children as they chased but threw snowballs after each other. The glow of the fluorescent acid orange snow brightened the garden.

CHAPTER 49

With his new responsibilities of a mortgage and two children, Raymond was finding things a bit more of a challenge than he thought it might be. Pam had a part time job as a receptionist at the local doctor's surgery. Both she and Raymond had moved from her flat on the Elementary Estate in Painsville, Lower Ghettoborough to Ghetto Heights, Higher Ghettoborough. It was on the border of Lower Greensborough. Raymond became tired of the *'poor'* life that caused him so many burdens. He had ditched most of his real friends. His new *colleagues* told him that he needed to *"get 'wise' before it was too late"*. What Raymond couldn't do is maintain a good relationship with his many women. He did care about Pam and his child but somehow the relationship between him and Pam had become jaded. They didn't go out as often as before because child minders were proving too expensive and friends were just as busy with their individual lifestyles. Pam had become ready to resort to nagging. She had tried using charm, patience, and many other combinations but Raymond was no longer staying in to help with the children. Pam grew more and more impatient with his *'lies'* that he made up as excuses for his regular absence from the home. Pam confronted him about his irresponsible attitude. "I could understand if you were out of work and struggling but I can't forgive you for not helping to look after the children. Each day you come home with just enough time to change and get to work. I have to plead with you for money. What kind of life do you call this", Pam asked him? Raymond was changing from the seemingly loving, caring man she *rescued* from her friend Sandra. Common sense was not a word that Raymond recognized any longer and his heavy drinking had started to tell on Pam. The normally jovial loving partner had started to become physically abusive since Pam forced him to marry her. She wore the bruises that resulted from his ill tempered assaults. Frequently, Raymond would push Pam around. He was becoming a bully; using his athletic build to overcome any form of defense that she could muster. On the day that Pam had come home to find Raymond and another woman in her house in a very compromising situation, the relationship was over. She wanted to leave him then but decided to stay despite the beatings.

On this visit to Spaceville, Carmen told her to move away but Pam had explained that she would stay because of the children. "I want my children to grow up with their daddy. That's the most important thing for any child", Pam submitted. "The relationship is dead but . . .", she added. Carmen empathised with Pam's reasons because she had witnessed how the children of single parents were treated differently to others. This happened both in her far off 5th rated exotic paradise island as well as here in the 1st rated Kingdom of Spaceville. "God kno sey ah tru yuh ah talk but how much more beating yuh can tek", she queried? "I can try to block out the verbal abuse but the physical is wearing me down", Pam confessed. The tears had already started to roll down her face. She looked a beaten woman. "Let it out sista, let it out. A man like dat is boun fi meet im match", Carmen said calmly. She used all her instincts to console her sad sister. "Is not like yuh fi ah cry dung di place . . . dat wicked man . . . im gwein feel it", Carmen added. She hugged Pam tightly but rocked her from side to side as if she was rocking a baby to sleep. They heard the keys as Raymond tried to open the door. Pam jumped and Carmen could hear her sister's heart thudding irregularly. Pam was alarmed by Raymond's return and she begged her sister not to intervene if Raymond started to moan. "Please don't say a word out of place especially if he smells of booze. That's when he acts like a man possessed", Pam pleaded. "But mi ah difrent smaddy from yuh an mi naw guh stan up and mek im batter yuh in yah", Carmen retorted. Raymond made several attempts at finding the right key. When he finally did, it took him a while before he could fit it into the door. As he pushed the door open, Pam and Carmen could hear giggling voices. They looked at each other questioningly. "Come in, come in", Raymond said. He was prompting the two women who were with him. They staggered through the door eventually. Their first attempts had been clumsy. Maybe it was the booze or maybe they were all uncoordinated through a different means but they somehow managed to negotiate the small hallway. As they entered the lounge, Carmen confronted Raymond. Pam was helpless because she knew that her sister was not as *'soft'* as her. "Ah who dem yah yuh ah bring inna mi sista house? Yuh nuh hav nuh rispek fi har an yuh children dem", Carmen challenged? She stood directly in front of Raymond and looked him squarely in the eyes. She didn't give him a chance to reply before asking him another question. "Yuh nuh waan try fi lick mi tuh . . . mad bwai", Carmen continued. She was much taller and more athletic than Pam. The two women, who had accompanied Raymond, stopped giggling but started to come to his defence. "Leave him nuh", one countered. Carmen's martial arts training came into full swing. Pam was surprised at how quickly the two women had hit the floor. They were now at the mercy of the ruthless streak of Carmen, the combatant. Strangely, Raymond did not attempt to intervene but encouraged the women to leave instead. "Catch you fillies later", he said as he ushered them through the door. The drunks were all a bit more sober than when they had first arrived. Pam told Carmen that she needed to have a straight discussion with Raymond. Carmen said it was the more reason for her to stay but Pam said she would be o.k. She called a minicab for her sister.

After Carmen left, Pam had dinner with the children then she helped Darsna with her homework before sending her and Rasdan to their rooms. Raymond had hardly said another word since Carmen left. He isolated himself from Pam and the children. In the bedroom, Raymond spent most of the time on his cell phone before he showered but left the house again. This was the new routine to which Pam had referred. She stayed up as long as she could. It was after midnight when she drifted off to sleep. When Raymond returned in the early hours of the morning, the children heard him and Pam squabbling. It was neither a discussion nor a debate where each would listen then respond. Each of the adults in the house was behaving poorly and not particularly sensitively towards one another. There were times when the children heard the threats from Raymond and the cries from Pam. Raymond's attempt to physically pummel his wife into submission was a most dastardly, cowardly exhibition of bullying at its worst. Pam's determined defiance meant that her torturous ordeal was prolonged. The children were wide awake now but nervously cowered in their bedrooms. They continued to hear wanton swearing being delivered by Raymond. It didn't take much for the children to imagine the intensity of force being delivered that occasioned the screams of despair from Pam. "You might as well kill me. Why don't you? If you hate me so much just go ahead and kill me", she shouted. Darsna and Rasdan had heard the commotion from Darsna's bedroom upstairs. Seven years old Rasdan rushed down to see what was going on. He pushed his parents' bedroom door open. Rasdan witnessed the whole *'movie'*. He saw his father with fist raised as he threatened to hit his mother again. Neither of them noticed Rasdan's presence. Pam challenged Raymond to strike her again. "I want you out of the house. Go to your women. They might want to put up with your anger tantrums but I won't. You have to leave or I'm going to get an injunction against you", she affirmed. Raymond delivered the blow that Rasdan witnessed. It smashed into her face but sent Pam flying across the room. She crumbled to the floor as the back of her head met with the wall behind her. It was when Raymond raised his foot to kick her that Rasdan spoke for the first time since his entry into his parents' bedroom. "Daddy, don't kick my mommy", he shouted. Raymond spun round to discover Rasdan standing there with a kitchen knife that he had gone to fetch from the kitchen next to the bedroom on the ground floor. Raymond felt the blade as it entered his thigh. Darsna witnessed it too but she stood at the entrance of the room instead. She was filming the scene on her cell phone. She quickly hid the cell phone as Raymond looked towards her. His embarrassment meant that he became even more unreasonable. "Go to your room. It has nothing to do with either of you. This is between me and your mother", he commented. Rasdan dropped the knife but ran up the stairs but Darsna stood in the doorway. "Move when I tell you to. You think you are a woman standing staring me in my face", he raged. Darsna looked him up and down but hissed under her breathe before moving towards the stairs. She could hear Raymond say, "I'm going to teach you a lesson you'll never forget", he threatened. Darsna had no idea what he meant by that but didn't care to take the chance to ask. Pam had been knocked out by the blow to the back of her head. She was not aware of the Raymond's behaviour towards the children while she was unconscious. Pam knew when she regained consciousness because she felt the excruciating pain and the throbbing at the back of her head. Her face was a mess and her body bore the bruises inflicted by the 6'4" muscular giant. Darsna and Rasdan discussed what they had each witnessed. He wondered what made adults so disagreeable among themselves. Rasdan was too young to understand the details involved but he would certainly retain the frightening experience his parents had created around him. Darsna still heard Raymond's threat reverberating in her head.

Pam and Raymond drifted even further apart when he accused her of interfering with his and Sandra's relationship. He told Pam that she had plotted and planned to take advantage at a time when he was at his most vulnerable. Pam was none too pleased about his cutting remarks. She felt Raymond was ungrateful but that he was emotionally confused about the events surrounding Sandra's preference for the financial security which she sought to enable her to live 'The Spacevillean Dream'. Though he was more than twice her age, Duke was the 'waggon' to which Sandra had chosen to hitch her 'star'. Raymond's worshipping of the tall, slim, lithe, busty, slim-waist, large backside, well formed proverbial acoustic guitar shaped body reflected how deeply mesmerised and obsessive he'd become. With Sandra's high cheekbones, 'highly kissable' full-lipped pouty-mouth, straight bridged nose, unusual large cornflower blue eyes, finely sculptured facial beauty with long 'relaxed' trendy straight hair had dazzled him but prolonged Raymond's addiction to the classic stereo-typical illusion. Her voice was so alluringly mesmerising but drove Raymond's emotionally insensitive neurotic behaviour. Sandra was the 'programmed' and 'conditioned' picture of his 'Cloned-Barbie Trophy Woman', 'Mrs Right'. At that time, Raymond had not audited his 'values and beliefs'. Without evaluating them, he had aspired to clone, practice and live those 'values and beliefs' he had come to was conditioned to accept as his own. Raymond was unaware how those same 'values and beliefs' had managed to contribute towards him forgetting the real heroine, who had rescued him when he was drowning in his humungous, tempestuous, whirlpool of cyclonical, spiralling, debilitating emotions. He seemed to have conveniently forgotten that he was submerged neck deep in self-pity when his 'ideal' 'Cloned-Barbie Trophy Woman', 'Mrs Right' had made a consciously, logically sequenced decision to abort their relationship. Sandra had again consciously sacrificed but sold her mind, body, soul and spirit to the 'highest bidder' of what seemed to be a 'no holds barred' self-auction for perceived 'privileges' over continuing to share an intimate relationship with him. Raymond could not bring himself to accept that he was in deep denial about being dumped by the strategically well informed ultra-devious Sandra. Her struggle was that she could not differentiate between her own set of 'values and beliefs' and those of her mother's. What Sandra seemed not to understand is that, much that money can provide a 'real' base for financial security, the road to 'real' happiness was not meant to come through perceived 'values and beliefs' provided by others. Instead, 'real' happiness comes through an individual's unique set of 'beliefs and values' on the pathway to a 'wealth of spiritual fulfillment'.

Both Pam and Raymond were having difficulties in their relationship because, since their marriage, they had each started to perceive *'ownership'* of the other instead of learning to become unconditionally interdependent. Each was going to bed with the *'want'* but awakening with the *'gimme'*. While they remained blinkered about their irresponsible behaviours around their children, neither can honestly say they showed the level of *'duty of care'* to their children that each needed. As with most individuals, Raymond and Pam demanded at least the minimum standard of *'duty of care'* from others but not themselves, necessarily! It was because of this situation that Pam was not aware that Raymond had been interfering with his stepdaughter,

Darsna was now 14 years old. Her physical maturity had seemed to *'blind'* Raymond about his responsibility as a father towards his stepdaughter. Instead, he made her a target for the madness that he and his paedophile colleagues considered a *'right'*. At first, the grooming came through the pretence to *"help Darsna with her homework"* but there was always an ulterior motive intended. Pam did not object to her husband helping his stepdaughter with her homework. Instead, Pam thought that it proved that they were bonding well, seemingly! Raymond pretended to be the *'caring'* parent and Darsna had felt that her non-biological *'daddy'* cared for her welfare, development and well being. After all, Pam would never have dreamed that Raymond could ever think in any other way about Darsna than as a parent. She never hid the fact from Raymond that Darsna's father, popular vocal artist and band leader, Horatio Magnificado, had run away from his responsibility the moment she had told him that she was pregnant with Darsna.

Pam, as a high flying naive young adult, had actively sought the *'special attention'* of the popular reggae artist. She, like every foolishly naive young female, wanted to be seen with the very impressive lead vocal singer of the popular band, 'The Sexual Expressions'. Horatio's voice was unusual and tantalizingly entrancing. Like an inspirational religious preacher, his *'love'* lyrics beckoned every female to come to his lair for the *"cleansing of their souls"*. Throngs of women, like Pam, in thongs and some daringly without, who had knowingly, willingly and deliberately tracked but hunted the wildly sexy performer, ached in those places that needed the type of sexual release they desired from their often frustrated experiences, which rendered them agonizingly unsatisfied with their intimate relationships. Through a carefully targeted subliminal method of auto-suggestions these women made themselves into *'converts'* to the *'stereo-hype'* about learning what was the true meaning of being *'sexually liberated'*. Those attending Horatio's Concerts demonstrated their *'sexual expressions'* by removing their panties/knickers and thongs but used them to decorate the stage on which Horatio appeared. Some behaved in such a manner as to turn their backs towards the stage, lifted their skimpy dresses but bent from the waist more than suggestively indicating what they were prepared to offer to the popular Reggae Superstar. His auto-suggestive techniques were well practiced subtle forms of subliminal suggestive intonations that made the female audience vulnerable to his commands. Pam too had succumbed to Horatio's sexual innuendos and magnetic charm until she became pregnant with Darsna.

In fact, Pam was hoping against hope that Raymond would become the type of *'Role Model'* father figure that Darsna was seeking. When she first arrived, the child trusted him. He had welcomed her to the family home without reservation. Over the last four years, Raymond had attended the obligatory Parents/Teachers Meetings and Sportsdays but had shown what appeared to be genuine interest like most parents do.

Sometimes, Raymond went to or phoned the School on Darsna's behalf whenever there was a need. He took her from and to piano lessons, plays, cinema and other activities as any other caring parent would do. Pam saw no reason to be suspicious of the relationship between Raymond and Darsna but she had noticed a change in the normally confident young girl. Like all mothers, Pam sensed there was something not quite right about Darsna's confidence but she had no idea how close to home that 'lack' had been initiated.

Darsna's ordeal started on the eve of her 14th birthday. Raymond had volunteered to go bowling with the teenager. Pam stayed at home with Rasdan because he was too young to stay out till when the Bowling Activity Centre evening session closed. Darsna and Raymond had a lot of fun together as parent and child should. It was during one of the unusually many hugs, that young Darsna's hand had brushed against the front of Raymond's jeans, accidentally. The young girl was startled by the rise in Raymond's passion. She had felt the bulge on her thigh during those hugs too. Darsna was naïve. She did not want to think beyond its firmness then but when Darsna felt the throbbing that was going on underneath the shield of Raymond's jeans, she backed off. Darsna became confused but was aware that something was not right. She refused the next hug that Raymond offered to her for accurately knocking over all the pins yet again.

This was déjà vu for Darsna. When she was eight years old, Darsna had had previous bad experiences in the exotic far off paradise islands where she grew up from the age of 2 years old until she arrived back in Spaceville when she was 10 years old. At 8 years old an adult male who had physically abused her had threatened to harm her if she told on him. Even though there was no penetration, the man had put his hand under Darsna's dress but abused her. Though this was not exclusive to the exotic 5th rated far off continents, countries and islands, it was very *'common' practice'* for some older individuals to think it was their *'right'* to 'interfere' with but abuse young children of both genders and pubescent young girls and boys also. Even young adult women were being targeted by adults with paedophilic mindsets, who chose to stalk, hunt and then *'conquer'* them through stealth but most times with force against their will. It was a type of cultural *'value and belief'* philosophy that had been passed along generations like a baton to the next generations but remained unquestioned, uninterrupted and unpunished with a nod and a wink by a deliberate *'cultural blindness'* that prolonged this paedophilic activity. This emotionally insensitive *'culturally accepted'* paedophilic activity seemed to reinforce the super-inflated egos of those, who not only practiced it but passed it on as a *'right'* to the next generation. These *'values and beliefs'* were initiated but belong to a time when *'slave masters'* chose to impose themselves upon the defenseless victims of their habitual lustful madness mindsets. This madness mindset was a practice that had never been acceptable to the victims. This type of ***'culturally accepted', 'serial stalking', neuro-profiling' and 'serial bullying' 'Slave-masters' rights'*** had never been accepted then or now as **paedophilia**. In the annals of the Science of Psychiatry, this category of madness was never catalogued let alone officially deemed as such on the parallel virtual planet, Earth nor had it been catalogued or deemed as such since the installation of the Science of Psychiatry had been introduced to the Royal Royal Dis-United Stately Kingdoms of Asteroidia.

Despite the threat from the adult male on the exotic island, Darsna, at 8 years old, had told her grandmother of her ordeal. She positively identified the perpetrator, who frequented the local AADC that her grandmother ran as a business. The child, Darsna, had learnt the non-verbal *'language'* of communication common to the exotic far off paradise island. With as little as the movement of her eyes and mouth, Darsna identified the adult offender. Pam's mother arranged for the man to have an *'experience'* he would always remember to the day he dies. Some of the local men, who objected to the man's abuse upon the child, ensured that the neuro-offender would never be able to use those fingers to *'fingering'* another child for as long as he lived. The mood of the opposition to the man's behaviour could have been more severe but they wanted him to live and be an example to any other locals or tourists, who thought they had a *'right'* to abuse children whether from the 5th rated exotic continents, countries, islands or anywhere in the World of Space.

On that night when Raymond took Darsna to the Bowling Activity Centre, his behaviour worsened before he brought the innocent teenager back to the house he shared with her, Rasdan and Pam. Raymond had pretended that he was unaware of Darsna's discovery about his being aroused by her presence. He drove from the Bowling Activity Centre but headed for the expressway. When Darsna asked why he had done so, Raymond said he wanted to discuss Darsna's future with her now that she was "becoming a young woman". She was suspicious but had no control over where they were heading. As the Series 6 high performance car hurtled along the expressway, Raymond asked Darsna what she was learning at school about sex education. At first, she didn't reply but eventually told Raymond some of the things she was being taught. He asked her how she felt about the things she was being taught. Darsna said that because sex was a taboo subject in schools back in the exotic far off paradise island, it was good to learn about it in her current school in Spaceville. They drove in silence until Raymond exited at a 'Fast Food' establishment along the expressway. There, he filled the car with petrol/gas then asked Darsna if she wanted something to eat. She said that she wanted to go to the toilet before they ate. Raymond watched the young girl as she walked away. He noticed how much more matured she was becoming and that her body was beginning to resemble that of a woman more so than a child. Raymond added to the madness of the picture he was painting in his mind. It had started to form but looked bad for Darsna. She would again become a victim of a perceived notion that ought to have been classified as a form of madness millennia before her birth. It was when Darsna had started to walk back towards the area where Raymond was sitting that his mind went into the overactive paedophilic state. His eyes jumped from her breasts to her thighs then back to her face. Raymond spotted Darsna's innocent beautiful young eyes, lips and developing body which sent him into the frenzied phase he seemed to recognize. He had been here before with other young girls. This was his new *'mission'*. He wanted every woman to pay for him being jilted by his *'Cloned-Barbie Trophy Woman'*, *'Mrs Right'*. As far as Raymond was concerned, all women would pay. He felt they each *'owed'* him but his focus was on the younger generation. As Darsna got closer to the table where Raymond was sitting, he could hardly control himself from the missiles of rapid firing sexual thoughts about making it with his step-daughter. They completely drove him further into the frenzied web of psychopathic madness, known as *'The Lust Factor'*, which haunted his psyche. It was then that Raymond realized his psychopathic urge for wanting to be sexually involved with his stepdaughter. He smiled at her as she approached the table but got up to pull out the chair for her to sit down. Darsna had no idea what made Raymond do that but it made her feel important. Raymond said Darsna could order anything she wanted. While she was looking at the menu, Darsna heard him talking to Pam on his cell phone. She particularly heard him say that he had decided to take her on the expressway in order to be able to catch up on a few things about the subjects being taught in school. Darsna felt more comfortable with Raymond now. Firstly, he had notified her mom where they were. Secondly, they were discussing at least one subject that was being taught at school. After the burger and fries came the milkshake, apple pie and ice cream. In fact, anything that a teenager might yearn for at a 'Fast Food' establishment, Darsna was allowed to have. Raymond just had a fish burger, fries and a milkshake. Darsna looked round but she didn't see many youngsters at the 'Fast Food' establishment at that time of night. It was nearly 00:00 hours by the time they were leaving. Raymond enquired whether Darsna had enjoyed the evening altogether. She said she had. Raymond rejoined the expressway but headed back in the direction from which they had come. At the speed with which Raymond was driving, it took about 50 minutes to get home from an hour and a half journey. Pam was waiting up. She greeted Darsna. "Happy birthday, sweetheart", Pam chimed. She hugged her daughter in an extended embrace that felt warm and comfortable for both. Raymond left mother and daughter to continue their celebration. Pam and Darsna heard the front door slam shut.

It wasn't long before Raymond joined his new colleagues in 'The Peacock and Peahen' AADC. Though not exclusively, it was mostly frequented by Raymond and his new colleagues. Some were gambling at cards, some were playing dominoes for booze and some were playing pool for fun, while some others were propping up the bar but eyeing the young girls, who flaunted themselves in front of them. Many were corralled into the AADC by GSE, Ghetto Sodomy Entrepreneurs who, it might be assumed, had no meaningful relationships with female members of family or none that they respected or valued beyond involvement in the *'art'* of whoredom, apparently! The Peacock and Peahen was an appropriate name for this particular AADC even if it wasn't so for others. It encouraged a diversity of cultures and ethnicity. While in one way that seemed quite politically correct, the ethos was specifically geared to appalling lewd acts performed by some individuals, who found those behaviours *'culturally normal'*, maybe! The brothel upstairs the large three story building was as busy as it had been throughout the day. The conveyor belt rotation was controlled by the resident Madame and Sire. They recruited on a daily basis but specialized in young girls and boys, some as young as 11 years old. The likes of Raymond and those others, who used the services of The Peacock and Peahen AADC, had to buy into membership in order to have the *'pick of the bunch'*. Membership Fees were very high indeed.

The green humanoid robotron owners of The Peacock and Peahen AADC, ex-vice squad detectives Mystery Madonna and Cravelle de Womanizer restricted membership to a weekly renewable. In doing so, they were able to manipulate the donations to membership. It didn't always mean that the prices went up. The owners were shrewd business people. When there was a *'sale'*, it meant that there was a surplus of young people being put up for auction by the Ghetto Sodomy Entrepreneurs, who worked hand in glove with the owners. A *'sale'* meant a rush for membership but then members had to book from two weeks to a month in advance. During that *'sale'* period, the reduced membership fees meant that individuals were allowed to choose two partners instead of one. These members were asked to choose from ID parades. In it, each partner displayed a card stating their ages. The younger the ages of the incumbent partners the more expensive the purchase. This was *'downtown'* business. The Peacock and Peahen AADC was situated in the aptly named Brazenborough.

Raymond had abandoned those friends, like DJ Herbie, who found the mere act of paedophilia disgusting. He had been brought up to respect his age but more than all to encourage young people to aspire to a better life. DJ Herbie encourage listeners to his radio show to debate the immature thinking behind those individuals, like Raymond, who found it attractive to stalk innocent children but felt the superlative urge to interfere with them. DJ Herbie gave up half his musical slot in order to enter into debate about the troubling psychopathic *'pastime'* that seemed to elude politicrats and poly-tricksters alike throughout millennia. When Raymond told DJ Herbie where he was hanging out nowadays, he told Raymond that their friendship had ended. 'Gold Digga' Herman and most of the others stayed loyal to DJ Herbie. Their own *'beliefs and values'* was the same as his. They told him to seek help before it was too late but Raymond told them he was fed up with living with the older Pam and that he still had Sandra on his mind. Raymond confessed that he couldn't live without her and he was unable to live with her so he might as well do something *'different'*. He also confided in DJ Herbie and others that a gang of gunmen had killed his mother, father and 10 other family members at a funeral they were attending of his younger cousin, who had got caught up in the Post/Zip Code War in the 5th rated exotic far off paradise island. Though DJ Herbie and those others, who were genuinely concerned for Raymond's well being, was willing to stand by him as a friend initially, they had to make a decision whether they wanted to be implicated in his new lifestyle. They had come to the conclusion that, if Raymond did not want to seek the help he so desperately needed, his old established friends were adamant that they might have been taking a risk too far, perhaps!

The truth is Raymond Wilberforce Oddball was having a very serious depressive mental breakdown but he might not have been aware of it. The people he had chosen to surround himself with were leeches who sought but ravished his vulnerability. These individuals had no hearts or consciences but rendered them of psychopathic mindsets and behaviours. Over time, they had become unemotionally cold but impervious to any other need but their own. Each night they went to bed with the *'want'* but awakened with the *'gimme'* each day. Their green humanoid robotrons' culturally accepted way of living amounted to a type of routine but individuals like Raymond were being mentally pollinated by being in their company. Their attitudes, mindsets and behaviours involved no sense of fairness, morals or scruples. These individuals cared nothing about themselves let alone others. They broke every law but had some politicrats or poly-tricksters on whom they depended to help defend them against being shut down. Some of politicrats and poly-tricksters were regular visitors to The Peacock and Peahen AADC too. Unscrupulous individuals continued to be ready to pounce at every financial opportunity despite the fact that the commodity was young innocent children whom they were leading into a life of debauchery. At The Peacock and Peahen AADC, Mystery Madonna and Cravelle de Womanizer knew that a great number of ethnicities were replicating the *'wrongdoings'* without legal consequences. In their minds, Mystery Madonna and Cravelle de Womanizer understood every loophole there was to exploit. Worse still, there were other individuals, some poly-tricksters in *'high places'*, who were just as committed to risking all in order to achieve their superlative urges. These irresponsible *'chancers'* were feeling safe in the belief that they might never get caught even if they had yet another lifetime in the World of Space.

Raymond was only just a mere novice amongst the plethora of 'seasoned' psychopathic practitioners of paedophilia. He drank heavily to numb his *'pain'* but drinking didn't seem to be enough. Raymond began to do something that, as an athlete, he had previously avoided with distinction for years but now he found himself being a compulsive smoker. It started with cigarettes but now he had graduated to other substances. Sitting in The Peacock and Peahen AADC night after night and sometimes all day and all night did bring Raymond into the focus of some women, who sought to satisfy their superlative urges, especially. This early morning had found Raymond drinking heavily and eating the stodgy foods which, through practicing proper nutrition, he had managed to keep away from during the previous years. Some of the food Raymond was eating now had not been prepared with hygiene in mind. It was more of a sloppy fry-up in a cockroach infested kitchen that was prone to salmonella poisoning. Pam was no longer preparing his meals. She could not afford to feed him as well as the children and herself on the part-time pay she received from the doctor's surgery. Raymond was fired from his job as personal trainer for failing to prepare for his sessions and for using inappropriate language while being in a drunken state. His employers had had enough complaints from the paying clients about his deterioration in hygiene also. After drinking and gambling till the early hours of the morning, Raymond drove his Series 6 top of the range car home recklessly. It was more by luck than skill that he found the key to the front door. He staggered his way along the hallway until he reached the bedroom.

CHAPTER 50

S tumbling into bed, Raymond lay in it. Half his body lay diagonally across its width. His feet hung between the edge of the mattress and the floor. The expression on his face was one of pensive mode yet with a silly half grin. Raymond's face resembled that of a smiling donkey on a holiday brochure. Pam had tried hard to awaken the drunken man who'd crept into bed at 05:10 hours. The smell of the stale smoke, booze and his unwashed body had abused her nostrils by its asphyxiating effect. Pam was now wide awake, sitting up in bed, wondering where their relationship was heading. For the past six months, Raymond's behaviour had deteriorated badly. It had worsened even more in recent weeks. Pam no longer knew whether Raymond was working or not. He'd still kept his side of the bills paid up to date except for the last two weeks. Raymond was displaying a type of behaviour that was directly opposite to his normal mode. It was as if he was in some sort of trance and was being led into this lifestyle by some outside force. Raymond was now a regular at the local betting shops and the AADCs. His closest friends had been avoiding him. One complained to Pam that Raymond had habitually borrowed money from him. He also complained that Raymond owed him a large sum of money. Pam gathered that Raymond was laying heavy bets not only in the betting shops and AADCs but also at illegal gambling Dens. The man warned that people, who often visited those places, were treating their lives with very little respect. There were known to be many altercations that took place in those illegal Dens. Some rumoured the Dens' reputation to be similar to those in the movies, in which the winner never survives to walk away with the *'winnings'*. Further rumours alleged arguments, threats of vicious revenge, personal intimidation, fights, stabbings, shootings and even more serious consequences most times.

Pam was beside herself with worry. Each day she found herself having to explain daddy's strange behaviours to the children. Raymond was never around until well after they'd gone to bed at night. Through her anguish, Pam stared at Raymond once again. She regained her composure at least for a moment or two. Pam recalled how things used to be between them. Raymond's gentle manner and common sense ways of dealing with everyday problems is what had made him attractive to her. There were times they just fooled around but laughed together and times when Raymond used to shower her with *'lyrics'* that made her feel desired. He cursed and swore all the time now, even in front of the children. Pam looked away from him, half feeling sorry she didn't leave Raymond to his *'Cloned-Barbie Trophy Woman', 'Mrs Right'*. Sandra and Raymond were similar, somehow. Each of them was living a particular *'vogue'* in life. Neither seemed capable enough of being able to impartially analyze the *'roles'* they were now playing. Pam looked across towards the bedroom door. She saw the figure of their 7 years old son, Rasdan, standing inside the door. Pam smiled. Using her hands to indicate, she beckoned for the child to come towards her. Raymond's presence did not interfere with the chemistry happening between mother and child. Pam stretched forward but encouraged her child unto the bed. There, they sat hugging and rocking in a total bliss state, oblivious of the world around them. Once they had disentangled themselves from their embrace, mother and child sat looking at Raymond. He lay on his back with mouth wide opened but started to snore heavily. This was the trigger that had put a stop to the long hugging moments earlier. Rasdan pointed towards Raymond. "Daddy is asleep", he said. Rasdan wanted to play with daddy. He wriggled away from Pam's supportive arms but lay with his head on Raymond's chest, reaching out with one hand until his fingers were just touching Raymond's chin. On contact, Rasdan moved his hand backwards and forwards. Pam watched intriguingly from her position on the bed. Rasdan closed his eyes, content that he was with his father. Raymond's snoring started again but seemed to spook Rasdan. Pam watched as he twitched but remained with his eyes closed. Rasdan fidgeted around, searching to find that degree of comfort that he'd experienced moments earlier. He shuffled until his head was nestling just under his father's chin. Rasdan reached upwards but only managed to put his fingers into Raymond's nostrils. When contact was made with the hairs in Raymond's nostrils, he instinctively moved his hands towards his face. Rasdan felt his father brushing his hands away. He opened his eyes but moved his hand back towards Raymond's face once again. He repeated his first behaviour but this time Raymond brushed the *'nuisance'* away with a bit more force. This action startled Rasdan. He felt pain and reacted by crying out. Rasdan had hardly seen his father around but longed to be close to him. The blow from Raymond made Rasdan think that his father was angry with him because he had stabbed him in his thigh when he saw Raymond beat his mother. Rasdan was frightened that he too might be treated the same if daddy became angry with him too. Pam saw the look on his face but assured him that daddy didn't mean to hit him. She hugged her son, cradling him in such a way that he was almost hidden from view. "Hush son, hush", Pam coaxed. She rocked back and forth in her effort to pacify the child. Raymond was still oblivious of his actions. Both Pam and Rasdan remained in the same position. In her mind she'd started to develop a strategy to deal with her situation. Pam had had enough but wanted to be sure how she and the children might survive in the future. She planned to be fair to Raymond. Pam knew no other way. Her upbringing had formed 'fairness' as a central social etiquette and that was that.

It was Raymond's groaning that broke into Pam's thoughts. She looked to her left. Pam saw the grimace on Raymond's face. He seemed to be in pain. Pam used her left hand to shake Raymond. "What's the matter with you", she asked? Raymond's only response was even more groaning. His normal deep voice had changed to a much higher pitch. Raymond was crying now. The tears that rolled down his face were real. He gripped his belly with both hands. "Aieeeeeeeee, Aaaaaaaaaah", he screamed. Rasdan started to cry. Pam couldn't tell whether he was crying because he was frightened or because Rasdan was sensing his father's pain. Only he knew why he was crying but Rasdan raised his tone by many decibels above Raymond's screams. Pam was concerned for Raymond. He was a tough individual. She reasoned that he needed help. Pam took Rasdan with her. She walked swiftly towards the lounge. It was situated 14 yards down the hallway, away from the bedroom. Pam hurried as best as she could. Raymond needed more care than she could offer.

Darsna, the 14 years old, had heard the uproar as well. Her bedroom was upstairs towards the back of the house. Darsna moved unsteadily along the landing. She was in a dazed stupor from sleep but used her hands as support to save her from stumbling into the walls. Darsna stopped. She opened her eyes then shut them again. Darsna repeated this action several times to make sure that she was awake. By the time she reached the top of the stairs, Darsna could see Pam and Rasdan. Pam was talking on the landline phone. The flex protruded from the lounge via the open door into the hallway. Darsna heard Pam giving directions to their address. "Mom, what's happening? I heard daddy crying", she said. Darsna's word's prompted Pam's attention. Suddenly, she realized that she couldn't hear Raymond anymore. "Hold on Darsna, I can't hear Raymond", Pam said. She raced away from them but ran towards their bedroom which was situated at the back of the house on the ground floor. The children followed as quickly as they could.

When Pam reached the bedroom, she saw Raymond in a prone position. Half his body hung precariously over the far edge of the bed. He was awake now but was feeling far too weak to shift another inch. Raymond was not comfortable but he preferred not to move. Pam sensed the reason for him to be in that position. The smell in the room had changed from stale beer and smoke to the sour scent of regurgitated undigested food and cigarette flavoured stale beer. Pam wafted her hands swiftly across her face to deter the full inhalation of the toxic fumes. Darsna reached the bedroom with Rasdan trailing behind her. Pam turned round swiftly. "Darsna, take Rasdan up to your room", Pam instructed. She used her hands to indicate that both the children should leave the room. The children looked over towards Raymond. He did not move or make another sound. Neither Rasdan nor Darsna could see Raymond's face. "Is daddy dead mommy", Rasdan asked? Pam looked away from the children but focused her attention towards Raymond. "Well, are you dead, daddy" Pam asked? The cynicism in her voice was enough to evoke Raymond to speak. "No, I'm not dead. Can a dead man talk to you", he asked? His voice was weak but defiant. Pam turned her attention back towards where the children were standing. "Something smells awful in this room", Darsna commented. Pam used this opportunity to remind the children that she'd told them to go out of the room.

The doorbell chimed. Pam was aroused by the sound of the bell. She grabbed her dressing gown that was draped over the back of the bedroom chair. Pam left the room swiftly. "Go upstairs", she reminded the children. "Who's it mommy", Rasdan asked? "I don't know. Go upstairs before I open the door", Pam scolded. She was a few paces away from the door when the bell began chiming again. Pam reached out but released the catch then opened the door. "Mrs Pamela Oddball", the female paramedic asked? Pam did not answer straight away. The male paramedic asked whether Pam had understood the question posed by his colleague. "Read my lips", the male paramedic said? He spoke slowly, using his hands to point towards his mouth. "What's—your—name", the male paramedic mimed? Pam had regained her composure but had still not answered. "I think he's alright now", she said. "Who is alright now", the female paramedic asked? "My husband was in great pain when I called but he has now vomited and has stopped crying", Pam explained. "Vomited you say. Well, we might as well look at him while we're here", the female paramedic offered? She stepped into the hallway. Pam led the way towards the bedroom. Raymond remained in the same position as when Pam and the children had left the room. As they got closer to the bedroom, the smell entered the paramedics' nostrils. "What's rotting in here", the male paramedic asked? Raymond didn't move but he queried the identity of the strangers' voices. "Who's that Pam", he asked? "I called the ambulance to take you to the Emergency Department at the hospital", Pam replied. "I don't need an ambulance", Raymond replied. "What do you need", the female paramedic asked? "I need painkillers. Have you got painkillers? My head is pounding a lot", Raymond stated. The male paramedic had made his way round the side of the bed where he could better observe Raymond. He saw the mess on the floor. The contents interested the male paramedic. There were streaks of yellow and specs of dark red mixed into the smelly patch on the white short piled carpet. The male paramedic commented. "Jesus Christ, what have you eaten? I can smell booze. Did you have a curry with it", he jeered? Raymond's response surprised the individuals in the room. "Aaaah, aaaah, aaaaaaaah", he screamed. His voice had raised itself by several decibels in both pitch and volume. All the individuals noticed that Raymond suddenly bent into the coiled foetus position, clasping his belly with his hands as if something in there was trying to escape. "Let's have a look at you", the female paramedic said. She'd stayed on the same side of the bed as Pam. The female paramedic beckoned for her colleague to help roll Raymond over toward her. Bennett, the male paramedic, inched his way along the trail of vomit then stood astride it to enable him to maintain balance. Raymond stayed in the coiled position that made him easier to move. Both paramedics pushed and pulled the very solidly built Raymond in the direction they wanted. The female paramedic spoke directly to him. "Do you feel like you want to do a number 2", she asked? "Yes", Raymond mumbled. "Can you get up", the female paramedic asked? "No", Raymond replied. His voice was feeble and weak. Raymond continued to groan but this time the groaning was intermittent. "Well, how are you going to get to the toilet", the male paramedic asked? Raymond mumbled yet another response but this time it wasn't clear. "Speak English. I can't understand your mumbo-jumbo", the male paramedic said. Pam could not be sure of the man's accent but his jibe at Raymond was unfair. The volume of his voice seemed to stir Raymond's headache. He cradled his head in his hands. Pam was not pleased with the behaviour of the male paramedic. She had allowed his earlier remark at the entrance door to pass. This time it was too much for her. "Why are you speaking to us as if we're beneath you? We speak English quite well. Your colleague don't seem to have any problem understanding us", Pam countered. She looked in the direction for support but the female paramedic from the 'Tribe of Hawke' deliberately chose to evade any involvement in the discourse between her green humanoid robotron colleague from the Tribe of Babylon and Pam. "I'm not getting involved", the female paramedic confirmed. Raymond began to make an effort to change from the coiled position. He moved slowly. Eventually, Raymond managed to get his feet on the floor. He sat on the side of the bed. Raymond felt much too weak to get himself to stand. His tummy rumbled angrily. It sounded more like rolling thunder. Raymond felt the movement of wind inside his belly. There was a wrenching pain that had located itself just underneath Raymond's navel. The wind was busily trying to find a way out. When it came, the release was loud but sounded like prolonged blasts on a Tuba. The female paramedic laughed. Raymond began passing wind downwards also. This time the sounds were wavering spasmodically like a rookie learning to play a trumpet badly but maintaining each note to uneven counts between one and four and sometimes sounded like the creaking of a door being opened but in need of oil to its hinges. Each individual took action to protect themselves from the stenches that invaded their nostrils. Raymond felt some relief though. The female paramedic asked Pam if she would take Raymond to the toilet. She moved round towards the other side of the bed. Raymond managed to struggle to his feet but he had to wait for a few moments before taking a step. His legs felt weak. Raymond's energy was pretty low but the urgency made him move his legs robotically onwards. Pam allowed Raymond to lean against her. She used her hand to support but guided him along towards the door from the bedroom. Once in the hallway they headed for the toilet. That was located just off the landing on the first floor. Raymond stopped at the bottom of the stairs but looked upwards. He pondered to himself whether he would make it to the toilet on time. Raymond tried to lift his legs but he was too weak to make such a big effort. He tried again but to no avail. "Come on Raymond", Pam encouraged. "I'm too weak to go upstairs. Someone will have to carry me up there", Raymond said. He slumped slightly. Pam was straining to keep Raymond standing upright. His body temperature changed swiftly from cold to hot then back again. Raymond was sweating profusely now. He was shaking. Pam put the back of her hand on Raymond's forehead. His temperature was very high yet he kept complaining that he was "freezing". Pam could no longer help to support Raymond's weight. He slipped from her grip. Raymond slumped his way down to the aqua blue carpet in the hallway. "Help", Pam shouted. The cry had carried to Darsna's bedroom. She ran from her bedroom into the hallway. Rasdan followed her. The female paramedic appeared from Raymond and Pam's bedroom fairly quickly. She moved swiftly towards the figure on the floor. "What happened", she queried? There was a look of concern on her face. Raymond looked almost lifeless. Pam noticed how pale he'd become. "He fainted", she replied. The female paramedic checked Raymond's pulse. "Bennett, bring the bag", she ordered. The male paramedic appeared from the bedroom. Darsna and Rasdan stood on the stairs. They looked concerned. It was

Rasdan that spoke first. "Is daddy dead, mommy", he asked? Darsna started to cry. "Oh, please God, don't let daddy die", she said. The female paramedic had finished taking Raymond's blood pressure. "Check this with me Bennett", she said. He started the procedure all over again. When he took the reading, Bennett whistled then commented. "What's his temperature like", Bennett queried? "It's 40.5. Let's take him to the hospital", the female paramedic replied. Pam said she was going to get herself and the children ready to travel in the ambulance with Raymond to the hospital. Bennett spoke directly to her. "You'll have to make your own way. We don't have enough space in the ambulance for you and your mob", he told her. Pam didn't want to make a fuss but she made a mental note of Bennett's remark. "I'll stay with him. Sheba you get the wheelchair" Bennett ordered. Sheba, the female paramedic, walked towards the front door.

When she opened it, she was shocked surprised to see that some people had gathered around the ambulance. The younger observers peered through the windows. Others rode around on their bikes. Some had seen Sheba as she exited the house. The woman with the bright orange headscarf was the first to ask a question. "Who's it? Is it the children", she asked? As if she'd answered her own question, the woman commented again. "Poor love", she said. Sheba had no time to answer the woman's question. She busied herself getting the wheelchair. Sheba left the rear doors of the ambulance open. She turned and walked away from the crowd but headed for the house. Inside, both she and Bennett managed to put Raymond in the wheelchair. They pushed Raymond in it but walked towards the front door. Darsna and Rasdan shared common moments of sadness. Triggered by his sisters crying, Rasdan started to cry too. Pam guided them back upstairs. "Come let's get ready to go with daddy to the hospital", Pam instructed. "Mom, what's wrong with daddy. He was breathing very fast", Darsna commented. "Yes, daddy's breathing fast", Rasdan added. "Get yourself cleaned up, Darsna. I'll get Rasdan ready", Pam said. All three of them went into the bathroom together. Fifteen minutes later they came out dressed and ready to go to the hospital. Pam, Rasdan and Darsna made their way down the stairs. She asked the children to wait in the hallway while she fetched the car keys and her handbag from her bedroom. Pam went swiftly towards it. As she got closer, the pungent smell attacked her nostrils again. It was getting stronger. The stale vomit was presenting itself as a barrier against which Pam had to struggle. She went past the bedroom to the kitchen that was also situated on the ground floor. It was the last room at the back of the house. Indeed, it was situated directly underneath Darsna's bedroom. Pam put on the bright yellow pair of rubber gloves. She picked up two old plastic bags and the scoop but left the brush behind. Instead, Pam took an empty margarine box with her. She made her way back to the bedroom but began the toil of scraping the stale vomit into the scoop. It was a disgusting job to clean up but Pam had no choice.

It was common knowledge that the average waiting time at the Emergency Department was 3 to 4 hours. The thought of being infested by a swarm of flies was enough to prompt Pam to clean up now rather than later. "Mom, they left the door open", Darsna said from the hallway. Pam acknowledged Darsna's message. She looked at the massive stain that discoloured the short pile white carpet. Pam opened the smaller horizontal shaped window that was positioned above the vertical shaped white UPV main double glazed windows. She went back and forth from the kitchen to the bedroom. This time Pam carried the carpet cleaner with the foam disinfectant mixed with warm water from the kitchen. She used it to clean the major stain plus all the other trails that led from it, especially the trail Raymond had caused by troding directly into the vomit when he'd stood up from the bed. When Pam started to clean up near the bottom of the stairs, the children said that they were hungry. Raymond's ordeal had completely taken away Pam's own hunger. She had clearly forgotten that the children had eaten nothing since they'd awakened.

After Raymond's recovery from gastroenteritis, he still pretended that he wasn't well. On the morning that Pam took Rasdan to Aunt Rose's house before she went off to work, Raymond called out for Darsna to make him a cup of tea. She made her way down the stairs but went to the kitchen to make her stepfather a cup of tea as requested. Darsna knocked on the bedroom door before she entered. Raymond acknowledged her request to enter the room. He was sitting up in bed. Darsna handed him the cup of tea. He took it but asked her what time she was going to school. "There is no school today daddy. It is half term holidays. We are off for a week", Darsna replied. "So what are you going to do today", he asked? "Me and my friends are going shopping this morning then do girlie things for the rest of the day", Darsna replied. Raymond thanked her for the tea. "Has your mother got to Aunt Rose yet", he queried? "No, mom said she's about 20 minutes away from Aunt Rose's house", Darsna replied. She looked at the time. "Is there anything else you want me to do daddy? I've got to start getting ready", she explained. He sipped the hot tea from the cup then told Darsna he would let her know if there was anything else he wanted before she left the house. She left the room but made her way upstairs. After about ten minutes, Raymond went upstairs to the toilet. He didn't want to use it. Instead, he sat there waiting to hear the shower in the bathroom. He could hear Darsna singing to herself as she showered. Raymond flushed the toilet then tapped the door of the bathroom. "You can't come in daddy, I'm in the shower", Darsna warned. "I just want to wash my hands. I've just used the toilet. Just pull the shower curtain", Raymond reasoned. He did not wait for a reply but instead pushed the door open. Raymond turned on the tap at the sink but left it running as he looked at Darsna's outline against the opaque shower curtain. He was excited but felt the rise below his waist. Raymond quickly removed his boxer shorts but pulled the curtain to reveal his stepdaughter's nakedness. Darsna was frightened. She remembered the firmness she had felt at the bowling alley but most of all she remembered his threat when she stood at the bedroom door when he had beaten her mom. The look on Raymond's face and his nudity exposed his intentions. "Daddy what are you doing", she screamed? "You got something I want and I'm going to get it", he replied. "It is not right what you are doing daddy", Darsna protested. She was helpless. There was no way she could escape from this monster but she resisted as best as she could. "No daddy, don't do it. I'm your daughter", she pleaded. Raymond ignored her plea for mercy. She cried for help but realized that there was no help to be had. All Darsna could do was cry. There was nothing Darsna had done to deserve this awful abuse but she had no idea that the man she called daddy had such intentions towards her. Raymond stood under the shower for awhile before stepping out but leaving Darsna alone. She felt dirty but stood under the shower wondering when Raymond had begun to plan this assault. Darsna's tears could not be separated from the water from the shower but cry she did. She scrubbed herself over and over but still felt invaded by Raymond's actions. Eventually, Darsna found the strength to leave the bathroom but return to her room. She lay on top of her bed crying,

crying and crying, contemplating what to do about her ordeal. Darsna considered that her virginity had been forcefully taken away from her by a mentally deranged monster that was meant to be her father but no longer deserved to be referred to as such. As the many thoughts rushed around her head, Darsna jumped when she saw Raymond reappear in her bedroom. She looked at him with disdain and scorn but didn't really care anymore about herself. He stood in the doorway of her bedroom but spoke. "If you tell anyone about this, something serious is going to happen to you", he threatened. She heard him but didn't know what else could be worst than what she had recently experienced. Darsna's cell phone rang. Raymond rushed over but pressed the red button. He then turned it off. Darsna was in freeze mode. She was suffering from latent shock. Darsna lay on top of the duvet with the large towel wrapped around her. Raymond mistook her not wanting to cover up as further encouragement. The crazed paedophile worked his way into another frenzied attack on the young girl. She was still so numb from the first experience that she just let him do what he wanted. This time he ravished her even more mercilessly than before. It was as if he wanted her to feel pain. Each time he looked at Darsna, she reminded Raymond of Pam. Physically, she was a mini version of her mother. It was as if Raymond was possessed by some evil spirits. He kept swearing but slapping Darsna around while he savaged her. He saw Darsna as one of the young girls at 'The Peacock and Peahen' AADC's motel. Darsna cried from the physical as well as psychological pain she was experiencing. Raymond went back into the shower. He returned to her bedroom to warn Darsna of what he would do to her if she ever told on him. Every second word was an expletive which Raymond used aggressively in order to degrade her gender but instill fear. This was followed by threat after threat with gesticulations which reinforced each threat. Darsna was shaking as if she had been exposed to artic conditions in only a bikini but with every flashback of being abused, the fire inside her raged out of control like flashback from a burning building. She heard when the front door slammed shut.

Darsna let out a blood-curdling cry that sounded more like that of a howling hound dog in a scary horror movie. At first, Darsna thought to end her life there and then. She felt soiled and unworthy but visited the type of low self-worth that drained her esteem and energy. The tears still flowed and Darsna was saddened with grief beyond anything she had experienced before. Thoughts of the possibility of her becoming pregnant from both actions of rape perpetrated upon her by her paedophile stepfather, was a real worry. She questioned how it was possible to bear that child or how guilty she might feel if she chose to abort the baby. It was a very tender and sensitive situation for the young adolescent to contemplate let alone decide on. In this situation there was no 'right' or 'wrong' answer but Darsna wondered what others might think about whatever decision she might have to choose to make. As from that moment of contemplation, Darsna realized she couldn't justify either decision. She was so preoccupied with how she was going to avenge the wrong that had been done to her. Darsna was unsure whether it was fear or the intense anger that made her tremble but she just couldn't stop doing so. The next issue she had to face was that she didn't see how she could continue to live under the same roof as the monster, who had savagely raped her not once but twice in a matter of hours? Darsna questioned herself about how she would explain to her mother what made her run away from home. There were no easy answers but Darsna was thinking of doing so. Raymond was unpredictable and dangerously so. He was also a bully and clearly mentally disturbed.

Darsna agonized but wondered how many other young girls he had raped? It was clear that he had done so before. Trying to cleanse herself from the piece of filth, who had forced himself on her, Darsna went back more times to shower again and again. After her fifth shower, Darsna picked up her cell phone from where Raymond had tossed it. She thought of calling her mom but then decided against it. When Darsna heard the doorbell ring, she jumped. Darsna tried to ignore the caller. The voices through the letterbox alerted her that her friends had called to collect her. She dragged on her dressing gown but walked slowly down the stairs. Darsna could hear the voices of her friends. One said she could see her coming towards the door. When she got there, Darsna chose to speak to them through the closed door. "Darsna you're late. Did you oversleep? We've been waiting for you", one voice said. "I've changed my mind. I don't want to go anywhere", Darsna replied. The friends insisted she tell them why she had changed her mind about going out with them. Darsna didn't want them to see her swollen face nor the tears which seemed to flow like an open tap. She was feeling listless and definitely not in the mood for shopping or conversation. "Why are you talking to us through the closed door? Open the door", the voices demanded. Darsna was adamant that she just wanted to be on her own. "I can't. Go away all of you. Just go away", she replied. This was a strange behaviour from the often jolly Darsna and the friends told her so. "Why don't you answer your phone", another voice queried? Darsna could not answer the questions in her mind let alone her friends'. "I'm just not in the mood. I want to be on my own. It's that time of the month", she lied. The friends left reluctantly but promised to call again later. Darsna went to the refrigerator but took some ice which she placed in a small rag. She applied it to the swelling on the left side of her face that Raymond had slapped her around. The cold compress was soothing but now anger had taken over Darsna's mind. She went back to lie on the bed. Darsna's head hurt but she was exhausted too. She lay there until she drifted off to sleep.

CHAPTER 51

When she had awakened, Darsna lay motionless on top of the duvet. Even though she was facing the only window in the room, she failed to hear the repetitive sounds of or see the hexagonal shaped crystals of sleet against the window pane. The golden sun reflected the sparkle of tangerine coloured quick-melting icicles but exposed the temperature outside. In her current mood, Darsna was still trying to fathom what had driven her stepfather to force himself upon her. Raymond had destroyed the **_core element of trust in their relationship_**. He had abused Darsna's physical body and made her feel unclean both inside and outside it. As she contemplated the entire ordeal, Darsna tried to figure out what she had done to encourage her weak-minded stepfather to be attracted to her in that way. She began to feel guilty but started to blame herself for the short, tight-fitting skimpy attire she wore as a teenager. Her thoughts were rolling around like storm clouds in the sky under the influence of high winds. No sooner did Darsna argue with herself that she might be guilty than, in another moment, she relinquished that train of thought. In some moments, Darsna reasoned that she was young and that what she chose to wear was her choice. At other times, Darsna was confused as to why she should be responsible for Raymond's twisted way of thinking. She debated with herself that, if Raymond had chosen to be turned on by the clothes she chose to wear as a teenager, there was something wrong about not only his mindset but also his mentality in making that choice. He could have chosen to behave responsibly. After all, she was just a child and he was meant to be a *'matured'* adult and her stepfather. It was his responsibility to behave like a parent and not her *'friend'* (lover). Darsna began to wonder whether Raymond would have been attracted to but raped her if he was her biological father! She didn't want to think that biological fathers' behaved in this way! None of what happened seemed to make any sense to her. Darsna wondered what made Raymond and other *'matured'*, so called, adults not be able to control their over-inflated egos, stinking attitudes and paedophilic mindsets. She concluded that their seemingly programmed and conditioned immensely vulgar, lecherous appetites for lust might well expose future generations of children to a type of *'culturally accepted'* sexual grooming and subsequent bullying as those children go through the various life stages. Darsna agonized whether being an adult meant that individuals were meant to be *'in a state of maturity'* or did it mean that advancing in age didn't guarantee individuals have matured attitudes, mindsets or behaviours, automatically, perhaps! She tried to stop the onrushing thoughts as they piled up. In her desperate quest to fathom Raymond's behaviour, there seemed to be millions more thoughts infiltrating her brain, all at the same time.

The lilac coloured mist that had descended earlier had now cleared sufficiently to announce how beautiful a day this was meant to be. The quick-melting tangerine hexagonal sleet had disappeared too but Darsna lay in her bedroom unaffected by the clarity of a most beautiful day weather-wise. For her, it might as well be a dreary extremely cold winter's day with thick mauve coloured fog and angry dark red clouds draping over Darsna to enable her to hide away from the chilling emotions which were descending rapidly like a shroud of darkness on a moonless night. Flashbacks of other moments of sexual abuse flooded back like repetitive tidal surges to the fore. Some of those flashbacks were abuses against her from as early as three years old when she lived on the exotic island. Being cast from as far back in early childhood that Darsna could recall, the giant shadows of those bizarre *'life'* experiences loomed large but pushed her towards an escape from sanity into the murky memories of wholesale pornographic and paedophilic insane acts in which she was forced to engage. Darsna didn't understand it then as such. Recalling those memories meant that Darsna replayed the lewd acts she was forcefully trained and conditioned to carry out. These she did while the so called *'adults'* indulged her further into their twisted psychopathic delusional behaviours in order to help them towards their mentally deranged form of *'satisfaction'*. Images of the strange masks of varying countenances and haunting groaning and grunting sounds signifying the releases Darsna's infantile presence was meant to trigger but seemingly augmented, kept appearing and re-appearing like consecutive holograms and resonant echoes into Darsna's visual and auditory recall of those memories. Even the different body odours still lingered as long as the threats and consequences to follow if the child Darsna dared to expose the *'secrets'* of those who pretended to be family, neighbours and friends. They often lived in or frequently visited the community in which she lived. Darsna clearly remembered when the local pastor played Santa Claus at Christmastimes. Being forced by her representative family member to sit in his lap in order to qualify for a Christmas gift, Darsna often felt the throbbing against her bum cheeks or upper thighs as the pastor position or repositioned her in order to receive his *'thrill'*. As a child, Darsna's acute sense of awareness meant that she had noticed that the local pastor did the same to boys too. Her little friend, Arcturius, told Darsna what his experience with the pastor had been like. Some other *'adults'* had used her conveniently for their *'thrills'* too. Darsna recalled how the woman, who lived a few houses away, used to stroke her body all over, often commenting about how lovely she was whilst committing to this premeditated ritual. When Darsna tried to escape the woman's grip, she was referred to as being *'rude'* and *'disrespectful'* or be pinched on either bum cheek or on an inner thigh. Both the woman and men like the pastor would often deliberately seek to kiss Darsna on her lips. The woman went even further by sticking her tongue into the child's mouth. It were those, seemingly *'matured'*, individuals, who had used her to relieve themselves sexually through a series of sick-minded crude practices, including kissing and touching the child Darsna in sensitive areas of her body but guiding her hands towards their genital areas in order for them to *'masturbate'* upon her childlike naivety and innocence. Situations, environments and past perpetrators against her person started to emanate from the central storage of memory. Darsna managed to construct a collage of scenarios including environments, situations and incidents that she had not even recognized as abuse then. Her current experience with her stepfather seemed to raise flashbacks of behaviours by others that Darsna had trusted or to whom she was forced to "*show 'respect'*". These memories exposed male and female family members alike, their friends, teachers, politicrats, as well as church and camp officials back on the exotic island where she grew up from two to ten years old. Collectively, the collage showed a common thread that seemed to highlight the behaviours of some *'adults'* who had abused her in some way or other in those tentative years. There was a common theme to their behaviours and the threats were not only meant to be a bullying tactic but also revealed the fears of those *'adults'* of being exposed. It seemed to Darsna that those behaviours formed a part of a mental impairment that was prevalent not only on the 5th rated exotic island but also here in the 1st rated Kingdom where she was born. She concluded that it appeared as if there was just nowhere to hide, physically. Mentally, Darsna rallied with how to carry these experiences around and for how long. She asked herself, what impact they might have on her in the long term! How much more heavy a burden might these uncomfortable experiences have on her relationships presently and in the future? Could she trust anyone again? The swelling on her face was also a more immediate worry. How would she be able to explain how the swelling came about without disclosing the other details to her mother and her brother? He was at that age where questioning enhanced his curious mind. Darsna got up slowly from the bed but went over towards the mirror in her bedroom. She stood in front of the full length mirror on the front of her wardrobe. The swelling had gone down a bit but was still making her face seem lopsided. As she touched the side of her face with her fingers, the puffy swelling from the bruised blood hurt but not as much as the memories that came flooding back to the physical experiences including the physical blows that had been administered to her jaw by the muscular giant insane bully.

Her mother, Pam, was beside herself with worry when she couldn't get through to Darsna. Instinctively, Pam's maternal instincts sensed that something was wrong. Darsna was not answering the landline phone and her cell phone was switched off. It was quite an unusual situation. Pam was not sure where Darsna might be. She had agreed for her to go shopping with her friends but knew, from the type of relationship they had, that Darsna would have sent her even a text message if she could not phone. As any mother in that type of situation might become worried about their child's whereabouts, Pam went on the instinctive intuition that guided her. She went in to tell the doctor, at the surgery where she worked, that she had an emergency that needed to be attended. Pam stated that there were enough staff members to cover for the next fifteen minutes before her shift was due to end. The doctor was empathic to Pam's concerns. She set off on her journey. First, Pam had to figure out whether to collect Rasdan from Aunt Rose's house but, by the urgency imposed upon her by her intuition, pressed to go straight home. Her motherly instinct could not endure the angst that she was experiencing with each passing moment. As she approached the bus stop, Pam noticed the huge crowd that seemed to surround someone on the pavement. The noise from the adolescent school children was raucous and their behaviours befitted hunters around a *'kill'*. Girls and boys alike were actively involved with the individual that was at the receiving end of their punishment. From Pam's observation, none of the adults at the bus stop became actively involved to stop the obvious one-sided assault on the trapped individual on the pavement. Because of the density of the crowd of youngsters milling around the individual on the pavement, Pam was unable to see the recipient of their assault. What she saw clearly was the kicking and stomping motions but heard the huge commotion that seemed to reverberate for at least half a mile away. Without knowing what made her do it, Pam shouted at the young rabble crowd, "Stop". She was unsure how she had managed to summon the courage to voice her disgust but there was something inside her that had prompted Pam's response. Some of the children looked at her in consternation. "I'm a social worker. What is going on here", Pam asked? One boy, who felt his bravado was being interrupted by the interfering woman, made a rude remark. "Shut up man", he growled. Pam looked at the boy, who was hardly much older than her daughter. He was about 15 years old. "Do not speak to me like that. I'm not one of your peers", Pam challenged. "Shame", some of the others remarked. They were rebuking the boy for not having any respect for the adult who was challenging their behaviours. Before he could recover to launch another rude remark at Pam, she spoke again. "I became a social worker because I care. That's my contribution. What's yours", she challenged. Pam's approach was assertive and she remained in charge. The boy was embarrassed in front of his friends. "You're acting as if you're my mother", he fired back. The words had hardly left his mouth when Pam responded. "You do realize that the way you're behaving does not only represent you but your family too. Is your mother aware of how you choose to behave when you're not at home", Pam pressed? The silence was deafening. "I want you to know that there are individuals like me who would like to work with you to bring out the best in you", she continued. What Pam had said impacted on the entire crowd of about 30 to 40 youngsters. Some started to drift away whilst others murmured amongst themselves over Pam's intervention. She seized the opportunity to reinforce her message. "Which one of you have done 'First Aid', she asked? When there was no answer, Pam made her final statement. "You would be better off learning how to save a life rather than taking one. That is more powerful, don't you think", she queried? The same boy who was being rude to her removed his cell phone but engaged in dialling a number.

Pam heard his conversation. "Please send an ambulance. There is a girl lying injured on the pavement", he stated. "Well done", Pam enthused. She walked over to the boy but hugged him. Pam told him how proud she was about the action he had chosen to take. The boy cried unashamedly in front of his friends. They were proud of him and the tears started to well up in their eyes too. As they began to disperse, the boy turned around but uttered two more words. "Thanks Miss", he said. The sound of the siren alerted that an ambulance was close by. The applause from the adult crowd at the bus stop made Pam feel proud of the action she had taken. The ambulance arrived just as the bus pulled up at the bus stop. Pam looked from the bus at the paramedics who attended the girl lying on the pavement. She wondered if the girl would survive! Pam's mind reflected back to her daughter. She selected but pressed Darsna's number logged in the cell phone. Again, there was no response. Pam felt her heart skip what seemed like a couple of beats then it started to race as if she was engaged in a strenuous physical activity. This continued along the entire bus journey.

As she walked up the pathway from her gate, Pam's heart raced at a tempo that was so quickened that she had to stop to inhale deeply a few times before opening the front door. "Darsna, are you alright", Pam queried? When there was no reply, Pam raced up the stairs, two steps at a time, until she reached Darsna's bedroom. She didn't knock but rather pushed hard against the door. It was locked from the inside. All kinds of images and thoughts combined to induce a depth of fear Pam had not experienced before. The questions came thick and fast. Why would Darsna lock her bedroom door? Was she alive? Pam panicked. "Darsna open the door", she demanded. Still, there was no response. Pam pulled back from the door but charged at it with her shoulders like she had seen in the films. Newton's Law about the reactive force being of equal force to the active force came into play. The deadlock on the chunky bedroom door felt no pain but Pam did. She could not decipher whether her guttural cry was from the physical pain or emotional exasperation. Pam felt the tears flooding down her face but felt the pangs of desperation which separated her from access to her daughter. She opined that, even if Darsna was asleep, she would have heard her thudding against the door and her loud pleas to open it. It was only then that Pam smelt the gas that had penetrated the entire house. Her whole focus had been so strong on Darsna that, on entry, Pam had hardly noticed the smell of gas. She raced into the bathroom, toilet and Rasdan's room to open the windows then slid down the banister to reach the ground floor in order to turn off the gas from the cooker. Pam then opened the windows to her own bedroom and the lounge but lastly Pam opened the front door. She was feeling the effects of being gassed too but had past out in the hallway temporarily. It was her neighbour's dog's howling that had caused her to stir back into consciousness but had sent shivers down her spine even in her unconscious state. Pam sat on the aqua blue carpet but wondered how she had got there. The smell of gas had disappeared and the draught from the open windows had slammed the front door shut. Pam raised herself but ran up the stairs once again. This time her strides allowed Pam to climb them three at a time. She banged hard on Darsna's bedroom door but demanded Darsna open it. This time Pam heard the key turn and then the door opened. Darsna stood there for a while before collapsing into her mother's arms. The mixture of being startled by Darsna's collapse and the joy of knowing her daughter was alive seemed to add to Pam's physical strength. Mother and daughter stood embraced in each others arms.

It seemed that they were embraced for hours but it was more like five minutes. Both were relieved to see each other but for different reasons. Pam's concern was about Darsna's change of mind from going shopping with her friends. "So, what happened? Why didn't you go shopping with your friends", Pam asked? Darsna hesitated. She couldn't decide if this was the appropriate time to tell her mother what Raymond had done or to disclose his sordid actions and live with the consequences that he had threatened. Pam noticed Darsna's reticence in responding. Like any mother, Pam fussed about her daughter but was careful to gently probe about her being at home on such a beautiful sunny day. "Is it that time of the month already", Pam suggested? "No mom but it feels like it" Darsna replied. "So you're feeling a bit moody today, are you", Pam searched? Darsna agreed. "Oh, never mind, moods do go away, don't they", Pam assured? Darsna stayed silent. "Your jaw looks a bit puffy. What happened", Pam searched? "Banged it against the toilet door", Darsna lied. "How did you do that", Pam asked? "I was bursting and got careless", Darsna affirmed. "What about the gas? Was that you being careless again", Pam queried? "Yes mom, it's just been one of those days. It seems I'm just clumsy and forgetful", Darsna offered. As she began to cry, Pam cradled Darsna in her arms. "What's wrong sweetheart? This is not like you. What's wrong", Pam enquired? Darsna just burst out into a full-bloodied bawling phase. She buried her head into her mother's bosom. "Oh mommy, I just want to die", Darsna sobbed. Pam knew then that her instinct and intuition about her daughter were right. "Oh angel, what could make you feel like that", Pam queried? She was aware that this situation, whatever it was, needed to be handled with kid gloves but Pam never expected the response she got from Darsna. "I want my daddy. Every child has a right to know their daddy. Why can't I", she cried? Pam was shocked into silence and was beginning to feel guilty for not encouraging Darsna to see her daddy. Because of their adult differences, Pam not only felt spurned by Horatio but also like an added extra to his Harem of women suitors. The magnetic charmer had no idea how many children he had. As a celebrity artiste and performer, Horatio was used to being surrounded by those women, who sought after his genes for the associative link with his DNA, prosperity or otherwise. Family members and close friends had warned him about the type of *'professional leeches',* who might be scheming to relieve him of his massive earnings. Horatio had laughed but dispelled their advice.

Pam, like the other hopefuls then, felt truly abandoned when Horatio had publicly announced his marriage to a green humanoid robotron socialite. After two years, the divorce was public knowledge also. The green humanoid robotron socialite, Mimi Steinking-Bitche, claimed half of Horatio's wealth. Even though they had only been together for the two years, the green humanoid robotron judge ruled in Mimi's favour. The tabloid newspapers and television 'Breaking News' headlines were different but the scandalous story was the same in context. It told of the final fight between Horatio and his green humanoid robotron wife. Pictures on STV, Spaceville Television, matched those in the newspapers. After a huge row, Mimi had chased Horatio on their grounds from the castle they had bought but threw several of his golden and platinum microphones at the windshield of his private jet. He was trying to escape yet another of her jealous tantrums. It was also reported that Mimi keyed the paintwork on the body of the light aircraft as well as shattering the windshield by the repetitive forces applied to it. Within hours of the 'Breaking News' and tabloid newspapers' scoop story, several other women came out in sympathy with Mimi. Some claimed that they had been in romantic situations with the affable, mesmeric charmer. Those women stated that Horatio had confided his preference for green humanoid women with lime green hair. Since his marriage to Mimi, Horatio was undergoing special skin treatment and physical body architecture. He had agreed to have his physical structure rebuilt. These superficial physical adjustments were meant to enable Horatio to become the perceived *'politically correct'* socially acceptable *'stereo-typical'* image of a socialite. His re-creation was being administered by the new **'Gods'** of images, 'HERO', the 'Human Engineering Re-sculpturing Organisation'. They had convinced Horatio that his re-appearance, after his **'resurrection'** from under the anaesthetics, would fit with the fast growing new population of **'collectable pawns'** all over the virtual planet of Asteroidia. The *'new look'* mega Reggae Star's appearance made Horatio seem much greener in shade than his original highly tanned melanin tone. There were whispers and other forms of gossip that supported the *'rumour mill'* which suggested that Horatio was suffering from an addiction to **'skin-tingency'**. His newly constructed face bore no resemblance to his original features. Even Horatio found it difficult to recognize his own reflection whenever he looked into the mirror. This stranger on the virtual side of the mirror was estranged from any association with Horatio's original personality traits. It seemed that every socialite from the 'Tribe of Hawke' wanted to look like the green humanoids from the 'Tribe of Babylon'. Socialites from the 'Tribe of Hawke' to the left and right of the political spectrum avidly usurped this delusional mindset about the preference for the greener skin tone and new adventures into physical reconstruction.

Professor Walynski's Research confirmed that over generations the 'Ghetto Mentality Engineering Scientists' invested heavily in the type of programming and conditioning which had brought about a new set of *'values and beliefs'*. These had brought about the hierarchy for greener skin tone and a penchant for being part of the *'collectable set of pawns'* as being more *'politically acceptable'*. Individuals, like Horatio, from the 'Tribe of Hawke' administered their self-inoculation of mental *'stereo-tripe'* and self-transfusion of mental *'stereo-hype'* in changing their natural skin colour, tones as well as hair textures, colours and styles. They did this by use of chemicals and sundry applications, to look more like the green humanoid robotrons. This was not only the completion of those individuals' psychopathic delusional neurotic imageries but also became the new *'fashionable'* trend. As *'politically correct'* socially acceptable *'stereo-types'*, these 'wannabee' socialites and their twisted mindsets were being offered as ideal *'role models'* for the younger generations of the 'Tribe of Hawke', especially. Professor Walynski referred to them as **"summary heirs to heirlooms of warped egos, psychotic attitudes and psychopathic mindsets"**. He said that **"they recycled, transplanted but managed to transcend the same perennial subservient messages much deeper into the psyche of the younger generations; poisoning their natural aptitude to live their natural traditions without feeling less than"**. Such was the level of Horatio's self-worth as he ascended into the mega-heights of stardom. He relented towards a lifestyle which beckoned but preyed upon his emotional state of low self-worth. GMES, Ghetto Mental Engineering Scientists inveigled but strategise the timed orchestration of techniques, which they applied to the naturally gifted musician. They assigned Horatio a personal nurse, who carefully applied the green 'skin-tinging' cream all over his melanin body to catalyse the transformation towards his new look features.

As part of the legal settlement, Horatio was being humiliated even further when his wife, Mimi, took over the castle but forced him out. The green robotron judge had sanctioned that Mimi's and Horatio's two children from their marriage "stay with their mother". Conditions for the limited visitation was "with supervision only" because Mimi had complained that Horatio might abscond with the children to his indigenous exotic island with which there was no extradition arrangements. On the news of the well publicised break-up between Mimi and Horatio, his sponsors were quick to relinquish any association with him after the scandalous public debacle. They hastily withdrew their support as early as when the newspaper and 'Breaking News' headlines had first been announced. 'The Chartbuster's Chronicle' and 'The Chartbuster's Association' jointly recommended that, unless Horatio publicly apologised to his green humanoid robotron wife for his *'unbearable'* behaviour, he be publicly belittled. This would be executed by withdrawing Horatio's name from the 'Honour Role' of 'Most Famous Musical Icons' at 'The Iconsville Museum', in the Kingdom of Spaceville where super-mega *'A' Blisters* were immortalized in perpetuity.

All that had happened before Darsna had come back to resettle in Spaceville. After Pam's reflection on Horatio's disappearance from the public, she was in a quandary as to how to contact the elusive celebrity. What could she do if she managed to contact Horatio? Would he even remember her let alone acknowledge that Darsna was his child? After all, it was Pam who had willingly joined the Harem of women. It was they who had flocked Horatio Magnificado's concerts. She had flung herself upon the impressive Reggae Star. It was Pam, the high flier then, who had a *'crush'* on the handsome magical charmer. During one of his superb performances at an auspicious elite venue, Pam soared above her competitors but exposed her willingness to have sexual intercourse with Horatio. She did this by throwing her thong, with her cell phone number imprinted on it, on stage amongst the others. With her loins on fire, Pam had spent a lot of money to secure an enviable position in the front row near the stage. She had planned it for months but saved enough money to purchase the high-priced ticket through auction. Pam had worn a very provocative outfit of which even Sandra might have approved and she was determined to outdo any competition for Horatio's attention.

After bedding her, Horatio called Pam a couple of times before moving on to another within his readily available Harem. That was par for the course as far as this super celebrity Reggae Star was concerned. Pam was doubtful that Horatio might even not remember her let alone own up to Darsna being his child. Now she was faced with a predicament that challenged her reputation. Pam couldn't find it in herself to tell her daughter that she was conceived in a *'one night stand'* relationship with the mesmeric Reggae Singer. She knew the risk and it was quite probable that the consequence for her deliberate behaviour was that she might become pregnant. How could Pam explain to her daughter that, at the time, she was on heat and that her *'Lust Factor'* had gone off the scale in favour of the infamous Cassanova?

After Pam's reflection on the conditions concerning her daughter's conception, it was Darsna's turn to be surprised by her mother's unusual behaviour. Pam sobbed unashamedly but snuggled up to her daughter like a pet to its empathic owner. "Mom, I didn't mean to upset you but I think I'm ready to meet my daddy now. I want to be able to ask the questions for which I need answers", Darsna assured. Pam felt so ashamed and rather embarrassed by her daughter's more than reasonable request. There was only one way for Pam to approach this situation and that was to tell Darsna the truth but which truth did she think was appropriate at this time! "I've had no contact with your daddy for some while now. I don't even know if he's still in this Kingdom", Pam confessed. She met Darsna's eyes to ensure that element of truth. "Doesn't he ask about me", Darsna enquired? "It wasn't that type of relationship", Pam confessed. Darsna searched her mother's countenance for what lay behind that statement. "What prompted you to ask to see your daddy now", Pam queried? Darsna hesitated then commented. "Is there a particular time that is convenient to ask", she searched? Pam was unsure what was causative to the cynical implications within Darsna's last question but she had to focus on her daughter's needs instead of the hurt she was feeling. "No sweetheart, it's just that I feel so inadequate not being able to tell you of your daddy's whereabouts. I wouldn't know where to start", Pam confessed. She managed to remain congruent but the feeling of guilt was killing her. "I know Raymond is not your biological father and I've not pretended that he is but he seems to want to play the daddy role. You two seem to get on well", Pam commented. Darsna did not want to discuss the rapist with her mother. She thought that if only her mother knew what he had done, she might not be so sure of his *'intentions'* as a father figure. Darsna switched tactics. Tell me about my real daddy. What was he like when you two were together? Did you live together? Pam was shocked surprised at how directly Darsna's questions were and the impact they were having on her. She decided to come clean so that there was no confusion in her daughter's mind. "No, we did not live together. Your daddy is a celebrity Reggae Star. He was always touring. That's why it so hard for me to tell you much about his whereabouts", Pam submitted. This was a huge disappointment for Darsna. She had images of her mother and father in a long termed loving relationship which probably drifted apart. Now, it seemed like they had hardly known each other. Darsna could see new tears welling up in her mother's eyes. She didn't want to see her mother cry anymore so she kissed her lightly on her forehead. "Don't cry mom. I didn't ask about my daddy to make you sad", she exclaimed.

CHAPTER 52

The phone rang for quite a while before Dian Bogus' feeble voice whispered into it, "Hello". "It's me", Sandra said softly. "Me who", Dian queried? Sandra was feeling a sense of disappointment that her mother did not recognize her voice. Even though she had not been in touch with her mother for such a long time, Sandra tried to tell herself that Dian would still welcome her. Sandra hesitated before she replied, "Sandra". "San-San, is that you", Dian enquired? "Yes", Sandra replied. Dian felt not only joy but also relief that her daughter would finally see her physical disablement and be available to hear of her mental anguish since her health took a turn for the worse. Conversely, Sandra recalled her mother's physical appearance within her mind. She remembered how Dian used to comment how younger men were attracted to her because she looked *'good'* for her age. Even though Sandra didn't know it, this image would be demolished whenever they met face to face. Apart from looking a little podgy around the chin and neck area, Dian retained her facial structure reasonably well. She still wore that flashing smile whenever she had a chance to but now her 'humped' back made her look like a female version of Quasimodo. Dian's gait was wobbly and greatly unstable. She was the first to break the silence that had forced itself into the brief hesitant conversation that had occurred previously between them. "Oh San-San, I'm glad to hear your voice. It's been a long time. You don't call anymore" Dian started. "Mom, don't let me feel worse than I do", Sandra replied. Her words were choked but sounded deeply sincere. She didn't give Dian anytime to respond. "I am not far away from you at the moment but I wanted to ask you if I could come round to see you", Sandra stressed. "Yes, how far away are you", Dian asked? The phone went dead. Dian looked at it but anticipated it ringing again. She placed it on the receiver but raised herself from the couch on which she was resting. Dian reached out for the walking stick that lent on the wall near the couch. She shifted but used the stick to help raise her huge frame into the crouch stance that had now become her new posture since her last operation at the local hospital. Sandra was unaware of her mother's failing health especially the chronic arthritis that had set in over the past year. Dian did not have access to any of Sandra's cell phone numbers previously but she welcomed the fact that her 'San-San' would be visiting. The landline phone rang again. Smiling happily to herself, Dian shuffled over towards it. Anticipating Sandra's call, Dian assumed it was her daughter ringing back to confirm how soon she might be arriving with her. "Hello San-San, where are you", Dian asked? The voice on the phone was not Sandra's. Dian soon recognized the 'crank' caller. He identified himself by the abuse that he spat down the line. "Get out, you black bitch. This is Higher Greensborough, Mid Suburbia. We don't want your 'lot' round here", the voice said. Dian ended the call. Since CB's death, Dian had bought a new house in a more secluded part of Higher Greensborough which she felt better reflected her status. She had been harassed by some individuals in that part of Greensborough. Dian had experienced a series of insults and assaults that was inexplicable but she chose to ignore these for as long as she could. Some of these assaults were quite bizarre. On several occasions, excrement was being posted through her letterbox. Random threatening notes were strewn across her lawn and along the pathway from the gate. Sometimes stones were thrown and pellet guns were used to break her windows. The closest Dian came to being physically injured was when her garage was set alight. She lost her brand new SUV but the cost to repair the damage to the house was quite a hefty sum too. Though the insurance company paid out, they warned Dian that her premium would rise steeply. Dian had cut off most of her friends and acquaintances but had pretended that, with time, she might be better accepted in her new community. This current phone call made Dian shake with rage. A cold chill ran up her spine. Her whole body trembled all over.

The walking stick slipped on the tatty carpet that had long past its lifespan. The threadbare patches far outnumbered the tufted areas. Crumbled rubberized underlay erupted through the threadbare areas but sent clouds of dust into the air as Dian's weight further pulverized whatever tufts of carpet that remained. The 'crank' phone call had thrown Dian somewhat. She was not only shaken physically but mentally too. The menacing phone calls were random before but lately they had become more frequent and more intimidating. Dian had made several complaints to the local police but they said they couldn't help her. When the phone rang again, Dian did not pick it up. She stared at it as it rang continuously. "Lord, I pray Sandra will arrive soon", Dian muttered. She could not take the ringing in her ears anymore. Dian shuffled over towards the small oak table but lifted the receiver from its cradle. She cut the call off then left the receiver dangling from the table. It was the rapid heavy knocking on the front door that alerted Dian. Again, she started to shake all over but this time there was no chill up her spine. Dian heard Sandra's voice calling through the letterbox. "Mom, open the door", she shouted. Sandra waited a few moments but still there were no sound. She peeked through the letterbox to see if she could see her mother. Dian was *'hurrying'* as fast as she could but it was not at the same pace as Sandra had anticipated. Struggling to get by the ornaments and those other items that had become collective barriers that cluttered the top landing of the house, Dian stared anxiously at the Deer's head that was placed on the wall facing the turn at the top of the stairs. Its protruding antlers were now a danger for the more obese Dian. She now had to be more cautious as she passed by them. As Dian started her decent down the stairs that led into the hallway, she heard the rapid knocking on the ornate gilded pig's head doorknocker that adorned the central area of the front door. She could hear her neigbours' voices. "Haven't seen her come out like she used to", one voice said. "She's had it rough for a while now, since the operation", another stated. "Old Dian use to be a laugh a minute but we don't see her now", the first voice said. Sandra's head was moving from side to side like someone at a Tennis Match. The word *'operation'* had registered into her brain. Of course, she wouldn't have known about her mother's operations. She simply didn't keep in touch except for the odd times like when she told her of Raymond's demise. The thought of her mother undergoing an operation rebounded enough to disturb even the *'uncaring'* Sandra. "What operation", she asked guardedly? The neighbours began to explain away what they knew of Dian's demise. Sandra stood numbed by the revelations. These neighbours were more informed about her mother than her. Sandra heard everything from the earlier days of the neighbours 'feastings' on "the exotic foods that Dian used to make" to the days Dian spent alone. The voices were loud enough for anyone to hear. Dian shook her head from side to side as she continued to negotiate the rest of the twelve steps into the hallway. Holding on tightly to the solid oak banister, Dian slipped one foot down unto the tread of stair in front of her, ensured her balance before attempting to bring the other foot down. Again she tested her balance before repeating the previous drill over and over again. This procedure took place each time Dian needed to go downstairs. The hammering of the ornate gilded pig against the matching gilded plate on the front door stopped Dian in her track. She looked directly at the front door. Dian heard the voice through the letterbox. "Are you in there Dian", the voice asked? She recognized the voice of the neighbour next door. "Yes", she replied. Dian's voice was a pitch or two higher than when she first answered the phone to Sandra. Amid the confused din outside the door, Dian's reply was not heard. She continued her journey down the stairs until she could place her foot onto the discoloured patch on the carpet that continued from the stairs into the hallway. Dian checked her balance once again even though both feet were now in the hallway. She huffed and puffed somewhat before trying to move again. This time she shuffled along towards the front door. There was still just over 18 ft for her to cover. The letterbox was raised and someone shouted through it. "You've got a visitor Dian". "I know", Dian shouted back. The neighbour looked through the letterbox. She could see Dian's distinctly varicose veined huge feet shuffling towards the door. "She's coming", the neighbour announced. The din had settled down to whispers. Sandra waited with the neigbours for the front door to open. "San-San are you really out there", Dian asked? There was a hint of anticipation in her voice. "Yes it's me", Sandra replied. Dian tried to shuffle a bit faster. She hadn't yet got used to walking with the stick but there was not much coordination without it either. Dian stopped at the dark oak hallstand that stood to one side of the wide hallway. Her shaking hands made contact with the small drawers in the hallstand. She fumbled with them but couldn't quite control how they came out. More than one set of keys flew into the air but spilt onto the worn carpet. "Oh dear, San-San I spilt the keys on the floor", Dian said aloud. There were two sets closer to her than the other yet it was more practical for Dian to retrieve the set furthest away from her. Dian's eyesight had deteriorated over the past eight months. Being shortsighted meant Dian had to get much closer to the keys to be able to identify them. With one hand on the walking stick to maintain her balance, she bent forwards to retrieve the keys closest to her. Dian's centre of gravity shifted. She overbalanced but plunged awkwardly towards the floor. It was at that moment that Sandra raised the letterbox to peak once again. For the first time Sandra felt real emotion towards the 6'3" figure lying awkwardly in the hallway. The very obese 'humped' back figure lay motionless on the floor. Sandra did not recognise the individual. She remembered her mother, Dian, as a tall buxom woman with a moderately trim figure not too dissimilar to her own. The woman with the "film star looks" that kept her husband, CB, mesmerized right up to the moment before he died, had changed both physically and mentally. Sandra could not bring herself to accept how much Dian had changed, physically. She wasn't aware that her mother had also spent four months in a Mental Home suffering from the depression brought on by the terrible deliberate harassment that had plagued her ever since she chose to move to this secluded part of Greensborough close to the border of Snideborough. CB's last Will & Testament had included a sizeable Lottery win which he had not told his wife about but helped him to leave Dian with the financial means to buy the current house. The mortgage on the previous house in Central Greensborough was fully paid up and CB had left sufficient insurance money to see Dian well into old age.

Dian's problems started when she applied for her work pension. She had been paying into the Fund for over 34 years. The company had lost the money from the Pension Fund by investing in more than risky shares on the Stockers Market. Financial depression over the previous five years meant that the value of the shares the Pension Fund had accumulated plummeted drastically. Workers like Dian, loss 'their' investments. She fought with the company about her rights to the pension but the legal fees soon ate up a great deal of the money she had available. Her State Pension Application was refused on the grounds that her declaration indicated that she was 'financially sound' and therefore did not qualify. Being alone, Dian thought about how she'd not only been cheated by her employers but also by the State as well. A glass or two of sherry turned into stronger alcoholic concoctions that ultimately caused her diseased liver. Arthritic joints and varicose veined legs meant hours of pain and anguish for who used to be 'the woman with the film star looks'. She needed to tell her San-San about her suffering. Dian was not aware of the shock surprise that confronted Sandra when she saw her physical increase in size. She stood back away from the letterbox not wanting to accept the individual on the floor as her mother. "There's a woman on the floor but it's not my mother", she exclaimed.

One neighbour took turn to peer through the letterbox. Dian lay motionless. "Oh my God, she's dead. Dian's dead", the woman screamed. "No, not Dian, no more of that lovely 'Rice and Peas', no more of that hot mouth-watering 'Curried Goat'", the other neighbour exclaimed. Dian could hear the cries coming from the other side of the front door. She was concerned about their perception of her state of health. "I'm not dead", she said loudly. "Shush, I could swear I heard Dian's voice", another neighbour exclaimed. The second neighbour peeked through the letterbox. She did not see Dian lying dead on the floor as had been thought by the first neighbour. Instead, she lay on her left side near to the dark oak hallstand. Dian was breathing and very much alive. She could see the keys that were first furthest away from her whilst she was in a standing position. Now they lay within reach. The walking stick had fallen from Dian's grasp, on her way down to the floor. It was even more accessible than the keys. She reached out but held the floor end of the walking stick. Dian used the crook end to pull the keys closer to her. To complete this feat, it meant she had to change position from resting on her left side to a full prone position. Dian held the keys close to her face, seeking to identify the correct ones that would open the front door. "These are the right ones", Dian said aloud. She smiled to herself then tried to get up from the floor. It was quite a sight to see a woman involuntarily mimicking the actions of a seal coming ashore. Dian pushed and groaned as much. She had made no progress going forward. Instead, the effort left Dian feeling breathless. She rested until her breathing became regular again. Dian placed her hands under her chest but pushed against the shoddy carpet covering the firm floor underneath as hard as she could but raised herself partially upwards onto her knees. Panting like a thirsty dog, Dian managed to hold onto the sturdy dark oak hallstand with her left hand. She used the walking stick in her right hand to support her effort. Dian could hear the clapping outside.

Each neighbour, who had taken an interest in what was going on, joined in celebration of her being alive. Sandra found herself clapping too but was surprised at her own action. She didn't want to clap necessarily but was swept up in the feeling of goodwill shown by her mother's neighbours. The letterbox was lifted once again and a running commentary of Dian's progression towards the front door was ongoing. The clapping had died down a bit in anticipation of the door opening. They heard the rattling of keys as Dian attempted to open the door. After the last of the five locks were open, the door opened slowly at first but then swung wide open. There, Dian stood crouched and grossly obese but ready to hug her San-San. She opened her arms but awaited Sandra's advance. Dian's physical change was a great shock for Sandra to witness. She froze where she was standing until one of Dian's neighbours pushed her gently towards Dian. "Go on duck", the neighbour encouraged. Sandra walked slowly at first then quickened her stride, as she got closer to Dian. She allowed herself to be hugged by her mother. They stood in deep embrace just inside the door as the neighbours cheered and clapped some more. "That's the daughter ain't it", one voice asked? "You don't mean her on the telly, do yah", another voice queried? "Naw, she's tastier than her", a male voice boomed. "Is this one a tasty bird? We could find out, couldn't we", a younger male voice enticed. "How're you gonna do that", a young female voice asked? The man with the suggestion was now in a corner. His bluff was called and he had no way out of the dare. He hesitated but the crowd that had now gathered jeered loudly. "Boo, boo, boo", the voices jeered. Someone replicated the sound of a chicken then the crowd joined in. "Cluck ... cluck, cluck ... cluck, cluck,

cluck, cluck ... cluck ...", the voices jeered. Embarrassed by the taunting, the man turned away from the crowd but walked swiftly towards Sandra. He walked up to her but stood at arms length from her then turned towards the crowd. The man gestured for them to cheer. He stooped bent at the knees but rose slowly, waving his hand with the control of a Maestro in charge of an Orchestra. Responding to his antics, the crowd responded with concerted understanding. The sound of their voices rose rapidly, octave by octave until it reached a sort of crescendo, then the crowd started again, ably led by their 'Orchestral Leader'. "W-h-e-e-h-e-y", the voices chanted repeatedly. It sounded more like Duke's way of celebrating. The chants seemed not to bother Sandra or Dian. They stood hugging just the same in the long embrace. "San-San, San-San", Dian repeated. Sandra did not speak but sobbed as she realized how long she had ignored her mother and the current state of her health. She had no excuse apart from the fact that her career and Duke occupied most hours of her days. The reality of her situation is that in Sandra's *'superficial world'* of the *'Neuro-stereo-type'* *'model'* lifestyle had been designed but choreographed by the green humanoid robotrons. Individuals like Sandra were controlled but determined to be the *'acceptable models'* to which other individual's must aspire, seemingly! No alternative *'models'* were tolerated. Sandra and her mother, Dian, broke their embrace, stood back but looked each other up and down. They turned, waved to the crowd then stepped further into the hallway.

Dian handed the keys to Sandra but asked her to lock the door. Sandra closed the solid oak door then fidgeted until she found the first of the keys that fitted a lock correctly. She turned the key but followed behind her mother. Dian was not satisfied that Sandra had turned the key in only one lock. "Make sure you lock the others, San-San". Dian warned. "Is it that bad round here", Sandra asked? "Yes, those that are desperate often prey on those that are destitute. It's in the News everyday" Dian advised before her voice trailed off. "Things are not the same as when you were growing up in Central Greenborough. All different kinds of old *'yagga'* *'yagga'* had moved into the area talking about they *"own territory"*. They had robbed, traded, stabbed and shot one another in gang fights openly in front of the CCTV cameras as if they were in some kind of a movie. It was one hell of a mix-up, mix-up. You don't know who to say hello to, nowadays", Dian preached. They walked down the hallway past the stairs but headed towards the kitchen. When Sandra opened the door a large ginger furred tabby cat rushed past them. "In this part of Greensborough, neighbours are watching out for strangers. Living in this secluded part of Higher Greensborough, I've been subjected to some very weird behaviours by some individuals, who see me as being out of my depth. As they keep pointing out, there's not many of my *'lot'* living round here", Dian continued to explain. "What about your neighbours? They seem to care about you", she replied. "They are just as fickle. A plastic smile here, comment about the weather there seem to be the depth of the conversation I've received so far in this secluded part of Greensborough. Apart from an invitation for a cup of tea or coffee, the preference seems to be limited to any excuse for an alcoholic drink everywhere. I've invited some of my neighbours to dinner and barbeques. At first, everyone seemed happy with me but over the last five years, I'm stunned at the array of insults and intimidation I've had to put up with", Dian explained. She used the opportunity to spill her frustrations and concerns about how she was being treated by the green humanoid robotrons, who were the majority in Higher Greensborough. Sandra listened keenly as her mother spilled her frustrations and disappointments. She recognized some of the feelings that Dian was conveying to her. Sandra noticed that the ginger cat was not the only one around. Her large cornflower blue eyes went searchingly around the room to the many voices of the twenty or so cats that had appeared. "Where did they all come from", Sandra asked? "These are the only true friends I've got nowadays. At least they don't discriminate nor humiliate me", Dian replied.

CHAPTER 53

Duke had chosen to spend a lot of time away from Sandra. He'd manage to keep telephone calls quite short. Duke seemed less keen than before to be in Sandra's company. Most of the time, he'd use his *'self-importance'* as the reason but Alan Baitman had reported to him that Raymond had been calling her often. Duke was jealous of what seemed like the rekindling of a relationship between Sandra and her ex-partner, Raymond. The quarrels between Sandra and Duke had become more frequent. His plan was to *"pull the plug"* to remind her that without his clout, Sandra's modelling and acting careers were as good as finished. She had climbed to the pinnacle of her careers with his and Grant Favours' astute leadership and creativity, respectively. Sandra was now the number one *'A' Blister*. She had come into the limelight with a huge explosive introduction featuring the famed *'Pum-Pum'* shorts episode at the Auditorium in the Hotel Welcome Complex. Billionaires fought for her signature while Duke orchestrated Sandra's rise to the top. Hollygoodyā's film directors and producers were eager to make her into an icon, the ideal *'role model'*. Duke had worked pretty cleverly with his contacts to bring Sandra to the attention of the entire Royal Royal Dis-United Stately Kingdoms of Asteroidia and beyond into the other Galaxies in the World of Space. He wanted his exotic bird to be the first incomparable 'Inter-Galactic Super Model Supreme' and for her to be nominated for and to win all the honours in the modeling and movie world.

All technological and physical magazines carried an editorially commanding, airbrushed, merchantable version of the delectable Sandra. Each portrayed her in a much greener complexion than was her natural highly melanin skin colour. Grant Favours had been working tirelessly with his contacts in Holygoodyā to arrange the *'Bests'* Awards for her. These nominations would consists of the *'Miss Best Legs'*, *'Miss Best Body'*, *'Miss Best Bimmer'*, *'Miss Best Breasts'*, *'Miss Best Kissable Lips'*, *'Miss Best Mouth'*, *'Miss Best High Cheekbones'*, *'Miss Best Nose'*, *'Miss Most Relaxed Hair'*, *'Miss Best Humanoid Robotron Barbie Look-a-Like'* and *'Miss Best Beautifully Mesmeric Eyes'* Awards. Duke and Grant were extremely confident Sandra would win all without comparison. Between them, they were most certain that it was more than just probable for Sandra to be the first and most likely the only Super Model and Movie Star Icon to claim a *'full house'* of Awards all at the same time in this millennium. *'The Inter-Galactic Guild of 'HERO'*, Human Engineering Re-sculpturing Organisation was amongst the major sponsors backing these Awards. Every female wanted to be a replica *'Role Model'* and become the *'Super Model'* and *'Movie Icon'*, Sandra look-a-like. Such were the demands for the services of body re-sculpturing that there was machinery actively being put into place to fast track the applications and training for more Human Engineering Re-sculpturing.

Advertising and Promotional Agencies had reported a huge surge in interest to help boost Duke's exotic bird into a much higher realm. The 'Extra Award Organisation', EAO, was planning to attract more major sponsors to participate in yet another new category of award, simply known as, TEA, 'The Extra Award'. This was a one off award which meant Sandra would go down in history as the only owner of that particular award. A new money machine was being birthed. The spin-offs would mean that Duke's venerable exotic bird, being one of the select few enabled by her magnanimous celebrity status and proven reputation, would be enabled to transition from The Village of Urgington to live in the most prestigious, idealistic, enviable, exclusive environment on the other side of the mountain known as Champagne Valley. As much as Duke had clout in most places, he, like most other residents living in the prestigious surroundings of the Village of Urgington, might have reached his maximal residential ambition. Without having that extra qualification, like Sandra, Duke would not be welcomed to make that transition into the most prestigiously enviable setting. Financial abundance was not enough. The 'Icon Status' was the core requirement to enable access to membership into the ultra exclusive, idealistic, enviable residency in the elitist, superb, Ultra-Suburban Champagne Valley environment, on the other side of the mountain. It was a preserve that was reserved for those more than privileged Mega Stars like Sandra, who were allowed to live in that much, much greener ultra-prestigious Champagne Valley. Living there would make Duke's clout even greater than that of the Most Honorable Prime Leaders of the Dis-United Stately Kingdoms of the virtual planet to date.

Sandra's head was in a spin. Because of her advanced status, she was being managed by the ruthlessly super-efficient task oriented new Agent, Andromeda Francescovic. She replaced Jane Dunnit. Andromeda Francescovic was nominated by Sir Ivanhoe Goldfeet and suitably sanctioned by Duke. Sandra became more aware of the autograph hunters and general *'back-slappers'*. They were now part of Sandra's daily life. Some meant it genuinely but there were others to whom *'back-slapping'* was a *'career'*. Some even invaded dinners arranged for selected listed VIP *'Invited Guests only'* functions but had daringly invited themselves. They miraculously managed to bluff their way into the inner sanctums of the residence of 'The Most Honorable Prime Leader' of Spaceville. The particular couple posed an embarrassment for the Security Arm of the Kingdom's elected leading official politicrats by breaching not only protocol but embarrassed the cordon of *'expert'* security staff, who were meant to ensure that no such breach could possibly happen. It was a security *'blip'* that could not be denied. The couple did not only pose for pictures with the Honorable Deputy Prime Leader and others but also shook hands with the Most Honorable Prime Leader to prove the authenticity of their planned caper. Alan Baitman used the same tactics to infiltrate but hover in and around the Prime Leaders' special guest, Sandra. He infiltrated her dressing room but planted a remote recording device in it. Alan Baitman posed as a member staff. He positioned himself in such a way as to be able to record some or parts of the conversations between Sandra and Raymond.

When he played the recordings back to Duke, he went completely berserk. The sexual innuendoes and the confirmation by Sandra that she had to remain beholden to Raymond forever because he had taken her virginity was a revelation that hurt Duke badly. He was truly sold on the *'values and beliefs'* that clout and riches were enough to distract from the needs of individuals like Sandra. What her message conveyed was that *'need'* far exceeds *'want'* every time. Raymond's sexual techniques were far superior to Duke's even with the aphrodisiac qualities of Champagne Urge Mark 3. No man wanted to hear that he is or had been a huge sexual disappointment but worse of all no man wanted to hear that he is just being used until . . . either. At first, Duke planned to take both Raymond and Sandra to the crypts to torture them in order to get them to confess that they had planned the whole thing prior to Sandra coming to work for DSI.

Even though Sandra had proven that she had been an excellent actor long before she was discovered by the movie moguls of Hollygoodyā, her version of events were quite different from Duke's. She was getting tired of being bullied by her agent, the notorious Andromeda Francescovic She told Sandra that as number one *'A' Blister* she had to "sleep around with the heads of huge corporations" in order to maintain her status. Sandra flatly refused. When she complained to Duke, he told her that if she wanted to stay at the top of the ladder, Sandra would have to be a Commercial Escort for the growing queue of influential moguls, who wanted to be seen in her company at the varied *'Pink and Green Tie'* Events. Sandra told Duke she wanted to be able to choose which events she attended and that she didn't want to be forced to sleep around. He told her those decisions were not in their hands. "You'll have to get off your bloody high horse. That is the price of fame". "You don't get something for nothing, there's no free lunch. You didn't think important people are giving their time free, do ya? Wake up and smell the coffee", Duke raged. Sandra was bitterly disappointed with Duke's manner. All of a sudden, he seemed to have changed from adoring his *'Sugarcake'* to this evil monster that had risen up from the heart of the cesspool sewers. Something about Duke had changed but Sandra could not understand what would make him despise her so much. In one of the many frequent quarrels, she dared to suggest that Duke was acting like someone with a split personality. She had done the research but discovered that his unstable behaviour matched a particular personality type known as *'bi-polar condition'*. It appeared that Duke was showing traits of this condition. His complex characteristics were reminding Sandra of a calm sea that, for no apparent reason, had suddenly erupted into swirling choppy raging tidal waves akin to that of a mini tsunami despite no apparent change in the weather, perhaps!

They agreed on nothing; not even to continue to the search for their missing dog, Tramp, on the exotic far off paradise island of Costa Del Shell. Duke's visits there and at other far off exotic continents, countries and islands were becoming more frequent too. Although he didn't spend much time in any of these destinations, Duke seemed to be more secretive about his visits to those other 5th rated exotic continents, countries and islands. Sandra had no idea what type of business had caused Duke to be *'touring'* these places as frequently as he was but they now seemed to be his priority. Whenever he was in Spaceville, Duke seemed to be avoiding her like the plague. Instead, he was spending more time with the rotund Doris Bendlow. They now seemed inseparable. When Sandra queried about what was going on between Duke and Doris, his comment was that *"birds of a feather stick together"*. Sandra began to wonder what she had done to deserve to be scorned by the man whom had sacrificed so much for her in the past. He had many critics when he flaunted with his prized *'catch'*, "the most exotic bird in the entire Kingdom of Spaceville", he had said. Now, she didn't seem to be the flavour of his moments anymore. After moving from the mansion in Poshborough and the house in the Village of Urgington, the last time Duke visited Sandra at their extremely spacious multi-acre grand mansion in Champagne Valley on the other side of the mountain, he voiced his gross disappointment with her none compliance to become an Escort to his billionaire and squillionaire contacts. It was as if she was contracted out in some type of negotiation from which she was absent. In the huge row they had whilst living in the exclusive Village of Urgington, even the neighbours could hear the loud discourse which took place between them. The villagers dubbed Duke and Sandra *"The Odd Couple from Hell"*. In an environment as close as a village, there were virtually no secrets. Everyone seemed to make it their business to know everyone else's business. The talk around the Village of Urgington was that Duke had told Sandra that when he met her she was *"nothink"*. It was him that had made her into the *'A' Blister* celebrity model and actress that she had become. He was grossly disappointed that by not acceding to his request to *"mingle"* with his contacts, Sandra had embarrassed him in front of all his friends in the World of Space. Children and adults alike whispered but pointed at Sandra wherever she went but criticized her for disappointing the popular magnate, Duke Stagg. "I don't know what he sees in her" were the latest jibe that circulated whenever she visited the prestige Village of Urgington where she often went to shop. Sandra had no real friends in the village but a few pretended to *'tolerate'* her. One woman in the local market had approached her but asked, "What have you done with our Duke"? Some of the children called her "the freak with blue eyes". Most of the comments were deliberately hurtful. One woman had boldly told her face to face what the village thought of her. "You and your *'type'* are not wanted round here. Sling your hook. You people need to go back to where you come from", she had advised. Sandra was reminded daily that she didn't fit in. Everyday, someone was hinting at her as being *"a stereo-typed misfit"*.

She still owned the house in the village. Whenever she stayed there, dog excrement was regularly *'delivered'* through her letterbox. That was such a disgusting experience for her but Sandra wondered what sort of mindset would think of doing such a thing and what sort of *'pleasure'* or *'satisfaction'* those individuals got from tasking themselves with such disgusting practices? Her most frightening experience was the smell of petrol that had been poured through her letterbox. That turned her into and becoming an insomniac. Notes were being posted through her letterbox too and the threats seemed to supersede the ones her mother Dian had told her that she was experiencing. Sandra seemed to believe that her fame would erase the prejudices which she faced in the village but it served as a reminder of those awesome times at St. Halo's High Apostolic Grammar School when she was younger. It was like re-living one's worst nightmare over and over again. They were like repeated encores after giving a performance. Sandra had no friends except for Pam and no family except for her mother, Dian, who never seemed to answer her phone anymore. Pam was having her own problems with Raymond and his lack of financial support. It seemed to have evaporated like water from a gulch, rendering it dry. Because Pam could not afford to pay the mortgage on a regular basis anymore, the threat of becoming homeless was imminent. The local government housing had told Pam that she had made herself and her children *'intentionally homeless'* by leaving Painsville, Lower Ghettoborough. Her children were at high risk of being taken over by Social Services. Although he was not taking responsibility of his children's basic needs, like ensuring they had a roof over their heads and the provision of food, Raymond was willing to listen to Sandra's *'trials'* and *'tribulations'* instead. She began to drink heavily and at times, Champagne Urge Mark 3 was the only form of *'sustenance'* that passed her lips for weeks. When Sandra complained to Duke about the treatment she was getting whenever she shopped or stayed in The Village of Urgington, he told her that she should stop complaining and that she *"needed to be more thick skinned"*.

It had been six months since she last saw or was contacted by Duke. Sandra had received a call from Hinton Fairly, the lawyer Duke had appointed to take care of her affairs. He advised her that Duke had instructed him to sever links with her. "What, how soon", Sandra asked? "Forthwith, I'm sorry," Hinton replied. This was like a bolt out of the blue. It was something Sandra could not have perceived happening. "Forthwith", Sandra queried? Her voice had changed to a slightly higher pitch and volume. The shock took the wind out her sails. "I need time", Sandra replied. Duke was listening to the conversation. The call was on loudspeaker mode. "That's not fair. Couldn't you wait until I find a replacement", Sandra asked? Duke scribbled swiftly on a note pad. He peeled off the top page from its place but handed it to Hinton. "Don't give her room to breathe Hinty", the note read. Hinton did not need Duke's encouragement but acknowledged his instruction all the same. He did not hesitate to reply. "My company's reputation is at stake if we loose Mr Staggs' business. We can't afford to ignore the wishes of our biggest client. It's as simple as that. I'm sure you'll understand", Hinton said firmly. Sandra was thrown aback not only by the swiftness of Hinton's response but also his eagerness to distance himself from her too. The implied tone was insensitively business-like and cold. Duke signalled to Hinton by passing his hand under his throat. The motion started from the right but continued to the left, horizontally. Sandra heard the buzz of the dial tone in her ear. Hinton had done his job. Sandra threw the cell phone on the table. She was feeling not only lonely but also unwanted. Sandra had noticed a pattern of strange behaviours, not only from Hinton but also from the few people who used to greet her in the streets. Now, they shied away from her but stated that they were always "in a hurry, love". The few that bothered to continue conversing with her were the ones Sandra thought of as boring. There was old Mrs Tibbs with her dozen cats, the man down the street that bred and owned Pit Bull Terrier dogs, the thin woman with the Alsatian 'Wolf' and old Miss Grumble who constantly went on about "holidays in the sun". The younger folk kept themselves to themselves. They pointed and whispered but would no longer engage with her.

Sandra had gone down to her local AADC for social interaction. To her disappointment she'd noticed that, since refusing to continue to pay for everyone's drinks like she used to, the atmosphere in the AADC entered into a monopoly of silent gestures and audible quips about ". . . these *'fancy'* women". Sandra's torment continued when she last spoke with Duke. She'd complained about the cold shouldered treatment she'd been experiencing but Duke had laughed and told her yet again that she was *"too bloody thin-skinned"*. In the past, he had said the same thing when she'd told him about the taunts when she had joined DSI. He didn't seem too interested then either. "What do you want me to do? I can't do nothink from here. Pull yourself together woman", Duke had warned. This made Sandra desperate for an outlet that would at least make her feel good about herself again. She tried the local Clubs but was refused, on occasions, for wearing "too much of a provocative outfit". "You, your fame and that outfit would be too much for our humble Club. Try down the road, they'd take anybody", the doorman had told her. It was the look of scorn on his face that triggered Sandra's frustration. Eventually, it turned to anger. "You admit you know who I am but you still refuse to let me in", Sandra seethed. Another doorman stepped forward. "We don't want your *'type'* in here, got it? That's plain enough, ain'it", he stated? "Sling your hook", the second doorman jeered? Out of sheer frustration from being dejected again and again, Sandra swung her highly decorated *'talons'* across his face. He yelped and squealed as the burning pain preceded the flow of blood. The front of his white shirt blotted the dripping droplets of burgundy coloured fluid. Sandra moved in this time with a high knee into the doorman's groin. She used her other hand to complete the incisions into the back of the doorman's neck. This time the blood soaked his collar but dripped down his back. Doubled over, the doorman tumbled in slow motion, to the floor. He lost his balance at the top of the twelve steps that led to the Club. The edges of the steps impacted with his body as he journeyed towards the pavement. Sandra was wild now with inner rage but sought to take on the first doorman as well. He dodged the issue by loosing himself in the crowd that had gathered to see the spectacle. Sandra heard the first of the police sirens. As the tyres screeched to a halt, she recalled a 'scene' from a previous news bulletin involving police. In it, she remembered a particular scene, where the police beat a man, relentlessly. There was no necessity for so many to keep him controlled. Sandra recalled the sounds of the sirens, the flashing lights and general chaos caused by *'Neuro-profiling'* and its influence. Now, it was her turn to face the *'blue music'* of the *'Siren Orchestra'* and its *'Conductors'* as they played their favourite, *'We're coming to get you'*, *'Overture'*. Soon, there seemed to be chaos everywhere. There were shouts from the men in acid yellow clothing. Shields, batons, horses and firearms were on display. Water cannons were aimed towards the entrance of the Club, 'The Left Handed Lobster'. "Come out with your hands up", said the voice over the megaphone. The wounded doorman embarrassed to be dismissed by the agile Sandra, remained at the foot of the steps where he had come to rest. He was breathing heavily and shouted a bit louder every now and then. The crowd was awkward but drifted across the path of the police. Each individual was vying for the best spot from which to view the imminent retribution. The police pushed one man to the floor after he refused to move. "F ... off", the man shouted. They ignored him. In trying to get up hastily, the man tripped one of the police, who was running towards the pavement leading to the steps. A number of other cops following too closely tripped or bumped into each other, causing a bit of laughter amongst the revellers who'd come out of the Club to witness the spectacle. Bottles started to crash onto the pavement as a set of drunken green humanoid robotron revellers took on the green humanoid robotron police. Tempers flared but the crowd and the police alike had lost their composure. Some nervous *'dealers'*, trying to dodge a *'search'*, got caught up in the rebellion that was to follow.

Sandra seized the opportunity to make good her escape from the scene outside The Left-Handed Lobster Night Club. When she told Duke about the whole event, he blamed her for inciting trouble amongst his friends. "You've ruined the good relationship the Club owners had with the police. You and them bloody nails (no pun intended), you're a spoilt, silly bitch", he scolded. Sandra tried to argue her point but Duke wouldn't listen. Another quarrel ensued between them. Soon they were trading *'choice'* phrases. Duke reminded Sandra how she ruined his relationship between him and his then wife, Dora.

"How did I do that Duke", Sandra asked icily? "You drove her away from me with your devious plan", Duke said. His tone carried more than a hint that he was loosing interest in her. This made Sandra feel even more unwanted. Duke twisted the metaphorical knife further. "I know you started to see your *'Mr Muscles'* again, haven't you? I don't know what he's got that I haven't but you're welcome to him", Duke hinted. "I have not been seeing Raymond", she defended. "You deceitful lying bitch, I've seen the texts messages on your phone", Duke declared. He was jealous. From Duke's point of view, that item of truth signified his lack of trust towards Sandra. It exposed that the core of Duke and Sandra's relationship was decaying from the inside but spreading outwardly. <u>**Trust had always been not only the core element but also the glue that was necessary to hold both sides of relationships together.**</u> There were no words that could better describe how Sandra was feeling in the moment. She was speechless from shock. "Cat got your tongue", Duke jibed. "I don't know quite what to say Duke. I'm a bit in shock at the moment. I don't know whether to feel disgusted that you are spying on me or to take it as a compliment that you're actually jealous. Which is it Duke", she queried? "Do you deny the love letters from him by e-mail too? You're such a conniving two-timing bitch. After all I did for you", he expressed. Sandra started to sob. She begun not only to hear the cold bitterness in Duke's voice being conveyed down the phone line towards her but sensed the deliberate inflections and intoned gross disappointment his message transmitted. Duke's words were pretty weighty and Sandra knew that they bore the hallmarks of finality as far as their relationship was concerned. She couldn't help but feel rejected. Loosing Duke, his clout and his contacts was not an option. During the exchange over the phone, Duke's words had had such devastating effect upon her. The impact felt like being awakened abruptly but with much force and urgent vigour from all that Sandra had dared to dream. Her world was fast collapsing now. It seemed more realistically delusional somewhat rather than the one-dimensional route towards leaving a legacy of becoming an iconic *'A' Blister*. Sandra's dream was to gain purposeful manifestation of becoming a seemingly successful socialite with Iconic Status.

The man they called 'The Professor' had often commented but deemed "this type of mindset as being in syncopation with the perceived *'politically correct'* definition of **'success'**. Research from the Walynski Institute stated that "compared to young males a disproportionate amount of young female adults but particularly adolescents were incessantly being subliminally programmed and conditioned to be extrinsically motivated towards aspiring to be part of the 'in-crowd'". He pointed out that . . . this green humanoid supersaturated, ego-inflating mental engineering scientific project had spread across the entire virtual planet quicker than a bushfire, perhaps! Except for those individuals, who had established traditional family-structured *'beliefs and values'* from childhood days, many had been attracted, like flies towards rotting flesh, to the new wasteful culture. It stank as much as decaying rotting flesh; evoking the representation of a typical *'class-ist status'* that had efficiently severed more meaningful traditional links. In exchange for *'playground politrickery'*, this type of *'elitist status'* had not only diminished the richness of quality communication but relegated invaluable traditional tribal heritage amongst indigenous peer groups into the abyss of fading memories. The lure of infinitesimal financial abundance of Champagne Urge was far too strong. It was like being sucked into riptide currents pulling away from safe shorelines but being swept outwards towards a tunnel of predictable disappointments which can lead to a bizarrely sensational, debilitating, perpetual, downward spiral into the seedy alleyways of doom and gloom. As Sandra was beginning to realise, the promise of *'elitist self-importance'* did not guarantee an automatic pathway to happiness.

The behaviours alluded to in Professor Walynski's Research meant that these individuals were being choreographed, directed and produced by individuals, who were less interested in the consequences of establishing such socially demoralising mindsets. They had no respect for any other traditional *'beliefs'*, *'values'* or *'cultures'* than their own, which they held up as the *'ideal template'* to the rest of the ironically named parallel virtual planet. In the archives of the Walynski Institute, there was more than proof that the *'ethos'* of the green humanoid robotrons transmitted their one and *only* mantra, "*you're either with us or against us*". Those individuals repeated this mantra as if it represented the planet's perennial *'cultural voicemail service'*! It seemed like something so antiquated that being an *'anorak'* appeared as if it was a modern phenomenon.

The Socialites' world seemed to be made up of petty arguments and unadulterated adolescent behaviours. These were classified by the man they called 'The Professor' as infantile *"carry-go-bring-come"* gossips being executed by *'calendar confirmed'* *'adults'*, so-called but whom had not yet seemed to either be emotionally intelligent or matured. These behaviours 'the man they called 'The Professor' explained was a sure sign of very low confidence, esteem and worst of all extreme lack of self-worth. The *'bitchy'* behaviours were "often triggered by a sense of the psychological behaviours known as *'the inner child'* or *'the inner adolescent'* but were mostly compounded by clinical (reactive) depression" and a cocktail of legal and illegal drugs, probably! These daily interactions amongst those socially approved or potential 'A' Blisters' were more commonplace than a pandemic of influenza around the geographical locations of the virtual planet. As portrayed by the media in which they were being *'used'* to influence others towards the lure for financial abundance, it seemed the established or aspiring novice socialite "developed confused states of minds. They practiced procrastination, felt fatigued, became insomniacs, comfort ate, took advantage of every opportunity to consistently abuse their bodies and suffered from OCR, Obsessive Craving to be Replicas, probably! Being angry, being in denial, globalising and apportioning blame were some of the other *'signpost's* from which individuals had to be aware", the man they called 'The Professor' stated. The self-imposed de-valuation of self worth was more difficult to come to terms with. It had plunged individuals from meteoric rise towards falling over the edge of a sheer cliff gathering momentum each second per second on the journey downwards. The pull towards the abyss of depression often meant that the 'A' Blister iconic socialite, like Sandra, might have sought cocktails of legal or illegal drugs in order to obliterate that sickeningly low feeling which had taken her to the precarious edge of the chasms of oblivion, until the crave for the next *'fix'*. What individuals like Sandra failed to understand is that "the type of *'buzz'* they crave can be made naturally by their own bodies", the man they call 'The Professor' explained. He said there is enough research available for individuals to access, in order to glean that information and confirm his pronouncement after seeking and gaining sobriety, probably! Even though Sandra was not aware, The Walynski Institute bore statistical witness that "some most famous icons had suffered greatly from dependency on legal and illegal drugs. After long sufferance of dependency, many addicts have had to go to rehabilitation establishments to regain sobriety".

Each of the wannabee socialites had a common theme. Often, to become the '*who's who*' socialite '*A*' *Blister* was to be assigned but accept and play a derogatory role in a television series or film in order to be accepted into the fold. The accumulation of the virtual currency, Champagne Urge not only reflected individuals like Sandra's financial abundance but justified and reinforced their acceptance of subservience towards the '*cause celeb*'. Financial abundance, by whatever means necessary, was their priority. Being extravagant was the accepted behavior amongst the socialites. Many before the likes of Sandra had already installed extravagance as the ideal '*model*' that fitted that '*role*'. She just followed in their wake, perhaps! Psychologically, Sandra was the ideal link in the continuity of the archetypical '*stereotype*' '*role model*' iconic image that had caught the attention of every young girl but especially those from the Tribe of Hawke, perhaps! Sandra wanted to maintain her reputation of being an iconic super model and actress but understood that without Duke his clout and contacts, her position was worsening the longer she and Duke's relationship remained damaged.

Now, his cryptic annunciations over the phone were having more impact than he was aware of. Sandra was desperate to keep the relationship between her and Duke alive that she resorted to begging his permission to rekindle the dying embers of their once inseparable relationship. "Couldn't you forgive me Duke", she begged? He hadn't told her that Doris Bendlow was snuggling in his arms but Sandra had heard the sniggling interspersing with their conversation. "Who's sniggling, Duke", Sandra demanded? "Never mind that, just quit the crocodile tears", he chided. "You're not being fair to me Duke. After all, our affair was not one-sided, was it", she asked? "What's that got to do with anythink", he retorted? Sandra was gutted. Her mind was confused by his cryptic remarks. They were unemotional and cold. In fact, Duke sounded as uninterested as he'd intended. Sandra didn't say anything for a while.

She reflected upon her fight with Doris Bendlow at 'The Pharmacy', a quaint old Club just 30 miles from Duke Stagg Incorporated, had caused a deep rift between Sandra and Duke. She remembered being driven to the exclusive Club by her chauffeur, Sam. When Sandra found out that Doris had travelled with Duke, this had made her jealous for Duke's attention. She wanted to settle with him but first Sandra's anger was directed at her rival, Doris Bendlow. It was during the Foxtrot sequence that Sandra and the teasing Doris bumped into each other on the dance floor, '*accidentally*', on purpose. "Bitch", Doris had commented. Sandra watched Duke and Doris dancing together but began to react to her jealous mood. Reeling away from her over-eager partner, Sandra advanced towards Doris. There was not a great deal of space for Sandra to manoeuvre her way through the animated dancers. Doris had kept on taunting Sandra from afar. There were familiar hand signals that indicated an element of annoyance. Duke was still struggling against Doris's round frame. It appeared as if they were having a wrestling bout. Two couples danced their way across Sandra's vision. By the time she pushed her way through, she'd lost sight of Doris and Duke, momentarily. Doris seized the opportunity to creep up behind Sandra. Grabbing her by her long flowing hair, Doris shouted some foul language at the struggling Sandra. "You cheap slut, leave us alone or I'll tear your hair out", Doris screamed. Sandra was caught off-guard and was at the mercy of her rival. She waited for Doris to get careless. Sandra placed both her hands on top of her head where Doris was holding her hair. Pressing both of Doris' hands hard against her skull, Sandra adjusted her legs much wider than the width of her shoulders. Suddenly, she lowered her body into a stooped position but arched her back then pulled herself forward whilst twisting anticlockwise, sharply. Doris was being pulled into the forwards motion which changed her centre of gravity immensely in Sandra's favour. Using Doris' weight against her, she was made to travel through the shape of an arc but was swiftly deposited very heavily onto the hard floor by the martial arts movement. It was a frame-by-frame well coordinated sequence of movements competently executed by the more agile Sandra. Doris might not have been aware of her destination until it was far too late for her to interrupt the well practiced techniques that were being applied. Someone commented but distracted Sandra's attention away from the bewildered Doris. Through embarrassment, she managed to get back on her feet. She looked round to the audience that had been privy to the live demonstration of Sandra's competent skill executions. They warned of her immense capabilities of physical accomplishments. Now Sandra could see Doris's feet, she kicked her hard in the shins quickly. Doris yelped but sounded more like a 'Town Crier' demanding attention. She bent forwards to attend her sore shins. That was a big mistake. Sandra's martial arts training came into good effect yet again. She swiftly chopped Doris in her nape at the back of her neck. As she fell forwards into a heap, Sandra danced around the figure on the floor but kicked Doris in her lower back. Her cries in response to the blows were like the sound a coyote as pictured against the moon in the old black and white movies. Sandra then finished off by jumping over Doris' rotund body so that she was now in front of her again. Taking a sideward stance, Sandra used the stiletto heel of her boots to stamp against one of Doris' knees. Everyone heard the loud cracking sound which preceded Doris' yelp as evidence of further agony as the excruciating pain shot through her shattered patella. "That's for you trying to steal my man", Sandra complained. Doris rolled around on the stone floor. It was similar to an uninjured Association Football Player who faked the intensity of an injury. Eventually, Doris managed to raise herself into a standing position. She looked more like a picture of her imitating the fabled Long John Silver of 'Treasure Island' but without the wooden crutch for support. Bearing most of her weight on one leg, Doris rested the damaged foot most precariously before grabbing hold of its thigh then entered into a type of one-footed hopping dance as if around a 'Totem Pole'. Doris knew she was beaten but showed some defiance despite the battering. "You might as well kill me but I'll never let you have Duke", she sobbed. Doris now stood bent at the one knee of the uninjured leg with the injured knee only slightly bent in front of the standing leg. In response to Doris' defiant recent rant, Sandra replied, "that's what you think". She used her foot to push the half-kneeling figure of Doris to the floor. Sandra had humiliated Doris enough. Two swift kicks to her ribs soon put Doris in a more submissive mood. Within minutes, she was pleading for Sandra to stop. As a last measure of intimidating power, Sandra brandished her sharp naturally grown hardened 'talons' but demonstrated to Doris how she might choose to use them to disfigure her face. Like animal specie, Sandra bared her teeth but snarled like any other feline aggressor waiting to pounce. "Grrrrrrrrrrrrrrrr", she growled aggressively. Her message was clear.

Duke had stood by without interfering. He didn't even try to stop the cameramen from the newspapers, who were there to record the live event. Doris was a sad sight as she lay on the floor, sobbing from the pains inflicted by the more agile Sandra. She looked towards Duke but he busied himself talking to another woman who was drinking Champagne Urge Mark 3. They stared but gestured towards the two combatants. "I told you she'd beat Doris. Now pay up", he demanded. The drunken woman opened her purse, placed her hand inside but handed Duke the winnings from their little side bet. Suddenly, some others walked up but paid Duke voluntarily.

The Host, Retired Brigadier General Sir Tank Alpino was the biggest loser. His *'values and beliefs'* had lured him into believing that, because of Doris' more rotund body shape she might have been more able to defeat the slimmer Sandra. He was most upset not only about loosing a huge some of money to his wily old pal, Duke but also the disgrace this fracas might bring to 'The Pharmacy'. It wasn't only that the reputation of The Pharmacy might sink to an all time low if rumours got out about 'fights' at this most exclusively prestigious established Club but also his extremely self-opinionated, prejudiced views which didn't allow him to accept that it was Doris, whom he regarded as "one of my own", who had initiated the fight. His facial features were grim and his jaws seemed to be set in stone. He sauntered over to where Sandra was standing. She'd noticed how the crowd meticulously shifted over to the other side of the dance floor away from her. Taunts of "troublemaker" were mild compared to some other comments that were being made. This segregation highlighted the awkward situation Sandra had got herself into. By the time the Host had got to where she was standing, his nasal toned voice sounded but shook the glasses on the table next to Sandra. One actually lost its balance but fell to the floor. That seemed to up the level of the Brigadier General's indignation. "What the bloody hell do you think you're doing? Who invited you here", he asked? The Brigadier General had a bad lisp. Not every word came out as he'd intended. In fact, his voice reminded Sandra of the cartoon with the cat and the mouse. She tried to keep a straight face but the poorly dubbed voice did not fit with the actions of the Brigadier General's regimented action of his jawbone. Sandra was feeling quite embarrassed by the intimidating way the Host was acting towards her. The Brigadier General was now ranting and raving like a lunatic. He threatened to have her removed by the hefty doormen that now stood either side of her. Sandra was tall but these men towered over her by at least 12 inches or so it seemed. She also noticed that they both had big bellies, almost similar in size to a 12 months pregnancy! Their huge forearms were darkened by graphic tattoos. Coincidentally, both men wore a drawing of a cross on their right forearms. When Brigadier General, Sir Tank Alpino removed his heavily decorated Tunic type Jacket, he rolled up his sleeve to challenge the woman he described as, "Amazon Woman". Sandra noticed the Brigadier General was wearing the tattoo with the drawing of the cross on his right hand too. His fists were raised and clenched like a pugilist from generations gone by. He danced lightly on his feet like a ballerina on a stage. Sir Tank Alpino stuck out a fast right jab that just missed Sandra by millimeters. "Put your mits up", the Brigadier General challenged. Sandra gathered what the Brigadier General meant by his action but the word like *'mits'* had no meaning to her. The two *'heavies'* made room for the bout to begin. Sandra looked all round for help but not one person stepped forward to stop the imminent fight. She looked over to where Duke and Doris Bendlow were sitting previously. When she didn't see Duke, there was a lump in Sandra's throat. "How could Duke abandon me in such a situation", she whispered to herself. The Brigadier General was 'high' on teaching "this young lassie a lesson". His first punch glanced along Sandra's face as she tried to dodge the blow. "Heh, Heh, you're not so brave now, are you Amazon Woman? Met your type during the war, what", the Brigadier General teased. The crowd hooted and jeered as Sandra backed away but slipped onto the floor. Further threatened by the oncoming Brigadier General, Sandra made herself into a ball but rolled forwards quickly, like tumbleweed in the wind, towards him. She accelerated so swiftly that it took the Brigadier General by surprise. He couldn't get out of the way quickly enough but proceeded to fall forwards over her, without control. There was a heavy thud as the Brigadier General hit the floor. Sandra's momentum had taken her just past where the Brigadier General had fallen. "I say, tricky little bastards, aren't they. These foreigners are a slippery lot", he bellowed. The crowd sanctioned the Brigadier General's description of the agile Sandra. By the time Brigadier General rose to a standing position again, Sandra climbed unto one of the tables. She cleared it of its contents with a couple of sweeping kicks that made the *'heavies'* a bit more cautious about approaching her. Reinforcing his embarrassment to being humiliated by a woman, made the Brigadier General jettisoned his anger to a much greater level of intensity. Sir Tank Alpino broke his army training but allowed his inner rage to take control. In this mode, he was quite vulnerable to the calmer, confident Sandra. As he rushed towards the table on which Sandra was standing, she sidestepped his poor effort to stab her in the leg with the broken glass that had fallen from the table. She could see the beads of sweat flowing from his now furrowed brow. Sir Tank Alpino's breathing was now extremely laboured but he felt he had to finish what he'd started out to do. He wouldn't be able to live down the *'dishonour'* of loosing to a woman. In these parts, women knew their places. Sandra snarled at the Brigadier General but showed him her highly decorated *'talons'*. The sequence of martial arts movement made Sandra seem quite an expert, especially to those who'd only seen the Bruce Lee Movies. Frustrated by Sandra's *"antics"*, the Brigadier General picked up a chair but swung it at her legs. With knees bent up towards her stomach, she leapt high into the air above the table then landed with a stamping motion that broke the leg of the chair before the Brigadier General could withdraw it to attempt another strike. There was a collective gasp that permeated the air. "OMG, Oh my God, did you see that", one woman asked another? Other comments now swiftly filled the room. Some of the women were quietly hoping that Sandra would beat the bullying retired Brigadier General. Nobody truly liked him as a person but he was considered by them as *"one of us"* because he said he'd fought for his country.

However, the people in that greener tree-lined community of castles, cottages, bungalows, farms, farmyards, barns, cattle, horses, peacocks, peahens, grouse, turkey, drakes, ducks, cocks, hens, streams, brooks, moats, meadows, vales, avenues, crescents, lanes, pathways, highways, by-ways, wooden bridges and thoroughfares which had remained un-spoilt by pavements, curbs, gutters, metal bridges, motor traffic, industrial pollution created by *'modern standards'*, ironically, had not quite forgotten his dear wife, Eliza Dumont, daughter of the mesmeric Aristocrat, Benji Armourite Dumont. He was a very rich man who earned his money as a Weapons Consultant; especially to the exotic continents, countries and islands. Eliza Dumont had disappeared without trace 14 months ago. Neighbours told the police that the Brigadier General was always heard bellowing at the frail bodied woman. Once they'd reported hearing him saying he would kill her but the Brigadier General told the police that he and his wife were rehearsing a Play they'd written together. She had concurred with her husband. About Eliza's absence, retired Brigadier General, Sir Tank Alpino told police that his wife was a counter spy for a foreign country. He had made it clear that he had no emotions about his wife's disappearance. The Brigadier General said he'd lived his life expecting her to just disappear as she did. The police was never encouraged to continue their investigations into Eliza Dumont's absence. The politicrats in the government departments, both incumbent and opposition, backed the Brigadier General's story. The poly-tricksters did a ten weeks spread in the media on the alleged double spy, Eliza. During the serialized 'Eliza-Gate' propaganda, there were pictures of a frail bodied woman with the 'Mother Theresa' sized build. It belied the claims that the fragile sqillionairess had played a double role in something as significant as the Spy game! It was rumoured that at the time of Eliza's disappearance, the Brigadier General had been seen leaving the local hardware store with a pickaxe, a shovel, box wood, a chainsaw, nails, bags of cement, sand and several plastic sheeting. Rumours had it that, apart from the digging on his grounds during the daytime, a chainsaw was heard late at night on more than one occasion. Activities from an individual of the same build as the Brigadier General but with face covered by a a a balaclava and in boiler suit going to and from the rear of the outbuilding at the rear of his bungalow was reported to the police but no action was taken against the brigadier.

By the time the Brigadier General had regained his composure at The Pharmacy Club, the two 'heavies' approached Sandra from different directions. She saw the first one from the corner of her right eye. Sandra went through the martial arts routine again. Without warning, she sprang from the table to confront the first of the heavies. Her left foot shot upwards much higher than a 'Can-Can' dancer's but collided with the man's chin. His huge frame went backwards like a cardboard 'cut-out' figure. There was very hard contact with the edge of the table and the man's head on his way down to the floor. Either way, he was knocked out before his body came to rest. Sandra shuffled her feet in a well-practiced manner somewhat like the 'Ali Shuffle' but shifted her stance to a crouched one as she awaited the man's next move. The other man, who had positioned himself back with the crowd, suddenly seized his chance to upset Sandra's dominance. He drew the serrated hunting knife from his right boot. His approach was crude. Swinging the knife wildly from side to side, like the famed actors in a black and white 'swordfight' movie, the heavily built giant swiftly positioned himself, ready to slash "Amazon Woman" to ribbons. The crowd's 'oohs' and 'aahs' directed Sandra's attention to the antics behind her. Without looking round, she first darted forwards then to the side before she turned to face the crazed 'security' personnel. Those few steps forwards had bought Sandra more space between her and the attacker. As the heavily 'tattoed' hand with the knife, began its decent towards its target, Sandra used her right hand against the man's left forearm to block the blow. During the sequence of that move, Sandra pushed the index and middle fingers of her left hand directly into the man's eyes. The knife fell immediately from his grasp. This sudden blindness disorientated the 'security' personnel and he began to panic. He screamed as the pain jerked at the damaged nerve ends in his eye sockets. There was some blood too, running down his face. Some of the people rushed forward to attend to the beaten pot-bellied giant 'security' personnel. Two men pulled the man's hands from his face. One of his eyes hung from the socket as if suspended by a broken spring mechanism but the other, though damaged, was still intact, somehow. One woman used table napkins in an attempt to stop the flow of blood. The man was still screaming like a child who'd been beaten by a drunken parent. His wailing drowned out the general hub-hub of murmurs and other comments. Sandra noticed that all the attention was focused on the wounded security personnel. The other hadn't moved after hitting the floor and the Brigadier General had changed his mind about "teaching 'Amazon Woman' a lesson". He mingled amongst the chaotic crowd. Sandra now had to reach the nearest exit but the three Doberman dogs, though chained, looked aroused enough to defeat any attempt of an escape.

The Band had stopped playing since Doris had grabbed Sandra by the hair. The musicians' instruments were still on the stage but they too had disappeared. Whilst the crowd was being distracted by the injured man's bellowing Sandra sidled up to the stage. She eased herself unto the raised platform then disappeared behind the thick curtains at the back of the stage. Sandra peered through where two edges of the curtains met in the middle of the stage. From her vantage point, she could see the people on the dance floor. She gasped when she saw Duke. His rough flat voice rose above the main din as he expressed his inner feelings. "That lot, they're not used to being treated well, are they", he commented. The Brigadier General grunted but was conspicuous by his actions. Sandra saw the Blunderbuss gun that he was toting. She heard him tell Duke that he intended to "blow 'Amazon woman' apart". "When I was in the Army" the Brigadier General started to say. "Give me the bloody gun. I'll do it for you. That woman has turned out to be nothink but a money-seeking parasite", Duke insisted. He tried to wrench the gun away from the Brigadier General. Duke struggled with him for possession of the gun. The explosion that followed deafened everyone in the hall including Sandra. She heard little bells ringing in her ears. The smell of the discharge was harsh but burnt the back of the people's throats. As the smoke drifted across the room, it slowly made its way over to where Sandra was hiding. The stench began to burn the inner part of her nose. She felt like sneezing. Pinching her nose between her index finger and thumb, Sandra managed to lessen the sound of her sneezing fit. Her eyes started to water as the acrid smoke enveloped the curtained area behind the stage. It was only by chance that the musicians returned to investigate the sound of the explosion. They could see Duke and the Brigadier General still in the motion of their fierce struggle for possession of the gun. "Tankie, gimme the f . . . . . g gun", Duke insisted. "No, it's my bloody gun, get your f . . . . . g hands off it", the Brigadier General protested. The musicians, not knowing the reason for the gun, raced towards the two men. They saw the bloodied napkins as well as the first Security personnel lying on the floor. While the people converged around the injured individuals, Sandra took her chance to exploit the vacated Musicians' Dressing Room. Once inside, she raced towards the window but climbed out into the yard. Sandra dodged between the fleet of parked limos as she sought to find her own.

Sam, the chauffeur was not in the car. He was standing a little distance away tucking into a huge plate of food that one of the staff from the kitchen had brought for him. Sam picked up the oversized chicken drumstick from the plate the size of a large tray. Sandra placed herself beside the limo he was standing next to. The other chauffeur had a champagne glass in this hand. He and Sam chatted but laughed about their jobs. "It's not such a bad job if you get food like this everyday", the other chauffeur commented. Sam chose not to speak but instead bowed his head several times while grunting his approval of the meal. He placed the half-bitten drumstick on top of the half-eaten food but kept his jaws moving swiftly. At first, Sandra whispered Sam's name but he was caught up in the conversation with his friend, Soljie, the other chauffeur. He was an ex-army man who had bought himself out after 11 years service. Soljie knew the Brigadier General since his army days. He was the retired Brigadier General's personal chauffeur now. Sam burped loudly. It sounded like thunder. The Doberman dogs inside the building heard the 'explosion'. They were disturbed by it but began to bark at the sudden noise. "Sound carries", Soljie joked. Both men laughed heartily together. Sandra spoke again. "Take me home Sam", she said sternly. This time the tone and volume of her voice had changed to one that was audible. Sam spun round swiftly as if being caught out. The large plate divorced itself from the hand holding it and the remainder of the food spilt randomly onto the grass. Sam tried to speak but his over-stuffed mouth denied any other sound from escaping except for the grunting that transpired. Sam was choking on his food now and began to cough violently as the sharp intake of breath caused the food to block his throat. Soljie rushed over but pounded Sam with open palm across his back several times. Sam spat the food from his mouth but continued to cough. "Water", Sam whispered. "Give me a little water", he pleaded. Sandra witnessed Sam's distress but she needed to escape. Anxious to avoid meeting with Duke or any of the others with whom she had fought. Sandra became impatient with her chauffeur. She remembered what Raymond had taught her about breathing. "Just breathe Sam, breathe", she ordered. Sandra held his head back but kept pressing him to breathe. After a while, Sam signalled that he was feeling better. He cleared his throat a few times before dutifully turning towards Sandra's limo. "I'm ok now ma'am", Sam said gratefully. He wiped his greasy hands on the leg of his trousers. When they reached the limo, Sandra didn't wait for Sam to open the door. She slipped into the back seat. "Give it some gas, Sam. Give it some gas", she ordered. Sam carefully turned the limo round then screeched away, leaving gravel and dust in his trail. Sandra heard the loud explosion again. She looked back as Sam whisked her towards the exit. She could see the diminutive, stocky figure of Duke with the Blunderbuss in his hand. It was pointed towards the limo.

That had happened six months ago. Since then, Duke has deliberately avoided Sandra altogether. Now, she found herself sitting at the other end of the phone, cold-shouldered by all the contacts that she'd dreamt of and made. Not even Duke wanted to know her now. She spoke again into the phone. "Have you gone off me Duke", Sandra asked? He didn't answer but instead slurped his beer from the Pewter Jug. Duke ended the call abruptly. He carried on joking with Doris and the others. That funny whirring sound started to distract Duke again from the frivolity happening around him. Doris was drunk. She started to swing her hips like she was mentally remembering her younger days as 'Hula Hoop' Champion. The men at the bar watched but seemed mesmerized by Doris gyrations. "You're making me dizzy Doris", one commented. All the voices carried a similar vein of being entertained by her rather round body. It rotated in slow motions but grew into more vigorous swishing from the hip. The circular motions rapidly increased until Doris' centrifugal movement indicated that the imaginary 'Hula Hoop' was at its top speed. At this stage Doris seemed to appear as a blur. Her audience found themselves unsteady on their feet partly because of the booze they had imbibed and partly because they were mesmerized by Doris' dynamic performance. The locomotion allowed Doris to reduce the movement from her waist into slow rhythmic trance movements that sometimes went back and forth, suggestively. These movements were similar to those performed on Planet Earth by exotic females in grass skirts. Uproar from the cheering crowd reached its maximal decibel crescendo but carried for at least half a mile distance and more depending when any of the doors were opened by those still trying to get into The Haunting Post AADC before "last orders" was called. Sandra was determined to contact Duke to try and make up for their latest fight. She decided to take the blame for the fight with Duke's friends but more importantly she wanted to know if he'd really intended to kill her when he fired the Blunderbuss towards the limo. Sandra had to know just what caused him to want to side with the man he called Tankie. After all, he'd deliberately set out not only to embarrass her but also to "teach her a lesson", as he had announced at the time.

She pressed the green button on her cell phone again. This time, amid the laughter and jollification, Duke picked up the whirring sound but was visually distracted by the movement of the phone as it danced to the rhythm of the vibrations. He had placed it on the table next to his large Pewter Jug. This time he spoke into the phone. "What", Duke asked? His tone was curt and there was an air of annoyance that carried over the airways. Sandra sensed the tenseness in his tone but spoke quickly. "I'm sorry Duke", Sandra submitted. There was a giggle then a guttural laugh from a female voice. This time Sandra was able to identify the owner of the voice. "You bastard", Sandra said down the phone. "Behave yourself Doris", Duke said deliberately. Sandra sensed that he too was giggling now. Sandra winced when she heard Doris's deriding remarks in the background. Her blood was fast approaching 'boiling point'. Her head pulsated as if to an irregular beat. Each beat registered even more anger. There she was sitting in the most expensive grand mansion in the mega-affluent Champagne Valley, alluding to the antics of Doris and Duke. They could have hung up the phone at anytime but they chose to play the 'mind' game on the naïve Sandra. This was only her second affair but it was quite different to the first relationship with Raymond. She had played the 'mind' games with him but King Karma had a way of reminding Sandra about 'mental farming'. The seeds she had sewn were beginning to break through. Their growth might help Sandra to further understand her current state of 'non compos mentis', probably! In this relationship with Duke, the 'role' was now being reversed. He was playing the 'mind game' and with greater success than Sandra had with Raymond. As she sat there in the King sized bed with the enormous down-filled Duvet hanging from the edge, Sandra realized how Raymond's friends must have felt when she had snubbed them. She'd become so used to having things her own way that this experience was ripping her apart. Sandra was chastened by it. She had been taught 'well' by her mother, Dian Bogus, to distance herself from people she despised. What Dian had failed to inform Sandra about was how much harder the fall might be if one should fall from a great height.

The man they called 'The Professor' had built a philosophy around that sort of thinking. He stated that "those whose super-inflated egos had initiated the type of attitude that manifested into a mindset of snobbery were more than likely to fall from a great height. Individuals who might think that, because of financial affluent status, they were in any way 'better' than those who were less fortunate than themselves might become more aware of their *'psychotic neurosis'* after they had landed from their fall, maybe"! Sandra was beginning to get a better understanding that striving for the taste of Champagne Urge was not only an acceptable principle but was more than reasonable even though it did not guaranteed satisfaction. The man they called 'The Professor' referred to the particular mindset about ". . . having a sound financial base is not only an excellent idea and is a stable resource for financial security but it does not guarantee fulfillment or meaningful relationships". Now, Sandra was being referred to as "the rich bitch with the manicured claws", by some individuals like Doris Bendlow.

Like the *'slights'* from most of the people in the Village of Urgington, the severing of contact by Hinton Fairly and Grant Favours amongst others meant that total isolation was a real *'fear'* that had begin to grow into mammoth proportions in Sandra's mind. It was a maddening situation for anyone to be in. Sandra's head was swimming and she felt unsteady as the huge round King-sized bed seemed to turn 360 degrees more rapidly in one direction like a merry-go-round that had been programmed to increase its speed rapidly. With an array of bottles tucked under both arms but clutching a couple of glasses between her fingers on one hand like she had learnt from Duke, Sandra stepped from the high bed unsteadily but staggered aimlessly towards the bathroom. There, she attempted to turn on the gold plated taps with the free hand. After several attempts, Sandra seemed, by luck or judgment, to figure out which were the real taps from the many which seemed to give her other options from which to choose. The powerful gushing water was released into the gigantic solid gold 'Roman' Bath. It stood on solid gold legs in the middle of a massive room. Sandra placed the glasses and bottles on the floor. She stooped to pour yet another drink while the bath was filling. Brooding over her *'loss'*, she needed something stronger than Champagne. She poured but mixed a cocktail of 'Overproof Rum' and Coffee Liqueurs from the far off exotic paradise island from which her mother, Dian had emigrated, Ouzo from an even more ancient past, Vodka, Brandy and Whisky from Spaceville all into the two glasses. Sandra gulped the lethal cocktail from each glass. It had an immediate effect upon the oversensitive, brokenhearted Sandra. She had enough time to contemplate Duke's influence as being the lifeblood of her career but that he seemed determined to drastically reduce his support. Sandra fought off the feelings of resentment and abandonment with even more booze. She continued to gulp the cocktail that had the potential energy to blow a hole in a wall. Sandra tossed the booze down her throat as if it was a prescribed drug of which she hated the taste. Soon the whole room was beginning to feel similar to the movements of the Speedboat during inclement weather in the choppy waters of the emerald green ocean. It had caused the boat to toss 'to and fro' in those choppy ocean waves in Costa Del Shell. This felt like freefall into an enormous void. Sandra spilled most of the other drink that she hastily poured into the glasses after *'gulping'* the previous ones. Her hands were visibly shaking like a heavy drug user in rehab facing withdrawal symptoms. The pulsing headache was still raging. There were tears flowing down Sandra's cheeks now. The headaches were enough to bring anyone to tears but she could not tell why she was crying. All Sandra knew was that she felt awful. Hunger wrenched her stomach but the raw liquor steamed its way through, scorching her throat as well as the thin inner walls of her intestines. Sandra felt the burning trail of 'over-acidic' fluids but she wanted to use the drink to 'numb' the headaches and dispel the busy thinking process that seemed to overwhelm her greatly. Since she was young, Sandra had heard of many cures for headaches. This one wasn't working. Sandra kept staggering around the bathroom aimlessly, wrapped up in the melee within her mind. It didn't seem as if there was any room for negotiations with Duke.

The new advert for planet-wide television viewing and the star *'role'* in two blockbuster movies, (1) ***'The Model that fits the Role'*** and (2) ***'The Role that fits the Model'***, backed by the Credit Card billionaire Mogul, Sir Ivanhoe Goldfeet and his billionaire colleagues were now in peril. Under his instructions, all of Duke's friends and contacts had started to shun Sandra now. None would dare to cross *'Mr Clout'*. With the burden of the enormity of the consequences bearing down heavily on her, Sandra started a conversation with herself. "What have I done? I've managed to blow a career", she commented aloud. Without any voluntary encouragement from her, the *'good times'*, when Sandra was flying high, flashed repetitively across her mind. She fell to the floor purposely, wailing and calling out Duke's name. "Duke, Duke . . . oh Duke, don't leave me . . . p-l-e-a-s-e", Sandra cried. The tears were real and her contorted face conjured an expression of acceptance of defeat. The mascara traced its way artistically down Sandra's face but met with the lipstick she had started using under the direction of her agent, Andromeda Francescovic. The coloured tears travelled until they found their way onto Sandra's very delicate mouth. Her large teary cornflower blue eyes look even wider as she stared further into oblivion as if she was contemplating infinity. Sandra had wandered back into the overlarge bedroom but fell onto the round bed more by accident than intentionally. Laying flat on her back didn't help too much. The mixture of 'booze' didn't settle too well. Sandra felt nauseous and faint. She tried to shake her head a few times to try to clear it but each time Sandra moved the pulsing increased. She turned slowly onto her stomach to see if there would be any relief from either the nauseous feeling or the pulsing headache. Sandra remembered the bath. As she arose gingerly to a standing position, Sandra felt the sogginess underfoot. Plodding around in the gigantic bathroom, she waved the unfinished bottles of Champagne Urge Mark 3 and the Overproof Rum carelessly around. She started another conversation with herself. Her voice was childlike and the tone flat and dull. "Who's a silly girl then", Sandra mimicked. She knew that's what Duke would have said. Sandra struggled into the bathroom to witness the devastation she'd caused. The damage to such an exquisite grand mansion could cost Sandra millions but that was the last thing on her mind. She had to concentrate hard on the arduous journey across the gigantic room. It seemed to take forever for her to reach the bath. The water was flowing over the edges in quite rapid motion like from a waterfall. Almost all the bubbles had disappeared from the bath unto the carpeted floor. 'Frothy' looking bubbles rested almost like snow on the ground. Sandra's bare feet slid every now and then on the supersaturated soapy surface, testing her further. She blinked rapidly as she reached out to turn the taps off. There seemed to be several taps in front of her. Sandra chose a couple but missed her target by a long way. She tried again to line up which were the real taps. These appeared to be even further away from her. Sandra moved her hands slowly but deliberately towards what appeared to be the correct taps. This time she overbalanced but plunged headlong into the bath. Miraculously, she didn't harm herself but instead became totally immersed. Sandra raised her head to get some air but held on to the side of the bath with one hand, the other was still holding one of the bottles. It was the unfinished bottle of Overproof Rum. She now drank directly from it. Her long flowing hair shrunk towards her skull but extended itself down her long slender back and into the water in the tub. Sandra was in a kneeling position now, almost as if she was about to pray. She re-balanced herself often as the movement of the slippery water tossed her from side to side. Finally, Sandra decided to sit in the bath. As she did so the warm water started to soothe her tired body. It had been a day she'd want to forget.

Before the *'pow-wow'* with Duke, someone had left a voicemail message to say her mother was admitted into the Slow Service General Hospital, Ghettoville, in Lower Ghettoborough. Dian was refused admission from hospitals in 'Higher', 'Central' and 'Lower' Greensborough, apparently! The caller did not specify what was wrong with Dian Bogus. Sandra had not yet called the hospital to enquire about her mother. Instead, she'd kept the last few appointments that were still going for her. The major agent, Grant Favours, was Duke's business partner. He'd told Sandra that morning that *'things'* were *"slowing down"*. Grant also suggested that she find herself a new major agent. There was no further conversation between them. Sandra noticed the tone used when Grant had told her the *'bad'* news. His comments were very formal and curt. Sandra did not get the *'habitual'* kiss on the cheek from Grant as he'd used to doing. Everything pointed to the finality of all associations with Duke and his connections. There was still another side to consider but Sandra, in her present state, could not think laterally. Nothing was clear-cut. In fact, everything seemed to merge into each other, rendering any possible positive solutions to disappear like the booze was down Sandra's throat. Each time she took a bigger swig from the bottle of Overproof Rum. Sandra had no recall of the bottle of Champagne Urge Mark 3 that lie at the bottom of the huge bath or even that the bottle of Overproof Rum had also immersed in the partially soapy water. She didn't even notice any difference in taste. Such was the state of her mind. The drunkenness had started to impact even more. As she began to drift off to sleep, Sandra sunk a little deeper into the tub. Her chin was touching the surface but she had no control over the convulsions in her head. It had dulled somewhat but her movements were not coordinated enough to maintain balance. Sandra placed the bottle to her mouth again and for the umpteenth time swigged from it. She held the near empty bottle over the side of the bath with one hand while she hugged herself with the other. The flashes across her mind now was not pictures of Duke but instead Raymond. Sandra savoured whatever memories she was recalling by hugging herself with both hands now. Memories of 'Mr. Right' and his ability to quench her fire loomed largely in her mind at this moment. The smile had returned to her face now and a calmer Sandra kept the dream going for longer than its initial appearance. The mascara stained face was looking more like the Sandra Raymond used to know. She raised herself enough to rest her head backwards on the rim at the back of her neck. Whatever dreams Sandra were having had other effects on the *'drunken'* woman. She could 'hear' Raymond's voice telling her to *"breathe"*. Sandra tossed the bottle and its remaining content onto the flooded carpet. She continued to *'hear'* Raymond's instructions in her mind. His voice projected purely from the process of 'recall'. "Breath inwards slowly Sandy, to the count of 4 then exhale gradually to the count of seven", he coached. "I can't do it Ray", Sandra could hear herself reply. She chanced to open her eyes for the first time since the *'apparition'*. Sandra squinted as the soft lights entered her vision. She tried again. This time she thought she saw Raymond sitting on the painted 'Rattan Basket Woven Style' circular stool. It was not too far away from the bath. "Oh Ray, you've come to rescue me. Thanks Ray, you're my hero", Sandra said aloud. She'd entered a different *'world'* now, adrift of the reality that impacted on her earlier. The water was still quite warm and welcoming. Sandra lay in the tub affixed to her vision. She stretched her left hand out but invited *'the apparition'* to engage in holding hands. The *'apparition'* smiled but reached forwards, gently touching Sandra's hand. Her body shook violently. She was experiencing rather *'fulfilling'* sensations that had buried themselves deep into Sandra's memory. Her headache was not fully gone but there was a great deal of relief. "You can do anything you want Sandy", the *'apparition'* said. "With you everything is possible Ray", Sandra replied aloud. "Ready when you feel comfortable Sandy", the *'apparition'* encouraged. "I'm always ready when you're around, Ray", Sandra replied. "O.K, start now", the *'apparition'* tasked. Sandra settled into a smooth rhythm of breathing patterns and soon the headache had disappeared. Sandra was sure of this because, when she made yet another adjustment to her posture, the water from her hair made her twitch her head fairly robustly. The next time Sandra looked the *'apparition'* had completely disappeared. She began to feel even more relaxed than she'd been before Raymond's *'apparition'* had materialised. Sandra could not have known which moment sleep had arrived but she was now feeling the full effect of the cocktail she had imbibed. Ventilation was poor inside the bathroom because Sandra had instructed that those windows should be kept closed at all times. Inside, the steam filled bathroom, huge mirrors along the walls were rendered 'useless' for reflecting any image clearly. An opaque image of the huge solid gold 'Roman' Bathtub with its solid gold taps and current occupant was there in the mirrors. As Sandra slide further and further down into the huge golden 'Roman' Bath, her heavy snoring confirmed that she was in a deep yet thoroughly drunken state of sleep.

CHAPTER 54

With Sandra out of the way, there was virtually no competition for the rotund, bubbly, matter-of-fact Doris Bendlow. She was enjoying more of Duke's company now, since the split up between him and Sandra. He took Doris with him every time he visited his old *'haunts'* and that was more often than he had done in a long time. She stuck closely to him but walked confidently hand in hand with the influential Duke. They were like two lovebirds. Doris didn't mind but in fact welcomed the jibes from the local people that she and Duke seemed like husband and wife. They often stopped to smooch or steal a long passionate kiss in public and without care. In these moments, Duke would grasp Doris' bum cheeks with his huge shovel-like hands then he would comment that he knew she "didn't mind a bit of rough". He wasn't only controlling the more than willing Doris. Duke was also being more open to acknowledge his status as the big time 'Don' in his childhood community. Recently, he was spending more time there than at the Office or at his new grand mansion in Champagne Valley on the other side of the mountain. His connections with *'shady'* characters were dragging him down deeper and deeper into the world of broken dreams. It wasn't that he needed to get involved but his rough upbringing had hardened his character in such a way that 'good advice' from well meaning friends were often swiftly swept aside. One of the places he visited regularly was his favourite AADC, The Haunting Post. Inside, he and his *'friends'* would gather to *'socialise'*.

Gambling and drinking were only part of the *'entertainment'* on offer at The Haunting Post AADC. The smoky den had huge wooden beams with barrels hanging from the heavy metal chains attached to them. A huge inflatable doll hung above the beam nearest the bar. Duke was the donator of the doll. He said it reminded him of Doris. She often giggled whenever Duke commented on it. The Haunting Post AADC reminded Duke of the black and white and Technicolor movies he used to watch as a child. The swinging wooden louvre half-doors led to the Saloon Bar. The Haunting Post AADC's worn wooden flooring echoed each footstep that contacted them and sounded as if special effects were being used to re-create the ambience of the old movies. The furniture and fittings were 'replicas' from those black and white and Technicolor movies that Duke recalled watching when he was a boy. The solid oak wooden tables and chairs with splayed legs were scattered around The Haunting Post AADC. Men sat with crumpled outdated suits, crushed hats, twisted peaked caps, braces, monocles and eye patches gambling as if there was a race on as to who could loose the largest amount of money on that particular day or night. Salaried and waged earners, the under-employed, pinstriped bowler-hat City Tycoons elect, got *'high'* together on their favourite legal *'liquid drug'* and more besides but swore at each other often. Duke was just as guilty of swearing as the others. Some chewed tobacco but spat the accumulated spittle onto the floor without reprimand.

Duke's Empire was slowly transforming itself into insolvency through a latent process. He began to embezzle funds from DSI, the company his father, Earl, had founded, established but willed to him in order to carry it on as a family business. Had he been alive, Earl Stagg would have been driven into one of his manic moods to see how his son, Duke, had managed to ruin the prestige company that he had worked so hard to remain solvent. Never in his time would Earl have treated his staff so poorly. As it was nigh on impossible to tell the difference between the identical twins, whenever it was convenient for them, they often swapped places without anyone else being the wiser. It was not clear whether it was Duke or Baron had brought in the *'hatchet'* accounting personnel whose job it was to terminate staff employment at a stroke. He used the type of practice that bore the hallmarks of a rabid hyena rummaging for food. There was no other word for the type of inhumane actions of the rapier-like way in which staff were being disposed of. Without warning, the disgustingly poor communications between management and staff reflected the type of treatment they suffered. Some were dismissed via letters strewn across their workstations, some via e-mails or texts even. Another form of insensitive communication was applied to those members of staff, who found themselves being escorted from the building by security personnel as soon as they had arrived for work. Even worst still, the most harshly insensitive form of communication was directed towards those members of staff, who were being forced to leave the building whilst they were using the toilets. They were warned that, if they didn't come out of the cubicles immediately, the doors would be opened by force and the occupants would be ejected in whichever state they were found to be in. Mary Allsorts, who had faithfully served as Earl's PA and continued throughout the transition period before Duke's incumbency, became his PA eventually. She was most shabbily treated by the accounting *'hatchet'* personnel. "FIFO" was all she was told. "I don't know what that means", Mary submitted. "FIRST IN, FIRST OUT, you've been here so long, the dust is settling on your wrinkled body. We have no further use for you. It is time you went. You're surplus to requirements, got it", the accounting *'hatchet'* personnel crowed. Though the staff understood the accounting *'hatchet'* personnel had a job to do, there was really no need to prove the mindless way he had gone about his job. His behaviour defined the *'hatchet'* personnel's *'values and beliefs'*. He had no heart, no soul and seemed impervious to emotional sensitivity but was being paid an enormous sum for reducing the staff number to a mere skeletal amount. Each individual remaining was being asked to do the job of three or four people. When they complained, the *'hatchet'* personnel showed them the door, literally. The state of DSI as a company was comparable only to that of a human having a sudden heavy stroke; the paralysis rendering them without the functionalities they once might have taken for granted, perhaps! DSI had called in the *'Receiver'*. The creditors were converging upon the company like vultures attracted to the stinking carcasses that lay openly exposed to the elements. Duke Stagg Incorporated was no longer the giant it had become over so many years. In those years, it had sat atop its rivals like a cap of snow on the apex of Mount Everest. Its competitors had rated DSI so highly that now that their shares had plummeted to an all time low, they wanted to amalgamate in order to take over the impressive 'goodwill' that had been *realised* in accounting terminology. It appeared as if Duke or Baron had drained the company in such a way that it was like a doctor giving up on a patient because the hemorrhaging was unstoppable, literally. He was no longer investing in stocks and shares but instead chose to *'invest'* heavily in drugs, arms and sodomy throughout the Royal Royal Dis-United Stately Kingdoms of Asteroidia as well as those 5th rated exotic far off continents, countries and islands. No longer was he imparting the type of *'spin'* that was healthy for the company. Instead, the type of *'spin'* that Duke or Baron found himself in had spun both *'clockwise'* and *'anticlockwise'*; one way then another. It was as massively destructive as a cyclone; spinning into ridiculous spirals, effectively. The *'overworld'* is where Duke's or Baron's *'Inter-Kingdom'* and *'Inter-Exotica'* personal armies of paedophiles deliberately hunted, but was openly allowed to seize and exploit childlike innocence repeatedly without mercy, care or *'politically accepted'* deliberately weakened structures of consequential *'deterrents'*, so-called. In the environments of the *'overworld'*, the subliminally charged programmed and conditioned pornographic mentality was embedded, sensitized and *'politically accepted'* with childlike glee by both young and old. It might even be considered a type of *'culture'* that had swept over the populations like the arrival of a plague of viral diseases of epidemic proportions.

Under the practical *'guidance'* of the GSE, Ghetto Sodomy Entrepreneurs on the Royal Royal Dis-United Stately Kingdoms of Asteroidia and including the exotic continents, countries and islands like Costa Del Shell where Kerri O'Ki and the rest of the young girls were vying to become *'The Dancehall Queenbees'*. These were classic examples of the influence of the Ghetto Sodomy Entrepreneurs, the Ghetto Celebrity Entrepreneurs and the Ghetto Celebrity CEOs. Each had captive audiences eagerly waiting to be converted and shaped into the *'stereo-typical'* *'models'* that befit the *'stereo-typical'* *'roles'*. The new *'converts'* were being forcibly mentally kidnapped by the Ghetto Mentality Terrorists, subliminally converted and programmed by the Ghetto Mentality Engineering Scientists, produced and directed by the Ghetto Mentality Practitioners and subsequently bullied, drilled and conditioned by the Ghetto Sodomy Entrepreneurs. Having been mentally battered into submission, the young girls accepted *slackness* with childlike glee and that being *'loose'* as a form of *'fun'* *'activity'* in which to be involved. This guaranteed them being acknowledged as Socialite *'A' Blisters* elect with altered egos which befitted their tunnel-vision cesspool mentalities.

At The Haunted Post AADC, women pranced but paraded themselves in *'loose'* fashion amongst the throng of drunken male revellers just like in the movies from three or four generations ago. Some clung to their partners as if to enable support to the various rooms upstairs. The Haunting Post AADC catered for and facilitated their varied superlative urges. Some of the props were huge wooden bedsteads with head and footboards, four posters with dusty curtains often with stained mattresses blended with antique escritoires, chaise lounges, large chests of drawers and the obligatory huge solid wooden *'distressed'* military chests at the foot of each bed like in the old movies. These military chests stored the various paraphernalia like costumes, whips, cuffs, ropes, leathers, feathers, furs and thongs that befitted the Motel section of The Haunting Post AADC. Grime was an accepted part of the antiquity of the quaint AADC and often men blew the falling dust off the froth of their beer. The *'over-world'* spiral included both legal and illegal drugs and arms aplenty.

A Documentary Report stated that a source from within 'The Interplanetary Police', InterPlanPol, alleged that "the revenue from the contraband arriving on the parallel virtual planet added to the GDP for each Kingdom throughout the entire Royal Royal Dis-United Stately Kingdoms of Asteroidia in the World of Space". Somehow, Duke or Baron had made a conscious decision to get involved in the transporting of contraband goods and the promotion of sodomy throughout the Royal Royal Dis-United Stately Kingdoms of Asteroidia and the far off exotic continents, countries and islands too in the World of Space. He was loosing interest in DSI. His preference for the new *'challenges'* that he found more exciting was sucking him into an awesome void which he found as a resource for spreading the *'risks'* across a destructive pathway of mind-bending *'thrills'* on the *'ultimate white-knuckled ride'*. Duke or Baron preferred to live on the edge and he found an association with hazardously high risks a similar experience when he was an adolescent in the fearsome gang called Clout. His backers then were the GOS, Gang Orientation Scientists, their colleagues the GOO, Gang Orientation Operators and the GOP, Gang Orientation Practitioners. They were the self-appointed oversight bodies. Emphasis was on the *'issue status'* of an ethnic gang formed under one common *'emotional banner'* like *'The Missing Fathers' Association'* which helped to bond the emotionally insensitive gang members together. Each gang had a singular *'issue status'* that glued them together but members did not migrate from one gang to another. Now, Duke or Baron was aware, like his experience in the adolescent gang Clout, that the younger generation was still entrapped in the UFO's *'Cult-Induced'* Post/Zip Code Wars. As advised and directed by the Gang Orientation Scientists, Operators and Practitioners, Duke or Baron concentrated on targeting the younger generations to sell drugs and arms at street level. This was turning out to be a lucrative business where GOS, Gang Orientation Scientists completed the conversion from *'groups'* sharing the same *sufferance* but transcended into marauding gangs that roamed the streets with impunity. In the Royal Royal Dis-United Stately Kingdoms of Asteroidia, corruption was rife but accepted as being the inevitable *"name of the game"*.

Politicrats and poly-tricksters chose to ignore the wanton waste of young lives at the expense of many grieving parents. It was their physical and emotional loss. No matter how many perished at the hands of the madness mentality called the UFO's *'Cult-Induced'* Post/

Zip Code Wars, politicrats as well as uniformed *'authority actors'* appeared and reappeared in the media stating the same old rhetoric that *"lessons were being learnt"*. The questions grieving parents kept asking were (1) how many more *"lessons had to be learnt"* before meaningful interventions were made to stymie the obvious schizophrenic behaviours brought on initially by fear and the repetitive symbolic glorification of violence? (2) What was being done with the *"lessons learnt"*? (3) How were those *'lessons'* being implemented by the authorities, so-called, to diminish at minimum but move to eradicate the repetition of this senseless mindset? (4) Was it the politicrats who could legislate that their uniformed representatives stop their prejudicial preferences for the lack of evaluation of the quality of lives of the ethnic populations wittingly or unwittingly? (5) Was it being left to the inherent, inveterate bigots, the poly-tricksters, to come forward but admit that it was hugely profitable for them to encourage violence amongst ethnic populations?

Apart from their loved ones, who had past on through the lack of and malaise to install meaningful preventative interventions, grieving parents had to finance the recurring huge costs of funerals on a daily basis. This continued to happen not only throughout the Dis-United Kingdoms of Asteroidia but also throughout the exotic continents, countries and islands that had been introduced but inveigled into the UFO's 'Cult-Induced' Post/Zip Code Wars. It appeared as if it was the latest trend, perhaps! Either Duke or Baron were *'investing'* hugely in Funeral Parlours as well as the associate businesses, which thrived off what had presently become the hourly slayings on the streets, perpetrated by the continuing *'gangland craze'* called the UFO's *'Cult-Induced'* Post/Zip Code Wars. It didn't matter whether it was way back when Clout was the most feared gang in Spaceville or now, the *"ride or die"* or *"die trying"* subliminal messages installed but reinforced by the GMT, Ghetto Mentality Terrorists, the GMES, Ghetto Mentality Engineering Scientists, the GMP, Ghetto Mentality Practitioners, the GOS, Gang Orientation Scientists and their subordinates the GOO, Gang Orientation Operators and GOP, Gang Orientation Practitioners, had riveted themselves to the underside of the youngsters' psyches. Both Duke and Baron had found that they never did let go of those post hypnotic commands, which rendered them the *'robotrons'* they had become. Still blinded by the influence of the *'stereo-hype'* and *'stereo-tripe'* that they had learnt in their earlier years, Duke and Baron chose to return to the corruptive gangland mentality. It had re-emerged to stifle their real potential and abilities as legitimate businessmen. The man they called 'The Professor' might have referred to this psychological condition as *'the inner adolescent'*. Replicating the gangland behaviour was as easy as the remaking of an object from the same mould. It was unfortunate that, over the years, neither Duke nor Baron had chosen to learn to raise their self-worth to levels whereby they could shape their own sets of *'values and beliefs'* instead of robotically living someone else's, assumedly!,

The twin brothers' childhood friends like Trojan, 'the horse', were known as hardened criminals. Trojan, 'the horse' had spent *'time'* in prison for the various vicious assaults he had committed during the UFO's *'Cult-Induced'* Post/Zip Code Wars in their teenage years. He was 6'4''' in height with an over-generous athletic build. Trojan 'the horse' was still a dedicated advocate of the *'three musketeers'* *"all for one, one for all"* philosophy. By his reputation, Trojan 'the horse' had been known to keep his rival, the shorter but heavy set 'crazy' Bobby, away from the *'honorary'* post of becoming Duke's number one *'bodyguard'*. Like the gangster he was, Trojan 'the horse' sent 'crazy' Bobby a *'Bereavement'* Card attached to a wreath of flowers. When 'crazy' Bobby received the wreath, he vouched to get Trojan 'the horse'. The warning had sent 'crazy Bobby' into another of his frenzied moments. They were never friends during their teenage years. There was a rumour that 'crazy' Bobby had snitched on the rest of his colleagues when they were members of the gang Clout. The fact that his alleged *'plea bargain'* had reduced his time served in prison did not go down well with the others, like Trojan 'the horse', who had to serve longer sentences. The enmity between those who backed either man had split the gang into two groups. 'Crazy Bobby' had denied *'grassing'* on his colleagues but the likes of Trojan 'the horse' did not believe him. There was no doubt that someone had grassed on the gang but each was a suspect. Duke had *'water-boarded'* most of them but was not convinced it was 'crazy' Bobby who had snitched on them. Trojan 'the horse' and 'crazy Bobby had never been the best of friends so it was inevitable that Trojan 'the horse' would judge him as the *'snitch'*.

That was then but now both men had gathered their own supporters for a confrontation. The potential for more unwanted violence was being tempered when both groups met at The Haunting Post AADC. Both 'crazy' Bobby and Trojan 'the horse' had chided and derided each other. "You keep blaming me", 'crazy' Bobby shouted. "It must have been you. The rest of us had to serve longer sentences, didn't we", Trojan 'the horse' said accusingly? Sparks flew but no fires were lit. "We are all strapped", 'crazy' Bobby warned. He removed the warlike weapon from his waist. His colleagues confirmed that they too were strapped by displaying their armoury. Trojan 'the horse' signalled to his colleagues to display their hardware too. Frigit 'the mouse' signalled to Henry 'the hook'. He moved closer to 'crazy' Bobby. "I haven't got any beef with you", 'crazy' Bobby said. The barman, who didn't want the 'shoot out' in 'The Haunting Post', threatened to send for Duke. All the posturing ceased immediately. "Where is he", a voice asked? It was filled with fear. "He is upstairs with his bit of rough. I don't think he is going to be pleased with you lot for disturbing him", the barman warned. Duke could not stand the bickering between Trojan 'the horse' and 'crazy' Bobby. He had often chastised one or the other for distracting him away from his treasured objective. Duke had found another way to make a lot of money and he didn't want to be distracted by internal squabbling or feuding within the gang. Even though, Duke and his colleagues were much older now, Clout was still very much alive. It was his brainchild and Duke wanted the kind of *'three musketeers'* unity that had served them well in the past. "Money is the only language people understand", he had often commented. Anyone but anyone who got in Duke's way while he was trying to *'earn'* money chanced not only their lives but their families too. He was truly an awesomely cold, unfeeling man when he was dishing out retribution. His methods were brutally crude. Loss of fingers, toes, ears, wounding by stabbings, shootings, beatings, kidnappings and sometimes fatalities were often linked to Duke, in some way. Being taken to a crypt to be tortured meant that not many were seen after their visit. Duke was shrewd enough to distance himself from all his initiations but he'd also been known to carry out some of these pistol whippings or other forms of torture himself. Both 'crazy' Bobby and Trojan, 'the horse' knew Duke since childhood. Neither would dare to take him on, one-on-one nor through their links with the *'under'* and *'over'* world. Trojan 'the horse' and 'crazy' Bobby had to swallow their pride and childlike bickering. They both knew that wily Duke dominated that community. From the large room above The Haunting Post AADC he was sharing with bubbly *'bird-of-a-feather'* Doris, Duke tapped the window pane with the fingers of his right hand while he pressed the cell phone hard up against his left ear with the other. He played an odd beat consisting of some long notes, some shorter and some very short indeed. The rapidity of his tapping indicated the measure of his impatience and frustration at not being able to contact Sandra. At times, there were no ringing tones from the window pane, only a very flat sound more like that of a snare drum being hit constantly rather in staccato style. He was furious with himself for making a most basic mistake. That was to treat Sandra like he did but still leaving her with the most dangerous weapon in her hands, the Marriage Certificate. Doris was pressing him to get married but he hadn't told her that Sandra was legally his wife. It was something that happened on the spur of the moment. Nothing was planned. Not even his best friend, Grant Favours, knew of the wedding. Duke being an astute businessman had to ensure the advertisers remain in the belief that Sandra was still single. As far as Duke was concerned, she was more marketable as a young single female. His nervous behaviour indicated to Doris that his sudden change of mood was an indication that he was going to try to win Sandra back again. "What's she got over you Duke? It's only a few hours ago everything was all right between me and you", Doris complained. "Shut it, just shut it Doris", Duke ordered. "What if I don't", she pressed. Duke reacted as he always does when he felt cornered. He struck Doris across her face with the back of the hand that had played percussion on the window pane moments before. Doris looked up from her position on the floor where Duke's blow had put her. Her face was already reddened and bruised by his roughened hands. At first, Doris thought it was one of Duke's rituals but the force was overwhelming enough to convince her of his intention. "You'll have to kill me. I won't shut up", Doris said defiantly. Duke ignored her but kept redialling the same number again and again. He was desperate to make contact with his wife. All sorts of imagined headlines appeared in his mind. His 'boozed' smile had turned to a more sombre, sour look. He was looking directly at Doris. It was the look of scorn. Now, Duke beat the wall of the room with the palm of his hand. "Come on you stubborn bitch, answer the phone, come on", he pleaded. "She doesn't want you anymore", Doris jeered. Duke went manic. "That's it, you've done it now", he shouted. "Don't like the truth, huh", Doris chanced. A volcanic eruption manifested between the two. Words frequently decorated with universally accepted extraordinary adjectives representing gross insensitivity were traded without regard. Things from the past were retrieved but were the main ingredients of the big pow-wow between them. For the duration of the quarrel, the volume of their voices rose to many decibels above what was tolerable. The universally accepted extraordinary adjectives interspersed the other drastically caustic words without mercy. Neither Doris nor Duke gave thought before speaking, rendering the confusion of cross-talk to threats, spite and desperation. Both Doris and Duke became aware of their shortcomings. Doris had got up from the floor now. She knew that she was as strong as Duke. Her rotund body identified itself as belonging to the 'endomorph' group. It was a mass that Duke would be foolish to miscalculate. Doris moved towards him. She held her hands behind her. The look in Doris's eyes was that not only of a woman scorned and frequently relegated in preference for the younger delectable Sandra but also one that Duke sensed was ready to gamble on an 'all' or 'nothing' basis. He dropped the cell phone but ducked when the glass vase was thrown at him. Doris' aim and direction were perfect except for the fact that Duke reacted quickly enough to avoid being hit. The force with which the glass vase hit the wall behind him then shattering into dozens of pieces carried its own message. "Have you gone mad woman", Duke asked? "You can't just use women and then dump them, Duke. You can't", Doris finished. She retrieved the onyx paperweight from the bedside table. Doris held it in her hand. She threatened to throw the paperweight at Duke but he dodged behind the first of the three antique red deeply buttoned leather Chesterfield Sofas. There were two three seat and one two seat Chesterfields in that large room. Duke hid behind one three seat Sofa. He crawled on both hands and knees to one end but peered around it. Duke couldn't see Doris. He looked behind him but again he couldn't see her. "Crawl around on all fours like the dog you are", Doris jeered. "You're bloody mad, that's what you are", Duke chimed. He didn't feel comfortable being on the other side of Doris' temper. She was normally even tempered but he remembered the fight between her and Sandra at the party at Sandra's house. Doris was desperate and ready to make Duke sweat. As long she kept quiet, Duke would have to keep guessing where she was positioned in the room. In that way, Duke was now the hunted. For the first time, Doris felt what it was like to have control over him. "You hide all you want. I'm gonna get you, you bastard. Think you can just walk out on 'plain old' Doris, do ya", she sneered. Her voice sounded like a 'bag of cats' but it carried a threat across the room. Doris stood far enough away from the three seat Chesterfield Sofa behind which Duke was hiding. He also knew that Doris' major weakness was naivety. He had to think fast. Duke switched tactics. "Doris lets make a deal" he offered. She decided to call his bluff. "Lets hear it then", Doris replied. "What would you say if I pitch in a nice car and that's just for starters", Duke chanced? "I can't live in a bleeding car, can I", Doris retorted? "You can keep the basement flat", Duke traded. "That old dump", Doris complained? "I'll have it decorated", Duke promised. "What, after 10 years", Doris replied? "I'll buy new furniture", Duke baited. "What about throwing in a teddy bear as a companion", she jeered. "Duke, you fail to understand the difference between need and want. You men are all alike. Always thinking you know what will satisfy us women", Doris complained. "Don't we", Duke queried? "No, you don't know. You only think you know. Ask any other women and you'll hear the same complaint", Doris said with disdain. "You never complained before", Duke said, nonchalantly. At first, Doris didn't respond to Duke's last comment. She was trying hard for the truth not to come out. She knew how tricky Duke was with his questions. Doris decided not to tell Duke the whole truth. "Sometimes you react badly, when I say I don't want to and worse if I say I can't. You men are clueless when it comes to understanding that us women are not geared up to say 'yes' all the time", Doris complained further. Duke remained quiet for a while and so did Doris. She was determined to get the best *deal* she could now she had the '*power*' to barter. Duke's phone rang. He lost his concentration but fished in his pocket for the small cell phone. It wan't there but it kept ringing. He saw it where he had dropped it on the floor but he didn't want Doris to answer it. Duke crawled towards the small cell phone which vibrated as it rung. He managed to get it but had exposed his position to the patient but still angry Doris. "Hello", he said. Duke felt when the paperweight thudded on the fleshy part of his shoulder. "Got ya", Doris said into the phone. Duke looked up from his position on the floor. The roles had been reversed. Doris held the nap hand. She used the whip that she had retrieved from the Military Chest at the foot of the bed. Duke lying on his back cowered but raised both of his hands to deter the three pronged whip from hitting him across his face. Doris dropped the whip but jumped from the top of the Chesterfield Settee. She did a belly flop but ended up on top of the defenseless Duke like a wrestler from the ropes onto to a helpless opponent. Even though he was quite fairly chunky himself, Doris' weight was not to be underestimated. Duke froze. Doris seized him by the wrist but twisted it suddenly and with purpose. Duke yelped like a wounded banshee. Doris continued to apply pressure on his now weakened wrist. "Surrender", Doris queried? Duke was a very stubborn man. "No. Get off me bitch", he shouted. "You have a right to call me a bitch. You even have a right to call me a slut because I let you but this time Duke Stagg I'm in charge. Say you surrender", Doris demanded. She now placed her body at a diagonal across Duke's body. There was no escape for the normally belligerent Duke. Doris had more or less squeezed most of the air from his tummy. He was gasping now and panting like Tramp did at the airport. Duke's tongue was hanging out much like the little dog's was then. He became reddened from the poundage on top of him and the technique being applied by Doris. "Say you surrender or I'll break your f ★ ★ ★ ★ ★ g wrist. Something went crack and the yelp must have been heard for at least a quarter of a mile away.

The barman looked up at the plastic doll hanging in front of the bar area but commented. "If she can make Duke yelp like that just think what she can do for us mere mortals", he quipped. Duke's prolonged groaning could also be heard above the din in the Saloon. They all heard when Duke and Doris shouted the word "Yes"? "Yes", "Yes"? "Yes" alternately then there was no sound. "He must be having a great time", Frigit 'the mouse' joined in. "Nobody has ever said that about me", she admitted. Back inside the room, Doris got up from the injured Duke. "Thought you were tough, didn't ya", she asked? Duke looked at Doris through new eyes. "Where did you learn to do that", he asked? He shook his hand vigorously. "I was going to do the same to Miss Fancy Pants at the party in her house until you saved her that night. She should kiss your feet for saving her from the kind of beating she was about to receive. Everyone sees me as plain old Doris but I was famous once. I fell unto hard times. Now I'm just a barmaid. Everyone uses and judges me but no one knows me like me, not even you, Duke Stagg. I play your game because I love you Duke but all you ever think of is you, you selfish bastard. Everything was going fine with me and you until Miss Fancy Pants came along", she lamented. Duke elected to keep quiet but observed Doris. "I was Brazenborough's Female Wrestling Champion before you came into my life", Doris advised.

CHAPTER 55

When he walked into the Haunting Post AADC, everyone froze as if they had seen a ghost. His uncanny resemblance to Duke was more than a replica. The only difference was that he seemed a bit thinner in body. 'Crazy' Bobby and Trojan 'the horse' stopped their bickering but used the language of the moving head to indicate their shocked surprise at the man who had just walk in. It was just like those *'Cowboy'* movies of the past when a tough new stranger came into the Saloon looking mean and mysterious. The bartender asked if he was an actor playing a part. "He's an interloper. Throw him out" the man sitting with Doris shouted. As some men in the Saloon started to approach him, the thinner man pointed towards the man with Doris but commented.

"He is the interloper. My name is Duke", he protested. It seemed so ridiculous that this stranger was coming into The Haunting Post AADC, to throw aspersions at *'The Gaffer's'* son, Duke. It was a crazy moment for all not least Doris. She, with her loud common laughter sounding more like a bag of cats, snuggled up to the man next to her but pointed at the stranger and his apparent stupidity. The thinner man stared at the man next to Doris. Their eyes remained fixed for what seemed an eternity but it was only a few minutes that had past.

When Grant Favours walked through the half wooden louvre swing doors of the Saloon, more complications arose. The man sitting with Doris looked absolutely shocked. The colour drained from his face altogether and Doris felt him go into spasms. "What's the matter Duke? Are you cold", she enquired? "Why is Grant here", the man muttered under his breath. This type of AADC wasn't Grant's type of surroundings. He would tend to visit the more upmarket swanky environments and Wine Bars. The man with Doris, purporting to be Duke, was very suspicious about Grant's entry but he pretended to be happy to see him. "Grant, you old bastard, come and have a drink. What's yours", he asked? The expression on Grant's face was one of consternation. He wanted to tell the man with Doris what he really thought of him but he was aware of what was yet to come and he didn't want to seem unfriendly or make him suspicious. "Mine's a brandy. How could you not know that? You must be loosing your marbles", Grant quipped. "Surely you mean a double don't you? Barman, give my good friend Grant a triple measure of brandy. Put it on my slate", the man sitting with Doris beamed. Grant walked over towards where Doris and the man, purporting to be Duke, were sitting. He greeted Doris. "What are you doing in these parts", Doris enquired. "I'm meeting a friend here. It's sort of a midway point, so I agreed", Grant lied. "So how is Costa Del Shell shaping up under your expertise", the man with Doris asked? Grant gave the sort of 'form' answer individuals get when they ring a hospital to find out how their relative or friend is progressing. "As best as can be expected", he replied. The man, purporting to be Duke, paused briefly to sip the beer from the Pewter Jug. The froth appeared above his top lip but seemed like a frothy moustache. Doris giggled at the sight. Oh Duke, you look so funny with that 'tache. Don't you think so Grant," she asked? Like in the *'Western'* movies, the man used the back of his hand to wipe the froth away but burped loudly. "Pardon", Doris prompted.

Grant raised the issue about the transformation of the 5th rated exotic island of Costa Del Shell. There was a deliberate plan in place to provide more *'activities'* in order to attract more tourists to it. Tourism was new to the island and had the potential to be a huge money making industry. With the blessings of the politicrats and poly-tricksters of the island and Duke, or so it seemed, had arranged to explore Costa Del Shell's potentiality for the expansion of tourism. He planned to introduce *'activities'* that might attract the attention of tourists. What was not clear to Grant and the others was what type of *'activities'* were agreed by both Duke, seemingly, and the politicrats and poly-tricksters of Spaceville and Costa Del Shell. Grant was not privy to the meetings at politicrats ministerial level. As requested by Duke, assumedly, Grant was able to confirm that hedonism, drugs, arms and paedophile rings were actively in place on the exotic island as ordered by Duke, apparently!

Costa Del Shell was previously an idyllic paradise. Indigenous as well as the earlier visitors to the exotic island used to be able to stroll around without fear on the *"paradise island"* at midnight in the bluish light of the moon or the golden rays of the early morning sun, which separated the darkness of night but announced the break of dawn. Since the introduction of the new *'activities'* on Costa Del Shell, some strange behaviours introduced by some visitors to the exotic island had started to impact greatly upon the indigenous population. Within three years of the increased number of tourists to the island, there were noticeable vast changes in some of the indigenous peoples' behaviours on the once idyllic island. The introduction of hardcore drugs and the availability of arms meant that the rate of violence had begun to rise steeply. Tourists as well as the indigenous population were no longer able to just wander from place to place even in the daytime. Each day, there were reports of kidnappings, robberies with violence and of local Posts/Zip Code gangs executing each other in the streets without regards for others. Drugs and arms cartels had begun to spring up all over Costa Del Shell. The other exotic islands, countries and continents were now replicating the madness mentality internally amongst the various *'Cult-Induced'* Post/Zip Code gangs. Intense rivalry had developed with the other exotic continents, countries and islands in the region as well.

The promise of the increase in employment was not forthcoming except for those few vacancies in Leisure and Tourism. Very few of the locals were involved with the building of new Hotels, Motels and Shopping Malls which were springing up rapidly on the shores of the exotic continents, countries and islands. Instead, workers from places like Spaceville were being imported but contracted to carry out that type of work on the 5th rated islands, countries and continents.

Grant and his team were not happy with the arrangements anymore as their lives were now in danger on the once idyllic island of Costa Del Shell and in the region generally. The number of tourists was fast dwindling with every item of news that told of the incessant violence that was happening on the exotic island. Grant was being used as the *Drug Ambassador* and the *Arms Mercenary* on Costa Del Shell. He thought he was working for Duke until Alan Baitman told him that it was Baron, a.k.a. Al Tuxedo that had been orchestrating all the moves. Costa Del Shell was only one of the exotic islands. They were fast getting reputations for being "too violent to visit". Spaceville's politicrats Minister for Foreign Affairs, Ali Gaitor Jnr, warned tourists that they travelled to those exotic destinations at their *"own risk"*.

Al Tuxedo had great influence at top level around the entire virtual planet of Asteroidia. Being sanctioned by the GOS, Gang Orientation Scientists, he converted to becoming a GOO, Gang Orientation Operator. Al Tuxedo was part of an international gang and had been given the thumbs up from some politicrats and poly-tricksters They were all benefiting from the proceeds of the multi-squillion abundance of Champagne Urge. This was happening all over the Royal Royal Dis-United Stately Kingdoms of Asteroidia. In the structure of the hierarchy of the United Fraternal Organisation, the GMP, Ghetto Mentality Practitioners, only purpose was to carry out the will of their *'puppeteers'*, the GMT, Ghetto Mentality Terrorists and the GMES, Ghetto Mentality Engineering Scientists They were above the GMP. In turn, they controlled the other subgroups like the GOS, Gang Orientation Scientists, the GOO, Gang Orientation Operators, like Al Tuxedo, and their subordinates, the Gang Orientation Practitioners. Each synchronized with the other under the umbrella of the head *'puppeteers'*, the UFO. The aim of each subgroup was to initially inoculate but make individuals dependent on drugs for the rest of their lives. Al Tuxedo's contact with the politicrats and poly-tricksters around the virtual planet of

Asteroidia was well chronicled by the media. There were footages of pictures of Al Tuxedo with very influential people from every possible walk of life.

At the Haunting Post AADC, each time the wooden louvre half swing doors opened, the man sitting with Doris seemed to be getting tenser by the minute. Doris and Grant observed his behaviour. When *'pretend'* government Private Investigator but Head of InterPlanPol, Alan Baitman entered The Haunting Post AADC, the man with Doris was shocked to see him too. Now he knew that there was something strange going on. The man with Doris was not feeling particularly powerful now. He sensed that he was being outnumbered. The man purporting to be Duke felt trapped but wanted to make a dash for the exit. When he made an attempt to leave The Haunting Post AADC the man sitting with Doris, on the instruction of Alan Baitman, was brought back into the Saloon by Geoff 'the rhino' and his colleagues. He seemed a bit bedraggled and was sweating even more profusely now. The thinner Duke 'look-a-like' smiled as if he was aware why the man had this dishevelled look. One of them was an impostor and they both knew it. When Henry 'the hook' and the others came back into the Saloon, despite his dishevelled look, the man who was with Doris bowed his head but kept a silly smile on his face. Henry 'the hook', Trojan 'the horse', Geoff 'the rhino', Pete 'the hammer' and Barney 'the owl' addressed the man as "Al Tuxedo".

When they had been arrested as part of the younger gang, Clout, it was them and their fellow prisoners who had named the man Al Tuxedo. It was rumoured that he was a notorious drug baron and arms dealer who had been ruling both the *'under'* and *'over'* worlds, apparently! Al Tuxedo had served his *'sentence'* in the same category 'A' prison as his colleagues, Geoff 'the rhino' and others. The difference was that he was a *'celebrity'* prisoner. Al Tuxedo actually was dressed in Tuxedos everyday while he was in prison. It was comical to see any prisoner wearing Tuxedos in prison. He was separated but protected by the prison establishment. All the prison staff, including the governor, bowed but saluted to him. He influenced but controlled the supply of drugs in prisons too. Al Tuxedo had some 'high level' contacts like politicrats, poly-tricksters, members of the police, and big business corporations like banks who laundered the money from drugs and arms. He was as ruthless as his namesake called 'Al Cap' in a previous generation on the parallel planet, Earth. Al Tuxedo was the head of a very well run *businesses* in the World of Space. He ran sophisticated *businesses* as well as sleazy joints. Al Tuxedo often recruited young girls like Kerri O'Ki through the subgroup named Ghetto Sodomy Entrepreneurs. He controlled the minds of both young boys and girls through the recruitment *'processes'* via the Ghetto Mentality Engineering Scientists and their subordinates, the Ghetto Mentality Practitioners. They delegated to the franchisee subgroups like the Ghetto Celebrity Entrepreneurs and the Ghetto Celebrity CEOs. Each of the named franchisees *'purpose'* was to supply the *'post-hypnotic'* subliminal messages in their Music, DVDs and Games. Their *'mission'* was to become the self-selected MIM, *'Mental Imagery Missionaries',* who tasked themselves to recruit but inveigle naive and vulnerable young minds into Al Tuxedo's lair. The GMT and the GMES were able to achieve this goal by strategising to systemically break down each tier of resistance whilst exploring the young people's emotional weaknesses. Through his puppeteers, the GMT, the GMES and subsequently the GMP, Al Tuxedo, taught the eager GSE, like Pimpè Ernel V1, how to become one of the MIM, *'Mental Imagery Mercenaries'.* They actively sought to physically and mentally kidnap but overwhelm young girls and boys by entrapment. Al Tuxedo knew that where young girls assembled young boys and those older males of paedophilic tendencies would follow, inevitably! He was trained by a multitude of religious *'Leaders'* from varying denominations who were experts in the psychology of *'conversion'* and *'post-hypnotic'* techniques. 'Al Tuxedo' thoroughly understood these subtler *'commands'* but became adept at activating *'the art of manipulating'* *'belief systems'*. In principle, the manipulation worked just like how *'worker'* bees seemed to be attracted to the *'honey'* bees. The *'paedophile mentality'* had, over millennia, long been not only etched but deeply grooved into the minds of individuals by a culture which encouraged it as part of ingrained philosophical *'politically accepted'* practices. These were particular toxic cultural mentalities which had been practiced but developed into cultural mindsets and approved by legislators, the so-called *'guardians'* against *'injustice'* under the umbrella of democracy, over those millennia. Even those in high offices, like police and Judges had often commented but ruled against many victims of paedophilia and rape because they said the victims had *"asked for it"*. This type of stone-aged way of thinking was still happening in the assumed more modern technological aged millennia within the 1st rated Royal Royal Dis-United Stately Kingdoms of Asteroidia, initially. The Walynski Institute produced research which concurred with other experts around the virtual planet of Asteroidia. Their findings were that, "through being thoroughly influenced by the 1st rated Royal Royal Dis-United Stately Kingdoms of Asteroidia's *'values and beliefs'* as being sacrosanct, individuals in the 5th rated exotic continents, countries and islands had come to accept, adopt but practice the culture of paedophilia and rape as their own. These disturbing systemic mental aberrations were part of a psychopathically-ill neuro-ritualistic mentality which had exploded but seemed to be carried like seeds being dispersed in the wind. This mentality exposed the mental inadequacies of *'adult'* individuals causing them to behave repetitively in a bizarrely unacceptable, mentally imbalanced manner, especially against vulnerable individuals and children alike". Professor Walynski's Research highlighted that, "over generations, psychiatrists had deliberately failed to declare the practices and behaviours of paedophilia and rapists as **_'mental illnesses'_** let alone publish any research to date of what made rapists target vulnerable, naïve individuals and paedophiles target children, in particular". Often, under the guise of being *'missionaries'* or using the umbrella of *'tourism'*, some visitors from the 1st rated Royal Royal Dis-United Stately Kingdoms deliberately targeted the children in the exotic continents, countries and islands for their *'pleasure'*, seemingly! They often use their 1st rated status to exploit the naivety and subservient mannerisms of the indigenous population of the exotic continents, countries and islands in order to exploit the children. Driven by their sickening mentalities and their super-hydrated thirst for Champagne Urge, the GSE provided innocent children to the paedophilic visitors to the exotic continents, countries and islands. This enabled the migration of their 1st rated lewd behaviours upon the 5th rated exotic continents, countries and islands. The serial paedophiles recruited but taught their new *'converts'* in these exotic environments what they had practiced on the parallel virtual planet of Asteroidia. In the exotic environments, the visiting active paedophiles' strategy was to seek out individuals without regular income but easily 'convert' them to buy in at GSE, Ghetto Sodomy Entrepreneur level within the Organisation. As part of their contracted commitment to become franchisees to their puppeteers, the indigenous GSE earned their money on *'commission only'* basis. The more young girls and boys they recruited, by whatever means, the more they earned. There were different tiers for entering into the *business*. Further recruitment of other GSE meant that *'recruiters'* rapidly moved up the ladder to higher levels. There was no bluffing in this type of *business*. The footfall to the massage parlours, strips joints, pole and lap dancing extravaganzas was evidence which indicated the *'success'* of the GSE. Some like Pimpè Ernel V1 became franchisees in the business but ran their own sleazy joints. It was alleged that through subordinates like the GSE, Al Tuxedo and his accomplices, often posing as VIPs, were involved in kidnapping young children but spirited them away from their indigenous exotic continents, countries and islands. He and his indigenous *'converts'* were actively organising Serial Rapists and Serial Paedophiles rings within the Royal Royal Dis-United Stately Kingdoms like Spaceville as well as in the exotic continents, countries and islands too.

Back in The Haunting Post AADC Saloon, the thinner man was still being referred to by the man sitting with Doris as the interloper. He stood his ground at the far end of the bar but ordered champagne. "Let us have a few bottles", he demanded. The barman was doubtful whether this stranger could afford it. "You'll have to pay up front. Nothing is chalked up here", the barman advised. The thinner Duke look-a-like told him that if he didn't do as he says then he might regret it. "Ha, ha, ha, ha, haaaaaa", did you hear that", the barman asked? He looked over towards Geoff 'the rhino' and the others. They wore serious countenances which suggested their moods. The barman laughed heartily but told the thinner man, who also looked like Duke, that he needed to understand just where he was and in whose company. "You actors don't know your limit do you? Champagne! Can you afford it? I'll give you a pint of beer", he teased. The barman pulled the pint of beer but spat in it in front of the stranger. "Count yourself lucky, I feel generous today. Here, this is on me.", he boasted. The thinner man at the bar took the pint of draught beer with the fast sinking lump of yellow mucus but threw it and the beer in the face of the barman. As the lump of yellow mucus slid down the barman's face, the thinner Duke look-alike spoke again but this time his deep baritone voice suggested his authority. "I only drink champagne", the man insisted. There was a harder edge to his deep voice than had been apparent before. It came through to the barman but he was still sceptical of the man's ability to pay. He tried a different line. "Celebrating something are we", he fished? The thinner man, who looked like Duke, ignored the jibe. The thinner man eased himself up onto one of the high stools but grabbed hold of the barman by the back of his neck. He pounded the barman's forehead into the hard solid wooden worktop of the bar. When the thinner Duke look-alike let the barman go, he asked him how many bottles he wanted. The thinner Duke look-alike just glared at him then commented. "As many as is needed", he snarled. The thinner Duke look-alike offered champagne to Geoff 'the rhino' and all his friends, Alan Baitman, Grant Favours, Doris and also to the man sitting with her. "What are we celebrating", Doris asked? Now, the thinner man spoke directly to the man who was sitting with her. "Hello Brov", he said. The man sitting with Doris looked like he had seen a ghost. He looked stunned because he thought that someone had paid an actor, who looked like his twin brother, to help him celebrate his birthday. "Happy birthday Brov, as you can see, I haven't forgotten what day it is. Let us celebrate our birthday together and also my freedom", the thinner man at the bar insisted. Corks from the bottles popped into the air and the champagne flowed freely. Even the barman, whose head was throbbing to an irregular beat from the battering that the thinner man at the bar had given him, toasted but drank champagne. The thinner man purporting to be the real Duke had been freed from the crypt on the basement floor of the Hotel Welcome but the man, Pete the 'hammer' and the others called Al Tuxedo, had no idea how he had managed to do so. "How did you get out", the man sitting with Doris asked? It was too late. The words had already been uttered. Everyone heard the question from the man sitting next to Doris to the thinner man at the bar purporting to be Duke. He remained calmer than the man sitting next to Doris.

This was a very interesting mind game being played. It might even have been as stimulating as watching a game of poker with two masterful bluffers with exceptional 'hands' who had developed an enormous thirst for the taste of Champagne Urge. Some of the other regulars stopped gambling but looked intriguingly at the two men one from the other. One was bluffing and the other was real. Which was the real Duke? No one really knew for sure. Even Geoff 'the rhino' and others were looking from one to the other unsure which was Duke and which was Baron. They would have never thought of Duke as Al Tuxedo. It was a huge coincidence that these two men looked so much like the twins they used to be with in the gang Clout. The two brothers had scars just below their left cheeks and broken noses. Both twin brothers had thick moustaches, eyebrows, hair pulled back with ponytails and were identical in height but, apart from these moments, were identical in weight, previously. Baron and Duke both had deep baritone voices that seemed to be tuned to the same frequency. Confusion reigned supreme in all the minds of the observers, except for the barman, who had earlier insisted that the man sitting next to Doris was the *'real'* Duke, maybe! No one had heard from Baron for a very long time. Alan Baitman was feeling quite alone now that Grant Favours seemed to have switched sides. He had agreed to give evidence against Baron Staveley, believed to be Al Tuxedo, who Alan Baitman had convinced him was the 'Drug Czar' of the entire virtual planet of Asteroidia. Although at the time, Grant thought he was working for Duke, the fact remains that InterPlanPol said they had irrefutable proof that Duke had not been involved at any level. They were convinced that it was his twin brother, Baron, who had posed as Duke. As Duke's *'Drug Ambassador'*, Grant Favours could not hide the fact about his involvement on the exotic island of Costa Del Shell. With Grant on board as a crucial prosecution witness, Alan Baitman was able to secure Sue Allen-Stokeley, Beth Tittye, Captain Plantain as additional witnesses against Duke's brother, Baron Staveley, apparently! Rather than serve long prison sentences for aiding and abetting in drug running, arms dealing, paedophilia and a catalogue of subsequent charges that were listed against him and his colleagues, Grant Favours and his minor players, caught up in the strategic dragnet cast by InterPlanPol, had agreed to become not just witnesses but agents for them also.

Alan Baitman said he could prove that Baron was impersonating Duke. He was answering the question posed by the man sitting with Doris earlier about how the thinner man standing at the bar had got out of the crypt on the basement floor of the Hotel Welcome. "Your brother got out because I freed him. It struck me as unusual that you would leave Costa Del Shell without your dog, Tramp" Alan Baitman challenged. "That's easy to explain. There was a reward set up to recover my dog", the man sitting with Doris fired back. Alan Baitman reacted swiftly to counter the man's reply. His job was to convince the likes of Henry 'the hook' and his colleagues to help him restrict the man with Doris, whom he believed to be Baron, from escaping before the militia from InterPlanPol, television and printed media arrived. The next set of details revealed by Alan

Baitman drew parallels with the characteristics of the man known as Al Tuxedo. "Getting back to Spaceville in time to ensure the haul of drugs was announced in the media was more important to you than anything else. That was the code you often used in order to alert your workers that the drugs and arms had landed in Spaceville but was ready for distribution. You prioritised that as more important to you than even the recovery of your own pet dog", Alan Baitman charged. There was immediate dialogue buzzing around The Haunting Post AADC. All eyes were focused on the man sitting with Doris. They seemed to condemn him to the charges being highlighted by Alan Baitman. Even Grant Favours was beginning to have doubts about whether the man sitting with Doris was the real Duke. Whilst the iron was hot, Alan Baitman struck again with more information. "You got careless but left a trail of evidence in your wake. Your trip to Costa Del Shell was your worst mistake but I suppose that greed was your stimulus as usual, was it", Alan Baitman asked? The man sitting with Doris fought back savagely. "How can you be sure I wasn't set up by my brother, Baron", he retorted?

The man sitting with Doris ordered a round of drinks for everyone present. Alan Baitman was still convinced that the real Duke would not have been involved with drugs, arms or paedophilia and he wanted to stay loyal to his friend. "I've known Duke for over 25 years. Everyone knows he has never pretended to be a saint but I'm convinced there is no way that he would get mixed up in this sort of business. It was you who sent Grant, Beth Tittye and Sue Allen-Stokeley to Costa Del Shell to establish the GMES for that island. I must say you train them well because it didn't take long before they recruited their own indigenous GOS, GOO, and GOP. They sought out the most naïve, vulnerable youngsters and young adult individuals, who had experienced rejection from educational establishments. Some had abandoned them a long time ago even from junior schools", Alan Baitman accused. The young adult indigenous population on the island of Costa Del Shell were being used by employers for statistical purposes only to say which employer attracted the most prospects for the same job. These were seldom short-listed. Even when they were, no employers wanted to employ them. "The young generations got tired of being used but saw themselves as more than capable of succeeding in the '*street business*'. They were attracted to it because they were no initial '*capital investment*' involved but '*earnings*' were many folds above the miserly '*politically correct*' '*minimum wage*' offered to them, set by '*political slave drivers*', who were in cahoots with heartless '*big business*' poly-tricksters. Those young generations also knew that, just like any other entrepreneur, they had the potential and abilities to become financially '*successful*'. All they needed was a commodity with which they could negotiate", Alan Baitman summarised. The man sitting next to Doris did not respond but waited to hear what else Alan Baitman had to say.

Those young '*potential geniuses*' were fodder for Al Tuxedo and his '*Gang Orientation*' colleagues. When they started their '*Recruitment Drive*', the vulnerable individuals were unaware of their intentions and so fell for the bait like fish at the end of fishing rods. They hadn't realised it then but were caught hook, line and sinker by volunteering to become franchisees like the GSE, GCCEO and the GCE. Those, who had gotten on their knees to the green humanoid robotrons' GMT and their subordinates like the GMES were as subservient as the historic obedient '*house slaves*' to their masters. They had made a conscious decision to, at least, compromise their traditional '*values and beliefs*' if not abandon them completely in favour of those of the green humanoid robotrons. They did this in order to achieve financial abundance far greater than the *'minimum wage'* or the *'National Benefit'* paid to the under-employed. Their decisions instigated but helped to form the partition between them and those they regarded as plebeian targets known as *'fodder'*, commonly. The GCCEO exchanged their *'elevation'* to Iconic Socialite Status for spitting out the explicit gangland *'stereo-tripe'* language to synchronise with the toxic violent technological games with identical subliminal instructions. Instead of using their God-given talents to inspire their peers towards bettering themselves, both the GCE and the GCCEO, used the *'alphabet'*, *'vocabulary'* and *'idioms'* of the green humanoid robotrons to degrade but debase their tribal heritage.

The man they called 'The Professor' stated that, "it seemed the GCE and GCCEO, accepted but volunteered to being used as *'acceptable pawns'* in the *'mentality chess'* game being played by the green humanoid robotrons". GCCEO set the trend for the GCE. They aspired to move from the status of *'wannabees'* to fully fledged Iconic peers. Both were showing how passionate they had become to wagering the deliberately selected subliminal *'learned helplessness'* messages. They chose to use effective lyrical instructional language to wage covert psychological war and hate against the targeted *'fodder'*; encouraging them to *"ride or die"* or at least to *"die trying"*. The Street Surveys from The Walynski Institute indicated that, having been sanctioned by their *'heroes'*, *'thuggery'* became *'trendy'*. Once approved, it made individuals *'majoring'* in *'Serial Bullying'* strive for a different type of goal than traditional moral *'values and beliefs'*. This *'pseudo-honour'* amongst *'thugs'* reeked of extremely low self-worth but achieving *'Street Credits'* for the most awesome crimes, seemed to be important to them, somewhat, perhaps! The avid recipients of the *'pseudo-honour'* *'Street Credits'* continued to implement their allegiance to an age old philosophy, "Ours are not to question why. Ours are to do or die". These *'City Cowboys'* and *'City Soldiers'* did not understand what that particular honourable philosophy really stood for. That particular philosophy was meant for those that had volunteered, as official soldiers, to die for and in defence of their respective countries, continents, islands and kingdoms. Serving as national soldiers was a huge statement of honour. Those who honoured thuggery were insulting the National Heroes. There seemed to be *'no justice'* in the thugs hijacking of the National Philosophy of the exotic continents, countries, islands and the kingdoms of Asteroidia's National Heroes. Instead, the *'City Cowboys'* and *'City Soldiers'* continued to commit *'suicide by gang violence'* through thuggery in the UFO's 'Cult-Induced' Post/ Zip Code Wars. Professor Walynski stated that, "it was an insult to each life of those *'Real Heroes'*. If these thugs really wanted to honour the National Philosophy then he challenged them to show how tough they were by signing up to go to real wars in order to help protect their kingdoms and exotic continents, countries and islands", he insisted. Of the GCCEO, the GCE and the technological purveyors of violent games, the eminent Professor Emeritus raged, "Stop the *'stereo-hype'* and the *'stereo-tripe'* that is promoting the *'politically accepted'* *'stereo-type'* imagery as being *'iconic'* as chronicled in those violent *'Western movies'*. Eliminate its glorification as being the most sought after *'heroic'*, *'thug'* image but which is fuelling *'Ethno-Genocidia'* amongst those, who are prosecuting the UFO's 'Cult-Induced' Post/Zip Code Wars in every kingdom, exotic continents, countries and islands". It was not the first time that the genial Professor had spoken so passionately about this one subject. He said that the evidence of the Research about the UFO's 'Cult-Induced' Post/Zip Code Wars over the last ten years had established some interesting facts.

He described these as *"the serial psychopathic mentality"*. It meant that the GCCEO, GCE and the serial technological violent games providers had been found to have secretly negotiated but formed honorary *'token'* ghoulish *'partnerships'* whilst boosting their investments in the likes of Funeral Parlours, Coffin Manufacturers and 'PODA', Private Organ Donors Association. GCE and GCCEO continued to show ineptitude to better understand the importance of the meaning behind emotional intelligence and emotional maturity. For this they were being rewarded handsomely by accepting the seemingly *'envious'* title of **'Honorary' Green Humanoid Robotrons.** Dazzled by their new superficial statuses and the obligatory pat on the head, like the proverbial pet, signified that they had been accepted into *'Club Exclusive'*. These modern subservient, wet behind the ears, converted honorary green humanoid robotron wimps insisted on bowing to the kind of **'stereo-imagery'** that had been chosen for them by the green humanoid robotrons, who were in charge of *'proceedings'*. The GCE and GCCEO soon became hopelessly addicted to but were much thirstier for the taste of Champagne Urge. They began to feel comfortable about being paraded, like the green humanoid robotrons' *'pet poodles'* at a *'Pet Show'* for what they perceived to be the many *'meaningful'* accolades like the perennial coveted *Judas Awards'* for which they aspired, so longingly, perhaps!

In the once exotic paradise continents, countries, islands and in the kingdoms of Asteroidia, there were mental storms brewing and the swirling winds of arguments had begun to come now at gale force propensities. At the stage of their initiation into the *'overworld'* of *'corruptive practices'*, assumedly, the generations of young adults potentials and abilities were being wasted by the governments of the kingdoms of Asteroidia including those exotic continents, countries and islands like Costa Del Shell. The traditionalists had lived in *'hope'* for far too long. They seemed not to sense the winds of change that had blown the metaphoric sandstorms into their faces; blotting out the stealthy removal, by sleight, by the use of subliminal terminologies, to rid those environments of traditional moral *'values and beliefs'*. These had been relegated to the dustbins of history by the likes of the GCE, the GCCEO but especially the GSE for a few Champagne Urges more. They were being *'guided'* to use debasing language and actions with which to address each other in order to gain kudos amongst the green humanoid robotrons. It was they who inveigled the hatred amongst the army of *'wannabees'*. The more degrading the language used the more likely it was for *'wannabees'* to reach their ultimate goal of becoming Ghetto Celebrity CEOs'. They did this so that they too could be lauded by their avid audiences but be *'elevated'* by the rumour mill brought on by the immense addiction to the greed mentality of which drove the malnutrition for their taste of Champagne Urge. In doing so, *'wannabees'* were guaranteed *success* but none wanted to take responsibility for the consequences of the UFO's 'Cult-Induced' Post/Zip Code Wars. These were being initiated but stirred up by emotionally unintelligent and immature mentalities. The Ghetto Celebrity CEOs choice of language of diatribe incited individuals to seek and destroy each other as efficiently as heat-seeking missiles in the **'Street Theatres of UFO's 'Cult-Induced' Post/Zip Code Wars'**. These *'human heat-seeking missiles'* were stirred into action by the GOO and GOP. As a consequence, young adolescents' errant behaviours chipped away at the tiers of traditional styles of living but established high levels of fear amongst themselves. The addiction to fear drove the chaos amongst peers from different streets or areas. The GOS persuaded the younger generation to ignore valuable support from immediate and extended family members alike too. Politicrats and poly-tricksters were just as culpable for the traditional family units de-construction of. Their structural model was fast being degraded by direct political intervention to stymie the respect for but inveigled the full-on destruction of value for heritage, traditional *'values and beliefs'*, morals, scruples and discipline as integral parts of the tried, tested structural teachings and the recognition of **ID**. Consequently, the void created by the parting of traditional family values, belittling disrespect of ethnic ethical cultural structure became much greater divide than the biblical "parting of the Red Sea".

In the exotic continents, countries and islands in particular, the older generation had been stubborn in their ways but failed to sense the infiltration which was presenting a new lifestyle that descended swifter than a flash of lightening. It would depend on when that generation felt able to hear the deafening clatter of thunder warning of the type of chaos about to flood their immediate physical and mental environments. Even the biblical Noah would have been hard-pressed at minimum but thoroughly overwhelmed by the sheer intensity of the flooding tactics that was being used to forge this new dishonourable mentality upon the children to *"ride or die"* or *"die trying"* even. The man they called 'The Professor' was actively mentoring a great number of those who became receptive *'hosts'* to the hugely destructive ugly mentality to hit those most vulnerable individuals referred to as *'fodder'*. He asked the questions, (1) "was it before or after the torrents of negative emotional showers had drenched those curiously parched minds on those exotic continents, countries, islands in particular but the kingdoms of Asteroidia too that these destructive mindsets of *'Ethno-Genocidia'* were determined? (2) Was it after the flood from the tempestuous tsunamis of drug induced behaviours that were threatening to diminish the quality of living for those populations who seemed less aware of the subtle subliminally induced changes in the mentality forecasts? (3) What indicated whether the forecast warning of *'Hurricane UFO'*, *'Tornado UFO'*, *'Earthquake UFO'*, *'Tempest UFO'* or *'Typhoon UFO'* was about to spell planet-wide disaster to the lives of all the vulnerable, naive younger generations"? Long before technological assistance, original *'mind-forecasters'* had developed some form of *'expertise'* to forecast *'inclement thoughts'* as well as what is considered *'acceptable thought patterns'*. Traditionally, these were sorted like the wheat from the chaffs in order to maintain meaningful traditional *'values and beliefs'*.

The traditionalist generations failed to see the heavily vapoured red clouds filled with anger hanging like drapes waiting to be unleashed via the 'Cult Induced' Post/Zip Code Wars. It had been prophesied in the biblical reference to **'Revelation'** whereby the prophesy stated that "in the last days", *children against children, children against parents, sons against daughters, sisters against sisters, fathers against mothers, brothers against sisters and brothers against brothers'*. On the virtual parallel planet of Asteroidia, this was manifesting currently amongst generations of ethnic populations practicing 'Ethno-Genocidia' through the enforced vicious UFO 'Cult Induced' Post/Zip Code Wars. Though the evidence was in their faces, the traditionalist thinkers thought that the younger generations might follow in their footsteps just like they had walked in the footsteps of the previous generations before them.

Being under-employed and with plenty of idle time, some of the younger generations were attracted to but actively got involved with petty crime until it seemed a *'worthy alternative career'* maybe! One that brought them quick money for high risks in the *'fast lane'* but which they seemed not to be able to resist or refuse. The young generations saw the *'offers'* being made by the GOS, the GOO and the GOP as alternative *'career pathways'*. They were influenced by the rise in popularity of the subgroup, the **_'artificial GCCEO'_**, who saw themselves as having been elevated in status but wore their upgraded **_'all sold out'_** badges with pseudo-honour and pride. Having escaped the harsh living conditions of *'dog eat dog'* street-life, the GCCEO were now superficially perched on higher branches of very tall trees indeed. Rather like parrots repeating the programmed and conditioned mantras to which they had agreed, been paid handsomely to help rivet the *'stereo-hype'* and *'stereo-tripe'* into the young generations' psyche via the *'subliminal mental highways'*.

Al Tuxedo managed to engage some children and some young adults with *'infantile mentality'* into his web of slackness and pornographic confusion through the GSE. They were guilty of establishing fertile ground for Al Tuxedo's paedophiles to gain access to children from poor families in the exotic continents, countries and islands and those from the poorer areas of the kingdoms of Asteroidia.

Back in The Haunted Posts AADC, the man who sat next to Doris stated once again that he was not the culprit but the victim instead. He fired his salvo of rhetoric but dared Alan Baitman to solve the mystery as to which of them was Duke? Alan Baitman went into overdrive mode. His insinuation seemed likely to not only narrow the odds but also to deliberately accuse the man he believed to be Al Tuxedo. "You drugged and kidnapped your own brother then locked him away in the crypt at the Hotel Welcome. As you see, he has lost a bit of weight but he is healthier than you expected, isn't he? I was suspicious of some of your actions but made a duplicate of the keys to enable me to free your brother from the hell you put him through", Alan Baitman finished. His resources of information began to sway the avid listeners yet again. Even Grant Favours was switching sides once again. The man sitting with Doris didn't know where to put his face. He didn't quite know how to refute these new allegations disclosed by Alan Baitman. Sweat was pouring off him now like water from a shower. His outer and under clothing were supersaturated. "I'm confused which of these bastards is Al Tuxedo", 'crazy' Bobby declared. He was stunned when Geoff 'the rhino' agreed with him. "I have never agreed with 'crazy' Bobby before but it is hard for any of us to take sides when we can't really tell which is Duke and which is Baron", he added. There was another pregnant pause then the thinner man commented. "I am happy to have a DNA test to prove who I am", he said calmly. "Yeah, I've heard them AND test don't lie", Frigit 'the mouse' exclaimed. She had hardly said anything before. Frigit 'the mouse' wasn't a very confident person hence her name. Everyone who knew Frigit 'the mouse' was aware that she often said things backward so they did not correct her obvious error. "I agree with Frigit 'the mouse' about the DNA test", Pete 'the hammer' declared. The man sitting next to Doris began mopping his face with what he thought was a large handkerchief he had recovered from his trouser pocket. It was only when the other occupants of The Haunting Post AADC started to laugh that the man sitting with Doris realised that he was mopping his brow with one of Doris' floral knickers/panties. The laughter was infectious. Some of the boisterous laughter helped to detract from the tenser moments they all had to endure in the previous moments. Even the man sitting with Doris saw the funny side. He laughed too.

Alan Baitman continued to reveal how long the man he referred to as Duke had to endure his imprisonment. "Duke saw Calvin Poser when he took the pictures of the men fighting in the garden at Miss Bogus' house but he didn't know why. Your man Calvin showed you the video of the actors you trained so well. It even got the local police thinking it was a real fight. You slipped into Miss Bogus' house when Duke was parting the fight with the men who were pretending to fight over Doris", he explained. Doris looked at the man sitting next to her, who others were referring to as Al Tuxedo. She had been spending time with him thinking he was Duke. Doris was more than perplexed. Even she couldn't really tell the difference between the brothers. Alan Baitman could sense that he was finally getting through to those who were transfixed at the mysterious happenings that were being revealed. "Nobody took notice when you slipped in during the confusion. You paid those men to create a diversion. It was meant to look like a real fight. We watched you slip by the distracted crowd then you walked through to the garden. You left the back door off the latch but pushed it back to make it look as if it was locked", Alan Baitman summarised. Each time he thought he had cornered the man they referred to as Al Tuxedo, he seemed to bounce right back with some retort that sounded if not totally but somewhat convincing. "You've got it wrong. I arranged the party. Ask Doris, she will vouch for me, won't you Doris", he appealed? She was totally shocked at being included in this strange game that was being played. The man they called Al Tuxedo was smart. He referred to the huge diamond ring on Sandra's hand. The man sitting with Doris said it was an engagement present. "Tell them Doris about the huge diamond ring that I bought Sandra for our engagement. You witnessed it, din't you Doris", the man sitting next to her asked? When Doris spoke in confirmation of the details disclosed about the huge diamond ring given to Sandra by Duke, all the heads swung but now stared at the thinner man at the bar. The balance swung like a pendulum from one brother to the other. The barman was the first to speak. "I knew there was something fishy about you", he accused. There was stone silence as others looked on at what reaction might come from the thinner man at the bar. So far no one had accused him of being Al Tuxedo but now they questioned how the man sitting with Doris could have such information as confirmed by her. After all, it had been established that she was present at the party. Henry 'the hook', Pete 'the hammer', Geoff 'the rhino' and even 'crazy Bobby' drew a bit closer towards the thinner man at the bar. He in particular wanted revenge for the supposed *'snitching'* that had taken place while they were in the category 'A' prison. The thinner man at the bar had said very little so far. All the suspicion was now focused on him. It was up to him to refute the accusations so cannily reflected back by the man sitting with Doris. The thinner man purporting to be Duke smiled wryly but did not speak. He just observed the movement of Pete 'the hammer' and the others towards him. Frigit 'the mouse' sensed a tension building and anticipated that her colleagues couldn't wait much longer to seek revenge on the *'snitch'*. She was the first to break the silence. "Hey guys, we'd better be careful. If we are not, I would hate to be a fly on the wall watching the repercussions let alone being involved in accusing the wrong man. I must tell you that I can't make up my mind which of them is lying", she commented. Alan Baitman looked towards Grant Favours for support but there wasn't any coming from him. He, like everyone else just wanted the mystery to end.

Alan Baitman had the experience of many years of detective work. He knew he had to go with his 'hunches'. Instinctively, he continued to defend the thinner man at the bar as being Duke and the man with Doris as Baron. "When everyone had left and Miss Bogus and your brother went to bed, you slipped in via the back door leading from the garden. It was then that you made your way upstairs. You knew they had had a lot to drink but you still used the ammonia on the rag to ensure they slept even deeper. You let your henchman, Calvin Poser in to help you get Duke down the stairs. The neighbours were not suspicious because they knew there had been a party. They thought it was just one more *'drunk'* being escorted to the limo", Alan Baitman explained. Everyone was dumbstruck when they heard Alan Baitman's observations and clever detective work. The man sitting with Doris either couldn't think of a counter immediately or he chose to tough it out. Alan Baitman lay into him again. "After getting Duke into the lift at the Hotel Welcome, you took him down to the basement floor and into the crypt. Calvin Poser drove you back to Miss Bogus' house where you replaced your brother in the bed. Clever but not smart enough to outwit the *'hound dog'* training and experience that I've got. I've been locked onto you, like radar, for a long time now. I knew your every move. When you used your cell phone to take the pictures on Costa Dell Shell was a great mistake. Even when you turned your phone off or swapped the Sim card from one phone to another, we were able to track you. In these moments of sophisticated technology we are able to track your every move via the satellite GPS system", Alan Baitman stated.

There were lots of 'ooohs' and 'aaahs' circumventing The Haunting Post AADC. Some of the more naïve individuals, who thought they could outsmart technological advancement, were getting a lesson from a real expert. The man sitting next to Doris openly denied all of the points Alan Baitman had brought into the public arena. "You don't know what you're talking about. I am Duke and he is Baron. I locked him in the crypt because he had stolen my identity. You can't know that wily old fox like me. He's been impersonating me ever since we were young. We realised that people couldn't tell the difference between us so, we used to take advantage. Even at our 18th birthday party, Geoff, 'the rhino' thought I was Baron and Baron was me", he declared. The man with Doris asked Geoff 'the rhino' if he remembered the incident. He didn't want to take sides but he did confirm what the man sitting next to Doris said. Being encouraged by Geoff 'the rhino's confirmation of a factual event, the man sitting next to Doris made yet another pronouncement. It threatened to rail against what Alan Baitman was alluding to be true. "Geoff 'the rhino' and all the others here can't tell you for sure which of us is Duke and which is Baron. Even our own grandfather can't tell the difference between us so what makes you think you can", he dared? The Haunted Post AADC went completely quiet. The only place quieter was a morgue. Doris started to cuddle up to the man sitting next to her once again. "This is Duke. I've known him for years" she supported. Alan Baitman and Grant Favours were flabbergasted by the counter arguments by the man sitting next to Doris. He began to order spirits instead of beer from the bar. Everything was a triple. The pressure was building up. Alan Baitman knew what he had arranged with the militia arm of InterPlanPol. There was no time to change anything now but he didn't want to arrest the wrong man. His job would just not be tenable if he arrested the wrong brother. All the others were having doubts about the legitimacy of evidence against the man sitting with Doris who they thought was Duke. Some were beginning to worry when he made his next comment. "For those who roughed me up earlier, beware of the repercussions to come", he challenged. There were some worried looks on the faces of those who had perpetrated the *'roughing up'* of the man they thought was the interloper. They looked from the man sitting with Doris to the thinner man standing at the bar. Alan Baitman was fast losing the support he needed so badly. He looked to Grant Favours for support but he started to withdraw his support when he heard of the words repercussions. Duke had backed him to the hilt while he built his business from being an under-employed competent creative artist to a magnate amongst his peers. The last thing Grant wanted to do was lose the unconditional support of the *'gift horse'* and solid friend, Duke, who had backed him over many years. He saw Duke regularly and he had not lost weight so he was now backing the man sitting with Doris as Duke. It was the other man who was now receiving the hard looks from the others. Finally, one of them cracked. "So you must be the bastard that snitched on us. Yeah, makes sense now. That's how you managed to wear Tuxedos while you're banged up and got all the other privileges we were not afforded", 'crazy Bobby shouted. He looked towards Trojan 'the horse' for confirmation. Although it seemed to make perfect sense what 'crazy' Bobby was saying, Trojan 'the horse' was finding it hard to agree for a second time with someone he still didn't like. He didn't know why he didn't like 'crazy' Bobby but he just didn't. The thinner man at the bar waited for the pregnant pause then commented. "My question is why you did what you did Brov? I shared everythink with you half and half. I didn't have to but I did. I could have chosen to have given you less or nothink at all but I chose to split everythink with you 50/50 everytime. You had to go and spoil what I thought we had. I love you brov. Apart from Grandad, you're the only family I've got. Look what you've done. You've chosen to drive a wedge between us. Why Brov, Why", the thinner man at the bar pleaded? There was a tense moment of awkward silence that felt eerie. It was as if a ghost had appeared to haunt the lot of them in the seemingly appropriately named The Haunting Post AADC. No one else said anything. Everyone was waiting with baited breathe for the man sitting with Doris to reply. He said nothing. Alan Baitman felt that he had to say something to reinforce support for the thinner man at the bar whom he believed to be Duke. He turned to the man sitting with Doris once again. "You know you are Al Tuxedo. Explain how you and your colleagues within the Travel Industry knowingly supplied tickets to convicted paedophiles on the national registers all over the virtual planet. They were allowed to go to the exotic destinations purposely to exploit those poor vulnerable children. Some were as young as 2 years old, toddlers and babies. You piece of filth", he charged.

Henry 'the hook' felt sick to the stomach when it was revealed that the man they called Al Tuxedo was guilty of establishing fertile ground for paedophiles to gain access to children as young as 2 years old, toddlers and babies throughout the entire 1st rated Royal Royal Stately Kingdoms. It mattered to him and his colleagues that this was happening to children in Spaceville and also in those exotic continents, countries and islands too. Henry 'the hook' had listened to the allegations and the exchanges between the two brothers but became angry at not being sure which of the two was really Al Tuxedo. Alan Baitman told the man sitting with Doris that he could prove his underhand practices beyond doubt. He told him that InterPlanPol, more than anyone else, knew of his contacts at ghetto as well as higher levels. Alan Baitman revealed that the man sitting with Doris current situation began initially when he started to send ransom notes to his own brother, Sandra and even Raymond via his recruits Andy Mann and Calvin Poser, requesting and extorting money with menacing threats. Ever since the gang Clout was formed, members like Henry 'the hook' and his colleagues thought they were working for Duke but they now realised that Baron had used them as pawns especially against the multi-coloured mixed DNA

Harbour-Shark Estate Gang. Having lost a number of close friends and family members themselves in the senseless UFO's 'Cult-Induced' Post/Zip Code Wars then, Henry 'the hook' can testify that he lost his arm by protecting one of the devious brothers he had mistaken for Duke. He now realised it could have been Baron. Henry 'the hook' and the other Clout members were still unable to tell the difference between the identical twin brothers. He and his colleagues were angry at Al Tuxedo for exploiting babies and children. Tough a life as they led, these seasoned criminals had children and grandchildren too. They did not agree with Al Tuxedo's sick association with paedophilia. Trojan 'the horse' and his colleagues knew how other prisoners felt about attacks on women, babies and children. The Clout members were not willing to sacrifice their lives or go back to prison for Al Tuxedo willingly. In prison, they had tried to kill the man they called Al Tuxedo, previously. He was protected from Trojan 'the horse' and his colleagues' wrath by prison officers, who were aware of how much damage he could do to their families even while he was in prison. Trojan 'the horse' and his colleagues believed that the man they called Al Tuxedo bore an uncanny resemblance to Duke and his brother Baron. Since the inception of Clout, Trojan 'the horse' and the others had assumed that, being identical twins from the same father, both Duke and Baron shared the same surname. They were not to know that Baron's surname was Staveley and that he was jealous of his own brother, Duke, seemingly, perhaps!

Ever since the revelation that Earl had left all of his riches to Duke, Baron had envied the position that his brother was in. It somehow was a reaction not so much against Duke but represented the anger Baron felt towards Earl, the father he had perceived had abandoned him. This might have been one way of getting back at his father through his own brother, Duke. It was a very confused and twisted mind that thought in this manner but all the same the execution of such spiteful delusional retribution had its impact on the relationship between the brothers. The irony was that, although they were meant to be identical, their *'values and beliefs'* were comparatively different. Even though, Duke had chosen to share with Baron equally, greed had already imprisoned his psyche but occupied his mindset. Such was his rage against his father, Earl, whom he still believes up to the present moment, had resented but abandoned him in preference for his brother Duke. Baron felt rejected but developed a psychological barrier that he reinforced rather than diminished. An equal share was not enough for Baron. He continued to convince himself that he was a *'victim'* though he couldn't adequately explain what made him turn against his own brother except for feeling bitter towards his father, Earl. Baron's connivance had been reinforced by the death of his only other parent, his mother, Enid Staveley. She had died in prison. Baron blamed Earl for abandoning her too. He felt guilty but was conscious that his non-attendance to school was a contributing factor and possibly causative for his mother ending up in prison. Added to all the confusion swirling around, like a mix of the rainbow colours without clear definitions in his mind, Baron also placed some of the blame on his mother for keeping him away from his father. What he wasn't aware of was his mother's awful ordeal at the moment of his conception on that night she was brutally raped by his father, Earl. Baron was on a mission to destroy himself and in so doing reneged on the only one who really cared for him, his brother Duke. He didn't pretend to be a saint himself but he truly wanted to share evenly with his brother, Baron. Instead of appreciating Duke's act of love and kind-heartedness, Baron decided that Duke was a show off and he had grown to envy him but showed contempt for his generosity. He used his brother's generosity but took his kindness for weakness. Baron plotted but schemed to ruin his brother. He abused Duke's genuine offer of love, caring and sharing. Baron used his identical features to bamboozle the likes of the naïve, bubbly, simple Doris Bendlow, the genial but *'earthy'* Dora Stagg, who eventually buried the beak of the wooden carving of the Doctor Bird into his temple. Most of all, Baron managed to thoroughly deceive Duke's exotic bird, the delectable, large cornflower blue eyed, naturally deeply tanned melanin skin, guitar shaped physique, stunningly beautiful, celebrity seeking 'A' Blister top model and movie icon, Sandra Bogus, just to name a few. Greed was the disease that had eventually totally overwhelmed Baron's psyche. It wasn't just Spaceville that was experiencing this epidemic of corruption, envy and greed that Baron had managed to initiate subliminally and reinforce amongst the massive criminal population throughout the entire virtual planet of Asteroidia including the exotic continents, countries and islands.

There was a pattern that was more prevalent than even Duke could imagine. All over the virtual planet of Asteroidia but especially in the exotic continents, countries and islands in particular, there was an overwhelming surge of similar disloyal mentalities amongst families too. They were feuding over wills, property and other material goods which seem to have taken precedence over basic human rights and needs. Envy drove awesomely powerful desires toward ownership of material goods in such a way that individuals became blinded and immune to the morals of fairness. Even when the deceased had clearly stated, who was to benefit after their deaths, the importance of obsession exposed the prioritised choices and true characters of some family members. They entered into feuding with each other like vultures over the remains of a carcass. This practice became so overwhelming that some visiting families to their far off exotic paradise continents, countries and islands were learning fast not to stay with family members. Instead, they became tourists in their exotic continents, countries and islands of origin for the lack of trust that had built up between them and those predictably envious family members. Properties were being sold off to foreigners. They had been given priority status especially over genuine family owners, who lived abroad. This was happening even when those lands and properties were being willed by the deceased to particular family members. Threats and sometimes actual harm would come to those, who dared to challenge the enraged, enviously possessive family members. In order to profit from other family member's heirlooms these envious family members falsified legal documents overtly. The Royal Dis-United Stately Kingdom's of Asteroidia had imploded upon itself and a plethora of crime and violence had become predominant but overwhelmed its entire population.

The thinner man at the bar spoke again but this time he laid into his brother for all the things he had done using his identity, allegedly. He accused him of conducting mayhem through DSI. The thinner man at the bar pointed out that his brother was being aptly supported by particular poly-tricksters and politicrats, whose behaviours were not dissimilar to his. They were often found to have used loopholes themselves. Whenever politicrats did so, they deliberately failed to declare their interest in companies like DSI or claimed money from taxpayers as expenses against properties, which they had never occupied. Whenever the scandals broke, these politicrats simply used their poly-tricksters' influence to join yet another company at Board Level. Al Tuxedo was part of that political merry-go-round. The politicrats and poly-tricksters saw themselves as being above the laws of the parallel virtual planet. DSI was an example of how huge financial organisations did manipulate even governments by using loopholes to nullify paying Tax in Kingdoms like Spaceville. When in his charge, Al Tuxedo had registered the company DSI, in an offshore tax haven. He was smart enough to engage the services of smart legal advisors and accountants to whom he paid handsome fees for their expertise in using the loopholes. These were designed by politicrats but sanctioned by their puppeteers, the poly-tricksters. Those were the channels being used by an elite group of lobbyists, who saw themselves as above the laws of the Royal Royal Dis-United Stately Kingdoms of Asteroidia.

Al Tuxedo had his fingers in many pies. Grant Favours argued that his influence in the music industry had been producing GCE, GSE and GCCEO. They would sell their souls for the moments of fame and celebrity status that they seemed to think were more important than the lives they had managed to help destroy, probably! Grant stressed that the views of GCE, GSE and the GCCEO were pretty narrow and utterly self serving. He spoke of those individuals as being fully engaged in the *'programming'* and *'conditioning'* that had rendered them impervious to caring one iota about the consequences of their collusion to plague the minds of the naïve young people to whom they were sending toxic subliminal messages. Those messages Grant argued were embedded in the psyche of the young generation. Grant Favours said that his experience in the creative industry had sharpened his observational skills. He stated that he couldn't help noticing how GCE and GCCEO were deliberately writing and using demeaning lyrics to *'thrill'* while they killed aspirations and opportunities to meaningfully nurture the talents of young children. He explained that he considered this type of abuse as a targeting strategy; being similar to that of the stalking predatory trait of paedophiles. "The enormity of the realisation of the lives Al Tuxedo had already managed to destroy but also that, by the consequences of his actions, he might well be impacting others lives for generations to come."

What Moralist Inc and Scruples United wanted to signpost was that Al Tuxedo and the likes of individuals like him, his GCCEO, GCE and especially his GSE like Pimpe Ernel V1, exist around the virtual planet of Asteroidia and beyond. They have no heart but suffer from a permanent mental state of denial that makes them impervious to empathy, respect, integrity, sensitivity, quality communication and trust. These are what the man they called 'The Professor' often referred to as "the basic tenets of what makes all relationships meaningful". As Grant Favours concurs, the GCCEO, GCE and GSE were one homogenous whole. Their lack of emotional intelligence and maturity made them seem unable to recognize these tenets which are applicable for meaningful relationships. The man they called 'The Professor' wondered, what makes some individuals like Al Tuxedo so cold and insensitive? Alan Baitman confirmed that Al Tuxedo had been moving drugs and arms into the exotic continents, countries and islands with immunity. The Inter Planetary Police further stated that they had been asked by the new Prime Leader of Spaceville, The Most Honourable Janette Brayhorne, to investigate but establish how the virtual planet of Asteroidia had managed to become so corrupted. Alan Baitman pointed out to the man they referred to as Al Tuxedo that InterPlanPol had more than enough evidence to put him, his confidants and accomplices away for life.

Doris Bendlow started to ask if all the time she thought she was sleeping with Duke that she might have been sleeping with his brother, Baron, unwittingly! She said that she felt used and abused. Dora might never find out that she too might have been duped on more than one occasion by the devious Baron. When his deeds hit the news, Dora might well be wondering, who fathered of her children? Are Buck and Ryan brothers or cousins? Sandra might never know whether (1) it was Duke or Baron, who had fired the Blunderbuss at her whilst she was making her escape from Sir Tank Alpino's exclusive Club, The Pharmacy, (2) with whom she had slept over the years, (3) to whom she had got engaged or (4) married! She had been heavily anesthetised by her imbibing of the *'legal'* drugs to which she had subliminally been addicted in her quest to gain Iconic Status as an *'A' Blister* Socialite. Sandra had managed to achieve her dream of awesome financial power and being able to rub shoulders with the *'who's who'* elite but to what end! She had managed to live in 'The Great Mansion' in the salubrious, exclusively prestigious, Greater Suburbia in the enviable Champagne Valley on the other side of the mountain. What her mother, Dian failed to tell her is how lonely it can be when individuals choose to isolate themselves but choose to live someone else's *'values and beliefs'* instead. Most of all, in the predicament in which she found herself, Sandra had entered into a slumberous state of sleep but sunk lower into the huge *'Golden Roman Bath'* from which she might never recover to celebrate her achievement, perhaps!

CHAPTER 56

There was a *'Breaking News'* announcement on television. When the individuals inside The Haunting Posts AADC saw the words Al Tuxedo on the screen, they all demanded for the barman to increase the volume. This he did. The television was tuned into IST, Independent Spacevillean Television. "We interrupt this programme to bring you some Breaking News. The notorious Extortionist, Arms Dealer, Drug Dealer, Head of the Inter Planetary Psychopathic Serial Rapists and Paedophiles Ring, Baron Staveley, aka Al Tuxedo', is wanted throughout The Royal Royal Dis-United Stately Kingdoms of Asteroidia, the exotic continents, countries and islands in the World of Space on these and several other extremely serious charges. Sources attached to the Inter Planetary Police, InterPlanPol, stated that Al Tuxedo was armed and dangerous and should not be approached by the general public".

A picture of the *'wanted'* man appeared on the screen. Both the man sitting next to Doris and his slightly thinner look-a-like standing next to the bar could not hide the look of consternation from their faces. There was a big uproar of excited voices coming from The Haunting Post AADC. It sounded more like that of an instantaneous eruption of voices which is normally associated with that of a crowd of thousands of dedicated partisan fans shouting in unison when a goal was scored against a Derby rival at an Association Football/Soccer Match. The noise was sickeningly deafening but must have broken all the *'noise nuisance'* rules within each Kingdom on the parallel virtual planet of Asteroidia. It could be heard in every direction a mile away at least, perhaps! All the voices sounded extremely discordant in pitch and tone. Even Frigit 'the mouse', with her shrill high pitched voice swore with intent at the look-a-likes. The identical twin brothers were both trapped in an environment where they would normally have had the upper hand. This was one of the AADC's, in which the brothers had heavily invested and owned. It was fitting that the deliberately antiquated looking *'Cowboy'* type Saloon seemed a fitting place for a lynching! The occupants on the other side of The Haunting Post AADC had heard the same *Breaking News* from the screen on the other side of the AADC building. They too joined in the awesomely chaotic overture but projected their taunts of revenge too. The occupants of the public bar were unaware that the twin brothers were present in the Saloon area of The Haunting Post AADC. Shouts of "lynch the bastard" came out in unison from both sides of The Haunting Post AADC. Those sentiments did not only represent their boozed states but it certainly didn't help. The commentators were merely reflecting their innermost feelings towards those from whom they sought revenge in spite of the severity of the offending actions. Even when they were sober, these individuals had a traditional cultural history of the "Hang 'em High" philosophy. It was ingrained into their psyche. They had often used it in the past to resolving issues by lynching. It was part of their *'values and beliefs'* but made it seem as if they were always armed with a length of rope in readiness for being part of a lynching party, perhaps!

On hearing the weight of disgust being aired on the News and now being surrounded by individuals eager to gain from passing on information in order to profit from the huge sums offered as *'Reward'*, both brothers now look nervously from one to another but was clearly concerned about the other's state of health. Seemingly trapped, each wondered how effective *'clout'* might be in such this situation! This dangerous environment reminded them and their gangster colleagues present of what it used to be like to feel trapped as in their younger days when they had carelessly wandered into another Post/Zip Code *'endz'* but were surrounded by rivals like the Harbour-Shark Estate Gang. It was Alan Baitman who waved his hands frantically like an orchestra's maestro bringing the piece to a climax. When that didn't work, he walked quickly over towards the bar but gesticulated that he wanted to hear the rest of the News. He had seen his nephew on the screen but wanted the crowd to hear the interview. As the crowd in the Saloon quietened down, Alan Baitman spoke urgently. "The drinks are on me. Barman, fill their glasses", he ordered. For that brief moment, Alan Baitman's actions proved how *'values and beliefs'* controlled the lives of those who shared the same culture. As they queued up to demand the *'free'* drinks, they heard that part of the interview by Alan Baitman's nephew, Hooke Baitman. He was also a member of InterPlanPol. Hooke stated in the interview on television that "irrefuteable proof existed that Baron Staveley, the man known as Al Tuxedo, is also wanted for a number of other charges which included him deliberately installing *'Sin Cities'*, *'Sin Islands'*, *'Sin Countries'* and *'Sin Continents'* on the parallel virtual Planet of Asteroidia". Hooke Baitman continued to add to the allegations against Al Tuxedo which linked his bosses, the UFO, United Fraternal Organisation, the UO DIS-UK, Union of Dis-United Kingdoms, their subordinates, co-workers and assistants as being involved altogether. He said that "the organisation had thumbed their noses at individuals who refused to share in their *'madness mentality'* known as *'greed'*, commonly. All were being rigorously pursued throughout the exotic continents, countries, islands as well as across all the Royal Royal Dis-United Stately Kingdoms that make up the parallel virtual planet of Asteroidia and across the entire World of Space. Anyone knowing of the whereabouts of Al Tuxedo, his confidants and accomplices must contact their local police or InterPlanPol immediately", he finished.

Spaceville's Deputy Attorney General, Ima Nightmāre-Constitutionious was the next person to be interviewed. The journalists seemed to have camped outside her

Office. There were hoards of them jostling amongst each other like impatient children in the queue at lunchtime in the cafeteria at school. Some had microphones with their representative labels attached to differentiate their importance. Others used digital recorders but, by their behaviours, it was obvious that this was *'hot news'*. Deputy Attorney General, Ima Nightmārè-Constitutionious warned that "'Extradition Requests' are being sought to bring each tier which makes up the hierarchical system of the Organisation back to the Dis-United Kingdoms to stand trial by Jury". Al Tuxedo and his notorious gangs had wreaked havoc both mentally and physically upon indigenous populations across the World of Space. "They will be prosecuted under the New Interplanetary Laws of the parallel virtual planet of Asteroidia. Under these new Laws could mean that, if found guilty, each individual might have to serve as many years as those they had taken away from the children they had managed to damage by coercing them mentally and physically into a life of sodomy, drugs, paedophilia and arms in particular", she concluded. The journalists continued to fire questions rapidly at her but Spaceville's Deputy Attorney General was a dab hand at interviews. "That will be all for now", she concluded.

Another senior member representing InterPlanPol, Squille Hawksbee, was the next individual to be interviewed on the News. She stated that the impact upon the communities in and around the entire parallel virtual planet was one of mass confusion. "We are beginning to understand a bit more about the running of the Organisation, its hierarchical levels and the impact it is having on the population around the Royal Royal Dis-United Stately Kingdoms. It seems that the Organisation is much bigger and more influential than was first thought. Our investigation has been going on for quite some years now. We are absolutely sure about the effect of their operation. The children from these communities are being deliberately pursued relentlessly by the likes of the Organisation's man, Al Tuxedo and his accomplices. Those children's minds were actively being observed, stalked, selected, kidnapped, isolated and tortured rigorously through the process of *'programming'* and *'conditioning'* by one tentacle, the GMT, Ghetto Mentality Terrorists. This they did before passing on these children to their co-workers, the GMES, Ghetto Mentality Engineering Scientists. They carried on the process by handing them over to the GMP, Ghetto Mentality Practitioners. Further along the chain of command their assistants and other subordinates, acting as *'models'* carried out their *'roles'* until the children from these communities spiralled downwards in self worth into ***'mental oblivion'*** but arrived at the depths of their respective ***'mental ravines'***. In this state of extremely low self worth, these children were at their most vulnerable mentality; rendering them no more than mere robotron *'puppets'* being readied to carry out the *'puppet masters'* *'ill-wills'*", she finished.

As they continued to take in the hour long extended news, the crowd of rabble-rousing drunks staggered back and forth from the bar to their seats. Some were more interested in the frequency of the *'free'* booze now rather than what was coming across from the giant TV screen. The *'legal'* drug was making its mark on those individuals who thrived on *'free'* booze. One or two had fallen asleep where they sat. Some were so drunk that they could not make out what was being said anymore. They separated themselves into groups babbling under their breaths as the News continued.

A more senior member of InterPlanPol, Icy Shiverington, further explained about "the might and influence of the *'upper'* levels of the hierarchy in the organisation". She further identified "the *'role'* of the *'middle'* level by the GOS, Gang Orientation Scientists. They gave instructions to their subordinates, the GOO, Gang Orientation Operators. In turn, they oversaw the GOP, Gang Orientation Practitioners. At the lower level, the self-important GCCEO, Ghetto Celebrity CEOs', their hopeful *'wannabees'*, the GCE, Ghetto Celebrity Entrepreneurs, the GSE, Ghetto Sodomy Entrepreneurs whose Serial Rapists and Serial Paedophiles were detailed to continue at the tail end to reinforce the globally encouraged *'stereo-typical imagery'* of the perennial *'stereo-type'*", she explained.

The News Presenter, Wata Ting stressed that the comments from the contributors dovetailed seamlessly with Professor Walynski's Studies over the years. It had confirmed all of the information already stated above but the Professor had clarified in his Report that the continuation of encouraging the *'stereo-typical imagery'* to produce the perennial *'stereo-type'* was a most deliberate foul act of *'serial discrimination'* via the awesomely powerful tool of *'disinformation'*. Professor Walynski's Report stated (1) it had managed to discover the initiation of what is said to be known psychologically "as *'the primed mind'*, commonly referred to as *'brain washing'* and how that impacts individuals' *'belief systems'*", (2) the effect of the *'primed mind'* means that *individuals' 'belief systems'* had been converted subliminally to believe the *'stereo-hype'* and the *'stereo-tripe'* dished out by the creators of the disinformation. The man they called 'The Professor' cited a typical example of the *'primed mind philosophy'*. "Imagine seeing a picture of a gorilla with bananas placed above its head. What are you thinking now", he asked? The perception drawn from that pointed *'stereo-type image'* had been deliberately created by *'association'* that gorillas eat bananas", he explained. The genial man they called 'The Professor' concurs with the Walynski Institute. Its research stated that "the *'association'* of the image that gorillas eat bananas bears no truth or relevancy to the gorilla's diet. (1) Gorillas do not eat bananas. Monkeys do, (2) the associative disinformation was not factual but appears to be so, (3) it was a deliberate strategy to send that subliminal message via that image to individuals' subconscious minds. This is an illusion like all other illusions. Magicians use sleight of hands to create illusion as entertainment and individuals approve it. The deliberate feeding of *'stereo-tripe'*, *'stereo-hype'* and the *'stereo-type'* imagery are foisted upon individuals' *'belief systems'* through what's known as *'sleight'*. It is a skilful, deliberate strategy to reinforce disinformation. This is done in order to persuade individuals to become *'converts'* to what is often referred to as *"just a little harmless 'white lie'"*, Professor Walynski concurred. The man they called 'The Professor' referred to the moral of a fable whereby a frog was being stoned by an adult aged *'fun-loving' 'animal lover'*. His seven year old son rebuked his father for the less than infantile behaviour. The father retorted by blaming the frog for his phobia about them. He related to his son that he remembered that his parents didn't know what made them fear frogs but their reactions led him to fear frogs too. Because they decided they didn't like frogs, throwing stones at them gave his parents some sort of twisted power over them, apparently. "What lessons are you teaching me, dad", the boy asked? His father remained silent but they both heard the voice of the frog. It was hiding in the thick undergrowth. "What is *'fun'* to you is death to me", it protested. "I guess we can all learn from that fable", the man they called 'The Professor' commented. "It's hard to shift an image that individuals are led to believe came from their own thinking", Professor Walynski concurred. The Walynski Institute stated that the UFO had been using the *'primed mind philosophy'* over generations about the imagery of the *'stereo-type'*. It had become embedded into the minds of the population across the 1st rated Kingdoms of Asteroidia and the 5th rated exotic continents, countries and islands. Both Moralists Inc and Scruples Unites complained about the perception of the *'stereo-type'* as being accepted globally as *'normal'*. They stated that politicrats and poly-tricksters used *'stereo-typical imagery'* and language often without regard for the damage it causes. The man they called 'The Professor' stated that, "it was now considered *'politically correct'* to wittingly or unwittingly refer to the doctrinal interpretation of the perennial *'stereo-types'* as an accepted image or belief. This imagery was being reinforced and riveted even more through repetition but maintained via other deliberate subliminal techniques. It not only brought about a level of subservient thinking but also behaviours too. Each individual with that *'stereo-typical mentality'* became mesmerised by the lure to the *'greed'* virus over morality. They found "working for the *'big man'* ", as normal as pets following instructions to *"fetch"* at a *'Pet Training Academy'* ", the research stated. It was carried out at the Walynski Institute but being used in line with and as part of InterPlanPol's investigation. The research brought about even more revelations. It found that "the UFO's Organisation's scientists and their subservient *'puppet'* collaborators, helped to induce but install the *'house-slave mentality'* through a psychological musical cocktail of *'pied piper'* entrancing rhythmic beats, lively tempos and haunting melodies. These haunting melodies kept young individuals spellbound by its repetitious, destructively degrading lyrical mantra and subliminal *'stereo-hyped'* embedded messages. They directed the young minds toward delusional mentalities. The GSE, Ghetto Sodomy Entrepreneurs, skilfully utilised the *'stereo-tripe'* to reinforce the entertainment *'stereo-hype'* in order to massage the egos of the vulnerable, naive youngsters", the research confirmed.

"The likes of Al Tuxedo and the Organisation for whom he represented and worked drove the youngsters into frenzied expectations. Empowered by the lure of the seemingly elusive virtual currency, Champagne Urge, the youngsters with guidance from the GOO, Gang Orientation Operators, helped to form a completely *'new culture'*. It promised huge earning potential without any capital outlay. Commodities were more specific than any from previous generations. Some business models like *'Bartering'* were carried over from previous generations to the current ones. Because of its *'franchisee'* element and the staged, progressive route to the top, the *'Pyramid' Sales Model* was the most favoured. Both exported themselves from the parallel planet Earth, travelled through several time zones but impacted upon the parallel virtual planet of Asteroidia, somehow! They were the preferred options which seemed to breed the onset of a new army of budding *'street entrepreneurs'*. As far as the youngsters were concerned, being in *'Sales'* was the only *'career'* into which they had been accepted as *'stakeholders'*. Each had a *'certified'*, *'street equivalent'* MBA, probably! Even *'Junior School'* students were working as *'Sales'* personnel in each community; selling drugs and arms, commonly. Some were earning more than their parents did but these high earnings potential were interspersed with sickening violence at every level. Selling particular *'very high risk'* *'preferred commodities'* was like being a *'bomb'* *'expert'*; **'Heroes' one moment, 'Zeroes' the next**, most likely, perhaps! Taking on such *'high risk'* carried its own unwritten *'health warnings'*, daily. The prospects for *'promotion'* were very precarious as that meant being admitted into *'The University of Crime'* via long custodial sentences or *'expiry'* if the individuals realised their ***'use by' date***, maybe! Sadly, each day there was an announcement of the terrible crimes being committed amongst the rivals. Intimidating behaviours such as ASPD known as bullying commonly were the only *'marketing techniques'* that was clearly understood by all but resulted in escalating the level of violence. Those who couldn't fight used their weapons, namely knives and guns as **the only language of communication** amongst the growing population foraging for the *'spoils'* of Champagne Urge. As the *'loan sharks'*, who financed their *'commodities'* turned the screws but demanded their *'pound of flesh'* as in the Shakespearean *'Twelfth Night'*, children, as instructed by GOPs, robbed from their own homes to settle their debts or Hoards of *'loyal devotees'* at the whisper of yet another *'rumour'* by cell phone, willingly showed their often temporary *'allegiance'* to their Post/Zip Code; defended their *'endz'* by displaying group cowardice openly in public. Often, they hunted then corralled but overpowered their singular quarry. They proceeded to kick and stamp on them as they lay on the streets, helpless. There was no discrimination whether their quarry was male or female. Irrespective whether the *'rumour'* was just an allegation or fact, either gender would be subjected to the same sort of punishing treatment. These intimidating episodes were commonplace but often led to even more serious outcomes. Quarries lives were ended immediately through *shanking* or by being shot sometimes, whilst others were left haemorrhaging internally from the mixture of schizophrenic ASPD, frenzied beatings, kicking or being trampled upon underfoot in the deliberate *'human'* stampede until death relieved those victims of the awesome physical and mental ordeal they had experienced. This Victorian type of unacceptable behaviour was typical of the daily occurrence which took place in the exotic continents, countries and islands as well as within the Royal Royal Dis-United Stately Kingdoms of the virtual planet of Asteroidia. It seemed that this was the only *'brand'* of mentality that was being embedded and reinforced under the specific instructions of the Ghetto Mentality Terrorists, GMT, but aptly applied by Ghetto Mentality Practitioners, GMP. This form of *'body'* *'language'* spread amongst the various 'Cult-Induced' Post/Zip Code gangs and was *'accepted'* as the *'norm'* but seemed to be the *'typical'* example of the *'designer street culture'* installed at the GOP, Gang Orientation Practitioners' level. The squabbling amongst the army of rival, maddening Post/Zip Code *'War Mongering'* *'City Cowboys'* and *'City Soldiers'* were actively instigated and encouraged by the GOP, Gang Orientation Practitioners too. At their level in the Organisation, both the GOO and the GOP received proportionate percentages of the payment that the Organisation received from PODA, the Private Organ Donor Association made available to the UFO. This financial arrangement came in the form of *commission*. It depended on the number of dead bodies produced by the violence. They also received a sizeable financial bonus for the number of prisoners that came from the particular *'endz'* they controlled, who were incarcerated in the privately funded *'Human Zoos'*.

Although Professor Walynski's in-depth Research managed to expose the inner workings of the UFO, the next set of details seemed to bring about oceans of emotions to the fore. The Research stated that, "over the last several generations, the *'Ethos'* of the Organisation had appeared to indicate that each child being born seemed pre-destined to reach their **'Expiry Date'** long before their parents", apparently! This was because some individuals chose to actively live the kind of *'lifestyle'* and sought the notoriety of Al Tuxedo. Thousands of young individuals all over the parallel virtual planet appeared to worship him as their ideal *'Role Model'*. Al Tuxedo's *'model'* seemed to fit the *'role'* being subliminally installed and reinforced by the intrepid UFO. This was done through other stimuli like what is perceived to be *'entertainment'*, maybe! The *'streets'* were the ideal backdrop in the seemingly perennial *'Life Movie'*. *'Pretenders'* had been given their individual *'scripts'* in order to live their momentary *'Star Roles'*. Despite the high levels of fearful challenges to which they were exposed each moment of each day, the **'pretenders'** actively sought to gain *'useless'* *'Street Credentials'* for their bizarre violent acts. The beatings, kicking, stampeding, shankings and the shootings were more than just discomforting. Sadly, they were real and far too frequent. Parents all over the parallel virtual planet suffered greatly. The addiction to fear had overwhelmed the population around the virtual planet of Asteroidia and the exotic continents, countries and islands but likened itself to the biblical infestation of swarms of locusts attacking all in their wake. While the young individuals set about on their "ride or die", "die trying", "live fast die fast" philosophical instructive pathways to destruction, many parents found themselves with huge bills for funeral expenses and the permanent physical loss of their children. There was nothing to compensate for that particular void which seemed as incomprehensible as staring into a hole which seemed like a bottomless pit. All were victims, who had been gripped so tightly with the addictive **'drug of fear'**. Some individuals became as addicted to both *'legal'* and *'illegal'* drugs. Each youngster was exposed to the Post/Zip Code madness whether they had conformed to the pressures being brought to bear upon them by the *'bullying'* award seeking *'converts'* of the Gang Orientation Operators, GOO. There were some youngsters, who chose not to succumb to the peer pressure but the Gang Orientation Practitioners were relentless in their condemnation against any resistance to their recruitment drive. The older *'converts'*, themselves possible *'franchisee entrepreneurs'*, GOP, were encouraged to seek and destroy, like heat seeking missiles, those youngsters who chose to avoid the perilous street madness *'lifestyle'*. Unfortunately, they became what the Post/Zip Coders referred to as *"targets"*. They were being hunted and harried like the foxes in a Foxhunt until they either relented or were **'extinguished'** like the light from Victorian street candles. These hired *'street assassins'* were *'programmed'* and *'conditioned'* but lived with the mentality of constant fear. They became so finely attuned that they remained in a *'hair-triggered'* edgy alert state. Their reaction in challenging situations and uncomfortable environments were so predictable that even the whispering of the breeze made their sensitivity so supersaturated with fear that their respective *'reaction times'* were more akin to that of an elite athlete. Whether they were young adults, youths or juniors, all the children, who had perpetrated these heinous crimes, were rounded up, herded but corralled into their new 7ft x 6ft *'luxury cages'* in the *'Human Zoos'* aptly prepared but anticipating their occupancy. There, they could be physically controlled, mentally manipulated but converted without much resistance. Their behaviours were the cause which brought about their physical expiry through unbridled violence. The perpetrators experienced enforced custodial sentences in mental and physical correctional establishments which were the consequences they had to pay but fear was the symptom which lay at the base of the explosion of maiming and killings in the ever violent UFO 'Cult-Induced' Post/Zip Code Street Wars. Some inmates found the regime of structure their first and only experience. Their particular parents or guardians had traded initiating structure at home at an early age for the materialistic mindsets that they too had sought but inveigled their children in which to partake.

Conversely, some other parents were genuinely busying themselves, slaving away at the two or three minimum waged jobs they had to attend in order to pay the bills to keep a roof over their families' heads and put food on their tables. Whilst they were so being occupied, there was a chance that, through being unsupervised and curious, their children too were subjected to being enticed into other *'pathways of interest'*, voluntarily. Some were being exposed to the bullying regime being encouraged by the GOP and their co-workers, the GSE into a life of criminal activities, probably"!

Professor Walynski's Research delved even further than any he had previously produced. It pointed out that "the GCCEOs had graduated from the infamous *'University of Pimpology and Madames'* but touted their *'stereo-hyped'* pornographic demeaning imagery and violent *'stereo-tripe'* lyrics which competed but matched with similar lyrics of their *'wannabee'* colleagues, the GCE, at local level. The GCCEOs had themselves chosen to be *'converted'* into becoming **'Honorary Green Humanoid Robotrons 'A' Blisters'** too. This position guaranteed they obey their *'puppeteer'* masters but consented to accept the perennial *'Judas Awards'* as an honour whenever they were being *'nominated'*. These *'A' Blisters* received the contracted financial abundant gratuities guaranteed with the *'package'*. They had decided to buy into the *'process'* as *'franchisees'*, through agreeing to degrade and relegate young girls to the status of being (Hoes) *"only meat"* and the young boys as *"fodder"* for the inhumane, robotron serial sexual predatory *'buzzards'* which visited their certifiable, un-natural, insane *'values and beliefs'* upon those vulnerable children. The GOS and their underlings the GOP added the *'stings'* in the tails into the mentalities of those youngsters abandoned from a structured upbringing by their parents but rejected by their schools as stakeholders. Having been initiated into the *'street culture'* by the slightly older young adults, the GOP, the entrapped youngsters had contracted into the seemingly lucrative *'street lifestyle business'* which was managed by the *'Operation Management Team'*, the GOO. Through a scheming systemic blueprint handed down from the GMT being at the *'upper'* levels of the hierarchical organisation, their *'middle'* and *'lower'* level subordinates tested the capabilities of the plethora of vulnerable youngsters' potential *'business acumen'*. They were young, keen, curious and eager to perform. In their situation, there was no need to question the *'commodities'* being offered as long as they were fast becoming financially abundant. Sales volume was their singular aim and they went about their business like any other keen *'Sales'* personnel. There was no inconvenience like tax to be paid. The young *franchisee entrepreneurs'* often squandered their earnings on things they *'wanted'* more than *'needed'* but what was important to them is that they considered what they were doing to be **'work'**! Since they were born, those youngsters had often been referred to as *'adults'* by their parents and the children had come to believe they had to provide like adults were meant to. Some ridiculous *'endearments'* like *"little men"*, *"kidhults"*, *"mini-adults"* were misguided at minimum but to treat those children as such made them have expectations and burdensome responsibilities of adults. Those parents might not have been aware of the devastating psychological effect that their choice of language might be having on the mindsets of their children, probably! To grow up thinking they were *'adults'* rather than recognising they were children meant they were easy targets for the Gang Orientation Operators.

Using sport as an example, some parents found it necessary to *'peddle'* their children from one venue to another *'touting'* them as *'sporting slaves'*. Except for corporal punishment, those parents behaviours were no different to the historic *'slave masters'*. In Asteroidia, children were no longer allowed to enjoy sport for the sake of it as an activity anymore. In fact, some were being coerced and sometimes bullied into becoming *'sporting slaves'* against their will for the benefit of those parents for whom it was too late for them to do anything about their own chances to impress their talents upon sporting audiences. Such was the enormity of thirst for the abundance of Champagne Urge that those parents were rumoured to take the view that their talented children should **earn them money** for the privilege of being born to them. It was a dangerous precedence to set but some were relentless in their pursuit of the urgency to accumulate the abundance of Champagne Urge via their children. Conversely, some other youngsters, who were determined to seek a career in sports, were being used as statistics in *'trials'* for fees to impress the level of demand for application to become *'sporting slaves'*. For those who were *'rejected'* at those *'trials'*, for one reason or another, were scouted by GOO, but passed on to their subordinates, the GOP to vent their anger through the UFO's *'Cult-Induced'* Post/Zip Code Wars. Once they were *'recruited'*, the GOP inveigled those youngsters towards becoming *'street entrepreneurs'*.

On the streets, having been given the *'commodities'* without capital outlay, this was a time in their young lives that anyone had given these children a chance to feel like a *'stakeholder'* in their respective communities. Once they were hooked onto the concept that they were accepted, their canny *'Street HR'*, the GOO began to install the fearful factor, the *'art'* of bullying as an essential *'business ethic'*. They supplied arms and drugs in bulk, in order to further corrupt the psyches of their new *'recruits'*. These were the children, who felt their *'needs'* were neither being acknowledged nor catered for within an old inflexible education system or a non-structured upbringing at home. The younger generations felt that they were neither previously included in the *'process'* nor were their particular *'needs'* being catered for within the antiquated approach by an educational system which had been the same for their great grand parents previously too, probably! The environment of the classrooms were anchored to a more ancient time and subjected to being referred to within the archives of educational practices but might best befit the environment of an **educational museum**, probably! What impacted most was that there was no provision for the children's feedback except for their errant behaviours for which they agreed they took no responsibility. The man they called 'The Professor' commented that "the youngsters' behaviours were *'a cry for attention'*. They didn't feel as if they were stakeholders in their schools, homes or communities. Their preferences for learning were being continuously marginalised at minimum, ignored or disregarded totally by systemic inflexibility of an archaic recurring *'one size fits all'* *'politically reinforced'* education system as being the *'only'* *'model'*", he commented.

As an eminent Coach, the man they called 'The Professor' continued his rant at the poor efforts being made at central and local government levels. He commented further that "as long as the *'only'* educational *'model'* was being forced upon the children and there was no consultation with them about the type of *'model'* from which they found easier to learn, education establishments would become progressively scantier in population but fade into oblivion more rapidly than water down a drain hole when cleared of obstructions", he continued. The man they called 'The Professor' highlighted the rather urgent need to "wanting to resolve the bullying issues in schools too". He pointed out that, "by not involving the same *'troubled'* youngsters in seeking to find solutions to their underlying feelings of low self-worth, local governments had wasted not only a lot of financial resources but also used interventions which helped to isolate the children further", he insisted. The man they called 'The Professor' stated further that "assigning the youngsters *'labels'*, incarcerating them in *'Holding Rooms'* within the schools was not only a bold statement but also confirmation that the particular educational establishments had made a decision to *'abandon'* the relationship with those children. Sending them to *'Referral Units'* outside the schools with *'chaperones'* who were not competent nor strategic enough to assist individuals to either address their behavioural challenges or to put the type of structure they needed in place in order for them to advance their personal development or performance was a further waste of financial resources that could be better utilised more meaningfully". The Walynski Institute's Research called it "a much stronger statement which equated to a dereliction of duty of care". Professor Walynski concurred with the man they called 'The Professor'. "Even with the best of intentions, the *'chaperones'*, chosen by the education establishments seemed to have no real commitment or leadership skills to install the type of *'behavioural structure'* required to affect the type of changes that might have been more meaningful to the students mental well being. Temporarily or permanently suspending or expelling youngsters from schools was clearly not the answer. That strategy was not working in the children's favour because all it did was to (a) isolate those children but made them vulnerable to hanging about on the streets (b) highlight those actions as a blight at minimum on the characters of the youngsters and their families but (c) stood out as a permanent stain on the reputations of all those, who were dedicated but being paid as teachers to educate those children", Professor Walynski reported. "When they were feeling abandoned as *'rejects'*, it was the spark of feeling *'included'* which ignited the youngsters' curiosities towards the dreaded *'street-life'*", he pressed. The man they called 'The Professor' agreed with Professor Walynski's Report about the Research. He commented further too, "left to their own devices, the youngsters were attracted/distracted but encouraged to look into the other *'windows of opportunities'*. They were being corralled onto the metaphorical prairie but being made ready and primed by the instigation of the chaotic mindset and *'street-lifestyle'* to which they became attracted", he commented. His observations portrayed a similarity to the western movies of *'the wild, wild west'*. These youngsters were the latter day *'City Cowboys'* as depicted by the epic cowboy movies. Each Post/Zip Code was the new *'Outpost'*. The cold-bloodied maiming and slayings were just as brutal and unwarranted. Strangers were not welcomed down their *'endz'* even if it was a family member they had not yet met or heard about. Chasing the victims elect would trigger an act of bullying often by more than one individual; resulting in boisterous chaotic scenes and unacceptable behaviours. As yet another one bit the dust or tarmac, the bodies of the youngsters lay strewn on the ground where they were felled by shanking or bullets. Posses now rode their metal horses but schemed to eliminate anyone of which they became fearfully suspicious", he concluded.

Another reference to Professor Walynski's Research and Report pointed to other practices which had become hugely prominent and was being investigated by InterPlanPol in concert with other agencies across the full spectrum of the exotic continents, countries and islands as well as the Royal Royal Dis-United Stately Kingdoms of Asteroidia. What resulted was another set of revelations that were indisputable. Apparently, "by maintaining the rivalry amongst the UFO's *'Cult-Induced'* Post/Zip Code Wars, the GOO and their accomplices the GOP sought to enhance but justify the *'politically-convenient'* imagery of the fashioned *'stereo-type'*. It was a clever psychological illusion which had served the agendas of the politicrats well throughout the history of the parallel virtual planet of Asteroidia. Driven by the financial clout of the poly-tricksters, corruption was not only a mentality but was also allowed to become rife. Each election cycle had the same plot repeated over and over again like repeats of the serials, soap operas and movies on television. The immigrant population was always the number one target. The ritualistic rhetoric of the politicrats and poly-tricksters confirmed the essence of an age old philosophy which stated that ". . . if you do the same thing over and over again expecting a different result, it is a sign of insanity". Despite the wisdom from that particular philosophy, the political cyclical mantra kept repeating the same pattern again and again as if it was encoded to repeat that particular behaviour by default (robotically). Political Scientists all over the World of Space had agreed to conclude that those politicrats and their seemingly Neuro-bigoted, financially powerful poly-tricksters master *'puppeteers'* were allowed to continue to chisel away at the emotions of the indigenous population until they too became entranced but repeated the mantra automatically. The politicrats and poly-tricksters' incessant attack throughout the months of the entire relentless political campaigning had often passed without redress from those significant others. They were charged with the responsibility to question or bring to account those who displayed insensitive behaviours through displaying their inveterate tunnel-viewed psychological instabilities. This was frequently brought on by a degree of fearful neurotic *'meltdowns'* often referred to as the psychopathic mental disease which drove the type of **_'psychotic mentality'_** known as **_'prejudice'_**, commonly. Poly-tricksters and politicrats alike pandered to the fears of the indigenous population by inventing or encouraging those, who wanted to identify with the *'values and beliefs'* about *'stereo-type'* imagery they had so painstakingly, purposely developed to hold up as **_'fodder'_**. This was proven by the proportionate population of those being incarcerated in the *'Human Zoos'*. Whenever it was convenient for the politicrats and poly-tricksters, they often referred to incarcerated *'stereo-types'* as justification to pommel single parenthood; themselves deliberately referred to as *'politically accepted'* *'stereo-types'*. Starting with the fear-mongering banter about *"dependency on State Benefits"* followed by the debasing of the *'immigrant'* population as "leeches and a burden upon the Royal Royal Dis-United Stately Kingdoms", these politicrats and poly-tricksters stealthily played with the emotions and the *'belief systems'* of those individuals whose *primed minds* were ready to be attracted to the carefully contrived ritualistic rhetoric of disinformation. The Neuro-bigoted poly-tricksters and politicrats had used that strategic ploy once too often. This time the majority, who were the poverty-stricken indigenous individuals and legal immigrants, decided to elect the New Prime Leader of Spaceville, the Most Honourable Janette Brayhorne. That concluded Professor Walynski's in depth Research and Report.

Sickened by the increase in Serial Rapists and Serial Paedophilia, Janet Brayhorne gambled her political career by commissioning the eminent *'Ghost Writer'*, Picha Bu, to write her Biography. In it, Janet Brayhorne revealed that at the age of 7 years old, she had herself been kidnapped by a paedophile on one occasion. At 12 years old, she had been gang raped by a mixed gang of emotionally unintelligent and emotionally immature boys and again at the age of 14 years old by adolescent emotionally unstable boys from one of the *'Cult-Induced'* Post/Zip Code gangs, who referred to her as *"only meat"*. Janette remembered those emotionally gruesome experiences most vividly even now as an adult. When she was 16 years old, she recalls that, because of what's known in early adolescent years as *'puppy fat'*, her body's development had seemingly driven a much older generation of *'male adults'*, with seemingly adolescent behaviours, into an emotionally immature frenzy. On this other occasion, these male *'adults'* visited an age old contrived *'accepted cultural practice'*, called *'battery'* upon her. *'Battery'* was a cultural pseudonym for rape. Janette remembered that one of the men used to visit the family home with one of her aunts. Although he was not a biological member of the family, she used to look to him as a cousin. On the day Stanley 'the jackal' pulled up beside her in his flashy brand new car, Janette accepted his invitation to go for a drive on the expressway. She was naïve enough to want to be seen in the trendy car. As soon as she climbed in, Stanley 'the jackal' told Janette that he was hungry and wanted to get some food. They headed for a nice quiet place called 'The Ethnic Eatery Restaurant'. It had a quaint looking façade but was a very trendy restaurant. They had eaten there before as a family so there was no reason for Janette to be alarmed about the invitation. Stanley 'the jackal' made and received quite a number of phone calls on his cell phone but again there was no reason for suspicion. He was a music producer of high repute and was in demand by artistes and music industry moguls alike. Stanley 'the jackal' had heard Janette's choir trained voice and, unknown to her, had found the youngster irresistibly physically appealing. He used to joke that he was mesmerised by her beauty but at 16 years old flattery was welcomed. As he was her aunt's boyfriend, there was no suspicion especially as it was coming from one who seemed so important. They enjoyed their meal but left 'The Ethnic Eatery Restaurant'. Soon, they entered the expressway. As the new model car hovered above the ground, it seemed to travel without making a sound. The teenager was impressed by the smoothness of the ride. It was only when they had been travelling for more than an hour that Janette began to show concern. "Where are we going", she asked? "I thought you might want to see the countryside. It's most beautiful at this time of year. You're not in a hurry, are you", Stanley asked? His tone was casual. "No", Janette replied. They must have travelled for more than 200 hundred miles before Stanley started to indicate that he was exiting the expressway. Janette began to notice that these dirt roads were leading into the bushes. "'Cousin' Stanley, are you lost", she enquired? "No, not really, I have a place I want to show you. It needs a bit of work but you'll like it, I'm sure", he replied. Janette soon saw the ramshackle building. It was a derelict building that seemed to be pleading to be razed to the ground. Something inside Janette's mind had sounded the alarm bell but it was too late. The car pulled up just a few feet away from the entrance. Stanley got out but beckoned for Janette to follow him inside. Even though her mind told her she shouldn't, Janette had to make a decision whether to sit in the car on her own. There were strange sounds coming from within the wooded surroundings. Janette was scared to stay in the car on her own. Her mind was busy with all kind of thoughts. She reached inside her bag for her cell phone but it wasn't there. In desperation, she threw all the contents on the seat but to no avail. It had disappeared. Janette tried to recall where she could have lost it but her mind was far too busy with other thoughts. Reluctantly, she came out of the car but headed for the entrance of the old wooden shack. Inside, all it had was a broken down little wooden bed. There were no tables, chairs or sofa. It was quite an eerie setting. Stanley sat patiently on the edge of the old wooden bed with the dusty threadbare red and grey plaid cover. "Come and sit down", he encouraged. "I'll stand", Janette said. "Suit yourself. Can I get you a drink", Stanley asked? He made his way through the only other door but returned with what looked like two large glasses of homemade lemonade. He handed one to Janette and he sipped from the other one. Although she was feeling a bit uncomfortable at first, Janette began to relax a little. Because she was very thirsty, she gulped rather than sipped from the big glass of homemade lemonade. It was when she awakened that she realised she had been drugged and raped. When Janette finally opened her eyes, she saw seven other men apart from Stanley 'the jackal' in the tiny room. Some were still without their clothes. None had noticed that she was awake but Janette heard them boasting about what they had done to her. Apart from the bluish moonlight that filtered through the cracks in the roof and through the only window, the light from the singular candle indicated that it was night. Stanley 'the jackal' gave her the first indication that they had decided to have another round. He told the others that they had to toss a coin to see the order of priority. Each took turns to savage her more than they had done before she had regained consciousness. They subjected Janette to a most violent vicious onslaught that made her feel emotionally pained and physically sore. The more she screamed the more they laughed but taunted that they were planning to do their deed since she had started to attend secondary school. Janette struggled against the serial rapists and paedophiles but they overwhelmed her resistance by beating her into submission. When they had had their fill, Stanley tossed her the missing cell phone but threatened that she should remember his influence. He reminded Janette that he would have her and her family eliminated if she told that he was involved in the gang rape. For years, Janette decided that she couldn't risk having her family being eliminated so she kept it all to herself for a very long time. Fortunately, she had heard about but consulted with the Coach, the man who they called 'The Professor'. Over a period of time, she had some sessions and had learned to use the tools to help her reach closure with her past bizarre ordeals.

Janette became empathic towards all other victims of paedophilia and rape. In her capacity as head of Spaceville's government, Janette Brayhorne's passion for all victims who had suffered similarly to herself was to bring about a sense of making perpetrators responsible for their actions. She had determined that there had to be more serious consequences for such inhumane, *'mentally insane psychopathic acts like rape and paedophilia'*. The new Prime Leader of Spaceville's National Survey had empowered her to propose new laws to combat not only the possibilities but also the probabilities of any individual having to suffer such indignities ever again. Janette Brayhorne stated that new Laws were passed a week ago unanimously by 'The House of Better Senses'. Not withstanding their disunities, all the Kingdoms of the virtual planet of Asteroidia was being represented in this Upper House of Senates. Having rid the Parliament of 'The House of Confusion', the new Prime Leader of Spaceville stated that the 'New Interplanetary Order' in the World of Space meant to bring out a new message to current offenders and those who were considering partaking in crime. This new 'Ethos of Law' addressed the crimes being committed but from new perspectives.

Spaceville's new Principal Attorney General, Genevieve Tugboat, stated that she was extremely confident that, with regard to Al Tuxedo and his associates, the corroborative evidence issued by InterPlanPol would be enough to convict all the individuals of the crimes already stated above."When found guilty, they will serve their time without parole or appeal, she explained. Genevieve Tugboat also stated that, under the 'New Interplanetary Order', sanctioned by all the Royal Royal Dis-Unitied Stately Kingdoms of Asteroidia, provisions were being made to address main areas of **'Criminal Acts against the Person'**. These are that paedophilia, rape, victims of rape, wounding, maiming with a weapon and bullying will be considered as being perpetrated by individuals who are mentally disturbed, allegedly. The new considerations came under the new **Asteroidian Kingdoms Mental Act**. It stated that PAEDOPHILEA—(1) paedophiles would have a battery of tests by neurologists to assess and determine whether they had any physical brain abnormalities, (1A) if there were no physical brain abnormalities found then the paedophiles would be taken to underground facilities where they would live permanently but be studied and treated by psychiatrists, (1B) the perpetrators would be placed on the national registry, named and shamed publicly, (1C) the paedophiles would be stripped naked. They would have their bodies sprayed with an acid yellow dye before being exposed to the 'Wasp Colony Crypts'. There, the paedophile would be exposed to be visited upon by swarms of wasps that would be released to stalk them as frequently as they had repeatedly stalked the innocent children around the parallel virtual planet of Asteroidia including those in the 5th rated exotic continents, countries and islands. The chances of their survival would be as slight as the chances they gave to the traumatised children. They might well begin to experience what it feels like to be kidnapped only their *'kidnapper'* would be anaphylactic shock. If they managed to survive, they might just feel the intensity of shock and desperation of each of their victims, perhaps! (1D) All victims of paedophilia would be given free counselling or coaching paid for by the local authorities in which the crime happened or by the perpetrators or in their absence or inability to pay, by their families, corporations, associations and other authorised bodies with whom the they were employed or currently associated, (1E) compensation on behalf of the victims would be sought from the perpetrators or in their absence or inability to pay, from their families, corporations, associations and other authorised bodies with whom they were employed or currently associated, (1F) individuals alleging paedophilia that was proven to be untrue would be assessed by psychiatrists whether they were insane, (1G) if they were not found to be insane, they would be sanctioned to spend time in the underground facilities too. The perpetrators would be named and shamed publicly, (1H) compensation on behalf of the victims would be sought from the perpetrators or in their absence or inability to pay, from their families, corporations, associations and other authorised bodies with whom the they were employed or currently associated. RAPISTS—(2) convicted rapists would have a battery of tests by neurologists to assess and determine whether they had any physical brain abnormalities, (2A) if there were no physical brain abnormalities found then the rapists would be taken to underground facilities, (2B) if the convicted rapists were men, they would be assessed by psychiatrists whether they were insane, (2C) if they were not assessed as being insane then they would be taken to the underground 'Beehive Colonies' where the nude rapists' hands and feet would be restricted by chains. The victims, wearing the appropriate protective clothing, would be enabled to paint or cover the offenders' penises with honey before releasing the bees from their hives, (2D) the perpetrators would be named and shamed publicly, (2E) if the convicted rapists were women, they too would be assessed by psychiatrists whether they were insane, (2F) if they were not assessed as being insane then they would be taken to underground 'Ants Colonies' where the nude rapists' hand and feet would be restricted by chains. The victims, wearing appropriate protective clothing, would be able to paint or cover the offenders' vaginas with honey before releasing the huge red ants from their ant hills, (2G) The perpetrators would be named and shamed publicly, (2H) Individuals alleging rape that was proven to be untrue would be assessed by psychiatrists whether they were insane, (2J) if they were not assessed to be insane, they would be sanctioned to spend time in the underground facilities too, (2K) the perpetrators would be named and shamed publicly. VICTIMS OF RAPE (3) all proven victims of rape would be given free counselling or coaching paid for by the local authorities in which the crime happened or by the perpetrators or in their absence or inability to pay, by their families, corporations, associations and other authorised bodies with whom the they were employed or currently associated, (3.1) compensation on behalf of the victims would be sought from the perpetrator(s) or in the absence or inability to pay, from their families, corporations, associations and other authorised bodies with whom they were employed or currently associated, (3A) all victims wrongly accused of rape would be given free counselling or coaching paid for by the local authorities in which the alleged crime happened or by the perpetrators or in their absence, by their families, corporations, associations and other authorised bodies with whom the they were employed or currently associated. WOUNDING OR MAIMING WITH A WEAPON (4) **Except for self-defence**, all forms of wounding and maiming with a weapon would be considered a mental aberration, (4A) the convicted perpetrators would be assessed mentally by psychiatrists whether they were insane, (4B) they would spend some time being assessed and treated for ASPD, bipolar and schizophrenia, (4C) all victims of wounding or maiming, who survived, would be given free counselling or coaching paid for by the local authorities in which the crime happened or by the perpetrators or in their absence or inability to pay, by their families, corporations, associations and other authorised bodies with whom they were employed or currently associated, (4D) compensation on behalf of the victims would be sought from the perpetrators or in their absence or inability to pay, from their families, corporations, associations and other authorised bodies with whom they were employed or currently associated. BULLYING including DOMESTIC VIOLENCE (5) all forms of bullying including domestic violence would be outlawed but *nipped in the bud* at every level and age group, (5A) to enable clear understanding as to what behaviours are classified as 'bullying' and domestic violence, there will be clear definitions which type of behaviours come under that particular category, (5B) all private and public establishments must enforce **nationally accepted anti-bullying strategies** in the form of counselling workshops via curricula and training, (5C) all cohabiting, married couples, parents and guardians of bullies must seek a grant from local authorities to provide counselling or coaching for themselves, partners, child/children who were actively being bullies and domestic abusers, (5D) all individuals/establishments alleging acts of bullying that is proven to be untrue will be publicly named and shamed, (5E) all individuals/establishments alleging acts of bullying that is proven to be untrue will have to pay compensation to the victims, (6F) all commercial and private as well as local government educational establishments have to provide counselling or coaching for their employees and students, respectively, who had become victims of bullying and violence on their premises, (5G)

Failure to carry out this function would result in the establishments being publicly named and shamed, (5H) compensation on behalf of the victims would be sought from the perpetrators or in their absence or inability to pay, from their families, corporations, associations and other authorised bodies who employed or were associated with the perpetrators. OVERSIGHT BODIES (6) 'Oversight Bodies' would by able to assess and grade the standards of interventions being actively implemented, (6A) one key area which the 'Oversight Bodies' would be assessing most stringently is that attention be focused on emotional sensitivity, (6B) initially, these assessments would be on a quarterly basis then progress to half yearly and subsequently yearly, (6C) that would be dependent on what degree of progress that was being made by the particular establishment. (6D) there would be a *'sweetener'* for those establishments that passionately showed concentrated commitment by way of incremental allowances in taxation according to the level of progression being attained each fiscal year, (6E) failure to implement these interventions would incur a heavy tax levy as penalty against the 'unwilling' establishment, (6F) the establishment would be publicly named and shamed.

Referring to the case against Al Tuxedo and his cronies, the New Prime Leader, the Most Honourable Janette Brayhorne said that, "in order to thwart any attempts by renegade groups of insurgents to rescue them, all prisoners found guilty will be unreachable. They will serve their sentences on the Floating Prisons far out at sea, sent to the Dungeons/Crypts or be transported to a vessel in the Interplanetary Galaxies somewhere in the World of Space but without the rights to visitation or any form of contact. Janette Brayhorne further stated that "the individuals found guilty in Spaceville will serve time at the pleasure of His Majesty 'King Karma' of the Kingdom of Spaceville".

The hour long News had thrown some unwanted attention not only on Al Tuxedo but also on his *'Puppeteer Masters'*, the UFO and OU DIS-UK as well as his confidants, accomplices and collaborators. They had aided and abetted Al Tuxedo and the others within the awesomely, finely tuned, efficiently run Organisation. The massive selection of authentic Research, Reports and Studies referenced by the eminent Professor Walynski and the man they called 'The Professor' archived by IST, Independent Spacevillean Television would be accepted and used as *'admissible evidence'* in the relevant cases against Al Tuxedo and the full hierarchy of the UFO. Interviews with the Prime Leader of Spaceville, Janette Brayhorne, her Biographer, the Attorney General, her Deputy as well as representatives of InterPlanPol, Inter Planetary Police were archived also and would also be made available as admissible evidence against Al Tuxedo and the hierarchy of the UFO too.

News Reader, Wata Ting, said, "InterPlanPol had generated a generous reward scheme in order for the general public to help them apprehend Al Tuxedo and his insurgent cronies from the Organisation. They had infiltrated the once united virtual planet of Asteroidia". "Contingent plans had been prepared and put in place well before the *'Breaking News'* announcement. With the size of the rewards, we expect to be executing some arrests within a matter of hours", Alan Baitman, Head of InterPlanPol, stated. The *'Reward List'* appeared on the screen. Even those that were buzzing from imbibing their *'legal' drugs* sobered up much faster when they saw the enormous sums of Champagne Urges that were being offered for unearthing the previously seemingly illusive Al Tuxedo and his cronies.

Throughout the announcement, the banner at the bottom of the screen kept rotating the words **Breaking News**—*"Unprecedented 'Reward List' posted at all Police Stations, Petrol/Gas Stations, Super Markets, Libraries, Cinemas, Night Clubs and all Social Websites for the capture of Al Tuxedo and his cronies"*—**Breaking News**—*"InterPlanPol put out advert with 'Rewards List'*—*Want to be an instant millionaire? Help us find these heinous criminals"*—**Breaking News**—*"The capture of Al Tuxedo and his accomplices are imminent"*, InterPlanPol states—**Breaking News**—*"Proof of the UFO's 'Cult-Induced' Post/Zip Code Wars"*—**Breaking News**—*"Walynski Institute Research, Reports and Studies support Professor Walynski's findings"*—**Breaking News**—*"UFO fund 'Cult-Induced' Post/Zip Code violent 'Theatres of War' to your Streets"*, InterPlanPol alleges—**Breaking News**—*"Serial Rapists and Paedophiles Rings destroying exotic islands, continents, countries and kingdoms"*, Moralist Inc announces on social websites.

Those in the Saloon Bar immediately abandoned all allegiance and pseudo friendships toward Duke and his twin brother, Baron. The lure of the sumptuous rewards ignited the biblical *'Judas'* characteristics within them. These might have remained unexposed or undiscovered for generations. For a few Champagne Urges more, these once seemingly dedicated colleagues and friends, like Trojan 'the horse' and the other members of the gang 'Clout', had abandoned their loyalties to Duke. They would have pretended their loyalty were genuine just like Brutus' pledge to Caesar. Previously, Brutus' pretence at "watching Caesar's back" might have made him appear to be worthy of being *'canonised'* as a saint by any ruling Sovereign Pontiff at the time. Brutus proved his disloyalty to Caesar by stabbing him in his back. The same comparison can be made of Judas's disloyalty when he accepted payment of thirty pieces of silver for selling the biblical Jesus Christi for crucifixion. Today, the price of disloyalty was a much more handsome proposition represented by an abundant sum much greater in quantity and of the highest value in modern currency terms. Champagne Urge was the preferred currency throughout the World of Space. The members of Clout would come to commit this same act of *'selling out'* to the highest bidder "for a few Champagne Urges more". They were ready in order to satiate their enormous voracious appetites or to quench their super dehydration for 'the taste of Champagne Urge', apparently!

Suddenly, the Saloon became alive again, as busy as the floors where stocks and shares were being bought and sold around the parallel virtual planet of Asteroidia. From an observer's point of view, it was as noisy as a common street market where individuals shouted for attention to what they were peddling. Individuals were busying themselves with receiving and relaying information to and from their respective *'brokers'* and *'prospects'*, urgently. Within the Saloon area of The Haunting Posts AADC, cell phones and their convenience were obviously imminent. Individuals were busy jamming the lines to the local Police Station in their respective communities, their local newspapers and the national news Media, severally. Servers were being overloaded but crashed by the enormity of the volume of emails. Texts, other messaging and social websites about Al Tuxedo's whereabouts were being circulated and broadcasted by the *'Hot Rumour Mill'* that was being created within the walls of The Haunting Posts AADC.

Having seen the extreme amounts of Champagne Urge being offered as reward for information on the character known as Al Tuxedo and witnessing the frantic explosion of activities within the Saloon, the man sitting with Doris had a sudden urge to go to the toilet. Earlier, although he had managed to plant the seeds of doubt about whether it was him or his thinner look-a-like standing at the bar that was Al Tuxedo into the minds of those present at The Haunting Post AADC, the pressure of suspicion seemed to be tipping the scale against him. His brother's loss of weight appeared to put the man at the bar rather slightly in favour as the victim. The man sitting with Doris knew there was a window from which he could escape. He decided it was time to do this. When he rose from the chair, Trojan 'the horse' nodded to Geoff 'the Rhino'. He nodded to Frigit 'the mouse'. She nodded to Barney 'the owl'. He signalled to Pete 'the hammer' then winked and nodded to Henry 'the hook'. They waited for the man, purporting to be Duke, to enter the toilet. Barney 'the owl' made a sound but motioned for the others to go outside to stand at the rear of The Haunting Post AADC where they could see the window. The weather was pretty overcast and the red clouds seemed to cover the moon. Only the light from the streetlamp on the other side of the level crossing was reflecting any light into the rear of The Haunting Post AADC. Alan Baitman joined the others in their pursuit of the man who had been sitting with Doris, purporting to be Duke. As soon as they heard the toilet was flushed, Pete 'the hammer', Frigit 'the mouse', Trojan 'the horse', Henry 'the hook' and Alan Baitman stayed watching as the man jumped from the window into the rear of The Haunting Post AADC. Barney 'the owl' made that sound again but much louder this time as he used to do to alert the gang 'Clout' when they had spotted their quarry.

On hearing the familiar alert, the man stopped but looked round. He didn't see anyone in the shadowy area at the rear of The Haunting Posts AADC but was sure that sound was made by Barney 'the owl'. The escapee broke into a quick dash towards the fence that separated the rear of The Haunting Post AADC and the railway lines. As the man started to scramble up the fence like the rat he seemed to be, Alan Baitman shouted, "Al Tuxedo". The man who had been sitting with Doris realised he had been spotted. It was then that Henry 'the hook' placed the metal hook against the man's shoulder blade but persuaded him to come down from the fence. 'Crazy' Bobby was waiting for his moment to prove to Trojan 'the horse' and others that it wasn't him that had snitched on them in prison. He couldn't control his temper. As soon as the man's legs touched the ground, 'crazy' Bobby pulled him to the ground. He began punching the man in the face then proceeded to attack him like a rabid pit-bull dog. 'Crazy' Bobby bit off a piece of the man's right ear. The other's piled in by kicking him in his crotch, the ribs and anywhere else on his body that they could but kept stamping on his head as they used to do to members of the Harbour-Shark Estate Mixed DNA Rainbow Gang and others. Alan Baitman shouted for them to stop. "We want him alive", he stated.

Doris, who had seen the procession of men who had headed towards the toilet, seemed more than a little perplexed. Something wasn't right and she could tell. Doris looked towards the barman but he just shrugged his shoulders. They had noticed that the thinner man, who was standing at the bar earlier had collapsed onto the floor. The man writhed, grunted but uttered the same sort of guttural sounds in unison with each blow and sounds that was coming from his twin at the rear of The Haunting Post AADC. It was as if it was the thinner man was being worked over by the angry raging mob outside. The barman, who had learnt his lesson from his earlier experience, chose not to comment. At the back of the Haunting Post AADC, Alan Baitman's plea was being ignored by those who sought revenge from the man they considered to be Al Tuxedo. Henry 'the hook' and others had done long sentences because of the man they called Al Tuxedo and they wanted him to know how they felt about his "snitching to the feds". The loud guttural sounds pleading for help were mixed in with the threats and exasperated uttering that came with each blow that registered on the man's body at the rear of The Haunting Post AADC. The man 'crazy' Bobby and others were convinced was Al Tuxedo had revealed himself by trying to escape, seemingly! Both the man on the ground at the rear of The Haunting Post AADC and that of the thinner man, who had collapsed onto the wooden floor inside it, uttered cries of anguish and pain. Their deep baritone voices harmonised but sounded more like a choir of wounded elephants sending out SOS messages in unison for the consideration of mercy before their inevitable fate at the hands of cold-blooded poachers.

It was greed that had made them thirst for the taste of the enviable virtual currency, Champagne Urge. Forged by their addiction to satisfy their perennial quest, the *'Reward List'* had awaken the *'Judas Spirit'* in each of them and there was no other consideration going through their minds but to switch to their judgemental mindsets even though they could not be convinced which of the twins was Al Tuxedo. Like in the 'Western Movies', which had helped to *'programme'* and *'condition'* their mindsets, the real Duke and his brother became the *'hunted'* by *'bounty hunters'* like Trojan 'the horse', his colleagues and Alan Baitman. The power of the *'programmed'* and *'conditioned'* mindset of materialism over humanity was in evidence. The information was now in the public domain. Across all the 1st rated Kingdoms and stretching as far as the 5th rated exotic continents, countries and islands, each individual was claiming sight of Al Tuxedo. Apart from the regular printed and television Media, the social websites were filled with *'novice'* as well as *'professional'* *'bounty hunters'* claiming to have sight of the now infamous Arms Dealer, Drug Dealer, head of the Serial Rapists and Serial Paedophile Rings, Al Tuxedo.

Though she was puzzled by the strange behaviour and sounds coming from the thinner man, who looked like Duke, on the floor near the bar, Doris was filled with remorse for the unfortunate individual outside at the back of The Haunting Post AADC. He was howling like a hound dog with every blow he received. The pitch of his voice had gotten shriller and shriller but bore an urgency for intervention in order to relieve him from the painful beating he was experiencing at the hands of those, who were once his trusted colleagues and in some cases believed to be friends. "What is going on", Doris asked the barman? In answer to her pained expression of concern for the man at the rear of The Haunting Post AADC, perpetrating to be Duke, the barman commented cynically, "Poor bastard, he must have piles! Painful when you're constipated, I'm told", he responded.

The Taste of Champagne Urge!

WIK-**ID**-FICTION

PART THREE

CHAPTER 57

Raymondo de Oddballo was the man with two brains named Hifle and Pifle. He was unaware he had two brains or how they had devised their Classy, Epic, Wik-**ID**-Fiction © Literary Docudrama Movie © made up of Fictional Virtual Realities Scenarios ©. He lay on the private hospital bed contemplating whether the scenes in his dream were real or fictional! His eyes were still closed but he was not asleep nor was he still in a coma. Raymondo had been awake for many hours but his nightmarish dream was so vivid and 'real-to-life' that he began to believe even the character and 'role' he had played to fit the incestuous stepfather 'model' in his own mind movie aptly directed and produced by his two brains. Even though Raymondo was aware of the presence of his long serving dedicated wife Pamela L'Brishè de Oddballo in the private room, Sandra Bogus still lingered on his mind representing his delusional 'Cloned-Barbie Trophy Woman', 'Mrs Right'. It was as if she had been indelibly stamped upon the inner recesses of his subconscious, unconscious and conscious minds. Even while Raymondo transitioned latently from his comatose state back to the state of conscious-mindedness, he still thought of Sandra Bogus as his 'Exotic Mona Lisa'. Raymondo's olfactory sense of smell searched his inner sense of awareness but registered the addictive scent of Sandra's perfumes, which seemed to be stuck to the 'mother-board' of his memory but suffused his entire being so much so that he still lust for Sandra, longingly. Her beautiful large cornflower blue eyes and soft, ultra-smooth peach textured melanin skin still clung so much closer to him than his shadow. Raymondo could not resist the temptress that had haunted him like a stalking ghost in his dream. His demise at the hands of the police was still as sobering and frightening even now that Raymondo was out of his comatose state. His torturous experience was at the hands of the green humanoid robotron Sergeant/ Deputy Sheriff Gruff and his rookies. The accusations by the police still hurt as much as the physical and psychological torturous pains which he had encountered.

Raymondo listened closely to the voices around him in the private room. He was aware of his two children, his son 16 years old Ras-Dan and his beautiful daughter 21 years old university 'Fine Art' student Darsna L'Brishè de Oddballo. He was more than relieved that the nightmare scenario of him committing incest with his daughter never happened. Even in his comatose state, he had felt more than ashamed to have seemingly committed such a dastardly act. When he reflected upon the nightmarish debacle, Raymondo could feel the beads of sweat that showered his entire body, dampened his spirit but flooded his soul. In real life, it was never the sort of thing that he would entertain as a thought let alone an act. Still, Raymondo felt guilty that it had happened at all even in the context of a nightmarish dream which had inadvertently acted as a counter shock but helped to bring him out of the coma. In their Classy, Epic, Wik-**ID**-Fiction © Literary Docudrama Movie © made up of 'real-to-life' Fictional Virtual Realities Scenarios © exploring what make up relationships on a virtual parallel planet, his two brains, Hifle and Pifle, had conjured up a finely woven tapestry of highly emotional life experiences. They tugged at the heartstrings but brought into focus an intergalactic debate on the importance of maintaining 'traditional values' like morals and scruples. Before his induced comatose state, Raymondo, in his investigative documentary film, had alleged that these once important *'traditional values'* were being deliberately diminished throughout the entire virtual planet of Asteroidia. These seemed to be targeted for obliteration by an alliance of heartless shadowy phantoms. They were bent on their *'minority'* organisations' insatiable appetite, unrelenting hunger but most conspicuously their development of un-quenching thirst for the taste of Champagne Urge. These parched palates were prioritised as being more important than the human needs of the *'majority'* of the population. In his extensive research over a period of 10 years, Raymondo had established that the then covert shadowy phantom characters were doing so in order to test the consistency and longevity of moral fibre amongst the population of the virtual planet of Asteroidia. These shadowy phantom characters aimed to seize the initiative but to ride roughshod over the laws and legislations they had targeted to influence or change undemocratically, apparently!

In Raymondo's dream movie, poly-tricksters, like Daryll Fastfamoussè, were becoming less caring about disguising their intent. His individual overt attempt not only to devalue the achievement of an ethnic poly-trickcian, The Most Honourable Prime Leader of Spaceville, Janette Brayhorne, but also to openly question her place of birth exposed the depth of his inveterate prejudice against her eminence, her gender and ethnicity. Daryll Fastfamoussè and his green humanoid robotron colleagues within the UFO, of which he was a fully paid up member, deliberately structured the type of onslaught that was more than political posturing. He and his sponsors, the once covert shadowy phantoms, rose from their pre-programmed mental entombments like the dire ogres they were but highlighted their preferences to diminish Janette Brayhorne's outstanding achievements. They chose to use every opportunity to bare their extended claws, talons, fangs and venomous vipers tongues to install incessant vicious attacks via a form of programming *'tool'* called *'disinformation'*. All the time, they sought opportunities to tear the metaphoric flesh away from Janette Brayhorne's skeletal frame but to deliberately destroy her reputation and to consistently debase her gender and ethnicity. Such was the level of fear that beset the minds of those spiteful, envious green humanoid robotrons from the Tribe of Babylon. Their parrot-ish repetitive mode had been preset at birth to a frequency, which was so precise and repetitive that individual beams of vitriolic hate, prejudice and Neuro-bigotry were deliberately aimed but found their target as precisely as heat-seeking missiles in the theatres of mental wars, not withstanding the *'collateral damages'*. Janette Brayhorne was not the first of the green humanoid robotrons' target and she most certainly would not be the last. Since their arrival on the virtual planet of Asteroidia from another planet amongst the galaxies in the World of Space, the green humanoid robotrons from the Tribe of Babylon had caused inter-galactic strife amongst those galaxies. They did this through their incessant attacks against, the brown, purple, pink, white, and blue Mixed DNA Rainbow Tribe, black from the Tribe of Hawke and yellow from the Tribe of Duke populations in the World of Space. Amongst the Tribes which exist within the parallel virtual planet, the Tribe of Babylon thought they were first in the *"Hierarchy of Class"*. They rendered all other Tribes as being inferior to them. The man they called 'The Professor' stated that, as a disciplined science, psychology had rendered this self-imposed *'ascent'* in hierarchical status, by the green humanoid robotrons, as *a sign of insecurity driven by deep-seated negative emotional actions and reactions mainly through fear.*

Janette Brayhorne's own ascent had defied all odds to become the first ethnic Prime Leader in the history of any of the Royal Royal Dis-United Stately Kingdoms of Asteroidia which exist on the parallel virtual planet. The scenes in Hifle and Pifle's Classic, Epic, Wik-**ID**-Fiction © Literary Docudrama Movie © made up of Fictional Virtual Realities Scenarios © saw all the Kingdoms of Asteroidia as being undivided in celebrating Janette Brayhorne's magnanimous, determined, rugged climb to the top of the political ladder. Of all the candidates, bookmakers had offered odds of one trillion to one against Janette Brayhorne becoming Prime Leader of Spaceville but the smart money of those whom she had managed to reach at local level in the Kingdom of Spaceville was an innovative concept that the big-headed green humanoid robotron members of the UFO had chosen to ignore. Even though it seemed impossible, some financially poor green humanoids from the Tribe of Babylon and ethnics from other tribes had bothered to chance their minimal bets on Janette Brayhorne, whom they saw as the most influential candidate. She had not only managed to influence but also to empower the younger population demographic to keep believing in the genuine democratic model. Their wagers were handsomely rewarded by her victory. Because of their *'values and beliefs'* some became *'instant'* Spacevillean Champagne Urge trillionaires and millionaires. Spaceville and the other Kingdoms had displayed their joy to witness such an emphatic victory and historic moment. Like spoilt children throwing a tantrum, the UFO and its more brazen members, who were politicrats and influential poly-trickster moguls, openly plotted, pledged to scheme but consistently oppose and disrupt the sanity that Janette Brayhorne was bringing into view for the entire population of the Kingdoms without exception. She aimed to influence other planets in the World of Space as well as the Kingdoms of Asteroidia. Janette Brayhorne had strategically sought to end and deter the intergalactic wars amongst the planets but was seen by the UFO as inteferring in their quests to accumulate even more Spacevillean Champagne Urges to fill their already overflowing coffers. Such was the green humanoid robotrons mindset, unbounded hunger and more than a parch-like thirst for Spacevillean Champagne Urge. They were becoming even more brazen with every moment that Janette Brayhorne remained as Prime Leader. The UFO and its *'puppet'* members exposed their singular ambition of total control over the administration and legislation of not only Spaceville but all the Royal Royal Dis-United Stately Kingdoms of Asteroidia.

In Raymondo's documentary film, these once shadowy phantoms were the main cause of the disunity amongst what was once called The Royal United Stately Kingdoms of Asteroidia. The UFO's *'spin doctors'* were exceptional in the art of installing the idea of succession away from the main body but had chipped away at the foundations which unified the Kingdoms. In order to gain absolute control, the UFO and their cronies managed to install their main philosophy, *"divide, conquer and rule"*, to separate the Kingdoms. Although the parallel virtual planet of Asteroidia was one Geo-Galactical location, breaking the Kingdoms into singular units gave greater leverage to the sinister gang. With the Kingdoms being disunited made the UFO's manipulation seamless. The unhinging of the Kingdoms into fragmented units made them more vulnerable to the type of access that the *'puppeteers'* needed to ride rough-shod through the unguarded thoroughfares. Having achieved their first objective, the shadowy phantoms were now becoming more daring in their quest to dominate how politicrats and associate poly-tricksters carried out their demands. The UFO and their associates had glaringly unmasked themselves but openly boasted that they had become powerful enough to influence even the political administrators and supreme legislators of the respective Kingdoms. Metaphorically, the tail began to wag the dog. Members of the UFO bought and sold the minds, spirits and souls of those who pandered to their every whim, isms or skisms. As long as the metaphoric *'carrot'*, the financial abundance of Champagne Urge, was being dangled in front of their eyes, those who were happy to be subservient *'puppets'* put up no resistance to the deviously manipulative *'puppeteers'*, the UFO. Waving their *'big sticks'*, they continued to auction their chosen candidates up and down the political expressways but imposed their will upon the population. They were seeking to become the overseers of all life form on the parallel virtual planet of Asteroidia, eventually. This gang of seemingly influential VIP lobbyists' poly-tricksters were able to determine but establish legally and otherwise that their organizations were more important than humans like the population from the Tribe of Duke, the Tribe of Hawke, the Mixed DNA Rainbow Tribe and the financially poor green humanoids from the Tribe of Babylon even. It was as if when the green humanoid robotrons from the Tribe of Babylon sneezed the entire parallel virtual planet was *obliged* to catch a cold, perhaps! Their psychological inoculation of the *'greed virus'* had become more than an epidemic but had graduated on an intensity scale rapidly moving from deep orange into the red danger zone alert system used to indicate the greed's *'viral status'* as a pandemic. This alert planted fear at a deeper level into the psyche of the population. It orchestrated chaos across the mental geo-galactic regions of the entire parallel virtual planet of Asteroidia. The fear seemed to have manifested itself hugely, particularly in the Kingdom of Spaceville.

Raymondo reasoned that the power-hungry green humanoid robotron *'vultures'* were no longer covert in their quest to have complete control of governments. He pointed out that they sought to re-enslave particular ethnics especially those, who had emigrated from the far off exotic continents, countries and islands as well as other planets. The green humanoid robotrons from the Tribe of Babylon openly stated that they were about to re-establish an apartheid system that might cause confusion between the *'aliens'* from those exotic geo-galactic locations and associate planets with the indigenous Mixed DNA Rainbow Tribe that were rapidly evolving within the Royal Royal Dis-United Stately Kingdoms of Asteroidia. In the final analysis, Raymondo had stated in his documentary film that he had technological evidence that the once shadowy phantoms were planning to mentally enslave and subsequently oversee the *'self-eradication'* of entire tribes around the parallel virtual planet of Asteroidia, eventually. The first of the *'Intergalactic Wars of the Tribes'* was very much being a planned project to be prosecuted across the World of Space in the *'Theatres of Inter-Galactic Wars'* between the green humanoid robotron *'Reptillian Vertibral Fins'*, RVF, from the Tribe of Babylon vs the purple coloured *'Mammalian Winged Fins'*, CMWF, from the Mixed DNA Rainbow Tribe. Through these wars, the green humanoid robotrons from the Tribe of Babylon planned to destroy most of the infrastructure on the galaxies of parallel virtual planets then forcefully claim the contracts to rebuild them for increased sums of Champagne Urge.

In Raymondo's documentary film, he claimed that he had quotes from prominent disgruntled *'inside sources'* from the UFO. With regards to eliciting the contracts to rebuild on virtual planets across the different galaxies, the UFO is quoted as saying, "It's like taking candies from babies". Triggered by the volume of evidence presented through Raymondo's mammoth research over ten years, this latest scandal had exploded the proverbial *'Pandora's Box'*. It threatened to scatter catalogues of proven generational practices of *'witting'* or *'unwitting'* prejudices and racism against the current exploding population of brown, purple, pink, white and blue Mixed DNA Rainbow Tribe. The original tribe on the parallel virtual planet of Asteroidia was the black Tribe of Hawke. It is fabled that the yellow Albino Tribe of Duke' was formed from traditional genetic scientific experiments carried out progressively over millennia by traditional scientific communities known as *'Yacoubians Genetics'*. These two tribes had populated the Royal Royal Dis-United Stately Kingdoms of Asteroidia long before even the Mixed DNA Rainbow Tribe existed or the arrival of the green humanoid robotrons. The green humanoid Tribe of Babylon were the interlopers from a different planet across the galaxies in the World of Space. If they were to be allowed to carry out their single-minded mission, the green humanoid robotrons from the Tribe of Babylon would become the only tribe reigning supreme over and above all other tribes on the parallel virtual planet of Asteroidia. Divisions of the geo-galactic regions had already been implemented. This ensured that, despite their rise in standards of financial abundance and academic achievements, individuals from the black Tribe of Hawke, the yellow Albino Tribe of Duke and the Mixed DNA Rainbow Tribe would be further isolated but discouraged from living in certain boroughs within the various Kingdoms. This meant that, despite the volume of their population, the black Tribe of Hawke, the yellow Albino Tribe of Duke in particular and those from the Mixed DNA Rainbow Tribe, who chose to affiliate with them culturally, were to be corralled into just two regions in each of the Royal Royal Dis-United Stately Kingdoms of Asteroidia, permanently. The Kingdom of Spaceville was the representative model which reflected the level of segregation that was taking place. Boroughs like Ghettoborough reflected the type of place individuals from the Tribe of Hawke and the Tribe of Duke would be allowed to live, be educated and to work in.

The inevitable massive consequences were reflected by the implications from the extended research by Raymondo. He pointed to how boroughs like Ghettoborough in the Kingdom of Spaceville had become as violent as it did. Raymondo had proof that *'Ghetto Engineering'* was a continuous scientific project implemented by the shadowy gang. They had managed to stay below the radar so far but were becoming more significant by their pomposity. The UFO would ensure that the statistics of high crime rate would be a perennially recurring constant theme. The GMT, drove their subordinates the GMES. Their remit was to recruit the GMP continuously. It was their responsibility to recruit the GOS, who activated the GOO and GOP. In turn, those tribes sub-contracted to their subordinates the GSE, GCCEO and GCE to coordinate the chaos but coordinate the pornographic mentality amongst the young generations from the Tribe of Duke, the Tribe of Hawke and the Mixed DNA Rainbow Tribe, latterly.

Like green shoots of plants learnt what it was like to experience enforced drought conditions, those tribes would begin to wilt from lack of essential nutrients, like water, that was required to establish but maintain healthy growth. Those green shoots withered and die, inevitably. Similarly, the young generation, stunted by the lack of essential mental nutrients, like structure, and social skills to better enable them to strive to learn to accept the principles of morals, scruples and become more emotionally sensitive, their mentalities were liable to wither but tend to remain emotionally unintelligent and immature. By their behaviours, these young generations were reflecting mentalities they had come to believe as their own. Unknown to them, they were being purposely observed, stalked, subliminally hijacked but violently submerged into cyclonic spirals of chaotic distractions/attractions being unleashed upon them under the conditions presented by the rise in negative emotional intensity levels involved in the senseless UFO's 'Cult-Induced' Post/Zip Code Wars. In the searing sauna-like intense heat of these uncomfortable humid mental temperate conditions of the UFO's 'Cult-Induced' Post/Zip Code Wars that had been brought to bear upon the naïve young generation by the full gambit of the GMT, the GMES, the GMP, GOS, GOO and GOP together with their franchisee underlings mentioned previously, some would perish either through direct confrontation, inevitably or be considered as *'collateral damage'* by the heartless, insensitive UFO. As if not satisfied with the madness mayhem they had already inveigled that had besieged the minds of the young generation, the *'bloodthirsty'*, *'organ-seeking'* UFO would unleash the *'thrill to kill'* mentality upon the *'survivors'* to react with overbearing toxic mixture of schizophrenic ASPD delirium but give *'post-hypnotic instructions'* to "finish them off". On receipt of those subliminal instructions, the robotron *'converts'* from the 'Cult-Induced' Post/Zip Code Gangs made up of the Mixed DNA Rainbow Tribe, the Tribes of Duke and Hawke, reverted to the *'self-induced'* *'panic attacks'* and *'anxiety'* behaviours. These addictive associations towards chaotic monochrome thinking launched the pandemonium in their busy minds but revisited their addiction to fear, sought their fixation on the *'buzz'* of earning not only *'Street Credits'* but also the sharing of the *'spoils'* of Champagne Urge from the sale of the newly provided *'body parts'* they had provided, through their actions and reactions, for their masters, the *'puppeteers'*. The 'Cult-Induced' Post/Zip Code Gangs carried out their acts of violence against their perceived *'enemies'* and *'frenemies'* alike, without feelings or remorse, indiscriminately, sometimes.

The young naïve, often confused, generations would come to forge the metaphoric alloy between the struggle to survive and the subliminal temptations, which manifested as the *'distractions or attractions'* that held their attention to ransom. They and their families paid these burdensome *'mental ransoms'* repeatedly to the UFO and their associates, who were gaining financially not only from each funeral that was caused by the UFO's 'Cult-Induced' Post/Zip Code Wars but also from the young generations' addition to the already bulging population of the ***privately owned*** 'Human Zoos'. They would keep on paying these *'mental ransoms'* through engaging in continually living the *'life of crime'* which appeared superficially to be their only alternative, seemingly! Most were more than over-committed to becoming the perceived *'stereotype'* by buying into the retention of false hopes. The vulnerable young generations consumed the *'bait'* of feasting on lashings of the seemingly mouth-watering menu of *'stereo-tripe'*. They did this because they had already become *'converts'* of the *'stereo-hype'* perpetrated by the *'politically correct'* *'acceptable'* enforced perception of the type of *'role models'* that they were being exposed to but compelled to follow. Some of these were from the streets whilst others were in the violent movies, and cartoons which they were subliminally instructed to watch, learn and emulate. Daily, the young generations on the parallel virtual planet of Asteroidia engaged in actively maiming, slaying or being *'finished off'* like in the *'fun'* games on their respective consoles. There were other influences like the subliminal messages from the mesmerising *'hook lines'* which they found highly irresistible. Those hauntingly entrancing melodies of the *'Pied Pipers Symphonies'*, which engaged their *'sympathetic nervous systems'*, were the *'mental organisations'* that had coerced yet embedded the sublime commands upon their psyche. With their already bloated egos being massaged by even more over-generous recurring *'helpings'* of the *'stereo-tripe'*, whilst being serenaded by the tempo, rhythms and flow of the verbal diatribe of highly inflammable *'stereo-hype'*, the young generations were on a one-way, tunnel-vision journey into the *'fast lanes'* along the *'mental expressways'* in which they found themselves. Young generations were heading nowhere, *"living fast"* and *"dying trying"* in order to acquire the seemingly elusive taste of Champagne Urge. They were being auditioned but cast in the extraordinary *'roles'* they were willing to and chose to play in the **'Life Street Movies'** in which they were engaged.

In his documentary film, Raymondo referred to the **'unexplained escalation'** of the most bizarre acts of ASPD known as bullying. The maiming and killings were being filmed by video on cell phones but posted on particular ironically named *'social'* websites. These acted as types of media but gave access to that toxic mixture of mindless schizophrenic ASPD behaviours, inadvertently perhaps! The number of *'hits'* indicated that there were interested parties keeping score whilst gaining financially from the *'mother of all explosions of recorded criminal activities'* to have infiltrated the parallel virtual planet of Asteroidia.

Raymond's documentary film included those parents, who seemed oblivious to any difference in the behaviours of their children but strove to become their *'friends'*, instead. Others, through *'over-protection'*, had chosen not to put any structure in place as *'guidelines'* for their youngsters. This rendered those parents as being deliberately *'clueless'* about their children's behaviours away from home until that inevitable knock at their front doors or those distressful telephone calls from the police to say their child or children had become victims of the horrendous street bullying madness known as the UFO's *'Cult-Induced'* Post/Zip Code Wars, commonly. Whether the inevitable telephone calls or the knock at the doors meant their children themselves had perpetrated an act of maiming, killing or had been brutally slain in the streets would mean a grief-stricken ride on the emotional roller coaster. Though most of the young generations were unaware, the man called 'The Professor' stressed that "other elements were being stacked, layer upon layer, against their psychological and physical well being". These young generations were being fed excess of the *'fast'*, *'convenient'* *'mental foods'* known as *'stereo-tripe'*. They had gorged themselves on the sickening diet of *'mentally toxic diatribe'* but had been overwhelmed by the enormity of the deafening coded language of recurring *'stereo-hype'* which triggered their automotive responses. These sensitive *'triggers'* were being *'trained'* and *'conditioned'* through *'game-play'* at a deeper psychological level but became an automatic response when challenged whether in virtual or real environments. This enabled the young generations to perform the perceived *'stereo-type'* behaviours. Lured by their voracious appetites and contrived parched dehydrated thirst for the taste of Champagne Urge, it was easy for the young generations to transition into becoming *'converts'* by the ruthless *'mental strategies'* of the UFO and their associates. Like their tortured minds, the young generations had accepted the repetitive constant *'conditioning'* commands that had been subtly implanted, embedded and nurtured into their psyche but was causative to them acting out the green humanoid robotron *'scripts of insanity'* until they were captured and caged in the *'Human Zoos'* or died on the streets in the *'uncivil'* UFO's *'Cult-Induced'* Post/Zip Code Wars, probably!

Raymondo's intense research exposed some previously little known facts. His investigative documentary film revealed but highlighted some very underhand tactics by the UFO and their associates, some of whom were from the Tribes of Hawke, Duke and the Mixed DNA Rainbow Tribe too. These came in the guise of *'educators'* as well as other technocrats working within *'trusted'* established resources. Bloated egos, stinking attitudes and judgemental mindsets did not belong to the green humanoid robotrons only. Raymondo's exclusive hard-hitting documentary film went beyond the main protagonists but reached into the corners, nooks, crannies and other hidden areas where other *'mental brooms'* couldn't or were dissuaded from reaching. Raymondo managed to glean other invaluable information from The Walynski Institute.

In his research, Professor Walynski's exclusive interviews revealed the patterns, as commented on by the young incumbents of the *'Correctional Establishments'* known as *'Human Zoos'*, commonly. In an attempt to stem the flow of errors they recognised that had rendered them emotionally unintelligent and immature, the young generations serving their calendar custodial sentences had poured out their hearts but uncluttered their minds, through a process devised by the man they called 'The Professor'. He referred to the process as *'Mental Vomiting'* ©. The interviewees spilled their mentally nauseous, undigested, griping rants from their minds in order to send messages of more than *'hope'* to the still younger generations, who they feared might get caught up in the network of webs designed to snare them. Adolescent as well as young adults appealed to parents to "***spend more 'quality time' with their children***" but trust that, through those all encompassing moments, parents use those opportunities to install but teach their youngsters about *"the value of structure"*. The new young inmates, and those, who were already incarcerated since their younger days but serving long sentences, agreed strongly that parents needed to consistently monitor and review the effectiveness of their individual styles but that it was more important to ask their individual children what was ***their "preference for learning"***. The young incarcerated incumbents stressed that although all parents intentions were pure, they needed to understand that each of their children are unique and therefore required *a different leadership style* rather than using a *'one size fit all'* approach. Many of the inmates revealed that was what had robbed them of their chance of living a decent family life.

In an online survey, Professor Walynski had recorded the following facts from the inmates he had contacted. (1) more than 60% stated that they grew up with only one parent, (2) more than 87% stated that they grew up with their mothers who had to play the dual parental role, (3) under 10% stated they grew up with their fathers as the sole parent who had to play the dual role (4) over 18% grew up with other family members who played the role of both parents (5) over 47% were adopted but did not know their original parents (6) over 37% wanted to make contact with their original parents (8) 93.8% suffered from low self-esteem issues (9) 77% had purposely committed crime to draw the attention of their families due to the lack of quality time that was missing from their lives and (10) due to the chaotic confusion in their minds about *'cultural values and beliefs'*, shockingly 100% had some form of **'ID'** issues.

The UFO *'puppeteers'* and their assigned associates (*'puppets'*) were the *'Mental Slave Masters'* who sold the *'hard sell'* *'scripts'* to the franchisees. They specifically targeted and played on the weaknesses but relentlessly exploited the young generations' naivety. Subliminally, they fed them corruptive *'ideas'* at a *'post-hypnotic level'* and treated them like fodder. Behaviours like *'mass individuation'* were achieved by using special psychological command elements via technological visual and audio techniques. It was no different or subtler than watching or hearing an advert on radio or television. Once the young generations were *'plugged in'*, they were being summoned but instructed via subliminal super-highway messaging towards a plethora of inadvertent commitment to a series of variable suicidal options. These were being referred to in the Post/Zip Code communities as **'bravado'**. The *'mental constructs'* drove the different categories of delusional suicidal thinking that most were not even aware of but which drove their stinking, toxic attitudes, schizophrenic mentalities and emotionally insensitive behaviours. *'Suicide by cop'* and *'suicide by slaying'* were as real as the à la carte menus of *'stereo-tripe'* or those subliminal messages being channelled through the *Pied Piper's* lyrics, virtual crime movies or game console commands, scenes or themes which had been used as resources embedding the *'love for violence'* *'stereo-hype'* the *'converts'* had consumed so willingly whilst having *'fun'*, apparently!. In their quest to accumulate the type of financial abundance they had been skilfully led to believe was available to them, the young generations were persuaded by the UFO and their associate franchisees. The GMP worked directly with the GOS, their subordinates the GOO, GOP and subsequently to those lower ranking *'models'* which obediently carried out the *'roles'* assigned them.

The process was well organised but appeared seamless. Young generations were being duped. In each Post/Zip Code gang, there was at least one infiltrator planted amongst each gang by the GOO. These individuals were GOP trained by their *'puppeteers'* how to infiltrate the 'Cult-Induced' Post/Zip Code gangs. First, those individual GOP infiltrators established the leaders of the gangs then worked with them until, they had learned about all the leaders' contacts. Once that had been established, the leader would be *'set up'*. Those leaders would be disposed of by being lured into environments of rivalry with another endz which had been triggered by something really trivial called *'pasa-pasa'* or *'beefs'*, which had been instigated by the *'rumour mill'* but was untrue 98% of the time. When settling *'pasa-pasa'* or *'beefs'*, leaders and their flock of *'sheep'* would be rounded up by Law Enforcement Personnel. They worked with and were being tipped off by the GOP who had infiltrated the gang. Those leaders would be *'ousted'* via custodial sentences. If another leader didn't step up, the infiltrator would encourage someone else to step up as leader. He would be encouraged to believe that there was a *'snitch'* within the gangs. The trust levels would now be at its lowest and all kinds of accusations would develop amongst the gang members. This ploy meant that individuals had to prove themselves to the new leaders or *'ride or die'* without any *'protection'* from other members of the gang. It is at this point where each gang member is inveigled to accept those *'roles'* given to them but had to prove themselves as the ideal *'models'* by slaying each other in the UFO 'Cult-Induced' Posts/Zip Code Wars. In pursuit of *'Street*

Credits', the younger generations carried out the embedded commands by *'living fast'* but *'died trying'* or were imprisoned in the same manner as their previous leaders, favourite characters or *'role model' 'heroes'*.

The UFO had created regions like Ghettoville, Painsville, Craterville and Odourville in Lower Ghettoborough. They were questioned by Media about the possibility of overcrowding in the limited spaces being provided. Representatives from the UFO said that overcrowding might force immigrants to *"self-repatriate"*. When pressed to decode their cryptic message, the green humanoid robotron representatives of the UFO in the Kingdom of Spaceville stated that the children of ethnic Spacevilleans were the probable *"self-repatriates"*. If they felt uncomfortable in the limited environments but had chosen to enter the criminal world, their choice was uncomplicated. They could choose either to be imprisoned on the *'Floating Prisons'* or select to be deported to the exotic continents, countries and islands of the original immigrant families, notwithstanding how far down the chain of generations or the fact that they might have been born in the relevant borough.

In contrast to the green humanoid UFO's influence with regards to inveigling young males into violence, there was another side to their unbridled depth of influence. They had a different strategy towards females. Their vulnerability were observed, noted, assesses, audited, reviewed but re-evaluated before a strategy was devised about how to best approach the female population of the Mixed DNA Rainbow Tribe and those of the Tribes of Duke and Hawke. The UFO was convinced that *'vanity'* was not only a common factor but also the major *'weakness'* of the majority of females from those tribes on the parallel virtual planet. Whilst in his comatose state, Raymondo's dream movie had placed Sandra into the limelight as achieving her dream of rubbing shoulders with the *'who's who'* in becoming an *'A' Blister Super Model*. Whilst accepting demeaning *'roles'* to fit the subservient, *'politically accepted'* perennial *'stereo-typical' 'model'*, she became an *'accomplished' Award Winning Celebrity Actress* but had been *'airbrushed'* to accommodate but reinforce the perceptions of the green humanoid robotron Tribe of Babylon. When it suited them to dethrone her, the scheming demons outcast Sandra as the *'misfit'* she had become. She had acceded to their ruse and finally *'crossed over'* to the *'other side'* of her perceived *'ideal'* but regretted the isolation she endured both in the Village of Urgington and on the other side of the mountain in the exquisite environs of Champagne Valley, subsequently. During her fall from the height of becoming an *'A' Blister Super Model* Socialite and *Award Winning Actress* to her slide into the enormous jaws of oblivion, Sandra's only companions in those moments in the solid gold Roman Bath were the apparition of her ideal *'Trophy Man Image'*, *'Mr Right'*, which she had been *'programmed'* and *'conditioned'* to perceive as *'ideal'* and the lethal cocktail of *'legal drugs'* she continued to imbibe in those moments.

Despite all the barriers, Sandra and Duke had managed to overcome them but the cost had been so immense that the relationships that they had formed along their individual journeys were proven to be not as genuine as they might have perceived or preferred. Even Duke's spiral from grace was alleged to be caused by his brother, Baron. He had openly welcomed and shared with his brother but least expected that Baron might seek to destroy the empire that their father, Earl, had established before his premature death from alcoholism. There still was no proof that it wasn't Duke who had framed Baron, probably! Even Sheila, their adopted grandmother, their biological grandfather, Raleigh, their friends from the gang Clout or the girls, Mari, Gordy and Joseté, who had helped them to continue to celebrate their eighteenth birthdays, could really not tell the difference between the twin brothers. Sandra's *'values and beliefs'* were as different to Duke's as his was to the Tribe of Babylon. Even so, both their experiences were different in content and context. On their individual journeys, Duke was allowed to *'merge'* because of his reputation and financial abundance. Sandra's experience had made her stand out in her modelling career only because she could be *'airbrushed'* into the *'commodity'* that was acceptably tolerated. Expectations of the green humanoid robotron Editors of Magazines and their *'preferred'* consumers demanded Sandra appear as green in colour as the green humanoid robotrons from the Tribe of Babylon. They saw themselves as being superior. From her conception to her seeming demise, Sandra was always what someone else wanted her to be, sadly. According to her *'values and beliefs'*, her mother, Dian, had planned and schemed what Sandra might become. During her career, Sandra was the *'model'* that was made to fit the *'role'* that everyone else wanted her to become according to their *'values and beliefs'*. When it suited others like Baron or Duke to scheme to isolate Sandra by using the *'tool'* of disinformation to besmirch her character, one or both of them ensured that, her resistance to refusing to become a *'Commercial Escort'* with one or either of them as her personal pimp, drove her to and over the edge of mental abyss, probably!

It seemed going over the edge of *'mental abyss'* was the only option Duke or Baron had left her. Sandra had become delirious with an avalanche of negative emotions, tempestuous mood swings and cyclonic *'mental spirals'*. It was like watching water disappearing swiftly down an unblocked drain. Collectively, these negative emotions and tempestuous mood swings ruptured her super-inflated ego but collapsed her seemingly valiant charge towards the robotic tunnel-vision pursuit of *'artificial mental decorations'*. Instead, Sandra's genius capabilities might have served her better had her goals been set **towards gaining more meaningful achievements with fulfilment,** probably!

While in a comatose state, Raymondo's dream of the highly controversial Classy, Epic Wik-**ID**-Fiction © Literary Docudrama Movie © made up of Fictional Virtual Realities Scenarios, © written, directed and produced by his two brains, Hifle and Pifle, had provided copious amounts of *'stereo-hype'*, *'stereo-tripe'* and *'stereo-types'*. Now that he was fully awake, the thought of Sandra drowning in that solid gold Roman Bath had sent spine-chilling spasms through his entire body but seemed to still make him shudder, somewhat!

There were attempts to undermine then block Raymondo de Oddballo's investigative documentary from being aired on television or be reported in traditional written Media. The best legal Eagles and Eaglets jostled to impose the will of the *'minority'* yet highly influential UFO upon the *'majority'*. Members of the most officious infamous 'Asteroidean Financial Alliance', the AFA, threatened the *"Mother of all Armageddon"* to befall the Television and Printed Media that dared to challenge the chain of poly-trickster led authorities with real political clout. They were involved in the reprehensible practices, which rendered the parallel virtual planet of Asteroidia as the most corrupted in the World of Space. What Raymondo's documentary had done was to present the researched *'facts'* but highlight how the heavily partisan UFO had managed to spread their most disgustingly odious *'mental viral pandemic'*. It had grown like bacteria in culture dishes and had mutated beyond control but been ingested by the metaphoric *'host octopuses'* that had managed to spread their tentacles across the Dis-United Kingdoms of the parallel virtual planet in the World of Space. Pamela, Ras-Dan and Darsna had watched the Investigative Documentary on the social websites but could not understand why the once shadowy phantoms raged vengeance against their husband and father, Raymondo. As far as they and those other individuals, who had seen the documentary film were concerned he was only doing his job like any other investigative journalist.

The objection raised by the UFO towards Raymondo's documentary film, had brought it to the attention of 'The Intergalactic Oversight Lords'. They were now in charge of the investigation but had charged specialist committees, chaired by seemingly *'non-partisan'* eminent Inter-Kingdom Supreme Court Judges from around the Royal Royal Dis-United Stately Kingdoms of Asteroidia, with the responsibilities to delve into the UFO's alleged malpractices referred to by Raymondo's highly controversial documentary film. Many other investigative journalists had been encouraged by Raymondo's passion for *'Justice'* but none had catered for the caustic responses from those guilt-stricken individuals and their cronies. Some of those were eminent Inter-Kingdom Supreme Court Judges themselves, who were active members of the UFO. Some were being paid large sums of Champagne Urge in offshore bank accounts to rule in favour of the septic-minded UFO. It was a matter of "you scratch my back and I'll scratch yours" and "the old school tie" philosophies. These were included in the behaviours being uploaded from planet Earth to the parallel virtual planet of Asteroidia. The UFO and their legal affiliates seemed hell-bent to prove beyond any element of doubt that *'Justice'* did not exist beyond *'Just This'* that Raymondo was experiencing.

The UFO's version of democracy had suffered its worst blow as social media provided for more *'whistleblowers'* under the guise of *'freedom of speech'* to step up to the plate but support their colleague, Raymondo. He was experiencing the type of backlash that proved there was a filter of political webs securely in place which seemingly caught the aspiring *'interfering flies'*, whom dared to test the strengths of those webs, probably! For Raymondo de Oddballo, the risk was not only to his career or reputation but also to the consequential incessant disinformation that seemed to be developing as rapidly as an avalanche down an extraordinarily steep decline. The total mass gathered like a humungous mudslide with such momentum which defied even the Laws of Physics. Raymondo was the scapegoat and he peered into the glare of the extremely bright full beamed headlights of not one but several dozen juggernauts all at once. He appeared to be as insignificant in proportion to the mighty UFO like a fly under the attention of several spotlights altogether. The UFO's appetite for vengeance probed unfairly into Raymondo's background but challenged his Spacevillean birth even. All the representatives of the UFO whom pretended to be more importantly *'worthier than thou'* openly demanded Raymondo prove the authenticity of his birthplace not once but incessantly so. His ethnicity was causative for those *'worthier than thou'* individuals and groups to question the authenticity of his qualifications as well as whether Raymondo's assumed *"smaller inferior brain"* was capable of the brilliance he had shown as an *'Ace'* *student* at the prestigiously exclusive Bastardé University from which he had graduated.

The proponents of disinformation seemed to want to enter into Raymondo's very soul, seeking to break his spirit and destroy his will. Six months earlier Raymondo's home in the leafier suburb of Upborough, which he had deservedly purchased for him and his family, was targeted for not one but a series of dawn raids by a *'Special Unit'*. They were ably assisted by television and printed Media on each occasion. When the *'Special Unit'* was being questioned by other investigative colleagues from around the parallel virtual planet, they said they were "just carrying out instructions". The Warrants were issued and was so authenticated by Eminent Judges, who were active members of the UFO. On each raid, the Forensic arm of the *'Special Unit'*, dressed in white boiler suits and gloves, removed items like computers and skeins of paper, books and files from the family home. Many of the neighbours blamed Raymondo and his family for bringing their seemingly *'peaceful'*, *'non-criminal'* environment into "gross disrepute". As part of their repertoire, the Special Unit brought trained mixed DNA laboratory produced Bull Mastiffs and Pit Bulls Terriers. They dragged their handlers along. The trained chained DNA laboratory produced Alligators salivated as their dual-handlers struggled to keep them from attacking Raymondo and his family.

The Militia *'Special Unit'* personnel dressed in helmets with visors and a swarm of acid yellow uniforms were the armed personnel that surrounded the de Oddballo's home on each occasion they chose to execute a dawn raid. They displayed assault weapons with clips that housed from 100 to 150 rounds of bullets, which were capable of exploding immediately after entering a body, as well as rocket launchers and shoulder held bazookas. Agents dressed in bespoke suits, straw hats and white patent spats, poised with shoulder holsters, liaised with the blue Mixed DNA Rainbow Tribe Captain with the huge shiny badge just above her left breast. She had given instructions to her subordinates to dress Raymondo and his family in bright orange colour coveralls with hands cuffed waist high but attached to body belts. He and his family wore foot chains which restricted them from "attempting to escape", apparently! All of these restrictions confirmed the mentality of the green humanoid robotrons, who had trained the blue Mixed DNA Rainbow Tribe Captain. The paranoid schizophrenic robotrons high levels of addiction to fear and their mentality towards choosing to treat individuals from the Tribe of Hawke especially in this way, was being observed by significant others. They observed the tactics that were being employed and could see that Raymondo, his wife and two young children posed no threat to the number of official attendees to their home. The children were traumatised but mystified what made them have to wear these implements of torture. They were far too young to know that in previous millennia this was *'normal'* for chattel slaves on the parallel planet Earth or even that some individuals in Human Zoos were wearing these *'restrictors'* daily in the parallel virtual planet of Asteroidia, *"for their own safety"*, apparently!

Raymondo and his family were hauled like bags of heavy posts along the floor but deposited into the back of the huge vehicles, hovering just above the ground that had arrived for their *'collection'*. Helicopters hovered overhead with thermal imaging devices whilst drones reconnoitred at a greater distance above ready to take out indigenous and foreign *'insurgents'* with precise accuracy. Space TV, STV, and the others fought to produce the most sensational headlines in the Media on the virtual planet of Asteroidia but present exclusive pictures that would accompany their *'breaking news'* on Television from Satellites hovering even further above the drones in the stratosphere into the World of Space. Raymondo de Oddballo protested against the harsh injustice but was physically discouraged from speaking at all.

He had managed to lift the heavy drapes that had been shielding the phantoms from their underhand practices that had devastated the lives of many generations including Raymondo's and his parents, who were now deceased. He had dedicated his efforts into becoming a brilliant political historian, analyst and relentless investigative journalist to his parents. Raymondo's precision on the finer details meant that the affiliations which were being formed against him had once appeared as separate entities, but could now be seen as a singular homogenous, wholesome plot to deceive not only the populations of the Royal Royal Dis-United Stately Kingdoms of Asteroidia but also the far off exotic continents, countries and islands, particularly. These were also a part of the parallel virtual planet of Asteroidia.

Some of Raymondo's comments had disturbed the political hornets' nests and he would be made to pay for prising open the *'fissures'* that were beginning to become much wider *'cracks'* into the seemingly rock-solid falsehoods that politicrats like Clovis Staccato and his colleagues had previously oversold to the populations around the World of Space. Clovis Staccato was a member of the opposition to the current ruling party led by The Most Honourable Prime Leader, Janet Brayhorne. He had been summoned to meet with his green humanoid robotron's most influential senior committee members of the UFO. They asked him to use his portfolio as Opposition Senate member for Spaceville to recommend what to do with *"the bothersome* Raymondo de Oddballo". The UFO had stressed to Clovis Staccato that they needed to come up with a strategy to dissuade Raymondo from carrying through his threat to expose them via his much researched documentary film. Clovis Staccato had been installed by the hugely influential VIP poly-tricksters, who were active senior members of the UFO. They had paid huge amounts of Spacevillean Champagne Urge to boost his chances of becoming a Senator. He owed them more than a *'favour'*. Clovis Staccato got in touch with Professor Frank Outstein. He knew that Professor Frank Outstein was an eccentric old codger but he was not aware that the genial Professor was now a victim of the *'burn out' syndrome* which was causative to his psychosis and that he was no longer a *'fit and proper'* person to carry out his function sanely. Instead, Clovis Staccato was really relying on the relationship they had had as friends since middle school.

CHAPTER 58

After the much publicised final dawn raid, Raymondo was taken to a nearby island to be investigated on a charge of treason. Pamela and the children were taken to another part of the same island but charged as his accomplices. They were placed into separate rooms in an old Fort but questioned on their knowledge of Raymondo's alleged crime. Whilst Pamela was being questioned, she was subjected to the type of interrogation that befitted the fabled 'Inquisition'. Restricted in the infamous Stock, only her head, two hands and legs could be viewed from the front. In that position, enforced insomnia greeted Pamela's many sleepless nights. Sleep depravation was a form of torture more commonplace with insurgents in times of war but none of the inquisitors cared. They applied it anyway. The inquisitors were instructed to be *"as relentless as they needed to be"* in order to secure a confession from Pamela against her husband. Raymondo suffered from sleep depravation too. He was also beaten on the soles of his feet, tazered and *'water-boarded'* at least twice per day but managed to steel his will against all odds. The children were questioned relentlessly about what they knew about their father. When they denied that their father was "an enemy of the Kingdom of Spaceville", they experienced psychoanalysis at a very deep level for their "own good". Darsna and Ras-Dan were threatened that they might be taken away from their parents but sent to separate Homes for "naughty children". The bullying tactics were meant to "break them" but acted as leverage by the inquisitors "to extract the *'truth'* from their parents". It was a most frightening experience for Raymondo and Pamela's children to endure but they stuck to the only story they knew and that was that their parents were not "enemies of the Kingdom of Spaceville".

Eventually, Pamela and the children were released but surveillance on their every move was a regular daily occurrence. Even their individual shadows could not be closer than the electronic bugs that tracked but displayed their every move. Raymondo was detailed to spend time on the island. He was being treated as the brown, pink, purple, white, blue and yellow combatants, who occupied it as alleged *'insurgents'*. Raymondo had not committed any crime yet his punishment was meant to be a *"deterrent"* to others, who might venture to dare to interfere or challenge the *'magnetic pull'* away from becoming members of the *'all mighty'* UFO, seemingly! All Raymondo had done was to use the social websites to tell of his discoveries as an investigative journalist. As a *'prisoner'* charged with the crime of treason *('free speech')*, he wore the cuffs, body belt and foot chains attached to heavy balls which made it difficult for him to walk. The metal ate into his flesh but caused infections to the sores which appeared underneath the metal shackles.

Raymondo heard the other inmates scream often but witnessed many of them being physically abused. The guards were made up of some from the Tribe of Hawke, the Tribe of Duke and the Mixed DNA Rainbow Tribe but mainly of the green humanoid robotrons from the Tribe of Babylon. They instigated but carried out beatings with fists as well as butts of guns, with sticks and odd-looking whips called *'cat-o-nine tails'* with razorwire attached to the ends. When it suited them, the green humanoid robotrons would delegate the use of the whips to the guards from the Tribe of Hawke. Raymondo noticed that this delegation took place whenever the individuals to be punished were from the Tribe of Hawke. He too had been beaten by both green humanoid robotron guards from the Tribe of Babylon and those from the Tribe of Hawke. Raymondo agreed that neither were pleasant experiences but there were extra efforts of force being inputted when the whips were in the hands of the guards from the Tribe of Hawke against inmates from their own tribe. With every stroke of the whip, the throaty sounds of ahmmm, ahmmm, ahmmm followed, indicating the magnification and expansion of effort being applied. It resonated but could be heard as far away as a quarter of a mile from where the whipping was taking place. These whippings were used to inflict the wrath of the guards whenever they were in bad moods or desired to *"show authority"*. It seemed the guards from the Tribe of Hawke chose to be in severely bad moods often or wanted to show their authority to individuals from their tribe more so than to any other tribes on the island. There was something about the guards from the Tribe of Hawke against their own tribe or that they believed they had a need to express their subservience by over-extending themselves as a kind of proof to their masters about their level of allegiance but defaulted commitment to the cause, perhaps! Raymondo noticed how the guards from the Tribe of Hawke took it upon themselves to administer punishment upon inmates from the Tribe of Hawke more cruelly than they did even to alleged insurgents. Those guards were often praised by their green humanoid robotron *'puppeteers'* from the Tribe of Babylon. The guards from the Tribe of Hawke accepted the eagerly anticipated obligatory pat on their bottoms, backs and heads, like household pets for showing their full commitment in admonishing particular inmates from the Tribe of Hawke, especially. As a result to the whippings, the smell of inmates, who had urinated or excreted on themselves because they had gone way beyond their pain thresholds, drifted across from one crypt to another or in the direction of the wind.

The food was minimal but disgusting when served. Many, like Raymondo, refused to eat the cockroach infested muck that was ill-prepared but was often spat upon or urinated into by the guards in front of the recipients before the *'meals'* were given to them. Most of the inmates had lost weight because of the lack of sustenance. There was one purple man, who was just skin and bones, literally. His skin looked like a thin purple sheet hanging on a skeleton. He had lost most of his musculature. The gaunt look upon his face accentuated by the sunken eye sockets, creased loose purple skin hanging from his high cheekbones drooped even further still under his chin like the folding of excess purple drapes hanging in suspense. When the wind blew, the sheet-like skin moved to its rhythmic impact like 'G-Forces' upon a motorist's face exposed to the elements in a vehicle, without a roof, moving at high speed. This powerful picture haunted Raymondo whilst he was awake but also in his sleep, whenever he was allowed to. The gaunt faced man was weakened by his ordeal but had shown defiance to his captors that rendered them powerless over his mental strength to carry out his hunger strike in opposition to their best efforts to conquer his mind. Raymondo was told by other inmates that, even when the captors force fed the man, his body system was so deteriorated that it could not process nor retain the liquid food even.

Each day one of the insurgents would be summoned but escorted by armed guards away from the group of inmates. One told Raymondo that there was a green humanoid robotron psychiatrist/psychoanalyst that was experimenting with the chosen individuals. As it was being explained to him, Raymondo heard his name being called by a guard. He felt an intense feeling of nervousness known as *'the collywobbles'*. Raymondo was escorted by five armed guards. The sixth one sat in the vehicle that had arrived to take him across the other side of the island. When he arrived there, Raymondo saw the wild look in the face of the psychiatrist/psychoanalyst. He introduced himself as Professor Frank Outstein. Raymondo felt a chill come over him but he did not recognise it as fear. Still, he could hear his heart thumping against his chest. The Professor said nothing but busied himself walking around Raymondo as if he were just taken from a *'slave'* ship but was being inspected for evaluation before being auctioned off to a plantation owner. Professor Frank Outstein wrote copious notes into the electronic *'Me-Pad'* © he carried with him. Raymondo observed the eccentric movements and behaviours of the psychiatrist/psychoanalyst.

The door opened and a nurse walked in. She was dressed in white uniform, white stockings, soft white shoes and huge triangular white headgear. The nurse had a receptacle with a huge syringe nearly a foot long and a needle, about nine inches long, attached to it. She put on some white plastic gloves before approaching the trolley-bed Raymondo was asked to sit on. The nurse approached him. Using both hands to support the unusually large syringe, she pressed the end of it but some of the clear fluid squirted from the large needle. Professor Frank Outstein looked from the nurse to Raymondo then nodded. She gave Raymondo a blue and white chequered gown. He placed his hands through the openings but left the streamers behind him untied. Neither the nurse nor Professor Frank Outstein spoke directly to him but they seemed to know the routine. She encouraged Raymondo to lie on his stomach in a prone position. He felt the jab of the long needle as it stabbed into one side of his bum cheek. Raymondo was unsure how much of the needle had entered his gluteus maximus. His bum cheek felt numb then the rest of his body seemed to follow. Raymondo tried to speak but there was no movement from his jaws. The nurse turned him over onto his back into the supine position.

It was the first time Raymondo noticed the spotlight which shone from the ceiling. It was positioned directly in line with his eyes but seemed to get brighter. Although the glare was almost blinding him, Raymondo could do nothing about it. Even the muscles around his eyes seemed not to work. He stared into the blinding beam without being able to squint. Eventually, the light became dimmer and dimmer until it went out. Professor Frank Outstein and the nurse left the room. The ceiling became a sea of psychedelic colours which seemed to change seamlessly. It was as if there was a lamp with these colours being shone unto the ceiling from the floor. Raymondo could not tell how long he had been in the room but he remembered going off unto a strange journey that was dreamlike.

As the numbness started to disappear, Raymondo realised he could now squint his eyes again. Even when he was able to close his eyes the psychedelic colours still stayed in his vision. Raymondo was feeling as if his body was not touching the trolley-bed anymore. As his body seemed to float above the trolley-bed, he felt completely full of new found energy. Raymondo recalled the nurse looking like an angel appearing in mid air and she didn't look like the dragon with the white tri-corn headgear but a more alluring being that beckoned him towards her. The nurse's pale green skin seemed as smooth as a peach. She appeared to be more alluring and beautiful than his wife, Pamela. Raymondo was tempted but felt lustful towards the angelic looking nurse. Her smile was mesmerising and he felt the urgency below his groin. All Raymondo could think of was entering the cavern between the nurse's crotch and resolving the need he wanted to fulfil, urgently. He rose into a sitting position but shook his head to see if this was a dream or was the nurse real. Time was of no essence. All he wanted to do was to satisfy the desires of the flesh. The apparition of the nurse started to fade and Raymondo struggled to understand how that was possible. He could hear himself shouting, "Please don't leave now", Raymondo pleaded.

Professor Frank Outstein's voice was quite pronounced but his question was quite specific. "Did you like how you feel", he enquired? "Yes. I like this feeling very much. I want that nurse", Raymondo confessed. He told of his dreamlike desire to become closer with the angelic apparition. Professor Frank Outstein couldn't hide the smile as he listened to Raymondo's acknowledgement of his weakness of the flesh. "You can choose to feel this way again but we have some work to do. It depends how you react. That lovely nurse can make you feel even better for longer. Do you understand", he queried? Raymondo heard himself responding to the Professor. "Now tell me about your hallucinations about those people who you write about", the Professor encouraged. Raymondo was almost back to full consciousness. "I've not been having any hallucinations. It's is a matter of investigative journalism", he defended. The Professor paused but reminded Raymondo about what he thought he saw in the room earlier on. "Tell me again about your experience earlier", the Professor queried. Raymondo repeated his experience. "So, where is the nurse now", the Professor challenged? "She faded away", Raymondo said. "There was no nurse floating towards you. That's what I mean by hallucinations", the Professor reinforced. Raymondo could not defend what he had described to the Professor but he was sure of what he thought he had seen. "I guess she was very alluring", the Professor confirmed? Before Raymondo could figure out what he thought he had seen, the Professor spoke again. "Was there anything else you thought you saw", he asked? "Yes", Raymondo replied. "Tell me about it", the Professor encouraged. Raymondo told of the psychedelic lights on the ceiling. The Professor smiled. "Look up at the ceiling. What colour is it", he asked? Without hesitation, Raymondo replied, "white". The Professor smiled. "So you realise what I'm saying about hallucinations, do you", he asked? Raymondo was feeling that the Professor was referring to someone other than him. He could not understand what happened earlier but he was sure he saw the psychedelic colours on the ceiling just as he'd seen the apparition of the nurse. Raymondo resolved that it was futile to argue with the Professor. He just lay on the trolley-bed wondering what was going on inside his head. "That will be all for today", the Professor said. Raymondo dressed himself just in time. The guards seem to know how long his ordeal would last. They took him back to the other side of the island where he shared a crypt with the alleged *'insurgents'*. Raymondo could not sleep that night. His mind was in turmoil. One of the things that he was wondering about is whether he was going out of his mind. The confusion played havoc with his thinking. What was happening to him? The visit to the Professor carried on for two weeks consistently. Each time the process and the experience was the same. By the end of the second week, Raymondo just wanted to clear the confusion from his mind.

His wish was about to happen but not in the way he might have preferred. On his next visit to the Professor, Raymondo told him that he too had started to believe that he was hallucinating and that he valued and bowed to the psychiatrist/psychoanalyst authoritative expertise. He was ready for the Professor to *"free"* him from the nightmarish hallucinations that he was experiencing. Raymondo begged the Professor to inject him with the same chemical that had given him the buzz he found himself craving. He was like a crazed drug addict, who found his addiction a *'comforter'* rather than a threat to his/her well being. The Professor winked at the nurse but smiled wryly in contemplation of his success in introducing the drug into Raymondo's bloodstream. Now, the Professor had Raymondo hooked on the hallucinary drug. He told Raymondo that he could help him to remove all hallucinations permanently. The Professor explained that there were two types of treatment. One was called the Electric Shock Therapy. He assured Raymondo that this had been used for years but he lied that it had been mostly successful.

Raymondo agreed to allow the Professor the latitude to administer his scientific expertise. "You should know what's best for me doctor", Raymondo submitted. The nurse was summoned by the Professor. He whispered into her ear then she left the room.

When she returned, there were four men with her. Each were like giants but looked solid and strong, as if they were honed from granite. They approached Raymondo but placed him on this special bed but strapped him down with six thick leather belts. One went across his chest and upper arms which lay by his side, one across his midriff and lower arms, one across his upper thighs just below his waist, one on his lower thighs just above his knees, one just under his knees and the smallest across both his ankles. The nurse asked Raymondo to open his mouth but stuck an irregular shaped hard leather stopper, which held his tongue in place but restricted Raymondo from biting it or his inner jaws. The end of the hard stopper kept his mouth open but stuck out of his mouth like a very thick Cuban cigar with a diameter of about four to five inches. Raymondo awaited the *fix* from the injection to satisfy his crave but it never came. Instead, he felt the probes being attached to the sides of his head. The sudden convulsions, which were severe enough to break bones, were all that Raymondo felt as the 2000 volts went through his head. He felt disoriented and was only aware of the second and third shocks because of their increase in voltage. The second shock had an intensity of 2500 volts and the third 3000 volts. Even the nurse shouted for Professor Frank Outstein to stop. His dedication to the phantom group to quieten the *"interfering headline seeking journalist"* was enough for the crazed scientist to want to apply a fourth increase in the severity of high voltage to Raymondo's brain. When it was applied, the voltage was a staggering 4000 volts. This time Raymondo's head twisted to one side but seemed to stay locked in that position as if it had made a voluntary autonomic *'correctional'* adjustment. A lopsided *'grimaced smile'* re-patterned the contours of Raymondo's once handsome feature into an awesome grotesque distorted mask befitting Professor Frank Outstein's grotesquely twisted mindset. Even the four granite looking men grimaced too as they witnessed the look of *'madness'* on the Professor's face. He was smiling now as if he was gaining some sort of crude satisfaction from the torturous applications of Electric Shock Therapy. Raymondo's stare was far beyond the ceiling. The look on his face was that of a zombie. His body was still convulsing to the irregular spasms that might have been more pronounced had they not been restricted by the *'safety'* belts. The nurse saw the foam oozing from the corners of Raymondo's mouth. She brought it to the attention of the Professor. "It's probably his hallucinations escaping", he joked cynically. He turned but walked out of the room. There was nothing the others could do so they left the room too. The shock treatment was administered to Raymondo every three days until he wore the stupor of a mentally disturbed individual, who had been given a mind-bending drug.

When he was being tortured by Sergeant Gruff and his rookies, Raymondo had worn that same silly smile which resembled that of a smiling donkey on a holiday postcard. It had reappeared. Even his walk seemed like that of a mentally ill patient who had been drugged up to the eyeballs on the type of medication which confused the alignment orientation between the top and bottom half of his body. The upper part of Raymondo's body twisted from the waist into a different direction to the bottom half. It made him seem crablike in his gait; walking sideward as if walking into strong gale force winds. Raymondo's head hung to one side as if his neck had been repositioned permanently and he wore the silly smirk which seemed to be not only painted on but also locked in place. He looked downwards rather bashfully towards the ground as if he was deliberately avoiding eye contact with another individual whose stare was more powerful than his.

Most of the alleged *'insurgents'* noticed the change in the genial character. Raymondo no longer held conversations with them but spent his time being an *'obedient servant'* instead. He was volunteering for more work from his captors. One alleged *'insurgent'* heard him asking, "Have you got anything else you want done master"? Raymondo had become the laughing stock of the guards but posed a threat to the alleged *'insurgents'*. They were unsure what game he might be playing. Raymondo ate the disgusting cockroach infested food on which the guards openly spat and pissed on before handing it too him. He would wolf it down but begged for more like the fabled 'Oliver', "please sir, can I have some more". Raymondo sat alone but did not involve himself in the limited exercises that he was afforded. He was a broken man. The next week the Professor told Raymondo that he had great news for him. He listened keenly like the ardent student he had become. "What have you got for me doctor", he asked? "You're now ready for the next phase of treatment", Professor Frank Outstein announced. It didn't seem to make Raymondo feel any better. He just said "OK, doctor, you know what's best for me". It was sad that there was no resistance coming from the previously frank speaking Raymondo but now it seemed that he was ready to be *'the human guinea pig'*, willingly!

The second procedure was what the Professor called a *"physical operation"*. It consisted of removing the top part of Raymondo's skull in order to access and use a probe to rid him of his seemingly *'delusional'* thoughts about the phantom gang around the virtual planet of Asteroidia. The only consensus of opinion was that of Professor Frank Outstein. No one else's seemed to matter to him. He had carte blanche freedom to do as he saw fit to these inmates without redress. Who would dare complain against one so eminent and revered? To whom would one address the complaint? Who could afford to take legal action against the moguls, who funded Professor Frank Outstein's torturous experiments but shared his *'values and beliefs'*? There were *'Think Tanks'* and large Institutions that backed the genial Professor but none was aware or even cared about his psychopathic psychosis. Who would dare question his *'ethical standards'* or lack of them, rather? Raymondo de Oddballo did not have the weight of financial clout behind him to take on a man, who already had buildings, streets, trophies and awards named after him. He seemed to have become one of the *'untouchables'*. Professor Frank Outstein of 'The Outstein Institute', was confident that he could rid Raymondo of his *'delusions'* about "the men of great steel", as he put it.

Raymondo was prepared by an anaesthetist but he sat strapped into a special chair. The whirring of the rotating blade sound did not disturb the anaesthetized, fully relaxed Raymondo but he could hear everything that was being said in the operating room. Professor Frank Outstein used the autopsy electric saw with the round blade to remove the top part of Raymondo's skull. "Now young man, I want you to tell me about the things you discussed in your documentary", the Professor probed. Raymondo obediently obliged. There was no pain but he could feel the heat from the probe that looked like a soldering iron as it burnt away the *'delusional memories'*. Each time the Professor asked Raymondo to recall the details relevant to the allegations he prodded an area in his brain to remove that particular memory. The procedure lasted for about thirty minutes. At the end, Professor Frank Outstein asked Raymondo if he could sing a little ditty but Raymond said he didn't know any. "I'll teach you one. When you come from under the anaesthetic you'll remember the little ditty I taught you", the Professor declared. Whilst using another probe, Professor Frank Outstein sang the little ditty to install it into Raymondo's memory. He fetched the top of Raymondo's skull from the table beside him but put it back in place then sewed the skull back on. "We can control humans", Professor Frank Outstein declared. He laughed uncontrollably as if the madness had begun to fully manifest. Raymondo was then sent to the recovery room. He spent three months in a private room. On one of his visits, Professor Frank Outstein asked Raymondo if he remembered any of the allegations. He said he didn't. The Professor asked him if he remembered the little ditty. Raymondo sang it over and over like a child in kindergarten then he commented. "I can't remember where I learnt that doctor", Raymondo submitted. Professor Frank Outstein knew that he was successful. He smiled broadly with pride before sauntering off to tell his *'bosses'* that they had nothing to fear from the *"interfering little guttersnipe"*, as he put it. The leader of the phantom gang praised Professor Frank Outstein but told him that there would be more funding for his organisation and a huge donation, in his name, to the charity of his choice. The Professor was also assured that he would receive a personal award publicly *"for services rendered to the parallel virtual planet of Asteroidia"*. It was later that afternoon that the nurse informed the Professor that Raymondo had fallen into a comatose state. He did not seem worried but asked if Raymondo was brain dead, maybe! The nurse said she didn't know. It was then that Professor Frank Outstein stated that Raymondo had to be hooked up to the relevant machines to keep him alive. He confided that Raymondo was a rare specimen. "What do you mean", the nurse queried? "He has two brains", the Professor whispered. "Two brains", the nurse asked? "Yes. One sits on top of the other", the Professor replied. He called some colleagues to come to see the man with the two brains. Professor Frank Outstein told them that Raymondo was both mammal and reptilian. "Quite unusual", they commented. With their curiosities raised to a very high level, scientists from across the World of Space started to arrive on the island. Raymondo could hear their comments but he could not respond. The anaesthetics had long gone from his system but he lay attached to several machines. The Professor told his colleagues that, in order to properly monitor the man with the two brains, Raymondo would have to be taken back to Spaceville University Teaching Hospital in Upborough. It was Professor Frank Outstein that had named the two brains 'Hifle' and 'Pifle'. Had it not been for them, the Professor would have declared Raymondo *'brain dead'* a long time ago, probably!

CHAPTER 59

Raymondo gently opened his eyes to confirm that he had not entered into another dreamlike state. Lying on his back, he surveyed the ceiling then rolled his eyes around generally. The eggshell white walls matched the white ceiling but his vision was interrupted by the busy contrast that the partially drawn floral screen offered. The colours seemed so vivid that Raymondo welcomed the burgundy red roses which stood out vividly amongst the mixture of shades of green foliage as well as the yellow stamens which seemed to burst from the insides of the crimson red hibiscus flowers. The golden honey coloured bees with their black hoop rings around there bodies attached themselves to the stamens but suggested the process of pollination taking place. A glimmer of golden sunlight reflecting through the spotless window panes made Raymondo conscious of the warm temperature in the room and soon his senses seemed to be switching themselves on again. The smell of antiseptic cleansing familiarised itself with the inner parts of his nostrils but evoked an associative lien towards the memory of such smells. It was distinctly separate from the pungent sense of stale urine which seemed to be in competition with the antiseptic smell of a hospital. Raymondo sensed the catheter that was attached to him at one end and to a plastic bag filled with deeply orange, yellowish coloured urine hanging from the side of the bed at the other end of the catheter. He closed his eyes once more but opened them immediately as if to assure himself that he was back from his bewildering dream whilst he was in a comatose state. The sound of voices around him permeated the room. Raymondo found them especially refreshingly familiar He turned his head slightly towards the sound of the voices. Raymondo recognised the voices as those of his immediate family members. They sat around discussing the research they had gathered about comatose states and the subsequent recoveries over different time frames by individuals all over the virtual planet of Asteroidia. He heard them discussing a woman, who was in a comatose state for years. Her family had not only the faith but also the financial abundance to rent a private room but provided first class care for 24 years. The woman's husband did not give in to the pressure being applied by all the so called *'well meaning'* medical *'experts'*, who had wanted him to "turn off" the machinery which was helping to keep his wife alive. The advice given by the experts demanded he agree to remove the artificial breathing support machines but abandon his wife; telling him that they were convinced his wife was "brain dead". This wasn't true of course but the administrators felt that another empty bed meant more revenue for the private hospice. The man, Captain Courageous Ignacionis had fought and won the legal battle with *'The Merciful Hospice'*, eventually. They had just wanted to administer more bromide to patients like his wife, Conswela, but were being thwarted from doing so by the feisty Captain Courageous Ignacionis. In order to dissuade the Captain from having his day in court, the private Hospice owners had deliberately dragged the case over 5 spells of four years period amounting to a total of 20 years. They were hoping to put great strain on Captain Courageous Ignacionis' resolve but drain his financial resources away too. He stood strong and against all odds won the right to maintain the life support machines while his wife Conswela was still in a comatose state. The insurance companies covering the particular *'health plan'* were also found to be in collusion with the privately owned Hospice. They had inconvenienced Captain Courageous by asking him to re-apply every six weeks in order for them to repetitively *re-assess* his wife's condition. The insurance companies did this to flaunt the new laws that had banned them from withdrawing responsibility for paying the Hospice fees against the claimant. During the final court case in the 20th year, Conswela Ignacionis came out from the comatose state. After two years of various therapies, she became fully physically active, subsequently. After another two years, Conswela had fully regained her mental faculties and was leading what one might describe as a *'normal life'*. The loss of the court case was a frustration for 'The Merciful Hospice' and the insurers of the 'health plan' but its adversity had damaged both their reputations hugely. It was a landmark beyond hope for significant others too. Even though it might have been referred to as "an isolated case" by commentators banging the drum for the cold, insensitive, inhumane green humanoid robotrons' inherently partisan *'status quo'* approach to comatose cases, the lessons about personal principles and *'values and beliefs'* seemed not only to eclipse but also triumphed over *'politically acceptable'* enforced practices, maybe!. What was important to Captain Courageous Ignacionis but especially to his wife, Conswela, was that the lessons from their case might seem to resonate like an influential roll of thunder around the parallel virtual planet. On the one hand, it should be a warning of greater awareness of the practices by trusted custodians of our health, who find it more convenient to pretend to have made important *'beneficial'* decisions for and on behalf of individuals afflicted by some unfortunate circumstances. On the other hand, there seemed to be a slavish dedication towards significant individuals, who were being deemed more worthy of their global medical expertise.

At first, none of Raymondo's visitors were aware of his re-entry into the world of consciousness but as Darsna casually looked away from the discussion group towards her father, she saw his eyes open. Darsna blinked rapidly as she struggled to come to terms with the reality of her discovery. Darsna started as if to speak but no sound came out. Tears welled up but started to seep from the sockets of her eyes as Darsna began to get up from the chair in which she was sitting. Ras-Dan saw her movements but asked his sister where she was going. Darsna could not speak but pointed towards their father instead. Ras-Dan shouted out the moment he saw his father's eyes and that smile which beckoned for them to come closer to him. "Daddy you're awake", Ras-Dan said enthusiastically. Pamela, Carmen, and Aunt Rose's heads seemed to turn around in unison as swiftly as the young girl in the film 'The Exorcist'. Their pleasant surprise was overwhelming enough to make their hearts race at a pace or two faster. Raymondo was smothered in kisses and hugs that made him appreciate the warmth emanating from each of them. "How long have you been awake", Pamela asked? Before he could answer her, the others were asking their own questions. They wanted answers too. "One at a time", Aunt Rose counselled. Raymondo was laughing now. The rapport was quite noisy but alerted the staff. A nurse peered around the door but saw that all the visitors were crowded around the figure on the bed. She was concerned whether she should call the doctor. "Is everything alright in here", the nurse queried? At first, none of the family members could hear the nurse's voice. Such was the heightened celebration in the room. It was the arrival of Dr Nathaniel Hawke, Phd. a.k.a. 'Natty' Hawke, which brought reassurance that the nurse need not be concerned. He soon sensed the mood was celebratory and not of mourning a bereavement. "It is a good sign nurse", he assured her. The nurse wanted to confirm the patient's condition. When she saw Raymondo smiling and joking with his family, the nurse left the room swiftly. Raymondo complained that he was hungry. His expressing the level of his hunger sounded more like the Raymondo they all knew. He always seemed to have a huge appetite. That brought a few laughs from the rest of the family. "I'm sure you didn't miss it but welcome back to our world", 'Natty' Hawke chimed. Raymondo told them that he desperately felt as if he wanted to pass urine. This was a sure sign that he was fully conscious. The research they had done had indicated that individuals in comatose states lost the ability to sense when they wanted to urinate. As a consequence, the bladder would increase in size but become distended. Raymondo's tummy was like that of a child suffering from malnutrition. That kind of picture was often seen on television, when there was a crisis or an appeal for funds to appease the longsuffering of indigenous populations from the 5th rated exotic continents, countries and islands, which were less fortunate than the wasteful culture of the indigenous population in the 1st rated Dis-United Kingdoms of Asteroidia. Pamela inspected the incontinence plastic bag. It was already full. She hurried away from Raymondo's bedside but went to fetch the nurse. As Pamela started to leave the room, she bumped into the nurse and a group of doctors, who seemed in a hurry to witness the *'miracle'* as they referred to Raymondo's recovery from his comatose state back to consciousness. Pamela explained about her husband's need. All the visitors were asked to leave the room while the medical staff attended to Raymondo. "Don't let them give him any injection. Even though they are qualified medical staff, you can't trust that they want the best for your husband", Aunt Rose warned. Pamela approached the senior doctor but told him that she did not want her husband to be given any medication without their knowledge. Most of the family waited just outside the room but Pamela and the children stayed just inside it. When the nurse started to pull the screen around Raymondo, Pamela stepped forward but said she wanted to witness what was happening behind the screen. She and other family members, who were present, did not trust the hospital or the medical staff who attended to Raymondo. At precisely that moment, it was fortunate that some of his journalists' colleagues and friends had arrived to visit with him but he was not yet aware of their arrival. There were five of them altogether. Some still had cameras hanging from their necks whilst others had secret recording audio machines and video cameras. They were mystified as to how Raymondo had become comatose. Pamela had alerted them to the strange things that were happening to them as a family. Ras-Dan and Darsna had complained of being followed. Pamela was aware of her other *'shadows'* too but International Barrister Carmen L'Brishe-Hawke had assured her sister that legal action against Professor Frank Outstein was being prepared.

Sam Cleverman was one of a number of secret agents working for InterPlanPol. He had tipped Carmen and Pamela off that Raymondo's documented revelations against the once shadowy phantoms were sticking in the craws of many politicrats and poly-tricksters, who were in active alliance with but hugely partisan to the biggest ever planetary gang, the UFO. Sam explained that they were the practitioners and prosecutors of political chicanery behind every *'leader'* on the parallel virtual planet. He further explained that competing factions within the organisation often battled amongst themselves in order to impose the *'will'* of the UFO. It operated below the radar but constructed, provided, implemented and executed the formulae by which the *'leader'* of each Kingdom, Continents, Countries and Islands could operate. Sam further stated that each *'leader'* in all the Dis-United Kingdoms, exotic continents, countries and islands across the entire parallel virtual planet in the World of Space genuinely thought that the electorate had determined their status. Clothed in their immense power-starved pomposity and self-righteousness, those *'leaders'* didn't seem to be aware of the machinery behind the *'veil of fraternal secrecy'*. The UFO gang had the clout to manipulate the political system, in order to provide the population with *'puppets'* who posed as *'leaders'*, despite their *'impressive titles'*. This Raymondo had established through his intense research and had made available now for public scrutiny in his documentary film. Sam reiterated Raymondo's findings but stressed that the UFO had always operated as the *'Directors of Political Operations'* throughout the planet's entire history. He warned Raymondo that the UFO was not an organisation that would take lightly to the type of exposure that he had brought into the public arena and that the only type of relationship they were interested in was that they dominated all proceedings, legal and illegal without sanctions. Sam stated that they were scheming to get rid of Raymondo and his evidence. He was fearful for him because InterPlanPol had established that many individuals and quangos had been formed at the highest levels outside and inside governments to deflect the current information within the documentary from being verified. They had deemed that type of information as "Classified". That meant the information could not be disclosed for many years after the deeds had been done. These quangos included combinations of politicrats with commercial interests as well as legislators and administrators from all parties, in each of the Dis-United Kingdoms. They were *'united'* in this regard but actively devoted to and in cahoots with their *'puppeteer masters'*, the UFO. Raymondo's documentary had the type of information that might embarrass many so-called *'powerful leaders'* but disclose how they had been packaged, bought and sold with many squillions of poly-tricksters' Spacevillean Champagne Urges. As active members of the UFO, these leaders together with their legislators, administrators and commercial interest personnel, groups and associations had been deliberately, strategically dispersed across the parallel virtual planet of Asteroidia.

Even though he was a few years younger than Aunt Rose, Sam Cleverman was her partner and had been for the last 20 years. They were not married but formed a stable partnership, which in this millennia, was *'politically correctly'* dubbed as *'co-habiting'* but previously was *'politically correctly'* described disdainfully as *"living in Sin"*, apparently! Aunt Rose and Sam's relationship started after the death of her husband, Daney Culture. He was deemed by the Media as "a radical, left-winged activist". Daney's disappearance was suspicious but the confirmation of his death was still linked but surrounded with mystique. InterPlanPol had a hunch that Daney Culture had stumbled across the UFO's plan to destabilise the unity between the then United Kingdoms of Asteroidia. He had stood on his *'soap-box'* but had disclosed what he suspected about the UFO. Using Daney's *'rants'* just before his disappearance and his subsequent death, InterPlanPol had established that the UFO had stated that their objective was to disable the current *'democratic model'* but replace it with a *'model'* that was diversely opposite to the *'original model'* and what it had implied. Sam Cleverman had gone underground in order to glean the information he had gathered steadily over the fifteen years he had been involved with InterPlanPol. Because they reported only to the Most Supreme Judges of the Inter-Galactic Court of Justice of Human Rights, Sam Cleverman had advised Carmen to seek that source rather than the seemingly corrupted judiciary which existed in Spaceville but also within the other individual Dis-United Kingdoms of Asteroidia too. There were some advantages to being independent but the disunity amongst the Kingdoms, being chasms apart, made the Prime Leader of Spaceville, The Most Honourable Janette Brayhorne's leadership less effective than a more united front might have gained for the parallel virtual planet and its population. The UFO hated the incumbent Prime Leader, The Most Honourable Janette Brayhorne with a vengeance. They despised her not only because of their bigotry towards Janette Brayhorne's ethnicity as well as the prejudice they held towards her gender but also for the difference in her political ethos against the perceived *'politically correct'* extremely inherent hugely partisan *'status quo'*. This, the green humanoid robotrons UFO had managed to manipulate without interference since its installation, previous to Janette Brayhorne's incumbency as Prime Leader of Spaceville. Her heart-felt empathy towards the less financially abundant population was seen by the greedy green humanoid robotrons as robbing them of the opportunities to fleece the majority of the less abundant population on the parallel virtual planet of Asteroidia.

The green humanoid robotrons and their corporations saw themselves as being protected from imprisonment by their allied recruits, who were *'insiders'* they had planted within the top echelon of the Dis-United Kingdom's Legislature. Manufacturing as well as service businesses and some individuals alike saw themselves as being "too important to be imprisoned". This was confirmed at a *'Pink Tie'* after dinner speech. One commentator boasted, "Only the little people go to prison". Another had all her colleagues rolling around with laughter at a similar gathering, the prestigious *'Green Tie'* Event. When someone warned that the UFO needed to be a bit more cautious about how blasé they were becoming, the Mistress of Ceremony, Adelia Confrontati, admonished her colleague, Arnold Rambo-Ski. "You're not worried that there could be such a thing as *'UFO-Gate'*, are you Arnold", she chided?

Another study by The Walynski Institute opined that, on the parallel virtual planet, social dynamics had taken on a new banner but announced a new fanfare of its arrival. Some individuals chose to refuse to hear the clarion call to accept the inevitable changes that were evolving. Even the advent of new technology challenged individual inflexibility towards change except for the financial abundance which compelled those individuals to take an over keen but rather sterile interest in the name of greed only. The man they called 'The Professor' added that it appeared that "the mainly green humanoid robotrons were so locked into their archaic, super-inflated, egotistical mindsets that they seemed to be denying themselves access to the use of the facilitations of their brains. It appeared that some individuals had remained in what is termed psychologically as a *'stuck state'* but in vibrating *'mind-warps'*, assumedly, perhaps! They didn't only think, believe but deliberately lived in millennia so antiquated, that made dinosaurs seem to be part of a modern discovery, seemingly! Despite the advancement towards generational changes, the mystery of the gung-ho political shenanigans used to maintain the grossly partisan *'status quo'* rendered relationships on the parallel virtual planet subject to being *'irretrievably broken down'* and most times *'incompatible'*. Under those extreme circumstances, those relationships provided opportunities to be intricately examined in depth. What was revealed is that there was a need for many metaphorical pixels as the important elements that were necessary in order to bring about the *'HD'* quality of the big picture of what *'values and beliefs'* made up relationships on the parallel virtual planet", he explained.

Raymondo's documentary disclosed the link amongst *'preferred'* politicrats, poly-tricksters and special interest groups that had stated their steadfast allegiance to the mighty UFO. Their influence was greater than had been known publicly prior to

Raymondo's documentary. It pointed out that the *'demons'* within each individual member of the UFO, their partisan legislators and subordinates in the Royal Royal Dis-United Stately Kingdoms had not only been unleashed upon the entire population of the parallel virtual planet of Asteroidia but also begun to express themselves with unbounded delirium. They extended their prejudices without redress from the *'pillars'* of a *'legal'* system that was meant to be representative of the population but instead openly sided with the viral madness of the UFO. Their agenda was to implant separation amongst the various ethnic populations and sometimes even among their own green humanoid robotron population through the chaotic in-fighting caused by the UFO's 'Cult-Induced' Post/Zip Code Wars. The supply of drugs and ammunition became more prevalent within communities but catalysed the reduction of the younger population in particular. Even their nutritional diets and eating habits had been pre-planned but choreographed through the media of advertising. The lure of the new toxic, unhealthy *'diet'* was seen by the youngsters as being more *'convenient'*. They had been *'programmed'* and *'conditioned'* that the *'convenience foods'* were *'preferred'* to the home cooked ethnic diets which, over generations, were proven to be more nutritious and balanced. As Raymondo pointed out in his tell-tale documentary film, the youngsters made no link to the rise in their blood pressures, their temper tantrums or the deterioration of their behaviours or health status even.

Alan Baitman and his agents from InterPlanPol had established that the philosophy of the UFO and their associates were quite clear. They wanted to keep promoting **'Ethno Genocidia'**. It was the quickest and most certain way of **'deleting'** entire tribes from the World of Space in general but Asteroidia in particular. The UFO had a *'dream'*. Their *'dream'* was to completely eliminate all other tribes. Whilst the youngsters destroyed themselves through the UFO's 'Cult-Induced' Post/Zip Code Wars, the *'baby boomers'* were advancing in age with each passing year and they would die from one disease or another, inevitably, perhaps! As the UFO's *'Cult-Induced'* Post/Zip Code Wars seemed to be a hugely magnetic attraction to the ethnic youngsters, who had been less than academically challenged at junior and secondary schools, they were more prone to get involved in the *"live fast"*, *"die trying"* philosophies of the GMES, GMP, GCCEO, GCE, GOS, GOO and GOP to the detriment of their ethnic longevity. GSE were, like in advertising, the supplementary strategy implemented to focus the mentality of the young women in particular. They were being inveigled to accept themselves as being degraded as *"only meat"*, *"bitches"* and *"hoes"*, repetitively via the subliminal messages encoded within the musical *'lyrics'* and *'videos'* to which they willingly subscribed, seemingly! This type of mindset was typical of the young generation, who fell prey but alluded to the gang culture. They knew no different but had been sold on that kind of green humanoid robotron *'training'* through the consistent *'programming'* and *'conditioning'* happening below the radar since junior school days. In contrast to their own traditional tribal *'values and beliefs'*, most had been fed largely on the specific **'toxic mentality'** alphabet, vocabulary of *'stereo-tripe'* and *'stereo-hype'* but morphed into the *'politically accepted'* *'stereo-type'* mould they had been shaped to become, probably! Having been bombarded by the contrasting chaotic mixed messages, the youngsters were trapped but became lost in the mire of translations of an *'alien language'* geared to install fear at a post-hypnotic level. This injection of high levels of fear embedded but reinforced the instructions to "self-destruct" through the divisive UFO's *'Cult-Induced'* Post/Zip Code Wars. Those active franchisee *'fully paid up' 'converts'* from all other tribes apart from the UFO's green humanoid robotrons' Tribe of Babylon, had chosen to *'cross over'* and had volunteered to become **'selected honorary green humanoid robotron affiliates'** of an apartheid-minded gang, the UFO. The trophies those *'honorary green humanoid robotron affiliates'* sought were no different to those *'accolades'* which Sandra had sought after too. It was the lure not only to become an Iconic *'A Blister'* Socialite but also to be nominated for the coveted *'Judas Awards'*.

These franchisee *'converts'* had been feasting on the *'A La Carté'* diets of *'stereo-tripe'* as supplied by representatives of the UFO. The *'honorary green humanoid robotrons affiliates'* continued to carry out their seemingly *'prestigious'* functions of supplying the *'stereo-hype'* to the desperately naïve vulnerable youngsters; knowingly enticing but leading them like lambs to the slaughterhouses. By their willingness to contribute to the destruction of generations of limitless potentialities and infinite volumes of abilities waiting to be tapped, these self-appointed simulated green humanoid robotrons from the Mixed DNA Rainbow Tribe and those from the Tribes of Hawke and Duke actively became converted *'Pied Pipers'*, by *'proxy'*. These *'converts'* made no reasonable contributions towards securing any form of meaningful advancement for the youngsters but were being selectively elevated by meaningless titles, trophies, awards and medals while being paid handsomely by their *'puppeteer masters'*, the UFO for doing a very bad job well, apparently!

Raymondo's research had established these *'facts'* about the drivers of the powerfully influential **'addictive mentality of fear'**, which was being embedded at subliminal levels on the young generations' minds. This was part of the psychological *'programming'* and *'conditioning'* which was to prove causative to the decisions that they made especially during confrontations with rival individuals and groups. What these self-appointed simulated green humanoid robotrons converted *'Pied Pipers'* by *'proxy'* might not have been aware of is that, when the biblical Judas Escariot realised that he was not impervious to developing a *'conscience'*, he hung himself. The biblical Judas Escariot did this out of sheer disgust at the realisation that he had chosen to *'sell'* his soul for the metaphorical 30 pieces of silver. "What price today, perhaps", Raymondo murmured!

The UFO was not perfect and while it summoned a lot of energy around young individuals discriminating amongst each other and jockeying for positions and titles, it was basically a money tree being nurtured by how much greed could be mustered or whipped up by those individuals no matter where on the hierarchical ladder they were positioned. New titles or levels could be bought or earned in one way or another. There was one thing that was sure about the UFO. For every advanced move up the rungs of the ladder by some individuals, others would be sliding down the slippery *'snakes'* that were set to entrap those careless enough to land on them. Disgruntled *'insiders'* within the UFO told Raymondo of the mega corruptive mindsets and practices which existed. Even more sinister though were the allegations that affiliates had to compete fiercely or be eliminated from the fraternity altogether.

Oversight Bodies, appointed by politicrats to monitor the UFO had no teeth but were soon being overcome by its awesome power and extremely influential allies, the poly-tricksters. Those Oversight Bodies had no gumption but wilted like dying flowers into insignificance because not only had they lost their beauty but also their allure. It was far easier for individuals on the Oversight Bodies to relent to the might of the UFO but conform to their philosophy by applying for membership. No one dared question the all mighty UFO otherwise they might end up like Raymondo on the island with insurgents and the totally loose cannon, Professor Frank Outstein. The question was how soon it might take the ex-members of the defunct Oversight Bodies to develop the *'Greed over Need Philosophy'*, perhaps!

During his ten years research project, Raymondo had interviewed many individuals about various issues. He wanted to get perspectives from various resources about how the UFO functioned and their influence, if any, at each level. This category exposed the *'Ethos'* of the medical industry and practices. They were littered with allegations. Some were from patients and workers on all levels including the extremes from ancillary to professionals within the industry and practices. Some allegations seemed so wild that Raymondo sometimes wondered whether he was being led with some of the extraordinary things he was being told. At each stage, he wanted to ensure there was concrete proof either way to stick as being factual. If not, they would be downgraded. With Raymondo's determination and curious mind, he strove to establish the arguments for or against the allegations. The next individual he interviewed about the allegations surrounding the medical industries and practices was Philpot J, Philpot Jnr. He was an expert on medication, how they should be administered and their effects. Philpot J, Philpot Jnr. was a walking encyclopaedia. His knowledge about the various types of drugs was amazing. He had commented on radio and television many times before and was said to be non-partisan in his views but wanted to share his knowledge to help educate individuals. Philpot J, Philpot Jnr. was famed to be a man with extraordinary knowledge of medical drugs, the industries and practices all over the parallel virtual planet. His speciality was being able to break down the terminologies into simpler formats for individuals to grasp easily. Raymondo started off by stating the allegations about *'politically correct'* *'treatments'* that were said to be forcefully administered by *'reputable'* medical authorities and institutions, so called, all over the Royal Royal Dis-United Stately Kingdoms of Asteroidia. After addressing the innovations of the medical drug industries, Philpot J, Philpot Jnr. addressed the ADR, Adverse Drug Reactions. "Sadly, the ADR are worse than the initial medication being taken to affect a *'cure'*", he stated. Philpot J, Philpot Jnr. said he started out as a Medical Sales Representative. He told of a case history of a doctor with a successful private medical practice who described himself as *"feeling like a drug dealer"*. Philpot J, Philpot Jnr. asked the doctor why? The doctor said that *"because of the ADR of the medications"* he had prescribed, he *"had to prescribe another 20 to 30 tablets to correct what the ADR were doing to the patients"*. Philpot J, Philpot Jnr. quoted the normally cheerful doctor as looking very sad and suffering from depression because he didn't see an end to the particular situation and he, the doctor, had no practical solutions he could offer anyway.

Frequent and strong allegations regarding biological germs being manufactured in laboratories all over the parallel virtual planet had appeared in Raymondo de Oddballo email inbox from eminent researchers but they wanted to know that they would not be exposed during the documentary film. Raymondo assured them of anonymity. Those eminent medical researchers did not want to be identified but fed Raymondo with the type of information that had lay dormant as being 'Classified' or 'Top Secret' information for at least the last 20 years. It was frightening to learn that what seemed like *'treatment'* from respected medical authorities were a deliberate act on behalf of the highly influential gang, the UFO, to help catalyse the further breakdown of finely tuned automotive systems. A retired MD told Raymondo of her concerns about the state of how medical practitioner standards were deteriorating. Dr Christine de Christians said that, although she "expected changes to occur", she "didn't expect the ethos or purpose for entering what was meant to be a worthwhile career to change as much as it had". She volunteered to be part of Raymondo's documentary. In it, she stated that she was "ashamed of what was taking place within the medical world". "When a national announcement was made and a campaign launched, it was meant for the good of those individuals who needed our expertise. Today, when a national announcement is made, it's hard to believe it's meant for the good of those who were suffering from particular illnesses that just happened". Raymondo stated that some allegations had come to him anonymously. He told Dr Christine de Christians that he didn't know whether the allegations were just that or whether there was any truth to them but he told her he was curious if she cared to comment. Raymondo read from one of the emails he had received. "Most diseases were being forcefully implanted into targeted ethnic populations, like the Tribe of Duke, the Mixed DNA Rainbow Tribe and the Tribe of Hawke, through a form of serial inoculation system. Deliberate efforts were being made to find targeted *'hosts'* for particular debilitating illnesses". He then quoted from another research about similar targeting of particular ethnicities. Raymondo asked the doctor if she could see a similar pattern in the email he had just read to what had been done previously by the infamous green humanoid robotron Doctor 'Death' and his enforced *'syphilis campaign'*. He said the only difference was how the germs entered the body. This implantation of harmful germs being initiated by the UFO was said to be spread by mouth, through the bloodstream by injection or by inhalation ensured that immune systems were being attacked, broken down or destroyed without regard. In answer to the allegations read to her by Raymondo, Dr Christine de Christians said there was no way she could say whether the allegations bore any truth. "On principle though, that cannot be right. Even though I'm retired from practice, I'm still an MD. I do not want to be associated with any kind of germs that is alleged to be purposely manufactured especially for a particular group of people. That would bring dishonour to what was meant to be an honourable career", Dr Christine de Christians finished. Raymondo and his colleagues were especially pleased with both contributions from Philpot J Philpot Jnr. and Dr Christine de Christians. He learned from his research what was being done in order to satiate the appetites of the gorging *'scientific buzzards'* awaiting the decaying corpse to claim their share of the abundance of Champagne Urge. This was being created by yet another funeral at minimum but the grand prize of expensive body parts were being made available for auctioning online as well as offline. Fingers and toes were fetching quite a price let alone major organs. Once again, emotions were being used to authenticate the demand. Raymondo posed this question. "Who was really gaining, the recipient, the donor's families or the seller, he challenged? One could empathise with individuals who needed the relevant body part. There was nothing wrong in receiving the necessary part but, if the donor did just that, *donate the body part*, why was any individual gaining financially from that donation?

It didn't take brain surgery to work that out. What price a liver or a heart", Raymondo asked? He was curious to find out if individuals found it disgusting to learn that because the UFO was gaining from the sale of body parts, they were actively soliciting for body parts to be made available through the crazy UFO's 'Cult-Induced' Post/Zip Code Wars. Some seemed to have ravenous appetites and purposes for the lifeless bodies. The research from the eminent medical researchers highlighted that of the innocent youngsters in particular, who had fallen victims to the senseless UFO's 'Cult-Induced' Post/Zip Code Wars were the perpetrators' targeted demographics. One source from within Spaceville's Coroners' Offices stated that there had always been a greater demand than availability of body parts from the UFO. "There's a higher turnover for younger body parts", one insider stated. These findings were being exposed by Raymondo's documentary film. All grieving parents choked even more when they saw Raymondo's documentary film on the social websites. It had made those parents more aware of better understanding behind the cold-hearted emotionally insensitive madness named the UFO's 'Cult-Induced' Post/Zip Code Wars and the morbid *'spin-offs'* gained by the UFO and their affiliates, the Gang Orientation Scientists, the Gang Orientation Operators and the Gang Orientation Practitioners, Ghetto Mentality Practitioners, Ghetto CEOs and Ghetto Celebrity Entrepreneurs, who shared the spoils proportionately. They were the members of the most influential gang, the UFO, on the parallel virtual planet, who were orchestrating, directing and administrating the precocious deaths of the youngsters within the 1st rated Dis-United Kingdoms and the 5th rated exotic continents, countries and islands. It was as if these grieving mothers were *'battery hens'* being impregnated by the fathers, the *'battery cocks'*, to produce and reproduce children for these reprobates, the UFO, with their hawkish mentalities to sacrifice these children like *'sacrificial lambs'* in some kind of mindless *'street game'* for their pleasure or otherwise, maybe! Each was gaining from the death of every child being killed or imprisoned in the brainless gang warfare between the Post/Zip Codes. Families living in the various Post/Zip Codes, who had never been identified as such, were eliminating each other through fear of being slaughtered themselves. The youngsters might not have been aware that they were working for the UFO but they were being paid as *'blood-thirsty assassins'* by their local contact, the Gang Orientation Operators and Practitioners each time they *'shanked'* or *'shot'* a rival to death. In doing so, they were providing body parts, the *'assets'*, required by the UFO. They had created a type of super-dehydration in those individuals' parched mouths to seek to quench their enormous thirst for the taste of Champagne Urge.

Raymondo's Documentary Film, 'Looking Inside their Crystal Brains©', had drawn individuals into sending him more and more bizarre case histories. There was one that had been hidden away for 55 years, apparently. It bore the official seal of the Kingdom of Spaceville and was marked 'Top Secret'. On breaking the seal, the information started to escape into Raymondo's consciousness. It was particularly painful but exploded his empathy towards the individuals, who were made to suffer not just the indignity but had left them exposed to the UFO's stinking mentalities which smelt more like cesspool drains. There was the cold, callous, unfeeling experimenter, Doctor Adulf Faust aka 'Doctor Death' and the woman who did the deed, Nursing Sister Contra Versiäle. The secret file showed that there was a deliberate effort to select men from the Tribe of Hawke to be subjected to a form of experimentation that was not only illegal and derogatory but against those men's human rights too. The UFO had purposely installed medical staff from the same ethnic tribe to lure the male *'volunteers'* into an experimentation that can only be described as *'medical induced torture'*. These *'volunteers'* were subjected to having a deadly disease called syphilis inoculated into their bloodstreams by Nursing Sister Contra Versiäle, from the Tribe of Hawke also. Over the period of those 55 years, many of the victims had suffered but died from their deliberately diseased bodies. Some individuals were still suffering but were alive, miraculously, perhaps! Raymondo's documentary featured him interviewing a survivor and 'Doctor Death', who had instigated the *'experiment'*. The survivor spoke of his tortured mind and his physical torturous agony over the 55 years. In contrast, 'Doctor Death's' response was more than a little inhumane. "He survived, didn't he? I can't see what the fuss is all about. He should be grateful he is alive", Doctor Adulf Faust replied. 'Doctor Death' as he was dubbed initially by his medical peers at the time of his psychopathic reign might have been more than a willing *'volunteer'* at Auswitch had he been around then, probably! His harsh un-empathising, insensitive tone, inhumane response and devaluation of the subjects' human rights were enough to confirm his psychopathic neurosis, schizophrenia and ASPD, which rendered him without remorse. By his deliberate actions and abuse of the authority entrusted to him in his *'role'* as a *'model'* medical practitioner, 'Doctor Death' seemed to indicate that the individual, who had survived for 55 years from the introduction of syphilis into his bloodstream was "making a fuss about nothing", seemingly! It was individuals like 'Doctor Death' and his dastardly deed that had raised the point about *'the importance of trust within relationships'*. "Dr Death was no different to any other psychopathic serial killers, was he", Raymondo asked? It was just that 'Doctor Death' had chosen to use injection needles, germs and another human as his chosen *'weapons'*. The debate raised by Raymondo's documentary film applied to all forms of relationships. In particular, the inference in the documentary was whether patients and the medical world had *'compatible relationships'* or had they *'irretrievable'* broken down, seemingly! The main questions were, (1) "how many medical staff saw their priority as the importance of the well being of the patient"? (2) "Did they see it from Nursing Sister Contra Versiäle perspective that the flow of pecuniary advances which increased individual financial abundance as being more important"? Survivors of the syphilis experimentation carried out by the serial psychopathic behaviour of Doctor Adulf Faust might want to prove the deliberate *'ill-will'* of the mentally deranged individual and his intention to eliminate those individuals by *'lethal injection'* even though their only crime seemed to have been their ethnicity! Raymondo wanted to raise the awareness of those, who might be lured into traps of other covert ambitions of individuals like 'Doctor Death' or groups who had chosen to abuse their authority from any professional perspective. His own experience at the hands of Professor Frank Outstein had taught Raymondo that the *'practice'* of medically induced torture had not gone away but was very much rife in the moments he had experienced. He was learning that there were stacks of Tomes which catalogued serial mental and physical psychopathic abusers like Professor Frank Outstein and Doctor Adulf Faust, aka 'Doctor Death', respectively. They were in positions of authority and trusted to carry out their functions of expertise fairly and evenly but without partisanship. Their abusive actions, triggered by their inveterate xenophobic *'values and beliefs'*, were deliberate but affected the physical and psychological well-being of the patients they attended.

Even though Doctor Adulf Faust, a.k.a. 'Doctor Death', and Professor Frank Outstein were from different generations, Raymondo's documentary film, when aired, would prove the link between them as staunch physical and mental mercenary members of the *'emotionally constipated'* UFO. The question posed by the documentary film was, "how many more 'Doctor Deaths' and Professor Frank Outsteins were at large and was ready to pounce upon vulnerable individuals within the population of the parallel virtual planet"? Raymondo declared that the extensive research he had carried out had proven that there was nothing *'new'* about 'The Old Order of Demigods', as issued by the UFO. It was announced repetitively by the UO DIS-UK perennially. As demonstrated over generations, they were the official voice of the UFO but parroted the same old ritual of rhetoric known commonly as mantra. Although the words were re-worked on each announcement, the message was synonymous in its meaning to the suffering brown, purple, pink, white, blue population from the Mixed DNA Rainbow Tribe, the Tribe of Duke and the Tribe of Hawke in particular but had been extended even to the financially *'poor'* indigenous green population. They were also being classed by the difference in the shade of their hair and a darker shade of green skin colour. This was a classic form of *'ethnic'* class-ism on the parallel virtual planet.

Sam Cleverman was a staunch supporter of the investigative project that Raymondo had undertaken. He thought it was about time that the population was made aware of the level of corruptive mentalities which were fast corroding the previous *'good'* intentions of the founding predecessors of the planet of Asteroidia. The sheer hunger and voracious appetites for living the 'Spacevillean Dream' not only led to but also drove the unquenchable thirst for Champagne Urge. It had opened up a void but exposed the character traits of many, who, on the surface, had seemed mentally stable but were, in fact, infected and affected by the viral mental reactions (madness) known commonly as greed. On this parallel virtual planet of Dis-United Kingdoms, individuals had been *'programmed'* and *'conditioned'* to accept the *'madness'* as normalcy. The greed madness had been long ignored with a nod and a wink until its pandemic infestation. It threatened to diminish the weight of *'value'*, importance of *'belief'* in scruples, morals and the concept of *'true'* democracy. Moralists Inc and Scruples United concurred with the man they called 'The Professor'. He went on record as referring to the necessity of maintaining scruples, morals and true democracy as the privilege of *'free speech'*, the art of *'quality communication'*, the power of *'trust'*, the deed of *'empathy'*, the desire to be *'flexible'* as being validated by *'integrity'*. These, he said, were to be universally accepted not only as *'tenets'* to be encouraged but also as the *'antidote'* to the toxicity of the *'mental derangement'* called greed. No matter the way of life chosen by individuals, these tenets were once the pillars with which each wanted to be associated, embraced and identified. *'True'* democracy, which was meant to be enjoyed by all the population on the parallel virtual planet of Asteroidia, the exotic continents, countries and islands was being deliberately and politically consumed but regurgitated as a political *'activity game'* of charades. The poly-tricksters' *'model'* of democracy was being presented as the only acceptable perspective, from which to view. Those players of this game were politicrats and poly-tricksters, who backed the 'Old Order of Demigods' as sanctioned by the green humanoid robotron UFO. They made the *'Rules'* but amended them accordingly by using the influence they had over Legislators at the highest level, who had conceptualised, designed but generated this systemic tunnel-viewed, greed-driven *'plot'* on behalf and under the direct instructions of the UFO. It seemed to be the main driver by which to establish power over another. The aim and objective of those practitioners were to *'program'*, *'condition'* but shape subliminally, delusional, greedy individuals' unquenchable thirst towards the taste of the virtual currency, Champagne Urge. With the greed mentality securely in place, individuals were being driven like thirsty animals towards a waterhole. The super-dehydrated humanoid robotrons' warped mentalities were being exposed to all and sundry by Raymondo de Oddballo's malnourished appetite and humungous hunger for justice. He and his family had earned the right to sue Professor Frank Outstein for an amount not less than 500 million SPCU, Spacevillean Champagne Urges. The difference is that this taste might be a bit more of a rewardingly thirst-quenching, re-hydrating elixir, perhaps!

CHAPTER 60

On finding out about Raymondo de Oddballo's recovery from his comatose state, Professor Frank Outstein was thoroughly stunned at Raymondo's ability to recover. Professor Frank Outstein's face became a very pale almost putrid shade of green. He fidgeted then heard himself repeat the word "recovered" several times whilst he puzzled to understand how it was possible for Raymondo to recover! No other of his patients had ever recovered to tell the tale about the torturous methods which he used to completely erase their ability to remember. He was frantic with fear that this very unusual man with two brains had defied not only the *'Laws of Possibilities'* but also the *'Laws of Probabilities'* too. As far as Professor Frank Outstein was concerned, no other of his patients had ever recovered from a comatose state after being the recipient of the *'Shock Therapy'* in the manner in which he had applied it; by massively increasing the voltage. Reluctantly, Professor Frank Outstein broke the news to his *'puppeteers'*, the UFO. After a very long discussion they plotted to send Raymondo to a *'Special Rehabilitation Centre'* manned by their chosen personnel. It was to be at a most remote location and he was not meant to be allowed to have any visitors. "You must ensure you don't foul up this time", the voice on the other end of the phone instructed. Professor Frank Outstein responded affirmatively but he was still stunned by Raymondo's recovery. It was affecting him at a much deeper level. He was forming a plot in his head. As far as he was concerned, Raymondo would not survive long enough to get to the *'Special Rehabilitation Centre'*. He instructed the hospital that Raymondo was not to be discharged until he had carried out his own *'assessment'* whether he was *"mentally 'well' enough to go home"*.

When Pamela and her family were told about Professor Frank Outstein's decision, they objected straight away. Within several moments, armed Special Security Officers, dressed in paramilitary attire arrived in the private room at the hospital. Four stood guard at the entrance of the room whilst the others stood in and around in the hallway leading to it. Raymondo's journalists colleagues started to film the scene but were quickly dissuaded from doing so by the gruff Special Security Officers. International Barrister Carmen L'Brishe-Hawke took notes but went outside to make a phone call to her colleagues about the current situation. There, she saw the enormous presence of Special Security Personnel just outside the hospital building and in the car park in the foreground. This unusual presence of the swarm of paramilitary Special Security Personnel signalled something sinister was either already happening or about to happen. When she returned to the room, Carmen whispered in Raymondo's ear. She told him that she had just learned that, with their impressive influence, the UFO had somehow managed to bring the case forward. It was scheduled for beginning within the next three days. Carmen told Raymondo she had to leave the hospital in order to prepare his deposition. Because of his impending absence, Carmen told Raymondo that she would submit it on his behalf. Carmen told the others that she had to leave but didn't tell them why. She was aware of the strange sudden request by the UFO to bring the case forwards but couldn't risk alerting the Special Security Personnel. Despite his miraculous recovery, Raymondo was told by the hospital staff officially that he was to remain in the hospital until Professor Frank Outstein had examined him. Pamela and the rest of the family were more than disappointed. It was just moments before they were celebrating Raymondo's recovery but hoping to take him home. Despite their gross disappointment, the family was asked to leave. This strange request alarmed them but the Special Security Personnel ensured that they left not only the room but the hospital grounds altogether.

The case against Al Tuxedo, his confidants, accomplices and the head of the Organisation, the UFO, started within the three days that Carmen had mentioned. Because he was restricted physically from attending The Highest Criminal Court of Justice in Spaceville, Raymondo's deposition was submitted by his International Barrister Carmen L'Brishe-Hawke. The Honourable Justice Prentice Noseworthy, presiding over the case, accepted Raymondo's deposition. The Judge had a reputation for his *'no nonsense'* approach. His function was to ensure that the interpretation of the Law was fully understood but applied by both prosecution and defence. Dressed in his blonde wig and Ermine trimmed gown, he and the barristers attending wore their attire with much pride. They too were bewigged but wore the black gowns which distinguished them by rank as compared to the learned Judge. Both his and the barristers' dress code reminded all present of the 'Charles Dickens' era. The Honourable Justice Prentice Noseworthy had worn that Ermine trimmed gown many times before and he might have felt not suitably dressed for the occasion if it was to be relegated to the era referred in which it had been originally in fashion. All the same, it reminded the public of the *'programmed'* and *'conditioned'* *'importance'* of uniform but adhered to the argument about *'values and beliefs'*, perhaps! After making pronouncements about how the case was to proceed and the latitude he would allow within this court, it was time for the prosecution to put its case forward. The court was full to capacity.

Earlier, the queue, four abreast, stretched for at least more than a mile directly outside the court building but carried on along the adjoining street at right angles to the High Street on which The Highest Criminal Court of Justice in Spaceville was positioned. It extended for at least another three quarters of a mile. Sundry observers compared that type of queue as similar to those when there was a massive winter sale at huge prestige department stores, when new electronic games or other electronic equipment, like technologically enhanced cell phones were made available for sale for the first time. Although this style of queuing was an imminent danger to the public thoroughfare, the National Security Service Personnel watched as other members of the public were forced to walk into the streets but mingled with the traffic in order to get to their place of work or educational establishments. It was evident that no *'risk assessment'* was being observed. What seemed to matter more to the National Security Service Personnel was that the printed and television Media had access to record the facts of the Case against Al Tuxedo, his 'puppeteer masters' and their accomplices. It had caused so much of a stir amongst the population of Spaceville. Ironically, it was the work of one of their colleague that was being put to the test. Raymondo's dedication as a celebrated, award winning investigative journalist was a representation of the sterling work that the Media sometimes managed to produce and was of meaningful benefit to the public, whom they acknowledged were the lifeblood of their existence. Case number 666 was of particular interest and **'Hot News'** all over the parallel virtual planet of Asteroidia, including the 5th rated exotic continents, countries and islands. Many of Raymondo's colleagues were present inside and outside The Highest Criminal Court of Justice. Some were there as witnesses whilst others were there to record this ultra significant legal event. They were in full support of their colleague's determination to expose Al Tuxedo and his *'puppeteer'* masters, the UFO.

International Barrister Carmen L'Brishe-Hawke was representing the prosecution. She and her battery of barristers were on one side of the court. The defence with their battery of barristers were on the other. Much to the annoyance of the green humanoid robotron barristers defending the UFO and their cronies, the jurors were made up of each of the five colours which was representative of the Mixed DNA Rainbow Tribe, three each from the Tribe of Duke and the Tribe of Hawke and one from the green humanoid Tribe of Babylon which was not necessarily a serial robotron. The defence barristers' objections to the proportional mix of the jurors were countered by the skilful ploy of International Barrister Carmen L'Brishe-Hawke. The defence barristers were used to stacking the odds in their favour by wanting to load nine green humanoid robotron jurors and one each from the Mixed DNA Rainbow Tribe, the Tribe of Duke and the Tribe of Hawke. In that way if the verdict could not be settled unanimously then, through partisanship, a majority verdict would most likely fall in their favour. With her international experience, Carmen said that the Laws from 'The Inter-Galactic Court of Justice for Human Rights' had precedence over the Dis-United Kingdoms. Their ruling stated that it was fair to use a proportionate balance according to what was considered not only representative but reflective of the population of the particular Dis-United Kingdom's population. Carmen pointed out that collectively, the three Tribes were the majority in Spaceville. Green humanoid robotrons represented only one twelfth of Spacville's population. The Honourable Justice Prentice Noseworthy told the defending barristers that he could not overrule 'The Inter-Galactic Court of Justice for Human Rights'. He also explained that the defence had the right to refer their case to that superior court if they so wished. After a lot of whispered communication amongst themselves, the defence barristers agreed to have their cases heard in this court, reluctantly. The jurors were duly sworn in. Carmen L'Brishe-Hawke opened with a very impressive set of arguments. She presented the case against Al Tuxedo primarily. Carmen inferred the involvement of his confidants and accomplices including the UFO. She said that she would prove that, although Al Tuxedo was all encompassed in his own importance, he too was a pawn in the *'mind game'* which was being played by the head of the Organisation, the UFO. They had engaged him to carry out a particular function. The international prosecuting barrister drew parallels but cited relevant legal case histories to remonstrate her intention. The Honourable Justice Prentice Noseworthy looked from above his strange looking half-lens spectacles at the inspiring young eagle as she cited the case histories.

The defence, representing the UFO spoke next. Their barrister was an eminent popular man named, Treis B Treye. His famous battles at the Bar were well documented and he was well known in chambers as "the shrew one". Al Tuxedo's barrister and the representatives for the others were acknowledged by the Judge and recognised by the public. The case was estimated to run for eight weeks altogether. During the course of those eight weeks, Raymondo had disappeared from the hospital. He had been spirited away from it mysteriously. Even InterPlanPol had no idea where he had been taken. The discovery was made by one of Raymondo's journalist colleague, Censiba Mc Intoba. She had infiltrated the hospital Security's high profile alertness by posing as an ancillary worker. Censiba posed as a *'stereo-typical'* ancillary worker, a cleaner. The name she used was Princess Cinderella Cinderella. It sounded so absurd that the Special Security Personnel made fun of her name but chided Princess Cinderella Cinderella about her infamous slippers but asked about her "Prince Charming". All the same, she had managed to infiltrate but breach the level of Security without suspicion. Princess Cinderella Cinderella began to document the careless talk, which took place amongst the Security Personnel and the hospital staff. She did this by recording them with the hidden camera and recording equipment she wore on her person. Princess Cinderella Cinderella carried out her cleaning duties alongside the other ancillary workers but actively continued to gather evidence about Raymondo's disappearance and how it was executed. He had been kidnapped by agents of the UFO but sent to a crypt where he was being tortured daily. The talk was that his health would deteriorate until he could be declared *'mentally unstable'* but be abandoned to a mental institution from which he would never be released. Professor Frank Outstein preferred for the hospital to say Raymondo had gone to a special rehabilitation establishment "for his own good".

Having been taken hostage, Raymondo was being injected with the same psychedelic drug that Professor Frank Outstein had used on the island on which Raymondo had shared with the insurgents. He had no idea where he was being held hostage but Raymondo was aware of the state of his environment. It was rough. There was not even a piece of cardboard to separate his body from the hard rough flooring inside the crypt which he occupied. The food was disgusting and it remained on the floor until the rotting stench reminded Raymondo that he was sharing the ghastly cave-like environment with rats bigger than cats. They were numerous but fought over the rotten scraps of food that lay around the stone tomb enclosure. Even though he could never escape, Raymondo wore foot chains similar to those worn by chattel slaves way back then on the parallel planet, Earth. As he moved about, the sound of the chains played a particular pattern. The stench of the dried as well as fresh excrement and the rancid, reeking smell of stale urine, which stained his ragged trouser, continued to attack his nostrils. Raymondo had lost quite a lot of weight and he felt less than strong. The daily visits from the staff left in charge of him meant that he was being tortured with a tazerlike *'cattle-prodder'* before being injected frequently each day. The staff handled him roughly but they scorned him just like how homeless people all over the Royal Royal Dis-United Stately Kingdoms of Asteroidia had been marginalised about their demise or those in *'Cardboard City'* on the parallel planet, Earth. Raymondo was not aware how he got to this hell hole but it was certainly much colder than the warmth of the hospital. He had developed a very troublesome cough. It sounded more like someone suffering from whooping cough. His chest was wheezy and his body had spells of shivering as if he was being exposed to temperature like that of the snow covered Alps without adequate clothing. As he shivered a bit more, the chains sounded more like tambourines being shaken. There was no one with which to converse. Raymondo longed for the comfort and warmth of his home but wondered if he would ever see his family again. He missed his wife Pamela and his two children, Ras-Dan and Darsna. At times, Raymondo had to abandon thinking about them as it seemed to be driving him insane. Whenever he was feeling down, he visualised the defiant thin purple man from the Mixed DNA Rainbow Tribe, whom he had met on the island when he stayed in those crypts with the insurgents. Raymondo drew strength from the purple man but wondered if he was still alive, despite his hunger strike protest. Inspired by the purple man's unselfish sacrifice to bring attention to the need for justice, he too was on hunger strike now. Raymondo wanted to force his captors to release him but they refused. They told him that they had orders to keep him alive. If he refused to eat, they threatened to force feed him.

It was time for his next torturous session with the tazer-like *'cattle-prodder'* and his hallucinatory injection. He felt nauseous when shocked by the tazer-like *'cattle prodder'* but the injection sent him into a spiral. It was as if he was moving backwards through different time zones. On this occasion, Raymondo saw the uncoordinated gait of Professor Frank Outstein. At least, that's whom he thought he saw. His physicality seemed the same from afar. In order to adjust to the poor lighting in the crypt, Raymondo eyes were squinted almost shut. He peered through the haze at the figure he perceived to be Professor Frank Outstein coming towards him. Eventually, when he was close enough, Raymondo saw the face of one of the men whom he had seen in his dream during his comatose state. That face reminded him of Sandra's boss Duke. Raymondo wondered how it was possible for Duke to be at this site. In his confusion, his thoughts were wild and random. They just kept popping into his consciousness. He figured that it must be Professor Frank Outstein but that he had had a *'face transplant'*, probably! Raymondo had no idea what made him think that was even possible! Nothing seemed to make sense anyway. Out of the corner of his eyes, he saw what seemed like a white tri-corn headgear similar to that of the nurse who had assisted Professor Frank Outstein on the island. The apparition appeared in his thought. Again, Raymondo witnessed her floating action as the psychedelic lights seemed to be shining from the floor towards the ceiling of the crypt. He lay on his back admiring the beauty of the apparition. As she came nearer towards him, Raymondo had almost surrendered to this ghostly figure. Again, peering through squinted eyes, he noticed that the nurse was a bit shapelier than before. She was slimmer too. Her skin was tanned melanin instead of green. As she came closer, Raymondo recognised the apparition to be Sandra. His eyes popped open and for a moment his hallucination confused him even more. Raymondo gazed into those large cornflower blue eyes which seemed much more familiar but he became even more mesmerised than he did when he was in the dreamlike comatose state. For a brief moment, Raymondo chose to feel jealous that Duke and Sandra were together. He also felt trapped as it seemed that she was working with Duke against him, seemingly! Raymondo shook his head from side to side as the thoughts seem to jeer him. He had no idea of how long this hallucination lasted but he started to come round from the effect of the injection. He blinked rapidly but shook his head violently from side to side to try to clear it from the experience. Raymondo's mouth and throat felt parched and the dehydration had begun to set in. The dizzy spells began to replace his hallucinations. As he struggled to see beyond the many stars which appeared before him but swarm his vision, Raymondo began drifting randomly in and out of consciousness.

Over the weeks, while he suffered even more at the hands of his captors and under the strict instructions of Professor Frank Outstein, Raymondo's sister-in-law, Barrister Carmen L'Brishe-Hawke toiled away to present his case. She used those witnesses like Beth Tittye, Sue Ellen-Stokeley, Grant Favours, Captain Plantain and others who had secured 'plea bargaining' but were now official agents for InterPlanPol. There were also Raymondo's journalists colleagues who had volunteered to be witnesses. Barrister Carmen L'Brishe-Hawke brought her great knowledge, poise and expertise but fought admirably against the eminent barrister, Treis B Treye. After the many *"objections"* and *"sustained"* comments between the Honourable Justice Prentice Noseworthy, the prosecution and defence barristers for and behalf of all parties that were being represented by them, both the defence and prosecution presented their final summing up speeches to the jury. International Barrister Carmen L'Brishe-Hawke's passionate factual presentation far outweighed the defence's parrot-like submissions to the weight of evidence against their clients, the Organisation, the UFO, individuals like Al Tuxedo and the number of others, who she had firmly established were proven to be franchisee agents in the employ of the UFO.

Honourable Justice Prentice Noseworthy found in favour of Raymondo de Oddballo's documentary. The eminent Honourable Justice Prentice Noseworthy said the weight of evidence against Al Tuxedo, the UFO and their franchisee cronies was "unquestionable" and that "Mr Raymondo de Oddballo had every right to use such genuine evidence to prove his case". He commented on International Barrister Carmen L'Brishe-Hawke's superb arguments and references to relevant case histories that reminded him of his younger days as a barrister. The Honourable Justice Prentice Noseworthy described the UFO, United Fraternal Organisation and the UO Dis-UK, Union of Dis-United Kingdoms as the "**Axes of Evil**" which had infiltrated an albeit imperfect but acceptable model of democracy. He said "the UFO had adapted it to represent their self-serving interests above the people's needs". The Honourable Justice Prentice Noseworthy stated further that "it was regrettable that the fines were limited to what the law deemed as the maximum amount allowable legally". He imposed the maximum fine of 750 million Champagne Urges on the UFO, the United Fraternal Organisation and 250 million Champagne Urges on the UO Dis-UK, Union of Dis-United Kingdoms but referred to them as being the *"head"* and *"neck"* of the Organisation. Although these fines seemed large, they would hardly have dented anything else apart from their reputation. None of the squillionaire elitist lobbyists or the billionaire poly-tricksters was individually being implicated or punished, regrettably!

The Honourable Justice Prentice Noseworthy commented that he too was confused as to which twin brother is Al Tuxedo or Baron Staveley even. He ordered that both brothers were to remain in custody until whenever the result of the DNA test determined the identity of the identical twins. He also stated that the New Interplanetary Laws as introduced by the current Prime Leader, the Honourable Janette Brayhorne, were being applied in this jurisdiction. These new Laws were being applied to all individuals, including those whom had to be extradited from outside the Dis-United Kingdoms but were involved in the cases currently before him. These Laws applied whether the crimes committed were cyber or physical. All individuals found guilty were sentenced severely from 50 to 75 years for the part they had played within the Organisation. The barristers for the Ghetto Celebrity CEO's were shocked that the Judge agreed that their clients were "guilty of poisoning and corrupting the minds of the young people", with their subliminal toxic lyrics.

Altiman Begi-Begi, the Tourism Minister, from Costa Del Shell, wept bitterly but begged the Judge to have mercy on him. He claimed that he didn't know Duke had a brother let alone an identical twin. Altiman Begi-Begi said that he had being duped by Al Tuxedo to helping to turn Costa Del Shell into a Sin City. The Judge reminded Altiman Begi-Begi that he had received and accepted payment. Referring to his plea, the Honourable Justice Prentice Noseworthy snapped, "that makes you part of the Organisation too". Altiman Begi-Begi was to serve his sentence in the outer Galaxy in the World of Space. Pimpernel V1 and several others, who were GSE, Ghetto Sodomy Entrepreneurs, Serial Rapists and Serial Paedophiles, would have to go through the battery of tests by Neurologists and Psychiatrists to establish their mental status. Afterwards, they would be taken to the ant, wasp and bee colonies to serve their sentences in the underground crypts in order to experience the *'antidote'* to their toxic thoughts and actions. The Honourable Justice Prentice Noseworthy praised Barrister Carmen L'Brishe-Hawke openly but advised that the UFO's barrister, Treis B Treye of his right to appeal to 'The Inter-Galactic Court of Human Rights' against his decisions if they so chose. All the media were celebrating the triumph of the case against the UFO and their cronies. Pamela and the children were delighted with the outcome of the cases. They were particular proud of Carmen. Natty Hawke was the most proud of them all but collectively their celebration as a family was marred by the fact that Raymondo was still missing. It was eight weeks of mental turmoil for him and his family in their different environments.

The next move was for Carmen to prosecute a case against the UFO in the Civil Court and to claim compensation from Professor Frank Outstein for his crude methodology which had rendered Raymondo into a comatose state. The case would be more difficult to prosecute in his mysterious absence but there was hope that Raymondo might be found before the case became active. All the same, Carmen had started the proceedings on his behalf.

The DNA tests ordered by Judge Prentice Noseworthy proved inconclusive. Unusually, both Duke's and Baron's DNA were very difficult to differentiate. Similarly, their fingerprints and toeprints were undistinguishable too. They were far too similar to differentiate. The legal eagles were at odds as to what to do to be able to identify which of the twin brothers was Baron Staveley. DNA taken from the seemingly illusive, notorious arms, drugs dealer, being responsible for establishing serial rapists and paedophile rings, **'Sin Kingdoms, Cities, Continents, Countries and Islands'** all over the World of Space was ready and available to be used in evidence against him but might prove whether indeed it was Baron Staveley or Duke Stagg who was Al Tuxedo! They called in Professor Walynski to find out if he could suggest a foolproof scientific way of ensuring how to identify the real Al Tuxedo believed to be Baron Staveley. He told them that he too was stumped as to how to go about it. He thought that the DNA test was foolproof but the oddity that two individuals shared the same pattern of DNA was unprecedented. He then addressed the next oddity about the two brothers' fingerprints and toe prints being so indistinguishable too. No technician could tell the difference between the two brothers' fingerprints or toe prints either. When the news got out into the public arena, there were lots of suggestions but most were regarded as hoax or just not practicably credible. All seem to be lost. It was not legal to commit these two men to prison for the same crime. Technically, only one was guilty. It was extremely scientifically uncanny that these oddities about the DNA and the fingerprints and toe prints existed. Legally, if there was no solution to be found, then both brothers would have to be released.

It was an email from the man they called 'The Professor' to Professor Walynski that raised an argument which was undisputable. He said that research had shown that based on individual belief systems there was a very good chance that the 'Lie Detector' Test might prove to present a genuine result. The man they called 'The Professor' said that if 'The Hifle and Pifle Theory' proved that individuals, who didn't believe that the 'Lie Detector Test' worked, then it is possible those individuals could cheat the test. Alternately, when individuals believe that the 'Lie Detector Test' can detect when one is lying then those individuals cannot cheat the test, perhaps! 'The Hifle and Pifle Theory' seemed so ludicrous but Professor Walynski decided to respect the genial man they called 'The Professor'. He knew of his reputation as a Coach/Practitioner besides. Professor Walinski believed in the old philosophy, "Nothing ventured, nothing gained". He had no idea which author had come up with such wise words. Professor Walynski decided to experiment with 50 volunteers. He tested but found that 25 of them were avid *'believers'* in the 'Lie Detector Test'. The other 25 individuals were like the biblical disciple, Thomas. Professor Walynski was not necessarily a religious man but he had learned that Thomas was referred to as a *'doubter'*. He carried out his experiment. The result was stunningly accurate. The *'believers'* all failed the test but the *'non-believers'* were able to cheat it. Professor Walynski rang the Honourable Justice Prentice Noseworthy to give him the result of his small sampled research. He asked the Judge if he wanted him to carry out the 'Lie Detector Test' on the twin brothers, Duke and Baron. "We have no alternative. If we don't, both men will be released and that would not only be a tradegy but also a travesty of justice because at least one of them is guilty of committing those awesome crimes", he finished. The Honourable Justice Prentice Nosworthy gave his permission for the twin brothers to be taken from prison to The Walynski Institute to have the test done. They were picked up from the prison by helicopter but taken to The Walynski Institute where they were tested. Duke thought that, because his father had encouraged him to lie, he might be able to cheat the tests, probably! His belief system had been *'programmed'* and *'conditioned'* to lie but under these controlled conditions would he be able to? Baron's upbringing was one with structure. In his household, telling lies was not acceptable. That had been riveted into him at a very young age by his mother. Under these controlled conditions, what might his reactions be? Strangely, both brothers were ill at ease throughout the tests but could not cheat it.

Professor Walynski notified the Honourable Justice Prentice about the irrefutable results. There were only two questions set but asked by the genial man they called 'The Professor'. Those were, "Are you Baron Staveley" and "Are you Duke Stagg"? These questions were being asked at random times in random order. Prior to the test, both Duke and Baron were prompted that any delay in answering would be construed as an attempt to deliberately lie. They seemed to have been outwitted by the genius of the man they called 'The Professor'. He had assured his colleague Professor Walynski that he would use a very simple method to illicit the truth. He did. The man they called 'The Professor' was given an Honorary Degree by The Walynski Institute for the sterling work he had put in over the years but particularly his massive contribution to The Walynski Institute.

Having identified himself via the Lie Detector Test, the thinner of the two brothers admitted he was Al Tuxedo. For the records, his name was also established. That man was flown by helicopter to one of the floating prisons on the high seas. The other man was taken back to the land based prison but released with the customary brown paper parcel and just about enough to pay his fare in order to get home. As he went through the gate to the walk of freedom, the prison guards watched him. The man turned to look at them before he walked off in one direction. He threw his head back but let out a big laugh. His deep baritone voice carried way beyond the prison gates. All who heard it was stunned into consternation then the man sung an operatic version of a very famous standard song which was a huge hit on the parallel planet, Earth. The title of which was *'I did it my way'*! The Opera Singer, Willard White would have been proud to have bellowed this rendition. As he walked along, the man, who had just been freed from prison, heard the sound of a motor vehicle behind him. He looked around in the direction from which the sound had come. The freed twin brother seemed to recognise the golden four wheel drive vehicle. It glided towards him. His heart began to play Beethoven's 'Chopsticks' on his chest. The man, assumed to be Duke, could not suppress his excitement.

All sort of thoughts raced through his mind. To be reunited with his *"exotic bird"* once again would mean more to him now than ever before. With his brother now permanently out of his and Sandra's life, he would reintroduce her to the parallel virtual planet. She would become more than just the 'A' 'Blister' Socialite but might remain as immortal an Icon as those significant others before her instead. Either as his *'Sugarcake'* or *'Commercial Escort'*, the surviving twin would now use clout to secure lead *'roles'* that suited the *'model'* he chose for her to be. No longer would Sandra be cast in subservient *'stereo-type'* *'roles'* as *'cook'*, *'housemaid'* or *'nanny'* or be perceived as just another *'ancillary supplement'* in the next movies in which she appeared. The freed surviving twin brother would want to secure *'roles'* of distinction for his iconic *"exotic bird"*. It might serve to help inspire younger generations from the Tribe of Hawke, who might want to *'model'* more deserved empowering *'roles'* instead of those demeaning ones deemed previously as being *'appropriate'* by the heavily partisan *'status quo'* for particular ethnicity. This identical twin figured that he would have even more impact now he had rid himself of his lifelong burdensome scourge, his twin brother, whom he had schemed to have confined to the Floating Prison, permanently.

The vehicle pulled up just a few yards past him. With his size 14 flat feet, the freed twin brother sauntered towards where the vehicle had stopped. When he opened the door, he saw the little IVF dwarf laboratory produced pit bull terrier dog, Tramp, but smelt the acrid smoke from the Cuban cigar. He also recognised the shiny, expensive, diamond encrusted chain he had given to the manager of the Marina, whom he'd named Garcia when he had tried to **buy his loyalty** in exchange for the unexplained disappearance of his friend, Alberto, as Duke had named him. The freed twin looked into the scrawny gaunt features of the man behind the steering wheel. He was aware that someone else was in the vehicle too but had no time to find out the identity of the individual sitting in the back seat. A singular shot was discharged. It followed its pathway from the metal chamber housing the bullet but rocketed via the silencer attached like the projectile it was until it found its mark in the stomach of the twin brother suspected to be Duke. The freed prisoner's features bore a mixture of the element of surprise, recognition, intrigue and indignation all at the same time. He grunted like a pig but grasped his stomach as if he was trying to protect something from escaping from it. The contorted phases of expression on the wounded man's face mirrored those often seen in violent movies. His knees started to buckle as he stumbled around on legs that wobbled like jelly but were unsteadily dragged along as if paralysed; leaving trails in the dirt. "That's for taking me for granted, beating me up and leaving me to drown, Mister Duke . . . Yes", the man Duke had named Alberto said scornfully! The wounded man sunk to his knees. He had just enough breathe to say who he really was. "My name is . . .". That is all he managed to say before collapsing into a crumpled heap on the ground. The scrawny man in the driver's seat reached across but patted Tramp on the head but commented, "Nasty man, that Mister Duke . . . Yes! He selected *'Hover'* then *'Glide'*. As the golden Four Wheel vehicle lifted off the ground but started to move forwards, the man named Alberto by Duke reached over but stroked Sandra's pregnant belly. "You have my baby . . . Yes! She caressed his strong slim sinewy melanin arm. Sandra looked down through the window to see if the body on the ground was moving. The pool of aquamarine blood crept slowly from under the man's body onto the dirt, like a snail slithering on the branch of a tree. "Let's go home Alberto . . . Yes", Sandra said cynically. They giggled together. With the man Sandra and Alberto referred to as Duke out of the way, they could live in the Palace in Champagne Valley. Together, they planned to have a large family. Sandra's mother, Dian, would have been proud of the status of the man with whom Sandra had chosen to have children. With Sandra being the only benefactor, her mother, Dian, had left her quite sizeable sums from Life Insurance Policies, her "rainy-day" savings and the accumulated sums she had placed in bonds for years from Sandra's early exploits since becoming *'Baby of the Month'* in her first six weeks of her arrival on the parallel virtual planet. Sandra was still not aware that CB was not her biological father and that the *'surrogate'* dad had been CB's younger brother, who had been fostered out by CB's snooty grandmother on his mother's side of the family. Dian had spent many enchanting hours with cornflower blue eyed Damien Bogus, an infamous gang leader, who was feared by everyone including the Civilian Security Services. He had grown tired of hearing his grandmother's racist comments to his grandfather. Each time he visited, all Damien could hear was the derogatory comments about his mother, father and his grandfather. Damien started to rebel since he was nine years old. It was his grandmother who had sent social workers to fetch Damien when he had killed her parrot. Young Damien had incriminated himself by leaving his grandmother a note to say he was sorry that he had killed the parrot but that the words the parrot uttered every time he was visiting reminded him of her. The boy had signed the note "I hate you", Damien. He even left a *'post script'*. It said, "don't ever call me your grandson again. You don't deserve me". Dian preferred the tough talking no-nonsense gang leader. Damien provided more physical security for her than the timid, affable CB. If only Sandra knew of her biological father's numerous custodial short sentences, severe drug addiction and her mother's involvement with being a *'drug mule'* on several occasions, she might never again look down upon any individual or dismiss the likes of DJ Herbie. He had far more respect for himself than her biological father. As Duke's wife, Sandra might gain even more from his Estate, perhaps! Duke also had lots of businesses as well as other assets all across the parallel virtual planet of Asteroidia which would be all hers now, seemingly!

The man driving the golden Four Wheel Drive vehicle was the legitimate son of the old King Karma from the Tribe of Hawke. He was Prince Karma Karma of Spaceville. The young Prince Karma Karma had requested but was allowed to live in one of the 5th rated exotic islands without revealing his real identity or crown. He chose Costa Del Shell and its then idyllic, paradise features and ambience. Young Prince Karma Karma wanted to experience living without all the trappings and restrictions of royalty away from the Kingdom of Spaceville. As he was able to keep his identity to himself, the young Prince's *'Life Experiences'*, gleaned invaluable information about social relationships from living amongst the 5th rated indigenous population of the 5th rated exotic island of Costa Del Shell. His way of living was enriched by his daily experiences. Prince Karma Karma witnessed what it was like to be marginalised, deliberately degraded and perceived as being *"unintelligent"* or being *"inferior"* because his brain was *"smaller"* and less capable of learning, apparently! He had lived what it felt like to be debased by those slurs. Prince Karma Karma had observed how the Mentality Terrorists had verbally and physically bullied the indigenous population of Costa Del Shell into subservience. He had studied how the *'programming'* and *'conditioning'* was part of a plot over millennia to use the *'language of hate'* to embed but populate the principles of *'mental torture'* by way of spreading deliberate disinformation about generations of individuals from the Tribe of Hawke. Prince Karma Karma had lived the class-ism that kept apartheid alive. It had been contrived but maintained by the type of cronyism that was rife within the political dogma that was still being belched out by the heavily partisan *'Neuro-bigoted'* gangs like the UFO. Prince Karma Karma knew that this wealth of experience was incomparable to any he could have gained growing up at the Palace. He was grateful for all those experiences he had gained from growing up on the once exotic island of Costa Del Shell. Prince Karma Karma was now a matured young adult Prince, who was ready to return to the Kingdom of Spaceville to take on the mantle of being King. In preparation to live the type of life he wanted for him and his family, the young King elect started to prepare Sandra for her life as a mother. Even though she would be waited on by her staff, the young King elect wanted her to learn how to cook like the indigenous people of the 5th rated exotic Continents, Countries and Islands like Costa Del Shell. It was an invaluable *'life skill'* that he wanted them not only to maintain throughout their relationship but also to transfer it to their children so that they never got tempted by, become attracted to or be dependable on *'Fast Foods'* as their staple diet.

As royalty, he also had more clout than Duke would ever have if he lived for another 50 years, probably! Sandra had learnt that submitting to the myth about choosing to hunt for the antiquated "brain washing" about the muscular *'Trophy Man Image'*, *'Mr Right' 'stereo-type'* 'bore little relevance to fulfilling her *'real'* rather than *'perceived'* needs. Sandra now knew that it was not just down to size of body or genitalia. It was more down to technique and how a *'craftsman'* used his *'tool'* that really mattered. At least, Sandra's experience with soon to be crowned King Karma Karma did not only quell her fire like Raymond used to but confirmed the legend about men from the exotic continents, countries and islands. She now bore testament it was true and that in their *'Kingdoms'*, those *'men'* ruled supreme in what they were *'Kings'* at . . . probably!

To be continued/discontinued . . . . SUBLIMINALLY, perhaps!!!!!!

From the Director's Chair, with the aid of the gigantic megaphone, Hifle shouts,

"CUT!!!!"

EPILOGUE

This book was written in order to identify what makes up relationships on a parallel virtual planet, and it questions whose 'values and beliefs' are you living?

Like all movies, literary filming on sets with character actors was important in order to justify the unbounded depths of creativity required for initiating some elements of curiosity whilst striving to maintain the complex, controversial, intriguing fictional moments. These had helped to build the extravagant, descriptive, documented narratives which oozed *'real-to-life'* issues, like the influence and importance of traditional or contemporary cultural *'values and beliefs'*. Establishing their importance had helped to frame but determined or documented different categories of relationships. They transitioned from the virtual framing latently into the *'real-to-life'* arena for debate, probably! The comparative magnetic feature of each relationship was a key factor used to ascertain the quality and longevity of those relationships. They were either mutually attractive or repugnantly repulsive.

As **'ID'** forms patterning of thinking towards which individuals demonstrate but strive to recognise the value of their uniqueness, the influence of indoctrination via *'programming'* and *'conditioning'* helped to create an oxymoron about equality. This type of thinking is in itself the singular example deemed to destroy the ability to assess and evaluate individual potentiality. It offers nothing but limitations, barriers and uncertainty about being able to strive to discover whether individuals can recognise or assess their capabilities. I wanted the story to establish consideration for the effect of the influence of perception of *'self'* by others as well as the individual's own perception of *'self'* upon the psyche. These corruptive influences drive individuals toward toxic mentalities, pungent attitudes but construct destructive monochrome mindsets. Most of all, individuals can learn that they are able to spend time to look within for the *'real'* self identification instead of being mentally enslaved but directed by either perception per se. Each individual or groups of characters bring a link in the chain of events within the context of the story.

The Fictional Virtual Realities Scenarios are there to titillate the controversial aspects within each scenario. Led by the 'Trailer', each chapter were pieces of literary portraiture. They portrayed invaluable content, context and concepts about the type of deeply emotional issues, situations, environments and life experiences which were highlighted for discussion or debate. Each scenario subscribed heavily but with the intent to give a subtle mix of metaphoric brushstrokes upon the minds of the audience. This was done in order to focus the audiences' attention on the conceptual 'golden ratio' embedded by the subliminal context in which the particular scenario was written.

Although the setting for this Literary Docudrama Movie © had been placed in a virtual space, this is not a Sci-Fi but rather a literary work of Art. Because of Asteroidia's virtual environment, there was only an imagined version of its physicality occupying that space. Whilst it might have been parallel to any planet in the universe, it was necessary to name one so as to have comparative references in order to establish similar physical locations and behaviours in that space. In doing so, the construct enabled comparable '*real-to-life*' content, context, concepts and experiential models. Geographic locations and weather patterns were inventive too. These added to the vividness of literary creativity through the concept of imaginative visualisation

The deconstruction of the once Royal Royal United Stately Kingdoms were created as a comparable metaphoric example of what influences determined the destruction of traditional values like structure, morals and scruples. The Kingdoms became 'Dis-United' not only because of the lack of strategic vision on behalf of those who were charged to protect and reinforce their unison but also exposed the level of unaccountability the extremely influential '*puppeteer masters*', the UFO, managed to exploit. They gained leverage through their hugely financially abundant lobbyist poly-tricksters, who were allowed to seize the initiative from the careless politicrats. They took the unity of the Royal Royal Stately Kingdoms for granted but succumbed to the super-hydrated corruptive thirst for the taste of Champagne Urge Each metaphoric atom of the UFO joined forces to form an extremely strong metaphoric molecular bond in order to usurp power from the weakened politicrats, who rendered themselves at the mercy of the 'Cult-Induced' Powerbrokers, the UFO. They were allowed to plan, initiate, establish but maintain and wield power over their '*puppets*', the politicrats and population, ultimately. The constant political in-fighting amongst the politicrats destroyed the Royal Royal United Stately Kingdoms' unity but established a type of sterile preference, which saw those Kingdoms succeeding from each other by the wedges driven between each of them. Those wedges helped to establish the new preferences by the self-appointed '*few*' over the '*majority*'; establishing the cult-driven '*greed*' over '*need*' philosophy. In doing so, '*fissures*' were allowed to deteriorate but had begun to widen into '*cracks*'. The metaphoric walls crumbled but separated the Kingdoms into the cult-induced political anarchy.

As for the beautiful exotic paradise continents, countries and islands, they too were being destroyed by the transference of the same philosophies which were destroying the 1st rated Kingdoms, effectively. Granted that the exotic continents, countries and islands had already accepted the title of being 5th rated as if it was an honour, the mentality of their population soon diminished but morphed into the type of subservient mindsets from which there was no chance of recovery. The indigenous '*new*' generations had taken to the concept of the '*crabs-in-a barrel*', '*dog*' eat '*dog*' philosophies by adopting the '*cultural trends*' of the 1st rated '*Powerbrokers*'. The 5th rated exotic continents, countries and islands even outdid the 1st rated Kingdoms by establishing a type of '*self-inoculation*', which rendered them immune towards their traditional '*values and beliefs*' and ways of living. Even though it was apparent what had caused the 1st rated Kingdoms to become 'Dis-United', the 5th rated exotic continents, countries and islands formed a strong bond of unity with the '*values and beliefs*' of the 1st rated Kingdoms instead but abandoned their traditional '*values and beliefs*', which had served their fore-parents millennia before the young generations' birth even. Their reckless choices had impacted upon them in a way they didn't understand nor cared to understand. Many generations in the 1st rated Kingdoms and 5th rated exotic continents, countries and islands found practicing **'*Ethno-Genocidia*'** an attraction, without preamble. The lunacy of the UFO's 'Cult-Induced' Post/Zip Code Wars seemed to have been dispersed but carried on the free-flowing mental air currents, seemingly. Each gust of mental wind blew the seeds of genetically engineered mental *'stereo-tripe'* foods across the expanse of space which established the physical distance between the 1st rated Kingdoms and the 5th rated exotic continents, countries and islands. The airwaves carried the neural-engineered *'stereo-hype'* subliminally induced melodies into their psyche across the vast mental oceans which divided them. Finally, the population of the 5th rated continents, countries and islands chose to commit to become the new wave *'politically-accepted'* Neuro-cultural *'stereo-types'*, seemingly, probably! How else could the level of *'programming'* and *'conditioning'* have had such mesmerising *'pied piper'* effect upon populations across the World of Space?

This compelling, highly controversial, Classy, Epic Wik-**ID**-Fiction © of *'real-to-life'*, Fictional Virtual Realities Scenarios © offered suspense, adventure and thrilling, ultra-intriguing, reflective, thoughtful, debateable views beset from different perspectives through this Creative, Literary Docudrama Movie © we've come to know as the perennial *'greed-induced'*, super-dehydrated *'mental thirst'* for 'The Taste of Champagne Urge'.

THE REWARD LIST

(A)

Wanted: Al Tuxedo
Arrest of Al Tuxedo = 7.5, 000, 000 SPCU (Spacevillean Champange Urges)
No tax apply
Conviction of Al Tuxedo = 15, 000, 000
SPCU (Spacevillean Champange Urges)
No tax apply

(B)

Wanted: Ghetto Mental Terrorists/Ghetto Mental Engineering Scientists
Arrest of GMT/GMES = 3.5, 000, 000 SPCU
(Spacevillean Champange Urges)
No tax apply
Conviction of GMT/GMES = 7.5, 000, 000
SPCU (Spacevillean Champange Urges)
No tax apply

(C)

Wanted: Ghetto Sodomy Entrepreneurs/Serial Rapists/
Active Registered/Unregistered Serial Paedophiles
Arrest of GSE/SR/ARSP/AUSP = 3.5, 000,
000 SPCU (Spacevillean Champange Urges)
No tax apply
Conviction of GSE/SR/ARSP/AUSP = 7.5, 000
000 SPCU (Spacevillean Champange Urges)
No tax apply

(D)

Wanted: Gang Mentality Practitioner/Gang Orientation Scientists
Arrest of GMP/GOS = 3.5, 000, 000 SPCU (Spacevillean Champange Urges)
No tax apply
Conviction of GMP/GOS = 7.5, 000 000
SPCU (Spacevillean Champange Urges)
No tax apply

(E)

Wanted: Ghetto Celebrity CEO/Gang Orientation Operators
Arrest of GCCEO/ GOO = 2.5, 000 000
SPCU (Spacevillean Champange Urges)
No tax apply
Conviction of GCCEO/ GOO = 5, 000, 000
SPCU (Spacevillean Champange Urges)
No tax apply

(F)

Wanted: Ghetto Celebrity Entrepreneurs/Gang Orientation Practitioners
Arrest of GCE/GOP = 1.5, 000, 000 SPCU (Spacevillean Champange Urges)
No tax apply
Conviction of GCE/GOP = 3, 000, 000 (Spacevillean Champange Urges)
No tax apply

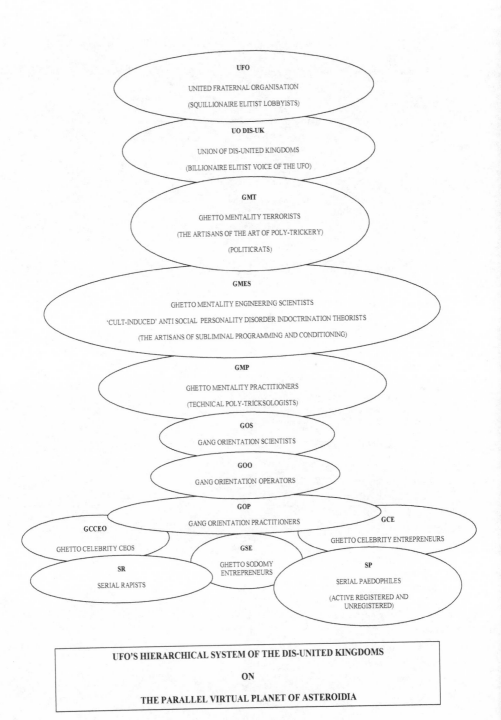

UFO
UNITED FRATERNAL ORGANISATION
(SQUILLIONAIRE ELITIST LOBBYISTS)

UO DIS-UK
UNION OF DIS-UNITED KINGDOMS
(BILLIONAIRE ELITIST VOICE OF THE UFO)

GMT
GHETTO MENTALITY TERRORISTS
(THE ARTISANS OF THE ART OF POLY-TRICKERY)
(POLITICRATS)

GMES
GHETTO MENTALITY ENGINEERING SCIENTISTS
'CULT-INDUCED' ANTI SOCIAL PERSONALITY DISORDER INDOCTRINATION THEORISTS
(THE ARTISANS OF SUBLIMINAL PROGRAMMING AND CONDITIONING)

GMP
GHETTO MENTALITY PRACTITIONERS
(TECHNICAL POLY-TRICKSOLOGISTS)

GOS
GANG ORIENTATION SCIENTISTS

GOO
GANG ORIENTATION OPERATORS

GOP
GANG ORIENTATION PRACTITIONERS

GCCEO
GHETTO CELEBRITY CEOS

GCE
GHETTO CELEBRITY ENTREPRENEURS

GSE
GHETTO SODOMY
ENTREPRENEURS

SR
SERIAL RAPISTS

SP
SERIAL PAEDOPHILES
(ACTIVE REGISTERED AND
UNREGISTERED)

UFO'S HIERARCHICAL SYSTEM OF THE DIS-UNITED KINGDOMS

ON

THE PARALLEL VIRTUAL PLANET OF ASTEROIDIA

ABOUT THE AUTHOR

Since he was 4 years old, Lyndon remembers his father describing him as a "word artist". He had no idea what was meant by such terminology but was impressed with the way it sounded. Whilst other children were being discouraged from 'day-dreaming', Lyndon remembers his mother encouraging him to day-dream as much as he wanted. With that level of encouragement, he continued to explore the potentiality of his imagination.

As he grew and progressed, Lyndon wrote mini plays, sang, danced, acted and recited monologues depicting various characters including birds, animals, and humans alike. As there was no radio or television at that time, each evening from twilight time, Lyndon often mesmerised his family with stories he often made up on the spot. He noticed that he could do this without having to set out the customary 'plot' at the beginning. Instead, Lyndon's unbridled imagination sometimes surprised him. Though, all he did was to describe what was happening in his boundless imaginary world, he managed to intricately weave the tale with spellbinding expertise.

Lyndon's use of language represents the choice of intensity of his 'literary brushstrokes' but renders the audiences' minds as his canvas. The artistic 'golden ratios' of his 'real-to-life' creations of 'Fictional Virtual Realities Scenarios' © become the focal point to which his audience is first attracted but become involuntarily curiously attached to the actions, thrills, suspense and twists. When his untamed imagination registers the seamless transfer of the potential effect of his 'literary artistry', it consumes him so wholesomely that every chapter becomes yet another scenario. Lyndon's sense of humour is obvious but his use of puns is sometimes cryptic.

His present occupation is 'I'-Coaching ©. It is a novel approach to coaching. This is his brainchild. Lyndon's specialty is Personal Development, Personal Performance and all Categories of Relationships.

Made in the USA
Middletown, DE
08 September 2017